STORY

Fictions Past and Present

STORY

Fictions Past and Present

Boyd Litzinger
Saint Bonaventure University

Joyce Carol Oates
Princeton University

D. C. HEATH AND COMPANY
Lexington, Massachusetts   Toronto

PREFACE

Story-telling, story-listening, and story-reading are among the oldest and most enduring of civilized, indeed human, pleasures. This book is meant to make those pleasures accessible to a new generation of readers and to renew those delights for the more experienced. Because the editors intend to represent the fullest possible range of short fiction, from the recognized achievements of its past masters to the vital experiments of its present practitioners, they have organized the book in two parts.

The first and larger part includes those writers who are often called "classic" and "modern"—men and women who brought the short story from its beginnings in the nineteenth century through its stages of definition and development down to our own generation. They are part of our literary heritage. Here you will find Poe and Hawthorne, James and Joyce, Woolf and Welty, Barth, Updike, and Bambara; many of these authors are represented by justly familiar works, some by stories that have been seldom or never before anthologized.

This section is arranged chronologically so that the beginning reader can begin to sense the development of this important literary form, the more experienced reader trace the influence of earlier writers on later ones, and the teacher conveniently support and exemplify various theories of writing practice and historical development. Writers from many different countries are represented, and the various sub-genres of the story—science fiction, fantasy, and detective fiction—are included as well.

The second section is an absorbing introduction to contemporary fiction. Twenty-seven stories representing short fiction as it is being written today have been selected by a writer whose authority in this field is substantial. The recognition Joyce Carol Oates has earned as author, critic, editor, and teacher of aspiring writers lends special weight to these selections. Her essay introducing Part II should prove especially interesting to students because it grows out of a ground of theory and practice that is exceptional, if not unique, among fiction editors.

Excellence and variety, leading to pleasure and knowledge, ought to mark an anthology of short stories—and we have made these qualities our criteria. But we have wanted as well to make a teachable book and have provided, beyond the two-part organization, a number of aids to make STORY useful. Notes to the stories are intended to be helpful, not intrusive; they have been kept to a minimum. The questions that follow each story are meant to arouse interest in technique and style as well as in content, to provide the groundwork for lectures and class discussion, and to help students develop habits of aesthetic judgment and appreciation. A glossary of critical terms and brief biographical notes are arranged alphabetically at the back of the book where they cannot interfere with the immediate pleasure of reading but where they are readily available for reference and can most easily lead the reader on to independent or assigned work beyond the text.

And that the reader will so be led is indeed our hope. For although among these hundred stories the reader will find God's plenty, the world of short fiction is virtually limitless and its exploration a source of almost inexhaustible delight. STORY, we trust, will be a window on that world.

Boyd Litzinger

ACKNOWLEDGEMENTS

Although Joyce Carol Oates and I cheerfully take responsibility for our selections, I have sought advice and received assistance from many people. Particular thanks are due to Leo E. Keenan, Jr., William A. Wehmeyer, James J. Martine, Alfred and Patricia Finocchio, John Mulryan, Paul Wood, Russell J. Jandoli, Walter Budzinski, Douglas Davis, Christopher Gary, Malcolm V.T. Wallace, and John Capozzi, O.F.M.—all of Saint Bonaventure University; James J. Gebhart of the Pennsylvania State University; Eugene F. Murphy of Hobart and William Smith Colleges; Daniel Barnes of Ohio State University; Thomas J. Collins and S.L. Dragland of Western Ontario University; Roy F. Montgomery, formerly of Spring Hill College; Jackie Unch, formerly of D. C. Heath & Company; and Theresa Covley and JoAnne Conroy of the Friedsam Memorial Library.

For research and clerical assistance, I want to thank Michelle Lawler, Lori Linderman, and Connie Tsujimoto. Holt Johnson of D. C. Heath and Company saw this book expertly through production. Paul Smith, my editor and still my friend, proposed this book, encouraged me at every turn, and has my gratitude.

More personally still, Toni, my wife, deserves more than the customary signs of thanks for her support. Finally, I want to dedicate my work on this book to Sara Litzinger and the late Boyd A. Litzinger who introduced me to the delights of reading and set me on a course I might otherwise have missed.

Boyd Litzinger

CONTENTS

Part I

Washington Irving
The Legend of Sleepy Hollow — 1

Honoré de Balzac
A Passion in the Desert — 19

Nathaniel Hawthorne
Young Goodman Brown — 28
My Kinsman, Major Molineux — 37

Nikolai Gogol
The Overcoat — 49

Edgar Allan Poe
The Fall of the House of Usher — 67
The Cask of Amontillado — 79
The Purloined Letter — 84

Herman Melville
Bartleby the Scrivener — 97

Fyodor Dostoevsky
The Grand Inquisitor — 120

Gustave Flaubert
A Simple Heart — 132

Leo Tolstoy
The Death of Ivan Ilych — 152

Mark Twain (Samuel L. Clemens)
The Celebrated Jumping Frog of Calaveras County — 187

Ambrose Bierce
Moxon's Master   192

Henry James
Four Meetings   199
Brooksmith   219
The Beast in the Jungle   229

Sarah Orne Jewett
Miss Tempy's Watchers   256

Kate Chopin
Désirée's Baby   263

Joseph Conrad
Heart of Darkness   268

Arthur Conan Doyle
The Red-Headed League   320

Anton Chekhov
Gooseberries   335
The Kiss   342

O. Henry (William Sydney Porter)
The Cop and the Anthem   353

Miguel de Unamuno
Juan Manso: A Dead Man's Tale   358

Saki (H. H. Munro)
The Open Window   362

Stephen Crane
The Open Boat   365

Willa Cather
Paul's Case   381

Thomas Mann
Disorder and Early Sorrow   394

Sherwood Anderson
I'm a Fool   415

James Joyce
The Dead   423
Araby   450
Ivy Day in the Committee Room   455

Virginia Woolf
Kew Gardens   466

Franz Kafka
    A Hunger Artist   471

D. H. Lawrence
    The Horse Dealer's Daughter   477
    The Rocking-Horse Winner   489

Agatha Christie
    Double Sin   500

Katherine Anne Porter
    Flowering Judas   510

Dorothy Parker
    You Were Perfectly Fine   518

James Thurber
    The Secret Life of Walter Mitty   521

F. Scott Fitzgerald
    Babylon Revisited   525

William Faulkner
    A Rose for Emily   540
    That Evening Sun   547

Ernest Hemingway
    A Clean, Well-Lighted Place   559

Jorge Luis Borges
    The Babylon Lottery   563

Sean O'Faolain
    The Man Who Invented Sin   568

Nathalie Sarraute
    Tropism XVIII   577

John Steinbeck
    Flight   578

Frank O'Connor
    Guests of the Nation   590

Isaac Bashevis Singer
    The Beard   599

Richard Wright
    The Man Who Killed a Shadow   605

Eudora Welty
    Why I Live at the P.O.   614

John Cheever
  The Swimmer   623

Ralph Ellison
  Flying Home   631

Bernard Malamud
  The Jewbird   643

Saul Bellow
  Looking for Mr. Green   650

Carson McCullers
  A Tree, A Rock, A Cloud   664

Arthur C. Clarke
  The Sentinel   670

Doris Lessing
  To Room Nineteen   677

Ray Bradbury
  The Golden Apples of the Sun   698

Mavis Gallant
  Acceptance of Their Ways   703

James Baldwin
  Sonny's Blues   709

William Gass
  In the Heart of the Heart of the Country   730

Flannery O'Connor
  Judgement Day   747
  Good Country People   759

Gabriel García Márquez
  A Very Old Man with Enormous Wings   772

Ursula K. Le Guin
  Schrödinger's Cat   777

John Barth
  Lost in the Funhouse   783

Donald Barthelme
  The Balloon   798

John Updike
  A & P   802

Joyce Carol Oates
  The Going-Away Party 807

Toni Cade Bambara
  Raymond's Run 821

Part II
  Preface, Joyce Carol Oates 829

Alice Adams
  Gift of Grass 835

Margaret Atwood
  The Man from Mars 841

Ann Beattie
  A Clever-Kids Story 854

Clark Blaise
  A Class of New Canadians 864

Paul Bowles
  A Distant Episode 871

Richard Brautigan
  Revenge of the Lawn 880
  A Short History of Religion in California 884

Hortense Calisher
  The Scream on Fifty-Seventh Street 886

Barry Callaghan
  The Black Queen 902

Raymond Carver
  Cathedral 905

John Gardner
  Redemption 915

Gail Godwin
  Dream Children 924

William Goyen
  Bridge of Music, River of Sand 933

John Hawkes
  Two Shoes for One Foot 937

Josephine Jacobsen
  The Mango Community   942

Alistair MacLeod
  In the Fall   955

Bobbie Ann Mason
  Graveyard Day   964

Alice Munro
  Spelling   972

Tim O'Brien
  Going After Cacciato   982

Cynthia Ozick
  The Shawl   996

Grace Paley
  The Used-Boy Raisers   1000

John Sayles
  Dillinger in Hollywood   1005

Lynne Sharon Schwartz
  Rough Strife   1014

Elizabeth Spencer
  The Girl Who Loved Horses   1027

Sean Virgo
  Home and Native Land   1039

Alice Walker
  Roselily   1043

Joy Williams
  The Farm   1047

Biographies of the Authors   1057
Glossary of Critical Terms   1071
Index of Authors and Titles   1075

PART 1

WASHINGTON IRVING

The Legend of Sleepy Hollow

FOUND AMONG THE PAPERS OF THE LATE DIEDRICH KNICKERBOCKER

A pleasing land of drowsy head it was,
Of dreams that wave before the half-shut eye,
And of gay castles in the clouds that pass,
For ever flushing round a summer sky.
CASTLE OF INDOLENCE

In the bosom of one of those spacious coves which indent the eastern shore of the Hudson, at that broad expansion of the river denominated by the ancient Dutch navigators the Tappan Zee, and where they always prudently shortened sail, and implored the protection of St. Nicholas when they crossed, there lies a small market-town or rural port, which by some is called Greensburgh, but which is more generally and properly known by the name of Tarry Town. This name was given, we are told, in former days, by the good housewives of the adjacent country, from the inveterate propensity of their husbands to linger about the village tavern on market days. Be that as it may, I do not vouch for the fact, but merely advert to it, for the sake of being precise and authentic. Not far from this village, perhaps about two miles, there is a little valley, or rather lap of land, among high hills, which is one of the quietest places in the whole world. A small brook glides through it, with just murmur enough to lull one to repose; and the occasional whistle of a quail, or tapping of a woodpecker, is almost the only sound that ever breaks in upon the uniform tranquillity.

I recollect that, when a stripling, my first exploit in squirrel-shooting was in a grove of tall walnut-trees that shades one side of the valley. I had wandered into it at noon time, when all nature is peculiarly quiet, and was startled by the roar of my own gun, as it broke the Sabbath stillness around, and was prolonged and reverberated by the angry echoes. If ever I should wish for a retreat, whither I might steal from the world and its distractions, and dream quietly away the remnant of a troubled life, I know of none more promising than this little valley.

From the listless repose of the place, and the peculiar character of its inhabitants, who are descendents from the original Dutch settlers, this sequestered glen has long been known by the name of SLEEPY HOLLOW, and its rustic lads are called the Sleepy Hollow Boys throughout all the neighboring country. A drowsy, dreamy influence seems to hang over the land, and to pervade the very atmosphere. Some say that the place was bewitched by a high German doctor, during the early days of the settlement; others, that an old Indian chief, the prophet or wizard of his tribe, held his powwows there before the country was discovered by Master Hendrick Hudson. Certain it is, the place still continues under the sway of some witching power, that holds a spell over the minds of the good people, causing them to walk in a continual reverie. They are given to all kinds of marvellous beliefs; are subject to trances and visions; and frequently see strange sights, and hear music and voices in the air. The whole neighborhood abounds with local tales, haunted spots, and twilight superstitions; stars shoot and meteors glare oftener across the valley than in any part of the country, and the nightmare, with her whole nine fold, seems to make it the favorite scene of her gambols.

The dominant spirit, however, that haunts this enchanted region, and seems to be commander-in-chief of all the powers of the air, is the apparition of a figure on horseback without a head. It is said by some to be the ghost of a Hessian trooper, whose head had been carried away by a cannon-ball, in some nameless battle during the revolutionary war; and who is ever and anon seen by the country folk, hurrying along in the gloom of night, as if on the wings of the wind. His haunts are not confined to the valley, but extend at times to the adjacent roads, and especially to the vicinity of a church at no great distance. Indeed, certain of the most authentic historians of those parts, who have been careful in collecting and collating the floating facts concerning this spectre, allege that the body of the trooper, having been buried in the church-yard, the ghost rides forth to the scene of battle in nightly quest of his head; and that the rushing speed with which he sometimes passes along the Hollow, like a midnight blast, is owing to his being belated, and in a hurry to get back to the church-yard before daybreak.

Such is the general purport of this legendary superstition, which has furnished materials for many a wild story in that region of shadows; and the spectre is known, at all the country firesides, by the name of the Headless Horseman of Sleepy Hollow.

It is remarkable that the visionary propensity I have mentioned is not confined to the native inhabitants of the valley, but is unconsciously imbibed by every one who resides there for a time. However wide awake they may have been before they entered that sleepy region, they are sure, in a little time, to inhale the witching influence of the air, and begin to grow imaginative — to dream dreams, and see apparitions.

I mention this peaceful spot with all possible laud; for it is in such little retired Dutch valleys, found here and there embosomed in the great State of New York, that population, manners, and customs, remain fixed; while the great torrent of migration and improvement, which is making such incessant changes in other parts of this restless country, sweeps by them unobserved. They are like those little nooks of still water which border a rapid stream; where we may see the straw and bubble riding quietly at anchor, or slowly revolving in their mimic harbor, undisturbed by the rush of the passing current. Though many years have elapsed since I trod the drowsy shades of Sleepy Hollow, yet I question whether I should not still find the same trees and the same families vegetating in its sheltered bosom.

In this by-place of nature, there abode, in a remote period of American history, that is to say, some thirty years since, a worthy wight of the name of Ichabod Crane; who sojourned, or, as he expressed it, "tarried," in Sleepy Hollow, for the purpose of instructing the children of the vicinity. He was a native of Connecticut; a State which supplies the Union with pioneers for the mind as well as for the forest, and sends forth yearly its legions of frontier woodsmen and country schoolmasters. The cognomen of Crane was not inapplicable to his person. He was tall, but exceedingly lank, with narrow shoulders, long arms and legs, hands that dangled a mile out of his sleeves, feet that might have served for shovels, and his whole frame most loosely hung together. His head was small, and flat at top, with huge ears, large green glassy eyes, and a long snipe nose, so that it looked like a weather-cock, perched upon his spindle neck, to tell which way the wind blew. To see him striding along the profile of a hill on a windy day, with his clothes bagging and fluttering about him, one might have mistaken him for the genius of famine descending upon the earth, or some scarecrow eloped from a cornfield.

His school-house was a low building of one large room, rudely constructed of logs; the windows partly glazed, and partly patched with leaves of old copy-books. It was most ingeniously secured at vacant hours, by a withe twisted in the handle of the door, and stakes set against the window shutters; so that, though a thief might get in with perfect ease, he would find some embarrassment in getting out; an idea most probably borrowed by the architect, Yost Van Houten, from the mystery of an eel-pot. The school-house stood in a rather lonely but pleasant situation, just at the foot of a woody hill, with a brook running close by, and a formidable birch tree growing at one end of it. From hence the low murmur of his pupils' voices, conning over their lessons, might be heard in a drowsy summer's day, like the hum of a bee-hive; interrupted now and then by the authoritative voice of the master, in the tone of menace or command; or, peradventure, by the appalling sound of the birch, as he urged some tardy loiterer along the flowery path of knowledge. Truth to say, he was a conscientious man, and ever bore in mind the golden maxim, "Spare the rod and spoil the child." — Ichabod Crane's scholars certainly were not spoiled.

I would not have it imagined, however, that he was one of those cruel potentates of the school, who joy in the smart of their subjects; on the contrary, he administered justice with discrimination rather than severity; taking the burthen off the backs of the weak, and laying it on those of the strong. Your mere puny stripling, that winced at the least flourish of the rod, was passed by with indulgence; but the claims of justice were satisfied by inflicting a double portion on some little, tough, wrong-headed, broad-skirted Dutch urchin, who sulked and swelled and grew dogged and sullen beneath the birch. All this he called "doing his duty by their parents"; and he never inflicted a chastisement without following it by the assurance, so consolatory to the smarting urchin, that "he would remember it, and thank him for it the longest day he had to live."

When school hours were over, he was even the companion and playmate of the larger boys; and on holiday afternoons would convoy some of the smaller ones home, who happened to have pretty sisters, or good housewives for mothers, noted for the comforts of the cupboard. Indeed it behooved him to keep on good terms with his pupils. The revenue arising from his school was small, and would have been scarcely sufficient to furnish him with daily bread, for he was a huge feeder, and though lank, had the dilating powers of an anaconda; but to help out his maintenance, he was, according to country custom in those parts, boarded and lodged at the houses of the farmers, whose children he instructed. With these he lived successively a week at a time; thus going the rounds of the neighborhood, with all his worldly effects tied up in a cotton handkerchief.

That all this might not be too onerous on the purses of his rustic patrons, who are apt to consider the costs of schooling a grievous burden, and schoolmasters as mere drones, he had various ways of rendering himself both useful and agreeable. He assisted the farmers occasionally in the lighter labors of their farms; helped to make hay; mended the fences; took the horses to water; drove the cows from pasture; and cut wood for the winter fire. He laid aside, too, all the dominant dignity and absolute sway with which he lorded it in his little empire, the school, and became wonderfully gentle and ingratiating. He found favor in the eyes of the mothers, by petting the children, particularly the youngest; and like the lion bold, which whilom so magnanimously the lamb did hold, he would sit with a child on one knee, and rock a cradle with his foot for whole hours together.

In addition to his other vocations, he was the singing-master of the neighborhood, and picked up many bright shillings by instructing the young folks in psalmody. It was a matter of no little vanity to him, on Sundays, to take his station in front of the church gallery, with a band of chosen singers; where, in his own mind, he completely carried away the psalm from the parson. Certain it is, his voice resounded far above all the rest of the congregation; and there are peculiar quavers still to be heard in that church, and which may even be heard half a mile off, quite to the opposite side of the mill-pond, on a still Sunday morning, which are said to be legitimately descended from the nose of Ichabod Crane. Thus, by divers little make-shifts in that ingenious way which is commonly denominated "by hook and by crook," the worthy pedagogue got on tolerably enough, and was thought, by all who understood nothing of the labor of headwork, to have a wonderfully easy life of it.

The schoolmaster is generally a man of some importance in the female circle of a rural neighborhood; being considered a kind of idle gentlemanlike personage, of vastly superior taste and accomplishments to the rough country swains, and, indeed, inferior in learning only to the parson. His appearance, therefore, is apt to occasion some little stir at the tea-table of a farmhouse, and the addition of a supernumerary dish of cakes or sweetmeats, or peradventure, the parade of a silver tea-pot. Our man of letters, therefore, was peculiarly happy in the smiles of all the country damsels. How he would figure among them in the church-yard, between services on Sundays! gathering grapes for them from the wild vines that overrun the surrounding trees; reciting for their amusement all the epitaphs on the tombstones; or sauntering, with a whole bevy of them, along the banks of the adjacent mill-pond; while the more bashful country bumpkins hung sheepishly back, envying his superior elegance and address.

From his half itinerant life, also, he was a kind of travelling gazette, carrying the whole budget of local gossip from house to house; so that his appearance was always greeted with satisfaction. He was, moreover, esteemed by the women as a man of great erudition, for he had read several books quite through, and was a perfect master of Cotton Mather's[1] History of New England Witchcraft, in which, by the way, he most firmly and potently believed.

He was, in fact, an odd mixture of small shrewdness and simple credulity. His appetite for the marvellous, and his powers of digesting it, were equally extraordinary; and both had been increased by his residence in this spellbound region. No tale was too gross or monstrous for his capacious swallow. It was often his delight, after his school was dismissed in the afternoon, to stretch himself on the rich bed of clover, bordering the little brook that whimpered by his school-house, and there con over old Mather's direful tales, until the gathering dusk of the evening made the printed page a mere mist before his eyes. Then, as he wended his way, by swamp and stream and awful woodland, to the farmhouse where he happened to be quartered, every sound of nature, at that witching hour, fluttered his excited imagination: the moan of the whip-poor-will from the hillside; the boding cry of the tree-toad, that harbinger of storm; the dreary hooting of the screech-owl, or the sudden rustling in the thicket of birds

---

[1] Cotton Mather (1663–1728), Puritan clergyman, theologian, and author, wrote two books dealing with witchcraft: *Memorable Providences, Relating to Witchcraft and Possessions* (1689) and *The Wonders of the Invisible World* (1693).

frightened from their roost. The fire-flies, too, which sparkled most vividly in the darkest places, now and then startled him, as one of uncommon brightness would stream across his path; and if, by chance, a huge blockhead of a beetle came winging his blundering flight against him, the poor varlet was ready to give up the ghost, with the idea that he was struck with a witch's token. His only resource on such occasions, either to drown thought, or drive away evil spirits, was to sing psalm tunes; — and the good people of Sleepy Hollow, as they sat by their doors of an evening, were often filled with awe, at hearing his nasal melody, "in linked sweetness long drawn out," floating from the distant hill, or along the dusky road.

Another of his sources of fearful pleasure was, to pass long winter evenings with the old Dutch wives, as they sat spinning by the fire, with a row of apples roasting and spluttering along the hearth, and listen to their marvellous tales of ghosts and goblins, and haunted fields, and haunted brooks, and haunted bridges, and haunted houses, and particularly of the headless horseman, or galloping Hessian of the Hollow, as they sometimes called him. He would delight them equally by his anecdotes of witchcraft, and of the direful omens and portentous sights and sounds in the air, which prevailed in the earlier times of Connecticut; and would frighten them wofully with speculations upon comets and shooting stars; and with the alarming fact that the world did absolutely turn round, and that they were half the time topsy-turvy!

But if there was a pleasure in all this, while snugly cuddling in the chimney corner of a chamber that was all of a ruddy glow from the crackling wood fire, and where, of course, no spectre dared to show his face, it was dearly purchased by the terrors of his subsequent walk homewards. What fearful shapes and shadows beset his path amidst the dim and ghastly glare of a snowy night! — With what wistful look did he eye every trembling ray of light streaming across the waste fields from some distant window! — How often was he appalled by some shrub covered with snow, which, like a sheeted spectre, beset his very path! — How often did he shrink with curdling awe at the sound of his own steps on the frosty crust beneath his feet; and dread to look over his shoulder, lest he should behold some uncouth being tramping close behind him! — and how often was he thrown into complete dismay by some rushing blast, howling among the trees, in the idea that it was the Galloping Hessian on one of his nightly scourings!

All these, however, were mere terrors of the night, phantoms of the mind that walk in darkness; and though he had seen many spectres in his time, and been more than once beset by Satan in divers shapes, in his lonely perambulations, yet daylight put an end to all these evils; and he would have passed a pleasant life of it, in despite of the devil and all his works, if his path had not been crossed by a being that causes more perplexity to mortal man than ghosts, goblins, and the whole race of witches put together, and that was — a woman.

Among the musical disciples who assembled, one evening in each week, to receive his instructions in psalmody, was Katrina Van Tassel, the daughter and only child of a substantial Dutch farmer. She was a blooming lass of fresh eighteen; plump as a partridge; ripe and melting and rosy cheeked as one of her father's peaches, and universally famed, not merely for her beauty, but her vast expectations. She was withal a little of a coquette, as might be perceived even in her dress, which was a mixture of ancient and modern fashions, as most suited to set off her charms. She wore the ornaments of pure yellow gold, which her great-great-grandmother had brought over from Saardam; the tempting stomacher[2] of the older time; and withal a provokingly short petticoat, to display the prettiest foot and ankle in the country round.

---

[2] A decorated garment worn over the stomach and breast, often under a woman's bodice.

Ichabod Crane had a soft and foolish heart towards the sex; and it is not to be wondered at, that so tempting a morsel soon found favor in his eyes; more especially after he had visited her in her paternal mansion. Old Baltus Van Tassel was a perfect picture of a thriving, contented, liberal-hearted farmer. He seldom, it is true, sent either his eyes or his thoughts beyond the boundaries of his own farm; but within those every thing was snug, happy, and well-conditioned. He was satisfied with his wealth, but not proud of it; and piqued himself upon the hearty abundance, rather than the style in which he lived. His stronghold was situated on the banks of the Hudson, in one of those green sheltered, fertile nooks, in which the Dutch farmers are so fond of nestling. A great elm-tree spread its broad branches over it; at the foot of which bubbled up a spring of the softest and sweetest water, in a little well, formed of a barrel; and then stole sparkling away through the grass, to a neighboring brook, that bubbled along among alders and dwarf willows. Hard by the farmhouse was a vast barn, that might have served for a church; every window and crevice of which seemed bursting forth with the treasures of the farm; the flail was busily resounding within it from morning to night; swallows and martins skimmed twittering about the eaves; and rows of pigeons, some with one eye turned up, as if watching the weather, some with their heads under their wings, or buried in their bosoms, and others swelling, and cooing, and bowing about their dames, were enjoying the sunshine on the roof. Sleek unwieldy porkers were grunting in the repose and abundance of their pens; whence sallied forth, now and then, troops of sucking pigs, as if to snuff the air. A stately squadron of snowy geese were riding in an adjoining pond, convoying whole fleets of ducks; regiments of turkeys were gobbling through the farmyard, and guinea fowls fretting about it, like ill-tempered housewives, with their peevish discontented cry. Before the barn door strutted the gallant cock, that pattern of a husband, a warrior, and a fine gentleman, clapping his burnished wings, and crowing in the pride and gladness of his heart — sometimes tearing up the earth with his feet, and then generously calling his ever-hungry family of wives and children to enjoy the rich morsel which he had discovered.

The pedagogue's mouth watered, as he looked upon this sumptuous promise of luxurious winter fare. In his devouring mind's eye, he pictured to himself every roasting-pig running about with a pudding in his belly, and an apple in his mouth; the pigeons were snugly put to bed in a comfortable pie, and tucked in with a coverlet of crust; the geese were swimming in their own gravy; and the ducks pairing cosily in dishes, like snug married couples, with a decent competency of onion sauce. In the porkers he saw carved out the future sleek side of bacon, and juicy relishing ham; not a turkey but he beheld daintily trussed up, with its gizzard under its wing, and, peradventure, a necklace of savory sausages; and even bright chanticleer himself lay sprawling on his back, in a side dish with uplifted claws, as if craving that quarter which his chivalrous spirit disdained to ask while living.

As the enraptured Ichabod fancied all this, and as he rolled his great green eyes over the fat meadowlands, the rich fields of wheat, of rye, of buckwheat, and Indian corn, and the orchards burthened with ruddy fruit, which surrounded the warm tenement of Van Tassel, his heart yearned after the damsel who was to inherit these domains, and his imagination expanded with the idea, how they might be readily turned into cash, and the money invested in immense tracts of wild land, and shingle palaces in the wilderness. Nay, his busy fancy already realized his hopes, and presented to him the blooming Katrina, with a whole family of children, mounted on the top of a wagon loaded with household trumpery, with pots and kettles dangling beneath; and he beheld himself bestriding a pacing mare, with a colt at her heels, setting out for Kentucky, Tennessee, or the Lord knows where.

When he entered the house the conquest of his heart was complete. It was one of those spacious farmhouses, with high-ridged, but lowly-sloping roofs, built in the style handed down from the first Dutch settlers; the low projecting eaves forming a piazza along the front, capable of being closed up in bad weather. Under this were hung flails, harness, various utensils of husbandry, and nets for fishing in the neighboring river. Benches were built along the sides for summer use; and a great spinning-wheel at one end, and a churn at the other, showed the various uses to which this important porch might be devoted. From this piazza the wondering Ichabod entered the hall, which formed the centre of the mansion and the place of usual residence. Here, rows of resplendent pewter, ranged on a long dresser, dazzled his eyes. In one corner stood a huge bag of wool ready to be spun; in another a quantity of linsey-woolsey just from the loom; ears of Indian corn, and strings of dried apples and peaches, hung in gay festoons along the walls, mingled with the gaud of red peppers; and a door left ajar gave him a peep into the best parlor, where the claw-footed chairs, and dark mahogany tables, shone like mirrors; andirons, with their accompanying shovel and tongs, glistened from their covert of asparagus tops; mock-oranges and conch-shells decorated the mantel-piece; strings of various colored birds' eggs were suspended above it: a great ostrich egg was hung from the centre of the room, and a corner cupboard, knowingly left open, displayed immense treasures of old silver and well-mended china.

From the moment Ichabod laid his eyes upon these regions of delight, the peace of his mind was at an end, and his only study was how to gain the affections of the peerless daughter of Van Tassel. In this enterprise, however, he had more real difficulties than generally fell to the lot of a knight-errant of yore, who seldom had any thing but giants, enchanters, fiery dragons, and such like easily-conquered adversaries, to contend with; and had to make his way merely through gates of iron and brass, and walls of adamant, to the castle keep, where the lady of his heart was confined; all which he achieved as easily as a man would carve his way to the centre of a Christmas pie; and then the lady gave him her hand as a matter of course. Ichabod, on the contrary, had to win his way to the heart of a country coquette, beset with a labyrinth of whims and caprices, which were for ever presenting new difficulties and impediments; and he had to encounter a host of fearful adversaries of real flesh and blood, and numerous rustic admirers, who beset every portal to her heart; keeping a watchful and angry eye upon each other, but ready to fly out in the common cause against any new competitor.

Among these the most formidable was a burly, roaring, roystering blade, of the name of Abraham, or, according to the Dutch abbreviation, Brom Van Brunt, the hero of the country round, which rang with his feats of strength and hardihood. He was broad-shouldered and double-jointed, with short curly black hair, and a bluff, but not unpleasant countenance, having a mingled air of fun and arrogance. From his Herculean frame and great powers of limb, he had received the nickname of BROM BONES, by which he was universally known. He was famed for great knowledge and skill in horsemanship, being as dexterous on horseback as a Tartar. He was foremost at all races and cock-fights; and, with the ascendency which bodily strength acquires in rustic life, was the umpire in all disputes, setting his hat on one side, and giving his decisions with an air and tone admitting of no gainsay or appeal. He was always ready for either a fight or a frolic; but had more mischief than ill-will in his composition; and, with all his over-bearing roughness, there was a strong dash of waggish good humor at bottom. He had three or four boon companions, who regarded him as their model, and at the head of whom he scoured the country, attending every scene of feud or merriment for miles round. In cold weather he was distinguished by a fur cap, surmounted with a flaunting fox's tail; and when folks at a country gathering described this well-known crest at a distance, whisking about among a squad of hard riders, they always stood by for a squall. Sometimes his crew would be heard dashing along past the farmhouses at midnight, with whoop and halloo, like a troop of Don Cossacks; and the old dames, startled out of their sleep, would listen for a moment till the hurry-scurry had clattered by, and then exclaim, "Ay, there goes Brom Bones and his gang!" The neighbors looked upon him with a mixture of awe, admiration, and good will; and when any madcap prank, or rustic brawl, occurred in the vicinity, always shook their heads, and warranted Brom Bones was at the bottom of it.

This rantipole[3] hero had for some time singled out the blooming Katrina for the object of his uncouth gallantries, and though his amorous toyings were something like the gentle caresses and endearments of a bear, yet it was whispered that she did not altogether discourage his hopes. Certain it is, his advances were signals for rival candidates to retire, who felt no inclination to cross a lion in his amours; insomuch, that when his horse was seen tied to Van Tassel's paling, on a Sunday night, a sure sign that his master was courting, or, as it is termed, "sparking," within, all other suitors passed by in despair, and carried the war into other quarters.

Such was the formidable rival with whom Ichabod Crane had to contend, and, considering all things, a stouter man than he would have shrunk from the competition, and a wiser man would have despaired. He had, however, a happy mixture of pliability and perserverance in his nature; he was in form and spirit like a supple-jack — yielding, but tough; though he bent, he never broke; and though he bowed beneath the slightest pressure, yet, the moment it was away — jerk! he was as erect, and carried his head as high as ever.

To have taken the field openly against his rival would have been madness; for he was not a man to be thwarted in his amours, any more than the stormy lover, Achilles.[4] Ichabod, therefore, made his advances in a quiet and gently-insinuating manner. Under cover of his character of singing-master, he made frequent visits at the farmhouse; not that he had any thing to apprehend from the meddlesome interference of parents, which is so often a stumbling-block in the path of lovers. Balt Van Tassel was an easy indulgent soul; he loved his daughter better even than his pipe, and like a reasonable man and an excellent father, let her have her way in every thing. His notable little wife, too, had enough to do to attend to her housekeeping and manage her poultry; for, as she sagely observed, ducks and geese are foolish things, and must be looked after, but girls can take care of themselves. Thus while the busy dame bustled about the house, or plied her spinning-wheel at one end of the piazza, honest Balt would sit smoking his evening pipe at the other, watching the achievements of a little wooden warrior, who, armed with a sword in each hand, was most valiantly fighting the wind on the pinnacle of the barn. In the mean time, Ichabod would carry on his suit with the daughter by the side of the spring under the great elm, or sauntering along in the twilight, that hour so favorable to the lover's eloquence.

I profess not to know how women's hearts are wooed and won. To me they have always been matters of riddle and admiration. Some seem to have but one vulnerable point, or door of access; while others have a thousand avenues, and may be captured in a thousand different ways. It is a great triumph of skill to gain the former, but a still greater proof of generalship to maintain possession of the latter, for the man must battle for his fortress at every door and window. He who wins a thousand common hearts is therefore entitled to some renown; but he who keeps undisputed sway over the heart of a coquette, is indeed a hero. Certain it is, that this was not the case with the redoubtable Brom Bones; and from the moment Ichabod Crane made his advances, the interests of the former evidently declined; his horse was no longer seen tied at the palings on Sunday nights, and a deadly feud gradually arose between him and the preceptor of Sleepy Hollow.

---

[3] Wild, unruly.

[4] The hero of Homer's *Iliad*.

Brom, who had a degree of rough chivalry in his nature, would fain have carried matters to open warfare, and have settled their pretensions to the lady, according to the mode of those most concise and simple reasoners, the knights-errant of yore — by single combat; but Ichabod was too conscious of the superior might of his adversary to enter the lists against him: he had overheard a boast of Bones, that he would "double the schoolmaster up, and lay him on a shelf of his own school-house"; and he was too wary to give him an opportunity. There was something extremely provoking in this obstinately pacific system; it left Brom no alternative but to draw upon the funds of rustic waggery in his disposition, and to play off boorish practical jokes upon his rival: Ichabod became the object of whimsical persecution to Bones, and his gang of rough riders. They harried his hitherto peaceful domains; smoked out his singing school, by stopping up the chimney; broke into the school-house at night, in spite of its formidable fastenings of withe and window stakes, and turned every thing topsy-turvy: so that the poor schoolmaster began to think all the witches in the country held their meetings there. But what was still more annoying, Brom took all opportunities of turning him into ridicule in presence of his mistress, and had a scoundrel dog whom he taught to whine in the most ludicrous manner, and introduced as a rival of Ichabod's to instruct her in psalmody.

In this way matters went on for some time, without producing any material effect on the relative situation of the contending powers. On a fine autumnal afternoon, Ichabod, in pensive mood, sat enthroned on the lofty stool whence he usually watched all the concerns of his little literary realm. In his hand he swayed a ferule, that sceptre of despotic power; the birch of justice reposed on three nails, behind the throne, a constant terror to evil doers; while on the desk before him might be seen sundry contraband articles, and prohibited weapons, detected upon the persons of idle urchins; such as half-munched apples, popguns, whirligigs, fly-cages, and whole legions of rampant little paper game-cocks. Apparently there had been some appalling act of justice recently inflicted, for his scholars were all busily intent upon their books, or slyly whispering behind them with one eye kept upon the master; and a kind of buzzing stillness reigned throughout the schoolroom. It was suddenly interrupted by the appearance of a negro, in tow-cloth jacket and trowsers, a round-crowned fragment of a hat, like the cap of Mercury,[5] and mounted on the back of a ragged, wild, half-broken colt, which he managed with a rope by way of halter. He came clattering up to the school door with an invitation to Ichabod to attend a merry-making or "quilting frolic," to be held that evening at Mynheer Van Tassel's; and having delivered his message with that air of importance, and effort at fine language, which a negro is apt to display on petty embassies of the kind, he dashed over the brook, and was seen scampering away up the hollow, full of the importance and hurry of his mission.

All was now bustle and hubbub in the late quiet schoolroom. The scholars were hurried through their lessons, without stopping at trifles; those who were nimble skipped over half with impunity, and those who were tardy, had a smart application now and then in the rear, to quicken their speed, or help them over a tall word. Books were flung aside without being put away on the shelves, inkstands were overturned, benches thrown down, and the whole school was turned loose an hour before the usual time, bursting forth like a legion of young imps, yelping and racketing about the green, in joy at their early emancipation.

The gallant Ichabod now spent at least an extra hour at his toilet, brushing and furbishing up his best, and indeed only suit of rusty black, and arranging his looks by a bit of broken looking-glass, that hung up in the school-house. That he might make his appearance before his mistress in the true style of a cavalier, he borrowed a horse from the farmer with

---

[5] The Roman messenger-god wore a winged helmet.

whom he was domiciliated, a choleric old Dutchman, of the name of Hans Van Ripper, and, thus gallantly mounted, issued forth, like a knight-errant in quest of adventures. But it is meet I should, in the true spirit of romantic story, give some account of the looks and equipments of my hero and his steed. The animal he bestrode was a broken-down plough-horse, that had outlived almost every thing but his viciousness. He was gaunt and shagged, with a ewe neck and a head like a hammer; his rusty mane and tail was tangled and knotted with burrs; one eye had lost its pupil, and was glaring and spectral; but the other had the gleam of a genuine devil in it. Still he must have had fire and mettle in his day, if we may judge from the name he bore of Gunpowder. He had, in fact, been a favorite steed of his master's, the choleric Van Ripper, who was a furious rider, and had infused, very probably, some of his own spirit into the animal; for, old and broken-down as he looked, there was more of the lurking devil in him than in any young filly in the country.

Ichabod was a suitable figure for such a steed. He rode with short stirrups, which brought his knees nearly up to the pommel of the saddle; his sharp elbows stuck out like grasshoppers'; he carried his whip perpendicularly in his hand, like a sceptre, and, as his horse jogged on, the motion of his arms was not unlike the flapping of a pair of wings. A small wool hat rested on the top of his nose, for so his scanty strip of forehead might be called; and the skirts of his black coat fluttered out almost to the horse's tail. Such was the appearance of Ichabod and his steed, as they shambled out of the gate of Hans Van Ripper, and it was altogether such an apparition as is seldom to be met with in broad daylight.

It was, as I have said, a fine autumnal day, the sky was clear and serene, and nature wore that rich and golden livery which we always associate with the idea of abundance. The forests had put on their sober brown and yellow, while some trees of the tenderer kind had been nipped by the frosts into brilliant dyes of orange, purple, and scarlet. Streaming files of wild ducks began to make their appearance high in the air; the bark of the squirrel might be heard from the groves of beech and hickory nuts, and the pensive whistle of the quail at intervals from the neighboring stubble-field.

The small birds were taking their farewell banquets. In the fulness of their revelry, they fluttered, chirping and frolicking, from bush to bush, and tree to tree, capricious from the very profusion and variety around them. There was the honest cock-robin, the favorite game of stripling sportsmen, with its loud querulous note; and the twittering blackbirds flying in sable clouds; and the golden-winged woodpecker, with his crimson crest, his broad black gorget, and splendid plumage; and the cedar bird, with its red-tipt wings and yellow-tipt tail, and its little monteiro cap of feathers; and the blue jay, that noisy coxcomb, in his gay light-blue coat and white underclothes; screaming and chattering, nodding and bobbing and bowing, and pretending to be on good terms with every songster of the grove.

As Ichabod jogged slowly on his way, his eye, ever open to every symptom of culinary abundance, ranged with delight over the treasures of jolly autumn. On all sides he beheld vast store of apples; some hanging in oppressive opulence on the trees; some gathered into baskets and barrels for the market; others heaped up in rich piles for the cider-press. Farther on he beheld great fields of Indian corn, with its golden ears peeping from their leafy coverts, and holding out the promise of cakes and hasty pudding; and the yellow pumpkins lying beneath them, turning up their fair round bellies to the sun, and giving ample prospects of the most luxurious of pies; and anon he passed the fragrant buckwheat fields, breathing the odor of the bee-hive, and as he beheld them, soft anticipations stole over his mind of dainty slapjacks, well buttered, and garnished with honey or treacle, by the delicate little dimpled hand of Katrina Van Tassel.

Thus feeding his mind with many sweet thoughts and "sugared suppositions," he journeyed along the sides of a range of hills which look out upon some of the goodliest scenes of the mighty Hudson. The sun gradually wheeled his broad disk down into the west. The wide bosom of the Tappan Zee lay motionless and glassy, excepting that here and there a gentle undulation waved and prolonged the blue shadow of the distant mountain. A few amber clouds floated in the sky, without a breath of air to move them. The horizon was of a fine golden tint, changing gradually into a pure apple green, and from that into the deep blue of the mid-heaven. A slanting ray lingered on the woody crests of the precipices that overhung some parts of the river, giving greater depth to the dark-gray and purple of their rocky sides. A sloop was loitering in the distance, dropping slowly down with the tide, her sail hanging uselessly against the mast; and as the reflection of the sky gleamed along the still water, it seemed as if the vessel was suspended in the air.

It was toward evening that Ichabod arrived at the castle of the Heer Van Tassel, which he found thronged with the pride and flower of the adjacent country. Old farmers, a spare leathern-faced race, in homespun coats and breeches, blue stockings, huge shoes, and magnificent pewter buckles. Their brisk withered little dames, in close crimped caps, long-waisted shortgowns, homespun petticoats, with scissors and pin-cushions, and gay calico pockets hanging on the outside. Buxom lasses, almost as antiquated as their mothers, excepting where a straw hat, a fine ribbon, or perhaps a white frock, gave symptoms of city innovation. The sons, in short square-skirted coats with rows of stupendous brass buttons, and their hair generally queued in the fashion of the times, especially if they could procure an eel-skin for the purpose, it being esteemed throughout the country, as a potent nourisher and strengthener of the hair.

Brom Bones, however, was the hero of the scene, having come to the gathering on his favorite steed Daredevil, a creature, like himself, full of mettle and mischief, and which no one but himself could manage. He was, in fact, noted for preferring vicious animals, given to all kinds of tricks, which kept the rider in constant risk of his neck, for he held a tractable well-broken horse as unworthy of a lad of spirit.

Fain would I pause to dwell upon the world of charms that burst upon the enraptured gaze of my hero, as he entered the state parlor of Van Tassel's mansion. Not those of the bevy of buxom lasses, with their luxurious display of red and white; but the ample charms of a genuine Dutch country tea-table, in the sumptuous time of autumn. Such heaped-up platters of cakes of various and almost indescribable kinds, known only to experienced Dutch housewives! There was the doughty dough-nut, the tenderer oly koek, and the crisp and crumbling cruller; sweet cakes and short cakes, ginger cakes and honey cakes, and the whole family of cakes. And then there were apple pies and peach pies and pumpkin pies; besides slices of ham and smoked beef; and moreover delectable dishes of preserved plums, and peaches, and pears, and quinces; not to mention broiled shad and roasted chicken; together with bowls of milk and cream, all mingled higgledy-piggledy, pretty much as I have enumerated them, with the motherly tea-pot sending up its clouds of vapor from the midst — Heaven bless the mark! I want breath and time to discuss this banquet as it deserves, and am too eager to get on with my story. Happily, Ichabod Crane was not in so great a hurry as his historian, but did ample justice to every dainty.

He was a kind and thankful creature, whose heart dilated in proportion as his skin was filled with good cheer; and whose spirits rose with eating as some men's do with drink. He could not help, too, rolling his large eyes round him as he ate, and chuckling with the possibility that he might one day be lord of all this scene of almost unimaginable luxury and splendor. Then, he thought, how soon he'd turn his back upon the old school-house; snap his fingers in the face of Hans Van Ripper, and every other niggardly patron, and kick any itinerant pedagogue out of doors that should dare to call him comrade!

Old Baltus Van Tassel moved about among his guests with a face dilated with content and good humor, round and jolly as the harvest moon. His hospitable attentions were brief, but expressive, being confined to a shake of a hand, a slap on the shoulder, a loud laugh, and a pressing invitation to "fall to, and help themselves."

And now the sound of the music from the common room, or hall, summoned to the dance. The musician was an old grayheaded negro, who had been the itinerant orchestra of the neighborhood for more than half a century. His instrument was as old and battered as himself. The greater part of the time he scraped on two or three strings, accompanying every movement of the bow with a motion of the head; bowing almost to the ground, and stamping with his foot whenever a fresh couple were to start.

Ichabod prided himself upon his dancing as much as upon his vocal powers. Not a limb, not a fibre about him was idle; and to have seen his loosely hung frame in full motion, and clattering about the room, you would have thought Saint Vitus himself, that blessed patron of the dance, was figuring before you in person. He was the admiration of all the negroes; who, having gathered, of all ages and sizes, from the farm and the neighborhood, stood forming a pyramid of shining black faces at every door and window, gazing with delight at the scene, rolling their white eye-balls, and showing grinning rows of ivory from ear to ear. How could the flogger of urchins be otherwise than animated and joyous? the lady of his heart was his partner in the dance, and smiling graciously in reply to all his amorous oglings; while Brom Bones, sorely smitten with love and jealousy, sat brooding by himself in one corner.

When the dance was at an end, Ichabod was attracted to a knot of the sager folks, who, with old Van Tassel, sat smoking at one end of the piazza, gossiping over former times, and drawing out long stories about the war.

This neighborhood, at the time of which I am speaking, was one of those highly-favored places which abound with chronicle and great men. The British and American line had run near it during the war; it had, therefore, been the scene of marauding, and infested with refugees, cow-boys, and all kinds of border chivalry. Just sufficient time had elapsed to enable each story-teller to dress up his tale with a little becoming fiction, and, in the indistinctness of his recollection, to make himself the hero of every exploit.

There was the story of Doffue Martling, a large blue-bearded Dutchman, who had nearly taken a British frigate with an old iron nine-pounder from a mud breastwork, only that his gun burst at the sixth discharge. And there was an old gentleman who shall be nameless, being too rich a mynheer[6] to be lightly mentioned, who, in the battle of Whiteplains, being an excellent master of defence, parried a musket ball with a small sword, insomuch that he absolutely felt it whiz round the blade, and glance off at the hilt: in proof of which he was ready at any time to show the sword, with the hilt a little bent. There were several more that had been equally great in the field, not one of whom but was persuaded that he had a considerable hand in bringing the war to a happy termination.

But all these were nothing to the tales of ghosts and apparitions that succeeded. The neighborhood is rich in legendary treasures of the kind. Local tales and superstitions thrive best in these sheltered long-settled retreats; but are trampled under foot by the shifting throng that forms the population of most of our country places. Besides, there is no encouragement for ghosts in most of our villages, for they have scarcely had time to finish their first nap, and

---

[6] Gentleman; sir.

turn themselves in their graves, before their surviving friends have travelled away from the neighborhood; so that when they turn out at night to walk their rounds, they have no acquaintance left to call upon. This is perhaps the reason why we so seldom hear of ghosts except in our long-established Dutch communities.

The immediate cause, however, of the prevalence of supernatural stories in these parts, was doubtless owing to the vicinity of Sleepy Hollow. There was a contagion in the very air that blew from that haunted region; it breathed forth an atmosphere of dreams and fancies infecting all the land. Several of the Sleepy Hollow people were present at Van Tassel's, and, as usual, were doling out their wild and wonderful legends. Many dismal tales were told about funeral trains, and mourning cries and wailings heard and seen about the great tree where the unfortunate Major André[7] was taken, and which stood in the neighborhood. Some mention was made also of the woman in white, that haunted the dark glen at Raven Rock, and was often heard to shriek on winter nights before a storm, having perished there in the snow. The chief part of the stories, however, turned upon the favorite spectre of Sleepy Hollow, the headless horseman, who had been heard several times of late, patrolling the country; and, it was said, tethered his horse nightly among the graves in the church-yard.

The sequestered situation of this church seems always to have made it a favorite haunt of troubled spirits. It stands on a knoll, surrounded by locust-trees and lofty elms, from among which its decent whitewashed walls shine modestly forth, like Christian purity beaming through the shades of retirement. A gentle slope descends from it to a silver sheet of water, bordered by high trees, between which, peeps may be caught at the blue hills of the Hudson. To look upon its grass-grown yard, where the sunbeams seem to sleep so quietly, one would think that there at least the dead might rest in peace. On one side of the church extends a wide woody dell, along which raves a large brook among broken rocks and trunks of fallen trees. Over a deep black part of the stream, not far from the church, was formerly thrown a wooden bridge; the road that led to it, and the bridge itself, were thickly shaded by overhanging trees, which cast a gloom about it, even in the daytime; but occasioned a fearful darkness at night. This was one of the favorite haunts of the headless horseman; and the place where he was most frequently encountered. The tale was told of old Brouwer, a most heretical disbeliever in ghosts, how he met the horseman returning from his foray into Sleepy Hollow, and was obliged to get up behind him; how they galloped over bush and brake, over hill and swamp, until they reached the bridge; when the horseman suddenly turned into a skeleton, threw old Brouwer into the brook, and sprang away over the tree-tops with a clap of thunder.

This story was immediately matched by a thrice marvellous adventure of Brom Bones, who made light of the galloping Hessian as an arrant jockey. He affirmed that, on returning one night from the neighboring village of Sing Sing, he had been overtaken by this midnight trooper; that he had offered to race with him for a bowl of punch, and should have won it too, for Daredevil beat the goblin-horse all hollow, but, just as they came to the church-bridge, the Hessian bolted, and vanished in a flash of fire.

All these tales, told in that drowsy undertone with which men talk in the dark, the countenances of the listeners only now and then receiving a casual gleam from the glare of a pipe, sank deep in the mind of Ichabod. He repaid them in kind with large extracts from his invaluable author, Cotton Mather, and added many marvellous events that had taken place in his native State of Connecticut, and fearful sights which he had seen in his nightly walks about Sleepy Hollow.

---

[7] John André was hanged as a British spy in the Revolutionary War.

The revel now gradually broke up. The old farmers gathered together their families in their wagons, and were heard for some time rattling along the hollow roads, and over the distant hills. Some of the damsels mounted on pillions behind their favorite swains, and their light-hearted laughter, mingling with the clatter of hoofs, echoed along the silent woodlands, sounding fainter and fainter until they gradually died away — and the late scene of noise and frolic was all silent and deserted. Ichabod only lingered behind, according to the custom of country lovers to have tête-à-tête with the heiress, fully convinced that he was now on the high road to success. What passed at this interview I will not pretend to say, for in fact I do not know. Something, however, I fear me, must have gone wrong, for he certainly sallied forth, after no very great interval, with an air quite desolate and chop-fallen. — Oh these women! these women! Could that girl have been playing off any of her coquettish tricks? — Was her encouragement of the poor pedagogue all a mere sham to secure her conquest of his rival? — Heaven only knows, not I! — Let it suffice to say, Ichabod stole forth with the air of one who had been sacking a hen-roost, rather than a fair lady's heart. Without looking to the right or left to notice the scene of rural wealth, on which he had so often gloated, he went straight to the stable, and with several hearty cuffs and kicks, roused his steed most uncourteously from the comfortable quarters in which he was soundly sleeping, dreaming of mountains of corn and oats, and whole valleys of timothy and clover.

It was the very witching time of night that Ichabod, heavy-hearted and crest-fallen, pursued his travel homewards, along the sides of the lofty hills which rise about Tarry Town, and which he had traversed so cheerily in the afternoon. The hour was as dismal as himself. Far below him, the Tappan Zee spread its dusky and indistinct waste of waters, with here and there the tall mast of a sloop, riding quietly at anchor under the land. In the dead hush of midnight, he could even hear the barking of the watchdog from the opposite shore of the Hudson; but it was so vague and faint as only to give an idea of his distance from this faithful companion of man. Now and then, too, the long-drawn crowing of a cock, accidentally awakened, would sound far, far off, from some farmhouse away among the hills — but it was like a dreaming sound in his ear. No signs of life occurred near him, but occasionally the melancholy chirp of a cricket, or perhaps the guttural twang of a bullfrog, from a neighboring marsh, as if sleeping uncomfortably, and turning suddenly in his bed.

All the stories of ghosts and goblins that he had heard in the afternoon, now came crowding upon his recollection. The night grew darker and darker; the stars seemed to sink deeper in the sky, and driving clouds occasionally hid them from his sight. He had never felt so lonely and dismal. He was, moreover, approaching the very place where many of the scenes of the ghost stories had been laid. In the centre of the road stood an enormous tulip-tree, which towered like a giant above all the other trees of the neighborhood, and formed a kind of landmark. Its limbs were gnarled, and fantastic, large enough to form trunks for ordinary trees, twisting down almost to the earth, and rising again into the air. It was connected with the tragical story of the unfortunate André, who had been taken prisoner hard by; and was universally known by the name of Major André's tree. The common people regarded it with a mixture of respect and superstition, partly out of sympathy for the fate of its ill-starred namesake, and partly from the tales of strange sights and doleful lamentations told concerning it.

As Ichabod approached this fearful tree, he began to whistle: he thought his whistle was answered — it was but a blast sweeping sharply through the dry branches. As he approached a little nearer, he thought he saw something white, hanging in the midst of the tree — he paused and ceased whistling; but on looking more narrowly, perceived that it was a place where the tree had been scathed by lightning, and the white wood laid bare. Suddenly he heard a groan — his teeth chattered and his knees smote against the saddle: it was but the rippling of one huge bough upon another, as they were swayed about by the breeze. He passed the tree in safety, but new perils lay before him.

About two hundred yards from the tree a small brook crossed the road, and ran into a marshy and thickly-wooded glen, known by the name of Wiley's swamp. A few rough logs, laid side by side, served for a bridge over this stream. On that side of the road where the brook entered the wood, a group of oaks and chestnuts, matted thick with wild grapevines, threw a cavernous gloom over it. To pass this bridge was the severest trial. It was at this identical spot that the unfortunate André was captured, and under the covert of those chestnuts and vines were the sturdy yeomen concealed who surprised him. This has ever since been considered a haunted stream, and fearful are the feelings of the schoolboy who has to pass it alone after dark.

As he approached the stream his heart began to thump; he summoned up, however, all his resolution, gave his horse half a score of kicks in the ribs, and attempted to dash briskly across the bridge; but instead of starting forward, the perverse old animal made a lateral movement, and ran broadside against the fence. Ichabod, whose fears increased with the delay, jerked the reins on the other side, and kicked lustily with the contrary foot: it was all in vain; his steed started, it is true, but it was only to plunge to the opposite side of the road into a thicket of brambles and alder bushes. The schoolmaster now bestowed both whip and heel upon the starveling ribs of old Gunpowder, who dashed forward, snuffling and snorting, but came to a stand just by the bridge, with a suddenness that had nearly sent his rider sprawling over his head. Just at this moment a plashy tramp by the side of the bridge caught the sensitive ear of Ichabod. In the dark shadow of the grove, on the margin of the brook, he beheld something huge, misshapen, black and towering. It stirred not, but seemed gathered up in the gloom, like some gigantic monster ready to spring upon the traveller.

The hair of the affrighted pedagogue rose upon his head with terror. What was to be done? To turn and fly was now too late; and besides, what chance was there of escaping ghost or goblin, if such it was, which could ride upon the wings of the wind? Summoning up, therefore, a show of courage, he demanded in stammering accents — "Who are you?" He received no reply. He repeated his demand in a still more agitated voice. Still there was no answer. Once more he cudgelled the sides of the inflexible Gunpowder, and, shutting his eyes, broke forth with involuntary fervor into a psalm tune. Just then the shadowy object of alarm put itself in motion, and, with a scramble and a bound, stood at once in the middle of the road. Though the night was dark and dismal, yet the form of the unknown might now in some degree be ascertained. He appeared to be a horseman of large dimensions, and mounted on a black horse of powerful frame. He made no offer of molestation or sociability, but kept aloof on one side of the road, jogging along on the blind side of old Gunpowder, who had now got over his fright and waywardness.

Ichabod, who had no relish for this strange midnight companion, and bethought himself of the adventure of Brom Bones with the Galloping Hessian, now quickened his steed, in hopes of leaving him behind. The stranger, however, quickened his horse to an equal pace. Ichabod pulled up, and fell into a walk, thinking to lag behind — the other did the same. His heart began to sink within him; he endeavored to resume his psalm tune, but his parched tongue clove to the roof of his mouth, and he could not utter a stave. There was something in the moody and dogged silence of this pertinacious companion, that was mysterious and appalling. It was soon fearfully accounted for. On mounting a rising ground, which brought the figure of his fellow-traveller in relief against the sky, gigantic in height, and muffled in a cloak, Ichabod was horror-struck, on perceiving that he was headless! — but his horror was still more increased, on observing that the head, which should have rested on his shoulders, was carried before him on the pommel of the saddle: his terror rose to desperation; he rained a shower of kicks and blows upon Gunpowder, hoping, by a sudden movement, to give his companion the slip — but the spectre started full jump with him. Away then they dashed, through thick and thin; stones flying, and sparks flashing at every bound. Ichabod's flimsy garments fluttered in the air, as he stretched his long lank body away over his horse's head, in the eagerness of his flight.

They had now reached the road which turns off to Sleepy Hollow; but Gunpowder, who seemed possessed with a demon, instead of keeping up it, made an opposite turn, and plunged headlong down hill to the left. This road leads through a sandy hollow, shaded by trees for about a quarter of a mile, where it crosses the bridge famous in goblin story, and just beyond swells the green knoll on which stands the whitewashed church.

As yet the panic of the steed had given his unskilful rider an apparent advantage in the chase; but just as he had got half way through the hollow, the girths of the saddle gave way, and he felt it slipping from under him. He seized it by the pommel, and endeavored to hold it firm, but in vain; and had just time to save himself by clasping old Gunpowder round the neck, when the saddle fell to the earth, and he heard it trampled under foot by his pursuer. For a moment the terror of Hans Van Ripper's wrath passed across his mind — for it was his Sunday saddle; but this was no time for petty fears; the goblin was hard on his haunches; and (unskilful rider that he was!) he had much ado to maintain his seat; sometimes slipping on one side, sometimes on another, and sometimes jolted on the high ridge of his horse's back-bone, with a violence that he verily feared would cleave him asunder.

An opening in the trees now cheered him with the hopes that the church bridge was at hand. The wavering reflection of a silver star in the bosom of the brook told him that he was not mistaken. He saw the walls of the church dimly glaring under the trees beyond. He recollected the place where Brom Bone's ghostly competitor had disappeared. "If I can but reach the bridge," thought Ichabod, "I am safe." Just then he heard the black steed panting and blowing close behind him; he even fancied that he felt his hot breath. Another convulsive kick in the ribs and old Gunpowder sprang upon the bridge; he thundered over the resounding planks; he gained the opposite side; and now Ichabod cast a look behind to see if his pursuer should vanish, according to rule, in a flash of fire and brimstone. Just then he saw the goblin rising in his stirrups, and in the very act of hurling his head at him. Ichabod endeavored to dodge the horrible missile, but too late. It encountered his cranium with a tremendous crash — he was tumbled headlong into the dust, and Gunpowder, the black steed, and the goblin rider, passed by like a whirlwind.

The next morning the old horse was found without his saddle, and with the bridle under his feet, soberly cropping the grass at his master's gate. Ichabod did not make his appearance at breakfast — dinner-hour came, but no Ichabod. The boys assembled at the school-house, and strolled idly about the banks of the brook; but no schoolmaster. Hans Van Ripper now began to feel some uneasiness about the fate of poor Ichabod, and his saddle. An inquiry was set on foot, and after diligent investigation they came upon his traces. In one part of the road leading to the church was found the saddle trampled in the dirt; the tracks of horses' hoofs deeply dented in the road, and evidently at furious speed, were traced to the bridge, beyond which, on the bank of a broad part of the brook, where the water ran deep and black, was found the hat of the unfortunate Ichabod, and close beside it a shattered pumpkin.

The brook was searched, but the body of the schoolmaster was not to be discovered. Hans Van Ripper, as executor of his estate, examined the bundle which contained all his worldly effects. They consisted of two shirts and a half; two stocks for the neck; a pair or two of worsted stockings; an old pair of corduroy small-clothes; a rusty razor; a book of psalm tunes, full of dogs' ears; and a broken pitch-pipe. As to the books and furniture of the schoolhouse, they belonged to the community, excepting Cotton Mather's History of Witchcraft, a New England Almanac, and a book of dreams and fortune-telling; in which last was a sheet of foolscap much scribbled and blotted in several fruitless attempts to make a copy of verses in honor of the heiress of Van Tassel. These magic books and the poetic scrawl were forthwith consigned to the flames by Hans Van Ripper; who from that time forward determined to send his children no more to school; observing, that he never knew any good come of this same reading and writing. Whatever money the schoolmaster possessed, and he had received his quarter's pay but a day or two before, he must have had about his person at the time of his disappearance.

The mysterious event caused much speculation at the church on the following Sunday. Knots of gazers and gossips were collected in the church-yard, at the bridge, and at the spot where the hat and pumpkin had been found. The stories of Brouwer, of Bones, and a whole budget of others, were called to mind; and when they had diligently considered them all, and compared them with the symptoms of the present case, they shook their heads, and came to the conclusion that Ichabod had been carried off by the Galloping Hessian. As he was a bachelor, and in nobody's debt, nobody troubled his head any more about him. The school was removed to a different quarter of the hollow, and another pedagogue reigned in his stead.

It is true, an old farmer, who had been down to New York on a visit several years after, and from whom this account of the ghostly adventure was received, brought home the intelligence that Ichabod Crane was still alive; that he had left the neighborhood, partly through fear of the goblin and Hans Van Ripper, and partly in mortification at having been suddenly dismissed by the heiress; that he had changed his quarters to a distant part of the country; had kept school and studied law at the same time, had been admitted to the bar, turned politician, electioneered, written for the newspapers, and finally had been made a justice of the Ten Pound Court. Brom Bones too, who, shortly after his rival's disappearance, conducted the blooming Katrina in triumph to the altar, was observed to look exceedingly knowing whenever the story of Ichabod was related, and always burst into a hearty laugh at the mention of the pumpkin; which led some to suspect that he knew more about the matter than he chose to tell.

The old country wives, however, who are the best judges of these matters, maintain to this day that Ichabod was spirited away by supernatural means; and it is a favorite story often told about the neighborhood round the winter evening fire. The bridge became more than ever an object of superstitious awe, and that may be the reason why the road has been altered of late years, so as to approach the church by the border of the mill-pond. The schoolhouse being deserted, soon fell to decay, and was reported to be haunted by the ghost of the unfortunate pedagogue; and the plough boy, loitering homeward of a still summer evening, has often fancied his voice at a distance, chanting a melancholy psalm tune among the tranquil solitudes of Sleepy Hollow.

POSTSCRIPT, FOUND IN THE HANDWRITING OF MR. KNICKERBOCKER

The preceding Tale is given, almost in the precise words in which I heard it related at a Corporation meeting of the ancient city of Manhattoes, at which were present many of its sagest and most illustrious burghers. The narrator was a pleasant, shabby, gentlemanly old fellow, in pepper-and-salt clothes, with a sadly humorous face; and one whom I strongly suspected of being poor, — he made such efforts to be entertaining. When his story was concluded, there was much laughter and approbation, particularly from two or three deputy aldermen, who had been asleep the greater part of the time. There was, however, one tall, dry-looking old gentleman, with beetling eyebrows, who maintained a grave and rather severe face throughout: now and then folding his arms, inclining his head, and looking down upon the floor, as if turning a doubt over in his mind. He was one of your wary men, who never laugh, but upon good grounds — when they have reason and the law on their side. When the mirth of the rest of the company had subsided, and silence was restored, he leaned one arm on the elbow of his chair, and sticking the other akimbo, demanded, with a slight, but exceedingly sage motion of the head, and contraction of the brow, what was the moral of the story, and what it went to prove?

The story-teller, who was just putting a glass of wine to his lips, as a refreshment after his toils, paused for a moment, looked at his inquirer with an air of infinite deference, and, lowering the glass slowly to the table, observed, that the story was intended most logically to prove: —

"That there is no situation in life but has its advantages and pleasures — providing we will but take a joke as we find it:

"That, therefore, he that runs races with goblin troopers is likely to have rough riding of it.

"Ergo, for a country schoolmaster to be refused the hand of a Dutch heiress, is a certain step to high preferment, in the state."

The cautious old gentleman knit his brows tenfold closer after this explanation, being sorely puzzled by the ratiocination of the syllogism; while, methought, the one in pepper-and-salt eyed him with something of a triumphant leer. At length he observed, that all this was very well, but still he thought the story a little on the extravagant — there were one or two points on which he had his doubts.

"Faith, sir," replied the story-teller, "as to that matter, I don't believe one-half of it myself."

D.K.

QUESTIONS

1. Irving claims that his story comes from the hand of one Diedrich Knickerbocker, who in turn "heard it related at a Corporation meeting." What is the effect of this double removal of the narrator from the story?

2. What is the setting of this story? How does the setting contribute to the difficulties Ichabod experiences? To what extent does the American Revolution impinge on the tale?

3. Ichabod Crane has become a memorable character in fiction. Why do you think this is so? Is he an entirely ridiculous person?

4. By what means does Irving make Ichabod a comic character? Are the Dutch less comic? Is the narrator's attitude toward his characters genial, or is it mocking? Do these old colonists and their occupations have redeeming qualities? Does Brom Bones?

5. How do the author's diction and tone contribute to the humorous effect of the story?

6. What actually happens to Ichabod in the graveyard? Does Irving leave any room for speculation?

HONORÉ DE BALZAC

A Passion in the Desert

Translated by Ellen Marriage

I was at the menagerie.

The first time I saw Monsieur Martin enter the cages I uttered an exclamation of surprise. I found myself next to an old soldier with the right leg amputated, who had come in with me. His face had attracted my attention. He had one of those intrepid heads, stamped with the seal of warfare, and on which the battles of Napoleon are written. Besides, he had that frank good-humored expression that always impresses me favorably. He was without doubt one of those troopers who are surprised at nothing, who find matter for laughter in the contortions of a dying comrade, who bury or plunder him quite lightheartedly, who stand intrepidly in the way of bullets; — in fact, one of those men who waste no time in deliberation, and would not hesitate to make friends with the devil himself. After looking very attentively at the proprietor of the menagerie getting out of his box, my companion pursed up his lips with an air of mockery and contempt, with that peculiar and expressive twist which superior people assume to show they are not taken in. Then, when I was expatiating on the courage of Monsieur Martin, he smiled, shook his head knowingly, and said, "Easy enough!"

"How 'easy enough'?" I said. "If you would only explain me the mystery I should be obliged."

After a few minutes, during which we made acquaintance, we went to dine at the first *restaurateur's* whose shop caught our eye. At dessert a bottle of champagne completely refreshed and brightened up the memories of this odd old soldier. He told me his story as follows: —

During the expedition in Upper Egypt under General Desaix, a Provençal soldier fell into the hands of the Mangrabins, and was taken by these Arabs into the deserts beyond the falls of the Nile.

In order to place a sufficient distance between themselves and the French army, the Mangrabins made forced marches and only rested during the night. They camped round a well overshadowed by palm trees under which they had previously concealed a store of provisions. Not surmising that the notion of flight would occur to their prisoner, they contented themselves with binding his hands, and after eating a few dates, and giving provender to their horses, went to sleep.

When the brave Provençal saw that his enemies were no longer watching him, he made use of his teeth to steal a scimitar, fixed the blade between his knees, and cut the cords which

19

prevented him using his hands; in a moment he was free. He at once seized a rifle and a dagger, then taking the precaution to provide himself with a sack of dried dates, oats, and powder and shot, and to fasten a scimitar to his waist, he leaped on to a horse and spurred on vigorously in the direction where he thought to find the French army. So impatient was he to see a bivouac again that he pressed on the already tired courser at such speed that its flanks were lacerated with his spurs, and at last the poor animal died, leaving the Frenchman alone in the desert.

After walking some time in the sand with all the courage of an escaped convict, the soldier was obliged to stop, as the day had already ended. In spite of the beauty of an oriental sky at night, he felt he had not strength enough to go on. Fortunately he had been able to find a small hill, on the summit of which a few palm trees shot up into the air; it was their verdure seen from afar which had brought hope and consolation to his heart. His fatigue was so great that he lay down upon a rock of granite, capriciously cut out like a camp-bed; there he fell asleep without taking any precaution to defend himself while he slept. He had made the sacrifice of his life. His last thought was one of regret. He repented having left the Mangrabins, whose nomad life seemed to smile on him now that he was far from them and without help. He was awakened by the sun, whose pitiless rays fell with all their force on the granite and produced an intolerable heat — for he had had the stupidity to place himself inversely to the shadow thrown by the verdant majestic heads of the palm trees. He looked at the solitary trees and shuddered — they reminded him of the graceful shafts crowned with foliage which characterize the Saracen columns in the cathedral of Arles.

But when, after counting the palm trees, he cast his eyes around him, the most horrible despair was infused into his soul. Before him stretched an ocean without limit. The dark sand of the desert spread further than sight could reach in every direction, and glittered like steel struck with bright light. It might have been a sea of looking-glass, or lakes melted together in a mirror. A fiery vapor carried up in streaks made a perpetual whirlwind over the quivering land. The sky was lit with an oriental splendor of insupportable purity, leaving naught for the imagination to desire. Heaven and earth were on fire.

The silence was awful in its wild and terrible majesty. Infinity, immensity, closed in upon the soul from every side. Not a cloud in the sky, not a breath in the air, not a flaw on the bosom of the sand, ever moving in diminutive waves; the horizon ended as at sea on a clear day, with one line of light, definite as the cut of a sword.

The Provençal threw his arms round the trunk of one of the palm trees, as though it were the body of a friend, and then in the shelter of the thin straight shadow that the palm cast upon the granite, he wept. Then sitting down he remained as he was, contemplating with profound sadness the implacable scene, which was all he had to look upon. He cried aloud, to measure the solitude. His voice, lost in the hollows of the hill, sounded faintly and aroused no echo — the echo was in his heart. The Provençal was twenty-two years old: — he loaded his carbine.

"There'll be time enough," he said to himself, laying on the ground the weapon which alone could bring him deliverance.

Looking by turns at the black expanse and the blue expanse, the soldier dreamed of France — he smelled with delight the gutters of Paris — he remembered the towns through which he had passed, the faces of his fellow-soldiers, the most minute details of his life. His southern fancy soon showed him the stones of his beloved Provence, in the play of the heat which waved over the spread sheet of the desert. Fearing the danger of this cruel mirage, he went down the opposite side of the hill to that by which he had come up the day before. The remains of a rug showed that this place of refuge had at one time been inhabited; at a short distance he saw some palm trees full of dates. Then the instinct which binds us to life awoke again in his heart. He hoped to live long enough to await the passing of some Arabs, or perhaps he might hear the sound of cannon; for at this time Bonaparte was traversing Egypt.

This thought gave him new life. The palm tree seemed to bend with the weight of the ripe fruit. He shook some of it down. When he tasted this unhoped-for manna, he felt sure that the palms had been cultivated by a former inhabitant — the savory, fresh meat of the dates was proof of the care of his predecessor. He passed suddenly from dark despair to an almost insane joy. He went up again to the top of the hill, and spent the rest of the day in cutting down one of the sterile palm trees, which the night before had served him for shelter. A vague memory made him think of the animals of the desert; and in case they might come to drink at the spring, visible from the base of the rocks but lost further down, he resolved to guard himself from their visits by placing a barrier at the entrance of his hermitage.

In spite of his diligence, and the strength which the fear of being devoured asleep gave him, he was unable to cut the palm in pieces, though he succeeded in cutting it down. At eventide the king of the desert fell; the sound of its fall resounded far and wide, like a sigh in the solitude; the soldier shuddered as though he had heard some voice predicting woe.

But like an heir who does not long bewail a deceased parent, he tore off from this beautiful tree the tall broad green leaves which are its poetic adornment, and used them to mend the mat on which he was to sleep.

Fatigued by the heat and his work, he fell asleep under the red curtains of his wet cave.

In the middle of the night his sleep was troubled by an extraordinary noise; he sat up, and the deep silence around allowed him to distinguish the alternative accents of a respiration whose savage energy could not belong to a human creature.

A profound terror, increased still further by the darkness, the silence, and his waking images, froze his heart within him. He almost felt his hair stand on end, when by straining his eyes to their utmost he perceived through the shadow two faint yellow lights. At first he attributed these lights to the reflection of his own pupils, but soon the vivid brilliance of the night aided him gradually to distinguish the objects around him in the cave, and he beheld a huge animal lying but two steps from him. Was it a lion, a tiger, or a crocodile?

The Provençal was not educated enough to know under what species his enemy ought to be classed; but his fright was all the greater, as his ignorance led him to imagine all terrors at once; he endured a cruel torture, noting every variation of the breathing close to him without daring to make the slightest movement. An odor, pungent like that of a fox, but more penetrating, profounder — so to speak — filled the cave, and when the Provençal became sensible of this, his terror reached its height, for he could no longer doubt the proximity of a terrible companion, whose royal dwelling served him for a shelter.

Presently the reflection of the moon descending on the horizon lit up the den, rendering gradually visible and resplendent the spotted skin of a panther.

This lion of Egypt slept, curled up like a big dog, the peaceful possessor of a sumptuous niche at the gate of a *hôtel;*[1] its eyes opened for a moment and closed again; its face was turned toward the man. A thousand confused thoughts passed through the Frenchman's mind; first he thought of killing it with a bullet from his gun, but he saw there was not enough distance between them for him to take proper aim — the shot would miss the mark. And if it were to wake! — the thought made his limbs rigid. He listened to his own heart beating in the midst of the silence, and cursed the too violent pulsations which the flow of blood brought on, fearing to disturb that sleep which allowed him time to think of some means of escape.

---

[1] Hotel or mansion.

Twice he placed his hand on his scimitar, intending to cut off the head of his enemy; but the difficulty of cutting the stiff short hair compelled him to abandon this daring project. To miss would be to die for *certain*, he thought; he preferred the chances of fair fight, and made up his mind to wait till morning; the morning did not leave him long to wait.

He could now examine the panther at ease; its muzzle was smeared with blood.

"She had a good dinner," he thought, without troubling himself as to whether her feast might have been on human flesh. "She won't be hungry when she gets up."

It was a female. The fur on her belly and flanks was glistening white; many small marks like velvet formed beautiful bracelets round her feet; her sinuous tail was also white, ending with black rings; the overpart of her dress, yellow like unburnished gold, very lissom and soft, had the characteristic blotches in the form of rosettes, which distinguish the panther from every other feline species.

This tranquil and formidable hostess snored in an attitude as graceful as that of a cat lying on a cushion. Her blood-stained paws, nervous and well armed, were stretched out before her face, which rested upon them, and from which radiated her straight slender whiskers, like threads of silver.

If she had been like that in a cage, the Provençal would doubtless have admired the grace of the animal, and the vigorous contrasts of vivid color which gave her robe an imperial splendor; but just then his sight was troubled by her sinister appearance.

The presence of the panther, even asleep, could not fail to produce the effect which the magnetic eyes of the serpent are said to have on the nightingale.

For a moment the courage of the soldier began to fail before this danger, though no doubt it would have risen at the mouth of a cannon charged with shell. Nevertheless, a bold thought brought daylight to his soul and sealed up the source of the cold sweat which sprang forth on his brow. Like men driven to bay, who defy death and offer their body to the smiter, so he, seeing in this merely a tragic episode, resolved to play his part with honor to the last.

"The day before yesterday the Arabs would have killed me perhaps," he said; so considering himself as good as dead already, he waited bravely, with excited curiosity, his enemy's awakening.

When the sun appeared, the panther suddenly opened her eyes; then she put out her paws with energy, as if to stretch them and get rid of cramp. At last she yawned, showing the formidable apparatus of her teeth and pointed tongue, rough as a file.

She licked off the blood which stained her paws and muzzle, and scratched her head with reiterated gestures full of prettiness.

"All right, make a little toilet," the Frenchman said to himself, beginning to recover his gayety with his courage; "we'll say good-morning to each other presently," and he seized the small short dagger which he had taken from the Mangrabins. At this moment the panther turned her head toward the man and looked at him fixedly without moving.

The rigidity of her metallic eyes and their insupportable luster made him shudder, especially when the animal walked toward him. But he looked at her caressingly, staring into her eyes in order to magnetize her, and let her come quite close to him; then with a movement both gentle and affectionate, as though he were caressing the most beautiful of women, he passed his hand over her whole body, from the head to the tail, scratching the flexible vertebrae which divided the panther's yellow back. The animal waved her tail, and her eyes grew gentle; and when for the third time the Frenchman accomplished this interested flattery, she gave forth one of those purrings by which our cats express their pleasure; but this murmur issued from a throat so powerful and so deep, that it resounded through the cave like the last vibrations of an organ in a church. The man, understanding the importance of his caresses, redoubled them. When he felt sure of having extinguished the ferocity of his capricious companion, whose hunger had so fortunately been satisfied the day before, he got up to go out of the cave; the panther let him go out, but when he had reached the summit of the hill she sprang with the lightness of a sparrow hopping from twig to twig, and rubbed herself against his legs, putting up her back after the manner of all the race of cats. Then regarding her guest with eyes whose glare had softened a little, she gave vent to that wild cry which naturalists compare to the grating of a saw.

"She is exacting," said the Frenchman, smiling.

He was bold enough to play with her ears; he scratched her head as hard as he could. When he saw he was successful he tickled her skull with the point of his dagger, watching for the moment to kill her, but the hardness of her bones made him tremble for his success.

The sultana of the desert showed herself gracious to her slave; she lifted her head, stretched out her neck, and manifested her delight by the tranquility of her attitude. It suddenly occurred to the soldier that to kill this savage princess with one blow he must poniard her in the throat.

He raised the blade, when the panther, satisfied, no doubt, laid herself gracefully at his feet, and cast up at him glances in which, in spite of their natural fierceness, was mingled confusedly a kind of goodwill. The poor Provençal ate his dates, leaning against one of the palm trees, and casting his eyes alternately on the desert in quest of some liberator and on his terrible companion to watch her uncertain clemency.

The panther looked at the place where the date stones fell, and every time that he threw one down, her eyes expressed an incredible mistrust.

She examined the man with an almost commercial prudence. However, this examination was favorable to him, for when he had finished his meager meal she licked his boots with her powerful rough tongue, brushing off with marvelous skill the dust gathered in the creases.

"Ah, but when she's really hungry!" thought the Frenchman.

In spite of the shudder this thought caused him, the soldier began to measure curiously the proportions of the panther, certainly one of the most splendid specimens of its race. She was three feet high and four feet long without counting her tail; this powerful weapon, rounded like a cudgel, was nearly three feet long. The head, large as that of a lioness, was distinguished by a rare expression of refinement. The cold cruelty of a tiger was dominant, it was true, but there was also a vague resemblance to the face of a sensual woman.

Indeed, the face of this solitary queen had something of the gayety of a drunken Nero: she had satiated herself with blood, and she wanted to play.

The soldier tried if he might walk up and down, and the panther left him free, contenting herself with following him with her eyes, less like a faithful dog than a big Angora cat, observing everything, and every movement of her master.

When he looked round, he saw, by the spring, the remains of his horse; the panther had dragged the carcass all that way; about two-thirds of it had been devoured already. The sight reassured him.

It was easy to explain the panther's absence, and the respect she had had for him while he slept. The first piece of good luck emboldened him to tempt the future, and he conceived the wild hope of continuing on good terms with the panther during the entire day, neglecting no means of taming her and remaining in her good graces.

He returned to her, and had the unspeakable joy of seeing her wag her tail with an almost imperceptible movement at his approach. He sat down then, without fear, by her side, and they began to play together; he took her paws and muzzle, pulled her ears, rolled her over on her back, stroked her warm, delicate flanks. She let him do whatever he liked, and when he began to stroke the hair on her feet she drew her claws in carefully.

The man, keeping the dagger in one hand, thought to plunge it into the belly of the too confiding panther, but he was afraid that he would be immediately strangled in her last convulsive struggle; besides, he felt in his heart a sort of remorse which bid him respect a creature that had done him no harm. He seemed to have found a friend, in a boundless desert; half unconsciously he thought of his first sweetheart, whom he had nicknamed "Mignonne"[2] by way of contrast, because she was so atrociously jealous, that all the time of their love he was in fear of the knife with which she had always threatened him.

This memory of his early days suggested to him the idea of making the young panther answer to this name, now that he began to admire with less terror her swiftness, suppleness, and softness. Toward the end of the day he had familiarized himself with his perilous position; he now almost liked the painfulness of it. At last his companion had got into the habit of looking up at him whenever he cried in a falsetto voice, "Mignonne."

At the setting of the sun Mignonne gave, several times running, a profound melancholy cry.

"She's been well brought up," said the light-hearted soldier; "she says her prayers." But this mental joke only occurred to him when he noticed what a pacific attitude his companion remained in. "Come, *ma petite blonde*,[3] I'll let you go to bed first," he said to her, counting on the activity of his own legs to run away as quickly as possible, directly she was asleep, and seek another shelter for the night.

The soldier awaited with impatience the hour of his flight, and when it had arrived he walked vigorously in the direction of the Nile; but hardly had he made a quarter of a league in the sand when he heard the panther bounding after him, crying with that saw-like cry, more dreadful even than the sound of her leaping.

"Ah!" he said, "then she's taken a fancy to me; she has never met any one before, and it is really quite flattering to have her first love."

That instant the man fell into one of those movable quicksands so terrible to travelers and from which it is impossible to save one's self. Feeling himself caught, he gave a shriek of alarm; the panther seized him with her teeth by the collar and, springing vigorously backward, drew him, as if by magic, out of the whirling sand.

"Ah, Mignonne!" cried the soldier, caressing her enthusiastically; "we're bound together for life and death — but no jokes, mind!" and he retraced his steps.

From that time the desert seemed inhabited. It contained a being to whom the man could talk, and whose ferocity was rendered gentle by him, though he could not explain to himself the reason for their strange friendship. Great as was the soldier's desire to stay up on guard, he slept.

On awakening he could not find Mignonne; he mounted the hill, and in the distance saw her springing toward him after the habit of these animals, who cannot run on account of the extreme flexibility of the vertebral column. Mignonne arrived, her jaws covered with blood; she received the wonted caress of her companion, showing with much purring how happy it made her. Her eyes, full of languor, turned still more gently than the day before toward the Provençal, who talked to her as one would to a tame animal.

"Ah! mademoiselle, you are a nice girl, aren't you? Just look at that! so we like to be made much of, don't we? Aren't you ashamed of yourself? So you have been eating some Arab or other, have you? that doesn't matter. They're animals just the same as you are; but don't you take to eating Frenchmen, or I shan't like you any longer."

---

[2] "Precious."

[3] "My little blonde."

She played like a dog with its master, letting herself be rolled over, knocked about, and stroked, alternately; sometimes she herself would provoke the soldier, putting up her paw with a soliciting gesture.

Some days passed in this manner. This companionship permitted the Provençal to appreciate the sublime beauty of the desert; now that he had a living thing to think about, alternations of fear and quiet, and plenty to eat, his mind became filled with contrasts, and his life began to be diversified.

Solitude revealed to him all her secrets, and enveloped him in her delights. He discovered in the rising and setting of the sun sights unknown to the world. He knew what it was to tremble when he heard over his head the hiss of a bird's wings, so rarely did they pass, or when he saw the clouds, changing and many-colored travelers, melt into one another. He studied in the night time the effects of the moon upon the ocean of sand, where the simoom[4] made waves swift of movement and rapid in their change. He lived the life of the Eastern day, marveling at its wonderful pomp; then, after having reveled in the sight of a hurricane over the plain where the whirling sands made red, dry mists and death-bearing clouds, he would welcome the night with joy, for then fell the healthful freshness of the stars, and he listened to imaginary music in the skies. Then solitude taught him to unroll the treasures of dreams. He passed whole hours in remembering mere nothings, and comparing his present life with his past.

At last he grew passionately fond of the tigress; for some sort of affection was a necessity.

Whether it was that his will powerfully projected had modified the character of his companion, or whether, because she found abundant food in her predatory excursions in the deserts, she respected the man's life, he began to fear for it no longer, seeing her so well tamed.

He devoted the greater part of his time to sleep, but he was obliged to watch like a spider in its web that the moment of his deliverance might not escape him, if any one should pass the line marked by the horizon. He had sacrificed his shirt to make a flag with, which he hung at the top of a palm tree, whose foliage he had torn off. Taught by necessity, he found the means of keeping it spread out, by fastening it with little sticks; for the wind might not be blowing at the moment when the passing traveler was looking through the desert.

It was during the long hours, when he had abandoned hope, that he amused himself with the panther. He had come to learn the different inflections of her voice, the expressions of her eyes; he had studied the capricious patterns of all the rosettes which marked the gold of her robe. Mignonne was not even angry when he took hold of the tuft at the end of her tail to count the rings, those graceful ornaments which glittered in the sun like jewelry. It gave him pleasure to contemplate the supple, fine outlines of her form, the graceful pose of her head. But it was especially when she was playing that he felt most pleasure in looking at her; the agility and youthful lightness of her movements were a continual surprise to him; he wondered at the supple way in which she jumped and climbed, washed herself and arranged her fur, crouched down and prepared to spring. However rapid her spring might be, however slippery the stone she was on, she would always stop short at the word "Mignonne."

One day, in a bright midday sun, an enormous bird coursed through the air. The man left his panther to look at this new guest; but after waiting a moment the deserted sultana growled deeply.

"My goodness! I do believe she's jealous," he cried, seeing her eyes become hard again; "the soul of Virginie has passed into her body, that's certain."

The eagle disappeared into the air, while the soldier admired the curved contour of the panther.

---

[4] A suffocating, sand-blowing desert wind.

But there was such youth and grace in her form! she was beautiful as a woman! the blond fur of her robe mingled well with the delicate tints of faint white which marked her flanks.

The profuse light cast down by the sun made this living gold, these russet markings, to burn in a way to give them an indefinable attraction.

The man and the panther looked at one another with a look full of meaning; the coquette quivered when she felt her friend stroke her head; her eyes flashed like lightning — then she shut them tightly.

"She has a soul," he said, looking at the stillness of this queen of the sands, golden like them, white like them, solitary and burning like them.

Ah! how did it all end?

Alas; as all great passions do end — in a misunderstanding. From some reason *one* suspects the other of treason; they don't come to an explanation through pride, and quarrel and part from sheer obstinacy. Yet sometimes at the best moments a single word or a look is enough.

"Well," the old fellow continued, "with her sharp teeth she one day caught hold of my leg — gently, I dare-say; but I, thinking she would devour me, plunged my dagger into her throat. She rolled over, giving a cry that froze my heart; and I saw her dying, still looking at me without anger. I would have given all the world — my cross even, which I had not got then — to have brought her to life again. It was as though I had murdered a real person; and the soldiers who had seen my flag, and were come to my assistance, found me in tears.   ⸱

"Well, sir," he said, after a moment of silence, "since then I have been in war in Germany, in Spain, in Russia, in France; I've certainly carried my carcass about a good deal, but never have I seen anything like the desert. Ah! yes, it is very beautiful!"

"What did you feel there?" I asked him.

"Oh! that can't be described, young man! Besides, I am not always regretting my palm trees and my panther. I should have to be very melancholy for that. In the desert, you see, there is everything, and nothing."

"Yes, but explain — "

"Well," he said, with an impatient gesture, "it is God without mankind."

QUESTIONS

1. What does Balzac gain by making the central narrative the story of "an old soldier, . . . one of those troopers who are surprised at nothing"? Would the story have been as effective had the soldier told the story directly, without the opening scene at the menagerie?

2. What is the effect of setting the story far from civilization? Does the setting lend plausibility to the events? Does it make them too strange and exotic to be credible?

3. "There'll be time enough," says the young soldier. For what?

4. What in the description of the panther tells us that this is no ordinary man-versus-wild-beast tale? Is the soldier's first reaction to the animal realistic?

5. What images convey the impression that the beast is an imperious woman? Trace the steps by which Balzac humanizes the panther.

6. Is Balzac relating a tall tale, or has he some other purpose? Is this an allegory of human love? If so, what are the parallels? Is it true that "all great passions" are ended "in a misunderstanding"?

7. Does the soldier's final comment about the desert shed light on the central narrative?

NATHANIEL HAWTHORNE ≡≡≡

Young Goodman Brown

Young Goodman Brown came forth at sunset into the street at Salem village; but put his head back, after crossing the threshold, to exchange a parting kiss with his young wife. And Faith, as the wife was aptly named, thrust her own pretty head into the street, letting the wind play with the pink ribbons of her cap while she called to Goodman Brown.

"Dearest heart," whispered she, softly and rather sadly, when her lips were close to his ear, "prithee put off your journey until sunrise and sleep in your own bed to-night. A lone woman is troubled with such dreams and such thoughts that she's afeard of herself sometimes. Pray tarry with me this night, dear husband, of all nights in the year."

"My love and my Faith," replied young Goodman Brown, "of all nights in the year, this one night must I tarry away from thee. My journey, as thou callest it, forth and back again, must needs be done 'twixt now and sunrise. What, my sweet, pretty wife, dost thou doubt me already, and we but three months married?"

"Then God bless you!" said Faith, with the pink ribbons; "and may you find all well when you come back."

"Amen!" cried Goodman Brown. "Say thy prayers, dear Faith, and go to bed at dusk, and no harm will come to thee."

So they parted; and the young man pursued his way until, being about to turn the corner by the meeting-house, he looked back and saw the head of Faith still peeping after him with a melancholy air, in spite of her pink ribbons.

"Poor little Faith!" thought he, for his heart smote him. "What a wretch am I to leave her on such an errand! She talks of dreams, too. Methought as she spoke there was trouble in her face, as if a dream had warned her what work is to be done to-night. But no, no; 't would kill her to think it. Well, she's a blessed angel on earth; and after this one night I'll cling to her skirts and follow her to heaven."

With this excellent resolve for the future, Goodman Brown felt himself justified in making more haste on his present evil purpose. He had taken a dreary road, darkened by all the gloomiest trees of the forest, which barely stood aside to let the narrow path creep through, and closed immediately behind. It was all as lonely as could be; and there is this peculiarity in such a solitude, that the traveller knows not who may be concealed by the innumerable trunks and the thick boughs overhead; so that with lonely footsteps he may yet be passing through an unseen multitude.

"There may be a devilish Indian behind every tree," said Goodman Brown to himself; and he glanced fearfully behind him as he added, "What if the devil himself should be at my very elbow!"

His head being turned back, he passed a crook of the road, and, looking forward again, beheld the figure of a man, in grave and decent attire, seated at the foot of an old tree. He arose at Goodman Brown's approach and walked onward side by side with him.

"You are late, Goodman Brown," said he. "The clock of the Old South was striking as I came through Boston, and that is full fifteen minutes agone."

"Faith kept me back a while," replied the young man, with a tremor in his voice, caused by the sudden appearance of his companion, though not wholly unexpected.

It was now deep dusk in the forest, and deepest in that part of it where these two were journeying. As nearly as could be discerned, the second traveller was about fifty years old, apparently in the same rank of life as Goodman Brown, and bearing a considerable resemblance to him, though perhaps more in expression than features. Still they might have been taken for father and son. And yet, though the elder person was as simply clad as the younger, and as simple in manner too, he had an indescribable air of one who knew the world, and who would not have felt abashed at the governor's dinner table or in King William's court, were it possible that his affairs should call him thither. But the only thing about him that could be fixed upon as remarkable was his staff, which bore the likeness of a great black snake, so curiously wrought that it might almost be seen to twist and wriggle itself like a living serpent. This, of course, must have been an ocular deception, assisted by the uncertain light.

"Come, Goodman Brown," cried his fellow-traveller, "this is a dull pace for the beginning of a journey. Take my staff, if you are so soon weary."

"Friend," said the other, exchanging his slow pace for a full stop, "having kept covenant by meeting thee here, it is my purpose now to return whence I came. I have scruples touching the matter thou wot'st of."

"Sayest thou so?" replied he of the serpent, smiling apart. "Let us walk on, nevertheless, reasoning as we go; and if I convince thee not thou shalt turn back. We are but a little way in the forest yet."

"Too far! too far!" exclaimed the goodman, unconsciously resuming his walk. "My father never went into the woods on such an errand, nor his father before him. We have been a race of honest men and good Christians since the days of the martyrs; and shall I be the first of the name of Brown that ever took this path and kept" —

"Such company, thou wouldst say," observed the elder person, interpreting his pause. "Well said, Goodman Brown! I have been as well acquainted with your family as with ever a one among the Puritans; and that's no trifle to say. I helped your grandfather, the constable, when he lashed the Quaker woman so smartly through the streets of Salem; and it was I that brought your father a pitch-pine knot, kindled at my own hearth, to set fire to an Indian village, in King Philip's war. They were my good friends, both; and many a pleasant walk have we had along this path, and returned merrily after midnight. I would fain be friends with you for their sake."

"If it be as thou sayest," replied Goodman Brown, "I marvel they never spoke of these matters; or, verily, I marvel not, seeing that the least rumor of the sort would have driven them from New England. We are a people of prayer, and good works to boot, and abide no such wickedness."

"Wickedness or not," said the traveller with the twisted staff, "I have a very general acquaintance here in New England. The deacons of many a church have drunk the communion wine with me; the selectmen of divers towns make me their chairman; and a majority of the Great and General Court are firm supporters of my interest. The governor and I, too — But these are state secrets."

"Can this be so?" cried Goodman Brown, with a stare of amazement at his undisturbed companion. "Howbeit, I have nothing to do with the governor and council; they have their own ways, and are no rule for a simple husbandman like me. But, were I to go on with thee, how should I meet the eye of that good old man, our minister, at Salem village? Oh, his voice would make me tremble both Sabbath day and lecture day."

Thus far the elder traveller had listened with due gravity; but now burst into a fit of irrepressible mirth, shaking himself so violently that his snake-like staff actually seemed to wriggle in sympathy.

"Ha! ha! ha!" shouted he again and again; then composing himself, "Well, go on, Goodman Brown, go on; but, prithee, don't kill me with laughing."

"Well, then, to end the matter at once," said Goodman Brown, considerably nettled, "there is my wife, Faith. It would break her dear little heart; and I'd rather break my own."

"Nay, if that be the case," answered the other, "e'en go thy ways, Goodman Brown. I would not for twenty old women like the one hobbling before us that Faith should come to any harm."

As he spoke he pointed his staff at a female figure on the path, in whom Goodman Brown recognized a very pious and exemplary dame, who had taught him his catechism in youth, and was still his moral and spiritual adviser, jointly with the minister and Deacon Gookin.

"A marvel, truly, that Goody Cloyse should be so far in the wilderness at nightfall," said he. "But with your leave, friend, I shall take a cut through the woods until we have left this Christian woman behind. Being a stranger to you, she might ask whom I was consorting with and whither I was going."

"Be it so," said his fellow-traveller. "Betake you the woods, and let me keep the path."

Accordingly the young man turned aside, but took care to watch his companion, who advanced softly along the road until he had come within a staff's length of the old dame. She, meanwhile, was making the best of her way, with singular speed for so aged a woman, and mumbling some indistinct words — a prayer, doubtless — as she went. The traveller put forth his staff and touched her withered neck with what seemed the serpent's tail.

"The devil!" screamed the pious old lady.

"Then Goody Cloyse knows her old friend?" observed the traveller, confronting her and leaning on his writhing stick.

"Ah, forsooth, and is it your worship indeed?" cried the good dame. "Yea, truly is it, and in the very image of my old gossip,[1] Goodman Brown, the grandfather of the silly fellow that now is. But — would your worship believe it? — my broomstick hath strangely disappeared, stolen, as I suspect, by that unhanged witch, Goody Cory, and that, too, when I was all anointed with the juice of smallage, and cinquefoil, and wolf's bane" —

"Mingled with fine wheat and the fat of a new-born babe," said the shape of old Goodman Brown.

"Ah, your worship knows the recipe," cried the old lady, cackling aloud. "So, as I was saying, being all ready for the meeting, and no horse to ride on, I made up my mind to foot it;

---

[1] Friend.

for they tell me there is a nice young man to be taken into communion to-night. But now your good worship will lend me your arm, and we shall be there in a twinkling."

"That can hardly be," answered her friend. "I may not spare you my arm, Goody Cloyse; but here is my staff, if you will."

So saying, he threw it down at her feet, where, perhaps, it assumed life, being one of the rods which its owner had formerly lent to the Egyptian magi.[2] Of this fact, however, Goodman Brown could not take cognizance. He had cast up his eyes in astonishment, and, looking down again, beheld neither Goody Cloyse nor the serpentine staff, but his fellow-traveller alone, who waited for him as calmly as if nothing had happened.

"That old woman taught me my catechism," said the young man; and there was a world of meaning in this simple comment.

They continued to walk onward, while the elder traveller exhorted his companion to make good speed and persevere in the path, discoursing so aptly that his arguments seemed rather to spring up in the bosom of his auditor than to be suggested by himself. As they went, he plucked a branch of maple to serve for a walking stick, and began to strip it of the twigs and little boughs, which were wet with evening dew. The moment his fingers touched them they became strangely withered and dried up as with a week's sunshine. Thus the pair proceeded, at a good free pace, until suddenly, in a gloomy hollow of the road, Goodman Brown sat himself down on the stump of a tree and refused to go any farther.

"Friend," said he, stubbornly, "my mind is made up. Not another step will I budge on this errand. What if a wretched old woman do choose to go to the devil when I thought she was going to heaven: is that any reason why I should quit my dear Faith and go after her?"

"You will think better of this by and by," said his acquaintance, composedly. "Sit here and rest yourself a while; and when you feel like moving again, there is my staff to help you along."

Without more words, he threw his companion the maple stick and was as speedily out of sight as if he had vanished into the deepening gloom. The young man sat a few moments by the roadside, applauding himself greatly, and thinking with how clear a conscience he should meet the minister in his morning walk, nor shrink from the eye of good old Deacon Gookin. And what calm sleep would be his that very night, which was to have been spent so wickedly, but so purely and sweetly now, in the arms of Faith! Amidst these pleasant and praiseworthy meditations, Goodman Brown heard the tramp of horses along the road, and deemed it advisable to conceal himself within the verge of the forest, conscious of the guilty purpose that had brought him thither, though now so happily turned from it.

On came the hoof tramps and the voices of the riders, two grave old voices, conversing soberly as they drew near. These mingled sounds appeared to pass along the road, within a few yards of the young man's hiding-place; but, owing doubtless to the depth of the gloom at that particular spot, neither the travellers nor their steeds were visible. Though their figures brushed the small boughs by the wayside, it could not be seen that they intercepted, even for a moment, the faint gleam from the strip of bright sky athwart which they must have passed. Goodman Brown alternately crouched and stood on tiptoe, pulling aside the branches and thrusting forth his head as far as he durst without discerning so much as a shadow. It vexed him the more, because he could have sworn, were such a thing possible, that he recognized the voices of the minister and Deacon Gookin, jogging along quietly, as they were wont to do,

---

[2] In the Old Testament, the Egyptian priests unsuccessfully matched their magic against the power God had given Moses.

when bound to some ordination or ecclesiastical council. While yet within hearing, one of the riders stopped to pluck a switch.

"Of the two, reverend sir," said the voice like the deacon's, "I had rather miss an ordination dinner than to-night's meeting. They tell me that some of our community are to be here from Falmouth and beyond, and others from Connecticut and Rhode Island, besides several of the Indian powwows, who, after their fashion, know almost as much deviltry as the best of us. Moreover, there is a goodly young woman to be taken into communion."

"Mighty well, Deacon Gookin!" replied the solemn old tones of the minister. "Spur up, or we shall be late. Nothing can be done, you know, until I get on the ground."

The hoofs clattered again; and the voices, talking so strangely in the empty air, passed on through the forest, where no church had ever been gathered or solitary Christian prayed. Whither, then, could these holy men be journeying so deep into the heathen wilderness? Young Goodman Brown caught hold of a tree for support, being ready to sink down on the ground, faint and overburdened with the heavy sickness of his heart. He looked up to the sky, doubting whether there really was a heaven above him. Yet there was the blue arch, and the stars brightening in it.

"With heaven above and Faith below, I will yet stand firm against the devil!" cried Goodman Brown.

While he still gazed upward into the deep arch of the firmament and had lifted his hands to pray, a cloud, though no wind was stirring, hurried across the zenith and hid the brightening stars. The blue sky was still visible, except directly overhead, where this black mass of cloud was sweeping swiftly northward. Aloft in the air, as if from the depths of the cloud, came a confused and doubtful sound of voices. Once the listener fancied that he could distinguish the accents of towns-people of his own, men and women, both pious and ungodly, many of whom he had met at the communion table, and had seen others rioting at the tavern. The next moment, so indistinct were the sounds, he doubted whether he had heard aught but the murmur of the old forest, whispering without a wind. Then came a stronger swell of those familiar tones, heard daily in the sunshine at Salem village, but never until now from a cloud of night. There was one voice, of a young woman, uttering lamentations, yet with an uncertain sorrow, and entreating for some favor, which, perhaps, it would grieve her to obtain; and all the unseen multitude, both saints and sinners, seemed to encourage her onward.

"Faith!" shouted Goodman Brown, in a voice of agony and desperation; and the echoes of the forest mocked him, crying, "Faith! Faith!" as if bewildered wretches were seeking her all through the wilderness.

The cry of grief, rage, and terror was yet piercing the night, when the unhappy husband held his breath for a response. There was a scream, drowned immediately in a louder murmur of voices, fading into far-off laughter, as the dark cloud swept away, leaving the clear and silent sky above Goodman Brown. But something fluttered lightly down through the air and caught on the branch of a tree. The young man seized it, and beheld a pink ribbon.

"My Faith is gone!" cried he, after one stupefied moment. "There is no good on earth; and sin is but a name. Come, devil; for to thee is this world given."

And, maddened with despair, so that he laughed loud and long, did Goodman Brown grasp his staff and set forth again, at such a rate that he seemed to fly along the forest path rather than to walk or run. The road grew wilder and drearier and more faintly traced, and vanished at length, leaving him in the heart of the dark wilderness, still rushing onward with the instinct that guides mortal man to evil. The whole forest was peopled with frightful sounds — the creaking of the trees, the howling of wild beasts, and the yell of Indians; while sometimes the wind tolled like a distant church bell, and sometimes gave a broad roar around the traveller, as if all Nature were laughing him to scorn. But he was himself the chief horror of the scene, and shrank not from its other horrors.

"Ha! ha! ha!" roared Goodman Brown when the wind laughed at him. "Let us hear which will laugh loudest. Think not to frighten me with your deviltry. Come witch, come wizard, come Indian powwow, come devil himself, and here comes Goodman Brown. You may as well fear him as he fear you."

In truth, all through the haunted forest there could be nothing more frightful than the figure of Goodman Brown. On he flew among the black pines, brandishing his staff with frenzied gestures, now giving vent to an inspiration of horrid blasphemy, and now shouting forth such laughter as set all the echoes of the forest laughing like demons around him. The fiend in his own shape is less hideous than when he rages in the breast of man. Thus sped the demoniac on his course, until, quivering among the trees, he saw a red light before him, as when the felled trunks and branches of a clearing have been set on fire, and throw up their lurid blaze against the sky, at the hour of midnight. He paused, in a lull of the tempest that had driven him onward, and heard the swell of what seemed a hymn, rolling solemnly from a distance with the weight of many voices. He knew the tune; it was a familiar one in the choir of the village meeting-house. The verse died heavily away, and was lengthened by a chorus, not of human voices, but of all the sounds of the benighted wilderness pealing in awful harmony together. Goodman Brown cried out, and his cry was lost to his own ear by its unison with the cry of the desert.

In the interval of silence he stole forward until the light glared full upon his eyes. At one extremity of an open space, hemmed in by the dark wall of the forest, arose a rock, bearing some rude, natural resemblance either to an altar or a pulpit, and surrounded by four blazing pines, their tops aflame, their stems untouched, like candles at an evening meeting. The mass of foliage that had overgrown the summit of the rock was all on fire, blazing high into the night and fitfully illuminating the whole field. Each pendent twig and leafy festoon was in a blaze. As the red light arose and fell, a numerous congregation alternately shone forth, then disappeared in shadow, and again grew, as it were, out of the darkness, peopling the heart of the solitary woods at once.

"A grave and dark-clad company," quoth Goodman Brown.

In truth they were such. Among them, quivering to and fro between gloom and splendor, appeared faces that would be seen next day at the council board of the province, and others which, Sabbath after Sabbath, looked devoutly heavenward, and benignantly over the crowded pews, from the holiest pulpits in the land. Some affirm that the lady of the governor was there. At least there were high dames well known to her, and wives of honored husbands, and widows, a great multitude, and ancient maidens, all of excellent repute, and fair young girls, who trembled lest their mothers should espy them. Either the sudden gleams of light flashing over the obscure field bedazzled Goodman Brown, or he recognized a score of the church members of Salem village famous for their especial sanctity. Good old Deacon Gookin had arrived, and waited at the skirts of that venerable saint, his revered pastor. But, irreverently consorting with these grave, reputable, and pious people, these elders of the church, these chaste dames and dewy virgins, there were men of dissolute lives and women of spotted fame, wretches given over to all mean and filthy vice, and suspected even of horrid crimes. It was strange to see that the good shrank not from the wicked, nor were the sinners abashed by the saints. Scattered also among their pale-faced enemies were the Indian priests, or powwows, who had often scared their native forest with more hideous incantations than any known to English witchcraft.

"But where is Faith?" thought Goodman Brown; and, as hope came into his heart, he trembled.

Another verse of the hymn arose, a slow and mournful strain, such as the pious love, but joined to words which expressed all that our nature can conceive of sin, and darkly hinted at far more. Unfathomable to mere mortals is the lore of fiends. Verse after verse was sung; and still the chorus of the desert swelled between like the deepest tone of a mighty organ; and with the final peal of that dreadful anthem there came a sound, as if the roaring wind, the rushing streams, the howling beasts, and every other voice of the unconcerted wilderness were mingling and according with the voice of guilty man in homage to the prince of all. The four blazing pines threw up a loftier flame, and obscurely discovered shapes and visages of horror on the smoke wreaths above the impious assembly. At the same moment the fire on the rock shot redly forth and formed a glowing arch above its base, where now appeared a figure. With reverence be it spoken, the figure bore no slight similitude, both in garb and manner, to some grave divine of the New England churches.

"Bring forth the converts!" cried a voice that echoed through the field and rolled into the forest.

At the word, Goodman Brown stepped forth from the shadow of the trees and approached the congregation, with whom he felt a loathful brotherhood by the sympathy of all that was wicked in his heart. He could have well-nigh sworn that the shape of his own dead father beckoned him to advance, looking downward from a smoke wreath, while a woman, with dim features of despair, threw out her hand to warn him back. Was it his mother? But he had no power to retreat one step, nor to resist, even in thought, when the minister and good old Deacon Gookin seized his arms and led him to the blazing rock. Thither came also the slender form of a veiled female, led between Goody Cloyse, that pious teacher of the catechism, and Martha Carrier,[3] who had received the devil's promise to be queen of hell. A rampant hag was she. And there stood the proselytes beneath the canopy of fire.

"Welcome, my children," said the dark figure, "to the communion of your race. Ye have found thus young your nature and your destiny. My children, look behind you!"

They turned; and flashing forth, as it were, in a sheet of flame, the fiend worshippers were seen; the smile of welcome gleamed darkly on every visage.

"There," resumed the sable form, "are all whom ye have reverenced from youth. Ye deemed them holier than yourselves, and shrank from your own sin, contrasting it with their lives of righteousness and prayerful aspirations heavenward. Yet here are they all in my worshipping assembly. This night it shall be granted you to know their secret deeds: how hoary-bearded elders of the church have whispered wanton words to the young maids of their households; how many a woman, eager for widows' weeds, has given her husband a drink at bedtime and let him sleep his last sleep in her bosom; how beardless youths have made haste to inherit their fathers' wealth; and how fair damsels — blush not, sweet ones — have dug little graves in the garden, and bidden me, the sole guest, to an infant's funeral. By the sympathy of your human hearts for sin ye shall scent out all the places — whether in church, bed-chamber, street, field, or forest — where crime has been committed, and shall exult to behold the whole earth one stain of guilt, one mighty blood spot. Far more than this. I shall be yours to penetrate, in every bosom, the deep mystery of sin, the fountain of all wicked arts, and which inexhaustibly supplies more evil impulses than human power — than my power at its utmost — can make manifest in deeds. And now, my children, look upon each other."

---

[3] One of the women of Salem who was put to death as a witch.

They did so; and, by the blaze of the hell-kindled torches, the wretched man beheld his Faith, and the wife her husband, trembling before that unhallowed altar.

"Lo, there ye stand, my children," said the figure, in a deep and solemn tone, almost sad with its despairing awfulness, as if his once angelic nature could yet mourn for our miserable race. "Depending upon one another's hearts, ye had still hoped that virtue were not all a dream. Now are ye undeceived. Evil is the nature of mankind. Evil must be your only happiness. Welcome again, my children, to the communion of your race."

"Welcome," repeated the fiend worshippers, in one cry of despair and triumph.

And there they stood, the only pair, as it seemed, who were yet hesitating on the verge of wickedness in this dark world. A basin was hollowed, naturally, in the rock. Did it contain water, reddened by the lurid light? or was it blood? or, perchance, a liquid flame? Herein did the shape of evil dip his hand and prepare to lay the mark of baptism upon their foreheads, that they might be partakers of the mystery of sin, more conscious of the secret guilt of others, both in deed and thought, than they could now be of their own. The husband cast one look at his pale wife, and Faith at him. What polluted wretches would the next glance show them to each other, shuddering alike at what they disclosed and what they saw!

"Faith! Faith!" cried the husband, "look up to heaven, and resist the wicked one."

Whether Faith obeyed he knew not. Hardly had he spoken when he found himself amid calm night and solitude, listening to a roar of the wind which died heavily away through the forest. He staggered against the rock, and felt it chill and damp; while a hanging twig, that had been all on fire, besprinkled his cheek with the coldest dew.

The next morning young Goodman Brown came slowly into the street of Salem village, staring around him like a bewildered man. The good old minister was taking a walk along the graveyard to get an appetite for breakfast and meditate his sermon, and bestowed a blessing, as he passed, on Goodman Brown. He shrank from the venerable saint as if to avoid an anathema. Old Deacon Gookin was at domestic worship, and the holy words of his prayer were heard through the open window. "What God doth the wizard pray to?" quoth Goodman Brown. Goody Cloyse, that excellent old Christian, stood in the early sunshine at her own lattice, catechizing a little girl who had brought her a pint of morning's milk. Goodman Brown snatched away the child as from the grasp of the fiend himself. Turning the corner by the meeting-house, he spied the head of Faith, with the pink ribbons, gazing anxiously forth, and bursting into such joy at sight of him that she skipped along the street and almost kissed her husband before the whole village. But Goodman Brown looked sternly and sadly into her face, and passed on without a greeting.

Had Goodman Brown fallen asleep in the forest and only dreamed a wild dream of a witch-meeting?

Be it so if you will; but, alas! it was a dream of evil omen for young Goodman Brown. A stern, a sad, a darkly meditative, a distrustful, if not a desperate man did he become from the night of that fearful dream. On the Sabbath day, when the congregation were singing a holy psalm, he could not listen because an anthem of sin rushed loudly upon his ear and drowned all the blessed strain. When the minister spoke from the pulpit with power and fervid eloquence, and, with his hand on the open Bible, of the sacred truths of our religion, and of saint-like lives and triumphant deaths, and of future bliss or misery unutterable, then did Goodman Brown turn pale, dreading lest the roof should thunder down upon the gray blasphemer and his hearers. Often, awaking suddenly at midnight, he shrank from the bosom of Faith; and at morning or eventide, when the family knelt down at prayer, he scowled and muttered to himself, and gazed sternly at his wife, and turned away. And when he had lived long, and was borne to his grave a hoary corpse, followed by Faith, an aged woman, and children and grandchildren, a goodly procession, besides neighbors not a few, they carved no hopeful verse upon his tombstone, for his dying hour was gloom.

QUESTIONS

1. Remembering that "Goodman" was an old form of address like "Mister," do you agree with commentators that the title character is symbolical? What does he symbolize?

2. What other evidence is there that this story is symbolical or allegorical? Consider the setting and action as well as names and characters.

3. Critics often say that Hawthorne is ambiguous, deliberately so, and they often cite as an example the "staff, which bore the likeness of a great black snake, so curiously wrought that it might almost be seen to twist and wriggle itself like a living serpent." Can you find other instances of ambiguity? Do you think Hawthorne's ambiguity is incidental or essential to the tale?

4. "Had Goodman Brown . . . only dreamed a wild dream of a witch-meeting?" Does Hawthorne imply that it doesn't matter whether or not it was only a dream? And yet, Goodman Brown seems to be a changed man. Has evil triumphed?

5. Is there evidence that Brown has been deceived? If so, by whom?

NATHANIEL HAWTHORNE

My Kinsman, Major Molineux

After the kings of Great Britain had assumed the right of appointing the colonial governors, the measures of the latter seldom met with the ready and general approbation which had been paid to those of their predecessors, under the original charters. The people looked with most jealous scrutiny to the exercise of power which did not emanate from themselves, and they usually rewarded their rulers with slender gratitude for the compliances by which, in softening their instructions from beyond the sea, they had incurred the reprehension of those who gave them. The annals of Massachusetts Bay will inform us, that of six governors in the space of about forty years from the surrender of the old charter, under James II., two were imprisoned by a popular insurrection; a third, as Hutchinson[1] inclines to believe, was driven from the province by the whizzing of a musket-ball; a fourth, in the opinion of the same historian, was hastened to his grave by continual bickerings with the House of Representatives; and the remaining two, as well as their successors, till the Revolution, were favored with few and brief intervals of peaceful sway. The inferior members of the court party, in times of high political excitement, led scarcely a more desirable life. These remarks may serve as a preface to the following adventures, which chanced upon a summer night, not far from a hundred years ago. The reader, in order to avoid a long and dry detail of colonial affairs, is requested to dispense with an account of the train of circumstances that had caused much temporary inflammation of the popular mind.

It was near nine o'clock of a moonlight evening, when a boat crossed the ferry with a single passenger, who had obtained his conveyance at that unusual hour by the promise of an extra fare. While he stood on the landing-place, searching in either pocket for the means of fulfilling his agreement, the ferryman lifted a lantern, by the aid of which, and the newly risen moon, he took a very accurate survey of the stranger's figure. He was a youth of barely eighteen years, evidently country-bred, and now, as it should seem, upon his first visit to town. He was clad in a coarse gray coat, well worn, but in excellent repair; his under garments were durably constructed of leather, and fitted tight to a pair of serviceable and well-shaped limbs; his stockings of blue yarn were the incontrovertible work of a mother or a sister; and on his head was a three-cornered hat, which in its better days had perhaps sheltered the graver brow of the lad's father. Under his left arm was a heavy cudgel formed of an oak sapling, and retaining a

---

[1] Thomas Hutchinson (1711–1780), historian and last royal governor of the Massachusetts Bay Colony.

part of the hardened root; and his equipment was completed by a wallet, not so abundantly stocked as to incommode the vigorous shoulders on which it hung. Brown, curly hair, well-shaped features, and bright, cheerful eyes were nature's gifts, and worth all that art could have done for his adornment.

The youth, one of whose names was Robin, finally drew from his pocket the half of a little province bill of five shillings, which, in the depreciation in that sort of currency, did but satisfy the ferryman's demand, with the surplus of a sexangular piece of parchment, valued at three pence. He then walked forward into the town, with as light a step as if his day's journey had not already exceeded thirty miles, and with as eager an eye as if he were entering London city, instead of the little metropolis of a New England colony. Before Robin had proceeded far, however, it occurred to him that he knew not whither to direct his steps; so he paused, and looked up and down the narrow street, scrutinizing the small and mean wooden buildings that were scattered on either side.

"This low hovel cannot be my kinsman's dwelling," thought he, "nor yonder house, where the moonlight enters at the broken casement; and truly I see none hereabouts that might be worthy of him. It would have been wise to inquire my way of the ferryman, and doubtless he would have gone with me, and earned a shilling from the Major for his pains. But the next man I meet will do as well."

He resumed his walk, and was glad to perceive that the street now became wider, and the houses more respectable in their appearance. He soon discerned a figure moving on moderately in advance, and hastened his steps to overtake it. As Robin drew nigh, he saw that the passenger was a man in years, with a full periwig of gray hair, a wide-skirted coat of dark cloth, and silk stockings rolled above his knees. He carried a long and polished cane, which he struck down perpendicularly before him at every step; and at regular intervals he uttered two successive hems, of a peculiarly solemn and sepulchral intonation. Having made these observations, Robin laid hold of the skirt of the old man's coat, just when the light from the open door and windows of a barber's shop fell upon both their figures.

"Good evening to you, honored sir," said he, making a low bow, and still retaining his hold of the skirt. "I pray you tell me whereabouts is the dwelling of my kinsman, Major Molineux."

The youth's question was uttered very loudly; and one of the barbers, whose razor was descending on a well-soaped chin, and another who was dressing a Ramillies wig,[2] left their occupations, and came to the door. The citizen, in the mean time, turned a long-favored countenance upon Robin, and answered him in a tone of excessive anger and annoyance. His two sepulchral hems, however, broke into the very centre of his rebuke, with most singular effect, like a thought of the cold grave obtruding among wrathful passions.

"Let go my garment, fellow! I tell you, I know not the man you speak of. What! I have authority, I have — hem, hem — authority; and if this be the respect you show for your betters, your feet shall be brought acquainted with the stocks by daylight, to-morrow morning!"

Robin released the old man's skirt, and hastened away, pursued by an ill-mannered roar of laughter from the barber's shop. He was at first considerably surprised by the result of his question, but, being a shrewd youth, soon thought himself able to account for the mystery.

"This is some country representative," was his conclusion, "who has never seen the inside of my kinsman's door, and lacks the breeding to answer a stranger civilly. The man is old, or verily — I might be tempted to turn back and smite him on the nose. Ah, Robin, Robin!

---

[2] A wig of fashionable style, named after a small city in Belgium.

even the barber's boys laugh at you for choosing such a guide! You will be wiser in time, friend Robin."

He now became entangled in a succession of crooked and narrow streets, which crossed each other, and meandered at no great distance from the water-side. The smell of tar was obvious to his nostrils, the masts of vessels pierced the moonlight above the tops of the buildings, and the numerous signs, which Robin paused to read, informed him that he was near the centre of business. But the streets were empty, the shops were closed, and lights were visible only in the second stories of a few dwelling-houses. At length, on the corner of a narrow lane, through which he was passing, he beheld the broad countenance of a British hero swinging before the door of an inn, whence proceeded the voices of many guests. The casement of one of the lower windows was thrown back, and a very thin curtain permitted Robin to distinguish a party at supper, round a well-furnished table. The fragrance of the good cheer steamed forth into the outer air, and the youth could not fail to recollect that the last remnant of his travelling stock of provision had yielded to his morning appetite, and that noon had found and left him dinnerless.

"Oh, that a parchment three-penny might give me a right to sit down at yonder table!" said Robin, with a sigh. "But the Major will make me welcome to the best of his victuals; so I will even step boldly in, and inquire my way to his dwelling."

He entered the tavern, and was guided by the murmur of voices and the fumes of tobacco to the public-room. It was a long and low apartment, with oaken walls, grown dark in the continual smoke, and a floor which was thickly sanded, but of no immaculate purity. A number of persons — the larger part of whom appeared to be mariners, or in some way connected with the sea — occupied the wooden benches, or leather-bottomed chairs, conversing on various matters, and occasionally lending their attention to some topic of general interest. Three or four little groups were draining as many bowls of punch, which the West India trade had long since made a familiar drink in the colony. Others, who had the appearance of men who lived by regular and laborious handicraft, preferred the insulated bliss of an unshared potation, and became more taciturn under its influence. Nearly all, in short, evinced a predilection for the Good Creature in some of its various shapes, for this is a vice to which, as Fast Day sermons of a hundred years ago will testify, we have a long hereditary claim. The only guests to whom Robin's sympathies inclined him were two or three sheepish countrymen, who were using the inn somewhat after the fashion of a Turkish caravansary; they had gotten themselves into the darkest corner of the room, and heedless of the Nicotian atmosphere, were supping on the bread of their own ovens, and the bacon cured in their own chimney-smoke. But though Robin felt a sort of brotherhood with these strangers, his eyes were attracted from them to a person who stood near the door, holding whispered conversation with a group of ill-dressed associates. His features were separately striking almost to grotesqueness, and the whole face left a deep impression on the memory. The forehead bulged out into a double prominence, with a vale between; the nose came boldly forth in an irregular curve, and its bridge was of more than a finger's breadth; the eyebrows were deep and shaggy, and the eyes glowed beneath them like fire in a cave.

While Robin deliberated of whom to inquire respecting his kinsman's dwelling, he was accosted by the innkeeper, a little man in a stained white apron, who had come to pay his professional welcome to the stranger. Being in the second generation from a French Protestant, he seemed to have inherited the courtesy of his parent nation; but no variety of circumstances was ever known to change his voice from the one shrill note in which he now addressed Robin.

"From the country, I presume, sir?" said he, with a profound bow. "Beg leave to congratulate you on your arrival, and trust you intend a long stay with us. Fine town here, sir, beautiful buildings, and much that may interest a stranger. May I hope for the honor of your commands in respect to supper?"

"The man sees a family likeness! the rogue has guessed that I am related to the Major!" thought Robin, who had hitherto experienced little superfluous civility.

All eyes were now turned on the country lad, standing at the door, in his worn three-cornered hat, gray coat, leather breeches, and blue yarn stockings, leaning on an oaken cudgel, and bearing a wallet on his back.

Robin replied to the courteous innkeeper, with such an assumption of confidence as befitted the Major's relative. "My honest friend," he said, "I shall make it a point to patronize your house on some occasion, when" — here he could not help lowering his voice — "when I may have more than a parchment three-pence in my pocket. My present business," continued he, speaking with lofty confidence, "is merely to inquire my way to the dwelling of my kinsman, Major Molineux."

There was a sudden and general movement in the room, which Robin interpreted as expressing the eagerness of each individual to become his guide. But the innkeeper turned his eyes to a written paper on the wall, which he read, or seemed to read, with occasional recurrences to the young man's figure.

"What have we here?" said he, breaking his speech into little dry fragments. " 'Left the house of the subscriber, bounden servant, Hezekiah Mudge, — had on, when he went away, gray coat, leather breeches, master's third-best hat. One pound currency reward to whosoever shall lodge him in any jail of the province.' Better trudge, boy; better trudge!"

Robin had begun to draw his hand towards the lighter end of the oak cudgel, but a strange hostility in every countenance induced him to relinquish his purpose of breaking the courteous innkeeper's head. As he turned to leave the room, he encountered a sneering glance from the bold-featured personage whom he had before noticed; and no sooner was he beyond the door, than he heard a general laugh, in which the innkeeper's voice might be distinguished, like the dropping of small stones into a kettle.

"Now, is it not strange," thought Robin, with his usual shrewdness, — "is it not strange that the confession of an empty pocket should outweigh the name of my kinsman, Major Molineux? Oh, if I had one of those grinning rascals in the woods, where I and my oak sapling grew up together, I would teach him that my arm is heavy though my purse be light!"

On turning the corner of the narrow lane, Robin found himself in a spacious street, with an unbroken line of lofty houses on each side, and a steepled building at the upper end, whence the ringing of a bell announced the hour of nine. The light of the moon, and the lamps from the numerous shop-windows, discovered people promenading on the pavement, and amongst them Robin hoped to recognize his hitherto inscrutable relative. The result of his former inquiries made him unwilling to hazard another, in a scene of such publicity, and he determined to walk slowly and silently up the street, thrusting his face close to that of every elderly gentleman, in search of the Major's lineaments. In his progress, Robin encountered many gay and gallant figures. Embroidered garments of showy colors, enormous periwigs, gold-laced hats, and silver-hilted swords glided past him and dazzled his optics. Travelled youths, imitators of the European fine gentlemen of the period, trod jauntily along, half dancing to the fashionable tunes which they hummed, and making poor Robin ashamed of his quiet and natural gait. At length, after many pauses to examine the gorgeous display of goods in the shop-windows, and after suffering some rebukes for the impertinence of his scrutiny into people's faces, the Major's kinsman found himself near the steepled building, still unsuccessful in his search. As yet, however, he had seen only one side of the thronged street; so Robin crossed, and continued the same sort of inquisition down the opposite pavement, with stronger hopes than the philosopher seeking an honest man, but with no better fortune. He had arrived about midway towards the lower end, from which his course began, when he overheard the approach of some one who struck down a can on the flag-stones at every step, uttering, at regular intervals, two sepulchral hems.

"Mercy on us!" quoth Robin, recognizing the sound.

Turning a corner, which chanced to be close at his right hand, he hastened to pursue his researches in some other part of the town. His patience now was wearing low, and he seemed to feel more fatigue from his rambles since he crossed the ferry, than from his journey of several days on the other side. Hunger also pleaded loudly within him, and Robin began to balance the propriety of demanding, violently, and with lifted cudgel, the necessary guidance from the first solitary passenger whom he should meet. While a resolution to this effect was gaining strength, he entered a street of mean appearance, on either side of which a row of ill-built houses was straggling towards the harbor. The moonlight fell upon no passenger along the whole extent, but in the third domicile which Robin passed there was a half-opened door, and his keen glance detected a woman's garment within.

"My luck may be better here," said he to himself.

Accordingly, he approached the door, and beheld it shut closer as he did so; yet an open space remained, sufficing for the fair occupant to observe the stranger, without a correspond-ing display on her part. All that Robin could discern was a strip of scarlet petticoat, and the occasional sparkle of an eye, as if the moonbeams were trembling on some bright thing.

"Pretty mistress," for I may call her so with a good conscience, thought the shrewd youth, since I know nothing to the contrary, — "my sweet pretty mistress, will you be kind enough to tell me whereabouts I must seek the dwelling of my kinsman, Major Molineux?"

Robin's voice was plaintive and winning, and the female, seeing nothing to be shunned in the handsome country youth, thrust open the door, and came forth into the moonlight. She was a dainty little figure, with a white neck, round arms, and a slender waist, at the extremity of which her scarlet petticoat jutted out over a hoop, as if she were standing in a balloon. Moreover, her face was oval and pretty, her hair dark beneath the little cap, and her bright eyes possessed a sly freedom, which triumphed over those of Robin.

"Major Molineux dwells here," said this fair woman.

Now, her voice was the sweetest Robin had heard that night, the airy counterpart of a stream of melted silver; yet he could not help doubting whether that sweet voice spoke Gospel truth. He looked up and down the mean street, and then surveyed the house before which they stood. It was a small, dark edifice of two stories, the second of which projected over the lower floor, and the front apartment had the aspect of a shop for petty commodities.

"Now, truly, I am in luck," replied Robin, cunningly, "and so indeed is my kinsman, the Major, in having so pretty a housekeeper. But I prithee trouble him to step to the door; I will deliver him a message from his friends in the country, and then go back to my lodgings at the inn."

"Nay, the Major has been abed this hour or more," said the lady of the scarlet petticoat; "and it would be to little purpose to disturb him to-night, seeing his evening draught was of the strongest. But he is a kind-hearted man, and it would be as much as my life's worth to let a kinsman of his turn away from the door. You are the good old gentleman's very picture, and I could swear that was his rainy-weather hat. Also he has garments very much resembling those leather smallclothes. But come in, I pray, for I bid you hearty welcome in his name."

So saying, the fair and hospitable dame took our hero by the hand; and the touch was light, and the force was gentleness, and though Robin read in her eyes what he did not hear in her words, yet the slender-waisted woman in the scarlet petticoat proved stronger than the athletic country youth. She had drawn his half-willing footsteps nearly to the threshold, when the opening of a door in the neighborhood startled the Major's housekeeper, and, leaving the Major's kinsman, she vanished speedily into her own domicile. A heavy yawn preceded the appearance of a man, who, like the Moonshine of Pyramus and Thisbe,[3] carried a lantern, needlessly aiding his sister luminary in the heavens. As he walked sleepily up the street, he turned his broad, dull face on Robin, and displayed a long staff, spiked at the end.

"Home, vagabond, home!" said the watchman, in accents that seemed to fall asleep as soon as they were uttered. "Home, or we'll set you in the stocks by peep of day!"

"This is the second hint of the kind," thought Robin. "I wish they would end my difficulties, by setting me there tonight."

Nevertheless, the youth felt an instinctive antipathy towards the guardian of midnight order, which at first prevented him from asking his usual question. But just when the man was about to vanish behind the corner, Robin resolved not to lose the opportunity, and shouted lustily after him, —

"I say, friend! will you guide me to the house of my kinsman, Major Molineux?"

The watchman made no reply, but turned the corner and was gone; yet Robin seemed to hear the sound of drowsy laughter stealing along the solitary street. At that moment, also, a pleasant titter saluted him from the open window above his head; he looked up, and caught the sparkle of a saucy eye; a round arm beckoned to him, and next he heard light footsteps descending the staircase within. But Robin, being of the household of a New England clergyman, was a good youth, as well as a shrewd one; so he resisted temptation, and fled away.

He now roamed desperately, and at random, through the town, almost ready to believe that a spell was on him, like that by which a wizard of his country had once kept three pursuers wandering, a whole winter night, within twenty paces of the cottage which they sought. The streets lay before him, strange and desolate, and the lights were extinguished in almost every house. Twice, however, little parties of men, among whom Robin distinguished individuals in outlandish attire, came hurrying along; but, though on both occasions they paused to address him, such intercourse did not at all enlighten his perplexity. They did but utter a few words in some language of which Robin knew nothing, and perceiving his inability to answer, bestowed a curse upon him in plain English and hastened away. Finally, the lad determined to knock at the door of every mansion that might appear worthy to be occupied by his kinsman, trusting that perseverance would overcome the fatality that had hitherto thwarted him. Firm in this resolve, he was passing beneath the walls of a church, which formed the corner of two streets, when, as he turned into the shade of its steeple, he encountered a bulky stranger, muffled in a cloak. The man was proceeding with the speed of earnest business, but Robin planted himself full before him, holding the oak cudgel with both hands across his body as a bar to further passage.

"Halt, honest man, and answer me a question," said he, very resolutely. "Tell me, this instant, whereabouts is the dwelling of my kinsman, Major Molineux!"

"Keep your tongue between your teeth, fool, and let me pass!" said a deep, gruff voice, which Robin partly remembered. "Let me pass, I say, or I'll strike you to the earth!"

"No, no, neighbor!" cried Robin, flourishing his cudgel, and then thrusting its larger end close to the man's muffled face. "No, no, I'm not the fool you take me for, nor do you pass till I have an answer to my question. Whereabouts is the dwelling of my kinsman, Major Molineux?"

---

[3] Reference to the comic interlude in Shakespeare's *A Midsummer Night's Dream.*

The stranger, instead of attempting to force his passage, stepped back into the moonlight, unmuffled his face, and stared full into that of Robin.

"Watch here an hour, and Major Molineux will pass by," said he.

Robin gazed with dismay and astonishment on the unprecedented physiognomy of the speaker. The forehead with its double prominence, the broad hooked nose, the shaggy eyebrows, and fiery eyes were those which he had noticed at the inn, but the man's complexion had undergone a singular, or, more properly, a twofold change. One side of the face blazed an intense red, while the other was black as midnight, the division line being in the broad bridge of the nose; and a mouth which seemed to extend from ear to ear was black or red, in contrast to the color of the cheek. The effect was as if two individual devils, a fiend of fire and a fiend of darkness, had united themselves to form this infernal visage. The stranger grinned in Robin's face, muffled his party-colored features, and was out of sight in a moment.

"Strange things we travellers see!" ejaculated Robin.

He seated himself, however, upon the steps of the church-door, resolving to wait the appointed time for his kinsman. A few moments were consumed in philosophical speculations upon the species of man who had just left him; but having settled this point shrewdly, rationally, and satisfactorily, he was compelled to look elsewhere for his amusement. And first he threw his eyes along the street. It was of more respectable appearance than most of those into which he had wandered; and the moon, creating, like the imaginative power, a beautiful strangeness in familiar objects, gave something of romance to a scene that might not have possessed it in the light of day. The irregular and often quaint architecture of the houses, some of whose roofs were broken into numerous little peaks, while others ascended, steep and narrow, into a single point, and others again were square; the pure snow-white of some of their complexions, the aged darkness of others, and the thousand sparklings, reflected from bright substances in the walls of many; these matters engaged Robin's attention for a while, and then began to grow wearisome. Next he endeavored to define the forms of distant objects, starting away, with almost ghostly indistinctness, just as his eye appeared to grasp them; and finally he took a minute survey of an edifice which stood on the opposite side of the street, directly in front of the church-door, where he was stationed. It was a large, square mansion, distinguished from its neighbors by a balcony, which rested on tall pillars, and by an elaborate Gothic window, communicating therewith.

"Perhaps this is the very house I have been seeking," thought Robin.

Then he strove to speed away the time, by listening to a murmur which swept continually along the street, yet was scarcely audible, except to an unaccustomed ear like his; it was a low, dull, dreamy sound, compounded of many noises, each of which was at too great a distance to be separately heard. Robin marvelled at this snore of a sleeping town, and marvelled more whenever its continuity was broken by now and then a distant shout, apparently loud where it originated. But altogether it was a sleep-inspiring sound, and, to shake off its drowsy influence, Robin arose, and climbed a window-frame, that he might view the interior of the church. There the moonbeams came trembling in, and fell down upon the deserted pews, and extended along the quiet aisles. A fainter yet more awful radiance was hovering around the pulpit, and one solitary ray had dared to rest upon the open page of the great Bible. Had nature, in that deep hour, become a worshipper in the house which man had builded? Or was that heavenly light the visible sanctity of the place, — visible because no earthly and impure feet were within the walls? The scene made Robin's heart shiver with a sensation of loneliness stronger than he had ever felt in the remotest depths of his native woods; so he turned away and sat down again before the door. There were graves around the church, and now an uneasy thought obtruded into Robin's breast. What if the object of his search, which had been so often and so strangely thwarted, were all the time mouldering in his shroud? What if his kinsman should glide through yonder gate, and nod and smile to him in dimly passing by?

"Oh that any breathing thing were here with me!" said Robin.

Recalling his thoughts from this uncomfortable track, he sent them over forest, hill, and stream, and attempted to imagine how that evening of ambiguity and weariness had been spent by his father's household. He pictured them assembled at the door, beneath the tree, the great old tree, which had been spared for its huge twisted trunk and venerable shade, when a thousand leafy brethren fell. There, at the going down of the summer sun, it was his father's custom to perform domestic worship, that the neighbors might come and join with him like brothers of the family, and that the wayfaring man might pause to drink at that fountain, and keep his heart pure by freshening the memory of home. Robin distinguished the seat of every individual of the little audience; he saw the good man in the midst, holding the Scriptures in the golden light that fell from the western clouds; he beheld him close the book and all rise up to pray. He heard the old thanksgivings for daily mercies, the old supplications for their continuance, to which he had so often listened in weariness, but which were now among his dear remembrances. He perceived the slight inequality of his father's voice when he came to speak of the absent one; he noted how his mother turned her face to the broad and knotted trunk; how his elder brother scorned, because the beard was rough upon his upper lip, to permit his features to be moved; how the younger sister drew down a low hanging branch before her eyes; and how the little one of all, whose sports had hitherto broken the decorum of the scene, understood the prayer for her playmate, and burst into clamorous grief. Then he saw them go in at the door; and when Robin would have entered also, the latch tinkled into its place, and he was excluded from his home.

"Am I here, or there?" cried Robin, starting; for all at once, when his thoughts had become visible and audible in a dream, the long, wide, solitary street shone out before him.

He aroused himself, and endeavored to fix his attention steadily upon the large edifice which he had surveyed before. But still his mind kept vibrating between fancy and reality; by turns, the pillars of the balcony lengthened into the tall, bare stems of pines, dwindled down to human figures, settled again into their true shape and size, and then commenced a new succession of changes. For a single moment, when he deemed himself awake, he could have sworn that a visage — one which he seemed to remember, yet could not absolutely name as his kinsman's — was looking towards him from the Gothic window. A deeper sleep wrestled with and nearly overcame him, but fled at the sound of footsteps along the opposite pavement. Robin rubbed his eyes, discerned a man passing at the foot of the balcony, and addressed him in a loud, peevish, and lamentable cry.

"Hallo, friend! must I wait here all night for my kinsman, Major Molineux?"

The sleeping echoes awoke, and answered the voice; and the passenger, barely able to discern a figure sitting in the oblique shade of the steeple, traversed the street to obtain a nearer view. He was himself a gentleman in his prime, of open, intelligent, cheerful, and altogether prepossessing countenance. Perceiving a country youth, apparently homeless and without friends, he accosted him in a tone of real kindness, which had become strange to Robin's ears.

"Well, my good lad, why are you sitting here?" inquired he. "Can I be of service to you in any way?"

"I am afraid not, sir," replied Robin, despondingly; "yet I shall take it kindly, if you'll answer me a single question. I've been searching, half the night, for one Major Molineux; now, sir, is there really such a person in these parts, or am I dreaming?"

"Major Molineux! The name is not altogether strange to me," said the gentleman, smiling. "Have you any objection to telling me the nature of your business with him?"

Then Robin briefly related that his father was a clergyman, settled on a small salary, at a long distance back in the country, and that he and Major Molineux were brothers' children. The Major, having inherited riches, and acquired civil and military rank, had visited his cousin, in great pomp, a year or two before; had manifested much interest in Robin and an elder brother, and, being childless himself, had thrown out hints respecting the future establishment of one of them in life. The elder brother was destined to succeed to the farm which his father cultivated in the interval of sacred duties; it was therefore determined that Robin should profit by his kinsman's generous intentions, especially as he seemed to be rather the favorite, and was thought to possess other necessary endowments.

"For I have the name of being a shrewd youth," observed Robin, in this part of his story.

"I doubt not you deserve it," replied his new friend, good-naturedly; "but pray proceed."

"Well, sir, being nearly eighteen years old, and well grown, as you see," continued Robin, drawing himself up to his full height, "I thought it high time to begin the world. So my mother and sister put me in handsome trim, and my father gave me half the remnant of his last year's salary, and five days ago I started for this place, to pay the Major a visit. But, would you believe it, sir! I crossed the ferry a little after dark, and have yet found nobody that would show me the way to his dwelling; only, an hour or two since, I was told to wait here, and Major Molineux would pass by."

"Can you describe the man who told you this?" inquired the gentleman.

"Oh, he was a very ill-favored fellow, sir," replied Robin, "with two great bumps on his forehead, a hook nose, fiery eyes; and, what struck me as the strangest, his face was of two different colors. Do you happen to know such a man, sir?"

"Not intimately," answered the stranger, "but I chanced to meet him a little time previous to your stopping me. I believe you may trust his word, and that the Major will very shortly pass through this street. In the mean time, as I have a singular curiosity to witness your meeting, I will sit down here upon the steps and bear you company."

He seated himself accordingly, and soon engaged his companion in animated discourse. It was but of brief continuance, however, for a noise of shouting, which had long been remotely audible, drew so much nearer that Robin inquired its cause.

"What may be the meaning of this uproar?" asked he. "Truly, if your town be always as noisy, I shall find little sleep while I am an inhabitant."

"Why, indeed, friend Robin, there do appear to be three or four riotous fellows abroad to-night," replied the gentleman. "You must not expect all the stillness of your native woods here in our streets. But the watch will shortly be at the heels of these lads and" —

"Ay, and set them in the stocks by peep of day," interrupted Robin, recollecting his own encounter with the drowsy lantern-bearer. "But, dear sir, if I may trust my ears, an army of watchmen would never make head against such a multitude of rioters. There were at least a thousand voices went up to make that one shout."

"May not a man have several voices, Robin, as well as two complexions?" said his friend.

"Perhaps a man may; but Heaven forbid that a woman should!" responded the shrewd youth, thinking of the seductive tones of the Major's housekeeper.

The sounds of a trumpet in some neighboring street now became so evident and continual, that Robin's curiosity was strongly excited. In addition to the shouts, he heard frequent bursts from many instruments of discord, and a wild and confused laughter filled up the intervals. Robin rose from the steps, and looked wistfully towards a point whither people seemed to be hastening.

"Surely some prodigious merry-making is going on," exclaimed he. "I have laughed very little since I left home, sir, and should be sorry to lose an opportunity. Shall we step round the corner by that darkish house, and take our share of the fun?"

"Sit down again, sit down, good Robin," replied the gentleman, laying his hand on the skirt of the gray coat. "You forget that we must wait here for your kinsman; and there is reason to believe that he will pass by, in the course of a very few moments."

The near approach of the uproar had now disturbed the neighborhood; windows flew open on all sides; and many heads, in the attire of the pillow, and confused by sleep suddenly broken, were protruded to the gaze of whoever had leisure to observe them. Eager voices hailed each other from house to house, all demanding the explanation, which not a soul could give. Half-dressed men hurried towards the unknown commotion, stumbling as they went over the stone steps that thrust themselves into the narrow foot-walk. The shouts, the laughter, and the tuneless bray, the antipodes of music, came onwards with increasing din, till scattered individuals, and then denser bodies, began to appear round a corner at the distance of a hundred yards.

"Will you recognize your kinsman, if he passes in this crowd?" inquired the gentleman.

"Indeed, I can't warrant it, sir; but I'll take my stand here, and keep a bright lookout," answered Robin, descending to the outer edge of the pavement.

A mighty stream of people now emptied into the street, and came rolling slowly towards the church. A single horseman wheeled the corner in the midst of them, and close behind him came a band of fearful wind-instruments, sending forth a fresher discord now that no intervening buildings kept it from the ear. Then a redder light disturbed the moonbeams, and a dense multitude of torches shone along the street, concealing, by their glare, whatever object they illuminated. The single horseman, clad in a military dress, and bearing a drawn sword, rode onward as the leader, and, by his fierce and variegated countenance, appeared like war personified; the red of one cheek was an emblem of fire and sword; the blackness of the other betokened the mourning that attends them. In his train were wild figures in the Indian dress, and many fantastic shapes without a model, giving the whole march a visionary air, as if a dream had broken forth from some feverish brain, and were sweeping visibly through the midnight streets. A mass of people, inactive, except as applauding spectators, hemmed the procession in; and several women ran along the sidewalk, piercing the confusion of heavier sounds with their shrill voices of mirth or terror.

"The double-faced fellow has his eye upon me," muttered Robin, with an indefinite but an uncomfortable idea that he was himself to bear a part in the pageantry.

The leader turned himself in the saddle, and fixed his glance full upon the country youth, as the steed went slowly by. When Robin had freed his eyes from those fiery ones, the musicians were passing before him, and the torches were close at hand; but the unsteady brightness of the latter formed a veil which he could not penetrate. The rattling of wheels over the stones sometimes found its way to his ear, and confused traces of a human form appeared at intervals, and then melted into the vivid light. A moment more, and the leader thundered a command to halt: the trumpets vomited a horrid breath, and then held their peace; the shouts and laughter of the people died away, and there remained only a universal hum, allied to silence. Right before Robin's eyes was an uncovered cart. There the torches blazed the brightest, there the moon shone out like day, and there, in tar-and-feathery dignity, sat his kinsman, Major Molineux!

He was an elderly man, of large and majestic person, and strong, square features, betokening a steady soul; but steady as it was, his enemies had found means to shake it. His face was pale as death, and far more ghastly; the broad forehead was contracted in his agony, so that his eyebrows formed one grizzled line; his eyes were red and wild, and the foam hung white upon his quivering lip. His whole frame was agitated by a quick and continual tremor, which his pride strove to quell, even in those circumstances of overwhelming humiliation. But perhaps the bitterest pang of all was when his eyes met those of Robin; for he evidently knew him on the instant, as the youth stood witnessing the foul disgrace of a head grown gray in honor. They stared at each other in silence, and Robin's knees shook, and his hair bristled, with a mixture of pity and terror. Soon, however, a bewildering excitement began to seize upon his mind; the preceding adventures of the night, the unexpected appearance of the crowd, the torches, the confused din and the hush that followed, the spectre of his kinsman reviled by that great multitude, — all this, and, more than all, a perception of tremendous ridicule in the whole scene, affected him with a sort of mental inebriety. At that moment a voice of sluggish merriment saluted Robin's ears; he turned instinctively, and just behind the corner of the church stood the lantern-bearer, rubbing his eyes, and drowsily enjoying the lad's amazement. Then he heard a peal of laughter like the ringing of silvery bells; a woman twitched his arm, a saucy eye met his, and he saw the lady of the scarlet petticoat. A sharp, dry cachinnation appealed to his memory, and, standing on tiptoe in the crowd, with his white apron over his head, he beheld the courteous little innkeeper. And lastly, there sailed over the heads of the multitude a great, broad laugh, broken in the midst by two sepulchral hems; thus, "Haw, haw, haw, — hem, hem, — haw, haw, haw, haw!"

The sound proceeded from the balcony of the opposite edifice, and thither Robin turned his eyes. In front of the Gothic window stood the old citizen, wrapped in a wide gown, his gray periwig exchanged for a nightcap, which was thrust back from his forehead, and his silk stockings hanging about his legs. He supported himself on his polished cane in a fit of convulsive merriment, which manifested itself on his solemn old features like a funny inscription on a tombstone. Then Robin seemed to hear the voices of the barbers, of the guests of the inn, and of all who had made sport of him that night. The contagion was spreading among the multitude, when all at once, it seized upon Robin, and he sent forth a shout of laughter that echoed through the street, — every man shook his sides, every man emptied his lungs, but Robin's shout was the loudest there. The cloud-spirits peeped from their silvery islands, as the congregated mirth went roaring up the sky! The Man in the Moon heard the far bellow. "Oho," quoth he, "the old earth is frolicsome to-night!"

When there was a momentary calm in that tempestuous sea of sound, the leader gave the sign, the procession resumed its march. On they went, like fiends that throng in mockery around some dead potentate, mighty no more, but majestic still in his agony. On they went, in counterfeited pomp, in senseless uproar, in frenzied merriment, trampling all on an old man's heart. On swept the tumult, and left a silent street behind.

"Well, Robin, are you dreaming?" inquired the gentleman, laying his hand on the youth's shoulder.

Robin started, and withdrew his arm from the stone post to which he had instinctively clung, as the living stream rolled by him. His cheek was somewhat pale, and his eye not quite as lively as in the earlier part of the evening.

"Will you be kind enough to show me the way to the ferry?" said he, after a moment's pause.

"You have, then, adopted a new subject of inquiry?" observed his companion, with a smile.

"Why, yes, sir," replied Robin, rather dryly. "Thanks to you, and to my other friends, I have at last met my kinsman, and he will scarce desire to see my face again. I begin to grow weary of a town life, sir. Will you show me the way to the ferry?"

"No, my good friend Robin, — not tonight, at least," said the gentleman. "Some few days hence, if you wish it, I will speed you on your journey. Or, if you prefer to remain with us, perhaps, as you are a shrewd youth, you may rise in the world without the help of your kinsman, Major Molineux."

QUESTIONS

1. How would you characterize Robin? Does his name suggest anything about him?

2. Robin arrives in town an innocent young fellow. How is he changed by the end of his visit? Is he better or worse for the change?

3. As Americans, we naturally side with the colonists who rebelled against England's rule. Does Hawthorne give us reasons to admire the insurrectionists? Does he give us reasons to despise Major Molineux?

4. Read carefully the paragraph beginning "He was an elderly man.... " Do you sympathize with the Major? Is there anything to admire about him?

5. When the mob shouts its laughter, "Robin's shout was the loudest there." What does Hawthorne want us to think about Robin at this point? Do you think Robin will decide — as the stranger advises him — to remain among the citizens of the town, or will he go back home?

NIKOLAI GOGOL

The Overcoat

Translated by Constance Garnett

In the department of . . . but I had better not mention in what department. There is nothing in the world more readily moved to wrath than a department, a regiment, a government office, and in fact any sort of official body. Nowadays every private individual considers all society insulted in his person. I have been told that very lately a petition was handed in from a police-captain of what town I don't recollect, and that in this petition he set forth clearly that the institutions of the State were in danger and that its sacred name was being taken in vain; and, in proof thereof, he appended to his petition an enormously long volume of some work of romance in which a police-captain appeared on every tenth page, occasionally, indeed, in an intoxicated condition. And so, to avoid any unpleasantness, we had better call the department of which we are speaking a certain department.

And so, in a certain department there was a government clerk; a clerk of whom it cannot be said that he was very remarkable; he was short, somewhat pock-marked, with rather reddish hair and rather dim, bleary eyes, with a small bald patch on the top of his head, with wrinkles on both sides of his cheeks and the sort of complexion which is usually associated with hæmorrhoids . . . no help for that, it is the Petersburg climate. As for his grade in the service (for among us the grade is what must be put first), he was what is called a perpetual titular councillor, a class at which, as we all know, various writers who indulge in the praiseworthy habit of attacking those who cannot defend themselves jeer and jibe to their hearts' content. This clerk's surname was Bashmatchkin. From the very name it is clear that it must have been derived from a shoe (*bashmak*); but when and under what circumstances it was derived from a shoe, it is impossible to say. Both his father and his grandfather and even his brother-in-law, and all the Bashmatchkins without exception wore boots, which they simply re-soled two or three times a year. His name was Akaky Akakyevitch. Perhaps it may strike the reader as a rather strange and far-fetched name, but I can assure him that it was not far-fetched at all, that the circumstances were such that it was quite out of the question to give him any other name. Akaky Akakyevitch was born towards nightfall, if my memory does not deceive me, on the twenty-third of March. His mother, the wife of a government clerk, a very good woman, made arrangements in due course to christen the child. She was still lying in bed, facing the door, while on her right hand stood the godfather, an excellent man called Ivan Ivanovitch Yeroshkin, one of the head clerks in the Senate, and the godmother, the wife of a police official, and a woman of rare qualities, Arina Semyonovna Byelobryushkov. Three names were offered to the happy mother for selection — Moky, Sossy, or the name of the martyr Hozdazat. "No," thought the poor lady, "they are all such names!" To satisfy her, they opened the calendar at another place, and the names which turned up were: Trifily, Dula, Varahasy. "What an infliction!" said the mother. "What names they all are! I really never heard such names. Varadat or Varuh would be bad enough, but Trifily and Varahasy!" They turned over another page and the names were: Pavsikahy and Vahtisy. "Well, I see," said the mother, "it is clear that it is his fate. Since that is how it is, he had better be called after his father, his father is Akaky, let the son be Akaky, too." This was how he came to be Akaky Akakyevitch. The baby was christened and cried and made wry faces during the ceremony, as though he foresaw that he would be a titular councillor. So that was how it all came to pass. We have recalled it here so that the reader may see for himself that it happened quite inevitably and that to give him any other name was out of the question. No one has been able to remember when and how long ago he entered the department, nor who gave him the job. However many directors and higher officials of all sorts came and went, he was always seen in the same place, in the same position, at the very same duty, precisely the same copying clerk, so that they used to declare that he must have been born a copying clerk in uniform all complete and with a bald patch on his head. No respect at all was shown him in the department. The porters, far from getting up from their seats when he came in, took no more notice of him than if a simple fly had flown across the vestibule. His superiors treated him with a sort of domineering chilliness. The head clerk's assistant used to throw papers under his nose without even saying: "Copy this" or "Here is an interesting, nice little case" or some agreeable remark of the sort, as is usually done in well-behaved offices. And he would take it, gazing only at the paper without looking to see who had put it there and whether he had the right to do so; he would take it and at once set to work to copy it. The young clerks jeered and made jokes at him to the best of their clerkly wit, and told before his face all sorts of stories of their own invention about him; they would say of his landlady, an old woman of seventy, that she beat him, would enquire when the wedding was to take place, and would scatter bits of paper on his head, calling them snow. Akaky Akakyevitch never answered a word, however, but behaved as though there were no one there. It had no influence on his work even; in the midst of all this teasing, he never made a single mistake in his copying. Only when the jokes were too unbearable, when they jolted his arm and prevented him from going on with his work, he would bring out: "Leave me alone! Why do you insult me?" and there was something strange in the words and in the voice in which they were uttered. There was a note in it of something that aroused compassion, so that one young man, new to the office, who, following the example of the rest, had allowed himself to mock at him, suddenly stopped as though cut to the heart, and from that time forth everything was, as it were, changed and appeared in a different light to him. Some unnatural force seemed to thrust him away from the companions with whom he had become acquainted, accepting them as well-bred, polished people. And long afterwards, at moments of the greatest gaiety, the figure of the humble little clerk with a bald patch on his head rose before him with his heart-rending words: "Leave me alone! Why do you insult me?" and in those heart-rending words he heard others: "I am your brother." And the poor young man hid his face in his hands, and many times afterwards in his life he shuddered, seeing how much inhumanity there is in man, how much savage brutality lies hidden under refined, cultured politeness, and, my God! even in a man whom the world accepts as a gentleman and a man of honour. . . .

It would be hard to find a man who lived in his work as did Akaky Akakyevitch. To say that he was zealous in his work is not enough; no, he loved his work. In it, in that copying, he found a varied and agreeable world of his own. There was a look of enjoyment on his face; certain letters were favourites with him, and when he came to them he was delighted; he chuckled to himself and winked and moved his lips, so that it seemed as though every letter his pen was forming could be read in his face. If rewards had been given according to the measure of zeal in the service, he might to his amazement have even found himself a civil councillor; but all he gained in the service, as the wits, his fellow-clerks expressed it, was a buckle in his button-hole and a pain in his back. It cannot be said, however, that no notice had ever been taken of him. One director, being a good-natured man and anxious to reward him for his long service, sent him something a little more important than his ordinary copying; he was instructed from a finished document to make some sort of report for another office, the work consisted only of altering the headings and in places changing the first person into the third. This cost him such an effort that it threw him into a regular perspiration: he mopped his brow and said at last, "No, better let me copy something."

From that time forth they left him to go on copying for ever. It seemed as though nothing in the world existed for him outside his copying. He gave no thought at all to his clothes; his uniform was — well, not green but some sort of rusty, muddy colour. His collar was very short and narrow, so that, although his neck was not particularly long, yet, standing out of the collar, it looked as immensely long as those of the plaster kittens that wag their heads and are carried about on trays on the heads of dozens of foreigners living in Russia. And there were always things sticking to his uniform, either bits of hay or threads; moreover, he had a special art of passing under a window at the very moment when various rubbish was being flung out into the street, and so was continually carrying off bits of melon rind and similar litter on his hat. He had never once in his life noticed what was being done and going on in the street, all those things at which, as we all know, his colleagues, the young clerks, always stare, carrying their sharp sight so far even as to notice any one on the other side of the pavement with a trouser strap hanging loose — a detail which always calls forth a sly grin. Whatever Akaky Akakyevitch looked at, he saw nothing anywhere but his clear, evenly written lines, and only perhaps when a horse's head suddenly appeared from nowhere just on his shoulder, and its nostrils blew a perfect gale upon his cheek, did he notice that he was not in the middle of his writing, but rather in the middle of the street.

On reaching home, he would sit down at once to the table, hurriedly sup his soup and eat a piece of beef with an onion; he did not notice the taste at all, but ate it all up together with the flies and anything else that Providence chanced to send him. When he felt that his stomach was beginning to be full, he would rise up from the table, get out a bottle of ink and set to copying the papers he had brought home with him. When he had none to do, he would make a copy expressly for his own pleasure, particularly if the document were remarkable not for the beauty of its style but for the fact of its being addressed to some new or important personage.

Even at those hours when the grey Petersburg sky is completely overcast and the whole population of clerks have dined and eaten their fill, each as best he can, according to the salary he receives and his personal tastes; when they are all resting after the scratching of pens and bustle of the office, their own necessary work and other people's, and all the tasks that an over-zealous man voluntarily sets himself even beyond what is necessary; when the clerks are hastening to devote what is left of their time to pleasure; some more enterprising are flying to the theatre, others to the street to spend their leisure, staring at women's hats, some to spend the evening paying compliments to some attractive girl, the star of a little official circle, while some — and this is the most frequent of all — go simply to a fellow-clerk's flat on the third or fourth storey, two little rooms with an entry or a kitchen, with some pretentions to style, with a lamp or some such article that has cost many sacrifices of dinners and excursions — at the time when all the clerks are scattered about the little flats of their friends, playing a tempestuous game of whist, sipping tea out of glasses to the accompaniment of farthing rusks, sucking in smoke from long pipes, telling, as the cards are dealt, some scandal that has floated down from higher circles, a pleasure which the Russian can never by any possibility deny himself, or, when there is nothing better to talk about, repeating the everlasting anecdote of the commanding officer who was told that the tail had been cut off the horse on the Falconet monument — in short, even when every one was eagerly seeking entertainment, Akaky Akakyevitch did not give himself up to any amusement. No one could say that they had ever seen him at an evening party. After working to his heart's content, he would go to bed, smiling at the thought of the next day and wondering what God would send him to copy! So flowed on the peaceful life of a man who knew how to be content with his fate on a salary of four hundred roubles, and so perhaps it would have flowed on to extreme old age, had it not been for the various calamities that bestrew the path through life, not only of titular, but even of privy, actual court and all other councillors, even those who neither give council to others nor accept it themselves.

There is in Petersburg a mighty foe of all who receive a salary of four hundred roubles or about that sum. that foe is none other than our northern frost, although it is said to be very good for the health. Between eight and nine in the morning, precisely at the hour when the streets are full of clerks going to their departments, the frost begins giving such sharp and stinging flips at all their noses indiscriminately that the poor fellows don't know what to do with them. At that time, when even those in the higher grade have a pain in their brows and tears in their eyes from the frost, the poor titular councillors are sometimes almost defenceless. Their only protection lies in running as fast as they can through five or six streets in a wretched, thin little overcoat and then warming their feet thoroughly in the porter's room, till all their faculties and qualifications for their various duties thaw again after being frozen on the way. Akaky Akakyevitch had for some time been feeling that his back and shoulders were particularly nipped by the cold, although he did try to run the regular distance as fast as he could. He wondered at last whether there were any defects in his overcoat. After examining it thoroughly in the privacy of his home, he discovered that in two or three places, to wit on the back and the shoulders, it had become a regular sieve; the cloth was so worn that you could see through it and the lining was coming out. I must observe that Akaky Akakyevitch's overcoat had also served as a butt for the jibes of the clerks. It had even been deprived of the honourable name of overcoat and had been referred to as the "dressing jacket." It was indeed of rather a strange make. Its collar had been growing smaller year by year as it served to patch the other parts. The patches were not good specimens of the tailor's art, and they certainly looked clumsy and ugly. On seeing what was wrong, Akaky Akakyevitch decided that he would have to take the overcoat to Petrovitch, a tailor who lived on a fourth storey up a back staircase, and, in spite of having only one eye and being pock-marked all over his face, was rather successful in repairing the trousers and coats of clerks and others — that is, when he was sober, be it understood, and had no other enterprise in his mind. Of this tailor I ought not, of course, to say much, but since it is now the rule that the character of every person in a novel must be completely drawn, well, there is no help for it, here is Petrovitch too. At first he was called simply Grigory, and was a serf belonging to some gentleman or other. He began to be called Petrovitch from the time that he got his freedom and began to drink rather heavily on every holiday, at first only on the chief holidays, but afterwards on all church holidays indiscriminately, wherever there is a cross in the calendar. On that side he was true to the customs of his forefathers, and when he quarrelled with his wife used to call her "a worldly woman and a German." Since we have now mentioned the wife, it will be necessary to say a few words about her too, but unfortunately not much is known about her, except indeed that Petrovitch had a wife and that she wore a cap and not a kerchief, but apparently she could not boast of beauty; anyway, none but soldiers of the Guards peeped under her cap when they met her, and they twitched their moustaches and gave vent to a rather peculiar sound.

As he climbed the stairs, leading to Petrovitch's — which, to do them justice, were all soaked with water and slops and saturated through and through with that smell of spirits which makes the eyes smart, and is, as we all know, inseparable from the back-stairs of Petersburg houses — Akaky Akakyevitch was already wondering how much Petrovitch would ask for the job, and inwardly resolving not to give more than two roubles. The door was open, for Petrovitch's wife was frying some fish and had so filled the kitchen with smoke that you could not even see the black-beetles. Akaky Akakyevitch crossed the kitchen unnoticed by the good woman, and walked at last into a room where he saw Petrovitch sitting on a big, wooden, unpainted table with his legs tucked under him like a Turkish Pasha. The feet, as is usual with tailors when they sit at work, were bare; and the first object that caught Akaky Akakyevitch's eye was the big toe, with which he was already familiar, with a misshapen nail as thick and strong as the shell of a tortoise. Round Petrovitch's neck hung a skein of silk and another of thread and on his knees was a rag of some sort. He had for the last three minutes been trying to thread his needle, but could not get the thread into the eye and so was very angry with the darkness and indeed with the thread itself, muttering in an undertone: "It won't go in, the savage! You wear me out, you rascal." Akaky Akakyevitch was vexed that he had come just at the minute when Petrovitch was in a bad humour; he liked to give him an order when he was a little "elevated," or, as his wife expressed it, "had fortified himself on fizz, the one-eyed devil." In such circumstances Petrovitch was as a rule very ready to give way and agree, and invariably bowed and thanked him, indeed. Afterwards, it is true, his wife would come wailing that her husband had been drunk and so had asked too little, but adding a single ten-kopeck piece would settle that. But on this occasion Petrovitch was apparently sober and consequently curt, unwilling to bargain, and the devil knows what price he would be ready to lay on. Akaky Akakyevitch perceived this, and was, as the saying is, beating a retreat, but things had gone too far, for Petrovitch was screwing up his solitary eye very attentively at him and Akaky Akakyevitch involuntarily brought out: "Good day, Petrovitch!" "I wish you a good day, sir," said Petrovitch, and squinted at Akaky Akakyevitch's hands, trying to discover what sort of goods he had brought.

"Here I have come to you, Petrovitch, do you see . . . !"

It must be noticed that Akaky Akakyevitch for the most part explained himself by apologies, vague phrases, and particles which have absolutely no significance whatever. If the subject were a very difficult one, it was his habit indeed to leave his sentences quite unfinished, so that very often after a sentence had begun with the words, "It really is, don't you know . . . " nothing at all would follow and he himself would be quite oblivious, supposing he had said all that was necessary.

"What is it?" said Petrovitch, and at the same time with his solitary eye he scrutinized his whole uniform from the collar to the sleeves, the back, the skirts, the button-holes — with all of which he was very familiar, they were all his own work. Such scrutiny is habitual with tailors, it is the first thing they do on meeting one.

"It's like this, Petrovitch . . . the overcoat, the cloth . . . you see everywhere else it is quite strong; it's a little dusty and looks as though it were old, but it is new and it is only in one place just a little . . . on the back, and just a little worn on one shoulder and on this shoulder, too, a little . . . do you see? that's all, and it's not much work. . . . "

Petrovitch took the "dressing jacket," first spread it out over the table, examined it for a long time, shook his head and put his hand out to the window for a round snuff-box with a portrait on the lid of some general — which precisely I can't say, for a finger had been thrust through the spot where a face should have been, and the hole had been pasted up with a square piece of paper. After taking a pinch of snuff, Petrovitch held the "dressing jacket" up in his hands and looked at it against the light, and again he shook his head; then he turned it with the lining upwards and once more shook his head; again he took off the lid with the general pasted up with paper and stuffed a pinch into his nose, shut the box, put it away and at last said: "No, it can't be repaired; a wretched garment!" Akaky Akakyevitch's heart sank at those words.

"Why can't it, Petrovitch?" he said, almost in the imploring voice of a child. "Why, the only thing is it is a bit worn on the shoulders; why, you have got some little pieces. . . . "

"Yes, the pieces will be found all right," said Petrovitch, "but it can't be patched, the stuff is quite rotten; if you put a needle in it, it would give way."

"Let it give way, but you just put a patch on it."

"There is nothing to put a patch on. There is nothing for it to hold on to; there is a great strain on it, it is not worth calling cloth, it would fly away at a breath of wind."

"Well, then, strengthen it with something — upon my word, really, this is . . . !

"No," said Petrovitch resolutely, "there is nothing to be done, the thing is no good at all. You had far better, when the cold winter weather comes, make yourself leg wrappings out of it, for there is no warmth in stockings, the Germans invented them just to make money." (Petrovitch was fond of a dig at the Germans occasionally.) "And as for the overcoat, it is clear that you will have to have a new one."

At the word "new" there was a mist before Akaky Akakyevitch's eyes, and everything in the room seemed blurred. He could see nothing clearly but the general with the piece of paper over his face on the lid of Petrovitch's snuff-box.

"A new one?" he said, still feeling as though he were in a dream; "why, I haven't the money for it."

"Yes, a new one," Petrovitch repeated with barbarous composure.

"Well, and if I did have a new one, how much would it . . . ?"

"You mean what will it cost?"

"Yes."

"Well, three fifty-rouble notes or more," said Petrovitch, and he compressed his lips significantly. He was very fond of making an effect, he was fond of suddenly disconcerting a man completely and then squinting sideways to see what sort of a face he made.

"A hundred and fifty roubles for an overcoat," screamed poor Akaky Akakyevitch — it was perhaps the first time he had screamed in his life, for he was always distinguished by the softness of his voice.

"Yes," said Petrovitch, "and even then it's according to the coat. If I were to put marten on the collar, and add a hood with silk linings, it would come to two hundred."

"Petrovitch, please," said Akaky Akakyevitch in an imploring voice, not hearing and not trying to hear what Petrovitch said, and missing all his effects, "do repair it somehow, so that it will serve a little longer."

"No, that would be wasting work and spending money for nothing," said Petrovitch, and after that Akaky Akakyevitch went away completely crushed, and when he had gone Petrovitch remained standing for a long time with his lips pursed up significantly before he took up his work again, feeling pleased that he had not demeaned himself nor lowered the dignity of the tailor's art.

When he got into the street, Akaky Akakyevitch was as though in a dream. "So that is how it is," he said to himself. "I really did not think it would be so . . . " and then after a pause he added, "So there it is! so that's how it is at last! and I really could never have supposed it would have been so. And there . . . " There followed another long silence, after which he brought out: "So there it is! well, it really is so utterly unexpected . . . who would have thought . . . what a circumstance. . . . " Saying this, instead of going home he walked off in quite the opposite direction without suspecting what he was doing. On the way a clumsy sweep brushed the whole of his sooty side against him and blackened all his shoulder; a regular hatful of plaster scattered upon him from the top of a house that was being built. He noticed nothing of this, and only after he had jostled against a sentry who had set his halberd down beside him and was shaking some snuff out of his horn into his rough fist, he came to himself a little and then only because the sentry said: "Why are you poking yourself right in one's face, haven't you the pavement to yourself?" This made him look round and turn homeward; only there he began to collect his thoughts, to see his position in a clear and true light and began talking to himself no longer incoherently but reasonably and openly as with a sensible friend with whom one can discuss the most intimate and vital matters. "No, indeed," said Akaky Akakyevitch, "it is no use talking to Petrovitch now; just now he really is . . . his wife must have been giving it to him. I had better go to him on Sunday morning; after the Saturday evening he will be squinting and sleepy, so he'll want a little drink to carry it off and his wife won't give him a penny. I'll slip ten kopecks into his hand and then he will be more accommodating and maybe take the overcoat. . . . "

So reasoning with himself, Akaky Akakyevitch cheered up and waited until the next Sunday; then, seeing from a distance Petrovitch's wife leaving the house, he went straight in. Petrovitch certainly was very tipsy after the Saturday. He could hardly hold his head up and was very drowsy: but, for all that, as soon as he heard what he was speaking about, it seemed as though the devil had nudged him. "I can't," he said, "you must kindly order a new one." Akaky Akakyevitch at once slipped a ten-kopeck piece into his hand. "I thank you, sir, I will have just a drop to your health, but don't trouble yourself about the overcoat; it is not a bit of good for anything. I'll make you a fine new coat, you can trust me for that."

Akaky Akakyevitch would have said more about repairs, but Petrovitch, without listening, said: "A new one now I'll make you without fail; you can rely upon that, I'll do my best. It could even be like the fashion that has come in with the collar to button with silver claws under appliqué."

Then Akaky Akakyevitch saw that there was no escape from a new overcoat and he was utterly depressed. How indeed, for what, with what money could he get it? Of course he could to some extent rely on the bonus for the coming holiday, but that money had long ago been appropriated and its use determined beforehand. It was needed for new trousers and to pay the cobbler an old debt for putting some new tops to some old boot-legs, and he had to order three shirts from a seamstress as well as two specimens of an undergarment which it is improper to mention in print; in short, all that money absolutely must be spent, and even if the director were to be so gracious as to assign him a gratuity of forty-five or even fifty, instead of forty roubles, there would be still left a mere trifle, which would be but as a drop in the ocean beside the fortune needed for an overcoat. Though, of course, he knew that Petrovitch had a strange craze for suddenly putting on the devil knows what enormous price, so that at times his own wife could not help crying out: "Why, you are out of your wits, you idiot! Another time he'll undertake a job for nothing, and here the devil has bewitched him to ask more than he is worth himself." Though, of course, he knew that Petrovitch would undertake to make it for eighty roubles, still where would he get those eighty roubles? He might manage half of that sum; half of it could be found, perhaps even a little more; but where could he get the other half? . . . But, first of all, the reader ought to know where that first half was to be found. Akaky Akakyevitch had the habit every time he spent a rouble of putting aside two kopecks in a little locked-up box with a slit in the lid for slipping the money in. At the end of every half-year he would inspect the pile of coppers there and change them for small silver. He had done this for a long time, and in the course of many years the sum had mounted up to forty roubles and so he had half the money in his hands, but where was he to get the other half, where was he to get another forty roubles? Akaky Akakyevitch pondered and pondered and decided at last that he would have to diminish his ordinary expenses, at least for a year; give up burning candles in the evening, and if he had to do anything he must go into the landlady's room and work by her candle; that as he walked along the streets he must walk as lightly and carefully as possible, almost on tiptoe, on the cobbles and flagstones, so that his soles might last a little longer than usual; that he must send his linen to the wash less frequently, and that, to preserve it from being worn, he must take it off every day when he came home and sit in a thin cotton-shoddy dressing-gown, a very ancient garment which Time itself had spared. To tell the truth, he found it at first rather hard to get used to these privations, but after a while it became a habit and went smoothly enough — he even became quite accustomed to being hungry in the evening; on the other hand, he had spiritual nourishment, for he carried ever in his thoughts the idea of his future overcoat. His whole existence had in a sense become fuller, as though he had married, as though some other person were present with him, as though he were no longer alone, but an agreeable companion had consented to walk the path of life hand in hand with him, and that companion was no other than the new overcoat with its thick wadding and its strong, durable lining. He became, as it were, more alive, even more strong-willed, like a man who has set before himself a definite aim. Uncertainty, indecision, in fact all the hesitating and vague characteristics vanished from his face and his manners. At times there was a gleam in his eyes, indeed, the most bold and audacious ideas flashed through his mind. Why not really have marten on the collar? Meditation on the subject always made him absent-minded. On one occasion when he was copying a document, he very nearly made a mistake, so that he almost cried out "ough" aloud and crossed himself. At least once every month he went to Petrovitch to talk about the overcoat, where it would be best to buy the cloth, and what colour it should be, and what price, and, though he returned home a little anxious, he was always pleased at the thought that at last the time was at hand when everything would be bought and the overcoat would be made. Things moved even faster than he had anticipated. Contrary to all expectations, the director bestowed on Akaky Akakyevitch a gratuity of no less than sixty roubles. Whether it was that he had an inkling that Akaky Akakyevitch needed a greatcoat, or whether it happened so by chance, owing to this he found he had twenty roubles extra. This circumstance hastened the course of affairs. Another two or three months of partial fasting and Akaky Akakyevitch had actually saved up nearly eighty roubles. His heart, as a rule very tranquil, began to throb. The very first day he set off in company with Petrovitch to the shops. They bought some very good cloth, and no wonder, since they had been thinking of it for more than six months before, and scarcely a month had passed without their going to the shop to compare prices; now Petrovitch himself declared that there was no better cloth to be had. For the lining they chose calico, but of a stout quality, which in Petrovitch's words was even better than silk, and actually as strong and handsome to look at. Marten they did not buy, because it certainly was dear, but instead they chose cat fur, the best to be found in the shop — cat which in the distance might almost be taken for marten. Petrovitch was busy over the coat for a whole fortnight, because there were a great many button-holes, otherwise it would have been ready sooner. Petrovitch asked twelve roubles for the work; less than that it hardly could have been, everything was sewn with silk, with fine double seams, and Petrovitch went over every seam afterwards with his own teeth imprinting various figures with them. It was . . . it is hard to say precisely on what day, but probably on the most triumphant day of the life of Akaky

Akakyevitch that Petrovitch at last brought the overcoat. He brought it in the morning, just before it was time to set off for the department. The overcoat could not have arrived more in the nick of time, for rather sharp frosts were just beginning and seemed threatening to be even more severe. Petrovitch brought the greatcoat himself as a good tailor should. There was an expression of importance on his face, such as Akaky Akakyevitch had never seen there before. He seemed fully conscious of having completed a work of no little moment and of having shown in his own person the gulf that separates tailors who only put in linings and do repairs from those who make up new materials. He took the greatcoat out of the pocket-handkerchief in which he had brought it (the pocket-handkerchief had just come home from the wash), he then folded it up and put it in his pocket for future use. After taking out the overcoat, he looked at it with much pride and, holding it in both hands, threw it very deftly over Akaky Akakyevitch's shoulders, then pulled it down and smoothed it out behind with his hands; then draped it about Akaky Akakyevitch with somewhat jaunty carelessness. The latter, as a man advanced in years, wished to try it with his arms in the sleeves. Petrovitch helped him to put it on, and it appeared that it looked splendid too with his arms in the sleeves. In fact it turned out that the overcoat was completely and entirely successful. Petrovitch did not let slip the occasion for observing that it was only because he lived in a small street and had no signboard, and because he had known Akaky Akakyevitch so long, that he had done it so cheaply, but on the Nevsky Prospect they would have asked him seventy-five roubles for the work alone. Akaky Akakyevitch had no inclination to discuss this with Petrovitch, besides he was frightened of the big sums that Petrovitch was fond of flinging airily about in conversation. He paid him, thanked him, and went off on the spot, with his new overcoat on, to the department. Petrovitch followed him out and stopped in the street, staring for a good time at the coat from a distance and then purposely turned off and, taking a short cut by a side street, came back into the street and got another view of the coat from the other side, that is, from the front.

Meanwhile Akaky Akakyevitch walked along with every emotion in its most holiday mood. He felt every second that he had a new overcoat on his shoulders, and several times he actually laughed from inward satisfaction. Indeed, it had two advantages, one that it was warm and the other that it was good. He did not notice the way at all and found himself all at once at the department; in the porter's room he took off the overcoat, looked it over and put it in the porter's special care. I cannot tell how it happened, but all at once every one in the department learned that Akaky Akakyevitch had a new overcoat and that the "dressing jacket" no longer existed. They all ran out at once into the porter's room to look at Akaky Akakyevitch's new overcoat, they began welcoming him and congratulating him so that at first he could do nothing but smile and afterwards felt positively abashed. When, coming up to him, they all began saying that he must "sprinkle" the new overcoat and that he ought at least to stand them all a supper, Akaky Akakyevitch lost his head completely and did not know what to do, how to get out of it, nor what to answer. A few minutes later, flushing crimson, he even began assuring them with great simplicity that it was not a new overcoat at all, that it was just nothing, that it was an old overcoat. At last one of the clerks, indeed the assistant of the head clerk of the room, probably in order to show that he was not proud and was able to get on with those beneath him, said: "So be it, I'll give a party instead of Akaky Akakyevitch and invite you all to tea with me this evening; as luck would have it, it is my name-day." The clerks naturally congratulated the assistant head clerk and eagerly accepted the invitation. Akaky Akakyevitch was beginning to make excuses, but they all declared that it was uncivil of him, that it was simply a shame and a disgrace and that he could not possibly refuse. However, he felt pleased about it afterwards when he remembered that through this he would have the opportunity of going out in the evening, too, in his new overcoat. That whole day was for Akaky Akakyevitch the most triumphant and festive day in his life. He returned home in the happiest frame of mind, took off the overcoat and hung it carefully on the wall, admiring the cloth and lining once more, and then pulled out his old "dressing jacket," now completely coming to pieces, on purpose to compare them. He glanced at it and positively laughed, the difference was so immense! And long afterwards he went on laughing at dinner, as the position in which the "dressing jacket" was placed recurred to his mind. He dined in excellent spirits and after dinner wrote nothing, no papers at all, but just took his ease for a little while on his bed, till it got dark, then, without putting things off, he dressed, put on his overcoat, and went out into the street. Where precisely the clerk who had invited him lived we regret to say that we cannot tell; our memory is beginning to fail sadly, and everything there is in Petersburg, all the streets and houses, are so blurred and muddled in our head that it is a very difficult business to put anything in orderly fashion. However that may have been, there is no doubt that the clerk lived in the better part of the town and consequently a very long distance from Akaky Akakyevitch. At first the latter had to walk through deserted streets, scantily lighted, but as he approached his destination the streets became more lively, more full of people, and more brightly lighted; passers-by began to be more frequent, ladies began to appear, here and there, beautifully dressed, beaver collars were to be seen on the men. Cabmen with wooden trellis-work sledges, studded with gilt nails, were less frequently to be met; on the other hand, jaunty drivers in raspberry coloured velvet caps with varnished sledges and bearskin rugs appeared, and carriages with decorated boxes dashed along the streets, their wheels crunching through the snow.

Akaky Akakyevitch looked at all this as a novelty; for several years he had not gone out into the streets in the evening. He stopped with curiosity before a lighted shop-window to look at a picture in which a beautiful woman was represented in the act of taking off her shoe and displaying as she did so the whole of a very shapely leg, while behind her back a gentleman with whiskers and a handsome imperial on his chin was putting his head in at the door. Akaky Akakyevitch shook his head and smiled and then went on his way. Why did he smile? Was it because he had come across something quite unfamiliar to him, though every man retains some instinctive feeling on the subject, or was it that he reflected, like many other clerks, as follows: "Well, upon my soul, those Frenchmen! it's beyond anything! if they try on anything of the sort, it really is . . . !" Though possibly he did not even think that; there is no creeping into a man's soul and finding out all that he thinks. At last he reached the house in which the assistant head clerk lived in fine style; there was a lamp burning on the stairs, and the flat was on the second floor. As he went into the entry Akaky Akakyevitch saw whole rows of goloshes. Amongst them in the middle of the room stood a samovar hissing and letting off clouds of steam. On the walls hung coats and cloaks, among which some actually had beaver collars or velvet revers. The other side of the wall there was noise and talk, which suddenly became clear and loud when the door opened and the footman came out with a tray full of empty glasses, a jug of cream, and a basket of biscuits. It was evident that the clerks had arrived long before and had already drunk their first glass of tea. Akaky Akakyevitch, after hanging up his coat with his own hands, went into the room, and at the same moment there flashed before his eyes a vision of candles, clerks, pipes, and card tables, together with the confused sounds of conversation rising up on all sides and the noise of moving chairs. He stopped very awkwardly in the middle of the room, looking about and trying to think what to do, but he was observed and received with a shout and they all went at once into the entry and again took a look at his overcoat. Though Akaky Akakyevitch was somewhat embarrassed, yet, being a simple-hearted man, he could not help being pleased at seeing how they all admired his coat.

Then of course they all abandoned him and his coat, and turned their attention as usual to the tables set for whist. All this — the noise, the talk, and the crowd of people — was strange and wonderful to Akaky Akakyevitch. He simply did not know how to behave, what to do with his arms and legs and his whole figure; at last he sat down beside the players, looked at the cards, stared first at one and then at another of the faces, and in a little while began to yawn and felt that he was bored — especially as it was long past the time at which he usually went to bed. He tried to take leave of his hosts, but they would not let him go, saying that he absolutely must have a glass of champagne in honour of the new coat. An hour later supper was served, consisting of salad, cold veal, a pasty, pies, and tarts from the confectioner's, and champagne. They made Akaky Akakyevitch drink two glasses, after which he felt that things were much more cheerful, though he could not forget that it was twelve o'clock and that he ought to have been home long ago. That his host might not take it into his head to detain him, he slipped out of the room, hunted in the entry for his greatcoat, which he found, not without regret, lying on the floor, shook it, removed some fluff from it, put it on, and went down the stairs into the street. It was still light in the streets. Some little general shops, those perpetual clubs for houseserfs and all sorts of people, were open; others which were closed showed, however, a long streak of light at every crack of the door, proving that they were not yet deserted, and probably maids and men-servants were still finishing their conversation and discussion, driving their masters to utter perplexity as to their whereabouts. Akaky Akakyevitch walked along in a cheerful state of mind; he was even on the point of running, goodness knows why, after a lady of some sort who passed by like lightning with every part of her frame in violent motion. He checked himself at once, however, and again walked along very gently, feeling positively surprised himself at the inexplicable impulse that had seized him. Soon the deserted streets, which are not particularly cheerful by day and even less so in the evening, stretched before him. Now they were still more dead and deserted; the light of street lamps was scantier, the oil was evidently running low; then came wooden houses and fences; not a soul anywhere; only the snow gleamed on the streets and the low-pitched slumbering hovels looked black and gloomy with their closed shutters. He approached the spot where the street was intersected by an endless square, which looked like a fearful desert with its houses scarcely visible on the further side.

In the distance, goodness knows where, there was a gleam of light from some sentry-box which seemed to be standing at the end of the world. Akaky Akakyevitch's light-heartedness grew somewhat sensibly less at this place. He stepped into the square, not without an involuntary uneasiness, as though his heart had a foreboding of evil. He looked behind him and to both sides — it was as though the sea were all round him. "No, better not look," he thought, and walked on, shutting his eyes, and when he opened them to see whether the end of the square were near, he suddenly saw standing before him, almost under his very nose, some men with moustaches; just what they were like he could not even distinguish. There was a mist before his eyes and a throbbing in his chest. "I say the overcoat is mine!" said one of them in a voice like a clap of thunder, seizing him by the collar. Akaky Akakyevitch was on the point of shouting "Help" when another put a fist the size of a clerk's head against his very lips, saying: "You just shout now." Akaky Akakyevitch felt only that they took the overcoat off, and gave him a kick with their knees, and he fell on his face in the snow and was conscious of nothing more. A few minutes later he came to himself and got on to his feet, but there was no one there. He felt that it was cold on the ground and that he had no overcoat, and began screaming, but it seemed as though his voice could not carry to the end of the square. Overwhelmed with despair and continuing to scream, he ran across the square straight to the sentry-box, beside which stood a sentry leaning on his halberd and, so it seemed, looking with curiosity to see who the devil the man was who was screaming and running towards him from the distance. As Akaky Akakyevitch reached him, he began breathlessly shouting that he was asleep and not looking after his duty not to see that a man was being robbed. The sentry answered that he had seen nothing, that he had only seen him stopped in the middle of the square by two men, and supposed that they were his friends, and that, instead of abusing him for nothing, he had better go the next day to the superintendent and that he would find out who had taken the overcoat. Akaky Akakyevitch ran home in a terrible state: his hair, which was still comparatively abundant on his temples and the back of his head, was completely dishevelled; his sides and chest and his trousers were all covered with snow. When his old landlady heard a fearful knock at the door she jumped hurriedly out of bed and, with only one slipper on, ran to open it, modestly holding her shift across her bosom; but when she opened it she stepped back, seeing what a state Akaky Akakyevitch was in. When he told her what had happened, she clasped her hands in horror and said that he must go straight to the superintendent, that the police constable of the quarter would deceive him, make promises and lead him a dance; that it would be best of all to go to the superintendent, and that she knew him indeed, because Anna the Finnish girl who was once her cook was now in service as a nurse at the superintendent's; and that she often saw him himself when he passed by their house, and that he used to be every Sunday at church too, saying his prayers and at the same time looking good-humouredly at every one, and that therefore by every token he must be a kind-hearted man. After listening to this advice, Akaky Akakyevitch made his way very gloomily to his room, and how he spent that night I leave to the imagination of those who are in the least able to picture the position of others. Early in the morning he set off to the police superintendent's, but was told that he was asleep. He came at ten o'clock, he was told again that he was asleep; he came at eleven and was told that tthe superintendent was not at home; he came at dinner-time, but the clerks in the ante-room would not let him in, and insisted on knowing what was the matter and what business had brought him and exactly what had happened; so that at last Akaky Akakyevitch for the first time in his life tried to show the strength of his character and said curtly that he must see the superintendent himself, that they dare not refuse to admit him, that he had come from the department on government business, and that if he made complaint of them they would see. The clerks dared to say nothing to this, and one of them went to summon the superintendent. The latter received his story of being robbed of his overcoat in an extremely strange way. Instead of attending to the main point, he began asking Akaky Akakyevitch questions, why had he been coming home so late? wasn't he going, or hadn't he been, to some house of ill-fame? so that Akaky Akakyevitch was overwhelmed with confusion, and went away without knowing whether or not the proper measures would be taken in regard to his overcoat. He was absent from the office all that day (the only time that it had happened in his life). Next day he appeared with a pale face, wearing his old "dressing jacket" which had become a still more pitiful sight. The tidings of the theft of the overcoat — though there were clerks who did not let even this chance slip of jeering at Akaky Akakyevitch — touched many of them. They decided on the spot to get up a subscription for him, but collected only a very trifling sum, because the clerks had already spent a good deal on subscribing to the director's portrait and on the purchase of a book, at the suggestion of the head of their department, who was a friend of the author, and so the total realised was very insignificant. One of the clerks, moved by compassion, ventured at any rate to assist Akaky Akakyevitch with good advice, telling him not to go to the district police inspector, because though it might happen that the latter might be sufficiently zealous of gaining the approval of his superiors to succeed in finding the overcoat, it would remain in the possession of the police unless he presented legal proofs that it belonged to him; he urged that far the best thing would be to appeal to a Person of Consequence; that the Person of Consequence, by writing and getting into communication with the proper authorities, could push the matter through more successfully. There was nothing else for it. Akaky Akakyevitch made up his mind to go to the Person of Consequence. What precisely was the nature of the functions of the Person of Consequence has remained a matter of uncertainty. It must be noted that this Person of Consequence had only lately become a person of consequence, and until recently had been a person of no consequence. Though, indeed, his position even now was not reckoned of consequence in comparison with others of still greater consequence. But there is always to be found a circle of persons to whom a person of little consequence in the eyes of others is a person of consequence. It is true that he did his utmost to increase the consequence of his position in various ways, for instance by insisting that his subordinates should come out on to the stairs to meet him when he arrived at his office; that no one should venture to approach him directly but all proceedings should be by the strictest order of precedence, that a collegiate registration clerk should report the matter to the provincial secretary, and the provincial secretary to the titular councillor or whomsoever it might be, and that business should only reach him by this channel. Every one in Holy Russia has a craze for imitation, every one apes and mimics his superiors. I have actually been told that a titular councillor who was put in charge of a small separate office, immediately partitioned off a special room for himself, calling it the head office, and set special porters at the door with red collars and gold lace, who took hold of the handle of the door and opened it for every one who went in, though the "head office" was so tiny that it was with difficulty that an ordinary writing table could be put into it. The manners and habits of the Person of Consequence were dignified and majestic, but not complex. The chief foundation of his system was strictness, "strictness, strictness, and — strictness!" he used to say, and at the last word he would look very significantly at the person he was addressing, though, indeed, he had no reason to do so, for the dozen clerks who made up the whole administrative mechanism of his office stood in befitting awe of him; any clerk who saw him in the distance would leave his work and remain standing at attention till his superior had left the room. His conversation with his subordinates was usually marked by severity and almost confined to three phrases: "How dare you? Do you know to whom you are speaking? Do you understand who I am?" He was, however, at heart a good-natured man, pleasant and obliging with his colleagues; but the grade of general had completely turned his head. When he received it, he was perplexed, thrown off his balance, and quite at a loss how to behave. If he chanced to be with his equals, he was still quite a decent man, a very gentlemanly man, in fact, and in many ways even an intelligent man, but as soon as he was in company with men who were even one grade below him, there was simply no doing anything with him: he sat silent and his position excited compassion, the more so as he himself felt that he might have been spending his time to incomparably more advantage. At times there could be seen in his eyes an intense desire to join in some interesting conversation, but he was restrained by the doubt whether it would not be too much on his part, whether it would not be too great a familiarity and lowering of his dignity, and in consequence of these reflections he remained everlastingly in the same mute condition, only uttering from time to time monosyllabic sounds, and in this way he gained the reputation of being a very tiresome man.

So this was the Person of Consequence to whom our friend Akaky Akakyevitch appealed, and he appealed to him at a most unpropitious moment, very unfortunate for himself, though fortunate, indeed, for the Person of Consequence. The latter happened to be in his study, talking in the very best of spirits with an old friend of his childhood who had only just arrived and whom he had not seen for several years. It was at this moment that he was informed that a man called Bashmatchkin was asking to see him. He asked abruptly, "What sort of man is he?" and received the answer, "A government clerk." "Ah! he can wait, I haven't time now," said the Person of Consequence. Here I must observe that this was a complete lie on the part of the Person of Consequence: he had time; his friend and he had long ago said all they had to say to each other and their conversation had begun to be broken by very long pauses during which they merely slapped each other on the knee, saying, "So that's how things are, Ivan Abramovitch!" — "There it is, Stepan Varlamovitch!" but, for all that, he told the clerk to wait in order to show his friend, who had left the service years before and was living at home in the country how long clerks had to wait in his ante-room. At last after they had talked, or rather been silent to their heart's content and had smoked a cigar in very comfortable arm-chairs with sloping backs, he seemed suddenly to recollect, and said to the secretary, who was standing at the door with papers for his signature: "Oh, by the way, there is a clerk waiting, isn't there? tell him he can come in." When he saw Akaky Akakyevitch's meek appearance and old uniform, he turned to him at once and said: "What do you want?" in a firm and abrupt voice, which he had purposely practised in his own room in solitude before the looking-glass for a week before receiving his present post and the grade of a general. Akaky Akakyevitch, who was overwhelmed with befitting awe beforehand, was somewhat confused and, as far as his tongue would allow him, explained to the best of his powers, with even more frequent "ers" than usual, that he had had a perfectly new overcoat and now he had been robbed of it in the most inhuman way, and that now he had come to beg him by his intervention either to correspond with his honour the head policemaster or anybody else, and find the overcoat. This mode of proceeding struck the general for some reason as taking a great liberty. "What next, sir," he went on as abruptly, "don't you know the way to proceed? To whom are you addressing yourself? Don't you know how things are done? You ought first to have handed in a petition to the office; it would have gone to the head clerk of the room, and to the head clerk of the section, then it would have been handed to the secretary and the secretary would have brought it to me. . . . "

"But, your Excellency," said Akaky Akakyevitch, trying to collect all the small allowance of presence of mind he possessed and feeling at the same time that he was getting into a terrible perspiration, "I ventured, your Excellency, to trouble you because secretaries . . . er . . . are people you can't depend on. . . . "

"What? what? what?" said the Person of Consequence, "where did you get hold of that spirit? where did you pick up such ideas? What insubordination is spreading among young men against their superiors and betters." The Person of Consequence did not apparently observe that Akaky Akakyevitch was well over fifty, and therefore if he could have been called a young man it would only have been in comparison with a man of seventy. "Do you know to whom you are speaking? do you understand who I am? do you understand that, I ask you?" At this point he stamped, and raised his voice to such a powerful note that Akaky Akakyevitch was not the only one to be terrified. Akaky Akakyevitch was positively petrified; he staggered, trembling all over, and could not stand; if the porters had not run up to support him, he would have flopped upon the floor; he was led out almost unconscious. The Person of Consequence, pleased that the effect had surpassed his expectations and enchanted at the idea that his words could even deprive a man of consciousness, stole a sideway glance at his friend to see how he was taking it, and perceived not without satisfaction that his friend was feeling very uncertain and even beginning to be a little terrified himself.

How he got downstairs, how he went out into the street — of all that Akaky Akakyevitch remembered nothing, he had no feeling in his arms or his legs. In all his life he had never been so severely reprimanded by a general, and this was by one of another department, too. He went out into the snowstorm, that was whistling through the streets, with his mouth open, and as he went he stumbled off the pavement; the wind, as its way is in Petersburg, blew upon him from all points of the compass and from every side street. In an instant it had blown a quinsy into his throat, and when he got home he was not able to utter a word; with a swollen face and throat he went to bed. So violent is sometimes the effect of a suitable reprimand!

Next day he was in a high fever. Thanks to the gracious assistance of the Petersburg climate, the disease made more rapid progress than could have been expected, and when the doctor came, after feeling his pulse he could find nothing to do but prescribe a fomentation,[1] and that simply that the patient might not be left without the benefit of medical assistance; however, two days later he informed him that his end was at hand, after which he turned to his landlady and said: "And you had better lose no time, my good woman, but order him now a deal coffin, for an oak one will be too dear for him." Whether Akaky Akakyevitch heard these fateful words or not, whether they produced a shattering effect upon him, and whether he regretted his pitiful life, no one can tell, for he was all the time in delirium and fever. Apparitions, each stranger than the one before, were continually haunting him: first, he saw Petrovitch and was ordering him to make a greatcoat trimmed with some sort of traps for robbers, who were, he fancied, continually under the bed, and he was calling his landlady every minute to pull out a thief who had even got under the quilt; then he kept asking why his old "dressing jacket" was hanging before him when he had a new overcoat, then he fancied he was standing before the general listening to the appropriate reprimand and saying "I am sorry, your Excellency," then finally he became abusive, uttering the most awful language, so that his old landlady positively crossed herself, having never heard anything of the kind from him before, and the more horrified because these dreadful words followed immediately upon the phrase "your Excellency." Later on, his talk was a mere medley of nonsense, so that it was quite unintelligible; all that could be seen was that his incoherent words and thoughts were concerned with nothing but the overcoat. At last poor Akaky Akakyevitch gave up the ghost. No seal was put upon his room nor upon his things, because, in the first place, he had no heirs and, in the second, the property left was very small, to wit, a bundle of goose-feathers, a quire of white government paper, three pairs of socks, two or three buttons that had come off his trousers, and the "dressing jacket" with which the reader is already familiar. Who came into all this wealth God only knows, even I who tell the tale must own that I have not troubled to enquire. And Petersburg remained without Akaky Akakyevitch, as though, indeed, he had never been in the city. A creature had vanished and departed whose cause no one had championed, who was dear to no one, of interest to no one, who never even attracted the attention of the student of natural history, though the latter does not disdain to fix a common fly upon a pin and look at him under the microscope — a creature who bore patiently the jeers of the office and for no particular reason went to his grave, though even he at the very end of his life was visited by a gleam of brightness in the form of an overcoat that for one instant brought colour into his poor life — a creature on whom calamity broke as insufferably as it breaks upon the heads of the mighty ones of this world . . . !

Several days after his death, the porter from the department was sent to his lodgings with instructions that he should go at once to the office, for his chief was asking for him; but the porter was obliged to return without him, explaining that he could not come, and to the enquiry "Why?" he added, "Well, you see: the fact is he is dead, he was buried three days ago." This was how they learned at the office of the death of Akaky Akakyevitch, and the next day there was sitting in his seat a new clerk who was very much taller and who wrote not in the same upright hand but made his letters more slanting and crooked.

---

[1] A medicinal ointment.

But who could have imagined that this was not all there was to tell about Akaky Akakyevitch, that he was destined for a few days to make a noise in the world after his death, as though to make up for his life having been unnoticed by any one? But so it happened, and our poor story unexpectedly finishes with a fantastic ending. Rumours were suddenly floating about Petersburg that in the neighbourhood of the Kalinkin Bridge and for a little distance beyond, a corpse had taken to appearing at night in the form of a clerk looking for a stolen overcoat, and stripping from the shoulders of all passers-by, regardless of grade and calling, overcoats of all descriptions — trimmed with cat fur, or beaver or wadded, lined with raccoon, fox and bear — made, in fact, of all sorts of skin which men have adapted for the covering of their own. One of the clerks of the department saw the corpse with his own eyes and at once recognized it as Akaky Akakyevitch; but it excited in him such terror, however, that he ran away as fast as his legs could carry him and so could not get a very clear view of him, and only saw him hold up his finger threateningly in the distance.

From all sides complaints were continually coming that backs and shoulders, not of mere titular councillors, but even of upper court councillors, had been exposed to taking chills, owing to being stripped of their greatcoats. Orders were given to the police to catch the corpse regardless of trouble or expense, alive or dead, and to punish him in the cruellest way, as an example to others, and, indeed, they very nearly succeeded in doing so. The sentry of one district police station in Kiryushkin Place snatched a corpse by the collar on the spot of the crime in the very act of attempting to snatch a frieze overcoat from a retired musician, who used in his day to play the flute. Having caught him by the collar, he shouted until he had brought two other comrades, whom he charged to hold him while he felt just a minute in his boot to get out a snuff-box in order to revive his nose which had six times in his life been frost-bitten, but the snuff was probably so strong that not even a dead man could stand it. The sentry had hardly had time to put his finger over his right nostril and draw up some snuff in the left when the corpse sneezed violently right into the eyes of all three. While they were putting their fists up to wipe them, the corpse completely vanished, so that they were not even sure whether he had actually been in their hands. From that time forward, the sentries conceived such a horror of the dead that they were even afraid to seize the living and confined themselves to shouting from the distance: "Hi, you there, be off!" and the dead clerk began to appear even on the other side of the Kalinkin Bridge, rousing no little terror in all timid people.

We have, however, quite deserted the Person of Consequence, who may in reality almost be said to be the cause of the fantastic ending of this perfectly true story. To begin with, my duty requires me to do justice to the Person of Consequence by recording that soon after poor Akaky Akakyevitch had gone away crushed to powder, he felt something not unlike regret. Sympathy was a feeling not unknown to him; his heart was open to many kindly impulses, although his exalted grade very often prevented them from being shown. As soon as his friend had gone out of his study, he even began brooding over poor Akaky Akakyevitch, and from that time forward, he was almost every day haunted by the image of the poor clerk who had succumbed so completely to the befitting reprimand. The thought of the man so worried him that a week later he actually decided to send a clerk to find out how he was and whether he really could help him in any way. And when they brought him word that Akaky Akakyevitch had died suddenly in delirium and fever, it made a great impression on him, his conscience reproached him and he was depressed all day. Anxious to distract his mind and to forget the unpleasant impression, he went to spend the evening with one of his friends, where he found a genteel company and, what was best of all, almost every one was of the same grade so that he was able to be quite free from restraint. This had a wonderful effect on his spirits, he expanded, became affable and genial — in short, spent a very agreeable evening. At supper he drank a couple of glasses of champagne — a proceeding which we all know has a happy effect in inducing good-humour. The champagne made him inclined to do something unusual, and he decided not to go home yet but to visit a lady of his acquaintance, one Karolina Ivanovna — a lady apparently of German extraction, for whom he entertained extremely friendly feelings. It must be noted that the Person of Consequence was a man no longer young, an excellent husband, and the respectable father of a family. He had two sons, one already serving in his office, and a nice-looking daughter of sixteen with a rather turned-up, pretty little nose, who used to come every morning to kiss his hand, saying: *"Bon jour, Papa."*[2] His wife, who was still blooming and decidedly good-looking, indeed, used first to give him her hand to kiss and then would kiss his hand, turning it the other side upwards. But though the Person of Consequence was perfectly satisfied with the kind amenities of his domestic life, he thought it proper to have a lady friend in another quarter of the town. This lady friend was not a bit better looking nor younger than his wife, but these mysterious facts exist in the world and it is not our business to criticise them. And so the Person of Consequence went downstairs, got into his sledge, and said to his coachman, "To Karolina Ivanovna," while luxuriously wrapped in his warm fur coat he remained in that agreeable frame of mind sweeter to a Russian than anything that could be invented, that is, when one thinks of nothing while thoughts come into the mind of themselves, one pleasanter than the other, without the labour of following them or looking for them. Full of satisfaction, he recalled all the amusing moments of the evening he had spent, all the phrases that had set the little circle laughing; many of them he repeated in an undertone and found them as amusing as before, and so, very naturally, laughed very heartily at them again. From time to time, however, he was disturbed by a gust of wind which, blowing suddenly, God knows whence and wherefore, cut him in the face, pelting him with flakes of snow, puffing out his coat-collar like a sack, or suddenly flinging it with unnatural force over his head and giving him endless trouble to extricate himself from it. All at once, the Person of Consequence felt that some one had clutched him very tightly by the collar. Turning round he saw a short man in a shabby old uniform, and not without horror recognized him as Akaky Akakyevitch. The clerk's face was white as snow and looked like that of a corpse, but the horror of the Person of Consequence was beyond all bounds when he saw the mouth of the corpse distorted into speech and, breathing upon him the chill of the grave, it uttered the following words: "Ah, so here you are at last! At last I've . . . er . . . caught you by the collar. It's your overcoat I want, you refused to help me and abused me into the bargain! So now give me yours!" The poor Person of Consequence very nearly died. Resolute and determined as he was in his office and before subordinates in general, and though any one looking at his manly air and figure would have said: "Oh, what a man of character!" yet in this plight he felt, like very many persons of athletic appearance, such terror that not without reason he began to be afraid he would have some sort of fit. He actually flung his overcoat off his shoulders as fast as he could and shouted to his coachman in a voice unlike his own: "Drive home and make haste!" The coachman, hearing the tone which he had only heard in critical moments and then accompanied by something even more rousing, hunched his shoulders up to his ears in case of worse following, swung his whip and flew on like an arrow. In a little over six minutes the Person of Consequence was at the entrance of his own house. Pale, panic-strickened, and without his overcoat, he arrived home instead of at Karolina Ivanovna's, dragged himself to his own room and spent the night in great perturbation, so that next morning his daughter said to him at breakfast, "You look quite pale to-day, Papa": but her papa remained mute and said not a word to any one of what happened to him, where he had been, and where he had been going. The incident made a great impression upon him. Indeed, it happened far more

---

2 "Good day, Father."

rarely that he said to his subordinates, "How dare you? do you understand who I am?" and he never uttered those words at all until he had first heard all the rights of the case.

What was even more remarkable is that from that time the apparition of the dead clerk ceased entirely: apparently the general's overcoat had fitted him perfectly, anyway nothing more was heard of overcoats being snatched from any one. Many restless and anxious people refused, however, to be pacified, and still maintained that in remote parts of the town the ghost of the dead clerk went on appearing. One sentry in Kolomna, for instance, saw with his own eyes a ghost appear from behind a house; but, being by natural constitution somewhat feeble — so much so that on one occasion an ordinary, well-grown pig, making a sudden dash out of some building, knocked him off his feet to the vast entertainment of the cabmen standing round, from whom he exacted two kopecks each for snuff for such rudeness — he did not dare to stop it, and so followed it in the dark until the ghost suddenly looked round and, stopping, asked him: "What do you want?" displaying a fist such as you never see among the living. The sentry said: "Nothing," and turned back on the spot. This ghost, however, was considerably taller and adorned with immense moustaches, and directing its steps apparently towards Obuhov Bridge, vanished into the darkness of the night.

QUESTIONS

1. Turgenev is supposed to have said, "We all came out from under Gogol's 'Overcoat.' " What do you see in this story that later writers might have found influential?

2. If Akaky is the protagonist, who is the antagonist? Is it the "Person of Consequence"? Bureaucracy? Life itself?

3. Is it Akaky's character or his situation that inspired Frank O'Connor to say that "The Overcoat" begins "the fiction of the Little Man"?

4. The narrator assumes a light, almost comic tone. Is he holding Akaky up to ridicule? If not, can you define his attitude toward the protagonist? Can you find admirable qualities in Akaky?

5. A recent U.S. President said, "Life is unfair." Is this story an illustration?

6. Many readers hold that the overcoat is more than a necessary article of clothing to Akaky. Do you agree?

The Fall of the House of Usher

Son cœur est un luth suspendu;
Sitôt qu'on le touche il résonne.[1]
DE BÉRANGER

During the whole of a dull, dark, and soundless day in the autumn of the year, when the clouds hung oppressively low in the heavens, I had been passing alone, on horseback, through a singularly dreary tract of country; and at length found myself, as the shades of the evening drew on, within view of the melancholy House of Usher. I know not how it was — but, with the first glimpse of the building, a sense of insufferable gloom pervaded my spirit. I say insufferable; for the feeling was unrelieved by any of that half-pleasurable, because poetic, sentiment, with which the mind usually receives even the sternest natural images of the desolate or terrible. I looked upon the scene before me — upon the mere house, and the simple landscape features of the domain — upon the bleak walls — upon the vacant eye-like windows — upon a few rank sedges — and upon a few white trunks of decayed trees — with an utter depression of soul which I can compare to no earthly sensation more properly than to the afterdream of the reveller upon opium — the bitter lapse into everyday life — the hideous dropping off of the veil. There was an iciness, a sinking, a sickening of the heart — an unredeemed dreariness of thought which no goading of the imagination could torture into aught of the sublime. What was it — I paused to think — what was it that so unnerved me in the contemplation of the House of Usher? It was a mystery all insoluble; nor could I grapple with the shadowy fancies that crowded upon me as I pondered. I was forced to fall back upon the unsatisfactory conclusion, that while, beyond doubt, there *are* combinations of very simple natural objects which have the power of thus affecting us, still the analysis of this power lies among considerations beyond our depth. It was possible, I reflected, that a mere different arrangement of the particulars of the scene, of the details of the picture, would be sufficient to modify, or perhaps to annihilate its capacity for sorrowful impression; and, acting upon this idea, I reined my horse to the precipitous brink of a black and lurid tarn that lay in unruffled lustre by the dwelling, and gazed down — but with a shudder even more thrilling than before

---

[1] "His heart is a strung lute;/ It resounds as soon as it is touched."

— upon the remodelled and inverted images of the gray sedge, and the ghastly tree-stems, and the vacant and eye-like windows.

Nevertheless, in this mansion of gloom I now proposed to myself a sojourn of some weeks. Its proprietor, Roderick Usher, had been one of my boon companions in boyhood; but many years had elapsed since our last meeting. A letter, however, had lately reached me in a distant part of the country — a letter from him — which, in its wildly importunate nature, had admitted of no other than a personal reply. The MS. gave evidence of nervous agitation. The writer spoke of acute bodily illness — of a mental disorder which oppressed him — and of an earnest desire to see me, as his best, and indeed his only personal friend, with a view of attempting, by the cheerfulness of my society, some alleviation of his malady. It was the manner in which all this, and much more, was said — it was the apparent *heart* that went with his request — which allowed me no room for hesitation; and I accordingly obeyed forthwith what I still considered a very singular summons.

Although, as boys, we had been even intimate associates, yet I really knew little of my friend. His reserve had been always excessive and habitual. I was aware, however, that his very ancient family had been noted, time out of mind, for a peculiar sensibility of temperament, displaying itself, through long ages, in many works of exalted art, and manifested, of late, in repeated deeds of munificent yet unobtrusive charity, as well as in a passionate devotion to the intricacies, perhaps even more than to the orthodox and easily recognizable beauties, of musical science. I had learned, too, the very remarkable fact, that the stem of the Usher race, all time-honoured as it was, had put forth, at no period, any enduring branch; in other words, that the entire family lay in the direct line of descent, and had always, with very trifling and very temporary variation, so lain. It was this deficiency, I considered, while running over in thought the perfect keeping of the character of the premises with the accredited character of the people, and while speculating upon the possible influence which the one, in the long lapse of centuries, might have exercised upon the other — it was this deficiency, perhaps, of collateral issue, and the consequent undeviating transmission, from sire to son, of the patrimony with the name, which had, at length, so identified the two as to merge the original title of the estate in the quaint and equivocal appellation of the "House of Usher" — an appellation which seemed to include, in the minds of the peasantry who used it, both the family and the family mansion.

I have said that the sole effect of my somewhat childish experiment — that of looking down within the tarn — had been to deepen the first singular impression. There can be no doubt that the consciousness of the rapid increase of my superstition — for why should I not so term it? — served mainly to accelerate the increase itself. Such, I have long known, is the paradoxical law of all sentiments having terror as a basis. And it might have been for this reason only, that, when I again uplifted my eyes to the house itself, from its image in the pool, there grew in my mind a strange fancy — a fancy so ridiculous, indeed, that I but mention it to show the vivid force of the sensations which oppressed me. I had so worked upon my imagination as really to believe that about the whole mansion and domain there hung an atmosphere peculiar to themselves and their immediate vicinity — an atmosphere which had no affinity with the air of heaven, but which had reeked up from the decayed trees, and the gray wall, and the silent tarn — a pestilent and mystic vapour, dull, sluggish, faintly discernible, and leaden-hued.

Shaking off from my spirit what *must* have been a dream, I scanned more narrowly the real aspect of the building. Its principal feature seemed to be that of an excessive antiquity. The discoloration of ages had been great. Minute fungi overspread the whole exterior, hanging in a fine tangled web-work from the eaves. Yet all this was apart from any extraordinary dilapidation. No portion of the masonry had fallen; and there appeared to be a wild inconsistency between its still perfect adaptation of parts, and the crumbling condition of the individual stones. In this there was much that reminded me of the specious totality of old wood-work which has rotted for long years in some neglected vault, with no disturbance from the breath of the external air. Beyond this indication of extensive decay, however, the fabric gave little token of instability. Perhaps the eye of a scrutinizing observer might have discovered a barely perceptible fissure, which, extending from the roof of the building in front, made its way down the wall in a zigzag direction, until it became lost in the sullen waters of the tarn.

Noticing these things, I rode over a short causeway to the house. A servant in waiting took my horse, and I entered the Gothic archway of the hall. A valet, of stealthy step, thence conducted me, in silence, through many dark and intricate passages in my progress to the *studio* of his master. Much that I encountered on the way contributed, I know not how, to heighten the vague sentiments of which I have already spoken. While the objects around me — while the carvings of the ceilings, the sombre tapestries of the walls, the ebon blackness of the floors, and the phantasmagoric armorial trophies which rattled as I strode, were but matters to which, or to such as which, I had been accustomed from my infancy — while I hesitated not to acknowledge how familiar was all this — I still wondered to find how unfamiliar were the fancies which ordinary images were stirring up. On one of the staircases, I met the physician of the family. His countenance, I thought, wore a mingled expression of low cunning and perplexity. He accosted me with trepidation and passed on. The valet now threw open a door and ushered me into the presence of his master.

The room in which I found myself was very large and lofty. The windows were long, narrow, and pointed, and at so vast a distance from the black oaken floor as to be altogether inaccessible from within. Feeble gleams of encrimsoned light made their way through the trellised panes, and served to render sufficiently distinct the more prominent objects around; the eye, however, struggled in vain to reach the remoter angles of the chamber, or the recesses of the vaulted and fretted ceiling. Dark draperies hung upon the walls. The general furniture was profuse, comfortless, antique, and tattered. Many books and musical instruments lay scattered about, but failed to give any vitality to the scene. I felt that I breathed an atmosphere of sorrow. An air of stern, deep, and irredeemable gloom hung over and pervaded all.

Upon my entrance, Usher arose from a sofa on which he had been lying at full length, and greeted me with a vivacious warmth which had much in it, I at first thought, of an overdone cordiality — of the constrained effort of the *ennuyé*[2] man of the world. A glance, however, at his countenance, convinced me of his perfect sincerity. We sat down; and for some moments, while he spoke not, I gazed upon him with a feeling half of pity, half of awe. Surely, man had never before so terribly altered, in so brief a period, as had Roderick Usher! It was with difficulty that I could bring myself to admit the identity of the wan being before me with the companion of my early boyhood. Yet the character of his face had been at all times remarkable. A cadaverousness of complexion; an eye large, liquid, and luminous beyond comparison; lips somewhat thin and very pallid, but of a surpassingly beautiful curve; a nose of a delicate Hebrew model, but with a breadth of nostril unusual in similar formations; a finely moulded chin, speaking, in its want of prominence, of a want of moral energy; hair of a more than web-like softness and tenuity; these features, with an inordinate expansion above the regions of the temple, made up altogether a countenance not easily to be forgotten. And

---

[2] Bored.

now in the mere exaggeration of the prevailing character of these features, and of the expression they were wont to convey, lay so much of change that I doubted to whom I spoke. The now ghastly pallor of the skin, and the now miraculous lustre of the eye, above all things startled and even awed me. The silken hair, too, had been suffered to grow all unheeded, and as, in its wild gossamer texture, it floated rather than fell about the face, I could not, even with effort, connect its Arabesque expression with any idea of simple humanity.

In the manner of my friend I was at once struck with an incoherence — an inconsistency; and I soon found this to arise from a series of feeble and futile struggles to overcome an habitual trepidancy — an excessive nervous agitation. For something of this nature I had indeed been prepared, no less by his letter, than by reminiscences of certain boyish traits, and by conclusions deduced from his peculiar physical conformation and temperament. His action was alternately vivacious and sullen. His voice varied rapidly from a tremulous indecision (when the animal spirits seemed utterly in abeyance) to that species of energetic concision — that abrupt, weighty, unhurried, and hollow-sounding enunciation — that leaden, self-balanced and perfectly modulated guttural utterance, which may be observed in the lost drunkard, or the irreclaimable eater of opium, during the periods of his most intense excitement.

It was thus that he spoke of the object of my visit, of his earnest desire to see me, and of the solace he expected me to afford him. He entered, at some length, into what he conceived to be the nature of his malady. It was, he said, a constitutional and a family evil, and one for which he despaired to find a remedy — a mere nervous affection, he immediately added, which would undoubtedly soon pass off. It displayed itself in a host of unnatural sensations. Some of these, as he detailed them, interested and bewildered me; although, perhaps, the terms, and the general manner of the narration had their weight. He suffered much from a morbid acuteness of the senses; the most insipid food was alone endurable; he could wear only garments of certain texture; the odours of all flowers were oppressive; his eyes were tortured by even a faint light; and there were but peculiar sounds, and these from stringed instruments, which did not inspire him with horror.

To an anomalous species of terror I found him a bounden slave. "I shall perish," said he, "I *must* perish in this deplorable folly. Thus, thus, and not otherwise, shall I be lost. I dread the events of the future, not in themselves, but in their results. I shudder at the thought of any, even the most trivial, incident, which may operate upon this intolerable agitation of soul. I have, indeed, no abhorrence of danger, except in its absolute effect — in terror. In this unnerved — in this pitiable condition — I feel that the period will sooner or later arrive when I must abandon life and reason together, in some struggle with the grim phantasm, FEAR."

I learned, moreover, at intervals, and through broken and equivocal hints, another singular feature of his mental condition. He was enchained by certain superstitious impressions in regard to the dwelling which he tenanted, and whence, for many years, he had never ventured forth — in regard to an influence whose supposititious force was conveyed in terms too shadowy here to be re-stated — an influence which some peculiarities in the mere form and substance of his family mansion, had, by dint of long sufferance, he said, obtained over his spirit — an effect which the *physique* of the gray walls and turrets, and of the dim tarn into which they all looked down, had, at length, brought about upon the *morale* of his existence.

He admitted, however, although with hesitation, that much of the peculiar gloom which thus afflicted him could be traced to a more natural and far more palpable origin — to the severe and long-continued illness — indeed to the evidently approaching dissolution — of a tenderly beloved sister — his sole companion for long years — his last and only relative on earth. "Her decease," he said, with a bitterness which I can never forget, "would leave him

(him the hopeless and the frail) the last of the ancient race of the Ushers." While he spoke, the lady Madeline (for so was she called) passed slowly through a remote portion of the apartment, and, without having noticed my presence, disappeared. I regarded her with an utter astonishment not unmingled with dread — and yet I found it impossible to account for such feelings. A sensation of stupor oppressed me, as my eyes followed her retreating steps. When a door, at length, closed upon her, my glance sought instinctively and eagerly the countenance of the brother — but he had buried his face in his hands, and I could only perceive that a far more than ordinary wanness had overspread the emaciated fingers through which trickled many passionate tears.

The disease of the lady Madeline had long baffled the skill of her physicians. A settled apathy, a gradual wasting away of the person, and frequent although transient affections of a partially cataleptical character, were the unusual diagnosis. Hitherto she had steadily borne up against the pressure of her malady, and had not betaken herself finally to bed; but, on the closing in of the evening of my arrival at the house, she succumbed (as her brother told me at night with inexpressible agitation) to the prostrating power of the destroyer; and I learned that the glimpse I had obtained of her person would thus probably be the last I should obtain — that the lady, at least while living, would be seen by me no more.

For several days ensuing, her name was unmentioned by either Usher or myself: and during this period I was busied in earnest endeavours to alleviate the melancholy of my friend. We painted and read together; or I listened, as if in a dream, to the wild improvisations of his speaking guitar. And thus, as a closer and still closer intimacy admitted me more unreservedly into the recesses of his spirit, the more bitterly did I perceive the futility of all attempt at cheering a mind from which darkness, as if an inherent positive quality, poured forth upon all objects of the moral and physical universe, in one unceasing radiation of gloom.

I shall ever bear about me a memory of the many solemn hours I thus spent alone with the master of the House of Usher. Yet I should fail in any attempt to convey an idea of the exact character of the studies, or of the occupations, in which he involved me, or led me the way. An excited and highly distempered ideality threw a sulphureous lustre over all. His long improvised dirges will ring forever in my ears. Among other things, I hold painfully in mind a certain singular perversion and amplification of the wild air of the last waltz of Von Weber. From the paintings over which his elaborate fancy brooded, and which grew, touch by touch, into vaguenesses at which I shuddered the more thrillingly, because I shuddered knowing not why; — from these paintings (vivid as their images now are before me) I would in vain endeavour to educe more than a small portion which should lie within the compass of merely written words. By the utter simplicity, by the nakedness of his designs, he arrested and overawed attention. If ever mortal painted an idea, that mortal was Roderick Usher. For me at least — in the circumstances then surrounding me — there arose out of the pure abstractions which the hypochondriac contrived to throw upon his canvas, an intensity of intolerable awe, no shadow of which felt I ever yet in the contemplation of the certainly glowing yet too concrete reveries of Fuseli.

One of the phantasmagoric conceptions of my friend, partaking not so rigidly of the spirit of abstraction, may be shadowed forth, although feebly, in words. A small picture presented the interior of an immensely long and rectangular vault or tunnel, with low walls, smooth, white, and without interruption or device. Certain accessory points of the design served well to convey the idea that this excavation lay at an exceeding depth below the surface of the earth. No outlet was observed in any portion of its vast extent, and no torch, or other artificial source of light was discernible; yet a flood of intense rays rolled throughout, and bathed the whole in a ghastly and inappropriate splendour.

I have just spoken of that morbid condition of the auditory nerve which rendered all music intolerable to the sufferer, with the exception of certain effects of stringed instruments. It was, perhaps, the narrow limits to which he thus confined himself upon the guitar, which gave birth, in great measure, to the fantastic character of his performances. But the fervid *facility* of his *impromptus* could not be so accounted for. They must have been, and were, in the notes, as well as in the words of his wild fantasias (for he not unfrequently accompanied himself with rhymed verbal improvisations), the result of that intense mental collectedness and concentration to which I have previously alluded as observable only in particular moments of the highest artificial excitement. The words of one of these rhapsodies I have easily remembered. I was, perhaps, the more forcibly impressed with it, as he gave it, because, in the under or mystic current of its meaning, I fancied that I perceived, and for the first time, a full consciousness on the part of Usher, of the tottering of his lofty reason upon her throne. The verses, which were entitled "The Haunted Palace,"[3] ran very nearly, if not accurately, thus:

I.

In the greenest of our valleys,
        By good angels tenanted,
Once a fair and stately palace —
        Radiant palace — reared its head.
In the monarch Thought's dominion —
        It stood there!
Never seraph spread a pinion
        Over fabric half so fair.

II.

Banners yellow, glorious, golden,
        On its roof did float and flow;
(This — all this — was in the olden
        Time long ago)
And every gentle air that dallied,
        In that sweet day,
Along the ramparts plumed and pallid,
        A winged odour went away.

III.

Wanderers in that happy valley
        Through two luminous windows saw
Spirits moving musically
        To a lute's well-tunèd law,
Round about a throne, where sitting
        (Porphyrogene!)
In state his glory well befitting,
        The ruler of the realm was seen.

---

[3] Poe's composition — this poem appeared in a magazine some months before "The Fall of the House of Usher" was published.

IV.

And all with pearl and ruby glowing
    Was the fair palace door,
Through which came flowing, flowing, flowing
    And sparkling evermore,
A troop of Echoes whose sweet duty
    Was but to sing,
In voices of surpassing beauty,
    The wit and wisdom of their king.

V.

But evil things, in robes of sorrow,
    Assailed the monarch's high estate;
(Ah, let us mourn, for never morrow
    Shall dawn upon him, desolate!)
And, round about his home, the glory
    That blushed and bloomed
Is but a dim-remembered story
    Of the old time entombed.

VI.

And travellers now within that valley,
    Through the red-litten windows, see
Vast forms that move fantastically
    To a discordant melody;
While, like a rapid ghastly river,
    Through the pale door,
A hideous throng rush out forever,
    And laugh — but smile no more.

I well remember that suggestions arising from this ballad, led us into a train of thought wherein there became manifest an opinion of Usher's which I mention not so much on account of its novelty (for other men have thought thus), as on account of the pertinacity with which he maintained it. This opinion, in its general form, was that of the sentience of all vegetable things. But, in his disordered fancy, the idea had assumed a more daring character, and trespassed, under certain conditions, upon the kingdom of inorganization. I lack words to express the full extent, or the earnest *abandon* of his persuasion. The belief, however, was connected (as I have previously hinted) with the gray stones of the home of his forefathers. The conditions of the sentience had been here, he imagined, fulfilled in the method of collocation of these stones — in the order of their arrangement, as well as in that of the many *fungi* which overspread them, and of the decayed trees which stood around — above all, in the long undisturbed endurance of this arrangement, and in its reduplication in the still waters of the tarn. Its evidence — the evidence of the sentience — was to be seen, he said, (and I here started as he spoke,) in the gradual yet certain condensation of an atmosphere of their own about the waters and the walls. The result was discoverable, he added, in that silent, yet importunate and terrible influence which for centuries had moulded the destinies of his family, and which made *him* what I now saw him — what he was. Such opinions need no comment, and I will make none.

Our books — the books which, for years, had formed no small portion of the mental existence of the invalid — were, as might be supposed, in strict keeping with this character of phantasm. We pored together over such works as the Ververt et Chartreuse of Gresset; the Belphegor of Machiavelli; the Heaven and Hell of Swedenborg; the Subterranean Voyage of Nicholas Klimm by Holberg; the Chiromancy of Robert Flud, of Jean D'Indaginé, and of De la Chambre; the Journey into the Blue Distance of Tieck; and the City of the Sun of Campanella. One favourite volume was a small octavo edition of the *Directorium Inquisitorum*, by the Dominican Eymeric de Gironne; and there were passages in Pomponius Mela, about the old African Satyrs and Ægipans, over which Usher would sit dreaming for hours. His chief delight, however, was found in the perusal of an exceedingly rare and curious book in quarto Gothic — the manual of a forgotten church — the *Vigiliæ Mortuorum secundum Chorum Ecclesiæ Maguntinæ*.

I could not help thinking of the wild ritual of this work, and of its probable influence upon the hypochondriac, when, one evening, having informed me abruptly that the lady Madeline was no more, he stated his intention of preserving her corpse for a fortnight, (previously to its final interment,) in one of the numerous vaults within the main walls of the building. The worldly reason, however, assigned for this singular proceeding, was one which I did not feel at liberty to dispute. The brother had been led to his resolution (so he told me) by consideration of the unusual character of the malady of the deceased, of certain obtrusive and eager inquiries on the part of her medical men, and of the remote and exposed situation of the burial-ground of the family. I will not deny that when I called to mind the sinister countenance of the person whom I met upon the staircase, on the day of my arrival at the house, I had no desire to oppose what I regarded as at best but a harmless, and by no means an unnatural, precaution.[4]

At the request of Usher, I personally aided him in the arrangements for the temporary entombment. The body having been encoffined, we two alone bore it to its rest. The vault in which we placed it (and which had been so long unopened that our torches, half smothered in its oppressive atmosphere, gave us little opportunity for investigation) was small, damp, and entirely without means of admission for light; lying, at great depth, immediately beneath that portion of the building in which was my own sleeping apartment. It had been used, apparently, in remote feudal times, for the worst purposes of a donjon-keep, and, in later days, as a place of deposit for powder, or some other highly combustible substance, as a portion of its floor, and the whole interior of a long archway through which we reached it, were carefully sheathed with copper. The door, of massive iron, had been, also, similarly protected. Its immense weight caused an unusually sharp grating sound, as it moved upon its hinges.

Having deposited our mournful burden upon tressels within this region of horror, we partially turned aside the yet unscrewed lid of the coffin, and looked upon the face of the tenant. A striking similitude between the brother and sister now first arrested my attention; and Usher, divining, perhaps, my thoughts, murmured out some few words from which I learned that the deceased and himself had been twins, and that sympathies of a scarcely intelligible nature had always existed between them. Our glances, however, rested not long upon the dead — for we could not regard her unawed. The disease which had thus entombed the lady in the maturity of youth, had left, as usual in all maladies of a strictly cataleptical character, the mockery of a faint blush upon the bosom and the face, and that suspiciously lingering smile upon the lip which is so terrible in death. We replaced and screwed down the

---

[4] Precaution against corpse-stealing for purposes of medical study.

lid, and, having secured the door of iron, made our way, with toil, into the scarcely less gloomy apartments of the upper portion of the house.

And now, some days of bitter grief having elapsed, an observable change came over the features of the mental disorder of my friend. His ordinary manner had vanished. His ordinary occupations were neglected or forgotten. He roamed from chamber to chamber with hurried, unequal, and objectless step. The pallor of his countenance had assumed, if possible, a more ghastly hue — but the luminousness of his eye had utterly gone out. The once occasional huskiness of his tone was heard no more; and a tremulous quaver, as if of extreme terror, habitually characterized his utterance. There were times, indeed, when I thought his unceasingly agitated mind was labouring with some oppressive secret, to divulge which he struggled for the necessary courage. At times, again, I was obliged to resolve all into the mere inexplicable vagaries of madness, for I beheld him gazing upon vacancy for long hours, in an attitude of the profoundest attention, as if listening to some imaginary sound. It was no wonder that his condition terrified — that it infected me. I felt creeping upon me, by slow yet certain degrees, the wild influences of his own fantastic yet impressive superstitions.

It was, especially, upon retiring to bed late in the night of the seventh or eighth day after the placing of the lady Madeline within the donjon, that I experienced the full power of such feelings. Sleep came not near my couch — while the hours waned and waned away. I struggled to reason off the nervousness which had dominion over me. I endeavoured to believe that much, if not all of what I felt, was due to the bewildering influence of the gloomy furniture of the room — of the dark and tattered draperies, which, tortured into motion by the breath of a rising tempest, swayed fitfully to and fro upon the walls, and rustled uneasily about the decorations of the bed. But my efforts were fruitless. An irrepressible tremour gradually pervaded my frame; and, at length, there sat upon my very heart an incubus[5] of utterly causeless alarm. Shaking this off with a gasp and a struggle, I uplifted myself upon the pillows, and, peering earnestly within the intense darkness of the chamber, hearkened — I know not why, except that an instinctive spirit prompted me — to certain low and indefinite sounds which came, through the pauses of the storm, at long intervals, I knew not whence. Overpowered by an intense sentiment of horror, unaccountable yet unendurable, I threw on my clothes with haste (for I felt that I should sleep no more during the night), and endeavoured to arouse myself from the pitiable condition into which I had fallen, by pacing rapidly to and fro through the apartment.

I had taken but few turns in this manner, when a light step on an adjoining staircase arrested my attention. I presently recognised it as that of Usher. In an instant afterward he rapped, with a gentle touch, at my door, and entered, bearing a lamp. His countenance was, as usual, cadaverously wan — but, moreover, there was a species of mad hilarity in his eyes — an evidently restrained *hysteria* in his whole demeanour. His air appalled me — but anything was preferable to the solitude which I had so long endured, and I even welcomed his presence as a relief.

"And you have not seen it?" he said abruptly, after having stared about him for some moments in silence — "you have not then seen it? — but, stay! you shall." Thus speaking, and having carefully shaded his lamp, he hurried to one of the casements, and threw it freely open to the storm.

The impetuous fury of the entering gust nearly lifted us from our feet. It was, indeed, a tempestuous yet sternly beautiful night, and one wildly singular in its terror and its beauty. A whirlwind had apparently collected its force in our vicinity; for there were frequent and

---

[5] A nightmarish fear.

violent alterations in the direction of the wind; and the exceeding density of the clouds (which hung so low as to press upon the turrets of the house) did not prevent our perceiving the life-like velocity with which they flew careering from all points against each other, without passing away into the distance. I say that even their exceeding density did not prevent our perceiving this — yet we had no glimpse of the moon or stars — nor was there any flashing forth of the lightning. But the under surfaces of the huge masses of agitated vapour, as well as all terrestrial objects immediately around us, were glowing in the unnatural light of a faintly luminous and distinctly visible gaseous exhalation which hung about and enshrouded the mansion.

"You must not — you shall not behold this!" said I, shudderingly, to Usher, as I led him, with a gentle violence, from the window to a seat. "These appearances, which bewilder you, are merely electrical phenomena not uncommon — or it may be that they have their ghastly origin in the rank miasma of the tarn. Let us close this casement; — the air is chilling and dangerous to your frame. Here is one of your favourite romances. I will read, and you shall listen; — and so we will pass away this terrible night together."

The antique volume which I had taken up was the "Mad Trist" of Sir Launcelot Canning; but I had called it a favourite of Usher's more in sad jest than in earnest; for, in truth, there is little in its uncouth and unimaginative prolixity which could have had interest for the lofty and spiritual ideality of my friend. It was, however, the only book immediately at hand; and I indulged a vague hope that the excitement which now agitated the hypochondriac, might find relief (for the history of mental disorder is full of similar anomalies) even in the extremeness of the folly which I should read. Could I have judged, indeed, by the wild overstrained air of vivacity with which he hearkened, or apparently hearkened, to the words of the tale, I might well have congratulated myself upon the success of my design.

I had arrived at that well-known portion of the story where Ethelred, the hero of the Trist, having sought in vain for peaceable admission into the dwelling of the hermit, proceeds to make good an entrance by force. Here, it will be remembered, the words of the narrative run thus:

"And Ethelred, who was by nature of a doughty heart, and who was now mighty withal, on account of the powerfulness of the wine which he had drunken, waited no longer to hold parley with the hermit, who, in sooth, was of an obstinate and maliceful turn, but, feeling the rain upon his shoulders, and fearing the rising of the tempest, uplifted his mace outright, and, with blows, made quickly room in the plankings of the door for his gauntleted hand; and now pulling therewith sturdily, he so cracked, and ripped, and tore all asunder, that the noise of the dry and hollow-sounding wood alarumed and reverberated throughout the forest."

At the termination of this sentence I started, and for a moment, paused; for it appeared to me (although I at once concluded that my excited fancy had deceived me) — it appeared to me that, from some very remote portion of the mansion, there came, indistinctly, to my ears, what might have been, in its exact similarity of character, the echo (but a stifled and dull one certainly) of the very cracking and ripping sound which Sir Launcelot had so particularly described. It was, beyond doubt, the coincidence alone which had arrested my attention; for, amid the rattling of the sashes of the casements, and the ordinary commingled noises of the still increasing storm, the sound, in itself, had nothing, surely, which should have interested or disturbed me. I continued the story:

"But the good champion Ethelred, now entering within the door, was sore enraged and amazed to perceive no signal of the maliceful hermit; but, in the stead thereof, a dragon of a scaly and prodigious demeanour, and of a fiery tongue, which sate in guard before a palace of gold, with a floor of silver; and upon the wall there hung a shield of shining brass with this legend enwritten —

Who entereth herein, a conqueror hath bin;
Who slayeth the dragon, the shield he shall win;

And Ethelred uplifted his mace, and struck upon the head of the dragon, which fell before him, and gave up his pesty breath, with a shriek so horrid and harsh, and withal so piercing, that Ethelred had fain to close his ears with his hands against the dreadful noise of it, the like whereof was never before heard."

Here again I paused abruptly, and now with a feeling of wild amazement — for there could be no doubt whatever that, in this instance, I did actually hear (although from what direction it proceeded I found it impossible to say) a low and apparently distant, but harsh, protracted, and most unusual screaming or grating sound — the exact counterpart of what my fancy had already conjured up for the dragon's unnatural shriek as described by the romancer.

Oppressed, as I certainly was, upon the occurrence of the second and most extraordinary coincidence, by a thousand conflicting sensations, in which wonder and extreme terror were predominant, I still retained sufficient presence of mind to avoid exciting, by any observation, the sensitive nervousness of my companion. I was by no means certain that he had noticed the sounds in question; although, assuredly, a strange alteration had, during the last few minutes, taken place in his demeanour. From a position fronting my own, he had gradually brought round his chair, so as to sit with his face to the door of the chamber; and thus I could but partially perceive his features, although I saw that his lips trembled as if he were murmuring inaudibly. His head had dropped upon his breast — yet I knew that he was not asleep, from the wide and rigid opening of the eye as I caught a glance of it in profile. The motion of his body, too, was at variance with this idea — for he rocked from side to side with a gentle yet constant and uniform sway. Having rapidly taken notice of all this, I resumed the narrative of Sir Launcelot, which thus proceeded:

"And now, the champion, having escaped from the terrible fury of the dragon, bethinking himself of the brazen shield, and of the breaking up of the enchantment which was upon it, removed the carcass from out of the way before him, and approached valorously over the silver pavement of the castle to where the shield was upon the wall; which in sooth tarried not for his full coming, but fell down at his feet upon the silver floor, with a mighty great and terrible ringing sound."

No sooner had these syllables passed my lips, than — as if a shield of brass had indeed, at the moment, fallen heavily upon a floor of silver — I became aware of a distinct, hollow, metallic, and clangorous, yet apparently muffled reverberation. Completely unnerved, I leaped to my feet; but the measured rocking movement of Usher was undisturbed. I rushed to the chair in which he sat. His eyes were bent fixedly before him, and throughout his whole countenance there reigned a stony rigidity. But, as I placed my hand upon his shoulder, there came a strong shudder over his whole person; a sickly smile quivered about his lips; and I saw that he spoke in a low, hurried, and gibbering murmur, as if unconscious of my presence. Bending closely over him, I at length drank in the hideous import of his words.

"Not hear it? — yes, I hear it, and *have* heard it. Long — long — long — many minutes, many hours, many days, have I heard it — yet I dared not — oh, pity me, miserable wretch that I am! — I dared not — I *dared* not speak! *We have put her living in the tomb!* Said I not that my senses were acute? I *now* tell you that I heard her first feeble movements in the hollow coffin. I heard them — many, many days ago — yet I dared not — I *dared not speak!* And now — to-night — Ethelred — ha! ha! — the breaking of the hermit's door, and the death-cry of the dragon, and the clangour of the shield! — say, rather, the rending of her coffin, and the grating of the iron hinges of her prison, and her struggles within the coppered archway of the vault! Oh whither shall I fly? Will she not be here anon? Is she not hurrying to upbraid me for my haste? Have I not heard her footstep on the stair? Do I not distinguish that heavy and horrible beating of her heart? MADMAN!" here he sprang furiously to his feet, and shrieked out his syllables, as if in the effort he were giving up his soul — "MADMAN! I TELL YOU THAT SHE NOW STANDS WITHOUT THE DOOR!"

As if in the superhuman energy of his utterance there had been found the potency of a spell — the huge antique panels to which the speaker pointed, threw slowly back, upon the instant, their ponderous and ebony jaws. It was the work of the rushing gust — but then without those doors there DID stand the lofty and enshrouded figure of the lady Madeline of Usher. There was blood upon her white robes, and the evidence of some bitter struggle upon every portion of her emaciated frame. For a moment she remained trembling and reeling to and fro upon the threshold, then, with a low moaning cry, fell heavily inward upon the person of her brother, and in her violent and now final death-agonies, bore him to the floor a corpse, and a victim to the terrors he had anticipated.

From that chamber, and from that mansion, I fled aghast. The storm was still abroad in all its wrath as I found myself crossing the old causeway. Suddenly there shot along the path a wild light, and I turned to see whence a gleam so unusual could have issued; for the vast house and its shadows were alone behind me. The radiance was that of the full, setting, and blood-red moon which now shone vividly through that once barely-discernible fissure of which I have before spoken as extending from the roof of the building, in a zigzag direction, to the base. While I gazed, this fissure rapidly widened — there came a fierce breath of the whirlwind — the entire orb of the satellite burst at once upon my sight — my brain reeled as I saw the mighty walls rushing asunder — there was a long tumultuous shouting sound like the voice of a thousand waters — and the deep and dank tarn at my feet closed suddenly and silently over the fragments of the "HOUSE OF USHER."

QUESTIONS

1. What does the epigraph imply about Roderick Usher?

2. Could the narrator have done anything to avert the tragic ending?

3. Some of the writers and composers mentioned, and some of their works, are real. Others, such as "the 'Mad Trist' of Sir Launcelot Canning," are Poe's invention. Does the difference matter? What do the names and titles have in common?

4. How does Poe make it plausible that Madeline has been buried alive? Can you describe the relationship between Madeline and Roderick?

5. Atmosphere is important in this story. How would you describe it? How does Poe go about creating it?

6. In what country does the story take place? What evidence supports your answer?

7. The condition of the Usher mansion is often called symbolic. But symbolic of what?

EDGAR ALLAN POE

The Cask of Amontillado

The thousand injuries of Fortunato I had borne as I best could, but when he ventured upon insult I vowed revenge. You, who so well know the nature of my soul, will not suppose, however, that I gave utterance to a threat. *At length* I would be avenged; this was a point definitely settled — but the very definitiveness with which it was resolved precluded the idea of risk. I must not only punish but punish with impunity. A wrong is unredressed when retribution overtakes its redresser. It is equally unredressed when the avenger fails to make himself felt as such to him who has done the wrong.

It must be understood that neither by word nor deed had I given Fortunato cause to doubt my good will. I continued, as was my wont, to smile in his face, and he did not perceive that my smile *now* was at the thought of his immolation.

He had a weak point — this Fortunato — although in other regards he was a man to be respected and even feared. He prided himself on his connoisseurship in wine. Few Italians have the true virtuoso spirit. For the most part their enthusiasm is adopted to suit the time and opportunity, to practise imposture upon the British and Austrian *millionaires*. In painting and gemmary, Fortunato, like his countrymen, was a quack, but in the matter of old wines he was sincere. In this respect I did not differ from him materially; — I was skillful in the Italian vintages myself, and bought largely whenever I could.

It was about dusk, one evening during the supreme madness of the carnival season, that I encountered my friend. He accosted me with excessive warmth, for he had been drinking much. The man wore motley. He had on a tight-fitting parti-striped dress, and his head was surmounted by the conical cap and bells. I was so pleased to see him that I thought I should never have done wringing his hand.

I said to him — "My dear Fortunato, you are luckily met. How remarkably well you are looking to-day. But I have received a pipe of what passes for Amontillado, and I have my doubts."

"How?" said he. "Amontillado? A pipe? Impossible! And in the middle of the carnival!"

"I have my doubts," I replied; "and I was silly enough to pay the full Amontillado price without consulting you in the matter. You were not to be found, and I was fearful of losing a bargain."

"Amontillado!"

"I have my doubts."

"Amontillado!"

"And I must satisfy them."

"Amontillado!"

"As you are engaged, I am on my way to Luchresi. If any one has a critical turn it is he. He will tell me — "

"Luchresi cannot tell Amontillado from Sherry."

"And yet some fools will have it that his taste is a match for your own."

"Come, let us go."

"Whither?"

"To your vaults."

"My friend, no; I will not impose upon your good nature. I perceive you have an engagement. Luchresi — "

"I have no engagement; — come."

"My friend, no. It is not the engagement, but the severe cold with which I perceive you are afflicted. The vaults are insufferably damp. They are encrusted with nitre."

"Let us go, nevertheless. The cold is merely nothing. Amontillado! You have been imposed upon. And as for Luchresi, he cannot distinguish Sherry from Amontillado."

Thus speaking, Fortunato possessed himself of my arm; and putting on a mask of black silk and drawing a *roquelaire*[1] closely about my person, I suffered him to hurry me to my palazzo.

There were no attendants at home; they had absconded to make merry in honor of the time. I had told them that I should not return until the morning, and had given them explicit orders not to stir from the house. These orders were sufficient, I well knew, to insure their immediate disappearance, one and all, as soon as my back was turned.

I took from their sconces two flambeaux, and giving one to Fortunato, bowed him through several suites of rooms to the archway that led into the vaults. I passed down a long and winding staircase, requesting him to be cautious as he followed. We came at length to the foot of the descent, and stood together upon the damp ground of the catacombs of the Montresors.

The gait of my friend was unsteady, and the bells upon his cap jingled as he strode.

"The pipe," he said.

"It is farther on," said I; "but observe the white web-work which gleams from these cavern walls."

He turned towards me, and looked into my eyes with two filmy orbs that distilled the rheum of intoxication.

"Nitre?" he asked at length.

"Nitre," I replied. "How long have you had that cough?"

"Ugh! ugh! ugh! — ugh! ugh! ugh! — ugh! ugh! ugh! — ugh! ugh! ugh! — ugh! ugh! ugh!"

My poor friend found it impossible to reply for many minutes.

"It is nothing," he said at last.

"Come," I said, with decision, "we will go back; your health is precious. You are rich, respected, admired, beloved; you are happy, as once I was. You are a man to be missed. For me it is no matter. We will go back; you will be ill, and I cannot be responsible. Besides, there is Luchresi — "

---

[1] A knee-length cloak.

"Enough," he said; "the cough is a mere nothing; it will not kill me. I shall not die of a cough."

"True — true," I replied; "and, indeed, I had no intention of alarming you unnecessarily — but you should use all proper caution. A draught of this Medoc will defend us from the damps."

Here I knocked off the neck of a bottle which I drew from a long row of its fellows that lay upon the mould.

"Drink," I said, presenting him the wine.

He raised it to his lips with a leer. He paused and nodded to me familiarly, while his bells jingled.

"I drink," he said, "to the buried that repose around us."

"And I to your long life."

He again took my arm, and we proceeded.

"These vaults," he said, "are extensive."

"The Montresors," I replied, "were a great and numerous family."

"I forget your arms."

"A huge human foot d'or, in a field azure; the foot crushes a serpent rampant whose fangs are imbedded in the heel."

"And the motto?"

"*Nemo me impune lacessit.*"[2]

"Good!" he said.

The wine sparkled in his eyes and the bells jingled. My own fancy grew warm with the Medoc. We had passed through long walls of piled skeletons, with casks and puncheons intermingling, into the inmost recesses of the catacombs. I paused again, and this time I made bold to seize Fortunato by an arm above the elbow.

"The nitre!" I said; "see, it increases. It hangs like moss upon the vaults. We are below the river's bed. The drops of moisture trickle among the bones. Come, we will go back ere it is too late. Your cough — "

"It is nothing," he said; "let us go on. But first, another draught of the Medoc."

I broke and reached him a flagon of De Grâve. He emptied it at a breath. His eyes flashed with a fierce light. He laughed and threw the bottle upwards with a gesticulation I did not understand.

I looked at him in surprise. He repeated the movement — a grotesque one.

"You do not comprehend?" he said.

"Not I," I replied.

"Then you are not of the brotherhood."

"How?"

"You are not of the masons."

"Yes, yes," I said; "yes, yes."

"You? Impossible! A mason?"

"A mason," I replied.

"A sign," he said, "a sign."

"It is this," I answered, producing from beneath the folds of my *roquelaire* a trowel.

"You jest," he exclaimed, recoiling a few paces. "But let us proceed to the Amontillado."

"Be it so," I said, replacing the tool beneath the cloak and again offering him my arm. He leaned upon it heavily. We continued our route in search of the Amontillado. We passed

---

[2] "No one attacks me with impunity."

through a range of low arches, descended, passed on, and descending again, arrived at a deep crypt, in which the foulness of the air caused our flambeaux rather to glow than flame.

At the most remote end of the crypt there appeared another less spacious. Its walls had been lined with human remains, piled to the vault overhead, in the fashion of the great catacombs of Paris. Three sides of this interior crypt were still ornamented in this manner. From the fourth side the bones had been thrown down, and lay promiscuously upon the earth, forming at one point a mound of some size. Within the wall thus exposed by the displacing of the bones, we perceived a still interior crypt or recess, in depth about four feet, in width three, in height six or seven. It seemed to have been constructed for no especial use within itself, but formed merely the interval between two of the colossal supports of the roof of the catacombs, and was backed by one of their circumscribing walls of solid granite.

It was in vain that Fortunato, uplifting his dull torch, endeavored to pry into the depth of the recess. Its termination the feeble light did not enable us to see.

"Proceed," I said; "herein is the Amontillado. As for Luchresi — "

"He is an ignoramus," interrupted my friend, as he stepped unsteadily forward, while I followed immediately at his heels. In an instant he had reached the extremity of the niche, and finding his progress arrested by the rock, stood stupidly bewildered. A moment more and I had fettered him to the granite. In its surface were two iron staples, distant from each other about two feet, horizontally. From one of these depended a short chain, from the other a padlock. Throwing the links about his waist, it was but the work of a few seconds to secure it. He was too much astounded to resist. Withdrawing the key I stepped back from the recess.

"Pass your hand," I said, "over the wall; you cannot help feeling the nitre. Indeed, it is *very* damp. Once more let me *implore* you to return. No? Then I must positively leave you. But I must first render you all the little attentions in my power."

"The Amontillado!" ejaculated my friend, not yet recovered from his astonishment.

"True," I replied; "the Amontillado."

As I said these words I busied myself among the pile of bones of which I have before spoken. Throwing them aside, I soon uncovered a quantity of building stone and mortar. With these materials and with the aid of my trowel, I began vigorously to wall up the entrance of the niche.

I had scarcely laid the first tier of the masonry when I discovered that the intoxication of Fortunato had in a great measure worn off. The earliest indication I had of this was a low moaning cry from the depth of the recess. It was *not* the cry of a drunken man. There was a long and obstinate silence. I laid the second tier, and the third, and the fourth; and then I heard the furious vibrations of the chain. The noise lasted for several minutes, during which, that I might hearken to it with the more satisfaction, I ceased my labors and sat down upon the bones. When at last the clanking subsided, I resumed the trowel, and finished without interruption the fifth, the sixth, and the seventh tier. The wall was now nearly upon a level with my breast. I again paused, and holding the flambeaux over the mason-work, threw a few feeble rays upon the figure within.

A succession of loud and shrill screams, bursting suddenly from the throat of the chained form, seemed to thrust me violently back. For a brief moment I hesitated, I trembled. Unsheathing my rapier, I began to grope with it about the recess; but the thought of an instant reassured me. I placed my hand upon the solid fabric of the catacombs, and felt satisfied. I reapproached the wall; I replied to the yells of him who clamoured. I re-echoed, I aided, I surpassed them in volume and in strength. I did this, and the clamourer grew still.

It was now midnight, and my task was drawing to a close. I had completed the eighth, the ninth and the tenth tier. I had finished a portion of the last and the eleventh; there remained but a single stone to be fitted and plastered in. I struggled with its weight; I placed it partially in its destined position. But now there came from out the niche a low laugh that erected the hairs upon my head. It was succeeded by a sad voice, which I had difficulty in recognizing as that of the noble Fortunato. The voice said —

"Ha! ha! ha! — he! he! he! — a very good joke, indeed — an excellent jest. We will have many a rich laugh about it at the palazzo — he! he! he! — over our wine — he! he! he!"

"The Amontillado!" I said.

"He! he! he! — he! he! he! — yes, the Amontillado. But is it not getting late? Will not they be awaiting us at the palazzo, the Lady Fortunato and the rest? Let us be gone."

"Yes," I said, "let us be gone."

"*For the love of God, Montresor!*"

"Yes," I said, "for the love of God."

But to these words I hearkened in vain for a reply. I grew impatient. I called aloud —

"Fortunato!"

No answer. I called again —

"Fortunato!"

No answer still. I thrust a torch through the remaining aperture and let it fall within. There came forth in return only a jingling of the bells. My heart grew sick; it was the dampness of the catacombs that made it so. I hastened to make an end of my labour. I forced the last stone into its position; I plastered it up. Against the new masonry I re-erected the old rampart of bones. For the half of a century no mortal has disturbed them. *In pace requiescat!*[3]

QUESTIONS

1. The opening sentence is a model of concision. Analyze it. Is too much information packed into it? What does the sentence tell you about the narrator?

2. Characterize the narrator. Does his character develop or remain static? Do the same for Fortunato.

3. What is the effect of setting this story in Italy at carnival time? When, approximately, is the story supposed to take place? in relatively modern times?

4. What is the significance of Montresor's coat of arms?

5. Montresor gives Fortunato several hints of what is to come. Does he secretly hope that Fortunato will catch on and escape vengeance? If not, why does Montresor give these veiled warnings?

6. Montresor's final words are a prayer for the dead Fortunato. Many readers assume them to be ironic. Do you see some other possibility?

---

[3] "May he rest in peace."

EDGAR ALLAN POE

The Purloined Letter

Nil sapientiae odiosius acumine nimio.[1]
SENECA

At Paris, just after dark one gusty evening in the autumn of 18—, I was enjoying the twofold luxury of meditation and a meerschaum, in company with my friend C. Auguste Dupin, in his little back library, or book-closet, *au troisième, No. 33, Rue Dunôt, Faubourg St. Germain.* For one hour at least we had maintained a profound silence; while each, to any casual observer, might have seemed intently and exclusively occupied with the curling eddies of smoke that oppressed the atmosphere of the chamber. For myself, however, I was mentally discussing certain topics which had formed matter for conversation between us at an earlier period of the evening; I mean the affair of the Rue Morgue, and the mystery attending the murder of Marie Rogêt.[2] I looked upon it, therefore, as something of a coincidence, when the door of our apartment was thrown open and admitted our old acquaintance, Monsieur G——, the Prefect of the Parisian police.

We gave him a hearty welcome; for there was nearly half as much of the entertaining as of the contemptible about the man, and we had not seen him for several years. We had been sitting in the dark, and Dupin now arose for the purpose of lighting a lamp, but sat down again, without doing so, upon G.'s saying that he had called to consult us, or rather to ask the opinion of my friend, about some official business which had occasioned a great deal of trouble.

"If it is any point requiring reflection," observed Dupin, as he forbore to enkindle the wick, "we shall examine it to better purpose in the dark."

"That is another of your odd notions," said the Prefect, who had a fashion of calling every thing "odd" that was beyond his comprehension, and thus lived amid an absolute legion of "oddities."

"Very true," said Dupin, as he supplied his visitor with a pipe, and rolled towards him a comfortable chair.

---

[1] "Nothing is more repugnant to good sense than too much cunning."

[2] "The Murders in the Rue Morgue" and "The Mystery of Marie Rogêt" were earlier detective stories by Poe. Dupin solved the Rue Morgue mystery.

"And what is the difficulty now?" I asked. "Nothing more in the assassination way, I hope?"

"Oh no; nothing of that nature. The fact is, the business is *very* simple indeed, and I make no doubt that we can manage it sufficiently well ourselves; but then I thought Dupin would like to hear the details of it, because it is so excessively *odd*."

"Simple and odd," said Dupin.

"Why, yes; and not exactly that, either. The fact is, we have all been a good deal puzzled because the affair *is* so simple, and yet baffles us altogether."

"Perhaps it is the very simplicity of the thing which puts you at fault," said my friend.

"What nonsense you *do* talk!" replied the Prefect, laughing heartily.

"Perhaps the mystery is a little *too* plain," said Dupin.

"Oh, good heavens! who ever heard of such an idea?"

"A little *too* self-evident."

"Ha! ha! ha! — ha! ha! ha! — ho! ho! ho!" — roared our visitor, profoundly amused, "oh, Dupin, you will be the death of me yet!"

"And what, after all, *is* the matter on hand?" I asked.

"Why, I will tell you," replied the Prefect, as he gave a long, steady, and contemplative puff, and settled himself in his chair. "I will tell you in a few words; but, before I begin, let me caution you that this is an affair demanding the greatest secrecy, and that I should most probably lose the position I now hold, were it known that I confided it to any one."

"Proceed," said I.

"Or not," said Dupin.

"Well then; I have received personal information, from a very high quarter, that a certain document of the last importance, has been purloined from the royal apartments. The individual who purloined it is known; this beyond a doubt; he was seen to take it. It is known, also, that it still remains in his possession."

"How is this known?" asked Dupin.

"It is clearly inferred," replied the Prefect, "from the nature of the document, and from the non-appearance of certain results which would at once arise from its passing *out* of the robber's possession; — that is to say, from his employing it as he must design in the end to employ it."

"Be a little more explicit," I said.

"Well, I may venture so far as to say that the paper gives its holder a certain power in a certain quarter where such power is immensely valuable." The Prefect was fond of the cant of diplomacy.

"Still I do not quite understand," said Dupin.

"No? Well; the disclosure of the document to a third person, who shall be nameless, would bring in question the honor of a personage of most exalted station; and this fact gives the holder of the document an ascendancy over the illustrious personage whose honor and peace are so jeopardized."

"But this ascendancy," I interposed, "would depend upon the robber's knowledge of the loser's knowledge of the robber. Who would dare—"

"The thief," said G., "is the Minister D——, who dares all things, those unbecoming as well as those becoming a man. The method of the theft was not less ingenious than bold. The document in question — a letter, to be frank — had been received by the personage robbed while alone in the royal *boudoir*.[3] During its perusal she was suddenly interrupted by the

---

[3] In this case, a sitting room.

entrance of the other exalted personage from whom especially it was her wish to conceal it. After a hurried and vain endeavor to thrust it in a drawer, she was forced to place it, open as it was, upon a table. The address, however, was uppermost, and, the contents thus unexposed, the letter escaped notice. At this juncture enters the Minister D——. His lynx eye immediately perceives the paper, recognises the handwriting of the address, observes the confusion of the personage addressed, and fathoms her secret. After some business transactions, hurried through in his ordinary manner, he produces a letter somewhat similar to the one in question, opens it, pretends to read it, and then places it in close juxtaposition to the other. Again he converses, for some fifteen minutes, upon the public affairs. At length, in taking leave, he takes also from the table the letter to which he had no claim. Its rightful owner saw, but, of course, dared not call attention to the act, in the presence of the third personage who stood at her elbow. The minister decamped; leaving his own letter — one of no importance — upon the table."

"Here, then," said Dupin to me, "you have precisely what you demand to make the ascendancy complete — the robber's knowledge of the loser's knowledge of the robber."

"Yes," replied the Prefect; "and the power thus attained has, for some months past, been wielded, for political purposes, to a very dangerous extent. The personage robbed is more thoroughly convinced, every day, of the necessity of reclaiming her letter. But this, of course, cannot be done openly. In fine, driven to despair, she has committed the matter to me."

"Than whom," said Dupin, amid a perfect whirlwind of smoke, "no more sagacious agent could, I suppose, be desired, or even imagined."

"You flatter me," replied the Prefect; "but it is possible that some such opinion may have been entertained."

"It is clear," said I, "as you observe, that the letter is still in possession of the minister; since it is in this possession, and not any employment of the letter, which bestows the power. With the employment the power departs."

"True," said G.; "and upon this conviction I proceeded. My first care was to make thorough search of the minister's hotel; and here my chief embarrassment lay in the necessity of searching without his knowledge. Beyond all things, I have been warned of the danger which would result from giving him reason to suspect our design."

"But," said I, "you are quite *au fait*[4] in these investigations. The Parisian police have done this thing often before."

"O yes; and for this reason I did not despair. The habits of the minister gave me, too, a great advantage. He is frequently absent from home all night. His servants are by no means numerous. They sleep at a distance from their master's apartment, and, being chiefly Neapolitans, are readily made drunk. I have keys, as you know, with which I can open any chamber or cabinet in Paris. For three months a night has not passed, during the greater part of which I have not been engaged, personally, in ransacking the D—— Hôtel. My honor is interested, and, to mention a great secret, the reward is enormous. So I did not abandon the search until I had become fully satisfied that the thief is a more astute man than myself. I fancy that I have investigated every nook and corner of the premises in which it is possible that the paper can be concealed."

"But is it not possible," I suggested, "that although the letter may be in possession of the minister, as it unquestionably is, he may have concealed it elsewhere than upon his own premises?"

---

[4] Expert.

"This is barely possible," said Dupin. "The present peculiar condition of affairs at court, and especially of those intrigues in which D—— is known to be involved, would render the instant availability of the document — its susceptibility of being produced at a moment's notice — a point of nearly equal importance with its possession."

"Its susceptibility of being produced?" said I.

"That is to say, of being *destroyed*," said Dupin.

"True," I observed; "the paper is clearly then upon the premises. As for its being upon the person of the minister, we may consider that as out of the question."

"Entirely," said the Prefect. "He has been twice waylaid, as if by footpads, and his person rigorously searched under my own inspection."

"You might have spared yourself this trouble," said Dupin. "D——, I presume, is not altogether a fool, and, if not, must have anticipated these waylayings, as a matter of course."

"Not *altogether* a fool," said G., "but then he's a poet, which I take to be only one remove from a fool."

"True," said Dupin, after a long and thoughtful whiff from his meerschaum, "although I have been guilty of certain doggerel myself."

"Suppose you detail," said I, "the particulars of your search."

"Why the fact is, we took our time, and we searched *every where*. I have had long experience in these affairs. I took the entire building, room by room; devoting the nights of a whole week to each. We examined, first, the furniture of each apartment. We opened every possible drawer; and I presume you know that, to a properly trained police agent, such a thing as a *secret* drawer is impossible. Any man is a dolt who permits a 'secret' drawer to escape him in a search of this kind. The thing is *so* plain. There is a certain amount of bulk — of space — to be accounted for in every cabinet. Then we have accurate rules. The fiftieth part of a line could not escape us. After the cabinets we took the chairs. The cushions we probed with the fine long needles you have seen me employ. From the tables we removed the tops."

"Why so?"

"Sometimes the top of a table, or other similarly arranged piece of furniture, is removed by the person wishing to conceal an article; then the leg is excavated, the article deposited within the cavity, and the top replaced. The bottoms and tops of bed-posts are employed in the same way."

"But could not the cavity be detected by sounding?" I asked.

"By no means, if, when the article is deposited, a sufficient wadding of cotton be placed around it. Besides, in our case, we were obliged to proceed without noise."

"But you could not have removed — you could not have taken to pieces *all* articles of furniture in which it would have been possible to make a deposit in the manner you mention. A letter may be compressed into a thin spiral roll, not differing much in shape or bulk from a large knitting-needle, and in this form it might be inserted into the rung of a chair, for example. You did not take to pieces all the chairs?"

"Certainly not; but we did better — we examined the rungs of every chair in the hotel, and, indeed, the jointings of every description of furniture, by the aid of a most powerful microscope.[5] Had there been any traces of recent disturbance we should not have failed to detect it instantly. A single grain of gimlet-dust, for example, would have been as obvious as an apple. Any disorder in the glueing — any unusual gaping in the joints — would have sufficed to insure detection."

---

[5] Magnifying glass.

"I presume you looked to the mirrors, between the boards and the plates, and you probed the beds and the bed-clothes, as well as the curtains and carpets."

"That of course; and when we had absolutely completed every particle of the furniture in this way, then we examined the house itself. We divided its entire surface into compartments, which we numbered, so that none might be missed; then we scrutinized each individual square inch throughout the premises, including the two houses immediately adjoining, with the microscope, as before."

"The two houses adjoining!" I exclaimed; "you must have had a great deal of trouble."

"We had; but the reward offered is prodigious."

"You include the *grounds* about the houses?"

"All the grounds are paved with brick. They gave us comparatively little trouble. We examined the moss between the bricks, and found it undisturbed."

"You looked among D——'s papers, of course, and into the books of the library?"

"Certainly; we opened every package and parcel; we not only opened every book, but we turned over every leaf in each volume, not contenting ourselves with a mere shake, according to the fashion of some of our police officers. We also measured the thickness of every book-*cover,* with the most accurate admeasurement, and applied to each the most jealous scrutiny of the microscope. Had any of the bindings been recently meddled with, it would have been utterly impossible that the fact should have escaped observation. Some five or six volumes, just from the hands of the binder, we carefully probed, longitudinally, with the needles."

"You explored the floors beneath the carpets?"

"Beyond doubt. We removed every carpet, and examined the boards with the microscope."

"And the paper on the walls?"

"Yes."

"You looked into the cellars?"

"We did."

"Then," I said, "you have been making a miscalculation, and the letter is *not* upon the premises, as you suppose."

"I fear you are right there," said the Prefect. "And now, Dupin, what would you advise me to do?"

"To make a thorough re-search of the premises."

"That is absolutely needless," replied G——. "I am not more sure that I breathe than I am that the letter is not at the Hôtel."

"I have no better advice to give you," said Dupin. "You have, of course, an accurate description of the letter?"

"Oh yes!" — And here the Prefect, producing a memorandum-book, proceeded to read aloud a minute account of the internal, and especially of the external appearance of the missing document. Soon after finishing the perusal of this description, he took his departure, more entirely depressed in spirits than I had ever known the good gentleman before.

In about a month afterwards he paid us another visit, and found us occupied very nearly as before. He took a pipe and a chair and entered into some ordinary conversation. At length I said, —

"Well, but G——, what of the purloined letter? I presume you have at last made up your mind that there is no such thing as overreaching the Minister?"

"Confound him, say I — yes; I made the re-examination, however, as Dupin suggested — but it was all labor lost, as I knew it would be."

"How much was the reward offered, did you say?" asked Dupin.

"Why, a very great deal — a *very* liberal reward — I don't like to say how much, precisely; but one thing I *will* say, that I wouldn't mind giving my individual check for fifty thousand francs to any one who could obtain me that letter. The fact is, it is becoming of more and more importance every day; and the reward has been lately doubled. If it were trebled, however, I could do no more than I have done."

"Why, yes," said Dupin, drawlingly, between the whiffs of his meerschaum, "I really — think, G——, you have not exerted yourself — to the utmost in this matter. You might — do a little more, I think, eh?"

"How? — in what way?"

"Why — puff, puff — you might — puff, puff — employ counsel in the matter, eh? — puff, puff, puff. Do you remember the story they tell of Abernethy?"

"No; hang Abernethy!"

"To be sure! hang him and welcome. But, once upon a time, a certain rich miser conceived the design of spunging upon this Abernethy for a medical opinion. Getting up, for this purpose, an ordinary conversation in a private company, he insinuated his case to the physician, as that of an imaginary individual.

" 'We will suppose,' said the miser, 'that his symptoms are such and such; now, doctor, what would *you* have directed him to take?' "

" 'Take!' said Abernethy, 'why, take *advice*, to be sure.' "

"But," said the Prefect, a little discomposed, "I am *perfectly* willing to take advice, and to pay for it. I would *really* give fifty thousand francs to any one who would aid me in the matter."

"In that case," replied Dupin, opening a drawer, and producing a checkbook, "you may as well fill me up a check for the amount mentioned. When you have signed it, I will hand you the letter."

I was astounded. The Prefect appeared absolutely thunder-stricken. For some minutes he remained speechless and motionless, looking incredulously at my friend with open mouth, and eyes that seemed starting from their sockets; then, apparently recovering himself in some measure, he seized a pen, and after several pauses and vacant stares, finally filled up and signed a check for fifty thousand francs, and handed it across the table to Dupin. The latter examined it carefully and deposited it in his pocketbook; then, unlocking an *escritoire*,[6] took thence a letter and gave it to the Prefect. This functionary grasped it in a perfect agony of joy, opened it with a trembling hand, cast a rapid glance at its contents, and then, scrambling and struggling to the door, rushed at length unceremoniously from the room and from the house, without having uttered a syllable since Dupin had requested him to fill up the check.

When he had gone, my friend entered into some explanations.

"The Parisian police," he said, "are exceedingly able in their way. They are persevering, ingenious, cunning, and thoroughly versed in the knowledge which their duties seem chiefly to demand. Thus, when G—— detailed to us his mode of searching the premises at the Hôtel D——, I felt entire confidence in his having made a satisfactory investigation — so far as his labors extended."

"So far as his labors extended?" said I.

"Yes," said Dupin. "The measures adopted were not only the best of their kind, but carried out to absolute perfection. Had the letter been deposited within the range of their search, these fellows would, beyond a question, have found it."

I merely laughed — but he seemed quite serious in all that he said.

---

[6] A writing desk.

"The measures, then," he continued, "were good in their kind, and well executed; their defect lay in their being inapplicable to the case, and to the man. A certain set of highly ingenious resources are, with the Prefect, a sort of Procrustean bed,[7] to which he forcibly adapts his designs. But he perpetually errs by being too deep or too shallow, for the matter in hand; and many a schoolboy is a better reasoner than he. I knew one about eight years of age, whose success at guessing in the game of 'even and odd' attracted universal admiration. This game is simple, and is played with marbles. One player holds in his hand a number of these toys, and demands of another whether that number is even or odd. If the guess is right, the guesser wins one; if wrong, he loses one. The boy to whom I allude won all the marbles of the school. Of course he had some principle of guessing; and this lay in mere observation and admeasurement of the astuteness of his opponents. For example, an arrant simpleton is his opponent, and, holding up his closed hand, asks, 'are they even or odd?' Our schoolboy replies, 'odd,' and loses; but upon the second trial he wins, for he then says to himself, 'the simpleton had them even upon the first trial, and his amount of cunning is just sufficient to make him have them odd upon the second; I will therefore guess odd;' — he guesses odd, and wins. Now, with a simpleton a degree above the first, he would have reasoned thus: 'This fellow finds that in the first instance I guessed odd, and, in the second, he will propose to himself upon the first impulse, a simple variation from even to odd, as did the first simpleton; but then a second thought will suggest that this is too simple a variation, and finally he will decide upon putting it even as before. I will therefore guess even;' — he guesses even, and wins. Now this mode of reasoning in the schoolboy, whom his fellows termed 'lucky,' — what, in its last analysis, is it?"

"It is merely," I said, "an identification of the reasoner's intellect with that of his opponent."

"It is," said Dupin; "and, upon inquiring of the boy by what means he effected the *thorough* identification in which his success consisted, I received answer as follows: 'When I wish to find out how wise, or how stupid, or how good, or how wicked is any one, or what are his thoughts at the moment, I fashion the expression of my face, as accurately as possible, in accordance with the expression of his, and then wait to see what thoughts or sentiments arise in my mind or heart, as if to match or correspond with the expression.' This response of the schoolboy lies at the bottom of all the spurious profundity which has been attributed to Rochefoucauld, to La Bougive, to Machiavelli, and to Campanella."

"And the identification," I said, "of the reasoner's intellect with that of his opponent, depends, if I understand you aright, upon the accuracy with which the opponent's intellect is admeasured."

"For its practical value it depends upon this," replied Dupin; "and the Prefect and his cohort fail so frequently, first, by default of this identification, and, secondly, by ill-admeasurement, or rather through non-admeasurement, of the intellect with which they are engaged. They consider only their *own* ideas of ingenuity; and, in searching for anything hidden, advert only to the modes in which *they* would have hidden it. They are right in this much — that their own ingenuity is a faithful representative of that of *the mass;* but when the cunning of the individual felon is diverse in character from their own, the felon foils them, of course. This always happens when it is above their own, and very usually when it is below. They have no variation of principle in their investigations; at best, when urged by some unusual emergency

---

[7] The Prefect, a man who tries to force the facts of every case to fit his single, fixed method of thinking, is like the legendary Procrustes, who had a bed to which he "fitted" all his victims: the short ones, he stretched; the long ones, he literally chopped down to size.

— by some extraordinary reward — they extend or exaggerate their old modes of *practice*, without touching their principles. What, for example, in this case of D——, has been done to vary the principle of action? What is all this boring, and probing, and sounding, and scrutinizing with the microscope, and dividing the surface of the building into registered square inches — what is it all but an exaggeration *of the application* of the one principle or set of principles of search, which are based upon the one set of notions regarding human ingenuity, to which the Prefect, in the long routine of his duty, has been accustomed? Do you not see he has taken it for granted that *all* men proceed to conceal a letter, — not exactly in a gimlet-hole bored in a chair-leg — but, at least, in *some* out-of-the-way hole or corner suggested by the same tenor of thought which would urge a man to secrete a letter in a gimlet-hole bored in a chair-leg? And do you not see also, that such *recherchés*[8] nooks for conceal-ment are adapted only for ordinary occasions, and would be adopted only by ordinary intellects; for, in all cases of concealment, a disposal of the article concealed — a disposal of it in this *recherché* manner, — is, in the very first instance, presumable and presumed; and thus its discovery depends, not at all upon the acumen, but altogether upon the mere care, patience, and determination of the seekers; and where the case is of importance — or, what amounts to the same thing in the political eyes, when the reward is of magnitude, — the qualities in question have *never* been known to fail. You will now understand what I meant in suggesting that, had the purloined letter been hidden any where within the limits of the Prefect's examination — in other words, had the principles of its concealment been comprehended within the principles of the Prefect — its discovery would have been a matter altogether beyond question. This functionary, however, has been thoroughly mystified; and the remote source of his defeat lies in the supposition that the Minister is a fool, because he has acquired renown as a poet. All fools are poets; this the Prefect *feels;* and he is merely guilty of a *non distributio medii*[9] in thence inferring that all poets are fools."

"But is this really the poet?" I asked. "There are two brothers, I know; and both have attained reputation in letters. The Minister I believe has written learnedly on the Differential Calculus. He is a mathematician, and no poet."

"You are mistaken; I know him well; he is both. As poet *and* mathematician, he would reason well; as mere mathematician, he could not have reasoned at all, and thus would have been at the mercy of the Prefect."

"You surprise me," I said, "by these opinions, which have been contradicted by the voice of the world. You do not mean to set at naught the well-digested idea of centuries. The mathematical reason has long been regarded as *the* reason *par excellence.*"

"'*Il y a à parier,*'" replied Dupin, quoting from Chamfort, "'*que toute idée publique, toute convention reçue, est une sottise, car elle a convenu au plus grand nombre.*'[10] The mathematicians, I grant you, have done their best to promulgate the popular error to which you allude, and which is none the less an error for its promulgation as truth. With an art worthy a better cause, for example, they have insinuated the term, 'analysis' into application to algebra. The French are the originators of this particular deception; but if a term is of any importance — if words derive any value from applicability — then 'analysis' conveys 'algebra' about as much as, in Latin, '*ambitus*' implies 'ambition,' '*religio*' 'religion,' or '*homines honesti,*' a set of *honorable* men."

---

[8] Carefully sought-out, cleverly chosen.

[9] Undistributed middle. In logic, a flaw of argument that leads to a false conclusion.

[10] From the *Maxims and Thoughts* of Sébastien R. N. Chamfort (1740–1810). "The odds are that every popular idea, every accepted convention, is folly because it is acceptable to the majority."

"You have a quarrel on hand, I see," said I, "with some of the algebraists of Paris; but proceed."

"I dispute the availability, and thus the value, of that reason which is cultivated in any especial form other than the abstractly logical. I dispute, in particular, the reason educed by mathematical study. The mathematics are the science of form and quantity; mathematical reasoning is merely logic applied to observation upon form and quantity. The great error lies in supposing that even the truths of what is called *pure* algebra, are abstract or general truths. And this error is so egregious that I am confounded at the universality with which it has been received. Mathematical axioms are *not* axioms of general truth. What is true of *relation* — of form and quantity — is often grossly false in regard to morals, for example. In this latter science it is very usually *un*true that the aggregated parts are equal to the whole. In chemistry also the axiom fails. In the consideration of motive it fails; for two motives, each of a given value, have not, necessarily, a value when united, equal to the sum of their values apart. There are numerous other mathematical truths which are only truths within the limits of *relation*. But the mathematician argues, from his *finite truths*, through habit, as if they were of an absolutely general applicability — as the world indeed imagines them to be. Bryant, in his very learned 'Mythology,' mentions an analogous source of error, when he says that 'although the Pagan fables are not believed, yet we forget ourselves continually, and make inferences from them as existing realities.' With the algebraists, however, who are Pagans themselves, the 'Pagan fables' *are* believed, and the inferences are made, not so much through lapse of memory, as through an unaccountable addling of the brains. In short, I never yet encountered the mere mathematician who could be trusted out of equal roots, or one who did not clandestinely hold it as a point of his faith that $x^2 + px$ was absolutely and unconditionally equal to q. Say to one of these gentlemen, by way of experiment, if you please, that you believe occasions may occur where $x^2 + px$ is *not* altogether equal to q, and, having made him understand what you mean, get out of his reach as speedily as convenient, for, beyond doubt, he will endeavor to knock you down.

"I mean to say," continued Dupin, while I merely laughed at his last observations, "that if the Minister had been no more than a mathematician, the Prefect would have been under no necessity of giving me this check. I knew him, however, as both mathematician and poet, and my measures were adapted to his capacity, with reference to the circumstances by which he was surrounded. I knew him as a courtier, too, and as a bold *intriguant*.[11] Such a man, I considered, could not fail to be aware of the ordinary policial modes of action. He could not have failed to anticipate — and events have proved that he did not fail to anticipate — the waylayings to which he was subjected. He must have foreseen, I reflected, the secret investigations of his premises. His frequent absences from home at night, which were hailed by the Prefect as certain aids to his success, I regarded only as *ruses*, to afford opportunity for thorough search to the police, and thus the sooner to impress them with the conviction to which G——, in fact, did finally arrive — the conviction that the letter was not upon the premises. I felt, also, that the whole train of thought, which I was at some pains in detailing to you just now, concerning the invariable principle of policial action in searches for articles concealed — I felt that this whole train of thought would necessarily pass through the mind of the Minister. It would imperatively lead him to despise all the ordinary *nooks* of concealment. *He* could not, I reflected, be so weak as not to see that the most intricate and remote recess of his hotel would be as open as his commonest closets to the eyes, to the probes, to the gimlets, and to the microscopes of the Prefect. I saw, in fine, that he would be driven, as a matter of

---

[11] Schemer.

course, to *simplicity*, if not deliberately induced to it as a matter of choice. You will remember, perhaps, how desperately the Prefect laughed when I suggested, upon our first interview, that it was just possible this mystery troubled him so much on account of its being so *very* self-evident."

"Yes," said I, "I remember his merriment well. I really thought he would have fallen into convulsions."

"The material world," continued Dupin, "abounds with very strict analogies to the immaterial; and thus some color of truth has been given to the rhetorical dogma, that metaphor, or simile, may be made to strengthen an argument, as well as to embellish a description. The principle of the *vis inertiae*,[12] for example, seems to be identical in physics and metaphysics. It is not more true in the former, that a large body is with more difficulty set in motion than a smaller one, and that its subsequent *momentum* is commensurate with this difficulty, than it is, in the latter, that intellects of the vaster capacity, while more forcible, more constant, and more eventful in their movements than those of inferior grade, are yet the less readily moved, and more embarrassed and full of hesitation in the first few steps of their progress. Again: have you ever noticed which of the street signs, over the shop doors, are the most attractive of attention?"

"I have never given the matter a thought," I said.

"There is a game of puzzles," he resumed, "which is played upon a map. One party playing requires another to find a given word — the name of town, river, state or empire — any word, in short, upon the motley and perplexed surface of the chart. A novice in the game generally seeks to embarrass his opponents by giving them the most minutely lettered names; but the adept selects such words as stretch, in large characters, from one end of the chart to the other. These, like the over-largely lettered signs and placards of the street, escape observation by dint of being excessively obvious; and here the physical oversight is precisely analogous with the moral inapprehension by which the intellect suffers to pass unnoticed those considerations which are too obtrusively and too palpably self-evident. But this is a point, it appears, somewhat above or beneath the understanding of the Prefect. He never once thought it probable, or possible, that the Minister had deposited the letter immediately beneath the nose of the whole world, by way of best preventing any portion of that world from perceiving it.

"But the more I reflected upon the daring, dashing, and discriminating ingenuity of D——; upon the fact that the document must always have been *at hand*, if he intended to use it to good purpose; and upon the decisive evidence, obtained by the Prefect, that it was not hidden within the limits of that dignitary's ordinary search — the more satisfied I became that, to conceal this letter, the Minister had resorted to the comprehensive and sagacious expedient of not attempting to conceal it at all.

"Full of these ideas, I prepared myself with a pair of green spectacles, and called one fine morning, quite by accident, at the Ministerial hotel. I found D—— at home, yawning, lounging, and dawdling, as usual, and pretending to be in the last extremity of *ennui*. He is, perhaps, the most really energetic human being now alive — but that is only when nobody sees him.

"To be even with him, I complained of my weak eyes, and lamented the necessity of the spectacles, under cover of which I cautiously and thoroughly surveyed the apartment, while seemingly intent only upon the conversation of my host.

---

[12] The power of inertia.

"I paid special attention to a large writing-table near which he sat, and upon which lay confusedly, some miscellaneous letters and other papers, with one or two musical instruments and a few books. Here, however, after a long and very deliberate scrutiny, I saw nothing to excite particular suspicion.

"At length my eyes, in going the circuit of the room, fell upon a trumpery fillagree card-rack of paste-board, that hung dangling by a dirty blue ribbon, from a little brass knob just beneath the middle of the mantel-piece. In this rack, which had three or four compartments, were five or six visiting cards and a solitary letter. This last was much soiled and crumpled. It was torn nearly in two, across the middle — as if a design, in the first instance, to tear it entirely up as worthless, had been altered, or stayed, in the second. It had a large black seal, bearing the D—— cipher *very* conspicuously, and was addressed, in a diminutive female hand, to D——, the minister, himself. It was thrust carelessly, and even, as it seemed, contemptuously, into one of the upper divisions of the rack.

"No sooner had I glanced at this letter, than I concluded it to be that of which I was in search. To be sure, it was, to all appearance, radically different from the one of which the Prefect had read us so minute a description. Here the seal was large and black, with the D—— cipher; there it was small and red, with the ducal arms of the S—— family. Here, the address, to the Minister, was diminutive and feminine; there the superscription, to a certain royal personage, was markedly bold and decided; the size alone formed a point of correspondence. But, then, the *radicalness* of these differences, which was excessive; the dirt; the soiled and torn condition of the paper, so inconsistent with the *true* methodical habits of D——, and so suggestive of a design to delude the beholder into an idea of the worthlessness of the document; these things, together with the hyperobtrusive situation of this document, full in the view of every visitor, and thus exactly in accordance with the conclusions to which I had previously arrived; these things, I say, were strongly corroborative of suspicion, in one who came with the intention to suspect.

"I protracted my visit as long as possible, and, while I maintained a most animated discussion with the Minister, on a topic which I knew well had never failed to interest and excite him, I kept my attention really riveted upon the letter. In this examination, I committed to memory its external appearance and arrangement in the rack; and also fell, at length, upon a discovery which set at rest whatever trivial doubt I might have entertained. In scrutinizing the edges of the paper, I observed them to be more *chafed* than seemed necessary. They presented the *broken* appearance which is manifested when a stiff paper, having been once folded and pressed with a folder, is refolded in a reversed direction, in the same creases or edges which had formed the original fold. This discovery was sufficient. It was clear to me that the letter had been turned, as a glove, inside out, re-directed, and re-sealed. I bade the Minister good morning, and took my departure at once, leaving a gold snuff-box upon the table.

"The next morning I called for the snuff-box, when we resumed, quite eagerly, the conversation of the preceding day. While thus engaged, however, a loud report, as if of a pistol, was heard immediately beneath the windows of the hotel, and was succeeded by a series of fearful screams, and the shoutings of a mob. D—— rushed to a casement, threw it open, and looked out. In the meantime, I stepped to the card-rack, took the letter, put it in my pocket, and replaced it by a *fac-simile*, (so far as regards externals,) which I had carefully prepared at my lodgings; imitating the D—— cipher, very readily, by means of a seal formed of bread.

"The disturbance in the street had been occasioned by the frantic behavior of a man with a musket. He had fired it among a crowd of women and children. It proved, however, to have been without ball, and the fellow was suffered to go his way as a lunatic or a drunkard. When he had gone, D—— came from the window, whither I had followed him immediately upon securing the object in view. Soon afterwards I bade him farewell. The pretended lunatic was a man in my own pay."

"But what purpose had you," I asked, "in replacing the letter by a *fac-simile*? Would it not have been better, at the first visit, to have seized it openly, and departed?"

"D——," replied Dupin, "is a desperate man, and a man of nerve. His hotel, too, is not without attendants devoted to his interests. Had I made the wild attempt you suggest, I might never have left the Ministerial presence alive. The good people of Paris might have heard of me no more. But I had an object apart from these considerations. You know my political prepossessions. In this matter, I act as a partisan of the lady concerned. For eighteen months the Minister has had her in his power. She has now him in hers; since, being unaware that the letter is not in his possession, he will proceed with his exactions as if it was. Thus will he inevitably commit himself, at once, to his political destruction. His downfall, too, will not be more precipitate than awkward. It is all very well to talk about the *facilis descensus Averni;*[13] but in all kinds of climbing, as Catalani said of singing, it is far more easy to get up than to come down. In the present instance I have no sympathy — at least no pity — for him who descends. He is that *monstrum horrendum,*[14] an unprincipled man of genius. I confess, however, that I should like very well to know the precise character of his thoughts, when, being defied by her whom the Prefect terms 'a certain personage,' he is reduced to opening the letter which I left for him in the card-rack."

"How? did you put any thing particular in it?"

"Why — it did not seem altogether right to leave the interior blank — that would have been insulting. D——, at Vienna once, did me an evil turn, which I told him, quite good-humoredly, that I should remember. So, as I knew he would feel some curiosity in regard to the identity of the person who had outwitted him, I thought it a pity not to give him a clue. He is well acquainted with my MS., and I just copied into the middle of the blank sheet the words —

——Un dessein si funeste,
S'il n'est digne d'Atrée, est digne de Thyeste.[15]

They are to be found in Crébillon's 'Atrée.' "

QUESTIONS

1. Poe is noted for creating tight plots. Is the plot of this story tight? Is the story spoiled by what follows Dupin's recovery of the stolen letter? If not, on what grounds can you defend the second half of the story?

2. If Dupin is the protagonist, who is the antagonist? What evidence supports your choice?

3. Consider the significance of the epigraph. Does it seem appropriate?

4. A mystery story depends in part for its effect on suspense and surprise. What elements of this story — plot, point of view, characterization — contribute to suspense? to surprise?

---

[13] The easy descent into Hell.

[14] Dreadful monster.

[15] "A design so deadly, if unworthy of Atreus, is worthy of Thyestes." In Greek legend and drama, Thyestes seduced Atreus's wife. Atreus murdered his nephews and served them at a banquet to Thyestes, their father.

5. What similarities do you find between the narrator here and Dr. Watson in "The Red-Headed League"? What differences?

6. Compare Dupin with Sherlock Holmes in "The Red-Headed League." Which character seems better-rounded, more real? Why?

HERMAN MELVILLE

Bartleby the Scrivener

A Story of Wall-Street

I am a rather elderly man. The nature of my avocations, for the last thirty years, has brought me into more than ordinary contact with what would seem an interesting and somewhat singular set of men, of whom, as yet, nothing, that I know of, has ever been written — I mean, the law-copyists, or scriveners. I have known very many of them, professionally and privately, and, if I pleased, could relate divers histories, at which good-natured gentlemen might smile, and sentimental souls might weep. But I waive the biographies of all other scriveners, for a few passages in the life of Bartleby, who was a scrivener, the strangest I ever saw, or heard of. While, of other law-copyists, I might write the complete life, of Bartleby nothing of that sort can be done. I believe that no materials exist, for a full and satisfactory biography of this man. It is an irreparable loss to literature. Bartleby was one of those beings of whom nothing is ascertainable, except from the original sources, and, in his case, those are very small. What my own astonished eyes saw of Bartleby, *that* is all I know of him, except, indeed, one vague report, which will appear in the sequel.

Ere introducing the scrivener, as he first appeared to me, it is fit I make some mention of myself, my employés, my business, my chambers, and general surroundings; because some such description is indispensable to an adequate understanding of the chief character about to be presented. Imprimis: I am a man who, from his youth upward, has been filled with a profound conviction that the easiest way of life is the best. Hence, though I belong to a profession proverbially energetic and nervous, even to turbulence, at times, yet nothing of that sort have I ever suffered to invade my peace. I am one of those unambitious lawyers who never addresses a jury, or in any way draws down public applause; but, in the cool tranquillity of a snug retreat, do a snug business among rich men's bonds, and mortgages, and title-deeds. All who know me, consider me an eminently *safe* man. The late John Jacob Astor, a personage little given to poetic enthusiasm, had no hesitation in pronouncing my first grand point to be prudence; my next, method. I do not speak it in vanity, but simply record the fact, that I was not unemployed in my profession by the late John Jacob Astor; a name which, I admit, I love to repeat; for it hath a rounded and orbicular sound to it, and rings like unto bullion. I will freely add, that I was not insensible to the late John Jacob Astor's good opinion.

Some time prior to the period at which this little history begins, my avocations had been largely increased. The good old office, now extinct in the State of New York, of a Master in

Chancery, had been conferred upon me. It was not a very arduous office, but very pleasantly remunerative. I seldom lose my temper; much more seldom indulge in dangerous indignation at wrongs and outrages; but, I must be permitted to be rash here, and declare, that I consider the sudden and violent abrogation of the office of Master in Chancery, by the new Constitution, as a — premature act; inasmuch as I had counted upon a life-lease of the profits, whereas I only received those of a few short years. But this is by the way.

My chambers were upstairs, at No. — Wall Street. At one end, they looked upon the white wall of the interior of a spacious skylight shaft, penetrating the building from top to bottom.

This view might have been considered rather tame than otherwise, deficient in what landscape painters call 'life.' But, if so, the view from the other end of my chambers offered, at least, a contrast, if nothing more. In that direction, my windows commanded an unobstructed view of a lofty brick wall, black by age and everlasting shade; which wall required no spy-glass to bring out its lurking beauties, but, for the benefit of all near-sighted spectators, was pushed up to within ten feet of my window panes. Owing to the great height of the surrounding buildings, and my chambers being on the second floor, the interval between this wall and mine not a little resembled a huge square cistern.

At the period just preceding the advent of Bartleby, I had two persons as copyists in my employment, and a promising lad as an office-boy. First, Turkey; second, Nippers; third, Ginger Nut. These may seem names, the like of which are not usually found in the Directory. In truth, they were nicknames, mutually conferred upon each other by my three clerks, and were deemed expressive of their respective persons or characters. Turkey was a short, pursy Englishman, of about my own age — that is, somewhere not far from sixty. In the morning, one might say, his face was of a fine florid hue, but after twelve o'clock, meridian — his dinner hour — it blazed like a grate full of Christmas coals; and continued blazing — but, as it were, with a gradual wane — till six o'clock, P.M., or thereabouts; after which, I saw no more of the proprietor of the face, which, gaining its meridian with the sun, seemed to set with it, to rise, culminate, and decline the following day, with the like regularity and undiminished glory. There are many singular coincidences I have known in the course of my life, not the least among which was the fact, that, exactly when Turkey displayed his fullest beams from his red and radiant countenance, just then, too, at that critical moment, began the daily period when I considered his business capacities as seriously disturbed for the remainder of the twenty-four hours. Not that he was absolutely idle, or averse to business, then; far from it. The difficulty was, he was apt to be altogether too energetic. There was a strange, inflamed, flurried, flighty recklessness of activity about him. He would be incautious in dipping his pen into his inkstand. All his blots upon my documents were dropped there after twelve o'clock, meridian. Indeed, not only would he be reckless, and sadly given to making blots in the afternoon, but, some days, he went further, and was rather noisy. At such times, too, his face flamed with augmented blazonry, as if cannel coal had been heaped on anthracite. He made an unpleasant racket with his chair; spilled his sand-box; in mending his pens, impatiently split them all to pieces, and threw them on the floor in a sudden passion; stood up, and leaned over his table, boxing his papers about in a most indecorous manner, very sad to behold in an elderly man like him. Nevertheless, as he was in many ways a most valuable person to me, and all the time before twelve o'clock, meridian, was the quickest, steadiest creature, too, accomplishing a great deal of work in a style not easily to be matched — for these reasons, I was willing to overlook his eccentricities, though, indeed, occasionally, I remonstrated with him. I did this very gently, however, because, though the civilest, nay, the blandest and most reverential of men in the morning, yet, in the afternoon, he was disposed, upon provocation, to be slightly rash with his tongue — in fact, insolent. Now, valuing his morning services as I did, and resolved not to lose them — yet, at the same time, made uncomfortable by his inflamed ways after twelve o'clock — and being a man of peace, unwilling by my admonitions to call forth unseemly retorts from him, I took upon me, one Saturday noon (he was always worse on Saturdays) to hint to him, very kindly, that, perhaps, now that he was growing old, it might be well to abridge his labours; in short, he need not come to my chambers after twelve o'clock, but, dinner over, had best go home to his lodgings, and rest himself till tea-time. But no; he insisted upon his afternoon devotions. His countenance became intolerably fervid, as he oratorically assured me — gesticulating with a long ruler at the other end of the room — that if his services in the morning were useful, how indispensable, then, in the afternoon?

"With submission, sir," said Turkey, on this occasion, "I consider myself your right-hand man. In the morning I but marshal and deploy my columns; but in the afternoon I put myself at their head, and gallantly charge the foe, thus" — and he made a violent thrust with the ruler.

"But the blots, Turkey," intimated I.

"True; but, with submission, sir, behold these hairs! I am getting old. Surely, sir, a blot or two of a warm afternoon is not to be severely urged against gray hairs. Old age — even if it blot the page — is honourable. With submission, sir, we *both* are getting old."

This appeal to my fellow-feeling was hardly to be resisted. At all events, I saw that go he would not. So, I made up my mind to let him stay, resolving, nevertheless, to see to it that, during the afternoon, he had to do with my less important papers.

Nippers, the second on my list, was a whiskered, sallow, and, upon the whole, rather piratical-looking young man, of about five-and-twenty. I always deemed him the victim of two evil powers — ambition and indigestion. The ambition was evinced by a certain impatience of the duties of a mere copyist, an unwarrantable usurpation of strictly professional affairs, such as the original drawing up of legal documents. The indigestion seemed betokened in an occasional nervous testiness and grinning irritability, causing the teeth to audibly grind together over mistakes committed in copying; unnecessary maledictions, hissed, rather than spoken, in the heat of business; and especially by a continual discontent with the height of the table where he worked. Though of a very ingenious mechanical turn, Nippers could never get this table to suit him. He put chips under it, blocks of various sorts, bits of pasteboard, and at last went so far as to attempt an exquisite adjustment, by final pieces of folded blotting-paper. But no invention would answer. If, for the sake of easing his back, he brought the table lid at a sharp angle well up toward his chin, and wrote there like a man using the steep roof of a Dutch house for his desk, then he declared that it stopped the circulation in his arms. If now he lowered the table to his waistbands, and stooped over it in writing, then there was a sore aching in his back. In short, the truth of the matter was, Nippers knew not what he wanted. Or, if he wanted anything, it was to be rid of a scrivener's table altogether. Among the manifestations of his diseased ambition was a fondness he had for receiving visits from certain ambiguous-looking fellows in seedy coats, whom he called his clients. Indeed, I was aware that not only was he, at times, considerable of a ward-politician, but he occasionally did a little business at the Justices' courts, and was not unknown on the steps of the Tombs. I have good reason to believe, however, that one individual who called upon him at my chambers, and who, with a grand air, he insisted was his client, was no other than a dun, and the alleged title-deed, a bill. But, with all his failings, and the annoyances he caused me, Nippers, like his compatriot Turkey, was a very useful man to me; wrote a neat, swift hand; and, when he chose, was not deficient in a gentlemanly sort of deportment. Added to this, he always dressed in a gentlemanly sort of way; and so, incidentally, reflected credit upon my chambers. Whereas, with respect to Turkey, I had much ado to keep him from being a reproach to me. His clothes were apt to look oily, and smell of eating-houses. He wore his pantaloons very loose and baggy in summer. His coats were execrable; his hat not to be handled. But while the hat was a thing of indifference to me, inasmuch as his natural civility and deference, as a dependent Englishman, always led him to doff it the moment he entered the room, yet his coat was another matter. Concerning his coats, I reasoned with him; but with no effect. The truth was, I suppose, that a man with so small an income could not afford to sport such a lustrous face and a lustrous coat at one and the same time. As Nippers once observed, Turkey's money went chiefly for red ink. One winter day, I presented Turkey with a highly respectable-looking coat of my own — a padded gray coat, of a most comfortable warmth, and which buttoned straight up from the knee to the neck. I thought Turkey would appreciate the favour, and abate his rashness and obstreperousness of afternoons. But no; I verily believe that buttoning himself up in so downy and blanket-like a coat had a pernicious effect upon him — upon the same principle that too much oats are bad for horses. In fact, precisely as a rash, restive horse is said to feel his oats, so Turkey felt his coat. It made him insolent. He was a man whom prosperity harmed.

Though, concerning the self-indulgent habits of Turkey, I had my own private surmises, yet, touching Nippers, I was well persuaded that, whatever might be his faults in other respects, he was, at least, a temperate young man. But, indeed, nature herself seemed to have been his vintner, and, at his birth, charged him so thoroughly with an irritable, brandy-like disposition, that all subsequent potations were needless. When I consider how, amid the stillness of my chambers, Nippers would sometimes impatiently rise from his seat, and stooping over his table, spread his arms wide apart, seize the whole desk, and move it, and jerk it, with a grim, grinding motion on the floor, as if the table were a perverse voluntary agent, intent on thwarting and vexing him, I plainly perceive that, for Nippers, brandy-and-water were altogether superfluous.

It was fortunate for me that, owing to its peculiar cause — indigestion — the irritability and consequent nervousness of Nippers were mainly observable in the morning, while in the afternoon he was comparatively mild. So that, Turkey's paroxysms only coming on about twelve o'clock, I never had to do with their eccentricities at one time. Their fits relieved each other, like guards. When Nippers's was on, Turkey's was off; and *vice versa*. This was a good natural arrangement, under the circumstances.

Ginger Nut, the third on my list, was a lad, some twelve years old. His father was a carman, ambitious of seeing his son on the bench instead of a cart, before he died. So he sent him to my office, as student at law, errand-boy, cleaner and sweeper, at the rate of one dollar a week. He had a little desk to himself, but he did not use it much. Upon inspection, the drawer exhibited a great array of the shells of various sorts of nuts. Indeed, to this quick-witted youth, the whole noble science of the law was contained in a nutshell. Not the least among the employments of Ginger Nut, as well as one which he discharged with the most alacrity, was his duty as cake and apple purveyor for Turkey and Nippers. Copying law-papers being prover-bially a dry, husky sort of business, my two scriveners were fain to moisten their mouths very often with Spitzenbergs, to be had at the numerous stalls nigh the Custom House and Post Office. Also, they sent Ginger Nut very frequently for that peculiar cake — small, flat, round, and very spicy — after which he had been named by them. Of a cold morning, when business was but dull, Turkey would gobble up scores of these cakes, as if they were mere wafers — indeed, they sell them at the rate of six or eight for a penny — the scrape of his pen blending with the crunching of the crisp particles in his mouth. Of all the fiery afternoon blunders and flurried rashnesses of Turkey, was his once moistening a ginger-cake between his lips, and clapping it on to a mortgage, for a seal. I came within an ace of dismissing him then. But he mollified me by making an oriental bow, and saying — "With submission, sir, it was generous of me to find you in stationery on my own account."

Now my original business — that of a conveyancer and title-hunter, and drawer-up of recondite documents of all sorts — was considerably increased by receiving the master's office. There was now great work for scriveners. Not only must I push the clerks already with me, but I must have additional help.

In answer to my advertisement, a motionless young man one morning stood upon my office threshold, the door being open, for it was summer. I can see that figure now — pallidly neat, pitiably respectable, incurably forlorn! It was Bartleby.

After a few words touching his qualifications, I engaged him, glad to have among my corps of copyists a man of so singularly sedate an aspect, which I thought might operate beneficially upon the flighty temper of Turkey, and the fiery one of Nippers.

I should have stated before that ground-glass folding doors divided my premises into two parts, one of which was occupied by my scriveners, the other by myself. According to my humour, I threw open these doors, or closed them. I resolved to assign Bartleby a corner by the folding-doors, but on my side of them, so as to have this quiet man within easy call, in case any trifling thing was to be done. I placed his desk close up to a small side-window in that part of the room, a window which originally had afforded a lateral view of certain grimy back-yards and bricks, but which, owing to subsequent erections, commanded at present no view at all, though it gave some light. Within three feet of the panes was a wall, and the light came down from far above, between two lofty buildings, as from a very small opening in a dome. Still further to a satisfactory arrangement, I procured a high green folding-screen, which might entirely isolate Bartleby from my sight, though not remove him from my voice. And thus, in a manner, privacy and society were conjoined.

At first, Bartleby did an extraordinary quantity of writing. As if long famishing for something to copy, he seemed to gorge himself on my documents. There was no pause for digestion. He ran a day and night line, copying by sun-light and by candle-light. I should have been quite delighted with his application, had he been cheerfully industrious. But he wrote on silently, palely, mechanically.

It is, of course, an indispensable part of a scrivener's business to verify the accuracy of his copy, word by word. Where there are two or more scriveners in an office, they assist each other in this examination, one reading from the copy, the other holding the original. It is a very dull, wearisome, and lethargic affair. I can readily imagine that, to some sanguine temperaments, it would be altogether intolerable. For example, I cannot credit that the mettlesome poet, Byron, would have contentedly sat down with Bartleby to examine a law document, of say, five hundred pages, closely written in a crimpy hand.

Now and then, in the haste of business, it had been my habit to assist in comparing some brief document myself, calling Turkey or Nippers for this purpose. One object I had, in placing Bartleby so handy to me behind the screen, was, to avail myself of his services on such trivial occasions. It was on the third day, I think, of his being with me, and before any necessity had arisen for having his own writing examined, that, being much hurried to complete a small affair I had in hand, I abruptly called to Bartleby. In my haste and natural expectancy of instant compliance, I sat with my head bent over the original on my desk, and my right hand sideways, and somewhat nervously extended with the copy, so that, immediately upon emerging from his retreat, Bartleby might snatch it and proceed to business without the least delay.

In this very attitude did I sit when I called to him, rapidly stating what it was I wanted him to do — namely, to examine a small paper with me. Imagine my surprise, nay, my consternation, when, without moving from his privacy, Bartleby, in a singularly mild, firm voice, replied, "I would prefer not to."

I sat a while in perfect silence, rallying my stunned faculties. Immediately it occurred to me that my ears had deceived me, or Bartleby had entirely misunderstood my meaning. I repeated my request in the clearest tone I could assume; but in quite as clear a one came the previous reply, "I would prefer not to."

"Prefer not to," echoed I, rising in high excitement, and crossing the room with a stride. "What do you mean? Are you moon-struck? I want you to help me compare this sheet here — take it," and I thrust it toward him.

"I would prefer not to," said he.

I looked at him steadfastly. His face was leanly composed; his gray eye dimly calm. Not a wrinkle of agitation rippled him. Had there been the least uneasiness, anger, impatience, or impertinence in his manner; in other words, had there been anything ordinarily human about him, doubtless I should have violently dismissed him from the premises. But as it was, I should have as soon thought of turning my pale plaster-of-paris bust of Cicero out of doors. I stood gazing at him a while, as he went on with his own writing, and then reseated myself at my desk. This is very strange, thought I. What had one best do? But my business hurried me. I concluded to forget the matter for the present, reserving it for my future leisure. So calling Nippers from the other room, the paper was speedily examined.

A few days after this, Bartleby concluded four lengthy documents, being quadruplicates of a week's testimony taken before me in my High Court of Chancery. It became necessary to examine them. It was an important suit, and great accuracy was imperative. Having all things arranged, I called Turkey, Nippers, and Ginger Nut, from the next room, meaning to place the four copies in the hands of my four clerks, while I should read from the original. Accordingly, Turkey, Nippers, and Ginger Nut had taken their seats in a row, each with his document in his hand, when I called to Bartleby to join this interesting group.

"Bartleby! quick, I am waiting."

I heard a slow scrape of his chair legs on the uncarpeted floor, and soon he appeared standing at the entrance of his hermitage.

"What is wanted?" said he mildly.

"The copies, the copies," said I hurriedly. "We are going to examine them. There" — and I held toward him the fourth quadruplicate.

"I would prefer not to," he said, and gently disappeared behind the screen.

For a few moments I was turned into a pillar of salt, standing at the head of my seated column of clerks. Recovering myself, I advanced toward the screen, and demanded the reason for such extraordinary conduct.

"*Why* do you refuse?"

"I would prefer not to."

With any other man I should have flown outright into a dreadful passion, scorned all further words, and thrust him ignominiously from my presence. But there was something about Bartleby that not only strangely disarmed me, but, in a wonderful manner, touched and disconcerted me. I began to reason with him.

"These are your own copies we are about to examine. It is labour saving to you, because one examination will answer for your four papers. It is common usage. Every copyist is bound to help examine his copy. Is it not so? Will you not speak? Answer!"

"I prefer not to," he replied in a flute-like tone. It seemed to me that, while I had been addressing him, he carefully revolved every statement that I made; fully comprehended the meaning; could not gainsay the irresistible conclusion; but, at the same time, some paramount consideration prevailed with him to reply as he did.

"You are decided, then, not to comply with my request — a request made according to common usage and common sense?"

He briefly gave me to understand, that on that point my judgment was sound. Yes: his decision was irreversible.

It is not seldom the case that, when a man is browbeaten in some unprecedented and violently unreasonable way, he begins to stagger in his own plainest faith. He begins, as it were, vaguely to surmise that, wonderful as it may be, all the justice and all the reason is on the other side. Accordingly, if any disinterested persons are present, he turns to them for some reinforcement for his own faltering mind.

"Turkey," said I, "what do you think of this? Am I not right?"

"With submission, sir," said Turkey, in his blandest tone, "I think that you are."

"Nippers," said I, "what do *you* think of it?"

"I think I should kick him out of the office."

(The reader, of nice perceptions, will here perceive that, it being morning, Turkey's answer is couched in polite and tranquil terms, but Nippers's replies in ill-tempered ones. Or, to repeat a previous sentence, Nippers's ugly mood was on duty, and Turkey's off.)

"Ginger Nut," said I, willing to enlist the smallest suffrage in my behalf, "what do *you* think of it?"

"I think, sir, he's a little *luny*," replied Ginger Nut, with a grin.

"You hear what they say," said I, turning toward the screen, "come forth and do your duty."

But he vouchsafed no reply. I pondered a moment in sore perplexity. But once more business hurried me. I determined again to postpone the consideration of this dilemma to my future leisure. With a little trouble we made out to examine the papers without Bartleby, though at every page or two Turkey deferentially dropped his opinion, that this proceeding was quite out of the common; while Nippers, twitching in his chair with a dyspeptic nervousness, ground out, between his set teeth, occasional hissing maledictions against the stubborn oaf behind the screen. And for his (Nippers's) part, this was the first and the last time he would do another man's business without pay.

Meanwhile Bartleby sat in his hermitage, oblivious to everything but his own peculiar business there.

Some days passed, the scrivener being employed upon another lengthy work. His late remarkable conduct led me to regard his ways narrowly. I observed that he never went to dinner; indeed, that he never went anywhere. As yet I had never, of my personal knowledge, known him to be outside of my office. He was a perpetual sentry in the corner. At about eleven o'clock though, in the morning, I noticed that Ginger Nut would advance toward the opening in Bartleby's screen, as if silently beckoned thither by a gesture invisible to me where I sat. The boy would then leave the office, jingling a few pence, and reappear with a handful of ginger-nuts, which he delivered in the hermitage, receiving two of the cakes for his trouble.

He lives, then, on ginger-nuts, thought I; never eats a dinner, properly speaking; he must be a vegetarian, then; but no; he never eats even vegetables, he eats nothing but ginger-nuts. My mind then ran on in reveries concerning the probable effects upon the human constitution of living entirely on ginger-nuts. Ginger-nuts are so called, because they contain ginger as one of their peculiar constituents, and the final flavouring one. Now, what was ginger? A hot, spicy thing. Was Bartleby hot and spicy? Not at all. Ginger, then, had no effect upon Bartleby. Probably he preferred it should have none.

Nothing so aggravates an earnest person as a passive resistance. If the individual so resisted be of a not inhumane temper, and the resisting one perfectly harmless in his passivity, then, in the better moods of the former, he will endeavour charitably to construe to his imagination what proves impossible to be solved by his judgment. Even so, for the most part, I regarded Bartleby and his ways. Poor fellow! thought I, he means no mischief; it is plain he intends no insolence; his aspect sufficiently evinces that his eccentricities are involuntary. He is useful to me. I can get along with him. If I turn him away, the chances are he will fall in with some less-indulgent employer, and then he will be rudely treated, and perhaps driven forth miserably to starve. Yes. Here I can cheaply purchase a delicious self-approval. To befriend Bartleby; to humour him in his strange wilfulness, will cost me little or nothing, while I lay up in my soul what will eventually prove a sweet morsel for my conscience. But this mood was not invariable with me. The passiveness of Bartleby sometimes irritated me. I felt strangely goaded on to encounter him in new opposition — to elicit some angry spark from him answerable to my own. But, indeed, I might as well have essayed to strike fire with my knuckles against a bit of Windsor soap. But one afternoon the evil impulse in me mastered me, and the following little scene ensued: —

"Bartleby," said I, "when those papers are all copied, I will compare them with you."

"I would prefer not to."

"How? Surely you do not mean to persist in that mulish vagary?"

No answer.

I threw open the folding-doors near by, and, turning upon Turkey and Nippers, exclaimed:

"Bartleby a second time says, he won't examine his papers. What do you think of it, Turkey?"

It was afternoon, be it remembered. Turkey sat glowing like a brass boiler; his bald head steaming; his hands reeling among his blotted papers.

"Think of it?" roared Turkey; "I think I'll just step behind his screen, and black his eyes for him!"

So saying, Turkey rose to his feet and threw his arms into a pugilistic position. He was hurrying away to make good his promise, when I detained him, alarmed at the effect of incautiously rousing Turkey's combativeness after dinner.

"Sit down, Turkey," said I, "and hear what Nippers has to say. What do you think of it, Nippers? Would I not be justified in immediately dismissing Bartleby?"

"Excuse me, that is for you to decide, sir. I think his conduct quite unusual, and, indeed, unjust, as regards Turkey and myself. But it may only be a passing whim."

"Ah," exclaimed I, "you have strangely changed your mind, then — you speak very gently of him now."

"All beer," cried Turkey; "gentleness is effects of beer — Nippers and I dined together to-day. You see how gentle *I* am, sir. Shall I go and black his eyes?"

"You refer to Bartleby, I suppose. No, not to-day, Turkey," I replied; "pray, put up your fists."

I closed the doors, and again advanced toward Bartleby. I felt additional incentives tempting me to my fate. I burned to be rebelled against again. I remembered that Bartleby never left the office.

"Bartleby," said I, "Ginger Nut is away; just step around to the Post Office, won't you? (it was but a three minutes' walk), and see if there is anything for me."

"I would prefer not to."

"You *will* not?"

"I *prefer* not."

I staggered to my desk, and sat there in a deep study. My blind inveteracy returned. Was there any other thing in which I could procure myself to be ignominiously repulsed by this lean, penniless wight? — my hired clerk? What added thing is there, perfectly reasonable, that he will be sure to refuse to do?

"Bartleby!"

No answer.

"Bartleby," in a louder tone.

No answer.

"Bartleby," I roared.

Like a very ghost, agreeably to the laws of magical invocation, at the third summons, he appeared at the entrance of his hermitage.

"Go to the next room, and tell Nippers to come to me."

"I prefer not to," he respectfully and slowly said, and mildly disappeared.

"Very good, Bartleby," said I, in a quiet sort of serenely-severe self-possessed tone, intimating the unalterable purpose of some terrible retribution very close at hand. At the moment I half intended something of the kind. But upon the whole, as it was drawing toward my dinner-hour, I thought it best to put on my hat and walk home for the day, suffering much from perplexity and distress of mind.

Shall I acknowledge it? The conclusion of this whole business was, that it soon became a fixed fact of my chambers, that a pale young scrivener, by the name of Bartleby, had a desk there; that he copied for me at the usual rate of four cents a folio (one hundred words); but he was permanently exempt from examining the work done by him, that duty being transferred to Turkey and Nippers, out of compliment, doubtless, to their superior acuteness; moreover, said Bartleby was never, on any account, to be dispatched on the most trivial errand of any sort; and that even if entreated to take upon him such a matter, it was generally understood that he would 'prefer not to' — in other words, that he would refuse point-blank.

As days passed on, I became considerably reconciled to Bartleby. His steadiness, his freedom from all dissipation, his incessant industry (except when he chose to throw himself into a standing revery behind his screen), his great stillness, his unalterableness of demeanour under all circumstances, made him a valuable acquisition. One prime thing was this — *he was always there* — first in the morning, continually through the day, and the last at night. I had a singular confidence in his honesty. I felt my most precious papers perfectly safe in his hands. Sometimes, to be sure, I could not, for the very soul of me, avoid falling into sudden spasmodic passions with him. For it was exceeding difficult to bear in mind all the time those strange peculiarities, privileges, and unheard-of exemptions, forming the tacit stipulations on Bartleby's part under which he remained in my office. Now and then, in the eagerness of dispatching pressing business, I would inadvertently summon Bartleby, in a short, rapid tone, to put his finger, say, on the incipient tie of a bit of red tape with which I was about compressing some papers. Of course, from behind the screen the usual answer, "I prefer not to," was sure to come; and then, how could a human creature, with the common infirmities of our nature, refrain from bitterly exclaiming upon such perverseness — such unreasonableness. However, every added repulse of this sort which I received only tended to lessen the probability of my repeating the inadvertence.

Here it must be said, that according to the custom of most legal gentlemen occupying chambers in densely populated law-buildings, there were several keys to my door. One was kept by a woman residing in the attic, which person weekly scrubbed and daily swept and dusted my apartments. Another was kept by Turkey for convenience sake. The third I sometimes carried in my own pocket. The fourth I knew not who had.

Now, one Sunday morning I happened to go to Trinity Church, to hear a celebrated preacher, and finding myself rather early on the ground I thought I would walk round to my chambers for a while. Luckily I had my key with me; but upon applying it to the lock, I found it resisted by something inserted from the inside. Quite surprised, I called out; when to my consternation a key was turned from within; and thrusting his lean visage at me, and holding the door ajar, the apparition of Bartleby appeared, in his shirt-sleeves, and otherwise in a strangely tattered dishabille, saying quietly that he was sorry, but he was deeply engaged just then, and — preferred not admitting me at present. In a brief word or two, he moreover added, that perhaps I had better walk round the block two or three times, and by that time he would probably have concluded his affairs.

Now, the utterly unsurmised appearance of Bartleby, tenanting my law-chambers of a Sunday morning, with his cadaverously gentlemanly nonchalance, yet withal firm and self-possessed, had such a strange effect upon me, that incontinently I slunk away from my own door, and did as desired. But not without sundry twinges of impotent rebellion against the mild effrontery of this unaccountable scrivener. Indeed, it was his wonderful mildness chiefly, which not only disarmed me, but unmanned me as it were. For I consider that one, for the time, is a sort of unmanned when he tranquilly permits his hired clerk to dictate to him, and order him away from his own premises. Furthermore, I was full of uneasiness as to what Bartleby could possibly be doing in my office in his shirt-sleeves, and in an otherwise dismantled condition of a Sunday morning. Was anything amiss going on? Nay, that was out of the question. It was not to be thought of for a moment that Bartleby was an immoral person. But what could he be doing there? — copying? Nay again, whatever might be his eccentricities, Bartleby was an eminently decorous person. He would be the last man to sit down to his desk in any state approaching to nudity. Besides, it was Sunday; and there was something about Bartleby that forbade the supposition that he would by any secular occupation violate the proprieties of the day.

Nevertheless, my mind was not pacified; and full of a restless curiosity, at last I returned to the door. Without hindrance I inserted my key, opened it, and entered. Bartleby was not to be seen. I looked round anxiously, peeped behind his screen; but it was very plain that he was gone. Upon more closely examining the place, I surmised that for an indefinite period Bartleby must have ate, dressed, and slept in my office, and that, too, without plate, mirror, or bed. The cushioned seat of a rickety old sofa in one corner bore the faint impress of a lean, reclining form. Rolled away under his desk, I found a blanket; under the empty grate a blacking box and brush; on a chair, a tin basin, with soap and a ragged towel; in a newspaper a few crumbs of ginger-nuts and a morsel of cheese. Yes, thought I, it is evident enough that Bartleby has been making his home here, keeping bachelor's hall all by himself. Immediately then the thought came sweeping across me, what miserable friendlessness and loneliness are here revealed! His poverty is great; but his solitude, how horrible! Think of it. Of a Sunday, Wall Street is deserted as Petra; and every night of every day it is an emptiness. This building, too, which of week-days hums with industry and life, at nightfall echoes with sheer vacancy, and all through Sunday is forlorn. And here Bartleby makes his home; sole spectator of a solitude which he has seen all-populous — a sort of innocent and transformed Marius[1] brooding among the ruins of Carthage!

For the first time in my life a feeling of overpowering stinging melancholy seized me. Before, I had never experienced aught but a not unpleasing sadness. The bond of a common humanity now drew me irresistibly to gloom. A fraternal melancholy! For both I and Bartleby were sons of Adam. I remembered the bright silks and sparkling faces I had seen that day, in

---

[1] Gaius Marius (157–86 B.C.), a Roman general who was exiled from Rome but later made a successful return to power.

gala trim, swan-like sailing down the Mississippi of Broadway; and I contrasted them with the pallid copyist, and thought to myself, Ah, happiness courts the light, so we deem the world is gay; but misery hides aloof, so we deem that misery there is none. These sad fancyings — chimeras, doubtless, of a sick and silly brain — led on to other and more special thoughts, concerning the eccentricities of Bartleby. Presentiments of strange discoveries hovered round me. The scrivener's pale form appeared to me laid out, among uncaring strangers, in its shivering winding-sheet.

Suddenly I was attracted by Bartleby's closed desk, the key in open sight left in the lock.

I mean no mischief, seek the gratification of no heartless curiosity, thought I; besides, the desk is mine, and its contents, too, so I will make bold to look within. Everything was methodically arranged, the papers smoothly placed. The pigeonholes were deep, and removing the files of documents, I groped into their recesses. Presently I felt something there, and dragged it out. It was an old bandanna handkerchief, heavy and knotted. I opened it, and saw it was a savings-bank.

I now recalled all the quiet mysteries which I had noted in the man. I remembered that he never spoke but to answer; that, though at intervals he had considerable time to himself, yet I had never seen him reading — no, not even a newspaper; that for long periods he would stand looking out, at his pale window behind the screen, upon the dead brick wall; I was quite sure he never visited any refectory or eating-house; while his pale face clearly indicated that he never drank beer like Turkey, or tea and coffee even, like other men; that he never went anywhere in particular that I could learn; never went out for a walk, unless, indeed, that was the case at present; that he had declined telling who he was, or whence he came, or whether he had any relatives in the world; that though so thin and pale, he never complained of ill health. And more than all, I remembered a certain unconscious air of pallid — how shall I call it? — of pallid haughtiness, say, or rather an austere reserve about him, which had positively awed me into my tame compliance with his eccentricities, when I had feared to ask him to do the slightest incidental thing for me, even though I might know, from his long-continued motionlessness, that behind his screen he must be standing in one of those dead-wall reveries of his.

Revolving all these things, and coupling them with the recently discovered fact, that he made my office his constant abiding-place and home, and not forgetful of his morbid moodiness; revolving all these things, a prudential feeling began to steal over me. My first emotions had been those of pure melancholy and sincerest pity; but just in proportion as the forlornness of Bartleby grew and grew to my imagination, did that same melancholy merge into fear, that pity into repulsion. So true it is, and so terrible, too, that up to a certain point the thought or sight of misery enlists our best affections; but, in certain special cases, beyond that point it does not. They err who would assert that invariably this is owing to the inherent selfishness of the human heart. It rather proceeds from a certain hopelessness of remedying excessive and organic ill. To a sensitive being, pity is not seldom pain. And when at last it is perceived that such pity cannot lead to effectual succour, commonsense bids the soul be rid of it. What I saw that morning persuaded me that the scrivener was the victim of innate and incurable disorder. I might give alms to his body; but his body did not pain him; it was his soul that suffered, and his soul I could not reach.

I did not accomplish the purpose of going to Trinity Church that morning. Somehow, the things I had seen disqualified me for the time from church-going. I walked homeward, thinking what I would do with Bartleby. Finally, I resolved upon this — I would put certain calm questions to him the next morning, touching his history, etc., and if he declined to answer them openly and unreservedly (and I supposed he would prefer not), then to give him a twenty-dollar bill over and above whatever I might owe him, and tell him his services were no longer required; but that if in any other way I could assist him, I would be happy to do so, especially if he desired to return to his native place, wherever that might be, I would willingly help to defray the expenses. Moreover, if, after reaching home, he found himself at any time in want of aid, a letter from him would be sure of a reply.

The next morning came.

"Bartleby," said I, gently calling to him behind his screen.

No reply.

"Bartleby," said I, in a still gentler tone, "come here; I am not going to ask you to do anything you would prefer not to do — I simply wish to speak to you."

Upon this he noiselessly slid into view.

"Will you tell me, Bartleby, where you were born?"

"I would prefer not to."

"Will you tell me *anything* about yourself?"

"I would prefer not to."

"But what reasonable objection can you have to speak to me? I feel friendly toward you."

He did not look at me while I spoke, but kept his glance fixed upon my bust of Cicero, which, as I then sat, was directly behind me, some six inches above my head.

"What is your answer, Bartleby?" said I, after waiting a considerable time for a reply, during which his countenance remained immovable, only there was the faintest conceivable tremor of the white attenuated mouth.

"At present I prefer to give no answer," he said, and retired into his hermitage.

It was rather weak in me, I confess, but his manner, on this occasion, nettled me. Not only did there seem to lurk in it a certain calm disdain, but his perverseness seemed ungrateful, considering the undeniable good usage and indulgence he had received from me.

Again I sat ruminating what I should do. Mortified as I was at his behaviour, and resolved as I had been to dismiss him when I entered my office, nevertheless I strangely felt something superstitious knocking at my heart, and forbidding me to carry out my purpose, and denouncing me for a villain if I dared to breathe one bitter word against this forlornest of mankind. At last, familiarly drawing my chair behind his screen, I sat down and said: "Bartleby, never mind, then, about revealing your history; but let me entreat you, as a friend, to comply as far as may be with the usages of this office. Say now, you will help to examine papers to-morrow or next day: in short, say now, that in a day or two you will begin to be a little reasonable: — say so, Bartleby."

"At present I would prefer not to be a little reasonable," was his mildly cadaverous reply.

Just then the folding doors opened, and Nippers approached. He seemed suffering from an unusually bad night's rest, induced by severer indigestion than common. He overheard those final words of Bartleby.

"*Prefer not*, eh?" gritted Nippers — "I'd *prefer* him; if I were you, sir," addressing me — "I'd *prefer* him; I'd give him preferences, the stubborn mule! What is it, sir, pray, that he *prefers* not to do now?"

Bartleby moved not a limb.

"Mr. Nippers," said I, "I'd prefer that you would withdraw for the present."

Somehow, of late, I had got into the way of involuntarily using this word "prefer" upon all sorts of not exactly suitable occasions. And I trembled to think that my contact with the scrivener had already and seriously affected me in a mental way. And what further and deeper aberration might it not yet produce? This apprehension had not been without efficacy in determining me to summary measures.

As Nippers, looking very sour and sulky, was departing, Turkey blandly and deferentially approached.

"With submission, sir," said he, "yesterday I was thinking about Bartleby here, and I think that if he would but prefer to take a quart of good ale every day, it would do much toward mending him, and enabling him to assist in examining his papers."

"So you have got the word too," said I, slightly excited.

"With submission, what word, sir," asked Turkey, respectfully crowding himself into the contracted space behind the screen, and by so doing, making me jostle the scrivener. "What word, sir?"

"I would prefer to be left alone here," said Bartleby, as if offended at being mobbed in his privacy.

"*That's* the word, Turkey," said I — "*that's* it."

"Oh, *prefer*? oh yes — queer word. I never use it myself. But, sir, as I was saying, if he would but prefer——"

"Turkey," interrupted I, "you will please withdraw."

"Oh certainly, sir, if you prefer that I should."

As he opened the folding-door to retire, Nippers at his desk caught a glimpse of me, and asked whether I would prefer to have a certain paper copied on blue paper or white. He did not in the least roguishly accent the word prefer. It was plain that it involuntarily rolled from his tongue. I thought to myself, surely I must get rid of a demented man, who already has in some degree turned the tongues, if not the heads of myself and clerks. But I thought it prudent not to break the dismission at once.

The next day I noticed that Bartleby did nothing but stand at his window in his dead-wall revery. Upon asking him why he did not write, he said that he had decided upon doing no more writing.

"Why, how now? what next?" exclaimed I, "do no more writing?"

"No more."

"And what is the reason?"

"Do you not see the reason for yourself?" he indifferently replied.

I looked steadfastly at him, and perceived that his eyes looked dull and glazed. Instantly it occurred to me, that his unexampled diligence in copying by his dim window for the first few weeks of his stay with me might have temporarily impaired his vision.

I was touched. I said something in condolence with him. I hinted that of course he did wisely in abstaining from writing for a while; and urged him to embrace that opportunity of taking wholesome exercise in the open air. This, however, he did not do. A few days after this, my other clerks being absent, and being in a great hurry to dispatch certain letters by the mail, I thought that having nothing else earthly to do, Bartleby would surely be less inflexible than usual, and carry these letters to the Post Office. But he blankly declined. So, much to my inconvenience, I went myself.

Still added days went by. Whether Bartleby's eyes improved or not, I could not say. To all appearance, I thought they did. But when I asked him if they did, he vouchsafed no answer. At all events, he would do no copying. At last, in reply to my urgings, he informed me that he had permanently given up copying.

"What!" exclaimed I; "suppose your eyes should get entirely well — better than ever before — would you not copy then?"

"I have given up copying," he answered, and slid aside.

He remained as ever, a fixture in my chamber. Nay — if that were possible — he became still more of a fixture than before. What was to be done? He would do nothing in the office;

why should he stay there? In plain fact, he had now become a millstone to me, not only useless as a necklace, but afflictive to bear. Yet I was sorry for him. I speak less than truth when I say that, on his own account, he occasioned me uneasiness. If he would but have named a single relative or friend, I would instantly have written, and urged their taking the poor fellow away to some convenient retreat. But he seemed alone, absolutely alone in the universe. A bit of wreck in the mid-Atlantic. At length, necessities connected with my business tyrannised over all other considerations. Decently as I could, I told Bartleby that in six days' time he must unconditionally leave the office. I warned him to take measures, in the interval, for procuring some other abode. I offered to assist him in this endeavour, if he himself would but take the first step toward a removal. "And when you finally quit me, Bartleby," added I, "I shall see that you go not away entirely unprovided. Six days from this hour, remember."

At the expiration of that period, I peeped behind the screen, and lo! Bartleby was there.

I buttoned up my coat, balanced myself; advanced slowly toward him, touched his shoulder, and said, "The time has come; you must quit this place; I am sorry for you; here is money; but you must go."

"I would prefer not," he replied, with his back still toward me.

"You *must*."

He remained silent.

Now I had an unbounded confidence in this man's common honesty. He had frequently restored to me sixpences and shillings carelessly dropped upon the floor, for I am apt to be very reckless in such shirt-button affairs. The proceeding, then, which followed will not be deemed extraordinary.

"Bartleby," said I, "I owe you twelve dollars on account; here are thirty-two; the odd twenty are yours — Will you take it?" and I handed the bills toward him.

But he made no motion.

"I will leave them here, then," putting them under a weight on the table. Then taking my hat and cane and going to the door, I tranquilly turned and added — "After you have removed your things from these offices, Bartleby, you will of course lock the door — since everyone is now gone for the day but you — and if you please, slip your key underneath the mat, so that I may have it in the morning. I shall not see you again; so good-bye to you. If, hereafter, in your new place of abode, I can be of any service to you, do not fail to advise me by letter. Good-bye, Bartleby, and fare you well."

But he answered not a word; like the last column of some ruined temple, he remained standing mute and solitary in the middle of the otherwise deserted room.

As I walked home in a pensive mood, my vanity got the better of my pity. I could not but highly plume myself on my masterly management in getting rid of Bartleby. Masterly I call it, and such it must appear to any dispassionate thinker. The beauty of my procedure seemed to consist in its perfect quietness. There was no vulgar bullying, no bravado of any sort, no choleric hectoring, and striding to and fro across the apartment, jerking out vehement commands for Bartleby to bundle himself off with his beggarly traps. Nothing of the kind. Without loudly bidding Bartleby depart — as an inferior genius might have done — I *assumed* the ground that depart he must; and upon that assumption built all I had to say. The more I thought over my procedure, the more I was charmed with it. Nevertheless, next morning, upon awakening, I had my doubts — I had somehow slept off the fumes of vanity. One of the coolest and wisest hours a man has, is just after he awakes in the morning. My procedure seemed as sagacious as ever — but only in theory. How it would prove in practice — there was the rub. It was truly a beautiful thought to have assumed Bartleby's departure; but, after all, that assumption was simply my own, and none of Bartleby's. The great point was, not whether I had assumed that he would quit me, but whether he would prefer so to do. He was more a man of preferences than assumptions.

After breakfast, I walked down town, arguing the probabilities *pro* and *con*. One moment I thought it would prove a miserable failure, and Bartleby would be found all alive at my office as usual; the next moment it seemed certain that I should find his chair empty. And so I kept veering about. At the corner of Broadway and Canal Street, I saw quite an excited group of people standing in earnest conversation.

"I'll take odds he doesn't," said a voice as I passed.

"Doesn't go? — done!" said I; "put up your money."

I was instinctively putting my hand in my pocket to produce my own, when I remembered that this was an election day. The words I had overheard bore no reference to Bartleby, but to the success or non-success of some candidate for the mayoralty. In my intent frame of mind, I had, as it were, imagined that all Broadway shared in my excitement, and were debating the same question with me. I passed on, very thankful that the uproar of the street screened my momentary absent-mindedness.

As I had intended, I was earlier than usual at my office door. I stood listening for a moment. All was still. He must be gone. I tried the knob. The door was locked. Yes, my procedure had worked to a charm; he indeed must be vanished. Yet a certain melancholy mixed with this: I was almost sorry for my brilliant success. I was fumbling under the doormat for the key, which Bartleby was to have left there for me, when accidentally my knee knocked against a panel, producing a summoning sound, and in response a voice came to me from within — "Not yet; I am occupied."

It was Bartleby.

I was thunderstruck. For an instant I stood like the man who, pipe in mouth, was killed one cloudless afternoon long ago in Virginia, by summer lightning; at his own warm open window he was killed, and remained leaning out there upon the dreamy afternoon, till someone touched him, when he fell.

"Not gone!" I murmured at last. But again obeying that wondrous ascendency which the inscrutable scrivener had over me, and from which ascendency, for all my chafing, I could not completely escape, I slowly went downstairs and out into the street, and while walking round the block, considered what I should next do in this unheard-of perplexity. Turn the man out by an actual thrusting I could not; to drive him away by calling him hard names would not do; calling in the police was an unpleasant idea; and yet, permit him to enjoy his cadaverous triumph over me — this, too, I could not think of. What was to be done? or, if nothing could be done, was there anything further that I could *assume* in the matter? Yes, as before I had prospectively assumed that Bartleby would depart, so now I might retrospectively assume that departed he was. In the legitimate carrying out of this assumption, I might enter my office in a great hurry, and pretending not to see Bartleby at all, walk straight against him as if he were air. Such a proceeding would in a singular degree have the appearance of a home-thrust. It was hardly possible that Bartleby could withstand such an application of the doctrine of assumptions. But upon second thoughts the success of the plan seemed rather dubious. I resolved to argue the matter over with him again.

"Bartleby," said I, entering the office, with a quietly severe expression, "I am seriously displeased. I am pained, Bartleby. I had thought better of you. I had imagined you of such a gentlemanly organisation, that in any delicate dilemma a slight hint would suffice — in short, an assumption. But it appears I am deceived. Why," I added, unaffectedly starting, "you have not even touched that money yet," pointing to it, just where I had left it the evening previous.

He answered nothing.

"Will you, or will you not, quit me?" I now demanded in a sudden passion, advancing close to him.

"I would prefer *not* to quit you," he replied, gently emphasising the *not*.

"What earthly right have you to stay here? Do you pay any rent? Do you pay my taxes? Or is this property yours?"

He answered nothing.

"Are you ready to go on and write now? Are your eyes recovered? Could you copy a small paper for me this morning? or help examine a few lines? or step round to the Post Office? In a word, will you do anything at all, to give a colouring to your refusal to depart the premises?"

He silently retired into his hermitage.

I was now in such a state of nervous resentment that I thought it but prudent to check myself at present from further demonstrations. Bartleby and I were alone. I remembered the tragedy of the unfortunate Adams and the still more unfortunate Colt in the solitary office of the latter; and how poor Colt, being dreadfully incensed by Adams, and imprudently permitting himself to get wildly excited, was at unawares hurried into his fatal act — an act which certainly no man could possibly deplore more than the actor himself.[2] Often it had occurred to me in my ponderings upon the subject, that had that altercation taken place in the public street, or at a private residence, it would not have terminated as it did. It was the circumstance of being alone in a solitary office, upstairs, of a building entirely unhallowed by humanising domestic associations — an uncarpeted office, doubtless, of a dusty, haggard sort of appearance — this it must have been, which greatly helped to enhance the irritable desperation of the hapless Colt.

But when this old Adam of resentment rose in me and tempted me concerning Bartleby, I grappled him and threw him. How? Why, simply by recalling the divine injunction: "A new commandment give I unto you, that ye love one another." Yes, this it was that saved me. Aside from higher considerations, charity often operates as a vastly wise and prudent principle — a great safeguard to its possessor. Men have committed murder for jealousy's sake, and anger's sake, and hatred's sake, and selfishness' sake, and spiritual pride's sake; but no man, that ever I heard of, ever committed a diabolical murder for sweet charity's sake. Mere self-interest, then, if no better motive can be enlisted, should, especially with high-tempered men, prompt all beings to charity and philanthropy. At any rate, upon the occasion in question, I strove to drown my exasperated feelings toward the scrivener by benevolently construing his conduct. Poor fellow, poor fellow! thought I, he don't mean anything; and besides, he has seen hard times, and ought to be indulged.

I endeavoured, also, immediately to occupy myself, and at the same time to comfort my despondency. I tried to fancy, that in the course of the morning, at such time as might prove agreeable to him, Bartleby, of his own free accord, would emerge from his hermitage and take up some decided line of march in the direction of the door. But no. Half-past twelve o'clock came; Turkey began to glow in the face, overturn his inkstand, and become generally obstreperous; Nippers abated down into quietude and courtesy; Ginger Nut munched his noon apple; and Bartleby remained standing at his window in one of his profoundest dead-wall reveries. Will it be credited? Ought I to acknowledge it? That afternoon I left the office without saying one further word to him.

Some days now passed, during which, at leisure intervals, I looked a little into "Edwards on the Will," and "Priestley on Necessity." Under the circumstances, those books induced a

---

[2] A notorious 1841 murder case in New York City. Colt killed Adams, but committed suicide before he could be executed for the crime.

salutary feeling. Gradually I slid into the persuasion that these troubles of mine, touching the scrivener, had been all predestinated from eternity, and Bartleby was billeted upon me for some mysterious purpose of an all-wise Providence, which it was not for a mere mortal like me to fathom. Yes, Bartleby, stay there behind your screen, thought I; I shall persecute you no more; you are harmless and noiseless as any of these old chairs; in short, I never feel so private as when I know you are here. At last I see it, I feel it; I penetrate to the predestinated purpose of my life. I am content. Others may have loftier parts to enact; but my mission in this world, Bartleby, is to furnish you with office-room for such period as you may see fit to remain.

I believe that this wise and blessed frame of mind would have continued with me, had it not been for the unsolicited and uncharitable remarks obtruded upon me by my professional friends who visited the rooms. But thus it often is, that the constant friction of illiberal minds wears out at last the best resolves of the more generous. Though to be sure, when I reflected upon it, it was not strange that people entering my office should be struck by the peculiar aspect of the unaccountable Bartleby, and so be tempted to throw out some sinister observations concerning him. Sometimes an attorney, having business with me, and calling at my office, and finding no one but the scrivener there, would undertake to obtain some sort of precise information from him touching my whereabouts; but without heeding his idle talk, Bartleby would remain standing immovable in the middle of the room. So after contemplating him in that position for a time, the attorney would depart, no wiser than he came.

Also, when a reference was going on, and the room full of lawyers and witnesses, and business driving fast, some deeply occupied legal gentleman present, seeing Bartleby wholly unemployed, would request him to run round to his (the legal gentleman's) office and fetch some papers for him. Thereupon, Bartleby would tranquilly decline, and yet remain idle as before. Then the lawyer would give a great stare, and turn to me. And what could I say? At last I was made aware that all through the circle of my professional acquaintance, a whisper of wonder was running round, having reference to the strange creature I kept at my office. This worried me very much. And as the idea came upon me of his possibly turning out a long-lived man, and keep occupying my chambers, and denying my authority; and perplexing my visitors; and scandalising my professional reputation; and casting a general gloom over the premises; keeping soul and body together to the last upon his savings (for doubtless he spent but half a dime a day), and in the end perhaps outlive me, and claim possession of my office by right of his perpetual occupancy: as all these dark anticipations crowded upon me more and more, and my friends continually intruded their relentless remarks upon the apparition in my room; a great change was wrought in me. I resolved to gather all my faculties together, and forever rid me of this intolerable incubus.

Ere revolving any complicated project, however, adapted to this end, I first simply suggested to Bartleby the propriety of his permanent departure. In a calm and serious tone, I commended the idea to his careful and mature consideration. But, having taken three days to meditate upon it, he apprised me, that his original determination remained the same; in short, that he still preferred to abide with me.

What shall I do? I now said to myself, buttoning up my coat to the last button. What shall I do? what ought I to do? what does conscience say I *should* do with this man, or, rather, ghost. Rid myself of him, I must; go, he shall. But how? You will not thrust him, the poor, pale, passive mortal — you will not thrust such a helpless creature out of your door? you will not dishonour yourself by such cruelty? No, I will not, I cannot do that. Rather would I let him live and die here, and then mason up his remains in the wall. What, then, will you do? For all your coaxing, he will not budge. Bribes he leaves under your own paperweight on your table; in short, it is quite plain that he prefers to cling to you.

Then something severe, something unusual must be done. What! surely you will not have him collared by a constable, and commit his innocent pallor to the common jail? And upon what ground could you procure such a thing to be done? — a vagrant, is he? What! he a vagrant, a wanderer, who refuses to budge? It is because he will *not* be a vagrant, then, that you seek to count him *as* a vagrant. That is too absurd. No visible means of support; there I have him. Wrong again: for indubitably he *does* support himself, and that is the only unanswerable proof that any man can show of his possessing the means so to do. No more, then. Since he will not quit me, I must quit him. I will change my offices; I will move elsewhere, and give him fair notice, that if I find him on my new premises I will then proceed against him as a common trespasser.

Acting accordingly, next day I thus addressed him: "I find these chambers too far from the City Hall; the air is unwholesome. In a word, I propose to remove my offices next week, and shall no longer require your services. I tell you this now, in order that you may seek another place."

He made no reply, and nothing more was said.

On the appointed day I engaged carts and men, proceeded to my chambers, and, having but little furniture, everything was removed in a few hours. Throughout, the scrivener remained standing behind the screen, which I directed to be removed the last thing. It was withdrawn; and, being folded up like a huge folio, left him the motionless occupant of a naked room. I stood in the entry watching him a moment, while something from within me upbraided me.

I re-entered, with my hand in my pocket — and — and my heart in my mouth.

"Good-bye, Bartleby; I am going — good-bye, and God some way bless you; and take that," slipping something in his hand. But it dropped upon the floor, and then — strange to say — I tore myself from him whom I had so longed to be rid of.

Established in my new quarters, for a day or two I kept the door locked, and started at every footfall in the passages. When I returned to my rooms, after any little absence, I would pause at the threshold for an instant, and attentively listen ere applying my key. But these fears were needless. Bartleby never came nigh me.

I thought all was going well, when a perturbed-looking stranger visited me, inquiring whether I was the person who had recently occupied rooms at No. — Wall Street.

Full of forebodings, I replied that I was.

"Then, sir," said the stranger, who proved a lawyer, "you are responsible for the man you left there. He refuses to do any copying; he refuses to do anything; he says he prefers not to; and he refuses to quit the premises."

"I am very sorry, sir," said I, with assumed tranquillity, but an inward tremor, "but, really, the man you allude to is nothing to me — he is no relation or apprentice of mine, that you should hold me responsible for him."

"In mercy's name, who is he?"

"I certainly cannot inform you. I know nothing about him. Formerly I employed him as a copyist; but he has done nothing for me now for some time past."

"I shall settle him, then — good morning, sir."

Several days passed, and I heard nothing more; and, though I often felt a charitable prompting to call at the place and see poor Bartleby, yet a certain squeamishness, of I know not what, withheld me.

All is over with him, by this time, thought I at last, when, through another week, no further intelligence reached me. But, coming to my room the day after, I found several persons waiting at my door in a high state of nervous excitement.

"That's the man — here he comes," cried the foremost one, whom I recognised as the lawyer who had previously called upon me alone.

"You must take him away, sir, at once," cried a portly person among them, advancing upon me, and whom I knew to be the landlord of No. — Wall Street. "These gentlemen, my tenants, cannot stand it any longer; Mr. B——," pointing to the lawyer, "has turned him out of his room, and he now persists in haunting the building generally, sitting upon the banisters of the stairs by day, and sleeping in the entry by night. Everybody is concerned; clients are leaving the offices; some fears are entertained of a mob; something you must do, and that without delay."

Aghast at this torrent, I fell back before it, and would fain have locked myself in my new quarters. In vain I persisted that Bartleby was nothing to me — no more than to anyone else. In vain — I was the last person known to have anything to do with him, and they held me to the terrible account. Fearful, then, of being exposed in the papers (as one person present obscurely threatened), I considered the matter, and, at length, said, that if the lawyer would give me a confidential interview with the scrivener, in his (the lawyer's) own room, I would, that afternoon, strive my best to rid them of the nuisance they complained of.

Going upstairs to my old haunt, there was Bartleby silently sitting upon the banister at the landing.

"What are you doing here, Bartleby?" said I.

"Sitting upon the bannister," he mildly replied.

I motioned him into the lawyer's room, who then left us.

"Bartleby," said I, "are you aware that you are the cause of great tribulation to me, by persisting in occupying the entry after being dismissed from the office?"

No answer.

"Now one of two things must take place. Either you must do something, or something must be done to you. Now what sort of business would you like to engage in? Would you like to re-engage in copying for someone?"

"No; I would prefer not to make any change."

"Would you like a clerkship in a dry-goods store?"

"There is too much confinement about that. No, I would not like a clerkship; but I am not particular."

"Too much confinement," I cried, "why, you keep yourself confined all the time!"

"I would prefer not to take a clerkship," he rejoined, as if to settle that little item at once.

"How would a bar-tender's business suit you? There is no trying of the eyesight in that."

"I would not like it at all; though, as I said before, I am not particular."

His unwonted wordiness inspirited me. I returned to the charge.

"Well, then, would you like to travel through the country collecting bills for the merchants? That would improve your health."

"No, I would prefer to be doing something else."

"How, then, would going as a companion to Europe, to entertain some young gentleman with your conversation — how would that suit you?"

"Not at all. It does not strike me that there is anything definite about that. I like to be stationary. But I am not particular."

"Stationary you shall be, then," I cried, now losing all patience, and, for the first time in all my exasperating connection with him, fairly flying into a passion. "If you do not go away from these premises before night, I shall feel bound — indeed, I *am* bound — to — to quit the premises myself!" I rather absurdly concluded, knowing not with what possible threat to try to frighten his immobility into compliance. Despairing of all further efforts, I was precipitately leaving him, when a final thought occurred to me — one which had not been wholly unindulged before.

"Bartleby," said I, in the kindest tone I could assume under such exciting circumstances, "will you go home with me now — not to my office, but my dwelling — and remain there till we can conclude upon some convenient arrangement for you at our leisure? Come, let us start now, right away."

"No; at present I would prefer not to make any change at all."

I answered nothing; but, effectually dodging everyone by the suddenness and rapidity of my flight, rushed from the building, ran up Wall Street toward Broadway, and, jumping into the first omnibus, was soon removed from pursuit. As soon as tranquillity returned, I distinctly perceived that I had now done all that I possibly could, both in respect to the demands of the landlord and his tenants, and with regard to my own desire and sense of duty, to benefit Bartleby, and shield him from rude persecution. I now strove to be entirely carefree and quiescent; and my conscience justified me in the attempt; though, indeed, it was not so successful as I could have wished. So fearful was I of being again hunted out by the incensed landlord and his exasperated tenants, that, surrendering my business to Nippers, for a few days, I drove about the upper part of the town and through the suburbs, in my rockaway; crossed over to Jersey City and Hoboken, and paid fugitive visits to Manhattanville and Astoria. In fact, I almost lived in my rockaway for the time.

When again I entered my office, lo, a note from the landlord lay upon the desk. I opened it with trembling hands. It informed me that the writer had sent to the police, and had Bartleby removed to the Tombs[3] as a vagrant. Moreover, since I knew more about him than anyone else, he wished me to appear at that place, and make a suitable statement of the facts. These tidings had a conflicting effect upon me. At first I was indignant; but, at last, almost approved. The landlord's energetic summary disposition had led him to adopt a procedure which I do not think I would have decided upon myself; and yet, as a last resort, under such peculiar circumstances, it seemed the only plan.

As I afterward learned, the poor scrivener, when told that he must be conducted to the Tombs, offered not the slightest obstacle, but, in his pale, unmoving way, silently acquiesced.

Some of the compassionate and curious bystanders joined the party; and headed by one of the constables arm in arm with Bartleby, the silent procession filed its way through all the noise, and heat, and joy of the roaring thoroughfares at noon.

The same day I received the note, I went to the Tombs, or, to speak more properly, the Halls of Justice. Seeking the right officer, I stated the purpose of my call, and was informed that the individual I described was, indeed, within. I then assured the functionary that Bartleby was a perfectly honest man, and greatly to be compassionated, however unaccountably eccentric. I narrated all I knew, and closed by suggesting the idea of letting him remain in as indulgent confinement as possible, till something less harsh might be done — though, indeed, I hardly knew what. At all events, if nothing else could be decided upon, the alms-house must receive him. I then begged to have an interview.

Being under no disgraceful charge, and quite serene and harmless in all his ways, they had permitted him freely to wander about the prison, and, especially, in the enclosed grass-platted yards thereof. And so I found him there, standing all alone in the quietest of the yards, his face toward a high wall, while all around, from the narrow slits of the jail windows, I thought I saw peering out upon him the eyes of murderers and thieves.

"Bartleby!"

---

[3] A prison.

"I know you," he said, without looking round — "and I want nothing to say to you."

"It was not I that brought you here, Bartleby," said I, keenly pained at his implied suspicion. "And to you, this should not be so vile a place. Nothing reproachful attaches to you by being here. And see, it is not so sad a place as one might think. Look, there is the sky, and here is the grass."

"I know where I am," he replied, but would say nothing more, and so I left him.

As I entered the corridor again, a broad meat-like man, in an apron, accosted me, and, jerking his thumb over his shoulder, said, "Is that your friend?"

"Yes."

"Does he want to starve? If he does, let him live on the prison fare, that's all."

"Who are you?" asked I, not knowing what to make of such an unofficially speaking person in such a place.

"I am the grub-man. Such gentlemen as have friends here, hire me to provide them with something good to eat."

"Is this so?" said I, turning to the turnkey.

He said it was.

"Well, then," said I, slipping some silver into the grub-man's hands (for so they called him), "I want you to give particular attention to my friend there; let him have the best dinner you can get. And you must be as polite to him as possible."

"Introduce me, will you?" said the grub-man, looking at me with an expression which seemed to say he was all impatience for an opportunity to give a specimen of his breeding.

Thinking it would prove of benefit to the scrivener, I acquiesced; and, asking the grub-man his name, went up with him to Bartleby.

"Bartleby, this is a friend; you will find him very useful to you."

"Your sarvant, sir, your sarvant," said the grub-man, making a low salutation behind his apron. "Hope you find it pleasant here, sir; nice grounds — cool apartments — hope you'll stay with us some time — try to make it agreeable. What will you have for dinner to-day?"

"I prefer not to dine to-day," said Bartleby, turning away. "It would disagree with me; I am unused to dinners." So saying, he slowly moved to the other side of the enclosure, and took up a position fronting the dead-wall.

"How's this?" said the grub-man, addressing me with a stare of astonishment. "He's odd, ain't he?"

"I think he is a little deranged," said I sadly.

"Deranged? deranged is it? Well, now, upon my word, I thought that friend of yourn was a gentleman forger; they are always pale and genteel-like, them forgers. I can't help pity 'em — can't help it, sir. Did you know Monroe Edwards?"[4] he added touchingly, and paused. Then, laying his hand piteously on my shoulder, sighed, "he died of consumption at Sing-Sing. So you weren't acquainted with Monroe?"

"No, I was never socially acquainted with any forgers. But I cannot stop longer. Look to my friend yonder. You will not lose by it. I will see you again."

Some few days after this, I again obtained admission to the Tombs, and went through the corridors in quest of Bartleby; but without finding him.

"I saw him coming from his cell not long ago," said a turnkey, "maybe he's gone to loiter in the yards."

So I went in that direction.

---

[4] Monroe Edwards (1808–1847) scandalized and shook Wall Street when it was found that he had forged credit documents to swindle clients. He was sent to prison as a result.

"Are you looking for the silent man?" said another turnkey, passing me. "Yonder he lies — sleeping in the yard there. 'Tis not twenty minutes since I saw him lie down."

The yard was entirely quiet. It was not accessible to the common prisoners. The surrounding walls, of amazing thickness, kept off all sounds behind them. The Egyptian character of the masonry weighed upon me with its gloom. But a soft imprisoned turf grew under foot. The heart of the eternal pyramids, it seemed, wherein, by some strange magic, through the clefts, grass-seed, dropped by birds, had sprung.

Strangely huddled at the base of the wall, his knees drawn up, and lying on his side, his head touching the cold stones, I saw the wasted Bartleby. But nothing stirred. I paused; then went close up to him; stooped over, and saw that his dim eyes were open; otherwise he seemed profoundly sleeping. Something prompted me to touch him. I felt his hand, when a tingling shiver ran up my arm and down my spine to my feet.

The round face of the grub-man peered upon me now. "His dinner is ready. Won't he dine to-day, either? Or does he live without dining?"

"Lives without dining," said I, and closed the eyes.

"Eh! — He's asleep, ain't he?"

"With kings and counsellors," murmured I.

There would seem little need for proceeding further in this history. Imagination will readily supply the meagre recital of poor Bartleby's interment. But, ere parting with the reader, let me say, that if this little narrative has sufficiently interested him, to awaken curiosity as to who Bartleby was, and what manner of life he led prior to the present narrator's making his acquaintance, I can only reply, that in such curiosity I fully share, but am wholly unable to gratify it. Yet here I hardly know whether I should divulge one little item of rumour, which came to my ear a few months after the scrivener's decease. Upon what basis it rested I could never ascertain; and hence, how true it is I cannot now tell. But, inasmuch as this vague report has not been without a certain suggestive interest to me, however sad, it may prove the same with some others; and so I will briefly mention it. The report was this: that Bartleby had been a subordinate clerk in the Dead Letter Office at Washington, from which he had been suddenly removed by a change in the administration. When I think over this rumour, hardly can I express the emotions which seize me. Dead letters! does it not sound like dead men? Conceive a man by nature and misfortune prone to a pallid hopelessness, can any business seem more fitted to heighten it than that of continually handling these dead letters, and assorting them for the flames? For by the cartload they are annually burned. Sometimes from out the folded paper the pale clerk takes a ring — the finger it was meant for, perhaps, moulders in the grave; a bank-note sent in swiftest charity — he whom it would relieve, nor eats nor hungers any more; pardon for those who died despairing; hope for those who died unhoping; good tidings for those who died stifled by unrelieved calamities. On errands of life, these letters speed to death.

Ah, Bartleby! Ah, humanity!

QUESTIONS

1. What significance do you find in the subtitle? Has Melville written an indictment of American commercial life?

2. Instead of saying, "I prefer not to," why doesn't Bartleby thunder out, "No!"? What does the repeated phrase suggest about his character?

3. A scrivener only copies, never creates, what he writes. Is this fact at the root of Bartleby's mild but persistent rebellion? Has he simply gone mad?

4. Is the narrator (who seems remarkably patient) an entirely admirable character? Why doesn't he fire Bartleby outright and have him removed bodily from the premises?

5. Is it fair of Bartleby finally to tell the narrator, "I know you . . . and I want nothing to say to you"? Has jail changed Bartleby?

6. If you were an employer with a Bartleby on your hands, what would you do about him? What would Melville's Bartleby likely do in return?

FYODOR DOSTOEVSKY

The Grand Inquisitor

Translated by Constance Garnett

"Do you know, Alyosha — don't laugh! I made a poem about a year ago. If you can waste another ten minutes on me, I'll tell it to you."

"You wrote a poem?"

"Oh, no, I didn't write it," laughed Ivan, "and I've never written two lines of poetry in my life. But I made up this poem in prose and I remembered it. I was carried away when I made it up. You will be my first reader — that is, listener. Why should an author forgo even one listener?" smiled Ivan. "Shall I tell it to you?"

"I am all attention," said Alyosha.

"My poem is called 'The Grand Inquisitor'; it's a ridiculous thing, but I want to tell it to you.

"Even this must have a preface — that is, a literary preface," laughed Ivan, "and I am a poor hand at making one. You see, my action takes place in the sixteenth century, and at that time, as you probably learnt at school, it was customary in poetry to bring down heavenly powers on earth. Not to speak of Dante, in France, clerks, as well as the monks in the monasteries, used to give regular performances in which the Madonna, the saints, the angels, Christ, and God Himself were brought on the stage. In those days it was done in all simplicity. In Victor Hugo's 'Notre Dame de Paris' an edifying and gratuitous spectacle was provided for the people in the Hôtel de Ville of Paris in the reign of Louis XI in honour of the birth of the dauphin. It was called *Le bon jugement de la très sainte et gracieuse Vierge Marie*;[1] and she appears herself on the stage and pronounces her *bon jugement*. Similar plays, chiefly from the Old Testament, were occasionally performed in Moscow too, up to the times of Peter the Great. But besides plays there were all sorts of legends and ballads scattered about the world, in which the saints and angels and all the powers of Heaven took part when required. In our monasteries the monks busied themselves in translating, copying, and even composing such poems — and even under the Tatars. There is, for instance, one such poem (of course, from the Greek), 'The Wanderings of Our Lady through Hell,' with descriptions as bold as Dante's. Our Lady visits Hell, and the Archangel Michael leads her through the torments. She sees the sinners and their punishments. There she sees among others one noteworthy set of sinners in a burning lake; some of them sink to the bottom of the lake so that they can't swim out, and 'these God forgets' — an expression of extraordinary depth and force. And so Our Lady,

---

[1] "The Right Judgment of the Most Holy and Gracious Virgin Mary."

shocked and weeping, falls before the throne of God and begs for mercy for all in Hell — for all she has seen there, indiscriminately. Her conversation with God is immensely interesting. She beseeches Him, she will not desist, and when God points to the hands and feet of her Son, nailed to the Cross, and asks: 'How can I forgive His tormentors?' she bids all the saints, all the martyrs, all the angels and archangels to fall down with her and pray for mercy on all without distinction. It ends by her winning from God a respite of suffering every year from Good Friday till Trinity day, and the sinners at once raise a cry of thankfulness from Hell, chanting: 'Thou art just, O Lord, in this judgment.' Well, my poem would have been of that kind if it had appeared at that time. He comes on the scene in my poem, but He says nothing, only appears and passes on. Fifteen centuries have passed since He promised to come in His glory, fifteen centuries since His prophet wrote, 'Behold, I come quickly'; 'Of that day and that hour knoweth no man, neither the Son, but the Father,' as He Himself predicted on earth. But humanity awaits him with the same faith and with the same love. Oh, with greater faith, for it is fifteen centuries since man has ceased to see signs from Heaven.

> No signs from Heaven come to-day
> To add to what the heart doth say.

There was nothing left but faith in what the heart doth say. It is true there were many miracles in those days. There were saints who performed miraculous cures; some holy people, according to their biographies, were visited by the Queen of Heaven herself. But the devil did not slumber, and doubts were already arising among men of the truth of these miracles. And just then there appeared in the north of Germany a terrible new heresy. 'A huge star like to a torch' (that is, to a church) 'fell on the sources of the waters and they became bitter.' These heretics began blasphemously denying miracles. But those who remained faithful were all the more ardent in their faith. The tears of humanity rose up to Him as before, awaited His coming, loved Him, hoped for Him, yearned to suffer and die for Him as before. And so many ages mankind had prayed with faith and fervour: 'O Lord our God, hasten Thy coming,' so many ages called upon Him, that in His infinite mercy He deigned to come down to His servants. Before that day He had come down, He had visited some holy men, martyrs and hermits, as is written in their 'Lives.' Among us, Tyutchev, with absolute faith in the truth of his words, bore witness that:

> Bearing the Cross, in slavish dress
> Weary and worn, the Heavenly King
> Our mother, Russia, came to bless
> And through our land went wandering.

And that certainly was so, I assure you.

"And behold, He deigned to appear for a moment to the people, to the tortured, suffering people, sunk in iniquity but loving Him like children. My story is laid in Spain, in Seville, in the most terrible time of the Inquisition, when fires were lighted every day to the glory of God, and 'in the splendid *auto da fé*[2] the wicked heretics were burnt.' Oh, of course, this was not the coming in which He will appear according to His promise at the end of time in all His heavenly glory, and which will be sudden 'as lightning flashing from east to west.' No, He visited His children only for a moment, and there where the flames were crackling round

---

[2] The "act of faith" by which the courts of the Spanish Inquisition condemned suspected heretics, and the secular arm executed the judgment, often by burning the condemned at the stake.

the heretics. In His infinite mercy He came once more among men in that human shape in which He walked among men for three years fifteen centuries ago. He came down to the 'hot pavements' of the southern town in which on the day before almost a hundred heretics had, *ad majorem gloriam Dei*,[3] been burnt by the cardinal, the Grand Inquisitor, in a magnificent *auto da fé*, in the presence of the king, the court, the knights, the cardinals, the most charming ladies of the court, and the whole population of Seville.

"He came softly, unobserved, and yet, strange to say, everyone recognised Him. That might be one of the best passages in the poem. I mean, why they recognised Him. The people are irresistibly drawn to Him, they surround Him, they flock about Him, follow Him. He moves silently in their midst with a gentle smile of infinite compassion. The sun of love burns in His heart, light and power shine from His eyes, and their radiance, shed on the people, stirs their hearts with responsive love. He holds out His hands to them, blesses them, and a healing virtue comes from contact with Him, even with His garments. An old man in the crowd, blind from childhood, cries out, 'O Lord, heal me and I shall see Thee!' and, as it were, scales fall from his eyes and the blind man sees Him. The crowd weeps and kisses the earth under His feet. Children throw flowers before Him, sing, and cry hosannah. 'It is He — it is He!' all repeat. 'It must be He, it can be no one but Him!' He stops at the steps of the Seville cathedral at the moment when the weeping mourners are bringing in a little open white coffin. In it lies a child of seven, the only daughter of a prominent citizen. The dead child lies hidden in flowers. 'He will raise your child,' the crowd shouts to the weeping mother. The priest, coming to meet the coffin, looks perplexed, and frowns, but the mother of the dead child throws herself at His feet with a wail. 'If it is Thou, raise my child!' she cries holding out her hands to Him. The procession halts, the coffin is laid on the steps at His feet. He looks with compassion, and His lips once more softly pronounce, 'Maiden, arise!' and the maiden arises. The little girl sits up in the coffin and looks round, smiling with wide-open wondering eyes, holding a bunch of white roses they had put in her hand.

"There are cries, sobs, confusion among the people, and at that moment, the cardinal himself, the Grand Inquisitor, passes by the cathedral. He is an old man, almost ninety, tall and erect, with a withered face and sunken eyes, in which there is still a gleam of light. He is not dressed in his gorgeous cardinal's robes, as he was the day before, when he was burning the enemies of the Roman Church — at that moment he was wearing his coarse, old, monk's cassock. At a distance behind him come his gloomy assistants and slaves and the 'holy guard.' He stops at the sight of the crowd and watches it from a distance. He sees everything; he sees them set the coffin down at His feet, sees the child rise up, and his face darkens. He knits his thick grey brows and his eyes gleam with a sinister fire. He holds out his finger and bids the guards take Him. And such is his power, so completely are the people cowed into submission and trembling obedience to him, that the crowd immediately make way for the guards, and in the midst of deathlike silence they lay hands on Him and lead Him away. The crowd instantly bows down to the earth, like one man, before the old inquisitor. He blesses the people in silence and passes on. The guards lead their prisoner to the close, gloomy vaulted prison in the ancient palace of the Holy Inquisition and shut Him in it. The day passes and is followed by the dark, burning 'breathless' night of Seville. The air is 'fragrant with laurel and lemon.' In the pitch darkness the iron door of the prison is suddenly opened and the Grand Inquisitor himself comes in with a light in his hand. He is alone; the door is closed at once behind him. He stands in the doorway and for a minute or two gazes into His face. At last he goes up slowly, sets the light on the table and speaks.

---

[3] "To the greater glory of God" — the motto of the Society of Jesus, or the Jesuits.

"'Is it Thou? Thou?' but receiving no answer, he adds at once: 'Don't answer, be silent. What canst Thou say, indeed? I know too well what Thou wouldst say. And Thou hast no right to add anything to what Thou hadst said of old. Why, then, art Thou come to hinder us? For Thou hast come to hinder us, and Thou knowest that. But dost Thou know what will be to-morrow? I know not who Thou art and care not to know whether it is Thou or only a semblance of Him, but to-morrow I shall condemn Thee and burn Thee at the stake as the worst of heretics. And the very people who have to-day kissed Thy feet, to-morrow at the faintest sign from me will rush to heap up the embers of Thy fire. Knowest Thou that? Yes, maybe Thou knowest it,' he added with thoughtful penetration, never for a moment taking his eyes off the Prisoner."

"I don't quite understand, Ivan. What does it mean?" Alyosha, who had been listening in silence, said with a smile. "Is it simply a wild fantasy, or a mistake on the part of the old man — some impossible *quid pro quo*?"[4]

"Take it as the last," said Ivan, laughing, "if you are so corrupted by modern realism and can't stand anything fantastic. If you like it to be a case of mistaken identity, let it be so. It is true," he went on, laughing, "the old man was ninety, and he might well be crazy over his set idea. He might have been struck by the appearance of the Prisoner. It might, in fact, be simply his ravings, the delusion of an old man of ninety, over-excited by the *auto da fé* of a hundred heretics the day before. But does it matter to us, after all, whether it was a mistake of identity or a wild fantasy? All that matters is that the old man should speak out, should speak openly of what he has thought in silence for ninety years."

"And the Prisoner too is silent? Does He look at him and not say a word?"

"That's inevitable in any case," Ivan laughed again. "The old man has told Him He hasn't the right to add anything to what He has said of old. One may say it is the most fundamental feature of Roman Catholicism, in my opinion at least. 'All has been given by Thee to the Pope,' they say, 'and all, therefore, is still in the Pope's hands, and there is no need for Thee to come now at all. Thou must not meddle for the time, at least.' That's how they speak and write too — the Jesuits, at any rate. I have read it myself in the works of their theologians. 'Hast Thou the right to reveal to us one of the mysteries of that world from which Thou hast come?' my old man asks Him, and answers the question for Him. 'No, Thou hast not; that Thou mayest not add to what has been said of old, and mayest not take from men the freedom which Thou didst exalt when thou wast on earth. Whatsoever Thou revealest anew will encroach on men's freedom of faith; for it will be manifest as a miracle, and the freedom of their faith was dearer to Thee than anything in those days fifteen hundred years ago. Didst Thou not often say then, "I will make you free"? But now Thou hast seen these "free" men,' the old man adds suddenly, with a pensive smile. 'Yes, we've paid dearly for it,' he goes on, looking sternly at Him, 'but at last we have completed that work in Thy name. For fifteen centuries we have been wrestling with Thy freedom, but now it is ended and over for good. Dost Thou not believe that it's over for good? Thou lookest meekly at me and deignest not even to be wroth with me. But let me tell Thee that now, to-day, people are more persuaded than ever that they have perfect freedom, yet they have brought their freedom to us and laid it humbly at our feet. But that has been our doing. Was this what Thou didst? Was this Thy freedom?'"

"I don't understand again," Alyosha broke in. "Is he ironical, is he jesting?"

"Not a bit of it! He claims it as a merit for himself and his Church that at last they have vanquished freedom and have done so to make men happy. 'For now' (he is speaking of the

---

[4] One thing in return for another; a fair exchange.

Inquisition, of course) 'for the first time it has become possible to think of the happiness of men. Man was created a rebel; and how can rebels be happy? Thou wast warned,' he says to Him. 'Thou hast had no lack of admonitions and warnings, but Thou didst not listen to those warnings; Thou didst reject the only way by which men might be made happy. But, fortunately, departing Thou didst hand on the work to us. Thou hast promised, Thou hast established by Thy word, Thou hast given to us the right to bind and to unbind, and now, of course, Thou canst not think of taking it away. Why, then, hast Thou come to hinder us?'"

"And what's the meaning of 'no lack of admonitions and warnings'?" asked Alyosha.

"Why, that's the chief part of what the old man must say.

"'The wise and dread Spirit, the spirit of self-destruction and non-existence,' the old man goes on, 'the great spirit talked with Thee in the wilderness, and we are told in the books that he "tempted" Thee. Is that so? And could anything truer be said than what he revealed to Thee in three questions and what Thou didst reject, and what in the books is called "the temptation"? And yet if there has ever been on earth a real stupendous miracle, it took place on that day, on the day of the three temptations. The statement of those three questions was itself a miracle. If it were possible to imagine simply for the sake of argument that those three questions of the dread spirit had perished utterly from the books, and that we had to restore them and to invent them anew, and to do so had gathered together all the wise men of the earth — rulers, chief priests, learned men, philosophers, poets — and had set them the task to invent three questions, such as would not only fit the occasion but express in three words, three human phrases, the whole future history of the world and of humanity — dost Thou believe that all the wisdom of the earth united could have invented anything in depth and force equal to the three questions which were actually put to Thee then by the wise and mighty spirit in the wilderness? From those questions alone, from the miracle of their statement, we can see that we have here to do not with the fleeting human intelligence but with the absolute and eternal. For in those three questions the whole subsequent history of mankind is, as it were, brought together into one whole, and foretold, and in them are united all the unsolved historical contradictions of human nature. At the time it could not be so clear, since the future was unknown; but now that fifteen hundred years have passed, we see that everything in those three questions was so justly divined and foretold, and has been so truly fulfilled, that nothing can be added to them or taken from them.

"'Judge Thyself who was right — Thou or he who questioned Thee then? Remember the first question; its meaning, in other words, was this: "Thou wouldst go into the world, and art going with empty hands, with some promise of freedom, which men in their simplicity and their natural unruliness cannot even understand, which they fear and dread — for nothing has ever been more insupportable for a man and a human society than freedom. But seest Thou these stones in this parched and barren wilderness? Turn them into bread, and mankind will run after Thee like a flock of sheep, grateful and obedient, though for ever trembling, lest Thou withdraw Thy hand and deny them Thy bread." But Thou wouldst not deprive man of freedom and didst reject the offer, thinking, what is that freedom worth, if obedience is bought with bread? Thou didst reply that man lives not by bread alone. But dost Thou know that for the sake of that earthly bread the spirit of the earth will rise up against Thee and will strive with Thee and overcome Thee, and all will follow him, crying, "Who can compare with this beast? He has given us fire from heaven!" Dost Thou know that the ages will pass, and humanity will proclaim by the lips of their sages that there is no crime, and therefore no sin; there is only hunger? "Feed men, and then ask of them virtue!" that's what they'll write on the banner, which they will raise against Thee, and with which they will destroy Thy temple. Where Thy temple stood will rise a new building; the terrible tower of Babel will be built again, and though, like the one of old, it will not be finished, yet Thou mightest have prevented that new tower and have cut short the sufferings of men for a thousand years; for they will come back to us after a thousand years of agony with their tower. They will seek us again, hidden underground in the catacombs, for we shall be again persecuted and tortured. They will find us and cry to us, "Feed us, for those who have promised us fire from heaven haven't given it!" And then we shall finish building their tower, for he finishes the building who feeds them. And we alone shall feed them in Thy name, declaring falsely that it is Thy name. Oh, never, never can they feed themselves without us! No science will give them bread so long as they remain free. In the end they will lay their freedom at our feet, and say to us, "Make us your slaves, but feed us." They will understand themselves, at last, that freedom and bread enough for all are inconceivable together, for never, never will they be able to share between them! They will be convinced, too, that they can never be free, for they are weak, vicious, worthless and rebellious. Thou didst promise them the bread of Heaven, but, I repeat again, can it compare with earthly bread in the eyes of the weak, ever-sinful and ignoble race of man? And if for the sake of the bread of Heaven thousands and ten of thousands shall follow Thee, what is to become of the millions and tens of thousands of millions of creatures who will not have the strength to forgo the earthly bread for the sake of the heavenly? Or dost Thou care only for the tens of thousands of the great and strong, while the millions, numerous as the sands of the sea, who are weak but love Thee, must exist only for the sake of the great and strong? No, we care for the weak too. They are sinful and rebellious, but in the end they too will become obedient. They will marvel at us and look on us as gods, because we are ready to endure the freedom which they have found so dreadful and to rule over them — so awful it will seem to them to be free. But we shall tell them that we are Thy servants and rule them in Thy name. We shall deceive them again, for we will not let Thee come to us again. That deception will be our suffering, for we shall be forced to lie.

"'This is the significance of the first question in the wilderness, and this is what Thou hast rejected for the sake of that freedom which Thou hast exalted above everything. Yet in this question lies hid the great secret of this world. Choosing "bread," Thou wouldst have satisfied the universal and everlasting craving of humanity — to find someone to worship. So long as man remains free he strives for nothing so incessantly and so painfully as to find someone to worship. But man seeks to worship what is established beyond dispute, so that all men would agree at once to worship it. For these pitiful creatures are concerned not only to find what one or the other can worship, but to find something that all would believe in and worship; what is essential is that all may be *together* in it. This craving for *community* of worship is the chief misery of every man individually and of all humanity from the beginning of time. For the sake of common worship they've slain each other with the sword. They have set up gods and challenged one another, "Put away your gods and come and worship ours, or we will kill you and your gods!" And so it will be to the end of the world, even when gods disappear from the earth; they will fall down before idols just the same. Thou didst know, Thou couldst not but have known, this fundamental secret of human nature, but Thou didst reject the one infallible banner which was offered Thee to make all men bow down to Thee alone — the banner of earthly bread; and Thou hast rejected it for the sake of freedom and the bread of Heaven. Behold what Thou didst further. And all again in the name of freedom! I tell Thee that man is tormented by no greater anxiety than to find someone quickly to whom he can hand over that gift of freedom with which the ill-fated creature is born. But only one who can appease their conscience can take over their freedom. In bread there was offered Thee an invincible banner; give bread, and man will worship thee, for nothing is more certain than bread. But if someone else gains possession of his conscience — oh! then he will cast away Thy bread and follow after him who has ensnared his conscience. In that Thou wast right. For the secret of man's being is not only to live but to have something to live for. Without a stable conception of the object of life, man would not consent to go on living, and would rather destroy himself than remain on earth, though he had bread in abundance. That is true. But what happened? Instead of taking men's freedom from them, Thou didst make it greater than ever! Didst Thou forget that man prefers peace, and even death, to freedom of choice in the knowledge of good and evil? Nothing is more seductive for man than his freedom of conscience, but nothing is a greater cause of suffering. And behold, instead of giving a firm foundation for setting the conscience of man at rest for ever, Thou didst choose all that is exceptional, vague and enigmatic; Thou didst choose what was utterly beyond the strength of men, acting as though Thou didst not love them at all — Thou who didst come to give Thy life for them! Instead of taking possession of men's freedom, Thou didst increase it, and burdened the spiritual kingdom of mankind with its sufferings for ever. Thou didst desire man's free love, that he should follow Thee freely, enticed and taken captive by Thee. In place of the rigid ancient law, man must hereafter with free heart decide for himself what is good and what is evil, having only Thy image before him as his guide. But didst Thou not know that he would at last reject even Thy image and Thy truth, if he is weighed down with the fearful burden of free choice? They will cry aloud at last that the truth is not in Thee, for they could not have been left in greater confusion and suffering than Thou hast caused, laying upon them so many cares and unanswerable problems.

"'So that, in truth, Thou didst Thyself lay the foundation for the destruction of Thy kingdom, and no one is more to blame for it. Yet what was offered Thee? There are three powers, three powers alone, able to conquer and to hold captive for ever the conscience of these impotent rebels for their happiness — those forces are miracle, mystery and authority. Thou hast rejected all three and hast set the example for doing so. When the wise and dread spirit set Thee on the pinnacle of the temple and said to Thee, "If Thou wouldst know whether Thou art the Son of God then cast Thyself down, for it is written: the angels shall hold him up lest he fall and bruise himself, and Thou shalt know then whether Thou art the son of God and shalt prove then how great is Thy faith in Thy Father." But Thou didst refuse and wouldst not cast Thyself down. Oh! of course, Thou didst proudly and well, like God; but the weak, unruly race of men, are they gods? Oh, Thou didst know then that in taking one step, in making one movement to cast Thyself down, Thou wouldst be tempting God and have lost all Thy faith in Him, and wouldst have been dashed to pieces against that earth which Thou didst come to save. And the wise spirit that tempted Thee would have rejoiced. But I ask again, are there many like Thee? And couldst Thou believe for one moment that men, too, could face such a temptation? Is the nature of men such, that they can reject miracle, and at the great moments of their life, the moments of their deepest, most agonising spiritual difficulties, cling only to the free verdict of the heart? Oh, Thou didst know that Thy deed would be recorded in books, would be handed down to remote times and the utmost ends of the earth, and Thou didst hope that man, following Thee, would cling to God and not ask for a miracle. But Thou didst not know that when man rejects miracle he rejects God too; for man seeks not so much God as the miraculous. And as man cannot bear to be without the miraculous, he will create new miracles of his own for himself, and will worship deeds of sorcery and witchcraft, though he might be a hundred times over a rebel, heretic and infidel. Thou didst not come down from the Cross when they shouted to Thee, mocking and reviling Thee, "Come down from the Cross and we will believe that Thou art He." Thou didst not come down, for again Thou wouldst not enslave man by a miracle, and didst crave faith given freely, not based on miracle. Thou didst crave for free love and not the base raptures of the slave before the might that has overawed him for ever. But Thou didst think too highly of men therein, for they are slaves, of course, though rebellious by nature. Look round and judge; fifteen centuries have passed, look upon them. Whom hast Thou raised up to Thyself? I swear, man is weaker and baser by nature than Thou hast believed him! Can he, can he do what Thou didst? By showing him so much respect, Thou didst, as it were, cease to feel for him, for Thou didst ask far too much from him — Thou who hast loved him more than Thyself! Respecting him less, Thou wouldst have asked less of him. That would have been more like love, for his burden would have been lighter. He is weak and vile. What though he is everywhere now rebelling against our power, and proud of his rebellion? It is the pride of a child and a schoolboy. They are little children rioting and barring out the teacher at school. But their childish delight will end; it will cost them dear. They will cast down temples and drench the earth with blood. But they will see at last, the foolish children, that, though they are rebels, they are impotent rebels, unable to keep up their own rebellion. Bathed in their foolish tears, they will recognise at last that He who created them rebels must have meant to mock at them. They will say this in despair, and their utterance will be a blasphemy which will make them more unhappy still, for man's nature cannot bear blasphemy, and in the end always avenges it on itself. And so unrest, confusion and unhappiness — that is the present lot of man after Thou didst bear so much for their freedom! Thy great prophet tells, in vision and in image, that he saw all those who took part in the first resurrection and that there were of each tribe twelve thousand. But if there were so many of them, they must have been no men but gods. They had borne Thy cross, they had endured scores of years in the barren, hungry wilderness, living upon locusts and roots — and Thou mayest indeed point with pride at those children of freedom, of free love, of free and splendid sacrifice for Thy name. But remember that they were only some thousands; and what of the rest? And how are the other weak ones to blame, because they could not endure what the strong have endured? How is the weak soul to blame that it is unable to receive such terrible gifts? Canst Thou have simply come to the elect and for the elect? But if so, it is a mystery and we cannot understand it. And if it is a mystery, we too have a right to preach a mystery, and to teach them that it's not the free judgment of their hearts, not love that matters, but a mystery which they must follow blindly, even against their conscience. So we have done. We have corrected Thy work and have founded it upon *miracle, mystery* and *authority*. And men rejoiced that they were again led like sheep, and that the terrible gift that had brought them such suffering was, at last, lifted from their hearts. Were we right teaching them this? Speak! Did we not love mankind, so meekly acknowledging their feebleness, lovingly lightening their burden, and permitting their weak nature even sin with our sanction? Why hast Thou come now to hinder us? And why dost Thou look silently and searchingly at me with Thy mild eyes? Be angry. I don't want Thy love, for I love Thee not. And what use is it for me to hide anything from Thee? Don't I know to Whom I am speaking? All that I can say is known to Thee already. And is it for me to conceal from Thee our mystery? Perhaps it is Thy will to hear it from my lips. Listen, then. We are not working with Thee but with *him* — that is our mystery. It's long — eight centuries — since we have been on *his* side and not on Thine. Just eight centuries ago we took from him what Thou didst reject with scorn, that last gift he offered Thee, showing Thee all the kingdoms of the earth. We took from him Rome and the sword of Cæsar, and proclaimed ourselves sole rulers of the earth, though hitherto we have not been able to complete our work. But whose fault is that? Oh, the work is only beginning, but it has begun. It has long to await completion and the earth has yet much to suffer, but we shall triumph and shall be Cæsars, and then we shall plan the universal happiness of man. But Thou mightest have taken even then the sword of Cæsar. Why didst Thou reject that last gift? Hadst Thou accepted that last counsel of the mighty spirit, Thou wouldst have accomplished all that man seeks on earth — that is, someone to worship, someone to keep his conscience, and some means of uniting all in one unanimous and harmonious ant-heap, for the craving for universal unity is the third and last anguish of men. Mankind as a whole has always striven to organise a universal state. There have been many great nations with great histories, but the more highly they were developed the more unhappy they were, for they felt more acutely than other people the craving for world-wide union. The great conquerors, Timours and Genghis Khans, whirled like hurricanes over the face of the earth striving to subdue its people, and they too were but the unconscious expression of the same craving for universal unity. Hadst Thou taken the world and Cæsar's purple, Thou wouldst have founded the universal state and have given universal peace. For who can rule men if not he who holds their conscience and their bread in his hands? We have taken the sword of Cæsar, and in taking it, of course have rejected Thee and followed *him*. Oh, ages are yet to come of the confusion of free thought, of their science and cannibalism. For having begun to build their tower of Babel without us, they will end, of course, with cannibalism. But then the beast will crawl to us and lick our feet and spatter them with tears of blood. And we shall sit upon the beast and raise the cup, and on it will be written, "Mystery." But then, and only then, the reign of peace and happiness will come for men. Thou art proud of Thine elect, but Thou hast only the elect, while we give rest to all. And besides, how many of those elect, those mighty ones who could become elect, have grown weary waiting for Thee, and have transferred and will transfer the powers of their spirit and the warmth of their heart to the other camp, and end by raising their *free* banner against Thee! Thou didst Thyself lift up that banner. But with us all will be happy and will no more rebel nor destroy one another as under Thy freedom. Oh, we shall persuade them that they will only become free when they renounce their freedom to us and submit to us. And shall we be right or shall we be lying? They will be convinced that we are right, for they will remember the horrors of slavery and confusion to which Thy freedom brought them. Freedom, free thought and science will lead them into such straits and will bring them face to face with such marvels and insoluble mysteries, that some of them, the fierce and rebellious, will destroy themselves; others, rebellious but weak, will destroy one another, while the rest, weak and unhappy, will crawl fawning to our feet and whine to us: "Yes, you were right, you alone possess His mystery, and we come back to you, save us from ourselves!"

"'Receiving bread from us, they will see clearly that we take the bread made by their hands from them, to give it to them, without any miracle. They will see that we do not change the stones to bread, but in truth they will be more thankful for taking it from our hands than for the bread itself! For they will remember only too well that in old days, without our help, even the bread they made turned to stones in their hands, while since they have come back to us, the very stones have turned to bread in their hands. Too, too well will they know the value of complete submission! And until men know that, they will be unhappy. Who is most to blame for their not knowing it, speak? Who scattered the flock and sent it astray on unknown paths? But the flock will come together again and will submit once more, and then it will be once for all. Then we shall give them the quiet humble happiness of weak creatures such as they are by nature. Oh, we shall persuade them at last not to be proud, for Thou didst lift them up and thereby taught them to be proud. We shall show them that they are weak, that they are only pitiful children, but that childlike happiness is the sweetest of all. They will become timid and will look to us and huddle close to us in fear, as chicks to the hen. They will marvel at us and will be awe-stricken before us, and will be proud at our being so powerful and clever, that we have been able to subdue such a turbulent flock of thousands of millions. They will tremble impotently before our wrath, their minds will grow fearful, they will be quick to shed tears like women and children, but they will be just as ready at a sign from us to pass to laughter and rejoicing, to happy mirth and childish song. Yes, we shall set them to work, but in their leisure hours we shall make their life like a child's game, with children's songs and innocent dance.

Oh, we shall allow them even sin, they are weak and helpless, and they will love us like children because we allow them to sin. We shall tell them that every sin will be expiated, if it is done with our permission, that we allow them to sin because we love them, and the punishment for these sins we take upon ourselves. And we shall take it upon ourselves, and they will adore us as their saviours who have taken on themselves their sins before God. And they will have no secrets from us. We shall allow or forbid them to live with their wives and mistresses, to have or not to have children — according to whether they have been obedient or disobedient — and they will submit to us gladly and cheerfully. The most painful secrets of their conscience, all, all they will bring to us, and we shall have an answer for all. And they will be glad to believe our answer, for it will save them from the great anxiety and terrible agony they endure at present in making a free decision for themselves. And all will be happy, all the millions of creatures except the hundred thousand who rule over them. For only we, we who guard the mystery, shall be unhappy. There will be thousands of millions of happy babes, and a hundred thousand sufferers who have taken upon themselves the curse of the knowledge of good and evil. Peacefully they will die, peacefully they will expire in Thy name, and beyond the grave they will find nothing but death. But we shall keep the secret, and for their happiness we shall allure them with the reward of heaven and eternity. Though if there were anything in the other world, it certainly would not be for such as they. It is prophesied that Thou wilt come again in victory, Thou wilt come with Thy chosen, the proud and strong, but we will say that they have only saved themselves, but we have saved all. We are told that the harlot who sits upon the beast, and holds in her hands the *mystery*, shall be put to shame, that the weak will rise up again, and will rend her royal purple and will strip naked her loathsome body. But then I will stand up and point out to Thee the thousand millions of happy children who have known no sin. And we who have taken their sins upon us for their happiness will stand up before Thee and say: "Judge us if Thou canst and darest." Know that I fear Thee not. Know that I too have been in the wilderness, I too have lived on roots and locusts, I too prized the freedom with which Thou hast blessed men, and I too was striving to stand among Thy elect, among the strong and powerful, thirsting "to make up the number." But I awakened and would not serve madness. I turned back and joined the ranks of those *who have corrected Thy work*. I left the proud and went back to the humble, for the happiness of the humble. What I say to Thee will come to pass, and our dominion will be built up. I repeat, to-morrow Thou shalt see that obedient flock who at a sign from me will hasten to heap up the hot cinders about the pile on which I shall burn Thee for coming to hinder us. For if anyone has ever deserved our fires, it is Thou. To-morrow I shall burn Thee. Dixi.'"[5]

Ivan stopped. He was carried away as he talked and spoke with excitement; when he had finished, he suddenly smiled.

Alyosha had listened in silence; towards the end he was greatly moved and seemed several times on the point of interrupting, but restrained himself. Now his words came with a rush.

"But . . . that's absurd!" he cried, flushing. "Your poem is in praise of Jesus, not in blame of Him — as you meant it to be. And who will believe you about freedom? Is that the way to understand it? That's not the idea of it in the Orthodox Church . . . That's Rome, and not even the whole of Rome, it's false — those are the worst of the Catholics, the Inquisitors, the Jesuits! . . . And there could not be such a fantastic creature as your Inquisitor. What are these sins of mankind they take on themselves? Who are these keepers of the mystery who have taken some curse upon themselves for the happiness of mankind? When have they been seen? We know the Jesuits, they are spoken ill of, but surely they are not what you describe? They are

---

[5] "I have spoken."

not that at all, not at all . . . They are simply the Romish army for the earthly sovereignty of the world in the future, with the Pontiff of Rome for Emperor . . . that's their ideal, but there's no sort of mystery or lofty melancholy about it . . . It's simple lust of power, of filthy earthly gain, of domination — something like a universal serfdom with them as masters — that's all they stand for. They don't even believe in God, perhaps. Your suffering inquisitor is a mere fantasy."

"Stay, stay," laughed Ivan, "how hot you are! A fantasy, you say, let it be so! Of course it's a fantasy. But allow me to say: do you really think that the Roman Catholic movement of the last centuries is actually nothing but the lust of power, of filthy earthly gain? Is that Father Païssy's teaching?"

"No, no, on the contrary, Father Païssy did once say something rather the same as you . . . but of course it's not the same, not a bit the same," Alyosha hastily corrected himself.

"A precious admission, in spite of your 'not a bit the same.' I ask you why your Jesuits and Inquisitors have united simply for vile material gain? Why can there not be among them one martyr oppressed by great sorrow and loving humanity? You see, only suppose that there was one such man among all those who desire nothing but filthy material gain — if there's only one like my old inquisitor, who had himself eaten roots in the desert and made frenzied efforts to subdue his flesh to make himself free and perfect. But yet all his life he loved humanity, and suddenly his eyes were opened, and he saw that it is no great moral blessedness to attain perfection and freedom, if at the same time one gains the conviction that millions of God's creatures have been created as a mockery, that they will never be capable of using their freedom, that these poor rebels can never turn into giants to complete the tower, that it was not for such geese that the great idealist dreamt his dream of harmony. Seeing all that he turned back and joined — the clever people. Surely that could have happened?"

"Joined whom, what clever people?" cried Alyosha, completely carried away. "They have no such great cleverness and no mysteries and secrets . . . Perhaps nothing but Atheism, that's all their secret. Your inquisitor does not believe in God, that's his secret!"

"What if it is so! At last you have guessed it. It's perfectly true, it's true that that's the whole secret, but isn't that suffering, at least for a man like that, who has wasted his whole life in the desert and yet could not shake off his incurable love of humanity? In his old age he reached the clear conviction that nothing but the advice of the great dread spirit could build up any tolerable sort of life for the feeble, unruly, 'incomplete, empirical creatures created in jest.' And so, convinced of this, he sees that he must follow the council of the wise spirit, the dread spirit of death and destruction, and therefore accept lying and deception, and lead men consciously to death and destruction, and yet deceive them all the way so that they may not notice where they are being led, that the poor blind creatures may at least, on the way, think themselves happy. And note, the deception is in the name of Him in Whose ideal the old man had so fervently believed all his life long. Is not that tragic? And if only one such stood at the head of the whole army 'filled with the lust of power only for the sake of filthy gain' — would not one such be enough to make a tragedy? More than that, one such standing at the head is enough to create the actual leading idea of the Roman Church, with all its armies and Jesuits, its highest idea. I tell you frankly that I firmly believe that there has always been such a man among those who stood at the head of the movement. Who knows, there may have been some such even among the Roman Popes. Who knows, perhaps the spirit of that accursed old man who loves mankind so obstinately in his own way, is to be found even now in a whole multitude of such old men, existing not by chance but by agreement, as a secret league formed long ago for the guarding of the mystery, to guard it from the weak and the unhappy, so as to make them happy. No doubt it is so, and so it must be indeed. I fancy that even among the

Masons there's something of the same mystery at the bottom, and that that's why the Catholics so detest the Masons as their rivals breaking up the unity of the idea, while it is so essential that there should be one flock and one shepherd . . . But from the way I defend my idea I might be an author impatient of your criticism. Enough of it."

"You are perhaps a Mason yourself!" broke suddenly from Alyosha. "You don't believe in God," he added, speaking this time very sorrowfully. He fancied besides that his brother was looking at him ironically. "How does your poem end?" he asked, suddenly looking down. "Or was it the end?"

"I meant to end it like this. When the Inquisitor ceased speaking he waited some time for his Prisoner to answer him. His silence weighed down upon him. He saw that the Prisoner had listened intently all the time, looking gently in his face and evidently not wishing to reply. The old man longed for Him to say something, however bitter and terrible. But He suddenly approached the old man in silence and softly kissed him on his bloodless aged lips. That was all his answer. The old man shuddered. His lips moved. He went to the door, opened it, and said to Him: 'Go, and come no more . . . come not at all, never, never!' And he let Him out into the dark alleys of the town. The Prisoner went away."

"And the old man?"

"The kiss glows in his heart, but the old man adheres to his idea."

"And you with him, you too?" cried Alyosha, mournfully.

Ivan laughed.

"Why, it's all nonsense, Alyosha. It's only a senseless poem of a senseless student, who could never write two lines of verse. Why do you take it so seriously?"

QUESTIONS

1. This is a kind of framework story: the tale of the Grand Inquisitor and Christ is told within the framework of another story, that of Ivan and his brother Alyosha. Does this fact reduce the impact of the clash between the Grand Inquisitor and Christ? Does the framework add anything to it?

2. What is Ivan's motive for telling the story to his brother? Do you sense a conflict here? Is there evidence of conflict?

3. Is there a relationship to be inferred between the brothers and the characters in Ivan's story? If so, how would you describe it?

4. Why is Christ under arrest?

5. Do you agree that mankind can be either free or secure, but not both? What arguments support the Grand Inquisitor's position? What arguments can be used against it?

6. What is the significance of the Prisoner's kiss? Why does the Grand Inquisitor free Christ?

7. Christ does not answer the Grand Inquisitor — not his charges, his bribes, or his version of man's destiny. Why not? And how, despite this silence, is Dostoevsky able to make Christ an effective, indeed a powerful, character?

GUSTAVE FLAUBERT ══════

A Simple Heart

Translated by Arthur McDowall

I

Madame Aubain's servant Félicité was the envy of the ladies of Pont-l'Évêque for half a century.

She received four pounds a year. For that she was cook and general servant, and did the sewing, washing, and ironing; she could bridle a horse, fatten poultry, and churn butter — and she remained faithful to her mistress, unamiable as the latter was.

Madame Aubain had married a gay bachelor without money who died at the beginning of 1809, leaving her with two small children and a quantity of debts. She then sold all her property except the farms of Toucques and Geffosses, which brought in two hundred pounds a year at most, and left her house in Saint-Melaine for a less expensive one that had belonged to her family and was situated behind the market.

This house had a slate roof and stood between an alley and a lane that went down to the river. There was an unevenness in the levels of the rooms which made you stumble. A narrow hall divided the kitchen from the "parlour" where Mme. Aubain spent her day, sitting in a wicker easy chair by the window. Against the panels, which were painted white, was a row of eight mahogany chairs. On an old piano under the barometer a heap of wooden and cardboard boxes rose like a pyramid. A stuffed armchair stood on either side of the Louis-Quinze chimney-piece, which was in yellow marble with a clock in the middle of it modelled like a temple of Vesta. The whole room was a little musty, as the floor was lower than the garden.

The first floor began with "Madame's" room: very large, with a pale-flowered wallpaper and a portrait of "Monsieur" as a dandy of the period. It led to a smaller room, where there were two children's cots without mattresses. Next came the drawing-room, which was always shut up and full of furniture covered with sheets. Then there was a corridor leading to a study. The shelves of a large bookcase were respectably lined with books and papers, and its three wings surrounded a broad writing-table in darkwood. The two panels at the end of the room were covered with pen-drawings, water-colour landscapes, and engravings by Audran, all relics of better days and vanished splendour. Félicité's room on the top floor got its light from a dormer-window, which looked over the meadows.

She rose at daybreak to be in time for Mass, and worked till evening without stopping. Then, when dinner was over, the plates and dishes in order, and the door shut fast, she thrust the log under the ashes and went to sleep in front of the hearth with her rosary in her hand. Félicité was the stubbornest of all bargainers; and as for cleanness, the polish on her saucepans was the despair of other servants. Thrifty in all things, she ate slowly, gathering off the table in her fingers the crumbs of her loaf — a twelve-pound loaf expressly baked for her, which lasted for three weeks.

At all times of year she wore a print handkerchief fastened with a pin behind, a bonnet that covered her hair, grey stockings, a red skirt, and a bibbed apron — such as hospital nurses wear — over her jacket.

Her face was thin and her voice sharp. At twenty-five she looked like forty. From fifty onwards she seemed of no particular age; and with her silence, straight figure, and precise movements she was like a woman made of wood, and going by clockwork.

II

She had had her love-story like another.

Her father, a mason, had been killed by falling off some scaffolding. Then her mother died, her sisters scattered, and a farmer took her in and employed her, while she was still quite little, to herd the cows at pasture. She shivered in rags and would lie flat on the ground to drink water from the ponds; she was beaten for nothing, and finally turned out for the theft of a shilling which she did not steal. She went to another farm, where she became dairy-maid; and as she was liked by her employers her companions were jealous of her.

One evening in August (she was then eighteen) they took her to the assembly at Colleville. She was dazed and stupefied in an instant by the noise of the fiddlers, the lights in the trees, the gay medley of dresses, the lace, the gold crosses, and the throng of people jigging all together. While she kept shyly apart a young man with a well-to-do air, who was leaning on the shaft of a cart and smoking his pipe, came up to ask her to dance. He treated her to cider, coffee, and cake, and bought her a silk handkerchief; and then, imagining she had guessed his meaning, offered to see her home. At the edge of a field of oats he pushed her roughly down. She was frightened and began to cry out; and he went off.

One evening later she was on the Beaumont road. A big hay-wagon was moving slowly along; she wanted to get in front of it, and as she brushed past the wheels she recognized Theodore. He greeted her quite calmly, saying she must excuse it all because it was "the fault of the drink." She could not think of any answer and wanted to run away.

He began at once to talk about the harvest and the worthies of the commune, for his father had left Colleville for the farm at Les Écots, so that now he and she were neighbours. "Ah!" she said. He added that they thought of settling him in life. Well, he was in no hurry; he was waiting for a wife to his fancy. She dropped her head; and then he asked her if she thought of marrying. She answered with a smile that it was mean to make fun of her.

"But I am not, I swear!" — and he passed his left hand round her waist. She walked in the support of his embrace; their steps grew slower. The wind was soft, the stars glittered, the huge wagon-load of hay swayed in front of them, and dust rose from the dragging steps of the four horses. Then, without a word of command, they turned to the right. He clasped her once more in his arms, and she disappeared into the shadow.

The week after Theodore secured some assignations with her.

They met at the end of farmyards, behind a wall, or under a solitary tree. She was not innocent as young ladies are — she had learned knowledge from the animals — but her reason and the instinct of her honour would not let her fall. Her resistance exasperated Theodore's passion; so much so that to satisfy it — or perhaps quite artlessly — he made her an offer of marriage. She was in doubt whether to trust him, but he swore great oaths of fidelity.

Soon he confessed to something troublesome; the year before his parents had bought him a substitute for the army, but any day he might be taken again, and the idea of serving was a terror to him. Félicité took this cowardice of his as a sign of affection, and it redoubled hers. She stole away at night to see him, and when she reached their meeting-place Theodore racked her with his anxieties and urgings.

At last he declared that he would go himself to the prefecture for information, and would tell her the result on the following Sunday, between eleven and midnight.

When the moment came she sped towards her lover. Instead of him she found one of his friends.

He told her that she would not see Theodore any more. To ensure himself against conscription he had married an old woman, Madame Lehoussais, of Toucques, who was very rich.

There was an uncontrollable burst of grief. She threw herself on the ground, screamed, called to the God of mercy, and moaned by herself in the fields till daylight came. Then she came back to the farm and announced that she was going to leave; and at the end of the month she received her wages, tied all her small belongings with a handkerchief, and went to Pont-l'Évêque.

In front of the inn there she made inquiries of a woman in a widow's cap, who, as it happened, was just looking for a cook. The girl did not know much, but her willingness seemed so great and her demands so small that Mme. Aubain ended by saying:

"Very well, then, I will take you."

A quarter of an hour afterwards Félicité was installed in her house.

She lived there at first in a tremble, as it were, at "the style of the house" and the memory of "Monsieur" floating over it all. Paul and Virginie, the first aged seven and the other hardly four, seemed to her beings of a precious substance; she carried them on her back like a horse; it was a sorrow to her that Mme. Aubain would not let her kiss them every minute. And yet she was happy there. Her grief had melted in the pleasantness of things all round.

Every Thursday regular visitors came in for a game of boston, and Félicité got the cards and foot-warmers ready beforehand. They arrived punctually at eight and left before the stroke of eleven.

On Monday mornings the dealer who lodged in the covered passage spread out all his old iron on the ground. Then a hum of voices began to fill the town, mingled with the neighing of horses, bleating of lambs, grunting of pigs, and the sharp rattle of carts along the street. About noon, when the market was at its height, you might see a tall, hook-nosed old countryman with his cap pushed back making his appearance at the door. It was Robelin, the farmer of Geffosses. A little later came Liébard, the farmer from Toucques — short, red, and corpulent — in a grey jacket and gaiters shod with spurs.

Both had poultry or cheese to offer their landlord. Félicité was invariably a match for their cunning, and they went away filled with respect for her.

At vague intervals Mme. Aubain had a visit from the Marquis de Gremanville, one of her uncles, who had ruined himself by debauchery and now lived at Falaise on his last remaining morsel of land. He invariably came at the luncheon hour, with a dreadful poodle whose paws left all the furniture in a mess. In spite of efforts to show his breeding, which he carried to the point of raising his hat every time he mentioned "my late father," habit was too strong for him; he poured himself out glass after glass and fired off improper remarks. Félicité edged him politely out of the house — "You have had enough, Monsieur de Gremanville! Another time!" — and she shut the door on him.

She opened it with pleasure to M. Bourais, who had been a lawyer. His baldness, his white stock, frilled shirt, and roomy brown coat, his way of rounding the arm as he took snuff — his whole person, in fact, created that disturbance of mind which overtakes us at the sight of extraordinary men.

As he looked after the property of "Madame" he remained shut up with her for hours in "Monsieur's" study, though all the time he was afraid of compromising himself. He respected the magistracy immensely, and had some pretensions to Latin.

To combine instruction and amusement he gave the children a geography book made up of a series of prints. They represented scenes in different parts of the world: cannibals with feathers on their heads, a monkey carrying off a young lady, Bedouins in the desert, the harpooning of a whale, and so on. Paul explained these engravings to Félicité; and that, in fact, was the whole of her literary education. The children's education was undertaken by Guyot, a poor creature employed at the town hall, who was famous for his beautiful hand and sharpened his penknife on his boots.

When the weather was bright the household set off early for a day at Geffosses Farm.

Its courtyard is on a slope, with the farmhouse in the middle, and the sea looks like a grey streak in the distance.

Félicité brought slices of cold meat out of her basket, and they breakfasted in a room adjoining the dairy. It was the only surviving fragment of a country house which was now no more. The wall-paper hung in tatters, and quivered in the draughts. Mme. Aubain sat with bowed head, overcome by her memories; the children became afraid to speak. "Why don't you play, then?" she would say, and off they went.

Paul climbed into the barn, caught birds, played at ducks and drakes over the pond, or hammered with his stick on the big casks which boomed like drums. Virginie fed the rabbits or dashed off to pick cornflowers, her quick legs showing their embroidered little drawers.

One autumn evening they went home by the fields. The moon was in its first quarter, lighting part of the sky; and mist floated like a scarf over the windings of the Toucques. Cattle, lying out in the middle of the grass, looked quietly at the four people as they passed. In the third meadow some of them got up and made a half-circle in front of the walkers. "There's nothing to be afraid of," said Félicité, as she stroked the nearest on the back with a kind of crooning song; he wheeled round and the others did the same. But when they crossed the next pasture there was a formidable bellow. It was a bull, hidden by the mist. Mme. Aubain was about to run. "No! no! don't go so fast!" They mended their pace, however, and heard a loud breathing behind them which came nearer. His hoofs thudded on the meadow grass like hammers; why, he was galloping now! Félicité turned round, and tore up clods of earth with both hands and threw them in his eyes. He lowered his muzzle, waved his horns, and quivered with fury, bellowing terribly. Mme. Aubain, now at the end of the pasture with her two little ones, was looking wildly for a place to get over the high bank. Félicité was retreating, still with her face to the bull, keeping up a shower of clods which blinded him, and crying all the time, "Be quick! be quick!"

Mme. Aubain went down into the ditch, pushed Virginie first and then Paul, fell several times as she tried to climb the bank, and managed it at last by dint of courage.

The bull had driven Félicité to bay against a rail-fence; his slaver was streaming into her face; another second, and he would have gored her. She had just time to slip between two of the rails, and the big animal stopped short in amazement.

This adventure was talked of at Pont-l'Évêque for many a year. Félicité did not pride herself on it in the least, not having the barest suspicion that she had done anything heroic.

Virginie was the sole object of her thoughts, for the child developed a nervous complaint as a result of her fright, and M. Poupart, the doctor, advised sea-bathing at Trouville. It was not a frequented place then. Mme. Aubain collected information, consulted Bourais, and made preparations as though for a long journey.

Her luggage started a day in advance, in Liébard's cart. The next day he brought round two horses, one of which had a lady's saddle with a velvet back to it, while a cloak was rolled up to make a kind of seat on the crupper of the other. Mme. Aubain rode on that, behind the farmer. Félicité took charge of Virginie, and Paul mounted M. Lechaptois' donkey, lent on condition that great care was taken of it.

The road was so bad that its five miles took two hours. The horses sank in the mud up to their pasterns, and their haunches jerked abruptly in the effort to get out; or else they stumbled in the ruts, and at other moments had to jump. In some places Liébard's mare came suddenly to a halt. He waited patiently until she went on again, talking about the people who had properties along the road, and adding moral reflections to their history. So it was that as they were in the middle of Toucques, and passed under some windows bowered with nasturtiums, he shrugged his shoulders and said: "There's a Mme. Lehoussais lives there; instead of taking a young man she ... " Félicité did not hear the rest; the horses were trotting and the donkey galloping. They all turned down a bypath; a gate swung open and two boys appeared; and the party dismounted in front of a manure-heap at the very threshold of the farmhouse door.

When Mme. Liébard saw her mistress she gave lavish signs of joy. She served her a luncheon with a sirloin of beef, tripe, black-pudding, a fricassee of chicken, sparkling cider, a fruit tart, and brandied plums; seasoning it all with compliments to Madame, who seemed in better health; Mademoiselle, who was "splendid" now; and Monsieur Paul, who had "filled out" wonderfully. Nor did she forget their deceased grandparents, whom the Liébards had known, as they had been in the service of the family for several generations. The farm, like them, had the stamp of antiquity. The beams on the ceiling were worm-eaten, the walls blackened with smoke, and the window-panes grey with dust. There was an oak dresser laden with every sort of useful article — jugs, plates, pewter bowls, wolf-traps, and sheep-shears; and a huge syringe made the children laugh. There was not a tree in the three courtyards without mushrooms growing at the bottom of it or a tuft of mistletoe on its boughs. Several of them had been thrown down by the wind. They had taken root again at the middle; and all were bending under their wealth of apples. The thatched roofs, like brown velvet and of varying thickness, withstood the heaviest squalls. The cart-shed, however, was falling into ruin. Mme. Aúbain said she would see about it, and ordered the animals to be saddled again.

It was another half-hour before they reached Trouville. The little caravan dismounted to pass Écores — it was an overhanging cliff with boats below it — and three minutes later they were at the end of the quay and entered the courtyard of the Golden Lamb, kept by good Mme. David.

From the first days of their stay Virginie began to feel less weak, thanks to the change of air and the effect of the sea-baths. These, for want of a bathing-dress, she took in her chemise; and her nurse dressed her afterwards in a coastguard's cabin which was used by the bathers.

In the afternoons they took the donkey and went off beyond the Black Rocks, in the direction of Hennequeville. The path climbed at first through ground with dells in it like the green sward of a park, and then reached a plateau where grass fields and arable lay side by side. Hollies rose stiffly out of the briary tangle at the edge of the road; and here and there a great withered tree made zigzags in the blue air with its branches.

They nearly always rested in a meadow, with Deauville on their left, Havre on their right, and the open sea in front. It glittered in the sunshine, smooth as a mirror and so quiet that its murmur was scarcely to be heard; sparrows chirped in hiding and the immense sky arched over it all. Mme. Aubain sat doing her needlework; Virginie plaited rushes by her side; Félicité pulled up lavender, and Paul was bored and anxious to start home.

Other days they crossed the Toucques in a boat and looked for shells. When the tide went out sea-urchins, starfish, and jelly-fish were left exposed; and the children ran in pursuit of the foam-flakes which scudded in the wind. The sleepy waves broke on the sand and unrolled all along the beach; it stretched away out of sight, bounded on the land-side by the dunes which parted it from the Marsh, a wide meadow shaped like an arena. As they came home that way, Trouville, on the hill-slope in the background, grew bigger at every step, and its miscellaneous throng of houses seemed to break into a gay disorder.

On days when it was too hot they did not leave their room. From the dazzling brilliance outside light fell in streaks between the laths of the blinds. There were no sounds in the village; and on the pavement below not a soul. This silence round them deepened the quietness of things. In the distance, where men were caulking, there was a tap of hammers as they plugged the hulls, and a sluggish breeze wafted up the smell of tar.

The chief amusement was the return of the fishing-boats. They began to tack as soon as they had passed the buoys. The sails came down on two of the three masts; and they drew on with the foresail swelling like a balloon, glided through the splash of the waves, and when they had reached the middle of the harbour suddenly dropped anchor. Then the boats drew up against the quay. The sailors threw quivering fish over the side; a row of carts was waiting, and women in cotton bonnets darted out to take the baskets and give their men a kiss.

One of them came up to Félicité one day, and she entered the lodgings a little later in a state of delight. She had found a sister again — and then Nastasie Barette, "wife of Leroux," appeared, holding an infant at her breast and another child with her right hand, while on her left was a little cabin boy with his hands on his hips and a cap over his ear.

After a quarter of an hour Mme. Aubain sent them off; but they were always to be found hanging about the kitchen, or encountered in the course of a walk. The husband never appeared.

Félicité was seized with affection for them. She bought them a blanket, some shirts, and a stove; it was clear that they were making a good thing out of her. Mme. Aubain was annoyed by this weakness of hers, and she did not like the liberties taken by the nephew, who said "thee" and "thou" to Paul. So as Virginie was coughing and the fine weather gone, she returned to Pont-l'Évêque.

There M. Bourais enlightened her on the choice of a boys' school. The one at Caen was reputed to be the best, and Paul was sent to it. He said his good-byes bravely, content enough at going to live in a house where he would have companions. Mme. Aubain resigned herself to her son's absence as a thing that had to be. Virginie thought about it less and less. Félicité missed the noise he made. But she found an occupation to distract her; from Christmas onward she took the little girl to catechism every day.

III

After making a genuflexion at the door she walked up between the double row of chairs under the lofty nave, opened Mme. Aubain's pew, sat down, and began to look about her. The choir stalls were filled with the boys on the right and the girls on the left, and the curé stood by the lectern. On a painted window in the apse the Holy Ghost looked down upon the Virgin.

Another window showed her on her knees before the child Jesus, and a group carved in wood behind the altar-shrine represented St. Michael overthrowing the dragon.

The priest began with a sketch of sacred history. The Garden, the Flood, the Tower of Babel, cities in flames, dying nations, and overturned idols passed like a dream before her eyes; and the dizzying vision left her with reverence for the Most High and fear of His wrath. Then she wept at the story of the Passion. Why had they crucified Him, when He loved the children, fed the multitudes, healed the blind, and had willed, in His meekness, to be born among the poor, on the dung-heap of a stable? The sowings, harvests, wine-presses, all the familiar things the Gospel speaks of, were a part of her life. They had been made holy by God's passing; and she loved the lambs more tenderly for her love of the Lamb, and the doves because of the Holy Ghost.

She found it hard to imagine Him in person, for He was not merely a bird, but a flame as well, and a breath at other times. It may be His light, she thought, which flits at night about the edge of the marshes, His breathing which drives on the clouds, His voice which gives harmony to the bells; and she would sit rapt in adoration, enjoying the cool walls and the quiet of the church.

Of doctrines, she understood nothing — did not even try to understand. The curé discoursed, the children repeated their lesson, and finally she went to sleep, waking up with a start when their wooden shoes clattered on the flagstones as they went away.

It was thus that Félicité, whose religious education had been neglected in her youth, learned the catechism by dint of hearing it; and from that time she copied all Virginie's observances, fasting as she did and confessing with her. On Corpus Christi Day they made a festal altar together.

The first communion loomed distractingly ahead. She fussed over the shoes, the rosary, the book and gloves; and how she trembled as she helped Virginie's mother to dress her!

All through the mass she was racked with anxiety. She could not see one side of the choir because of M. Bourais; but straight in front of her was the flock of maidens, with white crowns above their hanging veils, making the impression of a field of snow; and she knew her dear child at a distance by her dainty neck and thoughtful air. The bell tinkled. The heads bowed, and there was silence. As the organ pealed, singers and congregation took up the "Agnus Dei"[1]; then the procession of the boys began, and after them the girls rose. Step by step, with their hands joined in prayer, they went towards the lighted altar, knelt on the first step, received the sacrament in turn, and came back in the same order to their places. When Virginie's turn came Félicité leaned forward to see her; and with the imaginativeness of deep and tender feeling it seemed to her that she actually was the child; Virginie's face became hers, she was dressed in her clothes, it was her heart beating in her breast. As the moment came to open her mouth she closed her eyes and nearly fainted.

She appeared early in the sacristy next morning for Monsieur the curé to give her the communion. She took it with devotion, but it did not give her the same exquisite delight.

Mme. Aubain wanted to make her daughter into an accomplished person; and as Guyot could not teach her music or English she decided to place her in the Ursuline Convent at Honfleur as a boarder. The child made no objection. Félicité sighed and thought that Madame lacked feeling. Then she reflected that her mistress might be right; matters of this kind were beyond her.

So one day an old spring-van drew up at the door, and out of it stepped a nun to fetch the

---

[1] "Lamb of God" — a communal prayer offered at Mass.

young lady. Félicité hoisted the luggage on to the top, admonished the driver, and put six pots of preserves, a dozen pears, and a bunch of violets under the seat.

At the last moment Virginie broke into a fit of sobbing; she threw her arms round her mother, who kissed her on the forehead, saying over and over "Come, be brave! be brave!" The step was raised, and the carriage drove off.

Then Mme. Aubain's strength gave way; and in the evening all her friends — the Lormeau family, Mme. Lechaptois, the Rochefeuille ladies, M. de Houppeville, and Bourais — came in to console her.

To be without her daughter was very painful for her at first. But she heard from Virginie three times a week, wrote to her on the other days, walked in the garden, and so filled up the empty hours.

From sheer habit Félicité went into Virginie's room in the mornings and gazed at the walls. It was boredom to her not to have to comb the child's hair now, lace up her boots, tuck her into bed — and not to see her charming face perpetually and hold her hand when they went out together. In this idle condition she tried making lace. But her fingers were too heavy and broke the threads; she could not attend to anything, she had lost her sleep, and was, in her own words, "destroyed."

To "divert herself" she asked leave to have visits from her nephew Victor.

He arrived on Sundays after mass, rosy-cheeked, bare-chested, with the scent of the country he had walked through still about him. She laid her table promptly and they had lunch, sitting opposite each other. She ate as little as possible herself to save expense, but stuffed him with food so generously that at last he went to sleep. At the first stroke of vespers she woke him up, brushed his trousers, fastened his tie, and went to church, leaning on his arm with maternal pride.

Victor was always instructed by his parents to get something out of her — a packet of moist sugar, it might be, a cake of soap, spirits, or even money at times. He brought his things for her to mend and she took over the task, only too glad to have a reason for making him come back.

In August his father took him off on a coasting voyage. It was holiday time, and she was consoled by the arrival of the children. Paul, however, was getting selfish, and Virginie was too old to be called "thou" any longer; this put a constraint and barrier between them.

Victor went to Morlaix, Dunkirk, and Brighton in succession and made Félicité a present on his return from each voyage. It was a box made of shells the first time, a coffee cup the next, and on the third occasion a large gingerbread man. Victor was growing handsome. He was well made, had a hint of a moustache, good honest eyes, and a small leather hat pushed backwards like a pilot's. He entertained her by telling stories embroidered with nautical terms.

On a Monday, July 14, 1819 (she never forgot the date), he told her that he had signed on for the big voyage and next night but one he would take the Honfleur boat and join his schooner, which was to weigh anchor from Havre before long. Perhaps he would be gone two years.

The prospect of this long absence threw Félicité into deep distress; one more good-bye she must have, and on the Wednesday evening, when Madame's dinner was finished, she put on her clogs and made short work of the twelve miles between Pont-l'Évêque and Honfleur.

When she arrived in front of the Calvary she took the turn to the right instead of the left, got lost in the timber-yards, and retraced her steps; some people to whom she spoke advised her to be quick. She went all round the harbour basin, full of ships, and knocked against hawsers; then the ground fell away, lights flashed across each other, and she thought her wits had left her, for she saw horses up in the sky.

Others were neighing by the quay-side, frightened at the sea. They were lifted by a tackle and deposited in a boat, where passengers jostled each other among cider casks, cheese baskets, and sacks of grain; fowls could be heard clucking, the captain swore; and a cabin-boy stood leaning over the bows, indifferent to it all. Félicité, who had not recognized him, called "Victor!" and he raised his head; all at once, as she was darting forwards, the gangway was drawn back.

The Honfleur packet, women singing as they hauled it, passed out of harbour. Its framework creaked and the heavy waves whipped its bows. The canvas had swung round, no one could be seen on board now; and on the moon-silvered sea the boat made a black speck which paled gradually, dipped, and vanished.

As Félicité passed by the Calvary she had a wish to commend to God what she cherished most, and she stood there praying a long time with her face bathed in tears and her eyes towards the clouds. The town was asleep, coastguards were walking to and fro; and water poured without cessation through the holes in the sluice, with the noise of a torrent. The clocks struck two.

The convent parlour would not be open before day. If Félicité were late Madame would most certainly be annoyed; and in spite of her desire to kiss the other child she turned home. The maids at the inn were waking up as she came in to Pont-l'Évêque.

So the poor slip of a boy was going to toss for months and months at sea! She had not been frightened by his previous voyages. From England or Brittany you came back safe enough; but America, the colonies, the islands — these were lost in a dim region at the other end of the world.

Félicité's thoughts from that moment ran entirely on her nephew. On sunny days she was harassed by the idea of thirst; when there was a storm she was afraid of the lightning on his account. As she listened to the wind growling in the chimney or carrying off the slates she pictured him lashed by that same tempest, at the top of a shattered mast, with his body thrown backwards under a sheet of foam; or else (with a reminiscence of the illustrated geography) he was being eaten by savages, captured in a wood by monkeys, or dying on a desert shore. And never did she mention her anxieties.

Mme. Aubain had anxieties of her own, about her daughter. The good sisters found her an affectionate but delicate child. The slightest emotion unnerved her. She had to give up the piano.

Her mother stipulated for regular letters from the convent. She lost patience one morning when the postman did not come, and walked to and fro in the parlour from her armchair to the window. It was really amazing; not a word for four days!

To console Mme. Aubain by her own example Félicité remarked:

"As for me, Madame, it's six months since I heard … "

"From whom, pray?"

"Why … from my nephew," the servant answered gently.

"Oh! your nephew!" And Mme. Aubain resumed her walk with a shrug of the shoulders, as much as to say: "I was not thinking of him! And what is more, it's absurd! A scamp of a cabin-boy — what does he matter? … whereas my daughter … why, just think!"

Félicité, though she had been brought up on harshness, felt indignant with Madame — and then forgot. It seemed the simplest thing in the world to her to lose one's head over the little girl. For her the two children were equally important; a bond in her heart made them one, and their destinies must be the same.

She heard from the chemist that Victor's ship had arrived at Havana. He had read this piece of news in a gazette.

Cigars — they made her imagine Havana as a place where no one does anything but smoke, and there was Victor moving among the negroes in a cloud of tobacco. Could you, she wondered, "in case you needed," return by land? What was the distance from Pont-l'Évêque? She questioned M. Bourais to find out.

He reached for his atlas and began explaining the longitudes; Félicité's consternation provoked a fine pedantic smile. Finally he marked with his pencil a black, imperceptible point in the indentations of an oval spot, and said as he did so, "Here it is." She bent over the map; the maze of coloured lines wearied her eyes without conveying anything; and on an invitation from Bourais to tell him her difficulty, she begged him to show her the house where Victor was living. Bourais threw up his arms, sneezed, and laughed immensely: a simplicity like hers was a positive joy. And Félicité did not understand the reason; how could she when she expected, very likely, to see the actual image of her nephew — so stunted was her mind!

A fortnight afterwards Liébard came into the kitchen at market-time as usual and handed her a letter from her brother-in-law. As neither of them could read she took it to her mistress.

Mme. Aubain, who was counting the stitches in her knitting, put the work down by her side, broke the seal of the letter, started, and said in a low voice, with a look of meaning:

"It is bad news … that they have to tell you. Your nephew … "

He was dead. The letter said no more.

Félicité fell on to a chair, leaning her head against the wainscot; and she closed her eyelids, which suddenly flushed pink. Then with bent forehead, hands hanging, and fixed eyes, she said at intervals:

"Poor little lad! poor little lad!"

Liébard watched her and heaved sighs. Mme. Aubain trembled a little.

She suggested that Félicité should go to see her sister at Trouville. Félicité answered by a gesture that she had no need.

There was a silence. The worthy Liébard thought it was time for them to withdraw.

Then Félicité said:

"They don't care, not they!"

Her head dropped again; and she took up mechanically, from time to time, the long needles on her work-table.

Women passed in the yard with a barrow of dripping linen.

As she saw them through the window-panes she remembered her washing; she had put it to soak the day before, to-day she must wring it out; and she left the room.

Her plank and tub were at the edge of the Touques. She threw a pile of linen on the bank, rolled up her sleeves, and taking her wooden beater dealt lusty blows whose sound carried to the neighbouring gardens. The meadows were empty, the river stirred in the wind; and down below long grasses wavered, like the hair of corpses floating in the water. She kept her grief down and was very brave until the evening; but once in her room she surrendered to it utterly, lying stretched on the mattress with her face in the pillow and her hands clenched against her temples.

Much later she heard, from the captain himself, the circumstances of Victor's end. They had bled him too much at the hospital for yellow fever. Four doctors held him at once. He had died instantly, and the chief had said:

"Bah! there goes another!"

His parents had always been brutal to him. She preferred not to see them again; and they made no advances, either because they forgot her or from the callousness of the wretchedly poor.

Virginie began to grow weaker.

Tightness in her chest, coughing, continual fever, and veinings on her cheek-bones betrayed some deep-seated complaint. M. Poupart had advised a stay in Provence. Mme. Aubain determined on it, and would have brought her daughter home at once but for the climate of Pont-l'Évêque.

She made an arrangement with a job-master, and he drove her to the convent every Tuesday. There is a terrace in the garden, with a view over the Seine. Virginie took walks there over the fallen vine-leaves, on her mother's arm. A shaft of sunlight through the clouds made her blink sometimes, as she gazed at the sails in the distance and the whole horizon from the castle of Tancarville to the lighthouses at Havre. Afterwards they rested in the arbour. Her mother had secured a little cask of excellent Malaga; and Virginie, laughing at the idea of getting tipsy, drank a thimble-full of it, no more.

Her strength came back visibly. The autumn glided gently away. Félicité reassured Mme. Aubain. But one evening, when she had been out on a commission in the neighbourhood, she found M. Poupart's gig at the door. He was in the hall, and Mme. Aubain was tying her bonnet.

"Give me my foot-warmer, purse, gloves! Quicker, come!"

Virginie had inflammation of the lungs; perhaps it was hopeless.

"Not yet!" said the doctor, and they both got into the carriage under whirling flakes of snow. Night was coming on and it was very cold.

Félicité rushed into the church to light a taper. Then she ran after the gig, came up with it in an hour, and jumped lightly in behind. As she hung on by the fringes a thought came into her mind: "The courtyard has not been shut up; supposing burglars got in!" And she jumped down.

At dawn next day she presented herself at the doctor's. He had come in and started for the country again. Then she waited in the inn, thinking that a letter would come by some hand or other. Finally, when it was twilight, she took the Lisieux coach.

The convent was at the end of a steep lane. When she was about half-way up it she heard strange sounds — a death-bell tolling. "It is for someone else," thought Félicité, and she pulled the knocker violently.

After some minutes there was a sound of trailing slippers, the door opened ajar, and a nun appeared.

The good sister, with an air of compunction, said that "she had just passed away." On the instant the bell of St. Leonard's tolled twice as fast.

Félicité went up to the second floor.

From the doorway she saw Virginie stretched on her back, with her hands joined, her mouth open, and head thrown back under a black crucifix that leaned towards her, between curtains that hung stiffly, less pale than was her face. Mme. Aubain, at the foot of the bed which she clasped with her arms, was choking with sobs of agony. The mother superior stood on the right. Three candlesticks on the chest of drawers made spots of red, and the mist came whitely through the windows. Nuns came and took Mme. Aubain away.

For two nights Félicité never left the dead child. She repeated the same prayers, sprinkled holy water over the sheets, came and sat down again, and watched her. At the end of the first vigil she noticed that the face had grown yellow, the lips turned blue, the nose was sharper, and the eyes sunk in. She kissed them several times, and would not have been immensely surprised if Virginie had opened them again; to minds like hers the supernatural is quite simple. She made the girl's toilette, wrapped her in her shroud, lifted her down into her bier, put a garland on her head, and spread out her hair. It was fair, and extraordinarily long for her age. Félicité cut off a big lock and slipped half of it into her bosom, determined that she should never part with it.

The body was brought back to Pont-l'Évêque, as Mme. Aubain intended; she followed the hearse in a closed carriage.

It took another three-quarters of an hour after the mass to reach the cemetery. Paul walked in front, sobbing. M. Bourais was behind, and then came the chief residents, the women shrouded in black mantles, and Félicité. She thought of her nephew; and because she had not been able to pay these honours to him her grief was doubled, as though the one were being buried with the other.

Mme. Aubain's despair was boundless. It was against God that she first rebelled, thinking it unjust of Him to have taken her daughter from her — she had never done evil and her conscience was so clear! Ah, no! — she ought to have taken Virginie off to the south. Other doctors would have saved her. She accused herself now, wanted to join her child, and broke into cries of distress in the middle of her dreams. One dream haunted her above all. Her husband, dressed as a sailor, was returning from a long voyage, and shedding tears he told her that he had been ordered to take Virginie away. Then they consulted how to hide her somewhere.

the came in once from the garden quite upset. A moment ago — and she pointed out the place — the father and daughter had appeared to her, standing side by side, and they did nothing, but they looked at her.

For several months after this she stayed inertly in her room. Félicité lectured her gently; she must live for her son's sake, and for the other, in remembrance of "her."

"Her?" answered Mme. Aubain, as though she were just waking up. "Ah, yes! ... yes! ... You do not forget her!" this was an allusion to the cemetery, where she was strictly forbidden to go.

Félicité went there every day.

Precisely at four she skirted the houses, climbed the hill, opened the gate, and came to Virginie's grave. It was a little column of pink marble with a stone underneath and a garden plot enclosed by chains. the beds were hidden under a coverlet of flowers. She watered their leaves, freshened the gravel, and knelt down to break up the earth better. When Mme. Aubain was able to come there she felt a relief and a sort of consolation.

Then years slipped away, one like another, and their only episodes were the great festivals as they recurred — Easter, the Assumption, All Saints' Day. Household occurrences marked dates that were referred to afterwards. In 1825, for instance, two glaziers whitewashed the hall; in 1827 a piece of the roof fell into the courtyard and nearly killed a man. In the summer of 1828 it was Madame's turn to offer the consecrated bread; Bourais, about this time, mysteriously absented himself; and one by one the old acquaintances passed away: Guyot, Liébard, Mme. Lechaptois, Robelin, and Uncle Gremanville, who had been paralysed for a long time.

One night the driver of the mail-coach announced the Revolution of July in Pont-l'Évêque. A new sub-prefect was appointed a few days later — Baron de Larsonnière, who had been consul in America, and brought with him, besides his wife, a sister-in-law and three young ladies, already growing up. They were to be seen about on their lawn, in loose blouses, and they had a negro and a parrot. They paid a call on Mme. Aubain which she did not fail to return. The moment they were seen in the distance Félicité ran to let her mistress know. But only one thing could really move her feelings — the letters from her son.

He was swallowed up in a tavern life and could follow no career. She paid his debts, he made new ones; and the sighs that Mme. Aubain uttered as she sat knitting by the window reached Félicité at her spinning-wheel in the kitchen.

They took walks together along the espaliered wall, always talking of Virginie and wondering if such and such a thing would have pleased her and what, on some occasion, she would have been likely to say.

All her small belongings filled a cupboard in the two-bedded room. Mme. Aubain inspected them as seldom as she could. One summer day she made up her mind to it — and some moths flew out of the wardrobe.

Virginie's dresses were in a row underneath a shelf, on which there were three dolls, some hoops, a set of toy pots and pans, and the basin that she used. They took out her petticoats as well, and the stockings and handkerchiefs, and laid them out on the two beds before folding them up again. The sunshine lit up these poor things, bringing out their stains and the creases made by the body's movements. The air was warm and blue, a blackbird warbled, life seemed bathed in a deep sweetness. They found a little plush hat with thick, chestnut-coloured pile; but it was eaten all over by moths. Félicité begged it for her own. Their eyes met fixedly and filled with tears; at last the mistress opened her arms, the servant threw herself into them, and they embraced each other, satisfying their grief in a kiss that made them equal.

It was the first time in their lives, Mme. Aubain's nature not being expansive. Félicité was as grateful as though she had received a favour, and cherished her mistress from that moment with the devotion of an animal and a religious worship.

The kindness of her heart unfolded.

When she heard the drums of a marching regiment in the street she posted herself at the door with a pitcher of cider and asked the soldiers to drink. She nursed cholera patients and protected the Polish refugees; one of these even declared that he wished to marry her. They quarrelled, however; for when she came back from the Angelus one morning she found that he had got into her kitchen and made himself a vinegar salad which he was quietly eating.

After the Poles came Father Colmiche, an old man who was supposed to have committed atrocities in '93. He lived by the side of the river in the ruins of a pigsty. The little boys watched him through the cracks in the wall, and threw pebbles at him which fell on the pallet where he lay constantly shaken by a catarrh; his hair was very long, his eyes inflamed, and there was a tumour on his arm bigger than his head. She got him some linen and tried to clean up his miserable hole; her dream was to establish him in the bakehouse, without letting him annoy Madame. When the tumour burst she dressed it every day; sometimes she brought him cake, and would put him in the sunshine on a truss of straw. The poor old man, slobbering and trembling, thanked her in his worn-out voice, was terrified that he might lose her, and stretched out his hands when he saw her go away. He died; and she had a mass said for the repose of his soul.

That very day a great happiness befell her; just at dinner-time appeared Mme. de Larsonnière's negro, carrying the parrot in its cage, with perch, chain, and padlock. A note from the baroness informed Mme. Aubain that her husband had been raised to a prefecture and they were starting that evening; she begged her to accept the bird as a memento and mark of her regard.

For a long time he had absorbed Félicité's imagination, because he came from America; and that name reminded her of Victor, so much so that she made inquiries of the negro. She had once gone so far as to say, "How Madame would enjoy having him!"

The negro repeated the remark to his mistress; and as she could not take the bird away with her she chose this way of getting rid of him.

IV

His name was Loulou. His body was green and the tips of his wings rose-pink; his forehead was blue and his throat golden.

But he had the tiresome habits of biting his perch, tearing out his feathers, sprinkling his dirt about, and spattering the water of his tub. He annoyed Mme. Aubain, and she gave him to Félicité for good.

She endeavoured to train him; soon he could repeat "Nice boy! Your servant, sir! Good morning, Marie!" He was placed by the side of the door, and astonished several people by not answering to the name Jacquot, for all parrots are called Jacquot. People compared him to a turkey and a log of wood, and stabbed Félicité to the heart each time. Strange obstinacy on Loulou's part! — directly you looked at him he refused to speak.

None the less he was eager for society; for on Sundays, while the Rochefeuille ladies, M. de Houppeville, and new familiars — Onfroy the apothecary, Monsieur Varin, and Captain Mathieu — were playing their game of cards, he beat the windows with his wings and threw himself about so frantically that they could not hear each other speak.

Bourais' face, undoubtedly, struck him as extremely droll. Directly he saw it he began to laugh — and laugh with all his might. His peals rang through the couryard and were repeated by the echo; the neighbours came to their windows and laughed too; while M. Bourais, gliding along under the wall to escape the parrot's eye, and hiding his profile with his hat, got to the river and then entered by the garden gate. There was a lack of tenderness in the looks which he darted at the bird.

Loulou had been slapped by the butcher-boy for making so free as to plunge his head into his basket; and since then he was always trying to nip him through his shirt. Fabu threatened to wring his neck, although he was not cruel, for all his tattooed arms and large whiskers. Far from it; he really rather liked the parrot, and in a jovial humour even wanted to teach him to swear. Félicité, who was alarmed by such proceedings, put the bird in the kitchen. His little chain was taken off and he roamed about the house.

His way of going downstairs was to lean on each step with the curve of his beak, raise the right foot, and then the left; and Félicité was afraid that these gymnastics brought on fits of giddiness. He fell ill and could not talk or eat any longer. There was a growth under his tongue, such as fowls have sometimes. She cured him by tearing the pellicle off with her fingernails. Mr. Paul was thoughtless enough one day to blow some cigar smoke into his nostrils, and another time when Mme. Lormeau was teasing him with the end of her umbrella he snapped at the ferrule. Finally he got lost.

Félicité had put him on the grass to refresh him, and gone away for a minute, and when she came back — no sign of the parrot! She began by looking for him in the shrubs, by the waterside, and over the roofs, without listening to her mistress's cries of "Take care, do! You are out of your wits!" Then she investigated all the gardens in Pont-l'Évêque, and stopped the passers-by. "You don't ever happen to have seen my parrot, by any chance, do you?" And she gave a description of the parrot to those who did not know him. Suddenly, behind the mills at the foot of the hill she thought she could make out something green that fluttered. But on the top of the hill there was nothing. A hawker assured her that he had come across the parrot just before, at Saint-Melaine, in Mère Simon's shop. She rushed there; they had no idea of what she meant. At last she came home exhausted, with her slippers in shreds and despair in her soul; and as she was sitting in the middle of the garden-seat at Madame's side, telling the whole story of her efforts, a light weight dropped on to her shoulder — it was Loulou! What on earth had he been doing? Taking a walk in the neighbourhood, perhaps!

She had some trouble in recovering from this, or rather never did recover. As the result of a chill she had an attack of quinsy, and soon afterwards an earache. Three years later she was deaf; and she spoke very loud, even in church. Though Félicité's sins might have been published in every corner of the diocese without dishonour to her or scandal to anybody, his Reverence the priest thought it right now to hear her confession in the sacristy only.

Imaginary noises in the head completed her upset. Her mistress often said to her, "Heavens! how stupid you are!" "Yes, Madame," she replied, and looked about for something.

Her little circle of ideas grew still narrower; the peal of church-bells and the lowing of cattle ceased to exist for her. All living beings moved as silently as ghosts. One sound only reached her ears now — the parrot's voice.

Loulou, as though to amuse her, reproduced the click-clack of the turnspit, the shrill call of a man selling fish, and the noise of the saw in the joiner's house opposite; when the bell rang he imitated Mme. Aubain's "Félicité! the door! the door!"

They carried on conversations, he endlessly reciting the three phrases in his repertory, to which she replied with words that were just as disconnected but uttered what was in her heart. Loulou was almost a son and a lover to her in her isolated state. He climbed up her fingers, nibbled at her lips, and clung to her kerchief; and when she bent her forehead and shook her head gently to and fro, as nurses do, the great wings of her bonnet and the bird's wings quivered together.

When the clouds massed and the thunder rumbled Loulou broke into cries, perhaps remembering the downpours in his native forests. The streaming rain made him absolutely mad; he fluttered wildly about, dashed up to the ceiling, upset everything, and went out through the window to dabble in the garden; but he was back quickly to perch on one of the fire-dogs and hopped about to dry himself, exhibiting his tail and his beak in turn.

One morning in the terrible winter of 1837 she had put him in front of the fireplace because of the cold. She found him dead, in the middle of his cage: head downwards, with his claws in the wires. He had died from congestion, no doubt. But Félicité thought he had been poisoned with parsley, and though there was no proof of any kind her suspicions inclined to Fabu.

She wept so piteously that her mistress said to her, "Well, then, have him stuffed!"

She asked advice from the chemist, who had always been kind to the parrot. He wrote to Havre, and a person called Fellacher undertook the business. But as parcels sometimes got lost in the coach she decided to take the parrot as far as Honfleur herself.

Along the sides of the road were leafless apple-trees, one after the other. Ice covered the ditches. Dogs barked about the farms; and Félicité, with her hands under her cloak, her little black sabots and her basket, walked briskly in the middle of the road.

She crossed the forest, passed High Oak, and reached St. Gatien.

A cloud of dust rose behind her, and in it a mail-coach, carried away by the steep hill, rushed down at full gallop like a hurricane. Seeing this woman who would not get out of the way, the driver stood up in front and the postilion shouted too. He could not hold in his four horses, which increased their pace, and the two leaders were grazing her when he threw them to one side with a jerk of the reins. But he was wild with rage, and lifting his arm as he passed at full speed, gave her such a lash from waist to neck with his big whip that she fell on her back.

Her first act, when she recovered consciousness, was to open her basket. Loulou was happily none the worse. She felt a burn in her right cheek, and when she put her hands against it they were red; the blood was flowing.

She sat down on a heap of stones and bound up her face with her handkerchief. Then she ate a crust of bread which she had put in the basket as a precaution, and found a consolation for her wound in gazing at the bird.

When she reached the crest of Ecquemauville she saw the Honfleur lights sparkling in the night sky like a company of stars; beyond, the sea stretched dimly. Then a faintness overtook her and she stopped; her wretched childhood, the disillusion of her first love, her nephew's going away, and Virginie's death all came back to her at once like the waves of an oncoming tide, rose to her throat, and choked her.

Afterwards, at the boat, she made a point of speaking to the captain, begging him to take care of the parcel, though she did not tell him what was in it.

Fellacher kept the parrot a long time. He was always promising it for the following week. After six months he announced that a packing-case had started, and then nothing more was heard of it. It really seemed as though Loulou was never coming back. "Ah, they have stolen him!" she thought.

He arrived at last, and looked superb. There he was, erect upon a branch which screwed into a mahogany socket, with a foot in the air and his head on one side, biting a nut which the bird-stuffer — with a taste for impressiveness — had gilded.

Félicité shut him up in her room. It was a place to which few people were admitted, and held so many religious objects and miscellaneous things that it looked like a chapel and bazaar in one.

A big cupboard impeded you as you opened the door. Opposite the window commanding the garden a little round one looked into the court; there was a table by the folding-bed with a water-jug, two combs, and a cube of blue soap in a chipped plate. On the walls hung rosaries, medals, several benign Virgins, and a holy water vessel made out of coconut; on the chest of drawers, which was covered with a cloth like an altar, was the shell box that Victor had given her, and after that a watering-can, a toy-balloon, exercise-books, the illustrated geography, and a pair of young lady's boots; and, fastened by its ribbons to the nail of the looking-glass, hung the little plush hat! Félicité carried observances of this kind so far as to keep one of Monsieur's frock-coats. All the old rubbish which Mme. Aubain did not want any longer she laid hands on for her room. That was why there were artificial flowers along the edge of the chest of drawers and a portrait of the Comte d'Artois in the little window recess.

ıth the aid of a bracket Loulou was established over the chimney, which jutted into the room. Every morning when she woke up she saw him there in the dawning light, and recalled old days and the smallest details of insignificant acts in a deep quietness which knew no pain.

Holding, as she did, no communication with anyone, Félicité lived as insensibly as if she were walking in her sleep. The Corpus Christi processions roused her to life again. Then she went round begging mats and candlesticks from the neighbours to decorate the altar they put up in the street.

In church she was always gazing at the Holy Ghost in the window, and observed that there was something of the parrot in him. The likeness was still clearer, she thought, on a crude colour-print representing the baptism of Our Lord. With his purple wings and emerald body he was the very image of Loulou.

She bought him, and hung him up instead of the Comte d'Artois, so that she could see them both together in one glance. They were linked in her thoughts; and the parrot was consecrated by his association with the Holy Ghost, which became more vivid to her eye and more intelligible. The Father could not have chosen to express Himself through a dove, for such creatures cannot speak; it must have been one of Loulou's ancestors, surely. And though Félicité looked at the picture while she said her prayers she swerved a little from time to time towards the parrot.

She wanted to join the Ladies of the Virgin but Mme. Aubain dissuaded her.

And then a great event loomed up before them — Paul's marriage.

He had been a solicitor's clerk to begin with, and then tried business, the Customs, the Inland Revenue, and made efforts, even, to get into the Rivers and Forests. By an inspiration from heaven he had suddenly, at thirty-six, discovered his real line — the Registrar's Office. And there he showed such marked capacity that an inspector had offered him his daughter's hand and promised him his influence.

So Paul, grown serious, brought the lady to see his mother.

She sniffed at the ways of Pont-l'Évêque, gave herself great airs, and wounded Félicité's feelings. Mme. Aubain was relieved at her departure.

The week after came news of M. Bourais' death in an inn in Lower Brittany. The rumour of suicide was confirmed, and doubts arose as to his honesty. Mme. Aubain studied his accounts, and soon found out the whole tale of his misdoings — embezzled arrears, secret sales of wood, forged receipts, etc. Besides that he had an illegitimate child, and "relations with a person at Dozulé."

These shameful facts distressed her greatly. In March 1853 she was seized with a pain in the chest; her tongue seemed to be covered with film, and leeches did not ease the difficult breathing. On the ninth evening of her illness she died, just at seventy-two.

She passed as being younger, owing to the bands of brown hair which framed her pale, pock-marked face. There were few friends to regret her, for she had a stiffness of manner which kept people at a distance.

But Félicité mourned for her as one seldom mourns for a master. It upset her ideas and seemed contrary to the order of things, impossible and monstrous, that Madame should die before her.

Ten days afterwards, which was the time it took to hurry there from Besançon, the heirs arrived. The daughter-in-law ransacked the drawers, chose some furniture, and sold the rest; and then they went back to their registering.

Madame's armchair, her small round table, her foot-warmer, and the eight chairs were gone! Yellow patches in the middle of the panels showed where the engravings had hung. They had carried off the two little beds and the mattresses, and all Virginie's belongings had disappeared from the cupboard. Félicité went from floor to floor dazed with sorrow.

The next day there was a notice on the door, and the apothecary shouted in her ear that the house was for sale.

She tottered, and was obliged to sit down. What distressed her most of all was to give up her room, so suitable as it was for poor Loulou. She enveloped him with a look of anguish when she was imploring the Holy Ghost, and formed the idolatrous habit of kneeling in front of the parrot to say her prayers. Sometimes the sun shone in at the attic window and caught his glass eye, and a great luminous ray shot out of it and put her in an ecstasy.

She had a pension of fifteen pounds a year which her mistress had left her. The garden gave her a supply of vegetables. As for clothes, she had enough to last her to the end of her days, and she economized in candles by going to bed at dusk.

She hardly ever went out, as she did not like passing the dealer's shop, where some of the old furniture was exposed for sale. Since her fit of giddiness she dragged one leg; and as her strength was failing Mère Simon, whose grocery business had collapsed, came every morning to split the wood and pump water for her.

Her eyes grew feeble. The shutters ceased to be thrown open. Years and years passed, and the house was neither let nor sold.

Félicité never asked for repairs because she was afraid of being sent away. The boards on the roof rotted; her bolster was wet for a whole winter. After Easter she spat blood.

Then Mère Simon called in a doctor. Félicité wanted to know what was the matter with her. But she was too deaf to hear, and the only word which reached her was "pneumonia." It was a word she knew, and she answered softly "Ah! like Madame," thinking it natural that she should follow her mistress.

The time for the festal shrines was coming near. The first one was always at the bottom of the hill, the second in front of the post-office, and the third towards the middle of the street. There was some rivalry in the matter of this one, and the women of the parish ended by choosing Mme. Aubain's courtyard.

The hard breathing and fever increased. Félicité was vexed at doing nothing for the altar. If only she could at least have put something there! Then she thought of the parrot. The neighbours objected that it would not be decent. But the priest gave her permission, which so intensely delighted her that she begged him to accept Loulou, her sole possession, when she died.

From Tuesday to Saturday, the eve of the festival, she coughed more often. By the evening her face had shrivelled, her lips stuck to her gums, and she had vomitings; and at twilight next morning, feeling herself very low, she sent for a priest.

Three kindly women were round her during the extreme unction. Then she announced that she must speak to Fabu. He arrived in his Sunday clothes, by no means at his ease in the funereal atmosphere.

"Forgive me," she said, with an effort to stretch out her arm; "I thought it was you who had killed him."

What did she mean by such stories? She suspected him of murder — a man like him! He waxed indignant, and was on the point of making a row.

"There," said the women, "she is no longer in her senses, you can see it well enough!"

Félicité spoke to shadows of her own from time to time. The women went away, and Mère Simon had breakfast. A little later she took Loulou and brought him close to Félicité with the words:

"Come, now, say good-bye to him!"

Loulou was not a corpse, but the worms devoured him; one of his wings was broken, and the tow was coming out of his stomach. But she was blind now; she kissed him on the forehead and kept him close against her cheek. Mère Simon took him back from her to put him on the altar.

V

Summer scents came up from the meadows; flies buzzed; the sun made the river glitter and heated the slates. Mère Simon came back into the room and fell softly asleep.

She woke at the noise of bells; the people were coming out from vespers. Félicité's delirium subsided. She thought of the procession and saw it as if she had been there.

All the school children, the church-singers, and the firemen walked on the pavement, while in the middle of the road the verger armed with his hallebard and the beadle with a large cross advanced in front. Then came the schoolmaster, with an eye on the boys, and the sister, anxious about her little girls; three of the daintiest, with angelic curls, scattered rose-petals in the air; the deacon controlled the band with outstretched arms; and two censer-bearers turned back at every step towards the Holy Sacrament, which was borne by Monsieur the curé, wearing his beautiful chasuble, under a canopy of dark-red velvet held up by four churchwardens. A crowd of people pressed behind, between the white cloths covering the house walls, and they reached the bottom of the hill.

A cold sweat moistened Félicité's temples. Mère Simon sponged her with a piece of linen, saying to herself that one day she would have to go that way.

The hum of the crowd increased, was very loud for an instant, and then went further away.

A fusillade shook the window-panes. It was the postilions saluting the monstrance. Félicité rolled her eyes and said as audibly as she could: "Does he look well?" The parrot was weighing on her mind.

Her agony began. A death-rattle that grew more and more convulsed made her sides heave. Bubbles of froth came at the corners of her mouth and her whole body trembled.

Soon the booming of the ophicleides,[2] the high voices of the children, and the deep voices of the men were distinguishable. At intervals all was silent, and the tread of feet, deadened by the flowers they walked on, sounded like a flock pattering on grass.

The clergy appeared in the courtyard. Mère Simon clambered on to a chair to reach the attic window, and so looked down straight upon the shrine. Green garlands hung over the altar, which was decked with a flounce of English lace. In the middle was a small frame with relics in it; there were two orange-trees at the corners, and all along stood silver candlesticks and china vases, with sunflowers, lilies, peonies, foxgloves, and tufts of hortensia. This heap of blazing colour slanted from the level of the altar to the carpet which went on over the pavement; and some rare objects caught the eye. There was a silver-gilt sugar-basin with a crown of violets; pendants of Alençon stone glittered on the moss, and two Chinese screens displayed their landscapes. Loulou was hidden under roses, and showed nothing but his blue forehead, like a plaque of lapis lazuli.

The churchwardens, singers, and children took their places round the three sides of the court. The priest went slowly up the steps, and placed his great, radiant golden sun upon the lace. Everyone knelt down. There was a deep silence; and the censers glided to and fro on the full swing of their chains.

An azure vapour rose up into Félicité's room. Her nostrils met it; she inhaled it sensuously, mystically; and then closed her eyes. Her lips smiled. The beats of her heart lessened one by one, vaguer each time and softer, as a fountain sinks, an echo disappears; and when she sighed her last breath she thought she saw an opening in the heavens, and a gigantic parrot hovering above her head.

QUESTIONS

1. What does Flaubert imply by "simple"? Does he mean to be derogatory?

2. Not much "happens" in Félicité's life, but what does happen is significant to her, and Flaubert sees her as saintly. Pick out some of the incidents that illuminate her spiritual development.

3. What is the significance of the "Holy Ghost" window described at the beginning of Part III? How is the window symbolical? Is it meant to foreshadow the last paragraph of the story?

---

[2] A musical wind instrument.

4. Flaubert is famous for appealing to all our senses. Look closely at the opening paragraphs of Part IV for evidence that this is so. Now look closely at the final paragraph.

5. Does "A Simple Heart" depend for its effect more upon plot, tone, or characterization? Can you find evidence for your impression?

6. What is Félicité's relationship to the family she serves? Do they appreciate her adequately?

7. One interpreter has said that this story is "a drama of Christian renunciation" and one of its lessons is that "the simple and knowing heart can survive on scanty fare." Do you agree?

LEO TOLSTOY

The Death of Ivan Ilych

Translated by Louise and Aylmer Maude

I

During an interval in the Melvinski trial in the large building of the Law Courts the members and public prosecutor met in Ivan Egorovich Shebek's private room, where the conversation turned on the celebrated Krasovski case. Fedor Vasilievich warmly maintained that it was not subject to their jurisdiction, Ivan Egorovich maintained the contrary, while Peter Ivanovich, not having entered into the discussion at the start, took no part in it but looked through the *Gazette* which had just been handed in.

"Gentlemen," he said, "Ivan Ilych has died!"

"You don't say so!"

"Here, read it yourself," replied Peter Ivanovich, handing Fedor Vasilievich the paper still damp from the press. Surrounded by a black border were the words: "Praskovya Fedorovna Golovina, with profound sorrow, informs relatives and friends of the demise of her beloved husband Ivan Ilych Golovin, Member of the Court of Justice, which occurred on February the 4th of this year 1882. The funeral will take place on Friday at one o'clock in the afternoon."

Ivan Ilych had been a colleague of the gentlemen present and was liked by them all. He had been ill for some weeks with an illness said to be incurable. His post had been kept open for him, but there had been conjectures that in case of his death Alexeev might receive his appointment, and that either Vinnikov or Shtabel would succeed Alexeev. So on receiving the news of Ivan Ilych's death the first thought of each of the gentlemen in that private room was of the changes and promotions it might occasion among themselves or their acquaintances.

"I shall be sure to get Shtabel's place or Vinnikov's," thought Fedor Vasilievich. "I was promised that long ago, and the promotion means an extra eight hundred rubles a year for me besides the allowance."

"Now I must apply for my brother-in-law's transfer from Kaluga," thought Peter Ivanovich. "My wife will be very glad, and then she won't be able to say that I never do anything for her relations."

"I thought he would never leave his bed again," said Peter Ivanovich aloud. "It's very sad."

"But what really was the matter with him?"

"The doctors couldn't say — at least they could, but each of them said something different. When last I saw him I thought he was getting better."

"And I haven't been to see him since the holidays. I always meant to go."

"Had he any property?"

"I think his wife had a little — but something quite trifling."

"We shall have to go to see her, but they live so terribly far away."

"Far away from you, you mean. Everything's far away from your place."

"You see, he never can forgive my living on the other side of the river," said Peter Ivanovich, smiling at Shebek. Then, still talking of the distances between different parts of the city, they returned to the Court.

Besides considerations as to the possible transfers and promotions likely to result from Ivan Ilych's death, the mere fact of the death of a near acquaintance aroused, as usual, in all who heard of it the complacent feeling that, "it is he who is dead and not I."

Each one thought or felt, "Well, he's dead but I'm alive!" But the more intimate of Ivan Ilych's acquaintances, his so-called friends, could not help thinking also that they would now have to fulfil the very tiresome demands of propriety by attending the funeral service and paying a visit of condolence to the widow.

Fedor Vasilievich and Peter Ivanovich had been his nearest acquaintances. Peter Ivanovich had studied law with Ivan Ilych and had considered himself to be under obligations to him.

Having told his wife at dinner-time of Ivan Ilych's death, and of his conjecture that it might be possible to get her brother transferred to their circuit, Peter Ivanovich sacrificed his usual nap, put on his evening clothes, and drove to Ivan Ilych's house.

At the entrance stood a carriage and two cabs. Leaning against the wall in the hall downstairs near the cloak-stand was a coffin lid covered with cloth of gold, ornamented with gold cord and tassels, that had been polished up with metal powder. Two ladies in black were taking off their fur cloaks. Peter Ivanovich recognized one of them as Ivan Ilych's sister, but the other was a stranger to him. His colleague Schwartz was just coming downstairs, but on seeing Peter Ivanovich enter he stopped and winked at him, as if to say: "Ivan Ilych has made a mess of things — not like you and me."

Schwartz's face with his Piccadilly whiskers, and his slim figure in evening dress, had as usual an air of elegant solemnity which contrasted with the playfulness of his character and had a special piquancy here, or so it seemed to Peter Ivanovich.

Peter Ivanovich allowed the ladies to precede him and slowly followed them upstairs. Schwartz did not come down but remained where he was, and Peter Ivanovich understood that he wanted to arrange where they should play bridge that evening. The ladies went upstairs to the widow's room, and Schwartz with seriously compressed lips but a playful look in his eyes, indicated by a twist of his eyebrows the room to the right where the body lay.

Peter Ivanovich, like everyone else on such occasions, entered feeling uncertain what he would have to do. All he knew was that at such times it is always safe to cross oneself. But he was not quite sure whether one should make obeisances while doing so. He therefore adopted a middle course. On entering the room he began crossing himself and made a slight movement resembling a bow. At the same time, as far as the motion of his head and arm allowed, he surveyed the room. Two young men — apparently nephews, one of whom was a high-school pupil — were leaving the room, crossing themselves as they did so. An old woman was standing motionless, and a lady with strangely arched eyebrows was saying something to her in a whisper. A vigorous, resolute Church Reader, in a frock-coat, was reading something in a loud voice with an expression that precluded any contradiction. The butler's assistant,

Gerasim, stepping lightly in front of Peter Ivanovich, was strewing something on the floor. Noticing this, Peter Ivanovich was immediately aware of a faint odour of a decomposing body.

The last time he had called on Ivan Ilych, Peter Ivanovich had seen Gerasim in the study. Ivan Ilych had been particularly fond of him and he was performing the duty of a sick nurse.

Peter Ivanovich continued to make the sign of the cross slightly inclining his head in an intermediate direction between the coffin, the Reader, and the icons on the table in a corner of the room. Afterwards, when it seemed to him that this movement of his arm in crossing himself had gone on too long, he stoped and began to look at the corpse.

The dead man lay, as dead men always lie, in a specially heavy way, his rigid limbs sunk in the soft cushions of the coffin, with the head forever bowed on the pillow. His yellow waxen brow with bald patches over his sunken temples was thrust up in the way peculiar to the dead, the protruding nose seeming to press on the upper lip. He was much changed and had grown even thinner since Peter Ivanovich had last seen him, but, as is always the case with the dead, his face was handsomer and above all more dignified than when he was alive. The expression on the face said that what was necessary had been accomplished, and accomplished rightly. Besides this there was in that expression a reproach and a warning to the living. This warning seemed to Peter Ivanovich out of place, or at least not applicable to him. He felt a certain discomfort and so he hurriedly crossed himself once more and turned and went out of the door — too hurriedly and too regardless of propriety, as he himself was aware.

Schwartz was waiting for him in the adjoining room with legs spread wide apart and both hands toying with his top-hat behind his back. The mere sight of that playful, well-groomed, and elegant figure refreshed Peter Ivanovich. He felt that Schwartz was above all these happenings and would not surrender to any depressing influences. His very look said that this incident of a church service for Ivan Ilych could not be a sufficient reason for infringing the order of the session — in other words, that it would certainly not prevent his unwrapping a new pack of cards and shuffling them that evening while a footman placed four fresh candles on the table: in fact, that there was no reason for supposing that this incident would hinder their spending the evening agreeably. Indeed he said this in a whisper as Peter Ivanovich passed him, proposing that they should meet for a game at Fedor Vasilievich's. But apparently Peter Ivanovich was not destined to play bridge that evening. Praskovya Fedorovna (a short, fat woman who despite all efforts to the contrary had continued to broaden steadily from her shoulders downwards and who had the same extraordinarily arched eyebrows as the lady who had been standing by the coffin), dressed all in black, her head covered with lace, came out of her own room with some other ladies, conducted them to the room where the dead body lay, and said: "The service will begin immediately. Please go in."

Schwartz, making an indefinite bow, stood still, evidently neither accepting nor declining this invitation. Praskovya Fedorovna recognizing Peter Ivanovich, sighed, went close up to him, took his hand, and said: "I know you were a true friend to Ivan Ilych … " and looked at him awaiting some suitable response. And Peter Ivanovich knew that, just as it had been the right thing to cross himself in that room, so what he had to do here was to press her hand, sigh, and say, "Believe me … ." So he did all this and as he did it felt that the desired result had been achieved: that both he and she were touched.

"Come with me. I want to speak to you before it begins," said the widow. "Give me your arm."

Peter Ivanovich gave her his arm and they went to the inner rooms, passing Schwartz who winked at Peter Ivanovich compassionately.

"That does for our bridge! Don't object if we find another player. Perhaps you can cut in when you do escape," said his playful look.

Peter Ivanovich sighed still more deeply and despondently, and Praskovya Fedorovna pressed his arm gratefully. When they reached the drawing-room, upholstered in pink cretonne and lighted by a dim lamp, they sat down at the table — she on a sofa and Peter Ivanovich on a low pouffe, the springs of which yielded spasmodically under his weight. Praskovya Fedorovna had been on the point of warning him to take another seat, but felt that such a warning was out of keeping with her present condition and so changed her mind. As he sat down on the pouffe Peter Ivanovich recalled how Ivan Ilych had arranged this room and had consulted him regarding this pink cretonne with green leaves. The whole room was full of furniture and knick-knacks, and on her way to the sofa the lace of the widow's black shawl caught on the carved edge of the table. Peter Ivanovich rose to detach it, and the springs of the pouffe, relieved of his weight, rose also and gave him a push. The widow began detaching her shawl herself, and Peter Ivanovich again sat down, suppressing the rebellious springs of the pouffe under him. But the widow had not quite freed herself and Peter Ivanovich got up again, and again the pouffe rebelled and even creaked. When this was all over she took out a clean cambric handkerchief and began to weep. The episode with the shawl and the struggle with the pouffe had cooled Peter Ivanovich's emotions and he sat there with a sullen look on his face. This awkward situation was interrupted by Sokolov, Ivan Ilych's butler, who came to report that the plot in the cemetery that Praskovya Fedorovna had chosen would cost two hundred rubles. She stopped weeping and, looking at Peter Ivanovich with the air of a victim, remarked in French that it was very hard for her. Peter Ivanovich made a silent gesture signifying his full conviction that it must indeed be so.

"Please smoke," she said in a magnanimous yet crushed voice, and turned to discuss with Sokolov the price of the plot for the grave.

Peter Ivanovich while lighting his cigarette heard her inquiring very circumstantially into the prices of different plots in the cemetery and finally decide which she would take. When that was done she gave instructions about engaging the choir. Sokolov then left the room.

"I look after everything myself," she told Peter Ivanovich, shifting the albums that lay on the table; and noticing that the table was endangered by his cigarette-ash, she immediately passed him an ash-tray, saying as she did so: "I consider it an affectation to say that my grief prevents my attending to practical affairs. On the contrary, if anything can — I won't say console me, but — distract me, it is seeing to everything concerning him." She again took out her handkerchief as if preparing to cry, but suddenly, as if mastering her feeling, she shook herself and began to speak calmly. "But there is something I want to talk to you about."

Peter Ivanovich bowed, keeping control of the springs of the pouffe, which immediately began quivering under him.

"He suffered terribly the last few days."

"Did he?" said Peter Ivanovich.

"Oh, terribly! He screamed unceasingly, not for minutes but for hours. For the last three days he screamed incessantly. It was unendurable. I cannot understand how I bore it; you could hear him three rooms off. Oh, what I have suffered!"

"Is it possible that he was conscious all that time?" asked Peter Ivanovich.

"Yes," she whispered. "To the last moment. He took leave of us a quarter of an hour before he died, and asked us to take Volodya away."

The thought of the sufferings of this man he had known so intimately, first as a merry little boy, then as a school-mate, and later as a grown-up colleague, suddenly struck Peter Ivanovich with horror, despite an unpleasant consciousness of his own and this woman's dissimulation. He again saw that brow, and that nose pressing down on the lip, and felt afraid for himself.

"Three days of frightful suffering and then death! Why, that might suddenly, at any time, happen to me," he thought, and for a moment felt terrified. But — he did not himself know how — the customary reflection at once occurred to him that this had happened to Ivan Ilych and not to him, and that it should not and could not happen to him, and that to think that it could would be yielding to depression which he ought not to do, as Schwartz's expression plainly showed. After which reflection Peter Ivanovich felt reassured, and began to ask with interest about the details of Ivan Ilych's death, as though death was an accident natural to Ivan Ilych but certainly not to himself.

After many details of the really dreadful physical sufferings Ivan Ilych had endured (which details he learnt only from the effect those sufferings had produced on Praskovya Fedorovna's nerves) the widow apparently found it necessary to get to business.

"Oh, Peter Ivanovich, how hard it is! How terribly, terribly hard!" and she again began to weep.

Peter Ivanovich sighed and waited for her to finish blowing her nose. When she had done so he said, "Believe me ... ," and she again began talking and brought out what was evidently her chief concern with him — namely, to question him as to how she could obtain a grant of money from the government on the occasion of her husband's death. She made it appear that she was asking Peter Ivanovich's advice about her pension, but he soon saw that she already knew about that to the minutest detail, more even than he did himself. She knew how much could be got out of the government in consequence of her husband's death, but wanted to find out whether she could not possibly extract something more. Peter Ivanovich tried to think of some means of doing so, but after reflecting for a while and, out of propriety, condemning the government for its niggardliness, he said he thought that nothing more could be got. Then she sighed and evidently began to devise means of getting rid of her visitor. Noticing this, he put out his cigarette, rose, pressed her hand, and went out into the anteroom.

In the dining-room where the clock stood that Ivan Ilych had liked so much and had bought at an antique shop, Peter Ivanovich met a priest and a few acquaintances who had come to attend the service, and he recognized Ivan Ilych's daughter, a handsome young woman. She was in black and her slim figure appeared slimmer than ever. She had a gloomy, determined, almost angry expression, and bowed to Peter Ivanovich as though he were in some way to blame. Behind her, with the same offended look, stood a wealthy young man, an examining magistrate, whom Peter Ivanovich also knew and who was her fiancé, as he had heard. He bowed mournfully to them and was about to pass into the death-chamber, when from under the stairs appeared the figure of Ivan Ilych's schoolboy son, who was extremely like his father. He seemed a little Ivan Ilych, such as Peter Ivanovich remembered when they studied law together. His tear-stained eyes had in them the look that is seen in the eyes of boys of thirteen or fourteen who are not pure-minded. When he saw Peter Ivanovich he scowled morosely and shamefacedly. Peter Ivanovich nodded to him and entered the death-chamber. The service began: candles, groans, incense, tears, and sobs. Peter Ivanovich stood looking gloomily down at his feet. He did not look once at the dead man, did not yield to any depressing influence, and was one of the first to leave the room. There was no one in the anteroom, but Gerasim darted out of the dead man's room, rummaged with his strong hands among the fur coats to find Peter Ivanovich's and helped him on with it.

"Well, friend Gerasim," said Peter Ivanovich, so as to say something. "It's a sad affair, isn't it?"

"It's God's will. We shall all come to it some day," said Gerasim, displaying his teeth — the even, white teeth of a healthy peasant — and, like a man in the thick of urgent work, he briskly opened the front door, called the coachman, helped Peter Ivanovich into the sledge, and sprang back to the porch as if in readiness for what he had to do next.

Peter Ivanovich found the fresh air particularly pleasant after the smell of incense, the dead body, and carbolic acid.

"Where to, sir?" asked the coachman.

"It's not too late even now. ... I'll call round on Fedor Vasilievich."

He accordingly drove there and found them just finishing the first rubber, so that it was quite convenient for him to cut in.

II

Ivan Ilych's life had been most simple and most ordinary and therefore most terrible.

He had been a member of the Court of Justice, and died at the age of forty-five. His father had been an official who after serving in various ministries and departments in Petersburg had made the sort of career which brings men to positions from which by reason of their long service they cannot be dismissed, though they are obviously unfit to hold any responsible position, and for whom therefore posts are specially created, which though fictitious carry salaries of from six to ten thousand rubles that are not fictitious, and in receipt of which they live on to a great age.

Such was the Privy Councillor and superfluous member of various superfluous institutions, Ilya Epimovich Golovin.

He had three sons, of whom Ivan Ilych was the second. The eldest son was following in his father's footsteps only in another department, and was already approaching that stage in the service at which a similar sinecure would be reached. The third son was a failure. He had ruined his prospects in a number of positions and was now serving in the railway department. His father and brothers, and still more their wives, not merely disliked meeting him, but avoided remembering his existence unless compelled to do so. His sister had married Baron Greff, a Petersburg official of her father's type. Ivan Ilych was *le phénix de la famille* as people said. He was neither as cold and formal as his elder brother nor as wild as the younger, but was a happy mean between them — an intelligent, polished, lively and agreeable man. He had studied with his younger brother at the School of Law, but the latter had failed to complete the course and was expelled when he was in the fifth class. Ivan Ilych finished the course well. Even when he was at the School of Law he was just what he remained for the rest of his life: a capable, cheerful, good-natured, and sociable man, though strict in the fulfilment of what he considered to be his duty: and he considered his duty to be what was so considered by those in authority. Neither as a boy nor as a man was he a toady, but from early youth was by nature attracted to people of high station as a fly is drawn to the light, assimilating their ways and views of life and establishing friendly relations with them. All the enthusiasms of childhood and youth passed without leaving much trace on him; he succumbed to sensuality, to vanity, and latterly among the highest classes to liberalism, but always within limits which his instinct unfailingly indicated to him as correct.

At school he had done things which had formerly seemed to him very horrid and made him feel disgusted with himself when he did them; but when later on he saw that such actions were done by people of good position and that they did not regard them as wrong, he was able not exactly to regard them as right, but to forget about them entirely or not be at all troubled at remembering them.

Having graduated from the School of Law and qualified for the tenth rank of the civil service, and having received money from his father for his equipment, Ivan Ilych ordered himself clothes at Scharmer's, the fashionable tailor, hung a medallion inscribed *respice finem*[1] on his watch-chain, took leave of his professor and the prince who was patron of the school, had a farewell dinner with his comrades at Donon's first-class restaurant, and with his new and fashionable portmanteau, linen, clothes, shaving and other toilet appliances, and a travelling rug, all purchased at the best shops, he set off for one of the provinces where, through his father's influence, he had been attached to the Governor as an official for special service.

In the province Ivan Ilych soon arranged as easy and agreeable a position for himself as he had had at the School of Law. He performed his official tasks, made his career, and at the same time amused himself pleasantly and decorously. Occasionally he paid official visits to country districts, where he behaved with dignity both to his superiors and inferiors, and performed the duties entrusted to him, which related chiefly to the sectarians, with an exactness and incorruptible honesty of which he could not but feel proud.

In official matters, despite his youth and taste for frivolous gaiety, he was exceedingly reserved, punctilious, and even severe; but in society he was often amusing and witty, and always good-natured, correct in his manner, and *bon enfant*,[2] as the governor and his wife — with whom he was like one of the family — used to say of him.

In the province he had an affair with a lady who made advances to the elegant young lawyer, and there was also a milliner; and there were carousals with aides-de-camp who visited the district, and after-supper visits to a certain outlying street of doubtful reputation; and there was too some obsequiousness to his chief and even to his chief's wife, but all this was done with such a tone of good breeding that no hard names could be applied to it. It all came under the heading of the French saying: *"Il faut que jeunesse se passe."*[3] It was all done with clean hands, in clean linen, with French phrases, and above all among people of the best society and consequently with the approval of people of rank.

So Ivan Ilych served for five years and then came a change in his official life. The new and reformed judicial institutions were introduced, and new men were needed. Ivan Ilych became such a new man. He was offered the post of Examining Magistrate, and he accepted it though the post was in another province and obliged him to give up the connexions he had formed and to make new ones. His friends met to give him a send-off; they had a group-photograph taken and presented him with a silver cigarette-case, and he set off to his new post.

As examining magistrate Ivan Ilych was just as *comme il faut*[4] and decorous a man, inspiring general respect and capable of separating his official duties from his private life, as he had been when acting as an official on special service. His duties now as examining magistrate were far more interesting and attractive than before. In his former position it had been pleasant to wear an undress uniform made by Scharmer, and to pass through the crowd of petitioners and officials who were timorously awaiting an audience with the governor, and who envied him as with free and easy gait he went straight into his chief's private room to have a cup of tea and a cigarette with him. But not many people had then been directly dependent on him — Snly police officials and the sectarians when he went on special missions — and he liked to treat them politely, almost as comrades, as if he were letting them feel that he who had the

[1] "Look to the end"; that is, consider the consequences.
[2] Good company.
[3] "Youth must have its fling." (Translators' note.)
[4] Proper.

power to crush them was treating them in this simple, friendly way. There were then but few such people. But now, as an examining magistrate, Ivan Ilych felt that everyone without exception, even the most important and self-satisfied, was in his power, and that he need only write a few words on a sheet of paper with a certain heading, and this or that important, self-satisfied person would be brought before him in the role of an accused person or a witness, and if he did not choose to allow him to sit down, would have to stand before him and answer his questions. Ivan Ilych never abused his power; he tried on the contrary to soften its expression, but the consciousness of it and of the possibility of softening its effect, supplied the chief interest and attraction of his office. In his work itself, especially in his examinations, he very soon acquired a method of eliminating all considerations irrelevant to the legal aspect of the case, and reducing even the most complicated case to a form in which it would be presented on paper only in its externals, completely excluding his personal opinion of the matter, while above all observing every prescribed formality. The work was new and Ivan Ilych was one of the first men to apply the new Code of 1864.[5]

On taking up the post of examining magistrate in a new town, he made new acquaintances and connexions, placed himself on a new footing, and assumed a somewhat different tone. He took up an attitude of rather dignified aloofness towards the provincial authorities, but picked out the best circle of legal gentlemen and wealthy gentry living in the town and assumed a tone of slight dissatisfaction with the government, of moderate liberalism, and of enlightened citizenship. At the same time, without at all altering the elegance of his toilet, he ceased shaving his chin and allowed his beard to grow as it pleased.

Ivan Ilych settled down very pleasantly in this new town. The society there, which inclined towards opposition to the Governor, was friendly, his salary was larger, and he began to play *vint* [a form of bridge], which he found added not a little to the pleasure of life, for he had a capacity for cards, played good-humouredly, and calculated rapidly and astutely, so that he usually won.

After living there for two years he met his future wife, Praskovya Fedorovna Mikhel, who was the most attractive, clever, and brilliant girl of the set in which he moved, and among other amusements and relaxations from his labours as examining magistrate, Ivan Ilych established light and playful relations with her.

While he had been an official on special service he had been accustomed to dance, but now as an examining magistrate it was exceptional for him to do so. If he danced now, he did it as if to show that though he served under the reformed order of things, and had reached the fifth official rank, yet when it came to dancing he could do it better than most people. So at the end of an evening he sometimes danced with Praskovya Fedorovna, and it was chiefly during these dances that he captivated her. She fell in love with him. Ivan Ilych had at first no definite intention of marrying, but when the girl fell in love with him he said to himself: "Really, why shouldn't I marry?"

Praskovya Fedorovna came of a good family, was not bad looking, and had some little property. Ivan Ilych might have aspired to a more brilliant match, but even this was good. He had his salary, and she, he hoped, would have an equal income. She was well connected, and was a sweet, pretty, and thoroughly correct young woman. To say that Ivan Ilych married because he fell in love with Praskovya Fedorovna and found that she sympathized with his views of life would be as incorrect as to say that he married because his social circle approved of the match. He was swayed by both these considerations: the marriage gave him personal

---

[5] The emancipation of the serfs in 1861 was followed by a thorough all-round reform of judicial proceedings. (Translators' note.)

satisfaction, and at the same time it was considered the right thing by the most highly placed of his associates.

So Ivan Ilych got married.

The preparations for marriage and the beginning of married life, with its conjugal caresses, the new furniture, new crockery, and new linen, were very pleasant until his wife became pregnant — so that Ivan Ilych had begun to think that marriage would not impair the easy, agreeable, gay and always decorous character of his life, approved of by society and regarded by himself as natural, but would even improve it. But from the first months of his wife's pregnancy, something new, unpleasant, depressing, and unseemly, and from which there was no way of escape, unexpectedly showed itself.

His wife, without any reason — *de gaieté de coeur*[6] as Ivan Ilych expressed it to himself — began to disturb the pleasure and propriety of their life. She began to be jealous without any cause, expected him to devote his whole attention to her, found fault with everything, and made coarse and ill-mannered scenes.

At first Ivan Ilych hoped to escape from the unpleasantness of this state of affairs by the same easy and decorous relation to life that had served him heretofore: he tried to ignore his wife's disagreeable moods, continued to live in his usual easy and pleasant way, invited friends to his house for a game of cards, and also tried going out to his club or spending his evenings with friends. But one day his wife began upbraiding him so vigorously, using such coarse words, and continued to abuse him every time he did not fulfil her demands, so resolutely and with such evident determination not to give way till he submitted — that is, till he stayed at home and was bored just as she was — that he became alarmed. He now realized that matrimony — at any rate with Praskovya Fedorovna — was not always conducive to the pleasures and amenities of life but on the contrary often infringed both comfort and propriety, and that he must therefore entrench himself against such infringement. And Ivan Ilych began to seek for means of doing so. His official duties were the one thing that imposed upon Praskovya Fedorovna, and by means of his official work and the duties attached to it he began struggling with his wife to secure his own independence.

With the birth of their child, the attempts to feed it and the various failures in doing so, and with the real and imaginary illnesses of mother and child, in which Ivan Ilych's sympathy was demanded but about which he understood nothing, the need of securing for himself an existence outside his family life became still more imperative.

As his wife grew more irritable and exacting and Ivan Ilych transferred the centre of gravity of his life more and more to his official work, so did he grow to like his work better and became more ambitious than before.

Very soon, within a year of his wedding, Ivan Ilych had realized that marriage, though it may add some comforts to life, is in fact a very intricate and difficult affair towards which in order to perform one's duty, that is, to lead a decorous life approved of by society, one must adopt a definite attitude just as towards one's official duties.

And Ivan Ilych evolved such an attitude toward married life. He only required of it those conveniences — dinner at home, housewife, and bed — which it could give him, and above all that propriety of external forms required by public opinion. For the rest he looked for light-hearted pleasure and propriety, and was very thankful when he found them, but if he met with antagonism and querulousness he at once retired into his separate fenced-off world of official duties, where he found satisfaction.

---

[6] "From gaiety of heart."

Ivan Ilych was esteemed a good official, and after three years was made Assistant Public Prosecutor. His new duties, their importance, the possibility of indicting and imprisoning anyone he chose, the publicity his speeches received, and the success he had in all these things, made his work still more attractive.

More children came. His wife became more and more querulous and ill-tempered, but the attitude Ivan Ilych had adopted towards his home life rendered him almost impervious to her grumbling.

After seven years' service in that town he was transferred to another province as Public Prosecutor. They moved, but were short of money and his wife did not like the place they moved to. Though the salary was higher the cost of living was greater, besides which two of their children died and family life became still more unpleasant for him.

Praskovya Fedorovna blamed her husband for every inconvenience they encountered in their new home. Most of the conversations between husband and wife, especially as to the children's education, led to topics which recalled former disputes, and those disputes were apt to flare up again at any moment. There remained only those rare periods of amorousness which still came to them at times but did not last long. These were islets at which they anchored for a while and then again set out upon that ocean of veiled hostility which showed itself in their aloofness from one another. This aloofness might have grieved Ivan Ilych had he considered that it ought not to exist, but he now regarded the position as normal, and even made it the goal at which he aimed in family life. His aim was to free himself more and more from those unpleasantnesses and to give them a semblance of harmlessness and propriety. He attained this by spending less and less time with his family, and when obliged to be at home he tried to safeguard his position by the presence of outsiders. The chief thing however was that he had his official duties. The whole interest of his life now centred in the official world and that interest absorbed him. The consciousness of his power, being able to ruin anybody he wished to ruin, the importance, even the external dignity of his entry into court, or meetings with his subordinates, his success with superiors and inferiors, and above all his masterly handling of cases, of which he was conscious — all this gave him pleasure and filled his life, together with chats with his colleagues, dinners, and bridge. So that on the whole Ivan Ilych's life continued to flow as he considered it should do — pleasantly and properly.

So things continued for another seven years. His eldest daughter was already sixteen, another child had died, and only one son was left, a schoolboy and a subject of dissension. Ivan Ilych wanted to put him in the School of Law, but to spite him Praskovya Fedorovna entered him at the High School. The daughter had been educated at home and had turned out well: the boy did not learn badly either.

III

So Ivan Ilych lived for seventeen years after his marriage. He was already a Public Prosecutor of long standing, and had declined several proposed transfers while awaiting a more desirable post, when an unanticipated and unpleasant occurrence quite upset the peaceful course of his life. He was expecting to be offered the post of presiding judge in a University town, but Happe somehow came to the front and obtained the appointment instead. Ivan Ilych became irritable, reproached Happe, and quarrelled both with him and with his immediate superiors — who became colder to him and again passed him over when other appointments were made.

This was in 1880, the hardest year of Ivan Ilych's life. It was then that it became evident on the one hand that his salary was insufficient for them to live on, and on the other that he had been forgotten, and not only this, but that what was for him the greatest and most cruel injustice appeared to others a quite ordinary occurrence. Even his father did not consider it was his duty to help him. Ivan Ilych felt himself abandoned by everyone, and that they regarded his position with a salary of 3,500 roubles as quite normal and even fortunate. He alone knew that with the consciousness of the injustices done him, with his wife's incessant nagging, and with the debts he had contracted by living beyond his means, his position was far from normal.

In order to save money that summer he obtained leave of absence and went with his wife to live in the country at her brother's place.

In the country, without his work, he experienced *ennui*[7] for the first time in his life, and not only *ennui* but intolerable depression, and he decided that it was impossible to go on living like that, and that it was necessary to take energetic measures.

Having passed a sleepless night pacing up and down the veranda, he decided to go to Petersburg and bestir himself, in order to punish those who had failed to appreciate him and to get transferred to another ministry.

Next day, despite many protests from his wife and her brother, he started for Petersburg with the sole object of obtaining a post with a salary of five thousand rubles a year. He was no longer bent on any particular department, or tendency, or kind of activity. All he now wanted was an appointment to another post with a salary of five thousand rubles, either in the administration, in the banks, with the railways, in one of the Empress Marya's Institutions, or even in the customs — but it had to carry with it a salary of five thousand rubles and be in a ministry other than that in which they had failed to appreciate him.

And this quest of Ivan Ilych's was crowned with remarkable and unexpected success. At Kursk an acquaintance of his, F. I. Ilyin, got into the first-class carriage, sat down beside Ivan Ilych, and told him of a telegram just received by the Governor of Kursk announcing that a change was about to take place in the ministry: Peter Ivanovich was to be superseded by Ivan Semenovich.

The proposed change, apart from its significance for Russia, had a special significance for Ivan Ilych, because by bringing forward a new man, Peter Petrovich, and consequently his friend Zachar Ivanovich, it was highly favourable for Ivan Ilych, since Zachar Ivanovich was a friend and colleague of his.

In Moscow this news was confirmed, and on reaching Petersburg Ivan Ilych found Zachar Ivanovich and received a definite promise of an appointment in his former department of Justice.

A week later he telegraphed to his wife: "Zachar in Miller's place. I shall receive appointment on presentation of report."

Thanks to this change of personnel, Ivan Ilych had unexpectedly obtained an appointment in his former ministry which placed him two stages above his former colleagues besides giving him five thousand rubles salary and three thousand five hundred rubles for expenses connected with his removal. All his ill humour towards his former enemies and the whole department vanished, and Ivan Ilych was completely happy.

He returned to the country more cheerful and contented than he had been for a long time. Praskovya Fedorovna also cheered up and a truce was arranged between them. Ivan Ilych told of how he had been fêted by everybody in Petersburg, how all those who had been his enemies were put to shame and now fawned on him, how envious they were of his appointment, and how much everybody in Petersburg had liked him.

---

[7] Boredom.

Praskovya Fedorovna listened to all this and appeared to believe it. She did not contradict anything, but only made plans for their life in the town to which they were going. Ivan Ilych saw with delight that these plans were his plans, that he and his wife agreed, and that, after a stumble, his life was regaining its due and natural character of pleasant lightheartedness and decorum.

Ivan Ilych had come back for a short time only, for he had to take up his new duties on the 10th of September. Moreover, he needed time to settle into the new place, to move all his belongings from the province, and to buy and order many additional things: in a word, to make such arrangements as he had resolved on, which were almost exactly what Praskovya Fedorovna too had decided on.

Now that everything had happened so fortunately, and that he and his wife were at one in their aims and moreover saw so little of one another, they got on together better than they had done since the first years of marriage. Ivan Ilych had thought of taking his family away with him at once, but the insistence of his wife's brother and her sister-in-law, who had suddenly become particularly amiable and friendly to him and his family, induced him to depart alone.

So he departed, and the cheerful state of mind induced by his success and by the harmony between his wife and himself, the one intensifying the other, did not leave him. He found a delightful house, just the thing both he and his wife had dreamt of. Spacious, lofty reception rooms in the old style, a convenient and dignified study, rooms for his wife and daughter, a study for his son — it might have been specially built for them. Ivan Ilych himself superintended the arrangements, chose the wallpapers, supplemented the furniture (preferably with antiques which he considered particularly *comme il faut*[8]), and supervised the upholstering. Everything progressed and progressed and approached the ideal he had set himself: even when things were only half completed they exceeded his expectations. He saw what a refined and elegant character, free from vulgarity, it would all have when it was ready. On falling asleep he pictured to himself how the reception-room would look. Looking at the yet unfinished drawing-room he could see the fireplace, the screen, the what-not, the little chairs dotted here and there, the dishes and plates on the walls, and the bronzes, as they would be when everything was in place. He was pleased by the thought of how his wife and daughter, who shared his taste in this matter, would be impressed by it. They were certainly not expecting as much. He had been particularly successful in finding, and buying cheaply, antiques which gave a particularly aristocratic character to the whole place. But in his letters he intentionally understated everything in order to be able to surprise them. All this so absorbed him that his new duties — though he liked his official work — interested him less than he expected. Sometimes he even had moments of absent-mindedness during the Court Sessions, and would consider whether he should have straight or curved cornices for his curtains. He was so interested in it all that he often did things himself, rearranging the furniture, or rehanging the curtains. Once when mounting a step-ladder to show the upholsterer, who did not understand, how he wanted the hangings draped, he made a false step and slipped, but being a strong and agile man he clung on and only knocked his side against the knob of the window frame. The bruised place was painful but the pain soon passed, and he felt particularly bright and well just then. He wrote: "I feel fifteen years younger." He thought he would have everything ready by September, but it dragged on till mid-October. But the result was charming not only in his eyes but to everyone who saw it.

In reality it was just what is usually seen in the houses of people of moderate means who want to appear rich, and therefore succeed only in resembling others like themselves: there

---

[8] Stylish.

were damasks, dark wood, plants, rugs, and dull and polished bronzes — all the things people of a certain class have in order to resemble other people of that class. His house was so like the others that it would never have been noticed, but to him it all seemed to be quite exceptional. He was very happy when he met his family at the station and brought them to the newly furnished house all lit up, where a footman in a white tie opened the door into the hall decorated with plants, and when they went on into the drawing-room and the study uttering exclamations of delight. He conducted them everywhere, drank in their praises eagerly, and beamed with pleasure. At tea that evening, when Praskovya Fedorovna among other things asked him about his fall, he laughed, and showed them how he had gone flying and had frightened the upholsterer.

"It's a good thing I'm a bit of an athlete. Another man might have been killed, but I merely knocked myself, just here; it hurts when it's touched, but it's passing off already — it's only a bruise."

So they began living in their new home — in which, as always happens, when they got thoroughly settled in they found they were just one room short — and with the increased income, which as always was just a little (some five hundred rubles) too little, but it was all very nice.

Things went particularly well at first, before everything was finally arranged and while something had still to be done: this thing bought, that thing ordered, another thing moved, and something else adjusted. Though there were some disputes between husband and wife, they were both so well satisfied and had so much to do that it all passed off without any serious quarrels. When nothing was left to arrange it became rather dull and something seemed to be lacking, but they were then making acquaintances, forming habits, and life was growing fuller.

Ivan Ilych spent his mornings at the law court and came home to dinner, and at first he was generally in a good humour, though he occasionally became irritable just on account of his house. (Every spot on the tablecloth or the upholstery, and every broken window-blind string, irritated him. He had devoted so much trouble to arranging it all that every disturbance of it distressed him.) But on the whole his life ran its course as he believed life should do: easily, pleasantly, and decorously.

He got up at nine, drank his coffee, read the paper, and then put on his undress uniform and went to the law courts. There the harness in which he worked had already been stretched to fit him and he donned it without a hitch: petitioners, inquiries at the chancery, the chancery itself, and the sittings public and administrative. In all this the thing was to exclude everything fresh and vital, which always disturbs the regular course of official business, and to admit only official relations with people, and then only on official grounds. A man would come, for instance, wanting some information. Ivan Ilych, as one in whose sphere the matter did not lie, would have nothing to do with him: but if the man had some business with him in his official capacity, something that could be expressed on officially stamped paper, he would do everything, positively everything he could within the limits of such relations, and in doing so would maintain the semblance of friendly human relations, that is, would observe the courtesies of life. As soon as the official relations ended, so did everything else. Ivan Ilych possessed this capacity to separate his real life from the official side of affairs and not mix the two, in the highest degree, and by long practice and natural aptitude had brought it to such a pitch that sometimes, in the manner of a virtuoso, he would even allow himself to let the human and official relations mingle. He let himself do this just because he felt that he could at any time he chose resume the strictly official attitude again and drop the human relation. And he did it all easily, pleasantly, correctly, and even artistically. In the intervals between the sessions he smoked, drank tea, chatted a little about politics, a little about general topics, a little about cards, but most of all about official appointments. Tired, but with the feelings of a virtuoso — one of the first violins who has played his part in an orchestra with precision — he would return home to find that his wife and daughter had been out paying calls, or had a visitor, and that his son had been to school, had done his homework with his tutor, and was duly learning what is taught at High Schools. Everything was as it should be. After dinner, if they had no visitors, Ivan Ilych sometimes read a book that was being much discussed at the time, and in the evening settled down to work, that is, read official papers, compared the depositions of witnesses, and noted paragraphs of the Code applying to them. This was neither dull nor amusing. It was dull when he might have been playing bridge, but if no bridge was available it was at any rate better than doing nothing or sitting with his wife. Ivan Ilych's chief pleasure was giving little dinners to which he invited men and women of good social position, and just as his drawing-room resembled all other drawing-rooms so did his enjoyable little parties resemble all other such parties.

Once they even gave a dance. Ivan Ilych enjoyed it and everything went off well, except that it led to a violent quarrel with his wife about the cakes and sweets. Praskovya Fedorovna had made her own plans, but Ivan Ilych insisted on getting everything from an expensive confectioner and ordered too many cakes, and the quarrel occurred because some of those cakes were left over and the confectioner's bill came to forty-five rubles. It was a great and disagreeable quarrel. Praskovya Fedorovna called him "a fool and an imbecile," and he clutched at his head and made angry allusions to divorce.

But the dance itself had been enjoyable. The best people were there, and Ivan Ilych had danced with Princess Trufonova, a sister of the distinguished founder of the Society "Bear my Burden."

The pleasures connected with his work were pleasures of ambition; his social pleasures were those of vanity; but Ivan Ilych's greatest pleasure was playing bridge. He acknowledged that whatever disagreeable incident happened in his life, the pleasure that beamed like a ray of light above everything else was to sit down to bridge with good players, not noisy partners, and of course to four-handed bridge (with five players it was annoying to have to stand out, though one pretended not to mind), to play a clever and serious game (when the cards allowed it) and then to have supper and drink a glass of wine. After a game of bridge, especially if he had won a little (to win a large sum was unpleasant), Ivan Ilych went to bed in specially good humour.

So they lived. They formed a circle of acquaintances among the best people and were visited by people of importance and by young folk. In their views as to their acquaintances, husband and wife and daughter were entirely agreed, and tacitly and unanimously kept at arm's length and shook off the various shabby friends and relations who, with much show of affection, gushed into the drawing-room with its Japanese plates on the walls. Soon these shabby friends ceased to obtrude themselves and only the best people remained in the Golovins' set.

Young men made up to Lisa, and Petrischev, an examining magistrate and Dmitri Ivanovich Petrischev's son and sole heir, began to be so attentive to her that Ivan Ilych had already spoken to Praskovya Fedorovna about it, and considered whether they should not arrange a party for them, or get up some private theatricals.

So they lived, and all went well, without change, and life flowed pleasantly.

IV

They were all in good health. It could not be called ill health if Ivan Ilych sometimes said that he had a queer taste in his mouth and felt some discomfort in his left side.

But this discomfort increased and, though not exactly painful, grew into a sense of pressure in his side accompanied by ill humour. And his irritability became worse and worse and began to mar the agreeable, easy, and correct life that had established itself in the Golovin family. Quarrels between husband and wife became more and more frequent, and soon the ease and amenity disappeared and even the decorum was barely maintained. Scenes again became frequent, and very few of those islets remained on which husband and wife could meet without an explosion. Praskovya Fedorovna now had good reason to say that her husband's temper was trying. With characteristic exaggeration she said he had always had a dreadful temper, and that it had needed all her good nature to put up with it for twenty years. It was true that now the quarrels were started by him. His bursts of temper always came just before dinner, often just as he began to eat his soup. Sometimes he noticed that a plate or dish was chipped, or the food was not right, or his son put his elbow on the table, or his daughter's hair was not done as he liked it, and for all this he blamed Praskovya Fedorovna. At first she retorted and said disagreeable things to him, but once or twice he fell into such a rage at the beginning of dinner that she realized it was due to some physical derangement brought on by taking food, and so she restrained herself and did not answer, but only hurried to get the dinner over. She regarded this self-restraint as highly praiseworthy. Having come to the conclusion that her husband had a dreadful temper and made her life miserable, she began to feel sorry for herself, and the more she pitied herself the more she hated her husband. She began to wish he would die; yet she did not want him to die because then his salary would cease. And this irritated her against him still more. She considered herself dreadfully unhappy just because not even his death could save her, and though she concealed her exasperation, that hidden exasperation of hers increased his irritation also.

After one scene in which Ivan Ilych had been particularly unfair and after which he had said in explanation that he certainly was irritable but that it was due to his not being well, she said that if he was ill it should be attended to, and insisted on his going to see a celebrated doctor.

He went. Everything took place as he had expected and as it always does. There was the usual waiting and the important air assumed by the doctor, with which he was so familiar (resembling that which he himself assumed in court), and the sounding and listening, and the questions which called for answers that were foregone conclusions and were evidently unnecessary, and the look of importance which implied that "if only you put yourself in our hands we will arrange everything — we know indubitably how it has to be done, always in the same way for everybody alike." It was all just as it was in the law courts. The doctor put on just the same air towards him as he himself put on towards an accused person.

The doctor said that so-and-so indicated that there was so-and-so inside the patient, but if the investigation of so-and-so did not confirm this, then he must assume that and that. If he assumed that and that, then … and so on. To Ivan Ilych only one question was important: was his case serious or not? But the doctor ignored that inappropriate question. From his point of view it was not the one under consideration, the real question was to decide between a floating kidney, chronic catarrh, or appendicitis. It was not a question of Ivan Ilych's life or death, but one between a floating kidney and appendicitis. And that question the doctor solved brilliantly, as it seemed to Ivan Ilych, in favour of the appendix, with the reservation that should an examination of the urine give fresh indications the matter would be reconsidered. All this was just what Ivan Ilych had himself brilliantly accomplished a thousand times in dealing with men on trial. The doctor summed up just as brilliantly, looking over his spectacles triumphantly and even gaily at the accused. From the doctor's summing up Ivan Ilych concluded that things were bad, but that for the doctor, and perhaps for everybody else, it was a matter of indifference, though for him it was bad. And this conclusion struck him painfully, arousing in him a great feeling of pity for himself and of bitterness towards the doctor's indifference to a matter of such importance.

He said nothing of this, but rose, placed the doctor's fee on the table, and remarked with a sigh: "We sick people probably often put inappropriate questions. But tell me, in general, is this complaint dangerous, or not? ... "

The doctor looked at him sternly over his spectacles with one eye, as if to say: "Prisoner, if you will not keep to the questions put to you, I shall be obliged to have you removed from the court."

"I have already told you what I consider necessary and proper. The analysis may show something more." And the doctor bowed.

Ivan Ilych went out slowly, seated himself disconsolately in his sledge, and drove home. All the way home he was going over what the doctor had said, trying to translate those complicated, obscure, scientific phrases into plain language and find in them an answer to the question: "Is my condition bad? Is it very bad? Or is there as yet nothing much wrong?" And it seemed to him that the meaning of what the doctor had said was that it was very bad. Everything in the streets seemed depressing. The cabmen, the houses, the passers-by, and the shops, were dismal. His ache, this dull gnawing ache that never ceased for a moment, seemed to have acquired a new and more serious significance from the doctor's dubious remarks. Ivan Ilych now watched it with a new and oppressive feeling.

He reached home and began to tell his wife about it. She listened, but in the middle of his account his daughter came in with her hat on, ready to go out with her mother. She sat down reluctantly to listen to this tedious story, but could not stand it long, and her mother too did not hear him to the end.

"Well, I am very glad," she said. "Mind now to take your medicine regularly. Give me the prescription and I'll send Gerasim to the chemist's." And she went to get ready to go out.

While she was in the room Ivan Ilych had hardly taken time to breathe, but he sighed deeply when she left it.

"Well," he thought, "perhaps it isn't so bad after all."

He began taking his medicine and following the doctor's directions, which had been altered after the examination of the urine. But then it happened that there was a contradiction between the indications drawn from the examination of the urine and the symptoms that showed themselves. It turned out that what was happening differed from what the doctor had told him, and that he had either forgotten, or blundered, or hidden something from him. He could not, however, be blamed for that, and Ivan Ilych still obeyed his orders implicitly and at first derived some comfort from doing so.

From the time of his visit to the doctor, Ivan Ilych's chief occupation was the exact fulfilment of the doctor's instructions regarding hygiene and the taking of the medicine, and the observation of his pain and his excretions. His chief interests came to be people's ailments and people's health. When sickness, deaths, or recoveries, were mentioned in his presence, especially when the illness resembled his own, he listened with agitation which he tried to hide, asked questions, and applied what he heard to his own case.

The pain did not grow less, but Ivan Ilych made efforts to force himself to think that he was better. And he could do this so long as nothing agitated him. But as soon as he had any unpleasantness with his wife, any lack of success in his official work, or held bad cards at bridge, he was at once acutely sensible of his disease. He had formerly borne such mischances, hoping soon to adjust what was wrong, to master it and attain success, or make a grand slam. But now every mischance upset him and plunged him into despair. He would say to himself: "There now, just as I was beginning to get better and the medicine had begun to take effect, comes this accursed misfortune, or unpleasantness ... " And he was furious with the mishap, or with the people who were causing the unpleasantness and killing him, for he felt that this fury was killing him but could not restrain it. One would have thought that it should have been clear to him that this exasperation with circumstances and people aggravated his illness, and that he ought therefore to ignore unpleasant occurrences. But he drew the very opposite conclusion: he said that he needed peace, and he watched for everything that might disturb it and became irritable at the slightest infringement of it. His condition was rendered worse by the fact that he read medical books and consulted doctors. The progress of his disease was so gradual that he could deceive himself when comparing one day with another — the difference was so slight. But when he consulted the doctors it seemed to him that he was getting worse, and even very rapidly. Yet despite this he was continually consulting them.

That month he went to see another celebrity, who told him almost the same as the first had done but put his questions rather differently, and the interview with this celebrity only increased Ivan Ilych's doubts and fears. A friend of a friend of his, a very good doctor, diagnosed his illness again quite differently from the others, and though he predicted recovery, his questions and suppositions bewildered Ivan Ilych still more and increased his doubts. A homoeopathist diagnosed the disease in yet another way, and prescribed medicine which Ivan Ilych took secretly for a week. But after a week, not feeling any improvement and having lost confidence both in the former doctor's treatment and in this one's, he became still more despondent. One day a lady acquaintance mentioned a cure effected by a wonder-working icon. Ivan Ilych caught himself listening attentively and beginning to believe that it had occurred. This incident alarmed him. "Has my mind really weakened to such an extent?" he asked himself. "Nonsense! It's all rubbish. I mustn't give way to nervous fears but having chosen a doctor must keep strictly to his treatment. That is what I will do. Now it's all settled. I won't think about it, but will follow the treatment seriously till summer, and then we shall see. From now there must be no more of this wavering!" This was easy to say but impossible to carry out. The pain in his side oppressed him and seemed to grow worse and more incessant, while the taste in his mouth grew stranger and stranger. It seemed to him that his breath had a disgusting smell, and he was conscious of a loss of appetite and strength. There was no deceiving himself: something terrible, new, and more important than anything before in his life, was taking place within him of which he alone was aware. Those about him did not understand or would not understand it, but thought everything in the world was going on as usual. That tormented Ivan Ilych more than anything. He saw that his household, especially his wife and daughter who were in a perfect whirl of visiting, did not understand anything of it and were annoyed that he was so depressed and exacting, as if he were to blame for it. Though they tried to disguise it he saw that he was an obstacle in their path, and that his wife had adopted a definite line in regard to his illness and kept to it regardless of anything he said or did. Her attitude was this: "You know," she would say to her friends, "Ivan Ilych can't do as other people do, and keep to the treatment prescribed for him. One day he'll take his drops and keep strictly to his diet and go to bed in good time, but the next day unless I watch him he'll suddenly forget his medicine, eat sturgeon — which is forbidden — and sit up playing cards until one o'clock in the morning."

"Oh, come, when was that?" Ivan Ilych would ask in vexation. "Only once at Peter Ivanovich's."

"And yesterday with Shebek."

"Well, even if I hadn't stayed up, this pain would have kept me awake."

"Be that as it may you'll never get well like that, but will always make us wretched."

Praskovya Fedorovna's attitude to Ivan Ilych's illness, as she expressed it both to others and to him, was that it was his own fault and was another of the annoyances he caused her. Ivan Ilych felt that this opinion escaped her involuntarily — but that did not make it easier for him.

At the law courts too, Ivan Ilych noticed, or thought he noticed, a strange attitude towards himself. It sometimes seemed to him that people were watching him inquisitively as a man whose place might soon be vacant. Then again, his friends would suddenly begin to chaff him in a friendly way about his low spirits, as if the awful, horrible, and unheard-of thing that was going on within him, incessantly gnawing at him and irresistably drawing him away, was a very agreeable subject for jests. Schwartz in particular irritated him by his jocularity, vivacity, and *savoir-faire*,[9] which reminded him of what he himself had been ten years ago.

Friends came to make up a set and they sat down to cards. They dealt, bending the new cards to soften them, and he sorted the diamonds in his hand and found he had seven. His partner said "No trumps" and supported him with two diamonds. What more could be wished for? It ought to be jolly and lively. They would make a grand slam. But suddenly Ivan Ilych was conscious of that gnawing pain, that taste in his mouth, and it seemed ridiculous that in such circumstances he should be pleased to make a grand slam.

He looked at his partner Mikhail Mikhaylovich, who rapped the table with his strong hand and instead of snatching up the tricks pushed the cards courteously and indulgently towards Ivan Ilych that he might have the pleasure of gathering them up without the trouble of stretching out his hand for them. "Does he think I am too weak to stretch out my arm?" thought Ivan Ilych, and forgetting what he was doing he over-trumped his partner, missing the grand slam by three tricks. And what was most awful of all was that he saw how upset Mikhail Mikhaylovich was about it but did not himself care. And it was dreadful to realize why he did not care.

They all saw that he was suffering, and said: "We can stop if you are tired. Take a rest." Lie down? No, he was not at all tired, and he finished the rubber. All were gloomy and silent. Ivan Ilych felt that he had diffused this gloom over them and could not dispel it. They had supper and went away, and Ivan Ilych was left alone with the consciousness that his life was poisoned and was poisoning the lives of others, and that this poison did not weaken but penetrated more and more deeply into his whole being.

With this consciousness, and with physical pain besides the terror, he must go to bed, often to lie awake the greater part of the night. Next morning he had to get up again, dress, go to the law courts, speak, and write; or if he did not go out, spend at home those twenty-four hours a day each of which was a torture. And he had to live thus all alone on the brink of an abyss, with no one who understood or pitied him.

V

So one month passed and then another. Just before the New Year his brother-in-law came to town and stayed at their house. Ivan Ilych was at the law courts and Praskovya Fedorovna had gone shopping. When Ivan Ilych came home and entered his study he found his brother-in-law there — a healthy, florid man — unpacking his portmanteau himself. He raised his head on hearing Ivan Ilych's footsteps and looked up at him for a moment without a word. That stare told Ivan Ilych everything. His brother-in-law opened his mouth to utter an exclamation of surprise but checked himself, and that action confirmed all.

"I have changed, eh?"

"Yes, there is a change."

And after that, try as he would to get his brother-in-law to return to the subject of his looks, the latter would say nothing about it. Praskoyva Fedorovna came home and her brother went out to her. Ivan Ilych locked the door and began to examine himself in the glass, first full face, then in profile. He took up a portrait of himself taken with his wife, and compared it with what he saw in the glass. The change in him was immense. Then he bared his arms to the

---

[9] Adroitness.

elbow, looked at them, drew the sleeves down again, sat down on an ottoman, and grew blacker than night.

"No, no, this won't do!" he said to himself, and jumped up, went to the table, took up some law papers and began to read them, but could not continue. He unlocked the door and went into the reception-room. The door leading to the drawing-room was shut. He approached it on tiptoe and listened.

"No, you are exaggerating!" Praskovya Fedorovna was saying.

"Exaggerating! Don't you see it? Why, he's a dead man! Look at his eyes — there's no light in them. But what is it that is wrong with him?"

"No one knows. Nikolaevich [that was another doctor] said something, but I don't know what. And Leshchetitsky [this was the celebrated specialist] said quite the contrary ... "

Ivan Ilych walked away, went to his own room, lay down, and began musing: "The kidney, a floating kidney." He recalled all the doctors had told him of how it detached itself and swayed about. And by an effort of imagination he tried to catch that kidney and arrest it and support it. So little was needed for this, it seemed to him. "No, I'll go to see Peter Ivanovich again." [That was the friend whose friend was a doctor.] He rang, ordered the carriage, and got ready to go.

"Where are you going, Jean?" asked his wife, with a specially sad and exceptionally kind look.

This exceptionally kind look irritated him. He looked morosely at her.

"I must go to see Peter Ivanovich."

He went to see Peter Ivanovich, and together they went to see his friend, the doctor. He was in, and Ivan Ilych had a long talk with him.

Reviewing the anatomical and psychological details of what in the doctor's opinion was going on inside him, he understood it all.

There was something, a small thing, in the vermiform appendix. It might all come right. Only stimulate the energy of one organ and check the activity of another, then absorption would take place and everything would come right. He got home rather late for dinner, ate his dinner, and conversed cheerfully, but could not for a long time bring himself to go back to work in his room. At last, however, he went to his study and did what was necessary, but the consciousness that he had put something aside — an important, intimate matter which he would revert to when his work was done — never left him. When he had finished his work he remembered that this intimate matter was the thought of his vermiform appendix. But he did not give himself up to it, and went to the drawing-room for tea. There were callers there, including the examining magistrate who was a desirable match for his daughter, and they were conversing, playing the piano and singing. Ivan Ilych, as Praskovya Fedorovna remarked, spent that evening more cheerfully than usual, but he never for a moment forgot that he had postponed the important matter of the appendix. At eleven o'clock he said good-night and went to his bedroom. Since his illness he had slept in a small room next to his study. He undressed and took up a novel by Zola, but instead of reading it he fell into thought, and in his imagination that desired improvement in the vermiform appendix occurred. There was the absorption and evacuation and the re-establishment of normal activity. "Yes, that's it!" he said to himself. "One need only assist nature, that's all." He remembered his medicine, rose, took it, and lay down on his back watching for the beneficent action of the medicine and for it to lessen the pain. "I need only take it regularly and avoid all injurious influences. I am already feeling better, much better, much better." He began touching his side: it was not painful to the touch. "There, I really don't feel it. It's much better already." He put out the light and turned on his side ... "The appendix is getting better, absorption is occurring." Suddenly he felt the

old, familiar, dull, gnawing pain, stubborn and serious. There was the same familiar loathsome taste in his mouth. His heart sank and he felt dazed. "My God! My God!" he muttered.
"Again, again! And it will never cease." And suddenly the matter presented itself in a quite
different aspect. "Vermiform appendix! Kidney!" he said to himself. "It's not a question of
appendix or kidney, but of life and ... death. Yes, life was there and now it is going, going and I
cannot stop it. Yes. Why deceive myself? Isn't it obvious to everyone but me that I'm dying,
and that it's only a question of weeks, days ... it may happen this moment. There was light
and now there is darkness. I was here and now I'm going there! Where?" A chill came over
him, his breathing ceased, and he felt only the throbbing of his heart.

"When I am not, what will there be? There will be nothing. Then where shall I be when I
am no more? Can this be dying? No, I don't want to!" He jumped up and tried to light the
candle, felt for it with trembling hands, dropped candle and candlestick on the floor, and fell
back on his pillow.

"What's the use? It makes no difference," he said to himself, staring with wide-open eyes
into the darkness. "Death. Yes, death. And none of them know or wish to know it, and they
have no pity for me. Now they are playing." (He heard through the door the distant sound of a
song and its accompaniment.) "It's all the same to them, but they will die too! Fools! I first,
and they later, but it will be the same for them. And now they are merry ... the beasts!"

Anger choked him and he was agonizingly, unbearably miserable. "It is impossible that
all men have been doomed to suffer this awful horror!" He raised himself.

"Something must be wrong. I must calm myself — must think it all over from the
beginning." And he again began thinking. "Yes, the beginning of my illness: I knocked my
side, but I was still quite well that day and the next. It hurt a little, then rather more. I saw the
doctors, then followed despondency and anguish, more doctors, and I drew nearer to the
abyss. My strength grew less and I kept coming nearer and nearer, and now I have wasted away
and there is no light in my eyes. I think of the appendix — but this is death! I think of mending
the appendix, and all the while here is death! Can it really be death?" Again terror seized him
and he gasped for breath. He leant down and began feeling for the matches, pressing with his
elbow on the stand beside the bed. It was in his way and hurt him, he grew furious with it,
pressed on it still harder, and upset it. Breathless and in despair he fell on his back, expecting
death to come immediately.

Meanwhile the visitors were leaving. Praskovya Fedorovna was seeing them off. She
heard something fall and came in.

"What has happened?"

"Nothing. I knocked it over accidentally."

She went out and returned with a candle. He lay there panting heavily, like a man who
has run a thousand yards, and stared upwards at her with a fixed look.

"What is it, Jean?"

"No ... o ... thing. I upset it." ("Why speak of it? She won't understand," he thought.)

And in truth she did not understand. She picked up the stand, lit the candle, and hurried
away to see another visitor off. When she came back he still lay on his back, looking upwards.

"What is it? Do you feel worse?"

"Yes."

She shook her head and sat down.

"Do you know, Jean, I think we must ask Leshchetitsky to come and see you here."

This meant calling in the famous specialist, regardless of expense. He smiled malig-
nantly and said "No." She remained a little longer and then went up to him and kissed his
forehead.

While she was kissing him he hated her from the bottom of his soul and with difficulty refrained from pushing her away.

"Good-night. Please God you'll sleep."

"Yes."

VI

Ivan Ilych saw that he was dying, and he was in continual despair.

In the depth of his heart he knew he was dying, but not only was he not accustomed to the thought, he simply did not and could not grasp it.

The syllogism he had learnt from Kiezewetter's Logic: "Caius is a man, men are mortal, therefore Caius is mortal," had always seemed to him correct as applied to Caius, but certainly not as applied to himself. That Caius — man in the abstract — was mortal, was perfectly correct, but he was not Caius, not an abstract man, but a creature quite quite separate from all others. He had been little Vanya, with a mamma and a papa, with Mitya and Volodya, with the toys, a coachman and a nurse, afterwards with Katenka and with all the joys, griefs, and delights of childhood, boyhood, and youth. What did Caius know of the smell of that striped leather ball Vanya had been so fond of? Had Caius kissed his mother's hand like that, and did the silk of her dress rustle so for Caius? Had he rioted like that at school when the pastry was bad? Had Caius been in love like that? Could Caius preside at a session as he did? "Caius really was mortal, and it was right for him to die; but for me, little Vanya, Ivan Ilych, with all my thoughts and emotions, it's altogether a different matter. It cannot be that I ought to die. That would be too terrible."

Such was his feeling.

"If I had to die like Caius I should have known it was so. An inner voice would have told me so, but there was nothing of the sort in me and I and all my friends felt that our case was quite different from that of Caius. And now here it is!" he said to himself. "It can't be. It's impossible! But here it is. How is this? How is one to understand it?"

He could not understand it, and tried to drive this false, incorrect, morbid thought away and to replace it by other proper and healthy thoughts. But that thought, and not the thought only but the reality itself, seemed to come and confront him.

And to replace that thought he called up a succession of others, hoping to find in them some support. He tried to get back into the former current of thoughts that had once screened the thought of death from him. But strange to say, all that had formerly shut off, hidden, and destroyed, his consciousness of death, no longer had that effect. Ivan Ilych now spent most of his time in attempting to re-establish that old current. He would say to himself: "I will take up my duties again — after all I used to live by them." And banishing all doubts he would go to the law courts, enter into conversation with his colleagues, and sit carelessly as was his wont, scanning the crowd with a thoughtful look and leaning both his emaciated arms on the arms of his oak chair; bending over as usual to a colleague and drawing his papers nearer he would interchange whispers with him, and then suddenly raising his eyes and sitting erect would pronounce certain words and open the proceedings. But suddenly in the midst of those proceedings the pain in his side, regardless of the stage the proceedings had reached, would begin its own gnawing work. Ivan Ilych would turn his attention to it and try to drive the thought of it away, but without success. *It* would come and stand before him and look at him, and he would be petrified and the light would die out of his eyes, and he would again begin asking himself whether *It* alone was true. And his colleagues and subordinates would see with surprise and distress that he, the brilliant and subtle judge, was becoming confused and making mistakes. He would shake himself, try to pull himself together, manage somehow to bring the sitting to a close, and return home with the sorrowful consciousness that his judicial labours could not as formerly hide from him what he wanted them to hide, and could not deliver him from *It*. And what was worst of all was that *It* drew his attention to itself not in order to make him take some action but only that he should look at *It*, look it straight in the face: look at it and without doing anything, suffer inexpressibly.

And to save himself from this condition Ivan Ilych looked for consolations — new screens — and new screens were found and for a while seemed to save him, but then they immediately fell to pieces or rather became transparent, as if *It* penetrated them and nothing could veil *It*.

In these latter days he would go into the drawing-room he had arranged — that drawing-room where he had fallen and for the sake of which (how bitterly ridiculous it seemed) he had sacrificed his life — for he knew that his illness originated with that knock. He would enter and see that something had scratched the polished table. He would look for the cause of this and find that it was the bronze ornamentation of an album, that had got bent. He would take up the expensive album which he had lovingly arranged, and feel vexed with his daughter and her friends for their untidiness — for the album was torn here and there and some of the photographs turned upside down. He would put it carefully in order and bend the ornamentation back into position. Then it would occur to him to place all those things in another corner of the room, near the plants. He would call the footman, but his daughter or wife would come to help him. They would not agree, and his wife would contradict him, and he would dispute and grow angry. But that was all right, for then he did not think about *It*. *It* was invisible.

But then, when he was moving something himself, his wife would say: "Let the servants do it. You will hurt yourself again." And suddenly *It* would flash through the screen and he would see it. It was just a flash, and he hoped it would disappear, but he would involuntarily pay attention to his side. "It sits there as before, gnawing just the same!" And he could no longer forget *It*, but could distinctly see it looking at him from behind the flowers. "What is it all for?"

"It really is so! I lost my life over that curtain as I might have done when storming a fort. Is that possible? How terrible and how stupid. It can't be true! It can't, but it is."

He would go to his study, lie down, and again be alone with *It*: face to face with *It*. And nothing could be done with *It* except to look at it and shudder.

VII

How it happened it is impossible to say because it came about step by step, unnoticed, but in the third month of Ivan Ilych's illness, his wife, his daughter, his son, his acquaintances, the doctors, the servants, and above all he himself, were aware that the whole interest he had for other people was whether he would soon vacate his place, and at last release the living from the discomfort caused by his presence and be himself released from his sufferings.

He slept less and less. He was given opium and hypodermic injections or morphine, but this did not relieve him. The dull depression he experienced in a somnolent condition at first gave him a little relief, but only as something new, afterwards it became as distressing as the pain itself or even more so.

Special foods were prepared for him by the doctors' orders, but all those foods became increasingly distasteful and disgusting to him.

For his excretions also special arrangements had to be made, and this was a torment to him every time — a torment from the uncleanliness, the unseemliness, and the smell, and from knowing that another person had to take part in it.

But just through this most unpleasant matter Ivan Ilych obtained comfort. Gerasim, the butler's young assistant, always came in to carry the things out. Gerasim was a clean, fresh peasant lad, grown stout on town food and always cheerful and bright. At first the sight of him, in his clean Russian peasant costume, engaged on that disgusting task embarrassed Ivan Ilych.

Once when he got up from the commode too weak to draw up his trousers, he dropped into a soft armchair and looked with horror at his bare, enfeebled thighs with the muscles so sharply marked on them.

Gerasim with a firm light tread, his heavy boots emitting a pleasant smell of tar and fresh winter air, came in wearing a clean Hessian apron, the sleeves of his print shirt tucked up over his strong bare young arms and refraining from looking at his sick master out of consideration for his feelings, and restraining the joy of life that beamed from his face, he went up to the commode.

"Gerasim!" said Ivan Ilych in a weak voice.

Gerasim started, evidently afraid he might have committed some blunder, and with a rapid movement turned his fresh, kind, simple young face which just showed the first downy signs of a beard.

"Yes, sir?"

"That must be very unpleasant for you. You must forgive me. I am helpless."

"Oh, why, sir," and Gerasim's eyes beamed and he showed his glistening white teeth, "what's a little trouble? It's a case of illness with you, sir."

And his deft strong hands did their accustomed task, and he went out of the room stepping lightly. Five minutes later he as lightly returned.

Ivan Ilych was still sitting in the same position in the armchair.

"Gerasim," he said when the latter had replaced the freshly-washed utensil. "Please come here and help me." Gerasim went up to him. "Lift me up. It is hard for me to get up, and I have sent Dmitri away."

Gerasim went up to him, grasped his master with his strong arms deftly but gently, in the same way that he stepped — lifted him, supported him with one hand, and with the other drew up his trousers and would have set him down again, but Ivan Ilych asked to be led to the sofa. Gerasim, without an effort and without apparent pressure, led him, almost lifting him, to the sofa and placed him on it.

"Thank you. How easily and well you do it all!"

Gerasim smiled again and turned to leave the room. But Ivan Ilych felt his presence such a comfort that he did not want to let him go.

"One thing more, please move up that chair. No, the other one — under my feet. It is easier for me when my feet are raised."

Gerasim brought the chair, set it down gently in place, and raised Ivan Ilych's legs on to it. It seemed to Ivan Ilych that he felt better while Gerasim was holding up his legs.

"It's better when my legs are higher," he said. "Place that cushion under them."

Gerasim did so. He again lifted the legs and placed them, and again Ivan Ilych felt better while Gerasim held his legs. When he set them down Ivan Ilych fancied he felt worse.

"Gerasim," he said. "Are you busy now?"

"Not at all, sir," said Gerasim, who had learnt from the townfolk how to speak to gentlefolk.

"What have you still to do?"

"What have I to do? I've done everything except chopping the logs for tomorrow."

"Then hold my legs up a bit higher, can you?"

"Of course I can. Why not?" And Gerasim raised his master's legs higher and Ivan Ilych thought that in that position he did not feel any pain at all.

"And how about the logs?"

"Don't trouble about that, sir. There's plenty of time."

Ivan Ilych told Gerasim to sit down and hold his legs, and began to talk to him. And strange to say it seemed to him that he felt better while Gerasim held his legs up.

After that Ivan Ilych would sometimes call Gerasim and get him to hold his legs on his shoulders, and he liked talking to him. Gerasim did it all easily, willingly, simply, and with a good nature that touched Ivan Ilych. Health, strength, and vitality in other people were offensive to him, but Gerasim's strength and vitality did not mortify but soothed him.

What tormented Ivan Ilych most was the deception, the lie, which for some reason they all accepted, that he was not dying but was simply ill, and that he only need keep quiet and undergo a treatment and then something very good would result. He however knew that do what they would nothing would come of it, only still more agonizing suffering and death. This deception tortured him — their not wishing to admit what they all knew and what he knew, but wanting to lie to him concerning his terrible condition, and wishing and forcing him to participate in that lie. Those lies — lies enacted over him on the eve of his death and destined to degrade this awful, solemn act to the level of their visitings, their curtains, their sturgeon for dinner — were a terrible agony for Ivan Ilych. And strangely enough, many times when they were going through their antics over him he had been within a hairbreadth of calling out to them: "Stop lying! You know and I know that I am dying. Then at least stop lying about it!" But he had never had the spirit to do it. The awful terrible act of his dying was, he could see, reduced by those about him to the level of a casual, unpleasant, and almost indecorous incident (as if someone entered a drawing-room diffusing an unpleasant odor) and this was done by that very decorum which he had served all his life long. He saw that no one felt for him, because no one even wished to grasp his position. Only Gerasim recognized it and pitied him. And so Ivan Ilych felt at ease only with him. He felt comforted when Gerasim supported his legs (sometimes all night long) and refused to go to bed, saying: "Don't you worry, Ivan Ilych. I'll get sleep enough later on," or when he suddenly became familiar and exclaimed: "If you weren't sick it would be another matter, but as it is, why should I grudge a little trouble?" Gerasim alone did not lie; everything showed that he alone understood the facts of the case and did not consider it necessary to disguise them, but simply felt sorry for his emaciated and enfeebled master. Once when Ivan Ilych was sending him away he even said straight out: "We shall all of us die, so why should I grudge a little trouble?" — expressing the fact that he did not think his work burdensome, because he was doing it for a dying man and hoped someone would do the same for him when his time came.

Apart from this lying, or because of it, what most tormented Ivan Ilych was that no one pitied him as he wished to be pitied. At certain moments after prolonged suffering he wished most of all (though he would have been ashamed to confess it) for someone to pity him as a sick child is pitied. He longed to be petted and comforted. He knew he was an important functionary, that he had a beard turning grey, and that therefore what he longed for was impossible, but still he longed for it. And in Gerasim's attitude toward him there was something akin to what he wished for, and so that attitude comforted him. Ivan Ilych wanted to be petted and cried over, and then his colleague Shebek would come, and instead of weeping and being petted, Ivan Ilych would assume a serious, severe, and profound air, and by force of habit would express his opinion on a decision of the Court of Cassation and would stubbornly insist on that view. This falsity around him and within him did more than anything else to poison his last days.

VIII

It was morning. He knew it was morning because Gerasim had gone, and Peter the footman had come and put out the candles, drawn back one of the curtains, and began quietly to tidy up. Whether it was morning or evening, Friday or Sunday, made no difference, it was all just the same: the gnawing, unmitigated, agonizing pain, never ceasing for an instant, the consciousness of life inexorably waning but not yet extinguished, the approach of that ever dreaded and hateful Death which was the only reality, and always the same falsity. What were days, weeks, hours, in such a case?

"Will you have some tea, sir?"

"He wants things to be regular, and wishes the gentlefolk to drink tea in the morning," thought Ivan Ilych, and only said "No."

"Wouldn't you like to move onto the sofa, sir?"

"He wants to tidy up the room, and I'm in the way. I am uncleanliness and disorder," he thought, and said only:

"No, leave me alone."

The man went on bustling about. Ivan Ilych stretched out his hand. Peter came up, ready to help.

"What is it, sir?"

"My watch."

Peter took the watch which was close at hand and gave it to his master.

"Half-past eight. Are they up?"

"No sir, except Vladimir Ivanich" (the son) "who has gone to school. Praskovya Fedorovna ordered me to wake her if you asked for her. Shall I do so?"

"No, there's no need to." "Perhaps I'd better have some tea," he thought, and added aloud: "Yes, bring me some tea."

Peter went out. Left alone Ivan Ilych dreaded being left alone. "How can I keep him here? Oh yes, my medicine." "Peter, give me my medicine." "Why not? Perhaps it may still do me some good." He took a spoonful and swallowed it. "No, it won't help. It's all tomfoolery, all deception," he decided as soon as he became aware of the familiar, sickly, hopeless taste. "No, I can't believe in it any longer. But the pain, why this pain? If it would only cease just for a moment!" And he moaned. Peter turned towards him. "It's all right. Go and fetch me some tea."

Peter went out. Left alone Ivan Ilych groaned not so much with pain, terrible though that was, as from mental anguish. Always and for ever the same, always these endless days and nights. If only it would come quicker! If only *what* would come quicker? Death, darkness? ... No, no! Anything rather than death!

When Peter returned with the tea on a tray, Ivan Ilych stared at him for a time in perplexity, not realizing who and what he was. Peter was disconcerted by that look and his embarrassment brought Ivan Ilych to himself.

"Oh, tea! All right, put it down. Only help me to wash and put on a clean shirt."

And Ivan Ilych began to wash. With pauses for rest, he washed his hands and then his face, cleaned his teeth, brushed his hair, and looked in the glass. He was terrified by what he saw, especially by the limp way in which his hair clung to his pallid forehead.

While his shirt was being changed he knew that he would be still more frightened at the sight of his body, so he avoided looking at it. Finally he was ready. He drew on a dressing-gown, wrapped himself in a plaid, and sat down in the armchair to take his tea. For a moment he felt refreshed, but as soon as he began to drink the tea he was again aware of the same taste, and the pain also returned. He finished it with an effort, and then lay down stretching out his legs, and dismissed Peter.

Always the same. Now a spark of hope flashes up, then a sea of despair rages, and always pain; always pain, always despair, and always the same. When alone he had a dreadful and distressing desire to call someone, but he knew beforehand that with others present it would be still worse. "Another dose of morphine — to lose consciousness. I will tell him, the doctor, that he must think of something else. It's impossible, impossible, to go on like this."

An hour and another pass like that. But now there is a ring at the door bell. Perhaps it's the doctor? It is. He comes in fresh, hearty, plump, and cheerful, with that look on his face that seems to say: "There now, you're in a panic about something, but we'll arrange it all for you directly!" The doctor knows this expression is out of place here, but he has put it on once for all and can't take it off — like a man who has put on a frock-coat in the morning to pay a round of calls.

The doctor rubs his hands vigorously and reassuringly.

"Brr! How cold it is! There's such a sharp frost; just let me warm myself!" he says, as if it were only a matter of waiting till he was warm, and then he would put everything right.

"Well now, how are you?"

Ivan Ilych feels that the doctor would like to say: "Well, how are our affairs?" but that even he feels that this would not do, and says instead: "What sort of a night have you had?"

Ivan Ilych looks at him as much as to say: "Are you really never ashamed of lying?" But the doctor does not wish to understand this question, and Ivan Ilych says: "Just as terrible as ever. The pain never leaves me and never subsides. If only something ... "

"Yes, you sick people are always like that. ... There, now I think I am warm enough. Even Praskovya Fedorovna, who is so particular, could find no fault with my temperature. Well, now I can say good-morning," and the doctor presses his patient's hand.

Then, dropping his former playfulness, he begins with a most serious face to examine the patient, feeling his pulse and taking his temperature, and then begins the sounding and auscultation.

Ivan Ilych knows quite well and definitely that all this is nonsense and pure deception, but when the doctor, getting down on his knee, leans over him, putting his ear first higher then lower, and performs various gymnastic movements over him with a significant expression on his face, Ivan Ilych submits to it all as he used to submit to the speeches of the lawyers, though he knew very well that they were all lying and why they were lying.

The doctor, kneeling on the sofa, is still sounding him when Praskovya Fedorovna's silk dress rustles at the door and she is heard scolding Peter for not having let her know of the doctor's arrival.

She comes in, kisses her husband, and at once proceeds to prove that she has been up a long time already, and only owing to a misunderstanding failed to be there when the doctor arrived.

Ivan Ilych looks at her, scans her all over, sets against her the whiteness and plumpness and cleanness of her hands and neck, the gloss of her hair, and the sparkle of her vivacious eyes. He hates her with his whole soul. And the thrill of hatred he feels for her makes him suffer from her touch.

Her attitude towards him and his disease is still the same. Just as the doctor had adopted a certain relation to his patient which he could not abandon, so had she formed one towards him — that he was not doing something he ought to do and was himself to blame, and that she reproached him lovingly for this — and she could not now change that attitude.

"You see he doesn't listen to me and doesn't take his medicine at the proper time. And above all he lies in a position that is no doubt bad for him — with his legs up."

She described how he made Gerasim hold his legs up.

The doctor smiled with a contemptuous affability that said: "What's to be done? These sick people do have foolish fancies of that kind, but we must forgive them."

When the examination was over the doctor looked at his watch, and then Praskovya Fedorovna announced to Ivan Ilych that it was of course as he pleased, but she had sent to-day for a celebrated specialist who would examine him and have a consultation with Michael Danilovich (their regular doctor).

"Please don't raise any objections. I am doing this for my own sake," she said ironically, letting it be felt that she was doing it all for his sake and only said this to leave him no right to refuse. He remained silent, knitting his brows. He felt that he was so surrounded and involved in a mesh of falsity that it was hard to unravel anything.

Everything she did for him was entirely for her own sake, and she told him she was doing for herself what she actually was doing for herself, as if that was so incredible that he must understand the opposite.

At half-past eleven the celebrated specialist arrived. Again the sounding began and the significant conversations in his presence and in another room, about the kidneys and the appendix, and the questions and answers, with such an air of importance that again, instead of the real question of life and death which now alone confronted him, the question arose of the kidney and appendix which were not behaving as they ought to and would now be attacked by Michael Danilovich and the specialist and forced to amend their ways.

The celebrated specialist took leave of him with a serious though not hopeless look, and in reply to the timid question Ivan Ilych, with eyes glistening with fear and hope, put to him as to whether there was a chance of recovery, said that he could not vouch for it but there was a possibility. The look of hope with which Ivan Ilych watched the doctor out was so pathetic that Praskovya Fedorovna, seeing it, even wept as she left the room to hand the doctor his fee.

The gleam of hope kindled by the doctor's encouragement did not last long. The same room, the same pictures, curtains, wall-paper, medicine bottles, were all there, and the same aching suffering body, and Ivan Ilych began to moan. They gave him a subcutaneous injection and he sank into oblivion.

It was twilight when he came to. They brought his dinner and he swallowed some beef tea with difficulty, and then everything was the same again and night was coming on.

After dinner, at seven o'clock, Praskovya Fedorovna came into the room in evening dress, her full bosom pushed up by her corset, and with traces of powder on her face. She had reminded him in the morning that they were going to the theatre. Sarah Bernhardt[10] was visiting the town and they had a box, which he had insisted on their taking. Now he had forgotten about it and her toilet offended him, but he concealed his vexation when he

---

[10] Sarah Bernhardt (1845–1923), celebrated French actress.

remembered that he had himself insisted on their securing a box and going because it would be an instructive and aesthetic pleasure for the children.

Praskovya Fedorovna came in, self-satisfied but yet with a rather guilty air. She sat down and asked how he was but, as he saw, only for the sake of asking and not in order to learn about it, knowing that there was nothing to learn — and then went on to what she really wanted to say: that she would not on any account have gone but that the box had been taken and Helen and their daughter were going, as well as Petrishchev (the examining magistrate, their daughter's fiancé) and that it was out of the question to let them go alone; but that she would have much preferred to sit with him for a while; and he must be sure to follow the doctor's orders while she was away.

"Oh, and Fedor Petrovich" (the fiancé) "would like to come in. May he? And Lisa?"

"All right."

Their daughter came in in full evening dress, her fresh young flesh exposed (making a show of that very flesh which in his own case caused so much suffering), strong, healthy, evidently in love, and impatient with illness, suffering, and death, because they interfered with her happiness.

Fedor Petrovich came in too, in evening dress, his hair curled *à la Capoul*,[11] a tight stiff collar round his long sinewy neck, an enormous white shirt-front and narrow black trousers tightly stretched over his strong thighs. He had one white glove tightly drawn on, and was holding his opera hat in his hand.

Following him the schoolboy crept in unnoticed, in a new uniform, poor little fellow, and wearing gloves. Terribly dark shadows showed under his eyes, the meaning of which Ivan Ilych knew well.

His son had always seemed pathetic to him, and now it was dreadful to see the boy's frightened look of pity. It seemed to Ivan Ilych that Vasya was the only one besides Gerasim who understood and pitied him.

They all sat down and again asked how he was. A silence followed. Lisa asked her mother about the opera-glasses, and there was an altercation between mother and daughter as to who had taken them and where they had been put. This occasioned some unpleasantness.

Fedor Petrovich inquired of Ivan Ilych whether he had ever seen Sarah Bernhardt. Ivan Ilych did not at first catch the question, but then replied: "No, have you seen her before?"

"Yes, in *Adrienne Lecouvreur*."

Praskovya Fedorovna mentioned some rôles in which Sarah Bernhardt was particularly good. Her daughter disagreed. Conversation sprang up as to the elegance and realism of her acting — the sort of conversation that is always repeated and is always the same.

In the midst of the conversation Fedor Petrovich glanced at Ivan Ilych and became silent. The others also looked at him and grew silent. Ivan Ilych was staring with glittering eyes straight before him, evidently indignant with them. This had to be rectified, but it was impossible to do so. The silence had to be broken, but for a time no one dared to break it and they all became afraid that the conventional deception would suddenly become obvious and the truth become plain to all. Lisa was the first to pluck up courage and break that silence, but by trying to hide what everybody was feeling, she betrayed it.

"Well, if we are going it's time to start," she said, looking at her watch, a present from her father, and with a faint and significant smile at Fedor Petrovich relating to something known only to them. She got up with a rustle of her dress.

---

[11] A fashionable hair style of the period.

They all rose, said good-night, and went away.

When they had gone it seemed to Ivan Ilych that he felt better; the falsity had gone with them. But the pain remained — that same pain and that same fear that made everything monotonously alike, nothing harder and nothing easier. Everything was worse.

Again minute followed minute and hour followed hour. Everything remained the same and there was no cessation. And the inevitable end of it all became more and more terrible.

"Yes, send Gerasim here," he replied to a question Peter asked.

IX

His wife returned late at night. She came in on tiptoe, but he heard her, opened his eyes, and made haste to close them again. She wished to send Gerasim away and to sit with him herself, but he opened his eyes and said: "No, go away."

"Are you in great pain?"

"Always the same."

"Take some opium."

He agreed and took some. She went away.

Till about three in the morning he was in a state of stupified misery. It seemed to him that he and his pain were being thrust into a narrow, deep black sack, but though they were pushed further and further in they could not be pushed to the bottom. And this, terrible enough in itself, was accompanied by suffering. He was frightened yet wanted to fall through the sack, he struggled but yet co-operated. And suddenly he broke through, fell, and regained consciousness. Gerasim was sitting at the foot of the bed dozing quietly and patiently, while he himself lay with his emaciated stockinged legs resting on Gerasim's shoulders; the same shaded candle was there and the same unceasing pain.

"Go away, Gerasim," he whispered.

"It's all right, sir. I'll stay a while."

"No. Go away."

He removed his legs from Gerasim's shoulders, turned sideways onto his arm, and felt sorry for himself. He only waited till Gerasim had gone into the next room and then restrained himself no longer but wept like a child. He wept on account of his helplessness, his terrible loneliness, the cruelty of man, the cruelty of God, and the absence of God.

"Why hast Thou done all this? Why hast Thou brought me here? Why, why dost Thou torment me so terribly?"

He did not expect an answer and yet wept because there was no answer and could be none. The pain again grew more acute, but he did not stir and did not call. He said to himself: "Go on! Strike me! But what is it for? What have I done to Thee? What is it for?"

Then he grew quiet and not only ceased weeping but even held his breath and became all attention. It was as though he were listening not to an audible voice but to the voice of his soul, to the current of thoughts arising within him.

"What is it you want?" was the first clear conception capable of expression in words, that he heard.

"What do you want? What do you want?" he repeated to himself.

"What do I want? To live and not to suffer," he answered.

And again he listened with such concentrated attention that even his pain did not distract him.

"To live? How?" asked his inner voice.

"Why, to live as I used to — well and pleasantly."

"As you lived before, well and pleasantly?" the voice repeated.

And in imagination he began to recall the best moments of his pleasant life. But strange to say none of those best moments of his pleasant life now seemed at all what they had then seemed — none of them except the first recollections of childhood. There, in childhood, there had been something really pleasant with which it would be possible to live if it could return. But the child who had experienced that happiness existed no longer, it was like a reminiscence of somebody else.

As soon as the period began which had produced the present Ivan Ilych, all that had then seemed joys now melted before his sight and turned into something trivial and often nasty.

And the further he departed from childhood and the nearer he came to the present the more worthless and doubtful were the joys. This began with the School of Law. A little that was really good was still found there — there was light-heartedness, friendship, and hope. But in the upper classes there had already been fewer of such good moments. Then during the first years of his official career, when he was in the service of the Governor, some pleasant moments again occurred: they were the memories of love for a woman. Then all became confused and there was still less of what was good; later on again there was still less that was good, and the further he went the less there was. His marriage, a mere accident, then the disenchantment that followed it, his wife's bad breath and the sensuality and hypocrisy: then that deadly official life and those preoccupations about money, a year of it, and two, and ten, and twenty, and always the same thing. And the longer it lasted the more deadly it became. "It is as if I had been going downhill while I imagined I was going up. And that is really what it was. I was going up in public opinion, but to the same extent life was ebbing away from me. And now it is all done and there is only death."

"Then what does it mean? Why? It can't be that life is so senseless and horrible. But if it really has been so horrible and senseless, why must I die and die in agony? There is something wrong!"

"Maybe I did not live as I ought to have done," it suddenly occurred to him. "But how could that be, when I did everything properly?" he replied, and immediately dismissed from his mind this, the sole solution of all the riddles of life and death, as something quite impossible.

"Then what do you want now? To live? Live how? Live as you lived in the law courts when the usher proclaimed 'The judge is coming!' The judge is coming, the judge!" he repeated to himself. "Here he is, the judge. But I am not guilty!" he exclaimed angrily. "What is it for?" And he ceased crying, but turning his face to the wall continued to ponder on the same question: Why, and for what purpose, is there all this horror? But however much he pondered he found no answer. And whenever the thought occurred to him, as it often did, that it all resulted from his not having lived as he ought to have done, he at once recalled the correctness of his whole life and dismissed so strange an idea.

X

Another fortnight passed. Ivan Ilych now no longer left his sofa. He would not lie in bed but lay on the sofa, facing the wall nearly all the time. He suffered ever the same unceasing agonies and in his loneliness pondered always on the same insoluble question: "What is this? Can it be that it is Death?" And the inner voice answered: "Yes, it is Death."

"Why these sufferings?" And the voice answered, "For no reason — they just are so." Beyond and besides this there was nothing.

From the very beginning of his illness, ever since he had first been to see the doctor, Ivan Ilych's life had been divided between two contrary and alternating moods: now it was despair and the expectation of this uncomprehended and terrible death, and now hope and an intently interested observation of the functioning of his organs. Now before his eyes there was only a kidney or an intestine that temporarily evaded its duty, and now only that incomprehensible and dreadful death from which it was impossible to escape.

These two states of mind had alternated from the very beginning of his illness, but the further it progressed the more doubtful and fantastic became the conception of the kidney, and the more real the sense of impending death.

He had but to call to mind what he had been three months before and what he was now, to call to mind with what regularity he had been going downhill, for every possibility of hope to be shattered.

Latterly during that loneliness in which he found himself as he lay facing the back of the sofa, a loneliness in the midst of a populous town and surrounded by numerous acquaintances and relations but that yet could not have been more complete anywhere — either at the bottom of the sea or under the earth — during that terrible loneliness Ivan Ilych had lived only in memories of the past. Pictures of his past rose before him one after another. They always began with what was nearest in time and then went back to what was most remote — to his childhood — and rested there. If he thought of the stewed prunes that had been offered him that day, his mind went back to the raw shrivelled French plums of his childhood, their peculiar flavour and the flow of saliva when he sucked their stones, and along with the memory of that taste came a whole series of memories of those days: his nurse, his brother, and their toys. "No, I mustn't think of that. ... It is too painful," Ivan Ilych said to himself, and brought himself back to the present — to the button on the back of the sofa and the creases in its morocco. "Morocco is expensive, but it does not wear well: there had been a quarrel about it. It was a different kind of quarrel and a different kind of morocco that time when we tore father's portfolio and were punished, and mamma brought us some tarts. ... " And again his thoughts dwelt on his childhood, and again it was painful and he tried to banish them and fix his mind on something else.

Then again together with that chain of memories another series passed through his mind — of how his illness had progressed and grown worse. There also the further back he looked the more life there had been. There had been more of what was good in life and more of life itself. The two merged together. "Just as the pain went on getting worse and worse so my life grew worse and worse," he thought. "There is one bright spot there at the back, at the beginning of life, and afterwards all becomes blacker and blacker and proceeds more and more rapidly — in inverse ratio to the square of the distance from death," thought Ivan Ilych. And the example of a stone falling downwards with increasing velocity entered his mind. Life, a series of increasing sufferings, flies further and further towards its end — the most terrible suffering. "I am flying. ... " He shuddered, shifted himself, and tried to resist, but was already aware that resistance was impossible, and again with eyes weary of gazing but unable to cease seeing what was before them, he stared at the back of the sofa and waited — awaiting that dreadful fall and shock and destruction.

"Resistance is impossible!" he said to himself. "If I could only understand what it is all for! But that too is impossible. An explanation would be possible if it could be said that I have not lived as I ought to. But it is impossible to say that," and he remembered all the legality, correctitude, and propriety of his life. "That at any rate can certainly not be admitted," he thought, and his lips smiled ironically as if someone could see that smile and be taken in by it. "There is no explanation! Agony, death. ... What for?"

XI

Another two weeks went by in this way and during that fortnight an event occurred that Ivan Ilych and his wife had desired. Petrishchev formally proposed. It happened in the evening. The next day Praskovya Fedorovna came into her husband's room considering how best to inform him of it, but that very night there had been a fresh change for the worse in his condition. She found him still lying on the sofa but in a different position. He lay on his back, groaning and staring fixedly straight in front of him.

She began to remind him of his medicines, but he turned his eyes towards her with such a look that she did not finish what she was saying; so great an animosity, to her in particular, did that look express.

"For Christ's sake let me die in peace!" he said.

She would have gone away, but just then their daughter came in and went up to say good morning. He looked at her as he had done at his wife, and in reply to her inquiry about his health said dryly that he would soon free them all of himself. They were both silent and after sitting with him for a while went away.

"Is it our fault?" Lisa said to her mother. "It's as if we were to blame! I am sorry for papa, but why should we be tortured?"

The doctor came at his usual time. Ivan Ilych answered "Yes" and "No," never taking his angry eyes from him, and at last said: "You know you can do nothing for me, so leave me alone."

"We can ease your sufferings."

"You can't even do that. Let me be."

The doctor went into the drawing-room and told Praskovya Fedorovna that the case was very serious and that the only resource left was opium to allay her husband's sufferings, which must be terrible.

It was true, as the doctor said, that Ivan Ilych's physical sufferings were terrible, but worse than the physical sufferings were his mental sufferings which were his chief torture.

His mental sufferings were due to the fact that that night, as he looked at Gerasim's sleepy, good-natured face with its prominent cheek-bones, the question suddenly occurred to him: "What if my whole life has really been wrong?"

It occurred to him that what had appeared perfectly impossible before, namely that he had not spent his life as he should have done, might after all be true. It occurred to him that his scarcely perceptible attempts to struggle against what was considered good by the most highly placed people, those scarcely noticeable impulses which he had immediately suppressed, might have been the real thing, and all the rest false. And his professional duties and the whole arrangement of his life and of his family, and all his social and official interests, might all have been false. He tried to defend all those things to himself and suddenly felt the weakness of what he was defending. There was nothing to defend.

"But if that is so," he said to himself, "and I am leaving this life with the consciousness that I have lost all that was given me and it is impossible to rectify it — what then?"

He lay on his back and began to pass his life in review in quite a new way. In the morning when he saw first his footman, then his wife, then his daughter, and then the doctor, their every word and movement confirmed to him the awful truth that had been revealed to him during the night. In them he saw himself — all that for which he had lived — and saw clearly that it was not real at all, but a terrible and huge deception which had hidden both life and death. This consciousness intensified his physical suffering tenfold. He groaned and tossed about, and pulled at his clothing which choked and stifled him. And he hated them on that account.

He was given a large dose of opium and became unconscious, but at noon his sufferings began again. He drove everybody away and tossed from side to side.

His wife came to him and said:

"Jean, my dear, do this for me. It can't do any harm and often helps. Healthy people often do it."

He opened his eyes wide.

"What? Take communion? Why? It's unnecessary! However. ... "

She began to cry.

"Yes, do, my dear. I'll send for our priest. He is such a nice man."

"All right. Very well," he muttered.

When the priest came and heard his confession, Ivan Ilych was softened and seemed to feel a relief from his doubts and consequently from his sufferings, and for a moment there came a ray of hope. He again began to think of the vermiform appendix and the possibility of correcting it. He received the sacrament with tears in his eyes.

When they laid him down again afterwards he felt a moment's ease, and the hope that he might live awoke in him again. He began to think of the operation that had been suggested to him. "To live! I want to live!" he said to himself.

His wife came in to congratulate him after his communion, and when uttering the usual conventional words she added:

"You feel better, don't you?"

Without looking at her he said "Yes."

Her dress, her figure, the expression of her face, the tone of her voice, all revealed the same thing. "This is wrong, it is not as it should be. All you have lived for and still live for is falsehood and deception, hiding life and death from you." And as soon as he admitted that thought, his hatred and his agonizing physical suffering again sprang up, and with that suffering a consciousness of the unavoidable, approaching end. And to this was added a new sensation of grinding shooting pain and a feeling of suffocation.

The expression of his face when he uttered that "yes" was dreadful. Having uttered it, he looked her straight in the eyes, turned on his face with a rapidity extraordinary in his weak state and shouted:

"Go away! Go away and leave me alone!"

XII

From that moment the screaming began that continued for three days, and was so terrible that one could not hear it through two closed doors without horror. At the moment he answered his wife he realized that he was lost, that there was no return, that the end had come, the very end, and his doubts were still unsolved and remained doubts.

"Oh! Oh! Oh!" he cried in various intonations. He had begun by screaming "I won't!" and continued screaming on the letter "o."

For three whole days, during which time did not exist for him, he struggled in that black sack into which he was being thrust by an invisible, resistless force. He struggled as a man condemned to death struggles in the hands of the executioner, knowing that he cannot save himself. And every moment he felt that despite all his efforts he was drawing nearer and nearer to what terrified him. He felt that his agony was due to his being thrust into that black hole and still more to his not being able to get right into it. He was hindered from getting into it by his conviction that his life had been a good one. That very justification of his life held him fast and prevented his moving forward, and it caused him most torment of all.

Suddenly some force struck him in the chest and side, making it still harder to breathe, and he fell through the hole and there at the bottom was a light. What had happened to him was like the sensation one sometimes experiences in a railway carriage when one thinks one is going backwards while one is really going forwards and suddenly becomes aware of the real direction.

"Yes, it was all not the right thing," he said to himself, "but that's no matter. It can be done. But what *is* the right thing?" he asked himself, and suddenly grew quiet.

This occurred at the end of the third day, two hours before his death. Just then his schoolboy son had crept softly in and gone up to the bedside. The dying man was still screaming desperately and waving his arms. His hand fell on the boy's head, and the boy caught it, pressed it to his lips, and began to cry.

At that very moment Ivan Ilych fell through and caught sight of the light, and it was revealed to him that though his life had not been what it should have been, this could still be rectified. He asked himself, "What *is* the right thing?" and grew still, listening. Then he felt that someone was kissing his hand. He opened his eyes, looked at his son, and felt sorry for him. His wife came up to him and he glanced at her. She was gazing at him open-mouthed, with undried tears on her nose and cheek and a despairing look on her face. He felt sorry for her too.

"Yes, I am making them wretched," he thought. "They are sorry, but it will be better for them when I die." He wished to say this but had not the strength to utter it. "Besides, why speak? I must act," he thought. With a look at his wife he indicated his son and said: "Take him away ... sorry for him ... sorry for you too. ... " He tried to add, "forgive me," but said "forego" and waved his hand, knowing that He whose understanding mattered would understand.

And suddenly it grew clear to him that what had been oppressing him and would not leave him was all dropping away at once from two sides, from ten sides, and from all sides. He was sorry for them, he must act so as not to hurt them: release them and free himself from these sufferings. "How good and how simple!" he thought. "And the pain?" he asked himself. "What has become of it? Where are you, pain?"

He turned his attention to it.

"Yes, here it is. Well, what of it? Let the pain be."

"And death ... where is it?"

He sought his former accustomed fear of death and did not find it. "Where is it? What death?" There was no fear because there was no death.

In place of death there was light.

"So that's what it is!" he suddenly exclaimed aloud. "What joy!"

To him all this happened in a single instant, and the meaning of that instant did not change. For those present his agony continued for another two hours. Something rattled in his throat, his emaciated body twitched, then the gasping and rattle became less and less frequent.

"It is finished!" said someone near him.

He heard these words and repeated them in his soul.

"Death is finished," he said to himself. "It is no more!"

He drew in a breath, stopped in the midst of a sigh, stretched out, and died.

QUESTIONS

1. How do Ivan Ilych's colleagues react to the news of his death? Are their reactions believable? What about those of his widow?

2. "Ivan Ilych's life had been most simple and most ordinary and therefore most terrible." Is this the point of the story? Why "therefore"?

3. Félicité in "A Simple Heart" certainly lived an "ordinary" life; yet Flaubert portrayed her as happy and saintly. What distinguishes her simplicity from Ivan's?

4. Is the author telling us that we must not waste our lives? How should Ivan have acted differently? Could he have done so?

5. Is the flashback technique (opening with the news of Ivan's death and then going back to the story of his life) effective here? Doesn't it destroy suspense to know in advance that Ivan died?

6. The tone of this story is consistently somber. Does Tolstoy sustain this tone by language and imagery, or by the incidents and characters he creates? Do the characters around Ivan — look at Gerasim in particular — help color his character?

7. The deathbed scene is detailed, realistic, and painful. Does the moment when Ivan exclaims, "So that's what it is! ... What joy!" redeem the portrayal from utter darkness? Does Tolstoy mean to depress us with death's reality? Can you think of any other reason for his treatment of Ivan's deathbed scene?

MARK TWAIN
(SAMUEL L. CLEMENS)

The Celebrated Jumping Frog
of Calaveras County

In compliance with the request of a friend of mine, who wrote me from the East, I called on good-natured, garrulous old Simon Wheeler, and inquired about my friend's friend, Leonidas W. Smiley, as requested to do, and I hereunto append the result. I have a lurking suspicion that *Leonidas* W. Smiley is a myth; that my friend never knew such a personage; and that he only conjectured that if I asked old Wheeler about him, it would remind him of his infamous *Jim* Smiley, and he would go to work and bore me to death with some exasperating reminiscence of him as long and as tedious as it should be useless to me. If that was the design, it succeeded.

I found Simon Wheeler dozing comfortably by the bar-room stove of the dilapidated tavern in the decayed mining camp of Angel's, and I noticed that he was fat and bald-headed, and had an expression of winning gentleness and simplicity upon his tranquil countenance. He roused up, and gave me good day. I told him that a friend of mine had commissioned me to make some inquiries about a cherished companion of his boyhood named *Leonidas* W. Smiley — a young minister of the Gospel, who he had heard was at one time a resident of Angel's Camp. I added that if Mr. Wheeler could tell me anything about this Rev. Leonidas W. Smiley, I would feel under many obligations to him.

Simon Wheeler backed me into a corner and blockaded me there with his chair, and then sat down and reeled off the monotonous narrative which follows this paragraph. He never smiled, he never frowned, he never changed his voice from the gentle-flowing key to which he tuned his initial sentence, he never betrayed the slightest suspicion of enthusiasm; but all through the interminable narrative there ran a vein of impressive earnestness and sincerity, which showed me plainly that, so far from his imagining that there was anything ridiculous or funny about his story, he regarded it as a really important matter, and admired its two heroes as men of transcendent genius in *finesse*. I let him go on in his own way, and never interrupted him once.

"Rev. Leonidas W. H'm, Reverend Le — well, there was a feller here once by the name of *Jim* Smiley, in the winter of '49 — or maybe it was the spring of '50 — I don't recollect exactly, somehow, though what makes me think it was one or the other is because I remember the big flume warn't finished when he first came to the camp; but anyway, he was the curiousest man about always betting on anything that turned up you ever see, if he could get anybody to bet on the other side; and if he couldn't he'd change sides. Any way that suited the other man would suit *him* — any way just so's he got a bet, *he* was satisfied. But still he was lucky, uncommon lucky; he most always come out winner. He was always ready and laying for a chance; there couldn't be no solit'ry thing mentioned but that feller'd offer to bet on it, and take ary side you please, as I was just telling you. If there was a horse-race, you'd find him flush or you'd find him busted at the end of it; if there was a dog-fight, he'd bet on it; if there was a cat-fight, he'd bet on it; if there was a chicken fight, he'd bet on it; why, if there was two birds setting on a fence he would bet you which one would fly first; or if there was a camp meeting, he would be there reg'lar to bet on Parson Walker, which he judged to be the best exhorter about here, and so he was too, and a good man. If he even see a straddle-bug start to go anywheres, he would bet you how long it would take him to get to — to wherever he was going to, and if you took him up, he would foller that straddle-bug to Mexico but what he would find out where he was bound for and how long he was on the road. Lots of the boys here has seen that Smiley, and can tell you about him. Why, it never made no difference to *him* — he'd bet on *any* thing — the dangdest feller. Parson Walker's wife laid very sick once, for a good while and it seemed as if they warn't going to save her; but one morning he come in, and Smiley up and asked him how she was, and he said she was considerable better — thank the Lord for his inf'nite mercy — and coming on so smart that with the blessing of Prov'dence she'd get well yet; and Smiley, before he thought, says, 'Well, I'll resk two-and-a-half she don't anyway.'

"Thish-yer Smiley had a mare — the boys called her the fifteen-minute nag, but that was only in fun, you know, because of course she was faster than that — and he used to win money on that horse, for all she was so slow and always had the asthma, or the distemper, or the consumption, or something of that kind. They used to give her two or three hundred yards' start, and then pass her under way; but always at the fag end of the race she'd get excited and desperate like, and come cavorting and straddling up, and scattering her legs around limber, sometimes in the air, and sometimes out to one side among the fences, and kicking up m-o-r-e dust and raising m-o-r-e racket with her coughing and sneezing and blowing her nose — and *always* fetch up at the stand just about a neck ahead, as near as you could cipher it down.

"And he had a little small bull-pup, that to look at him you'd think he warn't worth a cent but to set around and look ornery and lay for a chance to steal something. But as soon as money was up on him he was a different dog; his under-jaw'd begin to stick out like the fo'castle of a steamboat, and his teeth would uncover and shine like the furnaces. And a dog might tackle him and bully-rag him, and bite him, and throw him over his shoulder two or three times, and Andrew Jackson — which was the name of the pup — Andrew Jackson would never let on but what *he* was satisfied, and hadn't expected nothing else — and the bets being doubled and doubled on the other side all the time, till the money was all up; and then all of a sudden he would grab that other dog jest by the j'int of his hind leg and freeze to it — not chaw, you understand, but only just grip and hang on till they throwed up the sponge, if it was a year. Smiley always come out winner on that pup, till he harnessed a dog once that didn't have no hind legs, because they'd been sawed off in a circular saw, and when the thing had gone along far enough, and the money was all up, and he come to make a snatch for his pet holt, he see in a minute how he'd been imposed on, and how the other dog had him in the door, so to speak, and he 'peared surprised, and then he looked sorter discouraged-like, and didn't try no more to win the fight, and so he got shucked out bad. He give Smiley a look, as much as to say his heart was broke, and it was *his* fault, for putting up a dog that hadn't no hind legs for him to take holt of, which was his main dependence in a fight, and then he limped off a piece and laid down and died. It was a good pup, was that Andrew Jackson, and would have made a name for hisself if he'd lived, for the stuff was in him and he had genius — I know it, because he hadn't no opportunities to speak of, and it don't stand to reason that a dog could make such a fight as he could under them circumstances if he hadn't no talent. It always makes me feel sorry when I think of that last fight of his'n, and the way it turned out.

"Well, thish-yer Smiley had rat-tarriers, and chicken cocks, and tom-cats and all them kind of things, till you couldn't rest, and you couldn't fetch nothing for him to bet on but he'd match you. He ketched a frog one day, and took him home, and said he cal'lated to educate him; and so he never done nothing for three months but set in his back yard and learn that frog to jump. And you bet you he *did* learn him, too. He'd give him a little punch behind, and the next minute you'd see that frog whirling in the air like a doughnut — see him turn one summerset, or maybe a couple, if he got a good start, and come down flat-footed and all right, like a cat. He got him up so in the matter of ketching flies, and kep' him in practice so constant, that he'd nail a fly every time as fur as he could see him. Smiley said all a frog wanted was education, and he could do 'most anything — and I believe him. Why, I've seen him set Dan'l Webster down here on this floor — Dan'l Webster was the name of the frog — and sing out, 'Flies, Dan'l, flies!' and quicker'n you could wink he'd spring straight up and snake a fly off'n the counter there, and flop down on the floor ag'in as solid as a gob of mud, and fall to scratching the side of his head with his hind foot as indifferent as if he hadn't no idea he'd been doin' any more'n any frog might do. You never see a frog so modest and straightfor'ard as he was, for all he was so gifted. And when it come to fair and square jumping on a dead level, he could get over more ground at one straddle than any animal of his breed you ever see. Jumping on a dead level was his strong suit, you understand; and when it come to that, Smiley would ante up money on him as long as he had a red. Smiley was monstrous proud of his frog, and well he might be, for fellers that had traveled and been everywheres, all said he laid over any frog that ever *they* see.

"Well, Smiley kep' the beast in a little lattice box, and he used to fetch him down-town sometimes and lay for a bet. One day a feller — a stranger in the camp, he was — come acrost him with his box, and says:

"'What might it be that you've got in the box?'

"And Smiley says, sorter indifferent-like, 'It might be a parrot, or it might be a canary, maybe, but it ain't — it's only just a frog.'

"And the feller took it, and looked at it careful, and turned it round this way and that, and says, 'H'm — so 'tis. Well, what's *he* good for?'

"'Well,' Smiley says, easy and careless, 'he's good enough for *one* thing, I should judge — he can outjump any frog in Calaveras County.'

"The feller took the box again, and took another long, particular look, and give it back to Smiley, and says, very deliberate, 'Well,' he says, 'I don't see no p'ints about that frog that's any better'n any other frog.'

"'Maybe you don't,' Smiley says. 'Maybe you understand frogs and maybe you don't understand 'em; maybe you've had experience, and maybe you ain't only a amature, as it were. Anyways, I've got *my* opinion, and I'll resk forty dollars that he can outjump any frog in Calaveras County.'

"And the feller studied a minute, and then says, kinder sadlike, 'Well, I'm only a stranger here, and I ain't got no frog; but if I had a frog, I'd bet you.'

"And then Smiley says, 'That's all right — that's all right — if you'll hold my box a minute, I'll go and get you a frog.' And so the feller took the box, and put up his forty dollars along with Smiley's, and set down to wait.

"So he set there a good while thinking and thinking to himself, and then he got the frog out and prized his mouth open and took a teaspoon and filled him full of quail-shot — filled him pretty near up to his chin — and set him on the floor. Smiley he went to the swamp and slopped around in the mud for a long time, and finally he ketched a frog, and fetched him in, and give him to this feller, and says:

"'Now, if you're ready, set him alongside of Dan'l, with his fore paws just even with Dan'l's, and I'll give the word.' Then he says, 'One — two — three — *git!*' and him and the feller touched up the frogs from behind, and the new frog hopped off lively, but Dan'l give a heave, and hysted up his shoulders — so — like a Frenchman, but it warn't no use — he couldn't budge; he was planted as solid as a church, and he couldn't no more stir than if he was anchored out. Smiley was a good deal surprised, and he was disgusted too, but he didn't have no idea what the matter was, of course.

"The feller took the money and started away; and when he was going out at the door, he sorter jerked his thumb over his shoulder — so — at Dan'l, and says again, very deliberate, 'Well,' he says, '*I* don't see no p'ints about that frog that's any better'n any other frog.'

"Smiley he stood scratching his head and looking down at Dan'l a long time, and at last he says, 'I do wonder what in the nation that frog throw'd off for — I wonder if there ain't something the matter with him — he 'pears to look mighty baggy, somehow.' And he ketched Dan'l by the nape of the neck, and hefted him, and says, 'Why blame my cats if he don't weigh five pound!' and turned him upside down and he belched out a double handful of shot. And then he see how it was, and he was the maddest man — he set the frog down and took out after that feller, but he never ketched him. And — "

[Here Simon Wheeler heard his name called from the front yard, and got up to see what was wanted.] And turning to me as he moved away, he said: "Just set where you are, stranger, and rest easy — I ain't going to be gone a second."

But, by your leave, I did not think that a continuation of the history of the enterprising vagabond *Jim* Smiley would be likely to afford me much information concerning the Rev. *Leonidas* W. Smiley, and so I started away.

At the door I met the sociable Wheeler returning, and he buttonholed me and recommenced:

"Well, thish-yer Smiley had a yaller one-eyed cow that didn't have no tail, only just a short stump like a bannanner, and — "

However, lacking both time and inclination, I did not wait to hear about the afflicted cow, but took my leave.

QUESTIONS

1. There are two narrators in this story, the first unnamed, the second Simon Wheeler, who tells us about the jumping frog. What differences can you see between them? Do you assume that Twain is the first? Why?

2. It takes Twain a while to get around to the story of Dan'l Webster. Does what comes before reduce or add to your pleasure?

3. What is the effect of giving the frog a name? Does Dan'l Webster have any other particularizing characteristics? any human ones?

4. What does the use of dialect contribute to Wheeler's tale?

5. Can you show that this "tall tale" is not meant to be a plausible story? What is your evidence?

6. Is the attraction of this story in its incidents, language, and imagery or in the characters portrayed?

7. How would you describe Wheeler's attitude toward the first narrator?

AMBROSE BIERCE ≡≡≡≡

Moxon's Master

"Are you serious? — do you really believe that a machine thinks?"

I got no immediate reply; Moxon was apparently intent upon the coals in the grate, touching them deftly here and there with the fire-poker till they signified a sense of his attention by a brighter glow. For several weeks I had been observing in him a growing habit of delay in answering even the most trivial of commonplace questions. His air, however, was that of preoccupation rather than deliberation; one might have said that he had "something on his mind."

Presently he said:

"What is a 'machine'? The word has been variously defined. Here is one definition from a popular dictionary: 'Any instrument or organization by which power is applied and made effective, or a desired effect produced.' Well, then, is not a man a machine? And you will admit that he thinks — or thinks he thinks."

"If you do not wish to answer my question," I said, rather testily, "why not say so? — all that you say is mere evasion. You know well enough that when I say 'machine' I do not mean a man, but something that man has made and controls."

"When it does not control him," he said, rising abruptly and looking out of a window, whence nothing was visible in the blackness of a stormy night. A moment later he turned about and with a smile said: "I beg your pardon; I had no thought of evasion. I considered the dictionary man's unconscious testimony suggestive and worth something in the discussion. I can give your question a direct answer easily enough; I do believe that a machine thinks about the work that it is doing."

That was direct enough, certainly. It was not altogether pleasing, for it tended to confirm a sad suspicion that Moxon's devotion to study and work in his machine-shop had not been good for him. I knew, for one thing, that he suffered from insomnia, and that is no light affliction. Had it affected his mind? His reply to my question seemed to me then evidence that it had; perhaps I should think differently about it now. I was younger then, and among the blessings that are not denied to youth is ignorance. Incited by that great stimulant to controversy, I said:

"And what, pray, does it think with — in the absence of a brain?"

The reply, coming with less than his customary delay, took his favorite form of counter-interrogation:

"With what does a plant think — in the absence of a brain?"

"Ah, plants also belong to the philosopher class! I should be pleased to know some of their conclusions; you may omit the premises."

"Perhaps," he replied, apparently unaffected by my foolish irony, "you may be able to infer their convictions from their acts. I will spare you the familiar examples of the sensitive mimosa, the several insectivorous flowers and those whose stamens bend down and shake their pollen upon the entering bee in order that he may fertilize their distant mates. But observe this. In an open spot in my garden I planted a climbing vine. When it was barely above the surface I set a stake into the soil a yard away. The vine at once made for it, but as it was about to reach it after several days I removed it a few feet. The vine at once altered in course, making an acute angle, and again made for the stake. This manœuvre was repeated several times, but finally, as if discouraged, the vine abandoned the pursuit and ignoring further attempts to divert it traveled to a small tree, further away, which it climbed.

"Roots of the eucalyptus will prolong themselves incredibly in search of moisture. A well-known horticulturist relates that one entered an old drain pipe and followed it until it came to a break, where a section of the pipe had been removed to make way for a stone wall that had been built across its course. The root left the drain and followed the wall until it found an opening where a stone had fallen out. It crept through and following the other side of the wall back to the drain, entered the unexplored part and resumed its journey."

"And all this?"

"Can you miss the significance of it? It shows the consciousness of plants. It proves that they think."

"Even if it did — what then? We were speaking, not of plants, but of machines. They may be composed partly of wood — wood that has no longer vitality — or wholly of metal. Is thought an attribute also of the mineral kingdom?"

"How else do you explain the phenomena, for example, of crystallization?"

"I do not explain them."

"Because you cannot without affirming what you wish to deny, namely, intelligent cooperation among the constituent elements of the crystals. When soldiers form lines, or hollow squares, you call it reason. When wild geese in flight take the form of a letter V you say instinct. When the homogeneous atoms of a mineral, moving freely in solution, arrange themselves into shapes mathematically perfect, or particles of frozen moisture into the symmetrical and beautiful forms of snowflakes, you have nothing to say. You have not even invented a name to conceal your heroic unreason."

Moxon was speaking with unusual animation and earnestness. As he paused I heard in an adjoining room known to me as his "machine-shop," which no one but himself was permitted to enter, a singular thumping sound, as of some one pounding upon a table with an open hand. Moxon heard it at the same moment and, visibly agitated, rose and hurriedly passed into the room whence it came. I thought it odd that any one else should be in there, and my interest in my friend — with doubtless a touch of unwarrantable curiosity — led me to listen intently, though, I am happy to say, not at the keyhole. There were confused sounds, as of a struggle or scuffle; the floor shook. I distinctly heard hard breathing and a hoarse whisper which said "Damn you!" Then all was silent, and presently Moxon reappeared and said, with a rather sorry smile:

"Pardon me for leaving you so abruptly. I have a machine in there that lost its temper and cut up rough."

Fixing my eyes steadily upon his left cheek, which was traversed by four parallel excoriations showing blood, I said:

"How would it do to trim its nails?"

I could have spared myself the jest; he gave it not attention, but seated himself in the chair that he had left and resumed the interrupted monologue as if nothing had occurred:

"Doubtless you do not hold with those (I need not name them to a man of your reading) who have taught that all matter is sentient, that every atom is a living, feeling, conscious being. *I* do. There is no such thing as dead, inert matter; it is all alive; all instinct with force, actual and potential; all sensitive to the same forces in its environment and susceptible to the contagion of higher and subtler ones residing in such superior organisms as it may be brought into relation with, as those of man when he is fashioning it into an instrument of his will. It absorbs something of his intelligence and purpose — more of them in proportion to the complexity of the resulting machine and that of its work.

"Do you happen to recall Herbert Spencer's[1] definition of 'Life'? I read it thirty years ago. He may have altered it afterward, for anything I know, but in all that time I have been unable to think of a single word that could profitably be changed or added or removed. It seems to me not only the best definition, but the only possible one.

" 'Life,' he says, 'is a definite combination of heterogeneous changes, both simultaneous and successive, in correspondence with external coexistences and sequences.' "

"That defines the phenomenon," I said, "but gives no hint of its cause."

"That," he replied, "is all that any definition can do. As Mill[2] points out, we know nothing of cause except as an antecedent — nothing of effect except as a consequent. Of certain phenomena, one never occurs without another, which is dissimilar: the first in point of time we call cause, the second, effect. One who had many times seen a rabbit pursued by a dog, and had never seen rabbits and dogs otherwise, would think the rabbit the cause of the dog.

"But I fear," he added, laughing naturally enough, "that my rabbit is leading me a long way from the track of my legitimate quarry: I'm indulging in the pleasure of the chase for its own sake. What I want you to observe is that in Herbert Spencer's definition of 'life' the activity of a machine is included — there is nothing in the definition that is not applicable to it. According to this sharpest of observers and deepest of thinkers, if a man during his period of activity is alive, so is a machine when in operation. As an inventor and constructor of machines I know that to be true."

Moxon was silent for a long time, gazing absently into the fire. It was growing late and I thought it time to be going, but somehow I did not like the notion of leaving him in that isolated house, all alone except for the presence of some person of whose nature my conjectures could go no further than that it was unfriendly, perhaps malign. Leaning toward him and looking earnestly into his eyes while making a motion with my hand through the door of his workshop I said:

"Moxon, whom have you in there?"

Somewhat to my surprise he laughed lightly and answered without hesitation:

"Nobody; the incident that you have in mind was caused by my folly in leaving a machine in action with nothing to act upon, while I undertook the interminable task of enlightening your understanding. Do you happen to know that Consciousness is the creature of Rhythm?"

---

[1] Herbert Spencer (1820–1903), English philosopher, much influenced by the theory of evolution.

[2] John Stuart Mill (1806–1873), English philosopher and economist.

"O bother them both!" I replied, rising and laying hold of my overcoat. "I'm going to wish you good night; and I'll add the hope that the machine which you inadvertently left in action will have her gloves on the next time you think it needful to stop her."

Without waiting to observe the effect of my shot I left the house.

Rain was falling, and the darkness was intense. In the sky beyond the crest of a hill toward which I groped my way along precarious plank sidewalks and across miry, unpaved streets I could see the faint glow of the city's lights, but behind me nothing was visible but a single window of Moxon's house. It glowed with what seemed to me a mysterious and fateful meaning. I knew it was an uncurtained aperture in my friend's "machine-shop," and I had little doubt that he had resumed the studies interrupted by his duties as my instructor in mechanical consciousness and the fatherhood of Rhythm. Odd, and in some degree humorous, as his convictions seemed to me at that time, I could not wholly divest myself of the feeling that they had some tragic relation to his life and character — perhaps to his destiny — although I no longer entertained the notion that they were the vagaries of a disordered mind. Whatever might be thought of his views, his exposition of them was too logical for that. Over and over, his last words came back to me: "Consciousness is the creature of Rhythm." Bald and terse as the statement was, I now found it infinitely alluring. At each recurrence it broadened in meaning and deepened in suggestion. Why, here, (I thought) is something upon which to found a philosophy. If consciousness is the product of rhythm all things *are* conscious, for all have motion, and all motion is rhythmic. I wondered if Moxon knew the significance and breadth of his thought — the scope of this momentous generalization; or had he arrived at his philosophic faith by the tortuous and uncertain road of observation?

That faith was then new to me, and all Moxon's expounding had failed to make me a convert; but now it seemed as if a great light shone about me, like that which fell upon Saul of Tarsus[3]; and out there in the storm and darkness and solitude I experienced what Lewes[4] calls "The endless variety and excitement of philosophic thought." I exulted in a new sense of knowledge, a new pride of reason. My feet seemed hardly to touch the earth; it was as if I were uplifted and borne through the air by invisible wings.

Yielding to an impulse to seek further light from him whom I now recognized as my master and guide, I had unconsciously turned about, and almost before I was aware of having done so found myself again at Moxon's door. I was drenched with rain, but felt no discomfort. Unable in my excitement to find the doorbell I instinctively tried the knob. It turned and, entering, I mounted the stairs to the room that I had so recently left. All was dark and silent; Moxon, as I had supposed, was in the adjoining room — the "machine-shop." Groping along the wall until I found the communicating door I knocked loudly several times, but got no response, which I attributed to the uproar outside, for the wind was blowing a gale and dashing the rain against the thin walls in sheets. The drumming upon the shingle roof spanning the unceiled room was loud and incessant.

I had never been invited into the machine-shop — had, indeed, been denied admittance, as had all others, with one exception, a skilled metal worker, of whom no one knew anything except that his name was Haley and his habit silence. But in my spiritual exaltation, discretion and civility were forgotten and I opened the door. What I saw took all philosophical speculation out of me in short order.

---

[3] The *Acts of the Apostles* tells us that Saul was violently converted from persecuting Christians when a bright light struck him from his horse. Thereafter, he was known as St. Paul, Apostle to the Gentiles.

[4] George Henry Lewes (1817–1878), English writer and literary critic.

Moxon sat facing me at the farther side of a small table upon which a single candle made all the light that was in the room. Opposite him, his back toward me, sat another person. On the table between the two was a chessboard; the men were playing. I knew little of chess, but as only a few pieces were on the board it was obvious that the game was near its close. Moxon was intensely interested — not so much, it seemed to me, in the game as in his antagonist, upon whom he had fixed so intent a look that, standing though I did directly in the line of his vision, I was altogether unobserved. His face was ghastly white, and his eyes glittered like diamonds. Of his antagonist I had only a back view, but that was sufficient; I should not have cared to see his face.

He was apparently not more than five feet in height, with proportions suggesting those of a gorilla — a tremendous breadth of shoulders, thick, short neck and broad, squat head, which had a tangled growth of black hair and was topped with a crimson fez. A tunic of the same color, belted tightly to the waist, reached the seat — apparently a box — upon which he sat; his legs and feet were not seen. His left forearm appeared to rest in his lap; he moved his pieces with his right hand, which seemed disproportionately long.

I had shrunk back and now stood a little to one side of the doorway and in shadow. If Moxon had looked farther than the face of his opponent he could have observed nothing now, except that the door was open. Something forbade me either to enter or to retire, a feeling — I know not how it came — that I was in the presence of an imminent tragedy and might serve my friend by remaining. With a scarcely conscious rebellion against the indelicacy of the act I remained.

The play was rapid. Moxon hardly glanced at the board before making his moves, and to my unskilled eye seemed to move the piece most convenient to his hand, his motions in doing so being quick, nervous and lacking in precision. The response of his antagonist, while equally prompt in the inception, was made with a slow, uniform, mechanical and, I thought, somewhat theatrical movement of the arm, that was a sore trial to my patience. There was something unearthly about it all, and I caught myself shuddering. But I was wet and cold.

Two or three times after moving a piece the stranger slightly inclined his head, and each time I observed that Moxon shifted his king. All at once the thought came to me that the man was dumb. And then that he was a machine — an automaton chess-player! Then I remembered that Moxon had once spoken to me of having invented such a piece of mechanism, though I did not understand that it had actually been constructed. Was all his talk about the consciousness and intelligence of machines merely a prelude to eventual exhibition of this device — only a trick to intensify the effect of its mechanical action upon me in my ignorance of its secret?

A fine end, this, of all my intellectual transports — my "endless variety and excitement of philosophic thought!" I was about to retire in disgust when something occurred to hold my curiosity. I observed a shrug of the thing's great shoulders, as if it were irritated: and so natural was this — so entirely human — that in my new view of the matter it startled me. Nor was that all, for a moment later it struck the table sharply with its clenched hand. At that gesture Moxon seemed even more startled than I: he pushed his chair a little backward, as in alarm.

Presently Moxon, whose play it was, raised his hand high above the board, pounced upon one of his pieces like a sparrow-hawk and with the exclamation "checkmate!" rose quickly to his feet and stepped behind his chair. The automaton sat motionless.

The wind had now gone down, but I heard, at lessening intervals and progressively louder, the rumble and roll of thunder. In the pauses between, I now became conscious of a low humming or buzzing which, like the thunder, grew momentarily louder and more distinct. It seemed to come from the body of the automaton, and was unmistakably a whirring of wheels. It gave me the impression of a disordered mechanism which had escaped the repressive and regulating action of some controlling part — an effect such as might be expected if a pawl should be jostled from the teeth of a ratchet-wheel. But before I had time for much conjecture as to its nature my attention was taken by the strange motions of the automaton itself. A slight but continuous convulsion appeared to have possession of it. In body and head it shook like a man with palsy or an ague chill, and the motion augmented every moment until the entire figure was in violent agitation. Suddenly it sprang to its feet and with a movement almost too quick for the eye to follow shot forward across table and chair, with both arms thrust forth to their full length — the posture and lunge of a diver. Moxon tried to throw himself backward out of reach, but he was too late: I saw the horrible thing's hands close upon his throat, his own clutch its wrists. Then the table was overturned, the candle thrown to the floor and extinguished, and all was black dark. But the noise of the struggle was dreadfully distinct, and most terrible of all were the raucous, squawking sounds made by the strangled man's efforts to breathe. Guided by the infernal hubbub, I sprang to the rescue of my friend, but had hardly taken a stride in the darkness when the whole room blazed with a blinding white light that burned into my brain and heart and memory a vivid picture of the combatants on the floor, Moxon underneath, his throat still in the clutch of those iron hands, his head forced backward, his eyes protruding, his mouth wide open and his tongue thrust out; and — horrible contrast! — upon the painted face of his assassin an expression of tranquil and profound thought, as in the solution of a problem in chess! This I observed, then all was blackness and silence.

Three days later I recovered consciousness in a hospital. As the memory of that tragic night slowly evolved in my ailing brain I recognized in my attendant Moxon's confidential workman, Haley. Responding to a look he approached, smiling.

"Tell me about it," I managed to say, faintly — "all about it."

"Certainly," he said; "you were carried unconscious from a burning house — Moxon's. Nobody knows how you came to be there. You may have to do a little explaining. The origin of the fire is a bit mysterious, too. My own notion is that the house was struck by lightning."

"And Moxon?"

"Buried yesterday — what was left of him."

Apparently this reticent person could unfold himself on occasion. When imparting shocking intelligence to the sick he was affable enough. After some moments of the keenest mental suffering I ventured to ask another question:

"Who rescued me?"

"Well, if that interests you — I did."

"Thank you, Mr. Haley, and may God bless you for it. Did you rescue, also, that charming product of your skill, the automaton chess-player that murdered its inventor"?

The man was silent a long time, looking away from me. Presently he turned and gravely said:

"Do you know that"?

"I do," I replied; "I saw it done."

That was many years ago. If asked to-day I should answer less confidently.

QUESTIONS

1. Is the emphasis in "Moxon's Master" on science, idea, or character?

2. What explanation might a modern botanist give for the instances of plant behavior that Moxon calls "thinking"? Do you agree that "the consciousness of plants ... proves that they think"?

3. Trace the steps by which the author prepares us for the appearance of the thinking machine. How is this machine characterized?

4. Are the narrator and Moxon rounded characters, or are they merely vehicles for ideas? Does Moxon's end suggest a moral?

5. What inferences do you draw from Mr. Haley's "answer" to the narrator's last question?

HENRY JAMES

Four Meetings

I saw her but four times, though I remember them vividly; she made her impression on me. I thought her very pretty and very interesting — a touching specimen of a type with which I had had other and perhaps less charming associations. I'm sorry to hear of her death, and yet when I think of it why *should* I be? The last time I saw her she was certainly not — ! But it will be of interest to take our meetings in order.

I

The first was in the country, at a small tea-party, one snowy night of some seventeen years ago. My friend Latouche, going to spend Christmas with his mother, had insisted on my company, and the good lady had given in our honour the entertainment of which I speak. To me it was really full of savour — it had all the right marks: I had never been in the depths of New England at that season. It had been snowing all day and the drifts were knee-high. I wondered how the ladies had made their way to the house; but I inferred that just those general rigours rendered any assembly offering the attraction of two gentlemen from New York worth a desperate effort.

Mrs. Latouche in the course of the evening asked me if I "didn't want to" show the photographs to some of the young ladies. The photographs were in a couple of great portfolios, and had been brought home by her son, who, like myself, was lately returned from Europe. I looked round and was struck with the fact that most of the young ladies were provided with an object of interest more absorbing than the most vivid sun-picture. But there was a person alone near the mantel-shelf who looked round the room with a small vague smile, a discreet, a disguised yearning, which seemed somehow at odds with her isolation. I looked at her a moment and then chose. "I should like to show them to that young lady."

"Oh yes," said Mrs. Latouche, "she's just the person. She doesn't care for flirting — I'll speak to her." I replied that if she didn't care for flirting she wasn't perhaps just the person; but Mrs. Latouche had already, with a few steps, appealed to her participation. "She's delighted," my hostess came back to report; "and she's just the person — so quiet and so bright." And she told me the young lady was by name Miss Caroline Spencer — with which she introduced me.

Miss Caroline Spencer was not quite a beauty, but was none the less, in her small odd way, formed to please. Close upon thirty, by every presumption, she was made almost like a little girl and had the complexion of a child. She had also the prettiest head, on which her hair was arranged as nearly as possible like the hair of a Greek bust, though indeed it was to be doubted if she had ever seen a Greek bust. She was "artistic," I suspected, so far as the polar influences of North Verona could allow for such yearnings or could minister to them. Her eyes were perhaps just too round and too inveterately surprised, but her lips had a certain mild decision and her teeth, when she showed them, were charming. About her neck she wore what ladies call, I believe, a "ruche" fastened with a very small pin of pink coral, and in her hand she carried a fan made of plaited straw and adorned with pink ribbon. She wore a scanty black silk dress. She spoke with slow soft neatness, even without smiles showing the prettiness of her teeth, and she seemed extremely pleased, in fact quite fluttered, at the prospect of my demonstrations. These went forward very smoothly after I had moved the portfolios out of their corner and placed a couple of chairs near a lamp. The photographs were usually things I knew — large views of Switzerland, Italy and Spain, landscapes, reproductions of famous buildings, pictures and statues. I said what I could for them, and my companion, looking at them as I held them up, sat perfectly still, her straw fan raised to her under-lip and gently, yet, as I could feel, almost excitedly, rubbing it. Occasionally, as I laid one of the pictures down, she said without confidence, which would have been too much: "Have you seen that place?" I usually answered that I had seen it several times — I had been a great traveller, though I was somehow particularly admonished not to swagger — and then I felt her look at me askance for a moment with her pretty eyes. I had asked her at the outset whether she had been to Europe; to this she had answered "No, no, no" — almost as much below her breath as if the image of such an event scarce, for solemnity, brooked phrasing. But after that, though she never took her eyes off the pictures, she said so little that I feared she was at last bored. Accordingly when we had finished one portfolio I offered, if she desired it, to desist. I rather guessed the exhibition really held her, but her reticence puzzled me and I wanted to make her speak. I turned round to judge better and then saw a faint flush in each of her cheeks. She kept waving her little fan to and fro. Instead of looking at me she fixed her eyes on the remainder of the collection, which leaned, in its receptacle, against the table.

"Won't you show me that?" she quavered, drawing the long breath of a person launched and afloat but conscious of rocking a little.

"With pleasure," I answered, "if you're really not tired."

"Oh I'm not tired a bit. I'm just fascinated." With which as I took up the other portfolio she laid her hand on it, rubbing it softly. "And have you been here too?"

On my opening the portfolio it appeared I had indeed been there. One of the first photographs was a large view of the Castle of Chillon by the Lake of Geneva. "Here," I said, "I've been many a time. Isn't it beautiful?" And I pointed to the perfect reflexion of the rugged rocks and pointed towers in the clear still water. She didn't say "Oh enchanting!" and push it away to see the next picture. She looked a while and then asked if it weren't where Bonnivard, about whom Byron wrote, had been confined. I assented, trying to quote Byron's verses, but not quite bringing it off.

She fanned herself a moment and then repeated the lines correctly, in a soft flat voice but with charming conviction. By the time she had finished, she was nevertheless blushing. I complimented her and assured her she was perfectly equipped for visiting Switzerland and Italy. She looked at me askance again, to see if I might be serious, and I added that if she wished to recognize Byron's descriptions she must go abroad speedily — Europe was getting sadly dis-Byronised. "How soon must I go?" she thereupon enquired.

"Oh I'll give you ten years."

"Well, I guess I can go in *that* time," she answered as if measuring her words.

"Then you'll enjoy it immensely," I said; "you'll find it of the highest interest." Just then I came upon a photograph of some nook in a foreign city which I had been very fond of and which recalled tender memories. I discoursed (as I suppose) with considerable spirit; my companion sat listening breathless.

"Have you been *very* long over there?" she asked some time after I had ceased.

"Well, it mounts up, put all the times together."

"And have you travelled everywhere?"

"I've travelled a good deal. I'm very fond of it and happily have been able."

Again she turned on me her slow shy scrutiny. "Do you know the foreign languages?"

"After a fashion."

"Is it hard to speak them?"

"I don't imagine you'd find it so," I gallantly answered.

"Oh I shouldn't want to speak — I should only want to listen." Then on a pause she added: "They say the French theatre's so beautiful."

"Ah the best in the world."

"Did you go there very often?"

"When I was first in Paris I went every night."

"Every night!" And she opened her clear eyes very wide. "That to me is" — and her expression hovered — "as if you tell me a fairy-tale." A few minutes later she put to me: "And which country do you prefer?"

"There's one I love beyond any. I think you'd do the same."

Her gaze rested as on a dim revelation and then she breathed "Italy?"

"Italy," I answered softly too; and for a moment we communed over it. She looked as pretty as if instead of showing her photographs I had been making love to her. To increase the resemblance she turned off blushing. It made a pause which she broke at last by saying: "That's the place which — in particular — I thought of going to."

"Oh that's the place — that's the place!" I laughed.

She looked at two or three more views in silence. "They say it's not very dear."

"As some other countries? Well, one gets back there one's money. That's not the least of the charms."

"But it's *all* very expensive, isn't it?"

"Europe, you mean?"

"Going there and travelling. That has been the trouble. I've very little money. I teach, you know," said Miss Caroline Spencer.

"Oh of course one must have money," I allowed; "but one can manage with a moderate amount judiciously spent."

"I think I should manage. I've saved and saved up, and I'm always adding a little to it. It's all for that." She paused a moment, and then went on with suppressed eagerness, as if telling me the story were a rare, but possibly an impure satisfaction. "You see it hasn't been only the money — it has been everything. Everything has acted against it. I've waited and waited. It has been my castle in the air. I'm almost afraid to talk about it. Two or three times it has come a little nearer, and then I've talked about it and it has melted away. I've talked about it too much," she said hypocritically — for I saw such talk was now a small tremulous ecstasy. "There's a lady who's a great friend of mine — she doesn't want to go, but I'm always at her about it. I think I must tire her dreadfully. She told me just the other day she didn't know what would become of me. She guessed I'd go crazy if I didn't sail, and yet certainly I'd go crazy if I did."

"Well," I laughed, "you haven't sailed up to now — so I suppose you *are* crazy."

She took everything with the same seriousness. "Well, I guess I must be. It seems as if I couldn't think of anything else — and I don't require photographs to work me up! I'm always right *on* it. It kills any interest in things nearer home — things I ought to attend to. That's a kind of craziness."

"Well then the cure for it's just to go," I smiled — "I mean the cure for this kind. Of course you may have the other kind worse," I added — "the kind you get over there."

"Well, I've a faith that I'll go *some* time all right!" she quite elatedly cried. "I've a relative right there on the spot," she went on, "and I guess he'll know how to control me." I expressed the hope that he would, and I forget whether we turned over more photographs; but when I asked her if she had always lived just where I found her, "Oh no sir," she quite eagerly replied; "I've spent twenty-two months and a half in Boston." I met it with the inevitable joke that in this case foreign lands might prove a disappointment to her, but I quite failed to alarm her. "I know more about them than you might think" — her earnestness resisted even that. "I mean by reading — for I've really read considerable. In fact I guess I've prepared my mind about as much as you *can* — in advance. I've not only read Byron — I've read histories and guide-books and articles and lots of things. I know I shall rave about everything."

"'Everything' is saying much, but I understand your case," I returned. "You've the great American disease, and you've got it 'bad' — the appetite, morbid and monstrous, for colour and form, for the picturesque and the romantic at any price. I don't know whether we come into the world with it — with the germs implanted and antecedent to experience; rather perhaps we catch it early, almost before developed consciousness — we *feel*, as we look about, that we're going (to save our souls, or at least our senses) to be thrown back on it hard. We're like travellers in the desert — deprived of water and subject to the terrible mirage, the torment of illusion, of the thirst-fever. They hear the plash of fountains, they see green gardens and orchards that are hundreds of miles away. So we with *our* thirst — except that with us it's *more* wonderful: we have before us the beautiful old things we've never seen at all, and when we do at last see them — if we're lucky! — we simply recognise them. What experience does is merely to confirm and consecrate our confident dream."

She listened with her rounded eyes. "The way you express it's too lovely, and I'm sure it will be just like that. I've dreamt of everything — I'll know it all!"

"I'm afraid," I pretended for harmless comedy, "that you've wasted a great deal of time."

"Oh yes, that has been my great wickedness!" The people about us had begun to scatter; they were taking their leave. She got up and put out her hand to me, timidly, but as if quite shining and throbbing.

"I'm going back there — one *has* to," I said as I shook hands with her. "I shall look out for you."

Yes, she fairly glittered with her fever of excited faith. "Well, I'll tell you if I'm disappointed." And she left me, fluttering all expressively her little straw fan.

II

A few months after this I crossed the sea eastward again and some three years elapsed. I had been living in Paris and, toward the end of October, went from that city to the Havre, to meet a pair of relatives who had written me they were about to arrive there. On reaching the Havre I found the steamer already docked — I was two or three hours late. I repaired directly to the hotel, where my travellers were duly established. My sister had gone to bed, exhausted and disabled by her voyage; she was the unsteadiest of sailors and her sufferings on this occasion had been extreme. She desired for the moment undisturbed rest and was able to see me but five minutes — long enough for us to agree to stop over, restoratively, till the morrow. My brother-in-law, anxious about his wife, was unwilling to leave her room; but she insisted on my taking him a walk for aid to recovery of his spirits and his land-legs.

The early autumn day was warm and charming, and our stroll through the bright-coloured busy streets of the old French seaport beguiling enough. We walked along the sunny noisy quays and then turned into a wide pleasant street which lay half in sun and half in shade — a French provincial street that resembled an old water-colour drawing: tall grey steep-roofed red-gabled many-storied houses; green shutters on windows and old scroll-work above them; flowerpots in balconies and white-capped women in doorways. We walked in the shade; all this stretched away on the sunny side of the vista and made a picture. We looked at it as we passed along; then suddenly my companion stopped — pressing my arm and staring. I followed his gaze and saw that we had paused just before reaching a café where, under an awning, several tables and chairs were disposed upon the pavement. The windows were open behind; half a dozen plants in tubs were ranged beside the door; the pavement was besprinkled with clean bran. It was a dear little quiet old-world café; inside, in the comparative dusk, I saw a stout handsome woman, who had pink ribbons in her cap, perched up with a mirror behind her back and smiling at some one placed out of sight. This, to be exact, I noted afterwards; what I first observed was a lady seated alone, outside, at one of the little marble-topped tables. My brother-in-law had stopped to look at her. Something had been put before her, but she only leaned back, motionless and with her hands folded, looking down the street and away from us. I saw her but in diminished profile; nevertheless I was sure I knew on the spot that we must already have met.

"The little lady of the steamer!" my companion cried.

"Was she on your steamer?" I asked with interest.

"From morning till night. She was never sick. She used to sit perpetually at the side of the vessel with her hands crossed that way, looking at the eastward horizon."

"And are you going to speak to her?"

"I don't know her. I never made acquaintance with her. I wasn't in form to make up to ladies. But I used to watch her and — I don't know why — to be interested in her. She's a dear little Yankee woman. I've an idea she's a school-mistress taking a holiday — for which her scholars have made up a purse."

She had now turned her face a little more into profile, looking at the steep grey house-fronts opposite. On this I decided. "I shall speak to her myself."

"I wouldn't — she's very shy," said my brother-in-law.

"My dear fellow, I know her. I once showed her photographs at a tea-party." With which I went up to her, making her, as she turned to look at me, leave me in no doubt of her identity. Miss Caroline Spencer had achieved her dream. But she was less quick to recognise me and showed a slight bewilderment. I pushed a chair to the table and sat down. "Well," I said, "I hope you're not disappointed!"

She stared, blushing a little — then gave a small jump and placed me. "It was you who showed me the photographs — at North Verona."

"Yes, it was I. This happens very charmingly, for isn't it quite for me to give you a formal reception here — the official welcome? I talked to you so much about Europe."

"You didn't say too much. I'm so intensely happy!" she declared.

Very happy indeed she looked. There was no sign of her being older; she was as gravely, decently, demurely pretty as before. If she had struck me then as a thin-stemmed mild-hued flower of Puritanism it may be imagined whether in her present situation this clear bloom was less appealing. Beside her an old gentleman was drinking absinthe; behind her the *dame de comptoir*[1] in the pink ribbons called "Alcibiade, Alcibiade!" to the long-aproned waiter. I explained to Miss Spencer that the gentleman with me had lately been her shipmate, and my brother-in-law came up and was introduced to her. But she looked at him as if she had never so much as seen him, and I remembered he had told me her eyes were always fixed on the eastward horizon. She had evidently not noticed him, and, still timidly smiling, made no attempt whatever to pretend the contrary. I staid with her on the little terrace of the café while he went back to the hotel and to his wife. I remarked to my friend that this meeting of ours at the first hour of her landing partook, among all chances, of the miraculous, but that I was delighted to be there and receive her first impressions.

"Oh I can't tell you," she said — "I feel so much in a dream. I've been sitting here an hour and I don't want to move. Everything's so delicious and romantic. I don't know whether the coffee has gone to my head — it's *so* unlike the coffee of my dead past."

"Really," I made answer, "if you're so pleased with this poor prosaic Havre you'll have no admiration left for better things. Don't spend your appreciation all the first day — remember it's your intellectual letter of credit. Remember all the beautiful places and things that are waiting for you. Remember that lovely Italy we talked about."

"I'm not afraid of running short," she said gaily, still looking at the opposite houses. "I could sit here all day — just saying to myself that here I am at last. It's so dark and strange — so old and different."

"By the way then," I asked, "how come you to be encamped in this odd place? Haven't you gone to one of the inns?" For I was half-amused, half-alarmed at the good conscience with which this delicately pretty woman had stationed herself in conspicuous isolation on the edge of the sidewalk.

"My cousin brought me here and — a little while ago — left me," she returned. "You know I told you I had a relation over here. He's still here — a real cousin. Well," she pursued with unclouded candour, "he met me at the steamer this morning."

It was absurd — and the case moreover none of my business; but I felt somehow disconcerted. "It was hardly worth his while to meet you if he was to desert you so soon."

"Oh he has only left me for half an hour," said Caroline Spencer. "He has gone to get my money."

I continued to wonder. "Where *is* your money?"

She appeared seldom to laugh, but she laughed for the joy of this. "It makes me feel very fine to tell you! It's in circular notes.[2]"

"And where are your circular notes?"

"In my cousin's pocket."

This statement was uttered with such clearness of candour that — I can hardly say why — it gave me a sensible chill. I couldn't at all at the moment have justified my lapse from ease, for I knew nothing of Miss Spencer's cousin. Since he stood in that relation to her — dear respectable little person — the presumption was in his favour. But I found myself wincing at the thought that half an hour after her landing her scanty funds should have passed into his hands. "Is he to travel with you?" I asked.

"Only as far as Paris. He's an art-student in Paris — I've always thought that so splendid. I wrote to him that I was coming, but I never expected him to come off to the ship. I supposed he'd only just meet me at the train in Paris. It's very kind of him. But he *is*," said Caroline Spencer, "very kind — and very bright."

---

[1] Cashier.

[2] The equivalent of travelers' checks.

I felt at once a strange eagerness to see this bright kind cousin who was an art-student. "He's gone to the banker's?" I enquired.

"Yes, to the banker's. He took me to an hotel — such a queer quaint cunning little place, with a court in the middle and a gallery all round, and a lovely landlady in such a beautifully fluted cap and such a perfectly fitting dress! After a while we came out to walk to the banker's, for I hadn't any French money. But I was very dizzy from the motion of the vessel and I thought I had better sit down. He found this place for me here — then he went off to the banker's himself. I'm to wait here till he comes back."

Her story was wholly lucid and my impression perfectly wanton, but it passed through my mind that the gentleman would never come back. I settled myself in a chair beside my friend and determined to await the event. She was lost in the vision and the imagination of everything near us and about us — she observed, she recognised and admired, with a touching intensity. She noticed everything that was brought before us by the movement of the street — the peculiarities of costume, the shapes of vehicles, the big Norman horses, the fat priests, the shaven poodles. We talked of these things, and there was something charming in her freshness of perception and the way her book-nourished fancy sallied forth for the revel.

"And when your cousin comes back what are you going to do?" I went on.

For this she had, a little oddly, to think. "We don't quite know."

"When do you go to Paris? If you go by the four o'clock train I may have the pleasure of making the journey with you."

"I don't think we shall do that." So far she was prepared. "My cousin thinks I had better stay here a few days."

"Oh!" said I — and for five minutes had nothing to add. I was wondering what our absentee was, in vulgar parlance, "up to." I looked up and down the street, but saw nothing that looked like a bright and kind American art-student. At last I took the liberty of observing that the Havre was hardly a place to choose as one of the æsthetic stations of a European tour. It was a place of convenience, nothing more; a place of transit, through which transit should be rapid. I recommended her to go to Paris by the afternoon train and meanwhile to amuse herself by driving to the ancient fortress at the mouth of the harbour — that remarkable circular structure which bore the name of Francis the First and figured a sort of small Castle of Saint Angelo. (I might really have foreknown that it was to be demolished.)

She listened with much interest — then for a moment looked grave. "My cousin told me that when he returned he should have something particular to say to me, and that we could do nothing or decide nothing till I should have heard it. But I'll make him tell me right off, and then we'll go to the ancient fortress. Francis the First, did you say? Why, that's lovely. There's no hurry to get to Paris; there's plenty of time."

She smiled with her softly severe little lips as she spoke those last words, yet, looking at her with a purpose, I made out in her eyes, I thought, a tiny gleam of apprehension. "Don't tell me," I said, "that this wretched man's going to give you bad news!"

She coloured as if convicted of a hidden perversity, but she was soaring too high to drop. "Well, I guess it's a *little* bad, but I don't believe it's *very* bad. At any rate I must listen to it."

I usurped an unscrupulous authority. "Look here; you didn't come to Europe to listen — you came to *see*!" But now I was sure her cousin would come back; since he had something disagreeable to say to her he'd infallibly turn up. We sat a while longer and I asked her about her plans of travel. She had them on her fingers' ends and told over the names as solemnly as a daughter of another faith might have told over the beads of a rosary: from Paris to Dijon and to Avignon, from Avignon to Marseilles and the Cornice road; thence to Genoa, to Spezia, to Pisa, to Florence, to Rome. It apparently had never occurred to her that there could be the least incommodity in her travelling alone; and since she was unprovided with a companion I of course civilly abstained from disturbing her sense of security.

At last her cousin came back. I saw him turn toward us out of a side-street, and from the moment my eyes rested on him I knew he could but be the bright, if not the kind, American art-student. He wore a slouch hat and a rusty black velvet jacket, such as I had often encountered in the Rue Bonaparte. His shirt-collar displayed a stretch of throat that at a distance wasn't strikingly statuesque. He was tall and lean, he had red hair and freckles. These items I had time to take in while he approached the café, staring at me with natural surprise from under his romantic brim. When he came up to us I immediately introduced myself as an old acquaintance of Miss Spencer's, a character she serenely permitted me to claim. He looked at me hard with a pair of small sharp eyes, then he gave me a solemn wave, in the "European" fashion, of his rather rusty sombrero.

"You weren't on the ship?" he asked.

"No, I wasn't on the ship. I've been in Europe these several years."

He bowed once more, portentously, and motioned me to be seated again. I sat down, but only for the purpose of observing him an instant — I saw it was time I should return to my sister. Miss Spencer's European protector was, by my measure, a very queer quantity. Nature hadn't shaped him for a Raphaelesque or Byronic attire, and his velvet doublet and exhibited though not columnar throat weren't in harmony with his facial attributes. His hair was cropped close to his head; his ears were large and ill-adjusted to the same. He had a lackadaisical carriage and a sentimental droop which were peculiarly at variance with his keen conscious strange-coloured eyes — of a brown that was almost red. Perhaps I was prejudiced, but I thought his eyes too shifty. He said nothing for some time; he leaned his hands on his stick and looked up and down the street. Then at last, slowly lifting the stick and pointing with it, "That's a very nice bit," he dropped with a certain flatness. He had his head to one side — he narrowed his ugly lids. I followed the direction of his stick; the object it indicated was a red cloth hung out of an old window. "Nice bit of colour," he continued; and without moving his head transferred his half-closed gaze to me. "Composes well. Fine old tone. Make a nice thing." He spoke in a charmless vulgar voice.

"I see you've a great deal of eye," I replied. "Your cousin tells me you're studying art." He looked at me in the same way, without answering, and I went on with deliberate urbanity: "I suppose you're at the studio of one of those great men." Still on this he continued to fix me, and then he named one of the greatest of that day; which led me to ask him if he liked his master.

"Do you understand French?" he returned.

"Some kinds."

He kept his little eyes on me; with which he remarked: "*Je suis fou de la peinture!*"[3]

"Oh I understand that kind!" I replied. Our companion laid her hand on his arm with a small pleased and fluttered movement; it was delightful to be among people who were on such easy terms with foreign tongues. I got up to take leave and asked her where, in Paris, I might have the honour of waiting on her. To what hotel would she go?

She turned to her cousin enquiringly and he favoured me again with his little languid leer. "Do you know the Hôtel des Princes?"

"I know where it is."

"Well, that's the shop."

---

[3] "I am mad about painting."

"I congratulate you," I said to Miss Spencer. "I believe it's the best inn in the world; but, in case I should still have a moment to call on you here, where are you lodged?"

"Oh it's such a pretty name," she returned gleefully. "A la Belle Normande."

"I guess I know my way round!" her kinsman threw in; and as I left them he gave me with his swaggering head-cover a great flourish that was like the wave of a banner over a conquered field.

III

My relative, as it proved, was not sufficiently restored to leave the place by the afternoon train; so that as the autumn dusk began to fall I found myself at liberty to call at the establishment named to me by my friends. I must confess that I had spent much of the interval in wondering what the disagreeable thing was that the less attractive of these had been telling the other. The *auberge* of the Belle Normande proved an hostelry in a shady by-street, where it gave me satisfaction to think Miss Spencer must have encountered local colour in abundance. There was a crooked little court, where much of the hospitality of the house was carried on; there was a staircase climbing to bedrooms on the outer side of the wall; there was a small trickling fountain with a stucco statuette set in the midst of it; there was a little boy in a white cap and apron cleaning copper vessels at a conspicuous kitchen door; there was a chattering landlady, neatly laced, arranging apricots and grapes into an artistic pyramid upon a pink plate. I looked about, and on a green bench outside of an open door labelled Salle-à-Manger, I distinguished Caroline Spencer. No sooner had I looked at her than I was sure something had happened since the morning. Supported by the back of her bench, with her hands clasped in her lap, she kept her eyes on the other side of the court where the landlady manipulated the apricots.

But I saw that, poor dear, she wasn't thinking of apricots or even of landladies. She was staring absently, thoughtfully; on a nearer view I could have certified she had been crying. I had seated myself beside her before she was aware; then, when she had done so, she simply turned round without surprise and showed me her sad face. Something very bad indeed had happened; she was completely changed, and I immediately charged her with it. "Your cousin has been giving you bad news. You've had a horrid time."

For a moment she said nothing, and I supposed her afraid to speak lest her tears should again rise. Then it came to me that even in the few hours since my leaving her she had shed them all — which made her now intensely, stoically composed. "My poor cousin has been having one," she replied at last. "He has had great worries. His news was bad." Then after a dismally conscious wait: "He was in dreadful want of money."

"In want of yours, you mean?"

"Of any he could get — honourably of course. Mine *is* all — well, that's available."

Ah it was as if I had been sure from the first! "And he has taken it from you?"

Again she hung fire, but her face meanwhile was pleading. "I gave him what I had."

I recall the accent of those words as the most angelic human sound I had ever listened to — which is exactly why I jumped up almost with a sense of personal outrage. "Gracious goodness, madam, do you call that his getting it 'honourably'?"

I had gone too far — she coloured to her eyes. "We won't speak of it."

"We *must* speak of it," I declared as I dropped beside her again. "I'm your friend — upon my word I'm your protector; it seems to me you need one. What's the matter with this extraordinary person?"

She was perfectly able to say, "He's just badly in debt."

"No doubt he is! But what's the special propriety of your — in such tearing haste! — paying for that?"

"Well, he has told me all his story. I *feel* for him so much."

"So do I, if you come to that! But I hope," I roundly added, "he'll give you straight back your money."

As to this she was prompt. "Certainly he will — as soon as ever he can."

"And when the deuce will that be?"

Her lucidity maintained itself. "When he has finished his great picture."

It took me full in the face. "My dear young lady, damn his great picture! Where is this voracious man?"

It was as if she must let me feel a moment that I did push her! — though indeed, as appeared, he was just where he'd naturally be. "He's having his dinner."

I turned about and looked through the open door into the salle-à-manger. There, sure enough, alone at the end of a long table, was the object of my friend's compassion — the bright, the kind young art-student. He was dining too attentively to notice me at first, but in the act of setting down a well-emptied wine-glass he caught sight of my air of observation. He paused in his repast and, with his head on one side and his meagre jaws slowly moving, fixedly returned my gaze. Then the landlady came brushing lightly by with her pyramid of apricots.

"And that nice little plate of fruit is for him?" I wailed.

Miss Spencer glanced at it tenderly. "They seem to arrange everything so nicely!" she simply sighed.

I felt helpless and irritated. "Come now, really," I said; "do you think it right, do you think it decent, that that long strong fellow should collar your funds?" She looked away from me — I was evidently giving her pain. The case was hopeless; the long strong fellow had "interested" her.

"Pardon me if I speak of him so unceremoniously," I said. "But you're really too generous, and he hasn't, clearly, the rudiments of delicacy. He made his debts himself — he ought to pay them himself."

"He has been foolish," she obstinately said — "of course I know that. He has told me everything. We had a long talk this morning — the poor fellow threw himself on my charity. He has signed notes to a large amount."

"The more fool he!"

"He's in real distress — and it's not only himself. It's his poor young wife."

"Ah he has a poor young wife?"

"I didn't know — but he made a clean breast of it. He married two years since — secretly."

"Why secretly?"

My informant took precautions as if she feared listeners. Then with low impressiveness: "She was a Countess!"

"Are you very sure of that?"

"She has written me the most beautiful letter."

"Asking you — whom she has never seen — for money?"

"Asking me for confidence and sympathy" — Miss Spencer spoke now with spirit. "She has been cruelly treated by her family — in consequence of what she has done for him. My cousin has told me every particular, and she appeals to me in her own lovely way in the letter, which I've here in my pocket. It's such a wonderful old-world romance," said my prodigious friend. "She was a beautiful young widow — her first husband was a Count, tremendously high-born, but really most wicked, with whom she hadn't been happy and whose death had left her ruined after he had deceived her in all sorts of ways. My poor cousin, meeting her in that situation and perhaps a little too recklessly pitying her and charmed with her, found her, don't you see?" — Caroline's appeal on this head was amazing! — "but too ready to trust a better man after all she had been through. Only when her 'people,' as he says — and I do like the word! — understood she *would* have him, poor gifted young American art-student though he simply was, because she just adored him, her great-aunt, the old Marquise, from whom she had expectations of wealth which she could yet sacrifice for her love, utterly cast her off and wouldn't so much as speak to her, much less to *him*, in their dreadful haughtiness and pride. They *can* be haughty over here, it seems," she ineffably developed— "there's no mistake about that! It's like something in some famous old book. The family, my cousin's wife's," she by this time almost complacently wound up, "are of the oldest Provençal noblesse."

I listened half-bewildered. The poor woman positively found it so interesting to be swindled by a flower of that stock — if stock or flower or solitary grain of truth was really concerned in the matter — as practically to have lost the sense of what the forfeiture of her hoard meant for her. "My dear young lady," I groaned, "you don't want to be stripped of every dollar for such a rigmarole!"

She asserted, at this, her dignity — much as a small pink shorn lamb might have done. "It isn't a rigmarole, and I shan't be stripped. I shan't live any worse than I *have* lived, don't you see? And I'll come back before long to stay with them. The Countess — he still gives her, he says, her title, as they do to noble widows, that is to 'dowagers,' don't you know? in England — insists on a visit from me *some* time. So I guess for *that* I can start afresh — and meanwhile I'll have recovered my money."

It was all too heart-breaking. "You're going home then at once?"

I felt the faint tremor of voice she heroically tried to stifle. "I've nothing left for a tour."

"You gave it *all* up?"

"I've kept enough to take me back."

I uttered, I think, a positive howl, and at this juncture the hero of the situation, the happy proprietor of my little friend's sacred savings and of the infatuated *grande dame* just sketched for me, reappeared with the clear consciousness of a repast bravely earned and consistently enjoyed. He stood on the threshold an instant, extracting the stone from a plump apricot he had fondly retained; then he put the apricot into his mouth and, while he let it gratefully dissolve there, stood looking at us with his long legs apart and his hands thrust into the pockets of his velvet coat. My companion got up, giving him a thin glance that I caught in its passage and which expressed at once resignation and fascination — the last dregs of her sacrifice and with it an anguish of upliftedness. Ugly vulgar pretentious dishonest as I thought him, and destitute of every grace of plausibility, he had yet appealed successfully to her eager and tender imagination. I was deeply disgusted, but I had no warrant to interfere, and at any rate felt that it would be vain. He waved his hand meanwhile with a breadth of appreciation. "Nice old court. Nice mellow old place. Nice crooked old staircase. Several pretty things."

Decidedly I couldn't stand it, and without responding I gave my hand to my friend. She looked at me an instant with her little white face and rounded eyes, and as she showed her pretty teeth I suppose she meant to smile. "Don't be sorry for me," she sublimely pleaded; "I'm very sure I shall see something of this dear old Europe yet."

I refused however to take literal leave of her — I should find a moment to come back next morning. Her awful kinsman, who had put on his sombrero again, flourished it off at me by way of a bow — on which I hurried away.

On the morrow early I did return, and in the court of the inn met the landlady, more loosely laced than in the evening. On my asking for Miss Spencer, "*Partie*,[4] monsieur," the

---

[4] Gone.

good woman said. "She went away last night at ten o'clock, with her — her — not her husband, eh? — in fine her Monsieur. They went down to the American ship." I turned off — I felt the tears in my eyes. The poor girl had been some thirteen hours in Europe.

IV

I myself, more fortunate, continued to sacrifice to opportunity as I myself met it. During this period — of some five years — I lost my friend Latouche, who died of a malarious fever during a tour in the Levant. One of the first things I did on my return to America was to go up to North Verona on a consolatory visit to his poor mother. I found her in deep affliction and sat with her the whole of the morning that followed my arrival — I had come in late at night — listening to her tearful descant and singing the praises of my friend. We talked of nothing else, and our conversation ended only with the arrival of a quick little woman who drove herself up to the door in a "carry-all" and whom I saw toss the reins to the horse's back with the briskness of a startled sleeper throwing off the bedclothes. She jumped out of the carry-all and she jumped into the room. She proved to be the minister's wife and the great town-gossip, and she had evidently, in the latter capacity, a choice morsel to communicate. I was as sure of this as I was that poor Mrs. Latouche was not absolutely too bereaved to listen to her. It seemed to me discreet to retire, and I described myself as anxious for a walk before dinner.

"And by the way," I added, "if you'll tell me where my old friend Miss Spencer lives I think I'll call on her."

The minister's wife immediately responded. Miss Spencer lived in the fourth house beyond the Baptist church; the Baptist church was the one on the right, with that queer green thing over the door; they called it portico, but it looked more like an old-fashioned bedstead swung in the air. "Yes, do look up poor Caroline," Mrs. Latouche further enjoined. "It will refresh her to see a strange face."

"I should think she had had enough of strange faces!" cried the minister's wife.

"To see, I mean, a charming visitor" — Mrs. Latouche amended her phrase.

"I should think she had had enough of charming visitors!" her companion returned. "But *you* don't mean to stay ten years," she added with significant eyes on me.

"Has she a visitor of that sort?" I asked in my ignorance.

"You'll make out the sort!" said the minister's wife. "She's easily seen; she generally sits in the front yard. Only take care what you say to her, and be very sure you're polite."

"Ah she's so sensitive?"

The minister's wife jumped up and dropped me a curtsey — a most sarcastic curtsey. "That's what she is, if you please. 'Madame la Comtesse!'"

And pronouncing these titular words with the most scathing accent, the little woman seemed fairly to laugh in the face of the lady they designated. I stood staring, wondering, remembering.

"Oh I shall be very polite!" I cried; and, grasping my hat and stick, I went on my way.

I found Miss Spencer's residence without difficulty. The Baptist church was easily identified, and the small dwelling near it, of a rusty white, with a large central chimney-stack and a Virginia creeper, seemed naturally and properly the abode of a withdrawn old maid with a taste for striking effects inexpensively obtained. As I approached I slackened my pace, for I had heard that some one was always sitting in the front yard, and I wished to reconnoitre. I looked cautiously over the low white fence that separated the small garden-space from the unpaved street, but I descried nothing in the shape of a Comtesse. A small straight path led up to the crooked door-step, on either side of which was a little grass-plot fringed with currant-bushes. In the middle of the grass, right and left, was a large quince-tree, full of antiquity and contortions, and beneath one of the quince-trees were placed a small table and a couple of light chairs. On the table lay a piece of unfinished embroidery and two or three books in bright-coloured paper covers. I went in at the gate and paused halfway along the path, scanning the place for some further token of its occupant, before whom — I could hardly have said why — I hesitated abruptly to present myself. Then I saw the poor little house to be of the shabbiest and felt a sudden doubt of my right to penetrate, since curiosity had been my motive and curiosity here failed of confidence. While I demurred a figure appeared in the open doorway and stood there looking at me. I immediately recognised Miss Spencer, but she faced me as if we had never met. Gently, but gravely and timidly, I advanced to the door-step, where I spoke with an attempt at friendly banter.

"I waited for you over there to come back, but you never came."

"Waited where, sir?" she quavered, her innocent eyes rounding themselves as of old. She was much older; she looked tired and wasted.

"Well," I said, "I waited at the old French port."

She stared harder, then recognised me, smiling, flushing, clasping her two hands together. "I remember you now — I remember that day." But she stood there, neither coming out nor asking me to come in. She was embarrassed.

I too felt a little awkward while I poked at the path with my stick. "I kept looking out for you year after year."

"You mean in Europe?" she ruefully breathed.

"In Europe of course! Here apparently you're easy enough to find."

She leaned her hand against the unpainted doorpost and her head fell a little to one side. She looked at me thus without speaking, and I caught the expression visible in women's eyes when tears are rising. Suddenly she stepped out on the cracked slab of stone before her threshold and closed the door. Then her strained smile prevailed and I saw her teeth were as pretty as ever. But there had been tears too. "Have you been there ever since?" she lowered her voice to ask.

"Until three weeks ago. And you — you never came back?"

Still shining at me as she could, she put her hand behind her and reopened the door. "I'm not very polite," she said. "Won't you come in?"

"I'm afraid I incommode you."

"Oh no!" — she wouldn't hear of it now. And she pushed back the door with a sign that I should enter.

I followed her in. She led the way to a small room on the left of the narrow hall, which I supposed to be her parlour, though it was at the back of the house, and we passed the closed door of another apartment which apparently enjoyed a view of the quince-trees. This one looked out upon a small wood-shed and two clucking hens. But I thought it pretty until I saw its elegance to be of the most frugal kind; after which, presently, I thought it prettier still, for I had never seen faded chintz and old mezzotint engravings, framed in varnished autumn leaves, disposed with so touching a grace. Miss Spencer sat down on a very small section of the sofa, her hands tightly clasped in her lap. She looked ten years older, and I needn't now have felt called to insist on the facts of her person. But I still thought them interesting, and at any rate I was moved by them. She was peculiarly agitated. I tried to appear not to notice it; but suddenly, in the most inconsequent fashion — it was an irresistible echo of our concentrated passage in the old French port — I said to her: "I do incommode you. Again you're in distress."

She raised her two hands to her face and for a moment kept it buried in them. Then taking them away, "It's because you remind me," she said.

"I remind you, you mean, of that miserable day at the Havre?"

She wonderfully shook her head. "It wasn't miserable. It was delightful."

Ah, was it? my manner of receiving this must have commented. "I never was so shocked as when, on going back to your inn the next morning, I found you had wretchedly retreated."

She waited an instant, after which she said: "Please let us not speak of that."

"Did you come straight back here?" I nevertheless went on.

"I was back here just thirty days after my first start."

"And here you've remained ever since?"

"Every minute of the time."

I took it in; I didn't know what to say, and what I presently said had almost the sound of mockery. "When then are you going to make that tour?" It might be practically aggressive; but there was something that irritated me in her depths of resignation, and I wished to extort from her some expression of impatience.

She attached her eyes a moment to a small sunspot on the carpet; then she got up and lowered the window-blind a little to obliterate it. I waited, watching her with interest — as if she had still something more to give me. Well, presently, in answer to my last question, she gave it. "Never!"

"I hope at least your cousin repaid you that money," I said.

At this again she looked away from me. "I don't care for it now."

"You don't care for your money?"

"For ever going to Europe."

"Do you mean you wouldn't go if you could?"

"I can't — I can't," said Caroline Spencer. "It's all over. Everything's different. I never think of it."

"The scoundrel never repaid you then!" I cried.

"Please, please — !" she began.

But she had stopped — she was looking toward the door. There had been a rustle and a sound of steps in the hall.

I also looked toward the door, which was open and now admitted another person — a lady who paused just within the threshold. Behind her came a young man. The lady looked at me with a good deal of fixedness — long enough for me to rise to a vivid impression of herself. Then she turned to Caroline Spencer and, with a smile and a strong foreign accent, "*Pardon, ma chère!*[5] I didn't know you had company," she said. "The gentleman came in so quietly." With which she again gave me the benefit of her attention. She was very strange, yet I was at once sure I had seen her before. Afterwards I rather put it that I had only seen ladies remarkably like her. But I had seen them very far away from North Verona, and it was the oddest of all things to meet one of them in that frame. To what quite other scene did the sight of her transport me? To some dusky landing before a shabby Parisian *quatrième*[6] — to an open door revealing a greasy ante-chamber and to Madame leaning over the banisters while she holds a faded wrapper together and bawls down to the portress to bring up her coffee. My friend's guest was a very large lady, of middle age, with a plump dead-white face and hair drawn back *à la chinoise*.[7] She had a small penetrating eye and what is called in French *le*

---

[5] "Excuse me, dear."

[6] The fourth floor above ground level.

[7] Chinese-style, that is, drawn back severely from the face.

sourire agréable.[8] She wore an old pink cashmere dressing-gown covered with white embroideries, and, like the figure in my momentary vision, she confined it in front with a bare rounded arm and a plump and deeply-dimpled hand.

"It's only to spick about my café," she said to her hostess with her *sourire agréable.* "I should like it served in the garden under the leetle tree."

The young man behind her had now stepped into the room, where he also stood revealed, though with rather less of a challenge. He was a gentleman of few inches but a vague importance, perhaps the leading man of the world of North Verona. He had a small pointed nose and a small pointed chin; also, as I observed, the most diminutive feet and a manner of no point at all. He looked at me foolishly and with his mouth open.

"You shall have your coffee," said Miss Spencer as if an army of cooks had been engaged in the preparation of it.

"C'est bien!" said her massive inmate. "Find your bouk" — and this personage turned to the gaping youth.

He gaped now at each quarter of the room. "My grammar, d'ye mean?"

The large lady however could but face her friend's visitor while persistently engaged with a certain laxity in the flow of her wrapper. "Find your bouk," she more absently repeated.

"My poetry, d'ye mean?" said the young man, who also couldn't take his eyes off me.

"Never mind your bouk" — his companion reconsidered. "To-day we'll just talk. We'll make some conversation. But we mustn't interrupt Mademoiselle's. Come, come" — and she moved off a step. "Under the leetle tree," she added for the benefit of Mademoiselle. After which she gave me a thin salutation, jerked a measured "Monsieur!" and swept away again with her swain following.

I looked at Miss Spencer, whose eyes never moved from the carpet, and I spoke, I fear, without grace. "Who in the world's that?"

"The Comtesse — that was: my *cousine*[9] as they call it in French."

"And who's the young man?"

"The Countess's pupil, Mr. Mixter." This description of the tie uniting the two persons who had just quitted us must certainly have upset my gravity; for I recall the marked increase of my friend's own as she continued to explain. "She gives lessons in French and music, the simpler sorts — "

"The simpler sorts of French?" I fear I broke in.

But she was still impenetrable, and in fact had now an intonation that put me vulgarly in the wrong. "She has had the worst reverses — with no one to look to. She's prepared for any exertion — and she takes her misfortunes with gaiety."

"Ah well," I returned — no doubt a little ruefully, "that's all I myself am pretending to do. If she's determined to be a burden to nobody, nothing could be more right and proper."

My hostess looked vaguely, though I thought quite wearily enough, about: she met this proposition in no other way. "I must go and get the coffee," she simply said.

"Has the lady many pupils?" I none the less persisted.

"She has only Mr. Mixter. She gives him all her time." It might have set me off again, but something in my whole impression of my friend's sensibility urged me to keep strictly decent. "He pays very well," she at all events inscrutably went on. "He's not very bright — as a pupil;

---

[8] The pleasant smile.

[9] Cousin.

but he's very rich and he's very kind. He has a buggy — with a back, and he takes the Countess to drive."

"For good long spells I hope," I couldn't help interjecting — even at the cost of her so taking it that she had still to avoid my eyes. "Well, the country's beautiful for miles," I went on. And then as she was turning away: "You're going for the Countess's coffee?"

"If you'll excuse me a few moments."

"Is there no one else to do it?"

She seemed to wonder who there should be. "I keep no servants."

"Then can't I help?" After which, as she but looked at me, I bettered it. "Can't she wait on herself?"

Miss Spencer had a slow headshake — as if that too had been a strange idea. "She isn't used to *manual* labour."

The discrimination was a treat, but I cultivated decorum. "I see — and you *are*." But at the same time I couldn't abjure curiosity. "Before you go, at any rate, please tell me this: who *is* this wonderful lady?"

"I told you just who in France — that extraordinary day. She's the wife of my cousin, whom you saw there."

"The lady disowned by her family in consequence of her marriage?"

"Yes; they've never seen her again. They've completely broken with her."

"And where's her husband?"

"My poor cousin's dead."

I pulled up, but only a moment. "And where's your money?"

The poor thing flinched — I kept her on the rack. "I don't know," she woefully said.

I scarce know what it didn't prompt me to — but I went step by step. "On her husband's death this lady at once came to you?"

It was as if she had had too often to describe it. "Yes, she arrived one day."

"How long ago?"

"Two years and four months."

"And has been here ever since?"

"Ever since."

I took it all in. "And how does she like it?"

"Well, not *very* much," said Miss Spencer divinely.

That too I took in. "And how do *you* — ?"

She laid her face in her two hands an instant as she had done ten minutes before. Then, quickly, she went to get the Countess's coffee.

Left alone in the little parlour I found myself divided between the perfection of my disgust and a contrary wish to see, to learn more. At the end of a few minutes the young man in attendance on the lady in question reappeared as for a fresh gape at me. He was inordinately grave — to be dressed in such particoloured flannels; and he produced with no great confidence on his own side the message with which he had been charged. "She wants to know if you won't come right out."

"Who wants to know?"

"The Countess. That French lady."

"She has asked you to bring me?"

"Yes sir," said the young man feebly — for I may claim to have surpassed him in stature and weight.

I went out with him, and we found his instructress seated under one of the small quince-trees in front of the house; where she was engaged in drawing a fine needle with a very fat hand through a piece of embroidery not remarkable for freshness. She pointed graciously to the chair beside her and I sat down. Mr. Mixter glanced about him and then accommodated himself on the grass at her feet; whence he gazed upward more gapingly than ever and as if convinced that between us something wonderful would now occur.

"I'm sure you spick French," said the Countess, whose eyes were singularly protuberant as she played over me her agreeable smile.

"I do, madam — *tant bien que mal*,"[10] I replied, I fear, more dryly.

"Ah voilà!" she cried as with delight. "I knew it as soon as I looked at you. You've been in my poor dear country."

"A considerable time."

"You love it then, *mon pays de France*?"[11]

"Oh it's an old affection." But I wasn't exuberant.

"And you know Paris well?"

"Yes, *sans me vanter*,[12] madam, I think I really do." And with a certain conscious purpose I let my eyes meet her own.

She presently, hereupon, moved her own and glanced down at Mr. Mixter. "What are we talking about?" she demanded of her attentive pupil.

He pulled his knees up, plucked at the grass, stared, blushed a little. "You're talking French," said Mr. Mixter.

"*La belle découverte*!"[13] mocked the Countess. "It's going on ten months," she explained to me, "since I took him in hand. Don't put yourself out not to say he's *la bêtise même*,"[14] she added in fine style. "He won't in the least understand you."

A moment's consideration of Mr. Mixter, awkwardly sporting at our feet, quite assured me that he wouldn't. "I hope your other pupils do you more honour," I then remarked to my entertainer.

"I have no others. They don't know what French — or what anything else — is in this place; they don't want to know. You may therefore imagine the pleasure it is to me to meet a person who speaks it like yourself." I could but reply that my own pleasure wasn't less, and she continued to draw the stitches through her embroidery with an elegant curl of her little finger. Every few moments she put her eyes, near-sightedly, closer to her work — this as if for elegance too. She inspired me with no more confidence than her late husband, if husband he was, had done, years before, on the occasion with which this one so detestably matched: she was coarse, common, affected, dishonest — no more a Countess than I was a Caliph. She had an assurance — based clearly on experience; but this couldn't have been the experience of "race." Whatever it was indeed it did now, in a yearning fashion, flare out of her. "Talk to me of Paris, *mon beau Paris*[15] that I'd give my eyes to see. The very name of it *me fait languir*.[16] How long since you were there?"

"A couple of months ago."

"*Vous avez de la chance*![17] Tell me something about it. What were they doing? Oh for an hour of the Boulevard!"

"They were doing about what they're always doing — amusing themselves a good deal."

---

[10] So-so.

[11] "My country of France."

[12] "Without bragging."

[13] "Wonderful discovery!"

[14] "Stupidity personified."

[15] "My lovely Paris."

[16] "Makes me pine."

[17] "Lucky you!"

"At the theatres, *hein?*"[18] sighed the Countess. "At the cafés-concerts? *sous ce beau ciel*[19] — at the little tables before the doors? *Quelle existence!*[20] You know I'm a Parisienne, monsieur," she added, "to my finger-tips."

"Miss Spencer was mistaken then," I ventured to return, "in telling me you're a Provençale."

She stared a moment, then put her nose to her embroidery, which struck me as having acquired even while we sat a dingier and more desultory air. "Ah I'm a Provençale by birth, but a Parisienne by — inclination." After which she pursued: "And by the saddest events of my life — as well as by some of the happiest, hélas!"

"In other words by a varied experience!" I now at last smiled.

She questioned me over it with her hard little salient eyes. "Oh experience! — I could talk of that, no doubt, if I wished. *On en a de toutes les sortes*[21] — and I never dreamed that mine, for example, would ever have *this* in store for me." And she indicated with her large bare elbow and with a jerk of her head all surrounding objects; the little white house, the pair of quince-trees, the rickety paling, even the rapt Mr. Mixter.

I took them all bravely in. "Ah if you mean you're decidedly in exile — !"

"You may imagine what it is. These two years of my *épreuve* — *elles m'en ont données, des heures, des heures!*[22] One gets used to things" — and she raised her shoulders to the highest shrug ever accomplished at North Verona; "so that I sometimes think I've got used to this. But there are some things that are always beginning again. For example my coffee."

I so far again lent myself. "Do you always have coffee at this hour?"

Her eyebrows went up as high as her shoulders had done. "At what hour would you propose to me to have it? I must have my little cup after breakfast."

"Ah you breakfast at this hour?"

"At mid-day — *comme cela se fait.*[23] Here they breakfast at a quarter past seven. That 'quarter past' is charming!"

"But you were telling me about your coffee," I observed sympathetically.

"My *cousine* can't believe in it; she can't understand it. *C'est une fille charmante,*[24] but that little cup of black coffee with a drop of '*fine,*'[25] served at this hour — they exceed her comprehension. So I have to break the ice each day, and it takes the coffee the time you see to arrive. And when it does arrive, monsieur — ! If I don't press it on *you* — though monsieur here sometimes joins me! — it's because you've drunk it on the Boulevard."

I resented extremely so critical a view of my poor friend's exertions, but I said nothing at all — the only way to be sure of my civility. I dropped my eyes on Mr. Mixter, who, sitting cross-legged and nursing his knees, watched my companion's foreign graces with an interest that familiarity had apparently done little to restrict. She became aware, naturally, of my mystified view of him and faced the question with all her boldness. "He adores me, you

---

[18] "What?"

[19] "Under the beautiful sky."

[20] "What a life!"

[21] "One has all sorts of them."

[22] "Suffering — they have given me hours and hours of it!"

[23] "As it's done."

[24] "She's a charming girl."

[25] Brandy.

know," she murmured with her nose again in her tapestry — "he dreams of becoming *mon amoureux*.[26] Yes, *il me fait une cour acharnée*[27] — such as you see him. That's what we've come to. He has read some French novel — it took him six months. But ever since that he has thought himself a hero and me — such as I am, monsieur — *je ne sais quelle dévergondée!*"[28]

Mr. Mixter may have inferred that he was to that extent the object of our reference; but of the manner in which he was handled he must have had small suspicion — preoccupied as he was, as to my companion, with the ecstasy of contemplation. Our hostess moreover at this moment came out of the house, bearing a coffee-pot and three cups on a neat little tray. I took from her eyes, as she approached us, a brief but intense appeal — the mute expression, as I felt, conveyed in the hardest little look she had yet addressed me, of her longing to know what, as a man of the world in general and of the French world in particular, I thought of these allied forces now so encamped on the stricken field of her life. I could only "act" however, as they said at North Verona, quite impenetrably — only make no answering sign. I couldn't intimate, much less could I frankly utter, my inward sense of the Countess's probable past, with its measure of her virtue, value and accomplishments, and of the limits of the considera-tion to which she could properly pretend. I couldn't give my friend a hint of how I myself personally "saw" her interesting pensioner — whether as the runaway wife of a too-jealous hair-dresser or of a too-morose pastry-cook, say; whether as a very small bourgeoise, in fine, who had vitiated her case beyond patching up, or even as some character, of the nomadic sort, less edifying still. I couldn't let in, by the jog of a shutter, as it were, a hard informing ray and then, washing my hands of the business, turn my back for ever. I could on the contrary but save the situation, my own at least, for the moment, by pulling myself together with a master hand and appearing to ignore everything but that the dreadful person between us *was* a "grande dame." This effort was possible indeed but as a retreat in good order and with all the forms of courtesy. If I couldn't speak, still less could I stay, and I think I must, in spite of everything, have turned black with disgust to see Caroline Spencer stand there like a waiting-maid. I therefore won't answer for the shade of success that may have attended my saying to the Countess, on my feet and as to leave her: "You expect to remain some time in these *parages?*"[29]

What passed between us, as from face to face, while she looked up at me, *that* at least our companion may have caught, that at least may have sown, for the aftertime, some seed of revelation. The Countess repeated her terrible shrug. "Who knows? I don't see my way — ! It isn't an existence, but when one's in misery — ! *Chère belle,*" she added as an appeal to Miss Spencer, "you've gone and forgotten the '*fine*'!"

I detained that lady as, after considering a moment in silence the small array, she was about to turn off in quest of this article. I held out my hand in silence — I had to go. Her wan set little face, severely mild and with the question of a moment before now quite cold in it, spoke of extreme fatigue, but also of something else strange and conceived — whether a desperate patience still, or at last some other desperation, being more than I can say. What was clearest on the whole was that she was glad I was going. Mr. Mixter had risen to his feet and was pouring out the Countess's coffee. As I went back past the Baptist church I could feel how right my poor friend had been in her conviction at the other, the still intenser, the now historic crisis, that she should still see something of that dear old Europe.

---

[26] "My lover."

[27] "He has pursued me relentlessly."

[28] "I don't know what sort of shameless person."

[29] Parts.

QUESTIONS

1. How would you characterize the narrator? Is there anything he should have done to help Caroline Spencer? Is there anything he could have done?

2. Does the four-part division of this story move the plot along or merely create the impression of four separate scenes? By what means has James tried to link the parts?

3. Is there anything in the first scene that foreshadows Miss Spencer's end?

4. James often portrays innocent Americans falling prey to experienced, cynical Europeans. He does so here. Whose fault is it that Miss Spencer is taken advantage of? Is it her own?

5. The narrator knows enough to recognize villainy when he sees it. Look closely at the scene between him and the "cousin." How does James convey the sense of recognition?

6. "Madame la Comtesse" is obviously not a countess. But how does James help us to see through her imposture without telling us in so many words that she is a fake?

7. What does the character Mr. Mixter contribute to our perception of the Countess? Is his name suggestive of his personality?

8. Consider the tone of the final sentence. What are we to make of the phrase "dear old Europe"?

HENRY JAMES

Brooksmith

We are scattered now, the friends of the late Mr Oliver Offord; but whenever we chance to meet I think we are conscious of a certain esoteric respect for each other. "Yes, you too have been in Arcadia," we seem not too grumpily to allow. When I pass the house in Mansfield Street I remember that Arcadia was there. I don't know who has it now, and I don't want to know; it's enough to be so sure that if I should ring the bell there would be no such luck for me as that Brooksmith should open the door. Mr Offord, the most agreeable, the most lovable of bachelors, was a retired diplomatist, living on his pension, confined by his infirmities to his fireside and delighted to be found there any afternoon in the year by such visitors as Brooksmith allowed to come up. Brooksmith was his butler and his most intimate friend, to whom we all stood, or I should say sat, in the same relation in which the subject of the sovereign finds himself to the prime minister. By having been for years, in foreign lands, the most delightful Englishman any one had ever known, Mr Offord had, in my opinion, rendered signal service to his country. But I suppose he had been too much liked — liked even by those who didn't like *it* — so that as people of that sort never get titles or dotations for the horrid things they have *not* done, his principal reward was simply that we went to see him.

Oh, we went perpetually, and it was not our fault if he was not overwhelmed with this particular honour. Any visitor who came once came again — to come merely once was a slight which nobody, I am sure, had ever put upon him. His circle, therefore, was essentially composed of *habitués*,[1] who were *habitués* for each other as well as for him, as those of a happy *salon*[2] should be. I remember vividly every element of the place, down to the intensely Londonish look of the grey opposite houses, in the gap of the white curtains of the high windows, and the exact spot where, on a particular afternoon, I put down my tea-cup for Brooksmith, lingering an instant, to gather it up as if he were plucking a flower. Mr Offord's drawing-room was indeed Brooksmith's garden, his pruned and tended human *parterre*,[3] and if we all flourished there and grew well in our places it was largely owing to his supervision.

Many persons have heard much, though most have doubtless seen little, of the famous institution of the *salon*, and many are born to the depression of knowing that this finest flower

---

[1] Regulars.

[2] A gathering of intellectuals in the reception room of a private house, usually a lady's.

[3] A flower garden arranged symmetrically.

of social life refuses to bloom where the English tongue is spoken. The explanation is usually that our women have not the skill to cultivate it — the art to direct, between suggestive shores, the course of the stream of talk. My affectionate, my pious memory of Mr Offord contradicts this induction only, I fear, more insidiously to confirm it. The very sallow and slightly smoked drawing-room in which he spent so large a portion of the last years of his life certainly deserved the distinguished name; but on the other hand it could not be said at all to owe its stamp to the soft pressure of the indispensable sex. The dear man had indeed been capable of one of those sacrifices to which women are deemed peculiarly apt; he had recognised (under the influence, in some degree, it is true, of physical infirmity), that if you wished people to find you at home you must manage not to be out. He had in short accepted the fact which many dabblers in the social art are slow to learn, that you must really, as they say, take a line and that the only way to be at home is to stay at home. Finally his own fireside had become a summary of his habits. Why should he ever have left it? — since this would have been leaving what was notoriously pleasantest in London, the compact charmed cluster (thinning away indeed into casual couples), round the fine old last century chimney-piece which, with the exception of the remarkable collection of miniatures, was the best thing the place contained. Mr Offord was not rich; he had nothing but his pension and the use for life of the somewhat superannuated house.

When I am reminded by some uncomfortable contrast of to-day how perfectly we were all handled there I ask myself once more what had been the secret of such perfection. One had taken it for granted at the time, for anything that is supremely good produces more acceptance than surprise. I felt we were all happy, but I didn't consider how our happiness was managed. And yet there were questions to be asked, questions that strike me as singularly obvious now that there is nobody to answer them. Mr Offord had solved the insoluble; he had, without feminine help (save in the sense that ladies were dying to come to him and he saved the lives of several), established a *salon*; but I might have guessed that there was a method in his madness — a law in his success. He had not hit it off by a mere fluke. There was an art in it all, and how was the art so hidden? Who, indeed, if it came to that, was the occult artist? Launching this inquiry the other day, I had already got hold of the tail of my reply. I was helped by the very wonder of some of the conditions that came back to me — those that used to seem as natural as sunshine in a fine climate.

How was it, for instance, that we never were a crowd, never either too many or too few, always the right people *with* the right people (there must really have been no wrong people at all), always coming and going, never sticking fast nor overstaying, yet never popping in or out with an indecorous familiarity? How was it that we all sat where we wanted and moved when we wanted and met whom we wanted and escaped whom we wanted; joining, according to the accident of inclination, the general circle or falling in with a single talker on a convenient sofa? Why were all the sofas so convenient, the accidents so happy, the talkers so ready, the listeners so willing, the subjects presented to you in a rotation as quickly fore-ordained as the courses at dinner? A dearth of topics would have been as unheard of as a lapse in the service. These speculations couldn't fail to lead me to the fundamental truth that Brooksmith had been somehow at the bottom of the mystery. If he had not established the *salon* at least he had carried it on. Brooksmith, in short, was the artist!

We felt this, covertly, at the time, without formulating it, and were conscious, as an ordered and prosperous community, of his evenhanded justice, untainted with flunkeyism. He had none of that vulgarity — his touch was infinitely fine. The delicacy of it was clear to me on the first occasion my eyes rested, as they were so often to rest again, on the domestic revealed, in the turbid light of the street, by the opening of the house-door. I saw on the spot that though he had plenty of school he carried it without arrogance — he had remained articulate and human. *L'Ecole Anglaise*,[4] Mr Offord used to call him, laughing, when, later, it happened more than once that we had some conversation about him. But I remember accusing Mr Offord of not doing him quite ideal justice. That he was not one of the giants of the school, however, my old friend, who really understood him perfectly and was devoted to him, as I shall show, quite admitted; which doubtless poor Brooksmith had himself felt, to his cost, when his value in the market was originally determined. The utility of his class in general is estimated by the foot and the inch, and poor Brooksmith had only about five feet two to put into circulation. He acknowledged the inadequacy of this provision, and I am sure was penetrated with the everlasting fitness of the relation between service and stature. If *he* had been Mr Offord he certainly would have found Brooksmith wanting, and indeed the laxity of his employer on this score was one of many things which he had had to condone and to which he had at last indulgently adapted himself.

I remember the old man's saying to me: "Oh, my servants, if they can live with me a fortnight they can live with me for ever. But it's the first fortnight that tries 'em." It was in the first fortnight, for instance, that Brooksmith had had to learn that he was exposed to being addressed as "my dear fellow" and "my poor child." Strange and deep must such a probation have been to him, and he doubtless emerged from it tempered and purified. This was written to a certain extent in his appearance; in his spare, brisk little person, in his cloistered white face and extraordinarily polished hair, which told of responsibility, looked as if it were kept up to the same high standard as the plate; in his small, clear, anxious eyes, even in the permitted, though not exactly encouraged tuft on his chin. "He thinks me rather mad, but I've broken him in, and now he likes the place, he likes the company," said the old man. I embraced this fully after I had become aware that Brooksmith's main characteristic was a deep and shy refinement, though I remember I was rather puzzled when, on another occasion, Mr Offord remarked: "What he likes is the talk — mingling in the conversation." I was conscious that I had never seen Brooksmith permit himself this freedom, but I guessed in a moment that what Mr Offord alluded to was a participation more intense than any speech could have repre- sented — that of being perpetually present on a hundred legitimate pretexts, errands, neces- sities, and breathing the very atmosphere of criticism, the famous criticism of life. "Quite an education, sir, isn't it, sir?" he said to me one day at the foot of the stairs, when he was letting me out; and I have always remembered the words and the tone as the first sign of the quickening drama of poor Brooksmith's fate. It was indeed an education, but to what was this sensitive young man of thirty-five, of the servile class, being educated?

Practically and inevitably, for the time, to companionship, to the perpetual, the even exaggerated reference and appeal of a person brought to dependence by his time of life and his infirmities and always addicted moreover (this was the exaggeration) to the art of giving you pleasure by letting you do things for him. There were certain things Mr Offord was capable of pretending he liked you to do, even when he didn't, if he thought *you* liked them. If it happened that you didn't either (this was rare, but it might be), of course there were cross- purposes; but Brooksmith was there to prevent their going very far. This was precisely the way he acted as moderator: he averted misunderstandings or cleared them up. He had been capable, strange as it may appear, of acquiring for this purpose an insight into the French

---

[4] The English School.

tongue, which was often used at Mr Offord's; for besides being habitual to most of the foreigners, and they were many, who haunted the place or arrived with letters (letters often requiring a little worried consideration, of which Brooksmith always had cognisance), it had really become the primary language of the master of the house. I don't know if all the *malentendus*[5] were in French, but almost all the explanations were, and this didn't a bit prevent Brooksmith from following them. I know Mr Offord used to read passages to him from Montaigne and Saint-Simon, for he read perpetually when he was alone — when they were alone, I should say — and Brooksmith was always about. Perhaps you'll say no wonder Mr Offord's butler regarded him as "rather mad." However, if I'm not sure what he thought about Montaigne I'm convinced he admired Saint-Simon. A certain feeling for letters must have rubbed off on him from the mere handling of his master's books, which he was always carrying to and fro and putting back in their places.

I often noticed that if an anecdote or a quotation, much more a lively discussion, was going forward, he would, if busy with the fire or the curtains, the lamp or the tea, find a pretext for remaining in the room till the point should be reached. If his purpose was to catch it you were not discreet to call him off, and I shall never forget a look, a hard, stony stare (I caught it in its passage), which, one day when there were a good many people in the room, he fastened upon the footman who was helping him in the service and who, in an undertone, had asked him some irrelevant question. It was the only manifestation of harshness that I ever observed on Brooksmith's part, and at first I wondered what was the matter. Then I became conscious that Mr Offord was relating a very curious anecdote, never before perhaps made so public, and imparted to the narrator by an eye-witness of the fact, bearing upon Lord Byron's life in Italy. Nothing would induce me to reproduce it here; but Brooksmith had been in danger of losing it. If I ever should venture to reproduce it I shall feel how much I lose in not having my fellow-auditor to refer to.

The first day Mr Offord's door was closed was therefore a dark date in contemporary history. It was raining hard and my umbrella was wet, but Brooksmith took it from me exactly as if this were a preliminary for going upstairs. I observed however that instead of putting it away he held it poised and trickling over the rug, and then I became aware that he was looking at me with deep, acknowledging eyes — his air of universal responsibility. I immediately understood; there was scarcely need of the question and the answer that passed between us. When I did understand that the old man had given up, for the first time, though only for the occasion, I exclaimed dolefully: "What a difference it will make — and to how many people!"

"I shall be one of them, sir!" said Brooksmith; and that was the beginning of the end.

Mr Offord came down again, but the spell was broken, and the great sign of it was that the conversation was, for the first time, not directed. It wandered and stumbled, a little frightened, like a lost child — it had let go the nurse's hand. "The worst of it is that now we shall talk about my health — *ç'est la fin de tout*,"[6] Mr Offord said, when he reappeared; and then I recognised what a sign of change that would be — for he had never tolerated anything so provincial. The talk became ours, in a word — not his; and as ours, even when *he* talked, it could only be inferior. In this form it was a distress to Brooksmith, whose attention now wandered from it altogether: he had so much closer a vision of his master's intimate conditions than our superficialities represented. There were better hours, and he was more in and out of the room, but I could see that he was conscious that the great institution was falling to pieces. He seemed to wish to take counsel with me about it, to feel responsible for its going on

---

[5] Misunderstandings.

[6] "It's all over."

in some form or other. When for the second period — the first had lasted several days — he had to tell me that our old friend didn't receive, I half expected to hear him say after a moment: "Do you think I ought to, sir, in his place?" — as he might have asked me, with the return of autumn, if I thought he had better light the drawing-room fire.

He had a resigned philosophic sense of what his guests — our guests, as I came to regard them in our colloquies — would expect. His feeling was that he wouldn't absolutely have approved of himself as a substitute for the host; but he was so saturated with the religion of habit that he would have made, for our friends, the necessary sacrifice to the divinity. He would take them on a little further, till they could look about them. I think I saw him also mentally confronted with the opportunity to deal — for once in his life — with some of his own dumb preferences, his limitations of sympathy, *weeding* a little, in prospect, and returning to a purer tradition. It was not unknown to me that he considered that toward the end of Mr Offord's career a certain laxity of selection had crept in.

At last it came to be the case that we all found the closed door more often than the open one; but even when it was closed Brooksmith managed a crack for me to squeeze through; so that practically I never turned away without having paid a visit. The difference simply came to be that the visit was to Brooksmith. It took place in the hall, at the familiar foot of the stairs, and we didn't sit down — at least Brooksmith didn't; moreover it was devoted wholly to one topic and always had the air of being already over — beginning, as it were, at the end. But it was always interesting — it always gave me something to think about. It is true that the subject of my meditation was ever the same — ever "It's all very well, but what *will* become of Brooksmith?" Even my private answer to this question left me still unsatisfied. No doubt Mr Offord would provide for him, but *what* would he provide? That was the great point. He couldn't provide society; and society had become a necessity of Brooksmith's nature. I must add that he never showed a symptom of what I may call sordid solicitude — anxiety on his own account. He was rather livid and intensely grave, as befitted a man before whose eyes the "shade of that which once was great" was passing away. He had the solemnity of a person winding up, under depressing circumstances, a long established and celebrated business; he was a kind of social executor or liquidator. But his manner seemed to testify exclusively to the uncertainty of *our* future. I couldn't in those days have afforded it — I lived in two rooms in Jermyn Street and didn't "keep a man;" but even if my income had permitted I shouldn't have ventured to say to Brooksmith (emulating Mr Offord), "My dear fellow, I'll take you on." The whole tone of our intercourse was so much more an implication that it was *I* who should now want a lift. Indeed there was a tacit assurance in Brooksmith's whole attitude that he would have me on his mind.

One of the most assiduous members of our circle had been Lady Kenyon, and I remember his telling me one day that her ladyship had, in spite of her own infirmities, lately much aggravated, been in person to inquire. In answer to this I remarked that she would feel it more than any one. Brooksmith was silent a moment; at the end of which he said, in a certain tone (there is no reproducing some of his tones), "I'll go and see her." I went to see her myself, and I learned that he had waited upon her; but when I said to her, in the form of a joke but with a core of earnest, that when all was over some of us ought to combine, to club together to set Brooksmith up on his own account, she replied a trifle disappointingly: "Do you mean in a public-house?" I looked at her in a way that I think Brooksmith himself would have approved, and then I answered: "Yes, the Offord Arms." What I had meant, of course, was that, for the love of art itself, we ought to look to it that such a peculiar faculty and so much acquired experience should not be wasted. I really think that if we had caused a few black-edged cards to be struck off and circulated— "Mr Brooksmith will continue to receive on the old premises from four to seven; business carried on as usual during the alterations" — the majority of us would have rallied.

Several times he took me upstairs — always by his own proposal — and our dear old friend, in bed, in a curious flowered and brocaded *casaque*[7] which made him, especially as his head was tied up in a handkerchief to match, look, to my imagination, like the dying Voltaire, held for ten minutes a sadly shrunken little *salon*. I felt indeed each time, as if I were attending the last *coucher*[8] of some social sovereign. He was royally whimsical about his sufferings and not at all concerned — quite as if the Constitution provided for the case — about his successor. He glided over *our* sufferings charmingly, and none of his jokes — it was a gallant abstention, some of them would have been so easy — were at our expense. Now and again, I confess, there was one at Brooksmith's, but so pathetically sociable as to make the excellent man look at me in a way that seemed to say: "Do exchange a glance with me, or I sha'n't be able to stand it." What he was not able to stand was not what Mr Offord said about him, but what he wasn't able to say in return. His notion of conversation, for himself, was giving you the convenience of speaking to him; and when he went to "see" Lady Kenyon, for instance, it was to carry her the tribute of his receptive silence. Where would the speech of his betters have been if proper service had been a manifestation of sound? In that case the fundamental difference would have had to be shown by *their* dumbness, and many of them, poor things, were dumb enough without that provision. Brooksmith took an unfailing interest in the preservation of the fundamental difference; it was the thing he had most on his conscience.

What had become of it, however, when Mr Offord passed away like any inferior person — was relegated to eternal stillness like a butler upstairs? His aspect for several days after the expected event may be imagined, and the multiplication by funeral observance of the things he didn't say. When everything was over — it was late the same day — I knocked at the door of the house of mourning as I so often had done before. I could never call on Mr Offord again, but I had come, literally, to call on Brooksmith. I wanted to ask him if there was anything I could do for him, tainted with vagueness as this inquiry could only be. My wild dream of taking him into my own service had died away: my service was not worth his being taken into. My offer to him could only be to help him to find another place, and yet there was an indelicacy, as it were, in taking for granted that his thoughts would immediately be fixed on another. I had a hope that he would be able to give his life a different form — though certainly not the form, the frequent result of such bereavements, of his setting up a little shop. That would have been dreadful; for I should have wished to further any enterprise that he might embark in, yet how could I have brought myself to go and pay him shillings and take back coppers over a counter? My visit then was simply an intended compliment. He took it as such, gratefully and with all the tact in the world. He knew I really couldn't help him and that I knew he knew I couldn't; but we discussed the situation — with a good deal of elegant generality — at the foot of the stairs, in the hall already dismantled, where I had so often discussed other situations with him. The executors were in possession, as was still more apparent when he made me pass for a few minutes into the dining-room, where various objects were muffled up for removal.

Two definite facts, however, he had to communicate; one being that he was to leave the house for ever that night (servants, for some mysterious reason, seem always to depart by night), and the other — he mentioned it only at the last, with hesitation — that he had already been informed his late master had left him a legacy of eighty pounds. "I'm very glad," I said, and Brooksmith rejoined: "It was so like him to think of me." This was all that passed between us on the subject, and I know nothing of his judgment of Mr Offord's memento. Eighty

---

[7] Bed jacket.

[8] Deathbed.

pounds are always eighty pounds, and no one has ever left *me* an equal sum; but, all the same, for Brooksmith, I was disappointed. I don't know what I had expected — in short I was disappointed. Eighty pounds might stock a little shop — a *very* little shop; but, I repeat, I couldn't bear to think of that. I asked my friend if he had been able to save a little, and he replied: "No, sir; I have had to do things." I didn't inquire what things he had had to do; they were his own affair, and I took his word for them as assentingly as if he had had the greatness of an ancient house to keep up; especially as there was something in his manner that seemed to convey a prospect of further sacrifice.

"I shall have to turn round a bit, sir — I shall have to look about me," he said; and then he added, indulgently, magnanimously: "If you should happen to hear of anything for me — "

I couldn't let him finish; this was, in its essence, too much in the really grand manner. It would be a help to my getting him off my mind to be able to pretend I *could* find the right place, and that help he wished to give me, for it was doubtless painful to him to see me in so false a position. I interposed with a few words to the effect that I was well aware that wherever he should go, whatever he should do, he would miss our old friend terribly — miss him even more than I should, having been with him so much more. This led him to make the speech that I have always remembered as the very text of the whole episode.

"Oh, sir, it's sad for *you*, very sad, indeed, and for a great many gentlemen and ladies; that it is, sir. But for me, sir, it is, if I may say so, still graver even than that: it's just the loss of something that was everything. For me, sir," he went on, with rising tears, "he was just *all*, if you know what I mean, sir. You have others, sir, I daresay — not that I would have you understand me to speak of them as in any way tantamount. But you have the pleasures of society, sir; if it's only in talking about him, sir, as I daresay you do freely — for all his blessed memory has to fear from it — with gentlemen and ladies who have had the same honour. That's not for me, sir, and I have to keep my associations to myself. Mr Offord was *my* society, and now I have no more. You go back to conversation, sir, after all, and I go back to my place," Brooksmith stammered, without exaggerated irony or dramatic bitterness, but with a flat, unstudied veracity and his hand on the knob of the street-door. He turned it to let me out and then he added: "I just go downstairs, sir, again, and I stay there."

"My poor child," I replied, in my emotion, quite as Mr Offord used to speak, "my dear fellow, leave it to me; we'll look after you, we'll all do something for you."

"Ah, if you could give me some one *like* him! But there ain't two in the world," said Brooksmith as we parted.

He had given me his address — the place where he would be to be heard of. For a long time I had no occasion to make use of the information; for he proved indeed, on trial, a very difficult case. In a word the people who knew him and had known Mr Offord, didn't want to take him, and yet I couldn't bear to try to thrust him among people who didn't know him. I spoke to many of our old friends about him, and I found them all governed by the odd mixture of feelings of which I myself was conscious, and disposed, further, to entertain a suspicion that he was "spoiled," with which I then would have nothing to do. In plain terms a certain embarrassment, a sensible awkwardness, when they thought of it, attached to the idea of using him as a menial: they had met him so often in society. Many of them would have asked him, and did ask him, or rather did ask me to ask him, to come and see them; but a mere visiting-list was not what I wanted for him. He was too short for people who were very particular; nevertheless I heard of an opening in a diplomatic household which led me to write him a note, though I was looking much less for something grand than for something human. Five days later I heard from him. The secretary's wife had decided, after keeping him waiting till then, that she couldn't take a servant out of a house in which there had not been a lady. The note had a P.S.: "It's a good job there wasn't, sir, such a lady as some."

A week later he came to see me and told me he was "suited" — committed to some highly respectable people (they were something very large in the City), who lived on the Bayswater side of the Park. "I daresay it will be rather poor, sir," he admitted; "but I've seen the fireworks, haven't I, sir? — it can't be fireworks *every* night. After Mansfield Street there ain't much choice." There was a certain amount, however, it seemed; for the following year, going one day to call on a country cousin, a lady of a certain age who was spending a fortnight in town with some friends of her own, a family unknown to me and resident in Chester Square, the door of the house was opened, to my surprise and gratification, by Brooksmith in person. When I came out I had some conversation with him, from which I gathered that he had found the large City people too dull for endurance, and I guessed, though he didn't say it, that he had found them vulgar as well. I don't know what judgment he would have passed on his actual patrons if my relative had not been their friend; but under the circumstances he abstained from comment.

None was necessary, however, for before the lady in question brought her visit to a close they honoured me with an invitation to dinner, which I accepted. There was a largeish party on the occasion, but I confess I thought of Brooksmith rather more than of the seated company. They required no depth of attention — they were all referable to usual, irredeemable, inevitable types. It was the world of cheerful commonplace and conscious gentility and prosperous density, a full-fed, material, insular world, a world of hideous florid plate and ponderous order and thin conversation. There was not a word said about Byron. Nothing would have induced me to look at Brooksmith in the course of the repast, and I felt sure that not even my overturning the wine would have induced him to meet my eye. We were in intellectual sympathy — we felt, as regards each other, a kind of social responsibility. In short we had been in Arcadia together, and we had both come to *this!* No wonder we were ashamed to be confronted. When he helped on my overcoat, as I was going away, we parted, for the first time since the earliest days in Mansfield Street, in silence. I thought he looked lean and wasted, and I guessed that his new place was not more "human" than his previous one. There was plenty of beef and beer, but there was no reciprocity. The question for him to have asked before accepting the position would have been not "How many footmen are kept?" but "How much imagination?"

The next time I went to the house — I confess it was not very soon — I encountered his successor, a personage who evidently enjoyed the good fortune of never having quitted his natural level. Could any be higher? he seemed to ask — over the heads of three footmen and even of some visitors. He made me feel as if Brooksmith were dead; but I didn't dare to inquire — I couldn't have borne his "I haven't the least idea, sir." I despatched a note to the address Brooksmith had given me after Mr Offord's death, but I received no answer. Six months later, however, I was favoured with a visit from an elderly, dreary, dingy person, who introduced herself to me as Mr Brooksmith's aunt and from whom I learned that he was out of place and out of health and had allowed her to come and say to me that if I could spare half-an-hour to look in at him he would take it as a rare honour.

I went the next day — his messenger had given me a new address — and found my friend lodged in a short sordid street in Marylebone, one of those corners of London that wear the last expression of sickly meanness. The room into which I was shown was above the small establishment of a dryer and cleaner who had inflated kid gloves and discoloured shawls in his shop-front. There was a great deal of grimy infant life up and down the place, and there was a hot, moist smell within, as of the "boiling" of dirty linen. Brooksmith sat with a blanket over his legs at a clean little window, where, from behind stiff bluish-white curtains, he could look across at a huckster's and a tinsmith's and a small greasy public-house. He had passed through an illness and was convalescent, and his mother, as well as his aunt, was in attendance on him. I liked the mother, who was bland and intensely humble, but I didn't much fancy the aunt, whom I connected, perhaps unjustly, with the opposite public-house (she seemed somehow to be greasy with the same grease), and whose furtive eye followed every movement of my hand, as if to see if it were not going into my pocket. It didn't take this direction — I couldn't, unsolicited, put myself at that sort of ease with Brooksmith. Several times the door of the room opened, and mysterious old women peeped in and shuffled back again. I don't know who they were; poor Brooksmith seemed encompassed with vague, prying, beery females.

He was vague himself, and evidently weak, and much embarrassed, and not an allusion was made between us to Mansfield Street. The vision of the *salon* of which he had been an ornament hovered before me, however, by contrast, sufficiently. He assured me that he was really getting better, and his mother remarked that he would come round if he could only get his spirits up. The aunt echoed this opinion, and I became more sure that in her own case she knew where to go for such a purpose. I'm afraid I was rather weak with my old friend, for I neglected the opportunity, so exceptionally good, to rebuke the levity which had led him to throw up honourable positions — fine, stiff, steady berths, with morning prayers, as I knew, attached to one of them — in Bayswater and Belgravia. Very likely his reasons had been profane and sentimental; he didn't want morning prayers, he wanted to be somebody's dear fellow; but I couldn't be the person to rebuke him. He shuffled these episodes out of sight — I saw that he had no wish to discuss them. I perceived further, strangely enough, that it would probably be a questionable pleasure for him to see me again: he doubted now even of my power to condone his aberrations. He didn't wish to have to explain; and his behaviour, in future, was likely to need explanation. When I bade him farewell he looked at me a moment with eyes that said everything: "How can I talk about those exquisite years in this place, before these people, with the old women poking their heads in? It was very good of you to come to see me — it wasn't my idea; *she* brought you. We've said everything; it's over; you'll lose all patience with me, and I'd rather you shouldn't see the rest." I sent him some money, in a letter, the next day, but I saw the rest only in the light of a barren sequel.

A whole year after my visit to him I became aware once, in dining out, that Brooksmith was one of the several servants who hovered behind our chairs. He had not opened the door of the house to me, and I had not recognised him in the cluster of retainers in the hall. This time I tried to catch his eye, but he never gave me a chance, and when he handed me a dish I could only be careful to thank him audibly. Indeed I partook of two *entrées*[9] of which I had my doubts, subsequently converted into certainties, in order not to snub him. He looked well enough in health, but much older, and wore, in an exceptionally marked degree, the glazed and expressionless mask of the British domestic *de race*.[10] I saw with dismay that if I had not known him I should have taken him, on the showing of his countenance, for an extravagant illustration of irresponsive servile gloom. I said to myself that he had become a reactionary, gone over to the Philistines, thrown himself into religion, the religion of his "place," like a foreign lady *sur le retour*.[11] I divined moreover that he was only engaged for the evening — he had become a mere waiter, had joined the band of the white-waistcoated who "go out." There was something pathetic in this fact, and it was a terrible vulgarisation of Brooksmith. It was the mercenary prose of butlerhood; he had given up the struggle for the poetry. If reciprocity was what he had missed, where was the reciprocity now? Only in the bottoms of the wine-glasses and the five shillings (or whatever they get), clapped into his hand by the permanent man. However, I supposed he had taken up a precarious branch of his profession because after all it

---

[9] Dishes served before the main course.

[10] Breed.

[11] On coming home.

sent him less downstairs. His relations with London society were more superficial, but they were of course more various. As I went away, on this occasion, I looked out for him eagerly among the four or five attendants whose perpendicular persons, fluting the walls of London passages, are supposed to lubricate the process of departure; but he was not on duty. I asked one of the others if he were not in the house, and received the prompt answer: "Just left, sir. Anything I can do for you, sir?" I wanted to say "Please give him my kind regards;" but I abstained; I didn't want to compromise him, and I never came across him again.

Often and often, in dining out, I looked for him, sometimes accepting invitations on purpose to multiply the chances of my meeting him. But always in vain; so that as I met many other members of the casual class over and over again, I at last adopted the theory that he always procured a list of expected guests beforehand and kept away from the banquets which he thus learned I was to grace. At last I gave up hope, and one day, at the end of three years, I received another visit from his aunt. She was drearier and dingier, almost squalid, and she was in great tribulation and want. Her sister, Mrs Brooksmith, had been dead a year, and three months later her nephew had disappeared. He had always looked after her a bit — since her troubles; I never knew what her troubles had been — and now she hadn't so much as a petticoat to pawn. She had also a niece, to whom she had been everything, before her troubles, but the niece had treated her most shameful. These were details; the great and romantic fact was Brooksmith's final evasion of his fate. He had gone out to wait one evening, as usual, in a white waistcoat she had done up for him with her own hands, being due at a large party up Kensington way. But he had never come home again, and had never arrived at the large party, or at any party that any one could make out. No trace of him had come to light — no gleam of the white waistcoat had pierced the obscurity of his doom. This news was a sharp shock to me, for I had my ideas about his real destination. His aged relative had promptly, as she said, guessed the worst. Somehow and somewhere he had got out of the way altogether, and now I trust that, with characteristic deliberation, he is changing the plates of the immortal gods. As my depressing visitant also said, he never *had* got his spirits up. I was fortunately able to dismiss her with her own somewhat improved. But the dim ghost of poor Brooksmith is one of those that I see. He had indeed been spoiled.

QUESTIONS

1. What effect does the narrator's occasional use of French have on the tone of this story? on the character of the narrator?

2. What is the essential difference between Brooksmith's position in Mr. Offord's home and those he holds after Mr. Offord's death?

3. Why doesn't the narrator employ Brooksmith himself?

4. Is Brooksmith a snob? What is the evidence for and against your position?

5. What does James mean by "the mercenary prose of butlerhood" as opposed to "the struggle for the poetry"? Has Brooksmith "indeed been spoiled"?

The Beast in the Jungle

I

What determined the speech that startled him in the course of their encounter scarcely matters, being probably but some words spoken by himself quite without intention — spoken as they lingered and slowly moved together after their renewal of acquaintance. He had been conveyed by friends an hour or two before to the house at which she was staying; the party of visitors at the other house, of whom he was one, and thanks to whom it was his theory, as always, that he was lost in the crowd, had been invited over to luncheon. There had been after luncheon much dispersal, all in the interest of the original motive, a view of Weatherend itself and the fine things, intrinsic features, pictures, heirlooms, treasures of all the arts, that made the place almost famous; and the great rooms were so numerous that guests could wander at their will, hang back from the principal group and in cases where they took such matters with the last seriousness give themselves up to mysterious appreciations and measurements. There were persons to be observed, singly or in couples, bending toward objects in out-of-the-way corners with their hands on their knees and their heads nodding quite as with the emphasis of an excited sense of smell. When they were two they either mingled their sounds of ecstasy or melted into silences of even deeper import, so that there were aspects of the occasion that gave it for Marcher much the air of the "look round," previous to a sale highly advertised, that excites or quenches, as may be, the dream of acquisition. The dream of acquisition at Weatherend would have had to be wild indeed, and John Marcher found himself, among such suggestions, disconcerted almost equally by the presence of those who knew too much and by that of those who knew nothing. The great rooms caused so much poetry and history to press upon him that he needed some straying apart to feel in a proper relation with them, though this impulse was not, as happened, like the gloating of some of his companions, to be compared to the movements of a dog sniffing a cupboard. It had an issue promptly enough in a direction that was not to have been calculated.

It led, briefly, in the course of the October afternoon, to his closer meeting with May Bartram, whose face, a reminder, yet not quite a remembrance, as they sat much separated at a very long table, had begun merely by troubling him rather pleasantly. It affected him as the sequel of something of which he had lost the beginning. He knew it, and for the time quite welcomed it, as a continuation, but didn't know what it continued, which was an interest or an amusement the greater as he was also somehow aware — yet without a direct sign from her — that the young woman herself hadn't lost the thread. She hadn't lost it, but she wouldn't give it back to him, he saw, without some putting forth of his hand for it; and he not only saw that, but saw several things more, things odd enough in the light of the fact that at the moment some accident of grouping brought them face to face he was still merely fumbling with the idea that any contact between them in the past would have had no importance. If it had had no importance he scarcely knew why his actual impression of her should so seem to have so much; the answer to which, however, was that in such a life as they all appeared to be leading for the moment one could but take things as they came. He was satisfied, without in the least being able to say why, that this young lady might roughly have ranked in the house as a poor relation; satisfied also that she was not there on a brief visit, but was more or less a part of the establishment — almost a working, a remunerated part. Didn't she enjoy at periods a protection that she paid for by helping, among other services, to show the place and explain it, deal with the tiresome people, answer questions about the dates of the building, the styles of the furniture, the authorship of the pictures, the favourite haunts of the ghost? It wasn't that she looked as if you could have given her shillings — it was impossible to look less so. Yet when she finally drifted toward him, distinctly handsome, though ever so much older — older than when he had seen her before — it might have been as an effect of her guessing that he had, within the couple of hours, devoted more imagination to her than to all the others put together, and had thereby penetrated to a kind of truth that the others were too stupid for. She *was* there on harder terms than any one; she was there as a consequence of things suffered, one way and another, in the interval of years; and she remembered him very much as she was remembered — only a good deal better.

By the time they at last thus came to speech they were alone in one of the rooms — remarkable for a fine portrait over the chimney-place — out of which their friends had passed, and the charm of it was that even before they had spoken they had practically arranged with each other to stay behind for talk. The charm, happily, was in other things too — partly in there being scarce a spot at Weatherend without something to stay behind for. It was in the way the autumn day looked into the high windows as it waned; the way the red light, breaking at the close from under a low sombre sky, reached out in a long shaft and played over old wainscots, old tapestry, old gold, old colour. It was most of all perhaps in the way she came to him as if, since she had been turned on to deal with the simpler sort, he might, should he choose to keep the whole thing down, just take her mild attention for a part of her general business. As soon as he heard her voice, however, the gap was filled up and the missing link supplied; the slight irony he divined in her attitude lost its advantage. He almost jumped at it to get there before her. "I met you years and years ago in Rome. I remember all about it." She confessed to disappointment — she had been so sure he didn't; and to prove how well he did he began to pour forth the particular recollections that popped up as he called for them. Her face and her voice, all at his service now, worked the miracle — the impression operating like the torch of a lamplighter who touches into flame, one by one, a long row of gas-jets. Marcher flattered himself the illumination was brilliant, yet he was really still more pleased on her showing him, with amusement, that in his haste to make everything right he had got most things rather wrong. It hadn't been at Rome — it had been at Naples; and it hadn't been eight years before — it had been more nearly ten. She hadn't been, either, with her uncle and aunt, but with her mother and her brother; in addition to which it was not with the Pembles *he* had been, but with the Boyers, coming down in their company from Rome — a point on which she insisted, a little to his confusion, and as to which she had her evidence in hand. The Boyers she had known, but didn't know the Pembles, though she had heard of them, and it was the people he was with who had made them acquainted. The incident of the thunderstorm that had raged round them with such violence as to drive them for refuge into an excavation — this incident had not occurred at the Palace of the Cæsars, but at Pompeii, on an occasion when they had been present there at an important find.

He accepted her amendments, he enjoyed her corrections, though the moral of them was, she pointed out, that he *really* didn't remember the least thing about her; and he only felt it as a drawback that when all was made strictly historic there didn't appear much of anything left. They lingered together still, she neglecting her office — for from the moment he was so clever she had no proper right to him — and both neglecting the house, just waiting as to see if a memory or two more wouldn't again breathe on them. It hadn't taken them many minutes, after all, to put down on the table, like the cards of a pack, those that constituted their respective hands; only what came out was that the pack was unfortunately not perfect — that the past, invoked, invited, encouraged, could give them, naturally, no more than it had. It had made them anciently meet — her at twenty, him at twenty-five; but nothing was so strange, they seemed to say to each other, as that, while so occupied, it hadn't done a little more for them. They looked at each other as with the feeling of an occasion missed; the present would have been so much better if the other, in the far distance, in the foreign land, hadn't been so stupidly meagre. There weren't apparently, all counted, more than a dozen little old things that had succeeded in coming to pass between them; trivialities of youth, simplicities of freshness, stupidities of ignorance, small possible germs, but too deeply buried — too deeply (didn't it seem?) to sprout after so many years. Marcher could only feel he ought to have rendered her some service — saved her from a capsized boat in the Bay or at least recovered her dressing-bag, filched from her cab in the streets of Naples by a lazzarone with a stiletto. Or it would have been nice if he could have been taken with fever all alone at his hotel, and she could have come to look after him, to write to his people, to drive him out in convalescence. *Then* they would be in possession of the something or other that their actual show seemed to lack. It yet somehow presented itself, this show, as too good to be spoiled; so that they were reduced for a few minutes more to wondering a little helplessly why — since they seemed to know a certain number of the same people — their reunion had been so long averted. They didn't use that name for it, but their delay from minute to minute to join the others was a kind of confession that they didn't quite want it to be a failure. Their attempted supposition of reasons for their not having met but showed how little they knew of each other. There came in fact a moment when Marcher felt a positive pang. It was vain to pretend she was an old friend, for all the communities were wanting, in spite of which it was as an old friend that he saw she would have suited him. He had new ones enough — was surrounded with them for instance on the stage of the other house; as a new one he probably wouldn't have so much as noticed her. He would have liked to invent something, get her to make-believe with him that some passage of a romantic or critical kind *had* originally occurred. He was really almost reaching out in imagination — as against time — for something that would do, and saying to himself that if it didn't come this sketch of a fresh start would show for quite awkwardly bungled. They would separate, and now for no second or no third chance. They would have tried and not succeeded. Then it was, just at the turn, as he afterwards made it out to himself, that, everything else failing, she herself decided to take up the case and, as it were, save the situation. He felt as soon as she spoke that she had been consciously keeping back what she said and hoping to get on without it; a scruple in her that immensely touched him when, by the end of three or four minutes more, he was able to measure it. What she brought out, at any rate, quite cleared the air and supplied the link — the link it was so odd he should frivolously have managed to lose.

"You know you told me something I've never forgotten and that again and again has made me think of you since; it was that tremendously hot day when we went to Sorrento, across the bay, for the breeze. What I allude to was what you said to me, on the way back, as we sat under the awning of the boat enjoying the cool. Have you forgotten?"

He had forgotten and was even more surprised than ashamed. But the great thing was that he saw in this no vulgar reminder of any "sweet" speech. The vanity of women had long memories, but she was making no claim on him of a compliment or a mistake. With another woman, a totally different one, he might have feared the recall possibly even of some imbecile "offer." So, in having to say that he had indeed forgotten, he was conscious rather of a loss than of a gain; he already saw an interest in the matter of her mention. "I try to think — but I give it up. Yet I remember the Sorrento day."

"I'm not very sure you do," May Bartram after a moment said; "and I'm not very sure I ought to want you to. It's dreadful to bring a person back at any time to what he was ten years before. If you've lived away from it," she smiled, "so much the better."

"Ah if *you* haven't why should I?" he asked.

"Lived away, you mean, from what I myself was?"

"From what *I* was. I was of course an ass," Marcher went on; "but I would rather know from you just the sort of ass I was than — from the moment you have something in your mind — not know anything."

Still, however, she hesitated. "But if you've completely ceased to be that sort — ?"

"Why I can then all the more bear to know. Besides, perhaps I haven't."

"Perhaps. Yet if you haven't," she added, "I should suppose you'd remember. Not indeed that *I* in the least connect with my impression the invidious name you use. If I had only thought you foolish," she explained, "the thing I speak of wouldn't so have remained with me. It was about yourself." She waited as if it might come to him; but as, only meeting her eyes in wonder, he gave no sign, she burnt her ships. "Has it ever happened?"

Then it was that, while he continued to stare, a light broke for him and the blood slowly came to his face, which began to burn with recognition. "Do you mean I told you — ?" But he faltered, lest what came to him shouldn't be right, lest he should only give himself away.

"It was something about yourself that it was natural one shouldn't forget — that is if one remembered you at all. That's why I ask you," she smiled, "if the thing you then spoke of has ever come to pass?"

Oh then he saw, but he was lost in wonder and found himself embarrassed. This, he also saw, made her sorry for him, as if her allusion had been a mistake. It took him but a moment, however, to feel it hadn't been, much as it had been a surprise. After the first little shock of it her knowledge on the contrary began, even if rather strangely, to taste sweet to him. She was the only other person in the world then who would have it, and she had had it all these years, while the fact of his having so breathed his secret had unaccountably faded from him. No wonder they couldn't have met as if nothing had happened. "I judge," he finally said, "that I know what you mean. Only I had strangely enough lost any sense of having taken you so far into my confidence."

"Is it because you've taken so many others as well?"

"I've taken nobody. Not a creature since then."

"So that I'm the only person who knows?"

"The only person in the world."

"Well," she quickly replied, "I myself have never spoken. I've never, never repeated of you what you told me." She looked at him so that he perfectly believed her. Their eyes met over it in such a way that he was without a doubt. "And I never will."

She spoke with an earnestness that, as if almost excessive, put him at ease about her possible derision. Somehow the whole question was a new luxury to him — that is from the moment she was in possession. If she didn't take the sarcastic view she clearly took the sympathetic, and that was what he had had, in all the long time, from no one whomsoever. What he felt was that he couldn't at present have begun to tell her, and yet could profit perhaps exquisitely by the accident of having done so of old. "Please don't then. We're just right as it is."

"Oh I am," she laughed, "if you are!" To which she added: "Then you do still feel in the same way?"

It was impossible he shouldn't take to himself that she was really interested, though it all kept coming as perfect surprise. He had thought of himself so long as abominably alone, and lo he wasn't alone a bit. He hadn't been, it appeared, for an hour — since those moments on the Sorrento boat. It was *she* who had been, he seemed to see as he looked at her — she who had been made so by the graceless fact of his lapse of fidelity. To tell her what he had told her — what had it been but to ask something of her? something that she had given, in her charity, without his having, by a remembrance, by a return of the spirit, failing another encounter, so much as thanked her. What he had asked of her had been simply at first not to laugh at him. She had beautifully not done so for ten years, and she was not doing so now. So he had endless gratitude to make up. Only for that he must see just how he had figured to her. "What, exactly, was the account I gave — ?"

"Of the way you did feel? Well, it was very simple. You said you had had from your earliest time, as the deepest thing within you, the sense of being kept for something rare and strange, possibly prodigious and terrible, that was sooner or later to happen to you, that you had in your bones the foreboding and the conviction of, and that would perhaps overwhelm you."

"Do you call that very simple?" John Marcher asked.

She thought a moment. "It was perhaps because I seemed, as you spoke, to understand it."

"You do understand it?" he eagerly asked.

Again she kept her kind eyes on him. "You still have the belief?"

"Oh!" he exclaimed helplessly. There was too much to say.

"Whatever it's to be," she clearly made out, "it hasn't yet come."

He shook his head in complete surrender now. "It hasn't yet come. Only, you know, it isn't anything I'm to *do*, to achieve in the world, to be distinguished or admired for. I'm not such an ass as *that*. It would be much better, no doubt, if I were."

"It's to be something you're merely to suffer?"

"Well, say to wait for — to have to meet, to face, to see suddenly break out in my life; possibly destroying all further consciousness, possibly annihilating me; possibly, on the other hand, only altering everything, striking at the root of all my world and leaving me to the consequences, however they shape themselves."

She took this in, but the light in her eyes continued for him not to be that of mockery. "Isn't what you describe perhaps but the expectation — or at any rate the sense of danger, familiar to so many people — of falling in love?"

John Marcher wondered. "Did you ask me that before?"

"No — I wasn't so free-and-easy then. But it's what strikes me now."

"Of course," he said after a moment, "it strikes you. Of course it strikes *me*. Of course what's in store for me may be no more than that. The only thing is," he went on, "that I think if it had been that I should by this time know."

"Do you mean because you've *been* in love?" And then as he looked at her in silence: "You've been in love, and it hasn't meant such a cataclysm, hasn't proved the great affair?"

"Here I am, you see. It hasn't been overwhelming."

"Then it hasn't been love," said May Bartram.

"Well, I at least thought it was. I took it for that — I've taken it till now. It was agreeable, it was delightful, it was miserable," he explained. "But it wasn't strange. It wasn't what *my* affair's to be."

"You want something all to yourself — something that nobody else knows or *has* known?"

"It isn't a question of what I 'want' — God knows I don't want anything. It's only a question of the apprehension that haunts me — that I live with day by day."

He said this so lucidly and consistently that he could see it further impose itself. If she hadn't been interested before she'd have been interested now. "Is it a sense of coming violence?"

Evidently now too again he liked to talk of it. "I don't think of it as — when it does come — necessarily violent. I only think of it as natural and as of course above all unmistakeable. I think of it simply as *the* thing. *The* thing will of itself appear natural."

"Then how will it appear strange?"

Marcher bethought himself. "It won't — to *me*."

"To whom then?"

"Well," he replied, smiling at last, "say to you."

"Oh then I'm to be present?"

"Why you *are* present — since you know."

"I see." She turned it over. "But I mean at the catastrophe."

At this, for a minute, their lightness gave way to their gravity; it was as if the long look they exchanged held them together. "It will only depend on yourself — if you'll watch with me."

"Are you afraid?" she asked.

"Don't leave me *now*," he went on.

"Are you afraid?" she repeated.

"Do you think me simply out of my mind?" he pursued instead of answering. "Do I merely strike you as a harmless lunatic?"

"No," said May Bartram. "I understand you. I believe you."

"You mean you feel how my obsession — poor old thing! — may correspond to some possible reality?"

"To some possible reality."

"Then you *will* watch with me?"

She hesitated, then for the third time put her question. "Are you afraid?"

"Did I tell you I was — at Naples?"

"No, you said nothing about it."

"Then I don't know. And I should *like* to know," said John Marcher. "You'll tell me yourself whether you think so. If you'll watch with me you'll see."

"Very good then." They had been moving by this time across the room, and at the door, before passing out, they paused as for the full wind-up of their understanding. "I'll watch with you," said May Bartram.

II

The fact that she "knew" — knew and yet neither chaffed him nor betrayed him — had in a short time begun to constitute between them a goodly bond, which became more marked when, within the year that followed their afternoon at Weatherend, the opportunities for meeting multiplied. The event that thus promoted these occasions was the death of the ancient lady her great-aunt, under whose wing, since losing her mother, she had to such an extent found shelter, and who, though but the widowed mother of the new successor to the property, had succeeded — thanks to a high tone and a high temper — in not forfeiting the supreme position at the great house. The deposition of this personage arrived but with her death, which, followed by many changes, made in particular a difference for the young woman in whom Marcher's expert attention had recognised from the first a dependent with a pride that might ache though it didn't bristle. Nothing for a long time had made him easier than the thought that the aching must have been much soothed by Miss Bartram's now finding herself able to set up a small home in London. She had acquired property, to an amount that made that luxury just possible, under her aunt's extremely complicated will, and when the whole matter began to be straightened out, which indeed took time, she let him know that the happy issue was at last in view. He had seen her again before that day, both because she had more than once accompanied the ancient lady to town and because he had paid another visit to the friends who so conveniently made of Weatherend one of the charms of their own hospitality. These friends had taken him back there; he had achieved there again with Miss Bartram some quiet detachment; and he had in London succeeded in persuading her to more than one brief absence from her aunt. They went together, on these latter occasions, to the National Gallery and the South Kensington Museum, where, among vivid reminders, they talked of Italy at large — not now attempting to recover, as at first, the taste of their youth and their ignorance. That recovery, the first day at Weatherend, had served its purpose well, had given them quite enough; so that they were, to Marcher's sense, no longer hovering about the headwaters of their stream, but had felt their boat pushed sharply off and down the current.

They were literally afloat together; for our gentleman this was marked, quite as marked as that the fortunate cause of it was just the buried treasure of her knowledge. He had with his own hands dug up this little hoard, brought to light — that is to within reach of the dim day constituted by their discretions and privacies — the object of value the hiding-place of which he had, after putting it into the ground himself, so strangely, so long forgotten. The rare luck of his having again just stumbled on the spot made him indifferent to any other question; he would doubtless have devoted more time to the odd accident of his lapse of memory if he hadn't been moved to devote so much to the sweetness, the comfort, as he felt, for the future, that this accident itself had helped to keep fresh. It had never entered into his plan that any one should "know," and mainly for the reason that it wasn't in him to tell any one. That would have been impossible, for nothing but the amusement of a cold world would have waited on it. Since, however, a mysterious fate had opened his mouth betimes, in spite of him, he would count that a compensation and profit by it to the utmost. That the right person *should* know tempered the asperity of his secret more even than his shyness had permitted him to imagine; and May Bartram was clearly right, because — well, because there she was. Her knowledge simply settled it; he would have been sure enough by this time had she been wrong. There was that in his situation, no doubt, that disposed him too much to see her as a mere confidant, taking all her light for him from the fact — the fact only — of her interest in his predicament; from her mercy, sympathy, seriousness, her consent not to regard him as the funniest of the funny. Aware, in fine, that her price for him was just in her giving him this constant sense of his being admirably spared, he was careful to remember that she had also a life of her own, with things that might happen to *her*, things that in friendship one should likewise take account of. Something fairly remarkable came to pass with him, for that matter, in this connexion — something represented by a certain passage of his consciousness, in the suddenest way, from one extreme to the other.

He had thought himself, so long as nobody knew, the most disinterested person in the world, carrying his concentrated burden, his perpetual suspense, ever so quietly, holding his tongue about it, giving others no glimpse of it nor of its effect upon his life, asking of them no allowance and only making on his side all those that were asked. He hadn't disturbed people with the queerness of their having to know a haunted man, though he had had moments of rather special temptation on hearing them say they were forsooth "unsettled." If they were as unsettled as he was — he who had never been settled for an hour in his life — they would know what it meant. Yet it wasn't, all the same, for him to make them, and he listened to them civilly enough. This was why he had such good — though possibly such rather colourless — manners; this was why, above all, he could regard himself, in a greedy world, as decently — as in fact perhaps even a little sublimely — unselfish. Our point is accordingly that he valued this character quite sufficiently to measure his present danger of letting it lapse, against which he promised himself to be much on his guard. He was quite ready, none the less, to be selfish just a little, since surely no more charming occasion for it had come to him. "Just a little," in a word, was just as much as Miss Bartram, taking one day with another, would let him. He never would be in the least coercive, and would keep well before him the lines on which consideration for her — the very highest — ought to proceed. He would thoroughly establish the heads under which her affairs, her requirements, her peculiarities — he went so far as to give them the latitude of that name — would come into their intercourse. All this naturally was a sign of how much he took the intercourse itself for granted. There was nothing more to be done about *that*. It simply existed; had sprung into being with her first penetrating question to him in the autumn light there at Weatherend. The real form it should have taken on the basis that stood out large was the form of their marrying. But the devil in this was that the very basis itself put marrying out of the question. His conviction, his apprehension, his obsession, in short, wasn't a privilege he could invite a woman to share; and that consequence of it was precisely what was the matter with him. Something or other lay in wait for him, amid the twists and the turns of the months and the years, like a crouching beast in the jungle. It signified little whether the crouching beast were destined to slay him or to be slain. The definite point was the inevitable spring of the creature; and the definite lesson from that was that a man of feeling didn't cause himself to be accompanied by a lady on a tiger-hunt. Such was the image under which he had ended by figuring his life.

They had at first, none the less, in the scattered hours spent together, made no allusion to that view of it; which was a sign he was handsomely alert to give that he didn't expect, that he in fact didn't care, always to be talking about it. Such a feature in one's outlook was really like a hump on one's back. The difference it made every minute of the day existed quite independently of discussion. One discussed of course *like* a hunchback, for there was always, if nothing else, the hunchback face. That remained, and she was watching him; but people watched best, as a general thing, in silence, so that such would be predominantly the manner of their vigil. Yet he didn't want, at the same time, to be tense and solemn; tense and solemn was what he imagined he too much showed for with other people. The thing to be, with the one person who knew, was easy and natural — to make the reference rather than be seeming to avoid it, to avoid it rather than be seeming to make it, and to keep it, in any case, familiar, facetious even, rather than pedantic and portentous. Some such consideration as the latter was doubtless in his mind for instance when he wrote pleasantly to Miss Bartram that perhaps the great thing he had so long felt as in the lap of the gods was no more than this circumstance, which touched him so nearly, of her acquiring a house in London. It was the first allusion they had yet again made, needing any other hitherto so little; but when she replied, after having given him the news, that she was by no means satisfied with such a trifle as the climax to so special a suspense, she almost set him wondering if she hadn't even a larger conception of singularity for him than he had for himself. He was at all events destined to become aware little by little, as time went by, that she was all the while looking at his life, judging it, measuring it, in the light of the thing she knew, which grew to be at last, with the consecration of the years, never mentioned between them save as "the real truth" about him. That had always been his own form of reference to it, but she adopted the form so quietly that, looking back at the end of a period, he knew there was no moment at which it was traceable that she had, as he might say, got inside his idea, or exchanged the attitude of beautifully indulging for that of still more beautifully believing him.

It was always open to him to accuse her of seeing him but as the most harmless of maniacs, and this, in the long run — since it covered so much ground — was his easiest description of their friendship. He had a screw loose for her, but she liked him in spite of it and was practically, against the rest of the world, his kind wise keeper, unremunerated but fairly amused and, in the absence of other near ties, not disreputably occupied. The rest of the world of course thought him queer, but she, she only, knew how, and above all why, queer; which was precisely what enabled her to dispose the concealing veil in the right folds. She took his gaiety from him — since it had to pass with them for gaiety — as she took everything else; but she certainly so far justified by her unerring touch his finer sense of the degree to which he had ended by convincing her. *She* at least never spoke of the secret of his life except as "the real truth about you," and she had in fact a wonderful way of making it seem, as such, the secret of her own life too. That was in fine how he so constantly felt her as allowing for him; he couldn't on the whole call it anything else. He allowed for himself, but she, exactly, allowed still more; partly because, better placed for a sight of the matter, she traced his unhappy perversion through reaches of its course into which he could scarce follow it. He knew how he felt, but, besides knowing that, she knew how he *looked* as well; he knew each of the things of importance he was insidiously kept from doing, but she could add up the amount they made, understand how much, with a lighter weight on his spirit, he might have done, and thereby establish how, clever as he was, he fell short. Above all she was in the secret of the difference between the forms he went through — those of his little office under Government, those of caring for his modest patrimony, for his library, for his garden in the country, for the people in London whose invitations he accepted and repaid — and the detachment that reigned beneath them and that made of all behaviour, all that could in the least be called behaviour, a long act of dissimulation. What it had come to was that he wore a mask painted with the social simper, out of the eye-holes of which there looked eyes of an expression not in the least matching the other features. This the stupid world, even after years, had never more than half-discovered. It was only May Bartram who had, and she achieved, by an art indescribable, the feat of at once — or perhaps it was only alternately — meeting the eyes from in front and mingling her own vision, as from over his shoulder, with their peep through the apertures.

So while they grew older together she did watch with him, and so she let this association give shape and colour to her own existence. Beneath *her* forms as well detachment had learned to sit, and behaviour had become for her, in the social sense, a false account of herself. There was but one account of her that would have been true all the while and that she could give straight to nobody, least of all to John Marcher. Her whole attitude was a virtual statement, but the perception of that only seemed called to take its place for him as one of the many things necessarily crowded out of his consciousness. If she had moreover, like himself, to make sacrifices to their real truth, it was to be granted that her compensation might have affected her as more prompt and more natural. They had long periods, in this London time, during which, when they were together, a stranger might have listened to them without in the least pricking up his ears; on the other hand the real truth was equally liable at any moment to rise to the surface, and the auditor would then have wondered indeed what they were talking about. They had from an early hour made up their mind that society was, luckily, unintelligent, and the margin allowed them by this had fairly become one of their commonplaces. Yet there were still moments when the situation turned almost fresh — usually under the effect of some expression drawn from herself. Her expressions doubtless repeated themselves, but her intervals were generous. "What saves us, you know, is that we answer so completely to so usual an appearance: that of the man and woman whose friendship has become such a daily habit — or almost — as to be at last indispensable." That for instance was a remark she had frequently enough had occasion to make, though she had given it at different times different developments. What we are especially concerned with is the turn it happened to take from her one afternoon when he had come to see her in honour of her birthday. This anniversary had fallen on a Sunday, at a season of thick fog and general outward gloom; but he had brought her his customary offering, having known her now long enough to have established a hundred small traditions. It was one of his proofs to himself, the present he made her on her birthday, that he hadn't sunk into real selfishness. It was mostly nothing more than a small trinket, but it was always fine of its kind, and he was regularly careful to pay for it more than he thought he could afford. "Our habit saves you at least, don't you see? because it makes you, after all, for the vulgar, indistinguishable from other men. What's the most inveterate mark of men in general? Why the capacity to spend endless time with dull women — to spend it I won't say without being bored, but without minding that they are, without being driven off at a tangent by it; which comes to the same thing. I'm your dull woman, a part of the daily bread for which you pray at church. That covers your tracks more than anything."

"And what covers yours?" asked Marcher, whom his dull woman could mostly to this extent amuse. "I see of course what you mean by your saving me, in this way and that, so far as other people are concerned — I've seen it all along. Only what is it that saves *you*? I often think, you know, of that."

She looked as if she sometimes thought of that too, but rather in a different way. "Where other people, you mean, are concerned?"

"Well, you're really so in with me, you know — as a sort of result of my being so in with yourself. I mean of my having such an immense regard for you, being so tremendously mindful of all you've done for me. I sometimes ask myself if it's quite fair. Fair I mean to have so involved and — since one may say it — interested you. I almost feel as if you hadn't really had time to do anything else."

"Anything else but be interested?" she asked. "Ah what else does one ever want to be? If I've been 'watching' with you, as we long ago agreed I was to do, watching's always in itself an absorption."

"Oh certainly," John Marcher said, "if you hadn't had your curiosity — ! Only doesn't it sometimes come to you as time goes on that your curiosity isn't being particularly repaid?"

May Bartram had a pause. "Do you ask that, by any chance, because you feel at all that yours isn't? I mean because you have to wait so long."

Oh he understood what she meant! "For the thing to happen that never does happen? For the beast to jump out? No, I'm just where I was about it. It isn't a matter as to which I can *choose*, I can decide for a change. It isn't one as to which there *can* be a change. It's in the lap of the gods. One's in the hands of one's law — there one is. As to the form the law will take, the way it will operate, that's its own affair."

"Yes," Miss Bartram replied; "of course one's fate's coming, of course it *has* come in its own form and its own way, all the while. Only, you know, the form and the way in your case were to have been — well, something so exceptional and, as one may say, so particularly *your* own."

Something in this made him look at her with suspicion. "You say 'were to *have* been,' as if in your heart you had begun to doubt."

"Oh!" she vaguely protested.

"As if you believed," he went on, "that nothing will now take place."

She shook her head slowly but rather inscrutably. "You're far from my thought."

He continued to look at her. "What then is the matter with you?"

"Well," she said after another wait, "the matter with me is simply that I'm more sure than ever my curiosity, as you call it, will be but too well repaid."

They were frankly grave now; he had got up from his seat, had turned once more about the little drawing-room to which, year after year, he brought his inevitable topic; in which he had, as he might have said, tasted their intimate community with every sauce, where every object was as familiar to him as the things of his own house and the very carpets were worn with his fitful walk very much as the desks in the old counting-houses are worn by the elbows of generations of clerks. The generations of his nervous moods had been at work there, and the place was the written history of his whole middle life. Under the impression of what his friend had just said he knew himself, for some reason, more aware of these things; which made him, after a moment, stop again before her. "Is it possibly that you've grown afraid?"

"Afraid?" He thought, as she repeated the word, that his question had made her, a little, change colour; so that, lest he should have touched on a truth, he explained very kindly: "You remember that that was what you asked *me* long ago — that first day at Weatherend."

"Oh yes, and you told me you didn't know — that I was to see for myself. We've said little about it since, even in so long a time."

"Precisely," Marcher interposed — "quite as if it were too delicate a matter for us to make free with. Quite as if we might find, on pressure, that I *am* afraid. For then," he said, "we shouldn't, should we? quite know what to do."

She had for the time no answer to this question. "There have been days when I thought you were. Only, of course," she added, "there have been days when we have thought almost anything."

"Everything. Oh!" Marcher softly groaned as with a gasp, half-spent, at the face, more uncovered just then than it had been for a long while, of the imagination always with them. It had always had its incalculable moments of glaring out, quite as with the very eyes of the very Beast, and, used as he was to them, they could still draw from him the tribute of a sigh that rose from the depths of his being. All they had thought, first and last, rolled over him; the past seemed to have been reduced to mere barren speculation. This in fact was what the place had just struck him as so full of — the simplification of everything but the state of suspense. That remained only by seeming to hang in the void surrounding it. Even his original fear, if fear it had been, had lost itself in the desert. "I judge, however," he continued, "that you see I'm not afraid now."

"What I see, as I make it out, is that you've achieved something almost unprecedented in the way of getting used to danger. Living with it so long and so closely you've lost your sense of it; you know it's there, but you're indifferent, and you cease even, as of old, to have to whistle in the dark. Considering what the danger is," May Bartram wound up, "I'm bound to say I don't think your attitude could well be surpassed."

John Marcher faintly smiled. "It's heroic?"

"Certainly — call it that."

It was what he would have liked indeed to call it. "I *am* then a man of courage?"

"That's what you were to show me."

He still, however, wondered. "But doesn't the man of courage know what he's afraid of — or *not* afraid of? I don't know *that*, you see. I don't focus it. I can't name it. I only know I'm exposed."

"Yes, but exposed — how shall I say? — so directly. So intimately. That's surely enough."

"Enough to make you feel then — as what we may call the end and the upshot of our watch — that I'm not afraid?"

"You're not afraid. But it isn't," she said, "the end of our watch. That is it isn't the end of yours. You've everything still to see."

"Then why haven't *you*?" he asked. He had had, all along, to-day, the sense of her keeping something back, and he still had it. As this was his first impression of that it quite made a date. The case was the more marked as she didn't at first answer; which in turn made him go on. "You know something I don't." Then his voice, for that of a man of courage, trembled a little. "You know what's to happen." Her silence, with the face she showed, was almost a confession — it made him sure. "You know, and you're afraid to tell me. It's so bad that you're afraid I'll find out."

All this might be true, for she did look as if, unexpectedly to her, he had crossed some mystic line that she had secretly drawn round her. Yet she might, after all, not have worried; and the real climax was that he himself, at all events, needn't. "You'll never find out."

III

It was all to have made, none the less, as I have said, a date; which came out in the fact that again and again, even after long intervals, other things that passed between them wore in relation to this hour but the character of recalls and results. Its immediate effect had been indeed rather to lighten insistence — almost to provoke a reaction; as if their topic had dropped by its own weight and as if moreover, for that matter, Marcher had been visited by one of his occasional warnings against egotism. He had kept up, he felt, and very decently on the whole, his consciousness of the importance of not being selfish, and it was true that he had never sinned in that direction without promptly enough trying to press the scales the other way. He often repaired his fault, the season permitting, by inviting his friend to accompany him to the opera; and it not infrequently thus happened that, to show he didn't wish her to have but one sort of food for her mind, he was the cause of her appearing there with him a dozen nights in the month. It even happened that, seeing her home at such times, he occasionally went in with her to finish, as he called it, the evening, and, the better to make his point, sat down to the frugal but always careful little supper that awaited his pleasure. His point was made, he thought, by his not eternally insisting with her on himself; made for instance, at such hours, when it befell that, her piano at hand and each of them familiar with it, they went over passages of the opera together. It chanced to be on one of these occasions, however, that he reminded her of her not having answered a certain question he had put to her during the talk that had taken place between them on her last birthday. "What is it that saves *you*?" — saved her, he meant, from that appearance of variation from the usual human type. If he had practically escaped remark, as she pretended, by doing, in the most important particular, what most men do — find the answer to life in patching up an alliance of a sort with a woman no better than himself — how had she escaped it, and how could the alliance, such as it was, since they must suppose it had been more or less noticed, have failed to make her rather positively talked about?

"I never said," May Bartram replied, "that it hadn't made me a good deal talked about."

"Ah well then you're not 'saved.'"

"It hasn't been a question for me. If you've had your woman I've had," she said, "my man."

"And you mean that makes you all right?"

Oh it was always as if there were so much to say! "I don't know why it shouldn't make me — humanly, which is what we're speaking of — as right as it makes you."

"I see," Marcher returned. " 'Humanly,' no doubt, as showing that you're living for something. Not, that is, just for me and my secret."

May Bartram smiled. "I don't pretend it exactly shows that I'm not living for you. It's my intimacy with you that's in question."

He laughed as he saw what she meant. "Yes, but since, as you say, I'm only, so far as people make out, ordinary, you're — aren't you? — no more than ordinary either. You help me to pass for a man like another. So if I *am*, as I understand you, you're not compromised. Is that it?"

She had another of her waits, but she spoke clearly enough. "That's it. It's all that concerns me — to help you to pass for a man like another."

He was careful to acknowledge the remark handsomely. "How kind, how beautiful, you are to me! How shall I ever repay you?"

She had her last grave pause, as if there might be a choice of ways. But she chose. "By going on as you are."

It was into this going on as he was that they relapsed, and really for so long a time that the day inevitably came for a further sounding of their depths. These depths, constantly bridged over by a structure firm enough in spite of its lightness and of its occasional oscillation in the somewhat vertiginous air, invited on occasion, in the interest of their nerves, a dropping of the plummet and a measurement of the abyss. A difference had been made moreover, once for all, by the fact that she had all the while not appeared to feel the need of rebutting his charge of an idea within her that she didn't dare to express — a charge uttered just before one of the fullest of their later discussions ended. It had come up for him then that she "knew" something and that what she knew was bad — too bad to tell him. When he had spoken of it as visibly so bad that she was afraid he might find it out, her reply had left the matter too equivocal to be let alone and yet, for Marcher's special sensibility, almost too formidable again to touch. He circled about it at a distance that alternately narrowed and widened and that still wasn't much affected by the consciousness in him that there was nothing she could "know," after all, any better than he did. She had no source of knowledge he hadn't equally — except of course that she might have finer nerves. That was what women had where they were interested; they made out things, where people were concerned, that the people often couldn't have made out for themselves. Their nerves, their sensibility, their imagination, were conductors and revealers, and the beauty of May Bartram was in particular that she had given herself so to his case. He felt in these days what, oddly enough, he had never felt before, the growth of a dread of losing her by some catastrophe — some catastrophe that yet wouldn't at all be *the* catastrophe: partly because she had almost of a sudden begun to strike him as more useful to him than ever yet, and partly by reason of an appearance of uncertainty in her health, coincident and equally new. It was characteristic of the inner detachment he had hitherto so successfully cultivated and to which our whole account of him is a reference, it was characteristic that his complications, such as they were, had never yet seemed so as at this crisis to thicken about him, even to the point of making him ask himself if he were, by any chance, of a truth, within sight or sound, within touch or reach, within the immediate jurisdiction, of the thing that waited.

When the day came, as come it had to, that his friend confessed to him her fear of a deep disorder in her blood, he felt somehow the shadow of a change and the chill of a shock. He immediately began to imagine aggravations and disasters, and above all to think of her peril as the direct menace for himself of personal privation. This indeed gave him one of those partial recoveries of equanimity that were agreeable to him — it showed him that what was still first in his mind was the loss she herself might suffer. "What if she should have to die before knowing, before seeing — ?" It would have been brutal, in the early stages of her trouble, to put that question to her; but it had immediately sounded for him to his own concern, and the possibility was what most made him sorry for her. If she did "know," moreover, in the sense of her having had some — what should he think? — mystical irresistible light, this would make the matter not better, but worse, inasmuch as her original adoption of his own curiosity had quite become the basis of her life. She had been living to see what would *be* to be seen, and it would quite lacerate her to have to give up before the accomplishment of the vision. These reflections, as I say, quickened his generosity; yet, make them as he might, he saw himself, with the lapse of the period, more and more disconcerted. It lapsed for him with a strange steady sweep, and the oddest oddity was that it gave him, independently of the threat of much inconvenience, almost the only positive surprise his career, if career it could be called, had yet offered him. She kept the house as she had never done; he had to go to her to see her — she could meet him nowhere now, though there was scarce a corner of their loved old London in which she hadn't in the past, at one time or another, done so; and he found her always seated by her fire in the deep old-fashioned chair she was less and less able to leave. He had been struck one day, after an absence exceeding his usual measure, with her suddenly looking much older to him than he had ever thought of her being; then he recognised that the suddenness was all on his side — he had just simply and suddenly noticed. She looked older because inevitably, after so many years, she *was* old, or almost; which was of course true in still greater measure of her companion. If she was old, or almost, John Marcher assuredly was, and yet it was her showing of the lesson, not his own, that brought the truth home to him. His surprises began here; when once they had begun they multiplied; they came rather with a rush: it was as if, in the oddest way in the world, they had all been kept back, sown in a thick cluster, for the late afternoon of life, the time at which for people in general, the unexpected has died out.

one of them was that he should have caught himself — for he *had* so done — *really* wondering if the great accident would take form now as nothing more than his being condemned to see this charming woman, this admirable friend, pass away from him. He had never so unreservedly qualified her as while confronted in thought with such a possibility; in spite of which there was small doubt for him that as answer to his long riddle the mere effacement of even so fine a feature of his situation would be an abject anticlimax. It would represent, as connected with his past attitude, a drop of dignity under the shadow of which his existence could only become the most grotesque of failures. He had been far from holding it a failure — long as he had waited for the appearance that was to make it a success. He had waited for quite another thing, not for such a thing as that. The breath of his good faith came short, however, as he recognised how long he had waited, or how long at least his companion had. That she, at all events, might be recorded as having waited in vain — this affected him sharply, and all the more because of his at first having done little more than amuse himself with the idea. It grew more grave as the gravity of her condition grew, and the state of mind it produced in him, which he himself ended by watching as if it had been some definite disfigurement of his outer person, may pass for another of his surprises. This conjoined itself still with another, the really stupefying consciousness of a question that he would have allowed to shape itself had he dared. What did everything mean — what, that is, did *she* mean, she and her vain waiting and her probable death and the soundless admonition of it all — unless that, at this time of day, it was simply, it was overwhelmingly too late? He had never at any stage of his queer consciousness admitted the whisper of such a correction; he had never till within these last few months been so false to his conviction as not to hold that what was to come to him had time, whether *he* struck himself as having it or not. That at last, at last, he certainly hadn't it, to speak of, or had it but in the scantiest measure — such, soon enough, as things went with him, became the inference with which his old obsession had to reckon: and this it was not helped to do by the more and more confirmed appearance that the great vagueness casting the long shadow in which he had lived had, to attest itself, almost no margin left. Since it was in Time that he was to have met his fate, so it was in Time that his fate was to have acted; and as he waked up to the sense of no longer being young, which was exactly the sense of being stale, just as that, in turn, was the sense of being weak, he waked up to another matter beside. It all hung together; they were subject, he and the great vagueness, to an equal and indivisible law. When the possibilities themselves had accordingly turned stale, when the secret of the gods had grown faint, had perhaps even quite evaporated, that, and that only, was failure. It wouldn't have been failure to be bankrupt, dishonoured, pilloried, hanged; it was failure not to be anything. And so, in the dark valley into which his path had taken its unlooked-for twist, he wondered not a little as he groped. He didn't care what awful crash might overtake him, with what ignominy or what monstrosity he might yet be associated — since he wasn't after all too utterly old to suffer — if it would only be decently proportionate to the posture he had kept, all his life, in the threatened presence of it. He had but one desire left — that he shouldn't have been "sold."

IV

Then it was that, one afternoon, while the spring of the year was young and new she met all in her own way his frankest betrayal of these alarms. He had gone in late to see her, but evening hadn't settled and she was presented to him in that long fresh light of waning April days which affects us often with a sadness sharper than the greyest hours of autumn. The week had been warm, the spring was supposed to have begun early, and May Bartram sat, for the first time in the year, without a fire, a fact that, to Marcher's sense, gave the scene of which she formed part a smooth and ultimate look, an air of knowing, in its immaculate order and cold meaningless cheer, that it would never see a fire again. Her own aspect — he could scarce have said why — intensified this note. Almost as white as wax, with the marks and signs in her face as numerous and as fine as if they had been etched by a needle, with soft white draperies relieved by a faded green scarf on the delicate tone of which the years had further refined, she was the picture of a serene and exquisite but impenetrable sphinx, whose head, or indeed all whose person, might have been powdered with silver. She was a sphinx, yet with her white petals and green fronds she might have been a lily too — only an artificial lily, wonderfully imitated and constantly kept, without dust or stain, though not exempt from a slight droop and a complexity of faint creases, under some clear glass bell. The perfection of household care, of high polish and finish, always reigned in her rooms, but they now looked most as if everything had been wound up, tucked in, put away, so that she might sit with folded hands and with nothing more to do. She was "out of it," to Marcher's vision; her work was over; she communicated with him as across some gulf or from some island of rest that she had already reached, and it made him feel strangely abandoned. Was it — or rather wasn't it — that if for so long she had been watching with him the answer to their question must have swum into her ken and taken on its name, so that her occupation was verily gone? He had as much as charged her with this in saying to her, many months before, that she even then knew something she was keeping from him. It was a point he had never since ventured to press, vaguely fearing as he did that it might become a difference, perhaps a disagreement, between them. He had in this later time turned nervous, which was what he in all the other years had never been; and the oddity was that his nervousness should have waited till he had begun to doubt, should have held off so long as he was sure. There was something, it seemed to him, that the wrong word would bring down on his head, something that would so at least ease off his tension. But he wanted not to speak the wrong word; that would make everything ugly. He wanted the knowledge he lacked to drop on him, if drop it could, by its own august weight. If she was to forsake him it was surely for her to take leave. This was why he didn't directly ask her again what she knew; but it was also why, approaching the matter from another side, he said to her in the course of his visit: "What do you regard as the very worst that at this time of day *can* happen to me?"

He had asked her that in the past often enough; they had, with the odd irregular rhythm of their intensities and avoidances, exchanged ideas about it and then had seen the ideas washed away by cool intervals, washed like figures traced in sea-sand. It had ever been the mark of their talk that the oldest allusions in it required but a little dismissal and reaction to come out again, sounding for the hour as new. She could thus at present meet his enquiry quite freshly and patiently. "Oh yes, I've repeatedly thought, only it always seemed to me of old that I couldn't quite make up my mind. I thought of dreadful things, between which it was difficult to choose; and so must you have done."

"Rather! I feel now as if I had scarce done anything else. I appear to myself to have spent my life in thinking of nothing *but* dreadful things. A great many of them I've at different times named to you, but there were others I couldn't name."

"They were too, too dreadful?"

"Too, too dreadful — some of them."

She looked at him a minute, and there came to him as he met it an inconsequent sense that her eyes, when one got their full clearness, were still as beautiful as they had been in youth, only beautiful with a strange cold light — a light that somehow was a part of the effect, if it wasn't rather a part of the cause, of the pale hard sweetness of the season and the hour. "And yet," she said at last, "there are horrors we've mentioned."

It deepened the strangeness to see her, as such a figure in such a picture, talk of "horrors," but she was to do in a few minutes something stranger yet — though even of this he was to take the full measure but afterwards — and the note of it already trembled. It was, for the matter of that, one of the signs that her eyes were having again the high flicker of their prime. He had to admit, however, what she said. "Oh yes, there were times when we did go far." He caught himself in the act of speaking as if it all were over. Well, he wished it were; and the consummation depended for him clearly more and more on his friend.

But she had now a soft smile. "Oh far — !"

It was oddly ironic. "Do you mean you're prepared to go further?"

She was frail and ancient and charming as she continued to look at him, yet it was rather as if she had lost the thread. "Do you consider that we went far?"

"Why I thought it the point you were just making — that we *had* looked most things in the face."

"Including each other?" She still smiled. "But you're quite right. We've had together great imaginations, often great fears; but some of them have been unspoken."

"Then the worst — we haven't faced that. I *could* face it, I believe, if I knew what you think it. I feel," he explained, "as if I had lost my power to conceive such things." And he wondered if he looked as blank as he sounded. "It's spent."

"Then why do you assume," she asked, "that mine isn't?"

"Because you've given me signs to the contrary. It isn't a question for you of conceiving, imagining, comparing. It isn't a question now of choosing." At last he came out with it. "You know something I don't. You've shown me that before."

These last words had affected her, he made out in a moment, exceedingly, and she spoke with firmness. "I've shown you, my dear, nothing."

He shook his head. "You can't hide it."

"Oh, oh!" May Bartram sounded over what she couldn't hide. It was almost a smothered groan.

"You admitted it months ago, when I spoke of it to you as of something you were afraid I should find out. Your answer was that I couldn't, that I wouldn't, and I don't pretend I have. But you had something therefore in mind, and I now see how it must have been, how it still is, the possibility that, of all possibilities, has settled itself for you as the worst. This," he went on, "is why I appeal to you. I'm only afraid of ignorance to-day — I'm not afraid of knowledge." And then as for a while she said nothing: "What makes me sure is that I see in your face and feel here, in this air and amid these appearances, that you're out of it. You've done. You've had your experience. You leave me to my fate."

Well, she listened, motionless and white in her chair, as on a decision to be made, so that her manner was fairly an avowal, though still, with a small fine inner stiffness, an imperfect surrender. "It *would* be the worst," she finally let herself say. "I mean the thing I've never said."

It hushed him a moment. "More monstrous than all the monstrosities we've named?"

"More monstrous. Isn't that what you sufficiently express," she asked, "in calling it the worst?"

Marcher thought. "Assuredly — if you mean, as I do, something that includes all the loss and all the shame that are thinkable."

"It would if it *should* happen," said May Bartram. "What we're speaking of, remember, is only my idea."

"It's your belief," Marcher returned. "That's enough for me. I feel your beliefs are right. Therefore if, having this one, you give me no more light on it, you abandon me."

"No, no!" she repeated. "I'm with you — don't you see? — still." And as to make it more vivid to him she rose from her chair — a movement she seldom risked in these days — and showed herself, all draped and all soft, in her fairness and slimness. "I haven't forsaken you."

It was really, in its effort against weakness, a generous assurance, and had the success of the impulse not, happily, been great, it would have touched him to pain more than pleasure. But the cold charm in her eyes had spread, as she hovered before him, to all the rest of her person, so that it was for the minute almost a recovery of youth. He couldn't pity her for that; he could only take her as she showed — as capable even yet of helping him. It was as if, at the same time, her light might at any instant go out; wherefore he must make the most of it. There passed before him with intensity the three or four things he wanted most to know; but the question that came of itself to his lips really covered the others. "Then tell me if I shall consciously suffer."

She promptly shook her head. "Never!"

It confirmed the authority he imputed to her, and it produced on him an extraordinary effect. "Well, what's better than that? Do you call that the worst?"

"You think nothing is better?" she asked.

She seemed to mean something so special that he again sharply wondered, though still with the dawn of a prospect of relief. "Why not, if one doesn't *know*?" After which, as their eyes, over his question, met in a silence, the dawn deepened and something to his purpose came prodigiously out of her very face. His own, as he took it in, suddenly flushed to the forehead, and he gasped with the force of a perception to which, on the instant, everything fitted. The sound of his gasp filled the air; then he became articulate. "I see — if I don't suffer!"

In her own look, however, was doubt. "You see what?"

"Why what you mean — what you've always meant."

She again shook her head. "What I mean isn't what I've always meant. It's different."

"It's something new?"

She hung back from it a little. "Something new. It's not what you think. I see what you think."

His divination drew breath then; only her correction might be wrong. "It isn't that I *am* a blockhead?" he asked between faintness and grimness. "It isn't that it's all a mistake?"

"A mistake?" she pityingly echoed. *That* possibility, for her, he saw, would be monstrous; and if she guaranteed him the immunity from pain it would accordingly not be what she had in mind. "Oh no," she declared; "it's nothing of that sort. You've been right."

Yet he couldn't help asking himself if she weren't, thus pressed, speaking but to save him. It seemed to him he should be most in a hole if his history should prove all a platitude. "Are you telling me the truth, so that I shan't have been a bigger idiot than I can bear to know? I *haven't* lived with a vain imagination, in the most besotted illusion? I haven't waited but to see the door shut in my face?"

She shook her head again. "However the case stands *that* isn't the truth. Whatever the reality, it *is* a reality. The door isn't shut. The door's open," said May Bartram.

"Then something's to come?"

She waited once again, always with her cold sweet eyes upon him. "It's never too late." She had, with her gliding step, diminished the distance between them, and she stood nearer to him, close to him, a minute, as if still charged with the unspoken. Her movement might have been for some finer emphasis of what she was at once hesitating and deciding to say. He had been standing by the chimney-piece, fireless and sparely adorned, a small perfect old French clock and two morsels of rosy Dresden constituting all its furniture; and her hand grasped the shelf while she kept him waiting, grasped it a little as for support and encouragement. She only kept him waiting, however; that is he only waited. It had become suddenly, from her movement and attitude, beautiful and vivid to him that she had something more to give him; her wasted face delicately shone with it — it glittered almost as with the white lustre of silver in her expression. She was right, incontestably, for what he saw in her face was the truth, and strangely, without consequence, while their talk of it as dreadful was still in the air, she appeared to present it as inordinately soft. This, prompting bewilderment, made him but gape the more gratefully for her revelation, so that they continued for some minutes silent, her face shining at him, her contact imponderably pressing, and his stare all kind but all expectant. The end, none the less, was that what he had expected failed to come to him. Something else took place instead, which seemed to consist at first in the mere closing of her eyes. She gave way at the same instant to a slow fine shudder, and though he remained staring — though he stared in fact but the harder — turned off and regained her chair. It was the end of what she had been intending, but it left him thinking only of that.

"Well, you don't say — ?"

She had touched in her passage a bell near the chimney and had sunk back strangely pale. "I'm afraid I'm too ill."

"Too ill to tell me?" It sprang up sharp to him, and almost to his lips, the fear she might die without giving him light. He checked himself in time from so expressing his question, but she answered as if she had heard the words.

"Don't you know — now?"

"'Now' — ?" She had spoken as if some difference had been made within the moment. But her maid, quickly obedient to her bell, was already with them. "I know nothing." And he was afterwards to say to himself that he must have spoken with odious impatience, such an impatience as to show that, supremely disconcerted, he washed his hands of the whole question.

"Oh!" said May Bartram.

"Are you in pain?" he asked as the woman went to her.

"No," said May Bartram.

Her maid, who had put an arm round her as if to take her to her room, fixed on him eyes that appealingly contradicted her; in spite of which, however, he showed once more his mystification. "What then has happened?"

She was once more, with her companion's help, on her feet, and, feeling withdrawal imposed on him, he had blankly found his hat and gloves and had reached the door. Yet he waited for her answer. "What *was* to," she said.

V

He came back the next day, but she was then unable to see him, and as it was literally the first time this had occurred in the long stretch of their acquaintance he turned away, defeated and sore, almost angry — or feeling at least that such a break in their custom was really the beginning of the end — and wandered alone with his thoughts, especially with the one he was least able to keep down. She was dying and he would lose her; she was dying and his life would end. He stopped in the Park, into which he had passed, and stared before him at his recurrent doubt. Away from her the doubt pressed again; in her presence he had believed her, but as he felt his forlornness he threw himself into the explanation that, nearest at hand, had most of a miserable warmth for him and least of a cold torment. She had deceived him to save him — to put him off with something in which he should be able to rest. What could the thing that was to happen to him be, after all, but just this thing that had begun to happen? Her dying, her death, his consequent solitude — *that* was what he had figured as the Beast in the Jungle, that was what had been in the lap of the gods. He had had her word for it as he left her — what else on earth could she have meant? It wasn't a thing of a monstrous order; not a fate rare and distinguished; not a stroke of fortune that overwhelmed and immortalised; it had only the stamp of the common doom. But poor Marcher at this hour judged the common doom sufficient. It would serve his turn, and even as the consummation of infinite waiting he would bend his pride to accept it. He sat down on a bench in the twilight. He hadn't been a fool. Something had *been*, as she had said, to come. Before he rose indeed it had quite struck him that the final fact really matched with the long avenue through which he had had to reach it. As sharing his suspense and as giving herself all, giving her life, to bring it to an end, she had come with him every step of the way. He had lived by her aid, and to leave her behind would be cruelly, damnably to miss her. What could be more overwhelming than that?

Well, he was to know within the week, for though she kept him a while at bay, left him restless and wretched during a series of days on each of which he asked about her only again to have to turn away, she ended his trial by receiving him where she had always received him. Yet she had been brought out at some hazard into the presence of so many of the things that were, consciously, vainly, half their past, and there was scant service left in the gentleness of her mere desire, all too visible, to check his obsession and wind up his long trouble. That was clearly what she wanted, the one thing more for her own peace while she could still put out her hand. He was so affected by her state that, once seated by her chair, he was moved to let everything go; it was she herself therefore who brought him back, took up again, before she dismissed him, her last word of the other time. She showed how she wished to leave their business in order. "I'm not sure you understood. You've nothing to wait for more. It *has* come."

Oh how he looked at her! "Really?"

"Really."

"The thing that, as you said, *was* to?"

"The thing that we began in our youth to watch for." Face to face with her once more he believed her; it was a claim to which he had so abjectly little to oppose. "You mean that it has come as a positive definite occurrence, with a name and a date?"

"Positive. Definite. I don't know about the 'name,' but oh with a date!"

He found himself again too helplessly at sea. "But come in the night — come and passed me by?"

May Bartram had her strange faint smile. "Oh no, it hasn't passed you by!"

"But if I haven't been aware of it and it hasn't touched me — ?"

"Ah your not being aware of it" — and she seemed to hesitate an instant to deal with this — "your not being aware of it is the strangeness *in* the strangeness. It's the wonder *of* the wonder." She spoke as with the softness almost of a sick child, yet now at last, at the end of all, with the perfect straightness of a sibyl. She visibly knew that she knew, and the effect on him was of something co-ordinate, in its high character, with the law that had ruled him. It was the true voice of the law; so on her lips would the law itself have sounded. "It *has* touched you," she went on. "It has done its office. It has made you all its own."

"So utterly without my knowing it?"

"So utterly without your knowing it." His hand, as he leaned to her, was on the arm of her chair, and, dimly smiling always now, she placed her own on it. "It's enough if *I* know it."

"Oh!" he confusedly breathed, as she herself of late so often had done.

"What I long ago said is true. You'll never know now, and I think you ought to be content. You've *had* it," said May Bartram.

"But had what?"

"Why what was to have marked you out. The proof of your law. It has acted. I'm too glad," she then bravely added, "to have been able to see what it's *not*."

He continued to attach his eyes to her, and with the sense that it was all beyond him, and that *she* was too, he would still have sharply challenged her hadn't he so felt it an abuse of her weakness to do more than take devoutly what she gave him, take it hushed as to a revelation. If he did speak, it was out of the foreknowledge of his loneliness to come. "If you're glad of what it's 'not' it might then have been worse?"

She turned her eyes away, she looked straight before her; with which after a moment: "Well, you know our fears."

He wondered. "It's something then we never feared?"

On this slowly she turned to him. "Did we ever dream, with all our dreams, that we should sit and talk of it thus?"

He tried for a little to make out that they had; but it was as if their dreams, numberless enough, were in solution in some thick cold mist through which thought lost itself. "It might have been that we couldn't talk?"

"Well" — she did her best for him — "not from this side. This, you see," she said, "is the *other* side."

"I think," poor Marcher returned, "that all sides are the same to me." Then, however, as she gently shook her head in correction: "We mightn't, as it were, have got across — ?"

"To where we are — no. We're *here*" — she made her weak emphasis.

"And much good does it do us!" was her friend's frank comment.

"It does us the good it can. It does us the good that *it* isn't here. It's past. It's behind," said May Bartram. "Before — " but her voice dropped.

He had got up, not to tire her, but it was hard to combat his yearning. She after all told him nothing but that his light had failed — which he knew well enough without her. "Before — ?" he blankly echoed.

"Before, you see, it was always to *come*. That kept it present."

"Oh I don't care what comes now! Besides," Marcher added, "it seems to me I liked it better present, as you say, than I can like it absent with *your* absence."

"Oh mine!" — and her pale hands made light of it.

"With the absence of everything." He had a dreadful sense of standing there before her for — so far as anything but this proved, this bottomless drop was concerned — the last time of their life. It rested on him with a weight he felt he could scarce bear, and this weight it apparently was that still pressed out what remained in him of speakable protest. "I believe you; but I can't begin to pretend I understand. *Nothing*, for me, is past; nothing *will* pass till I pass myself, which I pray my stars may be as soon as possible. Say, however," he added, "that I've eaten my cake, as you contend, to the last crumb — how can the thing I've never felt at all be the thing I was marked out to feel?"

She met him perhaps less directly, but she met him unperturbed. "You take your 'feelings' for granted. You were to suffer your fate. That was not necessarily to know it."

"How in the world — when what is such knowledge but suffering?"

She looked up at him a while in silence. "No — you don't understand."

"I suffer," said John Marcher.

"Don't, don't!"

"How can I help at least *that*?"

"*Don't!*" May Bartram repeated.

She spoke it in a tone so special, in spite of her weakness, that he stared an instant — stared as if some light, hitherto hidden, had shimmered across his vision. Darkness again closed over it, but the gleam had already become for him an idea. "Because I haven't the right — ?"

"Don't *know* — when you needn't," she mercifully urged. "You needn't — for we shouldn't."

"Shouldn't?" If he could but know what she meant!

"No — it's too much."

"Too much?" he still asked but, with a mystification that was the next moment of a sudden to give way. Her words, if they meant something, affected him in this light — the light also of her wasted face — as meaning *all*, and the sense of what knowledge had been for herself came over him with a rush which broke through into a question. "Is it of that then you're dying?"

She but watched him, gravely at first, as to see, with this, where he was, and she might have seen something or feared something that moved her sympathy. "I would live for you still — if I could." Her eyes closed for a little, as if, withdrawn into herself, she were for a last time trying. "But I can't!" she said as she raised them again to take leave of him.

She couldn't indeed, as but too promptly and sharply appeared, and he had no vision of her after this that was anything but darkness and doom. They had parted for ever in that strange talk; access to her chamber of pain, rigidly guarded, was almost wholly forbidden him; he was feeling now moreover, in the face of doctors, nurses, the two or three relatives attracted doubtless by the presumption of what she had to "leave," how few were the rights, as they were called in such cases, that he had to put forward, and how odd it might even seem that their intimacy shouldn't have given him more of them. The stupidest fourth cousin had more, even though she had been nothing in such a person's life. She had been a feature of features in *his*, for what else was it to have been so indispensable? Strange beyond saying were the ways of existence, baffling for him the anomaly of his lack, as he felt it to be, of producible claim. A woman might have been, as it were, everything to him, and it might yet present him in no connexion that any one seemed held to recognise. If this was the case in these closing weeks it was the case more sharply on the occasion of the last offices rendered, in the great grey London cemetery, to what had been mortal, to what had been precious, in his friend. The concourse at her grave was not numerous, but he saw himself treated as scarce more nearly concerned with it than if there had been a thousand others. He was in short from this moment face to face with the fact that he was to profit extraordinarily little by the interest May Bartram had taken in him. He couldn't quite have said what he expected, but he hadn't surely expected this approach to a double privation. Not only had her interest failed him, but he seemed to feel himself unattended — and for a reason he couldn't seize — by the distinction, the dignity, the propriety, if nothing else, of the man markedly bereaved. It was as if in the view of society he had not *been* markedly bereaved, as if there still failed some sign or proof of it, and as if none the less his character could never be affirmed nor the deficiency ever made up. There were moments as the weeks went by when he would have liked, by some almost aggressive act, to take his stand on the intimacy of his loss, in order that it *might* be questioned and his retort, to the relief of his spirit, so recorded; but the moments of an irritation more helpless followed fast on these, the moments during which, turning things over with a good conscience but with a bare horizon, he found himself wondering if he oughtn't to have begun, so to speak, further back.

He found himself wondering indeed at many things, and this last speculation had others to keep it company. What could he have done, after all, in her lifetime, without giving them both, as it were, away? He couldn't have made known she was watching him, for that would have published the superstition of the Beast. This was what closed his mouth now — now that the Jungle had been threshed to vacancy and that the Beast had stolen away. It sounded too foolish and too flat; the difference for him in this particular, the extinction in his life of the element of suspense, was such as in fact to surprise him. He could scarce have said what the effect resembled; the abrupt cessation, the positive prohibition, of music perhaps, more than anything else, in some place all adjusted and all accustomed to sonority and to attention. If he could at any rate have conceived lifting the veil from his image at some moment of the past (what had he done, after all, if not lift it to *her*?) so to do this to-day, to talk to people at large of the Jungle cleared and confide to them that he now felt it as safe, would have been not only to see them listen as to a goodwife's tale, but really to hear himself tell one. What it presently came to in truth was that poor Marcher waded through his beaten grass, where no life stirred, where no breath sounded, where no evil eye seemed to gleam from a possible lair, very much as if vaguely looking for the Beast, and still more as if acutely missing it. He walked about in an existence that had grown strangely more spacious, and, stopping fitfully in places where the undergrowth of life struck him as closer, asked himself yearningly, wondered secretly and sorely, if it would have lurked here or there. It would have at all events *sprung*; what was at least complete was his belief in the truth itself of the assurance given him. The change from his old sense to his new was absolute and final: what was to happen *had* so absolutely and finally happened that he was as little able to know a fear for his future as to know a hope; so absent in short was any question of anything still to come. He was to live entirely with the other question, that of his unidentified past, that of his having to see his fortune impenetrably muffled and masked.

The torment of this vision became then his occupation; he couldn't perhaps have consented to live but for the possibility of guessing. She had told him, his friend, not to guess; she had forbidden him, so far as he might, to know, and she had even in a sort denied the power in him to learn: which were so many things, precisely, to deprive him of rest. It wasn't that he wanted, he argued for fairness, that anything past and done should repeat itself; it was only that he shouldn't, as an anticlimax, have been taken sleeping so sound as not to be able to win back by an effort of thought the lost stuff of consciousness. He declared to himself at moments that he would either win it back or have done with consciousness for ever; he made this idea his one motive in fine, made it so much his passion that none other, to compare with it, seemed ever to have touched him. The lost stuff of consciousness became thus for him as a strayed or stolen child to an unappeasable father; he hunted it up and down very much as if he were knocking at doors and enquiring of the police. This was the spirit in which, inevitably, he set himself to travel; he started on a journey that was to be as long as he could make it; it danced before him that, as the other side of the globe couldn't possibly have less to say to him, it might, by a possibility of suggestion, have more. Before he quitted London, however, he made a pilgrimage to May Bartram's grave, took his way to it through the endless avenues of the grim suburban metropolis, sought it out in the wilderness of tombs, and, though he had come but for the renewal of the act of farewell, found himself, when he had at last stood by it, beguiled into long intensities. He stood for an hour, powerless to turn away and yet powerless to penetrate the darkness of death; fixing with his eyes her inscribed name and date, beating his forehead against the fact of the secret they kept, drawing his breath, while he waited, as if some sense would in pity of him rise from the stones. He kneeled on the stones, however, in vain; they kept what they concealed; and if the face of the tomb did become a face for him it was because her two names became a pair of eyes that didn't know him. He gave them a last long look, but no palest light broke.

VI

He stayed away, after this, for a year; he visited the depths of Asia, spending himself on scenes of romantic interest, of superlative sanctity; but what was present to him everywhere was that for a man who had known what *he* had known the world was vulgar and vain. The state of mind in which he had lived for so many years shone out to him, in reflexion, as a light that coloured and refined, a light beside which the glow of the East was garish cheap and thin. The terrible truth was that he had lost — with everything else — a distinction as well; the things he saw couldn't help being common when he had become common to look at them. He was simply now one of them himself — he was in the dust, without a peg for the sense of difference; and there were hours when, before the temples of gods and the sepulchres of kings, his spirit turned for nobleness of association to the barely discriminated slab in the London suburb. That had become for him, and more intensely with time and distance, his one witness of a past glory. It was all that was left to him for proof or pride, yet the past glories of Pharaohs were nothing to him as he thought of it. Small wonder then that he came back to it on the morrow of his return. He was drawn there this time as irresistibly as the other, yet with a confidence, almost, that was doubtless the effect of the many months that had elapsed. He had lived, in spite of himself, into his change of feeling, and in wandering over the earth had wandered, as might be said, from the circumference to the centre of his desert. He had settled to his safety and accepted perforce his extinction; figuring to himself, with some colour, in the likeness of certain little old men he remembered to have seen, of whom, all meagre and wizened as they might look, it was related that they had in their time fought twenty duels or been loved by ten princesses. They indeed had been wondrous for others while he was but wondrous for himself; which, however, was exactly the cause of his haste to renew the wonder by getting back, as he might put it, into his own presence. That had quickened his steps and checked his delay. If his visit was prompt it was because he had been separated so long from the part of himself that alone he now valued.

It's accordingly not false to say that he reached his goal with a certain elation and stood there again with a certain assurance. The creature beneath the sod *knew* of his rare experience, so that, strangely now, the place had lost for him its mere blankness of expression. It met him in mildness — not, as before, in mockery; it wore for him the air of conscious greeting that we find, after absence, in the things that have closely belonged to us and which seem to confess of themselves to the connexion. The plot of ground, the graven tablet, the tended flowers affected him so as belonging to him that he resembled for the hour a contented landlord reviewing a piece of property. Whatever had happened — well, had happened. He had not come back this time with the vanity of that question, his former worrying "What, *what?*" now practically so spent. Yet he would none the less never again so cut himself off from the spot; he would come back to it every month, for if he did nothing else by its aid he at least held up his head. It thus grew for him, in the oddest way, a positive resource; he carried out his idea of periodical returns, which took their place at last among the most inveterate of his habits. What it all amounted to, oddly enough, was that in his finally so simplified world this garden of death gave him the few square feet of earth on which he could still most live. It was as if, being nothing anywhere else for any one, nothing even for himself, he were just everything here, and if not for a crowd of witnesses or indeed for any witness but John Marcher, then by clear right of the register that he could scan like an open page. The open page was the tomb of his friend, and *there* were the facts of the past, there the truth of his life, there the backward reaches in which he could lose himself. He did this from time to time with such effect that he seemed to wander through the old years with his hand in the arm of a companion who was, in the most extraordinary manner, his other, his younger self; and to wander, which was more extraordinary yet, round and round a third presence — not wandering she, but stationary, still, whose eyes, turning with his revolution, never ceased to follow him, and whose seat was his point, so to speak, of orientation. Thus in short he settled to live — feeding all on the sense that he once *had* lived, and dependent on it not alone for a support but for an identity.

It sufficed him in its way for months and the year elapsed; it would doubtless even have carried him further but for an accident, superficially slight, which moved him, quite in another direction, with a force beyond any of his impressions of Egypt or of India. It was a thing of the merest chance — the turn, as he afterwards felt, of a hair, though he was indeed to live to believe that if light hadn't come to him in this particular fashion it would still have come in another. He was to live to believe this, I say, though he was not to live, I may not less definitely mention, to do much else. We allow him at any rate the benefit of the conviction, struggling up for him at the end, that, whatever might have happened or not happened, he would have come round of himself to the light. The incident of an autumn day had put the match to the train laid from of old by his misery. With the light before him he knew that even of late his ache had only been smothered. It was strangely drugged, but it throbbed; at the touch it began to bleed. And the touch, in the event, was the face of a fellow mortal. This face, one grey afternoon when the leaves were thick in the alleys, looked into Marcher's own, at the cemetery, with an expression like the cut of a blade. He felt it, that is, so deep down that he winced at the steady thrust. The person who so mutely assaulted him was a figure he had noticed, on reaching his own goal, absorbed by a grave a short distance away, a grave apparently fresh, so that the emotion of the visitor would probably match it for frankness. This fact alone forbade further attention, though during the time he stayed he remained vaguely conscious of his neighbour, a middle-aged man apparently, in mourning, whose bowed back, among the clustered monuments and mortuary yews, was constantly presented. Marcher's theory that these were elements in contact with which he himself revived, had suffered, on this occasion, it may be granted, a marked, an excessive check. The autumn day was dire for him as none had recently been, and he rested with a heaviness he had not yet known on the low stone table that bore May Bartram's name. He rested without power to move, as if some spring in him, some spell vouchsafed, had suddenly been broken for ever. If he could have done that moment as he wanted he would simply have stretched himself on the slab that was ready to take him, treating it as a place prepared to receive his last sleep. What in all the wide world had he now to keep awake for? He stared before him with the question, and it was then that, as one of the cemetery walks passed near him, he caught the shock of the face.

His neighbour at the other grave had withdrawn, as he himself, with force enough in him, would have done by now, and was advancing along the path on his way to one of the gates. This brought him close, and his pace was slow, so that — and all the more as there was a kind of hunger in his look — the two men were for a minute directly confronted. Marcher knew him at once for one of the deeply stricken — a perception so sharp that nothing else in the picture comparatively lived, neither his dress, his age, nor his presumable character and class; nothing lived but the deep ravage of the features he showed. He *showed* them — that was the point; he was moved, as he passed, by some impulse that was either a signal for sympathy or, more possibly, a challenge to an opposed sorrow. He might already have been aware of our friend, might at some previous hour have noticed in him the smooth habit of the scene, with which the state of his own senses so scantly consorted, and might thereby have been stirred as by an overt discord. What Marcher was at all events conscious of was in the first place that the imaged of scarred passion presented to him was conscious too — of something that profaned the air; and in the second that, roused, startled, shocked, he was yet the next moment looking after it, as it went, with envy. The most extraordinary thing that had happened to him — though he had given that name to other matters as well — took place, after his immediate vague stare, as a consequence of this impression. The stranger passed, but the raw glare of his grief remained, making our friend wonder in pity what wrong, what wound it expressed, what injury not to be healed. What had the man *had*, to make him by the loss of it so bleed and yet live?

Something — and this reached him with a pang — that *he*, John Marcher, hadn't; the proof of which was precisely John Marcher's arid end. No passion had ever touched him, for this was what passion meant; he had survived and maundered and pined, but where had been *his* deep ravage? The extraordinary thing we speak of was the sudden rush of the result of this question. The sight that had just met his eyes named to him, as in letters of quick flame, something he had utterly, insanely missed, and what he had missed made these things a train of fire, made them mark themselves in an anguish of inward throbs. He had seen *outside* of his life, not learned it within, the way a woman was mourned when she had been loved for herself:

such was the force of his conviction of the meaning of the stranger's face, which still flared for him as a smoky torch. It hadn't come to him, the knowledge, on the wings of experience; it had brushed him, jostled him, upset him, with the disrespect of chance, the insolence of accident. Now that the illumination had begun, however, it blazed to the zenith, and what he presently stood there gazing at was the sounded void of his life. He gazed, he drew breath, in pain; he turned in his dismay, and, turning, he had before him in sharper incision than ever the open page of his story. The name on the table smote him as the passage of his neighbour had done, and what it said to him, full in the face, was that *she* was what he had missed. This was the awful thought, the answer to all the past, the vision at the dread clearness of which he grew as cold as the stone beneath him. Everything fell together, confessed, explained, overwhelmed; leaving him most of all stupefied at the blindness he had cherished. The fate he had been marked for he had met with a vengeance — he had emptied the cup to the lees; he had been the man of his time, *the* man, to whom nothing on earth was to have happened. That was the rare stroke — that was his visitation. So he saw it, as we say, in pale horror, while the pieces fitted and fitted. So *she* had seen it while he didn't, and so she served at this hour to drive the truth home. It was the truth, vivid and monstrous, that all the while he had waited the wait was itself his portion. This the companion of his vigil had at a given moment made out, and she had then offered him the chance to baffle his doom. One's doom, however, was never baffled, and on the day she told him his own had come down she had seen him but stupidly stare at the escape she offered him.

The escape would have been to love her; then, *then* he would have lived. *She* had lived — who could say now with what passion? — since she had loved him for himself; whereas he had never thought of her (ah how it hugely glared at him!) but in the chill of his egotism and the light of her use. Her spoken words came back to him — the chain stretched and stretched. The Beast had lurked indeed, and the Beast, at its hour, had sprung; it had sprung in that twilight of the cold April when, pale, ill, wasted, but all beautiful, and perhaps even then recoverable, she had risen from her chair to stand before him and let him imaginably guess. It had sprung as he didn't guess; it had sprung as she hopelessly turned from him, and the mark, by the time he left her, had fallen where it *was* to fall. He had justified his fear and achieved his fate; he had failed, with the last exactitude, of all he was to fail of; and a moan now rose to his lips as he remembered she had prayed he mightn't know. This horror of waking — *this* was knowledge, knowledge under the breath of which the very tears in his eyes seemed to freeze. Through them, none the less, he tried to fix it and hold it; he kept it there before him so that he might feel the pain. That at least, belated and bitter, had something of the taste of life. But the bitterness suddenly sickened him, and it was as if, horribly, he saw, in the truth, in the cruelty of his image, what had been appointed and done. He saw the Jungle of his life and saw the lurking Beast; then, while he looked, perceived it, as by a stir of the air, rise, huge and hideous, for the leap that was to settle him. His eyes darkened — it was close; and, instinctively turning, in his hallucination, to avoid it, he flung himself, face down, on the tomb.

QUESTIONS

1. James has been called "the historian of fine consciences." Does this story bear out that judgment?

2. What do the names John Marcher and May Bartram suggest? What can you infer about their characters from the fact that "March" and "May" are in their names? Would "June" have served as well for Miss Bartram?

3. Look closely at the last sentence in each section of the story in light of the fact that James wrote plays as well as prose fiction. Do the sections correspond to the acts of a play?

4. Where does the climax occur?

5. Is Marcher cold and insensitive? What actions show that he does not intend to be so?

6. What incident brings Marcher to realize his utter failure?

7. "*She* had lived — who could say now with what passion?" Do you think this is true? Is it possible that May was fulfilled while Marcher remained unfulfilled? Can you find passages in Parts IV and V that suggest this?

8. Is Marcher characterized more by what he says and does or by what James tells us about him? Is the same true of May Bartram?

9. Nothing of a physically violent nature happens in "The Beast in the Jungle." Is the title misleading, then, or overdramatic? How would you defend James's choice of it?

SARAH ORNE JEWETT

Miss Tempy's Watchers

The time of year was April; the place was a small farming town in New Hampshire, remote from any railroad. One by one the lights had been blown out in the scattered houses near Miss Tempy Dent's; but as her neighbors took a last look out-of-doors, their eyes turned with instinctive curiosity toward the old house, where a lamp burned steadily. They gave a little sigh. "Poor Miss Tempy!" said more than one bereft acquaintance; for the good woman lay dead in her north chamber, and the light was a watcher's light. The funeral was set for the next day, at one o'clock.

The watchers were two of the oldest friends, Mrs. Crowe and Sarah Ann Binson. They were sitting in the kitchen, because it seemed less awesome than the unused best room, and they beguiled the long hours by steady conversation. One would think that neither topics nor opinions would hold out, at that rate, all through the long spring night; but there was a certain degree of excitement just then, and the two women had risen to an unusual level of expressiveness and confidence. Each had already told the other more than one fact that she had determined to keep secret; they were again and again tempted into statements that either would have found impossible by daylight. Mrs. Crowe was knitting a blue yarn stocking for her husband; the foot was already so long that it seemed as if she must have forgotten to narrow it at the proper time. Mrs. Crowe knew exactly what she was about, however; she was of a much cooler disposition than Sister Binson, who made futile attempts at some sewing, only to drop her work into her lap whenever the talk was most engaging.

Their faces were interesting, — of the dry, shrewd, quick-witted New England type, with thin hair twisted neatly back out of the way. Mrs. Crowe could look vague and benignant, and Miss Binson was, to quote her neighbors, a little too sharp-set; but the world knew that she had need to be, with the load she must carry of supporting an inefficient widowed sister and six unpromising and unwilling nieces and nephews. The eldest boy was at last placed with a good man to learn the mason's trade. Sarah Ann Binson, for all her sharp, anxious aspect, never defended herself, when her sister whined and fretted. She was told every week of her life that the poor children never would have had to lift a finger if their father had lived, and yet she had kept her steadfast way with the little farm, and patiently taught the young people many useful things, for which, as everybody said, they would live to thank her. However pleasureless her life appeared to outward view, it was brimful of pleasure to herself.

256

Mrs. Crowe, on the contrary, was well to do, her husband being a rich farmer and an easy-going man. She was a stingy woman, but for all that she looked kindly; and when she gave away anything, or lifted a finger to help anybody, it was thought a great piece of beneficence, and a compliment, indeed, which the recipient accepted with twice as much gratitude as double the gift that came from a poorer and more generous acquaintance. Everybody liked to be on good terms with Mrs. Crowe. Socially she stood much higher than Sarah Ann Binson. They were both old schoolmates and friends of Temperance Dent, who had asked them, one day, not long before she died, if they would not come together and look after the house, and manage everything, when she was gone. She may have had some hope that they might become closer friends in this period of intimate partnership, and that the richer woman might better understand the burdens of the poorer. They had not kept the house the night before; they were too weary with the care of their old friend, whom they had not left until all was over.

There was a brook which ran down the hillside very near the house, and the sound of it was much louder than usual. When there was silence in the kitchen, the busy stream had a strange insistence in its wild voice, as if it tried to make the watchers understand something that related to the past.

"I declare, I can't begin to sorrow for Tempy yet. I am so glad to have her at rest," whispered Mrs. Crowe. "It is strange to set here without her, but I can't make it clear that she has gone. I feel as if she had got easy and dropped off to sleep, and I'm more scared about waking her up than knowing any other feeling."

"Yes," said Sarah Ann, "it's just like that, ain't it? But I tell you we are goin' to miss her worse than we expect. She's helped me through with many a trial, has Temperance. I ain't the only one who says the same, neither."

These words were spoken as if there were a third person listening; somebody beside Mrs. Crowe. The watchers could not rid their minds of the feeling that they were being watched themselves. The spring wind whistled in the window crack, now and then, and buffeted the little house in a gusty way that had a sort of companionable effect. Yet, on the whole, it was a very still night, and the watchers spoke in a half-whisper.

"She was the freest-handed woman that ever I knew," said Mrs. Crowe, decidedly. "According to her means, she gave away more than anybody. I used to tell her 'twa'n't right. I used really to be afraid that she went without too much, for we have a duty to ourselves."

Sister Binson looked up in a half-amused, unconscious way, and then recollected herself.

Mrs. Crowe met her look with a serious face. "It ain't so easy for me to give as it is for some," she said simply, but with an effort which was made possible only by the occasion. "I should like to say, while Tempy is laying here yet in her own house, that she has been a constant lesson to me. Folks are too kind, and shame me with thanks for what I do. I ain't such a generous woman as poor Tempy was, for all she had nothin' to do with, as one may say."

Sarah Binson was much moved at this confession, and was even pained and touched by the unexpected humility. "You have a good many calls on you" — she began, and then left her kind little compliment half finished.

"Yes, yes, but I've got means enough. My disposition's more of a cross to me as I grow older, and I made up my mind this morning that Tempy's example should be my pattern henceforth." She began to knit faster than ever.

"'T ain't no use to get morbid; that's what Tempy used to say herself," said Sarah Ann, after a minute's silence. "Ain't it strange to say 'used to say'?" and her own voice choked a little. "She never did like to hear folks git goin' about themselves."

"''T was only because they're apt to do so as other folks will say 't wasn't so, an' praise 'em up," humbly replied Mrs. Crowe, "and that ain't my object. There wa'n't a child but what Tempy set herself to work to see what she could do to please it. One time my brother's folks had been stopping here in the summer, from Massachusetts. The children was all little, and they broke up a sight of toys, and left 'em when they were going away. Tempy come right up after they rode by, to see if she couldn't help me set the house to rights, and she caught me just as I was going to fling some of the clutter into the stove. I was kind of tired out, starting 'em off in season. 'Oh, give me them!' says she, real pleading; and she wropped 'em up and took 'em home with her when she went, and she mended 'em up and stuck 'em together, and made some young one or other happy with every blessed one. You'd thought I'd done her the biggest favor. 'No thanks to me. I should ha' burnt 'em, Tempy,' says I."

"Some of 'em came to our house, I know," said Miss Binson. "She'd take a lot o' trouble to please a child, 'stead o' shoving of it out o' the way, like the rest of us when we're drove."

"I can tell you the biggest thing she ever done, and I don't know's there's anybody left but me to tell it. I don't want it forgot," Sarah Binson went on, looking up at the clock to see how the night was going. "It was that pretty-looking Trevor girl, who taught the Corners school, and married so well afterwards, out in New York State. You remember her, I dare say?"

"Certain," said Mrs. Crowe, with an air of interest.

"She was a splendid scholar, folks said, and give the school a great start; but she'd overdone herself getting her education, and working to pay for it, and she all broke down one spring, and Tempy made her come and stop with her a while, — you remember that? Well, she had an uncle, her mother's brother, out in Chicago, who was well off and friendly, and used to write to Lizzie Trevor, and I dare say make her some presents; but he was a lively, driving man, and didn't take time to stop and think about his folks. He hadn't seen her since she was a little girl. Poor Lizzie was so pale and weakly that she just got through the term o' school. She looked as if she was just going straight off in a decline. Tempy, she cosseted her up a while, and then, next thing folks knew, she was tellin' round how Miss Trevor had gone to see her uncle, and meant to visit Niagary Falls on the way, and stop over night. Now I happened to know, in ways I won't dwell on to explain, that the poor girl was in debt for her schoolin' when she come here, and her last quarter's pay had just squared it off at last, and left her without a cent ahead, hardly; but it had fretted her thinking of it, so she paid it all; those might have dunned her that she owed it to. An' I taxed Tempy about the girl's goin' off on such a journey till she owned up, rather 'n have Lizzie blamed, that she'd given her sixty dollars, same's if she was rolling in riches, and sent her off to have a good rest and vacation."

"Sixty dollars!" exclaimed Mrs. Crowe. "Tempy only had ninety dollars a year that came in to her; rest of her livin' she got by helpin' about, with what she raised off this little piece o' ground, sand one side an' clay the other. An' how often I've heard her tell, years ago, that she'd rather see Niagary than any other sight in the world!"

The women looked at each other in silence; the magnitude of the generous sacrifice was almost too great for their comprehension.

"She was just poor enough to do that!" declared Mrs. Crowe at last, in an abandonment of feeling. "Say what you may, I feel humbled to the dust," and her companion ventured to say nothing. She never had given away sixty dollars at once, but it was simply because she never had it to give. It came to her very lips to say in explanation, "Tempy was so situated;" but she checked herself in time, for she would not betray her own loyal guarding of a dependent household.

"Folks say a great deal of generosity, and this one's being public-sperited, and that one free-handed about giving," said Mrs. Crowe, who was a little nervous in the silence. "I suppose we can't tell the sorrow it would be to some folks not to give, same's 't would be to me not to save. I seem kind of made for that, as if 't was what I'd got to do. I should feel sights better about it if I could make it evident what I was savin' for. If I had a child, now, Sarah Ann," and her voice was a little husky, — "if I had a child, I should think I was heapin' of it up because he was the one trained by the Lord to scatter it again for good. But here's Mr. Crowe and me, we can't do anything with money, and both of us like to keep things same's they've always been. Now Priscilla Dance was talking away like a mill-clapper, week before last. She'd think I would go right off and get one o' them new-fashioned gilt-and-white papers for the best room, and some new furniture, an' a marble-top table. And I looked at her, all struck up. 'Why,' says I, 'Priscilla, that nice old velvet paper ain't hurt a mite. I shouldn't feel 't was my best room without it. Dan'el says 't is the first thing he can remember rubbin' his little baby fingers on to it, and how splendid he thought them red roses was.' I maintain," continued Mrs. Crowe stoutly, "that folks wastes sights o' good money doin' just such foolish things. Tearin' out the insides o' meetin'-houses, and fixin' the pews different; 't was good enough as 't was with mendin'; then times come, an' they want to put it all back same's 't was before."

This touched upon an exciting subject to active members of that parish. Miss Binson and Mrs. Crowe belonged to opposite parties, and had at one time come as near hard feelings as they could, and yet escape them. Each hastened to speak of other things and to show her untouched friendliness.

"I do agree with you," said Sister Binson, "that few of us know what use to make of money, beyond every-day necessities. You've seen more o' the world than I have, and know what's expected. When it comes to taste and judgment about such things, I ought to defer to others;" and with this modest avowal the critical moment passed when there might have been an improper discussion.

In the silence that followed, the fact of their presence in a house of death grew more clear than before. There was something disturbing in the noise of a mouse gnawing at the dry boards of a closet wall near by. Both the watchers looked up anxiously at the clock; it was almost the middle of the night, and the whole world seemed to have left them alone with their solemn duty. Only the brook was awake.

"Perhaps we might give a look up-stairs now," whispered Mrs. Crowe, as if she hoped to hear some reason against their going just then to the chamber of death; but Sister Binson rose, with a serious and yet satisfied countenance, and lifted the small lamp from the table. She was much more used to watching than Mrs. Crowe, and much less affected by it. They opened the door into a small entry with a steep stairway; they climbed the creaking stairs, and entered the cold upper room on tiptoe. Mrs. Crowe's heart began to beat very fast as the lamp was put on a high bureau, and made long, fixed shadows about the walls. She went hesitatingly toward the solemn shape under its white drapery, and felt a sense of remonstrance as Sarah Ann gently, but in a business-like way, turned back the thin sheet.

"Seems to me she looks pleasanter and pleasanter," whispered Sarah Ann Binson impulsively, as they gazed at the white face with its wonderful smile. "To-morrow 't will all have faded out. I do believe they kind of wake up a day or two after they die, and it's then they go." She replaced the light covering, and they both turned quickly away; there was a chill in this upper room.

"'T is a great thing for anybody to have got through, ain't it?" said Mrs. Crowe softly, as she began to go down the stairs on tiptoe. The warm air from the kitchen beneath met them with a sense of welcome and shelter.

"I don' know why it is, but I feel as near again to Tempy down here as I do up there," replied Sister Binson. "I feel as if the air was full of her, kind of. I can sense things, now and then, that she seems to say. Now I never was one to take up with no nonsense of sperits and such, but I declare I felt as if she told me just now to put some more wood into the stove."

Mrs. Crowe preserved a gloomy silence. She had suspected before this that her companion was of a weaker and more credulous disposition than herself. "'T is a great thing to have got through," she repeated, ignoring definitely all that had last been said. "I suppose you know as well as I that Tempy was one that always feared death. Well, it's all put behind her now; she knows what 't is." Mrs. Crowe gave a little sigh, and Sister Binson's quick sympathies were stirred toward this other old friend, who also dreaded the great change.

"I'd never like to forget almost those last words Tempy spoke plain to me," she said gently, like the comforter she truly was. "She looked up at me once or twice, that last afternoon after I come to set by her, and let Mis' Owen go home; and I says, 'Can I do anything to ease you, Tempy?' and the tears come into my eyes so I couldn't see what kind of a nod she give me. 'No, Sarah Ann, you can't, dear,' says she; and then she got her breath again, and says she, looking at me real meanin', 'I'm only a-gettin' sleepier and sleepier; that's all there is,' says she, and smiled up at me kind of wishful, and shut her eyes. I knew well enough all she meant. She'd been lookin' out for a chance to tell me, and I don' know's she ever said much afterwards."

Mrs. Crowe was not knitting; she had been listening too eagerly. "Yes, 't will be a comfort to think of that sometimes," she said, in acknowledgment.

"I know that old Dr. Prince said once, in evenin' meetin', that he'd watched by many a dyin' bed, as we well knew, and enough o' his sick folks had been scared o' dyin' their whole lives through; but when they come to the last, he'd never seen one but was willin', and most were glad, to go. ''T is as natural as bein' born or livin' on,' he said. I don't know what had moved him to speak that night. You know he wa'n't in the habit of it, and 't was the monthly concert of prayer for foreign missions anyways," said Sarah Ann; "but 't was a great stay to the mind to listen to his words of experience."

"There never was a better man," responded Mrs. Crowe, in a really cheerful tone. She had recovered from her feeling of nervous dread, the kitchen was so comfortable with lamplight and firelight; and just then the old clock began to tell the hour of twelve with leisurely whirring strokes.

Sister Binson laid aside her work, and rose quickly and went to the cupboard. "We'd better take a little to eat," she explained. "The night will go fast after this. I want to know if you went and made some o' your nice cupcake, while you was home to-day?" she asked, in a pleased tone; and Mrs. Crowe acknowledged such a gratifying piece of thoughtfulness for this humble friend who denied herself all luxuries. Sarah Ann brewed a generous cup of tea, and the watchers drew their chairs up to the table presently, and quelled their hunger with good country appetites. Sister Binson put a spoon into a small, old-fashioned glass of preserved quince, and passed it to her friend. She was most familiar with the house, and played the part of hostess. "Spread some o' this on your bread and butter," she said to Mrs. Crowe. "Tempy wanted me to use some three or four times, but I never felt to. I know she'd like to have us comfortable now, and would urge us to make a good supper, poor dear."

"What excellent preserves she did make!" mourned Mrs. Crowe. "None of us has got her light hand at doin' things tasty. She made the most o' everything, too. Now, she only had that one old quince-tree down in the far corner of the piece, but she'd go out in the spring and tend to it, and look at it so pleasant, and kind of expect the old thorny thing into bloomin'."

"She was just the same with folks," said Sarah Ann. "And she'd never git more 'n a little apernful o' quinces, but she'd have every mite o' goodness out o' those, and set the glasses up onto her best-room closet shelf, *so* pleased. 'T wa'n't but a week ago to-morrow mornin' I fetched her a little taste o' jelly in a teaspoon; and she says 'Thank ye,' and took it, an' the minute she tasted it she looked up at me as worried as could be. 'Oh, I don't want to eat that,' says she. 'I always keep that in case o' sickness.' 'You're goin' to have the good o' one tumbler yourself,' says I. 'I'd just like to know who's sick now, if you ain't!' An' she couldn't help laughin', I spoke up so smart. Oh, dear me, how I shall miss talkin' over things with her! She always sensed things, and got just the p'int you meant."

"She didn't begin to age until two or three years ago, did she?" asked Mrs. Crowe. "I never saw anybody keep her looks as Tempy did. She looked young long after I begun to feel like an old woman. The doctor used to say 't was her young heart, and I don't know but what he was right. How she did do for other folks! There was one spell she wasn't at home a day to a fortnight. She got most of her livin' so, and that made her own potatoes and things last her through. None o' the young folks could get married without her, and all the old ones was disappointed if she wa'n't round when they was down with sickness and had to go. An' cleanin', or tailorin' for boys, or rug-hookin', — there was nothin' but what she could do as handy as most. 'I do love to work,' — ain't you heard her say that twenty times a week?"

Sarah Ann Binson nodded, and began to clear away the empty plates. "We may want a taste o' somethin' more towards mornin'," she said. "There's plenty in the closet here; and in case some comes from a distance to the funeral, we'll have a little table spread after we get back to the house."

"Yes, I was busy all the mornin'. I've cooked up a sight o' things to bring over," said Mrs. Crowe. "I felt 't was the last I could do for her."

They drew their chairs near the stove again, and took up their work. Sister Binson's rocking-chair creaked as she rocked; the brook sounded louder than ever. It was more lonely when nobody spoke, and presently Mrs. Crowe returned to her thoughts of growing old.

"Yes, Tempy aged all of a sudden. I remember I asked her if she felt as well as common, one day, and she laughed at me good. There, when Mr. Crowe begun to look old, I couldn't help feeling as if somethin' ailed him, and like as not 't was somethin' he was goin' to git right over, and I dosed him for it stiddy, half of one summer."

"How many things we shall be wanting to ask Tempy!" exclaimed Sarah Ann Binson, after a long pause. "I can't make up my mind to doin' without her. I wish folks could come back just once, and tell us how 't is where they've gone. Seems then we could do without 'em better."

The brook hurried on, the wind blew about the house now and then; the house itself was a silent place, and the supper, the warm fire, and an absence of any new topics for conversation made the watchers drowsy. Sister Binson closed her eyes first, to rest them for a minute; and Mrs. Crowe glanced at her compassionately, with a new sympathy for the hard-worked little woman. She made up her mind to let Sarah Ann have a good rest, while she kept watch alone; but in a few minutes her own knitting was dropped, and she, too, fell asleep. Overhead, the pale shape of Tempy Dent, the outworn body of that generous, loving-hearted, simple soul, slept on also in its white raiment. Perhaps Tempy herself stood near, and saw her own life and its surroundings with new understanding. Perhaps she herself was the only watcher.

Later, by some hours, Sarah Ann Binson woke with a start. There was a pale light of dawn outside the small windows. Inside the kitchen, the lamp burned dim. Mrs. Crowe awoke, too.

"I think Tempy'd be the first to say 't was just as well we both had some rest," she said, not without a guilty feeling.

Her companion went to the outer door, and opened it wide. The fresh air was none too cold, and the brook's voice was not nearly so loud as it had been in the midnight darkness. She could see the shapes of the hills, and the great shadows that lay across the lower country. The east was fast growing bright.

"'T will be a beautiful day for the funeral," she said, and turned again, with a sigh, to follow Mrs. Crowe up the stairs.

QUESTIONS

1. Explain the play on words in Sarah Orne Jewett's title. Is it an appropriate one?

2. Are we given too much background information on Mrs. Crowe and Sarah Ann Binson? What, for example, is gained by our knowing that Miss Binson supports "an inefficient widowed sister and six … nieces and nephews"?

3. Show that Miss Tempy's "watchers" are good women, but by no means perfect.

4. Narrative and descriptive passages alternate with scenes of dialogue and personal interplay. What effect does this alternation have on you? Can you explain why?

5. Which events of Miss Tempy's life seem most memorable to the two ladies? to you? Would they have seemed so to Miss Tempy?

6. What attitude toward death do you find in this story? How is this attitude conveyed? Does this attitude seem to be shared by the author as well as her characters?

KATE CHOPIN

Désirée's Baby

As the day was pleasant, Madame Valmondé drove over to L'Abri to see Désirée and the baby.

It made her laugh to think of Désirée with a baby. Why, it seemed but yesterday that Désirée was little more than a baby herself; when Monsieur in riding through the gateway of Valmondé had found her lying asleep in the shadow of the big stone pillar.

The little one awoke in his arms and began to cry for "Dada." That was as much as she could do or say. Some people thought she might have strayed there of her own accord, for she was of the toddling age. The prevailing belief was that she had been purposely left by a party of Texans, whose canvas-covered wagon, late in the day, had crossed the ferry that Coton Maïs kept, just below the plantation. In time Madame Valmondé abandoned every speculation but the one that Désirée had been sent to her by a beneficent Providence to be the child of her affection, seeing that she was without child of the flesh. For the girl grew to be beautiful and gentle, affectionate and sincere, — the idol of Valmondé.

It was no wonder, when she stood one day against the stone pillar in whose shadow she had lain asleep, eighteen years before, that Armand Aubigny riding by and seeing her there, had fallen in love with her. That was the way all the Aubignys fell in love, as if struck by a pistol shot. The wonder was that he had not loved her before; for he had known her since his father brought him home from Paris, a boy of eight, after his mother died there. The passion that awoke in him that day, when he saw her at the gate, swept along like an avalanche, or like a prairie fire, or like anything that drives headlong over all obstacles.

Monsieur Valmondé grew practical and wanted things well considered: that is, the girl's obscure origin. Armand looked into her eyes and did not care. He was reminded that she was nameless. What did it matter about a name when he could give her one of the oldest and proudest in Louisiana? He ordered the *corbeille*[1] from Paris, and contained himself with what patience he could until it arrived; then they were married.

Madame Valmondé had not seen Désirée and the baby for four weeks. When she reached L'Abri she shuddered at the first sight of it, as she always did. It was a sad looking place, which for many years had not known the gentle presence of a mistress, old Monsieur Aubigny having married and buried his wife in France, and she having loved her own land too well ever to leave it. The roof came down steep and black like a cowl, reaching out beyond the wide galleries that

---

[1] Wedding presents, literally a "basket" of them.

encircled the yellow stuccoed house. Big solemn oaks grew close to it, and their thick-leaved, far-reaching branches shadowed it like a pall. Young Aubigny's rule was a strict one, too, and under it his negroes had forgotten how to be gay, as they had been during the old master's easy-going and indulgent lifetime.

The young mother was recovering slowly, and lay full length, in her soft white muslins and laces, upon a couch. The baby was beside her, upon her arm, where he had fallen asleep, at her breast. The yellow nurse woman sat beside a window fanning herself.

Madame Valmondé bent her portly figure over Désirée and kissed her, holding her an instant tenderly in her arms. Then she turned to the child.

"This is not the baby!" she exclaimed, in startled tones. French was the language spoken at Valmondé in those days.

"I knew you would be astonished," laughed Désirée, "at the way he has grown. The little *cochon de lait*![2] Look at his legs, mamma, and his hands and fingernails, — real fingernails. Zandrine had to cut them this morning. Isn't it true, Zandrine?"

The woman bowed her turbaned head majestically, "*Mais si,*[3] Madame."

"And the way he cries," went on Désirée, "is deafening. Armand heard him the other day as far away as La Blanche's cabin."

Madame Valmondé had never removed her eyes from the child. She lifted it and walked with it over to the window that was lightest. She scanned the baby narrowly, then looked as searchingly at Zandrine, whose face was turned to gaze across the fields.

"Yes, the child has grown, has changed," said Madame Valmondé, slowly, as she replaced it beside its mother. "What does Armand say?"

Désirée's face became suffused with a glow that was happiness itself.

"Oh, Armand is the proudest father in the parish, I believe, chiefly because it is a boy, to bear his name; though he says not, — that he would have loved a girl as well. But I know it isn't true. I know he says that to please me. And mamma," she added, drawing Madame Valmondé's head down to her, and speaking in a whisper, "he hasn't punished one of them — not one of them — since baby is born. Even Négrillon, who pretended to have burnt his leg that he might rest from work — he only laughed, and said Négrillon was a great scamp. Oh, mamma, I'm so happy; it frightens me."

What Désirée said was true. Marriage, and later the birth of his son had softened Armand Aubigny's imperious and exacting nature greatly. This was what made the gentle Désirée so happy, for she loved him desperately. When he frowned she trembled, but loved him. When he smiled, she asked no greater blessing of God. But Armand's dark, handsome face had not often been disfigured by frowns since the day he fell in love with her.

When the baby was about three months old, Désirée awoke one day to the conviction that there was something in the air menacing her peace. It was at first too subtle to grasp. It had only been a disquieting suggestion; an air of mystery among the blacks; unexpected visits from far-off neighbors who could hardly account for their coming. Then a strange, an awful change in her husband's manner, which she dared not ask him to explain. When he spoke to her, it was with averted eyes, from which the old love-light seemed to have gone out. He absented himself from home; and when there, avoided her presence and that of her child, without excuse. And the very spirit of Satan seemed suddenly to take hold of him in his dealings with the slaves. Désirée was miserable enough to die.

---

[2] Piglet.

[3] "But of course."

She sat in her room, one hot afternoon, in her *peignoir*,[4] listlessly drawing through her fingers the strands of her long, silky brown hair that hung about her shoulders. The baby, half naked, lay asleep upon her own great mahogany bed, that was like a sumptuous throne, with its satin-lined half-canopy. One of La Blanche's little quadroon boys — half naked too — stood fanning the child slowly with a fan of peacock feathers. Désirée's eyes had been fixed absently and sadly upon the baby, while she was striving to penetrate the threatening mist that she felt closing about her. She looked from her child to the boy who stood beside him, and back again; over and over. "Ah!" It was a cry that she could not help; which she was not conscious of having uttered. The blood turned like ice in her veins, and a clammy moisture gathered upon her face.

She tried to speak to the little quadroon boy; but no sound would come, at first. When he heard his name uttered, he looked up, and his mistress was pointing to the door. He laid aside the great, soft fan, and obediently stole away, over the polished floor, on his bare tiptoes.

She stayed motionless, with gaze riveted upon her child, and her face the picture of fright.

Presently her husband entered the room, and without noticing her, went to a table and began to search among some papers which covered it.

"Armand," she called to him, in a voice which must have stabbed him, if he was human. But he did not notice. "Armand," she said again. Then she rose and tottered towards him. "Armand," she panted once more, clutching his arm, "look at our child. What does it mean? tell me."

He coldly but gently loosened her fingers from about his arm and thrust the hand away from him. "Tell me what it means!" she cried despairingly.

"It means," he answered lightly, "that the child is not white; it means that you are not white."

A quick conception of all that this accusation meant for her nerved her with unwonted courage to deny it. "It is a lie; it is not true, I am white! Look at my hair, it is brown; and my eyes are gray, Armand, you know they are gray. And my skin is fair," seizing his wrist. "Look at my hand; whiter than yours, Armand," she laughed hysterically.

"As white as La Blanche's," he returned cruelly; and went away leaving her alone with their child.

When she could hold a pen in her hand, she sent a despairing letter to Madame Valmondé.

"My mother, they tell me I am not white. Armand has told me I am not white. For God's sake tell them it is not true. You must know it is not true. I shall die. I must die. I cannot be so unhappy, and live."

The answer that came was as brief:

"My own Désirée: Come home to Valmondé; back to your mother who loves you. Come with your child."

When the letter reached Désirée she went with it to her husband's study, and laid it open upon the desk before which he sat. She was like a stone image: silent, white, motionless after she placed it there.

In silence he ran his cold eyes over the written words. He said nothing. "Shall I go, Armand?" she asked in tones sharp with agonized suspense.

"Yes, go."

"Do you want me to go?"

---

[4] A dressing gown.

"Yes, I want you to go."

He thought Almighty God had dealt cruelly and unjustly with him; and felt, somehow, that he was paying Him back in kind when he stabbed thus into his wife's soul. Moreover he no longer loved her, because of the unconscious injury she had brought upon his home and his name.

She turned away like one stunned by a blow, and walked slowly toward the door, hoping he would call her back.

"Good-by, Armand," she moaned.

He did not answer her. That was his last blow at fate.

Désirée went in search of her child. Zandrine was pacing the sombre gallery with it. She took the little one from the nurse's arms with no word of explanation, and descending the steps, walked away, under the live-oak branches.

It was an October afternoon; the sun was just sinking. Out in the still fields the negroes were picking cotton.

Désirée had not changed the thin white garment nor the slippers which she wore. Her hair was uncovered and the sun's rays brought a golden gleam from its brown meshes. She did not take the broad, beaten road which led to the far-off plantation of Valmondé. She walked across a deserted field, where the stubble bruised her tender feet, so delicately shod, and tore her thin gown to shreds.

She disappeared among the reeds and willows that grew thick along the banks of the deep, sluggish bayou; and she did not come back again.

Some weeks later there was a curious scene enacted at L'Abri. In the centre of the smoothly swept back yard was a great bonfire. Armand Aubigny sat in the wide hallway that commanded a view of the spectacle; and it was he who dealt out to a half dozen negroes the material which kept this fire ablaze.

A graceful cradle of willow, with all its dainty furbishings, was laid upon the pyre, which had already been fed with the richness of a priceless *layette*.[5] Then there were silk gowns, and velvet and satin ones added to these; laces, too, and embroideries; bonnets and gloves; for the *corbeille* had been of rare quality.

The last thing to go was a tiny bundle of letters; innocent little scribblings that Désirée had sent to him during the days of their espousal. There was the remnant of one back in the drawer from which he took them. But it was not Désirée's; it was part of an old letter from his mother to his father. He read it. She was thanking God for the blessing of her husband's love: —

"But, above all," she wrote, "night and day, I thank the good God for having so arranged our lives that our dear Armand will never know that his mother, who adores him, belongs to the race that is cursed with the brand of slavery."

QUESTIONS

1. What details help to establish the setting and to distinguish it from, say, an "ordinary" Southern setting?

2. Désirée is a foundling, her parentage unknown. How does this information color your expectations? Is it deliberately misleading?

3. How has the baby's presence changed Armand? Is this a clue to Armand's own heritage? Are there more substantial hints that Armand is of mixed racial stock?

---

[5] An outfit of linens for a baby.

4. Why doesn't Désirée return to her family home when Armand rejects her?

5. What would you expect Armand to do once he has learned the truth? Has the author given us enough information to allow a logical inference? Does the answer lie in the character of Armand or in the social attitudes of Chopin's Louisiana?

JOSEPH CONRAD

Heart of Darkness

I

The *Nellie*, a cruising yawl, swung to her anchor without a flutter of the sails, and was at rest. The flood had made, the wind was nearly calm, and being bound down the river, the only thing for it was to come to and wait for the turn of the tide.

The sea-reach of the Thames stretched before us like the beginning of an interminable waterway. In the offing the sea and the sky were welded together without a joint, and in the luminous space the tanned sails of the barges drifting up with the tide seemed to stand still in red clusters of canvas sharply peaked, with gleams of varnished spirits. A haze rested on the low shores that ran out to sea in vanishing flatness. The air was dark above Gravesend,[1] and farther back still seemed condensed into a mournful gloom, brooding motionless over the biggest, and the greatest, town on earth.

The Director of Companies was our captain and our host. We four affectionately watched his back as he stood in the bows looking to seaward. On the whole river there was nothing that looked half so nautical. He resembled a pilot, which to a seaman is trustworthiness personified. It was difficult to realize his work was not out there in the luminous estuary, but behind him, within the brooding gloom.

Between us there was, as I have already said somewhere, the bond of the sea. Besides holding our hearts together through long periods of separation, it had the effect of making us tolerant of each other's yarns — and even convictions. The Lawyer — the best of old fellows — had, because of his many years and many virtues, the only cushion on deck, and was lying on the only rug. The Accountant had brought out already a box of dominoes, and was toying architecturally with the bones. Marlow sat cross-legged right aft, leaning against the mizzen-mast. He had sunken cheeks, a yellow complexion, a straight back, an ascetic aspect, and, with his arms dropped, the palms of hands outwards, resembled an idol. The director, satisfied the anchor had good hold, made his way aft and sat down amongst us. We exchanged a few words lazily. Afterwards there was silence on board the yacht. For some reason or other we did not begin that game of dominoes. We felt meditative, and fit for nothing but placid

---

[1] A seaport on the Thames, east of London.

staring. The day was ending in a serenity of still and exquisite brilliance. The water shone pacifically; the sky, without a speck, was a benign immensity of unstained light; the very mist on the Essex marshes was like a gauzy and radiant fabric, hung from the wooded rises inland, and draping the low shores in diaphanous folds. Only the gloom to the west, brooding over the upper reaches, became more sombre every minute, as if angered by the approach of the sun.

And at last, in its curved and imperceptible fall, the sun sank low, and from glowing white changed to a dull red without rays and without heat, as if about to go out suddenly, stricken to death by the touch of that gloom brooding over a crowd of men.

Forthwith a change came over the waters, and the serenity became less brilliant but more profound. The old river in its broad reach rested unruffled at the decline of day, after ages of good service done to the race that peopled its banks, spread out in the tranquil dignity of a waterway leading to the uttermost ends of the earth. We looked at the venerable stream not in the vivid flush of a short day that comes and departs for ever, but in the august light of abiding memories. And indeed nothing is easier for a man who has, as the phrase goes, "followed the sea" with reverence and affection, than to evoke the great spirit of the past upon the lower reaches of the Thames. The tidal current runs to and fro in its unceasing service, crowded with memories of men and ships it had borne to the rest of home or to the battles of the sea. It had known and served all the men of whom the nation is proud, from Sir Francis Drake to Sir John Franklin, knights all, titled and untitled — the great knights-errant of the sea. It had borne all the ships whose names are like jewels flashing in the night of time, from the *Golden Hind* returning with her round flanks full of treasure, to be visited by the Queen's Highness and thus pass out of the gigantic tale, to the *Erebus* and *Terror*, bound on other conquests — and that never returned. It had known the ships and the men. They had sailed from Deptford, from Greenwich, from Erith — the adventurers and the settlers; kings' ships and the ships of men on 'Change; captains, admirals, the dark "interlopers" of the Eastern trade, and the commissioned "generals" of East India fleets. Hunters for gold or pursuers of fame, they all had gone out on that stream, bearing the sword, and often the torch, messengers of the might within the land, bearers of a spark from the sacred fire. What greatness had not floated on the ebb of that river into the mystery of an unknown earth! ... The dreams of men, the seed of commonwealths, the germs of empires.

The sun set; the dusk fell on the stream, and lights began to appear along the shore. The Chapman lighthouse, a three-legged thing erect on a mud-flat, shone strongly. Lights of ships moved in the fairway — a great stir of lights going up and going down. And farther west on the upper reaches the place of the monstrous town was still marked ominously on the sky, a brooding gloom in sunshine, a lurid glare under the stars.

"And this also," said Marlow suddenly, "has been one of the dark places of the earth."

He was the only man of us who still "followed the sea." The worst that could be said of him was that he did not represent his class. He was a seaman, but he was a wanderer, too, while most seamen lead, if one may so express it, a sedentary life. Their minds are of the stay-at-home order, and their home is always with them — the ship; and so is their country — the sea. One ship is very much like another, and the sea is always the same. In the immutability of their surroundings the foreign shores, the foreign faces, the changing immensity of life, glide past, veiled not by a sense of mystery but by a slightly disdainful ignorance; for there is nothing mysterious to a seaman unless it be the sea itself; which is the mistress of his existence and as inscrutable as Destiny. For the rest, after his hours of work, a casual stroll or a casual spree on shore suffices to unfold for him the secret of a whole continent, and generally he finds the secret not worth knowing. The yarns of seamen have a direct simplicity, the whole meaning of which lies within the shell of a cracked nut. But Marlow was not typical (if his propensity to spin yarns be excepted), and to him the meaning of an episode was not inside like a kernel but outside, enveloping the tale which brought it out only as a glow brings out a haze, in the likeness of one of these misty halos that sometimes are made visible by the spectral illumination of moonshine.

His remark did not seem at all surprising. It was just like Marlow. It was accepted in silence. No one took the trouble to grunt even; and presently he said, very slow —

"I was thinking of very old times, when the Romans first came here, nineteen hundred years ago — the other day. ... Light came out of this river since — you say Knights? Yes; but it is like a running blaze on a plain, like a flash of lightning in the clouds. We live in the flicker — may it last as long as the old earth keeps rolling! But darkness was here yesterday. Imagine the feelings of a commander of a fine — what d'ye call 'em? — trireme[2] in the Mediterranean, ordered suddenly to the north; run overland across the Gauls in a hurry; put in charge of one of these craft the legionaries — a wonderful lot of handy men they must have been, too — used to build, apparently by the hundred, in a month, or two, if we may believe what we read. Imagine him here — the very end of the world, a sea the colour of lead, a sky the colour of smoke, a kind of ship about as rigid as a concertina — and going up this river with stores, or orders, or what you like. Sandbanks, marshes, forests, savages, — precious little to eat fit for a civilized man, nothing but Thames water to drink. No Falernian wine[3] here, no going ashore. Here and there a military camp lost in a wilderness, like a needle in a bundle of hay — cold, fog, tempests, disease, exile, and death, — death skulking in the air, in the water, in the bush. They must have been dying like flies here. Oh, yes — he did it. Did it very well, too, no doubt, and without thinking much about it either, except afterwards to brag of what he had gone through in his time, perhaps. They were men enough to face the darkness. And perhaps he was cheered by keeping his eye on a chance of promotion to the fleet at Ravenna by-and-by, if he had good friends in Rome and survived the awful climate. Or think of a decent young citizen in a toga — perhaps too much dice, you know — coming out here in the train of some prefect, or tax-gatherer, or trader even, to mend his fortunes. Land in a swamp, march through the woods, and in some inland post feel the savagery, the utter savagery, had closed round him, — all that mysterious life of the wilderness that stirs in the forest, in the jungles, in the hearts of wild men. There's no initiation either into such mysteries. He has to live in the midst of the incomprehensible, which is also detestable. And it has a fascination, too, that goes to work upon him. The fascination of the abomination — you know, imagine the growing regrets, the longing to escape, the powerless disgust, the surrender, the hate."

He paused.

"Mind," he began again, lifting one arm from the elbow, the palm of the hand outwards, so that, with his legs folded before him, he had the pose of a Buddha preaching in European clothes and without a lotus-flower — "Mind, none of us would feel exactly like this. What saves us is efficiency — the devotion to efficiency. But these chaps were not much account, really. They were no colonists; their administration was merely a squeeze, and nothing more, I suspect. They were conquerors, and for that you want only brute force — nothing to boast of, when you have it, since your strength is just an accident arising from the weakness of others. They grabbed what they could get for the sake of what was to be got. It was just robbery with violence, aggravated murder on a great scale, and men going at it blind — as is very proper for those who tackle a darkness. The conquest of the earth, which mostly means the taking it away from those who have a different complexion or slightly flatter noses than ourselves, is not

---

[2] A Roman galley propelled by three tiers of oars.

[3] A wine much celebrated among the Romans.

a pretty thing when you look into it too much. What redeems it is the idea only. An idea at the back of it; not a sentimental pretence but an idea; and an unselfish belief in the idea — something you can set up, and bow down before, and offer a sacrifice to. ... "

He broke off. Flames glided in the river, small green flames, red flames, white flames, pursuing, overtaking, joining, crossing each other — then separating slowly or hastily. The traffic of the great city went on in the deepening night upon the sleepless river. We looked on, waiting patiently — there was nothing else to do till the end of the flood; but it was only after a long silence, when he said, in a hesitating voice, "I suppose you fellows remember I did once turn freshwater sailor for a bit," that we knew we were fated, before the ebb began to run, to hear about one of Marlow's inconclusive experiences.

"I don't want to bother you much with what happened to me personally," he began, showing in this remark the weakness of many tellers of tales who seem so often unaware of what their audience would best like to hear; "yet to understand the effect of it on me you ought to know how I got out there, what I saw, how I went up that river to the place where I first met the poor chap. It was the farthest point of navigation and the culminating point of my experience. It seemed somehow to throw a kind of light on everything about me — and into my thoughts. It was sombre enough, too — and pitiful — not extraordinary in any way — not very clear either. No, not very clear. And yet it seemed to throw a kind of light.

"I had then, as you remember, just returned to London after a lot of Indian Ocean, Pacific, China Seas — a regular dose of the East — six years or so, and I was loafing about, hindering you fellows in your work and invading your homes, just as though I had got a heavenly mission to civilize you. It was very fine for a time, but after a bit I did get tired of resting. Then I began to look for a ship — I should think the hardest work on earth. But the ships wouldn't even look at me. And I got tired of that game, too.

"Now when I was a little chap I had a passion for maps. I would look for hours at South America, or Africa, or Australia, and lose myself in all the glories of exploration. At that time there were many blank spaces on the earth, and when I saw one that looked particularly inviting on a map (but they all look that) I would put my finger on it and say, When I grow up I will go there. The North Pole was one of these places, I remember. Well, I haven't been there yet, and shall not try now. The glamour's off. Other places were scattered about the Equator, and in every sort of latitude all over the two hemispheres. I have been in some of them, and ... well, we won't talk about that. But there was one[4] yet — the biggest, the most blank, so to speak — that I had a hankering after.

"True, by this time it was not a blank space any more. It had got filled since my boyhood with rivers and lakes and names. It had ceased to be a blank space of delightful mystery — a white patch for a boy to dream gloriously over. It had become a place of darkness. But there was in it one river especially, a mighty big river, that you could see on the map, resembling an immense snake uncoiled, with its head in the sea, its body at rest curving afar over a vast country, and its tail lost in the depths of the land. And as I looked at the map of it in a shop-window, it fascinated me as a snake would a bird — a silly little bird. Then I remembered there was a big concern, a Company for trade on that river. Dash it all! I thought to myself, they can't trade without using some kind of craft on that lot of fresh water — steamboats! Why shouldn't I try to get charge of one? I went on along Fleet Street, but could not shake off the idea. The snake had charmed me.

"You understand it was a Continental concern, that Trading society; but I have a lot of relations living on the Continent, because it's cheap and not so nasty as it looks, they say.

---

[4] The Congo Free State, at the time the personal domain of the King of Belgium, centered on the Congo River basin. It is now Zaire.

"I am sorry to own I began to worry them. This was already a fresh departure for me. I was not used to get things that way, you know. I always went my own road and on my own legs where I had a mind to go. I wouldn't have believed it of myself; but, then — you see — I felt somehow I must get there by hook or by crook. So I worried them. The men said 'My dear fellow,' and did nothing. Then — would you believe it? — I tried the women. I, Charles Marlow, set the women to work — to get a job. Heavens! Well, you see, the notion drove me. I had an aunt, a dear enthusiastic soul. She wrote: 'It will be delightful. I am ready to do anything, anything for you. It is a glorious idea. I know the wife of a very high personage in the Administration, and also a man who has lots of influence with,' etc., etc. She was determined to make no end of fuss to get me appointed skipper of a river steamboat, if such was my fancy.

"I got my appointment — of course; and I got it very quick. It appears the Company had received news that one of their captains had been killed in a scuffle with the natives. This was my chance, and it made me the more anxious to go. It was only months and months afterwards, when I made the attempt to recover what was left of the body, that I heard the original quarrel arose from a misunderstanding about some hens. Yes, two black hens. Fresleven — that was the fellow's name, a Dane — thought himself wronged somehow in the bargain, so he went ashore and started to hammer the chief of the village with a stick. Oh, it didn't surprise me in the least to hear this, and at the same time to be told that Fresleven was the gentlest, quietest creature that ever walked on two legs. No doubt he was; but he had been a couple of years already out there engaged in the noble cause, you know, and he probably felt the need at last of asserting his self-respect in some way. Therefore he whacked the old nigger mercilessly, while a big crowd of his people watched him, thunderstruck, till some man — I was told the chief's son — in desperation at hearing the old chap yell, made a tentative jab with a spear at the white man — and of course it went quite easy between the shoulder blades. Then the whole population cleared into the forest, expecting all kinds of calamities to happen, while, on the other hand, the steamer Fresleven commanded left also in a bad panic, in charge of the engineer, I believe. Afterwards nobody seemed to trouble much about Fresleven's remains, till I got out and stepped into his shoes. I couldn't let it rest, though; but when an opportunity offered at last to meet my predecessor, the grass growing through his ribs was tall enough to hide his bones. They were all there. The supernatural being had not been touched after he fell. And the village was deserted, the huts gaped black, rotting, all askew within the fallen enclosures. A calamity had come to it, sure enough. The people had vanished. Mad terror had scattered them, men, women, and children, through the bush, and they had never returned. What became of the hens I don't know either. I should think the cause of progress got them, anyhow. However, through this glorious affair I got my appointment, before I had fairly begun to hope for it.

"I flew around like mad to get ready, and before forty-eight hours I was crossing the Channel to show myself to my employers, and sign the contract. In a very few hours I arrived in a city that always makes me think of a whited sepulchre.[5] Prejudice no doubt. I had no difficulty in finding the Company's offices. It was the biggest thing in the town, and everybody I met was full of it. They were going to run an over-sea empire, and make no end of coin by trade.

"A narrow and deserted street in deep shadow, high houses, innumerable windows with venetian blinds, a dead silence, grass sprouting between the stones, imposing carriage archways right and left, immense double doors standing ponderously ajar. I slipped through one of these cracks, went up a swept and ungarnished staircase, as arid as a desert, and opened

---

[5] Brussels.

the first door I came to. Two women, one fat and the other slim, sat on straw-bottomed chairs, knitting black wool. The slim one got up and walked straight at me — still knitting with down-cast eyes — and only just as I began to think of getting out of her way, as you would for a somnambulist, stood still, and looked up. Her dress was as plain as an umbrella-cover, and she turned round without a word and preceded me into a waiting-room. I gave my name, and looked about. Deal table in the middle, plain chairs all round the walls, on one end a large shining map, marked with all the colours of a rainbow.[6] There was a vast amount of red — good to see at any time, because one knows that some real work is done in there, a deuce of a lot of blue, a little green, smears of orange, and, on the East Coast, a purple patch, to show where the jolly pioneers of progress drink the jolly lager-beer. However, I wasn't going into any of these. I was going into the yellow. Dead in the centre. And the river was there — fascinating — deadly — like a snake. Ough! A door opened, a white-haired secretarial head, but wearing a compassionate expression, appeared, and a skinny forefinger beckoned me into the sanctuary. Its light was dim, and a heavy writing-desk squatted in the middle. From behind that structure came out an impression of pale plumpness in a frock-coat. The great man himself. He was five feet six, I should judge, and had his grip on the handle-end of ever so many millions. He shook hands, I fancy, murmured vaguely, was satisfied with my French. *Bon voyage.*[7]

"In about forty-five seconds I found myself again in the waiting-room with the compassionate secretary, who, full of desolation and sympathy, made me sign some document. I believe I undertook amongst other things not to disclose any trade secrets. Well, I am not going to.

"I began to feel slightly uneasy. You know I am not used to such ceremonies, and there was something ominous in the atmosphere. It was just as though I had been let into some conspiracy — I don't know — something not quite right; and I was glad to get out. In the outer room the two women knitted black wool feverishly. People were arriving, and the younger one was walking back and forth introducing them. The old one sat on her chair. Her flat cloth slippers were propped up on a foot-warmer, and a cat reposed on her lap. She wore a starched white affair on her head, had a wart on one cheek, and silver-rimmed spectacles hung on the tip of her nose. She glanced at me above the glasses. The swift and indifferent placidity of that look troubled me. Two youths with foolish and cheery countenances were being piloted over, and she threw at them the same quick glance of unconcerned wisdom. She seemed to know all about them and about me, too. An eerie feeling came over me. She seemed uncanny and fateful. Often far away there I thought of these two, guarding the door of Darkness, knitting black wool as for a warm pall, one introducing, introducing continuously to the unknown, the other scrutinizing the cheery and foolish faces with unconcerned old eyes. *Ave!* Old knitter of black wool. *Morituri te salutant.*[8] Not many of those she looked at ever saw her again — not half, by a long way.

"There was yet a visit to the doctor. 'A simple formality,' assured me the secretary, with an air of taking an immense part in all my sorrows. Accordingly a young chap wearing his hat over the left eyebrow, some clerk I suppose, — there must have been clerks in the business, though the house was as still as a house in a city of the dead — came from somewhere up-

---

[6] The map's colors represent the powers controlling each area: red for the British, blue for the French, green for the Italians, orange for the Portuguese, purple for the Germans, and yellow for the Belgians.

[7] "Have a good trip."

[8] The Roman gladiators were supposed to have greeted Caesar with "Hail! Those who are about to die salute you."

stairs, and led me forth. He was shabby and careless, with ink-stains on the sleeves of his jacket, and his cravat was large and billowy, under a chin shaped like the toe of an old boot. It was a little too early for the doctor, so I proposed a drink, and thereupon he developed a vein of joviality. As we sat over our vermuths he glorified the Company's business, and by-and-by I expressed casually my surprise at him not going out there. He became very cool and collected all at once. 'I am not such a fool as I look, quoth Plato to his disciples,' he said sententiously, emptied his glass with great resolution, and we rose.

"The old doctor felt my pulse, evidently thinking of something else the while. 'Good, good for there,' he mumbled, and then with a certain eagerness asked me whether I would let him measure my head. Rather surprised, I said Yes, when he produced a thing like calipers and got the dimensions back and front and every way, taking notes carefully. He was an unshaven little man in a threadbare coat like a gaberdine, with his feet in slippers, and I thought him a harmless fool. 'I always ask leave, in the interests of science, to measure the crania of those going out there,' he said. 'And when they come back, too?' I asked. 'Oh, I never see them,' he remarked; 'and, moreover, the changes take place inside, you know.' He smiled, as if at some quiet joke. 'So you are going out there. Famous. Interesting, too.' He gave me a searching glance, and made another note. 'Ever any madness in your family?' he asked, in a matter-of-fact tone. I felt very annoyed. 'Is that question in the interests of science, too?' 'It would be,' he said, without taking notice of my irritation, 'interesting for science to watch the mental changes of individuals, on the spot, but ...' 'Are you an alienist?'[9] I interrupted. 'Every doctor should be — a little,' answered that original, imperturbably. 'I have a little theory which you Messieurs who go out there must help me to prove. This is my share in the advantages my country shall reap from the possession of such a magnificent dependency. The mere wealth I leave to others. Pardon my questions, but you are the first Englishman coming under my observation ...' I hastened to assure him I was not in the least typical. 'If I were,' said I, 'I wouldn't be talking like this with you.' 'What you say is rather profound, and probably erroneous,' he said, with a laugh. 'Avoid irritation more than exposure to the sun. Adieu. How do you English say, eh? Good-bye. Ah! Good-bye. Adieu. In the tropics one must before everything keep calm.' ... He lifted a warning forefinger. ... 'Du calme, du calme. Adieu.'[10]

"One thing more remained to do — say good-bye to my excellent aunt. I found her triumphant. I had a cup of tea — the last decent cup of tea for many days — and in a room that most soothingly looked just as you would expect a lady's drawing-room to look, we had a long quiet chat by the fireside. In the course of these confidences it became quite plain to me I had been represented to the wife of the high dignitary, and goodness knows to how many more people besides, as an exceptional and gifted creature — a piece of good fortune for the Company — a man you don't get hold of every day . Good heavens; and I was going to take charge of a two-penny-half-penny river-steamboat with a penny whistle attached! It appeared, however, I was also one of the Workers, with a capital — you know. Something like an emissary of light, something like a lower sort of apostle. There had been a lot of such rot let loose in print and talk just about that time, and the excellent woman, living right in the rush of all that humbug, got carried off her feet. She talked about 'weaning those ignorant millions from their horrid ways,' till, upon my word, she made me quite uncomfortable. I ventured to hint that the Company was run for profit.

"'You forget, dear Charlie, that the labourer is worthy of his hire,' she said, brightly. It's queer how out of touch with truth women are. They live in a world of their own, and there had

---

[9] A physician who treats mental disorders.

[10] "Keep calm, keep calm. Good-bye."

never been anything like it, and never can be. It is too beautiful altogether, and if they were to set it up it would go to pieces before the first sunset. Some confounded fact we men have been living contentedly with ever since the day of creation would start up and knock the whole thing over.

"After this I got embraced, told to wear flannel, be sure to write often, and so on — and I left. In the street — I don't know why — a queer feeling came to me that I was an impostor. Odd thing that I, who used to clear out for any part of the world at twenty-four hours' notice, with less thought than most men give to the crossing of a street, had a moment — I won't say of hesitation, but of startled pause, before this commonplace affair. The best way I can explain it to you is by saying that, for a second or two, I felt as though, instead of going to the centre of a continent, I were about to set off for the centre of the earth.

"I left in a French steamer, and she called in every blamed port they have out there, for, as far as I could see, the sole purpose of landing soldiers and custom-house officers. I watched the coast. Watching a coast as it slips by the ship is like thinking about an enigma. There it is before you — smiling, frowning, inviting, grand, mean, insipid, or savage, and always mute with an air of whispering, Come and find out. This one was almost featureless, as if still in the making, with an aspect of monotonous grimness. The edge of a colossal jungle, so dark-green as to be almost black, fringed with white surf, ran straight, like a ruled line, far, far away along a blue sea whose glitter was blurred by a creeping mist. The sun was fierce, the land seemed to glisten and drip with steam. Here and there grayish-whitish specks showed up clustered inside the white surf, with a flag flying above them perhaps. Settlements some centuries old, and still no bigger than pin-heads on the untouched expanse of their background. We pounded along, stopped, landed soldiers; went on, landed custom-house clerks to levy toll in what looked like a God-forsaken wilderness, with a tin shed and a flag-pole lost in it; landed more soldiers — to take care of the custom-house clerks, presumably. Some, I heard, got drowned in the surf; but whether they did or not, nobody seemed particularly to care. They were just flung out there, and on we went. Every day the coast looked the same, as though we had not moved; but we passed various places — trading places — with names like Gran' Bassam, Little Popo; names that seemed to belong to some sordid farce acted in front of a sinister back-cloth. The idleness of a passenger, my isolation amongst all these men with whom I had no point of contact, the oily and languid sea, the uniform sombreness of the coast, seemed to keep me away from the truth of things, within the toil of a mournful and senseless delusion. The voice of the surf heard now and then was a positive pleasure, like the speech of a brother. It was something natural, that had its reason, that had a meaning. Now and then a boat from the shore gave one a momentary contact with reality. It was paddled by black fellows. You could see from afar the white of their eyeballs glistening. They shouted, sang; their bodies streamed with perspiration; they had faces like grotesque masks — these chaps; but they had bone, muscle, a wild vitality, an intense energy of movement, that was as natural and true as the surf along their coast. They wanted no excuse for being there. They were a great comfort to look at. For a time I would feel I belonged still to a world of straight-forward facts; but the feeling would not last long. Something would turn up to scare it away. Once, I remember, we came upon a man-of-war anchored off the coast. There wasn't even a shed there, and she was shelling the bush. It appears the French had one of their wars going on thereabouts. Her ensign dropped limp like a rag; the muzzles of the long six-inch guns stuck out all over the low hull; the greasy, slimy swell swung her up lazily and let her down, swaying her thin masts. In the empty immensity of earth, sky, and water, there she was, incomprehensible, firing into a continent. Pop, would go one of the six-inch guns; a small flame would dart and vanish, a little white smoke would disappear, a tiny projectile would give a feeble screech — and nothing happened. Nothing could happen. There was a touch of insanity in the proceeding, a sense of lugubrious drollery in the sight; and it was not dissipated by somebody on board assuring me earnestly there was a camp of natives — he called them enemies! — hidden out of sight somewhere.

"We gave her her letters (I heard the men in that lonely ship were dying of fever at the rate of three a-day) and went on. We called at some more places with farcical names, where the merry dance of death and trade goes on in a still and earthy atmosphere as of an overheated catacomb; all along the formless coast bordered by dangerous surf, as if Nature herself had tried to ward off intruders; in and out of rivers, streams of death in life, whose banks were rotting into mud, whose waters, thickened into slime, invaded the contorted mangroves, that seemed to writhe at us in the extremity of an impotent despair. Nowhere did we stop long enough to get a particularized impression, but the general sense of vague and oppressive wonder grew upon me. It was like a weary pilgrimage amongst hints for nightmares.

"It was upward of thirty days before I saw the mouth of the big river.[11] We anchored off the seat of the government. But my work would not begin till some two hundred miles farther on. So as soon as I could I made a start for a place thirty miles higher up.

"I had my passage on a little sea-going steamer. Her captain was a Swede, and knowing me for a seaman, invited me on the bridge. He was a young man, lean, fair, and morose, with lanky hair and a shuffling gait. As we left the miserable little wharf, he tossed his head contemptuously at the shore. 'Been living there?' he asked. I said, 'Yes.' 'Fine lot these government chaps — are they not?' he went on, speaking English with great precision and considerable bitterness. 'It is funny what some people will do for a few francs a-month. I wonder what becomes of that kind when it goes up country?' I said to him I expected to see that soon. 'So-o-o!' he exclaimed. He shuffled athwart, keeping one eye ahead vigilantly. 'Don't be too sure,' he continued. 'The other day I took up a man who hanged himself on the road. He was a Swede, too.' 'Hanged himself! Why, in God's name?' I cried. He kept on looking out watchfully. 'Who knows? The sun too much for him, or the country perhaps.'

"At last we opened a reach. A rocky cliff appeared, mounds of turned-up earth by the shore, houses on a hill, others with iron roofs, amongst a waste of excavations, or hanging to the declivity. A continuous noise of the rapids above hovered over this scene of inhabited devastation. A lot of people, mostly black and naked, moved about like ants. A jetty projected into the river. A blinding sunlight drowned all this at times in a sudden recrudescence of glare. 'There's your Company's station,' said the Swede, pointing to three wooden barrack-like structures on the rocky slope. 'I will send your things up. Four boxes did you say? So. Farewell.'

"I came upon a boiler wallowing in the grass, then found a path leading up the hill. It turned aside for the boulders, and also for an undersized railway-truck lying there on its back with its wheels in the air. One was off. The thing looked as dead as the carcass of some animal. I came upon more pieces of decaying machinery, a stack of rusty rails. To the left a clump of trees made a shady spot, where dark things seemed to stir feebly. I blinked, the path was steep. A horn tooted to the right, and I saw the black people run. A heavy and dull detonation shook the ground, a puff of smoke came out of the cliff, and that was all. No change appeared on the face of the rock. They were building a railway. The cliff was not in the way or anything; but this objectless blasting was all the work going on.

"A slight clinking behind me made me turn my head. Six black men advanced in a file, toiling up the path. They walked erect and slow, balancing small baskets full of earth on their

---

[11] The Congo River.

heads, and the clink kept time with their footsteps. Black rags were wound round their loins, and the short ends behind waggled to and fro like tails. I could see every rib, the joints of their limbs were like knots in a rope; each had an iron collar on his neck, and all were connected together with a chain whose bights swung between them, rhythmically clinking. Another report from the cliff made me think suddenly of that ship of war I had seen firing into a continent. It was the same kind of ominous voice; but these men could by no stretch of imagination be called enemies. They were called criminals, and the outraged law, like the bursting shells, had come to them, an insoluble mystery from the sea. All their meagre breasts panted together, the violently dilated nostrils quivered, the eyes stared stonily up-hill. They passed me within six inches, without a glance, with that complete, deathlike indifference of unhappy savages. Behind this raw matter one of the reclaimed, the product of the new forces at work, strolled despondently, carrying a rifle by its middle. He had a uniform jacket with one button off, and seeing a white man on the path, hoisted his weapon to his shoulder with alacrity. This was simple prudence, white men being so much alike at a distance that he could not tell who I might be. He was speedily reassured, and with a large, white, rascally grin, and a glance at his charge, seemed to take me into partnership in his exalted trust. After all, I also was a part of the great cause of these high and just proceedings.

"Instead of going up, I turned and descended to the left. My idea was to let that chain-gang get out of sight before I climbed the hill. You know I am not particularly tender; I've had to strike and to fend off. I've had to resist and to attack sometimes — that's only one way of resisting — without counting the exact cost, according to the demands of such sort of life as I had blundered into. I've seen the devil of violence, and the devil of greed, and the devil of hot desire; but, by all the stars! these were strong, lusty, red-eyed devils, that swayed and drove men — men, I tell you. But as I stood on this hillside, I foresaw that in the blinding sunshine of that land I would become acquainted with a flabby, pretending, weak-eyed devil of a rapacious and pitiless folly. How insidious he could be, too, I was only to find out several months later and a thousand miles farther. For a moment I stood appalled, as though by a warning. Finally I descended the hill, obliquely, towards the trees I had seen.

"I avoided a vast artificial hole somebody had been digging on the slope, the purpose of which I found it impossible to divine. It wasn't a quarry or a sandpit, anyhow. It was just a hole. It might have been connected with the philanthropic desire of giving the criminals something to do. I don't know. Then I nearly fell into a very narrow ravine, almost no more than a scar in the hillside. I discovered that a lot of imported drainage-pipes for the settlement had been tumbled in there. There wasn't one that was not broken. It was a wanton smash-up. At last I got under the trees. My purpose was to stroll into the shade for a moment; but no sooner within than it seemed to me I had stepped into the gloomy circle of some Inferno. The rapids were near, and an uninterrupted, uniform, headlong, rushing noise filled the mournful stillness of the grove, where not a breath stirred, not a leaf moved, with a mysterious sound — as though the tearing pace of the launched earth had suddenly become audible.

"Black shapes crouched, lay, sat between the trees leaning against the trunks, clinging to the earth, half coming out, half effaced within the dim light, in all the attitudes of pain, abandonment, and despair. Another mine on the cliff went off, followed by a slight shudder of the soil under my feet. The work was going on. The work! And this was the place where some of the helpers had withdrawn to die.

"They were dying slowly — it was very clear. They were not enemies, they were not criminals, they were nothing earthly now, — nothing but black shadows of disease and starvation, lying confusedly in the greenish gloom. Brought from all the recesses of the coast in all the legality of time contracts, lost in uncongenial surroundings, fed on unfamiliar food, they sickened, became inefficient, and were then allowed to crawl away and rest. These moribund shapes were free as air — and nearly as thin. I began to distinguish the gleam of the eyes under the trees. Then, glancing down, I saw a face near my hand. The black bones reclined at full length with one shoulder against the tree, and slowly the eyelids rose and the sunken eyes looked up at me, enormous and vacant, a kind of blind, white flicker in the depths of the orbs, which died out slowly. The man seemed young — almost a boy — but you know with them it's hard to tell. I found nothing else to do but to offer him one of my good Swede's ship's biscuits I had in my pocket. The fingers closed slowly on it and held — there was no other movement and no other glance. He had tied a bit of white worsted round his neck — Why? Where did he get it? Was it a badge — an ornament — a charm — a propitiatory act? Was there any idea at all connected with it? It looked startling round his black neck, this bit of white thread from beyond the seas.

"Near the same tree two more bundles of acute angles sat with their legs drawn up. One, with his chin propped on his knees, stared at nothing, in an intolerable and appalling manner: his brother phantom rested its forehead, as if overcome with a great weariness; and all about others were scattered in every pose of contorted collapse, as in some picture of a massacre or a pestilence. While I stood horror-struck, one of these creatures rose to his hands and knees, and went off on all-fours towards the river to drink. He lapped out of his hand, then sat up in the sunlight, crossing his shins in front of him, and after a time let his woolly head fall on his breastbone.

"I didn't want any more loitering in the shade, and I made haste towards the station. When near the buildings I met a white man, in such an unexpected elegance of get-up that in the first moment I took him for a sort of vision. I saw a high starched collar, white cuffs, a light alpaca jacket, snowy trousers, a clear necktie, and varnished boots. No hat. Hair parted, brushed, oiled, under a green-lined parasol held in a big white hand. He was amazing, and had a pen-holder behind his ear.

"I shook hands with this miracle, and I learned he was the Company's chief accountant, and that all the book-keeping was done at this station. He had come out for a moment, he said, 'to get a breath of fresh air.' The expression sounded wonderfully odd, with its suggestion of sedentary desk-life. I wouldn't have mentioned the fellow to you at all, only it was from his lips that I first heard the name of the man who is so indissolubly connected with the memories of that time. Moreover, I respected the fellow. Yes; I respected his collars, his vast cuffs, his brushed hair. His appearance was certainly that of a hairdresser's dummy; but in the great demoralization of the land he kept up his appearance. That's backbone. His starched collars and got-up shirt-fronts were achievements of character. He had been out nearly three years; and, later, I could not help asking him how he managed to sport such linen. He had just the faintest blush, and said modestly, 'I've been teaching one of the native women about the station. It was difficult. She had a distaste for the work.' Thus this man had verily accomplished something. And he was devoted to his books, which were in apple-pie order.

"Everything else in the station was in a muddle, — heads, things, buildings. Strings of dusty niggers with splay feet arrived and departed; a stream of manufactured goods, rubbishy cottons, beads, and brass-wire sent into the depths of darkness, and in return came a precious trickle of ivory.

"I had to wait in the station for ten days — an eternity. I lived in a hut in the yard, but to be out of the chaos I would sometimes get into the accountant's office. It was built of horizontal planks, and so badly put together that, as he bent over his high desk, he was barred from neck to heels with narrow strips of sunlight. There was no need to open the big shutter to see. It was hot there, too; big flies buzzed fiendishly, and did not sting, but stabbed. I sat generally on the floor, while, of faultless appearance (and even slightly scented), perching on a high stool, he wrote, he wrote. Sometimes he stood up for exercise. When a truckle-bed with a sick man (some invalid agent from upcountry) was put in there, he exhibited a gentle annoyance. 'The groans of this sick person,' he said, 'distract my attention. And without that it is extremely difficult to guard against clerical errors in this climate.'

"One day he remarked, without lifting his head, 'In the interior you will no doubt meet Mr. Kurtz.' On my asking who Mr. Kurtz was, he said he was a first-class agent; and seeing my disappointment at this information, he added slowly, laying down his pen, 'He is a very remarkable person.' Further questions elicited from him that Mr. Kurtz was at present in charge of a trading post, a very important one, in the true ivory-country, at 'the very bottom of there. Sends in as much ivory as all the others put together ...' He began to write again. The sick man was too ill to groan. The flies buzzed in a great peace.

"Suddenly there was a growing murmur of voices and a great tramping of feet. A caravan had come in. A violent babble of uncouth sounds burst out on the other side of the planks. All the carriers were speaking together, and in the midst of the uproar the lamentable voice of the chief agent was heard 'giving it up' tearfully for the twentieth time that day. ... He rose slowly. 'What a frightful row,' he said. He crossed the room gently to look at the sick man, and returning, said to me, 'He does not hear.' 'What! Dead?' I asked, startled. 'No, not yet,' he answered, with great composure. Then, alluding with a toss of the head to the tumult in the station-yard, 'When one has got to make correct entries, one comes to hate those savages — hate them to the death.' He remained thoughtful for a moment. 'When you see Mr. Kurtz,' he went on, 'tell him from me that everything here' — he glanced at the desk — 'is very satisfactory. I don't like to write to him — with those messengers of ours you never know who may get hold of your letter — at that Central Station.' He stared at me for a moment with his mild, bulging eyes. 'Oh, he will go far, very far,' he began again. 'He will be a somebody in the Administration before long. They, above — the Council in Europe, you know — mean him to be.'

"He turned to his work. The noise outside had ceased, and presently in going out I stopped at the door. In the steady buzz of flies the homeward-bound agent was lying flushed and insensible; the other, bent over his books, was making correct entries of perfectly correct transactions; and fifty feet below the door-step I could see the still tree-tops of the grove of death.

"Next day I left that station at last, with a caravan of sixty men, for a two-hundred-mile tramp.

"No use telling you much about that. Paths, paths, everywhere; a stamped-in network of paths spreading over the empty land, through long grass, through burnt grass, through thickets, down and up chilly ravines, up and down stony hills ablaze with heat; and a solitude, a solitude, nobody, not a hut. The population had cleared out a long time ago. Well, if a lot of mysterious niggers armed with all kinds of fearful weapons suddenly took to travelling on the road between Deal and Gravesend, catching the yokels right and left to carry heavy loads for them, I fancy every farm and cottage thereabouts would get empty very soon. Only here the dwellings were gone, too. Still I passed through several abandoned villages. There's something pathetically childish in the ruins of grass walls. Day after day, with the stamp and shuffle of sixty pair of bare feet behind me, each pair under a 60-lb. load. Camp, cook, sleep, strike camp, march. Now and then a carrier dead in harness, at rest in the long grass near the path, with an empty water-gourd and his long staff lying by his side. A great silence around and above. Perhaps on some quiet night the tremor of far-off drums, sinking, swelling, a tremor vast, faint; a sound weird, appealing, suggestive, and wild — and perhaps with as profound a meaning as the sound of bells in a Christian country. Once a white man in an unbuttoned uniform, camping on the path with an armed escort of lank Zanzibaris,[12] very hospitable and festive — not to say drunk. Was looking after the upkeep of the road he declared. Can't say I saw any road or any upkeep, unless the body of a middle-aged negro, with a bullet-hole in the forehead, upon which I absolutely stumbled three miles farther on, may be considered as a permanent improvement. I had a white companion, too, not a bad chap, but rather too fleshy and with the exasperating habit of fainting on the hot hillsides, miles away from the least bit of shade and water. Annoying, you know, to hold your own coat like a parasol over a man's head while he is coming-to. I couldn't help asking him once what he meant by coming there at all. 'To make money, of course. What do you think?' he said, scornfully. Then he got fever, and had to be carried in a hammock slung under a pole. As he weighed sixteen stones[13] I had no end of rows with the carriers. They jibbed, ran away, sneaked off with their loads in the night — quite a mutiny. So, one evening, I made a speech in English with gestures, not one of which was lost to the sixty pairs of eyes before me, and the next morning I started the hammock off in front all right. An hour afterwards I came upon the whole concern wrecked in a bush — man, hammock, groans, blankets, horrors. The heavy pole had skinned his poor nose. He was very anxious for me to kill somebody, but there wasn't the shadow of a carrier near. I remember the old doctor, — 'It would be interesting for science to watch the mental changes of individuals, on the spot.' I felt I was becoming scientifically interesting. However, all that is to no purpose. On the fifteenth day I came in sight of the big river again, and hobbled into the Central Station. It was on a back water surrounded by scrub and forest, with a pretty border of smelly mud on one side, and on the three others enclosed by a crazy fence of rushes. A neglected gap was all the gate it had, and the first glance at the place was enough to let you see the flabby devil was running that show. White men with long staves in their hands appeared languidly from amongst the buildings, strolling up to take a look at me, and then retired out of sight somewhere. One of them, a stout, excitable chap with black moustaches, informed me with great volubility and many digressions, as soon as I told him who I was, that my steamer was at the bottom of the river. I was thunderstruck. What, how, why? Oh, it was 'all right.' The 'manager himself' was there. All quite correct. 'Everybody had behaved splendidly! splendidly!' — 'you must,' he said in agitation, 'go and see the general manager at once. He is waiting!'

"I did not see the real significance of that wreck at once. I fancy I see it now, but I am not sure — not at all. Certainly the affair was too stupid — when I think of it — to be altogether natural. Still … But at the moment it presented itself simply as a confounded nuisance. The steamer was sunk. They had started two days before in a sudden hurry up the river with the manager on board, in charge of some volunteer skipper, and before they had been out three hours they tore the bottom out of her on stones, and she sank near the south bank. I asked myself what I was to do there, now my boat was lost. As a matter of fact, I had plenty to do in fishing my command out of the river. I had to set about it the very next day. That, and the repairs when I brought the pieces to the station, took some months.

"My first interview with the manager was curious. He did not ask me to sit down after my twenty-mile walk that morning. He was commonplace in complexion, in feature, in manners, and in voice. He was of middle size and of ordinary build. His eyes, of the usual blue, were perhaps remarkably cold, and he certainly could make his glance fall on one as trenchant and heavy as an axe. But even at these times the rest of his person seemed to disclaim

---

[12] Mercenaries from the island of Zanzibar.

[13] A stone is a British unit of weight equivalent to 14 pounds. The man weighed 224 pounds.

the intention. Otherwise there was only an indefinable, faint expression of his lips, something stealthy — a smile — not a smile — I remember it, but I can't explain. It was unconscious, this smile was, though just after he had said something it got intensified for an instant. It came at the end of his speeches like a seal applied on the words to make the meaning of the commonest phrase appear absolutely inscrutable. He was a common trader, from his youth up employed in these parts — nothing more. He was obeyed, yet he inspired neither love nor fear, nor even respect. He inspired uneasiness. That was it! Uneasiness. Not a definite mistrust — just uneasiness — nothing more. You have no idea how effective such a ... a ... faculty can be. He had no genius for organizing, for initiative, or for order even. That was evident in such things as the deplorable state of the station. He had no learning, and no intelligence. His position had come to him — why? Perhaps because he was never ill ... He had served three terms of three years out there ... Because triumphant health in the general rout of constitutions is a kind of power in itself. When he went home on leave he rioted on a large scale — pompously. Jack ashore[14] — with a difference — in externals only. This one could gather from his casual talk. He originated nothing, he could keep the routine going — that's all. But he was great. He was great by this little thing that it was impossible to tell what could control such a man. He never gave that secret away. Perhaps there was nothing within him. Such a suspicion made one pause — for out there there were no external checks. Once when various tropical diseases had laid low almost every 'agent' in the station, he was heard to say, 'Men who come out here should have no entrails.' He sealed the utterance with that smile of his, as though it had been a door opening into a darkness he had in his keeping. You fancied you had seen things — but the seal was on. When annoyed at meal-times by the constant quarrels of the white men about precedence, he ordered an immense round table to be made, for which a special house had to be built. This was the station's messroom. Where he sat was the first place — the rest were nowhere. One felt this to be his unalterable conviction. He was neither civil nor uncivil. He was quiet. He allowed his 'boy' — an overfed young negro from the coast — to treat the white men, under his very eyes, with provoking insolence.

"He began to speak as soon as he saw me. I had been very long on the road. He could not wait. Had to start without me. The up-river stations had to be relieved. There had been so many delays already that he did not know who was dead and who was alive, and how they got on — and so on, and so on. He paid no attention to my explanations, and, playing with a stick of sealing-wax, repeated several times that the situation was 'very grave, very grave.' There were rumours that a very important station was in jeopardy, and its chief, Mr. Kurtz, was ill. Hoped it was not true. Mr. Kurtz was ... I felt weary and irritable. Hang Kurtz, I thought. I interrupted him by saying I had heard of Mr. Kurtz on the coast. 'Ah! So they talk of him down there,' he murmured to himself. Then he began again, assuring me Mr. Kurtz was the best agent he had, an exceptional man, of the greatest importance to the Company; therefore I could understand his anxiety. He was, he said, 'very, very uneasy.' Certainly he fidgeted on his chair a good deal, exclaimed, 'Ah, Mr. Kurtz!' broke the stick of sealing-wax and seemed dumfounded by the accident. Next thing he wanted to know 'how long it would take to' ... I interrupted him again. Being hungry, you know, and kept on my feet, too, I was getting savage. 'How could I tell?' I said. 'I hadn't even seen the wreck yet — some months, no doubt.' All this talk seemed to me so futile. 'Some months,' he said. 'Well, let us say three months before we can make a start. Yes. That ought to do the affair.' I flung out of his hut (he lived all alone in a clay hut with a sort of verandah) muttering to myself my opinion of him. He was a chattering

---

[14] A sailor on shore leave.

idiot. Afterwards I took it back when it was borne in upon me startlingly with what extreme nicety he had estimated the time requisite for the 'affair.'

"I went to work the next day, turning, so to speak, my back on that station. In that way only it seemed to me I could keep my hold on the redeeming facts of life. Still, one must look about sometimes; and then I saw this station, these men strolling aimlessly about in the sunshine of the yard. I asked myself sometimes what it all meant. They wandered here and there with their absurd long staves in their hands, like a lot of faithless pilgrims bewitched inside a rotten fence. The word 'ivory' rang in the air, was whispered, was sighed. You would think they were praying to it. A taint of imbecile rapacity blew through it all, like a whiff from some corpse. By Jove! I've never seen anything so unreal in my life. And outside, the silent wilderness surrounding this clear speck on the earth struck me as something great and invincible, like evil or truth, waiting patiently for the passing away of this fantastic invasion.

"Oh, these months! Well, never mind. Various things happened. One evening a grass shed full of calico, cotton prints, beads, and I don't know what else, burst into a blaze so suddenly that you would have thought the earth had opened to let an avenging fire consume all that trash. I was smoking my pipe quietly by my dismantled steamer, and saw them all cutting capers in the light, with their arms lifted high, when the stout man with moustaches came tearing down to the river, a tin pail in his hand, assured me that everybody was 'behaving splendidly, splendidly,' dipped about a quart of water and tore back again. I noticed there was a hole in the bottom of his pail.

"I strolled up. There was no hurry. You see the thing had gone off like a box of matches. It had been hopeless from the very first. The flame had leaped high, driven everybody back, lighted up everything — and collapsed. The shed was already a heap of embers glowing fiercely. A nigger was being beaten near by. They said he had caused the fire in some way; be that as it may, he was screeching most horribly. I saw him, later, for several days, sitting in a bit of shade looking very sick and trying to recover himself: afterwards he arose and went out — and the wilderness without a sound took him into its bosom again. As I approached the glow from the dark I found myself at the back of two men, talking. I heard the name of Kurtz pronounced, then the words, 'take advantage of this unfortunate accident.' One of the men was the manager. I wished him a good evening. 'Did you ever see anything like it — eh? it is incredible,' he said, and walked off. The other man remained. He was a first-class agent, young, gentlemanly, a bit reserved, with a forked little beard and a hooked nose. He was stand-offish with the other agents, and they on their side said he was the manager's spy upon them. As to me, I had hardly ever spoken to him before. We got into talk, and by-and-by we strolled away from the hissing ruins. Then he asked me to his room, which was in the main building of the station. He struck a match, and I perceived that this young aristocrat had not only a silver-mounted dressing-case but also a whole candle all to himself. Just at that time the manager was the only man supposed to have any right to candles. Native mats covered the clay walls; a collection of spears, assegais,[15] shields, knives was hung up in trophies. The business intrusted to this fellow was the making of bricks — so I had been informed; but there wasn't a fragment of a brick anywhere in the station, and he had been there more than a year — waiting. It seems he could not make bricks without something, I don't know what — straw maybe. Anyways, it could not be found there, and as it was not likely to be sent from Europe, it did not appear clear to me what he was waiting for. An act of special creation perhaps. However, they were all waiting — all the sixteen or twenty pilgrims of them — for something; and upon my word it did not seem an uncongenial occupation, from the way they took it,

---

[15] Slender javelins.

though the only thing that ever came to them was disease — as far as I could see. They beguiled the time by backbiting and intriguing against each other in a foolish kind of way. There was an air of plotting about that station, but nothing came of it, of course. It was as unreal as everything else — as the philanthropic pretence of the whole concern, as their talk, as their government, as their show of work. The only real feeling was a desire to get appointed to a trading-post where ivory was to be had, so that they could earn percentages. They intrigued and slandered and hated each other only on that account, — but as to effectually lifting a little finger — oh, no. By heavens! there is something after all in the world allowing one man to steal a horse while another must not look at a halter. Steal a horse straight out. Very well. He has done it. Perhaps he can ride. But there is a way of looking at a halter that would provoke the most charitable of saints into a kick.

"I had no idea why he wanted to be sociable, but as we chatted in there it suddenly occurred to me the fellow was trying to get at something — in fact, pumping me. He alluded constantly to Europe, to the people I was supposed to know there — putting leading questions as to my acquaintances in the sepulchral city, and so on. His little eyes glittered like mica discs — with curiosity — though he tried to keep up a bit of superciliousness. At first I was astonished, but very soon I became awfully curious to see what he would find out from me. I couldn't possibly imagine what I had in me to make it worth his while. It was very pretty to see how he baffled himself, for in truth my body was full only of chills, and my head had nothing in it but that wretched steamboat business. It was evident he took me for a perfectly shameless prevaricator. At last he got angry, and, to conceal a movement of furious annoyance, he yawned. I rose. Then I noticed a small sketch in oils, on a panel, representing a woman, draped and blindfolded, carrying a lighted torch. The background was sombre — almost black. The movement of the woman was stately, and the effect of the torch-light on the face was sinister.

"It arrested me, and he stood by civilly, holding an empty half-pint champagne bottle (medical comforts) with the candle stuck in it. To my question he said Mr. Kurtz had painted this — in this very station more than a year ago — while waiting for means to go to his trading-post. 'Tell me, pray,' said I, 'who is this Mr. Kurtz?'

"'The chief of the Inner Station,' he answered in a short tone, looking away. 'Much obliged,' I said, laughing. 'And you are the brickmaker of the Central Station. Everyone knows that.' He was silent for a while. 'He is a prodigy,' he said at last. 'He is an emissary of pity, and science, and progress, and devil knows what else. We want,' he began to declaim suddenly, 'for the guidance of the cause intrusted to us by Europe, so to speak, higher intelligence, wide sympathies, a singleness of purpose.' 'Who says that?' I asked. 'Lots of them,' he replied. 'Some even write that; and so *he* comes here, a special being, as you ought to know.' 'Why ought I to know?' I interrupted, really surprised. He paid no attention. 'Yes. To-day he is chief of the best station, next year he will be assistant-manager, two years more and ... but I daresay you know what he will be in two years' time. You are of the new gang — the gang of virtue. The same people who sent him specially also recommended you. Oh, don't say no. I've my own eyes to trust.' Light dawned upon me. My dear aunt's influential acquaintances were producing an unexpected effect upon that young man. I nearly burst into a laugh. 'Do you read the Company's confidential correspondence?' I asked. He hadn't a word to say. It was great fun. 'When Mr. Kurtz,' I continued, severely, 'is General Manager, you won't have the opportunity.'

"He blew the candle out suddenly, and we went outside. The moon had risen. Black figures strolled about listlessly, pouring water on the glow, whence proceeded a sound of hissing; steam ascended in the moonlight, the beaten nigger groaned somewhere. 'What a row the brute makes!' said the indefatigable man with the moustaches, appearing near us. 'Serve him right. Transgression — punishment — bang! Pitiless, pitiless. That's the only way. This will prevent all conflagrations for the future. I was just telling the manager ... ' He noticed my companion, and became crestfallen all at once. 'Not in bed yet,' he said, with a kind of servile heartiness; 'it's so natural. Ha! Danger — agitation.' He vanished. I went on to the river-side, and the other followed me. I heard a scathing murmur at my ear, 'Heap of muffs — go to.' The pilgrims could be seen in knots gesticulating, discussing. Several had still their staves in their hands. I verily believe they took these sticks to bed with them. Beyond the fence the forest stood up spectrally in the moonlight, and through the dim stir, through the faint sounds of that lamentable courtyard, the silence of the land went home to one's very heart — its mystery, its greatness, the amazing reality of its concealed life. The hurt nigger moaned feebly somewhere near by, and then fetched a deep sigh that made me mend my pace away from there. I felt a hand introducing itself under my arm. 'My dear sir,' said the fellow. 'I don't want to be misunderstood, and especially by you, who will see Mr. Kurtz long before I can have that pleasure. I wouldn't like him to get a false idea of my disposition. ... '

"I let him run on, this papier-maché Mephistopheles, and it seemed to me that if I tried I could poke my forefinger through him, and would find nothing inside but a little loose dirt, maybe. He, don't you see, had been planning to be assistant-manager by-and-by under the present man, and I could see that the coming of that Kurtz had upset them both not a little. He talked precipitately, and I did not try to stop him. I had my shoulders against the wreck of my steamer, hauled up on the slope like a carcass of some big river animal. The smell of mud, of primeval mud, by Jove! was in my nostrils, the high stillness of primeval forest was before my eyes; there were shiny patches on the black creek. The moon had spread over everything a thin layer of silver — over the rank grass, over the mud, upon the wall of matted vegetation standing higher than the wall of a temple, over the great river I could see through a sombre gap glittering, glittering, as it flowed broadly by without a murmur. All this was great, expectant, mute, while the man jabbered about himself. I wondered whether the stillness on the face of the immensity looking at us two were meant as an appeal or as a menace. What were we who had strayed in here? Could we handle that dumb thing, or would it handle us? I felt how big, how confoundedly big, was that thing that couldn't talk, and perhaps was deaf as well. What was in there? I could see a little ivory coming out from there, and heard Mr. Kurtz was in there. I had heard enough about it, too — God knows! Yet somehow it didn't bring any image with it — no more than if I had been told an angel or a fiend was in there. I believed it in the same way one of you might believe there are inhabitants in the planet Mars. I knew once a Scotch sail-maker who was certain, dead sure, there were people in Mars. If you asked him for some idea how they looked and behaved, he would get shy and mutter something about 'walking on all-fours.' If you as much as smiled, he would — though a man of sixty — offer to fight you. I would not have gone so far as to fight for Kurtz, but I went for him near enough to a lie. You know I hate, detest, and can't bear a lie, not because I am straighter than the rest of us, but simply because it appals me. There is a taint of death, a flavour of mortality in lies — which is exactly what I hate and detest in the world — what I want to forget. It makes me miserable and sick, like biting something rotten would do. Temperament, I suppose. Well, I went near enough to it by letting the young fool there believe anything he liked to imagine as to my influence in Europe. I became in an instant as much of a pretence as the rest of the bewitched pilgrims. This simply because I had a notion it somehow would be of help to that Kurtz whom at the time I did not see — you understand. He was just a word for me. I did not see the man in the name any more than you do. Do you see him? Do you see the story? Do you see anything? It seems to me I am trying to tell you a dream — making a vain attempt, because no relation of a dream can convey the dream-sensation, that commingling of absurdity, surprise, and bewilderment in a tremor of struggling revolt, that notion of being captured by the incredible which is of the very essence of dreams. ... "

He was silent for a while.

" ... No, it is impossible; it is impossible to convey the life-sensation of any given epoch of one's existence — that which makes its truth, its meaning — its subtle and penetrating essence. It is impossible. We live, as we dream — alone. ... "

He paused again as if reflecting, then added —

"Of course in this you fellows see more than I could then. You see me, whom you know. ... "

It had become so pitch dark that we listeners could hardly see one another. For a long time already he, sitting apart, had been no more to us than a voice. There was not a word from anybody. The others might have been asleep, but I was awake. I listened, I listened on the watch for the sentence, for the word, that would give me the clue to the faint uneasiness inspired by this narrative that seemed to shape itself without human lips in the heavy night-air of the river.

" ... Yes — I let him run on," Marlow began again, "and think what he pleased about the powers that were behind me. I did! And there was nothing behind me! There was nothing but that wretched, old, mangled steamboat I was leaning against, while he talked fluently about 'the necessity for every man to get on.' 'And when one comes out here, you conceive, it is not to gaze at the moon.' Mr. Kurtz was a 'universal genius,' but even a genius would find it easier to work with 'adequate tools — intelligent men.' He did not make bricks — why, there was a physical impossibility in the way — as I was well aware; and if he did secretarial work for the manager, it was because 'no sensible man rejects wantonly the confidence of his superiors.' Did I see it? I saw it. What more did I want? What I really wanted was rivets, by heaven! Rivets. To get on with the work — to stop the hole. Rivets I wanted. There were cases of them down at the coast — cases — piled up — burst — split! You kicked a loose rivet at every second step in that station yard on the hillside. Rivets had rolled into the grove of death. You could fill your pockets with rivets for the trouble of stooping down — and there wasn't one rivet to be found where it was wanted. We had plates that would do, but nothing to fasten them with. And every week the messenger, a lone negro, letter-bag on shoulder and staff in hand, left our station for the coast. And several times a week a coast caravan came in with trade goods — ghastly glazed calico that made you shudder only to look at it, glass beads value about a penny a quart, confounded spotted cotton handkerchiefs. And no rivets. Three carriers could have brought all that was wanted to set that steamboat afloat.

"He was becoming confidential now, but I fancy my unresponsive attitude must have exasperated him at last, for he judged it necessary to inform me he feared neither God nor devil, let alone any mere man. I said I could see that very well, but what I wanted was a certain quantity of rivets — and rivets were what really Mr. Kurtz wanted, if he had only known it. Now letters went to the coast every week. ... 'My dear sir,' he cried, 'I write from dictation.' I demanded rivets. There was a way — for an intelligent man. He changed his manner; became very cold, and suddenly began to talk about a hippopotamus; wondered whether sleeping on board the steamer (I stuck to my salvage night and day) I wasn't disturbed. There was an old hippo that had the bad habit of getting out on the bank and roaming at night over the station grounds. The pilgrims used to turn out in a body and empty every rifle they could lay hands on at him. Some even had sat up o' nights for him. All this energy was wasted, though. 'That animal has a charmed life,' he said; 'but you can say this only of brutes in this country. No man — you apprehend me? — no man here bears a charmed life.' He stood there for a moment in the moonlight with his delicate hooked nose set a little askew, and his mica eyes glittering without a wink, then, with a curt Good-night, he strode off. I could see he was disturbed and considerably puzzled, which made me feel more hopeful than I had been for days. It was a great comfort to turn from that chap to my influential friend, the battered, twisted, ruined, tin-pot steamboat. I clambered on board. She rang under my feet like an empty Huntley & Palmer biscuit-tin kicked along a gutter; she was nothing so solid in make, and rather less pretty in shape, but I had expended enough hard work on her to make me love her. No influential friend would have served me better. She had given me a chance to come out a bit — to find out what I could do. No, I don't like work. I had rather laze about and think of all the fine things that can be done. I don't like work — no man does — but I like what is in the work, — the chance to find yourself. Your own reality — for yourself, not for others — what no other man can ever know. They can only see the mere show, and never can tell what it really means.

"I was not surprised to see somebody sitting aft, on the deck, with his legs dangling over the mud. You see I rather chummed with the few mechanics there were in that station, whom the other pilgrims naturally despised — on account of their imperfect manners, I suppose. This was the foreman — a boiler-maker by trade — a good worker. He was a lank, bony, yellow-faced man, with big intense eyes. His aspect was worried, and his head was as bald as the palm of my hand; but his hair in falling seemed to have stuck to his chin, and had prospered in the new locality, for his beard hung down to his waist. He was a widower with six young children (he had left them in charge of a sister of his to come out there), and the passion of his life was pigeon-flying. He was an enthusiast and a connoisseur. He would rave about pigeons. After work hours he used sometimes to come over from his hut for a talk about his children and his pigeons; at work, when he had to crawl in the mud under the bottom of the steamboat, he would tie up that beard of his in a kind of white serviette[16] he brought for the purpose. It had loops to go over his ears. In the evening he could be seen squatted on the bank rinsing that wrapper in the creek with great care, then spreading it solemnly on a bush to dry.

"I slapped him on the back and shouted 'We shall have rivets!' He scrambled to his feet exclaiming 'No! Rivets!' as though he couldn't believe his ears. Then in a low voice, 'You … eh?' I don't know why we behaved like lunatics. I put my finger to the side of my nose and nodded mysteriously. 'Good for you!' he cried, snapped his fingers above his head, lifting one foot. I tried a jig. We capered on the iron deck. A frightful clatter came out of that hulk, and the virgin forest on the other bank of the creek sent it back in a thundering roll upon the sleeping station. It must have made some of the pilgrims sit up in their hovels. A dark figure obscured the lighted doorway of the manager's hut, vanished, then, a second or so after, the doorway itself vanished, too. We stopped, and the silence driven away by the stamping of our feet flowed back again from the recesses of the land. The great wall of vegetation, an exuberant and entangled mass of trunks, branches, leaves, boughs, festoons, motionless in the moonlight, was like a rioting invasion of soundless life, a rolling wave of plants, piled up, crested, ready to topple over the creek, to sweep every little man of us out of his little existence. And it moved not. A deadened burst of mighty splashes and snorts reached us from afar, as though an ichthyosaurus[17] had been taking a bath of glitter in the great river. 'After all,' said the boiler-maker in a reasonable tone, 'why shouldn't we get the rivets?' Why not, indeed! I did not know of any reason why we shouldn't. 'They'll come in three weeks,' I said, confidently.

"But they didn't. Instead of rivets there came an invasion, an infliction, a visitation. It came in sections during the next three weeks, each section headed by a donkey carrying a white man in new clothes and tan shoes, bowing from that elevation right and left to the

---

[16] Napkin.

[17] An extinct marine reptile.

impressed pilgrims. A quarrelsome band of footsore sulky niggers trod on the heels of the donkey; a lot of tents, camp-stools, tin boxes, white cases, brown bales would be shot down in the courtyard, and the air of mystery would deepen a little over the muddle of the station. Five such instalments came, with their absurd air of disorderly flight with the loot of innumerable outfit shops and provision stores, that, one would think, they were lugging, after a raid, into the wilderness for equitable division. It was an inextricable mess of things decent in themselves but that human folly made look like spoils of thieving.

"This devoted band called itself the Eldorado Exploring Expedition, and I believe they were sworn to secrecy. Their talk, however, was the talk of sordid buccaneers: it was reckless without hardihood, greedy without audacity, and cruel without courage; there was not an atom of foresight or of serious intention in the whole batch of them, and they did not seem aware these things are wanted for the work of the world. To tear treasure out of the bowels of the land was their desire, with no more moral purpose at the back of it than there is in burglars breaking into a safe. Who paid the expenses of the noble enterprise I don't know; but the uncle of our manager was leader of that lot.

"In exterior he resembled a butcher in a poor neighbourhood, and his eyes had a look of sleepy cunning. He carried his fat paunch with ostentation on his short legs, and during the time his gang infested the station spoke to no one but his nephew. You could see these two roaming about all day long with their heads close together in an everlasting confab.

"I had given up worrying myself about the rivets. One's capacity for that kind of folly is more limited than you would suppose. I said Hang! — and let things slide. I had plenty of time for meditation, and now and then I would give some thought to Kurtz. I wasn't very interested in him. No. Still, I was curious to see whether this man, who had come out equipped with moral ideas of some sort, would climb to the top after all and how he would set about his work when there."

II

"One evening as I was lying flat on the deck of my steamboat, I heard voices approaching — and there were the nephew and the uncle strolling along the bank. I laid my head on my arm again, and had nearly lost myself in a doze, when somebody said in my ear, as it were: 'I am as harmless as a little child, but I don't like to be dictated to. Am I the manager — or am I not? I was ordered to send him there. It's incredible.' ... I became aware that the two were standing on the shore alongside the forepart of the steamboat, just below my head. I did not move; it did not occur to me to move: I was sleepy. 'It *is* unpleasant,' grunted the uncle. 'He has asked the Administration to be sent there,' said the other, 'with the idea of showing what he could do; and I was instructed accordingly. Look at the influence that man must have. Is it not frightful?' They both agreed it was frightful, then made several bizarre remarks: 'Make rain and fine weather — one man — the Council — by the nose' — bits of absurd sentences that got the better of my drowsiness, so that I had pretty near the whole of my wits about me when the uncle said, 'The climate may do away with this difficulty for you. Is he alone there?' 'Yes,' answered the manager; 'he sent his assistant down the river with a note to me in these terms: "Clear this poor devil out of the country, and don't bother sending more of that sort. I had rather be alone than have the kind of men you can dispose of with me." It was more than a year ago. Can you imagine such impudence!' 'Anything since then?' asked the other, hoarsely. 'Ivory,' jerked the nephew; 'lots of it — prime sort — lots — most annoying, from him.' 'And with that?' questioned the heavy rumble. 'Invoice,' was the reply fired out, so to speak. Then silence. They had been talking about Kurtz.

"I was broad awake by this time, but, lying perfectly at ease, remained still, having no inducement to change my position. 'How did that ivory come all this way?' growled the elder man, who seemed very vexed. The other explained that it had come with a fleet of canoes in charge of an English half-caste clerk Kurtz had with him; that Kurtz had apparently intended to return himself, the station being by that time bare of goods and stores, but after coming three hundred miles, had suddenly decided to go back, which he started to do alone in a small dugout with four paddlers, leaving the half-caste to continue down the river with the ivory. The two fellows there seemed astounded at anybody attempting such a thing. They were at a loss for an adequate motive. As to me, I seemed to see Kurtz for the first time. It was a distinct glimpse: the dugout, four paddling savages, and the lone white man turning his back suddenly on the headquarters, on relief, on thoughts of home — perhaps; setting his face towards the depths of the wilderness, towards his empty and desolate station. I did not know the motive. Perhaps he was just simply a fine fellow who stuck to his work for its own sake. His name, you understand, had not been pronounced once. He was 'that man.' The half-caste, who, as far as I could see, had conducted a difficult trip with great prudence and pluck, was invariably alluded to as 'that scoundrel.' The 'scoundrel' had reported that the 'man' had been very ill — had recovered imperfectly. ... The two below me moved away then a few paces, and strolled back and forth at some little distance. I heard: 'Military post — doctor — two hundred miles — quite alone now — unavoidable delays — nine months — no news — strange rumours.' They approached again, just as the manager was saying, 'No one, as far as I know, unless a species of wandering trader — a pestilential fellow, snapping ivory from the natives.' Who was it they were talking about now? I gathered in snatches that this was some man supposed to be in Kurtz's district, and of whom the manager did not approve. 'We will not be free from unfair competition till one of these fellows is hanged for an example,' he said. 'Certainly,' grunted the other; 'get him hanged! Why not? Anything — anything can be done in this country. That's what I say; nobody here, you understand, *here*, can endanger your position. And why? You stand the climate — you outlast them all. The danger is in Europe; but there before I left I took care to — ' They moved off and whispered, then their voices rose again. 'The extraordinary series of delays is not my fault. I did my best.' The fat man sighed. 'Very sad.' 'And the pestiferous absurdity of his talk,' continued the other; 'he bothered me enough when he was here. "Each station should be like a beacon on the road towards better things, a centre for trade of course, but also for humanizing, improving, instructing." Conceive you — that ass! And he wants to be manager! No, it's——' Here he got choked by excessive indignation, and I lifted my head the least bit. I was surprised to see how near they were — right under me. I could have spat upon their hats. They were looking on the ground, absorbed in thought. The manager was switching his leg with a slender twig: his sagacious relative lifted his head. 'You have been well since you came out this time?' he asked. The other gave a start. 'Who? I? Oh! Like a charm — like a charm. But the rest — oh, my goodness! All sick. They die so quick, too, that I haven't the time to send them out of the country — it's incredible!' 'H'm. Just so,' grunted the uncle. 'Ah! my boy, trust to this — I say, trust to this.' I saw him extend his short flipper of an arm for a gesture that took in the forest, the creek, the mud, the river, — seemed to beckon with a dishonouring flourish before the sunlit face of the land a treacherous appeal to the lurking death, to the hidden evil, to the profound darkness of its heart. It was so startling that I leaped to my feet and looked back at the edge of the forest, as though I had expected an answer of some sort to that black display of confidence. You know the foolish notions that come to one sometimes. The high stillness confronted these two figures with its ominous patience, waiting for the passing away of a fantastic invasion.

"They swore aloud together — out of sheer fright, I believe — then pretending not to know anything of my existence, turned back to the station. The sun was low; and leaning forward side by side, they seemed to be tugging painfully uphill their two ridiculous shadows of unequal length, that trailed behind them slowly over the tall grass without bending a single blade.

"In a few days the Eldorado Expedition went into the patient wilderness, that closed upon it as the sea closes over a diver. Long afterwards the news came that all the donkeys were dead. I know nothing as to the fate of the less valuable animals. They, no doubt, like the rest of us, found what they deserved. I did not inquire. I was then rather excited at the prospect of meeting Kurtz very soon. When I say very soon I mean it comparatively. It was just two months from the day we left the creek when we came to the bank below Kurtz's station.

"Going up that river was like travelling back to the earliest beginnings of the world, when vegetation rioted on the earth and the big trees were kings. An empty stream, a great silence, an impenetrable forest. The air was warm, thick, heavy, sluggish. There was no joy in the brilliance of sunshine. The long stretches of the waterway ran on, deserted, into the gloom of overshadowed distances. On silvery sandbanks hippos and alligators sunned themselves side by side. The broadening waters flowed through a mob of wooded islands; you lost your way on that river as you would in a desert, and butted all day long against shoals, trying to find the channel, till you thought yourself bewitched and cut off for ever from everything you had known once — somewhere — far away — in another existence perhaps. There were moments when one's past came back to one, as it will sometimes when you have not a moment to spare to yourself; but it came in the shape of an unrestful and noisy dream, remembered with wonder amongst the overwhelming realities of this strange world of plants, and water, and silence. And this stillness of life did not in the least resemble a peace. It was the stillness of an implacable force brooding over an inscrutable intention. It looked at you with a vengeful aspect. I got used to it afterwards; I did not see it any more; I had no time. I had to keep guessing at the channel; I had to discern, mostly by inspiration, the signs of hidden banks; I watched for sunken stones; I was learning to clap my teeth smartly before my heart flew out, when I shaved by a fluke some infernal sly old snag that would have ripped the life out of the tin-pot steamboat and drowned all the pilgrims; I had to keep a look-out for the signs of dead wood we could cut up in the night for next day's steaming. When you have to attend to things of that sort, to the mere incidents of the surface, the reality — the reality, I tell you — fades. The inner truth is hidden — luckily, luckily. But I felt it all the same; I felt often its mysterious stillness watching me at my monkey tricks, just as it watches you fellows performing on your respective tightropes for — what is it? half-a-crown a tumble——"

"Try to be civil, Marlow," growled a voice, and I knew there was at least one listener awake besides myself.

"I beg your pardon. I forgot the heartache which makes up the rest of the price. And indeed what does the price matter, if the trick be well done? You do your tricks very well. And I didn't do badly either, since I managed not to sink that steamboat on my first trip. It's a wonder to me yet. Imagine a blindfolded man set to drive a van over a bad road. I sweated and shivered over that business considerably, I can tell you. After all, for a seaman, to scrape the bottom of the thing that's supposed to float all the time under his care is the unpardonable sin. No one may know of it, but you never forget the thump — eh? A blow on the very heart. You remember it, you dream of it, you wake up at night and think of it — years after — and go hot and cold all over. I don't pretend to say that steamboat floated all the time. More than once she had to wade for a bit, with twenty cannibals splashing around and pushing. We had enlisted some of these chaps on the way for a crew. Fine fellows — cannibals — in their place. They were men one could work with, and I am grateful to them. And, after all, they did not eat each other before my face: they had brought along a provision of hippo-meat which went rotten, and made the mystery of the wilderness stink in my nostrils. Phoo! I can sniff it now. I had the manager on board and three or four pilgrims with their staves — all complete. Sometimes we came upon a station close by the bank, clinging to the skirts of the unknown, and the white men rushing out of a tumble-down hovel, with great gestures of joy and surprise and welcome, seemed very strange — had the appearance of being held there captive by a spell. The word ivory would ring in the air for a while — and on we went again into the silence, along empty reaches, round the still bends, between the high walls of our winding way, reverberating in hollow claps the ponderous beat of the stern-wheel. Trees, trees, millions of trees, massive, immense, running up high; and at their foot, hugging the bank against the stream, crept the little begrimed steamboat, like a sluggish beetle crawling on the floor of a lofty portico. It made you feel very small, very lost, and yet it was not altogether depressing, that feeling. After all, if you were small, the grimy beetle crawled on — which was just what you wanted it to do. Where the pilgrims imagined it crawled to I don't know. To some place where they expected to get something, I bet! For me it crawled towards Kurtz — exclusively; but when the steam-pipes started leaking we crawled very slow. The reaches opened before us and closed behind, as if the forest had stepped leisurely across the water to bar the way for our return. We penetrated deeper and deeper into the heart of darkness. It was very quiet there. At night sometimes the roll of drums behind the curtain of trees would run up the river and remain sustained faintly, as if hovering in the air high over our heads, till the first break of day. Whether it meant war, peace, or prayer we could not tell. The dawns were heralded by the descent of a chill stillness; the wood-cutters slept, their fires burned low; the snapping of a twig would make you start. We were wanderers on prehistoric earth, on an earth that wore the aspect of an unknown planet. We could have fancied ourselves the first of men taking possession of an accursed inheritance, to be subdued at the cost of profound anguish and of excessive toil. But suddenly, as we struggled round a bend, there would be a glimpse of rush walls, of peaked grass-roofs, a burst of yells, a whirl of black limbs, a mass of hands clapping, of feet stamping, of bodies swaying, of eyes rolling, under the droop of heavy and motionless foliage. The steamer toiled along slowly on the edge of a black and incomprehensible frenzy. The prehistoric man was cursing us, praying to us, welcoming us — who could tell? We were cut off from the comprehension of our surroundings; we glided past like phantoms, wondering and secretly appalled, as sane men would be before an enthusiastic outbreak in a madhouse. We could not understand because we were too far and could not remember, because we were travelling in the night of first ages, of those ages that are gone, leaving hardly a sign — and no memories.

"The earth seemed unearthly. We are accustomed to look upon the shackled form of a conquered monster, but there — there you could look at a thing monstrous and free. It was unearthly, and the men were——No, they were not inhuman. Well, you know, that was the worst of it — this suspicion of their not being inhuman. It would come slowly to one. They howled and leaped, and spun, and made horrid faces; but what thrilled you was just the thought of their humanity — like yours — the thought of your remote kinship with this wild and passionate uproar. Ugly. Yes, it was ugly enough; but if you were man enough you would admit to yourself that there was in you just the faintest trace of a response to the terrible frankness of that noise, a dim suspicion of there being a meaning in it which you — you so remote from the night of first ages — could comprehend. And why not? The mind of man is capable of anything — because everything is in it, all the past as well as all the future. What was there after all? Joy, fear, sorrow, devotion, valour, rage — who can tell? — but truth — truth stripped of its cloak of time. Let the fool gape and shudder — the man knows, and can look on without a wink. But he must at least be as much of a man as these on the shore. He must meet that truth with his own true stuff — with his own inborn strength. Principles won't do. Acquisitions, clothes, pretty rags — rags that would fly off at the first good shake. No; you want a deliberate belief. An appeal to me in this fiendish row — is there? Very well; I hear; I admit, but I have a voice, too, and for good or evil mine is the speech that cannot be silenced. Of course, a fool, what with sheer fright and fine sentiments, is always safe. Who's that grunting? You wonder I didn't go ashore for a howl and a dance? Well, no — I didn't. Fine sentiments, you say? Fine sentiments, be hanged! I had no time. I had to mess about with white-lead and strips of woollen blanket helping to put bandages on those leaky steampipes — I tell you. I had to watch the steering, and circumvent those snags, and get the tin-pot along by hook or by crook. There was surface-truth enough in these things to save a wiser man. And between whiles I had to look after the savage who was fireman. He was an improved specimen; he could fire up a vertical boiler. He was there below me, and, upon my word, to look at him was as edifying as seeing a dog in a parody of breeches and a feather hat, walking on his hind-legs. A few months of training had done for that really fine chap. He squinted at the steam-gauge and at the water-gauge with an evident effort of intrepidity — and he had filed teeth, too, the poor devil, and the wool of his pate shaved into queer patterns, and three ornamental scars on each of his cheeks. He ought to have been clapping his hands and stamping his feet on the bank, instead of which he was hard at work, a thrall to strange witchcraft, full of improving knowledge. He was useful because he had been instructed; and what he knew was this — that should the water in that transparent thing disappear, the evil spirit inside the boiler would get angry through the greatness of his thirst, and take a terrible vengeance. So he sweated and fired up and watched the glass fearfully (with an impromptu charm, made of rags, tied to his arm, and a piece of polished bone, as big as a watch, stuck flatways through his lower lip), while the wooded banks slipped past us slowly, the short noise was left behind, the interminable miles of silence — and we crept on, towards Kurtz. But the snags were thick, the water was treacherous and shallow, the boiler seemed indeed to have a sulky devil in it, and thus neither that fireman nor I had any time to peer into our creepy thoughts.

"Some fifty miles below the Inner Station we came upon a hut of reeds, an inclined and melancholy pole, with the unrecognizable tatters of what had been a flag of some sort flying from it, and a neatly stacked wood-pile. This was unexpected. We came to the bank, and on the stack of firewood found a flat piece of board with some faded pencil-writing on it. When deciphered it said: 'Wood for you. Hurry up. Approach cautiously.' There was a signature, but it was illegible — not Kurtz — a much longer word. Hurry up. Where? Up the river? 'Approach cautiously.' We had not done so. But the warning could not have been meant for the place where it could be only found after approach. Something was wrong above. But what — and how much? That was the question. We commented adversely upon the imbecility of that telegraphic style. The bush around said nothing, and would not let us look very far, either. A torn curtain of red twill hung in the doorway of the hut, and flapped sadly in our faces. The dwelling was dismantled; but we could see a white man had lived there not very long ago. There remained a rude table — a plank on two posts; a heap of rubbish reposed in a dark corner, and by the door I picked up a book. It had lost its covers, and the pages had been thumbed into a state of extremely dirty softness; but the back had been lovingly stitched afresh with white cotton thread, which looked clean yet. It was an extraordinary find. Its title was, *An Inquiry into some Points of Seamanship*, by a man Towser, Towson — some such name — Master in his Majesty's Navy. The matter looked dreary reading enough, with illustrative diagrams and repulsive tables of figures, and the copy was sixty years old. I handled this amazing antiquity with the greatest possible tenderness, lest it should dissolve in my hands. Within, Towson or Towser was inquiring earnestly into the breaking strain of ships' chains and tackle, and other such matters. Not a very enthralling book; but at the first glance you could see there a singleness of intention, an honest concern for the right way of going to work, which made these humble pages, thought out so many years ago, luminous with another than a professional light. The simple old sailor, with his talk of chains and purchases,[18] made me forget the jungle and the pilgrims in a delicious sensation of having come upon something unmistakably real. Such a book being there was wonderful enough; but still more astounding were the notes pencilled in the margin, and plainly referring to the text. I couldn't believe my eyes! They were in cipher! Yes, it looked like cipher. Fancy a man lugging with him a book of that description into this nowhere and studying it — and making notes — in cipher at that! It was an extravagant mystery.

"I had been dimly aware for some time of a worrying noise, and when I lifted my eyes I saw the wood-pile was gone, and the manager, aided by all the pilgrims, was shouting at me from the river-side. I slipped the book into my pocket. I assure you to leave off reading was like tearing myself away from the shelter of an old and solid friendship.

"I started the lame engine ahead. 'It must be this miserable trader — this intruder,' exclaimed the manager, looking back malevolently at the place we had left. 'He must be English,' I said. 'It will not save him from getting into trouble if he is not careful,' muttered the manager darkly. I observed with assumed innocence that no man was safe from trouble in this world.

"The current was more rapid now, the steamer seemed at her last gasp, the stern-wheel flopped languidly, and I caught myself listening on tiptoe for the next beat of the boat, for in sober truth I expected the wretched thing to give up every moment. It was like watching the last flickers of a life. But still we crawled. Sometimes I would pick out a tree a little way ahead to measure our progress towards Kurtz by, but I lost it invariably before we got abreast. To keep the eyes so long on one thing was too much for human patience. The manager displayed a beautiful resignation. I fretted and fumed and took to arguing with myself whether or no I would talk openly with Kurtz; but before I could come to any conclusion it occurred to me that my speech or my silence, indeed any action of mine, would be a mere futility. What did it matter what any one knew or ignored? What did it matter who was manager? One gets sometimes such a flash of insight. The essentials of this affair lay deep under the surface, beyond my reach, and beyond my power of meddling.

"Towards the evening of the second day we judged ourselves about eight miles from Kurtz's station. I wanted to push on; but the manager looked grave, and told me the navigation up there was so dangerous that it would be advisable, the sun being very low already, to wait where we were till next morning. Moreover, he pointed out that if the warning to approach cautiously were to be followed, we must approach in daylight — not at dusk, or in the dark. This was sensible enough. Eight miles meant nearly three hours' steaming for us, and I could also see suspicious ripples at the upper end of the reach. Nevertheless, I was annoyed beyond expression at the delay, and most unreasonably, too, since one night more could not matter much after so many months. As we had plenty of wood, and caution was the word, I brought up in the middle of the stream. The reach was narrow, straight, with high sides like a railway cutting. The dusk came gliding into it long before the sun had set. The current ran smooth and swift, but a dumb immobility sat on the banks. The living trees, lashed together by the creepers and every living bush of the undergrowth, might have been changed

---

[18] Rigging used to apply leverage.

into stone, even to the slenderest twig, to the lightest leaf. It was not sleep — it seemed unnatural, like a state of trance. Not the faintest sound of any kind could be heard. You looked on amazed, and began to suspect yourself of being deaf — then the night came suddenly, and struck you blind as well. About three in the morning some large fish leaped, and the loud splash made me jump as though a gun had been fired. When the sun rose there was a white fog, very warm and clammy, and more blinding than the night. It did not shift or drive; it was just there, standing all round you like something solid. At eight or nine, perhaps, it lifted as a shutter lifts. We had a glimpse of the towering multitude of trees, of the immense matted jungle, with the blazing little ball of the sun hanging over it — all perfectly still — and then the white shutter came down again, smoothly, as if sliding in greased grooves. I ordered the chain, which we had begun to heave in, to be paid out again. Before it stopped running with a muffled rattle, a cry, a very loud cry, as of infinite desolation, soared slowly in the opaque air. It ceased. A complaining clamour, modulated in savage discords, filled our ears. The sheer unexpectedness of it made my hair stir under my cap. I don't know how it struck the others; to me it seemed as though the mist itself had screamed, so suddenly, and apparently from all sides at once, did this tumultuous and mournful uproar arise. It culminated in a hurried outbreak of almost intolerably excessive shrieking, which stopped short, leaving us stiffened in a variety of silly attitudes, and obstinately listening to the nearly as appalling and excessive silence. 'Good God! What is the meaning——' stammered at my elbow one of the pilgrims, — a little fat man, with sandy hair and red whiskers, who wore side-spring boots, and pink pyjamas tucked into his socks. Two others remained open-mouthed a whole minute, then dashed into the little cabin, to rush out incontinently and stand darting scared glances, with Winchesters[19] at 'ready' in their hands. What we could see was just the steamer we were on, her outlines blurred as though she had been on the point of dissolving, and a misty strip of water, perhaps two feet broad, around her — and that was all. The rest of the world was nowhere, as far as our eyes and ears were concerned. Just nowhere. Gone, disappeared; swept off without leaving a whisper or a shadow behind.

"I went forward, and ordered the chain to be hauled in short, so as to be ready to trip the anchor and move the steamboat at once if necessary. 'Will they attack?' whispered an awed voice. 'We will be all butchered in this fog,' murmured another. The faces twitched with the strain, the hands trembled slightly, the eyes forgot to wink. It was very curious to see the contrast of expressions of the white men and of the black fellows of our crew, who were as much strangers to that part of the river as we, though their homes were only eight hundred miles away. The whites, of course greatly discomposed, had besides a curious look of being painfully shocked by such an outrageous row. The others had an alert, naturally interested expression; but their faces were essentially quiet, even those of the one or two who grinned as they hauled at the chain. Several exchanged short, grunting phrases, which seemed to settle the matter to their satisfaction. Their headman, a young, broad-chested black, severely draped in dark-blue fringed cloths, with fierce nostrils and his hair all done up artfully in oily ringlets, stood near me. 'Aha!' I said, just for good fellowship's sake. 'Catch 'im,' he snapped, with a bloodshot widening of his eyes and a flash of sharp teeth — 'catch 'im. Give 'im to us.' 'To you, eh?' I asked; 'what would you do with them?' 'Eat 'im!' he said, curtly, and, leaning his elbow on the rail, looked out into the fog in a dignified and profoundly pensive attitude. I would no doubt have been properly horrified, had it not occurred to me that he and his chaps must be very hungry: that they must have been growing increasingly hungry for at least this month past. They had been engaged for six months (I don't think a single one of them had any

---

[19] A Winchester is a famous repeating rifle, named for its American maker.

clear idea of time, as we at the end of countless ages have. They still belonged to the beginnings of time — had no inherited experience to teach them as it were), and of course, as long as there was a piece of paper written over in accordance with some farcical law or other made down the river, it didn't enter anybody's head to trouble how they would live. Certainly they had brought with them some rotten hippo-meat, which couldn't have lasted very long, anyway, even if the pilgrims hadn't, in the midst of a shocking hullabaloo, thrown a considerable quantity of it overboard. It looked like a high-handed proceeding; but it was really a case of legitimate self-defence. You can't breathe dead hippo waking, sleeping, and eating, and at the same time keep your precarious grip on existence. Besides that, they had given them every week three pieces of brass wire, each about nine inches long; and the theory was they were to buy their provisions with that currency in river-side villages. You can see how *that* worked. There were either no villages, or the people were hostile, or the director, who like the rest of us fed out of tins, with an occasional old he-goat thrown in, didn't want to stop the steamer for some more or less recondite reason. So, unless they swallowed the wire itself, or made loops of it to snare the fishes with, I don't see what good their extravagant salary could be to them. I must say it was paid with a regularity worthy of a large and honourable trading company. For the rest, the only thing to eat — though it didn't look eatable in the least — I saw in their possession was a few lumps of some stuff like hard-cooked dough, of a dirty lavender colour, they kept wrapped in leaves, and now and then swallowed a piece of, but so small that it seemed done more for the looks of the thing than for any serious purpose of sustenance. Why in the name of all the gnawing devils of hunger they didn't go for us — they were thirty to five — and have a good tuck-in[20] for once, amazes me now when I think of it. They were big powerful men, with not much capacity to weigh the consequences, with courage, with strength, even yet, though their skins were no longer glossy and their muscles no longer hard. And I saw that something restraining, one of those human secrets that baffle probability, had come into play there. I looked at them with a swift quickening of interest — not because it occurred to me I might be eaten by them before very long, though I own to you that just then I perceived — in a new light, as it were — how unwholesome the pilgrims looked, and I hoped, yes, I positively hoped, that my aspect was not so — what shall I say? — so — unappetizing: a touch of fantastic vanity which fitted well with the dream-sensation that pervaded all my days at that time. Perhaps I had a little fever, too. One can't live with one's finger everlastingly on one's pulse. I had often 'a little fever,' or a little touch of other things — the playful paw-strokes of the wilderness, the preliminary trifling before the more serious onslaught which came in due course. Yes; I looked at them as you would on any human being, with a curiosity of their impulses, motives, capacities, weaknesses, when brought to the test of an inexorable physical necessity. Restraint! What possible restraint? Was it superstition, disgust, patience, fear — or some kind of primitive honour? No fear can stand up to hunger, no patience can wear it out, disgust simply does not exist where hunger is; and as to superstition, beliefs, and what you may call principles, they are less than chaff in a breeze. Don't you know the devilry of lingering starvation, its exasperating torment, its black thoughts, its sombre and brooding ferocity? Well, I do. It takes a man all his inborn strength to fight hunger properly. It's really easier to face bereavement, dishonour, and the perdition of one's soul — than this kind of prolonged hunger. Sad, but true. And these chaps, too, had no earthly reason for any kind of scruple. Restraint! I would just as soon have expected restraint from a hyena prowling amongst the corpses of a battlefield. But there was the fact facing me — the fact dazzling, to be seen, like the foam on the depths of the sea, like a ripple on an unfathomable enigma, a mystery greater —

---

[20] A good meal.

when I thought of it — than the curious, inexplicable note of desperate grief in this savage clamour that had swept by us on the river-bank, behind the blind whiteness of the fog.

"Two pilgrims were quarreling in hurried whispers as to which bank. 'Left.' 'No, no; how can you? Right, right, of course.' 'It is very serious,' said the manager's voice behind me; 'I would be desolated if anything should happen to Mr. Kurtz before we came up.' I looked at him, and had not the slightest doubt he was sincere. He was just the kind of man who would wish to preserve appearances. That was his restraint. But when he muttered something about going on at once, I did not even take the trouble to answer him. I knew, and he knew, that it was impossible. Were we to let go our hold of the bottom, we would be absolutely in the air — in space. We wouldn't be able to tell where we were going to — whether up or down stream, or across — till we fetched against one bank or the other, — and then we wouldn't know at first which it was. Of course I made no move. I had no mind for a smash-up. You couldn't imagine a more deadly place for a shipwreck. Whether drowned at once or not, we were sure to perish speedily in one way or another. 'I authorize you to take all the risks,' he said, after a short silence. 'I refuse to take any,' I said, shortly; which was just the answer he expected, though its tone might have surprised him. 'Well, I must defer to your judgment. You are captain,' he said, with marked civility. I turned my shoulder to him in sign of my appreciation, and looked into the fog. How long would it last? It was the most hopeless look-out. The approach to this Kurtz grubbing for ivory in the wretched bush was beset by as many dangers as though he had been an enchanted princess sleeping in a fabulous castle. 'Will they attack, do you think?' asked the manager, in a confidential tone.

"I did not think they would attack, for several obvious reasons. The thick fog was one. If they left the bank in their canoes they would get lost in it, as we would be if we attempted to move. Still, I had also judged the jungle of both banks quite impenetrable — and yet eyes were in it, eyes that had seen us. The river-side bushes were certainly very thick; but the under-growth behind was evidently penetrable. However, during the short lift I had seen no canoes anywhere in the reach — certainly not abreast of the steamer. But what made the idea of attack inconceivable to me was the nature of the noise — of the cries we had heard. They had not the fierce character boding of immediate hostile intention. Unexpected, wild, and violent as they had been, they had given me an irresistible impression of sorrow. The glimpse of the steamboat had for some reason filled those savages with unrestrained grief. The danger, if any, I expounded, was from our proximity to a great human passion let loose. Even extreme grief may ultimately vent itself in violence — but more generally takes the form of apathy. ...

"You should have seen the pilgrims stare! They had no heart to grin, or even to revile me: but I believe they thought me gone mad — with fright, maybe. I delivered a regular lecture. My dear boys, it was no good bothering. Keep a look-out? Well, you may guess I watched the fog for the signs of lifting as a cat watches a mouse; but for anything else our eyes were of no more use to us than if we had been buried miles deep in a heap of cotton-wool. It felt like it, too — choking, warm, stifling. Besides, all I said, though it sounded extravagant, was absolutely true to fact. What we afterwards alluded to as an attack was really an attempt at repulse. The action was very far from being aggressive — it was not even defensive, in the usual sense: it was undertaken under the stress of desperation, and in its essence was purely protective.

"It developed itself, I should say, two hours after the fog lifted, and its commencement was at a spot, roughly speaking, about a mile and a half below Kurtz's station. We had just floundered and flopped round a bend, when I saw an islet, a mere grassy hummock of bright green, in the middle of the stream. It was the only thing of the kind; but as we opened the reach more, I perceived it was the head of a long sandbank, or rather of a chain of shallow patches stretching down the middle of the river. They were discoloured, just awash, and the whole lot was seen just under the water, exactly as a man's backbone is seen running down the middle of his back under the skin. Now, as far as I did see, I could go to the right or to the left of this. I didn't know either channel, of course. The banks looked pretty well alike, the depth appeared the same; but as I had been informed the station was on the west side, I naturally headed for the western passage.

"No sooner had we fairly entered it than I became aware it was much narrower than I had supposed. To the left of us there was the long uninterrupted shoal, and to the right a high, steep bank heavily overgrown with bushes. Above the bush the trees stood in serried ranks. The twigs overhung the current thickly, and from distance to distance a large limb of some tree projected rigidly over the stream. It was then well on in the afternoon, the face of the forest was gloomy, and a broad strip of shadow had already fallen on the water. In this shadow we steamed up — very slowly, as you may imagine. I sheered her well inshore — the water being deepest near the bank, as the sounding-pole informed me.

"One of my hungry and forbearing friends was sounding[21] in the bows just below me. This steamboat was exactly like a decked scow. On the deck, there were two little teak-wood houses, with doors and windows. The boiler was in the fore-end, and the machinery right astern. Over the whole there was a light roof, supported on stanchions. The funnel projected through that roof, and in front of the funnel a small cabin built of light planks served for a pilot-house. It contained a couch, two camp-stools, a loaded Martini-Henry[22] leaning in one corner, a tiny table, and the steering-wheel. It had a wide door in front and a broad shutter at each side. All these were always thrown open, of course. I spent my days perched up there on the extreme fore-end of that roof, before the door. At night I slept, or tried to, on the couch. An athletic black belonging to some coast tribe, and educated by my poor predecessor, was the helmsman. He sported a pair of brass earrings, wore a blue cloth wrapper from the waist to the ankles, and thought all the world of himself. He was the most unstable kind of fool I had ever seen. He steered with no end of a swagger while you were by; but if he lost sight of you, he became instantly the prey of an abject funk, and would let that cripple of a steamboat get the upper hand of him in a minute.

"I was looking down at the sounding-pole, and feeling much annoyed to see at each try a little more of it stick out of that river, when I saw my poleman give up the business suddenly, and stretch himself flat on the deck, without even taking the trouble to haul his pole in. He kept hold on it though, and it trailed in the water. At the same time the fireman, whom I could also see below me, sat down abruptly before his furnace and ducked his head. I was amazed. Then I had to look at the river mighty quick, because there was a snag in the fairway. Sticks, little sticks, were flying about — thick: they were whizzing before my nose, dropping below me, striking behind me against my pilot-house. All this time the river, the shore, the woods, were very quiet — perfectly quiet. I could only hear the heavy splashing thump of the stern-wheel and the patter of these things. We cleared the snag clumsily. Arrows, by Jove! We were being shot at! I stepped in quickly to close the shutter on the land-side. That fool-helmsman, his hands on the spokes, was lifting his knees high, stamping his feet, champing his mouth, like a reined-in horse. Confound him! And we were staggering within ten feet of the bank. I had to lean right out to swing the heavy shutter, and I saw a face amongst the leaves on the level with my own, looking at me very fierce and steady; and then suddenly, as though a veil had been removed from my eyes, I made out, deep in the tangled gloom, naked breasts, arms, legs, glaring eyes, — the bush was swarming with human limbs in movement, glistening, of bronze

---

[21] Gauging the water's depth by means of a weighted line.

[22] A make of military rifle.

colour. The twigs shook, swayed, and rustled, the arrows flew out of them, and then the shutter came to. 'Steer her straight,' I said to the helmsman. He held his head rigid, face forward; but his eyes rolled, he kept on, lifting and setting down his feet gently, his mouth foamed a little. 'Keep quiet!' I said in a fury. I might just as well have ordered a tree not to sway in the wind. I darted out. Below me there was a great scuffle of feet on the iron deck; confused exclamations; a voice screamed, 'Can you turn back?' I caught sight of a V-shaped ripple on the water ahead. What? Another snag! A fusillade burst out under my feet. The pilgrims had opened with their Winchesters, and were simply squirting lead into that bush. A deuce of a lot of smoke came up and drove slowly forward. I swore at it. Now I couldn't see the ripple or the snag either. I stood in the doorway, peering, and the arrows came in swarms. They might have been poisoned, but they looked as though they wouldn't kill a cat. The bush began to howl. Our wood-cutters raised a warlike whoop; the report of a rifle at my back deafened me. I glanced over my shoulder, and the pilot-house was yet full of noise and smoke when I made a dash at the wheel. The fool-nigger had dropped everything, to throw the shutter open and let off that Martini-Henry. He stood before the wide opening, glaring, and I yelled at him to come back, while I straightened the sudden twist out of that steamboat. There was no room to turn even if I had wanted to, the snag was somewhere very near ahead in that confounded smoke, there was no time to lose, so I just crowded her into the bank — right into the bank, where I knew the water was deep.

"We tore slowly along the overhanging bushes in a whirl of broken twigs and flying leaves. The fusillade below stopped short, as I had foreseen it would when the squirts got empty. I threw my head back to a glinting whizz that traversed the pilot-house, in at one shutter-hole and out at the other. Looking past that mad helmsman, who was shaking the empty rifle and yelling at the shore, I saw vague forms of men running bent double, leaping, gliding, distinct, incomplete, evanescent. Something big appeared in the air before the shutter, the rifle went overboard, and the man stepped back swiftly, looked at me over his shoulder in an extraordinary, profound, familiar manner, and fell upon my feet. The side of his head hit the wheel twice, and the end of what appeared a long cane clattered round and knocked over a little camp-stool. It looked as though after wrenching that thing from somebody ashore he had lost his balance in the effort. The thin smoke had blown away, we were clear of the snag, and looking ahead I could see that in another hundred yards or so I would be free to sheer off, away from the bank; but my feet felt so very warm and wet that I had to look down. The man had rolled on his back and stared straight up at me; both his hands clutched that cane. It was the shaft of a spear that, either thrown or lunged through the opening, had caught him in the side just below the ribs; the blade had gone in out of sight, after making a frightful gash; my shoes were full; a pool of blood lay very still, gleaming dark-red under the wheel; his eyes shone with an amazing lustre. The fusillade burst out again. He looked at me anxiously, gripping the spear like something precious, with an air of being afraid I would try to take it away from him. I had to make an effort to free my eyes from his gaze and attend to the steering. With one hand I felt above my head for the line of the steam whistle, and jerked out screech after screech hurriedly. The tumult of angry and warlike yells was checked instantly, and then from the depths of the woods went out such a tremulous and prolonged wail of mournful fear and utter despair as may be imagined to follow the flight of the last hope from the earth. There was a great commotion in the bush; the shower of arrows stopped, a few dropping shots rang out sharply — then silence, in which the languid beat of the stern-wheel came plainly to my ears. I put the helm hard a-starboard at the moment when the pilgrim in pink pyjamas, very hot and agitated, appeared in the doorway. 'The manager sends me——' he began in an official tone, and stopped short. 'Good God!' he said, glaring at the wounded man.

"We two whites stood over him, and his lustrous and inquiring glance enveloped us both. I declare it looked as though he would presently put to us some question in an understandable language; but he died without uttering a sound, without moving a limb, without twitching a muscle. Only in the very last moment, as though in response to some sign we could not see, to some whisper we could not hear, he frowned heavily, and that frown gave to his black death-mask an inconceivably sombre, brooding, and menacing expression. The lustre of inquiring glance faded swiftly into vacant glassiness. 'Can you steer?' I asked the agent eagerly. He looked very dubious; but I made a grab at his arm, and he understood at once I meant him to steer whether or no. To tell you the truth, I was morbidly anxious to change my shoes and socks. 'He is dead,' murmured the fellow, immensely impressed. 'No doubt about it,' said I, tugging like mad at the shoe-laces. 'And by the way, I suppose Mr. Kurtz is dead as well by this time.'

"For the moment that was the dominant thought. There was a sense of extreme disappointment, as though I had found out I had been striving after something altogether without substance. I couldn't have been more disgusted if I had travelled all this way for the sole purpose of talking with Mr. Kurtz. Talking with. ... I flung one shoe overboard, and became aware that that was exactly what I had been looking forward to — a talk with Kurtz. I made the strange discovery that I had never imagined him as doing, you know, but as discoursing. I didn't say to myself, 'Now I will never see him,' or 'Now I will never shake him by the hand,' but, 'now I will never hear him.' The man presented himself as a voice. Not of course that I did not connect him with some sort of action. Hadn't I been told in all the tones of jealousy and admiration that he had collected, bartered, swindled, or stolen more ivory than all the other agents together? That was not the point. The point was in his being a gifted creature, and that of all his gifts the one that stood out preëminently, that carried with it a sense of real presence, was his ability to talk, his words — the gift of expression, the bewildering, the illuminating, the most exalted and the most contemptible, the pulsating stream of light, or the deceitful flow from the heart of an impenetrable darkness.

"The other shoe went flying unto the devil-god of that river. I thought, By Jove! it's all over. We are too late; he has vanished — the gift has vanished, by means of some spear, arrow, or club. I will never hear that chap speak after all, — and my sorrow had a startling extravagance of emotion, even such as I had noticed in the howling sorrow of these savages in the bush. I couldn't have felt more of lonely desolation somehow, had I been robbed of a belief or had missed my destiny in life. ... Why do you sigh in this beastly way, somebody? Absurd? Well, absurd. Good Lord! mustn't a man ever——Here, give me some tobacco."

There was a pause of profound stillness, then a match flared, and Marlow's lean face appeared, worn, hollow, with downward folds and dropped eyelids, with an aspect of concentrated attention; and as he took vigorous draws at his pipe, it seemed to retreat and advance out of the night in the regular flicker of the tiny flame. The match went out.

"Absurd!" he cried. "This is the worst of trying to tell. ... Here you all are, each moored with two good addresses, like a hulk with two anchors, a butcher round one corner, a policeman round another, excellent appetites, and temperature normal — you hear — normal from year's end to year's end. And you say, Absurd! Absurd be — exploded! Absurd! My dear boys, what can you expect from a man who out of sheer nervousness had just flung overboard a pair of new shoes! Now I think of it, it is amazing I did not shed tears. I am, upon the whole, proud of my fortitude. I was cut to the quick at the idea of having lost the inestimable privilege of listening to the gifted Kurtz. Of course I was wrong. The privilege was waiting for me. Oh, yes, I heard more than enough. And I was right, too. A voice. He was very little more than a voice. And I heard — him — it — this voice — other voices — all of them were so little more than voices — and the memory of that time itself lingers around me, impalpable, like a dying vibration of one immense jabber, silly, atrocious, sordid, savage, or simply mean, without any kind of sense. Voices, voices — even the girl herself — now——"

He was silent for a long time.

"I laid the ghost of his gifts at last with a lie," he began, suddenly. "Girl! What? Did I mention a girl? Oh, she is out of it — completely. They — the women I mean — are out of it — should be out of it. We must help them to stay in that beautiful world of their own, lest ours gets worse. Oh, she had to be out of it. You should have heard the disinterred body of Mr. Kurtz saying, 'My Intended.' You would have perceived directly then how completely she was out of it. And the lofty frontal bone of Mr. Kurtz! They say the hair goes on growing sometimes, but this — ah — specimen, was impressively bald. The wilderness had patted him on the head, and, behold, it was like a ball — an ivory ball; it had caressed him, and — lo! — he had withered; it had taken him, loved him, embraced him, got into his veins, consumed his flesh, and sealed his soul to its own by the inconceivable ceremonies of some devilish initiation. He was its spoiled and pampered favourite. Ivory? I should think so. Heaps of it, stacks of it. The old mud shanty was bursting with it. You would think there was not a single tusk left either above or below the ground in the whole country. 'Mostly fossil,' the manager had remarked, disparagingly. It was no more fossil than I am; but they call it fossil when it is dug up. It appears these niggers do bury the tusks sometimes — but evidently they couldn't bury this parcel deep enough to save the gifted Mr. Kurtz from his fate. We filled the steamboat with it, and had to pile a lot on the deck. Thus he could see and enjoy as long as he could see, because the appreciation of this favour had remained with him to the last. You should have heard him say, 'My ivory.' Oh yes, I heard him. 'My Intended, my ivory, my station, my river, my——' everything belonged to him. It made me hold my breath in expectation of hearing the wilderness burst into a prodigious peal of laughter that would shake the fixed stars in their places. Everything belonged to him — but that was a trifle. The thing was to know what he belonged to, how many powers of darkness claimed him for their own. That was the reflection that made you creepy all over. It was impossible — it was not good for one either — trying to imagine. He had taken a high seat amongst the devils of the land — I mean literally. You can't understand. How could you? — with solid pavement under your feet, surrounded by kind neighbours ready to cheer you or to fall on you, stepping delicately between the butcher and the policeman, in the holy terror of scandal and gallows and lunatic asylums — how can you imagine what particular region of the first ages a man's untrammelled feet may take him into by the way of solitude — utter solitude without a policeman — by the way of silence — utter silence, where no warning voice of a kind neighbour can be heard whispering of public opinion? These little things make all the great difference. When they are gone you must fall back upon your own innate strength, upon your own capacity for faithfulness. Of course you may be too much of a fool to go wrong — too dull even to know you are being assaulted by the powers of darkness. I take it, no fool ever made a bargain for his soul with the devil: the fool is too much of a fool, or the devil too much of a devil — I don't know which. Or you may be such a thunderingly exalted creature as to be altogether deaf and blind to anything but heavenly sights and sounds. Then the earth for you is only a standing place — and whether to be like this is your loss or your gain I won't pretend to say. But most of us are neither one nor the other. The earth for us is a place to live in, where we must put up with sights, with sounds, with smells, too, by Jove! — breathe dead hippo, so to speak, and not be contaminated. And there, don't you see? your strength comes in, the faith in your ability for the digging of unosten-tatious holes to bury the stuff in — your power of devotion, not to yourself, but to an obscure, back-breaking business. And that's difficult enough. Mind, I am not trying to excuse or even explain — I am trying to account to myself for — for — Mr. Kurtz — for the shade of Mr. Kurtz. This initiated wraith from the back of Nowhere honoured me with its amazing confidence before it vanished altogether. This was because it could speak English to me. The original Kurtz had been educated partly in England, and — as he was good enough to say himself — his sympathies were in the right place. His mother was half-English, his father was half-French. All Europe contributed to the making of Kurtz; and by-and-by I learned that, most appropriately, the International Society for the Suppression of Savage Customs had intrusted him with the making of a report, for its future guidance. And he had written it, too. I've seen it. I've read it. It was eloquent, vibrating with eloquence, but too high-strung, I think. Seventeen pages of close writing he had found time for! But this must have been before his — let us say — nerves, went wrong, and caused him to preside at certain midnight dances ending with unspeakable rites, which — as far as I reluctantly gathered from what I heard at various times — were offered up to him — do you understand? — to Mr. Kurtz himself. But it was a beautiful piece of writing. The opening paragraph, however, in the light of later information, strikes me now as ominous. He began with the argument that we whites, from the point of development we had arrived at, 'must necessarily appear to them [savages] in the nature of supernatural beings — we approach them with the might as of a deity,' and so on, and so on. 'By the simple exercise of our will we can exert a power for good practically unbounded,' etc. etc. From that point he soared and took me with him. The peroration was magnificent, though difficult to remember, you know. It gave me the notion of an exotic Immensity ruled by an august Benevolence. It made me tingle with enthusiasm. This was the unbounded power of eloquence — of words — of burning noble words. There were no practical hints to interrupt the magic current of phrases, unless a kind of note at the foot of the last page, scrawled evidently much later, in an unsteady hand, may be regarded as the exposition of a method. It was very simple, and at the end of that moving appeal to every altruistic sentiment it blazed at you, luminous and terrifying, like a flash of lightning in a serene sky: 'Exterminate all the brutes!' The curious part was that he had apparently forgotten all about that valuable postscriptum, because, later on, when he in a sense came to himself, he repeatedly entreated me to take good care of 'my pamphlet' (he called it), as it was sure to have in the future a good influence upon his career. I had full information about all these things, and, besides, as it turned out, I was to have the care of his memory. I've done enough for it to give me the indisputable right to lay it, if I choose, for an everlasting rest in the dust-bin of progress, amongst all the sweepings and, figuratively speaking, all the dead cats of civilization. But then, you see, I can't choose. He won't be forgotten. Whatever he was, he was not common. He had the power to charm or frighten rudimentary souls into an aggravated witch-dance in his honour; he could also fill the small souls of the pilgrims with bitter misgivings: he had one devoted friend at least, and he had conquered one soul in the world that was neither rudimentary nor tainted with self-seeking. No; I can't forget him, though I am not prepared to affirm the fellow was exactly worth the life we lost in getting to him. I missed my late helmsman awfully, — I missed him even while his body was still lying in the pilot-house. Perhaps you will think it passing strange this regret for a savage who was no more account than a grain of sand in a black Sahara. Well, don't you see, he had done something, he had steered; for months I had him at my back — a help — an instrument. It was a kind of partnership. He steered for me — I had to look after him, I worried about his deficiencies, and thus a subtle bond had been created, of which I only became aware when it was suddenly broken. And the intimate profundity of that look he gave me when he received his hurt remains to this day in my memory — like a claim of distant kinship affirmed in a supreme moment.

"Poor fool! If he had only left that shutter alone. He had no restraint, no restraint — just like Kurtz — a tree swayed by the wind. As soon as I had put on a dry pair of slippers, I dragged him out, after first jerking the spear out of his side, which operation I confess I performed with my eyes shut tight. His heels leaped together over the little door-step; his shoulders were pressed to my breast; I hugged him from behind desperately. Oh! he was heavy, heavy; heavier than any man on earth, I should imagine. Then without more ado I tipped him overboard. The current snatched him as though he had been a wisp of grass, and I saw the body roll over twice before I lost sight of it for ever. All the pilgrims and the manager were then congregated on the awning-deck about the pilot-house, chattering at each other like a flock of excited magpies, and there was a scandalized murmur at my heartless promptitude. What they wanted to keep that body hanging about for I can't guess. Embalm it, maybe. But I had also heard another, and a very ominous, murmur on the deck below. My friends the wood-cutters, were likewise scandalized, and with a better show of reason — though I admit that the reason itself was quite inadmissible. Oh, quite! I had made up my mind that if my late helmsman was to be eaten, the fishes alone should have him. He had been a very second-rate helmsman while alive, but now he was dead he might have become a first-class temptation, and possibly cause some startling trouble. Besides, I was anxious to take the wheel, the man in pink pyjamas showing himself a hopeless duffer at the business.

"This I did directly the simple funeral was over. We were going half-speed, keeping right in the middle of the stream, and I listened to the talk about me. They had given up Kurtz, they had given up the station; Kurtz was dead, and the station had been burnt — and so on — and so on. The red-haired pilgrim was beside himself with the thought that at least this poor Kurtz had been properly avenged. 'Say! We must have made a glorious slaughter of them in the bush. Eh? What do you think? Say?' He positively danced, the bloodthirsty little gingery beggar. And he had nearly fainted when he saw the wounded man! I could not help saying, 'You made a glorious lot of smoke, anyhow.' I had seen, from the way the tops of the bushes rustled and flew, that almost all the shots had gone too high. You can't hit anything unless you take aim and fire from the shoulder; but these chaps fired from the hip with their eyes shut. The retreat, I maintained — and I was right — was caused by the screeching of the steam-whistle. Upon this they forgot Kurtz, and began to howl at me with indignant protests.

"The manager stood by the wheel murmuring confidentially about the necessity of getting well away down the river before dark at all events, when I saw in the distance a clearing on the river-side and the outlines of some sort of building. 'What's this?' I asked. He clapped his hands in wonder. 'The station!' he cried. I edged in at once, still going half-speed.

"Through my glasses I saw the slope of a hill interspersed with rare trees and perfectly free from undergrowth. A long decaying building on the summit was half buried in the high grass; the large holes in the peaked roof gaped black from afar; the jungle and the woods made a background. There was no enclosure or fence of any kind; but there had been one apparently, for near the house half-a-dozen slim posts remained in a row, roughly trimmed, and with their upper ends ornamented with round carved balls. The rails, or whatever there had been between, had disappeared. Of course the forest surrounded all that. The river-bank was clear, and on the water-side I saw a white man under a hat like a cart-wheel beckoning persistently with his whole arm. Examining the edge of the forest above and below, I was almost certain I could see movements — human forms gliding here and there. I steamed past prudently, then stopped the engines and let her drift down. The man on the shore began to shout, urging us to land. 'We have been attacked,' screamed the manager. 'I know — I know. It's all right,' yelled back the other, as cheerful as you please. 'Come along. It's all right. I am glad.'

"His aspect reminded me of something I had seen — something funny I had seen somewhere. As I manœuvred to get alongside, I was asking myself, 'What does this fellow look like?' Suddenly I got it. He looked like a harlequin. His clothes had been made of some stuff that was brown holland probably, but it was covered with patches all over, with bright patches, blue, red, and yellow, — patches on the back, patches on the front, patches on elbows, on knees; coloured binding around his jacket, scarlet edging at the bottom of his trousers; and the sunshine made him look extremely gay and wonderfully neat withal, because you could see how beautifully all this patching had been done. A beardless, boyish face, very fair, no features to speak of, nose peeling, little blue eyes, smiles and frowns chasing each other over that open countenance like sunshine and shadow on a wind-swept plain. 'Look out, captain!' he cried; 'there's a snag lodged in here last night.' What! Another snag? I confess I swore shamefully. I had nearly holed my cripple, to finish off that charming trip. The harlequin on the bank turned his little pug-nose up to me. 'You English?' he asked, all smiles. 'Are you?' I shouted from the wheel. The smiles vanished, and he shook his head as if sorry for my disappointment. Then he brightened up. 'Never mind!' he cried, encouragingly. 'Are we in time?' I asked. 'He is up there,' he replied, with a toss of the head up the hill, and becoming gloomy all of a sudden. His face was like the autumn sky, overcast one moment and bright the next.

"When the manager, escorted by the pilgrims, all of them armed to the teeth, had gone to the house this chap came on board. 'I say, I don't like this. These natives are in the bush,' I said. He assured me earnestly it was all right. 'They are simple people,' he added; 'well, I am glad you came. It took me all my time to keep them off.' 'But you said it was all right,' I cried. 'Oh, they meant no harm,' he said; and as I stared he corrected himself, 'Not exactly.' Then vivaciously, 'My faith, your pilot-house wants a clean up!' In the next breath he advised me to keep enough steam on the boiler to blow the whistle in case of any trouble. 'One good screech will do more for you than all your rifles. They are simple people,' he repeated. He rattled away at such a rate he quite overwhelmed me. He seemed to be trying to make up for lots of silence, and actually hinted, laughing, that such was the case. 'Don't you talk with Mr. Kurtz?' I said. 'You don't talk with that man — you listen to him,' he exclaimed with severe exaltation. 'But now — ' He waved his arm, and in the twinkling of an eye was in the uttermost depths of despondency. In a moment he came up again with a jump, possessed himself of both my hands, shook them continuously, while he gabbled: 'Brother sailor ... honour ... pleasure ... delight ... introduce myself ... Russian ... son of an arch-priest ... Government of Tambov ... What? Tobacco! English tobacco; the excellent English tobacco! Now, that's brotherly. Smoke? Where's a sailor that does not smoke?'

"The pipe soothed him, and gradually I made out he had run away from school, had gone to sea in a Russian ship; ran away again; served some time in English ships; was now reconciled with the arch-priest. He made a point of that. 'But when one is young one must see things, gather experience, ideas; enlarge the mind.' 'Here!' I interrupted. 'You can never tell! Here I met Mr. Kurtz,' he said, youthfully solemn and reproachful. I held my tongue after that. It appears he had persuaded a Dutch trading-house on the coast to fit him out with stores and goods, and had started for the interior with a light heart, and no more idea of what would happen to him than a baby. He had been wandering about that river for nearly two years alone, cut off from everybody and everything. 'I am not so young as I look. I am twenty-five,' he said. 'At first old Van Shuyten would tell me to go to the devil,' he narrated with keen enjoyment; 'but I stuck to him, and talked and talked, till at last he got afraid I would talk the hind-leg off his favourite dog, so he gave me some cheap things and a few guns, and told me he hoped he would never see my face again. Good old Dutchman, Van Shuyten. I've sent him one small lot of ivory a year ago, so that he can't call me a little thief when I get back. I hope he got it. And for the rest I don't care. I had some wood stacked for you. That was my old house. Did you see?'

"I gave him Towson's book. He made as though he would kiss me, but restrained himself. 'The only book I had left, and I thought I had lost it,' he said, looking at it ecstatically. 'So many accidents happen to a man going about alone, you know. Canoes get upset sometimes — and sometimes you've got to clear out so quick when the people get angry.' He thumbed the pages. 'You made notes in Russian?' I asked. He nodded. 'I thought they were written in cipher,' I said. He laughed, then became serious. 'I had lots of trouble to keep these people off,' he said. 'Did they want to kill you?' I asked. 'Oh, no!' he cried, and checked himself. 'Why did they attack us?' I pursued. He hesitated, then said shamefacedly, 'They don't want him to go.' 'Don't they?' I said, curiously. He nodded a nod full of mystery and wisdom. 'I tell you,' he cried, 'this man has enlarged my mind.' He opened his arms wide, staring at me with his little blue eyes that were perfectly round."

III

"I looked at him, lost in astonishment. There he was before me, in motley, as though he had absconded from a troupe of mimes, enthusiastic, fabulous. His very existence was improbable, inexplicable, and altogether bewildering. He was an insoluble problem. It was inconceivable how he had existed, how he had succeeded in getting so far, how he had managed to remain — why he did not instantly disappear. 'I went a little farther,' he said, 'then still a little farther — till I had gone so far that I don't know how I'll ever get back. Never mind. Plenty time. I can manage. You take Kurtz away quick — quick — I tell you.' The glamour of youth enveloped his particoloured rags, his destitution, his loneliness, the essential desolation of his futile wanderings. For months — for years — his life hadn't been worth a day's purchase; and there he was gallantly, thoughtlessly alive, to all appearance indestructible solely by the virtue of his few years and of his unreflecting audacity. I was seduced into something like admiration — like envy. Glamour urged him on, glamour kept him unscathed. He surely wanted nothing from the wilderness but space to breathe in and to push on through. His need was to exist, and to move onwards at the greatest possible risk, and with a maximum of privation. If the absolutely pure, uncalculating, unpractical spirit of adventure had ever ruled a human being, it ruled this be-patched youth. I almost envied him the possession of this modest and clear flame. It seemed to have consumed all thought of self so completely, that even while he was talking to you, you forgot that it was he — the man before your eyes — who had gone through these things. I did not envy him his devotion to Kurtz, though. He had not meditated over it. It came to him, and he accepted it with a sort of eager fatalism. I must say that to me it appeared about the most dangerous thing in every way he had come upon so far.

"They had come together unavoidably, like two ships becalmed near each other, and lay rubbing sides at last. I suppose Kurtz wanted an audience, because on a certain occasion, when encamped in the forest, they had talked all night, or more probably Kurtz had talked. 'We talked of everything,' he said, quite transported at the recollection. 'I forgot there was such a thing as sleep. The night did not seem to last an hour. Everything! Everything! ... Of love, too.' 'Ah, he talked to you of love!' I said, much amused. 'It isn't what you think,' he cried, almost passionately. 'It was in general. He made me see things. — things.'

"He threw his arms up. We were on deck at the time, and the headman of my wood-cutters, lounging near by, turned upon him his heavy and glittering eyes. I looked around, and I don't know why, but I assure you that never, never before, did this land, this river, this jungle, the very arch of this blazing sky, appear to me so hopeless and so dark, so impenetrable to human thought, so pitiless to human weakness. 'And, ever since, you have been with him, of course?' I said.

"On the contrary. It appears their intercourse had been very much broken by various causes. He had, as he informed me proudly, managed to nurse Kurtz through two illnesses (he alluded to it as you would to some risky feat), but as a rule Kurtz wandered alone, far in the depths of the forest. 'Very often coming to this station, I had to wait days and days before he would turn up,' he said. 'Ah, it was worth waiting for! — sometimes.' 'What was he doing? exploring or what?' I asked. 'Oh, yes, of course'; he had discovered lots of villages, a lake, too — he did not know exactly in what direction; it was dangerous to inquire too much — but mostly his expeditions had been for ivory. 'But he had no goods to trade with by that time,' I objected. 'There's a good lot of cartridges left even yet,' he answered, looking away. 'To speak plainly, he raided the country,' I said. He nodded. 'Not alone, surely!' He muttered something about the villages round that lake. 'Kurtz got the tribe to follow him, did he?' I suggested. He fidgeted a little. 'They adored him,' he said. The tone of these words was so extraordinary that I looked at him searchingly. It was curious to see his mingled eagerness and reluctance to speak of Kurtz. The man filled his life, occupied his thoughts, swayed his emotions. 'What can you expect?' he burst out; 'he came to them with thunder and lightning, you know — and they had never seen anything like it — and very terrible. He could be very terrible. You can't judge Mr. Kurtz as you would an ordinary man. No, no, no! Now — just to give you an idea — I don't mind telling you, he wanted to shoot me, too, one day — but I don't judge him.' 'Shoot you!' I cried. 'What for?' 'Well, I had a small lot of ivory the chief of that village near my house gave me. You see I used to shoot game for them. Well, he wanted it, and wouldn't hear reason. He declared he would shoot me unless I gave him the ivory and then cleared out of the country, because he could do so, and had a fancy for it, and there was nothing on earth to prevent him killing whom he jolly well pleased. And it was true, too. I gave him the ivory. What did I care! But I didn't clear out. No, no. I couldn't leave him. I had to be careful, of course, till we got friendly again for a time. He had his second illness then. Afterwards I had to keep out of the way; but I didn't mind. He was living for the most part in those villages on the lake. When he came down to the river, sometimes he would take to me, and sometimes it was better for me to be careful. This man suffered too much. He hated all this, and somehow he couldn't get away. When I had a chance I begged him to try and leave while there was time; I offered to go back with him. And he would say yes, and then he would remain; go off on another ivory hunt; disappear for weeks; forget himself amongst these people — forget himself — you know.' 'Why! he's mad,' I said. He protested indignantly. Mr. Kurtz couldn't be mad. If I had heard him talk, only two days ago, I wouldn't dare hint at such a thing. ... I had taken up my binoculars while we talked, and was looking at the shore, sweeping the limit of the forest at each side and at the back of the house. The consciousness of there being people in that bush, so silent, so quiet — as silent and quiet as the ruined house on the hill — made me uneasy. There was no sign on the face of nature of this amazing tale that was not so much told as suggested to me in desolate exclamations, completed by shrugs, in interrupted phrases, in hints ending in deep sighs. The woods were unmoved, like a mask — heavy, like the closed door of a prison — they looked with their air of hidden knowledge, of patient expectation, of unapproachable silence. The Russian was explaining to me that it was only lately that Mr. Kurtz had come down to the river, bringing along with him all the fighting men of that lake tribe. He had been absent for several months — getting himself adored, I suppose — and had come down unexpectedly, with the intention to all appearance of making a raid either across the river or down stream. Evidently the appetite for more ivory had got the better of the — what shall I say? — less material aspirations. However he had got much worse suddenly. 'I heard he was lying helpless, and so I came up — took my chance,' said the Russian. 'Oh, he is bad, very bad.' I directed my glass to the house. There were no signs of life, but there was the ruined roof, the long mud wall peeping above the grass, with three little square window-holes, no two of the same size; all this brought within reach of my hand, as it were. And then I made a brusque movement, and one of the remaining posts of that vanished fence leaped up in the field of my glass. You remember I told you I had been struck at the distance by certain attempts at ornamentation, rather remarkable in the ruinous aspect of the place. Now I had suddenly a nearer view, and its first result was to make me throw my head back as if before a blow. Then I went carefully from post to post with my glass, and I saw my mistake. These round knobs were not ornamental but symbolic; they were expressive and puzzling, striking and disturbing — food for thought and also for the vultures if there had been any looking down from the sky; but at all events for such ants as were industrious enough to ascend the pole. They would have been even more impressive, those heads on the stakes, if their faces had not been turned to the house. Only one, the first I had made out, was facing my way. I was not so shocked as you may think. The start back I had given was really nothing but a movement of surprise. I had expected to see a knob of wood there, you know. I returned deliberately to the first I had seen — and there it was, black, dried, sunken, with closed eyelids, — a head that seemed to sleep at the top of that pole, and, with the shrunken dry lips showing a narrow white line of the teeth, was smiling, too, smiling continuously at some endless and jocose dream of that eternal slumber.

"I am not disclosing any trade secrets. In fact, the manager said afterwards that Mr. Kurtz's methods had ruined the district. I have no opinion on that point, but I want you clearly to understand that there was nothing exactly profitable in these heads being there. They only showed that Mr. Kurtz lacked restraint in the gratification of his various lusts, that there was something wanting in him — some small matter which, when the pressing need arose, could not be found under his magnificent eloquence. Whether he knew of this deficiency himself I can't say. I think the knowledge came to him at last — only at the very last. But the wilderness had found him out early, and had taken on him a terrible vengeance for the fantastic invasion. I think it had whispered to him things about himself which he did not know, things of which he had no conception till he took counsel with this great solitude — and the whisper had proved irresistibly fascinating. It echoed loudly within him because he was hollow at the core. ... I put down the glass, and the head that had appeared near enough to be spoken to seemed at once to have leaped away from me into inaccessible distance.

"The admirer of Mr. Kurtz was a bit crestfallen. In a hurried, indistinct voice he began to assure me he had not dared to take these — say, symbols — down. He was not afraid of the natives; they would not stir till Mr. Kurtz gave the word. His ascendancy was extraordinary. The camps of these people surrounded the place, and the chiefs came every day to see him. They would crawl. ... 'I don't want to know anything of the ceremonies used when approaching Mr. Kurtz,' I shouted. Curious, this feeling that came over me that such details would be more intolerable than those heads drying on the stakes under Mr. Kurtz's windows. After all, that was only a savage sight, while I seemed at one bound to have been transported into some lightless region of subtle horrors, where pure, uncomplicated savagery was a positive relief, being something that had a right to exist — obviously — in the sunshine. The young man looked at me with surprise. I suppose it did not occur to him that Mr. Kurtz was no idol of mine. He forgot I hadn't heard any of these splendid monologues on, what was it? on love, justice, conduct of life — or what not. If it had come to crawling before Mr. Kurtz, he crawled as much as the veriest savage of them all. I had no idea of the conditions, he said: these heads were the heads of rebels. I shocked him excessively by laughing. Rebels! What would be the next definition I was to hear? There had been enemies, criminals, workers — and these were rebels. Those rebellious heads looked very subdued to me on their sticks. 'You don't know how such a life tries a man like Kurtz,' cried Kurtz's last disciple. 'Well, and you?' I said.

'I! I! I am a simple man. I have no great thoughts. I want nothing from anybody. How can you compare me to? ... ' His feelings were too much for speech, and suddenly he broke down. 'I don't understand,' he groaned. 'I've been doing my best to keep him alive, and that's enough. I had no hand in all this. I have no abilities. There hasn't been a drop of medicine or a mouthful of invalid food for months here. He was shamefully abandoned. A man like this, with such ideas. Shamefully! Shamefully! I — I — haven't slept for the last ten nights. ... '

"His voice lost itself in the calm of the evening. The long shadows of the forest had slipped down hill while we talked, had gone far beyond the ruined hovel, beyond the symbolic row of stakes. All this was in the gloom, while we down there were yet in the sunshine, and the stretch of the river abreast of the clearing glittered in a still and dazzling splendour, with a murky and overshadowed bend above and below. Not a living soul was seen on the shore. The bushes did not rustle.

"Suddenly round the corner of the house a group of men appeared, as though they had come up from the ground. They waded waist-deep in the grass, in a compact body, bearing an improvised stretcher in their midst. Instantly, in the emptiness of the landscape, a cry arose whose shrillness pierced the still air like a sharp arrow flying straight to the very heart of the land; and, as if by enchantment, streams of human beings — of naked human beings — with spears in their hands, with bows, with shields, with wild glances and savage movements, were poured into the clearing by the dark-faced and pensive forest. The bushes shook, the grass swayed for a time, and then everything stood still in attentive immobility.

"'Now, if he does not say the right thing to them we are all done for,' said the Russian at my elbow. The knot of men with the stretcher had stopped, too, halfway to the steamer, as if petrified. I saw the man on the stretcher sit up, lank and with an uplifted arm, above the shoulders of the bearers. 'Let us hope that the man who can talk so well of love in general will find some particular reason to spare us this time,' I said. I resented bitterly the absurd danger of our situation, as if to be at the mercy of that atrocious phantom had been a dishonouring necessity. I could not hear a sound, but through my glasses I saw the thin arm extended commandingly, the lower jaw moving, the eyes of that apparition shining darkly far in its bony head that nodded with grotesque jerks. Kurtz — Kurtz — that means short in German — don't it? Well, the name was as true as everything else in his life — and death. He looked at least seven feet long. His covering had fallen off, and his body emerged from it pitiful and appalling as from a winding-sheet. I could see the cage of his ribs all astir, the bones of his arm waving. It was as though an animated image of death carved out of old ivory had been shaking its hand with menaces at a motionless crowd of men made of dark and glittering bronze. I saw him open his mouth wide — it gave him a weirdly voracious aspect, as though he had wanted to swallow all the air, all the earth, all the men before him. A deep voice reached me faintly. He must have been shouting. He fell back suddenly. The stretcher shook as the bearers staggered forward again, and almost at the same time I noticed that the crowd of savages was vanishing without any perceptible movement of retreat, as if the forest that had ejected these beings so suddenly had drawn them in again as the breath is drawn in a long aspiration.

"Some of the pilgrims behind the stretcher carried his arms — two shotguns, a heavy rifle, and a light revolver-carbine — the thunderbolts of that pitiful Jupiter. The manager bent over him murmuring as he walked beside his head. They laid him down in one of the little cabins — just a room for a bedplace and a camp-stool or two, you know. We had brought his belated correspondence, and a lot of torn envelopes and open letters littered his bed. His hand roamed feebly amongst these papers. I was struck by the fire of his eyes and the composed languor of his expression. It was not so much the exhaustion of disease. He did not seem in pain. This shadow looked satiated and calm, as though for the moment it had had its fill of all the emotions.

"He rustled one of the letters, and looking straight in my face said, 'I am glad.' Somebody had been writing to him about me. These special recommendations were turning up again. The volume of tone he emitted without effort, almost without the trouble of moving his lips, amazed me. A voice! a voice! It was grave, profound, vibrating, while the man did not seem capable of a whisper. However, he had enough strength in him — factitious no doubt — to very nearly make an end of us, as you shall hear directly.

"The manager appeared silently in the doorway; I stepped out at once and he drew the curtain after me. The Russian, eyed curiously by the pilgrims, was staring at the shore. I followed the direction of his glance.

"Dark human shapes could be made out in the distance, flitting indistinctly against the gloomy border of the forest, and near the river two bronze figures, leaning on tall spears, stood in the sunlight under fantastic head-dresses of spotted skins, warlike and still in statuesque repose. And from right to left along the lighted shore moved a wild and gorgeous apparition of a woman.

"She walked with measured steps, draped in striped and fringed cloths, treading the earth proudly, with a slight jingle and flash of barbarous ornaments. She carried her head high; her hair was done in the shape of a helmet; she had brass leggings to the knee, brass wire gauntlets to the elbow, a crimson spot on her tawny cheek, innumerable necklaces of glass beads on her neck; bizarre things, charms, gifts of witch-men, that hung about her, glittered and trembled at every step. She must have had the value of several elephant tusks upon her. She was savage and superb, wild-eyed and magnificent; there was something ominous and stately in her deliberate progress. And in the hush that had fallen suddenly upon the whole sorrowful land, the immense wilderness, the colossal body of the fecund and mysterious life seemed to look at her, pensive, as though it had been looking at the image of its own tenebrous and passionate soul.

"She came abreast of the steamer, stood still, and faced us. Her long shadow fell to the water's edge. Her face had a tragic and fierce aspect of wild sorrow and of dumb pain mingled with the fear of some struggling, half-shaped resolve. She stood looking at us without a stir, and like the wilderness itself, with an air of brooding over an inscrutable purpose. A whole minute passed, and then she made a step forward. There was a low jingle, a glint of yellow metal, a sway of fringed draperies, and she stopped as if her heart had failed her. The young fellow by my side growled. The pilgrims murmured at my back. She looked at us all as if her life had depended upon the unswerving steadiness of her glance. Suddenly she opened her bared arms and threw them up rigid above her head, as though in an uncontrollable desire to touch the sky, and at the same time the swift shadows darted out on the earth, swept around on the river, gathering the steamer into a shadowy embrace. A formidable silence hung over the scene.

"She turned away slowly, walked on, following the bank, and passed into the bushes to the left. Once only her eyes gleamed back at us in the dusk of the thickets before she disappeared.

"'If she had offered to come aboard I really think I would have tried to shoot her,' said the man of patches, nervously. 'I had been risking my life every day for the last fortnight to keep her out of the house. She got in one day and kicked up a row about those miserable rags I picked up in the storeroom to mend my clothes with. I wasn't decent. At least it must have been that, for she talked like a fury to Kurtz for an hour, pointing at me now and then. I don't understand the dialect of this tribe. Luckily for me, I fancy Kurtz felt too ill that day to care, or there would have been mischief. I don't understand. ... No — it's too much for me. Ah, well, it's all over now.'

"At this moment I heard Kurtz's deep voice behind the curtain: 'Save me! — save the ivory, you mean. Don't tell me. Save *me*! Why, I've had to save you. You are interrupting my plans now. Sick! Sick! Not so sick as you would like to believe. Never mind. I'll carry my ideas out yet — I will return. I'll show you what can be done. You with your little peddling notions — you are interfering with me. I will return. I. ...'

"The manager came out. He did me the honour to take me under the arm and lead me aside. 'He is very low, very low,' he said. He considered it necessary to sigh, but neglected to be consistently sorrowful. 'We have done all we could for him — haven't we? But there is no disguising the fact, Mr. Kurtz has done more harm than good to the Company. He did not see the time was not ripe for vigorous action. Cautiously, cautiously — that's my principle. We must be cautious yet. The district is closed to us for a time. Deplorable! Upon the whole, the trade will suffer. I don't deny there is a remarkable quantity of ivory — mostly fossil. We must save it, at all events — but look how precarious the position is — and why? Because the method is unsound.' 'Do you,' said I, looking at the shore, 'call it "unsound method?"' 'Without doubt,' he exclaimed, hotly. 'Don't you?' ... 'No method at all,' I murmured after a while. 'Exactly,' he exulted. 'I anticipated this. Shows a complete want of judgment. It is my duty to point it out in the proper quarter.' 'Oh,' said I, 'that fellow — what's his name? — the brickmaker, will make a readable report for you.' He appeared confounded for a moment. It seemed to me I had never breathed an atmosphere so vile, and I turned mentally to Kurtz for relief — positively for relief. 'Nevertheless I think Mr. Kurtz is a remarkable man,' I said with emphasis. He started, dropped on me a cold heavy glance, said very quietly, 'he *was*,' and turned his back on me. My hour of favour was over; I found myself lumped along with Kurtz as a partisan of methods for which the time was not ripe: I was unsound! Ah! but it was something to have at least a choice of nightmares.

"I had turned to the wilderness really, not to Mr. Kurtz, who, I was ready to admit, was as good as buried. And for a moment it seemed to me as if I also were buried in a vast grave full of unspeakable secrets. I felt an intolerable weight oppressing my breast, the smell of the damp earth, the unseen presence of victorious corruption, the darkness of an impenetrable night. ... The Russian tapped me on the shoulder. I heard him mumbling and stammering something about 'brother seaman — couldn't conceal — knowledge of matters that would affect Mr. Kurtz's reputation.' I waited. For him evidently Mr. Kurtz was not in his grave; I suspect that for him Mr. Kurtz was one of the immortals. 'Well!' said I at last, 'speak out. As it happens, I am Mr. Kurtz's friend — in a way.'

"He stated with a good deal of formality that had we not been 'of the same profession,' he would have kept the matter to himself without regard to consequences. 'He suspected there was an active ill will towards him on the part of these white men that——' 'You are right,' I said, remembering a certain conversation I had overheard. 'The manager thinks you ought to be hanged.' He showed a concern at this intelligence which amused me at first. 'I had better get out of the way quietly,' he said, earnestly. 'I can do no more for Kurtz now, and they would soon find some excuse. What's to stop them? There's a military post three hundred miles from here.' 'Well, upon my word,' said I, 'perhaps you had better go if you have any friends amongst the savages near by.' 'Plenty,' he said. 'They are simple people — and I want nothing, you know.' He stood biting his lip, then: 'I don't want any harm to happen to these whites here, but of course I was thinking of Mr. Kurtz's reputation — but you are a brother seaman and——' 'All right,' said I, after a time. 'Mr. Kurtz's reputation is safe with me.' I did not know how truly I spoke.

"He informed me, lowering his voice, that it was Kurtz who had ordered the attack to be made on the steamer. 'He hated sometimes the idea of being taken away — and then again. ... But I don't understand these matters. I am a simple man. He thought it would scare you away — that you would give it up, thinking him dead. I could not stop him. Oh, I had an awful time of it this last month.' 'Very well,' I said. 'He is all right now.' 'Ye-e-es,' he muttered, not very convinced apparently. 'Thanks,' said I; 'I shall keep my eyes open.' 'But quiet — eh?' he urged, anxiously. 'It would be awful for his reputation if anybody here——' I promised a complete discretion with great gravity. 'I have a canoe and three black fellows waiting not very far. I am off. Could you give me a few Martini-Henry cartridges?' I could, and did, with proper secrecy. He helped himself, with a wink at me, to a handful of my tobacco. 'Between sailors — you know — good English tobacco.' At the door of the pilot-house he turned round — 'I say, haven't you a pair of shoes you could spare?' He raised one leg. 'Look.' The soles were tied with knotted strings sandal-wise under his bare feet. I rooted out an old pair, at which he looked with admiration before tucking it under his left arm. One of his pockets (bright red) was bulging with cartridges, from the other (dark blue) peeped 'Towson's Inquiry,' etc., etc. He seemed to think himself excellently well equipped for a renewed encounter with the wilderness. 'Ah! I'll never, never meet such a man again. You ought to have heard him recite poetry — his own, too, it was, he told me. Poetry!' He rolled his eyes at the recollection of these delights. 'Oh, he enlarged my mind!' 'Goodbye,' said I. He shook hands and vanished in the night. Sometimes I ask myself whether I had ever really seen him — whether it was possible to meet such a phenomenon! ...

"When I woke up shortly after midnight his warning came to my mind with its hint of danger that seemed, in the starred darkness, real enough to make me get up for the purpose of having a look round. On the hill a big fire burned, illuminating fitfully a crooked corner of the station-house. One of the agents with a picket of a few of our blacks, armed for the purpose, was keeping guard over the ivory; but deep within the forest, red gleams that wavered, that seemed to sink and rise from the ground amongst confused columnar shapes of intense blackness, showed the exact position of the camp where Mr. Kurtz's adorers were keeping their uneasy vigil. The monotonous beating of a big drum filled the air with muffled shocks and a lingering vibration. A steady droning sound of many men chanting each to himself some weird incantation came out from the black, flat wall of the woods as the humming of bees comes out of a hive, and had a strange narcotic effect upon my half-awake senses. I believe I dozed off leaning over the rail, till an abrupt burst of yells, an overwhelming outbreak of a pent-up and mysterious frenzy, woke me up in a bewildered wonder. It was cut short all at once, and the low droning went on with an effect of audible and soothing silence. I glanced casually into the little cabin. A light was burning within, but Mr. Kurtz was not there.

"I think I would have raised an outcry if I had believed my eyes. But I didn't believe them at first — the thing seemed so impossible. The fact is I was completely unnerved by a sheer blank fright, pure abstract terror, unconnected with any distinct shape of physical danger. What made this emotion so overpowering was — how shall I define it? — the moral shock I received, as if something altogether monstrous, intolerable to thought and odious to the soul, had been thrust upon me unexpectedly. This lasted of course the merest fraction of a second, and then the usual sense of commonplace, deadly danger, the possibility of a sudden onslaught and massacre, or something of the kind, which I saw impending, was positively welcome and composing. It pacified me, in fact, so much, that I did not raise an alarm.

"There was an agent buttoned up inside an ulster and sleeping on a chair on deck within three feet of me. The yells had not awakened him; he snored very slightly; I left him to his slumbers and leaped ashore. I did not betray Mr. Kurtz — it was ordered I should never betray him — it was written I should be loyal to the nightmare of my choice. I was anxious to deal with this shadow by myself alone, — and to this day I don't know why I was so jealous of sharing with any one the peculiar blackness of that experience.

"As soon as I got on the bank I saw a trail — a broad trail through the grass. I remember the exultation with which I said to myself, 'He can't walk — he is crawling on all-fours — I've got him.' The grass was wet with dew. I strode rapidly with clenched fists. I fancy I had some vague notion of falling upon him and giving him a drubbing. I don't know. I had some imbecile thoughts. The knitting old woman with the cat obtruded herself upon my memory as a most improper person to be sitting at the other end of such an affair. I saw a row of pilgrims squirting lead in the air out of Winchesters held to the hip. I thought I would never get back to the steamer, and imagined myself living alone and unarmed in the woods to an advanced age. Such silly things — you know. And I remember I confounded the beat of the drum with the beating of my heart, and was pleased at its calm regularity.

"I kept to the track though — then stopped to listen. The night was very clear; a dark blue space, sparkling with dew and starlight, in which black things stood very still. I thought I could see a kind of motion ahead of me. I was strangely cocksure of everything that night. I actually left the track and ran in a wide semicircle (I verily believe chuckling to myself) so as to get in front of that stir, of that motion I had seen — if indeed I had seen anything. I was circumventing Kurtz as though it had been a boyish game.

"I came upon him, and, if he had not heard me coming, I would have fallen over him, too, but he got up in time. He rose, unsteady, long, pale, indistinct, like a vapour exhaled by the earth, and swayed slightly, misty and silent before me; while at my back the fires loomed between the trees, and the murmur of many voices issued from the forest. I had cut him off cleverly; but when actually confronting him I seemed to come to my senses, I saw the danger in its right proportion. It was by no means over yet. Suppose he began to shout? Though he could hardly stand, there was still plenty of vigour in his voice. 'Go away — hide yourself,' he said, in that profound tone. It was very awful. I glanced back. We were within thirty yards from the nearest fire. A black figure stood up, strode on long black legs, waving long black arms, across the glow. It had horns — antelope horns, I think — on its head. Some sorcerer, some witch-man, no doubt: it looked fiend-like enough. 'Do you know what you are doing?' I whispered. 'Perfectly,' he answered, raising his voice for that single word: it sounded to me far off and yet loud, like a hail through a speaking-trumpet. If he makes a row we are lost, I thought to myself. This clearly was not a case for fisticuffs, even apart from the very natural aversion I had to beat that Shadow — this wandering and tormented thing. 'You will be lost,' I said — 'utterly lost.' One gets sometimes such a flash of inspiration, you know. I did say the right thing, though indeed he could not have been more irretrievably lost than he was at this very moment, when the foundations of our intimacy were being laid — to endure — to endure — even to the end — even beyond.

"'I had immense plans,' he muttered irresolutely. 'Yes,' said I; 'but if you try to shout I'll smash your head with——' There was not a stick or a stone near. 'I will throttle you for good,' I corrected myself. 'I was on the threshold of great things,' he pleaded, in a voice of longing, with a wistfulness of tone that made my blood run cold. 'And now for this stupid scoundrel——' 'Your success in Europe is assured in any case,' I affirmed, steadily. I did not want to have the throttling of him, you understand — and indeed it would have been very little use for any practical purpose. I tried to break the spell — the heavy, mute spell of the wilderness — that seemed to draw him to its pitiless breast by the awakening of forgotten and brutal instincts, by the memory of gratified and monstrous passions. This alone, I was convinced, had driven him out to the edge of the forest, to the bush, towards the gleam of fires, the throb of drums, the drone of weird incantations; this alone had beguiled his unlawful soul beyond the bounds of permitted aspirations. And, don't you see, the terror of the position was not in being knocked on the head — though I had a very lively sense of that danger, too — but in this, that I had to deal with a being to whom I could not appeal in the name of anything high or low. I had, even like the niggers, to invoke him — himself — his own exalted and incredible degradation. There was nothing either above or below him, and I knew it. He had kicked himself loose of the earth. Confound the man! he had kicked the very earth to pieces. He was alone, and I before him did not know whether I stood on the ground or floated in the air. I've been telling you what we said — repeating the phrases we pronounced — but what's the good? They were common everyday words — the familiar, vague sounds exchanged on every waking day of life. But what of that? They had behind them, to my mind, the terrific suggestiveness of words heard in dreams, of phrases spoken in nightmares. Soul! If anybody had ever struggled with a soul, I am the man. And I wasn't arguing with a lunatic either. Believe me or not, his intelligence was perfectly clear — concentrated, it is true, upon himself with horrible intensity, yet clear; and therein was my only chance — barring, of course, the killing him there and then, which wasn't so good, on account of unavoidable noise. But his soul was mad. Being alone in the wilderness, it had looked within itself, and, by heavens! I tell you, it had gone mad. I had — for my sins, I suppose — to go through the ordeal of looking into it myself. No eloquence could have been so withering to one's belief in mankind as his final burst of sincerity. He struggled with himself, too. I saw it, — I heard it. I saw the inconceivable mystery of a soul that knew no restraint, no faith, and no fear, yet struggling blindly with itself. I kept my head pretty well; but when I had him at last stretched on the couch, I wiped my forehead, while my legs shook under me as though I had carried half a ton on my back down that hill. And yet I had only supported him, his bony arm clasped round my neck — and he was not much heavier than a child.

"When next day we left at noon, the crowd, of whose presence behind the curtain of trees I had been acutely conscious all the time, flowed out of the woods again, filled the clearing, covered the slope with a mass of naked, breathing, quivering, bronze bodies. I steamed up a bit, then swung downstream, and two thousand eyes followed the evolutions of the splashing, thumping, fierce river-demon beating the water with its terrible tail and breathing black smoke into the air. In front of the first rank, along the river, three men, plastered with bright red earth from head to foot, strutted to and fro restlessly. When we came abreast again, they faced the river, stamped their feet, nodded their horned heads, swayed their scarlet bodies; they shook towards the fierce river-demon a bunch of black feathers, a mangy skin with a pendent tail — something that looked like a dried gourd; they shouted periodically together strings of amazing words that resembled no sounds of human language; and the deep murmurs of the crowd, interrupted suddenly, were like the responses of some satanic litany.

"We had carried Kurtz into the pilot-house: there was more air there. Lying on the couch, he stared through the open shutter. There was an eddy in the mass of human bodies, and the woman with helmeted head and tawny cheeks rushed out to the very brink of the stream. She put out her hands, shouted something, and all that wild mob took up the shout in a roaring chorus of articulated, rapid, breathless utterance.

"'Do you understand this?' I asked.

"He kept on looking out past me with fiery, longing eyes, with a mingled expression of wistfulness and hate. He made no answer, but I saw a smile, a smile of indefinable meaning, appear on his colourless lips that a moment after twitched convulsively. 'Do I not?' he said slowly, gasping, as if the words had been torn out of him by a supernatural power.

"I pulled the string of the whistle, and I did this because I saw the pilgrims on deck getting out their rifles with an air of anticipating a jolly lark. At the sudden screech there was a movement of abject terror through that wedged mass of bodies. 'Don't! don't you frighten them away,' cried someone on deck disconsolately. I pulled the string time after time. They broke and ran, they leaped, they crouched, they swerved, they dodged the flying terror of the sound. The three red chaps had fallen flat, face down on the shore, as though they had been shot dead. Only the barbarous and superb woman did not so much as flinch, and stretched tragically her bare arms after us over the sombre and glittering river.

"And then that imbecile crowd down on the deck started their little fun, and I could see nothing more for smoke.

"The brown current ran swiftly out of the heart of darkness, bearing us down towards the sea with twice the speed of our upward progress; and Kurtz's life was running swiftly, too, ebbing, ebbing out of his heart into the sea of inexorable time. The manager was very placid, he had no vital anxieties now, he took us both in with a comprehensive and satisfied glance: the 'affair' had come off as well as could be wished. I saw the time approaching when I would be left alone of the party of 'unsound method.' The pilgrims looked upon me with disfavour. I was, so to speak, numbered with the dead. It is strange how I accepted this unforeseen partnership, this choice of nightmares forced upon me in the tenebrous land invaded by these mean and greedy phantoms.

"Kurtz discoursed. A voice! a voice! It rang deep to the very last. It survived his strength to hide in the magnificent folds of eloquence the barren darkness of his heart. Oh, he struggled! he struggled! The wastes of his weary brain were haunted by shadowy images now — images of wealth and fame revolving obsequiously round his unextinguishable gift of noble and lofty expression. My Intended, my station, my career, my ideas — these were the subjects for the occasional utterances of elevated sentiments. The shade of the original Kurtz frequented the bedside of the hollow sham, whose fate it was to be buried presently in the mould of primeval earth. But both the diabolic love and the unearthly hate of the mysteries it had penetrated fought for the possession of that soul satiated with primitive emotions, avid of lying fame, of sham distinction, of all the appearances of success and power.

"Sometimes he was contemptibly childish. He desired to have kings meet him at railway-stations on his return from some ghastly Nowhere, where he intended to accomplish great things. 'You show them you have in you something that is really profitable, and then there will be no limits to the recognition of your ability,' he would say. 'Of course you must take care of the motives — right motives — always.' The long reaches that were like one and the same reach, monotonous bends that were exactly alike, slipped past the steamer with their multitude of secular[23] trees looking patiently after this grimy fragment of another world, the forerunner of change, of conquest, of trade, of massacres, of blessings. I looked ahead — piloting. 'Close the shutter,' said Kurtz suddenly one day; 'I can't bear to look at this.' I did so. There was a silence. 'Oh, but I will wring your heart yet!' he cried at the invisible wilderness.

"We broke down — as I had expected — and had to lie up for repairs at the head of an island. This delay was the first thing that shook Kurtz's confidence. One morning he gave me a packet of papers and a photograph — the lot tied together with a shoe-string. 'Keep this for me,' he said. 'This noxious fool' (meaning the manager) 'is capable of prying into my boxes

---

[23] Age-old.

when I am not looking.' In the afternoon I saw him. He was lying on his back with closed eyes, and I withdrew quietly, but I heard him mutter, 'Live rightly, die, die ... ' I listened. There was nothing more. Was he rehearsing some speech in his sleep, or was it a fragment of a phrase from some newspaper article? He had been writing for the papers and meant to do so again, 'for the furthering of my ideas. It's a duty.'

"His was an impenetrable darkness. I looked at him as you peer down at a man who is lying at the bottom of a precipice where the sun never shines. But I had not much time to give him, because I was helping the engine-driver to take to pieces the leaky cylinders, to straighten a bent connecting-rod, and in other such matters. I lived in an infernal mess of rust, filings, nuts, bolts, spanners, hammers, ratchet-drills — things I abominate, because I don't get on with them. I tended the little forge we fortunately had aboard; I toiled wearily in a wretched scrap-heap — unless I had the shakes too bad to stand.

"One evening coming in with a candle, I was startled to hear him say a little tremulously, 'I am lying here in the dark waiting for death.' The light was within a foot of his eyes. I forced myself to murmur, 'Oh, nonsense!' and stood over him as if transfixed.

"Anything approaching the change that came over his features I have never seen before, and hope never to see again. Oh, I wasn't touched. I was fascinated. It was as though a veil had been rent. I saw on that ivory face the expression of sombre pride, of ruthless power, of craven terror — of an intense and hopeless despair. Did he live his life again in every detail of desire, temptation, and surrender during that supreme moment of complete knowledge? He cried in a whisper at some image, at some vision — he cried out twice, a cry that was no more than a breath —

"'The horror! The horror!'

"I blew the candle out and left the cabin. The pilgrims were dining in the mess-room, and I took my place opposite the manager, who lifted his eyes to give me a questioning glance, which I successfully ignored. He leaned back, serene, with that peculiar smile of his sealing the unexpressed depths of his meanness. A continuous shower of small flies streamed upon the lamp, upon the cloth, upon our hands and faces. Suddenly the manager's boy put his insolent black head in the doorway, and said in a tone of scathing contempt —

"'Mistah Kurtz — he dead.'

"All the pilgrims rushed out to see. I remained, and went on with my dinner. I believe I was considered brutally callous. However, I did not eat much. There was a lamp in there — light, don't you know — and outside it was so beastly, beastly dark. I went no more near the remarkable man who had pronounced a judgment upon the adventures of his soul on this earth. The voice was gone. What else had been there? But I am of course aware that next day the pilgrims buried something in a muddy hole.

"And then they very nearly buried me.

"However, as you see, I did not go to join Kurtz there and then. I did not. I remained to dream the nightmare out to the end, and to show my loyalty to Kurtz once more. Destiny. My destiny! Droll thing life is — that mysterious arrangement of merciless logic for a futile purpose. The most you can hope from it is some knowledge of yourself — that comes too late — a crop of unextinguishable regrets. I have wrestled with death. It is the most unexciting contest you can imagine. It takes place in an impalpable grayness, with nothing underfoot, with nothing around, without spectators, without clamour, without glory, without the great desire of victory, without the great fear of defeat, in a sickly atmosphere of tepid scepticism, without much belief in your own right, and still less in that of your adversary. If such is the form of ultimate wisdom, then life is a greater riddle than some of us think it to be. I was within a hair's-breadth of the last opportunity for pronouncement, and I found with humiliation that probably I would have nothing to say. This is the reason why I affirm that Kurtz was a remarkable man. He had something to say. He said it. Since I had peeped over the edge myself, I understand better the meaning of his stare, that could not see the flame of the candle, but was wide enough to embrace the whole universe, piercing enough to penetrate all the hearts that beat in the darkness. He had summed up — he had judged. 'The horror!' He was a remarkable man. After all, this was the expression of some sort of belief; it had candour, it had conviction, it had a vibrating note of revolt in its whisper, it had the appalling face of a glimpsed truth — the strange commingling of desire and hate. And it is not my own extremity I remember best — a vision of grayness without form filled with physical pain, and a careless contempt for the evanescence of all things — even of this pain itself. No! It is his extremity that I seem to have lived through. True, he had made that last stride, he had stepped over the edge, while I had been permitted to draw back my hesitating foot. And perhaps in this is the whole difference; perhaps all the wisdom, and all truth, and all sincerity, are just compressed into that inappreciable moment of time in which we step over the threshold of the invisible. Perhaps! I like to think my summing-up would not have been a word of careless contempt. Better his cry — much better. It was an affirmation, a moral victory paid for by innumerable defeats, by abominable terrors, by abominable satisfactions. But it was a victory! That is why I have remained loyal to Kurtz to the last, and even beyond, when a long time after I heard once more, not his own voice, but the echo of his magnificent eloquence thrown to me from a soul as translucently pure as a cliff of crystal.

"No, they did not bury me, though there is a period of time which I remember mistily, with a shuddering wonder, like a passage through some inconceivable world that had no hope in it and no desire. I found myself back in the sepulchral city resenting the sight of people hurrying through the streets to filch a little money from each other, to devour their infamous cookery, to gulp their unwholesome beer, to dream their insignificant and silly dreams. They trespassed upon my thoughts. They were intruders whose knowledge of life was to me an irritating pretence, because I felt so sure they could not possibly know the things I knew. Their bearing, which was simply the bearing of commonplace individuals going about their business in the assurance of perfect safety, was offensive to me like the outrageous flauntings of folly in the face of a danger it is unable to comprehend. I had no particular desire to enlighten them, but I had some difficulty in restraining myself from laughing in their faces, so full of stupid importance. I daresay I was not very well at that time. I tottered about the streets — there were various affairs to settle — grinning bitterly at perfectly respectable persons. I admit my behaviour was inexcusable, but then my temperature was seldom normal in these days. My dear aunt's endeavours to 'nurse up my strength' seemed altogether beside the mark. It was not my strength that wanted nursing, it was my imagination that wanted soothing. I kept the bundle of papers given me by Kurtz, not knowing exactly what to do with it. His mother had died lately, watched over, as I was told, by his Intended. A clean-shaved man, with an official manner and wearing gold-rimmed spectacles, called on me one day and made inquiries, at first circuitous, afterwards suavely pressing, about what he was pleased to denominate certain 'documents.' I was not surprised, because I had had two rows with the manager on the subject out there. I had refused to give up the smallest scrap out of that package, and I took the same attitude with the spectacled man. He became darkly menacing at last, and with much heat argued that the Company had the right to every bit of information about its 'territories.' And said he, 'Mr. Kurtz's knowledge of unexplored regions must have been necessarily extensive and peculiar — owing to his great abilities and to the deplorable circumstances in which he had been placed: therefore——,' I assured him Mr. Kurtz's knowledge, however extensive, did not bear upon the problems of commerce or administration. He invoked then the name of science. 'It would be an incalculable loss if,' etc., etc. I offered him the report on the 'Suppression of Savage Customs,' with the postscriptum torn off. He took it up eagerly, but ended by sniffing at it with an air of contempt. 'This is not what we had a right to expect,' he remarked. 'Expect nothing else,' I said. 'There are only private letters.' He withdrew upon some threat of legal proceedings, and I saw him no more; but another fellow, calling himself Kurtz's cousin, appeared two days later, and was anxious to hear all the details about his dear relative's last moments. Incidentally he gave me to understand that Kurtz had been essentially a great musician. 'There was the making of an immense success,' said the man, who was an organist, I believe, with lank gray hair flowing over a greasy coat-collar. I had no reason to doubt his statement; and to this day I am unable to say what was Kurtz's profession, whether he ever had any — which was the greatest of his talents. I had taken him for a painter who wrote for the papers, or else for a journalist who could paint — but even the cousin (who took snuff during the interview) could not tell me what he had been — exactly. He was a universal genius — on that point I agreed with the old chap, who thereupon blew his nose noisily into a large cotton handkerchief and withdrew in senile agitation, bearing off some family letters and memoranda without importance. Ultimately a journalist anxious to know something of the fate of his 'dear colleague' turned up. This visitor informed me Kurtz's proper sphere ought to have been politics 'on the popular side.' He had furry straight eyebrows, bristly hair cropped short, an eye-glass on a broad ribbon, and, becoming expansive, confessed his opinion that Kurtz really couldn't write a bit — 'but heavens! how that man could talk. He electrified large meetings. He had faith — don't you see? — he had the faith. He could get himself to believe anything — anything. He would have been a splendid leader of an extreme party.' 'What party?' I asked. 'Any party,' answered the other. 'He was an — an — extremist.' Did I not think so? I assented. Did I know, he asked, with a sudden flash of curiosity, 'what it was that had induced him to go out there?' 'Yes,' said I, and forthwith handed him the famous Report for publication, if he thought fit. He glanced through it hurriedly, mumbling all the time, judged 'it would do,' and took himself off with this plunder.

"Thus I was left at last with a slim packet of letters and the girl's portrait. She struck me as beautiful — I mean she had a beautiful expression. I know that the sunlight can be made to lie, too, yet one felt that no manipulation of light and pose could have conveyed the delicate shade of truthfulness upon those features. She seemed ready to listen without mental reservation, without suspicion, without a thought for herself. I concluded I would go and give her back her portrait and those letters myself. Curiosity? Yes; and also some other feeling perhaps. All that had been Kurtz's had passed out of my hands: his soul, his body, his station, his plans, his ivory, his career. There remained only his memory and his Intended — and I wanted to give that up, too, to the past, in a way — to surrender personally all that remained of him with me to that oblivion which is the last word of our common fate. I don't defend myself. I had no clear perception of what it was I really wanted. Perhaps it was an impulse of unconscious loyalty, or the fulfilment of one of these ironic necessities that lurk in the facts of human existence. I don't know. I can't tell. But I went.

"I thought his memory was like the other memories of the dead that accumulate in every man's life — a vague impress on the brain of shadows that had fallen on it in their swift and final passage; but before the high and ponderous door, between the tall houses of a street as still and decorous as a well-kept alley in a cemetery, I had a vision of him on the stretcher, opening his mouth voraciously, as if to devour all the earth with all its mankind. He lived then before me; he lived as much as he had ever lived — a shadow insatiable of splendid appearances, of frightful realities; a shadow darker than the shadow of the night, and draped nobly in the folds of a gorgeous eloquence. The vision seemed to enter the house with me — the stretcher, the phantom-bearers, the wild crowd of obedient worshippers, the gloom of the forests, the glitter of the reach between the murky bends, the beat of the drum, regular and muffled like the beating of a heart — the heart of a conquering darkness. It was a moment of triumph for the wilderness, an invading and vengeful rush which, it seemed to me, I would have to keep back alone for the salvation of another soul. And the memory of what I had heard him say afar there, with the horned shapes stirring at my back, in the glow of fires, within the patient woods, those broken phrases came back to me, were heard again in their ominous and terrifying simplicity. I remembered his abject pleading, his abject threats, the colossal scale of his vile desires, the meanness, the torment, the tempestuous anguish of his soul. And later on I seemed to see his collected languid manner, when he said one day, 'This lot of ivory now is really mine. The Company did not pay for it. I collected it myself at a very great personal risk. I am afraid they will try to claim it as theirs though. H'm. It is a difficult case. What do you think I ought to do — resist? Eh? I want no more than justice.' ... He wanted no more than justice — no more than justice. I rang the bell before a mahogany door on the first floor, and while I waited he seemed to stare at me out of the glassy panel — stare with that wide and immense stare embracing, condemning, loathing all the universe. I seemed to hear the whispered cry, 'The horror! The horror!'

"The dusk was falling. I had to wait in a lofty drawing-room with three long windows from floor to ceiling that were like three luminous and bedraped columns. The bent gilt legs and backs of the furniture shone in indistinct curves. The tall marble fireplace had a cold and monumental whiteness. A grand piano stood massively in a corner; with dark gleams on the flat surfaces like a sombre and polished sarcophagus. A high door opened — closed. I rose.

"She came forward, all in black, with a pale head, floating towards me in the dusk. She was in mourning. It was more than a year since his death, more than a year since the news came; she seemed as though she would remember and mourn for ever. She took both my hands in hers and murmured, 'I had heard you were coming.' I noticed she was not very young — I mean not girlish. She had a mature capacity for fidelity, for belief, for suffering. The room seemed to have grown darker, as if all the sad light of the cloudy evening had taken refuge on her forehead. This fair hair, this pale visage, this pure brow, seemed surrounded by an ashy halo from which the dark eyes looked out at me. Their glance was guileless, profound, confident, and trustful. She carried her sorrowful head as though she were proud of that sorrow, as though she would say, I — I alone know how to mourn for him as he deserves. But while we were still shaking hands, such a look of awful desolation came upon her face that I perceived she was one of those creatures that are not the playthings of Time. For her he had died only yesterday. And, by Jove! the impression was so powerful that for me, too, he seemed to have died only yesterday — nay, this very minute. I saw her and him in the same instant of time — his death and her sorrow — I saw her sorrow in the very moment of his death. Do you understand? I saw them together — I heard them together. She had said, with a deep catch of the breath, 'I have survived' while my strained ears seemed to hear distinctly, mingled with her tone of despairing regret, the summing up whisper of his eternal condemnation. I asked myself what I was doing there, with a sensation of panic in my heart as though I had blundered into a place of cruel and absurd mysteries not fit for a human being to behold. She motioned me to a chair. We sat down. I laid the packet gently on the little table, and she put her hand over it. ... 'You knew him well,' she murmured, after a moment of mourning silence.

"'Intimacy grows quickly out there,' I said. 'I knew him as well as it is possible for one man to know another.'

"'And you admired him,' she said. 'It was impossible to know him and not to admire him. Was it?'

"'He was a remarkable man,' I said, unsteadily. Then before the appealing fixity of her gaze, that seemed to watch for more words on my lips, I went on, 'It was impossible not to——'

"'Love him,' she finished eagerly, silencing me into an appalled dumbness. 'How true! how true! But when you think that no one knew him so well as I! I had all his noble confidence. I knew him best.'

"'You knew him best,' I repeated. And perhaps she did. But with every word spoken the room was growing darker, and only her forehead, smooth and white, remained illumined by the unextinguishable light of belief and love.

"'You were his friend,' she went on. 'His friend,' she repeated, a little louder. 'You must have been, if he had given you this, and sent you to me. I feel I can speak to you — and oh! I must speak. I want you — you who have heard his last words — to know I have been worthy of him. ... It is not pride. ... Yes! I am proud to know I understood him better than any one on earth — he told me so himself. And since his mother died I have had no one — no one — to — to——'

"I listened. The darkness deepened. I was not even sure whether he had given me the right bundle. I rather suspect he wanted me to take care of another batch of his papers which, after his death, I saw the manager examining under the lamp. And the girl talked, easing her pain in the certitude of my sympathy; she talked as thirsty men drink. I had heard that her engagement with Kurtz had been disapproved by her people. He wasn't rich enough or something. And indeed I don't know whether he had not been a pauper all his life. He had given me some reason to infer that it was his impatience of comparative poverty that drove him out there.

"'... Who was not his friend who had heard him speak once?' she was saying. 'He drew men towards him by what was best in them.' She looked at me with intensity. 'It is the gift of the great,' she went on, and the sound of her low voice seemed to have the accompaniment of all the other sounds, full of mystery, desolation, and sorrow, I had ever heard — the ripple of the river, the soughing of the trees swayed by the wind, the murmurs of the crowds, the faint ring of incomprehensible words cried from afar, the whisper of a voice speaking from beyond the threshold of an eternal darkness. 'But you have heard him! You know!' she cried.

"'Yes, I know,' I said with something like despair in my heart, but bowing my head before the faith that was in her, before that great and saving illusion that shone with an unearthly glow in the darkness, in the triumphant darkness from which I could not have defended her — from which I could not even defend myself.

"'What a loss to me — to us!' — she corrected herself with beautiful generosity; then added in a murmur, 'To the world.' By the last gleams of twilight I could see the glitter of her eyes, full of tears — of tears that would not fall.

"'I have been very happy — very fortunate — very proud,' she went on. 'Too fortunate. Too happy for a little while. And now I am unhappy for — for life.'

"She stood up; her fair hair seemed to catch all the remaining light in a glimmer of gold. I rose, too.

"'And of all this,' she went on, mournfully, 'of all his promise, and of all his greatness, of his generous mind, of his noble heart, nothing remains — nothing but a memory. You and I——'

"'We shall always remember him,' I said, hastily.

"'No!' she cried. 'It is impossible that all this should be lost — that such a life should be sacrificed to leave nothing — but sorrow. You know what vast plans he had. I knew of them, too — I could not perhaps understand — but others knew of them. Something must remain. His words, at least, have not died.'

"'His words will remain,' I said.

"'And his example,' she whispered to herself. 'Men looked up to him — his goodness shone in every act. His example — '

"'True,' I said; 'his example, too. Yes, his example. I forgot that.'

"'But I do not. I cannot — I cannot believe — not yet. I cannot believe that I shall never see him again, that nobody will see him again, never, never, never.'

"She put out her arms as if after a retreating figure, stretching them black and with clasped pale hands across the fading and narrow sheen of the window. Never see him! I saw him clearly enough then. I shall see this eloquent phantom as long as I live, and I shall see her, too, a tragic and familiar Shade, resembling in this gesture another one, tragic also, and bedecked with powerless charms, stretching bare brown arms over the glitter of the infernal stream, the stream of darkness. She said suddenly very low, 'He died as he lived.'

"'His end,' said I, with dull anger stirring in me, 'was in every way worthy of his life.'

"'And I was not with him,' she murmured. My anger subsided before a feeling of infinite pity.

"'Everything that could be done——' I mumbled.

"'Ah, but I believed in him more than any one on earth — more than his own mother, more than — himself. He needed me! Me! I would have treasured every sigh, every word, every sign, every glance.'

"I felt like a chill grip on my chest. 'Don't,' I said, in a muffled voice.

"'Forgive me. I — I — have mourned so long in silence — in silence. ... You were with him — to the last? I think of his loneliness. Nobody near to understand him as I would have understood. Perhaps no one to hear. ...'

"'To the very end,' I said, shakily. 'I heard his very last words. ..." I stopped in a fright.

"'Repeat them,' she murmured in a heart-broken tone. 'I want — I want — something — something — to — to live with.'

"I was on the point of crying at her, 'Don't you hear them?' The dusk was repeating them in a persistent whisper all around us, in a whisper that seemed to swell menacingly like the first whisper of a rising wind. 'The horror! the horror!'

"'His last word — to live with,' she insisted. 'Don't you understand I loved him — I loved him — I loved him!'

"I pulled myself together and spoke slowly.

"'The last word he pronounced was — your name.'

"I heard a light sigh and then my heart stood still, stopped dead short by an exulting and terrible cry, by the cry of inconceivable triumph and of unspeakable pain. 'I knew it — I was sure!' ... She knew. She was sure. I heard her weeping; she had hidden her face in her hands. It seemed to me that the house would collapse before I could escape, that the heavens would fall upon my head. But nothing happened. The heavens do not fall for such a trifle. Would they have fallen, I wonder, if I had rendered Kurtz that justice which was his due? Hadn't he said he wanted only justice? But I couldn't. I could not tell her. It would have been too dark — too dark altogether. ..."

Marlow ceased, and sat apart, indistinct and silent, in the pose of a meditating Buddha. Nobody moved for a time. "We have lost the first of the ebb," said the Director, suddenly. I raised my head. The offing was barred by a black bank of clouds, and the tranquil waterway leading to the uttermost ends of the earth flowed sombre under an overcast sky — seemed to lead into the heart of an immense darkness.

QUESTIONS

1. Is this story about Marlow or about Kurtz? List the reasons for your answer. List the arguments against your position.

2. Marlow changes in the course of the story. Trace the major steps in his transformation. What causes them?

3. The Kurtz we come to know is not the Kurtz who first came to Africa. How has he changed? What has changed him?

4. Is the ivory symbolic of something more than a natural resource to be exploited? What effect does it have on the main characters?

5. Some readers think Conrad is commenting on colonialism. What evidence supports this contention?

6. At the Inner Station, Marlow finds that Kurtz is treated as a god and that "unspeakable rites ... were offered up to him." Has Kurtz "gone native," or has he become a human devil?

7. Which minor characters do most to move the plot forward? Which do most to give us insights into Kurtz? into Marlow?

8. What is the significance of Kurtz's last words, "The horror! The horror!"? What has Kurtz recognized? Is his recognition of it a sign of redemption?

9. How would you define the "immense darkness" with which the story ends?

ARTHUR CONAN DOYLE ═══

The Red-Headed League

I had called upon my friend, Mr. Sherlock Holmes, one day in the autumn of last year and found him in deep conversation with a very stout, florid-faced, elderly gentleman with fiery red hair. With an apology for my intrusion, I was about to withdraw when Holmes pulled me abruptly into the room and closed the door behind me.

"You could not possibly have come at a better time, my dear Watson," he said cordially.

"I was afraid that you were engaged."

"So I am. Very much so."

"Then I can wait in the next room."

"Not at all. This gentleman, Mr. Wilson, has been my partner and helper in many of my most successful cases, and I have no doubt that he will be of the utmost use to me in yours also."

The stout gentleman half rose from his chair and gave a bob of greeting, with a quick little questioning glance from his small, fat-encircled eyes.

"Try the settee," said Holmes, relapsing into his armchair and putting his fingertips together, as was his custom when in judicial moods. "I know, my dear Watson, that you share my love of all that is bizarre and outside the conventions and humdrum routine of everyday life. You have shown your relish for it by the enthusiasm which has prompted you to chronicle, and, if you will excuse my saying so, somewhat to embellish so many of my own little adventures."

"Your cases have indeed been of the greatest interest to me," I observed.

"You will remember that I remarked the other day, just before we went into the very simple problem presented by Miss Mary Sutherland, that for strange effects and extraordinary combinations we must go to life itself, which is always far more daring than any effort of the imagination."

"A proposition which I took the liberty of doubting."

"You did, Doctor, but none the less you must come round to my view, for otherwise I shall keep on piling fact upon fact on you until your reason breaks down under them and acknowledges me to be right. Now, Mr. Jabez Wilson here has been good enough to call upon me this morning, and to begin a narrative which promises to be one of the most singular which I have listened to for some time. You have heard me remark that the strangest and most unique things are very often connected not with the larger but with the smaller crimes, and occasionally, indeed, where there is room for doubt whether any positive crime has been committed. As far as I have heard it is impossible for me to say whether the present case is an instance of crime or not, but the course of events is certainly among the most singular that I have ever listened to. Perhaps, Mr. Wilson, you would have the great kindness to recommence your narrative. I ask you not merely because my friend Dr. Watson has not heard the opening part but also because the peculiar nature of the story makes me anxious to have every possible detail from your lips. As a rule, when I have heard some slight indication of the course of events, I am able to guide myself by the thousands of other similar cases which occur to my memory. In the present instance I am forced to admit that the facts are, to the best of my belief, unique."

The portly client puffed out his chest with an appearance of some little pride and pulled a dirty and wrinkled newspaper from the inside pocket of his great-coat. As he glanced down the advertisement column, with his head thrust forward and the paper flattened out upon his knee, I took a good look at the man and endeavoured, after the fashion of my companion, to read the indications which might be presented by his dress or appearance.

I did not gain very much, however, by my inspection. Our visitor bore every mark of being an average commonplace British tradesman, obese, pompous, and slow. He wore rather baggy gray shepherd's check trousers, a not over-clean black frock-coat, unbuttoned in the front, and a drab waistcoat with a heavy brassy Albert chain, and a square pierced bit of metal dangling down as an ornament. A frayed top-hat and a faded brown overcoat with a wrinkled velvet collar lay upon a chair beside him. Altogether, look as I would, there was nothing remarkable about the man save his blazing red head, and the expression of extreme chagrin and discontent upon his features.

Sherlock Holmes's quick eye took in my occupation, and he shook his head with a smile as he noticed my questioning glances. "Beyond the obvious facts that he has at some time done manual labour, that he takes snuff, that he is a Freemason, that he has been in China, and that he has done a considerable amount of writing lately, I can deduce nothing else."

Mr. Jabez Wilson started up in his chair, with his forefinger upon the paper, but his eyes upon my companion.

"How, in the name of good-fortune, did you know all that, Mr. Holmes?" he asked. "How did you know, for example, that I did manual labour? It's as true as gospel, for I began as a ship's carpenter."

"Your hands, my dear sir. Your right hand is quite a size larger than your left. You have worked with it, and the muscles are more developed."

"Well, the snuff, then, and the Freemasonry?"

"I won't insult your intelligence by telling you how I read that, especially as, rather against the strict rules of your order, you use an arc-and-compass breastpin."

"Ah, of course, I forgot that. But the writing?"

"What else can be indicated by that right cuff so very shiny for five inches, and the left one with the smooth patch near the elbow where you rest it upon the desk?"

"Well, but China?"

"The fish that you have tattooed immediately above your right wrist could only have been done in China. I have made a small study of tattoo marks and have even contributed to the literature of the subject. That trick of staining the fishes' scales of a delicate pink is quite peculiar to China. When, in addition, I see a Chinese coin hanging from your watch-chain, the matter becomes even more simple."

Mr. Jabez Wilson laughed heavily. "Well, I never!" said he. "I thought at first that you had done something clever, but I see that there was nothing in it, after all."

"I begin to think, Watson," said Holmes, "that I make a mistake in explaining. '*Omne ignotum pro magnifico,*'[1] you know, and my poor little reputation, such as it is, will suffer shipwreck if I am so candid. Can you not find the advertisement, Mr. Wilson?"

"Yes, I have got it now," he answered with his thick red finger planted halfway down the column. "Here it is. This is what began it all. You just read it for yourself, sir."

I took the paper from him and read as follows:

To the Red-headed League:

On account of the bequest of the late Ezekiah Hopkins, of Lebanon,Pennsylvania, U.S.A., there is now another vacancy open which entitles a member of the League to a salary of £4 a week for purely nominal services. All red-headed men who are sound in body and mind, and above the age of twenty-one years, are eligible. Apply in person on Monday, at eleven o'clock, to Duncan Ross, at the offices of the League, 7 Pope's Court, Fleet Street.

"What on earth does this mean?" I ejaculated after I had twice read over the extraordinary announcement.

Holmes chuckled and wriggled in his chair, as was his habit when in high spirits. "It is a little off the beaten track, isn't it?" said he. "And now, Mr. Wilson, off you go at scratch and tell us all about yourself, your household, and the effect which this advertisement had upon your fortunes. You will first make a note, Doctor, of the paper and the date."

"It is *The Morning Chronicle* of April 27, 1890. Just two months ago."

"Very good. Now, Mr. Wilson?"

"Well, it is just as I have been telling you, Mr. Sherlock Holmes," said Jabez Wilson, mopping his forehead; "I have a small pawnbroker's business at Coburg Square, near the City. It's not a very large affair, and of late years it has not done more than just give me a living. I used to be able to keep two assistants, but now I only keep one; and I would have a job to pay him but that he is willing to come for half wages so as to learn the business."

"What is the name of this obliging youth?" asked Sherlock Holmes.

"His name is Vincent Spaulding, and he's not such a youth, either. It's hard to say his age. I should not wish a smarter assistant, Mr. Holmes; and I know very well that he could better himself and earn twice what I am able to give him. But, after all, if he is satisfied, why should I put ideas in his head?"

"Why, indeed? You seem most fortunate in having an employee who comes under the full market price. It is not a common experience among employers in this age. I don't know that your assistant is not as remarkable as your advertisement."

"Oh, he has his faults, too," said Mr. Wilson. "Never was such a fellow for photography. Snapping away with a camera when he ought to be improving his mind, and then diving down into the cellar like a rabbit into its hole to develop his pictures. That is his main fault, but on the whole he's a good worker. There's no vice in him."

"He is still with you, I presume?"

"Yes, sir. He and a girl of fourteen, who does a bit of simple cooking and keeps the place clean — that's all I have in the house, for I am a widower and never had any family. We live very

---

[1] "Everything unknown passes for something splendid." From Tacitus, *Life of Agricola.*

quietly, sir, the three of us; and we keep a roof over our heads and pay our debts, if we do nothing more.

"The first thing that put us out was that advertisement. Spaulding, he came down into the office just this day eight weeks, with this very paper in his hand, and he says:

"'I wish to the Lord, Mr. Wilson, that I was a red-headed man.'

"'Why that?' I asks.

"'Why,' says he, 'here's another vacancy on the League of the Red-headed Men. It's worth quite a little fortune to any man who gets it, and I understand that there are more vacancies than there are men, so that the trustees are at their wits' end what to do with the money. If my hair would only change colour, here's a nice little crib all ready for me to step into.'

"'Why, what is it, then?' I asked. You see, Mr. Holmes, I am a very stay-at-home man, and as my business came to me instead of my having to go to it, I was often weeks on end without putting my foot over the door-mat. In that way I didn't know much of what was going on outside, and I was always glad of a bit of news.

"'Have you never heard of the League of the Red-headed Men?' he asked with his eyes open.

"'Never.'

"'Why, I wonder at that, for you are eligible yourself for one of the vacancies.'

"'And what are they worth?' I asked.

"'Oh, merely a couple of hundred a year, but the work is slight, and it need not interfere very much with one's other occupations.'

"Well, you can easily think that that made me prick up my ears, for the business has not been over-good for some years, and an extra couple of hundred would have been very handy.

"'Tell me all about it,' said I.

"'Well,' said he, showing me the advertisement, 'you can see for yourself that the League has a vacancy, and there is the address where you should apply for particulars. As far as I can make out, the League was founded by an American millionaire, Ezekiah Hopkins, who was very peculiar in his ways. He was himself red-headed, and he had a great sympathy for all red-headed men; so when he died it was found that he had left his enormous fortune in the hands of trustees, with instructions to apply the interest to the providing of easy berths to men whose hair is of that colour. From all I hear it is splendid pay and very little to do.'

"'But,' said I, 'there would be millions of red-headed men who would apply.'

"'Not so many as you might think,' he answered. 'You see it is really confined to Londoners, and to grown men. This American had started from London when he was young, and he wanted to do the old town a good turn. Then, again, I have heard it is no use your applying if your hair is light red, or dark red, or anything but real bright, blazing, fiery red. Now, if you cared to apply, Mr. Wilson, you would just walk in; but perhaps it would hardly be worth your while to put yourself out of the way for the sake of a few hundred pounds.'

"Now, it is a fact, gentlemen, as you may see for yourselves, that my hair is of a very full and rich tint, so that it seemed to me that if there was to be any competition in the matter I stood as good a chance as any man that I had ever met. Vincent Spaulding seemed to know so much about it that I thought he might prove useful, so I just ordered him to put up the shutters for the day and to come right away with me. He was very willing to have a holiday, so we shut the business up and started off for the address that was given us in the advertisement.

"I never hope to see such a sight as that again, Mr. Holmes. From north, south, east, and west every man who had a shade of red in his hair had tramped into the city to answer the advertisement. Fleet Street was choked with red-headed folk, and Pope's Court looked like a coster's orange barrow. I should not have thought there were so many in the whole country as were brought together by that single advertisement. Every shade of colour they were — straw, lemon, orange, brick, Irish-setter, liver, clay; but, as Spaulding said, there were not many who had the real vivid flame-coloured tint. When I saw how many were waiting, I would have given it up in despair; but Spaulding would not hear of it. How he did it I could not imagine, but he pushed and pulled and butted until he got me through the crowd, and right up to the steps which led to the office. There was a double stream upon the stair, some going up in hope, and some coming back dejected; but we wedged in as well as we could and soon found ourselves in the office."

"Your experience has been a most entertaining one," remarked Holmes as his client paused and refreshed his memory with a huge pinch of snuff. "Pray continue your very interesting statement."

"There was nothing in the office but a couple of wooden chairs and a deal table, behind which sat a small man with a head that was even redder than mine. He said a few words to each candidate as he came up, and then he always managed to find some fault in them which would disqualify them. Getting a vacancy did not seem to be such a very easy matter, after all. However, when our turn came the little man was much more favourable to me than to any of the others, and he closed the door as we entered, so that he might have a private word with us.

"'This is Mr. Jabez Wilson,' said my assistant, 'and he is willing to fill a vacancy in the League.'

"'And he is admirably suited for it,' the other answered. 'He has every requirement. I cannot recall when I have seen anything so fine.' He took a step backward, cocked his head on one side, and gazed at my hair until I felt quite bashful. Then suddenly he plunged forward, wrung my hand, and congratulated me warmly on my success.

"'It would be injustice to hesitate,' said he. 'You will, however, I am sure, excuse me for taking an obvious precaution.' With that he seized my hair in both his hands, and tugged until I yelled with the pain. 'There is water in your eyes,' said he as he released me. 'I perceive that all is as it should be. But we have to be careful, for we have twice been deceived by wigs and once by paint. I could tell you tales of cobbler's wax which would disgust you with human nature.' He stepped over to the window and shouted through it at the top of his voice that the vacancy was filled. A groan of disappointment came up from below, and the folk all trooped away in different directions until there was not a red-head to be seen except my own and that of the manager.

"'My name,' said he, 'is Mr. Duncan Ross, and I am myself one of the pensioners upon the fund left by our noble benefactor. Are you a married man, Mr. Wilson? Have you a family?'

"I answered that I had not.

"His face fell immediately.

"'Dear me!' he said gravely, 'that is very serious indeed! I am sorry to hear you say that. The fund was, of course, for the propagation and spread of the red-heads as well as for their maintenance. It is exceedingly unfortunate that you should be a bachelor.'

"My face lengthened at this, Mr. Holmes, for I thought that I was not to have the vacancy after all; but after thinking it over for a few minutes he said that it would be all right.

"'In the case of another,' said he, 'the objection might be fatal, but we must stretch a point in favour of a man with such a head of hair as yours. When shall you be able to enter upon your new duties?'

"'Well, it is a little awkward, for I have a business already,' said I.

"'Oh, never mind about that, Mr. Wilson!' said Vincent Spaulding. 'I should be able to look after that for you.'

"'What would be the hours?' I asked.

"'Ten to two.'

"Now a pawnbroker's business is mostly done of an evening, Mr. Holmes, especially Thursday and Friday evening, which is just before pay-day; so it would suit me very well to earn a little in the mornings. Besides, I knew that my assistant was a good man, and that he would see to anything that turned up.

"'That would suit me very well,' said I. 'And the pay?'

"'Is £4 a week.'

"'And the work?'

"'Is purely nominal.'

"'What do you call purely nominal?'

"'Well, you have to be in the office, or at least in the building, the whole time. If you leave, you forfeit your whole position forever. The will is very clear upon that point. You don't comply with the conditions if you budge from the office during that time.'

"'It's only four hours a day, and I should not think of leaving,' said I.

"'No excuse will avail,' said Mr. Duncan Ross; 'neither sickness nor business nor anything else. There you must stay, or you lose your billet.'

"'And the work?'

"'Is to copy out the Encyclopædia Britannica. There is the first volume of it in that press. You must find your own ink, pens, and blotting-paper, but we provide this table and chair. Will you be ready to-morrow?'

"'Certainly,' I answered.

"'Then, good-bye, Mr. Jabez Wilson, and let me congratulate you once more on the important position which you have been fortunate enough to gain.' He bowed me out of the room, and I went home with my assistant, hardly knowing what to say or do, I was so pleased at my own good fortune.

"Well, I thought over the matter all day, and by evening I was in low spirits again; for I had quite persuaded myself that the whole affair must be some great hoax or fraud, though what its object might be I could not imagine. It seemed altogether past belief that anyone could make such a will, or that they would pay such a sum for doing anything so simple as copying out the Encyclopædia Britannica. Vincent Spaulding did what he could to cheer me up, but by bedtime I had reasoned myself out of the whole thing. However, in the morning I determined to have a look at it anyhow, so I bought a penny bottle of ink, and with a quill-pen, and seven sheets of foolscap paper, I started off for Pope's Court.

"Well, to my surprise and delight, everything was as right as possible. The table was set out ready for me, and Mr. Duncan Ross was there to see that I got fairly to work. He started me off upon the letter A, and then he left me; but he would drop in from time to time to see that all was right with me. At two o'clock he bade me good-day, complimented me upon the amount that I had written, and locked the door of the office after me.

"This went on day after day, Mr. Holmes, and on Saturday the manager came in and planked down four golden sovereigns for my week's work. It was the same next week, and the same the week after. Every morning I was there at ten, and every afternoon I left at two. By degrees Mr. Duncan Ross took to coming in only once of a morning, and then, after a time, he did not come in at all. Still, of course, I never dared to leave the room for an instant, for I was not sure when he might come, and the billet was such a good one, and suited me so well, that I would not risk the loss of it.

"Eight weeks passed away like this, and I had written about Abbots and Archery and Armour and Architecture and Attica, and hoped with diligence that I might get on to the B's before very long. It cost me something in foolscap, and I had pretty nearly filled a shelf with my writings. And then suddenly the whole business came to an end."

"To an end?"

"Yes, sir. And no later than this morning. I went to my work as usual at ten o'clock, but the door was shut and locked, with a little square of card-board hammered on to the middle of the panel with a tack. Here it is, and you can read for yourself."

He held up a piece of white card-board about the size of a sheet of note-paper. It read in this fashion:

THE RED-HEADED LEAGUE

IS

DISSOLVED.

October 9, 1890.

Sherlock Holmes and I surveyed this curt announcement and the rueful face behind it, until the comical side of the affair so completely overtopped every other consideration that we both burst out into a roar of laughter.

"I cannot see that there is anything very funny," cried our client, flushing up to the roots of his flaming head. "If you can do nothing better than laugh at me, I can go elsewhere."

"No, no," cried Holmes, shoving him back into the chair from which he had half risen. "I really wouldn't miss your case for the world. It is most refreshingly unusual. But there is, if you will excuse my saying so, something just a little funny about it. Pray what steps did you take when you found the card upon the door?"

"I was staggered, sir. I did not know what to do. Then I called at the offices round, but none of them seemed to know anything about it. Finally, I went to the landlord, who is an accountant living on the ground-floor, and I asked him if he could tell me what had become of the Red-headed League. He said that he had never heard of any such body. Then I asked him who Mr. Duncan Ross was. He answered that the name was new to him.

"'Well,' said I, 'the gentleman at No. 4.'

"'What, the red-headed man?'

"'Yes.'

"'Oh,' said he, 'his name was William Morris. He was a solicitor and was using my room as a temporary convenience until his new premises were ready. He moved out yesterday.'

"'Where could I find him?'

"'Oh, at his new offices. He did tell me the address. Yes, 17 King Edward Street, near St. Paul's.'

"I started off, Mr. Holmes, but when I got to that address it was a manufactory of artificial knee-caps, and no one in it had ever heard of either Mr. William Morris or Mr. Duncan Ross."

"And what did you do then?" asked Holmes.

"I went home to Saxe-Coburg Square, and I took the advice of my assistant. But he could not help me in any way. He could only say that if I waited I should hear by post. But that was not quite good enough, Mr. Holmes. I did not wish to lose such a place without a struggle, so, as I had heard that you were good enough to give advice to poor folk who were in need of it, I came right away to you."

"And you did very wisely," said Holmes. "Your case is an exceedingly remarkable one, and I shall be happy to look into it. From what you have told me I think that it is possible that graver issues hang from it than might at first sight appear."

"Grave enough!" said Mr. Jabez Wilson. "Why, I have lost four pound a week."

"As far as you are personally concerned," remarked Holmes, "I do not see that you have any grievance against this extraordinary league. On the contrary, you are, as I understand, richer by some £30, to say nothing of the minute knowledge which you have gained on every subject which comes under the letter A. You have lost nothing by them."

"No, sir. But I want to find out about them, and who they are, and what their object was in playing this prank — if it was a prank — upon me. It was a pretty expensive joke for them, for it cost them two and thirty pounds."

"We shall endeavour to clear up these points for you. And, first, one or two questions, Mr. Wilson. This assistant of yours who first called your attention to the advertisement — how long had he been with you?"

"About a month then."

"How did he come?"

"In answer to an advertisement."

"Was he the only applicant?"

"No, I had a dozen."

"Why did you pick him?"

"Because he was handy and would come cheap."

"At half-wages, in fact."

"Yes."

"What is he like, this Vincent Spaulding?"

"Small, stout-built, very quick in his ways, no hair on his face, though he's not short of thirty. Has a white splash of acid upon his forehead."

Holmes sat up in his chair in considerable excitement. "I thought as much," said he. "Have you ever observed that his ears are pierced for earrings?"

"Yes, sir. He told me that a gypsy had done it for him when he was a lad."

"Hum!" said Holmes, sinking back in deep thought. "He is still with you?"

"Oh, yes, sir; I have only just left him."

"And has your business been attended to in your absence?"

"Nothing to complain of, sir. There's never very much to do of a morning."

"That will do, Mr. Wilson. I shall be happy to give you an opinion upon the subject in the course of a day or two. To-day is Saturday, and I hope that by Monday we may come to a conclusion."

"Well, Watson," said Holmes when our visitor had left us, "what do you make of it all?"

"I make nothing of it," I answered frankly. "It is a most mysterious business."

"As a rule," said Holmes, "the more bizarre a thing is the less mysterious it proves to be. It is your commonplace, featureless crimes which are really puzzling, just as a commonplace face is the most difficult to identify. But I must be prompt over this matter."

"What are you going to do, then?" I asked.

"To smoke," he answered. "It is quite a three pipe problem, and I beg that you won't speak to me for fifty minutes." He curled himself up in his chair, with his thin knes drawn up to his hawk-like nose, and there he sat with his eyes closed and his black clay pipe thrusting out like the bill of some strange bird. I had come to the conclusion that he had dropped asleep, and indeed was nodding myself, when he suddenly sprang out of his chair with the gesture of a man who has made up his mind and put his pipe down upon the mantelpiece.

"Sarasate plays at the St. James's Hall this afternoon," he remarked. "What do you think, Watson? Could your patients spare you for a few hours?"

"I have nothing to do to-day. My practice is never very absorbing."

"Then put on your hat and come. I am going through the City first, and we can have some lunch on the way. I observe that there is a good deal of German music on the programme, which is rather more to my taste than Italian or French. It is introspective, and I want to introspect. Come along!"

We travelled by the Underground as far as Aldersgate; and a short walk took us to Saxe-Coburg Square, the scene of the singular story which we had listened to in the morning. It was a poky, little, shabby-genteel place, where four lines of dingy two-storied brick houses looked out into a small railed-in enclosure, where a lawn of weedy grass and a few clumps of faded laurel-bushes made a hard fight against a smoke-laden and uncongenial atmosphere. Three gilt balls and a brown board with "JABEZ WILSON" in white letters, upon a corner house, announced the place where our red-headed client carried on his business. Sherlock Holmes stopped in front of it with his head on one side and looked it all over, with his eyes shining brightly between puckered lids. Then he walked slowly up the street, and then down again to the corner, still looking keenly at the houses. Finally he returned to the pawnbroker's, and, having thumped vigorously upon the pavement with his stick two or three times, he went up to the door and knocked. It was instantly opened by a bright-looking, clean-shaven young fellow, who asked him to step in.

"Thank you," said Holmes, "I only wished to ask you how you would go from here to the Strand."

"Third right, fourth left," answered the assistant promptly, closing the door.

"Smart fellow, that," observed Holmes as we walked away. "He is, in my judgment, the fourth smartest man in London, and for daring I am not sure that he has not a claim to be third. I have known something of him before."

"Evidently," said I, "Mr. Wilson's assistant counts for a good deal in this mystery of the Red-headed League. I am sure that you inquired your way merely in order that you might see him."

"Not him."

"What then?"

"The knees of his trousers."

"And what did you see?"

"What I expected to see."

"Why did you beat the pavement?"

"My dear doctor, this is a time for observation, not for talk. We are spies in an enemy's country. We know something of Saxe-Coburg Square. Let us now explore the parts which lie behind it."

The road in which we found ourselves as we turned round the corner from the retired Saxe-Coburg Square presented as great a contrast to it as the front of a picture does to the back. It was one of the main arteries which conveyed the traffic of the City to the north and west. The roadway was blocked with the immense stream of commerce flowing in a double tide inward and outward, while the footpaths were black with the hurrying swarm of pedestrians. It was difficult to realize as we looked at the line of fine shops and stately business premises that they really abutted on the other side upon the faded and stagnant square which we had just quitted.

"Let me see," said Holmes, standing at the corner and glancing along the line, "I should like just to remember the order of the houses here. It is a hobby of mine to have an exact knowledge of London. There is Mortimer's, the tobacconist, the little newspaper shop, the Coburg branch of the City and Suburban Bank, the Vegetarian Restaurant, and McFarlane's carriage-building depot. That carries us right on to the other block. And now, Doctor, we've done our work, so it's time we had some play. A sandwich and a cup of coffee, and then off to violin-land, where all is sweetness and delicacy and harmony, and there are no red-headed clients to vex us with their conundrums."

My friend was an enthusiastic musician, being himself not only a very capable performer but a composer of no ordinary merit. All the afternoon he sat in the stalls wrapped in the most perfect happiness, gently waving his long, thin fingers in time to the music, while his gently smiling face and his languid, dreamy eyes were as unlike those of Holmes, the sleuth-hound, Holmes the relentless, keen-witted, ready-handed criminal agent, as it was possible to conceive. In his singular character the dual nature alternately asserted itself, and his extreme exactness and astuteness represented, as I have often thought, the reaction against the poetic and contemplative mood which occasionally predominated in him. The swing of his nature took him from extreme languor to devouring energy; and, as I knew well, he was never so truly formidable as when, for days on end, he had been lounging in his armchair amid his improvisations and his black-letter editions. Then it was that the lust of the chase would suddenly come upon him, and that his brilliant reasoning power would rise to the level of intuition, until those who were unacquainted with his methods would look askance at him as on a man whose knowledge was not that of other mortals. When I saw him that afternoon so enwrapped in the music at St. James's Hall I felt that an evil time might be coming upon those whom he had set himself to hunt down.

"You want to go home, no doubt, Doctor," he remarked as we emerged.

"Yes, it would be as well."

"And I have some business to do which will take some hours. This business at Coburg Square is serious."

"Why serious?"

"A considerable crime is in contemplation. I have every reason to believe that we shall be in time to stop it. But to-day being Saturday rather complicates matters. I shall want your help to-night."

"At what time?"

"Ten will be early enough."

"I shall be at Baker Street at ten."

"Very well. And, I say, Doctor, there may be some little danger, so kindly put your army revolver in your pocket." He waved his hand, turned on his heel, and disappeared in an instant among the crowd.

I trust that I am not more dense than my neighbours, but I was always oppressed with a sense of my own stupidity in my dealings with Sherlock Holmes. Here I had heard what he had heard, I had seen what he had seen, and yet from his words it was evident that he saw clearly not only what had happened but what was about to happen, while to me the whole business was still confused and grotesque. As I drove home to my house in Kensington I thought over it all, from the extraordinary story of the red-headed copier of the Encyclopædia down to the visit to Saxe-Coburg Square, and the ominous words with which he had parted from me. What was this nocturnal expedition, and why should I go armed? Where were we going, and what were we to do? I had the hint from Holmes that this smooth-faced pawn-broker's assistant was a formidable man — a man who might play a deep game. I tried to puzzle it out, but gave it up in despair and set the matter aside until night should bring an explanation.

It was a quarter-past nine when I started from home and made my way across the Park, and so through Oxford Street to Baker Street. Two hansoms were standing at the door, and as I entered the passage I heard the sound of voices from above. On entering his room I found Holmes in animated conversation with two men, one of whom I recognized as Peter Jones, the official police agent, while the other was a long, thin, sad-faced man, with a very shiny hat and oppressively respectable frock-coat.

"Ha! our party is complete," said Holmes, buttoning up his pea-jacket and taking his heavy hunting crop from the rack. "Watson, I think you know Mr. Jones, of Scotland Yard? Let me introduce you to Mr. Merryweather, who is to be our companion in to-night's adventure."

"We're hunting in couples again, Doctor, you see," said Jones in his consequential way. "Our friend here is a wonderful man for starting a chase. All he wants is an old dog to help him to do the running down."

"I hope a wild goose may not prove to be the end of our chase," observed Mr. Merryweather gloomily.

"You may place considerable confidence in Mr. Holmes, sir," said the police agent loftily. "He has his own little methods, which are, if he won't mind my saying so, just a little too theoretical and fantastic, but he has the makings of a detective in him. It is not too much to say that once or twice, as in that business of the Sholto murder and the Agra treasure, he has been more nearly correct than the official force."

"Oh, if you say so, Mr. Jones, it is all right," said the stranger with deference. "Still, I confess that I miss my rubber. It is the first Saturday night for seven-and-twenty years that I have not had my rubber."

"I think you will find," said Sherlock Holmes, "that you will play for a higher take to-night than you have ever done yet, and that the play will be more exciting. For you, Mr. Merryweather, the stake will be some £30,000; and for you, Jones, it will be the man upon whom you wish to lay your hands."

"John Clay, the murderer, thief, smasher, and forger. He's a young man, Mr. Merryweather, but he is at the head of his profession, and I would rather have my bracelets on him than on any criminal in London. He's a remarkable man, is young John Clay. His grandfather was a royal duke, and he himself has been to Eton and Oxford. His brain is as cunning as his fingers, and though we meet signs of him at every turn, we never know where to find the man himself. He'll crack a crib in Scotland one week, and be raising money to build an orphanage in Cornwall the next. I've been on his track for years and have never set eyes on him yet."

"I hope that I may have the pleasure of introducing you to-night. I've had one or two little turns also with Mr. John Clay, and I agree with you that he is at the head of his profession. It is past ten, however, and quite time that we started. If you two will take the first hansom, Watson and I will follow in the second."

Sherlock Holmes was not very communicative during the long drive and lay back in the cab humming the tunes which he had heard in the afternoon. We rattled through an endless labyrinth of gas-lit streets until we emerged into Farrington Street.

"We are close there now," my friend remarked. "This fellow Merryweather is a bank director, and personally interested in the matter. I thought it as well to have Jones with us also. He is not a bad fellow, though an absolute imbecile in his profession. He has one positive virtue. He is as brave as a bulldog and as tenacious as a lobster if he gets his claws upon anyone. Here we are, and they are waiting for us."

We had reached the same crowded thoroughfare in which we had found ourselves in the morning. Our cabs were dismissed, and, following the guidance of Mr. Merryweather, we passed down a narrow passage and through a side door, which he opened for us. Within there was a small corridor, which ended in a very massive iron gate. This also was opened, and led down a flight of winding stone steps, which terminated at another formidable gate. Mr. Merryweather stopped to light a lantern, and then conducted us down a dark, earth-smelling passage, and so, after opening a third door, into a huge vault or cellar, which was piled all round with crates and massive boxes.

"You are not very vulnerable from above," Holmes remarked as he held up the lantern and gazed about him.

"Nor from below," said Mr. Merryweather, striking his stick upon the flags which lined the floor. "Why, dear me, it sounds quite hollow!" he remarked, looking up in surprise.

"I must really ask you to be a little more quiet!" said Holmes severely. "You have already imperilled the whole success of our expedition. Might I beg that you would have the goodness to sit down upon one of those boxes, and not to interfere?"

The solemn Mr. Merryweather perched himself upon a crate, with a very injured expression upon his face, while Holmes fell upon his knees upon the floor and, with the lantern and a magnifying lens, began to examine minutely the cracks between the stones. A few seconds sufficed to satisfy him, for he sprang to his feet again and put his glass in his pocket.

"We have at least an hour before us," he remarked, "for they can hardly take any steps until the good pawnbroker is safely in bed. Then they will not lose a minute, for the sooner they do their work the longer time they will have for their escape. We are at present, Doctor — as no doubt you have divined — in the cellar of the City branch of one of the principal London banks. Mr. Merryweather is the chairman of directors, and he will explain to you that there are reasons why the more daring criminals of London should take a considerable interest in this cellar at present."

"It is our French gold," whispered the director. "We have had several warnings that an attempt might be made upon it."

"Your French gold?"

"Yes. We had occasion some months ago to strengthen our resources and borrowed for that purpose 30,000 napoleons from the Bank of France. It has become known that we have never had occasion to unpack the money, and that it is still lying in our cellar. The crate upon which I sit contains 2,000 napoleons packed between layers of lead foil. Our reserve of bullion is much larger at present than is usually kept in a single branch office, and the directors have had misgivings upon the subject."

"Which were very well justified," observed Holmes. "And now it is time that we arranged our little plans. I expect that within an hour matters will come to a head. In the meantime, Mr. Merryweather, we must put the screen over that dark lantern."

"And sit in the dark?"

"I am afraid so. I had brought a pack of cards in my pocket, and I thought that, as we were a *partie carrée*,[2] you might have your rubber after all. But I see that the enemy's preparations have gone so far that we cannot risk the presence of a light. And, first of all, we must choose our positions. These are daring men, and though we shall take them at a disadvantage, they may do us some harm unless we are careful. I shall stand behind this crate, and do you conceal yourselves behind those. Then, when I flash a light upon them, close in swiftly. If they fire, Watson, have no compunction about shooting them down."

I placed my revolver, cocked, upon the top of the wooden case behind which I crouched. Holmes shot the slide across the front of his lantern and left us in pitch darkness — such an absolute darkness as I have never before experienced. The smell of hot metal remained to assure us that the light was still there, ready to flash out at a moment's notice. To me, with my nerves worked up to a pitch of expectancy, there was something depressing and subduing in the sudden gloom, and in the cold dank air of the vault.

"They have but one retreat," whispered Holmes. "That is back through the house into Saxe-Coburg Square. I hope that you have done what I asked you, Jones?"

"I have an inspector and two officers waiting at the front door."

"Then we have stopped all the holes. And now we must be silent and wait."

---

[2] A foursome.

What a time it seemed! From comparing notes afterwards it was but an hour and a quarter, yet it appeared to me that the night must have almost gone, and the dawn be breaking above us. My limbs were weary and stiff, for I feared to change my position; yet my nerves were worked up to the highest pitch of tension, and my hearing was so acute that I could not only hear the gentle breathing of my companions, but I could distinguish the deeper, heavier in-breath of the bulky Jones from the thin, sighing note of the bank director. From my position I could look over the case in the direction of the floor. Suddenly my eyes caught the glint of a light.

At first it was but a lurid spark upon the stone pavement. Then it lengthened out until it became a yellow line, and then, without any warning or sound, a gash seemed to open and a hand appeared; a white, almost womanly hand, which felt about in the centre of the little area of light. For a minute or more the hand, with its writhing fingers, protruded out of the floor. Then it was withdrawn as suddenly as it appeared, and all was dark again save the single lurid spark which marked a chink between the stones.

Its disappearance, however, was but momentary. With a rending, tearing sound, one of the broad, white stones turned over upon its side and left a square, gaping hole, through which streamed the light of a lantern. Over the edge there peeped a clean-out, boyish face, which looked keenly about it, and then, with a hand on either side of the aperture, drew itself shoulder-high and waist-high, until one knee rested upon the edge. In another instant he stood at the side of the hole and was hauling after him a companion, lithe and small like himself, with a pale face and a shock of very red hair.

"It's all clear," he whispered. "Have you the chisel and the bags? Great Scott! Jump, Archie, jump, and I'll swing for it!"

Sherlock Holmes had sprung out and seized the intruder by the collar. The other dived down the hole, and I heard the sound of rending cloth as Jones clutched at his skirts. The light flashed upon the barrel of a revolver, but Holmes's hunting crop came down on the man's wrist, and the pistol clinked upon the stone floor.

"It's no use, John Clay," said Holmes blandly. "You have no chance at all."

"So I see," the other answered with the utmost coolness. "I fancy that my pal is all right, though I see you have got his coat-tails."

"There are three men waiting for him at the door," said Holmes.

"Oh, indeed! You seem to have done the thing very completely. I must compliment you."

"And I you," Holmes answered. "Your red-headed idea was very new and effective."

"You'll see your pal again presently," said Jones. "He's quicker at climbing down holes than I am. Just hold out while I fix the derbies."

"I beg that you will not touch me with your filthy hands," remarked our prisoner as the handcuffs clattered upon his wrists. "You may not be aware that I have royal blood in my veins. Have the goodness, also, when you address me always to say 'sir' and 'please.'"

"All right," said Jones with a stare and a snigger. "Well, would you please, sir, march upstairs, where we can get a cab to carry your Highness to the police-station?"

"That is better," said John Clay serenely. He made a sweeping bow to the three of us and walked quietly off in the custody of the detective.

"Really, Mr. Holmes," said Mr. Merryweather as we followed them from the cellar, "I do not know how the bank can thank you or repay you. There is no doubt that you have detected and defeated in the most complete manner one of the most determined attempts at bank robbery that have ever come within my experience."

"I have had one or two little scores of my own to settle with Mr. John Clay," said Holmes. "I have been at some small expense over this matter, which I shall expect the bank to refund, but beyond that I am amply repaid by having had an experience which is in many ways unique, and by hearing the very remarkable narrative of the Red-headed League."

"You see, Watson," he explained in the early hours of the morning as we sat over a glass of whisky and soda in Baker Street, "it was perfectly obvious from the first that the only possible object of this rather fantastic business of the advertisement of the League, and the copying of the Encyclopædia, must be to get this not over-bright pawnbroker out of the way for a number of hours every day. It was a curious way of managing it, but, really, it would be difficult to suggest a better. The method was no doubt suggested to Clay's ingenious mind by the colour of his accomplice's hair. The £4 a week was a lure which must draw him, and what was it to them, who were playing for thousands? They put in the advertisement, one rogue has the temporary office, the other rogue incites the man to apply for it, and together they manage to secure his absence every morning in the week. From the time that I heard of the assistant having come for half wages, it was obvious to me that he had some strong motive for securing the situation."

"But how could you guess what the motive was?"

"Had there been women in the house, I should have suspected a mere vulgar intrigue. That, however, was out of the question. The man's business was a small one, and there was nothing in his house which could account for such elaborate preparations, and such an expenditure as they were at. It must, then, be something out of the house. What could it be? I thought of the assistant's fondness for photography, and his trick of vanishing into the cellar. The cellar! There was the end of this tangled clue. Then I made inquiries as to this mysterious assistant and found that I had to deal with one of the coolest and most daring criminals in London. He was doing something in the cellar — something which took many hours a day for months on end. What could it be, once more? I could think of nothing save that he was running a tunnel to some other building.

"So far I had got when we went to visit the scene of action. I surprised you by beating upon the pavement with my stick. I was ascertaining whether the cellar stretched out in front or behind. It was not in front. Then I rang the bell, and, as I hoped, the assistant answered it. We have had some skirmishes, but we had never set eyes upon each other before. I hardly looked at his face. His knees were what I wished to see. You must yourself have remarked how worn, wrinkled, and stained they were. They spoke of those hours of burrowing. The only remaining point was what they were burrowing for. I walked round the corner, saw the City and Suburban Bank abutted on our friend's premises, and felt that I had solved my problem. When you drove home after the concert I called upon Scotland Yard and upon the chairman of the bank directors, with the result that you have seen."

"And how could you tell that they would make their attempt to-night?" I asked.

"Well, when they closed their League offices that was a sign that they cared no longer about Mr. Jabez Wilson's presence — in other words, that they had completed their tunnel. But it was essential that they should use it soon, as it might be discovered, or the bullion might be removed. Saturday would suit them better than any other day, as it would give them two days for their escape. For all these reasons. I expected them to come to-night."

"You reasoned it out beautifully," I exclaimed in unfeigned admiration. "It is so long a chain, and yet every link rings true."

"It saved me from ennui," he answered, yawning. "Alas! I already feel it closing in upon me. My life is spent in one long effort to escape from the commonplaces of existence. These little problems help me to do so."

"And you are a benefactor of the race," said I.

He shrugged his shoulders. "Well, perhaps, after all, it is of some little use," he remarked. "'*L'homme c'est rien — l'œuvre c'est tout,*'[3] as Gustave Flaubert wrote to George Sand."

QUESTIONS

1. Is Jabez Wilson too gullible for belief? Is it gullibility or greed upon which the criminals depend for their plans?

2. What evidence is there in "The Red-Headed League" that Holmes and Watson are continuing characters rather than existing in this story only? Is this information necessary? What purpose does it serve?

3. Do you find the mystery or Sherlock Holmes of greater interest here? What does your answer suggest?

4. Holmes's brilliant deductions about Mr. Wilson's past have nothing to do with the plot. What, then, does this episode contribute to the story?

5. Compare Holmes with Agatha Christie's Poirot. What do they have in common? Are they characterized by the same methods?

6. Is the plot of this story logical and tight? Are any facts left unexplained? Has Conan Doyle played fair with the reader?

---

[3] "The man is nothing — the work is everything."

ANTON CHEKHOV

Gooseberries

Translated by Ivy Litvinov

The sky had been covered with rain-clouds ever since the early morning; it was a still day, cool and dull, one of those misty days when the clouds have long been lowering overhead and you keep thinking it is just going to rain, and the rain holds off. Ivan Ivanich, the veterinary surgeon, and Burkin, the high-school teacher, had walked till they were tired, and the way over the fields seemed endless to them. Far ahead they could just make out the windmill of the village of Mironositskoye, and what looked like a range of low hills at the right extending well beyond the village, and they both knew that this range was really the bank of the river, and that further on were meadows, green willow-trees, country-estates; if they were on top of these hills, they knew they would see the same boundless fields and telegraph-posts, and the train, like a crawling caterpillar in the distance, while in fine weather even the town would be visible. On this still day, when the whole of nature seemed kindly and pensive, Ivan Ivanich and Burkin felt a surge of love for this plain, and thought how vast and beautiful their country was.

"The last time we stayed in Elder Prokofy's hut," said Burkin, "you said you had a story to tell me."

"Yes. I wanted to tell you the story of my brother."

Ivan Ivanich took a deep breath and lighted his pipe as a preliminary to his narrative, but just then the rain came. Five minutes later it was coming down in torrents and nobody could say when it would stop. Ivan Ivanich and Burkin stood still, lost in thought. The dogs, already soaked, stood with drooping tails, gazing at them wistfully.

"We must try and find shelter," said Burkin. "Let's go to Alekhin's. It's quite near."

"Come on, then."

They turned aside and walked straight across the newly reaped field, veering to the right till they came to a road. Very soon poplars, an orchard, and the red roofs of barns came into sight. The surface of a river gleamed, and they had a view of an extensive reach of water, a windmill and a whitewashed bathing-shed. This was Sofyino, where Alekhin lived.

The mill was working, and the noise made by its sails drowned the sound of the rain; the whole dam trembled. Horses, soaking wet, were standing near some carts, their heads drooping, and people were moving about with sacks over their heads and shoulders. It was wet, muddy, bleak, and the water looked cold and sinister. Ivan Ivanich and Burkin were already experiencing the misery of dampness, dirt, physical discomfort, their boots were caked with mud, and when, having passed the mill-dam, they took the upward path to the landowner's barns, they fell silent, as if vexed with one another.

The sound of winnowing came from one of the barns; the door was open, and clouds of dust issued from it. Standing in the door-way was Alekhin himself, a stout man of some forty years, with longish hair, looking more like a professor or an artist than a landed proprietor. He was wearing a white shirt, greatly in need of washing, belted with a piece of string, and long drawers with no trousers over them. His boots, too, were caked with mud and straw. His eyes and nose were ringed with dust. He recognized Ivan Ivanich and Burkin, and seemed glad to see them.

"Go up to the house, gentlemen," he said, smiling. "I'll be with you in a minute."

It was a large two-storey house. Alekhin occupied the ground floor, two rooms with vaulted ceilings and tiny windows, where the stewards had lived formerly. They were poorly furnished, and smelled of rye-bread, cheap vodka, and harness. He hardly ever went into the upstairs rooms, excepting when he had guests. Ivan Ivanich and Burkin were met by a maid-servant, a young woman of such beauty that they stood still involuntarily and exchanged glances.

"You have no idea how glad I am to see you here, dear friends," said Alekhin, overtaking them in the hall. "It's quite a surprise! Pelageya," he said, turning to the maid, "find the gentlemen a change of clothes. And I might as well change, myself. But I must have a wash first, for I don't believe I've had a bath since the spring. Wouldn't you like to go and have a bathe while they get things ready here?"

The beauteous Pelageya, looking very soft and delicate, brought them towels and soap, and Alekhin and his guests set off for the bathing-house.

"Yes, it's a long time since I had a wash," he said, taking off his clothes. "As you see I have a nice bathing-place, my father had it built, but somehow I never seem to get time to wash."

He sat on the step, soaping his long locks and his neck, and all round him the water was brown.

"Yes, you certainly ... " remarked Ivan Ivanich, with a significant glance at his host's head.

"It's a long time since I had a wash ... " repeated Alekhin, somewhat abashed, and he soaped himself again, and now the water was dark-blue, like ink.

Ivan Ivanich emerged from the shed, splashed noisily into the water, and began swimming beneath the rain, spreading his arms wide, making waves all round him, and the white water-lilies rocked on the waves he made. He swam into the very middle of the river and then dived, a moment later came up at another place and swam further, diving constantly, and trying to touch the bottom. "Ah, my God," he kept exclaiming in his enjoyment. "Ah, my God. ... " He swam up to the mill, had a little talk with some peasants there and turned back, but when he got to the middle of the river, he floated, holding his face up to the rain. Burkin and Alekhin were dressed and ready to go, but he went on swimming and diving.

"God! God!" he kept exclaiming. "Dear God!"

"Come out!" Burkin shouted to him.

They went back to the house. And only after the lamp was lit in the great drawing-room on the upper floor, and Burkin and Ivan Ivanich, in silk dressing-gowns and warm slippers, were seated in arm-chairs, while Alekhin, washed and combed, paced the room in his new frock-coat, enjoying the warmth, the cleanliness, his dry clothes and comfortable slippers, while the fair Pelageya, smiling benevolently, stepped noiselessly over the carpet with her tray of tea and preserves, did Ivan Ivanich embark upon his yarn, the ancient dames, young ladies, and military gentlemen looking down at them severely from the gilded frames, as if they, too, were listening.

"There were two of us brothers," he began. "Ivan Ivanich (me), and my brother Nikolai Ivanich, two years younger than myself. I went in for learning and became a veterinary surgeon, but Nikolai started working in a government office when he was only nineteen. Our · father, Chimsha-Himalaisky, was educated in a school for the sons of private soldiers, but was later promoted to officer's rank, and was made a hereditary nobleman and given a small estate. After his death the estate had to be sold for debts, but at least our childhood was passed in the freedom of the countryside, where we roamed the fields and the woods like peasant children, taking the horses to graze, peeling bark from the trunks of lime-trees, fishing, and all that sort of thing. And anyone who has once in his life fished for perch, or watched the thrushes fly south in the autumn, rising high over the village on clear, cool days, is spoilt for town life, and will long for the country-side for the rest of his days. My brother pined in his government office. The years passed and he sat in the same place every day, writing out the same documents and thinking all the time of the same thing — how to get back to the country. And these longings of his gradually turned into a definite desire, into a dream of purchasing a little estate somewhere on the bank of a river or the shore of a lake.

"He was a meek, good-natured chap, I was fond of him, but could feel no sympathy with the desire to lock oneself up for life in an estate of one's own. They say man only needs six feet of earth. But it is a corpse, and not man, which needs these six feet. And now people are actually saying that it is a good sign for our intellectuals to yearn for the land and try to obtain country-dwellings. And yet these estates are nothing but those same six feet of earth. To escape from the town, from the struggle, from the noise of life, to escape and hide one's head on a country-estate, is not life, but egoism, idleness, it is a sort of renunciation, but renunciation without faith. It is not six feet of earth, not a country-estate, that man needs, but the whole globe, the whole of nature, room to display his qualities and the individual characteristics of his soul.

"My brother Nikolai sat at his office-desk, dreaming of eating soup made from his own cabbages, which would spread a delicious smell all over his own yard, of eating out of doors, on the green grass, of sleeping in the sun, sitting for hours on a bench outside his gate, and gazing at the fields and woods. Books on agriculture, and all those hints printed on calendars were his delight, his favourite spiritual nourishment. He was fond of reading newspapers, too, but all he read in them was advertisements of the sale of so many acres of arable and meadowland, with residence attached, a river, an orchard, a mill, and ponds fed by springs. His head was full of visions of garden paths, flowers, fruit, nesting-boxes, carp-ponds, and all that sort of thing. These visions differed according to the advertisements he came across, but for some reason gooseberry bushes invariably figured in them. He could not picture to himself a single estate or picturesque nook that did not have gooseberry bushes in it.

"'Country life has its conveniences,' he would say. 'You sit on the verandah, drinking tea, with your own ducks floating on the pond, and everything smells so nice, and ... and the gooseberries ripen on the bushes.'

"He drew up plans for his estate, and every plan showed the same features: a) the main residence, b) the servant's wing, c) the kitchen-garden, d) gooseberry bushes. He lived thriftily, never ate or drank his fill, dressed anyhow, like a beggar, and saved up all his money in the bank. He became terribly stingy. I could hardly bear to look at him, and whenever I gave him a little money, or sent him a present on some holiday, he put that away, too. Once a man gets an idea into his head, there's no doing anything with him.

"The years passed, he was sent to another gubernia,[1] he was over forty, and was still reading advertisements in the papers, and saving up. At last I heard he had married. All for the same purpose, to buy himself an estate with gooseberry bushes on it, he married an ugly elderly widow, for whom he had not the slightest affection, just because she had some money. After his marriage he went on living as thriftily as ever, half-starving his wife, and putting her money in his own bank account. Her first husband had been a postmaster, and she was used to pies and cordials, but with her second husband she did not even get enough black bread to eat. She began to languish under such a regime, and three years later yielded up her soul to God. Of course my brother did not for a moment consider himself guilty of her death. Money, like vodka, makes a man eccentric. There was a merchant in our town who asked for a plate of honey on his deathbed and ate up all his bank-notes and lottery tickets with the honey, so that no one else should get it. And one day when I was examining a consignment of cattle at a railway station, a drover fell under the engine and his leg was severed from his body. We carried him all bloody into the waiting-room, a terrible sight, and he did nothing but beg us to look for his leg, worrying all the time — there were twenty rubles in the boot, and he was afraid they would be lost."

"You're losing the thread," put in Burkin.

Ivan Ivanich paused for a moment, and went on: "After his wife's death my brother began to look about for an estate. You can search for five years, of course, and in the end make a mistake and buy something quite different from what you dreamed of. My brother Nikolai bought three hundred acres, complete with gentleman's house, servants' quarters, and a park, as well as a mortgage to be paid through an agent, but there were neither an orchard, gooseberry bushes, nor a pond with ducks on it. There was a river, but it was as dark as coffee, owing to the fact that there was a brick-works on one side of the estate, and bone-kilns on the other. Nothing daunted, however, my brother Nikolai Ivanich ordered two dozen gooseberry bushes and settled down as a landed proprietor.

"Last year I paid him a visit. I thought I would go and see how he was getting on there. In his letters my brother gave his address as Chumbaroklova Pustosh or Himalaiskoye. I arrived at Himalaiskoye in the afternoon. It was very hot. Everywhere were ditches, fences, hedges, rows of fir-trees, and it was hard to drive into the yard and find a place to leave one's carriage. As I went a fat ginger-coloured dog, remarkably like a pig, came out to meet me. It looked as if it would have barked if it were not so lazy. The cook, who was also fat and like a pig, came out of the kitchen, barefoot, and said her master was having his after-dinner rest. I made my way to my brother's room, and found him sitting up in bed, his knees covered by a blanket. He had aged, and grown stout and flabby. His cheeks, nose and lips protruded — I almost expected him to grunt into the blanket.

"We embraced and wept — tears of joy, mingled with melancholy — because we had once been young and were now both grey-haired and approaching the grave. He put on his clothes and went out to show me over his estate.

"'Well, how are you getting on here?' I asked.

"'All right, thanks be, I'm enjoying myself.'

"He was no longer the poor, timid clerk, but a true proprietor, a gentleman. He had settled down, and was entering with zest into country life. He ate a lot, washed in the bath-house, and put on flesh. He had already got into litigation with the village commune, the brick-works and the bone-kilns, and took offence if the peasants failed to call him 'Your Honour.' He went in for religion in a solid, gentlemanly way, and there was nothing casual

---

[1] District.

about his pretentious good works. And what were these good works? He treated all the diseases of the peasants with bicarbonate of soda and castor-oil, and had a special thanksgiving service held on his name-day, after which he provided half a pail of vodka, supposing that this was the right thing to do. Oh, those terrible half pails! Today the fat landlord hauls the peasants before the Zemstvo representative[2] for letting their sheep graze on his land, tomorrow, on the day of rejoicing, he treats them to half a pail of vodka, and they drink and sing and shout hurrah, prostrating themselves before him when they are drunk. Any improvement in his conditions, anything like satiety or idleness, develops the most insolent complacency in a Russian. Nikolai Ivanich, who had been afraid of having an opinion of his own when he was in the government service, was now continually coming out with axioms, in the most ministerial manner: 'Education is essential, but the people are not ready for it yet,' 'corporal punishment is an evil, but in certain cases it is beneficial and indispensable.'

"'I know the people and I know how to treat them,' he said. 'The people love me. I only have to lift my little finger, and the people will do whatever I want.'

"And all this, mark you, with a wise, indulgent smile. Over and over again he repeated: 'We the gentry,' or 'speaking as a gentleman,' and seemed to have quite forgotten that our grandfather was a peasant, and our father a common soldier. Our very surname — Chimsha-Himalaisky — in reality so absurd, now seemed to him a resounding, distinguished, and euphonious name.

"But it is of myself, and not of him, that I wish to speak. I should like to describe to you the change which came over me in those few hours I spent on my brother's estate. As we were drinking tea in the evening, the cook brought us a full plate of gooseberries. These were not gooseberries bought for money, they came from his own garden, and were the first fruits of the bushes he had planted. Nikolai Ivanich broke into a laugh and gazed at the gooseberries, in tearful silence for at least five minutes. Speechless with emotion, he popped a single gooseberry into his mouth, darted at me the triumphant glance of a child who has at last gained possession of a longed-for toy, and said:

"'Delicious!'

"And he ate them greedily, repeating over and over again:

"'Simply delicious! You try them.'

"They were hard and sour, but, as Pushkin[3] says: 'The lie which elates us is dearer than a thousand sober truths.' I saw before me a really happy man, one whose dearest wish had come true, who had achieved his aim in life, got what he wanted, and was content with his lot and with himself. There had always been a tinge of melancholy in my conception of human happiness, and now, confronted by a happy man, I was overcome by a feeling of sadness bordering on desperation. This feeling grew strongest of all in the night. A bed was made up for me in the room next to my brother's bedroom, and I could hear him moving about restlessly, every now and then getting up to take a gooseberry from a plate. How many happy, satisfied people there are, after all, I said to myself! What an overwhelming force! Just consider this life — the insolence and idleness of the strong, the ignorance and bestiality of the weak, all around intolerable poverty, cramped dwellings, degeneracy, drunkenness, hypocrisy, lying. ... And yet peace and order apparently prevail in all those homes and in the streets. Of the fifty thousand inhabitants of a town, not one will be found to cry out, to proclaim his indignation aloud. We see those who go to the market to buy food, who eat in the day-time and sleep at night, who prattle away, marry, grow old, carry their dead to the cemeteries. But

---

[2] A local magistrate.

[3] Alexander Pushkin (1799–1837), Russian poet, short story writer, and dramatist.

we neither hear nor see those who suffer, and the terrible things in life are played out behind the scenes. All is calm and quiet, only statistics, which are dumb, protest: so many have gone mad, so many barrels of drink have been consumed, so many children died of malnutrition. ... And apparently this is as it should be. Apparently those who are happy can only enjoy themselves because the unhappy bear their burdens in silence, and but for this silence happiness would be impossible. It is a kind of universal hypnosis. There ought to be a man with a hammer behind the door of every happy man, to remind him by his constant knocks that there are unhappy people, and that happy as he himself may be, life will sooner or later show him its claws, catastrophe will overtake him — sickness, poverty, loss — and nobody will see it, just as he now neither sees nor hears the misfortunes of others. But there is no man with a hammer, the happy man goes on living and the petty vicissitudes of life touch him lightly, like the wind in an aspen-tree, and all is well.

"That night I understood that I, too, was happy and content," continued Ivan Ivanich, getting up. "I, too, while out hunting, or at the dinner table, have held forth on the right way to live, to worship, to manage the people. I, too, have declared that without knowledge there can be no light, that education is essential, but that bare literacy is sufficient for the common people. Freedom is a blessing, I have said, one can't get on without it, any more than without air, but we must wait. Yes, that is what I said, and now I ask: In the name of what must we wait?" Here Ivan Ivanich looked angrily at Burkin. "In the name of what must we wait, I ask you. What is there to be considered? Don't be in such a hurry, they tell me, every idea materializes gradually, in its own time. But who are they who say this? What is the proof that it is just? You refer to the natural order of things, to the logic of facts, but according to what order, what logic do I, a living, thinking individual, stand on the edge of a ditch and wait for it to be gradually filled up, or choked with silt, when I might leap across it or build a bridge over it? And again, in the name of what must we wait? Wait, when we have not the strength to live, though live we must and to live we desire!

"I left my brother early the next morning, and ever since I have found town life intolerable. The peace and order weigh on my spirits, and I am afraid to look into windows, because there is now no sadder spectacle for me than a happy family seated around the tea-table. I am old and unfit for the struggle, I am even incapable of feeling hatred. I can only suffer inwardly, and give way to irritation and annoyance, at night my head burns from the rush of thoughts, and I am unable to sleep. ... Oh, if only I were young!"

Ivan Ivanich began pacing backwards and forwards, repeating:

"If only I were young still!"

Suddenly he went up to Alekhin and began pressing first one of his hands, and then the other.

"Pavel Konstantinich," he said in imploring accents. "Don't *you* fall into apathy, don't *you* let your conscience be lulled to sleep! While you are still young, strong, active, do not be weary of well-doing. There is no such thing as happiness, nor ought there to be, but if there is any sense or purpose in life, this sense and purpose are to be found not in our own happiness, but in something greater and more rational. Do good!"

Ivan Ivanich said all this with a piteous, imploring smile, as if he were asking for something for himself.

Then they all three sat in their arm-chairs a long way apart from one another, and said nothing. Ivan Ivanich's story satisfied neither Burkin or Alekhin. It was not interesting to listen to the story of a poor clerk who ate gooseberries, when from the walls generals and fine ladies, who seemed to come to life in the dark, were looking down from their gilded frames. It would have been much more interesting to hear about elegant people, lovely women. And the fact that they were sitting in a drawing-room in which everything — the swathed chandeliers, the arm-chairs, the carpet on the floor, proved that the people now looking out of the frames had once moved about here, sat in the chairs, drunk tea, where the fair Pelageya was now going noiselessly to and fro, was better than any story.

Alekhin was desperately sleepy. He had got up early, at three o'clock in the morning, to go about his work on the estate, and could now hardly keep his eyes open. But he would not go to bed, for fear one of his guests would relate something interesting after he was gone. He could not be sure whether what Ivan Ivanich had just told them was wise or just, but his visitors talked of other things besides grain, hay, or tar, of things which had no direct bearing on his daily life, and he liked this, and wanted them to go on. ...

"Well, time to go to bed," said Burkin, getting up. "Allow me to wish you a good night."

Alekhin said good night and went downstairs to his own room, the visitors remaining on the upper floor. They were allotted a big room for the night, in which were two ancient bedsteads of carved wood, and an ivory crucifix in one corner. There was a pleasant smell of freshly laundered sheets from the wide, cool beds which the fair Pelageya made up for them.

Ivan Ivanich undressed in silence and lay down.

"Lord have mercy on us, sinners," he said, and covered his head with the sheet.

There was a strong smell of stale tobacco from his pipe, which he put on the table, and Burkin lay awake a long time, wondering where the stifling smell came from.

The rain tapped on the window-panes all night.

QUESTIONS

1. What do the gooseberries symbolize for Nikolai? for his brother? Is Ivan right when he says that the story is about him, not Nikolai? Are the two brothers essentially alike or different?

2. How did estate life change Nikolai? What do his maxims tell you about his character? What does the animal imagery suggest about it?

3. "The lie which elates us is dearer than a thousand sober truths." Do you agree? What does this imply about the pursuit of happiness?

4. What has Ivan learned from his brother's experience? What lesson does he try to teach Alekhin? Does he succeed?

5. Is Ivan's night prayer appropriate in the circumstances?

ANTON CHEKHOV

The Kiss

Translated by Robert N. Linscott

On the evening of the twentieth of May, at eight o'clock, all six batteries of the N Artillery Brigade on their way to camp arrived at the village of Miestechky with the intention of spending the night.

The confusion was at its worst — some officers fussed about the guns, others in the church square arranged with the quartermaster — when from behind the church rode a civilian upon a most remarkable mount. The small, short-tailed bay with well-shaped neck progressed with a wobbly motion, all the time making dance-like movements with its legs as if some one were switching its hoofs. When he had drawn rein level with the officers the rider doffed his cap and said ceremoniously —

"His Excellency, General von Rabbek, whose house is close by, requests the honour of the officers' company at tea. ... "

The horse shook its head, danced, and wobbled to the rear; its rider again took off his cap, and, turning his strange steed, disappeared behind the church.

"The devil take it!" was the general exclamation as the officers dispersed to their quarters. "We can hardly keep our eyes open, yet along comes this von Rabbek with his tea! I know that tea!"

The officers of the six batteries had lively memories of a past invitation. During recent manœuvres they had been asked, together with their Cossack comrades, to tea at the house of a local country gentleman, an officer in retirement, by title a Count; and this hearty, hospitable Count overwhelmed them with attentions, fed them to satiety, poured vodka down their throats, and made them stay the night. All this, of course, they enjoyed. The trouble was that the old soldier entertained his guests too well. He kept them up till daybreak while he poured forth tales of past adventures; he dragged them from room to room to point out valuable paintings, old engravings, and rare arms; he read them holograph letters from celebrated men. And the weary officers, bored to death, listened, gaped, yearned for their beds, and yawned cautiously in their sleeves, until at last when their host released them it was too late for sleep.

Was von Rabbek another old Count? It might easily be. But there was no neglecting his invitation. The officers washed and dressed, and set out for von Rabbek's house. At the church square they learnt that they must descend the hill to the river, and follow the bank till they reached the general's gardens, where they would find a path direct to the house. Or, if they chose to go up hill, they would reach the general's barns half a verst from Miestechky. It was this route they chose.

"But who is this von Rabbek?" asked one. "The man who commanded the N Cavalry Division at Plevna?"

"No, that was not von Rabbek, but simply Rabbe — without the von."

"What glorious weather!"

At the first barn they came to, two roads diverged; one ran straight forward and faded in the dusk; the other turning to the right led to the general's house. As the officers drew near they talked less loudly. To right and left stretched rows of red-roofed brick barns, in aspect heavy and morose as the barracks of provincial towns. In front gleamed the lighted windows of von Rabbek's house.

"A good omen, gentlemen!" cried a young officer. "Our setter runs in advance. There is game ahead!"

On the face of Lieutenant Lobytko, the tall stout officer referred to, there was not one trace of hair though he was twenty-five years old. He was famed among comrades for the instinct which told him of the presence of women in the neighbourhood. On hearing his comrade's remark, he turned his head and said —

"Yes. There are women there. My instinct tells me."

A handsome, well-preserved man of sixty, in mufti, came to the hall door to greet his guests. It was von Rabbek. As he pressed their hands, he explained that though he was delighted to see them, he must beg pardon for not asking them to spend the night; as guests he already had his two sisters, their children, his brother, and several neighbours — in fact, he had not one spare room. And though he shook their hands and apologised and smiled, it was plain that he was not half as glad to see them as was last year's Count, and that he had invited them merely because good manners demanded it. The officers climbing the soft-carpeted steps and listening to their host understood this perfectly well; and realised that they carried into the house an atmosphere of intrusion and alarm. Would any man — they asked themselves — who had gathered his two sisters and their children, his brother and his neighbours, to celebrate, no doubt, some family festival, find pleasure in the invasion of nineteen officers whom he had never seen before?

A tall, elderly lady, with a good figure, and a long face with black eyebrows, who resembled closely the ex-Empress Eugenie, greeted them at the drawing-room door. Smiling courteously and with dignity, she affirmed that she was delighted to see the officers, and only regretted that she could not ask them to stay the night. But the courteous, dignified smile disappeared when she turned away, and it was quite plain that she had seen many officers in her day, that they caused not the slightest interest, and that she had invited them merely because an invitation was dictated by good breeding and by her position in the world.

In a big dining-room seated at a big table sat ten men and women, drinking tea. Behind them, veiled in cigar-smoke, stood several young men, among them one, red-whiskered and extremely thin, who spoke English loudly with a lisp. Through an open door the officers saw into a brightly lighted room with blue wall-paper.

"You are too many to introduce singly, gentlemen!" said the general loudly, with affected joviality. "Make one another's acquaintance, please — without formalities!"

The visitors, some with serious, even severe faces, some smiling constrainedly, all with a feeling of awkwardness, bowed, and took their seats at the table. Most awkward of all felt Staff-Captain Riabovich, a short, round-shouldered, spectacled officer, whiskered like a lynx. While his brother officers looked serious or smiled constrainedly, his face, his lynx whiskers, and his spectacles seemed to explain: "I am the most timid, modest, undistinguished officer in the whole brigade." For some time after he took his seat at the table he could not fix his attention on any single thing. Faces, dresses, the cut-glass cognac bottles, the steaming tumblers, the moulded cornices — all merged in a single, overwhelming sentiment which caused him intense fright and made him wish to hide his head. Like an inexperienced lecturer he saw everything before him, but could distinguish nothing, and was in fact the victim of what men of science diagnose as "psychical blindness."

But slowly conquering his diffidence, Riabovich began to distinguish and observe. As became a man both timid and unsocial, he remarked first of all the amazing temerity of his new friends. Von Rabbek, his wife, two elderly ladies, a girl in lilac, and the red-whiskered youth who, it appeared, was a young von Rabbek, sat down among the officers as unconcernedly as if they had held rehearsals, and at once plunged into various heated arguments in which they soon involved their guests. That artillerists have a much better time than cavalrymen or infantrymen was proved conclusively by the lilac girl, while von Rabbek and the elderly ladies affirmed the converse. The conversation became desultory. Riabovich listened to the lilac girl fiercely debating themes she knew nothing about and took no interest in, and watched the insincere smiles which appeared on and disappeared from her face.

While the von Rabbek family with amazing strategy inveigled their guests into the dispute, they kept their eyes on every glass and mouth. Had every one tea, was it sweet enough, why didn't one eat biscuits, was another fond of cognac? And the longer Riabovich listened and looked, the more pleased he was with this disingenuous, disciplined family.

After tea the guests repaired to the drawing-room. Instinct had not cheated Lobytko. The room was packed with young women and girls, and ere a minute had passed the setter-lieutenant stood beside a very young, fair-haired girl in black, and, bending down as if resting on an invisible sword, shrugged his shoulders coquettishly. He was uttering, no doubt, most unentertaining nonsense, for the fair girl looked indulgently at his sated face, and exclaimed indifferently, "Indeed!" And this indifferent "Indeed!" might have quickly convinced the setter that he was on a wrong scent.

Music began. As the notes of a mournful valse throbbed out of the open window, through the heads of all flashed the feeling that outside that window it was spring-time, a night of May. The air was odorous of young poplar leaves, of roses and lilacs — and the valse and the spring were sincere. Riabovich, with valse and cognac mingling tipsily in his head, gazed at the window with a smile; then began to follow the movements of the women; and it seemed that the smell of roses, poplars, and lilacs came not from the gardens outside, but from the women's faces and dresses.

They began to dance. Young von Rabbek valsed twice round the room with a very thin girl; and Lobytko, slipping on the parqueted floor, went up to the girl in lilac, and was granted a dance. But Riabovich stood near the door with the wall-flowers, and looked silently on. Amazed at the daring of men who in sight of a crowd could take unknown women by the waist, he tried in vain to picture himself doing the same. A time had been when he envied his comrades their courage and dash, suffered from painful heart-searchings, and was hurt by the knowledge that he was timid, round-shouldered, and undistinguished, that he had lynx whiskers, and that his waist was much too long. But with years he had grown reconciled to his own insignificance, and now looking at the dancers and loud talkers, he felt no envy, but only mournful emotions.

At the first quadrille von Rabbek junior approached and invited two non-dancing officers to a game of billiards. The three left the room; and Riabovich who stood idle, and felt impelled to join in the general movement, followed. They passed the dining-room, traversed a narrow glazed corridor, and a room where three sleepy footmen jumped from a sofa with a start; and after walking, it seemed, through a whole houseful of rooms, entered a small billiard-room.

Von Rabbek and the two officers began their game. Riabovich, whose only game was cards, stood near the table and looked indifferently on, as the players, with unbuttoned coats, wielded their cues, moved about, joked, and shouted obscure technical terms. Riabovich was ignored, save when one of the players jostled him or caught his cue, and turning towards him said briefly, "Pardon!" so that before the game was over he was thoroughly bored, and impressed by a sense of his superfluity, resolved to return to the drawing-room, and turned away.

It was on the way back that his adventure took place. Before he had gone far he saw that he had missed the way. He remembered distinctly the room with the three sleepy footmen; and after passing through five or six rooms entirely vacant, he saw his mistake. Retracing his steps, he turned to the left, and found himself in an almost dark room which he had not seen before; and after hesitating a minute, he boldly opened the first door he saw, and found himself in complete darkness. Through a chink of the door in front peered a bright light; from afar throbbed the dulled music of a mournful mazurka. Here, as in the drawing-room, the windows were open wide, and the smell of poplars, lilacs, and roses flooded the air.

Riabovich paused in irresolution. For a moment all was still. Then came the sound of hasty footsteps; then, without any warning of what was to come, a dress rustled, a woman's breathless voice whispered "At last!" and two soft, scented, unmistakably womanly arms met round his neck, a warm cheek impinged on his, and he received a sounding kiss. But hardly had the kiss echoed through the silence when the unknown shrieked loudly, and fled away — as it seemed to Riabovich — in disgust. Riabovich himself nearly screamed, and rushed headlong towards the bright beam in the door-chink.

As he entered the drawing-room his heart beat violently, and his hands trembled so perceptibly that he clasped them behind his back. His first emotion was shame, as if every one in the room already knew that he had just been embraced and kissed. He retired into his shell, and looked tearfully around. But finding that hosts and guests were calmly dancing or talking, he regained courage, and surrendered himself to sensations experienced for the first time in life. The unexampled had happened. His neck, fresh from the embrace of two soft, scented arms, seemed anointed with oil; near his left moustache, where the kiss had fallen, trembled a slight, delightful chill, as from peppermint drops; and from head to foot he was soaked in new and extraordinary sensations, which continued to grow and grow.

He felt that he must dance, talk, run into the garden, laugh unrestrainedly. He forgot altogether that he was round-shouldered, undistinguished, lynx-whiskered, that he had an "indefinite exterior" — a description from the lips of a woman he had happened to overhear. As Madame von Rabbek passed him he smiled so broadly and graciously that she came up and looked at him questioningly.

"What a charming house you have!" he said, straightening his spectacles.

And Madame von Rabbek smiled back, said that the house still belonged to her father, and asked were his parents alive, how long he had been in the Army, and why he was so thin. After hearing his answers she departed. But though the conversation was over, he continued to smile benevolently, and think what charming people were his new acquaintances.

At supper Riabovich ate and drank mechanically what was put before him, heard not a word of the conversation, and devoted all his powers to the unraveling of his mysterious, romantic adventure. What was the explanation? It was plain that one of the girls, he reasoned, had arranged a meeting in the dark room, and after waiting some time in vain had, in her nervous tension, mistaken Riabovich for her hero. The mistake was likely enough, for on entering the dark room Riabovich had stopped irresolutely as if he, too, were waiting for some one. So far the mystery was explained.

"But which of them was it?" he asked, searching the women's faces. She certainly was young, for old women do not indulge in such romances. Secondly, she was not a servant. That was proved unmistakably by the rustle of her dress, the scent, the voice …

When at first he looked at the girl in lilac she pleased him; she had pretty shoulders and arms, a clever face, a charming voice. Riabovich piously prayed that it was she. But, smiling insincerely, she wrinkled her long nose, and that at once gave her an elderly air. So Riabovich turned his eyes on the blonde in black. The blonde was younger, simpler, sincerer; she had charming kiss-curls, and drank from her tumbler with inexpressible grace. Riabovich hoped it was she — but soon he noticed that her face was flat, and bent his eyes on her neighbour.

"It is a hopeless puzzle," he reflected. "If you take the arms and shoulders of the lilac girl, add the blonde's curls, and the eyes of the girl on Lobytko's left, then——"

He composed a portrait of all these charms, and had a clear vision of the girl who had kissed him. But she was nowhere to be seen.

Supper over, the visitors, sated and tipsy, bade their entertainers good-bye. Both host and hostess again apologised for not asking them to spend the night.

"I am very glad, very glad, gentlemen!" said the general, and this time seemed to speak sincerely, no doubt because speeding the parting guest is a kindlier office than welcoming him unwelcomed. "I am very glad indeed! I hope you will visit me on your way back. Without ceremony, please! Which way will you go? Up the hill? No, go down the hill and through the garden. That way is shorter."

The officers took his advice. After the noise and glaring illumination within doors, the garden seemed dark and still. Until they reached the wicket-gate all kept silence. Merry, half tipsy, and content, as they were, the night's obscurity and stillness inspired pensive thoughts. Through their brains, as through Riabovich's, sped probably the same question: "Will the time ever come when I, like von Rabbek, shall have a big house, a family, a garden, the chance of being gracious — even insincerely — to others, of making them sated, tipsy, and content?"

But once the garden lay behind them, all spoke at once, and burst into causeless laughter. The path they followed led straight to the river, and then ran beside it, winding around bushes, ravines, and over-hanging willow-trees. The track was barely visible; the other bank was lost entirely in gloom. Sometimes the black water imaged stars, and this was the only indication of the river's speed. From beyond it sighed a drowsy snipe, and beside them in a bush, heedless of the crowd, a nightingale chanted loudly. The officers gathered in a group, and swayed the bush, but the nightingale continued his song.

"I like his cheek!" they echoed admiringly. "He doesn't care a kopeck![1] The old rogue!"

Near their journey's end the path turned up the hill, and joined the road not far from the church enclosure; and there the officers, breathless from climbing, sat on the grass and smoked. Across the river gleamed a dull red light, and for want of a subject they argued the problem, whether it was a bonfire, a window-light, or something else. Riabovich looked also at the light, and felt that it smiled and winked at him as if it knew about the kiss.

On reaching home, he undressed without delay, and lay upon his bed. He shared the cabin with Lobytko and a Lieutenant Merzliakov, a staid, silent little man, by repute highly cultivated, who took with him everywhere *The Messenger of Europe*, and read it eternally. Lobytko undressed, tramped impatiently from corner to corner, and sent his servant for beer.

---

[1] A small coin, like a penny.

Merzliakov lay down, balanced the candle on his pillow, and hid his head behind *The Messenger of Europe*.

"Where is she now?" muttered Riabovich, looking at the soot-blacked ceiling.

His neck still seemed anointed with oil, near his mouth still trembled the speck of peppermint chill. Through his brain twinkled successively the shoulders and arms of the lilac girl, the kiss-curls and honest eyes of the girl in black, the waists, dresses, brooches. But though he tried his best to fix these vagrant images, they glimmered, winked, and dissolved; and as they faded finally into the vast black curtain which hangs before the closed eyes of all men, he began to hear hurried footsteps, the rustle of petticoats, the sound of a kiss. A strong, causeless joy possessed him. But as he surrendered himself to this joy, Lobytko's servant returned with the news that no beer was obtainable. The lieutenant resumed his impatient march up and down the room.

"The fellow's an idiot," he exclaimed, stopping first near Riabovich and then near Merzliakov. "Only the worst numbskull and blockhead can't get beer! *Canaille!*"[2]

"Every one knows there's no beer here," said Merzliakov, without lifting his eyes from *The Messenger of Europe*.

"You believe that!" exclaimed Lobytko. "Lord in heaven, drop me on the moon, and in five minutes I'll find both beer and women! I will find them myself! Call me a rascal if I don't!"

He dressed slowly, silently lighted a cigarette, and went out.

"Rabbek, Grabbek, Labbek," he muttered, stopping in the hall. "I won't go alone, devil take me! Riabovich, come for a walk! What?"

As he got no answer, he returned, undressed slowly, and lay down. Merzliakov sighed, dropped *The Messenger of Europe*, and put out the light. "Well?" muttered Lobytko, puffing his cigarette in the dark.

Riabovich pulled the bed-clothes up to his chin, curled himself into a roll, and strained his imagination to join the twinkling images into one coherent whole. But the vision fled him. He soon fell asleep, and his last impression was that he had been caressed and gladdened, that into his life had crept something strange, and indeed ridiculous, but uncommonly good and radiant. And this thought did not forsake him even in his dreams.

When he awoke the feeling of anointment and peppermint chill were gone. But joy, as on the night before, filled every vein. He looked entranced at the window-panes gilded by the rising sun, and listened to the noises outside. Some one spoke loudly under the very window. It was Lebedetzky, commander of his battery, who had just overtaken the brigade. He was talking to the sergeant-major, loudly, owing to lack of practice in soft speech.

"And what next?" he roared.

"During yesterday's shoeing, your honour, *Golubtchik* was pricked. The *feldscher*[3] ordered clay and vinegar. And last night, your honour, mechanic Artemieff was drunk, and the lieutenant ordered him to be put on the limber of the reserve gun-carriage."

The sergeant-major added that Karpov had forgotten the tent-pegs and the new lanyards for the friction-tubes, and that the officers had spent the evening at General von Rabbek's. But here at the window appeared Lebedetzky's red-bearded face. He blinked his short-sighted eyes at the drowsy men in bed, and greeted them.

"Is everything all right?"

"The saddle wheeler galled his withers with the new yoke," answered Lobytko.

The commander sighed, mused a moment, and shouted —

---

[2] "Scoundrel!"

[3] Assistant medical officer.

"I am thinking of calling on Alexandra Yegorovna. I want to see her. Good-bye! I will catch you up before night."

Fifteen minutes later the brigade resumed its march. As he passed von Rabbek's barns Riabovich turned his head and looked at the house. The Venetian blinds were down; evidently all still slept. And among them slept she — she who had kissed him but a few hours before. He tried to visualise her asleep. He projected the bedroom window opened wide with green branches peering in, the freshness of the morning air, the smell of poplars, lilacs, and roses, the bed, a chair, the dress which rustled last night, a pair of tiny slippers, a ticking watch on the table — all these came to him clearly with every detail. But the features, the kind, sleepy smile — all, in short, that was essential and characteristic — fled his imagination as quicksilver flees the hand. When he had covered half a verst he again turned back. The yellow church, the house, gardens, and river were bathed in light. Imagining an azure sky, the green-banked river specked with silver sunshine flakes was inexpressibly fair; and, looking at Miestechky for the last time, Riabovich felt sad, as if parting for ever with something very near and dear.

By the road before him stretched familiar, uninteresting scenes; to the right and left, fields of young rye and buckwheat with hopping rooks; in front, dust and the napes of human necks; behind, the same dust and faces. Ahead of the column marched four soldiers with swords — that was the advance guard. Next came the bandsmen. Advance guard and bandsmen, like mutes in a funeral procession, ignored the regulation intervals and marched too far ahead. Riabovich, with the first gun of Battery No. 5, could see four batteries ahead.

To a layman, the long, lumbering march of an artillery brigade is novel, interesting, inexplicable. It is hard to understand why a single gun needs so many men; why so many, such strangely harnessed horses are needed to drag it. But to Riabovich, a master of all these things, it was profoundly dull. He had learned years ago why a solid sergeant-major rides beside the officer in front of each battery, why the sergeant-major is called the *unosni*,[4] and why the drivers of leaders and wheelers ride behind him. Riabovich knew why the near horses are called saddle-horses, and why the off horses are called led-horses — and all of this was interesting beyond words. On one of the wheelers rode a soldier still covered with yesterday's dust, and with a cumbersome, ridiculous guard on his right leg. But Riabovich, knowing the use of this leg-guard, found it in no way ridiculous. The drivers, mechanically and with occasional cries, flourished their whips. The guns in themselves were impressive. The limbers were packed with tarpaulin-covered sacks of oats; and the guns themselves, hung around with tea-pots and satchels, looked like harmless animals, guarded for some obscure reason by men and horses. In the lee of the gun tramped six gunners, swinging their arms; and behind each gun came more *unosniye*, leaders, wheelers; and yet more guns, each as ugly and uninspiring as the one in front. And as every one of the six batteries in the brigade had four guns, the procession stretched along the road at least half a verst. It ended with a wagon train, with which, its head bent in thought, walked the donkey Magar, brought from Turkey by a battery commander.

Dead to his surroundings, Riabovich marched onward, looking at the napes ahead or at the faces behind. Had it not been for last night's event, he would have been half asleep. But now he was absorbed in novel, entrancing thoughts. When the brigade set out that morning he had tried to argue that the kiss had no significance save as a trivial though mysterious adventure; that it was without real import; and that to think of it seriously was to behave himself absurdly. But logic soon flew away and surrendered him to his vivid imaginings. At times he

---

[4] Forerider.

saw himself in von Rabbek's dining-room, *tête-à-tête*[5] with a composite being, formed of the girl in lilac and the blonde in black. At times he closed his eyes, and pictured himself with a different, this time quite an unknown, girl of cloudy feature; he spoke to her, caressed her, bent over her shoulder; he imagined war and parting ... then reunion, the first supper together, children ... .

"To the brakes!" rang the command as they topped the brow of each hill.

Riabovich also cried "To the brakes!" and each time dread that the cry would break the magic spell, and recall him to realities.

They passed a big country house. Riabovich looked across the fence into the garden, and saw a long path, straight as a ruler, carpeted with yellow sand, and shaded by young birches. In an ecstasy of enchantment, he pictured little feminine feet treading the yellow sand; and, in a flash, imagination restored the woman who had kissed him, the woman he had visualised after supper the night before. The image settled in his brain and never afterwards forsook him.

The spell reigned until midday, when a loud command came from the rear of the column. "Attention! Eyes right! Officers!"

In a *calèche*[6] drawn by a pair of white horses appeared the general of brigade. He stopped at the second battery, and called out something which no one understood. Up galloped several officers, among them Riabovich.

"Well, how goes it?" The general blinked his red eyes, and continued, "Are there any sick?"

Hearing the answer, the little skinny general mused a moment, turned to an officer, and said —

"The driver of your third-gun wheeler has taken off his leg-guard and hung it on the limber. *Canaille!* Punish him!"

Then raising his eyes to Riabovich, he added —

"And in your battery, I think, the harness is too loose."

Having made several other equally tiresome remarks, he looked at Lobytko, and laughed.

"Why do you look so downcast, Lieutenant Lobytko? You are sighing for Madame Lopukhov, eh? Gentlemen, he is pining for Madame Lopukhov!"

Madame Lopukhov was a tall, stout lady, long past forty. Being partial to big women, regardless of age, the general ascribed the same taste to his subordinates. The officers smiled respectfully; and the general, pleased that he had said something caustic and laughable, touched the coachman's back and saluted. The *calèche* whirled away.

"All this, though it seems to me impossible and unearthly, is in reality very commonplace," thought Riabovich, watching the clouds of dust raised by the general's carriage. "It is an everyday event, and within every one's experience. ... this old general, for instance, must have loved in his day; he is married now, and has children. Captain Wachter is also married, and his wife loves him, though he has an ugly red neck and no waist. ... Salmanoff is coarse, and a typical Tartar, but he has had a romance ending in marriage. ... I, like the rest, must go through it all sooner or later."

And the thought that he was an ordinary man, and that his life was ordinary, rejoiced and consoled him. He boldly visualised *her* and his happiness, and let his imagination run mad.

Towards evening the brigade ended its march. While the other officers sprawled in their

---

[5] In intimate conversation.

[6] A carriage with a convertible top to protect the passengers from the weather.

tents, Riabovich, Merzliakov, and Lobytko sat around a packing-case and supped. Merzliakov ate slowly, and, resting *The Messenger of Europe* on his knees, read on steadily. Lobytko, chattering without cease, poured beer into his glass. But Riabovich, whose head was dizzy from uninterrupted day-dreams, ate in silence. When he had drunk three glasses he felt tipsy and weak; and an overmastering impulse forced him to relate his adventure to his comrades.

"A most extraordinary thing happened to me at von Rabbek's," he began, doing his best to speak in an indifferent, ironical tone. "I was on my way, you understand, from the billiard-room ... "

And he attempted to give a very detailed history of the kiss. But in a minute he had told the whole story. In that minute he had exhausted every detail; and it seemed to him terrible that the story required such a short time. It ought, he felt, to have lasted all the night. As he finished, Lobytko, who as a liar himself believed in no one, laughed incredulously. Merzliakov frowned, and, with his eyes still glued to *The Messenger of Europe*, said indifferently —

"God knows who it was! She threw herself on your neck, you say, and didn't cry out! Some lunatic, I expect!"

"It must have been a lunatic," agreed Riabovich.

"I, too, have had adventures of that kind," began Lobytko, making a frightful face. "I was on my way to Kovno. I travelled second class. The carriage was packed, and I couldn't sleep. So I gave the guard a ruble, and he took my bag, and put me in a *coupé*.[7] I lay down, and pulled my rug over me. It was pitch dark, you understand. Suddenly I felt some one tapping my shoulder and breathing in my face. I stretched out my hand and felt an elbow. Then I opened my eyes. Imagine! A woman! Coal-black eyes, lips red as good coral, nostrils breathing passion, breasts — buffers!"

"Draw it mild!" interrupted Merzliakov in his quiet voice. "I can believe about the breasts, but if it was pitch dark how could you see the lips?"

By laughing at Merzliakov's lack of understanding, Lobytko tried to shuffle out of the dilemma. The story annoyed Riabovich. He rose from the box, lay on his bed, and swore that he would never again take any one into his confidence.

Life in camp passed without event. The days flew by, each like the one before. But on every one of these days Riabovich felt, thought, and acted as a man in love. When at daybreak his servant brought him cold water, and poured it over his head, it flashed at once into his half-awakened brain that something good and warm and caressing had crept into his life.

At night when his comrades talked of love and of women, he drew in his chair, and his face was the face of an old soldier who talks of battles in which he has taken part. And when the rowdy officers, led by setter Lobytko, made Don Juanesque raids upon the neighbouring "suburb," Riabovich, though he accompanied them, was morose and conscience-struck, and mentally asked *her* forgiveness. In free hours and sleepless nights, when his brain was obsessed by memories of childhood, of his father, his mother, of everything akin and dear, he remembered always Miestechky, the dancing horse, von Rabbek, von Rabbek's wife, so like the ex-Empress Eugenie, the dark room, the chink in the door.

On the thirty-first of August he left camp, this time not with the whole brigade but with only two batteries. As an exile returning to his native land, he was agitated and enthralled by day-dreams. He longed passionately for the queer-looking horse, the church, the insincere von Rabbeks, the dark room; and that internal voice which cheats so often the love-lorn whispered

---

[7] A compartment.

an assurance that he should see *her* again. But doubt tortured him. How should he meet her? What must he say? Would she have forgotten the kiss? If it came to the worst — he consoled himself — if he never saw her again, he might walk once more through the dark room, and remember. ...

Towards evening the white barns and well-known church rose on the horizon. Riabovich's heart beat wildly. He ignored the remark of an officer who rode by, he forgot the whole world, and he gazed greedily at the river glimmering afar, at the green roofs, at the dove-cote, over which fluttered birds, dyed golden by the setting sun.

As he rode towards the church, and heard again the quartermaster's raucous voice, he expected every second a horseman to appear from behind the fence and invite the officers to tea. ... But the quartermaster ended his harangue, the officers hastened to the village, and no horseman appeared.

"When Rabbek hears from the peasants that we are back he will send for us," thought Riabovich. And so assured was he of this, that when he entered the hut he failed to understand why his comrades had lighted a candle, and why the servants were preparing the samovar.

A painful agitation oppressed him. He lay on his bed. A moment later he rose to look for the horseman. But no horseman was in sight. Again he lay down; again he rose; and this time, impelled by restlessness, went into the street, and walked towards the church. The square was dark and deserted. On the hill stood three silent soldiers. When they saw Riabovich they started and saluted, and he, returning their salute, began to descend the well-remembered path.

Beyond the stream, in a sky stained with purple, the moon slowly rose. Two chattering peasant women walked in a kitchen garden and pulled cabbage leaves; behind them their log cabins stood out black against the sky. The river bank was as it had been in May; the bushes were the same; things differed only in that the nightingale no longer sang, that it smelt no longer of poplars and young grass.

When he reached von Rabbek's garden Riabovich peered through the wicket-gate. Silence and darkness reigned. Save only the white birch trunks and patches of pathway, the whole garden merged in a black, impenetrable shade. Riabovich listened greedily, and gazed intent. For a quarter of an hour he loitered; then hearing no sound, and seeing no light, he walked wearily towards home.

He went down to the river. In front rose the general's bathing box; and white towels hung on the rail of the bridge. He climbed on to the bridge and stood still; then, for no reason whatever, touched a towel. It was clammy and cold. He looked down at the river which sped past swiftly, murmuring almost inaudibly against the bathing-box piles. Near the left bank glowed the moon's ruddy reflection, overrun by ripples which stretched it, tore it in two, and, it seemed, would sweep it away as twigs and shavings are swept.

"How stupid! How stupid!" thought Riabovich, watching the hurrying ripples. "How stupid everything is!"

Now that hope was dead, the history of the kiss, his impatience, his ardour, his vague aspirations and disillusion appeared in a clear light. It no longer seemed strange that the general's horseman had not come, and that he would never again see *her* who had kissed him by accident instead of another. On the contrary, he felt, it would be strange if he did ever see her again. ...

The water flew past him, whither and why no one knew. It had flown past in May; it had sped a stream into a great river; a river, into the sea; it had floated on high in mist and fallen again in rain; it might be, the water of May was again speeding past under Riabovich's eyes. For what purpose? Why?

And the whole world — life itself seemed to Riabovich an inscrutable, aimless mystification. ... Raising his eyes from the stream and gazing at the sky, he recalled how Fate in the shape of an unknown woman had once caressed him; he recalled his summer fantasies and images — and his whole life seemed to him unnaturally thin and colourless and wretched. ...

When he reached the cabin his comrades had disappeared. His servant informed him that all had set out to visit "General Fonrabbkin," who had sent a horseman to bring them. ... For a moment Riabovich's heart thrilled with joy. But that joy he extinguished. He cast himself upon his bed, and wroth with his evil fate, as if he wished to spite it, ignored the invitation.

QUESTIONS

1. Why are the officers reluctant to accept General von Rabbek's invitation?

2. The center of attention shifts back and forth between Lieutenant Lobytko and Captain Riabovich before finally settling on the latter. Why? Could the story have been told as effectively from a single point of view, say Lobytko's?

3. What effect does Chekhov achieve by telling us how well Riabovich knows the dull business of artillery service?

4. What is the immediate effect of the kiss on Riabovich? What are the effects over the longer term? in the end? Would the effects have been the same if he had discovered the women's identity?

5. Why does Lobytko's story about the girl on the train annoy Riabovich? Is he jealous?

6. At the end, Riabovich ignores the invitation from "General Fonrabbkin." Does this mark a change in his character or a return to his old self?

O. HENRY
(WILLIAM SYDNEY PORTER)

The Cop and the Anthem

On his bench in Madison Square Soapy moved uneasily. When wild geese honk high of nights, and when women without sealskin coats grow kind to their husbands, and when Soapy moves uneasily on his bench in the park, you may know that winter is near at hand.

A dead leaf fell in Soapy's lap. That was Jack Frost's card. Jack is kind to the regular denizens of Madison Square, and gives fair warning of his annual call. At the corners of four streets he hands his pasteboard to the North Wind, footman of the mansion of All Outdoors, so that the inhabitants thereof may make ready.

Soapy's mind became cognizant of the fact that the time had come for him to resolve himself into a singular Committee of Ways and Means to provide against the coming rigor. And therefore he moved uneasily on his bench.

The hibernatorial ambitions of Soapy were not of the highest. In them were no considerations of Mediterranean cruises, of soporific Southern skies or drifting in the Vesuvian Bay. Three months on the Island was what his soul craved. Three months of assured board and bed and congenial company, safe from Boreas and bluecoats, seemed to Soapy the essence of things desirable.

For years the hospitable Blackwell's had been his winter quarters. Just as his more fortunate fellow New Yorkers had bought their tickets to Palm Beach and the Riviera each winter, so Soapy had made his humble arrangements for his annual hegira to the Island. And now the time was come. On the previous night three Sabbath newspapers, distributed beneath his coat, about his ankles and over his lap, had failed to repulse the cold as he slept on his bench near the spurting fountain in the ancient square. So the Island loomed big and timely in Soapy's mind. He scorned the provisions made in the name of charity for the city's dependents. In Soapy's opinion the Law was more benign than Philanthropy. There was an endless round of institutions, municipal and eleemosynary, on which he might set out and receive lodging and food accordant with the simple life. But to one of Soapy's proud spirit the gifts of charity are encumbered. If not in coin you must pay in humiliation of spirit for every benefit received at the hands of philanthropy. As Cæsar had his Brutus, every bed of charity must have its toll of a bath, every loaf of bread its compensation of a private and personal inquisition. Wherefore it is better to be a guest of the law, which, though conducted by rules, does not meddle unduly with a gentleman's private affairs.

Soapy, having decided to go to the Island, at once set about accomplishing his desire. There were many easy ways of doing this. The pleasantest was to dine luxuriously at some expensive restaurant; and then, after declaring insolvency, be handed over quietly and without uproar to a policeman. An accommodating magistrate would do the rest.

Soapy left his bench and strolled out of the square and across the level sea of asphalt, where Broadway and Fifth Avenue flow together. Up Broadway he turned, and halted at a glittering café, where are gathered together nightly the choicest products of the grape, the silkworm, and the protoplasm.

Soapy had confidence in himself from the lowest button of his vest upward. He was shaven, and his coat was decent and his neat black, ready-tied four-in-hand had been presented to him by a lady missionary on Thanksgiving Day. If he could reach a table in the restaurant unsuspected success would be his. The portion of him that would show above the table would raise no doubt in the waiter's mind. A roasted mallard duck, thought Soapy, would be about the thing — with a bottle of Chablis, and then Camembert, a demi-tasse and a cigar. One dollar for the cigar would be enough. The total would not be so high as to call forth any supreme manifestation of revenge from the café management; and yet the meat would leave him filled and happy for the journey to his winter refuge.

But as Soapy set foot inside the restaurant door the head waiter's eye fell upon his frayed trousers and decadent shoes. Strong and ready hands turned him about and conveyed him in silence and haste to the sidewalk and averted the ignoble fate of the menaced mallard.

Soapy turned off Broadway. It seemed that his route to the coveted Island was not to be an epicurean one. Some other way of entering limbo must be thought of.

At a corner of Sixth Avenue electric lights and cunningly displayed wares behind plate-glass made a shop window conspicuous. Soapy took a cobblestone and dashed it through the glass. People came running around the corner, a policeman in the lead. Soapy stood still, with his hands in his pockets, and smiled at the sight of brass buttons.

"Where's the man that done that?" inquired the officer, excitedly.

"Don't you figure out that I might have had something to do with it?" said Soapy, not without sarcasm, but friendly, as one greets good fortune.

The policeman's mind refused to accept Soapy even as a clue. Men who smash windows do not remain to parley with the law's minions. They take to their heels. The policeman saw a man halfway down the block running to catch a car. With drawn club he joined in the pursuit. Soapy, with disgust in his heart, loafed along, twice unsuccessful.

On the opposite side of the street was a restaurant of no great pretensions. It catered to large appetites and modest purses. Its crockery and atmosphere were thick; its soup and napery thin. Into this place Soapy took his accusive shoes and telltale trousers without challenge. At a table he sat and consumed beefsteak, flapjacks, doughnuts and pie. And then to the waiter he betrayed the fact that the minutest coin and himself were strangers.

"Now, get busy and call a cop," said Soapy. "And don't keep a gentleman waiting."

"No cop for youse," said the waiter, with a voice like butter cakes and an eye like the cherry in a Manhattan cocktail. "Hey, Con!"

Neatly upon his left ear on the callous pavement two waiters pitched Soapy. He arose joint by joint, as a carpenter's rule opens, and beat the dust from his clothes. Arrest seemed but a rosy dream. The Island seemed very far away. A policeman who stood before a drug store two doors away laughed and walked down the street.

Five blocks Soapy travelled before his courage permitted him to woo capture again. This time the opportunity presented what he fatuously termed to himself a "cinch." A young woman of a modest and pleasing guise was standing before a show window gazing with sprightly interest at its display of shaving mugs and inkstands, and two yards from the window a large policeman of severe demeanor leaned against a water plug.

It was Soapy's design to assume the rôle of the despicable and execrated "masher." The refined and elegant appearance of his victim and the contiguity of the conscientious cop encouraged him to believe that he would soon feel the pleasant official clutch upon his arm that would insure his winter quarters on the right little, tight little isle.

Soapy straightened the lady missionary's ready-made tie, dragged his shrinking cuffs into the open, set his hat at a killing cant and sidled toward the young woman. He made eyes at her, was taken with sudden coughs and "hems," smiled, smirked and went brazenly through the impudent and contemptible litany of the "masher." With half an eye Soapy saw that the policeman was watching him fixedly. The young woman moved away a few steps, and again bestowed her absorbed attention upon the shaving mugs. Soapy followed, boldly stepping to her side, raised his hat and said:

"Ah there, Bedelia! Don't you want to come and play in my yard?"

The policeman was still looking. The persecuted young woman had but to beckon a finger and Soapy would be practically en route for his insular haven. Already he imagined he could feel the cozy warmth of the station-house. The young woman faced him and, stretching out a hand, caught Soapy's coat sleeve.

"Sure, Mike," she said, joyfully, "if you'll blow me to a pail of suds. I'd have spoke to you sooner, but the cop was watching."

With the young woman playing the clinging ivy to his oak Soapy walked past the policeman overcome with gloom. He seemed doomed to liberty.

At the next corner he shook off his companion and ran. He halted in the district where by night are found the lightest streets, hearts, vows and librettos. Women in furs and men in greatcoats moved gaily in the wintry air. A sudden fear seized Soapy that some dreadful enchantment had rendered him immune to arrest. The thought brought a little of panic upon it, and when he came upon another policeman lounging grandly in front of a transplendent theatre he caught at the immediate straw of "disorderly conduct."

On the sidewalk Soapy began to yell drunken gibberish at the top of his harsh voice. He danced, howled, raved, and otherwise disturbed the welkin.

The policeman twirled his club, turned his back to Soapy and remarked to a citizen:

"'Tis one of them Yale lads celebratin' the goose egg they give to the Hartford[1] College. Noisy; but no harm. We've instructions to lave them be."

Disconsolate, Soapy ceased his unavailing racket. Would never a policeman lay hands on him? In his fancy the Island seemed an unattainable Arcadia. He buttoned his thin coat against the chilling wind.

In a cigar store he saw a well-dressed man lighting a cigar at a swinging light. His silk umbrella he had set by the door on entering. Soapy stepped inside, secured the umbrella and sauntered off with it slowly. The man at the cigar light followed hastily.

"My umbrella," he said, sternly.

"Oh, is it?" sneered Soapy, adding insult to petit larceny. "Well, why don't you call a policeman? I took it. Your umbrella! Why don't you call a cop? There stands one on the corner."

The umbrella owner slowed his steps. Soapy did likewise, with a presentiment that luck would again run against him. The policeman looked at the two curiously.

"Of course," said the umbrella man — "that is — well, you know how these mistakes

---

[1] The cop's slip for "Harvard."

occur — I — if it's your umbrella I hope you'll excuse me — I picked it up this morning in a restaurant — If you recognize it as yours, why — I hope you'll——"

"Of course it's mine," said Soapy, viciously.

The ex-umbrella man retreated. The policeman hurried to assist a tall blonde in an opera cloak across the street in front of a street car that was approaching two blocks away.

Soapy walked eastward through a street damaged by improvements. He hurled the umbrella wrathfully into an excavation. He muttered against the men who wear helmets and carry clubs. Because he wanted to fall into their clutches, they seemed to regard him as a king who could do no wrong.

At length Soapy reached one of the avenues to the east where the glitter and turmoil was but faint. He set his face down this toward Madison Square, for the homing instinct survives even when the home is a park bench.

But on an unusually quiet corner Soapy came to a stand-still. Here was an old church, quaint and rambling and gabled. Through one violet-stained window a soft light glowed, where, no doubt, the organist loitered over the keys, making sure of his mastery of the coming Sabbath anthem. For there drifted out to Soapy's ears sweet music that caught and held him transfixed against the convolutions of the iron fence.

The moon was above, lustrous and serene; vehicles and pedestrians were few; sparrows twittered sleepily in the eaves — for a little while the scene might have been a country churchyard. And the anthem that the organist played cemented Soapy to the iron fence, for he had known it well in the days when his life contained such things as mothers and roses and ambitions and friends and immaculate thoughts and collars.

The conjunction of Soapy's receptive state of mind and the influences about the old church wrought a sudden and wonderful change in his soul. He viewed with swift horror the pit into which he had tumbled, the degraded days, unworthy desires, dead hopes, wrecked faculties and base motives that made up his existence.

And also in a moment his heart responded thrillingly to this novel mood. An instantaneous and strong impulse moved him to battle with his desperate fate. He would pull himself out of the mire; he would make a man of himself again; he would conquer the evil that had taken possession of him. There was time; he was comparatively young yet: he would resurrect his old eager ambitions and pursue them without faltering. Those solemn but sweet organ notes had set up a revolution in him. To-morrow he would go into the roaring downtown district and find work. A fur importer had once offered him a place as driver. He would find him to-morrow and ask for the position. He would be somebody in the world. He would——

Soapy felt a hand laid on his arm. He looked quickly around into the broad face of a policeman.

"What are you doin' here?" asked the officer.

"Nothin'," said Soapy.

"Then come along," said the policeman.

"Three months on the Island," said the Magistrate in the Police Court the next morning.

QUESTIONS

1. How is humor achieved in this story? in the characterization of Soapy? What is the effect of O. Henry's sophisticated vocabulary here?

2. What can we infer about Soapy's early years? Should we have been told more about his background?

3. What is his relationship with the police? with society at large? Is Soapy in conflict or in harmony with his environment?

4. Where does the climax of this story occur? What elements of imagery and narration heighten the ironic effect of the climax?

5. Is the setting appropriate to the action and the outcome?

MIGUEL DE UNAMUNO

Juan Manso:
A Dead Man's Tale

And now for a story.

While he was on this wicked earth Juan Manso was a simple soul, a harmless fellow who during his whole life had never hurt a fly. As a child, when he played donkey with his friends, he was always the donkey. Later, his comrades confided in him about their love affairs, and when he grew to full manhood his acquaintances still used to greet him with an affectionate "Hello, little Johnny!"

His favorite maxim was from the Chinese: "Never commit yourself, and stick to the person who can help you the most."

He loathed politics, hated business, and avoided everything that might upset the even tenor of his ways.

He lived on a small income which he spent in its entirety without ever touching the capital. He was quite devout, would never contradict anyone, and as he had a bad opinion of everybody he spoke well of them.

If you mentioned politics to him he would say: "I'm nothing — neither one side nor the other: I don't care which party runs the government. I'm just a poor sinner who wants to live at peace with everyone."

His meekness, however, was of no avail against the finality of death. It was the only definite thing he ever did in his life.

An angel armed with a great flaming sword was sorting out souls according to the sign made upon them as they went by an enrollment desk which they had to pass as they departed from this world and went through a kind of immigration control where angels and devils were sitting side by side in friendly fashion examining documents to see if they were all in order.

The entrance to the registration room looked like the scene outside the box office on the day of a big bullfight. There were so many people milling around, pushing and shoving, with everyone in such a hurry to learn his fate, and such was the hubbub raised by the curses, entreaties, insults and excuses in the thousands of languages, dialects and jargons of this world, that Juan Manso said to himself:

"Who says I have to get mixed up in all this? There must be some very rough characters around here."

He said this *sotto voce*, so no one could hear him. The fact is that the angel with the great flaming sword paid not the slightest attention to him, so he was able to slip past and start on his way to Heaven.

He walked along very quietly all by himself. From time to time happy groups would pass by, chanting litanies; some were dancing wildly, which seemed to him not quite a proper thing for the blessed to be doing on their way up to Heaven. When he reached the heights he found a long line of people standing beside the walls of Paradise, and a few angels keeping order like policemen on earth. Juan Manso got on the very end of the line.

Shortly a humble Franciscan friar came along, and he was so clever in advancing pathetic arguments as to why he was in such a hurry to get inside right away that Juan Manso gave him his place in line, saying to himself:

"It's a good idea to make friends for yourself even in Heaven."

The next man to come along, though not a Franciscan, wanted the same privilege, and the same thing happened. In short, there wasn't a pious soul who did not trick Juan Manso out of his place; his reputation for meekness ran along the whole line, and was handed down as a continuing tradition among the constantly-changing crowd there. And Juan Manso stayed where he was, the prisoner of his own good reputation.

Centuries went by — or so it seemed to Juan Manso, for it took that much time for the meek little lamb to begin to lose his patience. Finally one day he happened to meet a wise and saintly bishop who turned out to be the great-great-grandson of one of Manso's brothers. Juan voiced his complaints to his great-great-grandnephew, and the wise and saintly bishop offered to intercede for him when he came before the Eternal Father. On the strength of this, Juan yielded his place to the wise and saintly bishop who, when he entered Heaven, quite properly went straight to the Eternal Father to pay Him his respects. He concluded his little talk with The Almighty, who listened absent-mindedly and said:

"Wasn't there something else you wanted to say?"

And with His glance He searched the depths of the bishop's heart.

"Lord, permit me to intercede for one of Thy servants who is out there at the very tip end of the line. ... "

"Don't beat about the bush," thundered The Lord. "You mean Juan Manso."

"Yes, Lord, he is the one; Juan Manso, who. ... "

"All right! All right! Let him look out for himself, and don't you get mixed up again in other people's affairs!" And turning to the angel who was introducing souls, He added: "Let the next one in!"

If anything is capable of marring the eternal happiness of a soul in everlasting bliss, we could say that the soul of the wise and saintly bishop was troubled. But at least, moved by pity, he went to Heaven's walls, next to which the long line was standing. He climbed up, and calling to Juan Manso he said:

"Great-great-uncle, how sad I am about this — how very sad, my dear man! The Lord told me that you should look out for yourself, and that I shouldn't get mixed up in other people's affairs again. But ... are you still at the end of the line? Come now, my dear man! Summon up some courage and don't yield your place again."

"Now he tells me!" exclaimed Juan Manso, shedding tears as big as chick-peas. But it was too late, for the tragic tradition was now attached to him: people no longer even asked him for his place, they just took it.

Crestfallen, he abandoned the line and began to wander about the lonely wastelands beyond the grave until he came upon many people, all downcast, walking along a road. He followed their footsteps and found himself at the gates of Purgatory.

"It will be easier to get in here," he said to himself, "and once inside they will send me directly to Heaven after I have been purified."

"Hey! Where are you going, my friend?"

Juan Manso turned around and found himself face to face with an angel who was wearing an academic mortarboard and had a pen behind his ear. He looked at Juan over the top of his glasses, had him turn around, and after examining him from head to foot frowned and said:

"H-m-m! *Malorum causa* — the root of all ills! You are completely grey, and I'm afraid to put you through our procedures for fear you'll melt. You would do better to go to Limbo."

"To Limbo!"

Upon hearing this, Juan Manso became indignant for the first time, for no man is so patient and long-suffering that he will stand for having an angel treat him like a complete idiot.

In desperation, he set out for Hell. Here there was no waiting line, nor anything like one. It had a broad entrance, from which came puffs of thick smoke and an infernal din. At the door a poor devil was playing a hand-organ and shrieking at the top of his voice:

"Come inside, gentlemen, step inside ... Here you will see the human comedy ... Anyone may enter. ..."

Juan Manso closed his eyes.

"Hey, young man! Stop!" the poor devil said to him.

"Didn't you say that anyone might enter?"

"Yes, but ... Look," said the poor devil earnestly, as he stroked his tail, "we still have some slight spark of conscience ... and, after all ... you?"

"All right, all right!" said Juan Manso, turning away because he could not stand the smoke.

And he heard the devil mutter to himself, "Poor fellow!"

"Poor fellow? Even the devil pities me!"

Desperate now to the point of madness, he began to bob around like a cork in mid-ocean as he crossed the vast spaces beyond the grave. From time to time he would meet other legendary lost souls.

One day, attracted by the appetizing odor that was coming from Heaven, he approached its walls to see what they were cooking inside. It was about time for sunset, and he saw that The Lord was coming out to enjoy the cool air in the gardens of Paradise. Juan Manso waited for Him near the wall, and when he saw His noble head he opened his arms wide in supplication and said in a rather indignant tone:

"Lord, Lord, didst Thou not promise the Kingdom of Heaven to the meek?"

"Yes, but to the enterprising, not to the weak-kneed."

And He turned His back on Juan.

An old legend recounts that The Lord, taking pity on Juan Manso, let him return to this wicked world, and that when he got here again he began to push people around right and left. When he died a second time, he shoved his way right past the famous line and slipped boldly into Paradise.

Now inside, he keeps repeating:

"Man has to fight his way through life on earth!"

QUESTIONS

1. By what images does Unamuno try to make the process of final judgment look like an ordinary event? Does he succeed?

2. How do Juan's earthly habits carry over into the next world?

3. What is the author's purpose in making the "humble Franciscan friar" a seeker of privilege?

4. Were you surprised by the Lord's answer to the interceding bishop? by his last remark to Juan?

5. Jesus taught by parables. This story suggests that we should assert ourselves, even at the expense of the meek ones who are in our way. Is this Unamuno's message, or is he being ironic? What does the opening sentence suggest by way of an answer?

SAKI

(H. H. MUNRO)

The Open Window

"My aunt will be down presently, Mr. Nuttel," said a very self-possessed young lady of fifteen; "in the meantime you must try and put up with me."

Framton Nuttel endeavoured to say the correct something which should duly flatter the niece of the moment without unduly discounting the aunt that was to come. Privately he doubted more than ever whether these formal visits on a succession of total strangers would do much towards helping the nerve cure which he was supposed to be undergoing.

"I know how it will be," his sister had said when he was preparing to migrate to this rural retreat; "you will bury yourself down there and not speak to a living soul, and your nerves will be worse than ever from moping. I shall just give you letters of introduction to all the people I know there. Some of them, as far as I can remember, were quite nice."

Framton wondered whether Mrs. Sappleton, the lady to whom he was presenting one of the letters of introduction, came into the nice division.

"Do you know many of the people round here?" asked the niece, when she judged that they had had sufficient silent communion.

"Hardly a soul," said Framton. "My sister was staying here, at the Rectory, you know, some four years ago, and she gave me letters of introduction to some of the people here."

He made the last statement in a tone of distinct regret.

"Then you know practically nothing about my aunt?" pursued the self-possessed young lady.

"Only her name and address," admitted the caller. He was wondering whether Sappleton was in the married or widowed state. An undefinable something about the room seemed to suggest masculine habitation.

"Her great tragedy happened just three years ago," said the child; "that would be since your sister's time."

"Her tragedy?" asked Framton; somehow in this restful country spot tragedies seemed out of place.

"You may wonder why we keep that window wide open on an October afternoon," said the niece, indicating a large French window that opened on to a lawn.

"It is quite warm for the time of the year," said Framton; "but has that window got anything to do with the tragedy?"

"Out through that window, three years ago to a day, her husband and her two young brothers went off for their day's shooting. They never came back. In crossing the moor to their favourite snipe-shooting ground they were all three engulfed in a treacherous piece of bog. It had been that dreadful wet summer, you know, and places that were safe in other years gave way suddenly without warning. Their bodies were never recovered. That was the dreadful part of it." Here the child's voice lost its self-possessed note and became falteringly human. "Poor aunt always thinks that they will come back some day, they and the little brown spaniel that was lost with them, and walk in at that window just as they used to do. That is why the window is kept open every evening till it is quite dusk. Poor dear aunt, she has often told me how they went out, her husband with his white waterproof coat over his arm, and Ronnie, her youngest brother, singing, 'Bertie, why do you bound?' as he always did to tease her, because she said it got on her nerves. Do you know, sometimes on still, quiet evenings like this, I almost get a creepy feeling that they will all walk in through that window——"

She broke off with a little shudder. It was a relief to Framton when the aunt bustled into the room with a whirl of apologies for being late in making her appearance.

"I hope Vera has been amusing you?" she said.

"She has been very interesting," said Framton.

"I hope you don't mind the open window," said Mrs. Sappleton briskly; "my husband and brothers will be home directly from shooting, and they always come in this way. They've been out for snipe in the marshes today, so they'll make a fine mess over my poor carpets. So like you men-folk, isn't it?"

She rattled on cheerfully about the shooting and the scarcity of birds, and the prospects for duck in the winter. To Framton it was all purely horrible. He made a desperate but only partially successful effort to turn the talk on to a less ghastly topic; he was conscious that his hostess was giving him only a fragment of her attention, and her eyes were constantly straying past him to the open window and the lawn beyond. It was certainly an unfortunate coincidence that he should have paid his visit on this tragic anniversary.

"The doctors agree in ordering me complete rest, an absence of mental excitement, and avoidance of anything in the nature of violent physical exercise," announced Framton, who laboured under the tolerably wide-spread delusion that total strangers and chance acquaintances are hungry for the least detail of one's ailments and infirmities, their cause and cure. "On the matter of diet they are not so much in agreement," he continued.

"No?" said Mrs. Sappleton, in a voice which only replaced a yawn at the last moment. Then she suddenly brightened into alert attention — but not to what Framton was saying.

"Here they are at last!" she cried. "Just in time for tea, and don't they look as if they were muddy up to the eyes!"

Framton shivered slightly and turned towards the niece with a look intended to convey sympathetic comprehension. The child was staring out through the open window with dazed horror in her eyes. In a chill shock of nameless fear Framton swung round in his seat and looked in the same direction.

In the deepening twilight three figures were walking across the lawn towards the window; they all carried guns under their arms, and one of them was additionally burdened with a white coat hung over his shoulders. A tired brown spaniel kept close to their heels. Noiselessly they neared the house, and then a hoarse young voice chanted out of the dusk: "I said, Bertie, why do you bound?"

Framton grabbed wildly at his stick and hat; the hall-door, the gravel-drive, and the front gate were dimly noted stages in his headlong retreat. A cyclist coming along the road had to run into the hedge to avoid imminent collision.

"Here we are, my dear," said the bearer of the white mackintosh, coming in through the window; "fairly muddy, but most of it's dry. Who was that who bolted out as we came up?"

"A most extraordinary man, a Mr. Nuttel," said Mrs. Sappleton; "could only talk about his illnesses, and dashed off without a word of good-bye or apology when you arrived. One would think he had seen a ghost."

"I expect it was the spaniel," said the niece calmly; "he told me he had a horror of dogs. He was once hunted into a cemetery somewhere on the banks of the Ganges by a pack of pariah dogs, and had to spend the night in a newly dug grave with the creatures snarling and grinning and foaming just above him. Enough to make any one lose their nerve."

Romance at short notice was her speciality.

QUESTIONS

1. How does the second paragraph prepare the reader for what is to follow? What essential information is presented there?

2. Is Vera's name appropriate? At what point does she decide to tell Mr. Nuttel her ghost story? At what point did you realize she was playing a trick on him?

3. Notice that we enter only one mind, Mr. Nuttel's. Why should that be so? Could suspense have been maintained had the story been told from Vera's point of view?

4. Does the last sentence adequately express the point of "The Open Window"?

5. In terms of each author's ability to surprise, compare "The Open Window" with Agatha Christie's "Double Sin" and Arthur Conan Doyle's "The Red-Headed League."

STEPHEN CRANE

The Open Boat

*A Tale Intended to Be after the Fact: Being the
Experience of Four Men from the Sunk Steamer*
COMMODORE

I

None of them knew the color of the sky. Their eyes glanced level and were fastened upon the waves that swept toward them. These waves were of the hue of slate, save for the tops, which were of foaming white, and all of the men knew the colors of the sea. The horizon narrowed and widened, and dipped and rose, and at all times its edge was jagged with waves that seemed thrust up in points like rocks.

Many a man ought to have a bathtub larger than the boat which here rode upon the sea. These waves were most wrongfully and barbarously abrupt and tall, and each froth-top was a problem in small-boat navigation.

The cook squatted in the bottom, and looked with both eyes at the six inches of gunwale which separated him from the ocean. His sleeves were rolled over his fat forearms, and the two flaps of his unbuttoned vest dangled as he bent to bail out the boat. Often he said, "Gawd! that was a narrow clip." As he remarked it he invariably gazed eastward over the broken sea.

The oiler, steering with one of the two oars in the boat, sometimes raised himself suddenly to keep clear of water that swirled in over the stern. It was a thin little oar, and it seemed often ready to snap.

The correspondent, pulling at the other oar, watched the waves and wondered why he was there.

The injured captain, lying in the bow, was at this time buried in that profound dejection and indifference which comes, temporarily at least, to even the bravest and most enduring when, willy-nilly, the firm fails, the army loses, the ship goes down. The mind of the master of a vessel is rooted deep in the timbers of her, though he command for a day or a decade; and this captain had on him the stern impression of a scene in the grays of dawn of seven turned faces, and later a stump of a topmast with a white ball on it, that slashed to and fro at the waves, went low and lower, and down. Thereafter there was something strange in his voice. Although steady, it was deep with mourning, and of a quality beyond oration or tears.

"Keep'er a little more south, Billie," said he.

"A little more south, sir," said the oiler in the stern.

A seat in this boat was not unlike a seat upon a bucking broncho, and by the same token a broncho is not much smaller. The craft pranced and reared and plunged like an animal. As each wave came, and she rose for it, she seemed like a horse making at a fence outrageously high. The manner of her scramble over these walls of water is a mystic thing, and, moreover, at the top of them were ordinarily these problems in white water, the foam racing down from the summit of each wave requiring a new leap, and a leap from the air. Then, after scornfully bumping a crest, she would slide and race and splash down a long incline, and arrive bobbing and nodding in front of the next menace.

A singular disadvantage of the sea lies in the fact that after successfully surmounting one wave you discover that there is another behind it just as important and just as nervously anxious to do something effective in the way of swamping boats. In a ten-foot dinghy one can get an idea of the resources of the sea in the line of waves that is not probable to the average experience, which is never at sea in a dinghy. As each slaty wall of water approached, it shut all else from the view of the men in the boat, and it was not difficult to imagine that this particular wave was the final outburst of the ocean, the last effort of the grim water. There was a terrible grace in the move of the waves, and they came in silence, save for the snarling of the crests.

In the wan light the faces of the men must have been gray. Their eyes must have glinted in strange ways as they gazed steadily astern. Viewed from a balcony, the whole thing would, doubtless, have been weirdly picturesque. But the men in the boat had no time to see it, and if they had had leisure, there were other things to occupy their minds. The sun swung steadily up the sky, and they knew it was broad day because the color of the sea changed from slate to emerald-green streaked with amber lights, and the foam was like tumbling snow. The process of the breaking day was unknown to them. They were aware only of this effect upon the color of the waves that rolled toward them.

In disjointed sentences the cook and the correspondent argued as to the difference between a life-saving station and a house of refuge. The cook had said: "There's a house of refuge just north of the Mosquito Inlet Light, and as soon as they see us they'll come off in their boat and pick us up."

"As soon as who see us?" said the correspondent.

"The crew," said the cook.

"Houses of refuge don't have crews," said the correspondent. "As I understand them, they are only places where clothes and grub are stored for the benefit of shipwrecked people. They don't carry crews."

"Oh, yes, they do," said the cook.

"No, they don't," said the correspondent.

"Well, we're not there yet, anyhow," said the oiler, in the stern.

"Well," said the cook, "perhaps it's not a house of refuge that I'm thinking of as being near Mosquito Inlet Light; perhaps it's a life-saving station."

"We're not there yet," said the oiler in the stern.

II

As the boat bounced from the top of each wave the wind tore through the hair of the hatless men, and as the craft plopped her stern down again the spray slashed past them. The crest of each of these waves was a hill, from the top of which the men surveyed for a moment a broad tumultuous expanse, shining and wind-riven. It was probably splendid, it was probably glorious, this play of the free sea, wild with lights of emerald and white and amber.

"Bully good thing it's an on-shore wind," said the cook. "If not, where would we be? Wouldn't have a show."

"That's right," said the correspondent.

The busy oiler nodded his assent.

Then the captain, in the bow, chuckled in a way that expressed humor, contempt, tragedy, all in one. "Do you think we've got much of a show now, boys?" said he.

Whereupon the three were silent, save for a trifle of hemming and hawing. To express any particular optimism at this time they felt to be childish and stupid, but they all doubtless possessed this sense of the situation in their minds. A young man thinks doggedly at such times. On the other hand, the ethics of their condition was decidedly against any open suggestion of hopelessness. So they were silent.

"Oh, well," said the captain, soothing his children, "we'll get ashore all right."

But there was that in his tone which made them think; so the oiler quoth, "Yes! if this wind holds."

The cook was bailing. "Yes! if we don't catch hell in the surf."

Canton-flannel[1] gulls flew near and far. Sometimes they sat down on the sea, near patches of brown seaweed that rolled over the waves with a movement like carpets on a line in a gale. The birds sat comfortably in groups, and they were envied by some in the dinghy, for the wrath of the sea was no more to them than it was to a covey of prairie chickens a thousand miles inland. Often they came very close and stared at the men with black bead-like eyes. At these times they were uncanny and sinister in their unblinking scrutiny, and the men hooted angrily at them, telling them to be gone. One came, and evidently decided to alight on the top of the captain's head. The bird flew parallel to the boat and did not circle, but made short sidelong jumps in the air in chicken fashion. His black eyes were wistfully fixed upon the captain's head. "Ugly brute," said the oiler to the bird. "You look as if you were made with a jackknife." The cook and the correspondent swore darkly at the creature. The captain naturally wished to knock it away with the end of the heavy painter, but he did not dare do it, because anything resembling an emphatic gesture would have capsized this freighted boat; and so, with his open hand, the captain gently and carefully waved the gull away. After it had been discouraged from the pursuit the captain breathed easier on account of his hair, and others breathed easier because the bird struck their minds at this time as being somehow gruesome and ominous.

In the meantime the oiler and the correspondent rowed; and also they rowed. They sat together in the same seat, and each rowed an oar. Then the oiler took both oars; then the correspondent took both oars, then the oiler; then the correspondent. They rowed and they rowed. The very ticklish part of the business was when the time came for the reclining one in the stern to take his turn at the oars. By the very last star of truth, it is easier to steal eggs from under a hen than it was to change seats in the dinghy. First the man in the stern slid his hand

---

[1] A comparison to sturdy cotton flannel.

along the thwart and moved with care, as if he were of Sèvres.[2] Then the man in the rowing-seat slid his hand along the other thwart. It was all done with the most extraordinary care. As the two sidled past each other, the whole party kept watchful eyes on the coming wave, and the captain cried: "Look out, now! Steady, there!"

The brown mats of seaweed that appeared from time to time were like islands, bits of earth. They were travelling, apparently, neither one way nor the other. They were, to all intents, stationary. They informed the men in the boat that it was making progress slowly toward the land.

The captain, rearing cautiously in the bow after the dinghy soared on a great swell, said that he had seen the lighthouse at Mosquito Inlet. Presently the cook remarked that he had seen it. The correspondent was at the oars then, and for some reason he too wished to look at the lighthouse; but his back was toward the far shore, and the waves were important, and for some time he could not seize an opportunity to turn his head. But at last there came a wave more gentle than the others, and when at the crest of it he swiftly scoured the western horizon.

"See it?" said the captain.

"No," said the correspondent, slowly; "I didn't see anything."

"Look again," said the captain. He pointed. "It's exactly in that direction."

At the top of another wave the correspondent did as he was bid, and this time his eyes chanced on a small, still thing on the edge of the swaying horizon. It was precisely like the point of a pin. It took an anxious eye to find a lighthouse so tiny.

"Think we'll make it, Captain?"

"If this wind holds and the boat don't swamp, we can't do much else," said the captain.

The little boat, lifted by each towering sea and splashed viciously by the crests, made progress that in the absence of seaweed was not apparent to those in her. She seemed just a wee thing wallowing, miraculously top up, at the mercy of five oceans. Occasionally a great spread of water, like white flames, swarmed into her.

"Bail her, cook," said the captain, serenely.

"All right, Captain," said the cheerful cook.

III

It would be difficult to describe the subtle brotherhood of men that was here established on the seas. No one said that it was so. No one mentioned it. But it dwelt in the boat, and each man felt it warm him. They were a captain, an oiler, a cook, and a correspondent, and they were friends — friends in a more curiously iron-bound degree than may be common. The hurt captain, lying against the water jar in the bow, spoke always in a low voice and calmly; but he could never command a more ready and swiftly obedient crew than the motley three of the dinghy. It was more than a mere recognition of what was best for the common safety. There was surely in it a quality that was personal and heart-felt. And after this devotion to the commander of the boat, there was this comradeship, that the correspondent, for instance, who had been taught to be cynical of men, knew even at the time was the best experience of his life. But no one said that it was so. No one mentioned it.

"I wish we had a sail," remarked the captain. "We might try my overcoat on the end of an oar, and give you two boys a chance to rest." So the cook and the correspondent held the mast and spread wide the overcoat; the oiler steered; and the little boat made good way with her

---

[2] Delicate and expensive French china.

new rig. Sometimes the oiler had to scull sharply to keep a sea from breaking into the boat, but otherwise sailing was a success.

Meanwhile the lighthouse had been growing slowly larger. It had now almost assumed color, and appeared like a little gray shadow on the sky. The man at the oars could not be prevented from turning his head rather often to try for a glimpse of this little gray shadow.

At last, from the top of each wave, the men in the tossing boat could see land. Even as the lighthouse was an upright shadow on the sky, this land seemed but a long black shadow on the sea. It certainly was thinner than paper. "We must be about opposite New Smyrna,"[3] said the cook, who had coasted this shore often in schooners. "Captain, by the way, I believe they abandoned that life-saving station there about a year ago."

"Did they?" said the captain.

The wind slowly died away. The cook and the correspondent were not now obliged to slave in order to hold high the oar. But the waves continued their old impetuous swooping at the dinghy, and the little craft, no longer underway, struggled woundily over them. The oiler or the correspondent took the oars again.

Shipwrecks are *apropos* of nothing. If men could only train for them and have them occur when the men had reached pink condition, there would be less drowning at sea. Of the four in the dinghy none had slept any time worth mentioning for two days and two nights previous to embarking in the dinghy, and in the excitement of clambering about the deck of a foundering ship they had also forgotten to eat heartily.

For these reasons, and for others, neither the oiler nor the correspondent was fond of rowing at this time. The correspondent wondered ingenuously how in the name of all that was sane could there be people who thought it amusing to row a boat. It was not an amusement; it was a diabolical punishment, and even a genius of mental aberrations could never conclude that it was anything but a horror to the muscles and a crime against the back. He mentioned to the boat in general how the amusement of rowing struck him, and the weary-faced oiler smiled in full sympathy. Previously to the foundering, by the way, the oiler had worked a double watch in the engine-room of the ship.

"Take her easy now, boys," said the captain. "Don't spend yourselves. If we have to run a surf you'll need all your strength, because we'll sure have to swim for it. Take your time."

Slowly the land arose from the sea. From a black line it became a line of black and a line of white — trees and sand. Finally the captain said that he could make out a house on the shore. "That's the house of refuge, sure," said the cook. "They'll see us before long, and come out after us."

The distant lighthouse reared high. "The keeper ought to be able to make us out now, if he's looking through a glass," said the captain. "He'll notify the life-saving people."

"None of those other boats could have got ashore to give word of this wreck," said the oiler, in a low voice, "else the life-boat would be out hunting us."

Slowly and beautifully the land loomed out of the sea. The wind came again. It had veered from the northeast to the southeast. Finally a new sound struck the ears of the men in the boat. It was the low thunder of the surf on the shore. "We'll never be able to make the lighthouse now," said the captain. "Swing her head a little more north, Billie."

"A little more north, sir," said the oiler.

Whereupon the little boat turned her nose once more down the wind, and all but the oarsman watched the shore grow. Under the influence of this expansion doubt and direful

---

[3] A coastal town just south of Daytona Beach, Florida.

apprehension were leaving the minds of the men. The management of the boat was still most absorbing, but it could not prevent a quiet cheerfulness. In an hour, perhaps, they would be ashore.

Their backbones had become thoroughly used to balancing in the boat, and they now rode this wild colt of a dinghy like circus men. The correspondent thought that he had been drenched to the skin, but happening to feel in the top pocket of his coat, he found therein eight cigars. Four of them were soaked with sea-water; four were perfectly scatheless. After a search, somebody produced three dry matches; and thereupon the four waifs rode impudently in their little boat and, with an assurance of an impending rescue shining in their eyes, puffed at the big cigars, and judged well and ill of all men. Everybody took a drink of water.

IV

"Cook," remarked the captain, "there don't seem to be any signs of life about your house of refuge."

"No," replied the cook. "Funny they don't see us!"

A broad stretch of lowly coast lay before the eyes of the men. It was of low dunes topped with dark vegetation. The roar of the surf was plain, and sometimes they could see the white lip of a wave as it spun up the beach. A tiny house was blocked out black upon the sky. Southward, the slim lighthouse lifted its little gray length.

Tide, wind, and waves were swinging the dinghy northward. "Funny they don't see us," said the men.

The surf's roar was here dulled, but its tone was nevertheless thunderous and mighty. As the boat swam over the great rollers the men sat listening to this roar. "We'll swamp sure," said everybody.

It is fair to say here that there was not a life-saving station within twenty miles in either direction; but the men did not know this fact, and in consequence they made dark and opprobrious remarks concerning the eyesight of the nation's life-savers. Four scowling men sat in the dinghy and surpassed records in the invention of epithets.

"Funny they don't see us."

The light-heartedness of a former time had completely faded. To their sharpened minds it was easy to conjure pictures of all kinds of incompetency and blindness and, indeed, cowardice. There was the shore of the populous land, and it was bitter and bitter to them that from it came no sign.

"Well," said the captain, ultimately, "I suppose we'll have to make a try for ourselves. If we stay out here too long, we'll none of us have strength left to swim after the boat swamps."

And so the oiler, who was at the oars, turned the boat straight for the shore. There was a sudden tightening of muscles. There was some thinking.

"If we don't all get ashore," said the captain—"if we don't all get ashore, I suppose you fellows know where to send news of my finish?"

They then briefly exchanged some addresses and admonitions. As for the reflections of the men, there was a great deal of rage in them. Perchance they might be formulated thus: "If I am going to be drowned — if I am going to be drowned — if I am going to be drowned, why, in the name of the seven mad gods who rule the sea, was I allowed to come thus far and contemplate sand and trees? Was I brought here merely to have my nose dragged away as I was about to nibble the sacred cheese of life? It is preposterous. If this old ninny-woman, Fate, cannot do better than this, she should be deprived of the management of men's fortunes. She is an old hen who knows not her intention. If she has decided to drown me, why did she not do it in the beginning and save me all this trouble? The whole affair is absurd. ... But no; she cannot mean to drown me. She dare not drown me. She cannot drown me. Not after all this work." Afterward the man might have had an impulse to shake his fist at the clouds. "Just you drown me, now, and then hear what I call you!"

The billows that came at this time were more formidable. They seemed always just about to break and roll over the little boat in a turmoil of foam. There was a preparatory and long growl in the speech of them. No mind unused to the sea would have concluded that the dinghy could ascend these sheer heights in time. The shore was still afar. The oiler was a wily surfman. "Boys," he said swiftly, "she won't live three minutes more, and we're too far out to swim. Shall I take her to sea again, Captain?"

"Yes; go ahead!" said the captain.

This oiler, by a series of quick miracles and fast and steady oarsmanship, turned the boat in the middle of the surf and took her safely to sea again.

There was a considerable silence as the boat bumped over the furrowed sea to deeper water. Then somebody in gloom spoke: "Well, anyhow, they must have seen us from the shore by now."

The gulls went in slanting flight up the wind toward the gray, desolate east. A squall, marked by dingy clouds and clouds brick-red, like smoke from a burning building, appeared from the southeast.

"What do you think of those life-saving people? Ain't they peaches?"

"Funny they haven't seen us."

"Maybe they think we're out here for sport! Maybe they think we're fishin'. Maybe they think we're damned fools."

It was a long afternoon. A changed tide tried to force them southward, but wind and wave said northward. Far ahead, where coast-line, sea, and sky formed their mighty angle, there were little dots which seemed to indicate a city on the shore.

"St. Augustine?"

The captain shook his head. "Too near Mosquito Inlet."

And the oiler rowed, and then the correspondent rowed; then the oiler rowed. It was a weary business. The human back can become the seat of more aches and pains than are registered in books for the composite anatomy of a regiment. It is a limited area, but it can become the theater of innumerable muscular conflicts, tangles, wrenches, knots, and other comforts.

"Did you ever like to row, Billie?" asked the correspondent.

"No," said the oiler; "hang it!"

When one exchanged the rowing-seat for a place in the bottom of the boat, he suffered a bodily depression that caused him to be careless of everything save an obligation to wiggle one finger. There was cold sea-water swashing to and fro in the boat, and he lay in it. His head, pillowed on a thwart, was within an inch of the swirl of a wave-crest, and sometimes a particularly obstreperous sea came inboard and drenched him once more. But these matters did not annoy him. It is almost certain that if the boat had capsized he would have tumbled comfortably out upon the ocean as if he felt sure that it was a great soft mattress.

"Look! There's a man on the shore!"

"Where?"

"There! See 'im? See 'im?"

"Yes, sure! He's walking along."

"Now he's stopped. Look! He's facing us!"

"He's waving at us!"

"So he is! By thunder!"

"Ah, now we're all right! Now we're all right! There'll be a boat out here for us in half an hour."

"He's going on. He's running. He's going up to that house there."

The remote beach seemed lower than the sea, and it required a searching glance to discern the little black figure. The captain saw a floating stick, and they rowed to it. A bath towel was by some weird chance in the boat, and, tying this on the stick, the captain waved it. The oarsman did not dare turn his head, so he was obliged to ask questions.

"What's he doing now?"

"He's standing still again. He's looking, I think. ... There he goes again — toward the house. ... Now he's stopped again."

"Is he waving at us?"

"No, not now; he was, though."

"Look! There comes another man!"

"He's running."

"Look at him go, would you!"

"Why, he's on a bicycle. Now he's met the other man. They're both waving at us. Look!"

"There comes something up the beach."

"What the devil is that thing?"

"Why, it looks like a boat."

"Why, certainly, it's a boat."

"No; it's on wheels."

"Yes, so it is. Well, that must be the life-boat. They drag them along shore on a wagon."

"That's the life-boat, sure."

"No, by God, it's — it's an omnibus."

"I tell you it's a life-boat."

"It is not! It's an omnibus. I can see it plain. See? One of these big hotel omnibuses."

"By thunder, you're right. It's an omnibus, sure as fate. What do you suppose they are doing with an omnibus? Maybe they are going around collecting the life-crew, hey?"

"That's it, likely. Look! There's a fellow waving a little black flag. He's standing on the steps of the omnibus. There come those other two fellows. Now they're all talking together. Look at the fellow with the flag. Maybe he ain't waving it!"

"That ain't a flag, is it? That's his coat. Why, certainly, that's his coat."

"So it is; it's his coat. He's taken it off and is waving it around his head. But would you look at him swing it!"

"Oh, say, there isn't any life-saving station there. That's just a winter-resort hotel omnibus that has brought over some of the boarders to see us drown."

"What's that idiot with the coat mean? What's he signaling, anyhow?"

"It looks as if he were trying to tell us to go north. There must be a life-saving station up there."

"No; he thinks we're fishing. Just giving us a merry hand. See? Ah, there, Willie!"

"Well, I wish I could make something out of those signals. What do you suppose he means?"

"He don't mean anything; he's just playing."

"Well, if he'd just signal us to try the surf again, or to go to sea and wait, or go north, or go south, or go to hell, there would be some reason in it. But look at him! He just stands there and keeps his coat revolving like a wheel. The ass!"

"There come more people."

"Now there's quite a mob. Look! Isn't that a boat?"

"Where? Oh, I see where you mean. No, that's no boat."

"That fellow is still waving his coat."

"He must think we like to see him do that. Why don't he quit it? It don't mean anything."

"I don't know. I think he is trying to make us go north. It must be that there's a life-saving station there somewhere."

"Say, he ain't tired yet. Look at 'im wave!"

"Wonder how long he can keep that up. He's been revolving his coat ever since he caught sight of us. He's an idiot. Why aren't they getting men to bring a boat out? A fishing-boat — one of the those big yawls — could come out here all right. Why don't he do something?"

"Oh, it's all right now."

"They'll have a boat out here for us in less than no time, now that they've seen us."

A faint yellow tone came into the sky over the low land. The shadows on the sea slowly deepened. The wind bore coldness with it, and the men began to shiver.

"Holy smoke!" said one, allowing his voice to express his impious mood, "if we keep on monkeying out here! If we've got to flounder out here all night!"

"Oh, we'll never have to stay here all night! Don't you worry. They've seen us now, and it won't be long before they'll come chasing out after us."

The shore grew dusky. The man waving a coat blended gradually into this gloom, and it swallowed in the same manner the omnibus and the group of people. The spray, when it dashed uproariously over the side, made the voyagers shrink and swear like men who were being branded.

"I'd like to catch the chump who waved the coat. I feel like socking him one, just for luck."

"Why? What did he do?"

"Oh, nothing, but then he seemed so damned cheerful."

In the meantime the oiler rowed, and then the correspondent rowed, and then the oiler rowed. Gray-faced and bowed forward, they mechanically, turn by turn, plied the leaden oars. The form of the lighthouse had vanished from the southern horizon, but finally a pale star appeared, just lifting from the sea. The streaked saffron in the west passed before the all-merging darkness, and the sea to the east was black. The land had vanished, and was expressed only by the low and drear thunder of the surf.

"If I am going to be drowned — if I am going to be drowned — if I am going to be drowned, why, in the name of the seven mad gods who rule the sea, was I allowed to come thus far and contemplate sand and trees? Was I brought here merely to have my nose dragged away as I was about to nibble the sacred cheese of life?"

The patient captain, drooped over the water-jar, was sometimes obliged to speak to the oarsman.

"Keep her head up! Keep her head up!"

"Keep her head up, sir." The voices were weary and low.

This was surely a quiet evening. All save the oarsman lay heavily and listlessly in the boat's bottom. As for him, his eyes were just capable of noting the tall black waves that swept forward in a most sinister silence, save for an occasional subdued growl of a crest.

The cook's head was on a thwart, and he looked without interest at the water under his nose. He was deep in other scenes. Finally he spoke. "Billie," he murmured, dreamfully, "what kind of pie do you like best?"

V

"Pie!" said the oiler and the correspondent, agitatedly. "Don't talk about those things, blast you!"

"Well," said the cook, "I was just thinking about ham sandwiches, and — "

A night on the sea in an open boat is a long night. As darkness settled finally, the shine of the light, lifting from the sea in the south, changed to full gold. On the northern horizon a new light appeared, a small bluish gleam on the edge of the waters. These two lights were the furniture of the world. Otherwise there was nothing but waves.

Two men huddled in the stern, and distances were so magnificent in the dinghy that the rower was enabled to keep his feet partly warm by thrusting them under his companions. Their legs indeed extended far under the rowing-seat until they touched the feet of the captain forward. Sometimes, despite the efforts of the tired oarsman, a wave came piling into the boat, an icy wave of the night, and the chilling water soaked them anew. They would twist their bodies for a moment and groan, and sleep the dead sleep once more, while the water in the boat gurgled about them as the craft rocked.

The plan of the oiler and the correspondent was for one to row until he lost the ability, and then arouse the other from his sea-water couch in the bottom of the boat.

The oiler plied the oars until his head drooped forward and the overpowering sleep blinded him; and he rowed yet afterward. Then he touched a man in the bottom of the boat, and called his name. "Will you spell me for a little while?" he said meekly.

"Sure, Billie," said the correspondent, awaking and dragging himself to a sitting position. They exchanged places carefully, and the oiler, cuddling down in the sea-water at the cook's side, seemed to go to sleep instantly.

The particular violence of the sea had ceased. The waves came without snarling. The obligation of the man at the oars was to keep the boat headed so that the tilt of the rollers would not capsize her, and to preserve her from filling when the crests rushed past. The black waves were silent and hard to be seen in the darkness. Often one was almost upon the boat before the oarsman was aware.

In a low voice the correspondent addressed the captain. He was not sure that the captain was awake, although this iron man seemed to be always awake. "Captain, shall I keep her making for that light north, sir?"

The same steady voice answered him. "Yes. Keep it about two points off the port bow."

The cook had tied a life-belt around himself in order to get even the warmth which this clumsy cork contrivance could donate, and he seemed almost stove-like when a rower, whose teeth invariably chattered wildly as soon as he ceased his labor, dropped down to sleep.

The correspondent, as he rowed, looked down at the two men sleeping underfoot. The cook's arm was around the oiler's shoulders, and, with their fragmentary clothing and haggard faces, they were the babes of the sea — a grotesque rendering of the old babes in the wood.

Later he must have grown stupid at his work, for suddenly there was a growling of water, and a crest came with a roar and a swash into the boat, and it was a wonder that it did not set the cook afloat in his life-belt. The cook continued to sleep, but the oiler sat up, blinking his eyes and shaking with the new cold.

"Oh, I'm awful sorry, Billie," said the correspondent, contritely.

"That's all right, old boy," said the oiler, and lay down again and was asleep.

Presently it seemed that even the captain dozed, and the correspondent thought that he was the one man afloat on all the ocean. The wind had a voice as it came over the waves, and it was sadder than the end.

There was a long, loud swishing astern of the boat, and a gleaming trail of phosphorescence, like blue flame, was furrowed on the black waters. It might have been made by a monstrous knife.

Then there came a stillness, while the correspondent breathed with open mouth and looked at the sea.

Suddenly there was another swish and another long flash of bluish light, and this time it was alongside the boat, and might almost have been reached with an oar. The correspondent saw an enormous fin speed like a shadow through the water, hurling the crystalline spray and leaving the long glowing trail.

The correspondent looked over his shoulder at the captain. His face was hidden, and he seemed to be asleep. He looked at the babes of the sea. They certainly were asleep. So, being bereft of sympathy, he leaned a little way to one side and swore softly into the sea.

But the thing did not then leave the vicinity of the boat. Ahead or astern, on one side or the other, at intervals long or short, fled the long sparkling streak, and there was to be heard the *whirroo* of the dark fin. The speed and power of the thing was greatly to be admired. It cut the water like a gigantic and keen projectile.

The presence of this biding thing did not affect the man with the same horror that it would if he had been a picnicker. He simply looked at the sea dully and swore in an undertone.

Nevertheless, it is true that he did not wish to be alone with the thing. He wished one of his companions to awake by chance and keep him company with it. But the captain hung motionless over the water-jar, and the oiler and the cook in the bottom of the boat were plunged in slumber.

VI

"If I am going to be drowned — if I am going to be drowned — if I am going to be drowned, why, in the name of the seven mad gods who rule the sea, was I allowed to come thus far and contemplate sand and trees?"

During this dismal night, it may be remarked that a man would conclude that it was really the intention of the seven mad gods to drown him, despite the abominable injustice of it. For it was certainly an abominable injustice to drown a man who had worked so hard, so hard. The man felt it would be a crime most unnatural. Other people had drowned at sea since galleys swarmed with painted sails, but still —

When it occurs to a man that nature does not regard him as important, and that she feels she would not maim the universe by disposing of him, he at first wishes to throw bricks at the temple, and he hates deeply the fact that there are no bricks and no temples. Any visible expression of nature would surely be pelleted with his jeers.

Then, if there be no tangible thing to hoot, he feels, perhaps, the desire to confront a personification and indulge in pleas, bowed to one knee, and with hands supplicant, saying, "Yes, but I love myself."

A high cold star on a winter's night is the word he feels that she says to him. Thereafter he knows the pathos of his situation.

The men in the dinghy had not discussed these matters, but each had, no doubt, reflected upon them in silence and according to his mind. There was seldom any expression upon their faces save the general one of complete weariness. Speech was devoted to the business of the boat.

To chime the notes of his emotion, a verse mysteriously entered the correspondent's head. He had even forgotten that he had forgotten this verse, but it suddenly was in his mind.

A soldier of the Legion lay dying in Algiers;
There was lack of woman's nursing,
    there was dearth of woman's tears;
But a comrade stood beside him,
    and he took the comrade's hand,
And he said, "I never more shall see
    my own, my native land."[4]

In his childhood the correspondent had been made acquainted with the fact that a soldier of the Legion lay dying in Algiers, but he had never regarded it as important. Myriads of his schoolfellows had informed him of the soldier's plight, but the dinning had naturally ended by making him perfectly indifferent. He had never considered it his affair that a soldier of the Legion lay dying in Algiers, nor had it appeared to him as a matter for sorrow. It was less to him than the breaking of a pencil's point.

Now, however, it quaintly came to him as a human, living thing. It was no longer merely a picture of a few throes in the breast of a poet, meanwhile drinking tea and warming his feet at the grate; it was an actuality — stern, mournful, and fine.

The correspondent plainly saw the soldier. He lay on the sand with his feet out straight and still. While his pale left hand was upon his chest in an attempt to thwart the going of his life, the blood came between his fingers. In the far Algerian distance, a city of low square forms was set against a sky that was faint with the last sunset hues. The correspondent, plying the oars and dreaming of the slow and slower movements of the lips of the soldier, was moved by a profound and perfectly impersonal comprehension. He was sorry for the soldier of the Legion who lay dying in Algiers.

The thing which had followed the boat and waited had evidently grown bored at the delay. There was no longer to be heard the slash of the cutwater, and there was no longer the flame of the long trail. The light in the north still glimmered, but it was apparently no nearer to the boat. Sometimes the boom of the surf rang in the correspondent's ears, and he turned the craft seaward then and rowed harder. Southward, some one had evidently built a watch-fire on the beach. It was too low and too far to be seen, but it made a shimmering, roseate reflection upon the bluff in back of it, and this could be discerned from the boat. The wind came stronger, and sometimes a wave suddenly raged out like a mountain-cat, and there was to be seen the sheen and sparkle of a broken crest.

The captain, in the bow, moved on his water-jar and sat erect. "Pretty long night," he observed to the correspondent. He looked at the shore. "Those life-saving people take their time."

"Did you see that shark playing around?"

"Yes, I saw him. He was a big fellow, all right."

"Wish I had known you were awake."

Later the correspondent spoke into the bottom of the boat. "Billie!" There was a slow and gradual disentanglement. "Billie, will you spell me?"

"Sure," said the oiler.

As soon as the correspondent touched the cold, comfortable sea-water in the bottom of the boat and had huddled close to the cook's life-belt he was deep in sleep, despite the fact that

---

[4] From verses by Caroline Norton (1808–1877), a minor English writer.

his teeth played all the popular airs. This sleep was so good to him that it was but a moment before he heard a voice call his name in a tone that demonstrated the last stages of exhaustion.

"Will you spell me?"

"Sure, Billie."

The light in the north had mysteriously vanished, but the correspondent took his course from the wide-awake captain.

Later in the night they took the boat farther out to sea, and the captain directed the cook to take one oar at the stern and keep the boat facing the seas. He was to call out if he should hear the thunder of the surf. This plan enabled the oiler and the correspondent to get respite together. "We'll give those boys a chance to get into shape again," said the captain. They curled down and, after a few preliminary chatterings and trembles, slept once more the dead sleep. Neither knew they had bequeathed to the cook the company of another shark, or perhaps the same shark.

As the boat caroused on the waves, spray occasionally bumped over the side and gave them a fresh soaking, but this had no power to break their repose. The ominous slash of the wind and the water affected them as it would have affected mummies.

"Boys," said the cook, with the notes of every reluctance in his voice, "she's drifted in pretty close. I guess one of you had better take her to sea again." The correspondent, aroused, heard the crash of the toppled crests.

As he was rowing, the captain gave him some whiskey-and-water, and this steadied the chills out of him. "If I ever get ashore and anybody shows me even a photograph of an oar—"

At last there was a short conversation.

"Billie! . . . Billie, will you spell me?"

"Sure," said the oiler.

VII

When the correspondent again opened his eyes, the sea and the sky were each of the gray hue of the dawning. Later, carmine and gold was painted upon the waters. The morning appeared finally, in its splendor, with a sky of pure blue, and the sunlight flamed on the tips of the waves.

On the distant dunes were set many little black cottages, and a tall white windmill reared above them. No man, nor dog, nor bicycle appeared on the beach. The cottages might have formed a deserted village.

The voyagers scanned the shore. A conference was held in the boat. "Well," said the captain, "if no help is coming, we might better try a run through the surf right away. If we stay out here much longer we will be too weak to do anything for ourselves at all." The others silently acquiesced in this reasoning. The boat was headed for the beach. The correspondent wondered if none ever ascended the tall wind-tower, and if then they never looked seaward. This tower was a giant, standing with its back to the plight of the ants. It represented in a degree, to the correspondent, the serenity of nature amid the struggles of the individual — nature in the wind, and nature in the vision of men. She did not seem cruel to him then, nor beneficent, nor treacherous, nor wise. But she was indifferent, flatly indifferent. It is, perhaps, plausible that a man in this situation, impressed with the unconcern of the universe, should see the innumerable flaws of his life, and have them taste wickedly in his mind, and wish for another chance. A distinction between right and wrong seems absurdly clear to him, then, in this new ignorance of the grave-edge, and he understands that if he were given another opportunity he would mend his conduct and his words, and be better and brighter during an introduction or at a tea.

"Now, boys," said the captain, "she is going to swamp sure. All we can do is to work her in as far as possible, and then when she swamps, pile out and scramble for the beach. Keep cool now, and don't jump until she swamps sure."

The oiler took the oars. Over his shoulders he scanned the surf. "Captain," he said, "I think I'd better bring her about and keep her head-on to the seas and back her in."

"All right, Billie," said the captain. "back her in." The oiler swung the boat then, and, seated in the stern, the cook and the correspondent were obliged to look over their shoulders to contemplate the lonely and indifferent shore.

The monstrous inshore rollers heaved the boat high until the men were again enabled to see the white sheets of water scudding up the slanted beach. "We won't get in very close," said the captain. Each time a man could wrest his attention for the rollers, he turned his glance toward the shore, and in the expression of the eyes during this contemplation there was a singular quality. The correspondent, observing the others, knew that they were not afraid, but the full meaning of their glances was shrouded.

As for himself, he was too tired to grapple fundamentally with the fact. He tried to coerce his mind into thinking of it, but the mind was dominated at this time by the muscles, and the muscles said they did not care. It merely occurred to him that if he should drown it would be a shame.

There were no hurried words, no pallor, no plain agitation. The men simply looked at the shore. "Now, remember to get well clear of the boat when you jump," said the captain.

Seaward the crest of a roller suddenly fell with a thunderous crash, and the long white comber came roaring down upon the boat.

"Steady now," said the captain. The men were silent. They turned their eyes from the shore to the comber and waited. The boat slid up the incline, leaped at the furious top, bounced over it, and swung down the long back of the wave. Some water had been shipped, and the cook bailed it out.

But the next crest crashed also. The tumbling, boiling flood of white water caught the boat and whirled it almost perpendicular. Water swarmed in from all sides. The correspondent had his hands on the gunwale at this time, and when the water entered at that place he swiftly withdrew his fingers, as if he objected to wetting them.

The little boat, drunken with this weight of water, reeled and snuggled deeper into the sea. "Bail her out, cook! Bail her out!" said the captain.

"All right, Captain," said the cook.

"Now, boys, the next one will do for us sure," said the oiler. "Mind to jump clear of the boat."

The third wave moved forward, huge, furious, implacable. It fairly swallowed the dinghy, and almost simultaneously the men tumbled into the sea. A piece of life-belt had lain in the the bottom of the boat, and as the correspondent went overboard he held this to his chest with his left hand.

The January water was icy, and he reflected immediately that it was colder than he had expected to find it off the coast of Florida. This appeared to his dazed mind as a fact important enough to be noted at the time. The coldness of the water was sad; it was tragic. This fact was somehow mixed and confused with his opinion of his own situation, so that it seemed almost a proper reason for tears. The water was cold.

When he came to the surface he was conscious of little but the noisy water. Afterward he saw his companions in the sea. The oiler was ahead in the race. He was swimming strongly and rapidly. Off to the correspondent's left, the cook's great white and corked back bulged out of the water, and in the rear the captain was hanging with his one good hand to the keel of the overturned dinghy.

There is a certain immovable quality to a shore, and the correspondent wondered at it amid the confusion of the sea.

It seemed also very attractive; but the correspondent knew that it was a long journey, and he paddled leisurely. The piece of life-preserver lay under him, and sometimes he whirled down the incline of a wave as if he were on a hand-sled.

But finally he arrived at a place in the sea where travel was beset with difficulty. He did not pause swimming to inquire what manner of current had caught him, but there his progress ceased. The shore was set before him like a bit of scenery on a stage, and he looked at it and understood with his eyes each detail of it.

As the cook passed, much farther to the left, the captain was calling to him, "Turn over on your back, cook! Turn over on your back and use the oar."

"All right, sir." The cook turned on his back, and, paddling with an oar, went ahead as if he were a canoe.

Presently the boat also passed to the left of the correspondent, with the captain clinging with one hand to the keel. He would have appeared like a man raising himself to look over a board fence if it were not for the extraordinary gymnastics of the boat. The correspondent marvelled that the captain could still hold to it.

They passed on nearer to shore — the oiler, the cook, the captain — and following them went the water-jar, bouncing gaily over the seas.

The correspondent remained in the grip of this strange new enemy, a current. The shore, with its white slope of sand and its green bluff topped with little silent cottages, was spread like a picture before him. It was very near to him then, but he was impressed as one who, in a gallery, looks at a scene from Brittany or Algiers.

He thought: "I am going to drown? Can it be possible? Can it be possible? Can it be possible?" Perhaps an individual must consider his own death to be the final phenomenon of nature.

But later a wave perhaps whirled him out of this small deadly current, for he found suddenly that he could again make progress toward the shore. Later still he was aware that the captain, clinging with one hand to the keel of the dinghy, had his face turned away from the shore and toward him, and was calling his name. "Come to the boat! Come to the boat!"

In his struggle to reach the captain and the boat, he reflected that when one gets properly wearied drowning must really be a comfortable arrangement — a cessation of hostilities accompanied by a large degree of relief; and he was glad of it, for the main thing in his mind for some moments had been horror of the temporary agony; he did not wish to be hurt.

Presently he saw a man running along the shore. He was undressing with most remarkable speed. Coat, trousers, shirt, everything flew magically off him.

"Come to the boat!" called the captain.

"All right, Captain." As the correspondent paddled, he saw the captain let himself down to bottom and leave the boat. Then the correspondent performed his one little marvel of the voyage. A large wave caught him and flung him with ease and supreme speed completely over the boat and far beyond it. It struck him even then as an event in gymnastics and a true miracle of the sea. An overturned boat in the surf is not a plaything to a swimming man.

The correspondent arrived in water that reached only to his waist, but his condition did not enable him to stand for more than a moment. Each wave knocked him into a heap, and the undertow pulled at him.

Then he saw the man who had been running and undressing, and undressing and running, come bounding into the water. He dragged ashore the cook, and then waded toward the captain; but the captain waved him away and sent him to the correspondent. He was naked —naked as a tree in winter; but a halo was about his head, and he shone like a saint. He gave a strong pull, and a long drag, and a bully heave at the correspondent's hand. The correspondent, schooled in minor formulae, said, "Thanks, old man." But suddenly the man cried, "What's that?" He pointed a swift finger. The correspondent said, "Go."

In the shallows, face downward, lay the oiler. His forehead touched sand that was periodically, between each wave, clear of the sea.

The correspondent did not know all that transpired afterward. When he achieved safe ground he fell, striking the sand with each particular part of his body. It was as if he had drooped from a roof, but the thud was grateful to him.

It seems that instantly the beach was populated with men with blankets, clothes, and flasks, and women with coffee-pots and all the remedies sacred to their minds. The welcome of the land to the men from the sea was warm and generous; but a still and dripping shape was carried slowly up the beach, and the land's welcome for it could only be the different and sinister hospitality of the grave.

When it came night, the white waves paced to and fro in the moonlight, and the wind brought the sound of the great sea's voice to the men on the shore, and they felt that they could then be interpreters.

QUESTIONS

1. There is an alternation of panoramic and close-up views in "The Open Boat." How is this alternation accomplished? What is its effect?

2. This story is recognized as a masterpiece of realism. How does Crane achieve the sense of the real? Is it his language, his tone, or the action that contributes most?

3. "None of them knew the color of the sky." Why is this opening sentence more effective than, say, "A ship had gone down off the Carolinas, and four men were battling the sea for their lives"?

4. What images make you see and feel the predicament of the men? With which man do you most associate yourself?

5. Do you find it ironic that the oiler is the one person to die? Does this violate the realism of the story?

6. In Part IV, a great deal of dialogue is presented without speech tags. Do you find this confusing? Can you distinguish any of the speakers? How?

7. Some critics think that "The Open Boat" is an allegory of life and the boat, a microcosm. Assuming them to be right, what does Crane want us to conclude about life's meaning? Does it have a meaning? Whom do the four men represent? Are we abandoned by Providence and left at the mercy of natural forces?

8. Who is the protagonist? the antagonist? What case can be made for your choices?

9. Of what can the survivors now "be interpreters"?

WILLA CATHER

Paul's Case

It was Paul's afternoon to appear before the faculty of the Pittsburgh High School to account for his various misdemeanours. He had been suspended a week ago, and his father had called at the Principal's office and confessed his perplexity about his son. Paul entered the faculty room suave and smiling. His clothes were a trifle outgrown and the tan velvet on the collar of his open overcoat was frayed and worn; but for all that there was something of the dandy about him, and he wore an opal pin in his neatly knotted black four-in-hand, and a red carnation in his buttonhole. This latter adornment the faculty somehow felt was not properly significant of the contrite spirit befitting a boy under the ban of suspension.

Paul was tall for his age and very thin, with high, cramped shoulders and a narrow chest. His eyes were remarkable for a certain hysterical brilliancy and he continually used them in a conscious, theatrical sort of way, peculiarly offensive in a boy. The pupils were abnormally large, as though he were addicted to belladonna, but there was a glassy glitter about them which that drug does not produce.

When questioned by the Principal as to why he was there, Paul stated, politely enough, that he wanted to come back to school. This was a lie, but Paul was quite accustomed to lying; found it, indeed, indispensable for overcoming friction. His teachers were asked to state their respective charges against him, which they did with such a rancour and aggrievedness as evinced that this was not a usual case. Disorder and impertinence were among the offences named, yet each of his instructors felt that it was scarcely possible to put into words the real cause of the trouble, which lay in a sort of hysterically defiant manner of the boy's; in the contempt which they all knew he felt for them, and which he seemingly made not the least effort to conceal. Once, when he had been making a synopsis of a paragraph at the blackboard, his English teacher had stepped to his side and attempted to guide his hand. Paul had started back with a shudder and thrust his hands violently behind him. The astonished woman could scarcely have been more hurt and embarrassed had he struck at her. The insult was so involuntary and definitely personal as to be unforgettable. In one way and another, he had made all his teachers, men and women alike, conscious of the same feeling of physical aversion. In one class he habitually sat with his hand shading his eyes; in another he always looked out of the window during the recitation; in another he made a running commentary on the lecture, with humorous intention.

His teachers felt this afternoon that his whole attitude was symbolized by his shrug and his flippantly red carnation flower, and they fell upon him without mercy, his English teacher leading the pack. He stood through it smiling, his pale lips parted over his white teeth. (His lips were continually twitching, and he had a habit of raising his eyebrows that was contemptuous and irritating to the last degree.) Older boys than Paul had broken down and shed tears under that baptism of fire, but his set smile did not once desert him, and his only sign of discomfort was the nervous trembling of the fingers that toyed with the buttons of his overcoat, and an occasional jerking of the other hand that held his hat. Paul was always smiling, always glancing about him, seeming to feel that people might be watching him and trying to detect something. This conscious expression, since it was as far as possible from boyish mirthfulness, was usually attributed to insolence or "smartness."

As the inquisition proceeded, one of his instructors repeated an impertinent remark of the boy's, and the Principal asked him whether he thought that a courteous speech to have made a woman. Paul shrugged his shoulders slightly and his eyebrows twitched.

"I don't know," he replied. "I didn't mean to be polite or impolite, either. I guess it's a sort of way I have of saying things regardless."

The Principal, who was a sympathetic man, asked him whether he didn't think that a way it would be well to get rid of. Paul grinned and said he guessed so. When he was told that he could go, he bowed gracefully and went out. His bow was but a repetition of the scandalous red carnation.

His teachers were in despair, and his drawing master voiced the feeling of them all when he declared there was something about the boy which none of them understood. He added: "I don't really believe that smile of his comes altogether from insolence; there's something sort of haunted about it. The boy is not strong, for one thing. I happen to know that he was born in Colorado, only a few months before his mother died out there of a long illness. There is something wrong about the fellow."

The drawing master had come to realize that, in looking at Paul, one saw only his white teeth and the forced animation of his eyes. One warm afternoon the boy had gone to sleep at his drawing-board, and his master had noted with amazement what a white, blue-veined face it was; drawn and wrinkled like an old man's about the eyes, the lips twitching even in his sleep, and stiff with a nervous tension that drew them back from his teeth.

His teachers left the building dissatisfied and unhappy; humiliated to have felt so vindictive toward a mere boy, to have uttered this feeling in cutting terms, and to have set each other on, as it were, in the grewsome game of intemperate reproach. Some of them remembered having seen a miserable street cat set at bay by a ring of tormentors.

As for Paul, he ran down the hill whistling the Soldiers' Chorus from *Faust* looking wildly behind him now and then to see whether some of his teachers were not there to writhe under his light-heartedness. As it was now late in the afternoon and Paul was on duty that evening as usher at Carnegie Hall, he decided that he would not go home to supper. When he reached the concert hall the doors were not yet open and, as it was chilly outside, he decided to go up into the picture gallery — always deserted at this hour — where there were some of Raffelli's gay studies of Paris streets and an airy blue Venetian scene or two that always exhilarated him. He was delighted to find no one in the gallery but the old guard, who sat in one corner, a newspaper on his knee, a black patch over one eye and the other closed. Paul possessed himself of the place and walked confidently up and down, whistling under his breath. After a while he sat down before a blue Rico and lost himself. When he bethought him to look at his watch, it was after seven o'clock, and he rose with a start and ran downstairs, making a face at Augustus, peering out from the cast-room, and an evil gesture at the Venus of Milo as he passed her on the stairway.

When Paul reached the ushers' dressing-room half-a-dozen boys were there already, and he began excitedly to tumble into his uniform. It was one of the few that at all approached fitting, and Paul thought it very becoming — though he knew that the tight, straight coat accentuated his narrow chest, about which he was exceedingly sensitive. He was always considerably excited while he dressed, twanging all over to the tuning of the strings and the preliminary flourishes of the horns in the music-room; but to-night he seemed quite beside himself, and he teased and plagued the boys until, telling him that he was crazy, they put him down on the floor and sat on him.

Somewhat calmed by his suppression, Paul dashed out to the front of the house to seat the early comers. He was a model usher; gracious and smiling he ran up and down the aisles; nothing was too much trouble for him; he carried messages and brought programmes as though it were his greatest pleasure in life, and all the people in his section thought him a charming boy, feeling that he remembered and admired them. As the house filled, he grew more and more vivacious and animated, and the colour came to his cheeks and lips. It was very much as though this were a great reception and Paul were the host. Just as the musicians came out to take their places, his English teacher arrived with checks for the seats which a prominent manufacturer had taken for the season. She betrayed some embarrassment when she handed Paul the tickets, and a *hauteur*[1] which subsequently made her feel very foolish. Paul was startled for a moment, and had the feeling of wanting to put her out; what business had she here among all these fine people and gay colours? He looked her over and decided that she was not appropriately dressed and must be a fool to sit downstairs in such togs. The tickets had probably been sent her out of kindness, he reflected as he put down a seat for her, and she had about as much right to sit there as he had.

When the symphony began Paul sank into one of the rear seats with a long sigh of relief, and lost himself as he had done before the Rico. It was not that symphonies, as such, meant anything in particular to Paul, but the first sigh of the instruments seemed to free some hilarious and potent spirit within him; something that struggled there like the Genius in the bottle found by the Arab fisherman.[2] He felt a sudden zest of life; the lights danced before his eyes and the concert hall blazed into unimaginable splendour. When the soprano soloist came on, Paul forgot even the nastiness of his teacher's being there and gave himself up to the peculiar stimulus such personages always had for him. The soloist chanced to be a German woman, by no means in her first youth, and the mother of many children; but she wore an elaborate gown and a tiara, and above all she had that indefinable air of achievement, that world-shine upon her, which, in Paul's eyes, made her a veritable queen of Romance.

After a concert was over Paul was always irritable and wretched until he got to sleep, and to-night he was even more than usually restless. He had the feeling of not being able to let down, of its being impossible to give up this delicious excitement which was the only thing that could be called living at all. During the last number he withdrew and, after hastily changing his clothes in the dressing-room, slipped out to the side door where the soprano's carriage stood. Here he began pacing rapidly up and down the walk, waiting to see her come out.

---

[1] Haughtiness.

[2] A reference to Aladdin and his magic lamp.

Over yonder the Schenley, in its vacant stretch, loomed big and square through the fine rain, the windows of its twelve stories glowing like those of a lighted card-board house under a Christmas tree. All the actors and singers of the better class stayed there when they were in the city, and a number of the big manufacturers of the place lived there in the winter. Paul had often hung about the hotel, watching the people go in and out, longing to enter and leave school-masters and dull care behind him forever.

At last the singer came out, accompanied by the conductor, who helped her into her carriage and closed the door with a cordial *auf wiedersehen*[3] which set Paul to wondering whether she were not an old sweetheart of his. Paul followed the carriage over to the hotel, walking so rapidly as not to be far from the entrance when the singer alighted and disappeared behind the swinging glass doors that were opened by a negro in a tall hat and a long coat. In the moment that the door was ajar it seemed to Paul that he, too, entered. He seemed to feel himself go after her up the steps, into the warm, lighted building, into an exotic, a tropical world of shiny, glistening surfaces and basking ease. He reflected upon the mysterious dishes that were brought into the dining-room, the green bottles in buckets of ice, as he had seen them in the supper party pictures of the *Sunday World* supplement. A quick gust of wind brought the rain down with sudden vehemence, and Paul was startled to find that he was still outside in the slush of the gravel driveway; that his boots were letting in the water and his scanty overcoat was clinging wet about him; that the lights in front of the concert hall were out, and that the rain was driving in sheets between him and the orange glow of the windows above him. There it was, what he wanted — tangibly before him, like the fairy world of a Christmas pantomime, but mocking spirits stood guard at the doors, and, as the rain beat in his face, Paul wondered whether he were destined always to shiver in the black night outside, looking up at it.

He turned and walked reluctantly toward the car tracks. The end had to come some-time; his father in his night-clothes at the top of the stairs, explanations that did not explain, hastily improvised fictions that were forever tripping him up, his upstairs room and its horrible yellow wall-paper, the creaking bureau with the greasy plush collar-box, and over his painted wooden bed the pictures of George Washington and John Calvin, and the framed motto, "Feed my Lambs," which had been worked in red worsted by his mother.

Half an hour later, Paul alighted from his car and went slowly down one of the side streets off the main thoroughfare. It was a highly respectable street, where all the houses were exactly alike, and where businessmen of moderate means begot and reared large families of children, all of whom went to Sabbath-school and learned the shorter catechism, and were interested in arithmetic; all of whom were as exactly alike as their homes, and of a piece with the monotony in which they lived. Paul never went up Cordelia Street without a shudder of loathing. His home was next to the house of the Cumberland minister. He approached it to-night with the nerveless sense of defeat, the hopeless feeling of sinking back forever into ugliness and commonness that he had always had when he came home. The moment he turned into Cordelia Street he felt the waters close above his head. After each of these orgies of living, he experienced all the physical depression which follows a debauch; the loathing of respectable beds, of common food, of a house penetrated by kitchen odours; a shuddering repulsion for the flavourless, colourless mass of every-day existence; a morbid desire for cool things and soft lights and fresh flowers.

The nearer he approached the house, the more absolutely unequal Paul felt to the sight of it all; his ugly sleeping chamber; the cold bath-room with the grimy zinc tub, the cracked

---

[3] "Good-bye."

mirror, the dripping spiggots; his father, at the top of the stairs, his hairy legs sticking out from his night-shirt, his feet thrust into carpet slippers. He was so much later than usual that there would certainly be inquiries and reproaches. Paul stopped short before the door. He felt that he could not be accosted by his father to-night; that he could not toss again on that miserable bed. He would not go in. He would tell his father that he had no car fare, and it was raining so hard he had gone home with one of the boys and stayed all night.

Meanwhile, he was wet and cold. He went around to the back of the house and tried one of the basement windows, found it open, raised it cautiously, and scrambled down the cellar wall to the floor. There he stood, holding his breath, terrified by the noise he had made, but the floor above him was silent, and there was no creak on the stairs. He found a soap-box, and carried it over to the soft ring of light that streamed from the furnace door, and sat down. He was horribly afraid of rats, so he did not try to sleep, but sat looking distrustfully at the dark, still terrified lest he might have awakened his father. In such reactions, after one of the experiences which made days and nights out of the dreary blanks of the calendar, when his senses were deadened, Paul's head was always singularly clear. Suppose his father had heard him getting in at the window and had come down and shot him for a burglar? Then, again, suppose his father had come down, pistol in hand, and he had cried out in time to save himself, and his father had been horrified to think how nearly he had killed him? Then, again, suppose a day should come when his father would remember that night, and wish there had been no warning cry to stay his hand? With this last supposition Paul entertained himself until daybreak.

The following Sunday was fine; the sodden November chill was broken by the last flash of autumnal summer. In the morning Paul had to go to church and Sabbath-school, as always. On seasonable Sunday afternoons the burghers of Cordelia Street always sat out on their front "stoops," and talked to their neighbours on the next stoop, or called to those across the street in neighbourly fashion. The men usually sat on gay cushions placed upon the steps that led down to the sidewalk, while the women, in their Sunday "waists," sat in rockers on the cramped porches, pretending to be greatly at their ease. The children played in the streets; there were so many of them that the place resembled the recreation grounds of a kindergarten. The men on the steps — all in their shirt sleeves, their vests unbuttoned — sat with their legs well apart, their stomachs comfortably protruding, and talked of the prices of things, or told anecdotes of the sagacity of their various chiefs and overlords. They occasionally looked over the multitude of squabbling children, listened affectionately to their high-pitched, nasal voices, smiling to see their own proclivities reproduced in their offspring, and interspersed their legends of the iron kings with remarks about their sons' progress at school, their grades in arithmetic, and the amounts they had saved in their toy banks.

On this last Sunday of November, Paul sat all the afternoon on the lowest step of his "stoop," staring into the street, while his sisters, in their rockers, were talking to the minister's daughters next door about how many shirt-waists they had made in the last week, and how many waffles some one had eaten at the last church supper. When the weather was warm, and his father was in a particularly jovial frame of mind, the girls made lemonade, which was always brought out in a red-glass pitcher, ornamented with forget-me-nots in blue enamel. This the girls thought very fine, and the neighbours always joked about the suspicious colour of the pitcher.

To-day Paul's father sat on the top step, talking to a young man who shifted a restless baby from knee to knee. He happened to be the young man who was daily held up to Paul as a model, and after whom it was his father's dearest hope that he would pattern. This young man was of a ruddy complexion, with a compressed, red mouth, and faded, near-sighted eyes, over which he wore thick spectacles, with gold bows that curved about his ears. He was clerk to one of the magnates of a great steel corporation, and was looked upon in Cordelia Street as a young man with a future. There was a story that, some five years ago — he was now barely twenty-six — he had been a trifle dissipated but in order to curb his appetites and save the loss of time and strength that a sowing of wild oats might have entailed, he had taken his chief's advice, oft reiterated to his employees, and at twenty-one had married the first woman whom he could persuade to share his fortunes. She happened to be an angular school-mistress, much older than he, who also wore thick glasses, and who had now borne him four children, all near-sighted, like herself.

The young man was relating how his chief, now cruising in the Mediterranean, kept in touch with all the details of the business, arranging his office hours on his yacht just as though he were at home, and "knocking off work enough to keep two stenographers busy." His father told, in turn, the plan his corporation was considering, of putting in an electric railway plant at Cairo. Paul snapped his teeth; he had an awful apprehension that they might spoil it all before he got there. Yet he rather liked to hear these legends of the iron kings, that were told and retold on Sundays and holidays; these stories of palaces in Venice, yachts on the Mediterranean, and high play at Monte Carlo appealed to his fancy, and he was interested in the triumphs of these cash boys who had become famous, though he had no mind for the cash-boy stage.

After supper was over, and he had helped to dry the dishes, Paul nervously asked his father whether he could go to George's to get some help in his geometry, and still more nervously asked for car fare. This latter request he had to repeat, as his father, on principle, did not like to hear requests for money, whether much or little. He asked Paul whether he could not go to some boy who lived nearer, and told him that he ought not to leave his school work until Sunday; but he gave him the dime. He was not a poor man, but he had a worthy ambition to come up in the world. His only reason for allowing Paul to usher was, that he thought a boy ought to be earning a little.

Paul bounded upstairs, scrubbed the greasy odour of the dish-water from his hands with the ill-smelling soap he hated, and then shook over his fingers a few drops of violet water from the bottle he kept hidden in his drawer. He left the house with his geometry conspicuously under his arm, and the moment he got out of Cordelia Street and boarded a downtown car, he shook off the lethargy of two deadening days, and began to live again.

The leading juvenile of the permanent stock company which played at one of the downtown theatres was an acquaintance of Paul's, and the boy had been invited to drop in at the Sunday-night rehearsals whenever he could. For more than a year Paul had spent every available moment loitering about Charley Edwards's dressing-room. He had won a place among Edwards's following not only because the young actor, who could not afford to employ a dresser, often found him useful, but because he recognized in Paul something akin to what churchmen term "vocation."

It was at the theatre and at Carnegie Hall that Paul really lived; the rest was but a sleep and a forgetting. This was Paul's fairy tale, and it had for him all the allurement of a secret love. The moment he inhaled the gassy, painty, dusty odour behind the scenes, he breathed like a prisoner set free, and felt within him the possibility of doing or saying splendid, brilliant, poetic things. The moment the cracked orchestra beat out the overture from *Martha*, or jerked at the serenade from *Rigoletto*, all stupid and ugly things slid from him, and his senses were deliciously, yet delicately fired.

Perhaps it was because, in Paul's world, the natural nearly always wore the guise of ugliness, that a certain element of artificiality seemed to him necessary in beauty. Perhaps it was because his experience of life elsewhere was so full of Sabbath-school picnics, petty economics, wholesome advice as to how to succeed in life, and the unescapable odours of cooking, that he found this existence so alluring, these smartly-clad men and women so attractive, that he was so moved by these starry apple orchards that bloomed perennially under the lime-light.

It would be difficult to put it strongly enough how convincingly the stage entrance of that theatre was for Paul the actual portal of Romance. Certainly none of the company ever suspected it, least of all Charley Edwards. It was very like the old stories that used to float about London of fabulously rich Jews, who had subterranean halls there, with palms, and fountains, and soft lamps and richly apparelled women who never saw the disenchanting light of London day. So, in the midst of that smoke-palled city, enamoured of figures and grimy toil, Paul had his secret temple, his wishing carpet, his bit of blue-and-white Mediterranean shore bathed in perpetual sunshine.

Several of Paul's teachers had a theory that his imagination had been perverted by garish fiction, but the truth was that he scarcely ever read at all. The books at home were not such as would either tempt or corrupt a youthful mind, and as for reading the novels that some of his friends urged upon him — well, he got what he wanted much more quickly from music; any sort of music, from an orchestra to a barrel organ. He needed only the spark, the indescribable thrill that made his imagination master of his senses, and he could make plots and pictures enough of his own. It was equally true that he was not stage struck — not, at any rate, in the usual acceptation of that expression. He had no desire to become an actor, any more than he had to become a musician. He felt no necessity to do any of these things; what he wanted was to see, to be in the atmosphere, float on the wave of it, to be carried out, blue league after blue league, away from everything.

After a night behind the scenes, Paul found the school-room more than ever repulsive; the bare floors and naked walls; the prosy men who never wore frock coats, or violets in their buttonholes; the women with their dull gowns, shrill voices, and pitiful seriousness about prepositions that govern the dative. He could not bear to have the other pupils think, for a moment, that he took these people seriously; he must convey to them that he considered it all trivial, and was there only by way of a jest, anyway. He had autographed pictures of all the members of the stock company which he showed his classmates, telling them the most incredible stories of his familiarity with these people, of his acquaintance with the soloists who came to Carnegie Hall, his suppers with them and the flowers he sent them. When these stories lost their effect, and his audience grew listless, he became desperate and would bid all the boys good-bye, announcing that he was going to travel for a while; going to Naples, to Venice, to Egypt. Then, next Monday, he would slip back, conscious and nervously smiling; his sister was ill, and he should have to defer his voyage until spring.

Matters went steadily worse with Paul at school. In the itch to let his instructors know how heartily he despised them and their homilies, and how thoroughly he was appreciated elsewhere, he mentioned once or twice that he had no time to fool with theorems; adding — with a twitch of the eyebrows and a touch of that nervous bravado which so perplexed them — that he was helping the people down at the stock company; they were old friends of his.

The upshot of the matter was that the Principal went to Paul's father, and Paul was taken out of school and put to work. The manager at Carnegie Hall was told to get another usher in his stead; the doorkeeper at the theatre was warned not to admit him to the house; and Charley Edwards remorsefully promised the boy's father not to see him again.

The members of the stock company were vastly amused when some of Paul's stories reached them — especially the women. They were hardworking women, most of them supporting indigent husbands or brothers, and they laughed rather bitterly at having stirred the boy to such fervid and florid inventions. They agreed with the faculty and with his father that Paul's was a bad case.

The east-bound train was ploughing through a January snow-storm; the dull dawn was beginning to show grey when the engine whistled a mile out of Newark. Paul started up from the seat where he had lain curled in uneasy slumber, rubbed the breath-misted window glass with his hand, and peered out. The snow was whirling in curling eddies above the white bottom lands, and the drifts lay already deep in the fields and along the fences, while here and there the long dead grass and dried weed stalks protruded black above it. Lights shone from the scattered houses, and a gang of labourers who stood beside the track waved their lanterns.

Paul had slept very little, and he felt grimy and uncomfortable. He had made the all-night journey in a day coach, partly because he was ashamed, dressed as he was, to go into a Pullman, and partly because he was afraid of being seen there by some Pittsburgh business man, who might have noticed him in Denny & Carson's office. When the whistle awoke him, he clutched quickly at his breast pocket, glancing about him with an uncertain smile. But the little, clay-bespattered Italians were still sleeping, the slatternly women across the aisle were in open-mouthed oblivion, and even the crumby, crying babies were for the nonce stilled. Paul settled back to struggle with his impatience as best he could.

When he arrived at the Jersey City station, he hurried through his breakfast, manifestly ill at ease and keeping a sharp eye about him. After he reached the Twenty-third Street station, he consulted a cabman, and had himself driven to a men's furnishing establishment that was just opening for the day. He spent upward of two hours there, buying with endless reconsidering and great care. His new street suit he put on in the fitting-room; the frock coat and dress clothes he had bundled into the cab with his linen. Then he drove to a hatter's and a shoe house. His next errand was at Tiffany's, where he selected his silver and a new scarf-pin. He would not wait to have his silver marked, he said. Lastly, he stopped at a trunk shop on Broadway, and had his purchases packed into various travelling bags.

It was a little after one o'clock when he drove up to the Waldorf, and after settling with the cabman, went into the office. He registered from Washington; said his mother and father had been abroad, and that he had come down to await the arrival of their steamer. He told his story plausibly and had no trouble, since he volunteered to pay for them in advance, in engaging his rooms; a sleeping-room, sitting-room and bath.

Not once, but a hundred times Paul had planned this entry into New York. He had gone over every detail of it with Charley Edwards, and in his scrap book at home there were pages of description about New York hotels, cut from the Sunday papers. When he was shown to his sitting-room on the eighth floor, he saw at a glance that everything was as it should be; there was but one detail in his mental picture that the place did not realize, so he rang for the bell boy and sent him down for flowers. He moved about nervously until the boy returned, putting away his new linen and fingering it delightedly as he did so. When the flowers came, he put them hastily into water, and then tumbled into a hot bath. Presently he came out of his white bath-room, resplendent in his new silk underwear, and playing with the tassels of his red robe. The snow was whirling so fiercely outside his windows that he could scarcely see across the street, but within the air was deliciously soft and fragrant. He put the violets and jonquils on the taboret beside the couch, and threw himself down, with a long sigh, covering himself with a Roman blanket. He was thoroughly tired; he had been in such haste, he had stood up to such a strain, covered so much ground in the last twenty-four hours, that he wanted to think how it had all come about. Lulled by the sound of the wind, the warm air, and the cool fragrance of the flowers, he sank into deep, drowsy retrospection.

It had been wonderfully simple; when they had shut him out of the theatre and concert hall, when they had taken away his bone, the whole thing was virtually determined. The rest was a mere matter of opportunity. The only thing that at all surprised him was his own courage — for he realized well enough that he had always been tormented by fear, a sort of apprehensive dread that, of late years, as the meshes of the lies he had told closed about him, had been pulling the muscles of his body tighter and tighter. Until now, he could not remember the time when he had not been dreading something. Even when he was a little boy, it was always there — behind him, or before, or on either side. There had always been the shadowed corner, the dark place into which he dared not look, but from which something seemed always to be watching him — and Paul had done things that were not pretty to watch, he knew.

But now he had a curious sense of relief, as though he had at last thrown down the gauntlet to the thing in the corner.

Yet it was but a day since he had been sulking in the traces; but yesterday afternoon that he had been sent to the bank with Denny & Carson's deposit, as usual — but this time he was instructed to leave the book to be balanced. There was above two thousand dollars in checks, and nearly a thousand in the bank notes which he had taken from the book and quietly transferred to his pocket. At the bank he had made out a new deposit slip. His nerves had been steady enough to permit of his returning to the office, where he had finished his work and asked for a full day's holiday to-morrow, Saturday, giving a perfectly reasonable pretext. The bank book, he knew, would not be returned before Monday or Tuesday, and his father would be out of town for the next week. From the time he slipped the bank notes into his pocket until he boarded the night train for New York, he had not known a moment's hesitation. It was not the first time Paul had steered through treacherous waters.

How astonishingly easy it had all been; here he was, the thing done; and this time there would be no awakening, no figure at the top of the stairs. He watched the snow flakes whirling by his window until he fell asleep.

When he awoke, it was three o'clock in the afternoon. He bounded up with a start; half of one of his precious days gone already! He spent more than an hour in dressing, watching every stage of his toilet carefully in the mirror. Everything was quite perfect; he was exactly the kind of boy he had always wanted to be.

When he went downstairs, Paul took a carriage and drove up Fifth Avenue toward the Park. The snow had somewhat abated; carriages and tradesmen's wagons were hurrying soundlessly to and fro in the winter twilight; boys in woollen mufflers were shovelling off the doorsteps; the avenue stages made fine spots of colour against the white street. Here and there on the corners were stands, with whole flower gardens blooming under glass cases, against the sides of which the snow flakes stuck and melted; violets, roses, carnations, lilies of the valley — somehow vastly more lovely and alluring that they blossomed thus unnaturally in the snow. The Park itself was a wonderful stage winterpiece.

When he returned, the pause of the twilight had ceased, and the tune of the streets had changed. The snow was falling faster, lights streamed from the hotels that reared their dozen stories fearlessly up into the storm, defying the raging Atlantic winds. A long, black stream of carriages poured down the avenue, intersected here and there by other streams, tending horizontally. There were a score of cabs about the entrance of his hotel, and his driver had to wait. Boys in livery were running in and out of the awning stretched across the sidewalk, up and down the red velvet carpet laid from the door to the street. Above, about, within it all was the rumble and roar, the hurry and toss of thousands of human beings as hot for pleasure as himself, and on every side of him towered the glaring affirmation of the omnipotence of wealth.

The boy set his teeth and drew his shoulders together in a spasm of realization; the plot of all dramas, the text of all romances, the nerve-stuff of all sensations was whirling about him like the snow flakes. He burnt like a faggot in a tempest.

When Paul went down to dinner, the music of the orchestra came floating up the elevator shaft to greet him. His head whirled as he stepped into the thronged corridor, and he sank back into one of the chairs against the wall to get his breath. The lights, the chatter, the perfumes, the bewildering medley of colour — he had, for a moment, the feeling of not being able to stand it. But only for a moment; these were his own people, he told himself. He went slowly about the corridors, through the writing-rooms, smoking-rooms, reception-rooms, as though he were exploring the chambers of an enchanted palace, built and peopled for him alone.

When he reached the dining-room he sat down at a table near a window. The flowers, the white linen, the many-coloured wine glasses, the gay toilettes of the women, the low popping of corks, the undulating repetitions of the *Blue Danube* from the orchestra, all flooded Paul's dream with bewildering radiance. When the roseate tinge of his champagne was added — that cold, precious, bubbling stuff that creamed and foamed in his glass — Paul wondered that there were honest men in the world at all. This was what all the world was fighting for, he reflected; this was what all the struggle was about. He doubted the reality of his past. Had he ever known a place called Cordelia Street, a place where fagged-loking businessmen got on the early car; mere rivets in a machine they seemed to Paul, — sickening men, with combings of children's hair always hanging to their coats, and the smell of cooking in their clothes. Cordelia Street — Ah! that belonged to another time and country; had he not always been thus, had he not sat here night after night, from as far back as he could remember, looking pensively over just such shimmering textures, and slowly twirling the stem of a glass like this one between his thumb and middle finger? He rather thought he had.

He was not in the least abashed or lonely. He had no especial desire to meet or to know any of these people; all he demanded was the right to look on and conjecture, to watch the pageant. The mere stage properties were all he contended for. Nor was he lonely later in the evening, in his loge at the Metropolitan. He was now entirely rid of his nervous misgivings, of his forced aggressiveness, of the imperative desire to show himself different from his surroundings. He felt now that his surroundings explained him. Nobody questioned the purple; he had only to wear it passively. He had only to glance down at his attire to reassure himself that here it would be impossible for anyone to humiliate him.

He found it hard to leave his beautiful sitting-room to go to bed that night, and sat long watching the raging storm from his turret window. When he went to sleep it was with the lights turned on in his bedroom; partly because of his old timidity, and partly so that, if he should wake in the night, there would be no wretched moment of doubt, no horrible suspicion of yellow wall-paper, or of Washington and Calvin above his bed.

Sunday morning the city was practically snow-bound. Paul breakfasted late, and in the afternoon he fell in with a wild San Francisco boy, a freshman at Yale, who said he had run down for a "little flyer" over Sunday. The young man offered to show Paul the night side of the town, and the two boys went out together after dinner, not returning to the hotel until seven o'clock the next morning. They had started out in the confiding warmth of a champagne friendship, but their parting in the elevator was singularly cool. The freshman pulled himself together to make his train, and Paul went to bed. He awoke at two o'clock in the afternoon, very thirsty and dizzy, and rang for ice-water, coffee, and the Pittsburgh papers.

On the part of the hotel management, Paul excited no suspicion. There was this to be said for him, that he wore his spoils with dignity and in no way made himself conspicuous. Even under the glow of his wine he was never boisterous, though he found the stuff like a magician's wand for wonder-building. His chief greediness lay in his ears and eyes, and his excesses were not offensive ones. His dearest pleasures were the grey winter twilights in his sitting-room; his quiet enjoyment of his flowers, his clothes, his wide divan, his cigarette and his sense of power. He could not remember a time when he had felt so at peace with himself. The mere release from the necessity of petty lying, lying every day and every day, restored his self-respect. He had never lied for pleasure, even at school; but to be noticed and admired, to assert his difference from other Cordelia Street boys; and he felt a good deal more manly, more honest, even, now that he had no need for boastful pretensions, now that he could, as his actor friends used to say, "dress the part." It was characteristic that remorse did not occur to him. His golden days went by without a shadow, and he made each as perfect as he could.

On the eighth day after his arrival in New York, he found the whole affair exploited in the Pittsburgh papers, exploited with a wealth of detail which indicated that local news of a sensational nature was at a low ebb. The firm of Denny & Carson announced that the boy's father had refunded the full amount of the theft, and that they had no intention of prosecuting. The Cumberland minister had been interviewed, and expressed his hope of yet reclaiming the motherless lad, and his Sabbath-school teacher declared that she would spare no effort to that end. The rumour had reached Pittsburgh that the boy had been seen in a New York hotel, and his father had gone East to find him and bring him home.

Paul had just come in to dress for dinner; he sank into a chair, weak to the knees, and clasped his head in his hands. It was to be worse than jail, even; the tepid waters of Cordelia Street were to close over him finally and forever. The grey monotony stretched before him in hopeless, unrelieved years; Sabbath-school, Young People's Meeting, the yellow-papered room, the damp dish-towels; it all rushed back upon him with a sickening vividness. He had the old feeling that the orchestra had suddenly stopped, the sinking sensation that the play was over. The sweat broke out on his face, and he sprang to his feet, looked about him with his white, conscious smile, and winked at himself in the mirror. With something of the old childish belief in miracles with which he had so often gone to class, all his lessons unlearned, Paul dressed and dashed whistling down the corridor to the elevator.

He had no sooner entered the dining-room and caught the measure of the music than his remembrance was lightened by his old elastic power of claiming the moment, mounting with it, and finding it all sufficient. The glare and glitter about him, the mere scenic accessories had again, and for the last time, their old potency. He would show himself that he was game, he would finish the thing splendidly. He doubted, more than ever, the existence of Cordelia Street, and for the first time he drank his wine recklessly. Was he not, after all, one of those fortunate beings born to the purple, was he not still himself and in his own place? He drummed a nervous accompaniment to the Pagliacci music and looked about him, telling himself over and over that it had paid.

He reflected drowsily, to the swell of the music and the chill sweetness of his wine, that he might have done it more wisely. He might have caught an outbound steamer and been well out of their clutches before now. But the other side of the world had seemed too far away and too uncertain then; he could not have waited for it; his need had been too sharp. If he had to choose over again, he would do the same thing tomorrow. He looked affectionately about the dining-room, now gilded with a soft mist. Ah, it had paid indeed!

Paul was awakened next morning by a painful throbbing in his head and feet. He had thrown himself across the bed without undressing, and had slept with his shoes on. His limbs and hands were lead heavy, and his tongue and throat were parched and burnt. There came upon him one of those fateful attacks of clear-headedness that never occurred except when he was physically exhausted and his nerves hung loose. He lay still and closed his eyes and let the tide of things wash over him.

His father was in New York; "stopping at some joint or other," he told himself. The memory of successive summers on the front stoop fell upon him like a weight of black water. He had not a hundred dollars left; and he knew now, more than ever, that money was everything, the wall that stood between all he loathed and all he wanted. The thing was winding itself up; he had thought of that on his first glorious day in New York, and had even provided a way to snap the thread. It lay on his dressing-table now; he had got it out last night when he came blindly up from dinner, but the shiny metal hurt his eyes, and he disliked the looks of it.

He rose and moved about with a painful effort, succumbing now and again to attacks of nausea. It was the old depression exaggerated; all the world had become Cordelia Street. Yet somehow he was not afraid of anything, was absolutely calm; perhaps because he had looked into the dark corner at last and knew. It was bad enough, what he saw there, but somehow not so bad as his long fear of it had been. He saw everything clearly now. He had a feeling that he had made the best of it, that he had lived the sort of life he was meant to live, and for half an hour he sat staring at the revolver. But he told himself that was not the way, so he went downstairs and took a cab to the ferry.

When Paul arrived at Newark, he got off the train and took another cab, directing the driver to follow the Pennsylvania tracks out of the town. The snow lay heavy on the roadways and had drifted deep in the open fields. Only here and there the dead grass or dried weed stalks projected, singularly black, above it. Once well into the country, Paul dismissed the carriage and walked, floundering along the tracks, his mind a medley of irrelevant things. He seemed to hold in his brain an actual picture of everything he had seen that morning. He remembered every feature of both his drivers, of the toothless old woman from whom he had bought the red flowers in his coat, the agent from whom he had got his ticket, and all of his fellow-passengers on the ferry. His mind, unable to cope with vital matters near at hand, worked feverishly and deftly at sorting and grouping these images. They made for him a part of the ugliness of the world, of the ache in his head, and the bitter burning on his tongue. He stooped and put a handful of snow into his mouth as he walked, but that, too, seemed hot. When he reached a little hillside, where the tracks ran through a cut some twenty feet below him, he stopped and sat down.

The carnations in his coat were drooping with the cold, he noticed; their red glory all over. It occurred to him that all the flowers he had seen in the glass cases that first night must have gone the same way, long before this. It was only one splendid breath they had, in spite of their brave mockery at the winter outside the glass; and it was a losing game in the end, it seemed, this revolt against the homilies by which the world is run. Paul took one of the blossoms carefully from his coat and scooped a little hole in the snow, where he covered it up. Then he dozed a while, from his weak condition, seemingly insensible to the cold.

The sound of an approaching train awoke him, and he started to his feet, remembering only his resolution, and afraid lest he should be too late. He stood watching the approaching locomotive, his teeth chattering, his lips drawn away from them in a frightened smile; once or twice he glanced nervously sidewise, as though he were being watched. When the right moment came, he jumped. As he fell, the folly of his haste occurred to him with merciless clearness, the vastness of what he had left undone. There flashed through his brain, clearer than ever before, the blue of Adriatic water, the yellow of Algerian sands.

He felt something strike his chest, and that his body was being thrown swiftly through the air, on and on, immeasurably far and fast, while his limbs were gently relaxed. Then, because the picture making mechanism was crushed, the disturbing visions flashed into black, and Paul dropped back into the immense design of things.

QUESTIONS

1. What does the title suggest to you? In what sense is this a "case"?

2. What is Paul's relationship with society? How is this made apparent? Can you imagine a set of circumstances in which Paul might have turned out better? Has society caused his problems?

3. What does Paul's interest in music and art have to do with his crime and his flight to New York City? Are his purchases in the city in character?

4. When Paul jumps in front of the train, we are told " ... the folly of his haste occurred to him ... " Has he repented? Are other answers possible?

5. What does the final sentence suggest about the cause of Paul's problem?

THOMAS MANN

Disorder and Early Sorrow

Translated by H. T. Lowe-Porter

The principal dish at dinner had been croquettes made of turnip greens. So there follows a trifle, concocted out of one of those dessert powders we use nowadays, that taste like almond soap. Xaver, the youthful manservant, in his outgrown striped jacket, white woollen gloves, and yellow sandals, hands it round, and the "big folk" take this opportunity to remind their father, tactfully, that company is coming today.

The "big folk" are two, Ingrid and Bert. Ingrid is brown-eyed, eighteen, and perfectly delightful. She is on the eve of her exams, and will probably pass them, if only because she knows how to wind masters, and even headmasters, round her finger. She does not, however, mean to use her certificate once she gets it; having leanings towards the stage, on the ground of her ingratiating smile, her equally ingratiating voice, and a marked and irresistible talent for burlesque. Bert is blond and seventeen. He intends to get done with school somehow, anyhow, and fling himself into the arms of life. He will be a dancer, or a cabaret actor, possibly even a waiter — but not a waiter anywhere else save at the Cairo, the night-club, whither he has once already taken flight, at five in the morning, and been brought back crestfallen. Bert bears a strong resemblance to the youthful manservant Xaver Kleinsgutl, of about the same age as himself; not because he looks common — in features he is strikingly like his father, Professor Cornelius — but by reason of an approximation of types, due in its turn to far-reaching compromises in matters of dress and bearing generally. Both lads wear their heavy hair very long on top, with a cursory parting in the middle, and give their heads the same characteristic toss to throw it off the forehead. When one of them leaves the house, by the garden gate, bareheaded in all weathers, in a blouse rakishly girt with a leather strap, and sheers off bent well over with his head on one side; or else mounts his push-bike — Xaver makes free with his employers', of both sexes, or even, in acutely irresponsible mood, with the Professor's own — Dr. Cornelius from his bedroom window cannot, for the life of him, tell whether he is looking at his son or his servant. Both, he thinks, look like young moujiks.[1] And both are impassioned cigarette-smokers, though Bert has not the means to compete with Xaver, who smokes as many as thirty a day, of a brand named after a popular cinema star. The big folk call their father and mother the "old folk" — not behind their backs, but as a form of address and in all affection: "Hullo, old folks," they will say; though Cornelius is only forty-seven years old and his wife eight years younger. And the Professor's parents, who

---

[1] Peasants.

lead in his household the humble and hesitant life of the really old, are on the big folk's lips the "ancients." As for the "little folk," Ellie and Snapper, who take their meals upstairs with blue-faced Ann — so-called because of her prevailing facial hue — Ellie and Snapper follow their mother's example and address their father by his first name, Abel. Unutterably comic it sounds, in its pert, confiding familiarity; particularly on the lips, in the sweet accents, of five-year-old Eleanor, who is the image of Frau Cornelius's baby pictures and whom the Professor loves above everything else in the world.

"Darling old thing," says Ingrid affably, laying her large but shapely hand on his, as he presides in proper middle-class style over the family table, with her on his left and the mother opposite: "Parent mine, may I ever so gently jog your memory, for you have probably forgotten: this is the afternoon we were to have our little jollification, our turkey-trot with eats to match. You haven't a thing to do but just bear up and not funk it; everything will be over by nine o'clock."

"Oh — ah!" says Cornelius, his face falling. "Good!" he goes on, and nods his head to show himself in harmony with the inevitable. "I only meant — is this really the day? Thursday, yes. How time flies! Well, what time are they coming?"

"Half past four they'll be dropping in, I should say," answers Ingrid, to whom her brother leaves the major rôle in all dealings with the father. Upstairs, while he is resting, he will hear scarcely anything, and from seven to eight he takes his walk. He can slip out by the terrace if he likes.

"Tut!" says Cornelius deprecatingly, as who should say: "You exaggerate." But Bert puts in: "It's the one evening in the week Wanja doesn't have to play. Any other night he'd have to leave by half past six, which would be painful for all concerned."

Wanja is Ivan Herzl, the celebrated young leading man at the Stadttheater.[2] Bert and Ingrid are on intimate terms with him, they often visit him in his dressing-room and have tea. He is an artist of the modern school, who stands on the stage in strange and, to the Professor's mind, utterly affected dancing attitudes, and shrieks lamentably. To a professor of history, all highly repugnant; but Bert has entirely succumbed to Herzl's influence, blackens the lower rim of his eyelids — despite painful but fruitless scenes with the father — and with youthful carelessness of the ancestral anguish declares that not only will he take Herzl for his model if he becomes a dancer, in case he turns out to be a waiter at the Cairo he means to walk precisely thus.

Cornelius slightly raises his brows and makes his son a little bow — indicative of the unassumingness and self-abnegation that befits his age. You could not call it a mocking bow or suggestive in any special sense. Bert may refer it to himself or equally to his so talented friend.

"Who else is coming?" next inquires the master of the house. They mention various people, names all more or less familiar, from the city, from the suburban colony, from Ingrid's school. They still have some telephoning to do, they say. They have to phone Max. This is Max Hergesell, an engineering student; Ingrid utters his name in the nasal drawl which according to her is the traditional intonation of all the Hergesells. She goes on to parody it in the most abandonedly funny and lifelike way, and the parents laugh until they nearly choke over the wretched trifle. For even in these times when something funny happens people have to laugh.

From time to time the telephone bell rings in the Professor's study, and the big folk run across, knowing it is their affair. Many people had to give up their telephones the last time

---

[2] Town theater.

the price rose, but so far the Corneliuses have been able to keep theirs, just as they have kept their villa, which was built before the war, by dint of the salary Cornelius draws as professor of history — a million marks,[3] and more or less adequate to the chances and changes of post-war life. The house is comfortable, even elegant, though sadly in need of repairs that cannot be made for lack of materials, and at present disfigured by iron stoves with long pipes. Even so, it is still the proper setting of the upper middle class, though they themselves look odd enough in it, with their worn and turned clothing and altered way of life. The children, of course, know nothing else; to them it is normal and regular, they belong by birth to the "villa proletariat." The problem of clothing troubles them not at all. They and their like have evolved a costume to fit the time, by poverty out of taste for innovation: in summer it consists of scarcely more than a belted linen smock and sandals. The middle-class parents find things rather more difficult.

The big folk's table-napkins hang over their chair-backs, they talk with their friends over the telephone. These friends are the invited guests who have rung up to accept or decline or arrange; and the conversation is carried on in the jargon of the clan, full of slang and high spirits, of which the old folk understand hardly a word. These consult together meantime about the hospitality to be offered to the impending guests. The Professor displays a middle-class ambitiousness: he wants to serve a sweet — or something that looks like a sweet — after the Italian salad and brown-bread sandwiches. But Frau Cornelius says that would be going too far. The guests would not expect it, she is sure — and the big folk, returning once more to their trifle, agree with her.

The mother of the family is of the same general type as Ingrid, though not so tall. She is languid; the fantastic difficulties of the housekeeping have broken and worn her. She really ought to go and take a cure, but feels incapable; the floor is always swaying under her feet, and everything seems upside down. She speaks of what is uppermost in her mind: the eggs, they simply must be bought today. Six thousand marks apiece they are, and just so many are to be had on this one day of the week at one single shop fifteen minutes' journey away. Whatever else they do, the big folk must go and fetch them immediately after luncheon, with Danny, their neighbour's son, who will soon be calling for them; and Xaver Kleinsgutl will don civilian garb and attend his young master and mistress. For no single household is allowed more than five eggs a week; therefore the young people will enter the shop singly, one after another, under assumed names, and thus wring twenty eggs from the shopkeeper for the Cornelius family. This enterprise is the sporting event of the week for all participants, not excepting the moujik Kleinsgutl, and most of all for Ingrid and Bert, who delight in misleading and mystifying their fellowmen and would revel in the performance even if it did not achieve one single egg. They adore impersonating fictitious characters; they love to sit in a bus and carry on long lifelike conversations in a dialect which they otherwise never speak, the most commonplace dialogue about politics and people and the price of food, while the whole bus listens open-mouthed to this incredibly ordinary prattle, though with a dark suspicion all the while that something is wrong somewhere. The conversation waxes ever more shameless, it enters into revolting detail about these people who do not exist. Ingrid can make her voice sound ever so common and twittering and shrill as she impersonates a shop-girl with an illegitimate child, said child being a son with sadistic tendencies, who lately out in the country treated a cow with such unnatural cruelty that no Christian could have borne to see it. Bert nearly explodes at her twittering, but restrains himself and displays a grisly

---

[3] This huge sum was not extraordinary during the horrible inflation in Germany following World War I.

sympathy; he and the unhappy shop-girl entering into a long, stupid, depraved, and shuddery conversation over the particular morbid cruelty involved; until an old gentleman opposite, sitting with his ticket folded between his index finger and his seal ring, can bear it no more and makes public protest against the nature of the themes these young folk are discussing with such particularity. He uses the Greek plural: "themata." Whereat Ingrid pretends to be dissolving in tears, and Bert behaves as though his wrath against the old gentleman was with difficulty being held in check and would probably burst out before long. He clenches his fists, he gnashes his teeth, he shakes from head to foot; and the unhappy old gentleman, whose intentions had been of the best, hastily leaves the bus at the next stop.

Such are the diversions of the big folk. The telephone plays a prominent part in them: they ring up any and everybody — members of government, opera singers, dignitaries of the Church — in the character of shop assistants, or perhaps as Lord or Lady Doolittle. They are only with difficulty persuaded that they have the wrong number. Once they emptied their parents' card-tray[4] and distributed its contents among the neighbours' letter-boxes, wantonly, yet not without enough impish sense of the fitness of things to make it highly upsetting, God only knowing why certain people should have called where they did.

Xaver comes in to clear away, tossing the hair out of his eyes. Now that he has taken off his gloves you can see the yellow chain-ring on his left hand. And as the Professor finishes his watery eight-thousand-mark beer and lights a cigarette, the little folk can be heard scrambling down the stair, coming, by established custom, for their after-dinner call on Father and Mother. They storm the dining-room, after a struggle with the latch, clutched by both pairs of little hands at once; their clumsy small feet twinkle over the carpet, in red felt slippers with the socks falling down on them. With prattle and shoutings each makes for his own place: Snapper to Mother, to climb on her lap, boast of all he has eaten, and thump his fat little tum; Ellie to her Abel, so much hers because she is so very much his; because she consciously luxuriates in the deep tenderness — like all deep feeling, concealing a melancholy strain — with which he holds her small form embraced; in the love in his eyes as he kisses her little fairy hand or the sweet brow with its delicate tracery of tiny blue veins.

The little folk look like each other, with the strong undefined likeness of brother and sister. In clothing and hair-cut they are twins. Yet they are sharply distinguished after all, and quite on sex lines. It is a little Adam and a little Eve. Not only is Snapper the sturdier and more compact, he appears consciously to emphasize his four-year-old masculinity in speech, manner, and carriage, lifting his shoulders and letting the little arms hang down quite like a young American athlete, drawing down his mouth when he talks and seeking to give his voice a gruff and forthright ring. But all this masculinity is the result of effort rather than natively his. Born and brought up in these desolate, distracted times, he has been endowed by them with an unstable and hypersensitive nervous system and suffers greatly under life's disharmonies. He is prone to sudden anger and outbursts of bitter tears, stamping his feet at every trifle; for this reason he is his mother's special nursling and care. His round, round eyes are chestnut brown and already inclined to squint, so that he will need glasses in the near future. His little nose is long, the mouth small — the father's nose and mouth they are, more plainly than ever since the Professor shaved his pointed beard and goes smooth-faced. The pointed beard had become impossible — even professors must make some concession to the changing times.

But the little daughter sits on her father's knee, his Eleanorchen, his little Eve, so much more gracious a little being, so much sweeter-faced than her brother — and he holds his

---

4 On which visitors left calling cards.

cigarette away from her while she fingers his glasses with her dainty wee hands. The lenses are divided for reading and distance, and each day they tease her curiosity afresh.

At bottom he suspects that his wife's partiality may have a firmer basis than his own: that Snapper's refractory masculinity perhaps is solider stuff than his own little girl's more explicit charm and grace. But the heart will not be commanded, that he knows; and once and for all his heart belongs to the little one, as it has since the day she came, since the first time he saw her. Almost always when he holds her in his arms he remembers that first time: remembers the sunny room in the Women's Hospital, where Ellie first saw the light, twelve years after Bert was born. He remembers how he drew near, the mother smiling the while, and cautiously put aside the canopy of the diminutive bed that stood beside the large one. There lay the little miracle among the pillows: so well formed, so encompassed, as it were, with the harmony of sweet proportions, with little hands that even then, though so much tinier, were beautiful as now; with wide-open eyes blue as the sky and brighter than the sunshine — and almost in that very second he felt himself captured and held fast. This was love at first sight, love everlasting: a feeling unknown, unhoped for, unexpected — in so far as it could be a matter of conscious awareness; it took entire possession of him, and he understood, with joyous amazement, that this was for life.

But he understood more. He knows, does Dr. Cornelius, that there is something not quite right about his feeling, so unaware, so undreamed of, so involuntary. He has a shrewd suspicion that it is not by accident it has so utterly mastered him and bound itself up with his existence; that he had — even subconsciously — been preparing for it, or, more precisely, been prepared for it. There is, in short, something in him which at a given moment was ready to issue in such a feeling; and this something, highly extraordinary to relate, is his essence and quality as a professor of history. Dr. Cornelius, however, does not actually say this, even to himself; he merely realizes it, at odd times, and smiles a private smile. He knows that history professors do not love history because it is something that comes to pass, but only because it is something that *has* come to pass; that they hate a revolution like the present one because they feel it is lawless, incoherent, irrelevant — in a word, unhistoric; that their hearts belong to the coherent, disciplined, historic past. For the temper of timelessness, the temper of eternity — thus the scholar communes with himself when he takes his walk by the river before supper — that temper broods over the past; and it is a temper much better suited to the nervous system of a history professor than are the excesses of the present. The past is immortalized; that is to say, it is dead; and death is the root of all godliness and all abiding significance. Dr. Cornelius, walking alone in the dark, has a profound insight into this truth. It is this conservative instinct of his, his sense of the eternal, that has found in his love for his little daughter a way to save itself from the wounding inflicted by the times. For father love, and a little child on its mother's breast — are not these timeless, and thus very, very holy and beautiful? Yet Cornelius, pondering there in the dark, descries something not perfectly right and good in his love. Theoretically, in the interests of science, he admits it to himself. There is something ulterior about it, in the nature of it; that something is hostility, hostility against the history of today, which is still in the making and thus not history at all, in behalf of the genuine history that has already happened — that is to say, death. Yes, passing strange though all this is, yet it is true; true in a sense, that is. His devotion to this priceless little morsel of life and new growth has something to do with death, it clings to death as against life; and that is neither right nor beautiful — in a sense. Though only the most fanatical asceticism could be capable, on no other ground than such casual scientific perception, of tearing this purest and most precious of feelings out of his heart.

He holds his darling on his lap and her slim rosy legs hang down. He raises his brows as he talks to her, tenderly, with a half-teasing note of respect, and listens enchanted to her high, sweet little voice calling him Abel. He exchanges a look with the mother, who is caressing her Snapper and reading him a gentle lecture. He must be more reasonable, he must learn self-control; today again, under the manifold exasperations of life, he has given way to rage and behaved like a howling dervish. Cornelius casts a mistrustful glance at the big folk now and then, too; he thinks it not unlikely they are not unaware of those scientific preoccupations of his evening walks. If such be the case they do not show it. They stand there leaning their arms on their chair-backs and with a benevolence not untinctured with irony look on at the parental happiness.

The children's frocks are of a heavy, brick-red stuff, embroidered in modern "arty" style. They once belonged to Ingrid and Bert and are precisely alike, save that little knickers come out beneath Snapper's smock. And both have their hair bobbed. Snapper's is a streaky blond, inclined to turn dark. It is bristly and sticky and looks for all the world like a droll, badly fitting wig. But Ellie's is chestnut brown, glossy and fine as silk, as pleasing as her whole little personality. It covers her ears — and these ears are not a pair, one of them being the right size, the other distinctly too large. Her father will sometimes uncover this little abnormality and exclaim over it as though he had never noticed it before, which both makes Ellie giggle and covers her with shame. Her eyes are now golden brown, set far apart and with sweet gleams in them — such a clear and lovely look! The brows above are blond; the nose still unformed, with thick nostrils and almost circular holes; the mouth large and expressive, with a beautifully arching and mobile upper lip. When she laughs, dimples come in her cheeks and she shows her teeth like loosely strung pearls. So far she has lost but one tooth, which her father gently twisted out with his handkerchief after it had grown very wobbling. During this small operation she had paled and trembled very much. Her cheeks have the softness proper to her years, but they are not chubby; indeed, they are rather concave, due to her facial structure, with its somewhat prominent jaw. On one, close to the soft fall of her hair, is a downy freckle.

Ellie is not too well pleased with her looks — a sign that already she troubles about such things. Sadly she thinks it is best to admit it once for all, her face is "homely"; though the rest of her, "on the other hand," is not bad at all. She loves expressions like "on the other hand"; they sound choice and grown-up to her, and she likes to string them together, one after the other: "very likely," "probably," "after all." Snapper is self-critical too, though more in the moral sphere: he suffers from remorse for his attacks of rage and considers himself a tremendous sinner. He is quite certain that heaven is not for such as he; he is sure to go to "the bad place" when he dies, and no persuasions will convince him to the contrary — as that God sees the heart and gladly makes allowances. Obstinately he shakes his head, with a comic, crooked little peruke, and vows there is no place for him in heaven. When he has a cold he is immediately quite choked with mucus; rattles and rumbles from top to toe if you even look at him; his temperature flies up at once and he simply puffs. Nursy is pessimistic on the score of his constitution: such fat-blooded children as he might get a stroke any minute. Once she even thought she saw the moment at hand: Snapper had been in one of his berserker rages, and in the ensuing fit of penitence stood himself in the corner with his back to the room. Suddenly Nursy noticed that his face had gone all blue, far bluer, even, than her own. She raised the alarm, crying out that the child's all too rich blood had at length brought him to his final hour; and Snapper, to his vast astonishment, found himself, so far from being rebuked for evil-doing, encompassed in tenderness and anxiety — until it turned out that his colour was not caused by apoplexy but by the distempering on the nursery wall, which had come off on his tear-wet face.

Nursy has come downstairs too, and stands by the door, sleek-haired, owl-eyed, with her hands folded over her white apron, and a severely dignified manner born of her limited intelligence. She is very proud of the care and training she gives her nurslings and declares that they are "enveloping wonderfully." She has had seventeen suppurated teeth lately removed from her jaws and been measured for a set of symmetrical yellow ones in dark rubber gums; these now embellish her peasant face. She is obsessed with the strange conviction that these teeth of hers are the subject of general conversation, that, as it were, the sparrows on the house-tops chatter of them. "Everybody knows I've had a false set put in," she will say; "there has been a great deal of foolish talk about them." She is much given to dark hints and veiled innuendo: speaks, for instance, of a certain Dr. Bleifuss,[5] whom every child knows, and "there are even some in the house who pretend to be him." All one can do with talk like this is charitably to pass it over in silence. But she teaches the children nursery rhymes: gems like:

> *Puff, puff, here comes the train!*
> *Puff, puff, toot, toot,*
> *Away it goes again.*

Or that gastronomical jingle, so suited, in its sparseness, to the times, and yet seemingly with a blitheness of its own:

> *Monday we begin the week,*
> *Tuesday there's a bone to pick.*
> *Wednesday we're half way through,*
> *Thursday what a great to-do!*
> *Friday we eat what fish we're able,*
> *Saturday we dance round the table.*
> *Sunday brings us pork and greens —*
> *Here's a feast for kings and queens!*

Also a certain four-line stanza with a romantic appeal, unutterable and unuttered:

> *Open the gate, open the gate*
> *And let the carriage drive in.*
> *Who is it in the carriage sits:*
> *A lordly sir with golden hair.*

Or, finally that ballad about golden-haired Marianne who sat on a, sat on a, sat on a stone, and combed out her, combed out her hair; and about bloodthirsty Rudolph, who pulled out a, pulled out a, pulled out a knife — and his ensuing direful end. Ellie enunciates all these ballads charmingly, with her mobile little lips, and sings them in her sweet little voice — much better than Snapper. She does everything better than he does, and he pays her honest admiration and homage and obeys her in all things except when visited by one of his attacks. Sometimes she teaches him, instructs him upon the birds in the picture-book and tells him their proper names: "This is a chaffinch, Buddy, this is a bullfinch, this is a cowfinch." He has to repeat them after her. She gives him medical instruction too, teaches him the names of diseases, such as infammation of the lungs, infammation of the blood, infammation of the air. If he does not pay attention and cannot say the words after her, she stands him in the corner. Once she even boxed his ears, but was so ashamed that she stood

---

[5] Dr. Leadfoot, a fictional character.

herself in the corner for a long time. Yes, they are fast friends, two souls with but a single thought, and have all their adventures in common. They come home from a walk and relate as with one voice that they have seen two moollies and a teenty-weenty baby calf. They are on familiar terms with the kitchen, which consists of Xaver and the ladies Hinterhofer, two sisters once of the lower middle class who, in these evil days, are reduced to living *"au pair"*[6] as the phrase goes and officiating as cook and housemaid for their board and keep. The little ones have a feeling that Xaver and the Hinterhofers are on much the same footing with their father and mother as they are themselves. At least sometimes, when they have been scolded, they go downstairs and announce that the master and mistress are cross. But playing with the servants lacks charm compared with the joys of playing upstairs. The kitchen could never rise to the height of the games their father can invent. For instance, there is "four gentlemen taking a walk." When they play it Abel will crook his knees until he is the same height with themselves and go walking with them, hand in hand. They never get enough of this sport; they could walk round and round the dining-room a whole day on end, five gentlemen in all, counting the diminished Abel.

Then there is the thrilling cushion game. One of the children, usually Ellie, seats herself, unbeknownst to Abel, in his seat at table. Still as a mouse she awaits his coming. He draws near with his head in the air, descanting in loud, clear tones upon the surpassing comfort of his chair; and sits down on top of Ellie. "What's this, what's this?" says he. And bounces about, deaf to the smothered giggles exploding behind him. "Why have they put a cushion in my chair? And what a queer, hard, awkward-shaped cushion it is!" he goes on. "Frightfully uncomfortable to sit on!" And keeps pushing and bouncing about more and more on the astonishing cushion and clutching behind him into the rapturous giggling and squeaking, until at last he turns round, and the game ends with a magnificent climax of discovery and recognition. They might go through all this a hundred times without diminishing by an iota its power to thrill.

Today is no time for such joys. The imminent festivity disturbs the atmosphere, and besides there is work to be done, and, above all, the eggs to be got. Ellie has just time to recite "Puff, puff," and Cornelius to discover that her ears are not mates, when they are interrupted by the arrival of Danny, come to fetch Bert and Ingrid. Xaver, meantime, has exchanged his striped livery for an ordinary coat, in which he looks rather rough-and-ready, though as brisk and attractive as ever. So then Nursy and the children ascend to the upper regions, the Professor withdraws to his study to read, as always after dinner, and his wife bends her energies upon the sandwiches and salad that must be prepared. And she has another errand as well. Before the young people arrive she has to take her shopping-basket and dash into town on her bicycle, to turn into provisions a sum of money she has in hand, which she dares not keep lest it lose all value.

Cornelius reads, leaning back in his chair, with his cigar between his middle and index fingers. First he reads Macaulay on the origin of the English public debt at the end of the seventeeth century; then an article in a French periodical on the rapid increase in the Spanish debt towards the end of the sixteenth. Both these for his lecture on the morrow. He intends to compare the astonishing prosperity which accompanied the phenomenon in England with its fatal effects a hundred years earlier in Spain, and to analyse the ethical and psychological grounds of the difference in results. For that will give him a chance to refer back from the England of William III, which is the actual subject in hand, to the time of Philip II and the Counter-Reformation, which is his own special field. He has already written a valuable work

---

[6] Exchanging household services for room and board.

on this period; it is much cited and got him his professorship. While his cigar burns down and gets strong, he excogitates a few pensive sentences in a key of gentle melancholy, to be delivered before his class next day: about the practically hopeless struggle carried on by the belated Philip against the whole trend of history: against the new, the kingdom-disrupting power of the Germanic ideal of freedom and individual liberty. And about the persistent, futile struggle of the aristocracy, condemned by God and rejected of man, against the forces of progress and change. He savours his sentences; keeps on polishing them while he puts back the books he has been using; then goes upstairs for the usual pause in his day's work, the hour with drawn blinds and closed eyes, which he so imperatively needs. But today, he recalls, he will rest under disturbed conditions, amid the bustle of preparations for the feast. He smiles to find his heart giving a mild flutter at the thought. Disjointed phrases on the theme of black-clad Philip and his times mingle with a confused consciousness that they will soon be dancing down below. For five minutes or so he falls asleep.

As he lies and rests he can hear the sound of the garden gate and the repeated ringing at the bell. Each time a little pang goes through him, of excitement and suspense, at the thought that the young people have begun to fill the floor below. And each time he smiles at himself again — though even his smile is slightly nervous, is tinged with the pleasurable anticipations people always feel before a party. At half past four — it is already dark — he gets up and washes at the wash-stand. The basin has been out of repair for two years. It is supposed to tip, but has broken away from its socket on one side and cannot be mended because there is nobody to mend it; neither replaced because no shop can supply another. So it has to be hung up above the vent and emptied by lifting in both hands and pouring out the water. Cornelius shakes his head over this basin, as he does several times a day — whenever, in fact, he has occasion to use it. He finished his toilet with care, standing under the ceiling light to polish his glasses till they shine. Then he goes downstairs.

On his way to the dining-room he hears the gramophone already going, and the sound of voices. He puts on a polite, society air; at his tongue's end is the phrase he means to utter: "Pray don't let me disturb you," as he passes directly into the dining-room for his tea. "Pray don't let me disturb you" — it seems to him precisely the *mot juste;*[7] towards the guests cordial and considerate, for himself a very bulwark.

The lower floor is lighted up, all the bulbs in the chandelier are burning save one that has burned out. Cornelius pauses on a lower step and surveys the entrance hall. It looks pleasant and cosy in the bright light, with its copy of Marée over the brick chimney-piece, its wainscoted walls — wainscoted in soft wood — and red-carpeted floor, where the guests stand in groups, chatting, each with his teacup and slice of bread-and-butter spread with anchovy paste. There is a festal haze, faint scents of hair and clothing and human breath come to him across the room, it is all characteristic and familiar and highly evocative. The door into the dressing-room is open, guests are still arriving.

A large group of people is rather bewildering at first sight. The Professor takes in only the general scene. He does not see Ingrid, who is standing just at the foot of the steps, in a dark silk frock with a pleated collar falling softly over the shoulders, and bare arms. She smiles up at him, nodding and showing her lovely teeth.

"Rested?" she asks, for his private ear. With a quite unwarranted start he recognizes her, and she presents some of her friends.

"May I introduce Herr Zuber?" she says. "And this is Fräulein Plaichinger."

Herr Zuber is insignificant. But Fräulein Plaichinger is a perfect Germania, blond and

---

[7] The right word.

voluptuous, arrayed in floating draperies. She has a snub nose, and answers the Professor's salutation in the high, shrill pipe so many stout women have.

"Delighted to meet you," he says. "How nice of you to come! A classmate of Ingrid's, I suppose?"

And Herr Zuber is a golfing partner of Ingrid's. He is in business; he works in his uncle's brewery. Cornelius makes a few jokes about the thinness of the beer and professes to believe that Herr Zuber could easily do something about the quality if he would. "But pray don't let me disturb you," he goes on, and turns towards the dining-room.

"There comes Max," says Ingrid. "Max, you sweep, what do you mean by rolling up at this time of day?" For such is the way they talk to each other, offensively to an older ear; of social forms, of hospitable warmth, there is no faintest trace. They all call each other by their first names.

A young man comes up to them out of the dressing-room and makes his bow; he has an expanse of white shirt-front and a little black string tie. He is as pretty as a picture, dark, with rosy cheeks, clean-shaven of course, but with just a sketch of side-whisker. Not a ridiculous or flashy beauty, not like a gypsy fiddler, but just charming to look at, in a winning, well-bred way, with kind dark eyes. He even wears his dinner-jacket a little awkwardly.

"Please don't scold me, Cornelia," he says; "it's the idiotic lectures." And Ingrid presents him to her father as Herr Hergesell.

Well, and so this is Herr Hergesell. He knows his manners, does Herr Hergesell, and thanks the master of the house quite ingratiatingly for his invitation as they shake hands. "I certainly seem to have missed the bus," says he jocosely. "Of course I have lectures today up to four o'clock; I would have; and after that I had to go home to change." Then he talks about his pumps, with which he has just been struggling in the dressing-room.

"I brought them with me in a bag," he goes on. "Mustn't tramp all over the carpet in our brogues — it's not done. Well, I was ass enough not to fetch along a shoe-horn, and I find I simply can't get in! What a sell! They are the tightest I've ever had, the numbers don't tell you a thing, and all the leather today is just cast iron. It's not leather at all. My poor finger" — he confidingly displays a reddened digit and once more characterizes the whole thing as a "sell," and a putrid sell into the bargain. He really does talk just as Ingrid said he did, with a peculiar nasal drawl, not affectedly in the least, but merely because that is the way of all the Hergesells.

Dr. Cornelius says it is very careless of them not to keep a shoe-horn in the cloak-room and displays proper sympathy with the mangled finger. "But now you *really* must not let me disturb you any longer," he goes on. "*Auf wiedersehen!*"[8] And he crosses the hall into the dining-room.

There are guests there too, drinking tea; the family table is pulled out. But the Professor goes at once to his own little upholstered corner with the electric light bulb above it — the nook where he usually drinks his tea. His wife is sitting there talking with Bert and two other young men, one of them Herzl, whom Cornelius knows and greets; the other a typical "Wandervogel"[9] named Möller, a youth who obviously neither owns nor cares to own the correct evening dress of the middle classes (in fact, there is no such thing any more), nor to ape the manners of a gentleman (and, in fact, there is no such thing any more either). He has a wilderness of hair, horned spectacles, and a long neck, and wears golf stockings and a belted blouse. His regular occupation, the Professor learns, is banking, but he is by way of being an

---

[8] "Good-bye."
[9] "Bird of passage."

amateur folk-lorist and collects folk-songs from all localities and in all languages. He sings them, too, and at Ingrid's command has brought his guitar; it is hanging in the dressing-room in an oilcloth case. Herzl, the actor, is small and slight, but he has a strong growth of black beard, as you can tell by the thick coat of powder on his cheeks. His eyes are larger than life, with a deep and melancholy glow. He has put on rouge besides the powder — those dull carmine high-lights on the cheeks can be nothing but a cosmetic. "Queer," thinks the Professor. "You would think a man would be one thing or the other — not melancholic and use face paint at the same time. It's a psychological contradiction. How can a melancholy man rouge? But here we have a perfect illustration of the abnormality of the artist soul-form. It can make possible a contradiction like this — perhaps it even consists in the contradiction. All very interesting — and no reason whatever for not being polite to him. Politeness is a primitive convention — and legitimate. ... Do take some lemon, Herr Hofschauspieler!"[10]

Court actors and court theatres — there are no such things any more, really. But Herzl relishes the sound of the title, notwithstanding he is a revolutionary artist. This must be another contradiction inherent in his soul-form; so, at least, the Professor assumes, and he is probably right. The flattery he is guilty of is a sort of atonement for his previous hard thoughts about the rouge.

"Thank you so much — it's really too good of you, sir," says Herzl, quite embarrassed. He is so overcome that he almost stammers; only his perfect enunciation saves him. His whole bearing towards his hostess and the master of the house is exaggeratedly polite. It is almost as though he had a bad conscience in respect of his rouge; as though an inward compulsion had driven him to put it on, but now, seeing it through the Professor's eyes, he disapproves of it himself, and thinks, by an air of humility toward the whole of unrouged society, to mitigate its effect.

They drink their tea and chat; about Möller's folk-songs, about Basque folk-songs and Spanish folk-songs; from which they pass to the new production of *Don Carlos* at the Stadttheater, in which Herzl plays the title-rôle. He talks about his own rendering of the part and says he hopes his conception of the character has unity. They go on to criticize the rest of the cast, the setting, and the production as a whole; and Cornelius is struck, rather painfully, to find the conversation trending towards his own special province, back to Spain and the Counter-Reformation. He has done nothing at all to give it this turn, he is perfectly innocent, and hopes it does not look as though he has sought an occasion to play the professor. He wonders, and falls silent, feeling relieved when the little folk come up to the table. Ellie and Snapper have on their blue velvet Sunday frocks; they are permitted to partake in the festivities up to bedtime. They look shy and large-eyed as they say how-do-you-do to the strangers and, under pressure, repeat their names and ages. Herr Möller does nothing but gaze at them solemnly, but Herzl is simply ravished. He rolls his eyes up to heaven and puts his hands over his mouth; he positively blesses them. It all, no doubt, comes from his heart, but he is so addicted to theatrical methods of making an impression and getting an effect that both words and behaviour ring frightfully false. And even his enthusiasm for the little folk looks too much like part of his general craving to make up for the rouge on his cheeks.

The tea-table has meanwhile emptied of guests, and dancing is going on in the hall. The children run off, the Professor prepares to retire. "Go and enjoy yourselves," he says to Möller and Herzl, who have sprung from their chairs as he rises from his. They shake hands and he withdraws into his study, his peaceful kingdom, where he lets down the blinds, turns on the desk lamp, and sits down to his work.

---

[10] "Mr. Court Actor."

It is work which can be done, if necessary, under disturbed conditions: nothing but a few letters and a few notes. Of course, Cornelius's mind wanders. Vague impressions float through it: Herr Hergesell's refractory pumps, the high pipe in that plump body of the Plaichinger female. As he writes, or leans back in his chair and stares into space, his thoughts go back to Herr Möller's collection of Basque folk-songs, to Herzl's posings and humility, to "his" Carlos and the court of Philip II. There is something strange, he thinks, about conversations. They are so ductile, they will flow of their own accord in the direction of one's dominating interest. Often and often he has seen this happen. And while he is thinking, he is listening to the sounds next door — rather subdued, he finds them. He hears only voices, no sound of footsteps. The dancers do not glide or circle round the room; they merely walk about over the carpet, which does not hamper their movements in the least. Their way of holding each other is quite different and strange, and they move to the strains of the gramophone, to the weird music of the new world. He concentrates on the music and makes out that it is a jazz-band record, with various percussion instruments and the clack and clatter of castanets, which, however, are not even faintly suggestive of Spain, but merely jazz like the rest. No, not Spain. ... His thoughts are back at their old round.

Half an hour goes by. It occurs to him it would be no more than friendly to go and contribute a box of cigarettes to the festivities next door. Too bad to ask the young people to smoke their own — though they have probably never thought of it. He goes into the empty dining-room and takes a box from his supply in the cupboard: not the best ones, nor yet the brand he himself prefers, but a certain long, thin kind he is not averse to getting rid of — after all, they are nothing but youngsters. He takes the box into the hall, holds it up with a smile, and deposits it on the mantel-shelf. After which he gives a look round and returns to his own room.

There comes a lull in dance and music. The guests stand about the room in groups or round the table at the window or are seated in a circle by the fireplace. Even the built-in stairs, with their worn velvet carpet, are crowded with young folk as in an amphitheatre: Max Hergesell is there, leaning back with one elbow on the step above and gesticulating with his free hand as he talks to the shrill, voluptuous Plaichinger. The floor of the hall is nearly empty, save just in the centre: there, directly beneath the chandelier, the two little ones in their blue velvet frocks clutch each other in an awkward embrace and twirl silently round and round, oblivious of all else. Cornelius, as he passes, strokes their hair, with a friendly word; it does not distract them from their small solemn preoccupation. But at his own door he turns to glance round and sees young Hergesell push himself off the stair by his elbow — probably because he noticed the Professor. He comes down into the arena, takes Ellie out of her brother's arms, and dances with her himself. It looks very comic, without the music, and he crouches down just as Cornelius does when he goes walking with the four gentlemen, holding the fluttered Ellie as though she were grown up and taking little "shimmying" steps. Everybody watches with huge enjoyment, the gramophone is put on again, dancing becomes general. The Professor stands and looks, with his hand on the door-knob. He nods and laughs; when he finally shuts himself into his study the mechanical smile still lingers on his lips.

Again he turns over pages by his desk lamp, takes notes, attends to a few simple matters. After a while he notices that the guests have forsaken the entrance hall for his wife's drawing-room, into which there is a door from his own study as well. He hears their voices and the sounds of a guitar being tuned. Herr Möller, it seems, is to sing — and does so. He twangs the strings of his instrument and sings in a powerful bass a ballad in a strange tongue, possibly Swedish. The Professor does not succeed in identifying it, though he listens attentively to the end, after which there is great applause. The sound is deadened by the portière that hangs over the dividing door. The young bank-clerk begins another song. Cornelius goes softly in.

It is half-dark in the drawing-room; the only light is from the shaded standard lamp, beneath which Möller sits, on the divan, with his legs crossed, picking his strings. His audience is grouped easily about; as there are not enough seats, some stand, and more, among them many young ladies, are simply sitting on the floor with their hands clasped round their knees or even with their legs stretched out before them. Hergesell sits thus, in his dinner jacket, next the piano, with Fräulein Plaichinger beside him. Frau Cornelius is holding both children on her lap as she sits in her easy-chair opposite the singer. Snapper, the Boeotian,[11] begins to talk loud and clear in the middle of the song and has to be intimidated with hushings and finger-shakings. Never, never would Ellie allow herself to be guilty of such conduct. She sits there daintily erect and still on her mother's knee. The Professor tries to catch her eye and exchange a private signal with his little girl; but she does not see him. Neither does she seem to be looking at the singer. Her gaze is directed lower down.

Möller sings the "joli tambour"[12]:

Sire, mon roi, donnez-moi votre fille — [13]

They are all enchanted. "How good!" Hergesell is heard to say, in the odd, nasally condescending Hergesell tone. The next one is a beggar ballad, to a tune composed by young Möller himself; it elicits a storm of applause:

Gypsy lassie a-goin' to the fair,
Huzza!
Gypsy laddie a-goin' to be there —
Huzza, diddlety umpty dido!

Laughter and high spirits, sheer reckless hilarity, reigns after this jovial ballad. "Frightfully good!" Hergesell comments again, as before. Follows another popular song, this time a Hungarian one; Möller sings it in its own outlandish tongue, and most effectively. The Professor applauds with ostentation. It warms his heart and does him good, this outcropping of artistic, historic, and cultural elements all amongst the shimmying. He goes up to young Möller and congratulates him, talks about the songs and their sources, and Möller promises to lend him a certain annotated book of folk songs. Cornelius is the more cordial because all the time, as fathers do, he has been comparing the parts and achievements of this young stranger with those of his own son, and being gnawed by envy and chagrin. This young Möller, he is thinking, is a capable bank-clerk (though about Möller's capacity he knows nothing whatever) and has this special gift besides, which must have taken talent and energy to cultivate. "And here is my poor Bert, who knows nothing and can do nothing and thinks of nothing except playing the clown, without even talent for that!" He tries to be just; he tells himself that, after all, Bert has innate refinement; that probably there is a good deal more to him than there is to the successful Möller; that perhaps he has even something of the poet in him, and his dancing and table-waiting are due to mere boyish folly and the distraught times. But paternal envy and pessimism win the upper hand; when Möller begins another song, Dr. Cornelius goes back to his room.

---

[11] Ignorant clod.

[12] The "jolly drummer."

[13] "Lord, my king, give me your daughter."

He works as before, with divided attention, at this and that, while it gets on for seven o'clock. Then he remembers a letter he may just as well write, a short letter and not very important, but letter-writing is wonderful for the way it takes up the time, and it is almost half past when he has finished. At half past eight the Italian salad will be served; so now is the prescribed moment for the Professor to go out into the wintry darkness to post his letters and take his daily quantum of fresh air and exercise. They are dancing again, and he will have to pass through the hall to get his hat and coat; but they are used to him now, he need not stop and beg them not to be disturbed. He lays away his papers, takes up the letters he has written, and goes out. But he sees his wife sitting near the door of his room and pauses a little by her easy-chair.

She is watching the dancing. Now and then the big folk or some of their guests stop to speak to her; the party is at its height, and there are more onlookers than these two: blue-faced Ann is standing at the bottom of the stairs, in all the dignity of her limitations. She is waiting for the children, who simply cannot get their fill of these unwonted festivities, and watching over Snapper, lest his all too rich blood be churned to the danger-point by too much twirling round. And not only the nursery but the kitchen takes an interest: Xaver and the two ladies Hinterhofer are standing by the pantry door looking on with relish. Fräulein Walburga, the elder of the two sunken sisters (the culinary section — she objects to being called a cook), is a whimsical, good-natured sort, brown-eyed, wearing glasses with thick circular lenses; the nose-piece is wound with a bit of rag to keep it from pressing on her nose. Fräulein Cecilia is younger, though not so precisely young either. Her bearing is as self-assertive as usual, this being her way of sustaining her dignity as a former member of the middle class. For Fräulein Cecilia feels acutely her descent into the ranks of domestic service. She positively declines to wear a cap or other badge of servitude, and her hardest trial is on the Wednesday evening when she has to serve the dinner while Xaver has his afternoon out. She hands the dishes with averted face and elevated nose — a fallen queen; and so distressing is it to behold her degradation that one evening when the little folk happened to be at table and saw her they both with one accord burst into tears. Such anguish is unknown to young Xaver. He enjoys serving and does it with an ease born of practice as well as talent, for he was once a "piccolo."[14] But otherwise he is a thorough-paced good-for-nothing and windbag — with quite distinct traits of character of his own, as his long-suffering employers are always ready to concede, but perfectly impossible and a bag of wind for all that. One must just take him as he is, they think, and not expect figs from thistles. He is the child and product of the disrupted times, a perfect specimen of his generation, follower of the revolution, Bolshevist sympathizer. The Professor's name for him is the "minute-man," because he is always to be counted on in any sudden crisis, if only it address his sense of humour or love of novelty, and will display therein amazing readiness and resources. But he utterly lacks a sense of duty and can as little be trained to the performance of the daily round and common task as some kinds of dog can be taught to jump over a stick. It goes so plainly against the grain that criticism is disarmed. One becomes resigned. On grounds that appealed to him as unusual and amusing he would be ready to turn out of his bed at any hour of the night. But he simply cannot get up before eight in the morning, he cannot do it, he will not jump over the stick. Yet all day long the evidence of this free and untrammelled existence, the sound of his mouth-organ, his joyous whistle, or his raucous but expressive voice lifted in song, rises to the hearing of the world above-stairs; and the smoke of his cigarettes fills the pantry. While the Hinterhofer ladies work he stands and looks on. Of a morning while the Professor is breakfasting, he tears the leaf off the study calendar — but does not lift a finger to dust the room. Dr.

---

[14] An apprentice waiter; a bus boy.

Cornelius has often told him to leave the calendar alone, for he tends to tear off two leaves at a time and thus to add to the general confusion. But young Xaver appears to find joy in this activity, and will not be deprived of it.

Again, he is fond of children, a winning trait. He will throw himself into games with the little folk in the garden, make and mend their toys with great ingenuity, even read aloud from their books — and very droll it sounds in his thick-lipped pronunciation. With his whole soul he loves the cinema; after an evening spent there he inclines to melancholy and yearning and talking to himself. Vague hopes stir in him that some day he may make his fortune in that gay world and belong to it by rights — hopes based on his shock of hair and his physical agility and daring. He likes to climb the ash tree in the front garden, mounting branch by branch to the very top and frightening everybody to death who sees him. Once there he lights a cigarette and smokes it as he sways to and fro, keeping a look-out for a cinema director who might chance to come along and engage him.

If he changed his striped jacket for mufti,[15] he might easily dance with the others and no one would notice the difference. For the big folk's friends are rather anomalous in their clothing: evening dress is worn by a few, but it is by no means the rule. There is quite a sprinkling of guests, both male and female, in the same general style as Möller the ballad-singer. The Professor is familiar with the circumstances of most of this young generation he is watching as he stands beside his wife's chair; he has heard them spoken of by name. They are students at the high school or at the School of Applied Art; they lead, at least the masculine portion, that precarious and scrambling existence which is purely the product of the time. There is a tall, pale, spindling youth, the son of a dentist, who lives by speculation. From all the Professor hears, he is a perfect Aladdin. He keeps a car, treats his friends to champagne suppers, and showers presents upon them on every occasion, costly little trifles in mother-of-pearl and gold. So today he has brought gifts to the young givers of the feast: for Bert a gold lead-pencil, and for Ingrid a pair of ear-rings of barbaric size, great gold circlets that fortunately do not have to go through the little earlobe, but are fastened over it by means of a clip. The big folk come laughing to their parents to display these trophies; and the parents shake their heads even while they admire — Aladdin bowing over and over from afar.

The young people appear to be absorbed in their dancing — if the performance they are carrying out with so much still concentration can be called dancing. They stride across the carpet, slowly, according to some unfathomable prescript, strangely embraced; in the newest attitude, tummy advanced and shoulders high, waggling the hips. They do not get tired, because nobody could. There is no such thing as heightened colour or heaving bosoms. Two girls may dance together or two young men — it is all the same. They move to the exotic strains of the gramophone, played with the loudest needles to procure the maximum of sound: shimmies, foxtrots, one-steps, double foxes, African shimmies, Java dances, and Creole polkas, the wild musky melodies follow one another, now furious, now languishing, a monotonous Negro programme in unfamiliar rhythm, to a clacking, clashing, and strumming orchestral accompaniment.

"What is that record?" Cornelius inquires of Ingrid, as she passes him by in the arms of the pale young speculator, with reference to the piece then playing, whose alternate languors and furies he finds comparatively pleasing and showing a certain resourcefulness in detail.

"*Prince of Pappenheim:* 'Console thee, dearest child,'" she answers, and smiles pleasantly back at him with her white teeth.

---

[15] Plain clothes (not a servant's uniform).

The cigarette smoke wreathes beneath the chandelier. The air is blue with a festal haze compact of sweet and thrilling ingredients that stir the blood with memories of green-sick pains and are particularly poignant to those whose youth — like the Professor's own — has been over-sensitive. ... The little folk are still on the floor. They are allowed to stop up until eight, so great is their delight in the party. The guests have got used to their presence; in their own way, they have their place in the doings of the evening. They have separated, anyhow: Snapper revolves all alone in the middle of the carpet, in his little blue velvet smock, while Ellie is running after one of the dancing couples, trying to hold the man fast by his coat. It is Max Hergesell and Fräulein Plaichinger. They dance well, it is a pleasure to watch them. One has to admit that these mad modern dances, when the right people dance them, are not so bad after all — they have something quite taking. Young Hergesell is a capital leader, dances according to rule, yet with individuality. So it looks. With what aplomb can he walk backwards — when space permits! And he knows how to be graceful standing still in a crowd. And his partner supports him well, being unsuspectedly lithe and buoyant, as fat people often are. They look at each other, they are talking, paying no heed to Ellie, though others are smiling to see the child's persistence. Dr. Cornelius tries to catch up his little sweetheart as she passes and draw her to him. But Ellie eludes him, almost peevishly; her dear Abel is nothing to her now. She braces her little arms against his chest and turns her face away with a persecuted look. Then escapes to follow her fancy once more.

The Professor feels an involuntary twinge. Uppermost in his heart is hatred for this party, with its power to intoxicate and estrange his darling child. His love for her — that not quite disinterested, not quite unexceptionable love of his — is easily wounded. He wears a mechanical smile, but his eyes have clouded, and he stares fixedly at a point in the carpet, between the dancers' feet.

"The children ought to go to bed," he tells his wife. But she pleads for another quarter of an hour; she has promised already, and they do love it so! He smiles again and shakes his head, stands so a moment and then goes across to the cloak-room, which is full of coats and hats and scarves and overshoes. He has trouble in rummaging out his own coat, and Max Hergesell comes out of the hall, wiping his brow.

"Going out, sir?" he asks, in Hergesellian accents, dutifully helping the older man on with his coat. "Silly business this, with my pumps," he says. "They pinch like hell. The brutes are simply too tight for me, quite apart from the bad leather. They press just here on the ball of my great toe" — he stands on one foot and holds the other in his hand — "it's simply unbearable. There's nothing for it but to take them off; my brogues will have to do the business. ... Oh, let me help you, sir."

"Thanks," says Cornelius. "Don't trouble. Get rid of your own tormentors. ... Oh, thanks very much!" For Hergesell has gone on one knee to snap the fasteners of his snow-boots.

Once more the Professor expresses his gratitude; he is pleased and touched by so much sincere respect and youthful readiness to serve. "Go and enjoy yourself," he counsels. "Change your shoes and make up for what you have been suffering. Nobody can dance in shoes that pinch. Good-bye, I must be off to get a breath of fresh air."

"I'm going to dance with Ellie now," calls Hergesell after him. "She'll be a first-rate dancer when she grows up, and that I'll swear to."

"Think so?" Cornelius answers, already half out. "Well, you are a connoisseur, I'm sure. Don't get curvature of the spine with stooping."

He nods again and goes. "Fine lad," he thinks as he shuts the door. "Student of engineering. Knows what he's bound for, got a good clear head, and so well set up and pleasant too." And again paternal envy rises as he compares his poor Bert's status with this young man's, which he puts in the rosiest light that his son's may look the darker. Thus he sets out on his evening walk.

He goes up the avenue, crosses the bridge, and walks along the bank on the other side as far as the next bridge but one. The air is wet and cold, with a little snow now and then. He turns up his coat-collar and slips the crook of his cane over the arm behind his back. Now and then he ventilates his lungs with a long deep breath of the night air. As usual when he walks, his mind reverts to his professional preoccupations, he thinks about his lectures and the things he means to say tomorrow about Philip's struggle against the Germanic revolution, things steeped in melancholy and penetratingly just. Above all just, he thinks. For in one's dealings with the young it behooves one to display the scientific spirit, to exhibit the principles of enlightenment — not only for purposes of mental discipline, but on the human and individual side, in order not to wound them or indirectly offend their political sensibilities; particularly in these days, when there is so much tinder in the air, opinions are so frightfully split up and chaotic, and you may so easily incur attacks from one party or the other, or even give rise to scandal, by taking sides on a point of history. "And taking sides is unhistoric anyhow," so he muses. "Only justice, only impartiality is historic." And could not, properly considered, be otherwise. ... For justice can have nothing of youthful fire and blithe, fresh, loyal conviction. It is by nature melancholy. And, being so, has secret affinity with the lost cause and the forlorn hope rather than with the fresh and blithe and loyal — perhaps this affinity is its very essence and without it it would not exist at all! ... "And is there then no such thing as justice?" the Professor asks himself, and ponders the question so deeply that he absently posts his letters in the next box and turns round to go home. This thought of his is unsettling and disturbing to the scientific mind — but is it not after all itself scientific, psychological, conscientious, and therefore to be accepted without prejudice, no matter how upsetting? In the midst of which musings Dr. Cornelius finds himself back at his own door.

On the outer threshold stands Xaver, and seems to be looking for him.

"Herr Professor," says Xaver, tossing back his hair, "go upstairs to Ellie straight off. She's in a bad way."

"What's the matter?" asks Cornelius in alarm. "Is she ill?"

"No-o, not to say ill," answers Xaver. "She's just in a bad way and crying fit to bust her little heart. It's along o' that chap with the shirt-front that danced with her — Herr Hergesell. She couldn't be got to go upstairs peaceably, not at no price at all, and she's b'en crying bucketfuls."

"Nonsense," says the Professor, who has entered and is tossing off his things in the cloak-room. He says no more; opens the glass door and without a glance at the guests turns swiftly to the stairs. Takes them two at a time, crosses the upper hall and the small room leading into the nursery. Xaver follows at his heels, but stops at the nursery door.

A bright light still burns within, showing the gay frieze that runs all round the room, the large row of shelves heaped with a confusion of toys, the rocking-horse on his swaying platform, with red-varnished nostrils and raised hoofs. On the linoleum lie other toys — building blocks, railway trains, a little trumpet. The two white cribs stand not far apart, Ellie's in the window corner, Snapper's out in the room.

Snapper is asleep. He has said his prayers in loud, ringing tones, prompted by Nurse, and gone off at once into vehement, profound, and rosy slumber — from which a cannon-ball fired at close range could not rouse him. He lies with both fists flung back on the pillows on either side of the tousled head with its funny crooked little slumber-tossed wig.

A circle of females surrounds Ellie's bed: not only blue-faced Ann is there, but the Hinterhofer ladies too, talking to each other and to her. They make way as the Professor comes up and reveal the child sitting all pale among her pillows, sobbing and weeping more bitterly than he has ever seen her sob and weep in her life. Her lovely little hands lie on the coverlet in front of her, the nightgown with its narrow lace border has slipped down from her shoulder — such a thin, birdlike little shoulder — and the sweet head Cornelius loves so well, set on the neck like a flower on its stalk, her head is on one side, with the eyes rolled up to the corner between wall and ceiling above her head. For there she seems to envisage the anguish of her heart and even to nod to it — either on purpose or because her head wobbles as her body is shaken with the violence of her sobs. Her eyes rain down tears. The bow-shaped lips are parted, like a little *mater dolorosa's*,[16] and from them issue long, low wails that in nothing resemble the unnecessary and exasperating shrieks of a naughty child, but rise from the deep extremity of her heart and wake in the Professor's own a sympathy that is well-nigh intolerable. He has never seen his darling so before. His feelings find immediate vent in an attack on the ladies Hinterhofer.

"What about the supper?" he asks sharply. "There must be a great deal to do. Is my wife being left to do it alone?"

For the acute sensibilities of the former middle class this is quite enough. The ladies withdraw in righteous indignation, and Xaver Kleingutl jeers at them as they pass out. Having been born to low life instead of achieving it, he never loses a chance to mock at their fallen state.

"Childie, childie," murmurs Cornelius, and sitting down by the crib enfolds the anguished Ellie in his arms. "What is the trouble with my darling?"

She bedews his face with her tears.

"Abel ... Abel ..." she stammers between sobs. "Why — isn't Max — my brother? Max ought to be — my brother!"

Alas, alas! What mischance is this? Is this what the party has wrought, with its fatal atmosphere? Cornelius glances helplessly up at blue-faced Ann standing there in all the dignity of her limitations with her hands before her on her apron. She purses up her mouth and makes a long face. "It's pretty young," she says, "for the female instincts to be showing up."

"Hold your tongue," snaps Cornelius, in his agony. He has this much to be thankful for, that Ellie does not turn from him now; she does not push him away as she did downstairs, but clings to him in her need, while she reiterates her absurd, bewildered prayer that Max might be her brother, or with a fresh burst of desire demands to be taken downstairs so that he can dance with her again. But Max, of course, is dancing with Fräulein Plaichinger, that behemoth who is his rightful partner and has every claim upon him; whereas Ellie — never, thinks the Professor, his heart torn with the violence of his pity, never has she looked so tiny and birdlike as now, when she nestles to him shaken with sobs and all unaware of what is happening in her little soul. No, she does not know. She does not comprehend that her suffering is on account of Fräulein Plaichinger, fat, overgrown, and utterly within her rights in dancing with Max Hergesell, whereas Ellie may only do it once, by way of a joke, although she is incomparably the more charming of the two. Yet it would be quite mad to reproach young Hergesell with the state of affairs or to make fantastic demands upon him. No, Ellie's suffering is without help or healing and must be covered up. Yet just as it is without understanding, so it is also without restraint — and that is what makes it so horribly painful. Xaver and blue-faced Ann do not feel this pain, it does not affect them — either because of native callousness or because they accept it as the way of nature.

---

[16] "Sorrowful Mother" (of the crucified Jesus).

But the Professor's fatherly heart is quite torn by it, and by a distressful horror of this passion, so hopeless and so absurd.

Of no avail to hold forth to poor Ellie on the subject of the perfectly good little brother she already has. She only casts a distraught and scornful glance over at the other crib, where Snapper lies vehemently slumbering, and with fresh tears calls again for Max. Of no avail either the promise of a long, long walk tomorrow, all five gentlemen, round and round the dining-room table; or a dramatic description of the thrilling cushion games they will play. No, she will listen to none of all this, nor to lying down and going to sleep. She will not sleep, she will sit bolt upright and suffer. ... But on a sudden they stop and listen, Abel and Ellie; listen to something miraculous that is coming to pass, that is approaching by strides, two strides, to the nursery door, that now overwhelmingly appears. ...

It is Xaver's work, not a doubt of that. He has not remained by the door where he stood to gloat over the ejection of the Hinterhofers. No, he has bestirred himself, taken a notion; likewise steps to carry it out. Downstairs he has gone, twitched Herr Hergesell's sleeve, and made a thick-lipped request. So here they both are. Xaver, having done his part, remains by the door; but Max Hergesell comes up to Ellie's crib; in his dinner-jacket, with his sketchy side-whisker and charming black eyes; obviously quite pleased with his rôle of swan knight and fairy prince, as one who should say: "See, here am I, now all losses are restored and sorrows end."

Cornelius is almost as much overcome as Ellie herself.

"Just look," he says feebly, "look who's here. This is uncommonly good of you, Herr Hergesell."

"Not a bit of it," says Hergesell. "Why shouldn't I come to say good-night to my fair partner?"

And he approaches the bars of the crib, behind which Ellie sits struck mute. She smiles blissfully through her tears. A funny, high little note that is half a sigh of relief comes from her lips, then she looks dumbly up at her swan knight with her golden-brown eyes — tear-swollen though they are, so much more beautiful than the fat Plaichinger's. She does not put up her arms. Her joy, like her grief, is without understanding; but she does not do that. The lovely little hands lie quiet on the coverlet, and Max Hergesell stands with his arms leaning over the rail as on a balcony.

"And now," he says smartly, "she need not 'sit the livelong night and weep upon her bed'!" He looks at the Professor to make sure he is receiving due credit for the quotation. "Ha ha!" he laughs, "she's beginning young. 'Console thee, dearest child!' Never mind, you're all right! Just as you are you'll be wonderful! You've only got to grow up. ... And you'll lie down and go to sleep like a good girl, now I've come to say good-night? And not cry any more, little Lorelei?"[17]

Ellie looks up at him, transfigured. One birdlike shoulder is bare; the Professor draws the lace-trimmed nighty over it. There comes into his mind a sentimental story he once read about a dying child who longs to see a clown he had once, with unforgettable ecstasy, beheld in a circus. And they bring the clown to the bedside marvellously arrayed, embroidered before and behind with silver butterflies; and the child dies happy. Max Hergesell is not embroidered, and Ellie, thank God, is not going to die, she has only "been in a bad way." But, after all, the effect is the same. Young Hergesell leans over the bars of the crib and rattles on, more for the father's ear than the child's, but Ellie does not know that — and the father's

---

[17] Legendary Rhine nymph whose siren song draws sailors to shipwreck.

feelings towards him are a most singular mixture of thankfulness, embarrassment, and hatred.

"Good night, little Lorelei," says Hergesell, and gives her his hand through the bars. Her pretty, soft, white little hand is swallowed up in the grasp of his big, strong, red one. "Sleep well," he says, "and sweet dreams! But don't dream about me — God forbid! Not at your age — ha ha!" And then the fairy clown's visit is at an end. Cornelius accompanies him to the door. "No, no positively, no thanks called for, don't mention it," he large-heartedly protests; and Xaver goes downstairs with him, to help serve the Italian salad.

But Dr. Cornelius returns to Ellie, who is now lying down, with her cheek pressed into her flat little pillow.

"Well, wasn't that lovely?" he says as he smooths the covers. She nods, with one last little sob. For a quarter of an hour he sits beside her and watches while she falls asleep in her turn, beside the little brother who found the right way so much earlier than she. Her silky brown hair takes the enchanting fall it always does when she sleeps; deep, deep lie the lashes over the eyes that late so abundantly poured forth their sorrow; the angelic mouth with its bowed upper lip is peacefully relaxed and a little open. Only now and then comes a belated catch in her slow breathing.

And her small hands, like pink and white flowers, lie so quietly, one on the coverlet, the other on the pillow by her face — Dr. Cornelius, gazing, feels his heart melt with tenderness as with strong wine.

"How good," he thinks, "that she breathes in oblivion with every breath she draws! That in childhood each night is a deep, wide gulf between one day and the next. Tomorrow, beyond all doubt, young Hergesell will be a pale shadow, powerless to darken her little heart. Tomorrow, forgetful of all but present joy, she will walk with Abel and Snapper, all five gentlemen, round and round the table, will play the ever-thrilling cushion game."

Heaven be praised for that!

QUESTIONS

1. How does the use of the "historical present" tense — using the present tense to relate past events — affect your response to this story? Does it make the events seem more immediate, more "present" to you? Does it suit a story in which a past moment is remembered as clearly as if it had happened just today?

2. Why does Professor Cornelius doubt that his love for his daughter is quite what it should be? Is it really flawed or is he too critical of himself?

3. Is it significant that he is a professor? a history professor in particular?

4. The events take place after World War I, with Germany defeated and its economy ruined. How does this setting influence the story? How does the time affect the children differently than it affects the historian-father?

5. Cornelius is a specialist in the Counter-Reformation, an effort by the Catholic Church to counteract the spread of the Protestant Reformation. Have his studies made him more sympathetic to the changing times, or less?

6. In what ways is the party scene effective? Does it move the plot along, or is it mainly a way of dramatizing the conflict?

7. Where does the central conflict lie, in the professor's mind or between him and his daughter? How is it resolved?

SHERWOOD ANDERSON

I'm a Fool

It was a hard jolt for me, one of the most bitterest I ever had to face. And it all came about through my own foolishness, too. Even yet sometimes, when I think of it, I want to cry or swear or kick myself. Perhaps, even now, after all this time, there will be a kind of satisfaction in making myself look cheap by telling of it.

It began at three o'clock one October afternoon as I sat in the grand stand at the fall trotting and pacing meet at Sandusky, Ohio.

To tell the truth, I felt a little foolish that I should be sitting in the grand stand at all. During the summer before I had left my home town with Harry Whitehead and, with a nigger named Burt, had taken a job as swipe[1] with one of the two horses Harry was campaigning through the fall race meets that year. Mother cried and my sister Mildred, who wanted to get a job as a school teacher in our town that fall, stormed and scolded about the house all during the week before I left. They both thought it was something disgraceful that one of our family should take a place as a swipe with race horses. I've an idea Mildred thought my taking the place would stand in the way of her getting the job she'd been working so long for.

But after all I had to work, and there was no other work to be got. A big lumbering fellow of nineteen couldn't just hang around the house and I had got too big to mow people's lawns and sell newspapers. Little chaps who could get next to people's sympathies by their sizes were always getting jobs away from me. There was one fellow who kept saying to everyone who wanted a lawn mowed or a cistern cleaned, that he was saving money to work his way through college, and I used to lay awake nights thinking up ways to injure him without being found out. I kept thinking of wagons running over him and bricks falling on his head as he walked along the street. But never mind him.

I got the place with Harry and I liked Burt fine. We got along splendid together. He was a big nigger with a lazy sprawling body and soft, kind eyes, and when it came to a fight he could hit like Jack Johnson.[2] He had Bucephalus, a big black pacing stallion that could do 2.09 or 2.10, if he had to, and I had a little gelding named Doctor Fritz that never lost a race all fall when Harry wanted him to win.

---

[1] A groom.

[2] Heavyweight boxing champion, 1908–1915.

We set out from home late in July in a box car with the two horses and after that, until late November, we kept moving along to the race meets and the fairs. It was a peachey time for me, I'll say that. Sometimes now I think that boys who are raised regular in houses, and never have a fine nigger like Burt for best friend, and go to high schools and college, and never steal anything, or get drunk a little, or learn to swear from fellows who know how, or come walking up in front of a grand stand in their shirt sleeves and with dirty horsy pants on when the races are going on and the grand stand is full of people all dressed up — What's the use of talking about it? Such fellows don't know nothing at all. They've never had no opportunity.

But I did. Burt taught me how to rub down a horse and put the bandages on after a race and steam a horse out and a lot of valuable things for any man to know. He could wrap a bandage on a horse's leg so smooth that if it had been the same color you would think it was his skin, and I guess he'd have been a big driver, too, and got to the top like Murphy and Walter Cox and the others if he hadn't been black.

Gee whizz, it was fun. You got to a county seat town, maybe say on a Saturday or Sunday, and the fair began the next Tuesday and lasted until Friday afternoon. Doctor Fritz would be, say in the 2.25 trot on Tuesday afternoon and on Thursday afternoon Bucephalus would knock 'em cold in the "free-for-all" pace. It left you a lot of time to hang around and listen to horse talk, and see Burt knock some yap cold that got too gay, and you'd find out about horses and men and pick up a lot of stuff you could use all the rest of your life, if you had some sense and salted down what you heard and felt and saw.

And then at the end of the week when the race meet was over, and Harry had run home to tend up to his livery stable business, you and Burt hitched the two horses to carts and drove slow and steady across country, to the place for the next meeting, so as to not overheat the horses, etc., etc., you know.

Gee whizz, Gosh almighty, the nice hickorynut and beechnut and oaks and other kinds of trees along the roads, all brown and red, and the good smells, and Burt singing a song that was called Deep River, and all the country girls at the windows of houses and everything. You can stick your colleges up your nose for all me. I guess I know where I got my education.

Why, one of those little burgs of towns you come to on the way, say now on a Saturday afternoon, and Burt says, "let's lay up here." And you did.

And you took the horses to a livery stable and fed them, and you got your good clothes out of a box and put them on.

And the town was full of farmers gaping, because they could see you were race horse people, and the kids maybe never see a nigger before and was afraid and run away when the two of us walked down their main street.

And that was before prohibition and all that foolishness, and so you went into a saloon, the two of you, and all the yaps come and stood around, and there was always someone pretended he was horsy and knew things and spoke up and began asking questions, and all you did was to lie and lie all you could about what horses you had, and I said I owned them, and then some fellow said, "Will you have a drink of whiskey" and Burt knocked his eye out the way he could say, off-hand like, "Oh well, all right, I'm agreeable to a little nip. I'll split a quart with you." Gee whizz.

But that isn't what I want to tell my story about. We got home late in November and I promised mother I'd quit the race horses for good. There's a lot of things you've got to promise a mother because she don't know any better.

And so, there not being any work in our town any more than when I left there to go to the races, I went off to Sandusky and got a pretty good place taking care of horses for a man who owned a teaming and delivery and storage and coal and real estate business there. It was a pretty good place with good eats, and a day off each week, and sleeping on a cot in a big barn, and mostly just shovelling in hay and oats to a lot of big good-enough skates of horses, that couldn't have trotted a race with a toad. I wasn't dissatisfied and I could send money home.

And then, as I started to tell you, the fall races come to Sandusky and I got the day off and I went. I left the job at noon and had on my good clothes and my new brown derby hat, I'd just bought the Saturday before, and a stand-up collar.

First of all I went down-town and walked about with the dudes. I've always thought to myself, "put up a good front" and so I did it. I had forty dollars in my pocket and so I went into the West House, a big hotel, and walked up to the cigar stand. "Give me three twenty-five cent cigars," I said. There was a lot of horsemen and strangers and dressed-up people from other towns standing around in the lobby and in the bar, and I mingled amongst them. In the bar there was a fellow with a cane and a Windsor tie on, that it made me sick to look at him. I like a man to be a man and dress up, but not to go put on that kind of airs. So I pushed him aside, kind of rough, and had me a drink of whiskey. And then he looked at me, as though he thought maybe he'd get gay, but he changed his mind and didn't say anything. And then I had another drink of whiskey, just to show him something, and went out and had a hack[3] out to the races, all to myself, and when I got there I bought myself the best seat I could get up in the grand stand, but didn't go in for any of these boxes. That's putting on too many airs.

And so there I was, sitting up in the grand stand as gay as you please and looking down on the swipes coming out with their horses, and with their dirty horsy pants on and the horse blankets swung over their shoulders, same as I had been doing all the year before. I liked one thing about the same as the other, sitting up there and feeling grand and being down there and looking up at the yaps and feeling grander and more important, too. One thing's about as good as another, if you take it just right. I've often said that.

Well, right in front of me, in the grand stand that day, there was a fellow with a couple of girls and they was about my age. The young fellow was a nice guy all right. He was the kind maybe that goes to college and then comes to be a lawyer or maybe a newspaper editor or something like that, but he wasn't stuck on himself. There are some of that kind are all right and he was one of the ones.

He had his sister with him and another girl and the sister looked around over his shoulder, accidental at first, not intending to start anything — she wasn't that kind — and her eyes and mine happened to meet.

You know how it is. Gee, she was a peach! She had on a soft dress, kind of a blue stuff and it looked carelessly made, but was well sewed and made and everything. I knew that much. I blushed when she looked right at me and so did she. She was the nicest girl I've ever seen in my life. She wasn't stuck on herself and she could talk proper grammar without being like a school teacher or something like that. What I mean, is, she was O.K. I think maybe her father was well-to-do, but not rich to make her chesty because she was his daughter, as some are. Maybe he owned a drug store or a drygoods store in their home town, or something like that. She never told me and I never asked.

My own people are all O.K. too, when you come to that. My grandfather was Welsh and over in the old country, in Wales he was — But never mind that.

The first heat of the first race come off and the young fellow setting there with the two girls left them and went down to make a bet. I knew what he was up to, but he didn't talk big and noisy and let everyone around know he was a sport, as some do. He wasn't that kind.

---

[3] A taxi.

Well, he come back and I heard him tell the two girls what horse he'd bet on, and when the heat trotted they all half got to their feet and acted in the excited, sweaty way people do when they've got money down on a race, and the horse they bet on is up there pretty close at the end, and they think maybe he'll come on with a rush, but he never does because he hasn't got the old juice in him, come right down to it.

And then, pretty soon, the horses came out for the 2.18 pace and there was a horse in it I knew. He was a horse Bob French had in his string but Bob didn't own him. He was a horse owned by a Mr. Mathers down at Marietta, Ohio.

This Mr. Mathers had a lot of money and owned some coal mines or something and he had a swell place out in the country, and he was stuck on race horses, but was a Presbyterian or something, and I think more than likely his wife was one, too, maybe a stiffer one than himself. So he never raced his horses hisself, and the story round the Ohio race tracks was that when one of his horses got ready to go to the races he turned him over to Bob French and pretended to his wife he was sold.

So Bob had the horses and he did pretty much as he pleased and you can't blame Bob, at least, I never did. Sometimes he was out to win and sometimes he wasn't. I never cared much about that when I was swiping a horse. What I did want to know was that my horse had the speed and could go out in front, if you wanted him to.

And, as I'm telling you, there was Bob in this race with one of Mr. Mathers' horses, was named "About Ben Ahem" or something like that, and was fast as a streak. He was a gelding and had a mark of 2.21, but could step in .08 or .09.

Because when Burt and I were out, as I've told you, the year before, there was a nigger, Burt knew, worked for Mr. Mathers and we went out there one day when we didn't have no race on at the Marietta Fair and our boss Harry was gone home.

And so everyone was gone to the fair but just this one nigger and he took us all through Mr. Mathers' swell house and he and Burt tapped a bottle of wine Mr. Mathers had hid in his bedroom, back in a closet, without his wife knowing, and he showed us this Ahem horse. Burt was always stuck on being a driver but didn't have much chance to get to the top, being a nigger, and he and the other nigger gulped the whole bottle of wine and Burt got a little lit up.

So the nigger let Burt take this About Ben Ahem and step him a mile in a track Mr. Mathers had all to himself, right there on the farm. And Mr. Mathers had one child, a daughter, kinda sick and not very good looking, and she came home and we had to hustle and get About Ben Ahem stuck back in the barn.

I'm only telling you to get everything straight. At Sandusky, that afternoon I was at the fair, this young fellow with the two girls was fussed, being with the girls and losing his bet. You know how a fellow is that way. One of them was his girl and the other his sister. I had figured that out.

"Gee whizz," I says to myself, "I'm going to give him the dope."

He was mighty nice when I touched him on the shoulder. He and the girls were nice to me right from the start and clear to the end. I'm not blaming them.

And so he leaned back and I give him the dope on About Ben Ahem. "Don't bet a cent on this first heat because he'll go like an oxen hitched to a plow, but when the first heat is over go right down and lay on your pile." That's what I told him.

Well, I never saw a fellow treat any one sweller. There was a fat man sitting beside the little girl, that had looked at me twice by this time, and I at her, and both blushing, and what did he do but have the nerve to turn and ask the fat man to get up and change places with me so I could set with his crowd.

Gee whizz, craps amighty. There I was. What a chump I was to go and get gay up there in the West House bar, and just because that dude was standing there with a cane and that kind of a necktie on, to go and get all balled up and drink that whiskey, just to show off.

Of course she would know, me setting right beside her and letting her smell of my breath. I could have kicked myself right down out of that grand stand and all around that race track and made a faster record than most of the skates of horses they had there that year.

Because that girl wasn't any mutt of a girl. What wouldn't I have give right then for a stick of chewing gum to chew, or a lozenger, or some licorice, or most anything. I was glad I had those twenty-five cent cigars in my pocket and right away I give that fellow one and lit one myself. Then that fat man got up and we changed places and there I was, plunked right down beside her.

They introduced themselves and the fellow's best girl, he had with him, was named Miss Elinor Woodbury, and her father was a manufacturer of barrels from a place called Tiffin, Ohio. And the fellow himself was named Wilbur Wessen and his sister was Miss Lucy Wessen.

I suppose it was their having such swell names that got me off my trolley. A fellow just because he has been a swipe with a race horse, and works taking care of horses for a man in the teaming, delivery, and storage business isn't any better or worse than any one else. I've often thought that, and said it too.

But you know how a fellow is. There's something in that kind of nice clothes, and the kind of nice eyes she had, and the way she had looked at me, awhile before, over her brother's shoulder, and me looking back at her, and both of us blushing.

I couldn't show her up for a boob, could I?

I made a fool of myself, that's what I did. I said my name was Walter Mathers from Marietta, Ohio, and then I told all three of them the smashingest lie you ever heard. What I said was that my father owned the horse About Ben Ahem and that he had let him out to this Bob French for racing purposes, because our family was proud and had never gone into racing that way, in our own name, I mean. Then I had got started and they were all leaning over and listening, and Miss Lucy Wessen's eyes were shining, and I went the whole hog.

I told about our place down at Marietta, and about the big stables and the grand brick house we had on a hill, up above the Ohio River, but I knew enough not to do it in no bragging way. What I did was to start things and then let them drag the rest out of me. I acted just as reluctant to tell as I could. Our family hasn't got any barrel factory, and since I've known us, we've always been pretty poor, but not asking anything of any one at that, and my grandfather, over in Wales — but never mind that.

We set there talking like we had known each other for years and years, and I went and told them that my father had been expecting maybe this Bob French wasn't on the square, and had sent me up to Sandusky on the sly to find out what I could.

And I bluffed it through. I had found out all about the 2.18 pace, in which About Ben Ahem was to start.

I said he would lose the first heat by pacing like a lame cow and then he would come back and skin 'em alive after that. And to back up what I said I took thirty dollars out of my pocket and handed it to Mr. Wilbur Wessen and asked him, would he mind, after the first heat, to go down and place it on About Ben Ahem for whatever odds he could get. What I said was that I didn't want Bob French to see me and none of the swipes.

Sure enough the first heat come off and About Ben Ahem went off his stride, up the back stretch, and looked like a wooden horse or a sick one, and come in to be last. Then this Wilbur Wessen went down to the betting place under the grand stand and there I was with the two girls, and when that Miss Woodbury was looking the other way once, Lucy Wessen kinda, with her shoulder you know, kinda touched me. Not just tucking down, I don't mean. You know how a woman can do. They get close, but not getting gay either. You know what they do. Gee whizz.

And then they give me a jolt. What they had done, when I didn't know, was to get together, and they had decided Wilbur Wessen would bet fifty dollars, and the two girls had gone and put in ten dollars each, of their own money, too. I was sick then, but I was sicker later.

About the gelding, About Ben Ahem, and their winning their money, I wasn't worried a lot about that. It come out O.K. Ahem stepped the next three heats like a bushel of spoiled eggs going to market before they could be found out, and Wilbur Wessen had got nine to two for the money. There was something else eating at me.

Because Wilbur come back, after he had bet the money, and after that he spent most of his time talking to that Miss Woodbury, and Lucy Wessen and I was left alone together like on a desert island. Gee, if I'd only been on the square or if there had been any way of getting myself on the square. There ain't any Walter Mathers, like I said to her and them, and there hasn't ever been one, but if there was, I bet I'd go to Marietta, Ohio, and shoot him tomorrow.

There I was, big boob that I am. Pretty soon the race was over, and Wilbur had gone down and collected our money, and we had a hack down-town, and he stood us a swell supper at the West House, and a bottle of champagne beside.

And I was with that girl and she wasn't saying much, and I wasn't saying much either. One thing I know. She wasn't stuck on me because of the lie about my father being rich and all that. There's a way you know. ... Craps amighty. There's a kind of girl, you see just once in your life, and if you don't get busy and make hay, then you're gone for good and all, and might as well go jump off a bridge. They give you a look from inside of them somewhere, and it ain't no vamping, and what it means is — you want that girl to be your wife, and you want nice things around her like flowers and swell clothes, and you want her to have the kids you're going to have, and you want good music played and no ragtime. Gee whizz.

There's a place over near Sandusky, across a kind of bay, and it's called Cedar Point. And after we had supper we went over to it in a launch, all by ourselves. Wilbur and Miss Lucy and that Miss Woodbury had to catch a ten o'clock train back to Tiffin, Ohio, because, when you're out with girls like that you can't get careless and miss any trains and stay out all night, like you can with some kinds of Janes.

And Wilbur blowed himself to the launch and it cost him fifteen cold plunks, but I wouldn't never have knew if I hadn't listened. He wasn't no tin horn kind of a sport.

Over at the Cedar Point place, we didn't stay around where there was a gang of common kind of cattle at all.

There was big dance halls and dining places for yaps, and there was a beach you could walk along and get where it was dark, and we went there.

She didn't talk hardly at all and neither did I, and I was thinking how glad I was my mother was all right, and always made us kids learn to eat with a fork at table, and not swill soup, and not be noisy and rough like a gang you see around a race track that way.

Then Wilbur and his girl went away up the beach and Lucy and I sat down in a dark place, where there was some roots of old trees, the water had washed up, and after that the time, till we had to go back in the launch and they had to catch their trains, wasn't nothing at all. It went like winking your eye.

Here's how it was. The place we were setting in was dark, like I said, and there was the roots from that old stump sticking up like arms, and there was a watery smell, and the night was like — as if you could put your hand out and feel it — so warm and soft and dark and sweet like an orange.

I most cried and I most swore and I most jumped up and danced, I was so mad and happy and sad.

When Wilbur come back from being alone with his girl, and she saw him coming, Lucy she says, "we got to go to the train now," and she was most crying too, but she never knew nothing I knew, and she couldn't be so all busted up. And then, before Wilbur and Miss Woodbury got up to where we was, she put her face up and kissed me quick and put her head up against me and she was all quivering and — Gee whizz.

Sometimes I hope I have cancer and die. I guess you know what I mean. We went in the launch across the bay to the train like that, and it was dark, too. She whispered and said it was like she and I could get out of the boat and walk on the water, and it sounded foolish, but I knew what she meant.

And then quick we were right at the depot, and there was a big gang of yaps, the kind that goes to the fairs, and crowded and milling around like cattle, and how could I tell her? "It won't be long because you'll write and I'll write to you." That's all she said.

I got a chance like a hay barn afire. A swell chance I got.

And maybe she would write me, down at Marietta that way, and the letter would come back, and stamped on the front of it by the U. S. A. "there ain't any such guy," or something like that, whatever they stamp on a letter that way.

And me trying to pass myself off for a bigbug and a swell — to her, as decent a little body as God ever made. Craps amighty — a swell chance I got!

And then the train come in, and she got on it, and Wilbur Wessen, he come and shook hands with me, and that Miss Woodbury was nice too and bowed to me, and I at her, and the train went and I busted out and cried like a kid.

Gee, I could have run after that train and made Dan Patch[4] look like a freight train after a wreck but, socks amighty, what was the use? Did you ever see such a fool?

I'll bet you what — if I had an arm broke right now or a train had run over my foot — I wouldn't go to no doctor at all. I'd go set down and let her hurt and hurt — that's what I'd do.

I'll bet you what — if I hadn't drunk that booze I'd never been such a boob as to go tell such a lie — that couldn't never be made straight to a lady like her.

I wish I had that fellow right here that had on a Windsor tie and carried a cane. I'd smash him for fair. Gosh darn his eyes. He's a big fool — that's what he is.

And if I'm not another you just go find me one and I'll quit working and be a bum and give him my job. I don't care nothing for working, and earning money, and saving it for no such boob as myself.

QUESTIONS

1. Is the first-person point of view appropriate to this narrative? How does it color the events and characters? Could this story have been told as effectively from Harry's viewpoint?

---

[4] An almost legendary pacer. Dan Patch did a mile in 1:55¼ in 1905.

2. "But that isn't what I want to tell my story about," says the narrator. Have the first pages of the story been wasted? What do they accomplish?

3. The narrator's slang dates him, of course, but does it make him difficult to understand?

4. How would you characterize the narrator? What attempts has Anderson made to round out his characters? Has he succeeded?

5. Is the narrator too hard on himself?

JAMES JOYCE

The Dead

Lily, the caretaker's daughter, was literally run off her feet. Hardly had she brought one gentleman into the little pantry behind the office on the ground floor and helped him off with his overcoat than the wheezy hall-door bell clanged again and she had to scamper along the bare hallway to let in another guest. It was well for her she had not to attend to the ladies also. But Miss Kate and Miss Julia had thought of that and had converted the bathroom upstairs into a ladies' dressing-room. Miss Kate and Miss Julia were there, gossiping and laughing and fussing, walking after each other to the head of the stairs, peering down over the banisters and calling down to Lily to ask her who had come.

It was always a great affair, the Misses Morkan's annual dance. Everybody who knew them came to it, members of the family, old friends of the family, the members of Julia's choir, any of Kate's pupils that were grown up enough, and even some of Mary Jane's pupils too. Never once had it fallen flat. For years and years it had gone off in splendid style, as long as anyone could remember; ever since Kate and Julia, after the death of their brother Pat, had left the house in Stoney Batter and taken Mary Jane, their only niece, to live with them in the dark, gaunt house on Usher's Island, the upper part of which they had rented from Mr. Fulham, the corn-factor on the ground floor. That was a good thirty years ago if it was a day. Mary Jane, who was then a little girl in short clothes, was now the main prop of the household, for she had the organ in Haddington Road. She had been through the Academy and gave a pupils' concert every year in the upper room of the Antient Concert Rooms. Many of her pupils belonged to the better-class families on the Kingstown and Dalkey line. Old as they were, her aunts also did their share. Julia, though she was quite grey, was still the leading soprano in Adam and Eve's,[1] and Kate, being too feeble to go about much, gave music lessons to beginners on the old square piano in the back room. Lily, the caretaker's daughter, did housemaid's work for them. Though their life was modest, they believed in eating well; the best of everything: diamond-bone sirloins, three-shilling tea and the best bottled stout. But Lily seldom made a mistake in the orders, so that she got on well with her three mistresses. They were fussy, that was all. But the only thing they would not stand was back answers.

Of course, they had good reason to be fussy on such a night. And then it was long after

---

[1] One of Dublin's many Catholic churches.

ten o'clock and yet there was no sign of Gabriel and his wife. Besides they were dreadfully afraid that Freddy Malins might turn up screwed. They would not wish for worlds that any of Mary Jane's pupils should see him under the influence; and when he was like that it was sometimes very hard to manage him. Freddy Malins always came late, but they wondered what could be keeping Gabriel: and that was what brought them every two minutes to the banisters to ask Lily had Gabriel or Freddy come.

"O, Mr. Conroy," said Lily to Gabriel when she opened the door for him, "Miss Kate and Miss Julia thought you were never coming. Good-night, Mrs. Conroy."

"I'll engage they did," said Gabriel, "but they forget that my wife here takes three mortal hours to dress herself."

He stood on the mat, scraping the snow from his goloshes, while Lily led his wife to the foot of the stairs and called out:

"Miss Kate, here's Mrs. Conroy."

Kate and Julia came toddling down the dark stairs at once. Both of them kissed Gabriel's wife, said she must be perished alive, and asked was Gabriel with her.

"Here I am as right as the mail, Aunt Kate! Go on up. I'll follow," called out Gabriel from the dark.

He continued scraping his feet vigorously while the three women went upstairs, laughing, to the ladies' dressing-room. A light fringe of snow lay like a cape on the shoulders of his overcoat and like toecaps on the toes of his goloshes; and, as the buttons of his overcoat slipped with a squeaking noise through the snow-stiffened frieze, a cold fragrant air from out-of-doors escaped from crevices and folds.

"Is it snowing again, Mr. Conroy?" asked Lily.

She had preceded him into the pantry to help him off with his overcoat. Gabriel smiled at the three syllables she had given his surname and glanced at her. She was a slim, growing girl, pale in complexion and with hay-coloured hair. The gas in the pantry made her look still paler. Gabriel had known her when she was a child and used to sit on the lowest step nursing a rag doll.

"Yes, Lily," he answered, "and I think we're in for a night of it."

He looked up at the pantry ceiling, which was shaking with the stamping and shuffling of feet on the floor above, listened for a moment to the piano and then glanced at the girl, who was folding his overcoat carefully at the end of a shelf.

"Tell me, Lily," he said in a friendly tone, "do you still go to school?"

"O no, sir," she answered. "I'm done schooling this year and more."

"O, then," said Gabriel gaily, "I suppose we'll be going to your wedding one of these fine days with your young man, eh?"

The girl glanced back at him over her shoulder and said with great bitterness:

"The men that is now is only all palaver and what they can get out of you."

Gabriel coloured, as if he felt he had made a mistake and, without looking at her, kicked off his goloshes and flicked actively with his muffler at his patent-leather shoes.

He was a stout, tallish young man. The high colour of his cheeks pushed upwards even to his forehead, where it scattered itself in a few formless patches of pale red; and on his hairless face there scintillated restlessly the polished lenses and the bright gilt rims of the glasses which screened his delicate and restless eyes. His glossy black hair was parted in the middle and brushed in a long curve behind his ears where it curled slightly beneath the groove left by his hat.

When he had flicked lustre into his shoes he stood up and pulled his waistcoat down more tightly on his plump body. Then he took a coin rapidly from his pocket.

"O Lily," he said, thrusting it into her hands, "it's Christmas-time, isn't it? Just …here's a little. …"

He walked rapidly towards the door.

"O no, sir!" cried the girl, following him. "Really, sir, I wouldn't take it."

"Christmas-time! Christmas-time!" said Gabriel, almost trotting to the stairs and waving his hand to her in deprecation.

The girl, seeing that he had gained the stairs, called out after him:

"Well, thank you, sir."

He waited outside the drawing-room door until the waltz should finish, listening to the skirts that swept against it and to the shuffling of feet. He was still discomposed by the girl's bitter and sudden retort. It had cast a gloom over him which he tried to dispel by arranging his cuffs and the bows of his tie. He then took from his waistcoat pocket a little paper and glanced at the headings he had made for his speech. He was undecided about the lines from Robert Browning, for he feared they would be above the heads of his hearers. Some quotation that they would recognise from Shakespeare or from the Melodies[2] would be better. The indelicate clacking of the men's heels and the shuffling of their soles reminded him that their grade of culture differed from his. He would only make himself ridiculous by quoting poetry to them which they could not understand. They would think that he was airing his superior education. He would fail with them just as he had failed with the girl in the pantry. He had taken up a wrong tone. His whole speech was a mistake from first to last, an utter failure.

Just then his aunts and his wife came out of the ladies' dressing-room. His aunts were two small, plainly dressed old women. Aunt Julia was an inch or so the taller. Her hair, drawn low over the tops of her ears, was grey; and grey also, with darker shadows, was her large flaccid face. Though she was stout in build and stood erect, her slow eyes and parted lips gave her the appearance of a woman who did not know where she was or where she was going. Aunt Kate was more vivacious. Her face, healthier than her sister's, was all puckers and creases, like a shrivelled red apple, and her hair, braided in the same old-fashioned way, had not lost its ripe nut colour.

They both kissed Gabriel frankly. He was their favourite nephew, the son of their dead elder sister, Ellen, who had married T. J. Conroy of the Port and Docks.

"Gretta tells me you're not going to take a cab back to Monkstown tonight, Gabriel," said Aunt Kate.

"No," said Gabriel, turning to his wife, "we had quite enough of that last year, hadn't we? Don't you remember, Aunt Kate, what a cold Gretta got out of it? Cab windows rattling all the way, and the east wind blowing in after we passed Merrion. Very jolly it was. Gretta caught a dreadful cold."

Aunt Kate frowned severely and nodded her head at every word.

"Quite right, Gabriel, quite right," she said. "You can't be too careful."

"But as for Gretta there," said Gabriel, "she'd walk home in the snow if she were let." Mrs. Conroy laughed.

"Don't mind him, Aunt Kate," she said. "He's really an awful bother, what with green shades for Tom's eyes at night and making him do the dumb-bells, and forcing Eva to eat the stir-about.[3] The poor child! And she simply hates the sight of it! …O, but you'll never guess what he makes me wear now!"

---

[2] Thomas Moore's *Irish Melodies*, source of many popular songs.

[3] Porridge.

She broke out into a peal of laughter and glanced at her husband, whose admiring and happy eyes had been wandering from her dress to her face and hair. The two aunts laughed heartily, too, for Gabriel's solicitude was a standing joke with them.

"Goloshes!" said Mrs. Conroy. "That's the latest. Whenever it's wet underfoot I must put on my goloshes. Tonight even, he wanted me to put them on, but I wouldn't. The next thing he'll buy me will be a diving suit."

Gabriel laughed nervously and patted his tie reassuringly, while Aunt Kate nearly doubled herself, so heartily did she enjoy the joke. The smile soon faded from Aunt Julia's face and her mirthless eyes were directed towards her nephew's face. After a pause she asked:

"And what are goloshes, Gabriel?"

"Goloshes, Julia!" exclaimed her sister. "Goodness me, don't you know what goloshes are? You wear them over your ...over your boots, Gretta, isn't it?"

"Yes," said Mrs. Conroy. "Guttapercha things. We both have a pair now. Gabriel says everyone wears them on the Continent."

"O, on the Continent," murmured Aunt Julia, nodding her head slowly.

Gabriel knitted his brow and said, as if he were slightly angered:

"It's nothing very wonderful, but Gretta thinks it very funny because she says the word reminds her of Christy Minstrels."[4]

"But tell me, Gabriel," said Aunt Kate, with brisk tact. "Of course, you've seen about the room. Gretta was saying ..."

"O, the room is all right," replied Gabriel. "I've taken one in the Gresham."

"To be sure," said Aunt Kate, "by far the best thing to do. And the children, Gretta, you're not anxious about them?"

"O, for one night," said Mrs. Conroy. "Besides, Bessie will look after them."

"To be sure," said Aunt Kate again. "What a comfort it is to have a girl like that, one you can depend on! There's that Lily, I'm sure I don't know what has come over her lately. She's not the girl she was at all."

Gabriel was about to ask his aunt some questions on this point, but she broke off suddenly to gaze after her sister, who had wandered down the stairs and was craning her neck over the banisters.

"Now, I ask you," she said almost testily, "where is Julia going? Julia! Julia! Where are you going?"

Julia, who had gone half way down one flight, came back and announced blandly: "Here's Freddy."

At the same moment a clapping of hands and a final flourish of the pianist told that the waltz had ended. The drawing-room door was opened from within and some couples came out. Aunt Kate drew Gabriel aside hurriedly and whispered into his ear:

"Slip down, Gabriel, like a good fellow and see if he's all right, and don't let him up if he's screwed. I'm sure he's screwed. I'm sure he is."

Gabriel went to the stairs and listened over the banisters. He could hear two persons talking in the pantry. Then he recognised Freddy Malins' laugh. He went down the stairs noisily.

"It's such a relief," said Aunt Kate to Mrs. Conroy, "that Gabriel is here. I always feel easier in my mind when he's here. ... Julia, there's Miss Daly and Miss Power will take some refreshment. Thanks for your beautiful waltz, Miss Daly. It made lovely time."

---

[4] A troupe of American Negro minstrels, organized by Edwin Christy, famous on both sides of the Atlantic.

A tall wizen-faced man, with a stiff grizzled moustache and swarthy skin, who was passing out with his partner, said:

"And may we have some refreshment, too, Miss Morkan?"

"Julia," said Aunt Kate summarily, "and here's Mr. Browne and Miss Furlong. Take them in, Julia, with Miss Daly and Miss Power."

"I'm the man for the ladies," said Mr. Browne, pursing his lips until his moustache bristled and smiling in all his wrinkles. "You know, Miss Morkan, the reason they are so fond of me is——"

He did not finish his sentence, but, seeing that Aunt Kate was out of earshot, at once led the three young ladies into the back room. The middle of the room was occupied by two square tables placed end to end, and on these Aunt Julia and the caretaker were straightening and smoothing a large cloth. On the sideboard were arrayed dishes and plates, and glasses and bundles of knives and forks and spoons. The top of the closed square piano served also as a sideboard for viands and sweets. At a smaller sideboard in one corner two young men were standing, drinking hop-bitters.

Mr. Browne led his charges thither and invited them all, in jest, to some ladies' punch, hot, strong and sweet. As they said they never took anything strong, he opened three bottles of lemonade for them. Then he asked one of the young men to move aside, and, taking hold of the decanter, filled out for himself a goodly measure of whisky. The young men eyed him respectfully while he took a trial sip.

"God help me," he said, smiling, "it's the doctor's orders."

His wizened face broke into a broader smile, and the three young ladies laughed in musical echo to his pleasantry, swaying their bodies to and fro, with nervous jerks of their shoulders. The boldest said:

"O, now, Mr. Browne, I'm sure the doctor never ordered anything of the kind."

Mr. Browne took another sip of his whisky and said, with sidling mimicry:

"Well, you see, I'm like the famous Mrs. Cassidy, who is reported to have said: 'Now, Mary Grimes, if I don't take it, make me take it, for I feel I want it.'"

His hot face had leaned forward a little too confidentially and he had assumed a very low Dublin accent so that the young ladies, with one instinct, received his speech in silence. Miss Furlong, who was one of Mary Jane's pupils, asked Miss Daly what was the name of the pretty waltz she had played; and Mr. Browne, seeing that he was ignored, turned promptly to the two young men who were more appreciative.

A red-faced young woman, dressed in pansy, came into the room, excitedly clapping her hands and crying:

"Quadrilles! Quadrilles!"[5]

Close on her heels came Aunt Kate, crying:

"Two gentlemen and three ladies, Mary Jane!"

"O, here's Mr. Bergin and Mr. Kerrigan," said Mary Jane. "Mr. Kerrigan, will you take Miss Power? Miss Furlong, may I get you a partner, Mr. Bergin. O, that'll just do now."

"Three ladies, Mary Jane," said Aunt Kate.

The two young gentlemen asked the ladies if they might have the pleasure, and Mary Jane turned to Miss Daly.

"O, Miss Daly, you're really awfully good, after playing for the last two dances, but really we're so short of ladies tonight."

"I don't mind in the least, Miss Morkan."

---

[5] A quadrille is a square dance for four couples.

"But I've a nice partner for you, Mr. Bartell D'Arcy, the tenor. I'll get him to sing later on. All Dublin is raving about him."

"Lovely voice, lovely voice!" said Aunt Kate.

As the piano had twice begun the prelude to the first figure Mary Jane led her recruits quickly from the room. They had hardly gone when Aunt Julia wandered slowly into the room, looking behind her at something.

"What is the matter, Julia?" asked Aunt Kate anxiously. "Who is it?"

Julia, who was carrying in a column of table-napkins, turned to her sister and said, simply, as if the question had surprised her:

"It's only Freddy, Kate, and Gabriel with him."

In fact right behind her Gabriel could be seen piloting Freddy Malins across the landing. The latter, a young man of about forty, was of Gabriel's size and build, with very round shoulders. His face was fleshy and pallid, touched with colour only at the thick hanging lobes of his ears and at the wide wings of his nose. He had coarse features, a blunt nose, a convex and receding brow, tumid and protruded lips. His heavy-lidded eyes and the disorder of his scanty hair made him look sleepy. He was laughing heartily in a high key at a story which he had been telling Gabriel on the stairs and at the same time rubbing the knuckles of his left fist backwards and forwards into his left eye.

"Good-evening, Freddy," said Aunt Julia.

Freddy Malins bade the Misses Morkan good-evening in what seemed an offhand fashion by reason of the habitual catch in his voice and then, seeing that Mr. Browne was grinning at him from the sideboard, crossed the room on rather shaky legs and began to repeat in an undertone the story he had just told to Gabriel.

"He's not so bad, is he?" said Aunt Kate to Gabriel.

Gabriel's brows were dark but he raised them quickly and answered:

"O, no, hardly noticeable."

"Now, isn't he a terrible fellow!" she said. "And his poor mother made him take the pledge[6] on New Year's Eve. But come on, Gabriel, into the drawing-room."

Before leaving the room with Gabriel she signalled to Mr. Browne by frowning and shaking her forefinger in warning to and fro. Mr. Browne nodded in answer and, when she had gone, said to Freddy Malins:

"Now, then, Teddy, I'm going to fill you out a good glass of lemonade just to buck you up."

Freddy Malins, who was nearing the climax of his story, waved the offer aside impatiently but Mr. Browne, having first called Freddy Malins' attention to a disarray in his dress, filled out and handed him a full glass of lemonade. Freddy Malins' left hand accepted the glass mechanically, his right hand being engaged in the mechanical readjustment of his dress. Mr. Browne, whose face was once more wrinkling with mirth, poured out for himself a glass of whisky while Freddy Malins exploded, before he had well reached the climax of his story, in a kink of high-pitched bronchitic laughter and, setting down his untasted and overflowing glass, began to rub the knuckles of his left fist backwards and forwards into his left eye, repeating words of his last phrase as well as his fit of laughter would allow him.

Gabriel could not listen while Mary Jane was playing her Academy piece, full of runs and difficult passages, to the hushed drawing-room. He liked music but the piece she was playing had no melody for him and he doubted whether it had any melody for the other listeners, though they had begged Mary Jane to play something. Four young men, who had

---

[6] The teetotaler's promise to abstain from alcohol.

come from the refreshment-room to stand in the doorway at the sound of the piano, had gone away quietly in couples after a few minutes. The only persons who seemed to follow the music were Mary Jane herself, her hands racing along the key-board or lifted from it at the pauses like those of a priestess in momentary imprecation, and Aunt Kate standing at her elbow to turn the page.

Gabriel's eyes, irritated by the floor, which glittered with beeswax under the heavy chandelier, wandered to the wall above the piano. A picture of the balcony scene in *Romeo and Juliet* hung there and beside it was a picture of the two murdered princes in the Tower which Aunt Julia had worked in red, blue and brown wools when she was a girl. Probably in the school they had gone to as girls that kind of work had been taught for one year. His mother had worked for him as a birthday present a waistcoat of purple tabinet, with little foxes' heads upon it, lined with brown satin and having round mulberry buttons. It was strange that his mother had had no musical talent though Aunt Kate used to call her the brains carrier of the Morkan family. Both she and Julia had always seemed a little proud of their serious and matronly sister. Her photograph stood before the pierglass. She held an open book on her knees and was pointing out something in it to Constantine who, dressed in a man-o'-war suit, lay at her feet. It was she who had chosen the names for her sons for she was very sensible of the dignity of family life. Thanks to her, Constantine was now senior curate in Balbriggan and, thanks to her, Gabriel himself had taken his degree in the Royal University. A shadow passed over his face as he remembered her sullen opposition to his marriage. Some slighting phrases she had used still rankled in his memory; she had once spoken of Gretta as being country cute and that was not true of Gretta at all. It was Gretta who had nursed her during all her last long illness in their house at Monkstown.

He knew that Mary Jane must be near the end of her piece for she was playing against the opening melody with runs of scales after every bar and while he waited for the end the resentment died down in his heart. The piece ended with a trill of octaves in the treble and a final deep octave in the bass. Great applause greeted Mary Jane as, blushing and rolling up her music nervously, she escaped from the room. The most vigorous clapping came from the four young men in the doorway who had gone away to the refreshment-room at the beginning of the piece but had come back when the piano had stopped.

Lancers[7] were arranged. Gabriel found himself partnered with Miss Ivors. She was a frank-mannered talkative young lady, with a freckled face and prominent brown eyes. She did not wear a low-cut bodice and the large brooch which was fixed in the front of her collar bore on it an Irish device and motto.

When they had taken their places she said abruptly:

"I have a crow to pluck with you."

"With me?" said Gabriel.

She nodded her head gravely.

"What is it?" asked Gabriel, smiling at her solemn manner.

"Who is G. C.?" answered Miss Ivors, turning her eyes upon him.

Gabriel coloured and was about to knit his brows, as if he did not understand, when she said bluntly:

"O, innocent Amy! I have found out that you write for *The Daily Express*. Now, aren't you ashamed of yourself?"

"Why should I be ashamed of myself?" asked Gabriel, blinking his eyes and trying to smile.

---

[7] A set of quadrilles danced in sequence.

"Well, I'm ashamed of you," said Miss Ivors frankly. "To say you'd write for a paper like that. I didn't think you were a West Briton."[8]

A look of perplexity appeared on Gabriel's face. It was true that he wrote a literary column every Wednesday in *The Daily Express*, for which he was paid fifteen shillings. But that did not make him a West Briton surely. The books he received for review were almost more welcome than the paltry cheque. He loved to feel the covers and turn over the pages of newly printed books. Nearly every day when his teaching in the college was ended he used to wander down the quays to the second-hand booksellers, to Hickey's on Bachelor's Walk, to Web's or Massey's on Aston's Quay, or to O'Clohissey's in the by-street. He did not know how to meet her charge. He wanted to say that literature was above politics. But they were friends of many years' standing and their careers had been parallel, first at the University and then as teachers: he could not risk a grandiose phrase with her. He continued blinking his eyes and trying to smile and murmured lamely that he saw nothing political in writing reviews of books.

When their turn to cross had come he was still perplexed and inattentive. Miss Ivors promptly took his hand in a warm grasp and said in a soft friendly tone:

"Of course, I was only joking. Come, we cross now."

When they were together again she spoke of the University question and Gabriel felt more at ease. A friend of hers had shown her his review of Browning's poems. That was how she had found out the secret: but she liked the review immensely. Then she said suddenly:

"O, Mr. Conroy, will you come for an excursion to the Aran Isles this summer? We're going to stay there a whole month. It will be splendid out in the Atlantic. You ought to come. Mr. Clancy is coming, and Mr. Kilkelly and Kathleen Kearney. It would be splendid for Gretta too if she'd come. She's from Connacht, isn't she?"

"Her people are," said Gabriel shortly.

"But you will come, won't you?" said Miss Ivors, laying her warm hand eagerly on his arm.

"The fact is," said Gabriel, "I have just arranged to go——"

"Go where?" asked Miss Ivors.

"Well, you know, every year I go for a cycling tour with some fellows and so——"

"But where?" asked Miss Ivors.

"Well, we usually go to France or Belgium or perhaps Germany," said Gabriel awkwardly.

"And why do you go to France and Belgium," said Miss Ivors, "instead of visiting your own land?"

"Well," said Gabriel, "it's partly to keep in touch with languages and partly for a change."

"And haven't you your own language to keep in touch with — Irish?" asked Miss Ivors.

"Well," said Gabriel, "if it comes to that, you know, Irish is not my language."

Their neighbours had turned to listen to the cross examination. Gabriel glanced right and left nervously and tried to keep his good humour under the ordeal which was making a blush invade his forehead.

"And haven't you your own land to visit," continued Miss Ivors, "that you know nothing of, your own people, and your own country?"

"O, to tell you the truth," retorted Gabriel suddenly, "I'm sick of my own country, sick of it!"

"Why?" asked Miss Ivors.

---

[8] A teasing term for an Irishman who acts as though he would rather be English.

Gabriel did not answer for his retort had heated him.

"Why?" repeated Miss Ivors.

They had to go visiting together and, as he had not answered her, Miss Ivors said warmly:

"Of course, you've no answer."

Gabriel tried to cover his agitation by taking part in the dance with great energy. He avoided her eyes for he had seen a sour expression on her face. But when they met in the long chain he was surprised to feel his hand firmly pressed. She looked at him from under her brows for a moment quizzically until he smiled. Then, just as the chain was about to start again, she stood on tiptoe and whispered into his ear:

"West Briton!"

When the lancers were over Gabriel went away to a remote corner of the room where Freddy Malins' mother was sitting. She was a stout feeble old woman with white hair. Her voice had a catch in it like her son's and she stuttered slightly. She had been told that Freddy had come and that he was nearly all right. Gabriel asked her whether she had had a good crossing. She lived with her married daughter in Glasgow and came to Dublin on a visit once a year. She answered placidly that she had had a beautiful crossing and that the captain had been most attentive to her. She spoke also of the beautiful house her daughter kept in Glasgow, and of all the friends they had there. While her tongue rambled on Gabriel tried to banish from his mind all memory of the unpleasant incident with Miss Ivors. Of course the girl or woman, or whatever she was, was an enthusiast but there was a time for all things. Perhaps he ought not to have answered her like that. But she had no right to call him a West Briton before people, even in joke. She had tried to make him ridiculous before people, heckling him and staring at him with her rabbit's eyes.

He saw his wife making her way towards him through the waltzing couples. When she reached him she said into his ear:

"Gabriel, Aunt Kate wants to know won't you carve the goose as usual. Miss Daly will carve the ham and I'll do the pudding."

"All right," said Gabriel.

"She's sending in the younger ones first as soon as this waltz is over so that we'll have the table to ourselves."

"Were you dancing?" asked Gabriel.

"Of course I was. Didn't you see me? What row had you with Molly Ivors?"

"No row. Why? Did she say so?"

"Something like that. I'm trying to get that Mr. D'Arcy to sing. He's full of conceit, I think."

"There was no row," said Gabriel moodily, "only she wanted me to go for a trip to the west of Ireland and I said I wouldn't."

His wife clasped her hands excitedly and gave a little jump.

"O, do go, Gabriel," she said. "I'd love to see Galway again."

"You can go if you like," said Gabriel coldly.

She looked at him for a moment, then turned to Mrs. Malins and said:

"There's a nice husband for you, Mrs. Malins."

While she was threading her way back across the room Mrs. Malins, without adverting to the interruption, went on to tell Gabriel what beautiful places there were in Scotland and beautiful scenery. Her son-in-law brought them every year to the lakes and they used to go fishing. Her son-in-law was a splendid fisher. One day he caught a beautiful big fish and the man in the hotel cooked it for their dinner.

Gabriel hardly heard what she said. Now that supper was coming near he began to think again about his speech and about the quotation. When he saw Freddy Malins coming across the room to visit his mother Gabriel left the chair free for him and retired into the embrasure of the window. The room had already cleared and from the back room came the clatter of plates and knives. Those who still remained in the drawing-room seemed tired of dancing and were conversing quietly in little groups. Gabriel's warm trembling fingers tapped the cold pane of the window. How cool it must be outside! How pleasant it would be to walk out alone, first along by the river and then through the park! The snow would be lying on the branches of the trees and forming a bright cap on the top of the Wellington Monument. How much more pleasant it would be there than at the supper-table!

He ran over the headings of his speech: Irish hospitality, sad memories, the Three Graces, Paris, the quotation from Browning. He repeated to himself a phrase he had written in his review: "One feels that one is listening to a thought-tormented music." Miss Ivors had praised the review. Was she sincere? Had she really any life of her own behind all her propagandism? There had never been any ill-feeling between them until that night. It unnerved him to think that she would be at the supper-table, looking up at him while he spoke with her critical quizzing eyes. Perhaps she would not be sorry to see him fail in his speech. An idea came into his mind and gave him courage. He would say, alluding to Aunt Kate and Aunt Julia: "Ladies and Gentlemen, the generation which is now on the wane among us may have had its faults but for my part I think it had certain qualities of hospitality, of humour, of humanity, which the new and very serious and hypereducated generation that is growing up around us seems to me to lack." Very good: that was one for Miss Ivors. What did he care that his aunts were only two ignorant old women?

A murmur in the room attracted his attention. Mr. Browne was advancing from the door, gallantly escorting Aunt Julia, who leaned upon his arm, smiling and hanging her head. An irregular musketry of applause escorted her also as far as the piano and then, as Mary Jane seated herself on the stool, and Aunt Julia, no longer smiling, half turned so as to pitch her voice fairly into the room, gradually ceased. Gabriel recognised the prelude. It was that of an old song of Aunt Julia's — *Arrayed for the Bridal*. Her voice, strong and clear in tone, attacked with great spirit the runs which embellish the air and though she sang very rapidly she did not miss even the smallest of the grace notes. To follow the voice, without looking at the singer's face, was to feel and share the excitement of swift and secure flight. Gabriel applauded loudly with all the others at the close of the song and loud applause was borne in from the invisible supper-table. It sounded so genuine that a little colour struggled into Aunt Julia's face as she bent to replace in the music-stand the old leather-bound songbook that had her initials on the cover. Freddy Malins, who had listened with his head perched sideways to hear her better, was still applauding when everyone else had ceased and talking animatedly to his mother who nodded her head gravely and slowly in acquiescence. At last, when he could clap no more, he stood up suddenly and hurried across the room to Aunt Julia whose hand he seized and held in both his hands, shaking it when words failed him or the catch in his voice proved too much for him.

"I was just telling my mother," he said, "I never heard you sing so well, never. No, I never heard your voice so good as it is tonight. Now! Would you believe that now? That's the truth. Upon my word and honour that's the truth. I never heard your voice sound so fresh and so ... so clear and fresh, never."

Aunt Julia smiled broadly and murmured something about compliments as she released her hand from his grasp. Mr. Browne extended his open hand towards her and said to those who were near him in the manner of a showman introducing a prodigy to an audience:

"Miss Julia Morkan, my latest discovery!"

He was laughing very heartily at this himself when Freddy Malins turned to him and said:

"Well, Browne, if you're serious you might make a worse discovery. All I can say is I never heard her sing half so well as long as I am coming here. And that's the honest truth."

"Neither did I," said Mr. Browne. "I think her voice has greatly improved."

Aunt Julia shrugged her shoulders and said with meek pride:

"Thirty years ago I hadn't a bad voice as voices go."

"I often told Julia," said Aunt Kate emphatically, "that she was simply thrown away in that choir. But she never would be said by me."

She turned as if to appeal to the good sense of the others against a refractory child while Aunt Julia gazed in front of her, a vague smile of reminiscence playing on her face.

"No," continued Aunt Kate, "she wouldn't be said or led by anyone, slaving there in that choir night and day, night and day. Six o'clock on Christmas morning! And all for what?"

"Well, isn't it for the honour of God, Aunt Kate?" asked Mary Jane, twisting round on the piano-stool and smiling.

Aunt Kate turned fiercely on her niece and said:

"I know all about the honour of God, Mary Jane, but I think it's not at all honourable for the pope to turn out the women out of the choirs that have slaved there all their lives and put little whippersnappers of boys over their heads. I suppose it is for the good of the Church if the pope does it. But it's not just, Mary Jane, and it's not right."

She had worked herself into a passion and would have continued in defence of her sister for it was a sore subject with her but Mary Jane, seeing that all the dancers had come back, intervened pacifically:

"Now, Aunt Kate, you're giving scandal to Mr. Browne who is of the other persuasion."

Aunt Kate turned to Mr. Browne, who was grinning at this allusion to his religion, and said hastily:

"O, I don't question the pope's being right. I'm only a stupid old woman and I wouldn't presume to do such a thing. But there's such a thing as common everyday politeness and gratitude. And if I were in Julia's place I'd tell that Father Healey straight up to his face ..."

"And besides, Aunt Kate," said Mary Jane, "we really are all hungry and when we are hungry we are all very quarrelsome."

"And when we are thirsty we are also quarrelsome," added Mr. Browne.

"So that we had better go to supper," said Mary Jane, "and finish the discussion afterwards."

On the landing outside the drawing-room Gabriel found his wife and Mary Jane trying to persuade Miss Ivors to stay for supper. But Miss Ivors, who had put on her hat and was buttoning her cloak, would not stay. She did not feel in the least hungry and she had already overstayed her time.

"But only for ten minutes, Molly," said Mrs. Conroy. "That won't delay you."

"To take a pick itself," said Mary Jane, "after all your dancing."

"I really couldn't," said Miss Ivors.

"I am afraid you didn't enjoy yourself at all," said Mary Jane hopelessly.

"Ever so much, I assure you," said Miss Ivors, "but you really must let me run off now."

"But how can you get home?" asked Mrs. Conroy.

"O, it's only two steps up the quay."

Gabriel hesitated a moment and said:

"If you will allow me, Miss Ivors, I'll see you home if you are really obliged to go."

But Miss Ivors broke away from them.

"I won't hear it," she cried. "For goodness' sake go in to your suppers and don't mind me. I'm quite well able to take care of myself."

"Well, you're the comical girl, Molly," said Mrs. Conroy frankly.

"*Beannacht libh*,"[9] cried Miss Ivors, with a laugh, as she ran down the staircase.

Mary Jane gazed after her, a moody puzzled expression on her face, while Mrs. Conroy leaned over the banisters to listen for the hall-door. Gabriel asked himself was he the cause of her abrupt departure. But she did not seem to be in ill humour: she had gone away laughing. He stared blankly down the staircase.

At the moment Aunt Kate came toddling out of the supper-room, almost wringing her hands in despair.

"Where is Gabriel?" she cried. "Where on earth is Gabriel? There's everyone waiting in there, stage to let, and nobody to carve the goose!"

"Here I am, Aunt Kate!" cried Gabriel, with sudden animation, "ready to carve a flock of geese, if necessary."

A fat brown goose lay at one end of the table and at the other end, on a bed of creased paper strewn with sprigs of parsley, lay a great ham, stripped of its outer skin and peppered over with crust crumbs, a neat paper frill round its shin and beside this was a round of spiced beef. Between these rival ends ran parallel lines of side-dishes: two little minsters of jelly, red and yellow; a shallow dish full of blocks of blancmange and red jam, a large green leaf-shaped dish with a stalk-shaped handle, on which lay bunches of purple raisins and peeled almonds, a companion dish on which lay a solid rectangle of Smyrna figs, a dish of custard topped with grated nutmeg, a small bowl full of chocolates and sweets wrapped in gold and silver papers and a glass vase in which stood some tall celery stalks. In the centre of the table there stood, as sentries to a fruit-stand which upheld a pyramid of oranges and American apples, two squat old-fashioned decanters of cut glass, one containing port and the other dark sherry. On the closed square piano a pudding in a huge yellow dish lay in waiting and behind it were three squads of bottles of stout and ale and minerals, drawn up according to the colours of their uniforms, the first two black, with brown and red labels, the third and smallest squad white, with transverse green sashes.

Gabriel took his seat boldly at the head of the table and, having looked to the edge of the carver, plunged his fork firmly into the goose. He felt quite at ease now for he was an expert carver and liked nothing better than to find himself at the head of a well-laden table.

"Miss Furlong, what shall I send you?" he asked. "A wing or a slice of the breast?"

"Just a small slice of the breast."

"Miss Higgins, what for you?"

"O, anything at all, Mr. Conroy."

While Gabriel and Miss Daly exchanged plates of goose and plates of ham and spiced beef Lily went from guest to guest with a dish of hot floury potatoes wrapped in a white napkin. This was Mary Jane's idea and she had also suggested apple sauce for the goose but Aunt Kate had said that plain roast goose without any apple sauce had always been good

---

[9] "Blessings on you."

enough for her and she hoped she might never eat worse. Mary Jane waited on her pupils and saw that they got the best slices and Aunt Kate and Aunt Julia opened and carried across from the piano bottles of stout and ale for the gentlemen and bottles of minerals for the ladies. There was a great deal of confusion and laughter and noise, the noise of orders and counter-orders, of knives and forks, of corks and glass-stoppers. Gabriel began to carve second helpings as soon as he had finished the first round without serving himself. Everyone protested loudly so that he compromised by taking a long draught of stout for he had found the carving hot work. Mary Jane settled down quietly to her supper but Aunt Kate and Aunt Julia were still toddling round the table, walking on each other's heels, getting in each other's way and giving each other unheeded orders. Mr. Browne begged of them to sit down and eat their suppers and so did Gabriel but they said there was time enough, so that, at last Freddy Malins stood up and, capturing Aunt Kate, plumped her down on her chair amid general laughter.

When everyone had been well served Gabriel said, smiling:

"Now, if anyone wants a little more of what vulgar people call stuffing let him or her speak."

A chorus of voices invited him to begin his own supper and Lily came forward with three potatoes which she had reserved for him.

"Very well," said Gabriel amiably, as he took another preparatory draught, "kindly forget my existence, ladies and gentlemen, for a few minutes."

He set to his supper and took no part in the conversation with which the table covered Lily's removal of the plates. The subject of talk was the opera company which was then at the Theatre Royal. Mr. Bartell D'Arcy, the tenor, a dark-complexioned young man with a smart moustache, praised very highly the leading contralto of the company but Miss Furlong thought she had a rather vulgar style of production. Freddy Malins said there was a Negro chieftain singing in the second part of the Gaiety pantomime who had one of the finest tenor voices he had ever heard.

"Have you heard him?" he asked Mr. Bartell D'Arcy across the table.

"No," answered Mr. Bartell D'Arcy carelessly.

"Because," Freddy Malins explained, "now I'd be curious to hear your opinion of him. I think he has a grand voice."

"It takes Teddy to find out the really good things," said Mr. Browne familiarly to the table.

"And why couldn't he have a voice too?" asked Freddy Malins sharply. "Is it because he's only a black?"

Nobody answered this question and Mary Jane led the table back to the legitimate opera. One of her pupils had given her a pass for *Mignon*. Of course it was very fine, she said, but it made her think of poor Georgina Burns. Mr. Browne could go back farther still, to the old Italian companies that used to come to Dublin — Tietjens, Ilma de Murzka, Campanini, the great Trebelli, Giuglini, Ravelli, Aramburo. Those were the days, he said, when there was something like singing to be heard in Dublin. He told too of how the top gallery of the old Royal used to be packed night after night, of how one night an Italian tenor had sung five encores to *Let Me Like a Soldier Fall*, introducing a high C every time, and of how the gallery boys would sometimes in their enthusiasm unyoke the horses from the carriage of some great *prima donna* and pull her themselves through the streets to her hotel. Why did they never play the grand old operas now, he asked, *Dinorah, Lucrezia Borgia*? Because they could not get the voices to sing them: that was why.

"Oh, well," said Mr. Bartell D'Arcy, "I presume there are as good singers today as there were then."

"Where are they?" asked Mr. Browne defiantly.

"In London, Paris, Milan," said Mr. Bartell D'Arcy warmly. "I suppose Caruso, for example, is quite as good, if not better than any of the men you have mentioned."

"Maybe so," said Mr. Browne. "But I may tell you I doubt it strongly."

"O, I'd give anything to hear Caruso sing," said Mary Jane.

"For me," said Aunt Kate, who had been picking a bone, "there was only one tenor. To please me, I mean. But I suppose none of you ever heard of him."

"Who was he, Miss Morkan?" asked Mr. Bartell D'Arcy politely.

"His name," said Aunt Kate, "was Parkinson. I heard him when he was in his prime and I think he had then the purest tenor voice that was ever put into a man's throat."

"Strange," said Mr. Bartell D'Arcy. "I never even heard of him."

"Yes, yes, Miss Morkan is right," said Mr. Browne. "I remember hearing of old Parkinson but he's too far back for me."

"A beautiful, pure, sweet, mellow English tenor," said Aunt Kate with enthusiasm.

Gabriel having finished, the huge pudding was transferred to the table. The clatter of forks and spoons began again. Gabriel's wife served out spoonfuls of the pudding and passed the plates down the table. Midway down they were held up by Mary Jane, who replenished them with raspberry or orange jelly or with blancmange and jam. The pudding was of Aunt Julia's making and she received praises for it from all quarters. She herself said that it was not quite brown enough.

"Well, I hope, Miss Morkan," said Mr. Browne, "that I'm brown enough for you because, you know, I'm all brown."

All the gentlemen, except Gabriel, ate some of the pudding out of compliment to Aunt Julia. As Gabriel never ate sweets the celery had been left for him. Freddy Malins also took a stalk of celery and ate it with his pudding. He had been told that celery was a capital thing for the blood and he was just then under doctor's care. Mrs. Malins, who had been silent all through the supper, said that her son was going down to Mount Melleray[10] in a week or so. The table then spoke of Mount Melleray, how bracing the air was down there, how hospitable the monks were and how they never asked for a penny-piece from their guests.

"And do you mean to say," asked Mr. Browne incredulously, "that a chap can go down there and put up there as if it were a hotel and live on the fat of the land and then come away without paying anything?"

"O, most people give some donation to the monastery when they leave," said Mary Jane.

"I wish we had an institution like that in our Church," said Mr. Browne candidly.

He was astonished to hear that the monks never spoke, got up at two in the morning and slept in their coffins. He asked what they did it for.

"That's the rule of the order," said Aunt Kate firmly.

"Yes, but why?" asked Mr. Browne.

Aunt Kate repeated that it was the rule that was all. Mr. Browne still seemed not to understand. Freddy Malins explained to him, as best he could, that the monks were trying to make up for the sins committed by all the sinners in the outside world. The explanation was not very clear for Mr. Browne grinned and said:

---

[10] An Irish Trappist monastery.

"I like that idea very much but wouldn't a comfortable spring bed do them as well as a coffin?"

"The coffin," said Mary Jane, "is to remind them of their last end."

As the subject had grown lugubrious it was buried in a silence of the table during which Mrs. Malins could be heard saying to her neighbour in an indistinct undertone:

"They are very good men, the monks, very pious men."

The raisins and almonds and figs and apples and oranges and chocolates and sweets were now passed about the table and Aunt Julia invited all the guests to have either port or sherry. At first Mr. Bartell D'Arcy refused to take either but one of his neighbours nudged him and whispered something to him upon which he allowed his glass to be filled. Gradually as the last glasses were being filled the conversation ceased. A pause followed, broken only by the noise of the wine and by unsettlings of chairs. The Misses Morkan, all three, looked down at the tablecloth. Someone coughed once or twice and then a few gentlemen patted the table gently as a signal for silence. The silence came and Gabriel pushed back his chair and stood up.

The patting at once grew louder in encouragement and then ceased altogether. Gabriel leaned his ten trembling fingers on the tablecloth and smiled nervously at the company. Meeting a row of unturned faces he raised his eyes to the chandelier. The piano was playing a waltz tune and he could hear the skirts sweeping against the drawing-room door. People, perhaps, were standing in the snow on the quay outside, gazing up at the lighted windows and listening to the waltz music. The air was pure there. In the distance lay the park where the trees were weighted with snow. The Wellington Monument wore a gleaming cap of snow that flashed westward over the white field of Fifteen Acres.[11]

He began:

"Ladies and Gentlemen,

"It has fallen to my lot this evening, as in years past, to perform a very pleasing task but a task for which I am afraid my poor powers as a speaker are all too inadequate."

"No, no!" said Mr. Browne.

"But, however that may be, I can only ask you tonight to take the will for the deed and to lend me your attention for a few moments while I endeavour to express to you in words what my feelings are on this occasion.

"Ladies and Gentlemen, it is not the first time that we have gathered together under this hospitable roof, around this hospitable board. It is not the first time that we have been the recipients — or perhaps, I had better say, the victims — of the hospitality of certain good ladies."

He made a circle in the air with his arm and paused. Everyone laughed or smiled at Aunt Kate and Aunt Julia and Mary Jane who all turned crimson with pleasure. Gabriel went on more boldly:

"I feel more strongly with every recurring year that our country has no tradition which does it so much honour and which it should guard so jealously as that of its hospitality. It is a tradition that is unique as far as my experience goes (and I have visited not a few places abroad) among the modern nations. Some would say, perhaps, that with us it is rather a failing than anything to be boasted of. But granted even that, it is, to my mind, a princely failing, and one that I trust will long be cultivated among us. Of one thing, at least, I am sure. As long as this one roof shelters the good ladies aforesaid — and I wish from my heart it may do so for many and many a long year to come — the tradition of genuine warm-hearted

---

[11] A part of Dublin's Phoenix Park.

courteous Irish hospitality, which our forefathers have handed down to us and which we in turn must hand down to our descendants, is still alive among us."

A hearty murmur of assent ran round the table. It shot through Gabriel's mind that Miss Ivors was not there and that she had gone away discourteously: and he said with confidence in himself:

"Ladies and Gentlemen,

"A new generation is growing up in our midst, a generation actuated by new ideas and new principles. It is serious and enthusiastic for these new ideas and its enthusiasm, even when it is misdirected, is, I believe, in the main sincere. But we are living in a sceptical and, if I may use the phrase, a thought-tormented age: and sometimes I fear that this new generation, educated or hypereducated as it is, will lack those qualities of humanity, of hospitality, of kindly humour which belonged to an older day. Listening tonight to the names of all those great singers of the past it seemed to me, I must confess, that we were living in a less spacious age. Those days might, without exaggeration, be called spacious days: and if they are gone beyond recall let us hope, at least, that in gatherings such as this we shall still speak of them with pride and affection, still cherish in our hearts the memory of those dead and gone great ones whose fame the world will not willingly let die."

"Hear, hear!" said Mr. Browne loudly.

"But yet," continued Gabriel, his voice falling into a softer inflection, "there are always in gatherings such as this sadder thoughts that will recur to our minds: thoughts of the past, of youth, of changes, of absent faces that we miss here tonight. Our path through life is strewn with many such sad memories: and were we to brood upon them always we could not find the heart to go on bravely with our work among the living. We have all of us living duties and living affections which claim, and rightly claim, our strenuous endeavours.

"Therefore, I will not linger on the past. I will not let any gloomy moralising intrude upon us here tonight. Here we are gathered together for a brief moment from the bustle and rush of our everyday routine. We are met here as friends, in the spirit of good-fellowship, as colleagues, also to a certain extent, in the true spirit of *camaraderie*,[12] and as the guests of — what shall I call them — the Three Graces of the Dublin musical world."

The table burst into applause and laughter at this allusion. Aunt Julia vainly asked each of her neighbours in turn to tell her what Gabriel had said.

"He says we are the Three Graces, Aunt Julia," said Mary Jane.

Aunt Julia did not understand but she looked up, smiling, at Gabriel, who continued in the same vein:

"Ladies and Gentlemen,

"I will not attempt to play tonight the part that Paris played on another occasion. I will not attempt to choose between them. The task would be an invidious one and one beyond my poor powers. For when I view them in turn, whether it be our chief hostess herself, whose good heart, whose too good heart, has become a byword with all who know her, or her sister, who seems to be gifted with perennial youth and whose singing must have been a surprise and a revelation to us all tonight, or, last but not least, when I consider our youngest hostess, talented, cheerful, hard-working and the best of nieces, I confess, Ladies and Gentlemen, that I do not know to which of them I should award the prize."

Gabriel glanced down at his aunts and, seeing the large smile on Aunt Julia's face and the tears which had risen to Aunt Kate's eyes, hastened to his close. He raised his glass of port gallantly, while every member of the company fingered a glass expectantly, and said loudly:

---

[12] Comradeship.

"Let us toast them all three together. Let us drink to their health, wealth, long life, happiness and prosperity and may they long continue to hold the proud and self-won position which they hold in their profession and the position of honour and affection which they hold in our hearts."

All the guests stood up, glass in hand, and turning towards the three seated ladies, sang in unison, with Mr. Browne as leader:

For they are jolly gay fellows,
For they are jolly gay fellows,
For they are jolly gay fellows,
Which nobody can deny.

Aunt Kate was making frank use of her handkerchief and even Aunt Julia seemed moved. Freddy Malins beat time with his pudding-fork and the singers turned towards one another, as if in melodious conference, while they sang with emphasis:

Unless he tells a lie,
Unless he tells a lie,

Then, turning once more towards their hostesses, they sang:

For they are jolly gay fellows,
For they are jolly gay fellows,
For they are jolly gay fellows,
Which nobody can deny.

The acclamation which followed was taken up beyond the door of the supper-room by many of the other guests and renewed time after time, Freddy Malins acting as officer with his fork on high.

The piercing morning air came into the hall where they were standing so that Aunt Kate said:

"Close the door, somebody. Mrs. Malins will get her death of cold."

"Browne is out there, Aunt Kate," said Mary Jane.

"Browne is everywhere," said Aunt Kate, lowering her voice.

Mary Jane laughed at her tone.

"Really," she said archly, "he is very attentive."

"He has been laid on here like the gas," said Aunt Kate in the same tone, "all during the Christmas."

She laughed herself this time good-humouredly and then added quickly:

"But tell him to come in, Mary Jane, and close the door. I hope to goodness he didn't hear me."

At that moment the hall-door was opened and Mr. Browne came in from the doorstep, laughing as if his heart would break. He was dressed in a long green overcoat with mock astrakhan cuffs and collar and wore on his head an oval fur cap. He pointed down the snow-covered quay from where the sound of shrill prolonged whistling was borne in.

"Teddy will have all the cabs in Dublin out," he said.

Gabriel advanced from the little pantry behind the office, struggling into his overcoat and, looking round the hall, said:

"Gretta not down yet?"

"She's getting on her things, Gabriel," said Aunt Kate.

"Who's playing up there?" asked Gabriel.

"Nobody. They're all gone."

"O no, Aunt Kate," said Mary Jane. "Bartell D'Arcy and Miss O'Callaghan aren't gone yet."

"Someone is fooling at the piano anyhow," said Gabriel.

Mary Jane glanced at Gabriel and Mr. Browne and said with a shiver:

"It makes me feel cold to look at you two gentlemen muffled up like that. I wouldn't like to face your journey home at this hour."

"I'd like nothing better this minute," said Mr. Browne stoutly, "than a rattling fine walk in the country or a fast drive with a good spanking goer between the shafts."

"We used to have a very good horse and trap at home," said Aunt Julia sadly.

"The never-to-be-forgotten Johnny," said Mary Jane, laughing.

Aunt Kate and Gabriel laughed too.

"Why, what was wonderful about Johnny?" asked Mr. Browne.

"The late lamented Patrick Morkan, our grandfather, that is," explained Gabriel, "commonly known in his later years as the old gentleman, was a glue-boiler."

"O, now, Gabriel," said Aunt Kate, laughing, "he had a starch mill."

"Well, glue or starch," said Gabriel, "the old gentleman had a horse by the name of Johnny. And Johnny used to work in the old gentleman's mill, walking round and round in order to drive the mill. That was all very well; but now comes the tragic part about Johnny. One fine day the old gentleman thought he'd like to drive out with the quality to a military review in the park."

"The Lord have mercy on his soul," said Aunt Kate compassionately.

"Amen," said Gabriel. "So the old gentleman, as I said, harnessed Johnny and put on his very best tall hat and his very best stock collar and drove out in grand style from his ancestral mansion somewhere near Back Lane, I think."

Everyone laughed, even Mrs. Malins, at Gabriel's manner and Aunt Kate said:

"O, now, Gabriel, he didn't live in Back Lane, really. Only the mill was there."

"Out from the mansion of his forefathers," continued Gabriel, "he drove with Johnny. And everything went on beautifully until Johnny came in sight of King Billy's[13] statue: and whether he fell in love with the horse King Billy sits on or whether he thought he was back again in the mill, anyhow he began to walk round the statue."

Gabriel paced in a circle round the hall in his goloshes amid the laughter of the others.

"Round and round he went," said Gabriel, "and the old gentleman, who was a very pompous old gentleman, was highly indignant. 'Go on, sir! What do you mean, sir? Johnny! Johnny! Most extraordinary conduct! Can't understand the horse!'"

The peal of laughter which followed Gabriel's imitation of the incident was interrupted by a resounding knock at the hall door. Mary Jane ran to open it and let in Freddy Malins. Freddy Malins, with his hat well back on his head and his shoulders humped with cold, was puffing and steaming after his exertions.

"I could only get one cab," he said.

"O, we'll find another along the quay," said Gabriel.

"Yes," said Aunt Kate. "Better not keep Mrs. Malins standing in the draught."

Mrs. Malins was helped down the front steps by her son and Mr. Browne and, after many manœuvres, hoisted into the cab. Freddy Malins clambered in after her and spent a

---

[13] William of Orange, King of England from 1689 to 1702, and conqueror of Ireland in 1690.

long time settling her on the seat, Mr. Browne helping him with advice. At last she was settled comfortably and Freddy Malins invited Mr. Browne into the cab. There was a good deal of confused talk, and then Mr. Browne got into the cab. The cabman settled his rug over his knees, and bent down for the address. The confusion grew greater and the cabman was directed differently by Freddy Malins and Mr. Browne, each of whom had his head out through a window of the cab. The difficulty was to know where to drop Mr. Browne along the route, and Aunt Kate, Aunt Julia and Mary Jane helped the discussion from the doorstep with cross-directions and contradictions and abundance of laughter. As for Freddy Malins he was speechless with laughter. He popped his head in and out of the window every moment to the great danger of his hat, and told his mother how the discussion was progressing, till at last Mr. Browne shouted to the bewildered cabman above the din of everybody's laughter:

"Do you know Trinity College?"

"Yes, sir," said the cabman.

"Well, drive bang up against Trinity College gates," said Mr. Browne, "and then we'll tell you where to go. You understand now?"

"Yes, sir," said the cabman,

"Make like a bird for Trinity College."

"Right, sir," said the cabman.

The horse was whipped up and the cab rattled off along the quay amid a chorus of laughter and adieus.

Gabriel had not gone to the door with the others. He was in a dark part of the hall gazing up the staircase. A woman was standing near the top of the first flight, in the shadow also. He could not see her face but he could see the terra-cotta and salmon-pink panels of her skirt which the shadow made appear black and white. It was his wife. She was leaning on the banisters, listening to something. Gabriel was surprised at her stillness and strained his ear to listen also. But he could hear little save the noise of laughter and dispute on the front steps, a few chords struck on the piano and a few notes of a man's voice singing.

He stood still in the gloom of the hall, trying to catch the air that the voice was singing and gazing up at his wife. There was grace and mystery in her attitude as if she were a symbol of something. He asked himself what is a woman standing on the stairs in the shadow, listening to distant music, a symbol of. If he were a painter he would paint her in that attitude. Her blue felt hat would show off the bronze of her hair against the darkness and the dark panels of her skirt would show off the light ones. *Distant Music* he would call the picture if he were a painter.

The hall-door was closed; and Aunt Kate, Aunt Julia and Mary Jane came down the hall, still laughing.

"Well, isn't Freddy terrible?" said Mary Jane. "He's really terrible."

Gabriel said nothing but pointed up the stairs towards where his wife was standing. Now that the hall-door was closed the voice and the piano could be heard more clearly. Gabriel held up his hand for them to be silent. The song seemed to be in the old Irish tonality and the singer seemed uncertain both of his words and of his voice. The voice, made plaintive by distance and by the singer's hoarseness, faintly illuminated the cadence of the air with words expressing grief:

O, the rain falls on my heavy locks
And the dew wets my skin,
My babe lies cold ...

"O," exclaimed Mary Jane. "It's Bartell D'Arcy singing and he wouldn't sing all the night. O, I'll get him to sing a song before he goes."

"O, do, Mary Jane," said Aunt Kate.

Mary Jane brushed past the others and ran to the staircase, but before she reached it the singing stopped and the piano was closed abruptly.

"O, what a pity!" she cried. "Is he coming down, Gretta?"

Gabriel heard his wife answer yes and saw her come down towards them. A few steps behind her were Mr. Bartell D'Arcy and Miss O'Callaghan.

"O, Mr. D'Arcy," cried Mary Jane, "it's downright mean of you to break off like that when we were all in raptures listening to you."

"I have been at him all the evening," said Miss O'Callaghan, "and Mrs. Conroy, too, and he told us he had a dreadful cold and couldn't sing."

"O, Mr. D'Arcy," said Aunt Kate, "now that was a great fib to tell."

"Can't you see that I'm as hoarse as a crow?" said Mr. D'Arcy roughly.

He went into the pantry hastily and put on his overcoat. The others, taken aback by his rude speech, could find nothing to say. Aunt Kate wrinkled her brows and made signs to the others to drop the subject. Mr. D'Arcy stood swathing his neck carefully and frowning.

"It's the weather," said Aunt Julia, after a pause.

"Yes, everybody has colds," said Aunt Kate readily, "everybody."

"They say," said Mary Jane, "we haven't had snow like it for thirty years; and I read this morning in the newspapers that the snow is general all over Ireland."

"I love the look of snow," said Aunt Julia sadly.

"So do I," said Miss O'Callaghan. "I think Christmas is never really Christmas unless we have the snow on the ground."

"But poor Mr. D'Arcy doesn't like the snow," said Aunt Kate, smiling.

Mr. D'Arcy came from the pantry, fully swathed and buttoned, and in a repentant tone told them the history of his cold. Everyone gave him advice and said it was a great pity and urged him to be very careful of his throat in the night air. Gabriel watched his wife, who did not join in the conversation. She was standing right under the dusty fanlight and the flame of the gas lit up the rich bronze of her hair, which he had seen her drying at the fire a few days before. She was in the same attitude and seemed unaware of the talk about her. At last she turned towards them and Gabriel saw that there was colour on her cheeks and that her eyes were shining. A sudden tide of joy went leaping out of his heart.

"Mr. D'Arcy," she said, "what is the name of that song you were singing?"

"It's called *The Lass of Aughrim*," said Mr. D'Arcy, "but I couldn't remember it properly. Why? Do you know it?"

"*The Lass of Aughrim*," she repeated. "I couldn't think of the name."

"It's a very nice air," said Mary Jane. "I'm sorry you were not in voice tonight."

"Now, Mary Jane," said Aunt Kate, "don't annoy Mr. D'Arcy. I won't have him annoyed."

Seeing that all were ready to start she shepherded them to the door, where good-night was said:

"Well, good-night, Aunt Kate, and thanks for the pleasant evening."

"Good-night, Gabriel. Good-night, Gretta!"

"Good-night, Aunt Kate, and thanks ever so much. Good-night, Aunt Julia."

"O, good-night, Gretta, I didn't see you."

"Good-night, Mr. D'Arcy. Good-night, Miss O'Callaghan."

"Good-night, Miss Morkan."

"Good-night, again."

"Good-night, all. Safe home."

"Good-night. Good night."

The morning was still dark. A dull, yellow light brooded over the houses and the river; and the sky seemed to be descending. It was slushy underfoot; and only streaks and patches of snow lay on the roofs, on the parapets of the quay and on the area railings. The lamps were still burning redly in the murky air and, across the river, the palace of the Four Courts stood out menacingly against the heavy sky.

She was walking on before him with Mr. Bartell D'Arcy, her shoes in a brown parcel tucked under one arm and her hands holding her skirt up from the slush. She had no longer any grace of attitude, but Gabriel's eyes were still bright with happiness. The blood went bounding along his veins; and the thoughts went rioting through his brain, proud, joyful, tender, valorous.

She was walking on before him so lightly and so erect that he longed to run after her noiselessly, catch her by the shoulders and say something foolish and affectionate into her ear. She seemed to him so frail that he longed to defend her against something and then to be alone with her. Moments of their secret life together burst like stars upon his memory. A heliotrope envelope was lying beside his breakfast-cup and he was caressing it with his hand. Birds were twittering in the ivy and the sunny web of the curtain was shimmering along the floor: he could not eat for happiness. They were standing on the crowded platform and he was placing a ticket inside the warm palm of her glove. He was standing with her in the cold, looking in through a grated window at a man making bottles in a roaring furnace. It was very cold. Her face, fragrant in the cold air, was quite close to his; and suddenly he called out to the man at the furnace:

"Is the fire hot, sir?"

But the man could not hear with the noise of the furnace. It was just as well. He might have answered rudely.

A wave of yet more tender joy escaped from his heart and went coursing in warm flood along his arteries. Like the tender fire of stars moments of their life together, that no one knew of or would ever know of, broke upon and illumined his memory. He longed to recall to her those moments, to make her forget the years of their dull existence together and remember only their moments of ecstasy. For the years, he felt, had not quenched his soul or hers. Their children, his writing, her household cares had not quenched all their souls' tender fire. In one letter that he had written to her then he had said: "Why is it that words like these seem to me so dull and cold? Is it because there is no word tender enough to be your name?"

Like distant music these words that he had written years before were borne towards him from the past. He longed to be alone with her. When the others had gone away, when he and she were in the room in the hotel, then they would be alone together. He would call her softly:

"Gretta!"

Perhaps she would not hear at once: she would be undressing. Then something in his voice would strike her. She would turn and look at him. ...

At the corner of Winetavern Street they met a cab. He was glad of its rattling noise as it saved him from conversation. She was looking out of the window and seemed tired. The others spoke only a few words, pointing out some building or street. The horse galloped along wearily under the murky morning sky, dragging his old rattling box after his heels, and Gabriel was again in a cab with her, galloping to catch the boat, galloping to their honeymoon.

As the cab drove across O'Connell Bridge Miss O'Callaghan said:

"They say you never cross O'Connell Bridge without seeing a white horse."

"I see a white man[14] this time," said Gabriel.

"Where?" asked Mr. Bartell D'Arcy.

Gabriel pointed to the statue, on which lay patches of snow. Then he nodded familiarly to it and waved his hand.

"Good-night, Dan," he said gaily.

When the cab drew up before the hotel, Gabriel jumped out and, in spite of Mr. Bartell D'Arcy's protest, paid the driver. He gave the man a shilling over his fare. The man saluted and said:

"A prosperous New Year to you, sir."

"The same to you," said Gabriel cordially.

She leaned for a moment on his arm in getting out of the cab and while standing at the curbstone, bidding the others good-night. She leaned lightly on his arm, as lightly as when she had danced with him a few hours before. He had felt proud and happy then, happy that she was his, proud of her grace and wifely carriage. But now, after the kindling again of so many memories, the first touch of her body, musical and strange and perfumed, sent through him a keen pang of lust. Under cover of her silence he pressed her closely to his side; and, as they stood at the hotel door, he felt that they had escaped from their lives and duties, escaped from home and friends and run away together with wild and radiant hearts to a new adventure.

An old man was dozing in a great hooded chair in the hall. He lit a candle in the office and went before them to the stairs. They followed him in silence, their feet falling in soft thuds on the thickly carpeted stairs. She mounted the stairs behind the porter, her head bowed in the ascent, her frail shoulders curved as with a burden, her skirt girt tightly about her. He could have flung his arms about her hips and held her still, for his arms were trembling with desire to seize her and only the stress of his nails against the palms of his hands held the wild impulse of his body in check. The porter halted on the stairs to settle his guttering candle. They halted, too, on the steps below him. In the silence Gabriel could hear the falling of the molten wax into the tray and the thumping of his own heart against his ribs.

The porter led them along a corridor and opened a door. Then he set his unstable candle down on a toilet-table and asked at what hour they were to be called in the morning.

"Eight," said Gabriel.

The porter pointed to the tap of the electric-light and began a muttered apology, but Gabriel cut him short.

"We don't want any light. We have light enough from the street. And I say," he added, pointing to the candle, "you might remove that handsome article, like a good man."

The porter took up his candle again, but slowly, for he was surprised by such a novel idea. Then he mumbled good-night and went out. Gabriel shot the lock to.

A ghastly light from the street lamp lay in a long shaft from one window to the door. Gabriel threw his overcoat and hat on a couch and crossed the room towards the window. He looked down into the street in order that his emotion might calm a little. Then he turned and leaned against a chest of drawers with his back to the light. She had taken off her hat and cloak and was standing before a large swinging mirror, unhooking her waist. Gabriel paused for a few moments, watching her, and then said:

"Gretta!"

---

[14] Daniel O'Connell, Irish patriot and orator.

She turned away from the mirror slowly and walked along the shaft of light towards him. Her face looked so serious and weary that the words would not pass Gabriel's lips. No, it was not the moment yet.

"You looked tired," he said.

"I am a little," she answered.

"You don't feel ill or weak?"

"No, tired: that's all."

She went on to the window and stood there, looking out. Gabriel waited again and then, fearing that diffidence was about to conquer him, he said abruptly:

"By the way, Gretta!"

"What is it?"

"You know that poor fellow Malins?" he said quickly.

"Yes. What about him?"

"Well, poor fellow, he's a decent sort of chap, after all," continued Gabriel in a false voice. "He gave me back that sovereign I lent him, and I didn't expect it, really. It's a pity he wouldn't keep away from that Browne, because he's not a bad fellow, really."

He was trembling now with annoyance. Why did she seem so abstracted? He did not know how he could begin. Was she annoyed, too, about something? If she would only turn to him or come to him of her own accord! To take her as she was would be brutal. No, he must see some ardour in her eyes first. He longed to be master of her strange mood.

"When did you lend him the pound?" she asked, after a pause.

Gabriel strove to restrain himself from breaking out into brutal language about the sottish Malins and his pound. He longed to cry to her from his soul, to crush her body against his, to overmaster her. But he said:

"O, at Christmas, when he opened that little Christmas-card shop in Henry Street."

He was in such a fever of rage and desire that he did not hear her come from the window. She stood before him for an instant, looking at him strangely. Then, suddenly raising herself on tiptoe and resting her hands lightly on his shoulders, she kissed him.

"You are a very generous person, Gabriel," she said.

Gabriel, trembling with delight at her sudden kiss and at the quaintness of her phrase, put his hands on her hair and began smoothing it back, scarcely touching it with his fingers. The washing had made it fine and brilliant. His heart was brimming over with happiness. Just when he was wishing for it she had come to him of her own accord. Perhaps her thoughts had been running with his. Perhaps she had felt the impetuous desire that was in him, and then the yielding mood had come upon her. Now that she had fallen to him so easily, he wondered why he had been so diffident.

He stood, holding her head between his hands. Then, slipping one arm swiftly about her body and drawing her towards him, he said softly:

"Gretta, dear, what are you thinking about?"

She did not answer nor yield wholly to his arm. He said again, softly:

"Tell me what it is, Gretta. I think I know what is the matter. Do I know?"

She did not answer at once. Then she said in an outburst of tears:

"O, I am thinking about that song, *The Lass of Aughrim*."

She broke loose from him and ran to the bed and, throwing her arms across the bed-rail, hid her face. Gabriel stood stock-still for a moment in astonishment and then followed her. As he passed in the way of the cheval-glass he caught sight of himself in full length, his broad, well-filled shirt-front, the face whose expression always puzzled him when he saw it in a mirror, and his glimmering gilt-rimmed eyeglasses. He halted a few paces from her and said:

"What about the song? Why does that make you cry?"

She raised her head from her arms and dried her eyes with the back of her hand like a child. A kinder note than he had intended went into his voice.

"Why, Gretta?" he asked.

"I am thinking about a person long ago who used to sing that song."

"And who was the person long ago?" asked Gabriel, smiling.

"It was a person I used to know in Galway when I was living with my grandmother," she said.

The smile passed away from Gabriel's face. A dull anger began to gather again at the back of his mind and the dull fires of his lust began to glow angrily in his veins.

"Someone you were in love with?" he asked ironically.

"It was a young boy I used to know," she answered, "named Michael Furey. He used to sing that song, *The Lass of Aughrim*. He was very delicate."

Gabriel was silent. He did not wish her to think that he was interested in this delicate boy.

"I can see him so plainly," she said, after a moment. "Such eyes as he had: big, dark eyes! And such an expression in them — an expression!"

"O, then, you are in love with him?" said Gabriel.

"I used to go out walking with him," she said, "when I was in Galway."

A thought flew across Gabriel's mind.

"Perhaps that was why you wanted to go to Galway with that Ivors girl?" he said coldly.

She looked at him and asked in surprise:

"What for?"

Her eyes made Gabriel feel awkward. He shugged his shoulders and said:

"How do I know? To see him, perhaps."

She looked away from him along the shaft of light towards the window in silence.

"He is dead," she said at length. "He died when he was only seventeen. Isn't it a terrible thing to die so young as that?"

"What was he?" asked Gabriel, still ironically.

"He was in the gasworks," she said.

Gabriel felt humiliated by the failure of his irony and by the evocation of this figure from the dead, a boy in the gasworks. While he had been full of memories of their secret life together, full of tenderness and joy and desire, she had been comparing him in her mind with another. A shameful consciousness of his own person assailed him. He saw himself as a ludicrous figure, acting as a penny-boy[15] for his aunts, a nervous, well-meaning sentimentalist, orating to vulgarians and idealising his own clownish lusts, the pitiable fatuous fellow he had caught a glimpse of in the mirror. Instinctively he turned his back more to the light lest she might see the shame that burned upon his forehead.

He tried to keep up his tone of cold interrogation, but his voice when he spoke was humble and indifferent.

"I suppose you were in love with this Michael Furey, Gretta," he said.

"I was great with him at that time," she said.

Her voice was veiled and sad. Gabriel, feeling now how vain it would be to try to lead her whither he had purposed, caressed one of her hands and said, also sadly:

"And what did he die of so young, Gretta? Consumption, was it?"

---

[15] Errand boy.

"I think he died for me," she answered.

A vague terror seized Gabriel at this answer, as if, at that hour when he had hoped to triumph, some impalpable and vindictive being was coming against him, gathering forces against him in its vague world. But he shook himself free of it with an effort of reason and continued to caress her hand. He did not question her again, for he felt that she would tell him of herself. Her hand was warm and moist: it did not respond to his touch, but he continued to caress it just as he had caressed her first letter to him that spring morning.

"It was in the winter," she said, "about the beginning of the winter when I was going to leave my grandmother's and come up here to the convent. And he was ill at the time in his lodgings in Galway and wouldn't be let out, and his people in Oughterard were written to. He was in decline, they said, or something like that. I never knew rightly."

She paused for a moment and sighed.

"Poor fellow," she said. "He was very fond of me and he was such a gentle boy. We used to go out together, walking, you know, Gabriel, like the way they do in the country. He was going to study singing only for his health. He had a very good voice, poor Michael Furey."

"Well; and then?" asked Gabriel.

"And then when it came to the time for me to leave Galway and come up to the convent he was much worse and I wouldn't be let see him so I wrote him a letter saying I was going up to Dublin and would be back in the summer, and hoping he would be better then."

She paused for a moment to get her voice under control, and then went on:

"Then the night before I left, I was in my grandmother's house in Nuns' Island, packing up, and I heard gravel thrown up against the window. The window was so wet I couldn't see, so I ran downstairs as I was and slipped out the back into the garden and there was the poor fellow at the end of the garden, shivering."

"And did you not tell him to go back?" asked Gabriel.

"I implored of him to go home at once and told him he would get his death in the rain. But he said he did not want to live. I can see his eyes as well as well! He was standing at the end of the wall where there was a tree."

"And did he go home?" asked Gabriel.

"Yes, he went home. And when I was only a week in the convent he died and he was buried in Oughterard, where his people came from. O, the day I heard that, that he was dead!"

She stopped, choking with sobs, and, overcome by emotion, flung herself face downward on the bed, sobbing in the quilt. Gabriel held her hand for a moment longer, irresolutely, and then, shy of intruding on her grief, let it fall gently and walked to the window.

She was fast asleep.

Gabriel, leaning on his elbow, looked for a few moments unresentfully on her tangled hair and half-open mouth, listening to her deep-drawn breath. So she had had that romance in her life: a man had died for her sake. It hardly pained him now to think how poor a part he, her husband, had played in her life. He watched her while she slept, as though he and she had never lived together as man and wife. His curious eyes rested long upon her face and on her hair: and, as he thought of what she must have been then, in that time of her first girlish beauty, a strange, friendly pity for her entered his soul. He did not like to say even to himself that her face was no longer beautiful, but he knew that it was no longer the face for which Michael Furey had braved death.

Perhaps she had not told him all the story. His eyes moved to the chair over which she had thrown some of her clothes. A petticoat string dangled to the floor. One boot stood upright, its limp upper fallen down: the fellow of it lay upon its side. He wondered at his riot of emotions of an hour before. From what had it proceeded? From his aunt's supper, from his own foolish speech, from the wine and dancing, the merry-making when saying good-night in the hall, the pleasure of the walk along the river in the snow. Poor Aunt Julia! She, too, would soon be a shade with the shade of Patrick Morkan and his horse. He had caught that haggard look upon her face for a moment when she was singing *Arrayed for the Bridal*. Soon, perhaps, he would be sitting in that same drawing-room, dressed in black, his silk hat on his knees. The blinds would be drawn down and Aunt Kate would be sitting beside him, crying and blowing her nose and telling him how Julia had died. He would cast about in his mind for some words that might console her, and would find only lame and useless ones. Yes, yes: that would happen very soon.

The air of the room chilled his shoulders. He stretched himself cautiously along under the sheets and lay down beside his wife. One by one, they were all becoming shades. Better pass boldly into that other world, in the full glory of some passion, than fade and wither dismally with age. He thought of how she who lay beside him had locked in her heart for so many years that image of her lover's eyes when he had told her that he did not wish to live.

Generous tears filled Gabriel's eyes. He had never felt like that himself towards any woman, but he knew that such a feeling must be love. The tears gathered more thickly in his eyes and in the partial darkness he imagined he saw the form of a young man standing under a dripping tree. Other forms were near. His soul had approached that region where dwell the vast hosts of the dead. He was conscious of, but could not apprehend, their wayward and flickering existence. His own identity was fading out into a grey impalpable world: the solid world itself, which these dead had one time reared and lived in, was dissolving and dwindling.

A few light taps upon the pane made him turn to the window. It had begun to snow again. He watched sleepily the flakes, silver and dark, falling obliquely against the lamplight. The time had come for him to set out on his journey westward. Yes, the newspapers were right: snow was general all over Ireland. It was falling on every part of the dark central plain, on the treeless hills, falling softly upon the Bog of Allen and, farther westward, softly falling into the dark mutinous Shannon waves. It was falling, too, upon every part of the lonely churchyard on the hill where Michael Furey lay buried. It lay thickly drifted on the crooked crosses and headstones, on the spears of the little gate, on the barren thorns. His soul swooned slowly as he heard the snow falling faintly through the universe and faintly falling, like the descent of their last end, upon all the living and the dead.

QUESTIONS

1. One way that Joyce develops the character of Gabriel Conroy is to show him in contact with others. What do we learn about him through Lily, the maid? through Miss Ivors? through his aunts?

2. What idea of Dublin do you derive from the party scenes? How has Joyce created the sense of this society? Is it from the characters or the action that you get the sense of middle-class gentility?

3. Describe Gabriel's relationship with Gretta. What incidents show that his knowledge of her is shallow?

4. Trace the steps by which the snow grows from a mere physical detail to an encompassing symbol. What exactly does it come to symbolize?

5. What do you learn about Gabriel from the scene in which he reviews the "headings" of his speech? Is he condescending to, or properly considerate of, his audience?

6. Gabriel Conroy is a man in conflict — with society, his wife, perhaps himself. How does Joyce make us feel these conflicts? Are any of them resolved by the story's end?

7. Although he is long dead, young Michael Furey is an important figure in "The Dead." What function does he serve? What does he symbolize to Gretta? to Gabriel Conroy?

8. To whom does the title of this story refer?

JAMES JOYCE

Araby

North Richmond Street, being blind, was a quiet street except at the hour when the Christian Brothers' School set the boys free. An uninhabited house of two storeys stood at the blind end, detached from its neighbours in a square ground. The other houses of the street, conscious of decent lives within them, gazed at one another with brown imperturbable faces.

The former tenant of our house, a priest, had died in the back drawing-room. Air, musty from having been long enclosed, hung in all the rooms, and the waste room behind the kitchen was littered with old useless papers. Among these I found a few paper-covered books, the pages of which were curled and damp: *The Abbot*, by Walter Scott, *The Devout Communicant* and *The Memoirs of Vidocq*. I liked the last best because its leaves were yellow. The wild garden behind the house contained a central apple-tree and a few straggling bushes under one of which I found the late tenant's rusty bicycle-pump. He had been a very charitable priest; in his will he had left all his money to institutions and the furniture of his house to his sister.

When the short days of winter came dusk fell before we had well eaten our dinners. When we met in the street the houses had grown sombre. The space of sky above us was the colour of ever-changing violet and towards it the lamps of the street lifted their feeble lanterns. The cold air stung us and we played till our bodies glowed. Our shouts echoed in the silent street. The career of our play brought us through the dark muddy lanes behind the houses where we ran the gauntlet of the rough tribes from the cottages, to the back doors of the dark dripping gardens where odours arose from the ashpits, to the dark odorous stables where a coachman smoothed and combed the horse or shook music from the buckled harness. When we returned to the street light from the kitchen windows had filled the areas. If my uncle was seen turning the corner we hid in the shadow until we had seen him safely housed. Or if Mangan's sister came out on the doorstep to call her brother in to his tea we watched her from our shadow peer up and down the street. We waited to see whether she would remain or go in and, if she remained, we left our shadow and walked up to Mangan's steps resignedly. She was waiting for us, her figure defined by the light from the half-opened door. Her brother always teased her before he obeyed and I stood by the railings looking at her. Her dress swung as she moved her body and the soft rope of her hair tossed from side to side.

Every morning I lay on the floor in the front parlour watching her door. The blind was pulled down to within an inch of the sash so that I could not be seen. When she came out on the doorstep my heart leaped. I ran to the hall, seized my books and followed her. I kept her brown figure always in my eye and, when we came near the point at which our ways diverged, I quickened my pace and passed her. This happened morning after morning. I had never spoken to her, except for a few casual words, and yet her name was like a summons to all my foolish blood.

Her image accompanied me even in places the most hostile to romance. On Saturday evenings when my aunt went marketing I had to go to carry some of the parcels. We walked through the flaring streets, jostled by drunken men and bargaining women, amid the curse of labourers, the shrill litanies of shop-boys who stood on guard by the barrels of pigs' cheeks, the nasal chanting of street-singers, who sang a *come-all-you* about O'Donovan Rossa, or a ballad about the troubles in our native land. These noises converged in a single sensation of life for me: I imagined that I bore my chalice safely through a throng of foes. Her name sprang to my lips at moments in strange prayers and praises which I myself did not understand. My eyes were often full of tears (I could not tell why) and at times a flood from my heart seemed to pour itself out into my bosom. I thought little of the future. I did not know whether I would ever speak to her or not or, if I spoke to her, how I could tell her of my confused adoration. But my body was like a harp and her words and gestures were like fingers running upon the wires.

One evening I went into the back drawing-room in which the priest had died. It was a dark rainy evening and there was no sound in the house. Through one of the broken panes I heard the rain impinge upon the earth, the fine incessant needles of water playing in the sodden beds. Some distant lamp or lighted window gleamed below me. I was thankful that I could see so little. All my senses seemed to desire to veil themselves and, feeling that I was about to slip from them, I pressed the palms of my hands together until they trembled, murmuring: "*O love! O love!*" many times.

At last she spoke to me. When she addressed the first words to me I was so confused that I did not know what to answer. She asked me was I going to *Araby*. I forgot whether I answered yes or no. It would be a splendid bazaar, she said she would love to go.

"And why can't you?" I asked.

While she spoke she turned a silver bracelet round and round her wrist. She could not go, she said, because there would be a retreat[1] that week in her convent. Her brother and two other boys were fighting for their caps and I was alone at the railings. She held one of the spikes, bowing her head towards me. The light from the lamp opposite our door caught the white curve of her neck, lit up her hair that rested there and, falling, lit up the hand upon the railing. It fell over one side of her dress and caught the white border of a petticoat just visible as she stood at ease.

"It's well for you," she said.

"If I go," I said, "I will bring you something."

What innumerable follies laid waste my waking and sleeping thoughts after that evening! I wished to annihilate the tedious intervening days. I chafed against the work of school. At night in my bedroom and by day in the classroom her image came between me and the page I strove to read. The syllables of the word *Araby* were called to me through the silence in which my soul luxuriated and cast an Eastern enchantment over me. I asked for

---

[1] A religious exercise that consists of withdrawing for a time from ordinary activities to concentrate on one's spiritual growth.

leave to go to the bazaar on Saturday night. My aunt was surprised and hoped it was not some Freemason affair. I answered few questions in class. I watched my master's face pass from amiability to sternness; he hoped I was not beginning to idle. I could not call my wandering thoughts together. I had hardly any patience with the serious work of life which, now that it stood between me and my desire, seemed to me child's play, ugly monotonous child's play.

On Saturday morning I reminded my uncle that I wished to go to the bazaar in the evening. He was fussing at the hallstand, looking for the hat-brush, and answered me curtly:

"Yes, boy, I know."

As he was in the hall I could not go into the front parlour and lie at the window. I left the house in bad humour and walked slowly towards the school. The air was pitilessly raw and already my heart misgave me.

When I came home to dinner my uncle had not yet been home. Still it was early. I sat staring at the clock for some time and, when its ticking began to irritate me, I left the room. I mounted the staircase and gained the upper part of the house. The high cold empty gloomy rooms liberated me and I went from room to room singing. From the front window I saw my companions playing below in the street. Their cries reached me weakened and indistinct and, leaning my forehead against the cool glass, I looked over at the dark house where she lived. I may have stood there for an hour, seeing nothing but the brown-clad figure cast by my imagination, touched discreetly by the lamplight at the curved neck, at the hand upon the railings and at the border below the dress.

When I came downstairs again I found Mrs. Mercer sitting at the fire. She was an old garrulous woman, a pawnbroker's widow, who collected used stamps for some pious purpose. I had to endure the gossip of the tea-table. The meal was prolonged beyond an hour and still my uncle did not come. Mrs. Mercer stood up to go: she was very sorry she couldn't wait any longer, but it was after eight o'clock and she did not like to be out late, as the night air was bad for her. When she had gone I began to walk up and down the room, clenching my fists. My aunt said:

"I'm afraid you may put off your bazaar for this night of Our Lord."

At nine o'clock I heard my uncle's latchkey in the halldoor. I heard him talking to himself and heard the hallstand rocking when it had received the weight of his overcoat. I could interpret these signs. When he was midway through his dinner I asked him to give me the money to go to the bazaar. He had forgotten.

"The people are in bed and after their first sleep now," he said.

I did not smile. My aunt said to him energetically:

"Can't you give him the money and let him go? You've kept him late enough as it is."

My uncle said he was very sorry he had forgotten. He said he believed in the old saying: "All work and no play makes Jack a dull boy." He asked me where I was going and, when I had told him a second time he asked me did I know *The Arab's Farewell to his Steed*. When I left the kitchen he was about to recite the opening lines of the piece to my aunt.

I held a florin tightly in my hand as I strode down Buckingham Street towards the station. The sight of the streets thronged with buyers and glaring with gas recalled to me the purpose of my journey. I took my seat in a third-class carriage of a deserted train. After an intolerable delay the train moved out of the station slowly. It crept onward among ruinous houses and over the twinkling river. At Westland Row Station a crowd of people pressed to the carriage doors; but the porters moved them back, saying that it was a special train for the bazaar. I remained alone in the bare carriage. In a few minutes the train drew up beside an improvised wooden platform. I passed out on to the road and saw by the lighted dial of a clock that it was ten minutes to ten. In front of me was a large building which displayed the magical name.

I could not find any sixpenny entrance and, fearing that the bazaar would be closed, I passed quickly through a turnstile, handing a shilling to a weary-looking man. I found myself in a big hall girdled at half its height by a gallery. Nearly all the stalls were closed and the greater part of the hall was in darkness. I recognised a silence like that which pervades a church after a service. I walked into the centre of the bazaar timidly. A few people were gathered about the stalls which were still open. Before a curtain, over which the words *Café Chantant*[2] were written in coloured lamps, two men were counting money on a salver. I listened to the fall of the coins.

Remembering with difficulty why I had come I went over to one of the stalls and examined porcelain vases and flowered tea-sets. At the door of the stall a young lady was talking and laughing with two young gentlemen. I remarked their English accents and listened vaguely to their conversation.

"O, I never said such a thing!"

"O, but you did!"

"O, but I didn't!"

"Didn't she say that?"

"Yes. I heard her."

"O, there's a ...fib!"

Observing me the young lady came over and asked me did I wish to buy anything. The tone of her voice was not encouraging; she seemed to have spoken to me out of a sense of duty. I looked humbly at the great jars that stood like eastern guards at either side of the dark entrance to the stall and murmured:

"No, thank you."

The young lady changed the position of one of the vases and went back to the two young men. They began to talk of the same subject. Once or twice the young lady glanced at me over her shoulder.

I lingered before her stall, though I knew my stay was useless, to make my interest in her wares seem the more real. Then I turned away slowly and walked down the middle of the bazaar. I allowed the two pennies to fall against the six-pence in my pocket. I heard a voice call from one end of the gallery that the light was out. The upper part of the hall was now completely dark.

Gazing up into the darkness I saw myself as a creature driven and derided by vanity; and my eyes burned with anguish and anger.

QUESTIONS

1. The narrator is the young boy of the story, now grown older and looking back on an incident in his past. What is the effect of the distance Joyce has thereby created? Does this distance lessen the emotional impact of the boy's experience?

2. Do the boy's relationships with his uncle and aunt strike you as real? Are the adults clearly distinguished from each other? How does Joyce present them — by description, or speech, or action? Do you find the uncle an unsympathetic character?

---

[2] A café with musical entertainment.

3. List the signs that the boy is a romantic, rather than a realist, at the time the story takes place.

4. Why is the bazaar so important to the lad? As the narrator looks back to this minor tragedy in his life, does he mock or minimize it? Does he lay the blame for his disappointment in any particular quarter?

5. The last paragraph of "Araby" emphasizes the boy's humiliation and harsh opinion of himself. Does the older narrator share that opinion?

JAMES JOYCE

Ivy Day in the Committee Room

Old Jack raked the cinders together with a piece of cardboard and spread them judiciously over the whitening dome of coals. When the dome was thinly covered his face lapsed into darkness but, as he set himself to fan the fire again, his crouching shadow ascended the opposite wall and his face slowly re-emerged into light. It was an old man's face, very bony and hairy. The moist blue eyes blinked at the fire and the moist mouth fell open at times, munching once or twice mechanically when it closed. When the cinders had caught he laid the piece of cardboard against the wall, sighed and said:

"That's better now, Mr. O'Connor."

Mr. O'Connor, a grey-haired young man, whose face was disfigured by many blotches and pimples, had just brought the tobacco for a cigarette into a shapely cylinder but when spoken to he undid his handiwork meditatively. Then he began to roll the tobacco again meditatively and after a moment's thought decided to lick the paper.

"Did Mr. Tierney say when he'd be back?" he asked in a husky falsetto.

"He didn't say."

Mr. O'Connor put his cigarette into his mouth and began to search his pockets. He took out a pack of thin pasteboard cards.

"I'll get you a match," said the old man.

"Never mind, this'll do," said Mr. O'Connor.

He selected one of the cards and read what was printed on it:

MUNICIPAL ELECTIONS

ROYAL EXCHANGE WARD

Mr. Richard J. Tierney, P.L.G., respectfully solicits the favour of your vote and influence at the coming election in the Royal Exchange Ward.

Mr. O'Connor had been engaged by Tierney's agent to canvass one part of the ward but, as the weather was inclement and his boots let in the wet, he spent a great part of the day sitting by the fire in the Committee Room in Wicklow Street with Jack the old caretaker. They had been sitting thus since the short day had grown dark. It was the sixth of October, dismal and cold out of doors.

455

Mr. O'Connor tore a strip off the card and, lighting it, lit his cigarette. As he did so the flame lit up a leaf of dark glossy ivy in the lapel of his coat. The old man watched him attentively and then, taking up the piece of cardboard again, began to fan the fire slowly while his companion smoked.

"Ah, yes," he said, continuing, "it's hard to know what way to bring up children. Now who'd think he'd turn out like that! I sent him to the Christian Brothers and I done what I could for him, and there he goes boosing about. I tried to make him someway decent."

He replaced the cardboard wearily.

"Only I'm an old man now I'd change his tune for him. I'd take the stick to his back and beat him while I could stand over him — as I done many a time before. The mother, you know, she cocks him up with this and that. ..."

"That's what ruins children," said Mr. O'Connor.

"To be sure it is," said the old man. "And little thanks you get for it, only impudence. He takes th'upper hand of me whenever he sees I've a sup taken. What's the world coming to when sons speak that way to their fathers?"

"What age is he?" said Mr. O'Connor.

"Nineteen," said the old man.

"Why don't you put him to something?"

"Sure, amn't I never done at the drunken bowsy ever since he left school? 'I won't keep you,' I says. 'You must get a job for yourself.' But, sure, it's worse whenever he gets a job; he drinks it all."

Mr. O'Connor shook his head in sympathy, and the old man fell silent, gazing into the fire. Someone opened the door of the room and called out:

"Hello! Is this a Freemason's meeting?"

"Who's that?" said the old man.

"What are you doing in the dark?" asked a voice.

"Is that you, Hynes?" asked Mr. O'Connor.

"Yes. What are you doing in the dark?" said Mr. Hynes, advancing into the light of the fire.

He was a tall, slender young man with a light brown moustache. Imminent little drops of rain hung at the brim of his hat and the collar of his jacket-coat was turned up.

"Well, Mat," he said to Mr. O'Connor, "how goes it?"

Mr. O'Connor shook his head. The old man left the hearth, and after stumbling about the room returned with two candlesticks which he thrust one after the other into the fire and carried to the table. A denuded room came into view and the fire lost all its cheerful colour. The walls of the room were bare except for a copy of an election address. In the middle of the room was a small table on which papers were heaped.

Mr. Hynes leaned against the mantelpiece and asked:

"Has he paid you yet?"

"Not yet," said Mr. O'Connor. "I hope to God he'll not leave us in the lurch tonight."

Mr. Hynes laughed.

"O, he'll pay you. Never fear," he said.

"I hope he'll look smart about it if he means business," said Mr. O'Connor.

"What do you think, Jack?" said Mr. Hynes satirically to the old man.

The old man returned to his seat by the fire, saying:

"It isn't but he has it, anyway. Not like the other tinker."

"What other tinker?" said Mr. Hynes.

"Colgan," said the old man scornfully.

"It is because Colgan's a working-man you say that? What's the difference between a good honest bricklayer and a publican — eh? Hasn't the working-man as good a right to be in the Corporation as anyone else — ay, and a better right than those shoneens[1] that are always hat in hand before any fellow with a handle to his name? Isn't that so, Mat?" said Mr. Hynes, addressing Mr. O'Connor.

"I think you're right," said Mr. O'Connor.

"One man is a plain honest man with no hunker-sliding about him. He goes in to represent the labour classes. This fellow you're working for only wants to get some job or other."

"Of course, the working-classes should be represented," said the old man.

"The working-man," said Mr. Hynes, "gets all kicks and no halfpence. But it's labour produces everything. The working-man is not looking for fat jobs for his sons and nephews and cousins. The working-man is not going to drag the honour of Dublin in the mud to please a German monarch."

"How's that?" said the old man.

"Don't you know they want to present an address of welcome to Edward Rex if he comes here next year? What do we want kowtowing to a foreign king?"

"Our man won't vote for the address," said Mr. O'Connor. "He goes in on the Nationalist ticket."

"Won't he?" said Mr. Hynes. "Wait till you see whether he will or not. I know him. Is it Tricky Dicky Tierney?"

"By God! perhaps you're right, Joe," said Mr. O'Connor. "Anyway, I wish he'd turn up with the spondulics."[2]

The three men fell silent. The old man began to rake more cinders together. Mr. Hynes took off his hat, shook it and then turned down the collar of his coat, displaying, as he did so, an ivy leaf in the lapel.

"If this man was alive," he said, pointing to the leaf, "we'd have no talk of an address of welcome."

"That's true," said Mr. O'Connor.

"Musha,[3] God be with them times!" said the old man. "There was some life in it then."

The room was silent again. Then a bustling little man with a snuffling nose and very cold ears pushed in the door. He walked over quickly to the fire, rubbing his hands as if he intended to produce a spark from them.

"No money, boys," he said.

"Sit down here, Mr. Henchy," said the old man, offering him his chair.

"O, don't stir, Jack, don't stir," said Mr. Henchy.

He nodded curtly to Mr. Hynes and sat down on the chair which the old man vacated.

"Did you serve Aungier Street?" he asked Mr. O'Connor.

"Yes," said Mr. O'Connor, beginning to search his pockets for memoranda.

"Did you call on Grimes?"

"I did."

"Well? How does he stand?"

"He wouldn't promise. He said: 'I won't tell anyone what way I'm going to vote.' But I think he'll be all right."

"Why so?"

---

[1] Would-be gentlemen.

[2] Money; cash.

[3] An interjection showing strong feeling.

"He asked me who the nominators were; and I told him. I mentioned Father Burke's name. I think it'll be all right."

Mr. Henchy began to snuffle and to rub his hands over the fire at a terrific speed. Then he said:

"For the love of God, Jack, bring us a bit of coal. There must be some left."

The old man went out of the room.

"It's no go," said Mr. Henchy, shaking his head. "I asked the little shoeboy, but he said: 'O, now, Mr. Henchy, when I see the work going on properly I won't forget you, you may be sure.' Mean little tinker! 'Usha, how could he be anything else?"

"What did I tell you, Mat?" said Mr. Hynes. "Tricky Dicky Tierney."

"O, he's as tricky as they make 'em," said Mr. Henchy. "He hasn't got those little pigs' eyes for nothing. Blast his soul! Couldn't he pay up like a man instead of: 'O, now, Mr. Henchy, I must speak to Mr. Fanning. ... I've spent a lot of money'? Mean little schoolboy of hell! I suppose he forgets the time his little old father kept the hand-me-down shop in Mary's Lane."

"But is that a fact?" asked Mr. O'Connor.

"God, yes," said Mr. Henchy. "Did you never hear that? And the men used to go in on Sunday morning before the houses were open to buy a waistcoat or a trousers — moya! But Tricky Dicky's little old father always had a tricky little black bottle up in a corner. Do you mind now? That's that. That's where he first saw the light."

The old man returned with a few lumps of coal which he placed here and there on the fire.

"That's a nice how-do-you-do," said Mr. O'Connor. "How does he expect us to work for him if he won't stump up?"

"I can't help it," said Mr. Henchy. "I expect to find the bailiffs in the hall when I go home."

Mr. Hynes laughed and, shoving himself away from the mantelpiece with the aid of his shoulders, made ready to leave.

"It'll be all right when King Eddie comes," he said. "Well, boys, I'm off for the present. See you later. 'Bye, 'bye."

He went out of the room slowly. Neither Mr. Henchy nor the old man said anything, but, just as the door was closing, Mr. O'Connor, who had been staring moodily into the fire, called out suddenly:

"'Bye, Joe."

Mr. Henchy waited a few moments and then nodded in the direction of the door.

"Tell me," he said across the fire, "what brings our friend in here? What does he want?"

"'Usha, poor Joe!" said Mr. O'Connor, throwing the end of his cigarette into the fire, "he's hard up, like the rest of us."

Mr. Henchy snuffled vigorously and spat so copiously that he nearly put out the fire, which uttered a hissing protest.

"To tell you my private and candid opinion," he said, "I think he's a man from the other camp. He's a spy of Colgan's, if you ask me. Just go round and try and find out how they're getting on. They won't suspect you. Do you twig?"

"Ah, poor Joe is a decent skin," said Mr. O'Connor.

"His father was a decent, respectable man," Mr. Henchy admitted. "Poor old Larry Hynes! Many a good turn he did in his day! But I'm greatly afraid our friend is not nineteen carat. Damn it, I can understand a fellow being hard up, but what I can't understand is a fellow sponging. Couldn't he have some spark of manhood about him?"

"He doesn't get a warm welcome from me when he comes," said the old man. "Let him work for his own side and not come spying around here."

"I don't know," said Mr. O'Connor dubiously, as he took out cigarette-papers and tobacco. "I think Joe Hynes is a straight man. He's a clever chap, too, with the pen. Do you remember that thing he wrote ... ?"

"Some of these hillsiders and fenians are a bit too clever if you ask me," said Mr. Henchy. "Do you know what my private and candid opinion is about some of those little jokers? I believe half of them are in the pay of the Castle."

"There's no knowing," said the old man.

"O, but I know it for a fact," said Mr. Henchy. "They're Castle hacks. ... I don't say Hynes. ... No, damn it, I think he's a stroke above that. ... But there's a certain little nobleman with a cock-eye — you know the patriot I'm alluding to?"

Mr. O'Connor nodded.

"There's a lineal descendant of Major Sirr for you if you like! O, the heart's blood of a patriot! That's a fellow now that'd sell his country for fourpence — ay — and go down on his bended knees and thank the Almighty Christ he had a country to sell."

There was a knock at the door.

"Come in!" said Mr. Henchy.

A person resembling a poor clergyman or a poor actor appeared in the doorway. His black clothes were tightly buttoned on his short body and it was impossible to say whether he wore a clergyman's collar or a layman's, because the collar of his shabby frock-coat, the uncovered buttons of which reflected the candlelight, was turned up about his neck. He wore a round hat of hard black felt. His face, shining with raindrops, had the appearance of damp yellow cheese save where two rosy spots indicated the cheekbones. He opened his very long mouth suddenly to express disappointment and at the same time opened wide his very bright blue eyes to express pleasure and surprise.

"O Father Keon!" said Mr. Henchy, jumping up from his chair. "Is that you? Come in!"

"O, no, no, no!" said Father Keon quickly, pursing his lips as if he were addressing a child.

"Won't you come in and sit down?"

"No, no, no!" said Father Keon, speaking in a discreet, indulgent, velvety voice. "Don't let me disturb you now! I'm just looking for Mr. Fanning. ..."

"He's round at the *Black Eagle*," said Mr. Henchy. "But won't you come in and sit down a minute?"

"No, no, thank you. It was just a little business matter," said Father Keon. "Thank you, indeed."

He retreated from the doorway and Mr. Henchy, seizing one of the candlesticks, went to the door to light him downstairs.

"O, don't trouble, I beg!"

"No, but the stairs is so dark."

"No, no, I can see. ... Thank you, indeed."

"Are you right now?"

"All right, thanks. ... Thanks."

Mr. Henchy returned with the candlestick and put it on the table. He sat down again at the fire. There was silence for a few moments.

"Tell me, John," said Mr. O'Connor, lighting his cigarette with another pasteboard card.

"Hm?"

"What he is exactly?"

"Ask me an easier one," said Mr. Henchy.

"Fanning and himself seem to me very thick. They're often in Kavanagh's together. Is he a priest at all?"

"'Mmmyes, I believe so. … I think he's what you call a black sheep. We haven't many of them, thank God! but we have a few. … He's an unfortunate man of some kind. …'"

"And how does he knock it out?" asked Mr. O'Connor.

"That's another mystery."

"Is he attached to any chapel or church or institution or——"

"No," said Mr. Henchy, "I think he's travelling on his own account. … God forgive me," he added, "I thought he was the dozen of stout."

"Is there any chance of a drink itself?" asked Mr. O'Connor.

"I'm dry too," said the old man.

"I asked that little shoeboy three times," said Mr. Henchy, "would he send us a dozen of stout. I asked him again now, but he was leaning on the counter in his shirt-sleeves having a deep goster with Alderman Cowley."

"Why didn't you remind him?" said Mr. O'Connor.

"Well, I couldn't go over while he was talking to Alderman Cowley. I just waited till I caught his eye, and said: 'About that little matter I was speaking to you about. …' 'That'll be all right, Mr. H.,' he said. Yerra, sure the little hop-o'-my-thumb has forgotten all about it."

"There's some deal on in that quarter," said Mr. O'Connor thoughtfully. "I saw the three of them hard at it yesterday at Suffolk Street corner."

"I think I know the little game they're at," said Mr. Henchy. "You must owe the City Fathers money nowadays if you want to be made Lord Mayor. Then they'll make you Lord Mayor. By God! I'm thinking seriously of becoming a City Father myself. What do you think? Would I do for the job?"

Mr. O'Connor laughed.

"So far as owing money goes. …"

"Driving out of the Mansion House," said Mr. Henchy, "in all my vermin, with Jack here standing up behind me in a powdered wig — eh?"

"And make me your private secretary, John."

"Yes. And I'll make Father Keon my private chaplain. We'll have a family party."

"Faith, Mr. Henchy," said the old man, "you'd keep up better style than some of them. I was talking one day to old Keegan, the porter. 'And how do you like your new master, Pat?' says I to him. 'You haven't much entertaining now,' says I. 'Entertaining!' says he. 'He'd live on the smell of an oil-rag.' And do you know what he told me? Now, I declare to God I didn't believe him."

"What?" said Mr. Henchy and Mr. O'Connor.

"He told me: 'What do you think of a Lord Mayor of Dublin sending out for a pound of chops for his dinner? How's that for high living?' says he. 'Wisha! wisha,' says I. 'A pound of chops,' says he, 'coming into the Mansion House.' 'Wisha!' says I, 'what kind of people is going at all now?'"

At this point there was a knock at the door, and a boy put in his head.

"What is it?" said the old man.

"From the *Black Eagle*," said the boy, walking in sideways and depositing a basket on the floor with a noise of shaken bottles.

The old man helped the boy to transfer the bottles from the basket to the table and counted the full tally. After the transfer the boy put his basket on his arm and asked:

"Any bottles?"

"What bottles?" said the old man.

"Won't you let us drink them first?" said Mr. Henchy.

"I was told to ask for bottles."

"Come back to-morrow," said the old man.

"Here, boy!" said Mr. Henchy, "will you run over to O'Farrell's and ask him to lend us a corkscrew — for Mr. Henchy, say. Tell him we won't keep it a minute. Leave the basket there."

The boy went out and Mr. Henchy began to rub his hands cheerfully, saying:

"Ah, well, he's not so bad after all. He's as good as his word, anyhow."

"There's no tumblers," said the old man.

"O, don't let that trouble you, Jack," said Mr. Henchy. "Many's the good man before now drank out of the bottle."

"Anyway, it's better than nothing," said Mr. O'Connor.

"He's not a bad sort," said Mr. Henchy, "only Fanning has such a loan of him. He means well, you know, in his own tin-pot way."

The boy came back with the corkscrew. The old man opened three bottles and was handing back the corkscrew when Mr. Henchy said to the boy,

"Would you like a drink, boy?"

"If you please, sir," said the boy.

The old man opened another bottle grudgingly, and handed it to the boy.

"What age are you?" he asked.

"Seventeen," said the boy.

As the old man said nothing further, the boy took the bottle, said: "Here's my best respects, sir, to Mr. Henchy," drank the contents, put the bottle back on the table and wiped his mouth with his sleeve. Then he took up the corkscrew and went out of the door sideways, muttering some form of salutation.

"That's the way it begins," said the old man.

"The thin edge of the wedge," said Mr. Henchy.

The old man distributed the three bottles which he had opened and the men drank from them simultaneously. After having drank each placed his bottle on the mantelpiece within hand's reach and drew in a long breath of satisfaction.

"Well, I did a good day's work to-day," said Mr. Henchy, after a pause.

"That so, John?"

"Yes. I got him one or two sure things in Dawson Street, Crofton and myself. Between ourselves, you know, Crofton (he's a decent chap, of course), but he's not worth a damn as a canvasser. He hasn't a word to throw to a dog. He stands and looks at the people while I do the talking."

Here two men entered the room. One of them was a very fat man, whose blue serge clothes seemed to be in danger of falling from his sloping figure. He had a big face which resembled a young ox's face in expression, staring blue eyes and a grizzled moustache. The other man, who was much younger and frailer, had a thin, clean-shaven face. He wore a very high double collar and a wide-brimmed bowler hat.

"Hello, Crofton!" said Mr. Henchy to the fat man. "Talk of the devil ..."

"Where did the boose come from?" asked the young man. "Did the cow calve?"

"O, of course, Lyons spots the drink first thing!" said Mr. O'Connor, laughing.

"Is that the way you chaps canvass," said Mr. Lyons, "and Crofton and I out in the cold and rain looking for votes?"

"Why, blast your soul," said Mr. Henchy, "I'd get more votes in five minutes than you two'd get in a week."

"Open two bottles of stout, Jack," said Mr. O'Connor.

"How can I?" said the old man, "when there's no corkscrew?"

"Wait now, wait now!" said Mr. Henchy, getting up quickly. "Did you ever see this little trick?"

He took two bottles from the table and, carrying them to the fire, put them on the hob. Then he sat down again by the fire and took another drink from his bottle. Mr. Lyons sat on the edge of the table, pushed his hat towards the nape of his neck and began to swing his legs.

"Which is my bottle?" he asked.

"This, lad," said Mr. Henchy.

Mr. Crofton sat down on a box and looked fixedly at the other bottle on the hob. He was silent for two reasons. The first reason, sufficient in itself, was that he had nothing to say; the second reason was that he considered his companions beneath him. He had been a canvasser for Wilkins, the Conservative, but when the Conservatives had withdrawn their man and, choosing the lesser of two evils, given their support to the Nationalist candidate, he had been engaged to work for Mr. Tierney.

In a few minutes an apologetic "Pok!" was heard as the cork flew out of Mr. Lyons' bottle. Mr. Lyons jumped off the table, went to the fire, took his bottle and carried it back to the table.

"I was just telling them, Crofton," said Mr. Henchy, "that we got a good few votes to-day."

"Who did you get?" asked Mr. Lyons.

"Well, I got Parkes for one, and I got Atkinson for two, and I got Ward of Dawson Street. Fine old chap he is, too — regular old toff, old Conservative! 'But isn't your candidate a Nationalist?' said he. 'He's a respectable man,' said I. 'He's in favour of whatever will benefit this country. He's a big ratepayer,' I said. 'He has extensive house property in the city and three places of business and isn't it to his own advantage to keep down the rates? He's a prominent and respected citizen,' said I, 'and a Poor Law Guardian, and he doesn't belong to any party, good, bad, or indifferent.' That's the way to talk to 'em."

"And what about the address to the King?" said Mr. Lyons after drinking and smacking his lips.

"Listen to me," said Mr. Henchy. "What we want in this country, as I said to old Ward, is capital. The King's coming here will mean an influx of money into this country. The citizens of Dublin will benefit by it. Look at all the factories down by the quays there, idle! Look at all the money there is in the country if we only worked the old industries, the mills, the ship-building yards and factories. It's capital we want."

"But look here, John," said Mr. O'Connor. "Why should we welcome the King of England? Didn't Parnell himself ..."

"Parnell," said Mr. Henchy, "is dead. Now, here's the way I look at it. Here's this chap come to the throne after his old mother keeping him out of it till the man was grey. He's a man of the world, and he means well by us. He's a jolly fine decent fellow, if you ask me, and no damn nonsense about him. He just says to himself: 'The old one never went to see these wild Irish. By Christ, I'll go myself and see what they're like.' And are we going to insult the man when he comes over here on a friendly visit? Eh? Isn't that right, Crofton?"

Mr. Crofton nodded his head.

"But after all now," said Mr. Lyons argumentatively, "King Edward's life, you know, is not the very ..."

"Let bygones be bygones," said Mr. Henchy. "I admire the man personally. He's just an ordinary knockabout like you and me. He's fond of his glass of grog and he's a bit of a rake, perhaps, and he's a good sportsman. Damn it, can't we Irish play fair?"

"That's all very fine," said Mr. Lyons. "But look at the case of Parnell now."

"In the name of God," said Mr. Henchy, "where's the analogy between the two cases?"

"What I mean," said Mr. Lyons, "is we have our ideals. Why, now, would we welcome a man like that? Do you think now after what he did Parnell was a fit man to lead us? And why, then, would we do it for Edward the Seventh?"

"This is Parnell's anniversary," said Mr. O'Connor, "and don't let us stir up any bad blood. We all respect him now that he's dead and gone — even the Conservatives," he added, turning to Mr. Crofton.

Pok! The tardy cork flew out of Mr. Crofton's bottle. Mr. Crofton got up from his box and went to the fire. As he returned with his capture he said in a deep voice:

"Our side of the house respects him, because he was a gentleman."

"Right you are, Crofton!" said Mr. Henchy fiercely. "He was the only man that could keep that bag of cats in order. 'Down, ye dogs! Lie down, ye curs!' That's the way he treated them. Come in Joe! Come in!" he called out, catching sight of Mr. Hynes in the doorway.

Mr. Hynes came in slowly.

"Open another bottle of stout, Jack," said Mr. Henchy. "O, I forgot there's no corkscrew. Here, show me one here and I'll put it at the fire."

The old man handed him another bottle and he placed it on the hob.

"Sit down, Joe," said Mr. O'Connor, "we're just talking about the Chief."

"Ay, ay!" said Mr. Henchy.

Mr. Hynes sat on the side of the table near Mr. Lyons but said nothing.

"There's one of them, anyhow," said Mr. Henchy, "that didn't renege him. By God, I'll say for you, Joe! No, by God, you stuck to him like a man!"

"O, Joe," said Mr. O'Connor suddenly. "Give us that thing you wrote — do you remember? Have you got it on you?"

"O, ay!" said Mr. Henchy. "Give us that. Did you ever hear that, Crofton? Listen to this, now: splendid thing."

"Go on," said Mr. O'Connor. "Fire away, Joe."

Mr. Hynes did not seem to remember at once the piece to which they were alluding, but, after reflecting a while, he said:

"O, that thing is it. ... Sure, that's old now."

"Out with it, man!" said Mr. O'Connor.

"'Sh, 'sh," said Mr. Henchy. "Now, Joe!"

Mr. Hynes hesitated a little longer. Then amid the silence he took off his hat, laid it on the table and stood up. He seemed to be rehearsing the piece in his mind. After a rather long pause he announced:

THE DEATH OF PARNELL
   6th October, 1891
He cleared his throat once or twice and then began to recite:
He is dead. Our Uncrowned King is dead.
   O, Erin, mourn with grief and woe
For he lies dead whom the fell gang
   Of modern hypocrites laid low.

He lies slain by the coward hounds
　　He raised to glory from the mire;
And Erin's hopes and Erin's dreams
　　Perish upon her monarch's pyre.

In palace, cabin or in cot
　　The Irish heart where'er it be
Is bowed with woe — for he is gone
　　Who would have wrought her destiny.

He would have had his Erin famed,
　　The green flag gloriously unfurled,
Her statesmen, bards and warriors raised
　　Before the nations of the World.

He dreamed (alas, 'twas but a dream!)
　　Of Liberty: but as he strove
To clutch that idol, treachery
　　Sundered him from the thing he loved.

Shame on the coward, caitiff hands
　　That smote their Lord or with a kiss
Betrayed him to the rabble-rout
　　Of fawning priests — no friends of his.

May everlasting shame consume
　　The memory of those who tried
To befoul and smear the exalted name
　　Of one who spurned them in his pride.

He fell as fall the mighty ones,
　　Nobly undaunted to the last.
And death has now united him
　　With Erin's heroes of the past.

No sound of strife disturb his sleep!
　　Calmly he rests: no human pain
Or high ambition spurs him now
　　The peaks of glory to attain.

They had their way: they laid him low.
　　But Erin, list, his spirit may
Rise, like the Phœnix from the flames,
　　When breaks the dawning of the day,

The day that brings us Freedom's reign.
　　And on that day may Erin well
Pledge in the cup she lifts to Joy
　　One grief — the memory of Parnell.

Mr. Hynes sat down again on the table. When he had finished his recitation there was a silence and then a burst of clapping: even Mr. Lyons clapped. The applause continued for a little time. When it had ceased all the auditors drank from their bottles in silence.

Pok! The cork flew out of Mr. Hynes' bottle, but Mr. Hynes remained sitting flushed and bare-headed on the table. He did not seem to have heard the invitation.

"Good man, Joe!" said Mr. O'Connor, taking out his cigarette papers and pouch the better to hide his emotion.

"What do you think of that, Crofton?" cried Mr. Henchy. "Isn't that fine? What?"

Mr. Crofton said that it was a very fine piece of writing.

QUESTIONS

1. This is a story of contrasts — contrasts between modern Ireland (as represented by the political hacks in the committee room) and Ireland past (as represented by Charles Parnell, the dead "Chief" whom Ivy Day honors). Specify some of the ways by which Joyce makes the contrasts evident.

2. Joyce calls our attention frequently to the coal fire in the grate. Is he merely establishing a mood, or does this fire have some symbolic importance?

3. What is ironic about the possibility that the Irish will welcome a visit from King Edward VII? about giving a bottle of stout to the errand boy?

4. How does Joyce distinguish the characters from each other? What makes Joe Hynes, a relative late-comer, different from all the others? What does "The Death of Parnell" tell us about him? Who among his listeners has the greatest affinity of feeling with Joe Hynes?

5. How does Joyce make the long-dead Parnell a living presence in the story? Is it a gradual or a sudden matter?

6. What does the brief appearance of Father Keon contribute to the story?

7. How would you interpret the last sentence in this story?

VIRGINIA WOOLF

Kew Gardens

From the oval-shaped flower-bed there rose perhaps a hundred stalks spreading into heart-shaped or tongue-shaped leaves halfway up and unfurling at the tip red or blue or yellow petals marked with spots of colour raised upon the surface; and from the red, blue or yellow gloom of the throat emerged a straight bar, rough with gold dust and slightly clubbed at the end. The petals were voluminous enough to be stirred by the summer breeze, and when they moved, the red, blue and yellow lights passed one over the other, staining an inch of the brown earth beneath with a spot of the most intricate colour. The light fell either upon the smooth, grey back of a pebble, or, the shell of a snail with its brown, circular veins, or falling into a raindrop, it expanded with such intensity of red, blue and yellow the thin walls of water that one expected them to burst and disappear. Instead, the drop was left in a second silver grey once more, and the light now settled upon the flesh of a leaf, revealing the branching thread of fibre beneath the surface, and again it moved on and spread its illumination in the vast green spaces beneath the dome of the heart-shaped and tongue-shaped leaves. Then the breeze stirred rather more briskly overhead and the colour was flashed into the air above, into the eyes of the men and women who walk in Kew Gardens in July.

The figures of these men and women straggled past the flower-bed with a curiously irregular movement not unlike that of the white and blue butterflies who crossed the turf in zig-zag flights from bed to bed. The man was about six inches in front of the woman, strolling carelessly, while she bore on with greater purpose, only turning her head now and then to see that the children were not too far behind. The man kept this distance in front of the woman purposely, though perhaps unconsciously, for he wished to go on with his thoughts.

"Fifteen years ago I came here with Lily," he thought. "We sat somewhere over there by a lake and I begged her to marry me all through the hot afternoon. How the dragonfly kept circling round us: how clearly I see the dragonfly and her shoe with the square silver buckle at the toe. All the time I spoke I saw her shoe and when it moved impatiently I knew without looking up what she was going to say: the whole of her seemed to be in her shoe. And my love, my desire, were in the dragonfly; for some reason I thought that if it settled there, on that leaf, the broad one with the red flower in the middle of it, if the dragonfly settled on the leaf she would say 'Yes' at once. But the dragonfly went round and round: it never settled anywhere — of course not, happily not, or I shouldn't be walking here with Eleanor and the children. Tell me, Eleanor. D'you ever think of the past?"

"Why do you ask, Simon?"

"Because I've been thinking of the past. I've been thinking of Lily, the woman I might have married. ... Well, why are you silent? Do you mind my thinking of the past?"

"Why should I mind, Simon? Doesn't one always think of the past, in a garden with men and women lying under the trees. Aren't they one's past, all that remains of it, those men and women, those ghosts lying under the trees, ... one's happiness, one's reality?"

"For me, a square silver shoe buckle and a dragonfly — "

"For me, a kiss. Imagine six little girls sitting before their easels twenty years ago, down by the side of a lake, painting the water-lilies, the first red water-lilies I'd ever seen. And suddenly a kiss, there on the back of my neck. And my hand shook all the afternoon so that I couldn't paint. I took out my watch and marked the hour when I would allow myself to think of the kiss for five minutes only — it was so precious — the kiss of an old grey-haired woman with a wart on her nose, the mother of all my kisses all my life. Come, Caroline, come, Hubert."

They walked on past the flower-bed, now walking four abreast, and soon diminished in size among the trees and looked half transparent as the sunlight and shade swam over their backs in large trembling irregular patches.

In the oval flower-bed the snail, whose shell had been stained red, blue and yellow for the space of two minutes or so, now appeared to be moving very slightly in its shell, and next began to labour over the crumbs of loose earth which broke away and rolled down as it passed over them. It appeared to have a definite goal in front of it, differing in this respect from the singular high stepping angular green insect who attempted to cross in front of it, and waited for a second with its antennae trembling as if in deliberation, and then stepped off as rapidly and strangely in the opposite direction. Brown cliffs with deep green lakes in the hollows, flat, blade-like trees that waved from root to tip, round boulders of grey stone, vast crumpled surfaces of a thin crackling texture — all these objects lay across the snail's progress between one stalk and another to his goal. Before he had decided whether to circumvent the arched tent of a dead leaf or to breast it there came past the bed the feet of other human beings.

This time they were both men. The younger of the two wore an expression of perhaps unnatural calm; he raised his eyes and fixed them very steadily in front of him while his companion spoke, and directly his companion had done speaking he looked on the ground again and sometimes opened his lips only after a long pause and sometimes did not open them at all. The elder man had a curiously uneven and shaky method of walking, jerking his hand forward and throwing up his head abruptly, rather in the manner of an impatient carriage horse tired of waiting outside a house; but in the man these gestures were irresolute and pointless. He talked almost incessantly; he smiled to himself and again began to talk, as if the smile had been an answer. He was talking about spirits — the spirits of the dead, who, according to him, were even now telling him all sorts of odd things about their experiences in Heaven.

"Heaven was known to the ancients as Thessaly, William, and now, with this war, the spirit matter is rolling between the hills like thunder." He paused, seemed to listen, smiled, jerked his head and continued:

"You have a small electric battery and a piece of rubber to insulate the wire — isolate? — insulate? — well, we'll skip the details, no good going into details that wouldn't be understood — and in short the little machine stands in any convenient position by the head of the bed, we will say, on a neat mahogany stand. All arrangements being properly fixed by workmen under my direction, the widow applies her ear and summons the spirit by sign as agreed. Women! Widows! Women in black — "

Here he seemed to have caught sight of a woman's dress in the distance, which in the shade looked a purple black. He took off his hat, placed his hand upon his heart, and hurried towards her muttering and gesticulating feverishly. But William caught him by the sleeve and touched a flower with the tip of his walking-stick in order to divert the old man's attention. After looking at it for a moment in some confusion the old man bent his ear to it and seemed to answer a voice speaking from it, for he began talking about the forests of Uruguay which he had visited hundreds of years ago in company with the most beautiful young woman in Europe. He could be heard murmuring about forests of Uruguay blanketed with the wax petals of tropical roses, nightingales, sea beaches, mermaids, and women drowned at sea, as he suffered himself to be moved on by William, upon whose face the look of stoical patience grew slowly deeper and deeper.

Following his steps so closely as to be slightly puzzled by his gestures came two elderly women of the lower middle class, one stout and ponderous, the other rosy cheeked and nimble. Like most people of their station they were frankly fascinated by other signs of eccentricity betokening a disordered brain, especially in the well-to-do; but they were too far off to be certain whether the gestures were merely eccentric or genuinely mad. After they had scrutinized the old man's back in silence for a moment and given each other a queer, sly look, they went on energetically piecing together their very complicated dialogue:

"Nell, Bert, Lot, Cess, Phil, Pa, he says, I says, she says, I says, I says — "
"My Bert, Sis, Bill, Grandad, the old man, sugar,

> Sugar, flour, kippers, greens,
> Sugar, sugar, sugar."

The ponderous woman looked through the pattern of falling words at the flowers standing cool, firm, and upright in the earth, with a curious expression. She saw them as a sleeper waking from a heavy sleep sees a brass candlestick reflecting the light in an unfamiliar way, and closes his eyes and opens them, and seeing the brass candlestick again, finally starts broad awake and stares at the candlestick with all his powers. So the heavy woman came to a standstill opposite the oval-shaped flower-bed, and ceased even to pretend to listen to what the other woman was saying. She stood there letting the words fall over her, swaying the top part of her body slowly backwards and forwards, looking at the flowers. Then she suggested that they should find a seat and have their tea.

The snail had now considered every possible method of reaching his goal without going round the dead leaf or climbing over it. Let alone the effort needed for climbing a leaf, he was doubtful whether the thin texture which vibrated with such an alarming crackle when touched even by the tips of his horns would bear his weight; and this determined him finally to creep beneath it, for there was a point where the leaf curved high enough from the ground to admit him. He had just inserted his head in the opening and was taking stock of the high brown roof and was getting used to the cool brown light when two other people came past outside on the turf. This time they were both young, a young man and a young woman. They were both in the prime of youth, the season before the smooth pink folds of the flower have burst their gummy case, when the wings of the butterfly, though fully grown, are motionless in the sun.

"Lucky it isn't Friday," he observed.

"Why? D'you believe in luck?"

"They make you pay sixpence on Friday."

"What's a sixpence anyway? Isn't it worth sixpence?"

"What's 'it' — what do you mean by 'it'?"

"O, anything — I mean — you know what I mean."

Long pauses came between each of these remarks; they were uttered in toneless and monotonous voices. The couple stood still on the edge of the flower-bed, and together pressed the end of her parasol deep down into the soft earth. The action and the fact that his hand rested on the top of hers expressed their feelings in a strange way, as these short insignificant words also expressed something, words with short wings for their heavy body of meaning, inadequate to carry them far and thus alighting awkwardly upon the very common objects that surrounded them, and were to their inexperienced touch so massive; but who knows (so they thought as they pressed the parasol into the earth) what precipices aren't concealed in them, or what slopes of ice don't shine in the sun on the other side? Who knows? Who has ever seen this before? Even when she wondered what sort of tea they gave you at Kew, he felt that something loomed up behind her words, and stood vast and solid behind them; and the mist very slowly rose and uncovered — O, Heavens, what were those shapes? — little white tables, and waitresses who looked first at her and then at him; and there was a bill that he would pay with a real two-shilling piece, and it was real, all real, he assured himself, fingering the coin in his pocket, real to everyone except to him and to her; even to him it began to seem real; and then — but it was too exciting to stand and think any longer, and he pulled the parasol out of the earth with a jerk and was impatient to find the place where one had tea with other people, like other people.

"Come along, Trissie; it's time we had our tea."

"Wherever *does* one have one's tea?" she asked with the oddest thrill of excitement in her voice, looking vaguely round and letting herself be drawn on down the grass path, trailing her parasol; turning her head this way and that way forgetting her tea, wishing to go down there and then down there, remembering orchids and cranes among wild flowers, a Chinese pagoda and a crimson crested bird; but he bore her on.

Thus one couple after another with much the same irregular and aimless movement passed the flower-bed and were enveloped in layer after layer of green-blue vapour, in which at first their bodies had substance and a dash of colour, but later both substance and colour dissolved in the green-blue atmosphere. How hot it was! So hot that even the thrush chose to hop, like a mechanical bird, in the shadow of the flowers, with long pauses between one movement and the next; instead of rambling vaguely the white butterflies danced one above another, making with their white shifting flakes the outline of a shattered marble column above the tallest flowers; the glass roofs of the palm house shone as if a whole market full of shiny green umbrellas had opened in the sun; and in the drone of the aeroplane the voice of the summer sky murmured its fierce soul. Yellow and black, pink and snow white, shapes of all these colours, men, women, and children were spotted for a second upon the horizon, and then, seeing the breadth of yellow that lay upon the grass, they wavered and sought shade beneath the trees, dissolving like drops of water in the yellow and green atmosphere, staining it faintly with red and blue. It seemed as if all gross and heavy bodies had sunk down in the heat motionless and lay huddled upon the ground, but their voices went wavering from them as if they were flames lolling from the thick waxen bodies of candles. Voices. Yes, voices. Wordless voices, breaking the silence suddenly with such depth of contentment, such passion of desire, or, in the voices of children, such freshness of surprise; breaking the silence? But there was no silence; all the time the motor omnibuses were turning their wheels and changing their gear; like a vast nest of Chinese boxes all of wrought steel turning ceaselessly one within another the city murmured; on the top of which the voices cried aloud and the petals of myriads of flowers flashed their colours into the air.

QUESTIONS

1. Does this story have a plot in the conventional sense? Is there a logic to the sequence of characters and of miniature "dramas" that Woolf presents?

2. Why do we not learn more about the characters? Is enough suggested for us to picture them clearly?

3. Consider the imagery in "Kew Gardens." Is it consistent? Do any images from the descriptive passages carry over into the dramatic ones?

4. From what point of view is this story told? How would the story have been changed if it had been told in the first person?

5. Why is the snail personified? Does this violate the artistic integrity of the story?

6. How would you state the theme of "Kew Gardens"?

FRANZ KAFKA

A Hunger Artist

Translated by Willa and Edwin Muir

During these last decades the interest in professional fasting has markedly diminished. It used to pay very well to stage such great performances under one's own management, but today that is quite impossible. We live in a different world now. At one time the whole town took a lively interest in the hunger artist; from day to day of his fast the excitement mounted; everybody wanted to see him at least once a day; there were people who bought season tickets for the last few days and sat from morning till night in front of his small barred cage; even in the nighttime there were visiting hours, when the whole effect was heightened by torch flares; on fine days the cage was set out in the open air, and then it was the children's special treat to see the hunger artist; for their elders he was often just a joke that happened to be in fashion, but the children stood open-mouthed, holding each other's hands for greater security, marveling at him as he sat there pallid in black tights, with his ribs sticking out so prominently, not even on a seat but down among straw on the ground, sometimes giving a courteous nod, answering questions with a constrained smile, or perhaps stretching an arm through the bars so that one might feel how thin it was, and then again withdrawing deep into himself, paying no attention to anyone or anything, not even to the all-important striking of the clock that was the only piece of furniture in his cage, but merely staring into vacancy with half shut eyes, now and then taking a sip from a tiny glass of water to moisten his lips.

Besides casual onlookers there were also relays of permanent watchers selected by the public, usually butchers, strangely enough, and it was their task to watch the hunger artist day and night, three of them at a time, in case he should have some secret recourse to nourishment. This was nothing but a formality, instituted to reassure the masses, for the initiates knew well enough that during his fast the artist would never in any circumstances, not even under forcible compulsion, swallow the smallest morsel of food: the honor of his profession forbade it. Not every watcher, of course, was capable of understanding this, there were often groups of night watchers who were very lax in carrying out their duties and deliberately huddled together in a retired corner to play cards with great absorption, obviously intending to give the hunger artist the chance of a little refreshment, which they supposed he could draw from some private hoard. Nothing annoyed the artist more than such watchers; they made him miserable; they made his fast seem unendurable; sometimes he mastered his feebleness sufficiently to sing during their watch for as long as he could keep going, to show them how unjust their suspicions were. But that was of little use; they only wondered at his cleverness in being able to fill his mouth even while singing. Much more to his taste were the watchers who sat close up to the bars, who were not content with the dim night lighting of the hall but focused him in the full glare of the electric pocket torch given them by the impresario. The harsh light did not trouble him at all, in any case he could never sleep properly, and he could always drowse a little, whatever the light, at any hour, even when the hall was thronged with noisy onlookers. He was quite happy at the prospect of spending a sleepless night with such watchers; he was ready to exchange jokes with them, to tell them stories out of his nomadic life, anything at all to keep them awake and demonstrate to them again that he had no eatables in his cage and that he was fasting as not one of them could fast. But his happiest moment was when the morning came and an enormous breakfast was brought them, at his expense, on which they flung themselves with the keen appetite of healthy men after a weary night of wakefulness. Of course there were people who argued that this breakfast was an unfair attempt to bribe the watchers, but that was going rather too far, and when they were invited to take on a night's vigil without a breakfast, merely for the sake of the cause, they made themselves scarce, although they stuck stubbornly to their suspicions.

Such suspicions, anyhow, were a necessary accompaniment to the profession of fasting. No one could possibly watch the hunger artist continuously, day and night, and so no one could produce first-hand evidence that the fast had really been rigorous and continuous; only the artist himself could know that, he was therefore bound to be the sole completely satisfied spectator of his own fast. Yet for other reasons he was never satisfied; it was not perhaps mere fasting that had brought him to such skeleton thinness that many people had regretfully to keep away from his exhibitions, because the sight of him was too much for them, perhaps it was dissatisfaction with himself that had worn him down. For he alone knew, what no other initiate knew, how easy it was to fast. It was the easiest thing in the world. He made no secret of this, yet people did not believe him, at the best they set him down as modest, most of them, however, thought he was out for publicity or else was some kind of cheat who found it easy to fast because he had discovered a way of making it easy, and then had the impudence to admit the fact, more or less. He had to put up with all that, and in the course of time had got used to it, but his inner dissatisfaction always rankled, and never yet, after any term of fasting — this must be granted to his credit — had he left the cage of his own free will. The longest period of fasting was fixed by his impresario at forty days, beyond that term he was not allowed to go, not even in great cities, and there was good reason for it, too. Experience had proved that for about forty days the interest of the public could be stimulated by a steadily increasing pressure of advertisement, but after that the town began to lose interest, sympathetic support began notably to fall off; there were of course local variations as between one town and another or one country and another, but as a general rule forty days marked the limit. So on the fortieth day the flower-bedecked cage was opened, enthusiastic spectators filled the hall, a military band played, two doctors entered the cage to measure the results of the fast, which were announced through a megaphone, and finally two young ladies appeared, blissful at having been selected for the honor, to help the hunger artist down the few steps leading to a small table on which was spread a carefully chosen invalid repast. And at this very moment the artist always turned stubborn. True, he would entrust his bony arms to the outstretched helping hands of the ladies bending over him, but stand up he would not. Why stop fasting at this particular moment, after forty days of it? He had held out for a long time, an illimitably long time; why stop now, when he was in his best fasting form, or rather, not yet quite in his best fasting form? Why should he be cheated of the fame he would get for fasting longer, for being not only the record hunger artist of all time, which presumably he was already, but for beating his own record by a performance beyond human imagination, since he felt that there were no limits to his capacity for fasting? His public pretended to admire him so much, why should it have so little patience with him; if he could endure fasting longer, why shouldn't the public endure it? Besides, he was tired, he was comfortable sitting in the straw, and now he was supposed to lift himself to his full height and go down to a meal the very thought of which gave him a nausea that only the presence of the ladies kept him from betraying, and even that with an effort. And he looked up into the eyes of the ladies who were apparently so friendly and in reality so cruel, and shook his head, which felt too heavy on its strengthless neck. But then there happened yet again what always happened. The impresario came forward, without a word — for the band made speech impossible — lifted his arms in the air above the artist, as if inviting Heaven to look down upon its creature here in the straw, this suffering martyr, which indeed he was, although in quite another sense; grasped him round the emaciated waist, with exaggerated caution, so that the frail condition he was in might be appreciated; and committed him to the care of the blenching ladies, not without secretly giving him a shaking so that his legs and body tottered and swayed. The artist now submitted completely; his head lolled on his breast as if it had landed there by chance; his body was hollowed out; his legs in a spasm of self-preservation clung close to each other at the knees, yet scraped on the ground as if it were not really solid ground, as if they were only trying to find solid ground; and the whole weight of his body, a feather-weight after all, relapsed onto one of the ladies, who, looking round for help and panting a little — this post of honor was not at all what she had expected it to be — first stretched her neck as far as she could to keep her face at least free from contact with the artist, when finding this impossible, and her more fortunate companion not coming to her aid but merely holding extended on her own trembling hand the little bunch of knucklebones that was the artist's, to the great delight of the spectators burst into tears and had to be replaced by an attendant who had long been stationed in readiness. Then came the food, a little of which the impresario managed to get between the artist's lips, while he sat in a kind of half-fainting trance, to the accompaniment of cheerful patter designed to distract the public's attention from the artist's condition; after that, a toast was drunk to the public, supposedly prompted by a whisper from the artist in the impresario's ear; the band confirmed it with a mighty flourish, the spectators melted away, and no one had any cause to be dissatisfied with the proceedings, no one except the hunger artist himself, he only, as always.

So he lived for many years, with small regular intervals of recuperation, in visible glory, honored by the world, yet in spite of that troubled in spirit, and all the more troubled because no one would take his trouble seriously. What comfort could he possibly need? What more could he possibly wish for? And if some good-natured person, feeling sorry for him, tried to console him by pointing out that his melancholy was probably caused by fasting, it could happen, especially when he had been fasting for some time, that he reacted with an outburst of fury and to the general alarm began to shake the bars of his cage like a wild animal. Yet the impresario had a way of punishing these outbreaks which he rather enjoyed putting into operation. He would apologize publicly for the artist's behavior, which was only to be excused, he admitted, because of the irritability caused by fasting; a condition hardly to be understood by well-fed people; then by natural transition he went on to mention the artist's equally incomprehensible boast that he could fast for much longer than he was doing; he praised the high ambition, the good will, the great self-denial undoubtedly implicit in such a statement; and then quite simply countered it by bringing out photographs, which were also on sale to the public, showing the artist on the fortieth day of a fast lying in bed almost dead from exhaustion. This perversion of the truth, familiar to the artist though it was, always unnerved him afresh and proved too much for him. What was a consequence of the premature ending of his fast was here presented as the cause of it! To fight against this lack of understanding, against a whole world of nonunderstanding, was impossible. Time and again in good faith he stood by the bars listening to the impresario, but as soon as the photographs appeared he always let go and sank with a groan back on to his straw, and the reassured public could once more come close and gaze at him.

A few years later when the witnesses of such scenes called them to mind, they often failed to understand themselves at all. For meanwhile the aforementioned change in public interest had set in; it seemed to happen almost overnight; there may have been profound causes for it, but who was going to bother about that; at any rate the pampered hunger artist suddenly found himself deserted one fine day by the amusement seekers, who went streaming past him to other more favored attractions. For the last time the impresario hurried him over half Europe to discover whether the old interest might still survive here and there; all in vain; everywhere, as if by secret agreement, a positive revulsion from professional fasting was in evidence. Of course it could not really have sprung up so suddenly as all that, and many premonitory symptoms which had not been sufficiently remarked or suppressed during the rush and glitter of success now came retrospectively to mind, but it was now too late to take any countermeasures. Fasting would surely come into fashion again at some future date, yet that was no comfort for those living in the present. What, then, was the hunger artist to do? He had been applauded by thousands in his time and could hardly come down to showing himself in a street booth at village fairs, and as for adopting another profession, he was not only too old for that but too fanatically devoted to fasting. So he took leave of the impresario, his partner in an unparalleled career, and hired himself to a large circus; in order to spare his own feelings he avoided reading the conditions of his contract.

A large circus with its enormous traffic in replacing and recruiting men, animals and apparatus can always find a use for people at any time, even for a hunger artist, provided of course that he does not ask too much, and in this particular case anyhow it was not only the artist who was taken on but his famous and long-known name as well, indeed considering the peculiar nature of his performance, which was not impaired by advancing age, it could not be objected that here was an artist past his prime, no longer at the height of his professional skill, seeking a refuge in some quiet corner of a circus; on the contrary, the hunger artist averred that he could fast as well as ever, which was entirely credible, he even alleged that if he were allowed to fast as he liked, and this was at once promised him without more ado, he could astound the world by establishing a record never yet achieved, a statement which certainly provoked a smile among the other professionals, since it left out of account the change in public opinion, which the hunger artist in his zeal conveniently forgot.

He had not, however, actually lost his sense of the real situation and took it as a matter of course that he and his cage should be stationed, not in the middle of the ring as a main attraction, but outside, near the animal cages, on a site that was after all easily accessible. Large and gaily painted placards made a frame for the cage and announced what was to be seen inside it. When the public came thronging out in the intervals to see the animals, they could hardly avoid passing the hunger artist's cage and stopping there for a moment, perhaps they might even have stayed longer had not those pressing behind them in the narrow gangway, who did not understand why they should be held up on their way toward the excitements of the menagerie, made it impossible for anyone to stand gazing quietly for any length of time. And that was the reason why the hunger artist, who had of course been looking forward to these visiting hours as the main achievement of his life, began instead to shrink from them. At first he could hardly wait for the intervals; it was exhilarating to watch the crowds come streaming his way, until only too soon — not even the most obstinate self-deception, clung to almost consciously, could hold out against the fact — the conviction was borne in upon him that these people, most of them, to judge from their actions, again and again, without exception, were all on their way to the menagerie. And the first sight of them from the distance remained the best. For when they reached his cage he was at once deafened by the storm of shouting and abuse that arose from the two contending factions, which renewed themselves continuously, of those who wanted to stop and stare at him — he soon began to dislike them more than the others — not out of real interest but only out of obstinate self-assertiveness, and those who wanted to go straight on to the animals. When the first great rush was past, the stragglers came along, and these, whom nothing could have prevented from stopping to look at him as long as they had breath, raced past with long strides, hardly even glancing at him, in their haste to get to the menagerie in time. And all too rarely did it happen that he had a stroke of luck, when some father of a family fetched up before him with his children, pointed a finger at the hunger artist and explained at length what the phenomenon meant, telling stories of earlier years when he himself had watched similar but much more thrilling performances, and the children, still rather uncomprehending, since neither inside nor outside school had they been sufficiently prepared for this lesson — what did they care about fasting? — yet showed by the brightness of their intent eyes that new and better times might be coming. Perhaps, said the hunger artist to himself many a time, things would be a little better if his cage were set not quite so near the menagerie. That made it too easy for people to make their choice, to say nothing of what he suffered from the stench of the menagerie, the animals' restlessness by night, the carrying past of raw lumps of flesh for the beasts of prey, the roaring at feeding times, which depressed him continually. But he did not dare to lodge a complaint with the management; after all, he had the animals to thank for the troops of people who passed his cage, among whom there might always be one here and there to take an interest in him, and who could tell where they might seclude him if he called attention to his existence and thereby to the fact that, strictly speaking, he was only an impediment on the way to the menagerie.

A small impediment, to be sure, one that grew steadily less. People grew familiar with the strange idea that they could be expected, in times like these, to take an interest in a hunger artist, and with this familiarity the verdict went out against him. He might fast as much as he could, and he did so; but nothing could save him now, people passed him by. Just try to explain to anyone the art of fasting! Anyone who has no feeling for it cannot be made to understand it. The fine placards grew dirty and illegible, they were torn down; the little notice board telling the number of fast days achieved, which at first was changed carefully every day, had long stayed at the same figure, for after the first few weeks even this small task seemed pointless to the staff; and so the artist simply fasted on and on, as he had once dreamed of doing, and it was no trouble to him, just as he had always foretold, but no one counted the days, no one, not even the artist himself, knew what records he was already breaking, and his heart grew heavy. And when once in a time some leisurely passer-by stopped, made merry over the old figure on the board and spoke of swindling, that was in its way the stupidest lie ever invented by indifference and inborn malice, since it was not the hunger artist who was cheating; he was working honestly, but the world was cheating him of his reward.

Many more days went by, however, and that too came to an end. An overseer's eye fell on the cage one day and he asked the attendants why this perfectly good cage should be left standing there unused with dirty straw inside it; nobody knew, until one man, helped out by the notice board, remembered about the hunger artist. They poked into the straw with sticks and found him in it. "Are you still fasting?" asked the overseer. "When on earth do you mean to stop?" "Forgive me, everybody," whispered the hunger artist; only the overseer, who had his ear to the bars, understood him. "Of course," said the overseer, and tapped his forehead with a finger to let the attendants know what state the man was in, "we forgive you." "I always wanted you to admire my fasting," said the hunger artist. "We do admire it," said the overseer, affably. "But you shouldn't admire it," said the hunger artist. "Well, then we don't admire it," said the overseer, "but why shouldn't we admire it?" "Because I have to fast, I can't help it," said the hunger artist. "What a fellow you are," said the overseer, "and why can't you help it?" "Because," said the hunger artist, lifting his head a little and speaking, with his lips pursed, as if for a kiss, right into the overseer's ear, so that no syllable might be lost, "because I couldn't find the food I liked. If I had found it, believe me, I should have made no fuss and stuffed myself like you or anyone else." These were his last words, but in his dimming eyes remained the firm though no longer proud persuasion that he was still continuing to fast.

"Well, clear this out now!" said the overseer, and they buried the hunger artist, straw and all. Into the cage they put a young panther. Even the most insensitive felt it refreshing to see this wild creature leaping around the cage that had so long been dreary. The panther was all right. The food he liked was brought him without hesitation by the attendants; he seemed not even to miss his freedom; his noble body, furnished almost to the bursting point with all that it needed, seemed to carry freedom around with it too; somewhere in his jaws it seemed to lurk; and the joy of life streamed with such ardent passion from his throat that for the onlookers it was not easy to stand the shock of it. But they braced themselves, crowded round the cage, and did not want ever to move away.

QUESTIONS

1. What is your attitude toward the hunger artist? Can you discern Kafka's attitude?

2. Why does the impresario limit the artist's fasts to forty days? Is it significant that, when the artist is no longer limited, he loses track of the number?

3. How do the impresario and the overseer differ? Is one more humane than the other? more pragmatic?

4. What are the pros and cons of the artist's final location, near the menagerie?

5. The story invites an allegorical interpretation, the hunger artist a symbolical one. Can you construct such an interpretation?

6. Is the hunger artist representative of artists in general? Like other artists, he exhibits his work to the public; his fame fluctuates; he feels unappreciated and believes he is misunderstood. What other points of similarity can you suggest?

7. Is the artist diminished by his claim that he would not have fasted had he found any food he liked? Does this statement contradict anything we were told earlier?

8. At the end, the crowd watched the panther "and did not want ever to move away." Does Kafka prepare us to accept this as a judgment on people in general?

D. H. LAWRENCE

The Horse Dealer's Daughter

"Well, Mabel, and what are you going to do with yourself?" asked Joe, with foolish flippancy. He felt quite safe himself. Without listening for an answer, he turned aside, worked a grain of tobacco to the tip of his tongue, and spat it out. He did not care about anything, since he felt safe himself.

The three brothers and the sister sat round the desolate breakfast-table, attempting some sort of desultory consultation. The morning's post had given the final tap to the family fortunes, and all was over. The dreary dining-room itself, with its heavy mahogany furniture, looked as if it were waiting to be done away with.

But the consultation amounted to nothing. There was a strange air of ineffectuality about the three men, as they sprawled at table, smoking and reflecting vaguely on their own condition. The girl was alone, a rather short, sullen-looking young woman of twenty-seven. She did not share the same life as her brothers. She would have been good-looking, save for the impressive fixity of her face, 'bulldog,' as her brothers called it.

There was a confused tramping of horses' feet outside. The three men all sprawled round in their chairs to watch. Beyond the dark holly bushes that separated the strip of lawn from the high-road, they could see a cavalcade of shire horses swinging out of their own yard, being taken for exercise. This was the last time. These were the last horses that would go through their hands. The young men watched with critical, callous look. They were all frightened at the collapse of their lives, and the sense of disaster in which they were involved left them no inner freedom.

Yet they were three fine, well-set fellows enough. Joe, the eldest, was a man of thirty-three, broad and handsome in a hot, flushed way. His face was red, he twisted his black moustache over a thick finger, his eyes were shallow and restless. He had a sensual way of uncovering his teeth when he laughed, and his bearing was stupid. Now he watched the horses with a glazed look of helplessness in his eyes, a certain stupor of downfall.

The great draught-horses swung past. They were tied head to tail, four of them, and they heaved along to where a lane branched off from the high-road, planting their great hoofs floutingly in the fine black mud, swinging their great rounded haunches sumptuously, and trotting a few sudden steps as they were led into the lane, round the corner. Every movement showed a massive, slumbrous strength, and a stupidity which held them in subjection. The groom at the head looked back, jerking the leading rope. And the cavalcade moved out of sight up the lane, the tail of the last horse, bobbed up tight and stiff, held out taut from the swinging great haunches as they rocked behind the hedges in a motion-like sleep.

Joe watched with glazed hopeless eyes. The horses were almost like his own body to him. He felt he was done for now. Luckily he was engaged to a woman as old as himself, and therefore her father, who was steward of a neighbouring estate, would provide him with a job. He would marry and go into harness. His life was over, he would be a subject animal now.

He turned uneasily aside, the retreating steps of the horses echoing in his ears. Then, with foolish restlessness, he reached for the scraps of bacon-rind from the plates, and making a faint whistling sound, flung them to the terrier that lay against the fender. He watched the dog swallow them, and waited till the creature looked into his eyes. Then a faint grin came on his face, and in a high, foolish voice he said:

"You won't get much more bacon, shall you, you little b——?"

The dog faintly and dismally wagged its tail, then lowered its haunches, circled round, and lay down again.

There was another helpless silence at the table. Joe sprawled uneasily in his seat, not willing to go till the family conclave was dissolved. Fred Henry, the second brother, was erect, clean-limbed, alert. He had watched the passing of the horses with more *sang-froid*.[1] If he was an animal, like Joe, he was an animal which controls, not one which is controlled. He was master of any horse, and he carried himself with a well-tempered air of mastery. But he was not master of the situations of life. He pushed his coarse brown moustache upwards, off his lip, and glanced irritably at his sister, who sat impassive and inscrutable.

"You'll go and stop with Lucy for a bit, shan't you?" he asked. The girl did not answer.

"I don't see what else you can do," persisted Fred Henry.

"Go as a skivvy,"[2] Joe interpolated laconically.

The girl did not move a muscle.

"If I was her, I should go in for training for a nurse," said Malcolm, the youngest of them all. He was the baby of the family, a young man of twenty-two, with a fresh, jaunty *museau*.[3]

But Mabel did not take any notice of him. They had talked at her and round her for so many years, that she hardly heard them at all.

The marble clock on the mantelpiece softly chimed the half-hour, the dog rose uneasily from the hearth-rug and looked at the party at the breakfast-table. But still they sat on in ineffectual conclave.

"Oh, all right," said Joe suddenly, apropos of nothing. "I'll get a move on."

He pushed back his chair, straddled his knees with a downward jerk, to get them free, in horsey fashion, and went to the fire. Still he did not go out of the room; he was curious to know what the others would do or say. He began to charge his pipe, looking down at the dog and saying in a high, affected voice:

"Going wi' me? Going wi' me are ter? Tha'rt goin' further than tha counts on just now, dost hear?"

The dog faintly wagged its tail, the man stuck out his jaw and covered his pipe with his

---

[1] Composure.

[2] A household flunky.

[3] Face.

hands, and puffed intently, losing himself in the tobacco, looking down all the while at the dog with an absent brown eye. The dog looked up at him in mournful distrust. Joe stood with his knees stuck out, in real horsey fashion.

"Have you had a letter from Lucy?" Fred Henry asked of his sister.

"Last week," came the neutral reply.

"And what does she say?"

There was no answer.

"Does she *ask* you to go and stop there?" persisted Fred Henry.

"She says I can if I like."

"Well, then, you'd better. Tell her you'll come on Monday."

This was received in silence.

"That's what you'll do then, is it?" said Fred Henry, in some exasperation.

But she made no answer. There was a silence of futility and irritation in the room. Malcolm grinned fatuously.

"You'll have to make up your mind between now and next Wednesday," said Joe loudly, "or else find yourself lodgings on the kerbstone."

The face of the young woman darkened, but she sat on immutable.

"Here's Jack Fergusson!" exclaimed Malcolm, who was looking aimlessly out of the window.

"Where?" exclaimed Joe loudly.

"Just gone past."

"Coming in?"

Malcolm craned his neck to see the gate.

"Yes," he said.

There was a silence. Mabel sat on like one condemned, at the head of the table. Then a whistle was heard from the kitchen. The dog got up and barked sharply. Joe opened the door and shouted:

"Come on."

After a moment a young man entered. He was muffled up in overcoat and a purple woollen scarf, and his tweed cap, which he did not remove, was pulled down on his head. He was of medium height, his face was rather long and pale, his eyes looked tired.

"Hello, Jack! Well, Jack!" exclaimed Malcolm and Joe. Fred Henry merely said: "Jack."

"What's doing?" asked the newcomer, evidently addressing Fred Henry.

"Same. We've got to be out by Wednesday. Got a cold?"

"I have — got it bad, too."

"Why don't you stop in?"

"*Me* stop in? When I can't stand on my legs, perhaps I shall have a chance." The young man spoke huskily. He had a slight Scotch accent.

"It's a knock-out, isn't it," said Joe, boisterously, "if a doctor goes round croaking with a cold. Looks bad for the patients, doesn't it?"

The young doctor looked at him slowly.

"Anything the matter with *you*, then?" he asked sarcastically.

"Not as I know of. Damn your eyes, I hope not. Why?"

"I thought you were very concerned about the patients, wondered if you might be one yourself."

"Damn it, no, I've never been patient to no flaming doctor, and hope I never shall be," returned Joe.

At this point Mabel rose from the table, and they all seemed to become aware of her existence. She began putting the dishes together. The young doctor looked at her, but did not address her. He had not greeted her. She went out of the room with the tray, her face impassive and unchanged.

"When are you off then, all of you?" asked the doctor.

"I'm catching the eleven-forty," replied Malcolm. "Are you goin' down wi' th' trap, Joe?"

"Yes, I've told you I'm going down wi' th' trap, haven't I?"

"We'd better be getting her in then. So long, Jack, if I don't see you before I go," said Malcolm, shaking hands.

He went out, followed by Joe, who seemed to have his tail between his legs.

"Well, this is the devil's own," exclaimed the doctor, when he was left alone with Fred Henry. "Going before Wednesday, are you?"

"That's the orders," replied the other.

"Where, to Northampton?"

"That's it."

"The devil!" exclaimed Fergusson, with quiet chagrin.

And there was silence between the two.

"All settled up, are you?" asked Fergusson.

"About."

There was another pause.

"Well, I shall miss yer, Freddy, boy," said the young doctor.

"And I shall miss thee, Jack," returned the other.

"Miss you like hell," mused the doctor.

Fred Henry turned aside. There was nothing to say. Mabel came in again, to finish clearing the table.

"What are *you* going to do, then, Miss Pervin?" asked Fergusson. "Going to your sister's, are you?"

Mabel looked at him with her steady, dangerous eyes, that always made him uncomfortable, unsettling his superficial ease.

"No," she said.

"Well, what in the name of fortune *are* you going to do? Say what you mean to do," cried Fred Henry, with futile intensity.

But she only averted her head, and continued her work. She folded the white table-cloth, and put on the chenille cloth.

"The sulkiest bitch that ever trod!" muttered her brother.

But she finished her task with perfectly impassive face, the young doctor watching her interestedly all the while. Then she went out.

Fred Henry stared after her, clenching his lips, his blue eyes fixing in sharp antagonism, as he made a grimace of sour exasperation.

"You could bray her into bits, and that's all you'd get out of her," he said, in a small, narrowed tone.

The doctor smiled faintly.

"What's she *going* to do, then?" he asked.

"Strike me if *I* know!" returned the other.

There was a pause. Then the doctor stirred.

"I'll be seeing you to-night, shall I?" he said to his friend.

"Ay — where's it to be? Are we going over to Jessdale?"

"I don't know. I've got such a cold on me. I'll come round to the 'Moon and Stars,' anyway."

"Let Lizzie and May miss their night for once, eh?"

"That's it — if I feel as I do now."

"All's one —— "

The two young men went through the passage and down to the back door together. The house was large, but it was servant-less now, and desolate. At the back was a small bricked houseyard and beyond that a big square, gravelled fine and red, and having stables on two sides. Sloping, dank, winter-dark fields stretched away on the open sides.

But the stables were empty. Joseph Pervin, the father of the family, had been a man of no education, who had become a fairly large horse dealer. The stables had been full of horses, there was a great turmoil and come-and-go of horses and of dealers and grooms. Then the kitchen was full of servants. But of late things had declined. The old man had married a second time, to retrieve his fortunes. Now he was dead and everything was gone to the dogs, there was nothing but debt and threatening.

For months, Mabel had been servant-less in the big house, keeping the home together in penury for her ineffectual brothers. She had kept house for ten years. But previously it was with unstinted means. Then, however brutal and coarse everything was, the sense of money had kept her proud, confident. The men might be foul-mouthed, the women in the kitchen might have bad reputations, her brothers might have illegitimate children. But so long as there was money, the girl felt herself established, and brutally proud, reserved.

No company came to the house, save dealers and coarse men. Mabel had no associates of her own sex, after her sister went away. But she did not mind. She went regularly to church, she attended to her father. And she lived in the memory of her mother, who had died when she was fourteen, and whom she had loved. She had loved her father, too, in a different way, depending upon him, and feeling secure in him, until at the age of fifty-four he married again. And then she had set hard against him. Now he had died and left them all hopelessly in debt.

She had suffered badly during the period of poverty. Nothing, however, could shake the curious, sullen, animal pride that dominated each member of the family. Now, for Mabel, the end had come. Still she would not cast about her. She would follow her own way just the same. She would always hold the keys of her own situation. Mindless and persistent, she endured from day to day. Why should she think? Why should she answer anybody? It was enough that this was the end, and there was no way out. She need not pass any more darkly along the main street of the small town, avoiding every eye. She need not demean herself any more, going into the shops and buying the cheapest food. This was at an end. She thought of nobody, not even of herself. Mindless and persistent, she seemed in a sort of ecstasy to be coming nearer to her fulfilment, her own glorification, approaching her dead mother, who was glorified.

In the afternoon she took a little bag, with shears and sponge and a small scrubbing-brush, and went out. It was a grey, wintry day, with saddened, dark green fields and an atmosphere blackened by the smoke of foundries not far off. She went quickly, darkly along the causeway, heeding nobody, through the town to the churchyard.

There she always felt secure, as if no one could see her, although as a matter of fact she was exposed to the stare of everyone who passed along under the churchyard wall. Nevertheless, once under the shadow of the great looming church, among the graves, she felt immune from the world, reserved within the thick churchyard wall as in another country.

Carefully she clipped the grass from the grave, and arranged the pinky white, small chrysanthemums in the tin cross. When this was done, she took an empty jar from a neighbouring grave, brought water, and carefully, most scrupulously sponged the marble headstone and the coping-stone.

It gave her sincere satisfaction to do this. She felt in immediate contact with the world of her mother. She took minute pains, went through the park in a state bordering on pure happiness, as if in performing this task she came into a subtle, intimate connection with her mother. For the life she followed here in the world was far less real than the world of death she inherited from her mother.

The doctor's house was just by the church. Fergusson, being a mere hired assistant, was slave to the country-side. As he hurried now to attend to the out-patients in the surgery, glancing across the graveyard with his quick eye, he saw the girl at her task at the grave. She seemed so intent and remote, it was like looking into another world. Some mystical element was touched in him. He slowed down as he walked, watching her as if spellbound.

She lifted her eyes, feeling him looking. Their eyes met. And each looked again at once, each feeling, in some way, found out by the other. He lifted his cap and passed on down the road. There remained distinct in his consciousness, like a vision, the memory of her face, lifted from the tombstone in the churchyard, and looking at him with slow, large, portentous eyes. It *was* portentous, her face. It seemed to mesmerise him. There was a heavy power in her eyes which laid hold of his whole being, as if he had drunk some powerful drug. He had been feeling weak and done before. Now the life came back into him, he felt delivered from his own fretted, daily self.

He finished his duties at the surgery as quickly as might be, hastily filling up the bottles of the waiting people with cheap drugs. Then, in perpetual haste, he set off again to visit several cases in another part of his round, before tea-time. At all times he preferred to walk if he could, but particularly when he was not well. He fancied the motion restored him.

The afternoon was falling. It was grey, deadened, and wintry, with a slow, moist, heavy coldness sinking in and deadening all the faculties. But why should he think or notice? He hastily climbed the hill and turned across the dark green fields, following the black cinder-track. In the distance, across a shallow dip in the country, the small town was clustered like smouldering ash, a tower, a spire, a heap of low, raw, extinct houses. And on the nearest fringe of the town, sloping into the dip, was Oldmeadow, the Pervins' house. He could see the stables and the outbuildings distinctly, as they lay towards him on the slope. Well, he would not go there many more times! Another resource would be lost to him, another place gone: the only company he cared for in the alien, ugly little town he was losing. Nothing but work, drudgery, constant hastening from dwelling to dwelling among the colliers and the iron-workers. It wore him out, but at the same time he had a craving for it. It was a stimulant to him to be in the homes of the working people, moving, as it were, through the innermost body of their life. His nerves were excited and gratified. He could come so near, into the very lives of the rough, inarticulate, powerfully emotional men and women. He grumbled, he said he hated the hellish hole. But as a matter of fact it excited him, the contact with the rough, strongly-feeling people was a stimulant applied direct to his nerves.

Below Oldmeadow, in the green, shallow, soddened hollow of field, lay a square, deep pond. Roving across the landscape, the doctor's quick eye detected a figure in black passing through the gate of the field, down towards the pond. He looked again. It would be Mabel Pervin. His mind suddenly became alive and attentive.

Why was she going down there? He pulled up on the path on the slope above, and stood staring. He could just make sure of the small black figure moving in the hollow of the failing day. He seemed to see her in the midst of such obscurity, that he was like a clairvoyant, seeing rather with the mind's eye than with ordinary sight. Yet he could see her positively enough, whilst he kept his eye attentive. He felt, if he looked away from her, in the thick, ugly falling dusk, he would lose her altogether.

He followed her minutely as she moved, direct and intent, like something transmitted rather than stirring in voluntary activity, straight down the field towards the pond. There she stood on the bank for a moment. She never raised her head. Then she waded slowly into the water.

He stood motionless as the small black figure walked slowly and deliberately towards the centre of the pond, very slowly, gradually moving deeper into the motionless water, and still moving forward as the water got up to her breast. Then he could see her no more in the dusk of the dead afternoon.

"There!" he exclaimed. "Would you believe it?"

And he hastened straight down, running over the wet, soddened fields, pushing through the hedges, down into the depression of callous wintry obscurity. It took him several minutes to come to the pond. He stood on the bank, breathing heavily. He could see nothing. His eyes seemed to penetrate the dead water. Yes, perhaps that was the dark shadow of her black clothing beneath the surface of the water.

He slowly ventured into the pond. The bottom was deep, soft clay, he sank in, and the water clasped dead cold round his legs. As he stirred he could smell the cold, rotten clay that fouled up into the water. It was objectionable in his lungs. Still, repelled and yet not heeding, he moved deeper into the pond. The cold water rose over his thighs, over his loins, upon his abdomen. The lower part of his body was all sunk in the hideous cold element. And the bottom was so deeply soft and uncertain, he was afraid of pitching with his mouth underneath. He could not swim, and was afraid.

He crouched a little, spreading his hands under the water and moving them round, trying to feel for her. The dead cold pond swayed upon his chest. He moved again, a little deeper, and again, with his hands underneath, he felt all around under the water. And he touched her clothing. But it evaded his fingers. He made a desperate effort to grasp it.

And so doing he lost his balance and went under, horribly, suffocating in the foul earthy water, struggling madly for a few moments. At last, after what seemed an eternity, he got his footing, rose again into the air and looked around. He gasped, and knew he was in the world. Then he looked at the water. She had risen near him. He grasped her clothing, and drawing her nearer, turned to take his way to land again.

He went very slowly, carefully, absorbed in the slow progress. He rose higher, climbing out of the pond. The water was now only about his legs; he was thankful, full of relief to be out of the clutches of the pond. He lifted her and staggered on to the bank, out of the horror of wet, grey clay.

He laid her down on the bank. She was quite unconscious and running with water. He made the water come from her mouth, he worked to restore her. He did not have to work very long before he could feel the breathing begin again in her; she was breathing naturally. He worked a little longer. He could feel her live beneath his hands; she was coming back. He wiped her face, wrapped her in his overcoat, looked round into the dim, dark grey world, then lifted her and staggered down the bank and across the fields.

It seemed an unthinkably long way, and his burden so heavy he felt he would never get to the house. But at last he was in the stable-yard, and then in the houseyard. He opened the door and went into the house. In the kitchen he laid her down on the hearth-rug and called. The house was empty. But the fire was burning in the grate.

Then again he kneeled to attend to her. She was breathing regularly, her eyes were wide open and as if conscious, but there seemed something missing in her look. She was conscious in herself, but unconscious of her surroundings.

He ran upstairs, took blankets from a bed, and put them before the fire to warm. Then he removed her saturated, earthy-smelling clothing, rubbed her dry with a towel, and wrapped her naked in the blankets. Then he went into the dining-room, to look for spirits. There was a little whisky. He drank a gulp himself, and put some into her mouth.

The effect was instantaneous. She looked full into his face, as if she had been seeing him for some time, and yet had only just become conscious of him.

"Dr. Fergusson?" she said.

"What?" he answered.

He was divesting himself of his coat, intending to find some dry clothing upstairs. He could not bear the smell of the dead, clayey water, and he was mortally afraid for his own health.

"What did I do?" she asked.

"Walked into the pond," he replied. He had begun to shudder like one sick, and could hardly attend to her. Her eyes remained full on him, he seemed to be going dark in his mind, looking back at her helplessly. The shuddering became quieter in him, his life came back to him, dark and unknowing, but strong again.

"Was I out of my mind?" she asked, while her eyes were fixed on him all the time.

"Maybe, for the moment," he replied. He felt quiet, because his strength had come back. The strange fretful strain had left him.

"Am I out of my mind now?" she asked.

"Are you?" he reflected a moment. "No," he answered truthfully, "I don't see that you are." He turned his face aside. He was afraid now, because he felt dazed, and felt dimly that her power was stronger than his, in this issue. And she continued to look at him fixedly all the time. "Can you tell me where I shall find some dry things to put on?" he asked.

"Did you dive into the pond for me?" she asked.

"No," he answered. "I walked in. But I went in overhead as well."

There was silence for a moment. He hesitated. He very much wanted to go upstairs to get into dry clothing. But there was another desire in him. And she seemed to hold him. His will seemed to have gone to sleep, and left him, standing there slack before her. But he felt warm inside himself. He did not shudder at all, though his clothes were sodden on him.

"Why did you?" she asked.

"Because I didn't want you to do such a foolish thing," he said.

"It wasn't foolish," she said, still gazing at him as she lay on the floor, with a sofa cushion under her head. "It was the right thing to do. I knew best, then."

"I'll go and shift these wet things," he said. But still he had not the power to move out of her presence, until she sent him. It was as if she had the life of his body in her hands, and he could not extricate himself. Or perhaps he did not want to.

Suddenly she sat up. Then she became aware of her own immediate condition. She felt the blankets about her, she knew her own limbs. For a moment it seemed as if her reason were going. She looked round, with wild eye, as if seeking something. He stood still with fear. She saw her clothing lying scattered.

"Who undressed me?" she asked, her eyes resting full and inevitable on his face.

"I did," he replied, "to bring you round."

For some moments she sat and gazed at him awfully, her lips parted.

"Do you love me, then?" she asked.

He only stood and stared at her, fascinated. His soul seemed to melt.

She shuffled forward on her knees, and put her arms round him, round his legs, as he stood there, pressing her breasts against his knees and thighs, clutching him with strange, convulsive certainty, pressing his thighs against her, drawing him to her face, her throat, as she looked up at him with flaring, humble eyes of transfiguration, triumphant in first possession.

"You love me," she murmured, in strange transport, yearning and triumphant and confident. "You love me. I know you love me, I know."

And she was passionately kissing his knees, through the wet clothing, passionately and indiscriminately kissing his knees, his legs, as if unaware of everything.

He looked down at the tangled wet hair, the wild, bare, animal shoulders. He was amazed, bewildered, and afraid. He had never thought of loving her. He had never wanted to love her. When he rescued her and restored her, he was a doctor, and she was a patient. He had had no single personal thought of her. Nay, this introduction of the personal element was very distasteful to him, a violation of his professional honour. It was horrible to have her there embracing his knees. It was horrible. He revolted from it, violently. And yet — and yet — he had not the power to break away.

She looked at him again, with the same supplication of powerful love, and that same transcendent, frightening light of triumph. In view of the delicate flame which seemed to come from her face like a light, he was powerless. And yet he had never intended to love her. He had never intended. And something stubborn in him could not give way.

"You love me," she repeated, in a murmur of deep, rhapsodic assurance. "You love me."

Her hands were drawing him, drawing him down to her. He was afraid, even a little horrified. For he had, really, no intention of loving her. Yet her hands were drawing him towards her. He put out his hand quickly to steady himself, and grasped her bare shoulder. A flame seemed to burn the hand that grasped her soft shoulder. He had no intention of loving her: his whole will was against his yielding. It was horrible. And yet wonderful was the touch of her shoulders, beautiful the shining of her face. Was she perhaps mad? He had a horror of yielding to her. Yet something in him ached also.

He had been staring away at the door, away from her. But his hand remained on her shoulder. She had gone suddenly very still. He looked down at her. Her eyes were now wide with fear, with doubt, the light was dying from her face, a shadow of terrible greyness was returning. He could not bear the touch of her eyes' question upon him, and the look of death behind the question.

With an inward groan he gave way, and let his heart yield towards her. A sudden gentle smile came on his face. And her eyes, which never left his face, slowly, slowly filled with tears. He watched the strange water rise in her eyes, like some slow fountain coming up. And his heart seemed to burn and melt away in his breast.

He could not bear to look at her any more. He dropped on his knees and caught her head with his arms and pressed her face against his throat. She was very still. His heart, which seemed to have broken, was burning with a kind of agony in his breast. And he felt her slow, hot tears wetting his throat. But he could not move.

He felt the hot tears wet his neck and the hollows of his neck, and he remained motionless, suspended through one of man's eternities. Only now it had become indispensable to him to have her face pressed close to him; he could never let her go again. He could never let her head go away from the close clutch of his arm. He wanted to remain like that for ever, with his heart hurting him in a pain that was also life to him. Without knowing, he was looking down on her damp, soft brown hair.

Then, as it were suddenly, he smelt the horrid stagnant smell of that water. And at the same moment she drew away from him and looked at him. Her eyes were wistful and unfathomable. He was afraid of them, and he fell to kissing her, not knowing what he was doing. He wanted her eyes not to have that terrible, wistful, unfathomable look.

When she turned her face to him again, a faint delicate flush was glowing, and there was again dawning that terrible shining of joy in her eyes, which really terrified him, and yet which he now wanted to see, because he feared the look of doubt still more.

"You love me?" she said, rather faltering.

"Yes." The word cost him a painful effort. Not because it wasn't true. But because it was too newly true, the *saying* seemed to tear open again his newly-torn heart. And he hardly wanted it to be true, even now.

She lifted her face to him, and he bent forward and kissed her on the mouth, gently, with the one kiss that is an eternal pledge. And as he kissed her his heart strained again in his breast. He never intended to love her. But now it was over. He had crossed over the gulf to her, and all that he had left behind had shrivelled and become void.

After the kiss, her eyes again slowly filled with tears. She sat still, away from him, with her face drooped aside, and her hands folded in her lap. The tears fell very slowly. There was complete silence. He too sat there motionless and silent on the hearth-rug. The strange pain of his heart that was broken seemed to consume him. That he should love her? That this was love! That he should be ripped open in this way! Him, a doctor! How they would all jeer if they knew! It was agony to him to think they might know.

In the curious naked pain of the thought he looked again to her. She was sitting there drooped into a muse. He saw a tear fall, and his heart flared hot. He saw for the first time that one of her shoulders was quite uncovered, one arm bare, he could see one of her small breasts; dimly, because it had become almost dark in the room.

"Why are you crying?" he asked, in an altered voice.

She looked up at him, and behind her tears the consciousness of her situation for the first time brought a dark look of shame to her eyes.

"I'm not crying, really," she said, watching him, half frightened.

He reached his hand, and softly closed it on her bare arm.

"I love you! I love you!" he said in a soft, low vibrating voice, unlike himself.

She shrank, and dropped her head. The soft, penetrating grip of his hand on her arm distressed her. She looked up at him.

"I want to go," she said. "I want to go and get you some dry things."

"Why?" he said. "I'm all right."

"But I want to go," she said. "And I want you to change your things."

He released her arm, and she wrapped herself in the blanket, looking at him rather frightened. And still she did not rise.

"Kiss me," she said wistfully.

He kissed her, but briefly, half in anger.

Then, after a second, she rose nervously, all mixed up in the blanket. He watched her in her confusion as she tried to extricate herself and wrap herself up so that she could walk. He watched her relentlessly, as she knew. And as she went, the blanket trailing, and as he saw a glimpse of her feet and her white leg, he tried to remember her as she was when he had wrapped her in the blanket. But then he didn't want to remember, because she had been nothing to him then, and his nature revolted from remembering her as she was when she was nothing to him.

A tumbling, muffled noise from within the dark house startled him. Then he heard her voice: "There are clothes." He rose and went to the foot of the stairs, and gathered up the garments she had thrown down. Then he came back to the fire, to rub himself down and dress. He grinned at his own appearance when he had finished.

The fire was sinking, so he put on coal. The house was now quite dark, save for the light of a street-lamp that shone in faintly from beyond the holly trees. He lit the gas with matches he found on the mantelpiece. Then he emptied the pockets of his own clothes, and threw all his wet things in a heap into the scullery. After which he gathered up her sodden clothes, gently, and put them in a separate heap on the coppertop in the scullery.

It was six o'clock on the clock. His own watch had stopped. He ought to go back to the surgery. He waited, and still she did not come down. So he went to the foot of the stairs and called:

"I shall have to go."

Almost immediately he heard her coming down. She had on her best dress of black voile, and her hair was tidy, but still damp. She looked at him — and in spite of herself, smiled.

"I don't like you in those clothes," she said.

"Do I look a sight?" he answered.

They were shy of one another.

"I'll make you some tea," she said.

"No, I must go."

"Must you?" And she looked at him again with the wide, strained, doubtful eyes. And again, from the pain of his breast, he knew how he loved her. He went and bent to kiss her, gently, passionately, with his heart's painful kiss.

"And my hair smells so horrible," she murmured in distraction. "And I'm so awful, I'm so awful! Oh no, I'm too awful." And she broke into bitter, heartbroken sobbing. "You can't want to love me, I'm horrible."

"Don't be silly, don't be silly," he said, trying to comfort her, kissing her, holding her in his arms. "I want you, I want to marry you, we're going to be married, quickly, quickly — tomorrow if I can."

But she only sobbed terribly, and cried:

"I feel awful. I feel awful. I feel I'm horrible to you."

"No, I want you, I want you," was all he answered, blindly, with that terrible intonation which frightened her almost more than her horror lest he should *not* want her.

QUESTIONS

1. What is the effect of Lawrence's starting with a scene at the Pervin breakfast table? Why does he delay giving us the full background of the problem until this long scene is over? Are there elements in their scene that make it artistically effective for Lawrence to delay explaining the decline in the family's fortune?

2. How do the speech patterns of the brothers help establish the tone of the story? Could Lawrence have omitted their scene without affecting the rest of the story?

3. What effect did her father's second marriage have on Mabel? Is the memory of her mother a positive or a negative influence on her?

4. Is there any hint in Fergusson's first appearance at the Pervin house that he and Mabel are attracted to each other?

5. After Mabel tends to her mother's grave, Lawrence shifts the point of view to Fergusson. Was the shift necessary? Couldn't the entire tale have been told as well from Mabel's point of view?

6. Is Fergusson drawn to Mabel by pity? Is it gratitude or love that draws her to him?

7. Trace the steps by which Fergusson's reluctance to say "I love you" is overcome. Are these steps in character? What do these hesitating steps tell us about him?

8. Is this story Mabel's or Fergusson's? Consider both the title and the last sentence in the story for possible clues.

D. H. LAWRENCE

The Rocking-Horse Winner

There was a woman who was beautiful, who started with all the advantages, yet she had no luck. She married for love, and the love turned to dust. She had bonny children, yet she felt they had been thrust upon her, and she could not love them. They looked at her coldly, as if they were finding fault with her. And hurriedly she felt she must cover up some fault in herself. Yet what it was that she must cover up she never knew. Nevertheless, when her children were present, she always felt the centre of her heart go hard. This troubled her, and in her manner she was all the more gentle and anxious for her children, as if she loved them very much. Only she herself knew that at the centre of her heart was a hard little place that could not feel love, no, not for anybody. Everybody else said of her: "She is such a good mother. She adores her children." Only she herself, and her children themselves, knew it was not so. They read it in each other's eyes.

There were a boy and two little girls. They lived in a pleasant house, with a garden, and they had discreet servants, and felt themselves superior to anyone in the neighbourhood.

Although they lived in style, they felt always an anxiety in the house. There was never enough money. The mother had a small income, and the father had a small income, but not nearly enough for the social position which they had to keep up. The father went in to town to some office. But though he had good prospects, these prospects never materialized. There was always the grinding sense of the shortage of money, though the style was always kept up.

At last the mother said: "I will see if *I* can't make something." But she did not know where to begin. She racked her brains, and tried this thing and the other, but could not find anything successful. The failure made deep lines come into her face. Her children were growing up, they would have to go to school. There must be more money, there must be more money. The father, who was always very handsome and expensive in his tastes, seemed as if he never *would* be able to do anything worth doing. And the mother, who had a great belief in herself, did not succeed any better, and her tastes were just as expensive.

And so the house came to be haunted by the unspoken phrase: *There must be more money! There must be more money!* The children could hear it all the time, though nobody said it aloud. They heard it at Christmas, when the expensive and splendid toys filled the nursery. Behind the shining modern rocking-horse, behind the smart doll's-house, a voice would start whispering: "There *must* be more money! There *must* be more money!" And the children would stop playing, to listen for a moment. They would look into each other's eyes, to see if they had all heard. And each one saw in the eyes of the other two that they had heard. "There *must* be more money! There *must* be more money!"

It came whispering from the springs of the still-swaying rocking-horse, and even the horse, bending his wooden, champing head, heard it. The big doll, sitting so pink and smirking in her new pram,[1] could hear it quite plainly, and seemed to be smirking all the more self-consciously because of it. The foolish puppy, too, that took the place of the teddy-bear, he was looking so extraordinarily foolish for no other reason but that he heard the secret whisper all over the house: "There *must* be more money!"

Yet nobody ever said it aloud. The whisper was everywhere, and therefore no one spoke it. Just as no one ever says: "We are breathing!" in spite of the fact that breath is coming and going all the time.

"Mother," said the boy Paul one day, "why don't we keep a car of our own? Why do we always use uncle's, or else a taxi?"

"Because we're the poor members of the family," said the mother.

"But why *are* we, mother?"

"Well — I suppose," she said slowly and bitterly, "it's because your father has no luck."

The boy was silent for some time.

"Is luck money, mother?" he asked rather timidly.

"No, Paul. Not quite. It's what causes you to have money."

"Oh!" said Paul vaguely. "I thought when Uncle Oscar said *filthy lucker*, it meant money."

"*Filthy lucre* does mean money," said the mother. "But it's lucre, not luck."

"Oh!" said the boy. "Then what *is* luck, mother?"

"It's what causes you to have money. If you're lucky you have money. That's why it's better to be born lucky than rich. If you're rich, you may lose your money. But if you're lucky, you will always get more money."

"Oh! Will you? And is father not lucky?"

"Very unlucky, I should say," she said bitterly.

The boy watched her with unsure eyes.

"Why?" he asked.

"I don't know. Nobody ever knows why one person is lucky and another unlucky."

"Don't they? Nobody at all? Does *nobody* know?"

"Perhaps God. But He never tells."

"He ought to, then. And aren't you lucky either, mother?"

"I can't be, if I married an unlucky husband."

"But by yourself, aren't you?"

"I used to think I was, before I married. Now I think I am very unlucky indeed."

"Why?"

"Well — never mind! Perhaps I'm not really," she said.

The child looked at her, to see if she meant it. But he saw, by the lines of her mouth, that she was only trying to hide something from him.

"Well, anyhow," he said stoutly, "I'm a lucky person."

"Why?" said his mother, with a sudden laugh.

He stared at her. He didn't even know why he had said it.

---

[1] Baby carriage.

"God told me," he asserted, brazening it out.

"I hope He did, dear" she said, again with a laugh, but rather bitter.

"He did, mother!"

"Excellent!" said the mother, using one of her husband's exclamations.

The boy saw she did not believe him; or, rather, that she paid no attention to his assertion. This angered him somewhat, and made him want to compel her attention.

He went off by himself, vaguely, in a childish way, seeking for the clue to "luck." Absorbed, taking no heed of other people, he went about with a sort of stealth, seeking inwardly for luck. He wanted luck, he wanted it, he wanted it. When the two girls were playing dolls in the nursery, he would sit on his big rocking-horse, charging madly into space, with a frenzy that made the little girls peer at him uneasily. Wildly the horse careered, the waving dark hair of the boy tossed, his eyes had a strange glare in them. The little girls dared not speak to him.

When he had ridden to the end of his mad little journey, he climbed down and stood in front of his rocking-horse, staring fixedly into its lowered face. Its red mouth was slightly open, its big eye was wide and glassy-bright.

"Now!" he would silently command the snorting steed. "Now, take me to where there is luck! Now take me!"

And he would slash the horse on the neck with the little whip he had asked Uncle Oscar for. He *knew* the horse could take him to where there was luck, if only he forced it. So he would mount again, and start on his furious ride, hoping at last to get there. He knew he could get there.

"You'll break your horse, Paul!" said the nurse.

"He's always riding like that! I wish he'd leave off!" said his elder sister Joan.

But he only glared down on them in silence. Nurse gave him up. She could make nothing of him. Anyhow he was growing beyond her.

One day his mother and his Uncle Oscar came in when he was on one of his furious rides. He did not speak to them.

"Hallo, you young jockey! Riding a winner?" said his uncle.

"Aren't you growing too big for a rocking-horse? You're not a very little boy any longer, you know," said his mother.

But Paul only gave a blue glare from his big, rather close-set eyes. He would speak to nobody when he was in full tilt. His mother watched him with an anxious expression on her face.

At last he suddenly stopped forcing his horse into the mechanical gallop, and slid down.

"Well, I got there!" he announced fiercely, his blue eyes still flaring, and his sturdy long legs straddling apart.

"Where did you get to?" asked his mother.

"Where I wanted to go," he flared back at her.

"That's right, son!" said Uncle Oscar. "Don't you stop till you get there. What's the horse's name?"

"He doesn't have a name," said the boy.

"Gets on without all right?" asked the uncle.

"Well, he has different names. He was called Sansovino last week."

"Sansovino, eh? Won the Ascot.[2] How did you know his name?"

---

[2] A major race, equivalent perhaps to the American Preakness or Kentucky Derby. References to other race meetings—for example, the Grand National and the Derby—are scattered throughout the story.

"He always talks about horse-races with Bassett," said Joan.

The uncle was delighted to find that his small nephew was posted with all the racing news. Bassett, the young gardener, who had been wounded in the left foot in the war and had got his present job through Oscar Cresswell, whose batman he had been, was a perfect blade of the "turf." He lived in the racing events, and the small boy lived with him.

Oscar Cresswell got it all from Bassett.

"Master Paul comes and asks me, so I can't do more than tell him, sir," said Bassett, his face terribly serious, as if he were speaking of religious matters.

"And does he ever put anything on a horse he fancies?"

"Well — I don't want to give him away — he's a young sport, a fine sport, sir. Would you mind asking him himself? He sort of takes a pleasure in it, and perhaps he'd feel I was giving him away, sir, if you don't mind."

Bassett was serious as a church.

The uncle went back to his nephew and took him off for a ride in the car.

"Say, Paul, old man, do you ever put anything on a horse?" the uncle asked.

The boy watched the handsome man closely.

"Why, do you think I oughtn't to?" he parried.

"Not a bit of it! I thought perhaps you might give me a tip for the Lincoln."

The car sped on into the country, going down to Uncle Oscar's place in Hampshire.

"Honour bright?" said the nephew.

"Honour bright, son!" said the uncle.

"Well, then, Daffodil."

"Daffodil! I doubt it, sonny. What about Mirza?"

"I only know the winner," said the boy. "That's Daffodil."

"Daffodil, eh?"

There was a pause. Daffodil was an obscure horse comparatively.

"Uncle!"

"Yes, son?"

"You won't let it go any further, will you? I promised Bassett."

"Bassett be damned, old man! What's he got to do with it?"

"We're partners. We've been partners from the first. Uncle, he lent me my first five shillings, which I lost. I promised him, honour bright, it was only between me and him; only you gave me that ten-shilling note I started winning with, so I thought you were lucky. You won't let it go any further, will you?"

The boy gazed at his uncle from those big, hot, blue eyes, set rather close together. The uncle stirred and laughed uneasily.

"Right you are, son! I'll keep your tip private. Daffodil, eh? How much are you putting on him?"

"All except twenty pounds," said the boy. "I keep that in reserve."

The uncle thought it a good joke.

"You keep twenty pounds in reserve, do you, you young romancer? What are you betting, then?"

"I'm betting three hundred," said the boy, gravely. "But it's between you and me, Uncle Oscar! Honour bright?"

The uncle burst into a roar of laughter.

"It's between you and me all right, you young Nat Gould,"[3] he said, laughing. "But where's your three hundred?"

---

[3] A well-known British journalist and turfman.

"Bassett keeps it for me. We're partners."

"You are, are you! And what is Bassett putting on Daffodil?"

"He won't go quite as high as I do, I expect. Perhaps he'll go a hundred and fifty."

"What, pennies?" laughed the uncle.

"Pounds," said the child, with a surprised look at his uncle. "Bassett keeps a bigger reserve than I do."

Between wonder and amusement Uncle Oscar was silent. He pursued the matter no further, but he determined to take his nephew with him to the Lincoln races.

"Now, son," he said, "I'm putting twenty on Mirza, and I'll put five for you on any horse you fancy. What's your pick?"

"Daffodil, uncle."

"No, not the fiver on Daffodil!"

"I should if it was my own fiver," said the child.

"Good! Good! Right you are! A fiver for me and a fiver for you on Daffodil."

The child had never been to a race-meeting before, and his eyes were blue fire. He pursed his mouth tight, and watched. A Frenchman just in front had put his money on Lancelot. Wild with excitement, he flayed his arms up and down, yelling "*Lancelot! Lancelot!*" in his French accent.

Daffodil came in first, Lancelot second, Mirza third. The child, flushed and with eyes blazing, was curiously serene. His uncle brought him four five-pound notes, four to one.

"What am I to do with these?" he cried, waving them before the boy's eyes.

"I suppose we'll talk to Bassett," said the boy. "I expect I have fifteen hundred now; and twenty in reserve; and this twenty."

His uncle studied him for some moments.

"Look here, son!" he said. "You're not serious about Bassett and that fifteen hundred, are you?"

"Yes, I am. But it's between you amd me, uncle. Honour bright!"

"Honour bright all right, son! But I must talk to Bassett."

"If you'd like to be a partner, uncle, with Bassett and me, we could all be partners. Only, you'd have to promise, honour bright, uncle, not to let it go beyond us three. Bassett and I are lucky, and you must be lucky, because it was your ten shillings I started winning with. ...."

Uncle Oscar took both Bassett and Paul into Richmond Park for an afternoon, and there they talked.

"It's like this, you see, sir," Bassett said. "Master Paul would get me talking about racing events, spinning yarns, you know, sir. And he was always keen on knowing if I'd made or if I'd lost. It's about a year since, now, that I put five shillings on Blush of Dawn for him — and we lost. Then the luck turned, with that ten shillings he had from you, that we put on Singhalese. And since that time, it's been pretty steady, all things considering. What do you say, Master Paul?"

"We're all right when we're sure," said Paul. "It's when we're not quite sure that we go down."

"Oh, but we're careful then," said Bassett.

"But when are you *sure*?" smiled Uncle Oscar.

"It's Master Paul, sir," said Bassett, in a secret, religious voice.

"It's as if he had it from heaven. Like Daffodil, now, for the Lincoln. That was as sure as eggs."

"Did you put anything on Daffodil?" asked Oscar Cresswell.

"Yes, sir. I made my bit."

"And my nephew?"

Bassett was obstinately silent, looking at Paul.

"I made twelve hundred, didn't I, Bassett? I told uncle I was putting three hundred on Daffodil."

"That's right," said Bassett, nodding.

"But where's the money?" asked the uncle.

"I keep it safe locked up, sir. Master Paul he can have it any minute he likes to ask for it."

"What, fifteen hundred pounds?"

"And twenty! And *forty,* that is, with the twenty he made on the course."

"It's amazing!" said the uncle.

"If Master Paul offers you to be partners, sir, I would, if I were you; if you'll excuse me," said Bassett.

Oscar Cresswell thought about it.

"I'll see the money," he said.

They drove home again, and sure enough, Bassett came round to the garden-house with fifteen hundred pounds in notes. The twenty pounds reserve was left with Joe Glee, in the Turf Commission deposit.

"You see, it's all right, uncle, when I'm *sure!* Then we go strong, for all we're worth. Don't we, Bassett?"

"We do that, Master Paul."

"And when are you sure? said the uncle, laughing.

"Oh, well, sometimes I'm *absolutely* sure, like about Daffodil," said the boy; "and sometimes I have an idea; and sometimes I haven't even an idea, have I, Bassett? Then we're careful, because we mostly go down."

"You do, do you! And when you're sure, like about Daffodil, what makes you sure, sonny?"

"Oh, well, I don't know," said the boy uneasily. "I'm sure, you know, uncle; that's all."

"It's as if he had it from heaven, sir," Bassett reiterated.

"I should say so!" said the uncle.

But he became a partner. And when the Leger was coming on, Paul was "sure" about Lively Spark, which was a quite inconsiderable horse. The boy insisted on putting a thousand on the horse, Bassett went for five hundred, and Oscar Cresswell two hundred. Lively Spark came in first, and the betting had been ten to one against him. Paul had made ten thousand.

"You see," he said, "I was absolutely sure of him."

Even Oscar Cresswell had cleared two thousand.

"Look here, son," he said, "this sort of thing makes me nervous."

"It needn't, uncle! Perhaps I shan't be sure again for a long time."

"But what are you going to do with your money?" asked the uncle.

"Of course," said the boy, "I started it for mother. She said she had no luck, because father is unlucky, so I thought if *I* was lucky, it might stop whispering."

"What might stop whispering?"

"Our house. I *hate* our house for whispering."

"What does it whisper?"

"Why — why" — the boy fidgeted — "why, I don't know. But it's always short of money, you know, uncle."

"I know it, son, I know it."

"You know people send mother writs,[4] don't you, uncle?"

"I'm afraid I do," said the uncle.

"And then the house whispers, like people laughing at you behind your back. It's awful, that is! I thought if I was lucky ..."

"You might stop it," added the uncle.

The boy watched him with big blue eyes, that had an uncanny cold fire in them, and he said never a word.

"Well, then!" said the uncle. "What are we doing?"

"I shouldn't like mother to know I was lucky," said the boy.

"Why not, son?"

"She'd stop me."

"I don't think she would."

"Oh!" — and the boy writhed in an odd way — "I *don't* want her to know, uncle."

"All right, son! We'll manage it without her knowing."

They managed it very easily. Paul, at the other's suggestion, handed over five thousand pounds to his uncle, who deposited it with the family lawyer, who was then to inform Paul's mother that a relative had put five thousand pounds into his hands, which sum was to be paid out a thousand pounds at a time, on the mother's birthday, for the next five years.

"So she'll have a birthday present of a thousand pounds for five successive years," said Uncle Oscar. "I hope it won't make it all the harder for her later."

Paul's mother had her birthday in November. The house had been "whispering" worse than ever lately, and, even in spite of his luck, Paul could not bear up against it. He was very anxious to see the effect of the birthday letter, telling his mother about the thousand pounds.

When there were no visitors, Paul now took his meals with his parents, as he was beyond the nursery control. His mother went into town nearly every day. She had discovered that she had an odd knack of sketching furs and dress materials, so she worked secretly in the studio of a friend who was the chief "artist" for the leading drapers. She drew the figures of ladies in furs and ladies in silk and sequins for the newspaper advertisements. This young woman artist earned several thousand pounds a year, but Paul's mother only made several hundreds, and she was again dissatisfied. She so wanted to be first in something, and she did not succeed, even in making sketches for drapery advertisements.

She was down to breakfast on the morning of her birthday. Paul watched her face as she read her letters. He knew the lawyer's letter. As his mother read it, her face hardened and became more expressionless. Than a cold, determined look came on her mouth. She hid the letter under the pile of others, and said not a word about it.

"Didn't you have anything nice in the post for your birthday, mother?" said Paul.

"Quite moderately nice," she said, her voice cold and absent.

She went away to town without saying more.

But in the afternoon Uncle Oscar appeared. He said Paul's mother had had a long interview with the lawyer, asking if the whole five thousand could not be advanced at once, as she was in debt.

"What do you think, uncle?" said the boy.

"I leave it to you, son."

"Oh, let her have it, then! We can get some more with the other," said the boy.

"A bird in the hand is worth two in the bush, laddie!" said Uncle Oscar.

---

[4] Demands for payment.

"But I'm sure to *know* for the Grand National; or the Lincolnshire; or else the Derby. I'm sure to know for *one* of them," said Paul.

So Uncle Oscar signed the agreement, and Paul's mother touched the whole five thousand. Then something very curious happened. The voices in the house suddenly went mad, like a chorus of frogs on a spring evening. There were certain new furnishings, and Paul had a tutor. He was *really* going to Eton, his father's school, in the following autumn. There were flowers in the winter, and a blossoming of the luxury Paul's mother had been used to. And yet the voices in the house, behind the sprays of mimosa and almond blossom, and from under the piles of iridescent cushions, simply trilled and screamed in a sort of ecstasy: "There *must* be more money! Oh-h-h; there *must* be more money Oh, now, now-w! Now-w-w — there *must* be more money! — more than ever! More than ever!"

It frightened Paul terribly. He studied away at his Latin and Greek with his tutors. But his intense hours were spent with Bassett. The Grand National had gone by: he had not "known," and had lost a hundred pounds. Summer was at hand. He was in agony for the Lincoln. But even for the Lincoln he didn't "know," and he lost fifty pounds. He became wild-eyed and strange, as if something were going to explode in him.

"Let it alone, son! Don't you bother about it!" urged Uncle Oscar. But it was as if the boy really couldn't hear what his uncle was saying.

"I've got to know for the Derby! I've got to know for the Derby!" the child reiterated, his big blue eyes blazing with a sort of madness.

His mother noticed how overwrought he was.

"You'd better go to the seaside. Wouldn't you like to go now to the seaside, instead of waiting? I think you'd better," she said, looking down at him anxiously, her heart curiously heavy because of him.

But the child lifted his uncanny blue eyes.

"I couldn't possibly go before the Derby, mother!" he said. "I couldn't possibly!"

"Why not?" she said, her voice becoming heavy when she was opposed. "Why not? You can still go from the seaside to see the Derby with your Uncle Oscar, if that's what you wish. No need for you to wait here. Besides, I think you care too much about these races. It's a bad sign. My family has been a gambling family, and you won't know till you grow up how much damage it has done. But it has done damage. I shall have to send Bassett away, and ask Uncle Oscar not to talk racing to you, unless you promise to be reasonable about it; go away to the seaside and forget it. You're all nerves!"

"I'll do what you like, mother, so long as you don't send me away till after the Derby," the boy said.

"Send you away from where? Just from this house?"

"Yes," he said, gazing at her.

"Why, you curious child, what makes you care about this house so much, suddenly? I never knew you loved it."

He gazed at her without speaking. He had a secret within a secret, something he had not divulged, even to Bassett or to his Uncle Oscar.

But his mother, after standing undecided and a little bit sullen for some moments, said:

"Very well, then! Don't go to the seaside till after the Derby, if you don't wish it. But promise me you won't let your nerves go to pieces. Promise you won't think so much about horse-racing and events, as you call them!"

"Oh, no," said the boy casually. "I won't think much about them, mother. You needn't worry. I wouldn't worry, mother, if I were you."

"If you were me and I were you," said his mother, "I wonder what we *should* do!"

"But you know you needn't worry, mother, don't you?" the boy repeated.

"I should be awfully glad to know it," she said wearily.

"Oh, well, you *can*, you know. I mean, you *ought* to know you needn't worry," he insisted.

"Ought I? Then I'll see about it," she said.

Paul's secret of secrets was his wooden horse, that which had no name. Since he was emancipated from a nurse and a nursery-governess, he had had his rocking-horse removed to his own bedroom at the top of the house.

"Surely, you're too big for a rocking-horse!" his mother had remonstrated.

"Well, you see, mother, till I can have a *real* horse, I like to have *some* sort of animal about," had been his quaint answer.

"Do you feel he keeps you company?" she laughed.

"Oh, yes! He's very good, he always keeps me company, when I'm there," said Paul.

So the horse, rather shabby, stood in an arrested prance in the boy's bedroom.

The Derby was drawing near, and the boy grew more and more tense. He hardly heard what was spoken to him, he was very frail, and his eyes were really uncanny. His mother had sudden strange seizures of uneasiness about him. Sometimes, for half-an-hour, she would feel a sudden anxiety about him that was almost anguish. She wanted to rush to him at once, and know he was safe.

Two nights before the Derby, she was at a big party in town, when one of her rushes of anxiety about her boy, her first-born, gripped her heart till she could hardly speak. She fought with the feeling, might and main, for she believed in common-sense. But it was too strong. She had to leave the dance and go downstairs to telephone to the country. The children's nursery-governess was terribly surprised and startled at being rung up in the night.

"Are the children all right, Miss Wilmot?"

"Oh, yes, they are quite all right."

"Master Paul? Is he all right?"

"He went to bed as right as a trivet. Shall I run up and look at him?"

"No," said Paul's mother reluctantly. "No! Don't trouble. It's all right. Don't sit up. We shall be home fairly soon." She did not want her son's privacy intruded upon.

"Very good," said the governess.

It was about one o'clock when Paul's mother and father drove up to their house. All was still. Paul's mother went to her room and slipped off her white fur cloak. She had told her maid not to wait up for her. She heard her husband downstairs, mixing a whisky-and-soda.

And then, because of the strange anxiety at her heart, she stole upstairs to her son's room. Noiselessly she went along the upper corridor. Was there a faint noise? What was it?

She stood, with arrested muscles, outside his door, listening. There was a strange, heavy, and yet not loud noise. Her heart stood still. It was a soundless noise, yet rushing and powerful. Something huge, in violent, hushed motion. What was it? What in God's name was it? She ought to know. She felt that she knew the noise. She knew what it was.

Yet she could not place it. She couldn't say what it was. And on and on it went, like a madness.

Softly, frozen with anxiety and fear, she turned the door-handle.

The room was dark. Yet in the space near the window, she heard and saw something plunging to and fro. She gazed in fear and amazaement.

Then suddenly she switched on the light, and saw her son, in his green pyjamas, madly surging on the rocking-horse. The blaze of light suddenly lit him up, as he urged the wooden horse, and lit her up, as she stood, blonde, in her dress of pale green and crystal, in the doorway.

"Paul!" she cried. "Whatever are you doing?"

"It's Malabar!" he screamed, in a powerful, strange voice. "It's Malabar!"

His eyes blazed at her for one strange and senseless second, as he ceased urging his wooden horse. Then he fell with a crash to the ground, and she, all her tormented motherhood flooding upon her, rushed to gather him up.

But he was unconscious, and unconscious he remained, with some brain-fever. He talked and tossed, and his mother sat stonily by his side.

"Malabar! It's Malabar! Bassett, Bassett, I *know!* It's Malabar!"

So the child cried, trying to get up and urge the rocking-horse that gave him his inspiration.

"What does he mean by Malabar!" asked the heart-broken mother.

"I don't know," said the father stonily.

"What does he mean by Malabar?" she asked her brother Oscar.

"It's one of the horses running for the Derby," was the answer.

And, in spite of himself, Oscar Cresswell spoke to Bassett, and himself put a thousand on Malabar: at fourteen to one.

The third day of the illness was critical: they were waiting for a change. The boy, with his rather long, curly hair, was tossing ceaselessly on the pillow. He neither slept nor regained consciousness, and his eyes were like blue stones. His mother sat, feeling her heart had gone, turned actually into a stone.

In the evening, Oscar Cresswell did not come, but Bassett sent a message, saying could he come up for one moment, just one moment? Paul's mother was very angry at the intrusion, but on second thought she agreed. The boy was the same. Perhaps Bassett might bring him to consciousness.

The gardener, a shortish fellow with a little brown moustache, and sharp little brown eyes, tip-toed into the room, touched his imaginary cap to Paul's mother, and stole to the bedside, staring with glittering, smallish eyes, at the tossing, dying child.

"Master Paul!" he whispered. "Master Paul! Malabar came in first all right, a clean win. I did as you told me. You've made over seventy thousand pounds, you have; you've got over eighty thousand. Malabar came in all right, Master Paul."

"Malabar! Malabar! Did I say Malabar, mother? Did I say Malabar? Do you think I'm lucky, mother? I knew Malabar, didn't I? Over eighty thousand pounds! I call that lucky, don't you, mother? Over eighty thousand pounds! I knew, didn't I know I knew! Malabar came in all right. If I ride my horse till I'm sure, then I tell you, Bassett, you can go as high as you like. Did you go for all you were worth, Bassett?"

"I went a thousand on it, Master Paul."

"I never told you, mother, that if I can ride my horse, and *get there*, then I'm absolutely sure — oh absolutely! Mother, did I ever tell you? I *am* lucky!"

"No, you never did," said the mother.

But the boy died in the night.

And even as he lay dead, his mother heard her brother's voice saying to her: "My God, Hester, you're eighty-odd thousand to the good, and a poor devil of a son to the bad. But, poor devil, poor devil, he's best gone out of a life where he rides his rocking-horse to find a winner."

QUESTIONS

1. Whose story is this? Paul's? Considering the first and final paragraphs, can we argue that the story is the mother's? Or are these paragraphs simply a framework for Paul's tragedy?

2. Is the lack of money the root of the problem here? If it is, then why do things get worse after Paul's mother gets her five thousand pounds? If money is not the problem, what is?

3. What does the second paragraph tell us about the family?

4. Is the house haunted? Where do the voices come from?

5. Uncle Oscar and the gardener, Bassett, treat Paul differently than do the other adults. Can you show the difference?

6. The gardener and the uncle come from different strata of society. How does Lawrence dramatize the difference? Is it reflected in their speech?

7. Uncle Oscar has the last word. Is it in character? Does it reflect a lack of sympathy?

8. What, if anything, does the rocking horse symbolize?

AGATHA CHRISTIE ═══════

Double Sin

I had called in at my friend Poirot's rooms to find him sadly overworked. So much had he become the rage that every rich woman who had mislaid a bracelet or lost a pet kitten rushed to secure the services of the great Hercule Poirot. My little friend was a strange mixture of Flemish thrift and artistic fervour. He accepted many cases in which he had little interest owing to the first instinct being predominant.

He also undertook cases in which there was a little or no monetary reward sheerly because the problem involved interested him. The result was that, as I say, he was overworking himself. He admitted as much himself, and I found little difficulty in persuading him to accompany me for a week's holiday to that well-known South Coast resort, Ebermouth.

We had spent four very agreeable days when Poirot came to me, an open letter in his hand.

"*Mon ami,*[1] you remember my friend Joseph Aarons, the theatrical agent?"

I assented after a moment's thought. Poirot's friends are so many and so varied, and range from dustmen to dukes.

"*Eh bien,*[2] Hastings, Joseph Aarons finds himself at Charlock Bay. He is far from well, and there is a little affair that it seems is worrying him. He begs me to go over and see him. I think, *mon ami,* that I must accede to his request. He is a faithful friend, the good Joseph Aarons, and has done much to assist me in the past."

"Certainly, if you think so," I said. "I believe Charlock Bay is a beautiful spot, and as it happens, I've never been there."

"Then we combine business with pleasure," said Poirot. "You will inquire the trains, yes?"

"It will probably mean a change or two," I said with a grimace. "You know what these cross-country lines are. To go from the South Devon coast to the North Devon coast is sometimes a day's journey."

However, on inquiry, I found that the journey could be accomplished by only one change at Exeter and that the trains were good. I was hastening back to Poirot with the information when I happened to pass the offices of the Speedy cars and saw written up:

---

[1] "My friend."
[2] "Well."

Tomorrow. All-day excursion to Charlock Bay. Starting 8:30 through some most beautiful scenery in Devon.

I inquired a few particulars and returned to the hotel full of enthusiasm. Unfortunately, I found it hard to make Poirot share my feelings.

"My friend, why this passion for the motor coach? The train, see you, it is sure? The tires, they do not burst; the accidents, they do not happen. One is not incommoded by too much air. The windows can be shut and no draughts admitted."

I hinted delicately that the advantage of fresh air was what attracted me most to the motor-coach scheme.

"And if it rains? Your English climate is so uncertain."

"There's a hood and all that. Besides, if it rains badly, the excursion doesn't take place."

"Ah!" said Poirot. "Then let us hope that it rains."

"Of course, if you feel like that and ..."

"No, no, *mon ami*. I see that you have set your heart on the trip. Fortunately, I have my greatcoat with me and two mufflers." He sighed. "But shall we have sufficient time at Charlock Bay?"

"Well, I'm afraid it means staying the night there. You see, the tour goes round by Dartmoor. We have lunch at Monkhampton. We arrive at Charlock Bay about four o'clock, and the coach starts back at five, arriving here at ten o'clock."

"So!" said Poirot. "And there are people who do this for pleasure! We shall, of course, get a reduction of the fare since we do not make the return journey?"

"I hardly think that's likely."

"You must insist."

"Come now, Poirot, don't be mean. You know you're coining money."

"My friend, it is not the meanness. It is the business sense. If I were a millionaire, I would pay only what was just and right."

As I had foreseen, however, Poirot was doomed to fail in this respect. The gentleman who issued tickets at the Speedy office was calm and unimpassioned but adamant. His point was that we ought to return. He even implied that we ought to pay extra for the privilege of leaving the coach at Charlock Bay.

Defeated, Poirot paid over the required sum and left the office.

"The English, they have no sense of money," he grumbled. "Did you observe a young man, Hastings, who paid over the full fare and yet mentioned his intention of leaving the coach at Monkhampton?"

"I don't think I did. As a matter of fact ..."

"You were observing the pretty young lady who booked No. 5, the next seat to ours. Ah! Yes, my friend, I saw you. And that is why when I was on the point of taking seats No. 13 and 14 — which are in the middle and as well sheltered as it is possible to be — you rudely pushed yourself forward and said that 3 and 4 would be better."

"Really, Poirot," I said, blushing.

"Auburn hair — always the auburn hair!"

"At any rate, she was more worth looking at than an odd young man."

"That depends upon the point of view. To me, the young man was interesting."

Something rather significant in Poirot's tone made me look at him quickly. "Why? What do you mean?"

"Oh, do not excite yourself. Shall I say that he interested me because he was trying to grow a moustache and as yet the result is poor." Poirot stroked his own magnificent moustache tenderly. "It is an art," he murmured, "the growing of the moustache! I have sympathy for all who attempt it."

It is always difficult with Poirot to know when he is serious and when he is merely amusing himself at one's expense. I judged it safest to say no more.

The following morning dawned bright and sunny. A really glorious day! Poirot, however, was taking no chances. He wore a woolly waistcoat, a mackintosh, a heavy overcoat, and two mufflers, in addition to wearing his thickest suit. He also swallowed two tablets of "Anti-grippe" before starting and packed a further supply.

We took a couple of small suitcases with us. The pretty girl we had noticed the day before had a small suitcase, and so did the young man whom I gathered to have been the object of Poirot's sympathy. Otherwise, there was no luggage. The four pieces were stowed away by the driver, and we all took our places .

Poirot, rather maliciously, I thought, assigned me the outside place as "I had the mania for the fresh air" and himself occupied the seat next to our fair neighbour. Presently, however, he made amends. The man in seat 6 was a noisy fellow, inclined to be facetious and boisterous, and Poirot asked the girl in a low voice if she would like to change seats with him. She agreed gratefully, and, the change having been effected, she entered into conversation with us and we were soon all three chattering together merrily.

She was evidently quite young, not more than nineteen, and as ingenuous as a child. She soon confided to us the reason for her trip. She was going, it seemed, on business for her aunt who kept a most interesting antique shop in Ebermouth.

This aunt had been left in very reduced circumstances on the death of her father and had used her small capital and a houseful of beautiful things which her father had left to start in business. She had been extremely successful and had made quite a name for herself in the trade. This girl, Mary Durrant, had come to be with her aunt and learn the business and was very excited about it — much preferring it to the other alternative — becoming a nursery governess or companion.

Poirot nodded interest and approval to all this.

"Mademoiselle will be successful, I am sure," he said gallantly. "But I will give her a little word of advice. Do not be too trusting, mademoiselle. Everywhere in the world there are rogues and vagabonds, even it may be on this very coach of ours. One should always be on the guard, suspicious!"

She stared at him open-mouthed, and he nodded sapiently.

"But yes, it is as I say. Who knows? Even I who speak to you may be a malefactor of the worst description."

And he twinkled more than ever at her surprised face.

We stopped for lunch at Monkhampton, and, after a few words with the waiter, Poirot managed to secure us a small table for three close by the window. Outside, in a big courtyard, about twenty char-à-bancs[3] were parked — char-à-bancs which had come from all over the county. The hotel dining room was full, and the noise was rather considerable.

"One can have altogether too much of the holiday spirit," I said with a grimace.

Mary Durrant agreed. "Ebermouth is quite spoiled in the summers nowadays. My aunt says it used to be quite different. Now one can hardly get along the pavements for the crowd."

"But it is good for business, mademoiselle."

"Not for ours particularly. We sell only rare and valuable things. We do not go in for

---

[3] Sight-seeing buses.

cheap bric-à-brac. My aunt has clients all over England. If they want a particular period table or chair, or a certain piece of china, they write to her, and, sooner or later, she gets it for them. That is what has happened in this case."

We looked interested and she went on to explain. A certain American gentleman, Mr. J. Baker Wood, was a connoisseur and collector of miniatures. A very valuable set of miniatures had recently come into the market, and Miss Elizabeth Penn — Mary's aunt — had purchased them. She had written to Mr. Wood describing the miniatures and naming a price. He had replied at once, saying that he was prepared to purchase if the miniatures were as represented and asking that someone should be sent with them for him to see where he was staying at Charlock Bay. Miss Durrant had accordingly been despatched, acting as representative for the firm.

"They're lovely things, of course," she said. "But I can't imagine anyone paying all that money for them. Five hundred pounds! Just think of it! They're by Cosway. Is it Cosway I mean? I get so mixed up in these things."

Poirot smiled. "You are not yet experienced, eh, mademoiselle?"

"I've had no training," said Mary ruefully. "We weren't brought up to know about old things. It's a lot to learn."

She sighed. Then suddenly, I saw her eyes widen in surprise. She was sitting facing the window, and her glance now was directed out of that window, into the courtyard. With a hurried word, she rose from her seat and almost ran out of the room. She returned in a few moments, breathless and apologetic.

"I'm so sorry rushing off like that. But I thought I saw a man taking my suitcase out of the coach. I went flying after him, and it turned out to be his own. It's one almost exactly like mine. I felt like such a fool. It looked as though I were accusing him of stealing it."

She laughed at the idea.

Poirot, however, did not laugh. "What man was it, mademoiselle? Describe him to me."

"He had on a brown suit. A thin weedy young man with a very indeterminate moustache."

"Aha," said Poirot. "Our friend of yesterday, Hastings. You know this young man, mademoiselle? You have seen him before?"

"No, never. Why?"

"Nothing. It is rather curious — that is all."

He relapsed into silence and took no further part in the conversation until something Mary Durrant said caught his attention.

"Eh, mademoiselle, what is that you say?"

"I said that on my return journey I should have to be careful of 'malefactors,' as you call them. I believe Mr. Wood always pays for things in cash. If I have five hundred pounds in notes on me, I shall be worth some malefactor's attention."

She laughed but again Poirot did not respond. Instead, he asked her what hotel she proposed to stay at in Charlock Bay.

"The Anchor Hotel. It is small and not expensive, but quite good."

"So!" said Poirot. "The Anchor Hotel. Precisely where Hastings here has made up his mind to stay. How odd!"

He twinkled at me.

"You are staying long in Charlock Bay?" asked Mary.

"One night only. I have business there. You could not guess, I am sure, what my profession is, mademoiselle?"

I saw Mary consider several possibilities and reject them — probably from a feeling of caution. At last, she hazarded the suggestion that Poirot was a conjurer. He was vastly entertained.

"Ah! But it is an idea that! You think I take the rabbits out of the hat? No, mademoiselle. Me, I am the opposite of a conjurer. The conjurer, he makes things disappear. Me, I make things that have disappeared, reappear." He leaned forward dramatically so as to give the words full effect. "It is a secret, mademoiselle, but I will tell you, I am a detective!"

He leaned back in his chair pleased with the effect he had created. Mary Durrant stared at him spellbound. But any further conversation was barred, for the braying of various horns outside announced that the road monsters were ready to proceed.

As Poirot and I went out together, I commented on the charm of our luncheon companion. Poirot agreed.

"Yes, she is charming. But, also rather silly?"

"Silly?"

"Do not be outraged. A girl may be beautiful and have auburn hair and yet be silly. It is the height of foolishness to take two strangers into her confidence as she has done."

"Well, she could see we were all right."

"That is imbecile, what you say, my friend. Anyone who knows his job — naturally he will appear 'all right.' That little one she talked of being careful when she would have five hundred pounds in money with her. But she has five hundred pounds with her now."

"In miniatures."

"Exactly. In miniatures. And between one and the other, there is no great difference, *mon ami.*"

"But no one knows about them except us."

"And the waiter and the people at the next table. And, doubtless, several people in Ebermouth! Mademoiselle Durrant, she is charming, but, if I were Miss Elizabeth Penn, I would first of all instruct my new assistant in the common sense." He paused and then said in a different voice: "You know, my friend, it would be the easiest thing in the world to remove a suitcase from one of those char-à-bancs while we were all at luncheon."

"Oh, come, Poirot, somebody will be sure to see."

"And what would they see? Somebody removing his luggage. It would be done in an open and aboveboard manner, and it would be nobody's business to interfere."

"Do you mean — Poirot, are you hinting — But that fellow in the brown suit — it was his own suitcase?"

Poirot frowned. "So it seems. All the same, it is curious, Hastings, that he should have not removed his suitcase before, when the car first arrived. He has not lunched here, you notice."

"If Miss Durrant hadn't been sitting opposite the window, she wouldn't have seen him," I said slowly.

"And since it was his own suitcase, that would not have mattered," said Poirot. "So let us dismiss it from our thoughts, *mon ami.*"

Nevertheless, when we had resumed our places and were speeding along once more, he took the opportunity of giving Mary Durrant a further lecture on the dangers of indiscretion which she received meekly enough but with the air of thinking it all rather a joke.

We arrived at Charlock Bay at four o'clock and were fortunate enough to be able to get rooms at the Anchor Hotel — a charming old-world inn in one of the side streets.

Poirot had just unpacked a few necessaries and was applying a little cosmetic to his moustache preparatory to going out to call upon Joseph Aarons when there came a frenzied knocking at the door. I called "Come in," and, to my utter amazement, Mary Durrant appeared, her face white and large tears standing in her eyes.

"I do beg your pardon — but — but the most awful thing has happened. And you did say you were a detective?" This to Poirot.

"What has happened, mademoiselle?"

"I opened my suitcase. The miniatures were in a crocodile despatch case — locked, of course. Now, look!"

She held out a small square crocodile-covered case. The lid hung loose. Poirot took it from her. The case had been forced; great strength must have been used. The marks were plain enough. Poirot examined it and nodded.

"The miniatures?" he asked, though we both knew the answer well enough.

"Gone. They've been stolen. Oh, what shall I do?"

"Don't worry," I said. "My friend is Hercule Poirot. You must have heard of him. He'll get them back for you if anyone can."

"Monsieur Poirot. The great Monsieur Poirot."

Poirot was vain enough to be pleased at the obvious reverence in her voice. "Yes, my child," he said. "It is I, myself. And you can leave your little affair in my hands. I will do all that can be done. But I fear — I much fear — that it will be too late. Tell me, was the lock of your suitcase forced also?"

She shook her head.

"Let me see it, please."

We went together to her room, and Poirot examined the suitcase closely. It had obviously been opened with a key.

"Which is simple enough. These suitcase locks are all much of the same pattern. *Eh bien*, we must ring up the police and we must also get in touch with Mr. Baker Wood as soon as possible. I will attend to that myself."

I went with him and asked what he meant by saying it might be too late. "*Mon cher,*[4] I said today that I was the opposite of the conjurer — that I make the disappearing things reappear — but suppose someone has been beforehand with me. You do not understand? You will in a minute."

He disappeared into the telephone box. He came out five minutes later looking very grave. "It is as I feared. A lady called upon Mr. Wood with the miniatures half an hour ago. She represented herself as coming from Miss Elizabeth Penn. He was delighted with the miniatures and paid for them forthwith."

"Half an hour ago — before we arrived here."

Poirot smiled rather enigmatically. "The Speedy cars are quite speedy, but a fast motor from, say, Monkhampton would get here a good hour ahead of them at least."

"And what do we do now?"

"The good Hastings — always practical. We inform the police, do all we can for Miss Durrant, and — yes, I think decidedly, we have an interview with Mr. J. Baker Wood."

We carried out this programme. Poor Mary Durrant was terribly upset, fearing her aunt would blame her.

"Which she probably will," observed Poirot, as we set out for the Seaside Hotel where Mr. Wood was staying. "And with perfect justice. The idea of leaving five hundred pounds' worth of valuables in a suitcase and going to lunch! All the same, *mon ami*, there are one or two curious points about the case. That despatch box, for instance, why was it forced?"

"To get out the miniatures."

"But was not that a foolishness? Say our thief is tampering with the luggage at lunchtime under the pretext of getting out his own. Surely it is much simpler to open the

---

[4] "My dear [Hastings]."

suitcase, transfer the despatch case unopened to his own suitcase, and get away, than to waste the time forcing the lock?"

"He had to make sure the miniatures were inside."

Poirot did not look convinced, but, as we were just being shown into Mr. Wood's suite, we had no time for more discussion.

I took an immediate dislike to Mr. Baker Wood.

He was a large vulgar man, very much overdressed and wearing a diamond solitaire ring. He was blustering and noisy.

Of course, he'd not suspected anything amiss. Why should he? The woman said she had the miniatures all right. Very fine specimens, too! Had he the numbers of the notes? No, he hadn't. And who was Mr. — er — Poirot, anyway, to come asking him all these questions?

"I will not ask you anything more, monsieur, except for one thing. A description of the woman who called upon you. Was she young and pretty?"

"No, sir, she was not. Most emphatically not. A tall woman, middle-aged, grey hair, blotchy complexion and a budding moustache. A siren? Not on your life."

"Poirot," I cried, as we took our departure. "A moustache. Did you hear?"

"I have the use of my ears, thank you, Hastings."

"But what a very unpleasant man."

"He has not the charming manner, no."

"Well, we ought to get the thief all right," I remarked. "We can identify him."

"You are of such a naïve simplicity, Hastings. Do you not know that there is such a thing as an alibi?"

"You think he will have an alibi?"

Poirot replied unexpectedly: "I sincerely hope so."

"The trouble with you is," I said, "that you like a thing to be difficult."

"Quite right, *mon ami*. I do not like — how do you say it — the bird who sits!"

Poirot's prophecy was fully justified. Our travelling companion in the brown suit turned out to be a Mr. Norton Kane. He had gone straight to the George Hotel at Monkhampton and had been there during the afternoon. The only evidence against him was that of Miss Durrant, who declared that she had seen him getting out his luggage from the car while we were at lunch.

"Which in itself is not a suspicious act," said Poirot meditatively.

After that remark, he lapsed into silence and refused to discuss the matter any further, saying, when I pressed him, that he was thinking of moustaches in general, and that I should be well advised to do the same.

I discovered, however, that he had asked Joseph Aarons — with whom he spent the evening — to give him every detail possible about Mr. Baker Wood. As both men were staying at the same hotel, there was a chance of gleaning some stray crumbs of information. Whatever Poirot learned, he kept to himself, however.

Mary Durrant, after various interviews with the police, had returned to Ebermouth by an early morning train. We lunched with Joseph Aarons, and, after lunch, Poirot announced to me that he had settled the theatrical agent's problem satisfactorily, and that we could return to Ebermouth as soon as we liked. "But not by road, *mon ami*; we go by rail this time."

"Are you afraid of having your pocket picked, or of meeting another damsel in distress?"

"Both those affairs, Hastings, might happen to me on the train. No, I am in haste to be back in Ebermouth, because I want to proceed with our case."

"Our case?"

"But, yes, my friend. Mademoiselle Durrant appealed to me to help her. Because the matter is now in the hands of the police, it does not follow that I am free to wash my hands of it. I came here to oblige an old friend, but it shall never be said of Hercule Poirot that he deserted a stranger in need!" And he drew himself up grandiloquently.

"I think you were interested before that," I said shrewdly. "In the office of cars, when you first caught sight of that young man, though what drew your attention to him I don't know."

"Don't you, Hastings? You should. Well, well, that must remain my little secret."

We had a short conversation with the police inspector in charge of the case before leaving. He had interviewed Mr. Norton Kane, and told Poirot in confidence that the young man's manner had not impressed him favourably. He had blustered, denied, and contradicted himself.

"But just how the trick was done, I don't know," he confessed. "He could have handed the stuff to a confederate who pushed off at once in a fast car. But that's just theory. We've got to find the car and the confederate and pin the thing down."

Poirot nodded thoughtfully.

"Do you think that was how it was done?" I asked him, as we were seated in the train.

"No, my friend, that was not how it was done. It was cleverer than that."

"Won't you tell me?"

"Not yet. You know — it is my weakness — I like to keep my little secrets till the end."

"Is the end going to be soon?"

"Very soon now."

We arrived in Ebermouth a little after six and Poirot drove at once to the shop which bore the name "Elizabeth Penn." The establishment was closed, but Poirot rang the bell, and presently Mary herself opened the door and expressed surprise and delight at seeing us.

"Please come in and see my aunt," she said.

She led us into a back room. An elderly lady came forward to meet us; she had white hair and looked rather like a miniature herself with her pink-and-white skin and her blue eyes. Round her rather bent shoulders she wore a cape of priceless old lace.

"Is this the great Monsieur Poirot?" she asked in a low charming voice. "Mary has been telling me. I could hardly believe it. And you will really help us in our trouble. You will advise us?"

Poirot looked at her for a moment, then bowed.

"Mademoiselle Penn — the effect is charming. But you should really grow a moustache."

Miss Penn gave a gasp and drew back.

"You were absent from business yesterday, were you not?"

"I was here in the morning. Later I had a bad headache and went directly home."

"Not home, mademoiselle. For your headache you tried the change of air, did you not? The air of Charlock Bay is very bracing, I believe."

He took me by the arm and drew me towards the door. He paused there and spoke over his shoulder.

"You comprehend, I know everything. This little — farce — it must cease."

There was a menace in his tone. Miss Penn, her face ghastly white, nodded mutely. Poirot turned to the girl.

"Mademoiselle," he said gently, "you are young and charming. But participating in these little affairs will lead to that youth and charm being hidden behind prison walls — and I, Hercule Poirot, tell you that that will be a pity."

Then he stepped out into the street and I followed him, bewildered.

"From the first, *mon ami,* I was interested. When that young man booked his place as far as Monkhampton only, I saw the girl's attention suddenly riveted on him. Now why? He was not of the type to make a woman look at him for himself alone. When we started on that coach, I had a feeling that something would happen. Who saw the young man tampering with the luggage? Mademoiselle and mademoiselle only, and remember she chose that seat — a seat facing the window — a most unfeminine choice."

"And then she comes to us with the tale of robbery — the despatch box forced which makes not the common sense, as I told you at the time."

"And what is the result of it all? Mr. Baker Wood has paid over good money for stolen goods. The miniatures will be returned to Miss Penn. She will sell them and will have made a thousand pounds instead of five hundred. I make the discreet inquiries and learn that her business is in a bad state — touch and go. I say to myself — the aunt and niece are in this together."

"Then you never suspected Norton Kane?"

"*Mon ami!* With that moustache? A criminal is either clean-shaven or he has a proper moustache that can be removed at will. But what an opportunity for the clever Miss Penn — a shrinking elderly lady with a pink-and-white complexion as we saw her. But if she holds herself erect, wears large boots, alters her complexion with a few unseemly blotches and — crowning touch — adds a few sparse hairs to her upper lip. What then? A masculine woman, says Wood and — 'a man in disguise' say we at once."

"She really went to Charlock yesterday?"

"Assuredly. The train, as you may remember telling me, left here at eleven and got to Charlock Bay at two o'clock. Then the return train is even quicker — the one we came by. It leaves Charlock at four-five and gets here at six-fifteen. Naturally, the miniatures were never in the despatch case at all. That was artistically forced before being packed. Mademoiselle Mary has only to find a couple of mugs who will be sympathetic to her charm and champion beauty in distress. But one of the mugs was no mug — he was Hercule Poirot!"

I hardly liked the inference. I said hurriedly: "Then, when you said you were helping a stranger, you were wilfully deceiving me. That's exactly what you were doing."

"Never do I deceive you, Hastings. I only permit you to deceive yourself. I was referring to Mr. Baker Wood — a stranger to these shores." His face darkened. "Ah! When I think of that imposition, that iniquitous overcharge, the same fare single to Charlock as return, my blood boils to protect the visitor! Not a pleasant man, Mr. Baker Wood, not, as you would say, sympathetic. But a visitor! And we visitors, Hastings, must stand together. Me, I am all for the visitors!"

QUESTIONS

1. What similarities and differences do you find between Hastings and Poirot? To what extent does our knowledge of the one help us to define the other?

2. Hastings is both narrator and actor in this story. What advantages and disadvantages lie in his dual role?

3. Hastings and Poirot witness the same things, but only Poirot recognizes their significance. Is this because Hastings is dull-witted? Are his misreadings traceable to his character? How closely do you identify with his point of view?

4. Which apparently insignificant details in the first half of "Double Sin" later turn out

to be important? What details of Poirot's personal habits and character turn out to have a bearing on the solution of the mystery?

5. Compare Poirot's methods with those of Sherlock Holmes. Do those methods grow out of the characters of the two detectives, or do they represent tricks of plot?

KATHERINE ANNE PORTER =====

Flowering Judas

Braggioni sits heaped upon the edge of a straight-backed chair much too small for him, and sings to Laura in a furry, mournful voice. Laura has begun to find reasons for avoiding her own house until the latest possible moment, for Braggioni is there almost every night. No matter how late she is, he will be sitting there with a surly, waiting expression, pulling at his kinky yellow hair, thumbing the strings of his guitar, snarling a tune under his breath. Lupe the Indian maid meets Laura at the door, and says with a flicker of a glance towards the upper room, "He waits."

Laura wishes to lie down, she is tired of her hairpins and the feel of her long tight sleeves, but she says to him, "Have you a new song for me this evening?" If he says yes, she asks him to sing it. If he says no, she remembers his favorite one, and asks him to sing it again. Lupe brings her a cup of chocolate and a plate of rice, and Laura eats at the small table under the lamp, first inviting Braggioni, whose answer is always the same: "I have eaten, and besides, chocolate thickens the voice."

Laura says, "Sing, then," and Braggioni heaves himself into song. He scratches the guitar familiarly as though it were a pet animal, and sings passionately off key, taking the high notes in a prolonged painful squeal. Laura, who haunts the markets listening to the ballad singers, and stops every day to hear the blind boy playing his reed-flute in Sixteenth of September Street, listens to Braggioni with pitiless courtesy, because she dares not smile at his miserable performance. Nobody dares to smile at him. Braggioni is cruel to everyone, with a kind of specialized insolence, but he is so vain of his talents, and so sensitive to slights, it would require a cruelty and vanity greater than his own to lay a finger on the vast cureless wound of his self-esteem. It would require courage, too, for it is dangerous to offend him, and nobody has this courage.

Braggioni loves himself with such tenderness and amplitude and eternal charity that his followers — for he is a leader of men, a skilled revolutionist, and his skin has been punctured in honorable warfare — warm themselves in the reflected glow, and say to each other: "He has a real nobility, a love of humanity raised above mere personal affections." The excess of this self-love has flowed out, inconveniently for her, over Laura, who, with so many others, owes her comfortable situation and her salary to him. When he is in a very good humor, he tells her, "I am tempted to forgive you for being a *gringa, gringita!*[1] and Laura, burning,

---

[1] Disparaging terms for an American woman.

510

imagines herself leaning forward suddenly, and with a sound back-handed slap wiping the suety smile from his face. If he notices her eyes at these moments he gives no sign.

She knows what Braggioni would offer her, and she must resist tenaciously without appearing to resist, and if she could avoid it she would not admit even to herself the slow drift of his intention. During these long evenings which have spoiled a long month for her, she sits in her deep chair with an open book on her knees, resting her eyes on the consoling rigidity of the printed page when the sight and sound of Braggioni singing threaten to identify themselves with all her remembered afflictions and to add their weight to her uneasy premonitions of the future. The gluttonous bulk of Braggioni has become a symbol of her many disillusions, for a revolutionist should be lean, animated by heroic faith, a vessel of abstract virtues. This is nonsense, she knows it now and is ashamed of it. Revolution must have leaders, and leadership is a career for energetic men. She is, her comrades tell her, full of romantic error, for what she defines as cynicism in them is merely "a developed sense of reality." She is almost too willing to say, "I am wrong, I suppose I don't really understand the principles," and afterward she makes a secret truce with herself, determined not to surrender her will to such expedient logic. But she cannot help feeling that she has been betrayed irreparably by the disunion between her way of living and her feeling of what life should be, and at times she is almost contented to rest in this sense of grievance as a private store of consolation. Sometimes she wishes to run away, but she stays. Now she longs to fly out of this room, down the narrow stairs, and into the street where the houses lean together like conspirators under a single mottled lamp, and leave Braggioni singing to himself.

Instead she looks at Braggioni, frankly and clearly, like a good child who understands the rules of behavior. Her knees cling together under sound blue serge, and her round white collar is not purposely nun-like. She wears the uniform of an idea, and has renounced vanities. She was born Roman Catholic, and in spite of her fear of being seen by someone who might make a scandal of it, she slips now and again into some crumbling little church, kneels on the chilly stone, and says a Hail Mary on the gold rosary she bought in Tehuantepec. It is no good and she ends by examining the altar with its tinsel flowers and ragged brocades, and feels tender about the battered doll-shape of some male saint whose white, lace-trimmed drawers hang limply around his ankles below the hieratic dignity of his velvet robe. She has encased herself in a set of principles derived from her early training, leaving no detail of gesture or of personal taste untouched, and for this reason she will not wear lace made on machines. This is her private heresy, for in her special group the machine is sacred, and will be the salvation of the workers. She loves fine lace, and there is a tiny edge of fluted cobweb on this collar, which is one of twenty precisely alike, folded in blue tissue paper in the upper drawer of her clothes chest.

Braggioni catches her glance solidly as if he had been waiting for it, leans forward, balancing his paunch between his spread knees, and sings with tremendous emphasis, weighing his words. He has, the song relates, no father and no mother, nor even a friend to console him; lonely as a wave of the sea he comes and goes, lonely as a wave. His mouth opens round and yearns sideways, his balloon cheeks grow oily with the labor of song. He bulges marvelously in his expensive garments. Over his lavender collar, crushed upon a purple necktie, held by a diamond hoop: over his ammunition belt of tooled leather worked in silver, buckled cruelly around his gasping middle: over the tops of his glossy yellow shoes Braggioni swells with ominous ripeness, his mauve silk hose stretched taut, his ankles bound with the stout leather thongs of his shoes.

When he stretches his eyelids at Laura she notes again that his eyes are the true tawny yellow cat's eyes. He is rich, not in money, he tells her, but in power, and this power brings with it the blameless ownership of things, and the right to indulge his love of small luxuries.

"I have a taste for the elegant refinements," he said once, flourishing a yellow silk handkerchief before her nose. "Smell that? It is Jockey Club, imported from New York." Nonetheless he is wounded by life. He will say so presently. "It is true everything turns to dust in the hand, to gall on the tongue." He sighs and his leather belt creaks like a saddle girth. "I am disappointed in everything as it comes. Everything." He shakes his head. "You, poor thing, you will be disappointed too. You are born for it. We are more alike than you realize in some things. Wait and see. Some day you will remember what I have told you, you will know that Braggioni was your friend."

Laura feels a slow chill, a purely physical sense of danger, a warning in her blood that violence, mutilation, a shocking death, wait for her with lessening patience. She has translated this fear into something homely, immediate, and sometimes hesitates before crossing the street. "My personal fate is nothing, except as the testimony of a mental attitude," she reminds herself, quoting from some forgotten philosophic primer, and is sensible enough to add, "Anyhow, I shall not be killed by an automobile if I can help it."

"It may be true I am as corrupt, in another way, as Braggioni," she thinks in spite of herself, "as callous, as incomplete," and if this is so, any kind of death seems preferable. Still she sits quietly, she does not run. Where could she go? Uninvited she has promised herself to this place; she can no longer imagine herself as living in another country, and there is no pleasure in remembering her life before she came here.

Precisely what is the nature of this devotion, its true motives, and what are its obligations? Laura cannot say. She spends part of her days in Xochimilco, near by, teaching Indian children to say in English, "The cat is on the mat." When she appears in the classroom they crowd about her with smiles on their wise, innocent, clay-colored faces, crying, "Good morning, my titcher!" in immaculate voices, and they make of her desk a fresh garden of flowers every day.

During her leisure she goes to union meetings and listens to busy important voices quarreling over tactics, methods, internal politics. She visits the prisoners of her own political faith in their cells, where they entertain themselves with counting cockroaches, repenting of their indiscretions, composing their memoirs, writing out manifestoes and plans for their comrades who are still walking about free, hands in pockets, sniffing fresh air. Laura brings them food and cigarettes and a little money, and she brings messages disguised in equivocal phrases from the men outside who dare not set foot in the prison for fear of disappearing into the cells kept empty for them. If the prisoners confuse night and day, and complain, "Dear little Laura, time doesn't pass in this infernal hole, and I won't know when it is time to sleep unless I have a reminder," she brings them their favorite narcotics, and says in a tone that does not wound them with pity, "Tonight will really be night for you," and though her Spanish amuses them they find her comforting, useful. If they lose patience and all faith, and curse the slowness of their friends in coming to their rescue with money and influence, they trust her not to repeat everything, and if she inquires, "Where do you think we can find money, or influence?" they are certain to answer, "Well, there is Braggioni, why doesn't he do something?"

She smuggles letters from headquarters to men hiding from firing squads in back streets in mildewed houses, where they sit in tumbled beds and talk bitterly as if all Mexico were at their heels, when Laura knows positively they might appear at the band concert in the Alameda on Sunday morning, and no one would notice them. But Braggioni says, "Let them sweat a little. The next time they may be careful. It is very restful to have them out of the way for a while." She is not afraid to knock on any door in any street after midnight, and enter in the darkness, and say to one of these men who is really in danger: "They will be looking for you — seriously — tomorrow morning after six. Here is some money from Vicente. Go to Vera Cruz and wait."

She borrows money from the Roumanian agitator to give to his bitter enemy the Polish agitator. The favor of Braggioni is their disputed territory, and Braggioni holds the balance nicely, for he can use them both. The Polish agitator talks love to her over café tables, hoping to exploit what he believes is her secret sentimental preference for him, and he gives her misinformation which he begs her to repeat as the solemn truth to certain persons. The Roumanian is more adroit. He is generous with his money in all good causes, and lies to her with an air of ingenuous candor, as if he were her good friend and confidant. She never repeats anything they may say. Braggioni never asks questions. He has other ways to discover all that he wishes to know about them.

Nobody touches her, but all praise her gray eyes, and the soft, round under lip which promises gayety, yet is always grave, nearly always firmly closed: and they cannot understand why she is in Mexico. She walks back and forth on her errands, with puzzled eyebrows, carrying her little folder of drawings and music and school papers. No dancer dances more beautifully than Laura walks, and she inspires some amusing, unexpected ardors, which cause little gossip, because nothing comes of them. A young captain who had been a soldier in Zapata's army attempted, during a horseback ride near Cuernavaca, to express his desire for her with the noble simplicity befitting a rude folk-hero: but gently, because he was gentle. This gentleness was his defeat, for when he alighted, and removed her foot from the stirrup, and essayed to draw her down into his arms, her horse, ordinarily a tame one, shied fiercely, reared and plunged away. The young hero's horse careened blindly after his stable-mate, and the hero did not return to the hotel until rather late that evening. At breakfast he came to her table in full charro dress, gray buckskin jacket and trousers with strings of silver buttons down the leg, and he was in a humorous, careless mood. "May I sit with you?" and "You are a wonderful rider. I was terrified that you might be thrown and dragged. I should never have forgiven myself. But I cannot admire you enough for your riding."

"I learned to ride in Arizona," said Laura.

"If you will ride with me again this morning, I promise you a horse that will not shy with you," he said. But Laura remembered that she must return to Mexico City at noon.

Next morning the children made a celebration and spent their playtime writing on the blackboard, "We lov ar titcher," and with tinted chalks they drew wreaths of flowers around the words. The young hero wrote her a letter: "I am a very foolish, wasteful, impulsive man. I should have first said I love you, and then you would not have run away. But you shall see me again." Laura thought, "I must send him a box of colored crayons," but she was trying to forgive herself for having spurred her horse at the wrong moment.

A brown shock-haired youth came and stood in her patio one night and sang like a lost soul for two hours, but Laura could think of nothing to do about it. The moonlight spread a wash of gauzy silver over the clear spaces of the garden, and the shadows were cobalt blue. The scarlet blossoms of the Judas tree[2] were dull purple, and the names of the colors repeated themselves automatically in her mind, while she watched not the boy, but his shadow, fallen like a dark garment across the fountain rim, trailing in the water. Lupe came silently and whispered expert counsel in her ear: "If you will throw him one little flower, he will sing another song or two and go away." Laura threw the flower, and he sang a last song and went away with the flower tucked in the band of his hat. Lupe said, "He is one of the organizers of

---

[2] *Cercis siliquastrum*, the purple-flowered tree on which legend says that Judas hanged himself after betraying Christ.

the Typographers Union, and before that he sold corridos[3] in the Merced market, and before that, he came from Guanajuato, where I was born. I would not trust any man, but I trust least those from Guanajuato."

She did not tell Laura that he would be back again the next day, and the next, nor that he would follow her at a certain fixed distance around the Merced market, through the Zocolo, up Francesco I. Madero Avenue, and so along the Paseo de la Reforma to Chapultepec Park, and into the Philosopher's Footpath, still with that flower withering in his hat, and an indivisible attention in his eyes.

Now Laura is accustomed to him, it means nothing except that he is nineteen years old and is observing a convention with all propriety, as though it were founded on a law of nature, which in the end it might very well prove to be. He is beginning to write poems which he prints on a wooden press, and he leaves them stuck like handbills in her door. She is pleasantly disturbed by the abstract, unhurried watchfulness of his black eyes which will in time turn easily towards another object. She tells herself that throwing the flower was a mistake, for she is twenty-two years old and knows better; but she refuses to regret it, and persuades herself that her negation of all external events as they occur is a sign that she is gradually perfecting herself in the stoicism she strives to cultivate against that disaster she fears, though she cannot name it.

She is not at home in the world. Every day she teaches children who remain strangers to her, though she loves their tender round hands and their charming opportunistic savagery. She knocks at unfamiliar doors not knowing whether a friend or a stranger shall answer, and even if a known face emerges from the sour gloom of that unknown interior, still it is the face of a stranger. No matter what this stranger says to her, nor what her message to him, the very cells of her flesh reject knowledge and kinship in one monotonous word. No. No. No. She draws her strength from this one holy talismanic word which does not suffer her to be led into evil. Denying everything, she may walk anywhere in safety, she looks at everything without amazement.

No, repeats this firm unchanging voice of her blood; and she looks at Braggioni without amazement. He is a great man, he wishes to impress this simple girl who covers her great round breasts with thick dark cloth, and who hides long, invaluably beautiful legs under a heavy skirt. She is almost thin except for the incomprehensible fullness of her breasts, like a nursing mother's, and Braggioni, who considers himself a judge of women, speculates again on the puzzle of her notorious virginity, and takes the liberty of speech which she permits without a sign of modesty, indeed, without any sort of sign, which is disconcerting.

"You think you are so cold, *gringita!* Wait and see. You will surprise yourself someday! May I be there to advise you!" He stretches his eyelids at her, and his ill-humored cat's eyes waver in a separate glance for the two points of light marking the opposite ends of a smoothly drawn path between the swollen curve of her breasts. He is not put off by that blue serge, nor by her resolutely fixed gaze. There is all the time in the world. His cheeks are bellying with the wind of song. "O girl with the dark eyes," he sings, and reconsiders. "But yours are not dark. I can change all that. O girl with the green eyes, you have stolen my heart away." Then his mind wanders to the song, and Laura feels the weight of his attention being shifted elsewhere. Singing thus, he seems harmless, he is quite harmless, there is nothing to do but sit patiently and say "No," when the moment comes. She draws a full breath, and her mind wanders also, but not far. She dares not wander too far.

Not for nothing has Braggioni taken pains to be a good revolutionist and a professional

---

[3] Tickets to bullfights.

lover of humanity. He will never die of it. He has the malice, the cleverness, the wickedness, the sharpness of wit, the hardness of heart, stipulated for loving the world profitably. He *will never die of it*. He will live to see himself kicked out from his feeding trough by other hungry world-saviours. Traditionally he must sing in spite of his life which drives him to bloodshed, he tells Laura, for his father was a Tuscany peasant who drifted to Yucatan and married a Maya woman: a woman of race, an aristocrat. They gave him the love and knowledge of music, thus: and under the rip of his thumbnail, the strings of the instrument complain like exposed nerves.

Once he was called Delgadito by all the girls and married women who ran after him; he was so scrawny all his bones showed under his thin cotton clothing, and he could squeeze his emptiness to the very backbone with his two hands. He was a poet and the revolution was only a dream then; too many women loved him and sapped away his youth, and he could never find enough to eat anywhere, anywhere! Now he is a leader of men, crafty men who whisper in his ear, hungry men who wait for hours outside his office for a word with him, emaciated men with wild faces who waylay him at the street gate with a timid, "Comrade, let me tell you ..." and they blow the foul breath from their empty stomachs in his face.

He is always sympathetic. He gives them handfuls of small coins from his own pockets, he promises them work, there will be demonstrations, they must join the unions and attend the meetings, above all they must be on the watch for spies. They are closer to him than his own brothers, without them he can do nothing — until tomorrow, comrade!

Until tomorrow. "They are stupid, they are lazy, they are treacherous, they would cut my throat for nothing," he says to Laura. He has good food and abundant drink, he hires an automobile and drives in the Paseo on Sunday morning, and enjoys plenty of sleep in a soft bed beside a wife who dares not disturb him; and he sits pampering his bones in easy billows of fat, singing to Laura, who knows and thinks these things about him. When he was fifteen, he tried to drown himself because he loved a girl, his first love, and she laughed at him. "A thousand women have paid for that," and his tight little mouth turns down at the corners. Now he perfumes his hair with Jockey Club, and confides to Laura: "One woman is really as good as another for me in the dark. I prefer them all."

His wife organizes unions among the girls in the cigarette factories, and walks in picket lines, and even speaks at meetings in the evening. But she cannot be brought to acknowledge the benefits of true liberty. "I tell her I must have my freedom, net. She does not understand my point of view." Laura has heard this many times. Braggioni scratches the guitar and meditates. "She is an instinctively virtuous woman, pure gold, no doubt of that. If she were not, I should lock her up, and she knows it."

His wife, who works so hard for the good of the factory girls, employs part of her leisure lying on the floor weeping because there are so many women in the world, and only one husband for her, and she never knows where nor when to look for him. He told her: "Unless you can learn to cry when I am not here, I must go away for good." That day he went away and took a room at the Hotel Madrid.

It is this month of separation for the sake of higher principles that has been spoiled not only for Mrs. Braggioni, whose sense of reality is beyond criticism, but for Laura, who feels herself bogged in a nightmare. Tonight Laura envies Mrs. Braggioni, who is alone, and free to weep as much as she pleases about a concrete wrong. Laura has just come from a visit to the prison, and she is waiting for tomorrow with a bitter anxiety as if tomorrow may not come, but time may be caught immovably in this hour, with herself transfixed, Braggioni singing on forever, and Eugenio's body not yet discovered by the guard.

Braggioni says: "Are you going to sleep?" Almost before she can shake her head, he begins telling her about the May-day disturbances coming on in Morelia, for the Catholics hold a festival in honor of the Blessed Virgin, and the Socialists celebrate their martyrs on that day. "There will be two independent processions, starting from either end of town, and they will march until they meet, and the rest depends ..." He asks her to oil and load his pistols. Standing up, he unbuckles his ammunition belt, and spreads it laden across her knees. Laura sits with the shells slipping through the cleaning cloth dipped in oil, and he says again he cannot understand why she works so hard for the revolutionary idea unless she loves some man who is in it. "Are you not in love with someone?" "No," says Laura. "And no one is in love with you?" "No." "Then it is your own fault. No woman need go begging. Why, what is the matter with you? The legless beggar woman in the Alameda has a perfectly faithful lover. Did you know that?"

Laura peers down the pistol barrel and says nothing, but a long, slow faintness rises and subsides in her; Braggioni curves his swollen fingers around the throat of the guitar and softly smothers the music out of it, and when she hears him again he seems to have forgotten her, and is speaking in the hypnotic voice he uses when talking in small rooms to a listening, close-gathered crowd. Some day this world, now seemingly so composed and eternal, to the edges of every sea shall be merely a tangle of gaping trenches, of crashing walls and broken bodies. Everything must be torn from its accustomed place where it has rotted for centuries, hurled skyward and distributed, cast down again clean as rain, without separate identity. Nothing shall survive that the stiffened hands of poverty have created for the rich and no one shall be left alive except the elect spirits destined to procreate a new world cleansed of cruelty and injustice, ruled by benevolent anarchy: "Pistols are good, I love them, cannon are even better, but in the end I pin my faith to good dynamite," he concludes, and strokes the pistol lying in her hands. "Once I dreamed of destroying this city, in case it offered resistance to General Ortiz, but it fell into his hands like an overripe pear."

He is made restless by his own words, rises and stands waiting. Laura holds up the belt to him: "Put that on, and go kill somebody in Morelia, and you will be happier," she says softly. The presence of death in the room makes her bold. "Today, I found Eugenio going into a stupor. He refused to allow me to call the prison doctor. He had taken all the tablets I brought him yesterday. He said he took them because he was bored."

"He is a fool, and his death is his own business," says Braggioni, fastening his belt carefully.

"I told him if he had waited only a little while longer, you would have got him set free," says Laura. "He said he did not want to wait."

"He is a fool and we are well rid of him," says Braggioni, reaching for his hat.

He goes away. Laura knows his mood has changed, she will not see him anymore for a while. He will send word when he needs her to go on errands into strange streets, to speak to the strange faces that will appear, like clay masks with the power of human speech, to mutter their thanks to Braggioni for his help. Now she is free, and she thinks, I must run while there is time. But she does not go.

Braggioni enters his own house where for a month his wife has spent many hours every night weeping and tangling her hair upon her pillow. She is weeping now, and she weeps more at the sight of him, the cause of all her sorrows. He looks about the room. Nothing is changed, the smells are good and familiar, he is well acquainted with the woman who comes toward him with no reproach except grief on her face. He says to her tenderly: "You are so good, please don't cry any more, you dear good creature." She says, "Are you tired, my angel? Sit here and I will wash your feet." She brings a bowl of water, and kneeling, unlaces his shoes, and when from her knees she raises her sad eyes under her blackened lids, he is sorry for everything, and bursts into tears. "Ah, yes, I am hungry, I am tired, let us eat something together," he says, between sobs. His wife leans her head on his arm and says, "Forgive me!" and this time he is refreshed by the solemn, endless rain of her tears.

Laura takes off her serge dress and puts on a white linen nightgown and goes to bed. She turns her head a little to one side, and lying still, reminds herself that it is time to sleep. Numbers tick in her brain like little clocks, soundless doors close of themselves around her. If you would sleep, you must not remember anything, the children will say tomorrow, good morning, my teacher, the poor prisoners who come every day bringing flowers to their jailor. 1–2–3–4–5 — it is monstrous to confuse love with revolution, night with day, life with death — ah Eugenio!

The tolling of the midnight bell is a signal, but what does it mean? Get up, Laura, and follow me: come out of your sleep, out of your bed, out of this strange house. What are you doing in this house? Without a word, without fear she rose and reached for Eugenio's hand, but he eluded her with a sharp, sly smile and drifted away. This is not all, you shall see — Murderer, he said, follow me, I will show you a new country, but it is far away and we must hurry. No, said Laura, not unless you take my hand, no; and she clung first to the stair rail, and then to the topmost branch of the Judas tree that bent down slowly and set her upon the earth, and then to the rocky ledge of a cliff, and then to the jagged wave of a sea that was not water but a desert of crumbling stone. Where are you taking me? she asked in wonder but without fear. To death, and it is a long way off, and we must hurry, said Eugenio. No, said Laura, not unless you take my hand. Then eat these flowers, poor prisoner, said Eugenio in a voice of pity, take and eat: and from the Judas tree he stripped the warm bleeding flowers, and held them to her lips. She saw that his hand was fleshless, a cluster of small white petrified branches, and his eye sockets were without light, but she ate the flowers greedily for they satisfied both hunger and thirst. Murderer! said Eugenio, and Cannibal! This is my body and my blood. Laura cried No! and at the sound of her own voice, she awoke trembling, and was afraid to sleep again.

QUESTIONS

1. What are the differences between Laura's attitude toward Braggioni and her attitude toward Eugenio? Are there any points of similarity?

2. What does it mean that Braggioni "has ... taken pains to be a good revolutionist and a professional lover of humanity"? Does his wife understand this? Why does she weep?

3. Laura is "perfecting herself in the stoicism she strives to cultivate against that disaster she fears, though she cannot name it." Do the events of the story show that she has succeeded?

4. What does her relationship with the school children tell you about Laura's character? Her relationship with the prisoners?

5. Many of Porter's stories grow out of her strong religious sense, and "Flowering Judas" invites allegorical interpretation. Braggioni's wife washes his feet, as Mary Magdalen washed Christ's. In Laura's dream, Eugenio speaks Christ's words, "This is my body and my blood." Are both Braggioni and Eugenio Savior symbols? Does the title lead us to look for correspondences with the Last Supper and the betrayal of Jesus? Are we to equate Laura with Judas?

DOROTHY PARKER

You Were Perfectly Fine

The pale young man eased himself carefully into the low chair, and rolled his head to the side, so that the cool chintz comforted his cheek and temple.

"Oh, dear," he said. "Oh, dear, oh, dear, oh, dear. Oh."

The clear-eyed girl, sitting light and erect on the couch, smiled brightly at him.

"Not feeling so well today?" she said.

"Oh, I'm great," he said. "Corking, I am. Know what time I got up? Four o'clock this afternoon, sharp. I kept trying to make it, and every time I took my head off the pillow, it would roll under the bed. This isn't my head I've got on now. I think this is something that used to belong to Walt Whitman. Oh, dear, oh, dear, oh, dear."

"Do you think maybe a drink would make you feel better?" she said.

"The hair of the mastiff that bit me?" he said. "Oh, no thank you. Please never speak of anything like that again. I'm through. I'm all, all through. Look at that hand; steady as a humming-bird. Tell me, was I very terrible last night?"

"Oh, goodness," she said, "everybody was feeling pretty high. You were all right."

"Yeah," he said. "I must have been dandy. Is everybody sore at me?"

"Good heavens, no," she said. "Everyone thought you were terribly funny. Of course, Jim Pierson was a little stuffy, there for a minute at dinner. But people sort of held him back in his chair, and got him calmed down. I don't think anybody at the other tables noticed it at all. Hardly anybody."

"He was going to sock me?" he said. "Oh, Lord. What did I do to him?"

"Why, you didn't do a thing," she said. "You were perfectly fine. But you know how silly Jim gets, when he thinks anybody is making too much fuss over Elinor."

"Was I making a pass at Elinor?" he said. "Did I do that?"

"Of course you didn't," she said. "You were only fooling, that's all. She thought you were awfully amusing. She was having a marvelous time. She only got a little tiny bit annoyed just once, when you poured the clam-juice down her back."

"My God," he said. "Clam-juice down that back. And every vertebra a little Cabot. Dear God. What'll I ever do?"

"Oh, she'll be all right," she said. "Just send her some flowers, or something. Don't worry about it. It isn't anything."

518

"No, I won't worry," he said. "I haven't got a care in the world. I'm sitting pretty. Oh, dear, oh, dear. Did I do any other fascinating tricks at dinner?"

"You were fine," she said. "Don't be so foolish about it. Everybody was crazy about you. The maître d'hôtel was a little worried because you wouldn't stop singing, but he really didn't mind. All he said was, he was afraid they'd close the place again, if there was so much noise. But he didn't care a bit, himself. I think he loved seeing you have such a good time. Oh, you were just singing away, there, for about an hour. It wasn't so terribly loud, at all."

"So I sang," he said. "That must have been a treat. I sang."

"Don't you remember?" she said. "You just sang one song after another. Everybody in the place was listening. They loved it. Only you kept insisting that you wanted to sing some song about some kind of fusiliers or other, and everybody kept shushing you, and you'd keep trying to start it again. You were wonderful. We were all trying to make you stop singing for a minute, and eat something, but you wouldn't hear of it. My, you were funny."

"Didn't I eat any dinner?" he said.

"Oh, not a thing," she said. "Every time the waiter would offer you something, you'd give it right back to him, because you said that he was your long-lost brother, changed in the cradle by a gypsy band, and that anything you had was his. You had him simply roaring at you."

"I bet I did," he said. "I bet I was comical. Society's Pet, I must have been. And what happened then, after my overwhelming success with the waiter?"

"Why, nothing much," she said. "You took a sort of dislike to some old man with white hair, sitting across the room, because you didn't like his necktie and you wanted to tell him about it. But we got you out, before he got really mad."

"Oh, we got out," he said. "Did I walk?"

"Walk! Of course you did," she said. "You were absolutely all right. There was that nasty stretch of ice on the sidewalk, and you did sit down awfully hard, you poor dear. But good heavens, that might have happened to anybody."

"Oh, sure," he said. "Louisa Alcott[1] or anybody. So I fell down on the sidewalk. That would explain what's the matter with my — Yes. I see. And then what, if you don't mind?"

"Ah, now, Peter!" she said. "You can't sit there and say you don't remember what happened after that! I did think that maybe you were just a little tight at dinner — oh, you were perfectly all right, and all that, but I did know you were feeling pretty gay. But you were so serious, from the time you fell down — I never knew you to be that way. Don't you know, how you told me I had never seen your real self before? Oh, Peter, I just couldn't bear it, if you didn't remember that lovely long ride we took together in the taxi! Please, you do remember that, don't you? I think it would simply kill me, if you didn't.

"Oh, yes," he said. "Riding in the taxi. Oh, yes, sure. Pretty long ride, hmm?"

"Round and round and round the park," she said. "Oh, and the trees were shining so in the moonlight. And you said you never knew before that you really had a soul."

"Yes," he said. "I said that. That was me."

"You said such lovely, lovely things," she said. "And I'd never known, all this time, how you had been feeling about me, and I'd never dared to let you see how I felt about you. And then last night — oh, Peter dear, I think that taxi ride was the most important thing that ever happened to us in in our lives."

"Yes," he said. "I guess it must have been."

"And we're going to be so happy," she said. "Oh, I just want to tell everybody! But I don't know — I think maybe it would be sweeter to keep it all to ourselves."

---

[1] The author of *Little Women* and other proper books for children.

"I think it would be," he said.

"Isn't it lovely?" she said.

"Yes," he said. "Great."

"Lovely!" she said.

"Look here," he said, "do you mind if I have a drink? I mean, just medicinally, you know. I'm off the stuff for life, so help me. But I think I feel a collapse coming on."

"Oh, I think it would do you good," she said. "You poor boy, it's a shame you feel so awful. I'll go make you a whiskey and soda."

"Honestly," he said, "I don't see how you could ever want to speak to me again, after I made such a fool of myself, last night. I think I'd better go join a monastery in Tibet."

"You crazy idiot!" she said. "As if I could ever let you go away now! Stop talking like that. You were perfectly fine."

She jumped up from the couch, kissed him quickly on the forehead, and ran out of the room.

The pale young man looked after her and shook his head long and slowly, then dropped it in his damp and trembling hands.

"Oh, dear," he said. "Oh, dear, oh, dear, oh, dear."

QUESTIONS

1. Like the "pale young man," we learn the story of last night a bit at a time. We are more nearly in his shoes than in those of the "clear-eyed girl." How does this fact affect your response to the story?

2. This is an example of objective, third-person narration. We do not enter the mind of either character, and we are not told how to take the story. We know that the young man has a hangover, but can we be certain that he has forgotten the events of the night before? Are we sure that the girl is telling the truth?

3. What is his attitude towards her? What does the dialogue suggest about her?

4. Does the story's irony depend upon *what* the girl says or upon the *way* she says it?

5. At first, the young man declines a drink. Later, he asks for one. What changed his mind? What does this change tell you?

JAMES THURBER

The Secret Life of Walter Mitty

"We're going through!" The Commander's voice was like thin ice breaking. He wore his full-dress uniform, with the heavily braided white cap pulled down rakishly over one cold gray eye. "We can't make it, sir. It's spoiling for a hurricane, if you ask me." "I'm not asking you, Lieutenant Berg," said the Commander. "Throw on the power light! Rev her up to 8,500! We're going through!" The pounding of the cylinders increased: ta-pocketa-pocketa-pocketa-*pocketa-pocketa*. The Commander stared at the ice forming on the pilot window. He walked over and twisted a row of complicated dials. "Switch on No. 8 auxiliary!" he shouted. "Switch on No. 8 auxiliary!" repeated Lieutenant Berg. "Full strength in No. 3 turret!" shouted the Commander. "Full strength in No. 3 turret!" The crew, bending to their various tasks in the huge, hurtling eight-engined Navy hydroplane, looked at each other and grinned. "The Old Man'll get us through," they said to one another. "The Old Man ain't afraid of Hell!" ...

"Not so fast! You're driving too fast!" said Mrs. Mitty. "What are you driving so fast for?"

"Hmm?" said Walter Mitty. He looked at his wife, in the seat beside him, with shocked astonishment. She seemed grossly unfamiliar, like a strange woman who had yelled at him in a crowd. "You were up to fifty-five," she said. "You know I don't like to go more than forty. You were up to fifty-five." Walter Mitty drove on toward Waterbury in silence, the roaring of the SN202 through the worst storm in twenty years of Navy flying fading in the remote, intimate airways of his mind. "You're tensed up again," said Mrs. Mitty. "It's one of your days. I wish you'd let Dr. Renshaw look you over."

Walter Mitty stopped the car in front of the building where his wife went to have her hair done. "Remember to get those overshoes while I'm having my hair done," she said. "I don't need overshoes," said Mitty. She put her mirror back into her bag. "We've been all through that," she said, getting out of the car. "You're not a young man any longer." He raced the engine a little. "Why don't you wear your gloves? Have you lost your gloves?" Walter Mitty reached in a pocket and brought out the gloves. He put them on, but after she had turned and gone into the building and he had driven on to a red light, he took them off again. "Pick it up, brother!" snapped a cop as the light changed, and Mitty hastily pulled on his gloves and lurched ahead. He drove around the streets aimlessly for a time, and then he drove past the hospital on his way to the parking lot.

...“It’s the millionaire banker, Wellington McMillan,” said the pretty nurse. “Yes?” said Walter Mitty, removing his gloves slowly. “Who has the case?” “Dr. Renshaw and Dr. Benbow, but there are two specialists here, Dr. Remington from New York and Mr. Pritchard-Mitford from London. He flew over.” A door opened down a long, cool corridor and Dr. Renshaw came out. He looked distraught and haggard. “Hello, Mitty,” he said. “We’re having the devil’s own time with McMillan, the millionaire banker and close personal friend of Roosevelt. Obstreosis of the ductal tract. Tertiary. Wish you’d take a look at him.” “Glad to,” said Mitty.

In the operating room there were whispered introductions: “Dr. Remington, Dr. Mitty. Mr. Pritchard-Mitford, Dr. Mitty.” “I’ve read your book on streptothricosis,” said Pritchard-Mitford, shaking hands. “A brilliant performance, sir.” “Thank you,” said Walter Mitty. “Didn’t know you were in the States, Mitty,” grumbled Remington. “Coals to Newcastle, bringing Mitford and me up here for a tertiary.” “You are very kind,” said Mitty. A huge, complicated machine, connected to the operating table, with many tubes and wires, began at this moment to go pocketa-pocketa-pocketa. “The new anesthetizer is giving way!” shouted an intern. “There is no one in the East who knows how to fix it!” “Quiet, man!” said Mitty, in a low, cool voice. He sprang to the machine, which was now going pocketa-pocketa-queep-pocketa-queep. He began fingering delicately a row of glistening dials. “Give me a fountain pen!” he snapped. Someone handed him a fountain pen. He pulled a faulty piston out of the machine and inserted the pen in its place. “That will hold for ten minutes,” he said. “Get on with the operation.” A nurse hurried over and whispered to Renshaw, and Mitty saw the man turn pale. “Coreopsis has set in,” said Renshaw nervously. “If you would take over, Mitty?” Mitty looked at him and at the craven figure of Benbow, who drank, and at the grave, uncertain faces of the two great specialists. “If you wish,” he said. They slipped a white gown on him; he adjusted a mask and drew on thin gloves; nurses handed him shining ...

“Back it up, Mac! Look out for that Buick!” Walter Mitty jammed on the brakes. “Wrong lane, Mac,” said the parking-lot attendant, looking at Mitty closely. “Gee, Yeh,” muttered Mitty. He began cautiously to back out of the lane marked “Exit Only.” “Leave her sit there,” said the attendant. “I’ll put her away.” Mitty got out of the car. “Hey, better leave the key.” “Oh,” said Mitty, handing the man the ignition key. The attendant vaulted into the car, backed it up with insolent skill, and put it where it belonged.

They’re so damn cocky, thought Walter Mitty, walking along Main Street; they think they know everything. Once he had tried to take his chains off, outside New Milford, and he had got them wound around the axles. A man had had to come out in a wrecking car and unwind them, a young, grinning garageman. Since then Mrs. Mitty always made him drive to a garage to have the chains taken off. The next time, he thought, I’ll wear my right arm in a sling; they won’t grin at me then. I’ll have my right arm in a sling and they’ll see I couldn’t possibly take the chains off myself. He kicked at the slush on the sidewalk. “Overshoes,” he said to himself, and he began looking for a shoe store.

When he came out into the street again, with the overshoes in a box under his arm, Walter Mitty began to wonder what the other thing was his wife had told him to get. She had told him twice, before they set out from their house for Waterbury. In a way he hated these weekly trips to town — he was always getting something wrong. Kleenex, he thought, Squibb’s, razor blades? No. Toothpaste, toothbrush, bicarbonate, carborundum, initiative and referendum? He gave it up. But she would remember it. “Where’s the what’s-its-name?”

she would ask. "Don't tell me you forgot the what's-its-name." A newsboy went by shouting something about the Waterbury trial.

...."Perhaps this will refresh your memory." The District Attorney suddenly thrust a heavy automatic at the quiet figure on the witness stand. "Have you ever seen this before?" Walter Mitty took the gun and examined it expertly. "This is my Webley-Vickers 50.80," he said calmly. An excited buzz ran around the courtroom. The judge rapped for order. "You are a crack shot with any sort of firearms, I believe?" said the District Attorney, insinuatingly. "Objection!" shouted Mitty's attorney. "We have shown that the defendant could not have fired the shot. We have shown that he wore his right arm in a sling on the night of the fourteenth of July." Walter Mitty raised his hand briefly and the bickering attorneys were stilled. "With any known make of gun," he said evenly, "I could have killed Gregory Fitzhurst at three hundred feet *with my left hand*." Pandemonium broke loose in the courtroom. A woman's scream rose above the bedlam and suddenly a lovely, dark-haired girl was in Walter Mitty's arms. The District Attorney struck at her savagely. Without rising from his chair, Mitty let the man have it on the point of the chin. "You miserable cur!" ...

"Puppy biscuit," said Walter Mitty. He stopped walking and the buildings of Waterbury rose up out of the misty courtroom and surrounded him again. A woman who was passing laughed. "He said 'Puppy biscuit,'" she said to her companion. "That man said 'Puppy biscuit' to himself." Walter Mitty hurried on. He went into an A. & P., not the first one he came to but a smaller one farther up the street. "I want some biscuit for small, young dogs," he said to the clerk. "Any special brand, sir?" The greatest pistol shot in the world thought a moment. "It says 'Puppies Bark for It' on the box," said Walter Mitty.

His wife would be through at the hairdresser's in fifteen minutes, Mitty saw in looking at his watch, unless they had trouble drying it; sometimes they had trouble drying it. She didn't like to get to the hotel first; she would want him to be there waiting for her as usual. He found a big leather chair in the lobby, facing a window, and he put the overshoes and the puppy biscuit on the floor beside it. He picked up an old copy of *Liberty* and sank down into the chair. "Can Germany Conquer the World Through the Air?" Walter Mitty looked at the pictures of bombing planes and of ruined streets.

...."The cannonading has got the wind up in young Raleigh, sir," said the sergeant. Captain Mitty looked up at him through tousled hair. "Get him to bed," he said wearily. "With the others. I'll fly alone." "But you can't, sir," said the sergeant anxiously. "It takes two men to handle that bomber and the Archies are pounding hell out of the air. Von Richtman's circus is between here and Saulier." "Somebody's got to get that ammunition dump," said Mitty. "I'm going over. Spot of brandy?" He poured a drink for the sergeant and one for himself. War thundered and whined around the dugout and battered at the door. There was a rending of wood and splinters flew through the room. "A bit of a near thing," said Captain Mitty carelessly. "The box barrage is closing in," said the sergeant. "We only live once, Sergeant," said Mitty, with his faint, fleeting smile. "Or do we?" He poured another brandy and tossed it off. "I never see a man could hold his brandy like you, sir," said the sergeant. "Begging your pardon, sir." Captain Mitty stood up and strapped on his huge Webley-Vickers automatic. "It's forty kilometers through hell, sir," said the sergeant. Mitty finished one last brandy. "After all," he said softly, "what isn't?" The pounding of the cannon increased; there was the rat-tat-tatting of machine guns, and from somewhere came the menacing pocketa-pocketa-pocketa of the new flame throwers. Walter Mitty walked to the door of the dugout humming "Auprès de Ma Blonde." He turned and waved to the sergeant. "Cheerio!" he said. ...

Something struck his shoulder. "I've been looking all over this hotel for you," said Mrs.

Mitty. "Why do you have to hide in this old chair? How did you expect me to find you?" "Things close in," said Walter Mitty vaguely. "What?" Mrs. Mitty said. "Did you get the what's-its-name? The puppy biscuit? What's in that box?" "Overshoes," said Mitty. "Couldn't you have put them on in the store?" "I was thinking," said Walter Mitty. "Does it ever occur to you that I am sometimes thinking?" She looked at him. "I'm going to take your temperature when I get you home," she said.

They went out through the revolving doors that made a faintly derisive whistling sound when you pushed them. It was two blocks to the parking lot. At the drugstore on the corner she said, "Wait here for me. I forgot something. I won't be a minute." She was more than a minute. Walter Mitty lighted a cigarette. It began to rain, rain with sleet in it. He stood up against the wall of the drugstore, smoking. ...He put his shoulders back and his heels together. "To hell with the handkerchief," said Walter Mitty scornfully. He took one last drag on his cigarette and snapped it away. Then, with that faint, fleeting smile playing about his lips, he faced the firing squad; erect and motionless, proud and disdainful, Walter Mitty the Undefeated, inscrutable to the last.

QUESTIONS

1. What is the effect of Thurber's inventing such medical problems as "obstreosis" and "streptothricosis"? What difference would it have made had he used difficult names of real diseases?

2. There is a pattern to the alternation of "dream" and "reality" sequences. Is there also a pattern to the shifts in tone? Can you describe it?

3. Why will Mitty wear his arm in a sling?

4. What logical links can you find between Mitty's experiences and his fantasies? Do these seem plausible?

5. How well do the Mittys understand each other? To what extent can you argue that Mitty's marriage is the real focal point of this story?

6. Thurber's humor arises from many causes. How would you weight character, tone, invention, and incident in terms of their contribution to the humor of "The Secret Life of Walter Mitty"?

F. SCOTT FITZGERALD

Babylon Revisited

I

"And where's Mr. Campbell?" Charlie asked.

"Gone to Switzerland. Mr. Campbell's a pretty sick man, Mr. Wales."

"I'm sorry to hear that. And George Hardt?" Charlie inquired.

"Back in America, gone to work."

"And where is the Snow Bird?"

"He was in here last week. Anyway, his friend, Mr. Schaeffer, is in Paris."

Two familiar names from the long list of a year and a half ago. Charlie scribbled an address in his notebook and tore out the page.

"If you see Mr. Schaeffer, give him this," he said. "It's my brother-in-law's address. I haven't settled on a hotel yet."

He was not really disappointed to find Paris was so empty. But the stillness in the Ritz bar was strange and portentous. It was not an American bar any more — he felt polite in it, and not as if he owned it. It had gone back into France. He felt the stillness from the moment he got out of the taxi and saw the doorman, usually in a frenzy of activity at this hour, gossiping with a *chasseur*[1] by the servants' entrance.

Passing through the corridor, he heard only a single, bored voice in the once-clamorous women's room. When he turned into the bar he traveled the twenty feet of green carpet with his eyes fixed straight ahead by old habit; and then, with his foot firmly on the rail, he turned and surveyed the room, encountering only a single pair of eyes that fluttered up from a newspaper in the corner. Charlie asked for the head barman, Paul, who in the latter days of the bull market had come to work in his own custom-built car — disembarking, however, with due nicety at the nearest corner. But Paul was at his country house today and Alix giving him information.

"No, no more," Charlie said, "I'm going slow these days."

Alix congratulated him: "You were going pretty strong a couple of years ago."

"I'll stick to it all right," Charlie assured him. "I've stuck to it for over a year and a half now."

---

[1] A footman.

"How do you find conditions in America?"

"I haven't been to America for months. I'm in business in Prague, representing a couple of concerns there. They don't know about me down there."

Alix smiled.

"Remember the night of George Hardt's bachelor dinner here?" said Charlie. "By the way, what's become of Claude Fessenden?"

Alix lowered his voice confidentially: "He's in Paris, but he doesn't come here any more. Paul doesn't allow it. He ran up a bill of thirty thousand francs, charging all his drinks and his lunches, and usually his dinner, for more than a year. And when Paul finally told him he had to pay, he gave him a bad check."

Alix shook his head sadly.

"I don't understand it, such a dandy fellow. Now he's all bloated up — " He made a plump apple of his hands.

Charlie watched a group of strident queens installing themselves in a corner.

"Nothing affects them," he thought. "Stocks rise and fall, people loaf or work, but they go on forever." The place oppressed him. He called for the dice and shook with Alix for the drink.

"Here for long, Mr. Wales?"

"I'm here for four or five days to see my little girl."

"Oh-h! You have a little girl?"

Outside, the fire-red, gas-blue, ghost-green signs shone smokily through the tranquil rain. It was late afternoon and the streets were in movement; the *bistros*[2] gleamed. At the corner of the Boulevard des Capucines he took a taxi. The Place de la Concorde moved by in pink majesty; they crossed the logical Seine, and Charlie felt the sudden provincial quality of the Left Bank.

Charlie directed his taxi to the Avenue de l'Opera, which was out of his way. But he wanted to see the blue hour spread over the magnificent façade, and imagine that the cab horns, playing endlessly the first few bars of *Le Plus que Lent*,[3] were the trumpets of the Second Empire. They were closing the iron grill in front of Brentano's Book-store, and people were already at dinner behind the trim little bourgeois hedge of Duval's. He had never eaten at a really cheap restaurant in Paris. Five-course dinner, four francs fifty, eighteen cents, wine included. For some odd reason he wished that he had.

As they rolled on to the Left Bank and he felt its sudden provincialism, he thought, "I spoiled this city for myself. I didn't realize it, but the days came along one after another, and then two years were gone, and everything was gone, and I was gone."

He was thirty-five, and good to look at. The Irish mobility of his face was sobered by a deep wrinkle between his eyes. As he rang his brother-in-law's bell in the Rue Palatine, the wrinkle deepened till it pulled down his brows; he felt a cramping sensation in his belly. From behind the maid who opened the door darted a lovely little girl of nine who shrieked "Daddy!" and flew up, struggling like a fish, into his arms. She pulled his head around by one ear and set her cheek against his.

"My old pie," he said.

"Oh, daddy, daddy, daddy, daddy, dads, dads, dads!"

She drew him into the salon, where the family waited, a boy and a girl his daughter's

---

[2] Pubs.

[3] "Slower than Slow" — from a Debussy composition.

age, his sister-in-law and her husband. He greeted Marion with his voice pitched carefully to avoid either feigned enthusiasm or dislike, but her response was more frankly tepid, though she minimized her expression of unalterable distrust by directing her regard toward his child. The two men clasped hands in a friendly way and Lincoln Peters rested his for a moment on Charlie's shoulder.

The room was warm and comfortably American. The three children moved intimately about, playing through the yellow oblongs that led to other rooms; the cheer of six o'clock spoke in the eager smacks of the fire and the sounds of French activity in the kitchen. But Charlie did not relax; his heart sat up rigidly in his body and he drew confidence from his daughter, who from time to time came close to him, holding in her arms the doll he had brought.

"Really extremely well," he declared in answer to Lincoln's question. "There's a lot of business there that isn't moving at all, but we're doing even better than ever. In fact, damn well. I'm bringing my sister over from America next month to keep house for me. My income last year was bigger than it was when I had money. You see, the Czechs —— "

His boasting was for a specific purpose; but after a moment, seeing a faint restiveness in Lincoln's eye, he changed the subject:

"Those are fine children of yours, well brought up, good manners."

"We think Honoria's a great little girl too."

Marion Peters came back from the kitchen. She was a tall woman with worried eyes, who had once possessed a fresh American loveliness. Charlie had never been sensitive to it and was always surprised when people spoke of how pretty she had been. From the first there had been an instinctive antipathy between them.

"Well, how do you find Honoria?" she asked.

"Wonderful. I was astonished how much she's grown in ten months. All the children are looking well."

"We haven't had a doctor for a year. How do you like being back in Paris?"

"It seems very funny to see so few Americans around."

"I'm delighted," Marion said vehemently. "Now at least you can go into a store without their assuming you're a millionaire. We've suffered like everybody, but on the whole it's a good deal pleasanter."

"But it was nice while it lasted," Charlie said. "We were a sort of royalty, almost infallible, with a sort of magic around us. In the bar this afternoon" — he stumbled, seeing his mistake — "there wasn't a man I knew."

She looked at him keenly. "I should think you'd have had enough of bars."

"I only stayed a minute. I take one drink every afternoon, and no more."

"Don't you want a cocktail before dinner?" Lincoln asked.

"I take only one drink every afternoon, and I've had that."

"I hope you keep to it," said Marion.

Her dislike was evident in the coldness with which she spoke, but Charlie only smiled; he had larger plans. Her very aggressiveness gave him an advantage, and he knew enough to wait. He wanted them to initiate the discussion of what they knew had brought him to Paris.

At dinner he couldn't decide whether Honoria was most like him or her mother. Fortunate if she didn't combine the traits of both that had brought them to disaster. A great wave of protectiveness went over him. He thought he knew what to do for her. He believed in character; he wanted to jump back a whole generation and trust in character again as the eternally valuable element. Everything else wore out.

He left soon after dinner, but not to go home. He was curious to see Paris by night with clearer and more judicious eyes than those of other days. He bought a *strapontin*[4] for the Casino and watched Josephine Baker go through her chocolate arabesques.

After an hour he left and strolled toward Montmartre, up the Rue Pigalle into the Place Blanche. The rain had stopped and there were a few people in evening clothes disembarking from taxis in front of cabarets, and *cocottes*[5] prowling singly or in pairs, and many Negroes. He passed a lighted door from which issued music, and stopped with the sense of familiarity; it was Bricktop's, where he had parted with so many hours and so much money. A few doors farther on he found another ancient rendezvous and incautiously put his head inside. Immediately an eager orchestra burst into sound, a pair of professional dancers leaped to their feet and a maître d'hôtel swooped toward him, crying, "Crowd just arriving, sir!" But he withdrew quickly.

"You have to be damn drunk," he thought.

Zelli's was closed, the bleak and sinister cheap hotels surrounding it were dark; up in the Rue Blanche there was more light and a local, colloquial French crowd. The Poet's Cave had disappeared, but the two great mouths of the Café of Heaven and the Café of Hell still yawned — even devoured, as he watched, the meager contents of a tourist bus — a German, a Japanese, and an American couple who glanced at him with frightened eyes.

So much for the effort and ingenuity of Montmartre. All the catering to vice and waste was on an utterly childish scale, and he suddenly realized the meaning of the word "dissipate" — to dissipate into thin air; to make nothing out of something. In the little hours of the night every move from place to place was an enormous human jump, an increase of paying for the privilege of slower and slower motion.

He remembered thousand-franc notes given to an orchestra for playing a single number, hundred-franc notes tossed to a doorman for calling a cab.

But it hadn't been given for nothing.

It had been given, even the most wildly squandered sum, as an offering to destiny that he might not remember the things most worth remembering, the things that now he would always remember — his child taken from his control, his wife escaped to a grave in Vermont.

In the glare of a *brasserie*[6] a woman spoke to him. He bought her some eggs and coffee, and then, eluding her encouraging stare, gave her a twenty-franc note and took a taxi to his hotel.

II

He woke upon a fine fall day — football weather. The depression of yesterday was gone and he liked the people on the streets. At noon he sat opposite Honoria at Le Grand Vatel, the only restaurant he could think of not reminiscent of champagne dinners and long luncheons that began at two and ended in a blurred and vague twilight.

"Now, how about vegetables? Oughtn't you to have some vegetables?"

"Well, yes."

"Here's *épinards* and *chou-fleur* and carrots and *haricots*."[7]

---

[4] A folding chair.

[5] Streetwalkers.

[6] A small restaurant, usually serving beer and wine.

[7] Spinach; cauliflower; kidney beans.

"I'd like *chou-fleur*."

"Wouldn't you like to have two vegetables?"

"I usually only have one at lunch."

The waiter was pretending to be inordinately fond of children. "*Qu'elle est mignonne la petite! Elle parle exactement comme une Française.*"[8]

"How about dessert? Shall we wait and see?"

The waiter disappeared. Honoria looked at her father expectantly.

"What are we going to do?"

"First, we're going to that toy store in the Rue Saint-Honoré and buy you anything you like. And then we're going to the vaudeville at the Empire."

She hesitated. "I like it about the vaudeville, but not the toy store."

"Why not?"

"Well, you brought me this doll." She had it with her. "And I've got lots of things. And we're not rich any more, are we?"

"We never were. But today you are to have anything you want."

"All right," she agreed resignedly.

When there had been her mother and a French nurse he had been inclined to be strict; now he extended himself, reached out for a new tolerance; he must be both parents to her and not shut any of her out of communication.

"I want to get to know you," he said gravely. "First let me introduce myself. My name is Charles J. Wales, of Prague."

"Oh, daddy!" her voice cracked with laughter.

"And who are you, please?" he persisted, and she accepted a rôle immediately: "Honoria Wales, Rue Palatine, Paris."

"Married or single?"

"No, not married. Single."

He indicated the doll. "But I see you have a child, madame."

Unwilling to disinherit it, she took it to her heart and thought quickly: "Yes, I've been married, but I'm not married now. My husband is dead."

He went on quickly, "And the child's name?"

"Simone. That's after my best friend at school."

"I'm very pleased that you're doing so well at school."

"I'm third this month," she boasted. "Elsie" — that was her cousin — "is only about eighteenth, and Richard is about at the bottom."

"You like Richard and Elsie, don't you?"

"Oh, yes. I like Richard quite well and I like her all right."

Cautiously and casually he asked: "And Aunt Marion and Uncle Lincoln — which do you like best?"

"Oh, Uncle Lincoln, I guess."

He was increasingly aware of her presence. As they came in, a murmur of ". . . adorable" followed them, and now the people at the next table bent all their silences upon her, staring as if she were something no more conscious than a flower.

"Why don't I live with you?" she asked suddenly. "Because mamma's dead?"

"You must stay here and learn more French. It would have been hard for daddy to take care of you so well."

---

[8] "What a pretty little girl! She speaks exactly as if she were French!"

"I don't really need much taking care of any more. I do everything for myself."

Going out of the restaurant, a man and a woman unexpectedly hailed him.

"Well, the old Wales!"

"Hello there, Lorraine. ... Dunc."

Sudden ghosts out of the past: Duncan Schaeffer, a friend from college. Lorraine Quarrles, a lovely, pale blonde of thirty; one of a crowd who had helped them make months into days in the lavish times of three years ago.

"My husband couldn't come this year," she said, in answer to his question. "We're poor as hell. So he gave me two hundred a month and told me I could do my worst on that. ... This your little girl?"

"What about coming back and sitting down?" Duncan asked.

"Can't do it." He was glad for an excuse. As always, he felt Lorraine's passionate, provocative attraction, but his own rhythm was different now.

"Well, how about dinner?" she asked.

"I'm not free. Give me your address and let me call you."

"Charlie, I believe you're sober," she said judicially. "I honestly believe he's sober, Dunc. Pinch him and see if he's sober."

Charlie indicated Honoria with his head. They both laughed.

"What's your address?" said Duncan skeptically.

He hesitated, unwilling to give the name of his hotel.

"I'm not settled yet. I'd better call you. We're going to see the vaudeville at the Empire."

"There! That's what I want to do," Lorraine said. "I want to see some clowns and acrobats and jugglers. That's just what we'll do, Dunc."

"We've got to do an errand first," said Charlie. "Perhaps we'll see you there."

"All right, you snob. ... Good-by, beautiful little girl."

"Good-by."

Honoria bobbed politely.

Somehow, an unwelcome encounter. They liked him because he was functioning, because he was serious; they wanted to see him, because he was stronger than they were now, because they wanted to draw a certain sustenance from his strength.

At the Empire, Honoria proudly refused to sit upon her father's folded coat. She was already an individual with a code of her own, and Charlie was more and more absorbed by the desire of putting a little of himself into her before she crystallized utterly. It was hopeless to try to know her in so short a time.

Between the acts they came upon Duncan and Lorraine in the lobby where the band was playing.

"Have a drink?"

"All right, but not up at the bar. We'll take a table."

"The perfect father."

Listening abstractedly to Lorraine, Charlie watched Honoria's eyes leave their table, and he followed them wistfully about the room, wondering what they saw. He met her glance and she smiled.

"I liked that lemonade," she said.

What had she said? What had he expected? Going home in a taxi afterward, he pulled her over until her head rested against his chest.

"Darling, do you ever think about your mother?"

"Yes, sometimes," she answered vaguely.

"I don't want you to forget her. Have you got a picture of her?"

"Yes, I think so. Anyhow, Aunt Marion has. Why don't you want me to forget her?"

"She loved you very much."

"I loved her too."

They were silent for a moment.

"Daddy, I want to come and live with you," she said suddenly.

His heart leaped; he had wanted it to come like this.

"Aren't you perfectly happy?"

"Yes, but I love you better than anybody. And you love me better than anybody, don't you, now that mummy's dead?"

"Of course I do. But you won't always like me best, honey. You'll grow up and meet somebody your own age and go marry him and forget you ever had a daddy."

"Yes, that's true," she agreed tranquilly.

He didn't go in. He was coming back at nine o'clock and he wanted to keep himself fresh and new for the thing he must say then.

"When you're safe inside, just show yourself in that window."

"All right. Good-by, dads, dads, dads, dads."

He waited in the dark street until she appeared, all warm and glowing, in the window above and kissed her fingers out into the night.

III

They were waiting. Marion sat behind the coffee service in a dignified black dinner dress that just faintly suggested mourning. Lincoln was walking up and down with the animation of one who had already been talking. They were as anxious as he was to get into the question. He opened it almost immediately:

"I suppose you know what I want to see you about — why I really came to Paris."

Marion played with the black stars on her necklace and frowned.

"I'm awfully anxious to have a home," he continued. "And I'm awfully anxious to have Honoria in it. I appreciate your taking in Honoria for her mother's sake, but things have changed now" — he hesitated and then continued more forcibly — "changed radically with me, and I want to ask you to reconsider the matter. It would be silly for me to deny that about three years ago I was acting badly ——"

Marion looked up at him with hard eyes.

" — but all that's over. As I told you, I haven't had more than a drink a day for over a year, and I take that drink deliberately, so that the idea of alcohol won't get too big in my imagination. You see the idea?"

"No," said Marion succinctly.

"It's a sort of stunt I set myself. It keeps the matter in proportion."

"I get you," said Lincoln. "You don't want to admit it's got any attraction for you."

"Something like that. Sometimes I forget and don't take it. But I try to take it. Anyhow, I couldn't afford to drink in my position. The people I represent are more than satisfied with what I've done, and I'm bringing my sister over from Burlington to keep house for me, and I want awfully to have Honoria too. You know that even when her mother and I weren't getting along well we never let anything that happened touch Honoria. I know she's fond of me and I know I'm able to take care of her and — well, there you are. How do you feel about it?"

He knew that now he would have to take a beating. It would last an hour or two hours, and it would be difficult, but if he modulated his inevitable resentment to the chastened attitude of the reformed sinner, he might win his point in the end.

Keep your temper, he told himself. You don't want to be justified. You want Honoria.

Lincoln spoke first: "We've been talking it over ever since we got your letter last month. We're happy to have Honoria here. She's a dear little thing, and we're glad to be able to help her, but of course that isn't the question ——"

Marion interrupted suddenly. "How long are you going to stay sober, Charlie?" she asked.

"Permanently, I hope."

"How can anybody count on that?"

"You know I never did drink heavily until I gave up business and came over here with nothing to do. Then Helen and I began to run around with ——"

"Please leave Helen out of it. I can't bear to hear you talk about her like that."

He stared at her grimly; he had never been certain how fond of each other the sisters were in life.

"My drinking only lasted about a year and a half — from the time we came over until I — collapsed."

"It was time enough."

"It was time enough," he agreed.

"My duty is entirely to Helen," she said. "I try to think what she would have wanted me to do. Frankly, from the night you did that terrible thing you haven't really existed for me. I can't help 2hat. She was my sister."

"Yes."

"When she was dying she asked me to look out for Honoria. If you hadn't been in a sanitarium then, it might have helped matters."

He had no answer.

"I'll never in my life be able to forget the morning when Helen knocked at my door, soaked to the skin and shivering and said you'd locked her out."

Charlie gripped the sides of the chair. This was more difficult than he expected; he wanted to launch out into a long expostulation and explanation, but he only said: "The night I locked her out — " and she interrupted, "I don't feel up to going over that again."

After a moment's silence Lincoln said: "We're getting off the subject. You want Marion to set aside her legal guardianship and give you Honoria. I think the main point for her is whether she has confidence in you or not."

"I don't blame Marion," Charlie said slowly, "but I think she can have entire confidence in me. I had a good record up to three years ago. Of course, it's within human possibilities I might go wrong any time. But if we wait much longer I'll lose Honoria's childhood and my chance for a home." He shook his head, "I'll simply lose her, don't you see?"

"Yes, I see," said Lincoln.

"Why didn't you think of all this before?" Marion asked.

"I suppose I did, from time to time, but Helen and I were getting along badly. When I consented to the guardianship, I was flat on my back in a sanitarium and the market had cleaned me out. I knew I'd acted badly, and I thought if it would bring any peace to Helen, I'd agree to anything. But now it's different. I'm functioning, I'm behaving damn well, so far as ——"

"Please don't swear at me," Marion said.

He looked at her, startled. With each remark the force of her dislike became more and more apparent. She had built up all her fear of life into one wall and faced it toward him. This trivial reproof was possibly the result of some trouble with the cook several hours before. Charlie became increasingly alarmed at leaving Honoria in this atmosphere of hostility against himself; sooner or later it would come out, in a word here, a shake of the head there, and some of that distrust would be irrevocably implanted in Honoria. But he pulled his temper down out of his face and shut it up inside him; he had won a point, for Lincoln realized the absurdity of Marion's remark and asked her lightly since when she had objected to the word "damn."

"Another thing," Charlie said: "I'm able to give her certain advantages now. I'm going to take a French governess to Prague with me. I've got a lease on a new apartment ——"

He stopped, realizing that he was blundering. They couldn't be expected to accept with equanimity the fact that his income was again twice as large as their own.

"I suppose you can give her more luxuries than we can," said Marion. "When you were throwing away money we were living along watching every ten francs. ... I suppose you'll start doing it again."

"Oh, no," he said. "I've learned. I worked hard for ten years, you know — until I got lucky in the market, like so many people. Terribly lucky. It won't happen again."

There was a long silence. All of them felt their nerves straining, and for the first time in a year Charlie wanted a drink. He was sure now that Lincoln Peters wanted him to have his child.

Marion shuddered suddenly; part of her saw that Charlie's feet were planted on the earth now, and her own maternal feeling recognized the naturalness of his desire; but she had lived for a long time with a prejudice — a prejudice founded on a curious disbelief in her sister's happiness, and which, in the shock of one terrible night, had turned to hatred for him. It had all happened at a point in her life where the discouragement of ill health and adverse circumstances made it necessary for her to believe in tangible villainy and a tangible villain.

"I can't help what I think!" she cried out suddenly. "How much you were responsible for Helen's death, I don't know. It's something you'll have to square with your own conscience."

An electric current of agony surged through him; for a moment he was almost on his feet, an unuttered sound echoing in his throat. He hung on to himself for a moment, another moment.

"Hold on there," said Lincoln uncomfortably. "I never thought you were responsible for that."

"Helen died of heart trouble," Charlie said dully.

"Yes, heart trouble." Marion spoke as if the phrase had another meaning for her.

Th2n, in the flatness that followed her outburst, she saw him plainly and she knew he had somehow arrived at control over the situation. Glancing at her husband, she found no help from him, and as abruptly as if it were a matter of no importance, she threw up the sponge.

"Do what you like!" she cried, springing up from her chair. "She's your child. I'm not the person to stand in your way. I think if it were my child I'd rather see her— " She managed to check herself. "You two decide it. I can't stand this. I'm sick. I'm going to bed."

She hurried from the room; after a moment Lincoln said:

"This has been a hard day for her. You know how strongly she feels— " His voice was almost apologetic: "When a woman gets an idea in her head."

"Of course."

"It's going to be all right. I think she sees now that you— can provide for the child, and so we can't very well stand in your way or Honoria's way."

"I'd better go along and see how she is."

"I'm going."

He was still trembling when he reached the street, but a walk down the Rue Bonaparte to the *quais*[9] set him up, and as he crossed the Seine, fresh and new by the *quai* lamps, he felt exultant. But back in his room he couldn't sleep. The image of Helen haunted him. Helen whom he had loved so until they had senselessly begun to abuse each other's love, tear it into shreds. On that terrible February night that Marion remembered so vividly, a slow quarrel had gone on for hours. There was a scene at the Florida, and then he attempted to take her home, and then she kissed young Webb at a table; after that there was what she had hysterically said. When he arrived home alone he turned the key in the lock in wild anger. How could he know she would arrive an hour later alone, that there would be a snowstorm in which she wandered about in slippers, too confused to find a taxi? Then the aftermath, her escaping pneumonia by a miracle, and all the attendant horror. They were "reconciled," but that was the beginning of the end, and Marion, who had seen with her own eyes and who imagined it to be one of many scenes from her sister's martyrdom, never forgot.

Going over it again brought Helen nearer, and in the white, soft light that steals upon half sleep near morning he found himself talking to her again. She said that he was perfectly right about Honoria and that she wanted Honoria to be with him. She said she was glad he was being good and doing better. She said a lot of other things — very friendly things — but she was in a swing in a white dress, and swinging faster and faster all the time, so that at the end he could not hear clearly all that she said.

IV

He woke up feeling happy. The door of the world was open again. He made plans, vistas, futures for Honoria and himself, but suddenly he grew sad, remembering all the plans he and Helen had made. She had not planned to die. The present was the thing — work to do and someone to love. But not to love too much, for he knew the injury that a father can do to a daughter or a mother to a son by attaching them too closely: afterward, out in the 2orld, the child would seek in the marriage partner the same blind tenderness and, failing probably to find it, turn against love and life.

It was another bright, crisp day. He called Lincoln Peters at the bank where he worked and asked if he could count on taking Honoria when he left for Prague. Lincoln agreed that there was no reason for delay. One thing — the legal guardianship. Marion wanted to retain that a while longer. She was upset by the whole matter, and it would oil things if she felt that the situation was still in her control for another year. Charlie agreed, wanting only the tangible, visible child.

Then the question of a governess. Charles sat in a gloomy agency and talked to a cross Béarnaise and to a buxom Breton peasant, neither of whom he could have endured. There were others whom he would see tomorrow.

He lunched with Lincoln Peters at Griffons, trying to keep down his exultation.

"There's nothing quite like your own child," Lincoln said. "But you understand how Marion feels too."

"She's forgotten how hard I worked for seven years there," Charlie said. "She just remembers one night."

"There's another thing." Lincoln hesitated. "While you and Helen were tearing around

---

[9] Quays; wharfs.

Europe throwing money away, we were just getting along. I didn't touch any of the prosperity because I never got ahead enough to carry anything but my insurance. I think Marion felt there was some kind of injustice in it — you not even working toward the end, and getting richer and richer."

"It went just as quick as it came," said Charlie.

"Yes, a lot of it stayed in the hands of *chasseurs* and saxophone players and maîtres d'hôtel — well, the big party's over now. I just said that to explain Marion's feeling about those crazy years. If you drop in about six o'clock tonight before Marion's too tired, we'll settle the details on the spot."

Back at his hotel, Charlie found a *pneumatique*[10] that had been redirected from the Ritz bar where Charlie had left his address for the purpose of finding a certain man.

> DEAR CHARLIE: You were so strange when we saw you the other day that I wondered if I did something to offend you. If so, I'm not conscious of it. In fact, I have thought about you too much for the last year, and it's always been in the back of my mind that I might see you if I came over here. We *did* have such good times that crazy spring, like the night you and I stole the butcher's tricycle, and the time we tried to call on the president and you had the old derby rim and the wire cane. Everybody seems so old lately, but I don't feel old a bit. Couldn't we get together some time today for old time's sake? I've got a vile hang-over for the moment, but will be feeling better this afternoon and will look for you about five in the sweatshop at the Ritz.
>
> Always devotedly,
> Lorraine

His first feeling was one of awe that he had actually, in his mature years, stolen a tricycle and pedaled Lorraine all over the Étoile between the small hours and dawn. In retrospect it was a nightmare. Locking out Helen didn't fit in with any other act of his life, but the tricycle incident did — it was one of many. How many weeks or months of dissipation to arrive at that condition of utter irresponsibility?

He tried to picture how Lorraine had appeared to him then — very attractive; Helen was unhappy about it, though she said nothing. Yesterday, in the restaurant, Lorraine had seemed trite, blurred, worn away. He emphatically did not want to see her, and he was glad Alix had not given away his hotel address. It was a relief to think, instead, of Honoria, to think of Sundays spent with her and of saying good morning to her and of knowing she was there in his house at night, drawing her breath in the darkness.

At five he took a taxi and bought presents for all the Peters — a piquant cloth doll, a box of Roman soldiers, flowers for Marion, big linen handkerchiefs for Lincoln.

He saw, when he arrived in the apartment, that Marion had accepted the inevitable. She greeted him now as though he were a recalcitrant member of the family, rather than a menacing outsider. Honoria had been told she was going; Charlie was glad to see that her tact made her conceal her excessive happiness. Only on his lap did she whisper her delight and the question "When?" before she slipped away with the other children.

He and Marion were alone for a minute in the room, and on an impulse he spoke out boldly:

"Family quarrels are bitter things. They don't go according to any rules. They're not

---

[10] Special express letter.

like aches or wounds; they're more like splits in the skin that won't heal because there's not enough material. I wish you and I could be on better terms."

"Some things are hard to forget," she answered. "It's a question of confidence." There was no answer to this and presently she asked, "When do you propose to take her?"

"As soon as I can get a governess. I hoped the day after tomorrow."

"That's impossible. I've got to get her things in shape. Not before Saturday."

He yielded. Coming back into the room, Lincoln offered him a drink.

"I'll take my daily whisky," he said.

It was warm here, it was a home, people together by a fire. The children felt very safe and important; the mother and father were serious, watchful. They had things to do for the children more important than his visit here. A spoonful of medicine was, after all, more important than the strained relations between Marion and himself. They were not dull people, but they were very much in the grip of life and circumstances. He wondered if he couldn't do something to get Lincoln out of his rut at the bank.

A long peal at the door-bell; the *bonne à tout faire*[11] passed through and went down the corridor. The door opened upon another long ring, and then voices, and the three in the salon looked up expectantly; Richard moved to bring the corridor within his range of vision, and Marion rose. Then the maid came back along the corridor, closely followed by the voices, which developed under the light into Duncan Schaeffer and Lorraine Quarrles.

They were gay, they were hilarious, they were roaring with laughter. For a moment Charlie was astounded; unable to understand how they ferreted out the Peters' address.

"Ah-h-h!" Duncan wagged his finger roguishly at Charlie. "Ah-h-h!"

They both slid down another cascade of laughter. Anxious and at a loss, Charlie shook hands with them quickly and presented them to Lincoln and Marion. Marion nodded, scarcely speaking. She had drawn back a step toward the fire; her little girl stood beside her, and Marion put an arm about her shoulder.

With growing annoyance at the intrusion, Charlie waited for them to explain themselves. After some concentration Duncan said:

"We came to invite you out to dinner. Lorraine and I insist that all this shishi, cagy business 'bout your address got to stop."

Charlie came closer to them, as if to force them backward down the corridor.

"Sorry, but I can't. Tell me where you'll be and I'll phone you in half an hour."

This made no impression. Lorraine sat down suddenly on the side of a chair, and focusing her eyes on Richard, cried, "Oh, what a nice little boy! Come here, little boy." Richard glanced at his mother, but did not move. With a perceptible shrug of her shoulders, Lorraine turned back to Charlie:

"Come and dine. Sure your cousins won' mine. See you so sel'om. Or solemn."

"I can't," said Charlie sharply. "You two have dinner and I'll phone you."

Her voice became suddenly unpleasant. "All right, we'll go. But I remember once when you hammered on my door at four A.M. I was enough of a good sport to give you a drink. Come on, Dunc."

Still in slow motion, with blurred, angry faces, with uncertain feet, they retired along the corridor.

"Good night," Charlie said.

"Good night!" responded Lorraine emphatically.

---

[11] The maid.

When he went back into the salon Marion had not moved, only now her son was standing in the circle of her other arm. Lincoln was still swinging Honoria back and forth like a pendulum from side to side.

"What an outrage!" Charlie broke out. "What an absolute outrage!"

Neither of them answered. Charlie dropped into an armchair, picked up his drink, set it down again and said:

"People I haven't seen for two years having the colossal nerve ——"

He broke off. Marion had made the sound "Oh!" in one swift, furious breath, turned her body from him with a jerk and left the room.

Lincoln set down Honoria carefully.

"You children go in and start your soup," he said, and when they obeyed, he said to Charlie:

"Marion's not well and she can't stand shocks. That kind of people make her really physically sick."

"I didn't tell them to come here. They wormed your name out of somebody. They deliberately ——"

"Well, it's too bad. It doesn't help matters. Excuse me a minute."

Left alone, Charlie sat tense in his chair. In the next room he could hear the children eating, talking in monosyllables, already oblivious to the scene between their elders. He heard a murmur of conversation from a farther room and then the ticking bell of a telephone receiver picked up, and in a panic he moved to the other side of the room and out of earshot.

In a minute Lincoln came back. "Look here, Charlie. I think we'd better call off dinner for tonight. Marion's in bad shape."

"Is she angry with me?"

"Sort of," he said, almost roughly. "She's not strong and ——"

"You mean she's changed her mind about Honoria?"

"She's pretty bitter right now. I don't know. You phone me at the bank tomorrow."

"I wish you'd explain to her I never dreamed these people would come here. I'm just as sore as you are."

"I couldn't explain anything to her now."

Charlie got up. He took his coat and hat and started down the corridor. Then he opened the door of the dining room and said in a strange voice, "Good night, children."

Honoria rose and ran around the table to hug him.

"Good night, sweetheart," he said vaguely, and then trying to make his voice more tender, trying to conciliate something. "Good night, dear children."

V

Charlie went directly to the Ritz bar with the furious idea of finding Lorraine and Duncan, but they were not there, and he realized that in any case there was nothing he could do. He had not touched his drink at the Peters, and now he ordered a whisky-and-soda. Paul came over to say hello.

"It's a great change," he said sadly. "We do about half the business we did. So many fellows I hear about back in the States lost everything, maybe not in the 2irst crash, but then in the second. Your friend George Hardt lost every cent, I hear. Are you back in the States?"

"No, I'm in business in Prague."

"I heard that you lost a lot in the crash."

"I did," and he added grimly, "but I lost everything I wanted in the boom."

"Selling short."

"Something like that."

Again the memory of those days swept over him like a nightmare — the people they had met travelling; then people who couldn't add a row of figures or speak a coherent sentence. The little man Helen had consented to dance with at the ship's party, who had insulted her ten feet from the table; the women and girls carried screaming with drink or drugs out of public places ——

— The men who locked their wives out in the snow, because the snow of twenty-nine wasn't real snow. If you didn't want it to be snow, you just paid some money.

He went to the phone and called the Peters' apartment; Lincoln answered.

"I called up because this thing is on my mind. Has Marion said anything definite?"

"Marion's sick," Lincoln answered shortly. "I know this thing isn't altogether your fault, but I can't have her go to pieces about it. I'm afraid we'll have to let it slide for six months; I can't take the chance of working her up to this state again."

"I see."

"I'm sorry, Charlie."

He went back to his table. His whisky glass was empty, but he shook his head when Alix looked at it questioningly. There wasn't much he could do now except send Honoria some things; he would send her a lot of things tomorrow. He thought rather angrily that this was just money — he had given so many people money. ...

"No, no more," he said to another waiter. "What do I owe you?"

He would come back some day; they couldn't make him pay forever. But he wanted his child, and nothing was much good now, beside that fact. He wasn't young any more, with a lot of nice thoughts and dreams to have by himself. He was absolutely sure Helen wouldn't have wanted him to be so alone.

QUESTIONS

1. The central story is told between two scenes in the Ritz bar. What effect is achieved by this framing of Charlie's attempt to recover his child?

2. For the most part, we see into only one mind, Charlie's. But on p. 533 we move briefly into Marion's consciousness: "Marion shuddered suddenly; part of her saw that Charlie's feet were planted on the earth now, ..." Does this shift in point of view break the unity of the story? Does it serve an important purpose?

3. How do Marion's and Lincoln's attitudes toward Charlie differ? their attitudes toward the child?

4. Although Charlie is reformed and the "bad old days" are in the past, Fitzgerald still manages to recreate the sense of the Roaring Twenties. How does he do this?

5. What is Charlie's conception of fatherhood? Does the last sentence of the story tell you anything about it?

6. Trace Fitzgerald's use of action scenes and dialogue scenes. Is there a pattern?

7. Fitzgerald is a master of dialogue. How does dialogue contribute to the tone of the story? to characterization?

8. Is Marion's opposition to Charlie entirely emotional? Which of her fears are based on logical evidence?

9. Is it purely bad luck, or is it the past catching up with him, that undercuts Charlie just when he is about to regain Honoria?

WILLIAM FAULKNER

A Rose for Emily

I

When Miss Emily Grierson died, our whole town went to her funeral: the men through a sort of respectful affection for a fallen monument, the women mostly out of curiosity to see the inside of her house, which no one save an old manservant — a combined gardener and cook — had seen in at least ten years.

It was a big, squarish frame house that had once been white, decorated with cupolas and spires and scrolled balconies in the heavily lightsome style of the seventies, set on what had once been our most select street. But garages and cotton gins had encroached and obliterated even the august names of that neighborhood; only Miss Emily's house was left, lifting its stubborn and coquettish decay above the cotton wagons and the gasoline pumps — an eyesore among eyesores. And now Miss Emily had gone to join the representatives of those august names where they lay in the cedar-bemused cemetery among the ranked and anonymous graves of Union and Confederate soldiers who fell at the battle of Jefferson.

Alive, Miss Emily had been a tradition, a duty, and a care; a sort of hereditary obligation upon the town, dating from that day in 1894 when Colonel Sartoris, the mayor — he who fathered the edict that no Negro woman should appear on the streets without an apron — remitted her taxes, the dispensation dating from the death of her father on into perpetuity. Not that Miss Emily would have accepted charity. Colonel Sartoris invented an involved tale to the effect that Miss Emily's father had loaned money to the town, which the town, as a matter of business, preferred this way of repaying. Only a man of Colonel Sartoris' generation and thought could have invented it, and only a woman could have believed it.

When the next generation, with its more modern ideas, became mayors and aldermen, this arrangement created some little dissatisfaction. On the first of the year they mailed her a tax notice. February came, and there was no reply. They wrote her a formal letter, asking her to call at the sheriff's office at her convenience. A week later the mayor wrote her himself, offering to call or to send his car for her, and received in reply a note on paper of an archaic shape, in a thin, flowing calligraphy in faded ink, to the effect that she no longer went out at all. The tax notice was also enclosed, without comment.

They called a special meeting of the Board of Aldermen. A deputation waited upon her, knocked at the door through which no visitor had passed since she ceased giving china-painting lessons eight or ten years earlier. They were admitted by the old Negro into a dim hall from which a stairway mounted into still more shadow. It smelled of dust and disuse — a close, dank smell. The Negro led them into the parlor. It was furnished in heavy, leather-covered furniture. When the Negro opened the blinds of one window, they could see that the leather was cracked; and when they sat down, a faint dust rose sluggishly about their thighs, spinning with slow motes in the single sun-ray. On a tarnished gilt easel before the fireplace stood a crayon portrait of Miss Emily's father.

They rose when she entered — a small, fat woman in black, with a thin gold chain descending to her waist and vanishing into her belt, leaning on an ebony cane with a tarnished gold head. Her skeleton was small and spare; perhaps that was why what would have been merely plumpness in another was obesity in her. She looked bloated, like a body long submerged in motionless water, and of that pallid hue. Her eyes, lost in the fatty ridges of her face, looked like two small pieces of coal pressed into a lump of dough as they moved from one face to another while the visitors stated their errand.

She did not ask them to sit. She just stood in the door and listened quietly until the spokesman came to a stumbling halt. Then they could hear the invisible watch ticking at the end of the gold chain.

Her voice was dry and cold. "I have no taxes in Jefferson. Colonel Sartoris explained it to me. Perhaps one of you can gain access to the city records and satisfy yourselves."

"But we have. We are the city authorities, Miss Emily. Didn't you get a notice from the sheriff, signed by him?"

"I received a paper, yes," Miss Emily said. "Perhaps he considers himself the sheriff ... I have no taxes in Jefferson."

"But there is nothing on the books to show that, you see. We must go by the — "

"See Colonel Sartoris. I have no taxes in Jefferson."

"But, Miss Emily — "

"See Colonel Sartoris." (Colonel Sartoris had been dead almost ten years.) "I have no taxes in Jefferson. Tobe!" The Negro appeared. "Show these gentlemen out."

II

So she vanquished them, horse and foot, just as she had vanquished their fathers thirty years before about the smell. That was two years after her father's death and a short time after her sweetheart — the one we believed would marry her — had deserted her. After her father's death she went out very little; after her sweetheart went away, people hardly saw her at all. A few of the ladies had the temerity to call, but were not received, and the only sign of life about the place was the Negro man — a young man then — going in and out with a market basket.

"Just as if a man — any man — could keep a kitchen properly," the ladies said; so they were not surprised when the smell developed. It was another link between the gross, teeming world and the high and mighty Griersons.

A neighbor, a woman, complained to the mayor, Judge Stevens, eighty years old.

"But what will you have me do about it, madam?" he said.

"Why, send her word to stop it," the woman said. "Isn't there a law?"

"I'm sure that won't be necessary," Judge Stevens said. "It's probably just a snake or a rat that nigger of hers killed in the yard. I'll speak to him about it."

The next day he received two more complaints, one from a man who came in diffident deprecation. "We really must do something about it, Judge. I'd be the last one in the world to bother Miss Emily, but we've got to do something." That night the Board of Aldermen met — three graybeards and one younger man, a member of the rising generation.

"It's simple enough," he said. "Send her word to have her place cleaned up. Give her a certain time to do it in, and if she don't ..."

"Dammit, sir," Judge Stevens said, "will you accuse a lady to her face of smelling bad?"

So the next night, after midnight, four men crossed Miss Emily's lawn and slunk about the house like burglars, sniffing along the base of the brickwork and at the cellar openings while one of them performed a regular sowing motion with his hand out of a sack slung from his shoulder. They broke open the cellar door and sprinkled lime there, and in all the out-buildings. As they recrossed the lawn, a window that had been dark was lighted and Miss Emily sat in it, the light behind her, and her upright torso motionless as that of an idol. They crept quietly across the lawn and into the shadow of the locusts that lined the street. After a week or two the smell went away.

That was when people had begun to feel really sorry for her. People in our town, remembering how old lady Wyatt, her great-aunt, had gone completely crazy at last, believed that the Griersons held themselves a little too high for what they really were. None of the young men were quite good enough for Miss Emily and such. We had long thought of them as a tableau, Miss Emily a slender figure in white in the background, her father a spraddled silhouette in the foreground, his back to her and clutching a horsewhip, the two of them framed by the back-flung front door. So when she got to be thirty and was still single, we were not pleased exactly, but vindicated; even with insanity in the family she wouldn't have turned down all of her chances if they had really materialized.

When her father died, it got about that the house was all that was left to her; and in a way, people were glad. At last they could pity Miss Emily. Being left alone, and a pauper, she had become humanized. Now she too would know the old thrill and the old despair of a penny more or less.

The day after his death all the ladies prepared to call at the house and offer condolence and aid, as is our custom. Miss Emily met them at the door, dressed as usual and with no trace of grief on her face. She told them that her father was not dead. She did that for three days, with the ministers calling on her, and the doctors, trying to persuade her to let them dispose of the body. Just as they were about to resort to law and force, she broke down, and they buried her father quickly.

We did not say she was crazy then. We believed she had to do that. We remembered all the young men her father had driven away, and we knew that with nothing left, she would have to cling to that which had robbed her, as people will.

III

She was sick for a long time. When we saw her again, her hair was cut short, making her look like a girl, with a vague resemblance to those angels in colored church windows — sort of tragic and serene.

The town had just let the contracts for paving the sidewalks, and in the summer after her father's death they began the work. The construction company came with niggers and mules and machinery, and a foreman named Homer Barron, a Yankee — a big, dark, ready man, with a big voice and eyes lighter than his face. The little boys would follow in groups to hear him cuss the niggers, and the niggers singing in time to the rise and fall of picks. Pretty soon he knew everybody in town. Whenever you heard a lot of laughing anywhere about the square, Homer Barron would be in the center of the group. Presently we began to see him and

Miss Emily on Sunday afternoons driving in the yellow-wheeled buggy and the matched team of bays from the livery stable.

At first we were glad that Miss Emily would have an interest, because the ladies all said, "Of course a Grierson would not think seriously of a Northerner, a day laborer." But there were still others, older people, who said that even grief could not cause a real lady to forget *noblesse oblige*[1] — without calling it *noblesse oblige*. They just said, "Poor Emily. Her kinsfolk should come to her." She had some kin in Alabama; but years ago her father had fallen out with them over the estate of old lady Wyatt, the crazy woman, and there was no communication between the two families. They had not even been represented at the funeral.

And as soon as the old people said, "Poor Emily," the whispering began. "Do you suppose it's really so?" they said to one another. "Of course it is. What else could ..." This behind their hands; rustling of craned silk and satin behind jalousies closed upon the sun of Sunday afternoon as the thin, swift clop-clop-clop of the matched team passed: "Poor Emily."

She carried her head high enough — even when we believed that she was fallen. It was as if she demanded more than ever the recognition of her dignity as the last Grierson; as if it had wanted that touch of earthiness to reaffirm her imperviousness. Like when she bought the rat poison, the arsenic. That was over a year after they had begun to say "Poor Emily," and while the two female cousins were visiting her.

"I want some poison," she said to the druggist. She was over thirty then, still a slight woman, though thinner than usual, with cold, haughty black eyes in a face the flesh of which was strained across the temples and about the eyesockets as you imagine a lighthouse-keeper's face ought to look. "I want some poison," she said.

"Yes, Miss Emily. What kind? For rats and such? I'd recom — "

"I want the best you have. I don't care what kind."

The druggist named several. "They'll kill anything up to an elephant. But what you want is — "

"Arsenic," Miss Emily said. "Is that a good one?"

"Is ... arsenic? Yes, ma'am. But what you want — "

"I want arsenic."

The druggist looked down at her. She looked back at him, erect, her face like a strained flag. "Why, of course," the druggist said. "If that's what you want. But the law requires you to tell what you are going to use it for."

Miss Emily just stared at him, her head tilted back in order to look him eye for eye, until he looked away and went and got the arsenic and wrapped it up. The Negro delivery boy brought her the package; the druggist didn't come back. When she opened the package at home there was written on the box, under the skull and bones: "For rats."

IV

So the next day we all said, "She will kill herself"; and we said it would be the best thing. When she had first begun to be seen with Homer Barron, we had said, "She will marry him." Then we said, "She will persuade him yet," because Homer himself had remarked — he liked men, and it was known that he drank with the younger men in the Elks' Club — that he was

---

[1] "Rights imply duties"; that is, the upper classes have responsibilities toward the lower.

not a marrying man. Later we said, "Poor Emily" behind the jalousies as they passed on Sunday afternoon in the glittering buggy, Miss Emily with her head high and Homer Barron with his hat cocked and a cigar in his teeth, reins and whip in a yellow glove.

Then some of the ladies began to say that it was a disgrace to the town and a bad example to the young people. The men did not want to interfere, but at last the ladies forced the Baptist minister — Miss Emily's people were Episcopal — to call upon her. He would never divulge what happened during that interview, but he refused to go back again. The next Sunday they again drove about the streets, and the following day the minister's wife wrote to Miss Emily's relations in Alabama.

So she had blood-kin under her roof again and we sat back to watch developments. At first nothing happened. Then we were sure that they were to be married. We learned that Miss Emily had been to the jeweler's and ordered a man's toilet set in silver, with the letters H. B. on each piece. Two days later we learned that she had bought a complete outfit of men's clothing, including a nightshirt, and we said, "They are married." We were really glad. We were glad because the two female cousins were even more Grierson than Miss Emily had ever been.

So we were not surprised when Homer Barron — the streets had been finished some time since — was gone. We were a little disappointed that there was not a public blowing-off, but we believed that he had gone on to prepare for Miss Emily's coming, or to give her a chance to get rid of the cousins. (By that time it was a cabal, and we were all Miss Emily's allies to help circumvent the cousins.) Sure enough, after another week they departed. And, as we had expected all along, within three days Homer Barron was back in town. A neighbor saw the Negro man admit him at the kitchen door at dusk one evening.

And that was the last we saw of Homer Barron. And of Miss Emily for some time. The Negro man went in and out with the market basket, but the front door remained closed. Now and then we would see her at a window for a moment, as the men did that night when they sprinkled the lime, but for almost six months she did not appear on the streets. Then we knew that this was to be expected too; as if that quality of her father which had thwarted her woman's life so many times had been too virulent and too furious to die.

When we next saw Miss Emily, she had grown fat and her hair was turning gray. During the next few years it grew grayer and grayer until it attained an even pepper-and-salt iron-gray, when it ceased turning. Up to the day of her death at seventy-four it was still that vigorous iron-gray, like the hair of an active man.

From that time on her front door remained closed, save for a period of six or seven years, when she was about forty, during which she gave lessons in china-painting. She fitted up a studio in one of the downstairs rooms, where the daughters and granddaughters of Colonel Sartoris' contemporaries were sent to her with the same regularity and in the same spirit that they were sent to church on Sundays with a twenty-five-cent piece for the collection plate. Meanwhile her taxes had been remitted.

Then the newer generation became the backbone and the spirit of the town, and the painting pupils grew up and fell away and did not send their children to her with boxes of color and tedious brushes and pictures cut from the ladies' magazines. The front door closed upon the last one and remained closed for good. When the town got free postal delivery, Miss Emily alone refused to let them fasten the metal numbers above her door and attach a mailbox to it. She would not listen to them.

Daily, monthly, yearly we watched the Negro grow grayer and more stooped, going in and out with the market basket. Each December we sent her a tax notice, which would be returned by the post office a week later, unclaimed. Now and then we would see her in one of the downstairs windows — she had evidently shut up the top floor of the house — like the carven torso of an idol in a niche, looking or not looking at us, we could never tell which. Thus she passed from generation to generation — dear, inescapable, impervious, tranquil, and perverse.

And so she died. Fell ill in the house filled with dust and shadows, with only a doddering Negro man to wait on her. We did not even know she was sick; we had long since given up trying to get any information from the Negro. He talked to no one, probably not even to her, for his voice had grown harsh and rusty, as if from disuse.

She died in one of the downstairs rooms, in a heavy walnut bed with a curtain, her gray head propped on a pillow yellow and moldy with age and lack of sunlight.

V

The Negro met the first of the ladies at the front door and let them in, with their hushed, sibilant voices and their quick, curious glances, and then he disappeared. He walked right through the house and out the back and was not seen again.

The two female cousins came at once. They held the funeral on the second day, with the town coming to look at Miss Emily beneath a mass of bought flowers, with the crayon face of her father musing profoundly above the bier and the ladies sibilant and macabre; and the very old men — some in their brushed Confederate uniforms — on the porch and the lawn, talking of Miss Emily as if she had been a contemporary of theirs, believing that they had danced with her and courted her perhaps, confusing time with its mathematical progression, as the old do, to whom all the past is not a diminishing road but, instead, a huge meadow which no winter ever quite touches, divided from them now by the narrow bottle-neck of the most recent decade of years.

Already we knew that there was one room in that region above stairs which no one had seen in forty years, and which would have to be forced. They waited until Miss Emily was decently in the ground before they opened it.

The violence of breaking down the door seemed to fill this room with pervading dust. A thin, acrid pall as of the tomb seemed to lie everywhere upon this room decked and furnished as for a bridal: upon the valance curtains of faded rose color, upon the rose-shaded lights, upon the dressing table, upon the delicate array of crystal and the man's toilet things backed with tarnished silver, silver so tarnished that the monogram was obscured. Among them lay a collar and tie, as if they had just been removed, which, lifted, left upon the surface a pale crescent in the dust. Upon a chair hung the suit, carefully folded; beneath it the two mute shoes and the discarded socks.

The man himself lay in the bed.

For a long while we just stood there, looking down at the profound and fleshless grin. The body had apparently once lain in the attitude of an embrace, but now the long sleep that outlasts love, that conquers even the grimace of love, had cuckolded him. What was left of him, rotted beneath what was left of the nightshirt, had become inextricable from the bed in which he lay; and upon him and upon the pillow beside him lay that even coating of the patient and biding dust.

Then we noticed that in the second pillow was the indentation of a head. One of us lifted something from it, and leaning forward, that faint and invisible dust dry and acrid in the nostrils, we saw a long strand of iron-gray hair.

QUESTIONS

1. Does the division of this story into five parts interrupt the continuity? Are the divisions logical or chronological; that is, do they mark significant developments or mainly the passage of time?

2. What is the narrator's relationship to Miss Emily? to the town?

3. What is the significance of the title? Is it affectionate or ironic?

4. Which of Miss Emily's actions are most revealing of her character? Does it seem within her character to murder Homer Barron?

5. Faulkner often contrasts the present and the past by means of characters who are symbols as well as actors in his stories. Is Miss Emily such a symbol? Is the narrator?

6. What is your emotional response to the three concluding paragraphs? By what means has Faulkner elicited that response?

WILLIAM FAULKNER

That Evening Sun

I

Monday is no different from any other weekday in Jefferson now. The streets are paved now, and the telephone and electric companies are cutting down more and more of the shade trees — the water oaks, the maples and locusts and elms — to make room for iron poles bearing clusters of bloated and ghostly and bloodless grapes, and we have a city laundry which makes the rounds on Monday morning, gathering the bundles of clothes into bright-colored, specially-made motor cars: the soiled wearing of a whole week now flees apparitionlike behind alert and irritable electric horns, with a long diminishing noise of rubber and asphalt like tearing silk, and even the Negro women who still take in white people's washing after the old custom, fetch and deliver it in automobiles.

But fifteen years ago, on Monday morning the quiet, dusty, shady streets would be full of Negro women with, balanced on their steady, turbaned heads, bundles of clothes tied up in sheets, almost as large as cotton bales, carried so without touch of hand between the kitchen door of the white house and the blackened washpot beside a cabin door in Negro Hollow.

Nancy would set her bundle on the top of her head, then upon the bundle in turn she would set the black straw sailor hat which she wore winter and summer. She was tall, with a high, sad face sunken a little where her teeth were missing. Sometimes we would go a part of the way down the lane and across the pasture with her, to watch the balanced bundle and the hat that never bobbed nor wavered, even when she walked down into the ditch and up the other side and stooped through the fence. She would go down on her hands and knees and crawl through the gap, her head rigid, uptilted, the bundle steady as a rock or a balloon, and rise to her feet again and go on.

Sometimes the husbands of the washing women would fetch and deliver the clothes, but Jesus never did that for Nancy, even before father told him to stay away from our house, even when Dilsey was sick and Nancy would come to cook for us.

And then about half the time we'd have to go down the lane to Nancy's cabin and tell her to come on and cook breakfast. We would stop at the ditch, because father told us to not have anything to do with Jesus — he was a short black man, with a razor scar down his face — and we would throw rocks at Nancy's house until she came to the door, leaning her head around it without any clothes on.

"What yawl mean, chunking my house?" Nancy said. "What you little devils mean?"

"Father says for you to come on and get breakfast," Caddy said. "Father says it's over a half an hour now, and you've got to come this minute."

"I aint studying no breakfast," Nancy said. "I going to get my sleep out."

"I bet you're drunk," Jason said. "Father says you're drunk. Are you drunk, Nancy?"

"Who says I is?" Nancy said. "I got to get my sleep out. I aint studying no breakfast."

So after a while we quit chunking the cabin and went back home. When she finally came, it was too late for me to go to school. So we thought it was whisky until that day they arrested her again and they were taking her to jail and they passed Mr Stovall. He was the cashier in the bank and a deacon in the Baptist church, and Nancy began to say:

"When you going to pay me, white man? When you going to pay me, white man? It's been three times now since you paid me a cent — " Mr Stovall knocked her down, but she kept on saying, "When you going to pay me, white man? It's been three times now since — " until Mr Stovall kicked her in the mouth with his heel and the marshal caught Mr Stovall back, and Nancy lying in the street, laughing. She turned her head and spat out some blood and teeth and said, "It's been three times now since he paid me a cent."

That was how she lost her teeth, and all that day they told about Nancy and Mr Stovall, and all that night the ones that passed the jail could hear Nancy singing and yelling. They could see her hands holding to the window bars, and a lot of them stopped along the fence, listening to her and to the jailer trying to make her stop. She didn't shut up until almost daylight, when the jailer began to hear a bumping and scraping upstairs and he went up there and found Nancy hanging from the window bar. He said that it was cocaine and not whisky, because no nigger would try to commit suicide unless he was full of cocaine, because a nigger full of cocaine wasn't a nigger any longer.

The jailer cut her down and revived her; then he beat her, whipped her. She had hung herself with her dress. She had fixed it all right, but when they arrested her she didn't have on anything except a dress and so she didn't have anything to tie her hands with and she couldn't make her hands let go of the window ledge. So the jailer heard the noise and ran up there and found Nancy hanging from the window, stark naked, her belly already swelling out a little, like a little balloon.

When Dilsey was sick in her cabin and Nancy was cooking for us, we could see her apron swelling out; that was before father told Jesus to stay away from the house. Jesus was in the kitchen, sitting behind the stove, with his razor scar on his black face like a piece of dirty string. He said it was a watermelon that Nancy had under her dress.

"It never come off of your vine, though," Nancy said.

"Off of what vine?" Caddy said.

"I can cut down the vine it did come off of," Jesus said.

"What makes you want to talk like that before these chillen?" Nancy said. "Whyn't you go on to work? You done et. You want Mr Jason to catch you hanging around his kitchen, talking that way before these chillen?"

"Talking what way?" Caddy said. "What vine?"

"I cant hang around white man's kitchen," Jesus said. "But white man can hang around mine. White man can come in my house, but I cant stop him. When white man want to come in my house, I aint got no house. I cant stop him, but he cant kick me outen it. He cant do that."

Dilsey was still sick in her cabin. Father told Jesus to stay off our place. Dilsey was still sick. It was a long time. We were in the library after supper.

"Isn't Nancy through in the kitchen yet?" mother said. "It seems to me that she has had plenty of time to have finished the dishes."

"Let Quentin go and see," father said. "Go and see if Nancy is through, Quentin. Tell her she can go on home."

I went to the kitchen. Nancy was through. The dishes were put away and the fire was out. Nancy was sitting in a chair, close to the cold stove. She looked at me.

"Mother wants to know if you are through," I said.

"Yes," Nancy said. She looked at me. "I done finished." She looked at me.

"What is it?" I said. "What is it?"

"I aint nothing but a nigger," Nancy said. "It aint none of my fault."

She looked at me, sitting in the chair before the cold stove, the sailor hat on her head. I went back to the library. It was the cold stove and all, when you think of a kitchen being warm and busy and cheerful. And with a cold stove and the dishes all put away, and nobody wanting to eat at that hour.

"Is she through?" mother said.

"Yessum," I said.

"What is she doing?" mother said.

"She's not doing anything. She's through."

"I'll go and see," father said.

"Maybe she's waiting for Jesus to come and take her home," Caddy said.

"Jesus is gone," I said. Nancy told us how one morning she woke up and Jesus was gone.

"He quit me," Nancy said. "Done gone to Memphis, I reckon. Dodging them city police for a while, I reckon."

"And a good riddance," father said. "I hope he stays there."

"Nancy's scaired of the dark," Jason said.

"So are you," Caddy said.

"I'm not," Jason said.

"Scairy cat," Caddy said.

"I'm not," Jason said.

"You, Candace!" mother said. Father came back.

"I am going to walk down the lane with Nancy," he said. "She says that Jesus is back."

"Has she seen him?" mother said.

"No. Some Negro sent her word that he was back in town. I wont be long."

"You'll leave me alone, to take Nancy home?" mother said. "Is her safety more precious to you than mine?"

"I wont be long," father said.

"You'll leave these children unprotected, with that Negro about?"

"I'm going too," Caddy said. "Let me go, Father."

"What would he do with them, if he were unfortunate enough to have them?" father said.

"I want to go, too," Jason said.

"Jason!" mother said. She was speaking to father. You could tell that by the way she said the name. Like she believed that all day father had been trying to think of doing the thing she wouldn't like the most, and that she knew all the time that after a while he would think of it. I stayed quiet, because father and I both knew that mother would want him to make me stay with her if she just thought of it in time. So father didn't look at me. I was the oldest. I was nine and Caddy was seven and Jason was five.

"Nonsense," father said. "We wont be long."

Nancy had her hat on. We came to the lane. "Jesus always been good to me," Nancy said. "Whenever he had two dollars, one of them was mine." We walked in the lane. "If I can just get through the lane," Nancy said, "I be all right then."

The lane was always dark. "This is where Jason got scared on Hallowe'en," Caddy said.

"I didn't," Jason said.

"Cant Aunt Rachel do anything with him?" father said. Aunt Rachel was old. She lived in a cabin beyond Nancy's, by herself. She had white hair and she smoked a pipe in the door, all day long; she didn't work any more. They said she was Jesus' mother. Sometimes she said she was and sometimes she said she wasn't any kin to Jesus.

"Yes, you did," Caddy said. "You were scairder than Frony. You were scairder than T.P. even. Scairder than niggers."

"Cant nobody do nothing with him," Nancy said. "He say I done woke up the devil in him and aint but one thing going to lay it down again."

"Well, he's gone now," father said. "There's nothing for you to be afraid of now. And if you'd just let white men alone."

"Let what white men alone?" Caddy said. "How let them alone?"

"He aint gone nowhere," Nancy said. "I can feel him. I can feel him now, in this lane. He hearing us talk, every word, hid somewhere, waiting. I aint seen him, and I aint going to see him again but once more, with that razor in his mouth. That razor on that string down his back, inside his shirt. And then I aint going to be even surprised."

"I wasn't scaired," Jason said.

"If you'd behave yourself, you'd have kept out of this," father said. "But it's all right now. He's probably in St. Louis now. Probably got another wife by now and forgot all about you."

"If he has, I better not find out about it," Nancy said. "I'd stand there right over them, and every time he wropped her, I'd cut that arm off. I'd cut his head off and I'd slit her belly and I'd shove — "

"Hush," father said.

"Slit whose belly, Nancy?" Caddy said.

"I wasn't scaired," Jason said. "I'd walk right down this lane by myself."

"Yah," Caddy said. "You wouldn't dare to put your foot down in it if we were not here too."

II

Dilsey was still sick, so we took Nancy home every night until mother said, "How much longer is this going on? I to be left alone in this big house while you take home a frightened Negro?"

We fixed a pallet in the kitchen for Nancy. One night we waked up, hearing the sound. It was not singing and it was not crying, coming up the dark stairs. There was a light in mother's room and we heard father going down the hall, down the back stairs, and Caddy and I went into the hall. The floor was cold. Our toes curled away from it while we listened to the sound. It was like singing and it wasn't like singing, like the sounds that Negroes make.

Then it stopped and we heard father going down the back stairs, and we went to the head of the stairs. Then the sound began again, in the stairway, not loud, and we could see

Nancy's eyes halfway up the stairs, against the wall. They looked like cat's eyes do, like a big cat against the wall, watching us. When we came down the steps to where she was, she quit making the sound again, and we stood there until father came back up from the kitchen, with his pistol in his hand. He went back down with Nancy and they came back with Nancy's pallet.

We spread the pallet in our room. After the light in mother's room went off, we could see Nancy's eyes again. "Nancy," Caddy whispered, "are you asleep, Nancy?"

Nancy whispered something. It was oh or no, I dont know which. Like nobody had made it, like it came from nowhere and went nowhere, until it was like Nancy was not there at all; that I had looked so hard at her eyes on the stairs that they had got printed on my eyeballs, like the sun does when you have closed your eyes and there is no sun. "Jesus," Nancy whispered. "Jesus."

"Was it Jesus?" Caddy said. "Did he try to come into the kitchen?"

"Jesus," Nancy said. Like this: Jeeeeeeeeeeeeeeeeesus, until the sound went out, like a match or a candle does.

"It's the other Jesus she means," I said.

"Can you see us, Nancy?" Caddy whispered. "Can you see our eyes too?"

"I aint nothing but a nigger," Nancy said. "God knows. God knows."

"What did you see down there in the kitchen?" Caddy whispered. "What tried to get in?"

"God knows," Nancy said. We could see her eyes. "God knows."

Dilsey got well. She cooked dinner. "You'd better stay in bed a day or two longer," father said.

"What for?" Dilsey said. "If I had been a day later, this place would be to rack and ruin. Get on out of here now, and let me get my kitchen straight again."

Dilsey cooked supper too. And that night, just before dark, Nancy came into the kitchen.

"How do you know he's back?" Dilsey said. "You aint seen him."

"Jesus is a nigger," Jason said.

"I can feel him," Nancy said. "I can feel him laying yonder in the ditch."

"Tonight?" Dilsey said. "Is he there tonight?"

"Dilsey's a nigger too," Jason said.

"You try to eat something," Dilsey said.

"I dont want nothing," Nancy said.

"I aint a nigger," Jason said.

"Drink some coffee," Dilsey said. She poured a cup of coffee for Nancy. "Do you know he's out there tonight? How come you know it's tonight?"

"I know," Nancy said. "He's there, waiting. I know. I done lived with him too long. I know what he is fixing to do fore he know it himself."

"Drink some coffee," Dilsey said. Nancy held the cup to her mouth and blew into the cup. Her mouth pursed out like a spreading adder's, like a rubber mouth, like she had blown all the color out of her lips with blowing the coffee.

"I aint a nigger," Jason said. "Are you a nigger, Nancy?"

"I hellborn, child," Nancy said. "I wont be nothing soon. I going back where I come from soon."

III

She began to drink the coffee. While she was drinking, holding the cup in both hands, she began to make the sound again. She made the sound into the cup and the coffee sploshed out onto her hands and her dress. Her eyes looked at us and she sat there, her elbows on her knees, holding the cup in both hands, looking at us across the wet cup, making the sound. "Look at Nancy," Jason said. "Nancy cant cook for us now. Dilsey's got well now."

"You hush up," Dilsey said. Nancy held the cup in both hands, looking at us, making the sound, like there were two of them: one looking at us and the other making the sound. "Whyn't you let Mr Jason telefoam the marshal?" Dilsey said. Nancy stopped then, holding the cup in her long brown hands. She tried to drink some coffee again, but it sploshed out of the cup, onto her hands and her dress, and she put the cup down. Jason watched her.

"I cant swallow it," Nancy said. "I swallows but it wont go down me."

"You go down to the cabin," Dilsey said. "Frony will fix you a pallet and I'll be there soon."

"Wont no nigger stop him," Nancy said.

"I aint a nigger," Jason said. "Am I, Dilsey?"

"I reckon not," Dilsey said. She looked at Nancy. "I dont reckon so. What you going to do, then?"

Nancy looked at us. Her eyes went fast, like she was afraid there wasn't time to look, without hardly moving at all. She looked at us, at all three of us at one time. "You member that night I stayed in yawls' room?" she said. She told about how we waked up early the next morning, and played. We had to play quiet, on her pallet, until father woke up and it was time to get breakfast. "Go and ask your maw to let me stay here tonight," Nancy said. "I wont need no pallet. We can play some more."

Caddy asked mother. Jason went too. "I cant have Negroes sleeping in the bedrooms," mother said. Jason cried. He cried until mother said he couldn't have any dessert for three days if he didn't stop. Then Jason said he could stop if Dilsey would make a chocolate cake. Father was there.

"Why dont you do something about it?" mother said. "What do we have officers for?"

"Why is Nancy afraid of Jesus?" Caddy said. "Are you afraid of father, mother?"

"What could the officers do?" father said. "If Nancy hasn't seen him, how could the officers find him?"

"Then why is she afraid?" mother said.

"She says he is there. She says she knows he is there tonight."

"Yet we pay taxes," mother said. "I must wait here alone in this big house while you take a Negro woman home."

"You know that I am not lying outside with a razor," father said.

"I'll stop if Dilsey will make a chocolate cake," Jason said. Mother told us to go out and father said he didn't know if Jason would get a chocolate cake or not, but he knew what Jason was going to get in about a minute. We went back to the kitchen and told Nancy.

"Father said for you to go home and lock the door, and you'll be all right," Caddy said. "All right from what, Nancy? Is Jesus mad at you?" Nancy was holding the coffee cup in her hands again, her elbows on her knees and her hands holding the cup between her knees. She was looking into the cup. "What have you done that made Jesus mad?" Caddy said. Nancy let the cup go. It didn't break on the floor, but the coffee spilled out, and Nancy sat there with her hands still making the shape of the cup. She began to make the sound again, not loud. Not singing and not unsinging. We watched her.

"Here," Dilsey said. "You quit that, now. You get aholt of yourself. You wait here. I going to get Versh to walk home with you." Dilsey went out.

We looked at Nancy. Her shoulders kept shaking, but she quit making the sound. We watched her. "What's Jesus going to do to you?" Caddy said. "He went away."

Nancy looked at us. "We had fun that night I stayed in yawls' room, didn't we?"

"I didn't," Jason said. "I didn't have any fun."

"You were asleep in mother's room," Caddy said. "You were not there."

"Let's go down to my house and have some more fun," Nancy said.

"Mother wont let us," I said "It's too late now."

"Dont bother her," Nancy said. "We can tell her in the morning. She wont mind."

"She wouldn't let us," I said.

"Dont ask her now," Nancy said. "Dont bother her now."

"She didn't say we couldn't go," Caddy said.

"We didn't ask," I said.

"If you go, I'll tell," Jason said.

"We'll have fun," Nancy said. "They wont mind, just to my house. I been working for yawl a long time. They wont mind."

"I'm not afraid to go," Caddy said. "Jason is the one that's afraid. He'll tell."

"I'm not," Jason said.

"Yes, you are," Caddy said. "You'll tell."

"I wont tell," Jason said. "I'm not afraid."

"Jason aint afraid to go with me," Nancy said. "Is you, Jason?"

"Jason is going to tell," Caddy said. The lane was dark. We passed the pasture gate. "I bet if something was to jump out from behind that gate, Jason would holler."

"I wouldn't," Jason said. We walked down the lane. Nancy was talking loud.

"What are you talking so loud for, Nancy?" Caddy said.

"Who; me?" Nancy said. "Listen at Quentin and Caddy and Jason saying I'm talking loud."

"You talk like there was five of us here," Caddy said. "You talk like father was here too."

"Who; me talking loud, Mr Jason?" Nancy said.

"Nancy called Jason 'Mister,'" Caddy said.

"Listen how Caddy and Quentin and Jason talk," Nancy said.

"We're not talking loud," Caddy said. "You're the one that's talking like father — "

"Hush," Nancy said; "hush, Mr Jason."

"Nancy called Jason 'Mister' aguh — "

"Hush," Nancy said. She was talking loud when we crossed the ditch and stooped through the fence where she used to stoop through with the clothes on her head. Then we came to her house. We were going fast then. She opened the door. The smell of the house was like the lamp and the smell of Nancy was like the wick, like they were waiting for one another to begin to smell. She lit the lamp and closed the door and put the bar up. Then she quit talking loud, looking at us.

"What're we going to do?" Caddy said.

"What do yawl want to do?" Nancy said.

"You said we would have some fun," Caddy said.

There was something about Nancy's house; something you could smell besides Nancy and the house. Jason smelled it, even. "I dont want to stay here," he said. "I want to go home."

"Go home, then," Caddy said.

"I dont want to go by myself," Jason said.

"We're going to have some fun," Nancy said.

"How?" Caddy said.

Nancy stood by the door. She was looking at us, only it was like she had emptied her eyes, like she had quit using them. "What do you want to do?" she said.

"Tell us a story," Caddy said. "Can you tell a story?"

"Yes," Nancy said.

"Tell it," Caddy said. We looked at Nancy. "You dont know any stories."

"Yes," Nancy said. "Yes, I do."

She came and sat in a chair before the hearth. There was a little fire there. Nancy built it up, when it was already hot inside. She built up a good blaze. She told a story. She talked like her eyes looked, like her eyes watching us and her voice talking to us did not belong to her. Like she was living somewhere else, waiting somewhere else. She was outside the cabin. Her voice was inside and the shape of her, the Nancy that could stoop under a barbed wire fence with a bundle of clothes balanced on her head as though without weight, like a balloon, was there. But that was all. "And so this here queen come walking up to the ditch, where that bad man was hiding. She was walking up to the ditch, and she say, 'If I can just get past this here ditch,' was what she say …"

"What ditch?" Caddy said. "A ditch like that one out there? Why did a queen want to go into a ditch?"

"To get to her house," Nancy said. She looked at us. "She had to cross the ditch to get into her house quick and bar the door."

"Why did she want to go home and bar the door?" Caddy said.

IV

Nancy looked at us. She quit talking. She looked at us. Jason's legs stuck straight out of his pants where he sat on Nancy's lap. "I don't think that's a good story," he said. "I want to go home."

"Maybe we had better," Caddy said. She got up from the floor. "I bet they are looking for us right now." She went toward the door.

"No," Nancy said. "Dont open it." She got up quick and passed Caddy. She didn't touch the door, the wooden bar.

"Why not?" Caddy said.

"Come back to the lamp," Nancy said. "We'll have fun. You dont have to go."

"We ought to go," Caddy said. "Unless we have a lot of fun." She and Nancy came back to the fire, the lamp.

"I want to go home," Jason said. "I'm going to tell."

"I know another story," Nancy said. She stood close to the lamp. She looked at Caddy, like when your eyes look up at a stick balanced on your nose. She had to look down to see Caddy, but her eyes looked like that, like when you are balancing a stick.

"I wont listen to it," Jason said. "I'll bang on the floor."

"It's a good one," Nancy said. "It's better than the other one."

"What's it about?" Caddy said. Nancy was standing by the lamp. Her hand was on the lamp, against the light, long and brown.

"Your hand is on that hot globe," Caddy said. "Dont it feel hot to your hand?"

Nancy looked at her hand on the lamp chimney. She took her hand away, slow. She stood there, looking at Caddy, wringing her long hand as though it were tied to her wrist with a string.

"Let's do something else," Caddy said.

"I want to go home," Jason said.

"I got some popcorn," Nancy said. She looked at Caddy and then at Jason and then at me and then at Caddy again. "I got some popcorn."

"I dont like popcorn," Jason said. "I'd rather have candy."

Nancy looked at Jason. "You can hold the popper." She was still wringing her hand; it was long and limp and brown.

"All right," Jason said. "I'll stay a while if I can do that. Caddy cant hold it. I'll want to go home again if Caddy holds the popper."

Nancy built up the fire. "Look at Nancy putting her hands in the fire," Caddy said. "What's the matter with you, Nancy?"

"I got popcorn," Nancy said. "I got some." She took the popper from under the bed. It was broken. Jason began to cry.

"Now we cant have any popcorn," he said.

"We ought to go home, anyway," Caddy said. "Come on, Quentin."

"Wait," Nancy said; "wait. I can fix it. Dont you want to help me fix it?"

"I dont think I want any," Caddy said. "It's too late now."

"You help me, Jason," Nancy said. "Dont you want to help me?"

"No," Jason said. "I want to go home."

"Hush," Nancy said; "hush. Watch. Watch me. I can fix it so Jason can hold it and pop the corn." She got a piece of wire and fixed the popper.

"It wont hold good," Caddy said.

"Yes, it will," Nancy said. "Yawl watch. Yawl help me shell some corn."

The popcorn was under the bed too. We shelled it into the popper and Nancy helped Jason hold the popper over the fire.

"It's not popping," Jason said. "I want to go home."

"You wait," Nancy said. "It'll begin to pop. We'll have fun then." She was sitting close to the fire. The lamp was turned up so high it was beginning to smoke.

"Why dont you turn it down some?" I said.

"It's all right," Nancy said. "I'll clean it. Yawl wait. The popcorn will start in a minute."

"I dont believe it's going to start," Caddy said. "We ought to start home, anyway. They'll be worried."

"No," Nancy said. "It's going to pop. Dilsey will tell um yawl with me. I been working for yawl long time. They won't mind if yawl at my house. You wait, now. It'll start popping any minute now."

Then Jason got some smoke in his eyes and he began to cry. He dropped the popper into the fire. Nancy got a wet rag and wiped Jason's face, but he didn't stop crying.

"Hush," she said. "Hush." But he didn't hush. Caddy took the popper out of the fire.

"It's burned up," she said. "You'll have to get some more popcorn, Nancy."

"Did you put all of it in?" Nancy said.

"Yes," Caddy said. Nancy looked at Caddy. Then she took the popper and opened it and poured the cinders into her apron and began to sort the grains, her hands long and brown, and we watching her.

"Haven't you got any more?" Caddy said.

"Yes," Nancy said; "yes. Look. This here ain't burnt. All we need to do is — "

"I want to go home," Jason said. "I'm going to tell."

"Hush," Caddy said. We all listened. Nancy's head was already turned toward the barred door, her eyes filled with red lamplight. "Somebody is coming," Caddy said.

Then Nancy began to make that sound again, not loud, sitting there above the fire, her long hands dangling between her knees; all of a sudden water began to come out on her face in big drops, running down her face, carrying in each one a little turning ball of firelight like a spark until it dropped off her chin. "She's not crying," I said.

"I aint crying," Nancy said. Her eyes were closed. "I aint crying. Who is it?"

"I dont know," Caddy said. She went to the door and looked out. "We've got to go now," she said. "Here comes father."

"I'm going to tell," Jason said. "Yawl made me come."

The water still ran down Nancy's face. She turned in her chair. "Listen. Tell him. Tell him we going to have fun. Tell him I take good care of yawl until in the morning. Tell him to let me come home with yawl and sleep on the floor. Tell him I won't need no pallet. We'll have fun. You member last time how we had so much fun?"

"I didn't have fun," Jason said. "You hurt me. You put smoke in my eyes. I'm going to tell."

V

Father came in. He looked at us. Nancy did not get up.

"Tell him," she said.

"Caddy made us come down here," Jason said. "I didn't want to."

Father came to the fire. Nancy looked up at him. "Cant you go to Aunt Rachel's and stay?" he said. Nancy looked up at father, her hands between her knees. "He's not here," father said. "I would have seen him. There's not a soul in sight."

"He in the ditch," Nancy said. "He waiting in the ditch yonder."

"Nonsense," father said. He looked at Nancy. "Do you know he's there?"

"I got the sign," Nancy said.

"What sign?"

"I got it. It was on the table when I come in. It was a hogbone, with blood meat still on it, laying by the lamp. He's out there. When yawl walk out that door, I gone."

"Gone where, Nancy?" Caddy said.

"I'm not a tattletale," Jason said.

"Nonsense," father said.

"He out there," Nancy said. "He looking through that window this minute, waiting for yawl to go. Then I gone."

"Nonsense," father said. "Lock up your house and we'll take you on to Aunt Rachel's"

"Twont do no good," Nancy said. She didn't look at father now, but he looked down at her, at her long, limp, moving hands. "Putting it off wont do no good."

"Then what do you want to do?" father said.

"I dont know," Nancy said. "I cant do nothing. Just put it off. And that dont do no good. I reckon it belong to me. I reckon what I going to get aint no more than mine."

"Get what?" Caddy said. "What's yours?"

"Nothing," father said. "You all must get to bed."

"Caddy made me come," Jason said.

"Go on to Aunt Rachel's," father said.

"It wont do no good," Nancy said. She sat before the fire, her elbows on her knees, her long hands between her knees. "When even your own kitchen wouldn't do no good. When even if I was sleeping on the floor in the room with your chillen, and the next morning there I am, and blood — "

"Hush," father said. "Lock the door and put out the lamp and go to bed."

"I scared of the dark," Nancy said. "I scared for it to happen in the dark."

"You mean you're going to sit right here with the lamp lighted?" father said. Then Nancy began to make the sound again, sitting before the fire, her long hands between her knees. "Ah, damnation," father said. "Come along, chillen. It's past bedtime."

"When yawl go home, I gone," Nancy said. She talked quieter now, and her face looked quiet, like her hands. "Anyway, I got my coffin money saved up with Mr Lovelady." Mr Lovelady was a short, dirty man who collected the Negro insurance, coming around to the cabins or the kitchens every Saturday morning, to collect fifteen cents. He and his wife lived at the hotel. One morning his wife committed suicide. They had a child, a little girl. He and the child went away. After a week or two he came back alone. We would see him going along the lanes and the back streets on Saturday mornings.

"Nonsense," father said. "You'll be the first thing I'll see in the kitchen tomorrow morning."

"You'll see what you'll see, I reckon," Nancy said. "But it will take the Lord to say what that will be."

VI

We left her sitting before the fire.

"Come and put the bar up," father said. But she didn't move. She didn't look at us again, sitting quietly there between the lamp and the fire. From some distance down the lane we could look back and see her through the open door.

"What, Father?" Caddy said. "What's going to happen?"

"Nothing," father said. Jason was on father's back, so Jason was the tallest of all of us. We went down into the ditch. I looked at it, quiet. I couldn't see much where the moonlight and the shadows tangled.

"If Jesus is hid here, he can see us, cant he?" Caddy said.

"He's not there," father said. "He went away a long time ago."

"You made me come," Jason said, high; against the sky it looked like father had two heads, a little one and a big one. "I didn't want to."

We went up out of the ditch. We could still see Nancy's house and the open door, but we couldn't see Nancy now, sitting before the fire with the door open, because she was tired. "I just done got tired," she said. "I just a nigger. It aint no fault of mine."

But we could hear her, because she began just after we came up out of the ditch, the sound that was not singing and not unsinging. "Who will do our washing now, Father?" I said.

"I'm not a nigger," Jason said, high and close above father's head.

"You're worse," Caddy said, "you are a tattletale. If something was to jump out, you'd be scairder than a nigger."

"I wouldn't," Jason said.

"You'd cry," Caddy said.

"Caddy," father said.

"I wouldn't!" Jason said.

"Scairy cat," Caddy said.

"Candace!" father said.

QUESTIONS

1. How has Faulkner created the atmosphere of impending doom in "That Evening Sun"?

2. Who is the protagonist in this story? Can you make a case for some other character?

3. What is the nature of the conflict in the mind of the children's father? At what point does it reach a crisis? How is it resolved?

4. Faulkner names his characters with considerable care. Do these names reflect their places in society? Is this true of Jesus, too?

5. Who is the narrator of the story? How long after the event does the narrator tell the story?

6. Is the incident between Nancy and Mr. Stovall essential to the story? What does it contribute?

7. Are the children adequately distinguished from each other? From what Faulkner's story tells us about them, are they likely to grow up like the father or like Mr. Stovall?

8. The children do not grasp everything that goes on around them. Are they too innocent to be credible? How does Faulkner show that they sense something is wrong?

9. What is the relationship between Nancy and Dilsey? between the two women and the children?

10. What, if anything, does the popcorn incident contribute to the plot? Does it interrupt the flow of action? Does it build suspense?

11. Why doesn't Faulkner tell what happens to Nancy? Is the present ending effective?

ERNEST HEMINGWAY

A Clean, Well-Lighted Place

It was late and every one had left the café except an old man who sat in the shadow the leaves of the tree made against the electric light. In the daytime the street was dusty, but at night the dew settled the dust and the old man liked to sit late because he was deaf and now at night it was quiet and he felt the difference. The two waiters inside the café knew that the old man was a little drunk, and while he was a good client they knew that if he became too drunk he would leave without paying, so they kept watch on him.

"Last week he tried to commit suicide," one waiter said.

"Why?"

"He was in despair."

"What about?"

"Nothing."

"How do you know it was nothing?"

"He has plenty of money."

They sat together at a table that was close against the wall near the door of the café and looked at the terrace where the tables were all empty except where the old man sat in the shadow of the leaves of the tree that moved slightly in the wind. A girl   a soldier went by in the street. The street light shone on the brass number on his collar. The girl wore no head covering and hurried beside him.

"The guard will pick him up," one waiter said.

"What does it matter if he gets what he's after?"

"He had better get off the street now. The guard will get him. They went by five minutes ago."

The old man sitting in the shadow rapped on his saucer with his glass. The younger waiter went over to him.

"What do you want?"

The old man looked at him. "Another brandy," he said.

"You'll be drunk," the waiter said. The old man looked at him. The waiter went away.

"He'll stay all night," he said to his colleague. "I'm sleepy now. I never get into bed before three o'clock. He should have killed himself last week."

The waiter took the brandy bottle and another saucer from the counter inside the café and marched out to the old man's table. He put down the saucer and poured the glass full of brandy.

"You should have killed yourself last week," he said to the deaf man. The old man motioned with his finger. "A little more," he said. The waiter poured on into the glass so that the brandy slopped over and ran down the stem into the top saucer of the pile. "Thank you," the old man said. The waiter took the bottle back inside the café. He sat down at the table with his colleague again.

"He's drunk now," he said.

"He's drunk every night."

"What did he want to kill himself for?"

"How should I know."

"How did he do it?"

"He hung himself with a rope."

"Who cut him down?"

"His niece."

"Why did they do it?"

"Fear for his soul."

"How much money has he got?"

"He's got plenty."

"He must be eighty years old."

"Anyway I should say he was eighty."

"I wish he would go home. I never get to bed before three o'clock. What kind of hour is that to go to bed?"

"He stays up because he likes it."

"He's lonely. I'm not lonely. I have a wife waiting in bed for me."

"He had a wife once too."

"A wife would be no good to him now."

"You can't tell. He might be better with a wife."

"His niece looks after him."

"I know. You said she cut him down."

"I wouldn't want to be that old. An old man is a nasty thing."

"Not always. This old man is clean. He drinks without spilling. Even now, drunk. Look at him."

"I don't want to look at him. I wish he would go home. He has no regard for those who must work."

The old man looked from his glass across the square, then over at the waiters.

"Another brandy," he said, pointing to his glass. The waiter who was in a hurry came over.

"Finished," he said, speaking with that omission of syntax stupid people employ when talking to drunken people or foreigners. "No more tonight. Close now."

"Another," said the old man.

"No. Finished." The waiter wiped the edge of the table with a towel and shook his head.

The old man stood up, slowly counted the saucers, took a leather coin purse from his pocket and paid for the drinks, leaving half a peseta tip.

The waiter watched him go down the street, a very old man walking unsteadily but with dignity.

"Why didn't you let him stay and drink?" the unhurried waiter asked. They were putting up the shutters. "It is not half-past two."

"I want to go home to bed."

"What is an hour?"

"More to me than to him."

"An hour is the same."

"You talk like an old man yourself. He can buy a bottle and drink at home."

"It's not the same."

"No, it is not," agreed the waiter with a wife. He did not wish to be unjust. He was only in a hurry.

"And you? You have no fear of going home before your usual hour?"

"Are you trying to insult me?"

"No, hombre,[1] only to make a joke."

"No," the waiter who was in a hurry said, rising from pulling down the metal shutters. "I have confidence. I am all confidence."

"You have youth, confidence, and a job," the older waiter said. "You have everything."

"And what do you lack?"

"Everything but work."

"You have everything I have."

"No. I have never had confidence and I am not young."

"Come on. Stop talking nonsense and lock up."

"I am of those who like to stay late at the café," the older waiter said. "With all those who do not want to go to bed. With all those who need a light for the night."

"I want to go home and into bed."

"We are of two different kinds," the older waiter said. He was now dressed to go home. "It is not only a question of youth and confidence although those things are very beautiful. Each night I am reluctant to close up because there may be some one who needs the café"

"Hombre, there are bodegas[2] open all night long."

"You do not understand. This is a clean and pleasant café. It is well lighted. The light is very good and also, now, there are shadows of the leaves."

"Good night," said the younger waiter.

"Good night," the other said. Turning off the electric light he continued the conversation with himself. It is the light of course but it is necessary that the place be clean and pleasant. You do not want music. Certainly you do not want music. Nor can you stand before a bar with dignity although that is all that is provided for these hours. What did he fear? It was not fear or dread. It was a nothing that he knew too well. It was all a nothing and a man was nothing too. It was only that and light was all it needed and a certain cleanness and order. Some lived in it and never felt it but he knew it all was nada y pues nada y nada y pues nada.[3] Our nada who art in nada, nada be thy name thy kingdom nada thy will be nada in nada as it is in nada. Give us this nada our daily nada and nada us our nada as we nada our nadas and nada us not into nada but deliver us from nada; pues nada. Hail nothing full of

---

[1] Man.

[2] Wine shops.

[3] "... nothing and then nothing and nothing and then nothing." What follows is a parody of "The Lord's Prayer" and "Hail Mary."

nothing, nothing is with thee. He smiled and stood before a bar with a shining steam pressure coffee machine.

"What's yours?" asked the barman.

"Nada."

"Otro loco mas,"[4] said the barman and turned away.

"A little cup," said the waiter.

The barman poured it for him.

"The light is very bright and pleasant but the bar is unpolished," the waiter said.

The barman looked at him but did not answer. It was too late at night for conversation.

"You want another copita?"[5] the barman asked.

"No, thank you," said the waiter and went out. He disliked bars and bodegas. A clean, well-lighted café was a very different thing. Now, without thinking further, he would go home to his room. He would lie in the bed and finally, with daylight, he would go to sleep. After all, he said to himself, it is probably only insomnia. Many must have it.

QUESTIONS

1. Does this story have a plot? If so, what are its elements? What are its conflicts? What is the resolution? Does "A Clean, Well-Lighted Place" have a structure?

2. Hemingway was famous for economy. Why, then, did he include the passing soldier and the girl in this story? What purpose do they serve?

3. What is the relationship between the two waiters? Is this relationship affected by their separate attitudes toward the old man?

4. Why did the old man attempt suicide?

5. Hemingway frequently omits speech tags in this story. Can you distinguish the speakers by what they say? by their tone and manner of speech? Is this how real people talk?

6. Is this a story of the clash between generations, the new and the old? Does Hemingway show a preference for one or the other?

7. Why is it important to drink in "a clean, well-lighted place"? Why is this more important to one waiter than to the other?

8. What does the parody of the "The Lord's Prayer" and "Hail Mary" suggest to you? Why these particular prayers? Is this part of a message Hemingway wants to convey, or is it a means of characterizing the older waiter? Are there other possibilities?

9. What is your emotional response to "A Clean, Well-Lighted Place"? How can you account for it?

---

[4] "Another crazy one."

[5] A little cup.

JORGE LUIS BORGES

The Babylon Lottery

Translated by Emece Editores, S.A.

Like all men in Babylon I have been a proconsul; like all, a slave; I have also known omnipotence, opprobrium, jail. Look: the index finger of my right hand is missing. Look again: through this rent in my cape you can see a ruddy tatoo on my belly. It is the second symbol, Beth.[1] This letter, on nights of full moon, gives me power over men whose mark is Ghimel; but it also subordinates me to those marked Aleph, who on moonless nights owe obedience to those marked Ghimel. In a cellar at dawn, I have severed the jugular vein of sacred bulls against a black rock. During one lunar year, I have been declared invisible: I shrieked and was not heard, I stole my bread and was not decapitated. I have known what the Greeks did not: uncertainty. In a bronze chamber, faced with the silent handkerchief of a strangler, hope has been faithful to me; in the river of delights, panic has not failed me. Heraclitus of Pontica admiringly relates that Pythagoras recalled having been Pyrrho, and before that Euphorbus, and before that some other mortal. In order to recall analogous vicissitudes I do not need to have recourse to death, nor even to imposture.

I owe this almost atrocious variety to an institution which other republics know nothing about, or which operates among them imperfectly and in secret: the lottery. I have not delved into its history; I do know that the wizards have been unable to come to any agreement; of its powerful designs I know what a man not versed in astrology might know of the moon. I come from a vertiginous country where the lottery forms a principal part of reality: until this very day I have thought about all this as little as I have about the behavior of the indecipherable gods or about the beating of my own heart. Now, far from Babylon and its beloved customs, I think of the lottery with some astonishment and ponder the blasphemous conjectures murmured by men in the shadows at twilight.

My father related that anciently — a matter of centuries; of years? — the lottery in Babylon was a game of plebeian character. He said (I do not know with what degree of truth) that barbers gave rectangular bits of bone or decorated parchment in exchange for copper coins. A drawing of the lottery was held in the middle of the day: the winners received, without further corroboration from chance, silver-minted coins. The procedure, as you see, was elemental.

Naturally, these "lotteries" failed. Their moral virtue was nil. They did not appeal to all

---

[1] The second letter of the Hebrew alphabet. In the next sentence, Ghimel and Aleph are, respectively, the third and the first.

the faculties of men: only to their hope. In the face of public indifference, the merchants who established these venal lotteries began to lose money. Someone attempted to introduce a slight reform: the interpolation of a certain small number of adverse outcomes among the favored numbers. By means of this reform, the purchasers of numbered rectangles stood the double chance of winning a sum or of paying a fine often considerable in size. This slight danger — for each thirty favored numbers there would be one adverse number — awoke, as was only natural, the public's interest. The Babylonians gave themselves up to the game. Anyone who did not acquire lots was looked upon as pusillanimous, mean-spirited. In time, this disdain multiplied. The person who did not play was despised, but the losers who paid the fine were also scorned. The Company (thus it began to be known at that time) was forced to take measures to protect the winners, who could not collect their prizes unless nearly the entire amount of the fines was already collected. The Company brought suit against the losers: the judge condemned them to pay the original fine plus costs or to spend a number of days in jail. Every loser chose jail, so as to defraud the Company. It was from this initial bravado of a few men that the all-powerful position of the Company — its ecclesiastical, metaphysical strength — was derived.

A short while later, the reports on the drawings omitted any enumeration of fines and limited themselves to publishing the jail sentences corresponding to each adverse number. This laconism, almost unnoticed at the time, became of capital importance. *It constituted the first appearance in the lottery of nonpecuniary elements.* Its success was great. Pushed to such a measure by the players, the Company found itself forced to increase its adverse numbers.

No one can deny that the people of Babylonia are highly devoted to logic, even to symmetry. It struck them as incoherent that the fortunate numbers should be computed in round figures of money while the unfortunate should be figured in terms of days and nights in jail. Some moralists argued that the possession of money does not determine happiness and that other forms of fortune are perhaps more immediate.

There was another source of restlessness in the lower depths. The members of the sacerdotal college multiplied the stakes and plumbed the vicissitudes of terror and hope; the poor, with reasonable or inevitable envy, saw themselves excluded from this notoriously delicious exhiliration. The just anxiety of all, poor and rich alike, to participate equally in the lottery, inspired an indignant agitation, the memory of which the years have not erased. Certain obstinate souls did not comprehend, or pretended not to comprehend, that a new order had come, a necessary historical stage. ... A slave stole a crimson ticket, a ticket which earned him the right to have his tongue burned in the next drawing. The criminal code fixed the same penalty for the theft of a ticket. A number of Babylonians argued that he deserved a red-hot poker by virtue of the theft; others, more magnanimous, held that the public executioner should apply the penalty of the lottery, since chance had so determined. ...

Disturbances broke out, there was a lamentable shedding of blood; but the people of Babylon imposed their will at last, over the opposition of the rich. That is: the people fully achieved their magnanimous ends. In the first place, it made the Company accept complete public power. (This unification was necessary, given the vastness and complexity of the new operations.) In the second place, it forced the lottery to be secret, free, and general. The sale of tickets for money was abolished. Once initiated into the mysteries of Bel, every free man automatically participated in the sacred drawings of lots, which were carried out in the labyrinths of the gods every seventy nights and which determined every man's fate until the next exercise. The consequences were incalculable. A happy drawing might motivate his elevation to the council of wizards or his condemnation to the custody of an enemy (notorious or intimate), or to find, in the peaceful shadows of a room, the woman who had begun to disquiet him or whom he had never expected to see again. An adverse drawing might mean mutilation, a varied infamy, death. Sometimes a single event — the tavern killing of C, the mysterious glorification of B — might be the brilliant result of thirty or forty drawings. But it must be recalled that the individuals of the Company were (and are) all-powerful and astute as well. In many cases, the knowledge that certain joys were the simple doing of chance might have detracted from their excellence; to avoid this inconvenience the Company's agents made use of suggestion and magic. Their moves, their management, were secret. In the investigation of people's intimate hopes and intimate terrors, they made use of astrologers and spies. There were certain stone lions, there was a sacred privy called Qaphqa, there were fissures in a dusty aqueduct which, according to general opinion, *lead to the Company;* malign or benevolent people deposited accusations in these cracks. These denunciations were incorporated into an alphabetical archive of variable veracity.

Incredibly enough, there were still complaints. The Company, with its habitual discretion, did not reply directly. It preferred to scribble a brief argument — which now figures among sacred scriptures — in the debris of a mask factory. That doctrinal piece of literature observed that the lottery is an interpolation of chance into the order of the world and that to accept errors is not to contradict fate but merely to corroborate it. It also observed that those lions and that sacred recipient, though not unauthorized by the Company (which did not renounce the right to consult them), functioned without official guaranty.

This declaration pacified the public unease. It also produced other effects, not foreseen by the author. It deeply modified the spirit and operations of the Company. (I have little time left to tell what I know; we have been warned that the ship is ready to sail; but I will attempt to explain it.)

Improbable as it may be, no one had until then attempted to set up a general theory of games. A Babylonian is not highly speculative. He reveres the judgments of fate, he hands his life over to them, he places his hopes, his panic terror in them, but it never occurs to him to investigate their labyrinthian laws nor the giratory spheres which disclose them. Nevertheless, the unofficial declaration which I have mentioned inspired many discussions of a juridico-mathematical nature. From one of these discussions was born the following conjecture: if the lottery is an intensification of chance, a periodic infusion of chaos into the cosmos, would it not be desirable for chance to intervene at all stages of the lottery and not merely in the drawing? Is it not ridiculous for chance to dictate the death of someone, while the circumstances of his death — its silent reserve or publicity, the time limit of one hour or one century — should remain immune to hazard? These eminently just scruples finally provoked a considerable reform, whose complexities (intensified by the practice of centuries) are not understood except by a handful of specialists, but which I will attempt to summarize, even if only in a symbolic manner.

Let us imagine a first drawing, which eventuates in a sentence of death against some individual. To carry out the sentence, another drawing is set up, and this drawing proposes (let us say) nine possible executioners. Of these executioners, four can initiate a third drawing which will reveal the name of the actual executioner, two others can replace the adverse order with a fortunate order (the finding of a treasure, let us say), another may exacerbate the death sentence (that is: make it infamous or enrich it with torture), still others may refuse to carry it out. ...

Such is the symbolic scheme. In reality, *the number of drawings is infinite.* No decision is final, all diverge into others. The ignorant suppose that an infinite number of drawings require an infinite amount of time; in reality, it is quite enough that time be infinitely subdivisible, as is the case in the famous parable of the Tortoise and the Hare. This infinitude harmonizes in an admirable manner with the sinuous numbers of Chance and of the Celestial Archetype of the Lottery adored by the Platonists. ...

A certain distorted echo of our ritual seems to have resounded along the Tiber: Aelius Lampridius, in his *Life of Antoninus Heliogabalus*, tells of how this emperor wrote down the lot of his guests on seashells, so that one would receive ten pounds of gold and another ten flies, ten dormice, ten bears. It is only right to remark that Heliogabalus was educated in Asia Minor, among the priests of the eponymous god.

There are also impersonal drawings, of undefined purpose: one drawing will decree that a sapphire from Taprobane be thrown into the waters of the Euphrates; another, that a bird be released from a tower roof; another, that a grain of sand be withdrawn (or added) to the innumerable grains on a beach. The consequences, sometimes, are terrifying.

Under the beneficent influence of the Company, our customs have become thoroughly impregnated with chance. The buyer of a dozen amphoras of Damascus wine will not be surprised if one of them contains a talisman or a viper. The scribe who draws up a contract scarcely ever fails to introduce some erroneous datum; I myself, in making this hasty declaration, have falsified or invented some grandeur, some atrocity; perhaps, too, a certain mysterious monotony. ...

Our historians, the most discerning in the world, have invented a method for correcting chance. It is well known that the operations of this method are (in general) trustworthy; although, naturally, they are not divulged without a measure of deceit. In any case, there is nothing so contaminated with fiction as the history of the Company. ...

A paleographic document, unearthed in a temple, may well be the work of yesterday's drawing or that of one lasting a century. No book is ever published without some variant in each copy. Scribes take a secret oath to omit, interpolate, vary.

The Company, with divine modesty, eludes all publicity. Its agents, as is only natural, are secret. The orders which it is continually sending out do not differ from those lavishly issued by imposters. Besides, who can ever boast of being a mere imposter? The inebriate who improvises an absurd mandate, the dreamer who suddenly awakes to choke the woman who lies at his side to death, do they not both, perhaps, carry out a secret decision by the Company? This silent functioning, comparable to that of God, gives rise to all manner of conjectures. One of them, for instance, abominably insinuates that the Company is eternal and that it will last until the last night of the world, when the last god annihilates the cosmos. Still another conjecture declares that the Company is omnipotent, but that it exerts its influence only in the most minute matters: in a bird's cry, in the shades of rust and the hues of dust, in the cat naps of dawn. There is one conjecture, spoken from the mouths of masked heresiarchs, to the effect that *the Company has never existed and never will*. A conjecture no less vile argues that it is indifferently inconsequential to affirm or deny the reality of the shadowy corporation, because Babylon is nothing but an infinite game of chance.

QUESTIONS

1. Trace the stages by which the lottery changed from its first form to its last. What was the most important change?

2. What is the Company? Is it a symbol for bureaucracy? for something more?

3. Is nothing certain in Babylon; is everything subject to chance?

4. The narrator tells us that "the ship is ready to sail." Where is it going? Why is it leaving Babylon?

5. Who is the narrator of this story? Is he a trustworthy reporter? What evidence supports your answer?

6. Is "The Babylon Lottery" a fantasy? a nightmare? an allegory? If it is an allegory, what is the moral of the tale?

SEAN O'FAOLAIN

The Man Who Invented Sin

In our youth when we used to pour into the mountains to learn Irish, places that were lonely and silent for the rest of the year became full of gaiety during the summer months. Every day there were picnics and expeditions; every night there were dances, moonlight boating parties, singsongs in the cottages. The village street became a crowded promenade; its windows never went black before one in the morning; the pub was never empty. Where once you could have been utterly alone half a mile off the road, in the bog or up the mountain, you could not now be sure of privacy anywhere. If you went up the mountain to bathe naked in some tiny loch you might suddenly see a file of young students like Alpineers coming laughing down on you over the next scarp; you might turn the corner of a lonely mountain pass courting your girl and burst upon a bevy of nuns sedately singing choruses among the rocks — for every kind of teacher, laymen and women, nuns, priests, and monks were encouraged in those years to come out into the hills.

How we all got accommodation I do not know. The priests took lodgings in the villages. The monks and nuns purchased derelict houses which had been abandoned by the landlords after the Revolution. The people gave up their best rooms to the rest of us, turned lofts into dormitories, one or two even set up secondhand bell tents. One July, so stifling was the house where I stayed — six at least to every room — that I used to take a rug every night and climb into the high hay in the barn; and there were always four or five like me who preferred to be bitten by the ticks and waked early by the birds and the mountain air than to be half suffocated in featherbeds under the baking slates. By the end of the month, however, I got so tired of digging the little crablike ticks from under my skin that I moved two miles out the road to a place called Ryder's, a small house on the lower lake, which usually took nobody at all. Indeed, only by great cajoling did I persuade Mrs. Ryder to take me in. My only fear, then, was that I might be lonely. But before she knew what had happened Mrs. Ryder had not merely one lodger but five; for with the beginning of August the monks' hostel overflowed, and the nuns' hostel overflowed, and she had to take in two of the monks and two of the nuns.

There was nothing remarkable about my fellow students, except, perhaps, that little Sister Magdalen was so dainty and gay and spirited that it seemed a shame to lock her away from the world in a convent. Sister Chrysostom was tall, delicate, with big hands and a blotchy skin, and she walked with her toes turned in. She was a bit of a Miss Prim, and I think she had been chosen as companion for Sister Magdalen because she was so prim. Brother Virgilius was a countryman with a powerful frame and a powerful voice, round red cheeks, and no nerves, and why he had chosen to be a monk was hard to understand. It seemed to me that he would have made a better farmer than a teacher. However, I found that he was a fine hurler and I am sure the boys loved him for his natural ways. Brother Majellan was very different, a gentle, apple-cheeked man with big glasses, a complexion like a girl's, teeth as white as a hound's, and soft, beaming eyes. He was an intelligent, sensitive man. I took to him immediately.

At first we saw very little of one another. They had their principal meal at their own hostels, were studying most of the day, and the only time we all met was in the evenings, when we sat in the little garden and passed discreet remarks across the path about politics or the weather; or, if there was rain, we would meet in the drawing room, where there was a turf fire, and talk of the day's lessons. They kept convent hours, were off to their rooms by nine at the latest, and long before I rose were gone down to the village to morning Mass. That year, however, the weather broke suddenly in the middle of August so that we found ourselves in the drawing room almost every evening, over our notebooks and dictionaries and grammars. We had, by then, become like travelers on a long railway journey who have broken the silence and are beginning to chat companionably. We might still sit silent for, say, a quarter of an hour, but then somebody would say something and we would all get going. One night, for instance, Majellan lifted his eager, earnest, doggy eyes, and said:

"Sister Magdalen, how do you pronounce the word which I call *cearrbhach*?"

"Oh, Brother Majellan," she laughed, shocked at herself, entertained by her own folly, "I am afraid I do not even know what the word means!"

Virgilius clapped his two big countryman's paws together and roared out laughing.

"Sister Magdalen, I'm surprised at you! I'm surprised at you! Not know the word *cearrbhach*." It means a card player or a gambler."

"And is that what it means? *Cearrbhach*." And she pronounced the guttural word as daintily as if it rhymed with *peruke*.

She was a city girl and had never before heard Irish spoken by anybody but city people.

"No! You're not saying it right at all. You're too ladylike about it. Say it the way the people say it. *This* way."

"I see." And again the dainty pronunciation like *peruke*. "Like that?"

"Listen, Sister. I'll show you the way to talk Irish. If you'll pardon the expression, make a great big shpit inside in your mouth and gurgle it. Like this: *carrrwoochhhk*."

Chrysostom immediately protested.

"Please, Brother Virgilius! If we cannot speak our own language like ladies let us not speak it at all."

"But," from Majellan, "that really is the way the people speak. It is a guttural language. Like German."

"Not Bavarian German. It is true that the Prussians ..."

And off they went into a heated argument — the sort of argument we were always having in those days, about whether Ireland must always be a peasant country, and what other countries had achieved, and Virgilius, who hated arguments, blew out his lips and looked gloomily at his two big feet stretched out before him, and Majellan and Magdalen got so excited that Chrysostom had to stop it with her usual:

"Sister, I really think it is our hour to retire."

One day at the college, as we called the sun-baked tin building where we studied from ten to one, we were asked to write an essay on a proverb to which the nearest Saxon equivalent is "The child is father to the man." I remember, that evening, how the mists lifted from the hills, and the sun began to raise gentle wisps of steam from the rocks, and the trout were leaping from a lake as blue as the patches of sky between the dissolving clouds. We spread newspapers on the two damp garden seats, and as we discussed the proper Irish terms to be used, the four of them began, without noticing it, to speak of their own childhood; where they had been born, where they went to school, and so on. Sister Magdalen sucked the end of her silver pencil and said:

"I know the Gaelic for 'I was born.' That is *Do rugadh mé*. And the place — Templemore. Of course, that is *An Teampall Môr*. The Great Temple. Or The Big Church. Though the Lord knows there's no big temple in Templemore." She sighed. Then she cocked her head suddenly. "I suppose you were never in Templemore, Brother Majellan? But, sure, why would you! It's an out-of-the-way little place."

Chrysostom tapped my fingers irritably with her pencil. I was idly pulling a fuchsia flower to pieces.

"How would you say that, Sister?"

"Which? What? What was it you said, Sister Chrysostom?"

"'It's an out-of-the-way little place.' You see, I want to say that, too. I was born in a small little place like Templemore."

"Where was that?" asked Virgilius idly. He had been staring solemnly at the fuchsia that I threw into his lap.

"Kilfinnane," said Chrysostom, "in County Limerick."

At once Virgilius whirled and slapped her thigh.

"Yerrah, Chrysostom, do you mean to tell me that you come from Kilfinnane!"

"Brother!" And she held his arm excitedly. "Do you know Kilfinnane?"

"Do I know my own father? Wasn't I born just below in Kilmallock? Oh, wisha, then, 'tis many the fine Sunday I took the old bicycle out to Kilfinnane hunting hares behind the rath. If you come from Kilfinnane you must surely know the rath?"

"The rath is on our land!"

"Ah, no?" — in a huge childish delight.

"Often and often I stood on the rath and looked down at the smoke of the train coming into Kilmallock — in and out of the woods — the little white smoke. And I could watch it again for another half an hour after it left Kilmallock, puffing away down towards Cork."

"I well believe you! It's a wonderful view. They say you can see six counties!"

"For a whole hour," she remembered. "The little white smoke. I used to wonder who might be in it, and would I ever travel away in it myself."

"Didn't I go every night to meet it at the station and gather the Dublin papers, for my uncle kept a paper shop in the Main Street? The Cork train we called it. Majellan, you're a Corkman, aren't you?"

Majellan was not listening to us. He was gazing across the darkening lake whose headlands were faint as smoke.

"My father," said Sister Magdalen thoughtfully, "was a doctor. I know how to say that, too. My mother died when I was fourteen. ... I was a lone child. ... My father married a second time."

Majellan kept staring over the lake. She said something about a notebook and flitted indoors. I got tired of listening to Virgilius and Chrysostom and got up to go to the dance. It was only then I noticed that Majellan and Magdalen were in the hall. She was dabbing her eyes with his big red handkerchief.

When I came back from the dance the half-moon had vaporized the moist land with a melancholy, filmy light. The house was black and silent.

I think it was Virgilius who first began to play pitch-and-toss along the garden path, and it was that evening that Magdalen called Majellan "Jelly." I came on them laughing over the game, which Brother Virgilius was trying to teach to the other three. Brother Majellan was, by then, calling Sister Magdalen "Maggie," Chrysostom naturally became "Chrissy," and Virgilius, of course, joined Jelly as "Jilly." How they laughed over that! I crowned the night for them by taking them up to the drawing-room piano and teaching them all a song with a chorus: *"Bab Eró'gus O mo mhíle grá."*

And Chrissy so surprised us by the strength and sweetness of her voice that at the end Virgilius clapped his hands and shouted, "I wouldn't doubt you, Chrissy. I knew you had it in you," and made her sing the song again alone. As she sang we heard a clear echo: it was a boating party out on the lake. They took up the chorus and gave it back to her until they faded around a headland still singing.

"But you know," gurgled Magdalen, "I really don't know what it all means. Can you translate it for me, Jelly?"

"No trouble at all," said Majellan. "It is a young fellow singing a song to his lady and this is what he says."

As he translated he gradually blushed redder and redder, and Virgilius winked at the big, rolling eyes of Magdalen, and her rounded little mouth, just ready to burst into laughter. When Majellan stuck his head right out through the window to look at the lake Magdalen burst. Chrysostom said, "I really think, Sister, it is our hour to retire."

"Jelly," said Virgilius, when they were gone, "you big gom! You have as much sense as a child of two."

When monks and nuns quarrel, I found, they seem to be astonished and shocked rather than angry: like children who have bumped against a door or a calf who has tried his first nettle. Grown men would have ended it with a curse or a clout. I escaped down to the kitchen to practice my Irish on Mrs. Ryder. She was baking a cake, and humming *"Bab Eró ..."* Her cousin, who was the clerk in the post office, was sitting on the settle. She asked me which had the lovely voice. Mrs. Ryder said her house was blessed.

"The creatures! Isn't it grand to hear them enjoying themselves! Four saints I have in the house."

"Only four?" I protested.

"What time did *you* come in last night?" she asked, and the conversation became exuberantly coarse.

The next evening, too, was exquisitely silent. The tiny trout splashes could be heard clearly, and the cattle lying on the dry strand across the water chewing the cud. We were all upstairs, I playing the piano, Virgilius seated in the open window singing and beating time with a silver tankard that young Ryder won in a tug of war, Jelly and Maggie trying to waltz, and when Chrissy was not laughing at poor Jelly's efforts to learn the steps she, too, was singing, at *Bab Eró*," like a blackbird. The music must have carried a long way over the water.

The door was slashed open with a bang that made the piano hum, and there was our local curate's black barrel of a body blocking the opening: for though he was not more than twenty-five — I believe it was his first parish — he was very fat. He was also pompous and cocksure. In the college we called him Lispeen, which is the Irish for a frog. For that second it was as if a cinema reel stopped dead — the tankard held in the air, the two dancers like a waxworks, and Chrissy with her mouth open.

"Glory be to God," he moaned. "So I have been informed correctly." (It was only after that I thought of the postmistress on the settle the night before; you might as well talk to a microphone as to a postmistress.) "To think that this kind of thing has been going on under my nose for weeks." He let his voice fall solemnly, even secretively. "Unknown to anybody!" He roared then. "To think I cannot go for a summer walk to read my office without hearing this kind of caterwauling!" His voice fell again. "If Martin Luther could only see this! What's your name?" he stabbed at Chrissy. She had turned as pale as her coif.

"Sissster Chryssossostom, Father."

"And your name, Sister?"

"My name is Sister Mary Magdalen," said Maggie, very dignified and entirely self-possessed, and looking very angry.

"Well named," he growled. I saw Jelly grow red with fury. "Go to your rooms, please. I'll talk to these gentlemen." With a scornful emphasis on the last word.

They fluttered out obediently, Magdalen with her head in the air, Chrysostom with terror in her eyes. Majellan turned on him. I held his arm. He was only a monk, and no match for a curate in his own parish.

"You had no right, Father, to talk to the sisters like that."

The curate swelled.

"Are you daring to answer me back, young man?"

Majellan's voice shook, but he held his ground.

"We were doing no harm."

Even Virgilius spoke up, though more respectfully — he knew the power before him.

"Sure we were only having a bit of singsong, Father?"

The curate gasped, melodramatically — I swear he had taken a prize for elocution at his seminary — then dropped into a wonderful tone of sarcasm.

"Only having a bit of a singsong? *Only* having a bit of a singsong? Well, well!" He put his stick behind him like a shooting stick and teetered back and fro on it. He was very sure of himself. "Perhaps, gentlemen, we think that we are back in the days of the Reformation?" Then he did his roar again. "Singing? Dancing? Drinking?" He whirled his stick and cracked the tankard.

Virgilius stared into the tankard, and sighed. "Shweepstake tickets."

That sent the blood to Lispeen's forehead.

"I'll talk to you young bucks in the morning when I've had a word with your superior. Good evening to you."

The door slammed. We heard him go downstairs. His voice boomed in the kitchen at the Ryders. Then we saw his shadow passing across the paling sheen of the lake.

"The bosthoon," hissed Majellan.

"Jelly," moaned Virgilius, who had seized the situation at once, "we're for the long drop!"

With that we stole down the corridor and tapped at the sisters' doors and conferred in a huddle, and Virgilius and Chrysostom blamed Majellan for speaking back, but Magdalen said, "You were quite right, Brother. He is no gentleman." But Chrysostom kept pulling her fingers and looking at each of us in turn. She knew, too, how all this would appear back in the city, where the bishop and their superiors would say, "What is this! Nuns and monks living in the same house? Dancing together? Singing choruses? Playing pitch-and-toss out in the garden? And what's all this about *a tankard*?"

Magdalen said next morning that she heard Chrysostom crying late into the night.

Actually nothing at all happened. Old Ryder and the parish priest between them must have put a stop to the curate's gallop. After all, curates come and curates go but parish priests, like the brook, go on forever. But the story spread, and the students gathered around the four to comfort and encourage them, and of evenings people started to walk out to Ryder's and, in spite of Sister Chrysostom's warnings and tremors, we began to have regular concerts in the garden. The four even began to go out on surreptitious boating parties, and the bed-at-nine rule gradually became bed at ten, and even bed at eleven, until they were soon having as happy a time as anybody. Or should have, if their consciences were at ease. But were they? For, looking back at it now, I think I understand what had occurred. The Serpent had come into the garden with the most wily of temptations. He had said, "How dare you eat this apple?" And straightaway they began to eat it. They swallowed the last morsel of their apple the night before they were due to return to the city, perhaps for a lifetime, among the smelly slums about their schools.

We were moody that evening in the garden.

"I suppose this will be the last time we'll see the moon on the lake," said Sister Magdalen.

But the moon would not be up until after eleven, and a fairy wind in the reeds, ruffling the stars in the water into a fuzz, meant that even then there might be a clouded night.

"Our bus goes at seven," said Sister Chrysostom. "When does yours go, Brother Virgilius?"

By anticipation they were already becoming formal with one another.

"Half past seven," said Brother Virgilius.

"Who'll walk as far as the lake?" suggested Brother Majellan.

They went down the white road. Autumn was coming already. A white mist hung low over the river. The lake was breathed upon. They stood at the edge of it and looked at the low hills beyond.

"Sure, we can be looking forward to next year," said Brother Virgilius cheerfully.

"If there are any summer courses next year," murmured Sister Magdalen.

The soft sound of oars was heard and a boat appeared out on the water. The people in it were singing quietly; a last boating party. It was one of those big bargelike boats built for excursion parties, and there must have been twenty people in it, crushed shoulder to shoulder. Majellan hailed them and they approached and when they invited the four out for a row even Chrissy hardly demurred. The presence of the two monks and the two nuns seemed to cheer them up, for as they rowed away towards the narrows, making for the upper lake, the songs became louder and more merry. The lights of the village overflowed into the lake. Promenaders there heard them and sang back. Doubtless the curate heard them, too, and thanked God they would all be gone in the morning.

Time ceases to exist on a lake: every fisherman knows that. Somebody said that the moon would be up at eleven and would light them home. Chrissy whispered to Maggie that that would be very late, and what would happen if some message came from the hostel? But Maggie hushed her passionately, and Virgilius cried, "Let the last night be the longest."

It was much later than eleven before they got through the narrows — the old barge stuck there as it always did. Then the gray mountain slowly swelled up like a ghost against the spreading moon, and the whole land became black and white. On the bright side of the land the white cottages shone under their tarry roofs, and on the dark hills their scattered yellow lights invited us home. It became cold on the water. Rowing back against the current was a slow business. Heavy drops of phosphorescence fell from the blades. Presently a voice said, "It is near twelve, lads, put your backs into it." Now they were not singing at all; nor did they sing again until they saw the remaining village lights — only one or two left now. And they did not sing Irish songs, which are nearly all melancholy, but old music-hall songs like "Daisy, Daisy," and "The Girls You Can't Forget," and "I'm One of the Knuts of Barcelona." The barge was not much more than twelve feet from the shore when they saw, clear in the moonlight, the black figure standing on the causeway. Majellan yelled, "Back-water!" The barge slewed around.

"I suppose, my dear ladies and gentlemen, that it does not matter to you that you are keeping the whole village awake?"

Nobody replied. The rowers set off for the opposite shore. The two brothers turned up their coat collars to hide their Roman collars. The two nuns hid their gimps and coifs with borrowed coats. Everybody was feeling cross and tired. As they neared the far shore the same black figure awaited them. He had raced round by the bridge, and gone leaping over heather and bog pool.

"You won't land here tonight until I have the name of every person on that boat!"

The midnight mountain cried back, "On — that — boat."

The boat pushed off again and in mid-lake they held a conference: for even lay teachers do not like falling out with a priest. And the four religious? There was only one thing to do. It was easy to disguise Majellan and Virgilius: caps for black hats, and the Roman collars ripped off. The nuns had to remove gimps, and cowls, put on kerchiefs and pin up their skirts. Then the boat again rowed to the landing place, the men crushed around the priest arguing loudly, and the rest ran. In five minutes he was alone on the causeway. At his feet he saw a white object on the stones: a nun's starched gimp. As he looked at it he trembled like a dog.

He was no longer alone by the moon-flooded lake. He was roaring in the pulpit, holding up the gimp: he was in the bishop's palace quietly unfolding a pale linen object out of brown paper: he was in the parish priest's sitting room and the white thing lay between them on the table: he was knocking at Ryder's door — yes, even if it was nearly one o'clock in the morning. He might have done all these things if, when he got back to his cottage, there had not been a sick call before him, and he had to get out his car and drive at once three and a half miles into the heart of the hills. Half an hour later he was tearing back. He had been hoaxed. The window of his cottage was open. The gimp was gone. It was the one good deed I did for my four friends.

I was awakened by the supernaturally bright light: it was not the sunrise: it was the sinking moon. My watch showed me that it was barely turned five o'clock. Dew and mist were all around the silent house: the lake was frosty; the sky pallid. The trees were weighted with sleep. Only the ceaseless mountain stream and the deceived birds made a sweet noise. Below in the garden, by the wooden gate, stood Majellan and Magdalen, talking. ...

I never saw Magdalen again; I never saw Virgilius again; I never saw Chrysostom again.

That was 1920, and not for twenty-three years did I meet Majellan. He was, of course, still a monk, and will always be: he was graying, and a little stooped, and much thinner. His eager, doggy eyes lit up for me: until I began to joke about those days, and then the light faded. I asked him about the others, and he told me that Virgilius was now a principal somewhere. He had not heard of the two nuns since that night on the lake.

"Ah!" I sighed. "Great days! But nobody wants to learn the language now. The mountains are empty."

"Yes. The mountains are empty."

"What a shame!"

"Mind you," he said, after a moment, "I'm not sure that I altogether approve of young people going out to these places. I hope I'm not being puritanical or anything like that, but ... well, you know the sort of thing that goes on there."

I was so shocked that I could not reply for a moment.

"But, surely, it's all very harmless?"

He shook his head seriously.

"Maybe. You *never* know."

I said something idle. Then I asked him did he go out there at all nowadays.

"That was our last year."

"I hope it wasn't any trouble with your superiors?" I asked anxiously.

"Oh, nothing like that. No. It was just ..." He looked away. Then he said over his shoulder, "I didn't much want to, really." Then he looked at me, and in a little gush of confidence he said, "You mightn't understand it, now! But it's not good to take people out of their rut. I didn't enjoy that summer."

I said I understood that. After a few more words, we parted. He smiled, said he was delighted to see I was looking so well, and went off, stooping his way back to his monastery in the slum.

By coincidence, two hours later, I found myself side by side with Lispeen, looking into a bookshop window. He was scarcely changed, except for a faint brush of gray at each ear; he wore a tall silk hat and carried a silver-headed umbrella. When I spoke to him and he turned, the sunset struck his rosy face and lit the sides of his hat so that they glowed and shone. With difficulty I brought his mind back to those years, but when I did he greeted me as heartily as if I was his best friend, and laughed so merrily at the memory of those old days that I almost expected him to clap me on the back.

"Of course, you know," he confided, with wide eyes, "they were only children. Such innocents!" He laughed at the thought of the innocents. "Of course, I *had* to frighten them!" And he laughed again, and then threw up his head and said "Heigh-ho" in a big sigh. Then he shook my hand, and beamed at me, told me I was looking grand, and went his cheerful way. He bowed benevolently to every respectful salute along the glowing street, and, when he did, his elongated shadow waved behind him like a tail.

QUESTIONS

1. What does the title mean? Who is the "man"? Is it sin or guilt that has been invented?

2. Is it important that all the principals, except Lispeen, are boarding with Mrs. Ryder?

3. How would you describe the relationship among the five student boarders?

4. "... they were only children. Such innocents!" says Lispeen at the end. Why, then, does he say he "*had* to frighten them"?

5. The narrator looks back from a distance of many years to the events of the story.

Have the years changed him much? Have they changed the other characters? Was Majellan honest when he said, "I didn't enjoy that summer"?

6. In this story, the sense of nostalgia suggests that the past was somehow better than the present. On what elements of that long-ago summer does nostalgia depend here?

7. Is "The Man Who Invented Sin" an allegory, a kind of *Paradise Lost* brought up to date? How well does the parallel hold? Are there important points at which the stories diverge?

Tropism XVIII

Translated by Maria Jolas

On the outskirts of London, in a little cottage with percale curtains, its little back lawn sunny and all wet with rain.

The big, wisteria-framed window in the studio, opens on to this lawn.

A cat with its eyes closed, is seated quite erect on the warm stone.

A spinster lady with white hair, and pink cheeks that tend towards purple, is reading an English magazine in front of the door.

She sits there, very stiff, very dignified, quite sure of herself and of others, firmly settled in her little universe. She knows that in a few moments the bell will ring for tea.

Down below, the cook, Ada, is cleaning vegetables at a table covered with white oilcloth. Her face is motionless, she appears to be thinking of nothing. She knows that it will soon be time to toast the buns, and ring the bell for tea.

QUESTIONS

1. Is this a story or only the setting for a story? No action seems to take place, but two characters — and a cat — are sitting in their places. What connects them?

2. Consider the idea of conflict, often called "the life of fiction." Is conflict suggested here? If so, how would you describe it?

3. Several verbal and structural parallels appear in "Tropism XVIII." What is their effect? Can you explain that effect?

JOHN STEINBECK

Flight

About fifteen miles below Monterey, on the wild coast, the Torres family had their farm, a few sloping acres above a cliff that dropped to the brown reefs and to the hissing white waters of the ocean. Behind the farm the stone mountains stood up against the sky. The farm buildings huddled like little clinging aphids on the mountain skirts, crouched low to the ground as though the wind might blow them into the sea. The little shack, the rattling, rotting barn were gray-bitten with sea salt, beaten by the damp wind until they had taken on the color of the granite hills. Two horses, a red cow and a red calf, half a dozen pigs and a flock of lean, multicolored chickens stocked the place. A little corn was raised on the sterile slope, and it grew short and thick under the wind, and all the cobs formed on the landward sides of the stalks.

Mama Torres, a lean, dry woman with ancient eyes, had ruled the farm for ten years, ever since her husband tripped over a stone in the field one day and fell full length on a rattlesnake. When one is bitten on the chest there is not much that can be done.

Mama Torres had three children, two undersized black ones of twelve and fourteen, Emilio and Rosy, whom Mama kept fishing on the rocks below the farm when the sea was kind and when the truant officer was in some distant part of Monterey County. And there was Pepé, the tall smiling son of nineteen, a gentle, affectionate boy, but very lazy. Pepé had a tall head, pointed at the top, and from its peak, coarse black hair grew down like a thatch all around. Over his smiling little eyes, Mama cut a straight bang so he could see. Pepé had sharp Indian cheek bones and an eagle nose, but his mouth was as sweet and shapely as a girl's mouth, and his chin was fragile and chiseled. He was loose and gangling, all legs and feet and wrists, and he was very lazy. Mama thought him fine and brave, but she never told him so. She said, "Some lazy cow must have got into thy father's family, else how could I have a son like thee." And she said, "When I carried thee, a sneaking lazy coyote came out of the brush and looked at me one day. That must have made thee so."

Pepé smiled sheepishly and stabbed at the ground with his knife to keep the blade sharp and free from rust. It was his inheritance, that knife, his father's knife. The long heavy blade folded back into the black handle. There was a button on the handle. When Pepé pressed the button, the blade leaped out ready for use. The knife was with Pepé always, for it had been his father's knife.

One sunny morning when the sea below the cliff was glinting and blue and the white surf creamed on the reef, when even the stone mountains looked kindly, Mama Torres called out the door of the shack, "Pepé, I have a labor for thee."

There was no answer. Mama listened. From behind the barn she heard a burst of laughter. She lifted her full long skirt and walked in the direction of the noise.

Pepé was sitting on the ground with his back against a box. His white teeth glistened. On either side of him stood the two black ones, tense and expectant. Fifteen feet away a redwood post was set in the ground. Pepé's right hand lay limply in his lap, and in the palm the big black knife rested. The blade was closed back into the handle. Pepé looked smiling at the sky.

Suddenly Emilio cried, "Ya!"

Pepé's wrist flicked like the head of a snake. The blade seemed to fly open in mid-air, and with a thump the point dug into the redwood post, and the black handle quivered. The three burst into excited laughter. Rosy ran to the post and pulled out the knife and brought it back to Pepé. He closed the blade and settled the knife carefully in his listless palm again. He grinned self-consciously at the sky.

"Ya!"

The heavy knife lanced out and sunk into the post again. Mama moved forward like a ship and scattered the play.

"All day you do foolish things with the knife, like a toy-baby," she stormed. "Get up on thy huge feet that eat up shoes. Get up!" She took him by one loose shoulder and hoisted at him. Pepé grinned sheepishly and came half-heartedly to his feet. "Look!" Mama cried. "Big lazy, you must catch the horse and put on him thy father's saddle. You must ride to Monterey. The medicine bottle is empty. There is no salt. Go thou now, Peanut! Catch the horse."

A revolution took place in the relaxed figure of Pepé. "To Monterey, me? Alone? *Sí,*[1] Mama."

She scowled at him. "Do not think, big sheep, that you will buy candy. No, I will give you only enough for the medicine and the salt."

Pepé smiled. "Mama, you will put the hatband on the hat?"

She relented then. "Yes, Pepé. You may wear the hatband."

His voice grew insinuating, "And the green handkerchief, Mama?"

"Yes, if you go quickly and return with no trouble, the silk green handkerchief will go. If you make sure to take off the handkerchief when you eat so no spot may fall on it. ..."

"*Sí,* Mama. I will be careful. I am a man."

"Thou? A man? Thou art a peanut."

He went into the rickety barn and brought out a rope, and he walked agilely enough up the hill to catch the horse.

When he was ready and mounted before the door, mounted on his father's saddle that was so old that the oaken frame showed through torn leather in many places, then Mama brought out the round black hat with the tooled leather band, and she reached up and knotted the green silk handkerchief about his neck. Pepé's blue denim coat was much darker than his jeans, for it had been washed much less often.

Mama handed up the big medicine bottle and the silver coins. "That for the medicine," she said, "and that for the salt. That for a candle to burn for the papa. That for *dulces*[2] for the little ones. Our friend Mrs. Rodriguez will give you dinner and maybe a bed for the night.

---

[1] Yes.

[2] Sweets.

When you go to the church say only ten Paternosters and only twenty-five Ave Marias. Oh! I know, big coyote. You would sit there flapping your mouth over Aves all day while you looked at the candles and the holy pictures. That is not good devotion to stare at the pretty things."

The black hat, covering the high pointed head and black thatched hair of Pepé, gave him dignity and age. He sat the rangy horse well. Mama thought how handsome he was, dark and lean and tall. "I would not send thee now alone, thou little one, except for the medicine," she said softly. "It is not good to have no medicine, for who knows when the toothache will come, or the sadness of the stomach. These things are."

"Adios, Mama," Pepé cried. "I will come back soon. You may send me often alone. I am a man."

"Thou art a foolish chicken."

He straightened his shoulders, flipped the reins against the horse's shoulder and rode away. He turned once and saw that they still watched him, Emilio and Rosy and Mama. Pepé grinned with pride and gladness and lifted the tough buckskin horse to a trot.

When he had dropped out of sight over a little dip in the road, Mama turned to the black ones, but she spoke to herself. "He is nearly a man now," she said. "It will be a nice thing to have a man in the house again." Her eyes sharpened on the children. "Go to the rocks now. The tide is going out. There will be abalones to be found." She put the iron hooks into their hands and saw them down the steep trail to the reefs. She brought the smooth stone *metate*[3] to the doorway and sat grinding her corn to flour and looking occasionally at the road over which Pepé had gone. The noonday came and then the afternoon, when the little ones beat the abalones on a rock to make them tender and Mama patted the tortillas to make them thin. They ate their dinner as the red sun was plunging down toward the ocean. They sat on the doorsteps and watched the big white moon come over the mountain tops.

Mama said, "He is now at the house of our friend Mrs. Rodriguez. She will give him nice things to eat and maybe a present."

Emilio said, "Some day I too will ride to Monterey for medicine. Did Pepé come to be a man today?"

Mama said wisely, "A boy gets to be a man when a man is needed. Remember this thing. I have known boys forty years old because there was no need for a man."

Soon afterwards they retired, Mama in her big oak bed on one side of the room, Emilio and Rosy in their boxes full of straw and sheepskins on the other side of the room.

The moon went over the sky and the surf roared on the rocks. The roosters crowed the first call. The surf subsided to a whispering surge against the reef. The moon dropped toward the sea. The roosters crowed again.

The moon was near down to the water when Pepé rode on a winded horse to his home flat. His dog bounced out and circled the horse yelping with pleasure. Pepé slid off the saddle to the ground. The weathered little shack was silver in the moonlight and the square shadow of it was black to the north and east. Against the east the piling mountains were misty with light; their tops melted into the sky.

Pepé walked wearily up the three steps and into the house. It was dark inside. There was a rustle in the corner.

Mama cried out from her bed. "Who comes? Pepé, is it thou?"

"*Sí*, Mama."

"Did you get the medicine?"

---

[3] A large, flat stone on which corn is ground.

"*Sí*, Mama."

"Well, go to sleep, then. I thought you would be sleeping at the house of Mrs. Rodriguez." Pepé stood silently in the dark room. "Why do you stand there, Pepé? Did you drink wine?"

"*Sí*, Mama."

"Well, go to bed then and sleep out the wine."

His voice was tired and patient, but very firm. "Light the candle, Mama. I must go away into the mountains."

"What is this, Pepé? You are crazy." Mama struck a sulphur match and held the little blue burr until the flame spread up the stick. She set light to the candle on the floor beside her bed. "Now, Pepé, what is this you say?" She looked anxiously into his face.

He was changed. The fragile quality seemed to have gone from his chin. His mouth was less full than it had been, the lines of the lips were straighter, but in his eyes the greatest change had taken place. There was no laughter in them any more, nor any bashfulness. They were sharp and bright and purposeful.

He told her in a tired monotone, told her everything just as it had happened. A few people came into the kitchen of Mrs. Rodriguez. There was wine to drink. Pepé drank wine. The little quarrel — the man started toward Pepé and then the knife — it went almost by itself. It flew, it darted before Pepé knew it. As he talked, Mama's face grew stern, and it seemed to grow more lean. Pepé finished. "I am a man now, Mama. The man said names to me I could not allow."

Mama nodded. "Yes, thou art a man, my poor little Pepé. Thou art a man. I have seen it coming on thee. I have watched you throwing the knife into the post, and I have been afraid." For a moment her face had softened, but now it grew stern again. "Come! We must get you ready. Go. Awaken Emilio and Rosy. Go quickly."

Pepé stepped over to the corner where his brother and sister slept among the sheepskins. He leaned down and shook them gently. "Come, Rosy! Come, Emilio! The mama says you must arise."

The little black ones sat up and rubbed their eyes in the candlelight. Mama was out of bed now, her long black skirt over her nightgown. "Emilio," she cried. "Go up and catch the other horse for Pepé. Quickly, now! Quickly." Emilio put his legs in his overalls and stumbled sleepily out the door.

"You heard no one behind you on the road?" Mama demanded.

"No, Mama. I listened carefully. No one was on the road."

Mama darted like a bird about the room. From a nail on the wall she took a canvas water bag and threw it on the floor. She stripped a blanket from her bed and rolled it into a tight tube and tied the ends with string. From a box beside the stove she lifted a flour sack half full of black stringy jerky. "Your father's black coat, Pepé. Here, put it on."

Pepé stood in the middle of the floor watching her activity. She reached behind the door and brought out the rifle, a long 38-56, worn shiny the whole length of the barrel. Pepé took it from her and held it in the crook of his elbow. Mama brought a little leather bag and counted the cartridges into his hand. "Only ten left," she warned. "You must not waste them."

Emilio put his head in the door. "*Qui'st 'l caballo*, Mama."[4]

"Put on the saddle from the other horse. Tie on the blanket. Here, tie the jerky to the saddle horn."

Still Pepé stood silently watching his mother's frantic activity. His chin looked hard,

---

[4] "Here's the horse, Mama."

and his sweet mouth was drawn and thin. His little eyes followed Mama about the room almost suspiciously.

Rosy asked softly, "Where goes Pepé?"

Mama's eyes were fierce. "Pepé goes on a journey. Pepé is a man now. He has a man's thing to do."

Pepé straightened his shoulders. His mouth changed until he looked very much like Mama.

At last the preparation was finished. The loaded horse stood outside the door. The water bag dripped a line of moisture down the bay shoulder.

The moonlight was being thinned by the dawn and the big white moon was near down to the sea. The family stood by the shack. Mama confronted Pepé. "Look, my son! Do not stop until it is dark again. Do not sleep even though you are tired. Take care of the horse in order that he may not stop of weariness. Remember to be careful with the bullets — there are only ten. Do not fill thy stomach with jerky or it will make thee sick. Eat a little jerky and fill thy stomach with grass. When thou comest to the high mountains, if thou seest any of the dark watching men, go not near to them nor try to speak to them. And forget not thy prayers." She put her lean hands on Pepé's shoulders, stood on her toes and kissed him formally on both cheeks, and Pepé kissed her on both cheeks. Then he went Emilio and Rosy and kissed both of their cheeks.

Pepé turned back to Mama. He seemed to look for a little softness, a little weakness in her. His eyes were searching, but Mama's face remained fierce. "Go now," she said. "Do not wait to be caught like a chicken."

Pepé pulled himself into the saddle. "I am a man," he said.

It was the first dawn when he rode up the hill toward the little canyon which let a trail into the mountains. Moonlight and daylight fought with each other, and the two warring qualities made it difficult to see. Before Pepé had gone a hundred yards, the outlines of his figure were misty; and long before he entered the canyon, he had become a gray, indefinite shadow.

Mama stood stiffly in front of her doorstep, and on either side of her stood Emilio and Rosy. They cast furtive glances at Mama now and then.

When the gray shape of Pepé melted into the hillside and disappeared, Mama relaxed. She began the high, whining keen of the death wail. "Our beautiful — our brave," she cried. "Our protector, our son is gone." Emilio and Rosy moaned beside her. "Our beautiful — our brave, he is gone." It was the formal wail. It rose to a high piercing whine and subsided to a moan. Mama raised it three times and then she turned and went into the house and shut the door.

Emilio and Rosy stood wondering in the dawn. They heard Mama whimpering in the house. They went out to sit on the cliff above the ocean. They touched shoulders. "When did Pepé come to be a man?" Emilio asked.

"Last night," said Rosy. "Last night in Monterey." The ocean clouds turned red with the sun that was behind the mountains.

"We will have no breakfast," said Emilio. "Mama will not want to cook." Rosy did not answer him. "Where is Pepé gone?" he asked.

Rosy looked around at him. She drew her knowledge from the quiet air. "He has gone on a journey. He will never come back."

"Is he dead? Do you think he is dead?"

Rosy looked back at the ocean again. A little steamer, drawing a line of smoke sat on the edge of the horizon. "He is not dead," Rosy explained. "Not yet."

Pepé rested the big rifle across the saddle in front of him. He let the horse walk up the hill and he didn't look back. The stony slope took on a coat of short brush so that Pepé found the entrance to a trail and entered it.

When he came to the canyon opening, he swung once in his saddle and looked back, but the houses were swallowed in the misty light. Pepé jerked forward again. The high shoulder of the canyon closed in on him. His horse stretched out its neck and sighed and settled to the trail.

It was a well-worn path, dark soft leaf-mould earth strewn with broken pieces of sandstone. The trail rounded the shoulder of the canyon and dropped steeply into the bed of the stream. In the shallows the water ran smoothly, glinting in the first morning sun. Small round stones on the bottom were as brown as rust with sun moss. In the sand along the edges of the stream the tall, rich wild mint grew, while in the water itself the cress, old and tough, had gone to heavy seed.

The path went into the stream and emerged on the other side. The horse sloshed into the water and stopped. Pepé dropped his bridle and let the beast drink of the running water.

Soon the canyon sides became steep and the first giant sentinel redwoods guarded the trail, great round red trunks bearing foliage as green and lacy as ferns. Once Pepé was among the trees, the sun was lost. A perfumed and purple light lay in the pale green of the underbrush. Gooseberry bushes and blackberries and tall ferns lined the stream, and overhead the branches of the redwoods met and cut off the sky.

Pepé drank from the water bag, and he reached into the flour sack and brought out a black string of jerky. His white teeth gnawed at the string until the tough meat parted. He chewed slowly and drank occasionally from the water bag. His little eyes were slumberous and tired, but the muscles of his face were hard set. The earth of the trail was black now. It gave up a hollow sound under the walking hoofbeats.

The stream fell more sharply. Little waterfalls splashed on the stones. Five-fingered ferns hung over the water and dripped spray from their fingertips. Pepé rode half over in his saddle, dangling one leg loosely. He picked a bay leaf from a tree beside the way and put it into his mouth for a moment to flavor the dry jerky. He held the gun loosely across the pommel.

Suddenly he squared in his saddle, swung the horse from the trail and kicked it hurriedly up behind a big redwood tree. He pulled up the reins tight against the bit to keep the horse from whinnying. His face was intent and his nostrils quivered a little.

A hollow pounding came down the trail, and a horseman rode by, a fat man with red cheeks and a white stubble beard. His horse put down its head and blubbered at the trail when it came to the place where Pepé had turned off. "Hold up!" said the man and he pulled up his horse's head.

When the last sound of the hoofs died away, Pepé came back into the trail again. He did not relax in the saddle any more. He lifted the big rifle and swung the lever to throw a shell into the chamber, and then he let down the hammer to half cock.

The trail grew very steep. Now the redwood trees were smaller and their tops were dead, bitten dead where the wind reached them. The horse plodded on; the sun went slowly overhead and started down toward the afternoon.

Where the stream came out of a side canyon, the trail left it. Pepé dismounted and watered his horse and filled up his water bag. As soon as the trail had parted from the stream, the trees were gone and only the thick brittle sage and manzanita and chaparral edged the trail. And the soft black earth was gone, too, leaving only the light tan broken rock for the trail bed. Lizards scampered away into the brush as the horse rattled over the little stones.

Pepé turned in his saddle and looked back. He was in the open now: he could be seen from a distance. As he ascended the trail the country grew more rough and terrible and dry. The way wound about the bases of great square rocks. Little gray rabbits skittered in the brush. A bird made a monotonous high creaking. Eastward the bare rock mountaintops were pale and powder-dry under the dropping sun. The horse plodded up and up the trail toward a little V in the ridge which was the pass.

Pepé looked suspiciously back every minute or so, and his eyes sought the tops of the ridges ahead. Once, on a white barren spur, he saw a black figure for a moment, but he looked quickly away, for it was one of the dark watchers. No one knew who the watchers were, nor where they lived, but it was better to ignore them and never to show interest in them. They did not bother one who stayed on the trail and minded his own business.

The air was parched and full of light dust blown by the breeze from the eroding mountains. Pepé drank sparingly from his bag and corked it tightly and hung it on the horn again. The trail moved up the dry shale hillside, avoiding rocks, dropping under clefts, climbing in and out of old water scars. When he arrived at the little pass he stopped and looked back for a long time. No dark watchers were to be seen now. The trail behind was empty. Only the high tops of the redwoods indicated where the stream flowed.

Pepé rode on through the pass. His little eyes were nearly closed with weariness, but his face was stern, relentless and manly. The high mountain wind coasted sighing through the pass and whistled on the edges of the big blocks of broken granite. In the air, a red-tailed hawk sailed over close to the ridge and screamed angrily. Pepé went slowly through the broken jagged pass and looked down on the other side.

The trail dropped quickly, staggering among broken rock. At the bottom of the slope there was a dark crease, thick with brush, and on the other side of the crease a little flat, in which a grove of oak trees grew. A scar of green grass cut across the flat. And behind the flat another mountain rose, desolate with dead rocks and starving little black bushes. Pepé drank from the bag again for the air was so dry that it encrusted his nostrils and burned his lips. He put the horse down the trail. The hooves slipped and struggled on the steep way, starting little stones that rolled off into the brush. The sun was gone behind the westward mountain now, but still it glowed brilliantly on the oaks and on the grassy flat. The rocks and the hillsides still sent up waves of the heat they had gathered from the day's sun.

Pepé looked up to the top of the next dry withered ridge. He saw a dark form against the sky, a man's figure standing on top of a rock, and he glanced away quickly not to appear curious. When a moment later he looked up again, the figure was gone.

Downward the trail was quickly covered. Sometimes the horse floundered for footing, sometimes set his feet and slid a little way. They came at last to the bottom where the dark chaparral was higher than Pepé's head. He held up his rifle on one side and his arm on the other to shield his face from the sharp brittle fingers of the brush.

Up and out of the crease he rode, and up a little cliff. The grassy flat was before him, and the round comfortable oaks. For a moment he studied the trail down which he had come, but there was no movement and no sound from it. Finally he rode out over the flat, to the green streak, and at the upper end of the damp he found a little spring welling out of the earth and dropping into a dug basin before it seeped out over the flat.

Pepé filled his bag first, and then he let the thirsty horse drink out of the pool. He led the horse to the clump of oaks, and in the middle of the grove, fairly protected from sight on all sides, he took off the saddle and the bridle and laid them on the ground. The horse stretched his jaws sideways and yawned. Pepé knotted the lead rope about the horse's neck and tied him to a sapling among the oaks, where he could graze in a fairly large circle.

When the horse was gnawing hungrily at the dry grass, Pepé went to the saddle and took a black string of jerky from the sack and strolled to an oak tree on the edge of the grove, from under which he could watch the trail. He sat down in the crisp dry oak leaves and automatically felt for his big black knife to cut the jerky, but he had no knife. He leaned back on his elbow and gnawed at the tough strong meat. His face was blank, but it was a man's face.

The bright evening light washed the eastern ridge, but the valley was darkening. Doves flew down from the hills to the spring, and the quail came running out of the brush and joined them, calling clearly to one another.

Out of the corner of his eye Pepé saw a shadow grow out of the bushy crease. He turned his head slowly. A big spotted wildcat was creeping toward the spring, belly to the ground, moving like thought.

Pepé cocked his rifle and edged the muzzle slowly around. Then he looked apprehensively up the trail and dropped the hammer again. From the ground beside him he picked an oak twig and threw it toward the spring. The quail flew up with a roar and the doves whistled away. The big cat stood up: for a long moment he looked at Pepé with cold yellow eyes, and then fearlessly walked back into the gulch.

The dusk gathered quickly in the deep valley. Pepé muttered his prayers, put his head down on his arm and went instantly to sleep.

The moon came up and filled the valley with cold blue light, and the wind swept rustling down from the peaks. The owls worked up and down the slopes looking for rabbits. Down in the brush of the gulch a coyote gabbled. The oak trees whispered softly in the night breeze.

Pepé started up, listening. His horse had whinnied. The moon was just slipping behind the western ridge, leaving the valley in darkness behind it. Pepé sat tensely gripping his rifle. From far up the trail he heard an answering whinny and the crash of shod hooves on the broken rock. He jumped to his feet, ran to his horse and led it under the trees. He threw on the saddle and cinched it tight for the steep trail, caught the unwilling head and forced the bit into the mouth. He felt the saddle to make sure the water bag and the sack of jerky were there. Then he mounted and turned up the hill.

It was velvet dark. The horse found the entrance to the trail where it left the flat, and started up, stumbling and slipping on the rocks. Pepé's hand rose up to his head. His hat was gone. He had left it under the oak tree.

The horse had struggled far up the trail when the first change of dawn came into the air, a steel grayness as light mixed thoroughly with dark. Gradually the sharp snaggled edge of the ridge stood out above them, rotten granite tortured and eaten by the winds of time. Pepé had dropped his reins on the horn, leaving direction to the horse. The brush grabbed at his legs in the dark until one knee of his jeans was ripped.

Gradually the light flowed down over the ridge. The starved brush and rocks stood out in the half light, strange and lonely in high perspective. Then there came warmth into the light. Pepé drew up and looked back, but he could see nothing in the darker valley below. The sky turned blue over the coming sun. In the waste of the mountainside, the poor dry brush grew only three feet high. Here and there, big outcroppings of unrotted granite stood up like mouldering houses. Pepé relaxed a little. He drank from his water bag and bit off a piece of jerky. A single eagle flew over, high in the light.

Without warning Pepé's horse screamed and fell on its side. He was almost down before the rifle crash echoed up from the valley. From a hole behind the struggling shoulder, a stream of bright crimson blood pumped and stopped and pumped and stopped. The hooves threshed on the ground. Pepé lay half stunned beside the horse. He looked slowly down the hill. A piece of sage clipped off beside his head and another crash echoed up from side to side of the canyon. Pepé flung himself frantically behind a bush.

He crawled up the hill on his knees and one hand. His right hand held the rifle up off the ground and pushed it ahead of him. He moved with the instinctive care of an animal. Rapidly he wormed his way toward one of the big outcroppings of granite on the hill above him. Where the brush was high he doubled up and ran, but where the cover was slight he wiggled forward on his stomach, pushing the rifle ahead of him. In the last little distance there was no cover at all. Pepé poised and then he darted across the space and flashed around the corner of the rock.

He leaned panting against the stone. When his breath came easier he moved along behind the big rock until he came to a narrow split that offered a thin section of vision down the hill. Pepé lay on his stomach and pushed the rifle barrel through the slit and waited.

The sun reddened the western ridges now. Already the buzzards were settling down toward the place where the horse lay. A small brown bird scratched in the dead sage leaves directly in front of the rifle muzzle. The coasting eagle flew back toward the rising sun.

Pepé saw a little movement in the brush far below. His grip tightened on the gun. A little brown doe stepped daintily out on the trail and crossed it and disappeared into the brush again. For a long time Pepé waited. Far below he could see the little flat and the oak trees and the slash of green. Suddenly his eyes flashed back at the trail again. A quarter of a mile down there had been a quick movement in the chaparral. The rifle swung over. The front sight nestled in the v of the rear sight. Pepé studied for a moment and then raised the rear sight a notch. The little movement in the brush came again. The sight settled on it. Pepé squeezed the trigger. The explosion crashed down the mountain and up the other side, and came rattling back. The whole side of the slope grew still. No more movement. And then a white streak cut into the granite of the slit and a bullet whined away and a crash sounded up from below. Pepé felt a sharp pain in his right hand. A sliver of granite was sticking out from between his first and second knuckles and the point protruded from his palm. Carefully he pulled out the sliver of stone. The wound bled evenly and gently. No vein nor artery was cut.

Pepé looked into a little dusty cave in the rock and gathered a handful of spider web, and he pressed the mass into the cut, plastering the soft web into the blood. The flow stopped almost at once.

The rifle was on the ground. Pepé picked it up, levered a new shell into the chamber. And then he slid into the brush on his stomach. Far to the right he crawled, and then up the hill, moving slowly and carefully, crawling to cover and resting and then crawling again.

In the mountains the sun is high in its arc before it penetrates the gorges. The hot face looked over the hill and brought instant heat with it. The white light beat on the rocks and reflected from them and rose up quivering from the earth again, and the rocks and bushes seemed to quiver behind the air.

Pepé crawled in the general direction of the ridge peak, zig-zagging for cover. The deep cut between his knuckles began to throb. He crawled close to a rattlesnake before he saw it, and when it raised its dry head and made a soft beginning whirr, he backed up and took another way. The quick gray lizards flashed in front of him, raising a tiny line of dust. He found another mass of spider web and pressed it against his throbbing hand.

Pepé was pushing the rifle with his left hand now. Little drops of sweat ran to the ends of his coarse black hair and rolled down his cheeks. His lips and tongue were growing thick and heavy. His lips writhed to draw saliva into his mouth. His little dark eyes were uneasy and suspicious. Once when a gray lizard paused in front of him on the parched ground and turned its head sideways he crushed it flat with a stone.

When the sun slid past noon he had not gone a mile. He crawled exhaustedly a last hundred yards to a patch of high sharp manzanita, crawled desperately, and when the patch was reached he wriggled in among the tough gnarly trunks and dropped his head on his left arm. There was little shade in the meager brush, but there was cover and safety. Pepé went to sleep as he lay and the sun beat on his back. A few little birds hopped close to him and peered and hopped away. Pepé squirmed in his sleep and he raised and dropped his wounded hand again and again.

The sun went down behind the peaks and the cool evening came, and then the dark. A coyote yelled from the hillside, Pepé started awake and looked about with misty eyes. His hand was swollen and heavy; a little thread of pain ran up the inside of his arm and settled in a pocket in his armpit. He peered about and then stood up, for the mountains were black and the moon had not yet risen. Pepé stood up in the dark. The coat of his father pressed on his arm. His tongue was swollen until it nearly filled his mouth. He wriggled out of the coat and dropped it in the brush, and then he struggled up the hill, falling over rocks and tearing his way through the brush. The rifle knocked against stones as he went. Little dry avalanches of gravel and shattered stone went whispering down the hill behind him.

After a while the old moon came up and showed the jagged ridge top ahead of him. By moonlight Pepé traveled more easily. He bent forward so that his throbbing arm hung away from his body. The journey uphill was made in dashes and rests, a frantic rush up a few yards and then a rest. The wind coasted down the slope rattling the dry stems of the bushes.

The moon was at meridian when Pepé came at last to the sharp backbone of the ridge top. On the last hundred yards of the rise no soil had clung under the wearing winds. The way was on solid rock. He clambered to the top and looked down on the other side. There was a draw like the last below him, misty with moonlight, brushed with dry struggling sage and chaparral. On the other side the hill rose up sharply and at the top the jagged rotten teeth of the mountain showed against the sky. At the bottom of the cut the brush was thick and dark.

Pepé stumbled down the hill. His throat was almost closed with thirst. At first he tried to run, but immediately he fell and rolled. After that he went more carefully. The moon was just disappearing behind the mountains when he came to the bottom. He crawled into the heavy brush feeling with his fingers for water. There was no water in the bed of the stream, only damp earth. Pepé laid his gun down and scooped up a handful of mud and put it in his mouth, and then he spluttered and scraped the earth from his tongue with his finger, for the mud drew at his mouth like a poultice. He dug a hole in the stream bed with his fingers, dug a little basin to catch water; but before it was very deep his head fell forward on the damp ground and he slept.

The dawn came and the heat of the day fell on the earth, and still Pepé slept. Late in the afternoon his head jerked up. He looked slowly around. His eyes were slits of wariness. Twenty feet away in the heavy brush a big tawny mountain lion stood looking at him. Its long thick tail waved gracefully, its ears were erect with interest, not laid back dangerously. The lion squatted down on its stomach and watched him.

Pepé looked at the hole he had dug in the earth. A half inch of muddy water had collected in the bottom. He tore the sleeve from his hurt arm, with his teeth ripped out a little square, soaked it in the water and put it in his mouth. Over and over he filled the cloth and sucked it.

Still the lion sat and watched him. The evening came down but there was no movement on the hills. No birds visited the dry bottom of the cut. Pepé looked occasionally at the lion. The eyes of the yellow beast drooped as though he were about to sleep. He yawned and his long thin red tongue curled out. Suddenly his head jerked around and his nostrils quivered. His big tail lashed. He stood up and slunk like a tawny shadow into the thick brush.

A moment later Pepé heard the sound, the faint far crash of horses' hooves on gravel. And he heard something else, a high whining yelp of a dog.

Pepé took his rifle on his left hand and he glided into the brush almost as quietly as the lion had. In the darkening evening he crouched up the hill toward the next ridge. Only when the dark came did he stand up. His energy was short. Once it was dark he fell over the rocks and slipped to his knees on the steep slope, but he moved on and on up the hill, climbing and scrabbling over the broken hillside.

When he was far up toward the top, he lay down and slept for a little while. The withered moon, shining on his face, awakened him. He stood up and moved up the hill. Fifty yards away he stopped and turned back, for he had forgotten his rifle. He walked heavily down and poked about in the brush, but he could not find his gun. At last he lay down to rest. The pocket of pain in his armpit had grown more sharp. His arm seemed to swell out and fall with every heartbeat. There was no position lying down where the heavy arm did not press against his armpit.

With the effort of a hurt beast, Pepé got up and moved again toward the top of the ridge. He held his swollen arm away from his body with his left hand. Up the steep hill he dragged himself, a few steps and a rest, and a few more steps. At last he was nearing the top. The moon showed the uneven sharp back of it against the sky.

Pepé's brain spun in a big spiral up and away from him. He slumped to the ground and lay still. The rock ridge top was only a hundred feet above him.

The moon moved over the sky. Pepé half turned on his back. His tongue tried to make words, but only a thick hissing came from between his lips.

When the dawn came, Pepé pulled himself up. His eyes were sane again. He drew his great puffed arm in front of him and looked at the angry wound. The black line ran up from his waist to his armpit. Automatically he reached in his pocket for the big black knife, but it was not there. His eyes searched the ground. He picked up a sharp blade of stone and scraped at the wound, sawed at the proud flesh and then squeezed the green juice out in big drops. Instantly he threw back his head and whined like a dog. His whole right side shuddered at the pain, but the pain cleared his head.

In the gray light he struggled up the last slope to the ridge and crawled over and lay down behind a line of rocks. Below him lay a deep canyon exactly like the last, waterless and desolate. There was no flat, no oak trees, not even heavy brush in the bottom of it. And on the other side a sharp ridge stood up, thinly brushed with starving sage, littered with broken granite. Strewn over the hill there were giant outcroppings, and on the top the granite teeth stood out against the sky.

The new day was light now. The flame of the sun came over the ridge and fell on Pepé where he lay on the ground. His coarse black hair was littered with twigs and bits of spider web. His eyes had retreated back into his head. Between his lips the tip of his black tongue showed.

He sat up and dragged his great arm into his lap and nursed it, rocking his body and moaning in his throat. He threw back his head and looked up into the pale sky. A big black bird circled nearly out of sight, and far to the left another was sailing near.

He lifted his head to listen, for a familiar sound had come to him from the valley he had climbed out of; it was the crying yelp of hounds, excited and feverish, on a trail.

Pepé bowed his head quickly. He tried to speak rapid words but only a thick hiss came from his lips. He drew a shaky cross on his breast with his left hand. It was a long struggle to get to his feet. He crawled slowly and mechanically to the top of a big rock on the ridge peak. Once there, he arose slowly, swaying to his feet, and stood erect. Far below he could see the dark brush where he had slept. He braced his feet and stood there, black against the morning sky.

There came a ripping sound at his feet. A piece of stone flew up and a bullet droned off into the next gorge. The hollow crash echoed up from below. Pepé looked down for a moment and then pulled himself straight again.

His body jarred back. His left hand fluttered helplessly toward his breast. The second crash sounded from below. Pepé swung forward and toppled from the rock. His body struck and rolled over and over, starting a little avalanche. And when at last he stopped against a bush, the avalanche slid slowly down and covered up his head.

QUESTIONS

1. What does the knife mean to Pepé?

2. At several points Pepé's laziness is emphasized. Is this a clue to his fate?

3. What actions define the difference between Pepé and his mother? Does she understand her son? What do her directions to Pepé as he sets out for Monterey suggest about her knowledge of his character? What do they suggest about her own character?

4. What role do the younger children play in the tragedy?

5. What causes Pepé's mother to admit he has become a man? Is it the killing or the consequences that change her mind?

6. The knife "flew, it darted before Pepé knew it." Does Steinbeck not blame Pepé for his actions? If not, who or what is to blame? Pepé's mother? the concept of *machismo*? the man who insulted him? fate?

7. Steinbeck does not identify Pepé's pursuers. What is the effect of this omission?

8. Pepé's period of manhood is brief, encompassed really by his flight. Are there signs that he has matured?

9. Is the ending appropriate? Is there a positive thrust to this story, or is it simply a naturalistic narrative? What does the final sentence contribute to your answer?

FRANK O'CONNOR

Guests of the Nation

I

At dusk the big Englishman, Belcher, would shift his long legs out of the ashes and say "Well, chums, what about it?" and Noble or me would say "All right, chum" (for we had picked up some of their curious expressions), and the little Englishman, Hawkins, would light the lamp and bring out the cards. Sometimes Jeremiah Donovan would come up and supervise the game and get excited over Hawkins's cards, which he always played badly, and shout at him as if he was one of our own "Ah, you divil, you, why didn't you play the tray?"

But ordinarily Jeremiah was a sober and contented poor devil like the big Englishman, Belcher, and was looked up to only because he was a fair hand at documents, though he was slow enough even with them. He wore a small cloth hat and big gaiters over his long pants, and you seldom saw him with his hands out of his pockets. He reddened when you talked to him, tilting from toe to heel and back, and looking down all the time at his big farmer's feet. Noble and me used to make fun of his broad accent, because we were from the town.

I couldn't at the time see the point of me and Noble guarding Belcher and Hawkins at all, for it was my belief that you could have planted that pair down anywhere from this to Claregalway and they'd have taken root there like a native weed. I never in my short experience seen two men to take to the country as they did.

They were handed on to us by the Second Battalion when the search for them became too hot, and Noble and myself, being young, took over with a natural feeling of responsibility, but Hawkins made us look like fools when he showed that he knew the country better than we did.

"You're the bloke they calls Bonaparte," he says to me. "Mary Brigid O'Connell told me to ask you what you done with the pair of her brother's socks you borrowed."

For it seemed, as they explained it, that the Second used to have little evenings, and some of the girls of the neighbourhood turned in, and, seeing they were such decent chaps, our fellows couldn't leave the two Englishmen out of them. Hawkins learned to dance "The Walls of Limerick," "The Siege of Ennis," and "The Waves of Tory" as well as any of them, though, naturally, he couldn't return the compliment, because our lads at that time did not dance foreign dances on principle.

So whatever privileges Belcher and Hawkins had with the Second they just naturally took with us, and after the first day or two we gave up all pretence of keeping a close eye on them. Not that they could have got far, for they had accents you could cut with a knife and wore khaki tunics and overcoats with civilian pants and boots. But it's my belief that they never had any idea of escaping and were quite content to be where they were.

It was a treat to see how Belcher got off with the old woman of the house where we were staying. She was a great warrant to scold, and cranky even with us, but before ever she had a chance of giving our guests, as I may call them, a lick of her tongue, Belcher had made her his friend for life. She was breaking sticks, and Belcher, who hadn't been more than ten minutes in the house, jumped up from his seat and went over to her.

"Allow me, madam," he says, smiling his queer little smile, "please allow me"; and he takes the bloody hatchet. She was struck too paralytic to speak, and after that, Belcher would be at her heels, carrying a bucket, a basket, or a load of turf, as the case might be. As Noble said, he got into looking before she leapt, and hot water, or any little thing she wanted, Belcher would have it ready for her. For such a huge man (and though I am five foot ten myself I had to look up at him) he had an uncommon shortness — or should I say lack? — of speech. It took us some time to get used to him, walking in and out, like a ghost, without a word. Especially because Hawkins talked enough for a platoon, it was strange to hear big Belcher with his toes in the ashes come out with a solitary "Excuse me, chum," or "That's right, chum." His one and only passion was cards, and I will say for him that he was a good card-player. He could have fleeced myself and Noble, but whatever we lost to him Hawkins lost to us, and Hawkins played with the money Belcher gave him.

Hawkins lost to us because he had too much old gab, and we probably lost to Belcher for the same reason. Hawkins and Noble would spit at one another about religion into the early hours of the morning, and Hawkins worried the soul out of Noble, whose brother was a priest, with a string of questions that would puzzle a cardinal. To make it worse even in treating of holy subjects, Hawkins had a deplorable tongue. I never in all my career met a man who could mix such a variety of cursing and bad language into an argument. He was a terrible man, and a fright to argue. He never did a stroke of work, and when he had no one else to talk to, he got stuck in the old woman.

He met his match in her, for one day when he tried to get her to complain profanely of the drought, she gave him a great come-down by blaming it entirely on Jupiter Pluvius (a deity neither Hawkins nor I had ever heard of, though Noble said that among the pagans it was believed that he had something to do with the rain). Another day he was swearing at the capitalists for starting the German war[1] when the old lady laid down her iron, puckered up her little crab's mouth, and said: "Mr. Hawkins, you can say what you like about the war, and think you'll deceive me because I'm only a simple poor countrywoman, but I know what started the war. It was the Italian Count that stole the heathen divinity out of the temple in Japan. Believe me, Mr. Hawkins, nothing but sorrow and want can follow the people that disturb the hidden powers."

A queer old girl, all right.

II

We had our tea one evening, and Hawkins lit the lamp and we all sat into cards. Jeremiah Donovan came in too, and sat down and watched us for a while, and it suddenly struck me that he had no great love for the two Englishmen. It came as a great surprise to me, because I hadn't noticed anything about him before.

---

[1] World War I.

Late in the evening a really terrible argument blew up between Hawkins and Noble, about capitalists and priests and love of your country.

"The capitalists," says Hawkins with an angry gulp, "pays the priests to tell you about the next world so as you won't notice what the bastards are up to in this."

"Nonsense, man!" says Noble, losing his temper. "Before ever a capitalist was thought of, people believed in the next world."

Hawkins stood up as though he was preaching a sermon.

"Oh, they did, did they?" he says with a sneer. "They believed all the things you believe, isn't that what you mean? And you believe that God created Adam, and Adam created Shem, and Shem created Jehoshophat.[2] You believe all that silly old fairytale about Eve and Eden and the apple. Well, listen to me, chum. If you're entitled to hold a silly belief like that, I'm entitled to hold my silly belief — which is that the first thing your God created was a bleeding capitalist, with morality and Rolls-Royce complete. Am I right, chum?" he says to Belcher.

"You're right, chum," says Belcher with his amused smile, and got up from the table to stretch his long legs into the fire and stroke his moustache. So, seeing that Jeremiah Donovan was going, and that there was no knowing when the argument about religion would be over, I went out with him. We strolled down to the village together, and then he stopped and started blushing and mumbling and saying I ought to be behind, keeping guard on the prisoners. I didn't like the tone he took with me, and anyway I was bored with life in the cottage, so I replied by asking him what the hell we wanted guarding them at all for. I told him I'd talked it over with Noble, and that we'd both rather be out with a fighting column.

"What use are those fellows to us?" says I.

He looked at me in surprise and said: "I thought you knew we were keeping them as hostages."

"Hostages?" I said.

"The enemy have prisoners belonging to us," he says, "and now they're talking of shooting them. If they shoot our prisoners, we'll shoot theirs."

"Shoot them?" I said.

"What else did you think we were keeping them for?" he says.

"Wasn't it very unforeseen of you not to warn Noble and myself of that in the beginning?" I said.

"How was it?" says he. "You might have known it."

"We couldn't know it, Jeremiah Donovan," says I. "How could we when they were on our hands so long?"

"The enemy have our prisoners as long and longer," says he.

"That's not the same thing at all," says I.

"What difference is there?" says he.

I couldn't tell him, because I knew he wouldn't understand. If it was only an old dog that was going to the vet's, you'd try and not get too fond of him, but Jeremiah Donovan wasn't a man that would ever be in danger of that.

"And when is this thing going to be decided?" says I.

"We might hear tonight," he says. "Or tomorrow or the next day at latest. So if it's only hanging round here that's a trouble to you, you'll be free soon enough."

It wasn't the hanging round that was a trouble to me at all by this time. I had worse things to worry about. When I got back to the cottage the argument was still on. Hawkins was holding forth in his best style, maintaining that there was no next world, and Noble was maintaining that there was; but I could see that Hawkins had had the best of it.

---

[2] Hawkins's sense of Bible history is somewhat shaky.

"Do you know what, chum?" he was saying with a saucy smile. "I think you're just as big a bleeding unbeliever as I am. You say you believe in the next world, and you know just as much about the next world as I do, which is sweet damn-all. What's heaven? You don't know. Where's heaven? You don't know. You know sweet damn-all! I ask you again, do they wear wings?"

"Very well, then," says Noble, "they do. Is that enough for you? They do wear wings."

"Where do they get them, then? Who makes them? Have they a factory for wings? Have they a sort of store where you hands in your chit and takes your bleeding wings?"

"You're an impossible man to argue with," says Noble. "Now, listen to me — " And they were off again.

It was long after midnight when we locked up and went to bed. As I blew out the candle I told Noble what Jeremiah Donovan was after telling me. Noble took it very quietly. When we'd been in bed about an hour he asked me did I think we ought to tell the Englishmen. I didn't think we should, because it was more than likely that the English wouldn't shoot our men, and even if they did, the brigade officers, who were always up and down with the Second Battalion and knew the Englishmen well, wouldn't be likely to want them plugged. "I think so too," says Noble. "It would be great cruelty to put the wind up them now."

"It was very unforeseen of Jeremiah Donovan anyhow," says I.

It was next morning that we found it so hard to face Belcher and Hawkins. We went about the house all day scarcely saying a word. Belcher didn't seem to notice; he was stretched into the ashes as usual, with his usual look of waiting in quietness for something unforeseen to happen, but Hawkins noticed and put it down to Noble's being beaten in the argument of the night before.

"Why can't you take a discussion in the proper spirit?" he says severely. "You and your Adam and Eve! I'm a Communist, that's what I am. Communist or anarchist, it all comes to much the same thing." And for hours he went round the house, muttering when the fit took him. "Adam and Eve! Adam and Eve! Nothing better to do with their time than picking bleeding apples!"

III

I don't know how we got through that day, but I was very glad when it was over, the tea things were cleared away, and Belcher said in his peaceable way: "Well, chums, what about it?" We sat round the table and Hawkins took out the cards, and just then I heard Jeremiah Donovan's footstep on the path and a dark presentiment crossed my mind. I rose from the table and caught him before he reached the door.

"What do you want?" I asked.

"I want those two soldier friends of yours," he says, getting red.

"Is that the way, Jeremiah Donovan?" I asked.

"That's the way. There were four of our lads shot this morning, one of them a boy of sixteen."

"That's bad," I said.

At that moment Noble followed me out, and the three of us walked down the path together, talking in whispers. Feeney, the local intelligence officer, was standing by the gate.

"What are you going to do about it?" I asked Jeremiah Donovan.

"I want you and Noble to get them out; tell them they're being shifted again; that'll be the quietest way."

"Leave me out of that," says Noble under his breath.

Jeremiah Donovan looks at him hard.

"All right," he says. "You and Feeney get a few tools from the shed and dig a hole by the far end of the bog. Bonaparte and myself will be after you. Don't let anyone see you with the tools. I wouldn't like it to go beyond ourselves."

We saw Feeney and Noble go round to the shed and went in ourselves. I left Jeremiah Donovan to do the explanations. He told them that he had orders to send them back to the Second Battalion. Hawkins let out a mouthful of curses, and you could see that though Belcher didn't say anything, he was a bit upset too. The old woman was for having them stay in spite of us, and she didn't stop advising them until Jeremiah Donovan lost his temper and turned on her. He had a nasty temper, I noticed. It was pitch-dark in the cottage by this time, but no one thought of lighting the lamp, and in the darkness the two Englishmen fetched their topcoats and said good-bye to the old woman.

"Just as a man makes a home of a bleeding place, some bastard at headquarters thinks you're too cushy and shunts you off," says Hawkins, shaking her hand.

"A thousand thanks, madam," says Belcher. "A thousand thanks for everything" — as though he'd made it up.

We went round to the back of the house and down towards the bog. It was only then that Jeremiah Donovan told them. He was shaking with excitement.

"There were four of our fellows shot in Cork this morning and now you're to be shot as a reprisal."

"What are you talking about?" snaps Hawkins. "It's bad enough being mucked about as we are without having to put up with your funny jokes."

"It isn't a joke," says Donovan. "I'm sorry, Hawkins, but it's true," and begins on the usual rigmarole about duty and how unpleasant it is.

I never noticed that people who talk a lot about duty find it much of a trouble to them.

"Oh, cut it out!" says Hawkins.

"Ask Bonaparte," says Donovan, seeing that Hawkins isn't taking him seriously. "Isn't it true, Bonaparte?"

"It is," I say, and Hawkins stops.

"Ah, for Christ's sake, chum!"

"I mean it, chum," I say.

"You don't sound as if you meant it."

"If he doesn't mean it, I do," says Donovan, working himself up.

"What have you against me, Jeremiah Donovan?"

"I never said I had anything against you. But why did your people take out four of our prisoners and shoot them in cold blood?"

He took Hawkins by the arm and dragged him on, but it was impossible to make him understand that we were in earnest. I had the Smith and Wesson[3] in my pocket and I kept fingering it and wondering what I'd do if they put up a fight for it or ran, and wishing to God they'd do one or the other. I knew if they did run for it, that I'd never fire on them. Hawkins wanted to know was Noble in it, and when we said yes, he asked us why Noble wanted to plug him. Why did any of us want to plug him? What had he done to us? Weren't we all chums? Didn't we understand him and didn't he understand us? Did we imagine for an instant that he'd shoot us for all the so-and-so officers in the so-and-so British Army?

By this time we'd reached the bog, and I was so sick I couldn't even answer him. We walked along the edge of it in the darkness, and every now and then Hawkins would call a halt and begin all over again, as if he was wound up, about our being chums, and I knew that nothing but the sight of the grave would convince him that we had to do it. And all the time I

---

[3] An American revolver.

was hoping that something would happen; that they'd run for it or that Noble would take over the responsibility from me. I had the feeling that it was worse on Noble than on me.

IV

At last we saw the lantern in the distance and made towards it. Noble was carrying it, and Feeney was standing somewhere in the darkness behind him, and the picture of them so still and silent in the bogland brought it home to me that we were in earnest, and banished the last bit of hope I had.

Belcher, on recognizing Noble, said: "Hallo, chum," in his quiet way, but Hawkins flew at him at once, and the argument began all over again, only this time Noble had nothing to say for himself and stood with his head down, holding the lantern between his legs.

It was Jeremiah Donovan who did the answering. For the twentieth time, as though it was haunting his mind, Hawkins asked if anybody thought he'd shoot Noble.

"Yes, you would," says Jeremiah Donovan.

"No, I wouldn't, damn you!"

"You would, because you'd know you'd be shot for not doing it."

"I wouldn't, not if I was to be shot twenty times over. I wouldn't shoot a pal. And Belcher wouldn't — isn't that right, Belcher?"

"That's right, chum," Belcher said, but more by way of answering the question than of joining in the argument. Belcher sounded as though whatever unforeseen thing he'd always been waiting for had come at last.

"Anyway, who says Noble would be shot if I wasn't? What do you think I'd do if I was in his place, out in the middle of a blasted bog?"

"What would you do?" asks Donovan.

"I'd go with him wherever he was going, of course. Share my last bob with him and stick by him through thick and thin. No one can ever say of me that I let down a pal."

"We had enough of this," says Jeremiah Donovan, cocking his revolver. "Is there any message you want to send?"

"No, there isn't."

"Do you want to say your prayers?"

Hawkins came out with a cold-blooded remark that even shocked me and turned on Noble again.

"Listen to me, Noble," he says. "You and me are chums. You can't come over to my side, so I'll come over to your side. That show you I mean what I say? Give me a rifle and I'll go along with you and the other lads."

Nobody answered him. We knew that was no way out.

"Hear what I'm saying?" he says. "I'm through with it. I'm a deserter or anything else you like. I don't believe in your stuff, but it's no worse than mine. That satisfy you?"

Noble raised his head, but Donovan began to speak and he lowered it again without replying.

"For the last time, have you any messages to send?" says Donovan in a cold, excited sort of voice.

"Shut up, Donovan! You don't understand me, but these lads do. They're not the sort to make a pal and kill a pal. They're not the tools of any capitalist."

I alone of the crowd saw Donovan raise his Webley[4] to the back of Hawkins's neck, and as he did so I shut my eyes and tried to pray. Hawkins had begun to say something else when

---

[4] An English pistol.

Donovan fired, and as I opened my eyes at the bang, I saw Hawkins stagger at the knees and lie out flat at Noble's feet, slowly and as quiet as a kid falling asleep, with the lantern-light on his lean legs and bright farmer's boots. We all stood very still, watching him settle out in the last agony.

Then Belcher took out a handkerchief and began to tie it about his own eyes (in our excitement we'd forgotten to do the same for Hawkins), and, seeing it wasn't big enough, turned and asked for the loan of mine. I gave it to him and he knotted the two together and pointed with his foot at Hawkins.

"He's not quite dead," he says. "Better give him another."

Sure enough, Hawkins's left knee is beginning to rise. I bend down and put my gun to his head; then, recollecting myself, I get up again. Belcher understands what's in my mind.

"Give him his first," he says. "I don't mind. Poor bastard, we don't know what's happening to him now."

I knelt and fired. By this time I didn't seem to know what I was doing. Belcher, who was fumbling a bit awkwardly with the handkerchiefs, came out with a laugh as he heard the shot. It was the first time I heard him laugh and it sent a shudder down my back; it sounded so unnatural.

"Poor bugger!" he said quietly. "And last night he was so curious about it all. It's very queer, chums, I always think. Now he knows as much about it as they'll ever let him know, and last night he was all in the dark."

Donovan helped him to tie the handkerchiefs about his eyes. "Thanks, chum," he said. Donovan asked if there were any messages he wanted sent.

"No, chum," he says. "Not for me. If any of you would like to write to Hawkins's mother, you'll find a letter from her in his pocket. He and his mother were great chums. But my missus left me eight years ago. Went away with another fellow and took the kid with her. I like the feeling of a home, as you may have noticed, but I couldn't start again after that."

It was an extraordinary thing, but in those few minutes Belcher said more than in all the weeks before. It was just as if the sound of the shot had started a flood of talk in him and he could go on the whole night like that, quite happily, talking about himself. We stood round like fools now that he couldn't see us any longer. Donovan looked at Noble, and Noble shook his head. Then Donovan raised his Webley, and at that moment Belcher gives his queer laugh again. He may have thought we were talking about him, or perhaps he noticed the same thing I'd noticed and couldn't understand it.

"Excuse me, chums," he says. "I feel I'm talking the hell of a lot, and so silly, about my being so handy about a house and things like that. But this thing came on me suddenly. You'll forgive me, I'm sure."

"You don't want to say a prayer?" asks Donovan.

"No, chum," he says. "I don't think it would help. I'm ready, and you boys want to get 2t over."

"You understand that we're only doing our duty?" says Donovan.

Belcher's head was raised like a blind man's, so that you could only see his chin and the tip of his nose in the lantern-light.

"I never could make out what duty was myself," he said. "I think you're all good lads, if that's what you mean. I'm not complaining."

Noble, just as if he couldn't bear any more of it, raised his fist at Donovan, and in a flash Donovan raised his gun and fired. The big man went over like a sack of meal, and this time there was no need of a second shot.

I don't remember much about the burying, but that it was worse than all the rest because we had to carry them to the grave. It was all mad lonely with nothing but a patch of lantern-light between ourselves and the dark, and birds hooting and screeching all round, disturbed by the guns. Noble went through Hawkins's belongings to find the letter from his mother, and then joined his hands together. He did the same with Belcher. Then, when we'd filled in the grave, we separated from Jeremiah Donovan and Feeney and took our tools back to the shed. All the way we didn't speak a word. The kitchen was dark and cold as we'd left it, and the old woman was sitting over the hearth, saying her beads. We walked past her into the room, and Noble struck a match to light the lamp. She rose quietly and came to the doorway with all her cantankerousness gone.

"What did ye do with them?" she asked in a whisper, and Noble started so that the match went out in his hand.

"What's that?" he asked without turning round.

"I heard ye," she said.

"What did you hear?" asked Noble.

"I heard ye. Do ye think I didn't hear ye, putting the spade back in the houseen?"[5]
Noble struck another match and this time the lamp lit for him.

"Was that what ye did to them?" she asked.

Then, by God, in the very doorway, she fell on her knees and began praying, and after looking at her for a minute or two Noble did the same by the fireplace. I pushed my way out past her and left them at it. I stood at the door, watching the stars and listening to the shrieking of the birds dying out over the bogs. It is so strange what you feel at times like that that you can't describe it. Noble says he saw everything ten times the size, as though there were nothing in the whole world but that little patch of bog with the two Englishmen stiffening into it, but with me it was as if the patch of bog where the Englishmen were was a million miles away, and even Noble and the old woman, mumbling behind me, and the birds and the bloody stars were all far away, and I was somehow very small and very lost and lonely like a child astray in the snow. And anything that happened me afterwards, I never felt the same about again.

QUESTIONS

1. Is the title too frivolous for what actually takes place in the story?

2. This is a first-person narrative. What sort of character tells the story? To what extent does his personality color the story? How does his voice control the tone?

3. The four men — two prisoners, two guards — have developed a relationship. How would you describe it? How does the relationship complicate the plot?

4. Is Hawkins expressing cowardice when he offers to "come over to your side"?

5. Who is the protagonist of the story? Who or what is the antagonist?

6. What justification is there for the killing of Hawkins and Belcher? What should have, or could have, been done?

7. Belcher's character seems to grow as the story goes on. What does he do and say that fills out the bare outlines of his character?

---

[5] Toolshed.

8. The last paragraph is powerfully written. How does imagery contribute to its effect on you? Consider the words "mumbling" and "bloody" in this context. How do they color the narrator's final sentence?

9. How would you describe the author's attitude toward the Irish-English conflict? Is this attitude the theme of "Guests of the Nation," or is the theme something broader still?

The Beard

Translated by Isaac Bashevis Singer
and Herbert R. Lottman

That a Yiddish writer should become rich, and in his old age to boot, seemed unbelievable. But it happened to Bendit Pupko, a little man, sick, pockmarked, with one blind eye and a game leg.

While he struggled with his physical handicaps, the plays he could not finish, the poetry which no one read, and novels which no one was willing to publish, he followed a relative's advice and bought a thousand dollars' worth of over-the-counter stock for two dollars a share. He got the capital in the first place from generous patrons and benevolent societies. The stock went up to almost one hundred times its original value in a matter of months.

Later on, the same relative advised him to buy some half-ruined buildings on Third Avenue in New York. A construction company wanted the land and paid him an enormous sum for it.

No one in the cafeteria which we all frequented ever learned the identity of the mysterious advicegiver, but we knew that Bendit Pupko became richer from day to day. He himself admitted that he wasn't very far away from his first million. Nevertheless, he wore the same shabby clothes he always wore. He sat with us at the table, smoked cigarettes, coughed, ate rice pudding, and complained "What can I do with my money? Nothing."

"Give it to me," said Pelta Mannes, a writer of fables.

"What will you do with it? Take an egg cookie and a cup of coffee on my check."

Bendit Pupko was the kind of primitive writer who could never learn how to construct a correct sentence, had no notion of grammar, but was talented just the same. I often looked into his published works. They lacked any sense of organization, but on every page I found some lines to surprise me.

He described half-crazed people, chronic misers, old country quarrels which had gone on for so many years that no one knew how they began or what they were about, and complicated love affairs which started in the Polish villages and were carried over to the East Side tenement houses of New York and later to the hotels for old people in Miami Beach. His paragraphs went on for pages. He would insert himself into the middle of his hero's dialogue.

In the United States Pupko learned about Freud for the first time, and he tried to explain his characters according to Freudian theory. He needed an editor, but he never allowed anyone to correct even his punctuation.

Once, when I edited a small literary magazine, he brought me a story which began: "The day was cloudy and the sky loyal." When I asked him what he meant by "loyal," his good eye looked at me with anger and suspicion, and he exclaimed, "Don't bother me with this bookish nonsense. Either publish it or go to hell."

He grabbed his manuscript and ran away.

He had lived in America for forty years and never learned more than a handful of English words. He never read anything besides his Yiddish newspapers. Psychology he pronounced "pyschology." Someone told me that a dictionary could be compiled of Pupko's errors. But at times he spoke like a sage. He lived somewhere in Brownsville and had no children.

A man told me that Bendit Pupko's wife had a thick beard which used to be black but had since turned gray. He never took her anywhere. Nobody knew why she didn't shave off her beard.

In my circle I learned long ago never to look for explanations. A comedian of the Yiddish theater who was known for his salty language suddenly became religious, let his sidelocks grow, and settled down in Jerusalem in the Mea Shearim quarter, where the most zealous Jews lived. An Orthodox rabbi divorced his wife, left his synagogue, and went over to the Communists. Two Hebrew teachers divorced their husbands and went to live together as lesbian lovers. Even Pupko's getting rich would not have surprised us too much, but he never let us forget about it. Every day he came and told us about his latest financial accomplishments. He began to advise us how to invest our savings.

One day he boasted to us that the critic Gabriel Weitz was writing a book about him. This we could not believe. Weitz had written unfavorably about Pupko's work at every opportunity. He called him an ignoramus, a village philosopher, and a contriver.

We all asked, "How is this possible?" Bendit Pupko winked with his bad eye and smiled cunningly. "When you grease the wheels, you ride well." Then he quoted a saying from the Talmud: "Money can purify a bastard."

Pupko spoke to us openly. "All these literary faultfinders can be bought for a pittance." He, Pupko, had talked business to Gabriel Weitz. "How much would it cost, buddy?" And the critic had given him a price — five thousand dollars.

We were all shocked. Gabriel Weitz had the reputation of a serious writer. We had all decided that Bendit Pupko was bluffing. But then a magazine appeared with an essay by Gabriel Weitz about Bendit Pupko, which was announced as a fragment of a longer work. In it Gabriel Weitz spoke of Bendit Pupko as a classic. He called him a genius. He was eloquent concerning Pupko's importance to Yiddish literature. Bendit Pupko did not lie: Gabriel Weitz had let himself be bought for five thousand dollars.

I said to Bendit Pupko, "What do you gain by paying for such things? What is the value of such fame?" And Bendit Pupko replied, "You must buy everything. If you have a wife you have to provide for her. If not, she'll sue you. If you have a mistress you have to take her to a restaurant, pay for her hotel, and shower her with presents. Your own children would become your enemies if you stopped supporting them. Sooner or later everybody sends you a bill. In that case, why should fame be different?"

He said to me, "You too will praise me one day."

These words made me shudder and I replied, "I have a high opinion of you, but there isn't enough money in the world to make me write about you."

He laughed and immediately became serious. "Not even for ten thousand dollars?"

"Not even for ten million."

Someone at the table remarked, "Bendit, you spoil your own business. He might have written about you sooner or later."

"Yes, it may be," I said. "But now it's finished."

Bendit Pupko nodded. "Still, if you knew that writing a favorable review of me would keep you in comfort for the rest of your life, you wouldn't have to scribble your articles and could live somewhere in California, you would think twice. Why is it such a sin to say that Bendit Pupko has talent?"

"It's not a sin and you do have talent. But since you have begun to bribe critics, I wouldn't write about you for anything in the world."

"What if somebody put a gun to your temple? Would you give in then?"

"Yes, it certainly doesn't pay to die for something like this," I replied in our cafeteria style of conversation.

"Well, eat your rice pudding. I'm not offering you ten thousand yet. You'll make it a lot cheaper." And he laughed, showing his teeth, crooked and black like rusted nails.

A year passed, perhaps a little more or less. One day I entered the cafeteria and sat down at our usual table. For a while we chatted about a poem which a colleague had published in a magazine. One of us said it was a work of genius and another that it contained nothing but empty phrases. For a while we were engrossed in this controversial subject. Then the writer of fables asked, "Did you hear about Bendit Pupko?"

"What happened?"

"He has cancer."

"So this is the end of all his fortunes," someone remarked. We ate our rice pudding, drank coffee, and the question of whether the poem was excellent or a worthless compilation lost its importance. One of us said, "We are disappearing and younger writers don't appear. Twenty years from now no one will know we ever existed."

"And if they do know, how will this help us?"

After a while, I went home to my bachelor quarters. My desk was cluttered with manuscripts, stories, and novels I had never finished. Dust covered everything. I had a Negro woman who cleaned for me once a week, but I had forbidden her to touch my papers. Besides, she was old and half paralyzed. Often when she came I paid her for the day and sent her home because I saw that she had no strength to work. I worried that she might collapse while working in my apartment.

This time I lay down on the sofa and read a letter, the date of which showed that I had received it two years earlier. I found it while rummaging in my inside breast pocket. The sender's address could no longer be read. Then someone knocked at my door. I opened it and what I saw was like a nightmare. Outside stood a woman dressed in a shabby black dress, men's shoes and a hat, with a white beard. She leaned on a cane. I knew at once who she was — Mrs. Pupko. I was afraid my spying neighbors might see her and have something to laugh about. I said, "Come in, Mrs. Pupko."

She looked at me with astonishment. Her cane passed the door first. She said with a mannish voice, "Your elevator doesn't function. I had to climb five flights of stairs."

"I'm sorry, it's an old house. Sit down."

"May I smoke?"

"Yes, certainly."

She took out a cigar and lit it. Perhaps it's a man, I thought. But I saw that she had a large bust. Probably androgynous, I thought.

She said, "My husband is very sick."

"Yes, I heard. I'm very sorry."

"You are responsible for his illness," she said in a strong voice.

Shaken, I asked her, "What are you saying?"

"I know what I'm saying. You told him some time ago that you wouldn't write about him for all the money in the world. For you this was just talk to make yourself sound important. But there is a proverb, 'A blow is forgotten, but a word never.' You hurt him with those words more than you can imagine. How did he deserve it?

"My husband has great talent. Gabriel Weitz calls him a genius. Bendit has a high opinion of you. When you told him that you would never write about him, he took it very badly. You will never know how this affected him. He came home as yellow as wax. I asked him what was the matter and in the beginning he didn't want to tell me, but I got it out of him. You won't believe me, but from that day on he was never the same. Sick as he was, he was always full of joy. He used to make plans for years in advance. But since that day he never lifted a pen. He began to suffer from cramps in his stomach — "

"Mrs. Pupko, this cannot be true," I interrupted her.

"God knows that it's the truth."

"I'm not a critic. Gabriel Weitz is writing a whole book about him."

"He doesn't think much of Gabriel Weitz. We all know who he is, an intellectual bore. All brain, no feeling. He understands literature like my left foot. Don't think that one can fool Bendit. He may deceive himself but he knows the truth. You are different. He reads every word you write. Sometimes we read you together. We are both insomniacs. We lie awake at nights, and whenever we talk about you he says the same thing, 'He's genuine.'

"Then you had to strike such a blow. He's more sensitive than you imagine. Literature is his whole life. I've been with Bendit for over forty years. Do you realize what it is to share a life for forty years? He reads me every line he writes. Whatever problem he has in his work he asks for my advice.

"We have no children, but his works are our children. You never shared anything with anyone, so you don't understand such things. You write about love, but you don't know what it is. Forgive me, but you describe passion, not love which makes sacrifices and ripens with the years. In this respect Bendit is ten heads taller than you. Do you have an ashtray?"

I brought her an ashtray and she shook the cigar ash into it. She lifted her bushy brows and I saw dark eyes, almost all pupil. I thought the witches who flew on brooms to attend Black Mass on Saturday nights and were later burned at the stake must have looked like this.

"Why do you stare at me like that? I'm a woman, not a man."

"May I ask you why — "

"I know what you want to ask. I grew a beard when I was still a young girl. You may not believe it but I was beautiful then. I tried to shave it or even to burn out the roots, but the more I tried the quicker it grew. Don't think that I'm the only one. Thousands of women grow beards. A beard isn't only a man's privilege.

"When I met Bendit and he kissed my cheek, he exclaimed, 'Zelda, you're growing a beard!' And he fell into a strange rapture. He was in love with my beard. Unbelievable? I didn't believe myself that this could be true. He spoke to me clearly. He was willing to marry me, but on one condition — that I let my beard grow. It wasn't easy to promise a thing like that. I thought he was insane."

"He must have homosexual inclinations," I said.

"Oh, I knew you'd say that. That is what everyone said. From you I expected something more original. He's not a homosexual. People have idiosyncrasies which can't be explained by any theories. It wasn't a small matter for me to comply. It meant complete loneliness. When my mother came to visit me in Odessa after our marriage and she saw me with a beard, she literally passed out.

"I became a hermit. But Bendit's wish was more important to me than any comforts. This is the kind of love which you cannot appreciate. Here in America my isolation became even more complete. I could tell you a lot, but I didn't come here to explain my beard but to warn you that you're killing Bendit."

"Please don't say such things. Bendit is my friend."

"In that case, you are killing your friend."   `

We continued to talk for some time. I gave Mrs. Pupko my word that I would write about her husband. She said to me, "It may be too late to save him, but I want him to have the satisfaction of seeing something written about him by you."

"May I ask why you smoke cigars?"

"*Nu*,[1] one mustn't know everything."

In my mind I prayed to God that none of the neighbors would see her leave my rooms, but when I opened the door for Mrs. Pupko, I saw my neighbor the spinster lurking in the hall. The elevator was still not working, and Mrs. Pupko had to walk down the stairs. She called out to me, "Be a gentleman and help me down."

She grasped my arm and her breast touched my elbow. For some reason, all the neighbors on all the floors had their doors open as we descended. I heard children screaming, "Mama, look! A woman with a beard!" A barking dog ran out of one apartment and caught Mrs. Pupko's dress in his teeth, and I barely succeeded in driving him away.

That evening I sat down to reread Pupko's works. A few weeks later I had written an article about him, but the editor of the magazine to which I sent it delayed its publication so long that Bendit Pupko died in the meantime. He had just managed to read the proofs and on the margin of the last page he had written in a trembling hand: "Didn't I tell you?"

Once when I sat in the Automat on Sixth Avenue, not far from the public library, the door opened and Mrs. Pupko came in. She was supported by a cane and a crutch. Though a widow for two years, she still had her beard and wore a man's hat and shoes. She immediately limped over to my table and sat down as if she had an appointment with me.

All the customers in the Automat stared, winked at their neighbors, laughed. I wanted to ask Mrs. Pupko why, since her husband was no longer alive, she had kept her beard, but I remembered her words: "*Nu*, one mustn't know everything."

QUESTIONS

1. What is ironic about Bendit Pupko's becoming rich? Why doesn't wealth alter his living habits? Is the narrator surprised by this fact?

2. How well does the narrator know Pupko? Are there gaps in his understanding of Pupko? Does he like the man?

3. Most of the characters in this story are writers. How do Pupko, Weitz, and the narrator differ from each other? Is this story in part a commentary on the craft and profession of writing? Do you see the making of an allegory here?

4. The narrator refuses to write favorably about Pupko after it becomes clear that Gabriel Weitz has accepted a bribe to do so. Are there circumstances under which he will change his mind? Does this bring him down to Weitz's level? What is different about the "bribe" he accepts?

---

[1] A Yiddish interjection used in many contexts; here it means something like "Well-l-l ..."

5. Why do you think Mrs. Pupko kept her beard? Is she to be pitied?

6. Pupko, we are told, is a Yiddish writer who writes about odd folk: "half-crazed people, chronic misers, old country quarrels ..." Singer is a Yiddish writer who in this case writes about some rather odd characters of his own. Are we supposed to make a connection? Does some of the humor in this tale derive from some sort of ironic identification of the author with his characters?

RICHARD WRIGHT

The Man Who
Killed a Shadow

It all began long ago when he was a tiny boy who was already used, in a fearful sort of way, to living with shadows. But what were the shadows that made him afraid? Surely they were not those beautiful silhouettes of objects cast upon the earth by the sun. Shadows of that kind are innocent and he loved trying to catch them as he ran along sunlit paths in summer. But there were subtler shadows which he saw and which others could not see: the shadows of his fears. And this boy had such shadows and he lived to kill one of them.

Saul Saunders was born black in a little Southern town, not many miles from Washington, the nation's capital, which means that he came into a world that was split in two, a white world and a black one, the white one being separated from the black by a million psychological miles. So, from the very beginning, Saul looking timidly out from his black world, saw the shadowy outlines of a white world that was unreal to him and not his own.

It so happened that even Saul's mother was but a vague, shadowy thing to him, for she died long before his memory could form an image of her. And the same thing happened to Saul's father, who died before the boy could retain a clear picture of him in his mind.

People really never became personalities to Saul, for hardly had he ever got to know them before they vanished. So people became for Saul symbols of uneasiness, 2f a deprivation that evoked in him a sense of the transitory quality of life, which always made him feel that some invisible, unexplainable event was about to descend upon him.

He had five brothers and two sisters who remained strangers to him. There was, of course, no adult in his family with enough money to support them all, and the children were rationed out to various cousins, uncles, aunts, and grandparents.

It fell to Saul to live with his grandmother who moved constantly from one small Southern town to another, and even physical landscapes grew to have but little emotional meaning for the boy. Towns were places you lived in for a while, and then you moved on. When he had reached the age of twelve, all reality seemed to him to be akin to his mother and father, like the white world that surrounded the black island of his life, like the parade of dirty little towns that passed forever before his eyes, things that had names but not substance, things that happened and then retreated into an incomprehensible nothingness.

Saul was not dumb or lazy, but it took him seven years to reach the third grade in school. None of the people who came and went in Saul's life had ever prized learning and

Saul did likewise. It was quite normal in his environment to reach the age of fourteen and still be in the third grade, and Saul liked being normal, liked being like other people.

Then the one person — his grandmother — who Saul had thought would endure forever, passed suddenly from his life, and from that moment on Saul did not ever quite know what to do. He went to work for the white people of the South and the shadowlike quality of his world became terribly manifest, continuously present. He understood nothing of this white world into which he had been thrown; it was just there, a faint and fearful shadow cast by some object that stood between him and a hidden and powerful sun.

He quickly learned that the strange white people for whom he worked considered him inferior; he did not feel inferior and he did not think that he was. But when he looked about him he saw other black people accepting this definition of themselves, and who was he to challenge it? Outwardly he grew to accept it as part of that vast shadow-world that came and went, pulled by forces which he nor nobody he knew understood.

Soon all of Saul's anxieties, fears, and irritations became focused upon this white shadow-world which gave him his daily bread in exchange for his labor. Feeling unhappy and not knowing why, he projected his misery out from himself and upon the one thing that made him most constantly anxious. If this had not happened, if Saul had not found a way of putting his burden upon others, he would have early thought of suicide. He finally did, in the end, think of killing himself, but then it was too late ...

At the age of fifteen Saul knew that the life he was then living was to be his lot, that there was no way to rid himself of his plaguing sense of unreality, no way to relax and forget. He was most self-forgetful when he was with black people, and that made things a little easier for him. But as he grew older, he became more afraid, yet none of his friends noticed it. Indeed, many of Saul's friends liked him very much. Saul was always kind, attentive; but no one suspected that his kindness, his quiet, waiting loyalty came from his being afraid.

Then Saul changed. Maybe it was luck or misfortune; it is hard to tell. When he took a drink of whisky, he found that it helped to banish the shadows, lessened his tensions, made the world more reasonably three-dimensional, and he grew to like drinking. When he was paid off on a Saturday night, he would drink with his friends and he would feel better. He felt that whisky made life complete, that it stimulated him. But, of course, it did not. Whisky really depressed him, numbed him somewhat, reduced the force and number of the shadows that made him tight inside.

When Saul was sober, he almost never laughed in the presence of the white shadow-world, but when he had a drink or two he found that he could. Even when he was told about the hard lives that all Negroes lived, it did not worry him, for he would take a drink and not feel too badly. It did not even bother him when he heard that if you were alone with a white woman and she screamed, it was as good as hearing your death sentence, for, though you had done nothing, you would be killed. Saul got used to hearing the siren of the police car screaming in the Black Belt, got used to seeing white cops dragging Negroes off to jail. Once he grew wildly angry about it, felt that the shadows would some day claim him as he had seen them claim others, but his friends warned him that it was dangerous to feel that way, that always the black man lost, and the best thing to do was to take a drink. He did, and in a little while they were all laughing.

One night when he was mildly drunk — he was thirty years old and living in Washington at the time — he got married. The girl was good for Saul, for she too liked to drink and she was pretty and they got along together. Saul now felt that things were not so bad; as long as he could stifle the feeling of being hemmed in, as long as he could conquer the anxiety about the unexpected happening, life was bearable.

Saul's jobs had been many and simple. First he had worked on a farm. When he was fourteen he had gone to Washington, after his grandmother had died, where he did all kinds of odd jobs. Finally he was hired by an old white army colonel as chauffeur and butler and he averaged about twenty dollars every two weeks. He lived in and got his meals and uniform and remained with the colonel for five years. The colonel too liked to drink, and sometimes they would both get drunk. But Saul never forgot that the colonel, though drunk and feeling fine, was still a shadow, unreal, and might suddenly change toward him.

One day, when whisky was making him feel good, Saul asked the colonel for a raise in salary, told him that he did not have enough to live on, and that prices were rising. But the colonel was sober and hard that day and said no. Saul was so stunned that he quit the job that instant. While under the spell of whisky he had for a quick moment felt that the world of shadows was over, but when he had asked for more money and had been refused, he knew that he had been wrong. He should not have asked for money; he should have known that the colonel was a no-good guy, a shadow.

Saul was next hired as an exterminator by a big chemical company and he found that there was something in his nature that made him like going from house to house and putting down poison for rats and mice and roaches. He liked seeing concrete evidence of his work and the dead bodies of rats were no shadows. They were real. He never felt better in his life than when he was killing with the sanction of society. And his boss even increased his salary when he asked for it. And he drank as much as he liked and no one cared.

But one morning, after a hard night of drinking which had made him irritable and high-strung, his boss said something that he did not like and he spoke up, defending himself against what he thought was a slighting remark. There was an argument and Saul left.

Two weeks of job hunting got him the position of janitor in the National Cathedral, a church and religious institution. It was the solitary kind of work he liked; he reported for duty each morning at seven o'clock and at eleven he was through. He first cleaned the Christmas card shop, next he cleaned the library; and his final chore was to clean the choir room.

But cleaning the library, with its rows and rows of books, was what caught Saul's attention, for there was a strange little shadow woman there who stared at him all the time in a most peculiar way. The library was housed in a separate building and, whenever he came to clean it, he and the white woman would be there alone. She was tiny, blonde, blue-eyed, weighing about 110 pounds, and standing about five feet three inches. Saul's boss had warned him never to quarrel with the lady in charge of the library. "She's a crackpot," he had told Saul. And naturally Saul never wanted any trouble, in fact, he did not even know the woman's name. Many times, however, he would pause in his work, feeling that his eyes were being drawn to her and he would turn around and find her staring at him. Then she would look away quickly, as though ashamed. "What in hell does she want from me?" he wondered uneasily. The woman never spoke to him except to say good morning and she even said that as though she did not want to say it. Saul thought that maybe she was afraid of him; but how could that be? He could not recall when anybody had ever been afraid of him, and he had never been in any trouble in his life.

One morning while sweeping the floor he felt his eyes being drawn toward her and he paused and turned and saw her staring at him. He did not move, neither did she. They stared at each other for about ten seconds, then she went out of the room, walking with quick steps, as though angry or afraid. He was frightened, but forgot it quickly. "What the hell's wrong with that woman?" he asked himself.

Next morning Saul's boss called him and told him, in a nice quiet tone — but it made him scared and mad just the same — that the woman in the library had complained about him, had said that he never cleaned under her desk.

"Under her desk?" Saul asked, amazed.

"Yes," his boss said, amused at Saul's astonishment.

"But I clean under her desk every morning," Saul said.

"Well, Saul, remember, I told you she was a crackpot," his boss said soothingly. "Don't argue with her. Just do your work."

"Yes, sir," Saul said.

He wanted to tell his boss how the woman always stared at him, but he could not find courage enough to do so. If he had been talking with his black friends, he would have done so quite naturally. But why talk to one shadow about another queer shadow?

That day being payday, he got his weekly wages and that night he had a hell of a good time. He drank until he was drunk, until he blotted out almost everything from his consciousness. He was getting regularly drunk now whenever he had the money. He liked it and he bothered nobody and he was happy while doing it. But dawn found him broke, exhausted, and terribly depressed, full of shadows and uneasiness, a way he never liked it. The thought of going to his job made him angry. He longed for deep, heavy sleep. But, no, he had a good job and he had to keep it. Yes, he would go.

After cleaning the Christmas card shop — he was weak and he sweated a lot — he went to the library. No one was there. He swept the floor and was about to dust the books when he heard the footsteps of the woman coming into the room. He was tired, nervous, half asleep; his hands trembled and his reflexes were overquick. "So you're the bitch who snitched on me, hunh?" he said irritably to himself. He continued dusting and all at once he had the queer feeling that she was staring at him. He fought against the impulse to look at her, but he could not resist it. He turned slowly and saw that she was sitting in her chair at her desk, staring at him with unblinking eyes. He had the impression that she was about to speak. He could not help staring back at her, waiting.

"Why don't you clean under my desk?" she asked him in a tense but controlled voice.

"Why, ma'am," he said slowly, "I just did."

"Come here and look," she said, pointing downward.

He replaced the book on the shelf. She had never spoken so many words to him before. He went and stood before her and his mind protested against what his eyes saw, and then his senses leaped in wonder. She was sitting with her knees sprawled apart and her dress was drawn halfway up her legs. He looked from her round blue eyes to her white legs whose thighs thickened as they went to a V clothed in tight, sheer, pink panties; then he looked quickly again into her eyes. Her face was a beet red, but she sat very still, rigid, as though she was being impelled into an act which she did not want to perform but was being driven to perform. Saul was so startled that he could not move.

"I just cleaned under your desk this morning," he mumbled, sensing that he was not talking about what she meant.

"There's dust there now," she said sternly, her legs still so wide apart that he felt that she was naked.

He did not know what to do; he was so baffled, humiliated, and frightened that he grew angry. But he was afraid to express his anger openly.

"Look, ma'am," he said in a tone of suppressed rage and hate, "you're making trouble for me!"

"Why don't you do your work?" she blazed at him. "That's what you're being paid to do, you black nigger!" Her legs were still spread wide and she was sitting as though about to spring upon him and throw her naked thighs about his body.

For a moment he was still and silent. Never before in his life had he been called a "black nigger." He had heard that white people used that phrase as their supreme humiliation of black people, but he had never been treated so. As the insult sank in, as he stared at her gaping thighs, he felt overwhelmed by a sense of wild danger.

"I don't like that," he said and before he knew it he had slapped her flat across her face.

She sucked in her breath, sprang up, and stepped away from him. Then she screamed sharply, and her voice was like a lash cutting into his chest. She screamed again and he backed away from her. He felt helpless, strange; he knew what he had done, knew its meaning for him; but he knew that he could not have helped it. It seemed that some part of him was there in that room watching him do things that he should not do. He drew in his breath and for a moment he felt that he could not stand upon his legs. His world was now full of all the shadows he had ever feared. He was in the worst trouble that a black man could imagine.

The woman was screaming continuously now and he was running toward the stairs. Just as he put his foot on the bottom step, he paused and looked over his shoulder. She was backing away from him, toward an open window at the far end of the room, still screaming. Oh God! In her scream he heard the sirens of the police cars that hunted down black men in the Black Belts and he heard the shrill whistles of white cops running after black men and he felt again in one rush of emotion all the wild and bitter tales he had heard of how whites always got the black who did a crime and this woman was screaming as though he had raped her.

He ran on up the steps, but her screams were coming so loud that when he neared the top of the steps he slowed. Those screams would not let him run any more, they weakened him, tugged and pulled him. His chest felt as though it would burst. He reached the top landing and looked round aimlessly. He saw a fireplace and before it was a neat pile of wood and while he was looking at that pile of wood the screams tore at him, unnerved him. With a shaking hand he reached down and seized in his left hand — for he was lefthanded — a heavy piece of oaken firewood that had jagged, sharp edges where it had been cut with an ax. He turned and ran back down the steps to where the woman stood screaming. He lifted the stick of wood as he confronted her, then paused. He wanted her to stop screaming. If she had stopped, he would have fled, but while she screamed all he could feel was a hotness bubbling in him and urging him to do something. She would fill her lungs quickly and deeply and her breath would come out at full blast. He swung down his left arm and hit her a swinging blow on the side of her head, not to hurt her, not to kill her, but to stop that awful noise, to stop that shadow from screaming a scream that meant death ... He felt her skull crack and give as she sank to the floor, but she still screamed. He trembled from head to feet. Goddamn that woman ... Why didn't she stop that yelling? He lifted his arm and gave her another blow, feeling the oaken stick driving its way into her skull. But still she screamed. He was about to hit her again when he became aware that the stick he held was light. He looked at it and found that half of it had broken off, was lying on the floor. But she screamed on, with blood running down her dress, her legs sprawled nakedly out from under her. He dropped the remainder of the stick and grabbed her throat and choked her to stop her screams. That seemed to quiet her; she looked as though she had fainted. He choked her for a long time, not trying to kill her, but just to make sure that she would not scream again and make him wild and hot inside. He was not reacting to the woman, but to the feelings that her screams evoked in him.

The woman was limp and silent now and slowly he took his hands from her throat. She was quiet. He waited. He was not certain. Yes, take her downstairs into the bathroom and if she screamed again no one would hear her ... He took her hands in his and started dragging her away from the window. His hands were wet with sweat and her hands were so tiny and soft that time and again her little fingers slipped out of his palms. He tried holding her hands tighter and only succeeded in scratching her. Her ring slid off into his hand while he was dragging her and he stood still for a moment, staring in a daze at the thin band of shimmering gold, then mechanically he put it into his pocket. Finally he dragged her down the steps to the bathroom door.

He was about to take her in when he saw that the floor was spotted with drippings of blood. That was bad ... He had been trained to keep floors clean, just as he had been trained to fear shadows. He propped her clumsily against a wall and went into the bathroom and took wads of toilet paper and mopped up the red splashes. He even went back upstairs where he had first struck her and found blood spots and wiped them up carefully. He stiffened; she was hollering again. He ran downstairs and this time he recalled that he had a knife in his pocket. He took it out, opened it, and plunged it deep into her throat; he was frantic to stop her from hollering ... He pulled the knife from her throat and she was quiet.

He stood, his eyes roving. He noticed a door leading down to a recess in a wall through which steam pipes ran. Yes, it would be better to put her there; then if she started yelling no one would hear her. He was not trying to hide her; he merely wanted to make sure that she would not be heard. He dragged her again and her dress came up over her knees to her chest and again he saw her pink panties. It was too hard dragging her and he lifted her in his arms and while carrying her down the short flight of steps he thought that the pink panties, if he would wet them, would make a good mop to clean up the blood. Once more he sat her against the wall, stripped her of her pink panties — and not once did he so much as glance at her groin — wetted them and swabbed up the spots, then pushed her into the recess under the pipes. She was in full view, easily seen. He tossed the wet ball of panties in after her.

He sighed and looked around. The floor seemed clean. He went back upstairs. That stick of broken wood ... He picked up the two shattered ends of wood and several splinters; he carefully joined the ends together and then fitted the splinters into place. He laid the mended stick back upon the pile before the fireplace. He stood listening, wondering if she would yell again, but there was no sound. It never occurred to him that he could help her, that she might be in pain; he never wondered even if she were dead. He got his coat and hat and went home.

He was nervously tired. It seemed that he had just finished doing an old and familiar job of dodging the shadows that were forever around him, shadows that he could not understand. He undressed, but paid no attention to the blood on his trousers and shirt; he was alone in the room; his wife was at work. When he pulled out his billfold, he saw the ring. He put it in the drawer of his night table, more to keep his wife from seeing it than to hide it. He climbed wearily into bed and at once fell into a deep, sound sleep from which he did not awaken until late afternoon. He lay blinking bloodshot eyes and he could not remember what he had done. Then the vague, shadowlike picture of it came before his eyes. He was puzzled, and for a moment he wondered if it had happened or had someone told him a story of it. He could not be sure. There was no fear or regret in him.

When at last the conviction of what he had done was real in him, it came only in terms of flat memory, devoid of all emotion, as though he were looking when very tired and sleepy at a scene being flashed upon the screen of a movie house. Not knowing what to do, he remained in bed. He had drifted off to sleep again when his wife came home late that night from her cooking job.

Next morning he ate the breakfast his wife prepared, rose from the table and kissed her, and started off toward the Cathedral as though nothing had happened. It was not until he actually got to the Cathedral steps that he became shaky and nervous. He stood before the door for two or three minutes, and then he realized that he could not go back in there this morning. Yet it was not danger that made him feel this way, but a queer kind of repugnance. Whether the woman was alive or not did not enter his mind. He still did not know what to do. Then he remembered that his wife, before she had left for her job, had asked him to buy some groceries. Yes, he would do that. He wanted to do that because he did not know what else on earth to do.

He bought the groceries and took them home, then spent the rest of the day wandering from bar to bar. Not once did he think of fleeing. He would go home, sit, turn on the radio, then go out into the streets and walk. Finally he would end up at a bar, drinking. On one of his many trips into the house, he changed his clothes, rolled up his bloody shirt and trousers, put the blood-stained knife inside the bundle, and pushed it into a far corner of a closet. He got his gun and put it into his pocket, for he was nervously depressed.

But he still did not know what to do. Suddenly he recalled that some months ago he had bought a cheap car which was now in a garage for repairs. He went to the garage and persuaded the owner to take it back for twenty-five dollars; the thought that he could use the car for escape never came to his mind. During that afternoon and early evening he sat in bars and drank. What he felt now was no different from what he had felt all his life.

Toward eight o'clock that night he met two friends of his and invited them for a drink. He was quite drunk now. Before him on the table was a sandwich and a small glass of whisky. He leaned forward, listening sleepily to one of his friends tell a story about a girl, and then he heard:

"Aren't you Saul Saunders?"

He looked up into the faces of two white shadows.

"Yes," he admitted readily. "What do you want?"

"You'd better come along with us. We want to ask you some questions," one of the shadows said.

"What's this all about?" Saul asked.

They grabbed his shoulders and he stood up. Then he reached down and picked up the glass of whisky and drank it. He walked steadily out of the bar to a waiting auto, a policeman to each side of him, his mind a benign blank. It was not until they were about to put him into the car that something happened and whipped his numbed senses to an apprehension of danger. The policeman patted his waist for arms; they found nothing because his gun was strapped to his chest. Yes, he ought to kill himself ... The thought leaped into his mind with such gladness that he shivered. It was the answer to everything. Why had he not thought of it before?

Slowly he took off his hat and held it over his chest to hide the movement of his left hand, then he reached inside of his shirt and pulled out the gun. One of the policemen pounced on him and snatched the gun.

"So, you're trying to kill us too, hunh?" one asked.

"Naw, I was trying to kill myself," he answered simply.

"Like hell you were!"

A fist came onto his jaw and he sank back limp.

Two hours later, at the police station, he told them everything, speaking in a low, listless voice without a trace of emotion, vividly describing every detail, yet feeling that it was utterly hopeless for him to try to make them understand how horrible it was for him to hear that woman screaming. His narrative sounded so brutal that the policemen's faces were chalky.

Weeks later a voice droned in a court room and he sat staring dully.

" ... The Grand Jurors of the United States of America, in and for the District of Columbia aforesaid, upon their oath, do present:

"That one Saul Saunders, on, to wit, the first day of March, 19 —, and at and within the District of Columbia aforesaid, contriving and intending to kill one Maybelle Eva Houseman ..."

"So *that's* her name," he said to himself in amazement.

" ... Feloniously, wilfully, purposefully, and of his deliberate and premeditated malice did strike, beat, and wound the said Maybelle Eva Houseman, in and upon the front of the head and in and upon the right side of the head of her, the said Maybelle Eva Houseman, two certain mortal wounds and fractures; and did fix and fasten about the neck and throat of her, the said Maybelle Eva Houseman, his hand or hands — but whether it was one of his hands or both of his hands is to the Grand Jury aforesaid unknown — and that he, the said Saul Saunders, with his hand or hands as aforesaid fixed and fastened about the throat of her, did choke and strangle the said Maybelle Eva Houseman, of which said choking and strangling the said Maybelle Eva Houseman, on, to wit, the said first day of March, 19 —, and at and within the said District of Columbia, did die."

He longed for a drink, but that was impossible now. Then he took a deep breath and surrendered to the world of shadows about him, the world he had feared so long; and at once the tension went from him and he felt better than he had felt in a long time. He was amazed at how relaxed and peaceful it was when he stopped fighting the world of shadows.

" ... By force and violence and against resistance and by putting in fear, did steal, take, and carry away, from and off the person and from the immediate, actual possession of one Maybelle Eva Houseman, then and there being, a certain finger ring, of the value of, to wit, ten dollars."

He listened now with more attention but no anxiety:

"And in and while perpetrating robbery aforesaid did kill and murder the said Maybelle Eva Houseman; against the form of the statute in such case made and provided, and against the peace and government of the said United States of America."

P.S. Thereupon Dr. Herman Stein was called as a witness and being first duly sworn testified as follows:

" ... On examination of the genital organs there was no evidence of contusion, abrasion, or trauma, and the decedent's hymen ring was intact. This decedent had not been criminally assaulted or attempted to be entered. It has been ascertained that the decedent's age was 40."

QUESTIONS

1. Is Saul responsible for any of his actions, or is he only a victim of circumstances?

2. Are the shadows in this story real or only figments of Saul's imagination? Is it white society or fate (or both) that isolated Saul from reality? Is there a single antagonist?

3. Is the narrator of this story emotionally engaged with Saul? How does he manage to engage your sympathy?

4. Are the librarian's actions believable? Has Wright prepared us for them?

5. Saul performs several self-incriminating acts at the scene of the "murder." Which are the most damaging to him? Are they credible, or are they too "pat" for the reader to accept?

6. What is the effect of Dr. Stein's testimony? Why does Wright end the story with it?

7. Is Wright's purpose to explain Saul's case or to indict the society that allows his situation to occur?

EUDORA WELTY

Why I Live at the P.O.

I was getting along fine with Mama, Papa-Daddy and Uncle Rondo until my sister Stella-Rondo just separated from her husband and came back home again. Mr. Whitaker! Of course I went with Mr. Whitaker first, when he first appeared here in China Grove, taking "Pose Yourself" photos, and Stella-Rondo broke us up. Told him I was one-sided. Bigger on one side than the other, which is a deliberate, calculated falsehood: I'm the same. Stella-Rondo is exactly twelve months to the day younger than I am and for that reason she's spoiled.

She's always had anything in the world she wanted and then she'd throw it away. Papa-Daddy gave her this gorgeous Add-A-Pearl necklace when she was eight years old and she threw it away playing baseball when she was nine, with only two pearls.

So as soon as she got married and moved away from home the first thing she did was separate! From Mr. Whitaker! This photographer with the popeyes she said she trusted. Came home from one of those towns up in Illinois and to our complete surprise brought this child of two.

Mama said she like to make her drop dead for a second. "Here you had this marvelous blonde child and never so much as wrote your mother a word about it," says Mama. "I'm thoroughly ashamed of you." But of course she wasn't.

Stella-Rondo just calmly takes off this *hat*, I wish you could see it. She says, "Why, Mama, Shirley-T.'s adopted, I can prove it."

"How?" says Mama, but all I says was, "H'm!" There I was over the hot stove, trying to stretch two chickens over five people and a completely unexpected child into the bargain, without one moment's notice.

"What do you mean — 'H'm!'?" says Stella-Rondo, and Mama says, "I heard that, Sister."

I said that oh, I didn't mean a thing, only that whoever Shirley-T. was, she was the spit-image of Papa-Daddy if he'd cut off his beard, which of course he'd never do in the world. Papa-Daddy's Mama's papa and sulks.

Stella-Rondo got furious! She said, "Sister, I don't need to tell you you got a lot of nerve and always did have and I'll thank you to make no future reference to my adopted child whatsoever."

"Very well," I said. "Very well, very well. Of course I noticed at once she looks like Mr. Whitaker's side too. That frown. She looks like a cross between Mr. Whitaker and Papa-Daddy."

"Well, all I can say is she isn't."

"She looks exactly like Shirley Temple to me," says Mama, but Shirley-T. just ran away from her.

So the first thing Stella-Rondo did at the table was turn Papa-Daddy against me.

"Papa-Daddy," she says. He was trying to cut up his meat. "Papa-Daddy!" I was taken completely by surprise. Papa-Daddy is about a million years old and's got this long-long beard. "Papa-Daddy, Sister says she fails to understand why you don't cut off your beard."

So Papa-Daddy l-a-y-s down his knife and fork! He's real rich. Mama says he is, he says he isn't. So he says, "Have I heard correctly? You don't understand why I don't cut off my beard?"

"Why," I says, "Papa-Daddy, of course I understand, I did not say any such of a thing, the idea!"

He says, "Hussy!"

I says, "Papa-Daddy, you know I wouldn't any more want you to cut off your beard than the man in the moon. It was the farthest thing from my mind! Stella-Rondo sat there and made that up while she was eating breast of chicken."

But he says, "So the postmistress fails to understand why I don't cut off my beard. Which job I got you through my influence with the government. 'Bird's nest' — is that what you call it?"

Not that it isn't the next to smallest P.O. in the entire state of Mississippi.

I says, "Oh, Papa-Daddy," I says, "I didn't say any such of a thing, I never dreamed it was a bird's nest, I have always been grateful though this is the next to smallest P.O. in the state of Mississippi, and I do not enjoy being referred to as a hussy by my own grandfather."

But Stella-Rondo says, "Yes, you did say it too. Anybody in the world could of heard you, that had ears."

"Stop right there," says Mama, looking at *me*.

So I pulled my napkin straight back through the napkin ring and left the table.

As soon as I was out of the room Mama says, "Call her back, or she'll starve to death," but Papa-Daddy says, "This is the beard I started growing on the Coast when I was fifteen years old." He would of gone on till nightfall if Shirley-T. hadn't lost the Milky Way she ate in Cairo.

So Papa-Daddy says, "I am going out and lie in the hammock, and you can all sit here and remember my words: I'll never cut off my beard as long as I live, even one inch, and I don't appreciate it in you at all." Passed right by me in the hall and went straight out and got in the hammock.

It would be a holiday. It wasn't five minutes before Uncle Rondo suddenly appeared in the hall in one of Stella-Rondo's flesh-colored kimonos, all cut on the bias, like something Mr. Whitaker probably thought was gorgeous.

"Uncle Rondo!" I says. "I didn't know who that was! Where are you going?"

"Sister," he says, "get out of my way, I'm poisoned."

"If you're poisoned stay away from Papa-Daddy," I says. "Keep out of the hammock. Papa-Daddy will certainly beat you on the head if you come within forty miles of him. He thinks I deliberately said he ought to cut off his beard after he got me the P.O., and I've told him and told him and told him, and he acts like he just don't hear me. Papa-Daddy must of gone stone deaf."

"He picked a fine day to do it then," says Uncle Rondo, and before you could say "Jack Robinson" flew out in the yard.

What he'd really done, he'd drunk another bottle of that prescription. He does it every single Fourth of July as sure as shooting, and it's horribly expensive. Then he falls over in the hammock and snores. So he insisted on zigzagging right on out to the hammock, looking like a half-wit.

Papa-Daddy woke up with this horrible yell and right there without moving an inch he tried to turn Uncle Rondo against me. I heard every word he said. Oh, he told Uncle Rondo I didn't learn to read till I was eight years old and he didn't see how in the world I ever got the mail put up at the P.O., much less read it all, and he said if Uncle Rondo could only fathom the lengths he had gone to to get me that job! And he said on the other hand he thought Stella-Rondo had a brilliant mind and deserved credit for getting out of town. All the time he was just lying there swinging as pretty as you please and looping out his beard, and poor Uncle Rondo was *pleading* with him to slow down the hammock, it was making him as dizzy as a witch to watch it. But that's what Papa-Daddy likes about a hammock. So Uncle Rondo was too dizzy to get turned against me for the time being. He's Mama's only brother and is a good case of a one-track mind. Ask anybody. A certified pharmacist.

Just then I heard Stella-Rondo raising the upstairs window. While she was married she got this peculiar idea that it's cooler with the windows shut and locked. So she has to raise the window before she can make a soul hear her outdoors.

So she raises the window and says, "*Oh!*" You would have thought she was mortally wounded.

Uncle Rondo and Papa-Daddy didn't even look up, but kept right on with what they were doing. I had to laugh.

I flew up the stairs and threw the door open! I says, "What in the wide world's the matter, Stella-Rondo? You mortally wounded?"

"No," she says, "I am not mortally wounded but I wish you would do me the favor of looking out that window there and telling me what you see."

So I shade my eyes and look out the window.

"I see the front yard," I says.

"Don't you see any human beings?" she says.

"I see Uncle Rondo trying to run Papa-Daddy out of the hammock," I says. "Nothing more. Naturally, it's so suffocating-hot in the house, with all the windows shut and locked, everybody who cares to stay in their right mind will have to go out and get in the hammock before the Fourth of July is over."

"Don't you notice anything different about Uncle Rondo?" asks Stella-Rondo.

"Why, no, except he's got on some terrible-looking flesh-colored contraption I wouldn't be found dead in, is all I can see," I says.

"Never mind, you won't be found dead in it, because it happens to be part of my trousseau, and Mr. Whitaker took several dozen photographs of me in it," says Stella-Rondo. "What on earth could Uncle Rondo *mean* by wearing part of my trousseau out in the broad, open daylight without saying so much as 'Kiss my foot,' *knowing* I only got home this morning after my separation and hung my negligee up on the bathroom door, just as nervous as I could be?"

"I'm sure I don't know, and what do you expect me to do about it?" I says. "Jump out the window?"

"No, I expect nothing of the kind. I simply declare that Uncle Rondo looks like a fool in it, that's all," she says. "It makes me sick to my stomach."

"Well, he looks as good as he can," I says. "As good as anybody in reason could." I stood up for Uncle Rondo, please remember. And I said to Stella-Rondo, "I think I would do well not to criticize so freely if I were you and came home with a two-year-old child I had never said a word about, and no explanation whatever about my separation."

"I asked you the instant I entered this house not to refer one more time to my adopted child, and you gave me your word of honor you would not," was all Stella-Rondo would say, and started pulling out every one of her eyebrows with some cheap Kress tweezers.

So I merely slammed the door behind me and went down and made some green-tomato pickle. Somebody had to do it. Of course Mama had turned both the niggers loose; she always said no earthly power could hold one anyway on the Fourth of July, so she wouldn't even try. It turned out that Jaypan fell in the lake and came within a very narrow limit of drowning.

So Mama trots in. Lifts up the lid and says, "H'm! Not very good for your Uncle Rondo in his precarious condition, I must say. Or poor little adopted Shirley-T. Shame on you!"

That made me tired. I says, "Well, Stella-Rondo had better thank her lucky stars it was her instead of me came trotting in with that very peculiar-looking child. Now if it had been me that trotted in from Illinois and brought a peculiar-looking child of two, I shudder to think of the reception I'd of got, much less controlled the diet of an entire family."

"But you must remember, Sister, that you were never married to Mr. Whitaker in the first place and didn't go up to Illinois to live," says Mama, shaking a spoon in my face. "If you had I would of been just as overjoyed to see you and your little adopted girl as I was to see Stella-Rondo, when you wound up with your separation and came on back home."

"You would not," I says.

"Don't contradict me, I would," says Mama.

But I said she couldn't convince me though she talked till she was blue in the face. Then I said, "Besides, you know as well as I do that that child is not adopted."

"She most certainly is adopted," says Mama, stiff as a poker.

I says, "Why, Mama, Stella-Rondo had her just as sure as anything in this world, and just too stuck up to admit it."

"Why, Sister," said Mama. "Here I thought we were going to have a pleasant Fourth of July, and you start right out not believing a word your own baby sister tells you!"

"Just like Cousin Annie Flo. Went to her grave denying the facts of life," I remind Mama.

"I told you if you ever mentioned Annie Flo's name I'd slap your face," says Mama, and slaps my face.

"All right, you wait and see," I says.

"I," says Mama, "*I* prefer to take my children's word for anything when it's humanly possible." You ought to see Mama, she weighs two hundred pounds and has real tiny feet.

Just then something perfectly horrible occurred to me.

"Mama," I says, "can that child talk?" I simply had to whisper! "Mama, I wonder if that child can be — you know — in any way? Do you realize," I says, "that she hasn't spoken one single, solitary word to a human being up to the minute? This is the way she looks," I says, and I looked like this.

Well, Mama and I just stood there and stared at each other. It was horrible!

"I remember well that Joe Whitaker frequently drank like a fish," says Mama. "I believed to my soul he drank *chemicals*." And without another word she marches to the foot of the stairs and calls Stella-Rondo.

"Stella-Rondo? O-o-o-o-o! Stella-Rondo!"

"What?" says Stella-Rondo from upstairs. Not even the grace to get up off the bed.

"Can that child of yours talk?" asks Mama.

Stella-Rondo says, "Can she what?"

"Talk! Talk!" says Mama. "Burdyburdyburdyburdy!"

So Stella-Rondo yells back, "Who says she can't talk?"

"Sister says so," says Mama.

"You didn't have to tell me, I know whose word of honor don't mean a thing in this house," says Stella-Rondo.

And in a minute the loudest Yankee voice I ever heard in my life yells out, "OE'm Pop-OE the Sailor-r-r-r Ma-a-an!" and then somebody jumps up and down in the upstairs hall. In another second the house would of fallen down.

"Not only talks, she can tap-dance!" calls Stella-Rondo. "Which is more than some people I won't name can do."

"Why, the little precious darling thing!" Mama says, so surprised. "Just as smart as she can be!" Starts talking baby talk right there. Then she turns on me. "Sister, you ought to be thoroughly ashamed! Run upstairs this instant and apologize to Stella-Rondo and Shirley-T."

"Apologize for what?" I says. "I merely wondered if the child was normal, that's all. Now that she's proved she is, why, I have nothing further to say."

But Mama just turned on her heel and flew out, furious. She ran right upstairs and hugged the baby. She believed it was adopted. Stella-Rondo hadn't done a thing but turn her against me from upstairs while I stood there helpless over the hot stove. So that made Mama, Papa-Daddy and the baby all on Stella-Rondo's side.

Next, Uncle Rondo.

I must say that Uncle Rondo has been marvelous to me at various times in the past and I was completely unprepared to be made to jump out of my skin, the way it turned out. Once Stella-Rondo did something perfectly horrible to him — broke a chain letter from Flanders Field — and he took the radio back he had given her and gave it to me. Stella-Rondo was furious! For six months we all had to call her Stella instead of Stella-Rondo, or she wouldn't answer. I always thought Uncle Rondo had all the brains of the entire family. Another time he sent me to Mammoth Cave, with all expenses paid.

But this would be the day he was drinking that prescription, the Fourth of July.

So at supper Stella-Rondo speaks up and says she thinks Uncle Rondo ought to try to eat a little something. So finally Uncle Rondo said he would try a little cold biscuits and ketchup, but that was all. So *she* brought it to him.

"Do you think it wise to disport with ketchup in Stella-Rondo's flesh-colored kimono?" I says. Trying to be considerate! If Stella-Rondo couldn't watch out for her trousseau, somebody had to.

"Any objections?" asks Uncle Rondo, just about to pour out all the ketchup.

"Don't mind what she says, Uncle Rondo," says Stella-Rondo. "Sister has been devoting this solid afternoon to sneering out my bedroom window at the way you look."

"What's that?" says Uncle Rondo. Uncle Rondo has got the most terrible temper in the world. Anything is liable to make him tear the house down if it comes at the wrong time.

So Stella-Rondo says, "Sister says, 'Uncle Rondo certainly does look like a fool in that pink kimono!'"

Do you remember who it was really said that?

Uncle Rondo spills out all the ketchup and jumps out of his chair and tears off the kimono and throws it down on the dirty floor and puts his foot on it. It had to be sent all the way to Jackson to the cleaners and re-pleated.

"So that's your opinion of your Uncle Rondo, is it?" he says. "I look like a fool, do I? Well, that's the last straw. A whole day in this house with nothing to do, and then to hear you come out with a remark like that behind my back!"

"I didn't say any such of a thing, Uncle Rondo," I says, "and I'm not saying who did, either. Why, I think you look all right. Just try to take care of yourself and not talk and eat at the same time," I says. "I think you better go lie down."

"Lie down my foot," says Uncle Rondo. I ought to of known by that he was fixing to do something perfectly horrible.

So he didn't do anything that night in the precarious state he was in — just played Casino with Mama and Stella-Rondo and Shirley-T. and gave Shirley-T. a nickel with a head on both sides. It tickled her nearly to death, and she called him "Papa." But at 6:30 A.M. the next morning, he threw a whole five-cent package of some unsold one-inch firecrackers from the store as hard as he could into my bedroom and they every one went off. Not one bad one in the string. Anybody else, there'd be one that wouldn't go off.

Well, I'm just terribly susceptible to noise of any kind, the doctor has always told me I was the most sensitive person he had ever seen in his whole life, and I was simply prostrated. I couldn't eat! People tell me they heard it as far as the cemetery, and old Aunt Jep Patterson, that had been holding her own so good, thought it was Judgment Day and she was going to meet her whole family. It's usually so quiet here.

And I'll tell you it didn't take me any longer than a minute to make up my mind what to do. There I was with the whole entire house on Stella-Rondo's side and turned against me. If I have anything at all I have pride.

So I just decided I'd go straight down to the P.O. There's plenty of room there in the back, I says to myself.

Well! I made no bones about letting the family catch on to what I was up to. I didn't try to conceal it.

The first thing they knew, I marched in where they were all playing Old Maid and pulled the electric oscillating fan out by the plug, and everything got real hot. Next I snatched the pillow I'd done the needlepoint on right off the davenport from behind Papa-Daddy. He went "Ugh!" I beat Stella-Rondo up the stairs and finally found my charm bracelet in her bureau drawer under a picture of Nelson Eddy.

"So that's the way the land lies," says Uncle Rondo. There he was, piecing on the ham. "Well, Sister, I'll be glad to donate my army cot if you got any place to set it up, providing you'll leave right this minute and let me get some peace." Uncle Rondo was in France.

"Thank you kindly for the cot and 'peace' is hardly the word I would select if I had to resort to firecrackers at 6:30 A.M. in a young girl's bedroom," I says back to him. "And as to where I intend to go, you seem to forget my position as postmistress of China Grove, Mississippi," I says. "I've always got the P.O."

Well, that made them all sit up and take notice.

I went out front and started digging up some four-o'clocks to plant around the P.O.

"Ah-ah-ah!" says Mama, raising the window. "Those happen to be my four-o'clocks. Everything planted in that star is mine. I've never known you to make anything grow in your life."

"Very well," I says. "But I take the fern. Even you, Mama, can't stand there and deny that I'm the one watered that fern. And I happen to know where I can send in a box top and get a packet of one thousand mixed seeds, no two the same kind, free."

"Oh, where?" Mama wants to know.

But I says, "Too late. You 'tend to your house, and I'll 'tend to mine. You hear things like that all the time if you know how to listen to the radio. Perfectly marvelous offers. Get anything you want free."

So I hope to tell you I marched in and got that radio, and they could of all bit a nail in two, especially Stella-Rondo, that it used to belong to, and she well knew she couldn't get it back, I'd sue for it like a shot. And I very politely took the sewing-machine motor I helped pay the most on to give Mama for Christmas back in 1929, and a good big calendar, with the first-aid remedies on it. The thermometer and the Hawaiian ukulele certainly were rightfully mine, and I stood on the step-ladder and got all my watermelon-rind preserves and every fruit and vegetable I'd put up, every jar. Then I began to pull the tacks out of the bluebird wall vases on the archway to the dining room.

"Who told you you could have those, Miss Priss?" says Mama, fanning as hard as she could.

"I bought 'em and I'll keep track of 'em," I says. "I'll tack 'em up one on each side the post-office window, and you can see 'em when you come to ask me for your mail, if you're so dead to see 'em."

"Not I! I'll never darken the door to that post office again if I live to be a hundred," Mama says. "Ungrateful child! After all the money we spent on you at the Normal."

"Me either," says Stella-Rondo. "You can just let my mail lie there and *rot*, for all I care. I'll never come and relieve you of a single, solitary piece."

"I should worry," I says. "And who you think's going to sit down and write you all those big fat letters and postcards, by the way? Mr. Whitaker? Just because he was the only man ever dropped down in China Grove and you got him — unfairly — is he going to sit down and write you a lengthy correspondence after you come home giving no rhyme nor reason whatsoever for your separation and no explanation for the presence of that child? I may not have your brilliant mind, but I fail to see it."

So Mama says, "Sister, I've told you a thousand times that Stella-Rondo simply got homesick, and this child is far too big to be hers," and she says, "Now, why don't you all just sit down and play Casino?"

Then Shirley-T. sticks out her tongue at me in this perfectly horrible way. She has no more manners than the man in the moon. I told her she was going to cross her eyes like that some day and they'd stick.

"It's too late to stop me now," I says. "You should have tried that yesterday. I'm going to the P.O. and the only way you can possibly see me is to visit me there."

So Papa-Daddy says, "You'll never catch me setting foot in that post office, even if I should take a notion into my head to write a letter some place." He says, "I won't have you reachin' out of that little old window with a pair of shears and cuttin' off any beard of mine. I'm too smart for you!"

"We all are," says Stella-Rondo.

But I said, "If you're so smart, where's Mr. Whitaker?"

So then Uncle Rondo says, "I'll thank you from now on to stop reading all the orders I get on postcards and telling everybody in China Grove what you think is the matter with them," but I says, "I draw my own conclusions and will continue in the future to draw them." I says, "If people want to write their inmost secrets on penny postcards, there's nothing in the wide world you can do about it, Uncle Rondo."

"And if you think we'll ever *write* another postcard you're sadly mistaken," says Mama.

"Cutting off your nose to spite your face then," I says. "But if you're all determined to have no more to do with the U.S. mail, think of this: What will Stella-Rondo do now, if she wants to tell Mr. Whitaker to come after her?"

"Wah!" says Stella-Rondo. I knew she'd cry. She had a conniption fit right there in the kitchen.

"It will be interesting to see how long she holds out," I says. "And now — I am leaving."

"Good-bye," says Uncle Rondo.

"Oh, I declare," says Mama, "to think that a family of mine should quarrel on the Fourth of July, or the day after, over Stella-Rondo leaving old Mr. Whitaker and having the sweetest little adopted child! It looks like we'd all be glad!"

"Wah!" says Stella-Rondo, and has a fresh conniption fit.

"*He* left *her* — you mark my words," I says. "That Mr. Whitaker. I know Mr. Whitaker. After all, I knew him first. I said from the beginning he'd up and leave her. I foretold every single thing that's happened."

"Where'd he go?" asks Mama.

"Probably to the North Pole, if he knows what's good for him," I says.

But Stella-Rondo just bawled and wouldn't say another word. She flew to her room and slammed the door.

"Now look what you've gone and done, Sister," says Mama. "You go apologize."

"I haven't got time, I'm leaving," I says.

"Well, what are you waiting around for?" asks Uncle Rondo.

So I just picked up the kitchen clock and marched off without saying "Kiss my foot" or anything, and never did tell Stella-Rondo good-bye.

There was a nigger girl going along on a little wagon right in front.

"Nigger girl," I says, "come help me haul these things down the hill. I'm going to live in the post office."

Took her nine trips in her express wagon. Uncle Rondo came out on the porch and threw her a nickel.

And that's the last I've laid eyes on any of my family or my family laid eyes on me for five solid days and nights. Stella-Rondo may be telling the most horrible tales in the world about Mr. Whitaker, but I haven't heard them. As I tell everybody, I draw my own conclusions.

But oh, I like it here. It's ideal, as I've been saying. You see, I've got everything cater-cornered, the way I like it. Hear the radio? All the war news. Radio, sewing machine, book ends, ironing board and that great big piano lamp — peace, that's what I like. Butter-bean vines planted all along the front where the strings are.

Of course, there's not much mail. My family are naturally the main people in China Grove, and if they prefer to vanish from the face of the earth, for all the mail they get or the mail they write, why, I'm not going to open my mouth. Some of the folks here in town are taking up for me and some turned against me. I know which is which. There are always people who will quit buying stamps just to get on the right side of Papa-Daddy.

But here I am, and here I'll stay. I want the world to know I'm happy.

And if Stella-Rondo should come to me this minute, on bended knees, and *attempt* to explain the incidents of her life with Mr. Whitaker, I'd simply put my fingers in both my ears and refuse to listen.

QUESTIONS

1. Is the narrator entirely trustworthy? Is there another side to the story she tells? How would you characterize her? Is she happy living at the P.O.?

2. What is the effect of the narrator's adding information about her relatives almost haphazardly? Consider the paragraph ending with Mama's "real tiny feet." What is the function of such irrelevancies? Or *are* they irrelevant?

3. Are these small-town Mississippians naive?

4. Where does the humor of this famous story lie? in the action? the characters? the language? the tone?

5. What similarities do you see between "Why I Live at the P.O." and the parable of the Prodigal Son?

JOHN CHEEVER

The Swimmer

It was one of those midsummer Sundays when everyone sits around saying, "I *drank* too much last night." You might have heard it whispered by the parishioners leaving church, heard it from the lips of the priest himself, struggling with his cassock in the *vestiarium,*[1] heard it from the golf links and the tennis courts, heard it from the wildlife preserve where the leader of the Audubon group was suffering from a terrible hangover. "I *drank* too much," said Donald Westerhazy. "We all *drank* too much," said Lucinda Merrill. "It must have been the wine," said Helen Westerhazy. "I *drank* too much of that claret."

This was at the edge of the Westerhazys' pool. The pool, fed by an artesian well with a high iron content, was a pale shade of green. It was a fine day. In the west there was a massive stand of cumulus cloud so like a city seen from a distance — from the bow of an approaching ship — that it might have had a name. Lisbon. Hackensack. The sun was hot. Neddy Merrill sat by the green water, one hand in it, one around a glass of gin. He was a slender man — he seemed to have the especial slenderness of youth — and while he was far from young he had slid down his banister that morning and given the bronze backside of Aphrodite on the hall table a smack, as he jogged toward the smell of coffee in his dining room. He might have been compared to a summer's day, particularly the last hours of one, and while he lacked a tennis racket or a sail bag the impression was definitely one of youth, sport, and clement weather. He had been swimming and now he was breathing deeply, stertorously as if he could gulp into his lungs the components of that moment, the heat of the sun, the intenseness of his pleasure. It all seemed to flow into his chest. His own house stood in Bullet Park, eight miles to the south, where his four beautiful daughters would have had their lunch and might be playing tennis. Then it occurred to him that by taking a dogleg to the southwest he could reach his home by water.

His life was not confining and the delight he took in this observation could not be explained by its suggestion of escape. He seemed to see, with a cartographer's eye, that string of swimming pools, that quasi-subterranean stream that curved across the county. He had made a discovery, a contribution to modern geography; he would name the stream Lucinda after his wife. He was not a practical joker nor was he a fool but he was determinedly original

---

[1] Sacristy.

623

and had a vague and modest idea of himself as a legendary figure. The day was beautiful and it seemed to him that a long swim might enlarge and celebrate its beauty.

He took off a sweater that was hung over his shoulders and dove in. He had an inexplicable contempt for men who did not hurl themselves into pools. He swam a choppy crawl, breathing either with every stroke or every fourth stroke and counting somewhere well in the back of his mind the one-two one-two of a flutter kick. It was not a serviceable stroke for long distances but the domestication of swimming had saddled the sport with some customs and in his part of the world a crawl was customary. To be embraced and sustained by the light green water was less a pleasure, it seemed, than the resumption of a natural condition, and he would have liked to swim without trunks, but this was not possible, considering his project. He hoisted himself up on the far curb — he never used the ladder — and started across the lawn. When Lucinda asked where he was going he said he was going to swim home.

The only maps and charts he had to go by were remembered or imaginary but these were clear enough. First there were the Grahams, the Hammers, the Lears, the Howlands, and the Crosscups. He would cross Ditmar Street to the Bunkers and come, after a short portage, to the Levys, the Welchers, and the public pool in Lancaster. Then there were the Hallorans, the Sachses, the Biswangers, Shirley Adams, the Gilmartins, and the Clydes. The day was lovely, and that he lived in a world so generously supplied with water seemed like a clemency, a beneficence. His heart was high and he ran across the grass. Making his way home by an uncommon route gave him the feeling that he was a pilgrim, an explorer, a man with a destiny, and he knew that he would find friends all along the way; friends would line the banks of the Lucinda River.

He went through a hedge that separated the Westerhazys' land from the Grahams', walked under some flowering apple trees, passed the shed that housed their pump and filter, and came out at the Grahams' pool. "Why, Neddy," Mrs. Graham said, "what a marvelous surprise. I've been trying to get you on the phone all morning. Here, let me get you a drink." He saw then, like any explorer, that the hospitable customs and traditions of the natives would have to be handled with diplomacy if he was ever going to reach his destination. He did not want to mystify or seem rude to the Grahams nor did he have the time to linger there. He swam the length of their pool and joined them in the sun and was rescued, a few minutes later, by the arrival of two carloads of friends from Connecticut. During the uproarious reunions he was able to slip away. He went down by the front of the Grahams' house, stepped over a thorny hedge, and crossed a vacant lot to the Hammers'. Mrs. Hammer, looking up from her roses, saw him swim by although she wasn't quite sure who it was. The Lears heard him splashing past the open windows of their living room. The Howlands and the Crosscups were away. After leaving the Howlands' he crossed Ditmar Street and started for the Bunkers', where he could hear, even at that distance, the noise of a party.

The water refracted the sound of voices and laughter and seemed to suspend it in midair. The Bunkers' pool was on a rise and he climbed some stairs to a terrace where twenty-five or thirty men and women were drinking. The only person in the water was Rusty Towers, who floated there on a rubber raft. Oh, how bonny and lush were the banks of the Lucinda River! Prosperous men and women gathered by the sapphire-colored waters while caterer's men in white coats passed them cold gin. Overhead a red de Haviland trainer was circling around and around and around in the sky with something like the glee of a child in a swing. Ned felt a passing affection for the scene, a tenderness for the gathering, as if it was something he might touch. In the distance he heard thunder. As soon as Enid Bunker saw him she began to scream: "Oh, look who's here! What a marvelous surprise! When Lucinda said that you couldn't come I thought I'd *die*." She made her way to him through the crowd, and when they had finished kissing she led him to the bar, a progress that was slowed by the fact that he stopped to kiss eight or ten other women and shake the hands of as many men. A smiling bartender he had seen at a hundred parties gave him a gin and tonic and he stood by the bar for a moment, anxious not to get stuck in any conversation that would delay his voyage. When he seemed about to be surrounded he dove in and swam close to the side to avoid colliding with Rusty's raft. At the far end of the pool he bypassed the Tomlinsons with a broad smile and jogged up the garden path. The gravel cut his feet but this was the only unpleasantness. The party was confined to the pool, and as he went toward the house he heard the brilliant, watery sound of voices fade, heard the noise of a radio from the Bunkers' kitchen, where someone was listening to a ball game. Sunday afternoon. He made his way through the parked cars and down the grassy border of their driveway to Alewives Lane. He did not want to be seen on the road in his bathing trunks but there was no traffic and he made the short distance to the Levys' driveway, marked with a PRIVATE PROPERTY sign and a green tube for *The New York Times*. All the doors and windows of the big house were open but there were no signs of life; not even a dog barked. He went around the side of the house to the pool and saw that the Levys had only recently left. Glasses and bottles and dishes of nuts were on a table at the deep end, where there was a bathhouse or gazebo, hung with Japanese lanterns. After swimming the pool he got himself a glass and poured a drink. It was his fourth or fifth drink and he had swum nearly half the length of the Lucinda River. He felt tired, clean, and pleased at that moment to be alone; pleased with everything.

It would storm. The stand of cumulus cloud — that city — had risen and darkened, and while he sat there he heard the percussiveness of thunder again. The de Haviland trainer was still circling overhead and it seemed to Ned that he could almost hear the pilot laugh with pleasure in the afternoon; but when there was another peal of thunder he took off for home. A train whistle blew and he wondered what time it had gotten to be. Four? Five? He thought of the provincial station at that hour, where a waiter, his tuxedo concealed by a raincoat, a dwarf with some flowers wrapped in newspaper, and a woman who had been crying would be waiting for the local. It was suddenly growing dark; it was that moment when the pin-headed birds seem to organize their song into some acute and knowledgeable recognition of the storm's approach. Then there was a fine noise of rushing water from the crown of an oak at his back, as if a spigot there had been turned. Then the noise of fountains came from the crowns of all the tall trees. Why did he love storms, what was the meaning of his excitement when the door sprang open and the rain wind fled rudely up the stairs, why had the simple task of shutting the windows of an old house seemed fitting and urgent, why did the first watery notes of a storm wind have for him the unmistakable sound of good news, cheer, glad tidings? Then there was an explosion, a smell of cordite, and rain lashed the Japanese lanterns that Mrs. Levy had bought in Kyoto the year before last, or was it the year before that?

He stayed in the Levys' gazebo until the storm had passed. The rain had cooled the air and he shivered. The force of the wind had stripped a maple of its red and yellow leaves and scattered them over the grass and the water. Since it was midsummer the tree must be blighted, and yet he felt a peculiar sadness at this sign of autumn. He braced his shoulders, emptied his glass, and started for the Welchers' pool. This meant crossing the Lindleys' riding ring and he was surprised to find it overgrown with grass and all the jumps dismantled. He wondered if the Lindleys had sold their horses or gone away for the summer and put them out to board. He seemed to remember having heard something about the Lindleys and their horses but the memory was unclear. On he went, barefoot through the wet grass, to the Welchers', where he found their pool was dry.

This breach in his chain of water disappointed him absurdly, and he felt like some explorer who seeks a torrential headwater and finds a dead stream. He was disappointed and mystified. It was common enough to go away for the summer but no one ever drained his pool. The Welchers had definitely gone away. The pool furniture was folded, stacked, and covered with a tarpaulin. The bathhouse was locked. All the windows of the house were shut, and when he went around to the driveway in front he saw a FOR SALE sign nailed to a tree. When had he last heard from the Welchers — when, that is, had he and Lucinda last regretted an invitation to dine with them? It seemed only a week or so ago. Was his memory failing or had he so disciplined it in the repression of unpleasant facts that he had damaged his sense of the truth? Then in the distance he heard the sound of a tennis game. This cheered him, cleared away all his apprehensions and let him regard the overcast sky and the cold air with indifference. This was the day that Neddy Merrill swam across the county. That was the day! He started off then for his most difficult portage.

Had you gone for a Sunday afternoon ride that day you might have seen him, close to naked, standing on the shoulders of Route 424, waiting for a chance to cross. You might have wondered if he was the victim of foul play, had his car broken down, or was he merely a fool. Standing barefoot in the deposits of the highway — beer cans, rags, and blowout patches — exposed to all kinds of ridicule, he seemed pitiful. He had known when he started that this was a part of his journey — it had been on his maps — but confronted with the lines of traffic, worming through the summery light, he found himself unprepared. He was laughed at, jeered at, a beer can was thrown at him, and he had no dignity or humor to bring to the situation. He could have gone back, back to the Westerhazys', where Lucinda would still be sitting in the sun. He had signed nothing, vowed nothing, pledged nothing, not even to himself. Why, believing as he did, that all human obduracy was susceptible to common sense, was he unable to turn back? Why was he determined to complete his journey even if it meant putting his life in danger? At what point had this prank, this joke, this piece of horseplay become serious? He could not go back, he could not even recall with any clearness the green water at the Westerhazys', the sense of inhaling the day's components, the friendly and relaxed voices saying that they had *drunk* too much. In the space of an hour, more or less, he had covered a distance that made his return impossible.

An old man, tooling down the highway at fifteen miles an hour, let him get to the middle of the road, where there was a grass divider. Here he was exposed to the ridicule of the northbound traffic, but after ten or fifteen minutes he was able to cross. From here he had only a short walk to the Recreation Center at the edge of the village of Lancaster, where there were some handball courts and a public pool.

The effect of the water on voices, the illusion of brilliance and suspense, was the same here as it had been at the Bunkers' but the sounds here were louder, harsher, and more shrill, and as soon as he entered the crowded enclosure he was confronted with regimentation. "ALL SWIMMERS MUST TAKE A SHOWER BEFORE USING THE POOL. ALL SWIMMERS MUST USE THE FOOTBATH. ALL SWIMMERS MUST WEAR THEIR IDENTIFICATION DISKS." He took a shower, washed his feet in a cloudy and bitter solution, and made his way to the edge of the water. It stank of chlorine and looked to him like a sink. A pair of lifeguards in a pair of towers blew police whistles at what seemed to be regular intervals and abused the swimmers through a public address system. Neddy remembered the sapphire water at the Bunkers' with longing and thought that he might contaminate himself — damage his own prosperousness and charm — by swimming in this murk, but he reminded himself that he was an explorer, a pilgrim, and that this was merely a stagnant bend in the Lucinda River. He dove, scowling with distaste, into the chlorine and had to swim with his head above water to avoid collisions, but even so he was bumped into, splashed, and jostled. When he got to the shallow end both lifeguards were shouting at him: "Hey, you, you without the identification disk, get outa the water." He did, but they had no way of pursuing him and he went through the reek of suntan oil and chlorine out through the hurricane fence and passed the handball courts. By crossing the road he entered the wooded part of the Halloran estate. The woods were not cleared and the footing was treacherous and difficult until he reached the lawn and the clipped beech hedge that encircled their pool.

The Hallorans were friends, an elderly couple of enormous wealth who seemed to bask in the suspicion that they might be Communists. They were zealous reformers but they were not Communists, and yet when they were accused, as they sometimes were, of subversion, it seemed to gratify and excite them. Their beech hedge was yellow and he guessed this had been blighted like the Levys' maple. He called hullo, hullo, to warn the Hallorans of his approach, to palliate his invasion of their privacy. The Hallorans, for reasons that had never been explained to him, did not wear bathing suits. No explanations were in order, really. Their nakedness was a detail in their uncompromising zeal for reform and he stepped politely out of his trunks before he went through the opening in the hedge.

Mrs. Halloran, a stout woman with white hair and a serene face, was reading the *Times*. Mr. Halloran was taking beech leaves out of the water with a scoop. They seemed not surprised or displeased to see him. Their pool was perhaps the oldest in the country, a fieldstone rectangle, fed by a brook. It had no filter or pump and its waters were the opaque gold of the stream.

"I'm swimming across the county," Ned said.

"Why, I didn't know one could," exclaimed Mrs. Halloran.

"Well, I've made it from the Westerhazys'," Ned said. "That must be about four miles."

He left his trunks at the deep end, walked to the shallow end, and swam this stretch. As he was pulling himself out of the water he heard Mrs. Halloran say, "We've been *terribly* sorry to hear about all your misfortunes, Neddy."

"My misfortunes?" Ned asked. "I don't know what you mean."

"Why, we heard that you'd sold the house and that your poor children ..."

"I don't recall having sold the house," Ned said, "and the girls are at home."

"Yes," Mrs. Halloran sighed. "Yes ..." Her voice filled the air with an unseasonable melancholy and Ned spoke briskly. "Thank you for the swim."

"Well, have a nice trip," said Mrs. Halloran.

Beyond the hedge he pulled on his trunks and fastened them. They were loose and he wondered if, during the space of an afternoon, he could have lost some weight. He was cold and he was tired and the naked Hallorans and their dark water had depressed him. The swim was too much for his strength but how could he have guessed this, sliding down the banister that morning and sitting in the Westerhazys' sun? His arms were lame. His legs felt rubbery and ached at the joints. The worst of it was the cold in his bones and the feeling that he might never be warm again. Leaves were falling down around him and he smelled wood smoke on the wind. Who would be burning wood at this time of year?

He needed a drink. Whiskey would warm him, pick him up, carry him through the last of his journey, refresh his feeling that it was original and valorous to swim across the county. Channel swimmers took brandy. He needed a stimulant. He crossed the lawn in front of the

Hallorans' house and went down a little path to where they had built a house for their only daughter, Helen, and her husband, Eric Sachs. The Sachses' pool was small and he found Helen and her husband there.

"Oh, *Neddy*," Helen said. "Did you lunch at Mother's?"

"Not *really*," Ned said. "I *did* stop to see your parents." This seemed to be explanation enough. "I'm terribly sorry to break in on you like this but I've taken a chill and I wonder if you'd give me a drink."

"Why, I'd *love* to," Helen said, "but there hasn't been anything in this house to drink since Eric's operation. That was three years ago."

Was he losing his memory, had his gift for concealing painful facts let him forget that he had sold his house, that his children were in trouble, and that his friend had been ill? His eyes slipped from Eric's face to his abdomen, where he saw three pale, sutured scars, two of them at least a foot long. Gone was his navel, and what, Neddy thought, would the roving hand, bed-checking one's gifts at 3 A.M., make of a belly with no navel, no link to birth, this breach in the succession?

"I'm sure you can get a drink at the Biswangers'," Helen said. "They're having an enormous do. You can hear it from here. Listen!"

She raised her head and from across the road, the lawns, the gardens, the woods, the fields, he heard again the brilliant noise of voices over water. "Well, I'll get wet," he said, still feeling that he had no freedom of choice about his means of travel. He dove into the Sachses' cold water and, gasping, close to drowning, made his way from one end of the pool to the other. "Lucinda and I want *terribly* to see you," he said over his shoulder, his face set toward the Biswangers'. "We're sorry it's been so long and we'll call you *very* soon."

He crossed some fields to the Biswangers' and the sounds of revelry there. They would be honored to give him a drink, they would be happy to give him a drink. The Biswangers invited him and Lucinda for dinner four times a year, six weeks in advance. They were always rebuffed and yet they continued to send out their invitations, unwilling to comprehend the rigid and undemocratic realities of their society. They were the sort of people who discussed the price of things at cocktails, exchanged market tips during dinner, and after dinner told dirty stories to mixed company. They did not belong to Neddy's set — they were not even on Lucinda's Christmas-card list. He went toward their pool with feelings of indifference, charity, and some unease, since it seemed to be getting dark and these were the longest days of the year. The party when he joined it was noisy and large. Grace Biswanger was the kind of hostess who asked the optometrist, the veterinarian, the real-estate dealer, and the dentist. No one was swimming and the twilight, reflected on the water of the pool, had a wintry gleam. There was a bar and he started for this. When Grace Biswanger saw him she came toward him, not affectionately as he had every right to expect, but bellicosely.

"Why, this party has everything," she said loudly, "including a gate crasher."

She could not deal him a social blow — there was no question about this and he did not flinch. "As a gate crasher," he asked politely, "do I rate a drink?"

"Suit yourself," she said. "You don't seem to pay much attention to invitations."

She turned her back on him and joined some guests, and he went to the bar and ordered a whiskey. The bartender served him but he served him rudely. His was a world in which the caterer's men kept the social score, and to be rebuffed by a part-time barkeep meant that he had suffered some loss of social esteem. Or perhaps the man was new and uninformed. Then he heard Grace at his back say: "They went for broke overnight — nothing but income — and he showed up drunk one Sunday and asked us to loan him five thousand dollars. ..." She was always talking about money. It was worse than eating your peas off a knife. He dove into the pool, swam its length and went away.

The next pool on his list, the last but two, belonged to his old mistress, Shirley Adams. If he had suffered any injuries at the Biswangers' they would be cured here. Love — sexual roughhouse in fact — was the supreme elixir, the pain killer, the brightly colored pill that would put the spring back into his step, the joy of life in his heart. They had had an affair last week, last month, last year. He couldn't remember. It was he who had broken it off, his was the upper hand, and he stepped through the gate of the wall that surrounded her pool with nothing so considered as self-confidence. It seemed in a way to be his pool, as the lover, particularly the illicit lover, enjoys the possessions of his mistress with an authority unknown to holy matrimony. She was there, her hair the color of brass, but her figure, at the edge of the lighted, cerulean water, excited in him no profound memories. It had been, he thought, a lighthearted affair, although she had wept when he broke it off. She seemed confused to see him and he wondered if she was still wounded. Would she, God forbid, weep again?

"What do you want?" she asked.

"I'm swimming across the county."

"Good Christ. Will you ever grow up?"

"What's the matter?"

"If you've come here for money," she said, "I won't give you another cent."

"You could give me a drink."

"I could but I won't. I'm not alone."

"Well, I'm on my way."

He dove in and swam the pool, but when he tried to haul himself up onto the curb he found that the strength in his arms and shoulders had gone, and he paddled to the ladder and climbed out. Looking over his shoulder he saw, in the lighted bathhouse, a young man. Going out onto the dark lawn he smelled chrysanthemums or marigolds — some stubborn autumnal fragrance — on the night air, strong as gas. Looking overhead he saw that the stars had come out, but why should he seem to see Andromeda, Cepheus, and Cassiopeia? What had become of the constellations of midsummer? He began to cry.

It was probably the first time in his adult life that he had ever cried, certainly the first time in his life that he had ever felt so miserable, cold, tired, and bewildered. He could not understand the rudeness of the caterer's barkeep or the rudeness of a mistress who had come to him on her knees and showered his trousers with tears. He had swum too long, he had been immersed too long, and his nose and his throat were sore from the water. What he needed then was a drink, some company, and some clean, dry clothes, and while he could have cut directly across the road to his home he went on to the Gilmartins' pool. Here, for the first time in his life, he did not dive but went down the steps into the icy water and swam a hobbled sidestroke that he might have learned as a youth. He staggered with fatigue on his way to the Clydes' and paddled the length of their pool, stopping again and again with his hand on the curb to rest. He climbed up the ladder and wondered if he had the strength to get home. He had done what he wanted, he had swum the county, but he was so stupefied with exhaustion that his triumph seemed vague. Stooped, holding on to the gateposts for support, he turned up the driveway of his own house.

The place was dark. Was it so late that they had all gone to bed? Had Lucinda stayed at the Westerhazys' for supper? Had the girls joined her there or gone someplace else? Hadn't they agreed, as they usually did on Sunday, to regret all their invitations and stay at home?

He tried the garage doors to see what cars were in but the doors were locked and rust came off the handles onto his hands. Going toward the house, he saw that the force of the thunderstorm had knocked one of the rain gutters loose. It hung down over the front door like an umbrella rib, but it could be fixed in the morning. The house was locked, and he thought that the stupid cook or the stupid maid must have locked the place up until he remembered that it had been some time since they had employed a maid or a cook. He shouted, pounded on the door, tried to force it with his shoulder, and then, looking in at the windows, saw that the place was empty.

QUESTIONS

1. What does Cheever gain by opening with a paragraph written in the omniscient-author style? Does the shift, in the second paragraph, to the consciousness of Neddy Merrill seem abrupt? How has Cheever attempted to make the transition smooth?

2. Trace the explorer-discoverer image through the story. Is it appropriate? Is it consistent?

3. Does Neddy have moments of doubt about his sanity? At what point were your suspicions aroused? Does the author lay clues for us? Can you find any in the reactions of the people he meets on his swim home? What evidence is there that he is not completely incapable?

4. What do we learn about the neighborhood as he makes his way home? Is Neddy a typical resident? worse? better?

5. The author reverts to the omniscient stance while Neddy waits to cross Route 424. Does this mark a turning point in the story? How do you know? Note how the tone of the narration becomes more somber, perhaps crueler at this point.

6. What does his encounter with the Biswangers contribute to our knowledge of Merrill?

RALPH ELLISON

Flying Home

When Todd came to, he saw two faces suspended above him in a sun so hot and blinding that he could not tell if they were black or white. He stirred, feeling a pain that burned as though his whole body had been laid open to the sun which glared into his eyes. For a moment an old fear of being touched by white hands seized him. Then the very sharpness of the pain began slowly to clear his head. Sounds came to him dimly. He done come to. Who are they? he thought. Naw he ain't, I coulda sworn he was white. Then he heard clearly:

"You hurt bad?"

Something within him uncoiled. It was a Negro sound.

"He's still out," he heard.

"Give 'im time. ... Say, son, you hurt bad?"

Was he? There was that awful pain. He lay rigid, hearing their breathing and trying to weave a meaning between them and his being stretched painfully upon the ground. He watched them warily, his mind traveling back over a painful distance. Jagged scenes, swiftly unfolding as in a movie trailer, reeled through his mind, and he saw himself piloting a tailspinning plane and landing and falling from the cockpit and trying to stand. Then, as in a great silence, he remembered his accomplishments and they came to shame and embarrass him, like the distasteful praise of an idiot. A part of the meaning of flying had gone then, and he had not been able to regain it. If I were a prizefighter I would be more human, he thought. Not a monkey doing tricks, but a man. They were pleased simply that he was a Negro who could fly, and that was not enough. He felt cut off from them by age, by understanding, by sensibility, by technology and by his need to measure himself against the mirror of other men's appreciation. Somehow he felt betrayed, as he had when as a child he grew to discover that his father was dead. Now for him any real appreciation lay with his white officers; and with them he could never be sure. Between ignorant black men and condescending whites, his course of flight seemed mapped by the nature of things away from all needed and natural landmarks. Under some sealed orders, couched in ever more technical and mysterious terms, his path curved swiftly away from both the shame the old man symbolized and the cloudy terrain of white men's regard. Flying blind, he knew but one point of landing and there he would receive his wings. After that the enemy would appreciate his skill and he would assume his deepest meaning, he thought sadly, neither from those who condescended nor from those who praised without understanding, but from the enemy who would recognize his manhood and skill in terms of hate. ...

He sighed, seeing the oxen making queer, prehistoric shadows against the dry brown earth.

"You just take it easy, son," the old man soothed. "That boy won't take long. Crazy as he is about airplanes."

"I can wait," he said.

"What kinda airplane you call this here'n?"

"An Advanced Trainer," he said, seeing the old man smile. His fingers were like gnarled dark wood against the metal as he touched the low-slung wing.

"'Bout how fast can she fly?"

"Over two hundred an hour."

"Lawd! That's so fast I bet it don't seem like you moving!"

Holding himself rigid, Todd opened his flying suit. The shade had gone and he lay in a ball of fire.

"You mind if I take a look inside? I was always curious to see. ..."

"Help yourself. Just don't touch anything."

He heard him climb upon the metal wing, grunting. Now the questions would start. Well, so you don't have to think to answer. ...

He saw the old man looking over into the cockpit, his eyes bright as a child's.

"You must have to know a lot to work all these here things."

He was silent, seeing him step down and kneel beside him.

"Son, how come you want to fly way up there in the air?"

Because it's the most meaningful act in the world ... because it makes me less like you, he thought.

But he said: "Because I like it, I guess. It's as good a way to fight and die as I know."

"Yeah? I guess you right," the old man said. "But how long you think before they gonna let you all fight?"

He tensed. This was the question all Negroes asked, put with the same timid hope-fulness and longing that always opened a greater void within him than that he had felt beneath the plane the first time he had flown. He felt light-headed. It came to him suddenly that there was something sinister about the conversation, that he was flying unwillingly into unsafe and uncharted regions. If he could only be insulting and tell this old man who was trying to help him to shut up!

"I bet you one thing ..."

"Yes?"

"That you was plenty scared coming down."

He did not answer. Like a dog on a trail the old man seemed to smell out his fears and he felt anger bubble within him.

"You sho' scared me. When I seen you coming down in that thing with it a-rollin' and a-jumpin' like a pitchin' hoss, I thought sho' you was a goner. I almost had me a stroke!"

He saw the old man grinning, "Ever'thin's been happening round here this morning, come to think of it."

"Like what?" he asked.

"Well, first thing I know, here come two white fellers looking for Mister Rudolph, that's Mister Graves's cousin. That got me worked up right away. ..."

"Why?"

"Why? 'Cause he done broke outta the crazy house, that's why. He liable to kill somebody," he said. "They oughta have him by now though. Then here you come. First I think it's one of them white boys. Then doggone if you don't fall outta there. Lawd, I'd done heard about you boys but I haven't never seen one o' you-all. Cain't tell you how it felt to see somebody what look like me in a airplane!"

The old man talked on, the sound streaming around Todd's thoughts like air flowing over the fuselage of a flying plane. You were a fool, he thought, remembering how before the spin the sun had blazed bright against the billboard signs beyond the town, and how a boy's blue kite had bloomed beneath him, tugging gently in the wind like a strange, odd-shaped flower. He had once flown such kites himself and tried to find the boy at the end of the invisible cord. But he had been flying too high and too fast. He had climbed steeply away in exultation. Too steeply, he thought. And one of the first rules you learn is that if the angle of thrust is too steep the plane goes into a spin. And then, instead of pulling out of it and going into a dive you let a buzzard panic you. A lousy buzzard!

"Son, what made all that blood on the glass?"

"A buzzard," he said, remembering how the blood and feathers had sprayed back against the hatch. It had been as though he had flown into a storm of blood and blackness.

"Well, I declare! They's lots of 'em around here. They after dead things. Don't eat nothing what's alive."

"A little bit more and he would have made a meal out of me," Todd said grimly.

"They bad luck all right. Teddy's got a name for 'em, calls 'em jimcrows," the old man laughed.

"It's a damned good name."

"They the damnedest birds. Once I seen a hoss all stretched out like he was sick, you know. So I hollers, 'Gid up from there, suh!' Just to make sho! An' doggone, son, if I don't see two ole jimcrows come flying right up outa that hoss's insides! Yessuh! The sun was shinin' on 'em and they couldn't a been no greasier if they'd been eating barbecue."

Todd thought he would vomit, his stomach quivered.

"You made that up," he said.

"Nawsuh! Saw him just like I see you."

"Well, I'm glad it was you."

"You see lots a funny things down here, son."

"No, I'll let you see them," he said.

"By the way, the white folks round here don't like to see you boys up there in the sky. They ever bother you?"

"No."

"Well, they'd like to."

"Someone always wants to bother someone else," Todd said. "How do you know?"

"I just know."

"Well," he said defensively, "no one has bothered us."

Blood pounded in his ears as he looked away into space. He tensed, seeing a black spot in the sky, and strained to confirm what he could not clearly see.

"What does that look like to you?" he asked excitedly.

"Just another bad luck, son."

Then he saw the movement of wings with disappointment. It was gliding smoothly down, wings outspread, tail feathers gripping the air, down swiftly — gone behind the green screen of trees. It was like a bird he had imagined there, only the sloping branches of the pines remained, sharp against the pale stretch of sky. He lay barely breathing and stared at the point where it had disappeared, caught in a spell of loathing and admiration. Why did they make them so disgusting and yet teach them to fly so well? It's like when I was up in heaven, he heard, starting.

The old man was chuckling, rubbing his stubbled chin.

"What did you say?"

"Sho', I died and went to heaven ... maybe by time I tell you about it they be done come after you."

"I hope so," he said wearily.

"You boys ever sit around and swap lies?"

"Not often. Is this going to be one?"

"Well, I ain't so sho', on account of it took place when I was dead."

The old man paused, "That wasn't no lie 'bout the buzzards, though."

"All right," he said.

"Sho' you want to hear 'bout heaven?"

"Please," he answered, resting his head upon his arm.

"Well, I went to heaven and right away started to sproutin' me some wings. Six good ones, they was. Just like them the white angels had. I couldn't hardly believe it. I was so glad that I went off on some clouds by myself and tried 'em out. You know, 'cause I didn't want to make a fool outta myself the first thing. ..."

It's an old tale, Todd thought. Told me years ago. Had forgotten. But at least it will keep him from talking about buzzards.

He closed his eyes, listening.

"... First thing I done was to git up on a low cloud and jump off. And doggone, boy, if them wings didn't work! First I tried the right; then I tried the left; then I tried 'em both together. Then Lawd, I started to move on out among the folks. I let 'em see me. ..."

He saw the old man gesturing flight with his arms, his face full of mock pride as he indicated an imaginary crowd, thinking, It'll be in the newspapers, as he heard, "... so I went out and found me some colored angels — somehow I didn't believe I was an angel till I seen a real black one, ha, yes! Then I was sho' — but they tole me I better come down 'cause us colored folks had to wear a special kin' a harness when we flew. That was how come they wasn't flyin'. Oh yes, an' you had to be extra strong for a black man even, to fly with one of them harnesses. ..."

This is a new turn, Todd thought, what's he driving at?

"So I said to myself, I ain't gonna be bothered with no harness! Oh naw! 'Cause if God let you sprout wings you oughta have sense enough not to let nobody make you wear something what gits in the way of flyin'. So I starts to flyin'. Heck, son," he chuckled, his eyes twinkling, "you know I had to let eve'ybody know that old Jefferson could fly good as anybody else. And I could too, fly smooth as a bird! I could even loop-the-loop — only I had to make sho' to keep my long white robe down roun' my ankles. ..."

Todd felt uneasy. He wanted to laugh at the joke, but his body refused, as of an independent will. He felt as he had as a child when after he had chewed a sugar-coated pill which his mother had given him, she had laughed at his efforts to remove the terrible taste.

"... Well," he heard, "I was doing all right 'til I got to speeding. Found out I could fan up a right strong breeze, I could fly so fast. I could do all kin'sa stunts too. I started flying up to the stars and divin' down and zooming roun' the moon. Man, I like to scare the devil outa some ole white angels. I was raisin' hell. Not that I meant any harm, son. But I was just feeling good. It was so good to know I was free at last. I accidentally knocked the tips offa some stars and they tell me I caused a storm and a coupla lynchings down here in Macon County — though I swear I believe them boys what said that was making up lies on me. ..."

He's mocking me, Todd thought angrily. He thinks it's a joke. Grinning down at me ... His throat was dry. He looked at his watch; why the hell didn't they come? Since they had to, why? One day I was flying down one of them heavenly streets. You got yourself into it, Todd thought. Like Jonah in the whale.

"Justa throwin' feathers in everybody's face. An' ole Saint Peter called me in. Said, 'Jefferson, tell me two things, what you doin' flyin' without a harness; an' how come you flyin' so fast?' So I tole him I was flyin' without a harness 'cause it got in my way, but I couldn'ta been flyin' so fast, 'cause I wasn't usin' but one wing. Saint Peter said, 'You wasn't flyin' with but one wing?' 'Yessuh,' I says, scared-like. So he says, 'Well, since you got sucha extra fine pair of wings you can leave off yo' harness awhile. But from now on none of that there one-wing flyin', 'cause you gittin' up too damn much speed!'"

And with one mouth full of bad teeth you're making too damned much talk, thought Todd. Why don't I send him after the boy? His body ached from the hard ground and seeking to shift his position he twisted his ankle and hated himself for crying out.

"It gittin' worse?"

"I ... I twisted it," he groaned.

"Try not to think about it, son. That's what I do."

He bit his lip, fighting pain with counter-pain as the voice resumed its rhythmical droning. Jefferson seemed caught in his own creation.

"... After all that trouble I just floated roun' heaven in slow motion. But I forgot, like colored folks will do, and got to flyin' with one wing again. This time I was restin' my old broken arm and got to flyin' fast enough to shame the devil. I was comin' so fast, Lawd, I got myself called befo' ole Saint Peter again. He said, 'Jeff, didn't I warn you 'bout that speedin'?' 'Yessuh,' I says, 'but it was an accident.' He looked at me sad-like and shook his head and I knowed I was gone. He said, 'Jeff, you and that speedin' is a danger to the heavenly community. If I was to let you keep on flyin', heaven wouldn't be nothin' but uproar. Jeff, you got to go!' Son, I argued and pleaded with that old white man, but it didn't do a bit of good. They rushed me straight to them pearly gates and gimme a parachute and a map of the state of Alabama ..."

Todd heard him laughing so that he could hardly speak, making a screen between them upon which his humiliation glowed like fire.

"Maybe you'd better stop awhile," he said, his voice unreal.

"Ain't much more," Jefferson laughed. "When they gimme the parachute ole Saint Peter ask me if I wanted to say a few words before I went. I felt so bad I couldn't hardly look at him, specially with all them white angels standin' around. Then somebody laughed and made me mad. So I tole him, 'Well, you done took my wings. And you puttin' me out. You got charge of things so's I can't do nothin' about it. But you got to admit just this: While I was up here I was the flyinest sonofabitch what ever hit heaven!'"

At the burst of laughter Todd felt such an intense humiliation that only great violence would wash it away. The laughter which shook the old man like a boiling purge set up vibrations of guilt within him which not even the intricate machinery of the plane would have been adequate to transform and he heard himself screaming, "Why do you laugh at me this way?"

He hated himself at that moment, but he had lost control. He saw Jefferson's mouth fall open, "What — ?"

"Answer me!"

His blood pounded as though it would surely burst his temples and he tried to reach the old man and fell, screaming, "Can I help it because they won't let us actually fly? Maybe we are a bunch of buzzards feeding on a dead horse, but we can hope to be eagles, can't we? Can't we?"

He fell back, exhausted, his ankle pounding. The saliva was like straw in his mouth. If he had the strength he would strangle this old man. This grinning, gray-headed clown who made him feel as he felt when watched by the white officers at the field. And yet this old man had neither power, prestige, rank nor technique. Nothing that could rid him of this terrible feeling. He watched him, seeing his face struggle to express a turmoil of feeling.

"What you mean, son? What you talking 'bout ... ?"

"Go away. Go tell your tales to the white folks."

"But I didn't mean nothing like that. ... I ... I wasn't tryin' to hurt your feelings. ..."

"Please. Get the hell away from me!"

"But I didn't, son. I didn't mean all them things a-tall."

Todd shook as with a chill, searching Jefferson's face for a trace of the mockery he had seen there. But now the face was somber and tired and old. He was confused. He could not be sure that there had ever been laughter there, that Jefferson had ever really laughed in his whole life. He saw Jefferson reach out to touch him and shrank away, wondering if anything except the pain, now causing his vision to waver, was real. Perhaps he had imagined it all.

"Don't let it get you down, son," the voice said pensively.

He heard Jefferson sigh wearily, as though he felt more than he could say. His anger ebbed, leaving only the pain.

"I'm sorry," he mumbled.

"You just wore out with pain, was all. ..."

He saw him through a blur, smiling. And for a second he felt the embarrassed silence of understanding flutter between them.

"What you was doin' flyin' over this section, son? Wasn't you scared they might shoot you for a cow?"

Todd tensed. Was he being laughed at again? But before he could decide, the pain shook him and a part of him was lying calmly behind the screen of pain that had fallen between them, recalling the first time he had ever seen a plane. It was as though an endless series of hangars had been shaken ajar in the air base of his memory and from each, like a young wasp emerging from its cell, arose the memory of a plane.

The first time I ever saw a plane I was very small and planes were new in the world. I was four-and-a-half and the only plane that I had ever seen was a model suspended from the ceiling of the automobile exhibit at the State Fair. But I did not know that it was only a model. I did not know how large a real plane was, nor how expensive. To me it was a fascinating toy, complete in itself, which my mother said could only be owned by rich little white boys. I stood rigid with admiration, my head straining backwards as I watched the gray little plane describing arcs above the gleaming tops of the automobiles. And I vowed that, rich or poor, someday I would own such a toy. My mother had to drag me out of the exhibit and not even the merry-go-round, the Ferris wheel, or the racing horses could hold my attention for the rest of the Fair. I was too busy imitating the tiny drone of the plane with my lips, and imitating with my hands the motion, swift and circling, that it made in flight.

After that I no longer used the pieces of lumber that lay about our back yard to construct wagons and autos ... now it was used for airplanes. I built biplanes, using pieces of board for wings, a small box for the fuselage, another piece of wood for the rudder. The trip to the Fair had brought something new into my small world. I asked my mother repeatedly when the Fair would come back again. I'd lie in the grass and watch the sky, and each fighting bird became a soaring plane. I would have been good a year just to have seen a plane again. I became a nuisance to everyone with my questions about airplanes. But planes were new to the old folks, too, and there was little that they could tell me. Only my uncle knew some of the answers. And better still, he could carve propellers from pieces of wood that would whirl rapidly in the wind, wobbling noisily upon oiled nails.

I wanted a plane more than I'd wanted anything; more than I wanted the red wagon with rubber tires, more than the train that ran on a track with its train of cars. I asked my mother over and over again:

"Mamma?"

"What do you want, boy?" she'd say.

"Mamma, will you get mad if I ask you?" I'd say.

"What do you want now? I ain't got time to be answering a lot of fool questions. What you want?"

"Mamma, when you gonna get me one ... ?" I'd ask.

"Get you one what?" she'd say.

"You know, Mamma; what I been asking you. ..."

"Boy," she'd say, "if you don't want a spanking you better come on an' tell me what you talking about so I can get on with my work."

"Aw, Mamma, you know. ..."

"What I just tell you?" she'd say.

"I mean when you gonna buy me a airplane."

"AIRPLANE! Boy, is you crazy? How many times I have to tell you to stop that foolishness. I done told you them things cost too much. I bet I'm gon' wham the living daylight out of you if you don't quit worrying me 'bout them things!"

But this did not stop me, and a few days later I'd try all over again.

Then one day a strange thing happened. It was spring and for some reason I had been hot and irritable all morning. It was a beautiful spring. I could feel it as I played barefoot in the backyard. Blossoms hung from the thorny black locust trees like clusters of fragrant white grapes. Butterflies flickered in the sunlight above the short new dew-wet grass. I had gone in the house for bread and butter and coming out I heard a steady unfamiliar drone. It was unlike anything I had ever heard before. I tried to place the sound. It was no use. It was a sensation like that I had when searching for my father's watch, heard ticking unseen in a room. It made me feel as though I had forgotten to perform some task that my mother had ordered ... then I located it, overhead. In the sky, flying quite low and about a hundred yards off was a plane! It came so slowly that it seemed barely to move. My mouth hung wide; my bread and butter fell into the dirt. I wanted to jump up and down and cheer. And when the idea struck I trembled with excitement: "Some little white boy's plane's done flew away and all I got to do is stretch out my hands and it'll be mine!" It was a little plane like that at the Fair, flying no higher than the eaves of our roof. Seeing it come steadily forward I felt the world grow warm with promise. I opened the screen and climbed over it and clung there, waiting. I would catch the plane as it came over and swing down fast and run into the house before anyone could see me. Then no one could come to claim the plane. It droned nearer. Then when it hung like a silver cross in the blue directly above me I stretched out my hand and grabbed. It was like sticking my finger through a soap bubble. The plane flew on, as though I had simply blown my breath after it. I grabbed again, frantically, trying to catch the tail. My fingers clutched the air and disappointment surged tight and hard in my throat.

Giving one last desperate grasp, I strained forward. My fingers ripped from the screen. I was falling. The ground burst hard against me. I drummed the earth with my heels and when my breath returned, I lay there bawling.

My mother rushed through the door.

"What's the matter, chile! What on earth is wrong with you?"

"It's gone! It's gone!"

"What gone?"

"The airplane ..."

"Airplane?"

"Yessum, jus' like the one at the Fair. ... I ... I tried to stop it an' it kep' right on going. ..."

"When, boy?"

"Just now," I cried, through my tears.

"Where it go, boy, what way?"

"Yonder, there ..."

She scanned the sky, her arms akimbo and her checkered apron flapping in the wind as I pointed to the fading plane. Finally she looked down at me, slowly shaking her head.

"It's gone! It's gone!" I cried.

"Boy, is you a fool?" she said. "Don't you see that there's a real airplane 'stead of one of them toy ones?"

"Real ... ?" I forgot to cry. "Real?"

"Yass, real. Don't you know that thing you reaching for is bigger'n a auto? You here trying to reach for it and I bet it's flying 'bout two hundred miles higher'n this roof." She was disgusted with me. "You come on in this house before somebody else sees what a fool you done turned out to be. You must think these here lil ole arms of you'n is mighty long. ..."

I was carried into the house and undressed for bed and the doctor was called. I cried bitterly, as much from the disappointment of finding the plane so far beyond my reach as from the pain.

When the doctor came I heard my mother telling him about the plane and asking if anything was wrong with my mind. He explained that I had had a fever for several hours. But I was kept in bed for a week and I constantly saw the plane in my sleep, flying just beyond my fingertips, sailing so slowly that it seemed barely to move. And each time I'd reach out to grab it I'd miss and through each dream I'd hear my grandma warning:

Young man, young man,
Yo' arms too short
To box with God. ...

"Hey, son!"

At first he did not know where he was and looked at the old man pointing, with blurred eyes.

"Ain't that one of you-all's airplanes coming after you?"

As his vision cleared he saw a small black shape above a distant field, soaring through waves of heat. But he could not be sure and with the pain he feared that somehow a horrible recurring fantasy of being split in twain by the whirling blades of a propeller had come true.

"You think he sees us?" he heard.

"See? I hope so."

"He's coming like a bat outa hell!"

Straining, he heard the faint sound of a motor and hoped it would soon be over.

"How you feeling?"

"Like a nightmare," he said.

"Hey, he's done curved back the other way!"

"Maybe he saw us," he said. "Maybe he's gone to send out the ambulance and ground crew." And, he thought with despair, maybe he didn't even see us.

"Where did you send the boy?"

"Down to Mister Graves," Jefferson said. "Man what owns this land."

"Do you think he phoned?"

Jefferson looked at him quickly.

"Aw sho'. Dabney Graves is got a bad name on accounta them killings but he'll call though. ..."

"What killings?"

"Them five fellers ... ain't you heard?" he asked with surprise.

"No."

"Everybody knows 'bout Dabney Graves, especially the colored. He done killed enough of us."

Todd had the sensation of being caught in a white neighborhood after dark.

"What did they do?" he asked.

"Thought they was men," Jefferson said. "An' some he owed money, like he do me. ..."

"But why do you stay here?"

"You black, son."

"I know, but. ..."

"You have to come by the white folks, too."

He turned away from Jefferson's eyes, at once consoled and accused. And I'll have to come by them soon, he thought with despair. Closing his eyes, he heard Jefferson's voice as the sun burned blood-red upon his lips.

"I got nowhere to go," Jefferson said, "an' they'd come after me if I did. But Dabney Graves is a funny fellow. He's all the time making jokes. He can be mean as hell, then he's liable to turn right around and back the colored against the white folks. I seen him do it. But me, I hates him for that more'n anything else. 'Cause just as soon as he gits tired helping a man he don't care what happens to him. He just leaves him stone cold. And then the other white folks is double hard on anybody he done helped. For him it's just a joke. He don't give a hilla beans for nobody — but hisself. ..."

Todd listened to the thread of detachment in the old man's voice. It was as though he held his words arm's length before him to avoid their destructive meaning.

"He'd just as soon do you a favor and then turn right around and have you strung up. Me, I stays outa his way 'cause down here that's what you gotta do."

If my ankle would only ease for a while, he thought. The closer I spin toward the earth the blacker I become, flashed through his mind. Sweat ran into his eyes and he was sure that he would never see the plane if his head continued whirling. He tried to see Jefferson, what was it that Jefferson held in his hand? It was a little black man, another Jefferson! A little black Jefferson that shook with fits of belly-laughter while the other Jefferson looked on with detachment. Then Jefferson looked up from the thing in his hand and turned to speak, but Todd was far away, searching the sky for a plane in a hot dry land on a day and age he had long forgotten. He was going mysteriously with his mother through empty streets where black faces peered from behind drawn shades and someone was rapping at a window and he was looking back to see a hand and a frightened face frantically beckoning from a cracked door and his mother was looking down the empty perspective of the street and shaking her head and hurrying him along and at first it was only a flash he saw and a motor was droning as through the sun-glare he saw it gleaming silver as it circled and he was seeing a burst like a puff of white smoke and hearing his mother yell. Come along, boy, I got no time for them fool airplanes, I got no time, and he saw it a second time, the plane flying high, and the burst appeared suddenly and fell slowly, billowing out and sparkling like fireworks and he was watching and being hurried along as the air filled with a flurry of white pinwheeling cards that caught in the wind and scattered over the rooftops and into the gutters and a woman was running and snatching a card and reading it and screaming and he darted into the shower, grabbing as in winter he grabbed for snowflakes and bounding away at his mother's, Come on here, boy! Come on, I say! and he was watching as she took the card away, seeing her face grow puzzled and turning taut as her voice quavered, "Niggers Stay From The Polls," and died to a moan of terror as he saw the eyeless sockets of a white hood staring at him from the card and above he saw the plane spiraling gracefully, agleam in the sun like a fiery sword. And seeing it soar he was caught, transfixed between a terrible horror and a horrible fascination.

The sun was not so high now, and Jefferson was calling and gradually he saw three figures moving across the curving roll of the field.

"Look like some doctors, all dressed in white," said Jefferson.

They're coming at last, Todd thought. And he felt such a release of tension within him that he thought he would faint. But no sooner did he close his eyes than he was seized and he was struggling with three white men who were forcing his arms into some kind of coat. It was too much for him, his arms were pinned to his sides and as the pain blazed in his eyes, he realized that it was a straitjacket. What filthy joke was this?

"That oughta hold him, Mister Graves," he heard.

His total energies seemed focused in his eyes as he searched their faces. That was Graves; the other two wore hospital uniforms. He was poised between two poles of fear and hate as he heard the one called Graves saying, "He looks kinda purty in that there suit, boys. I'm glad you dropped by."

"This boy ain't crazy, Mister Graves," one of the others said. "He needs a doctor, not us. Don't see how you led us way out here anyway. It might be a joke to you, but your cousin Rudolph liable to kill somebody. White folks or niggers, don't make no difference. ..."

Todd saw the man turn red with anger. Graves looked down upon him, chuckling.

"This niggah belongs in a straitjacket, too, boys. I knowed that the minit Jeff's kid said something 'bout a nigguh flyer. You all know you cain't let the nigguh git up that high without his going crazy. The nigguh brain ain't built right for high altitudes. ..."

Todd watched the drawling red face, feeling that all the unnamed horror and obscenities that he had ever imagined stood materialized before him.

"Let's git outta here," one of the attendants said.

Todd saw the other reach toward him, realizing for the first time that he lay upon a stretcher as he yelled.

"Don't put your hands on me!"

They drew back, surprised.

"What's that you say, nigguh?" asked Graves.

He did not answer and thought that Graves's foot was aimed at his head. It landed on his chest and he could hardly breathe. He coughed helplessly, seeing Graves's lips stretch taut over his yellow teeth, and tried to shift his head. It was as though a half-dead fly was dragging slowly across his face and a bomb seemed to burst within him. Blasts of hot, hysterical laughter tore from his chest, causing his eyes to pop and he felt that the veins in his neck would surely burst. And then a part of him stood behind it all, watching the surprise in Graves's red face and his own hysteria. He thought he would never stop, he would laugh himself to death. It rang in his ears like Jefferson's laughter and he looked for him, centering his eyes desperately upon his face, as though somehow he had become his sole salvation in an insane world of outrage and humiliation. It brought a certain relief. He was suddenly aware that although his body was still contorted it was an echo that no longer rang in his ears. He heard Jefferson's voice with gratitude.

"Mister Graves, the Army done tole him not to leave his airplane."

"Nigguh, Army or no, you gittin' off my land! That airplane can stay 'cause it was paid for by taxpayers' money. But you gittin' off. An' dead or alive, it don't make no difference to me."

Todd was beyond it now, lost in a world of anguish.

"Jeff," Graves said, "you and Teddy come and grab holt. I want you to take this here black eagle over to that nigguh airfield and leave him."

Jefferson and the boy approached him silently. He looked away, realizing and doubting at once that only they could release him from his overpowering sense of isolation.

They bent for the stretcher. One of the attendants moved toward Teddy.

"Think you can manage it, boy?"

"I think I can, suh," Teddy said.

"Well, you better go behind then, and let yo' pa go ahead so's to keep that leg elevated."

He saw the white men walking ahead as Jefferson and the boy carried him along in silence. Then they were pausing and he felt a hand wiping his face; then he was moving again. And it was as though he had been lifted out of his isolation, back into the world of men. A new current of communication flowed between the man and boy and himself. They moved him gently. Far away he heard a mockingbird liquidly calling. He raised his eyes, seeing a buzzard poised unmoving in space. For a moment the whole afternoon seemed suspended and he waited for the horror to seize him again. Then like a song within his head he heard the boy's soft humming and saw the dark bird glide into the sun and glow like a bird of flaming gold.

QUESTIONS

1. Todd is an isolated man, and images of isolation run through "Flying Home." List several of these images, and explain how they work to define Todd's plight. What actually ends his isolation?

2. Why does Todd not want to relate to the old man who has found him? Is his reluctance deliberate or conditioned? Does Todd learn anything from him? Does the old man learn anything from Todd?

3. Explain the difference between Todd's idea of humiliation and the idea of humiliation expressed by the old man.

4. What does the old man's story about his "experiences" in heaven contribute to "Flying Home"? Is it more than a means of getting Todd's mind off his pain?

5. Is the flashback to Todd's childhood an exercise in sentimentality? What, if anything, keeps it from being an unnecessary interruption?

6. Is Mr. Graves a character or a caricature of the Simon Legree type? Is the old man a caricature like Uncle Tom?

7. The story ends with positive images. Has the ending been adequately prepared for, or does it seem tacked on? What now do you understand as the "home" of the story's title?

BERNARD MALAMUD

The Jewbird

The window was open so the skinny bird flew in. Flappity-flap with its frazzled black wings. That's how it goes. It's open, you're in. Closed, you're out and that's your fate. The bird wearily flapped through the open kitchen window of Harry Cohen's top-floor apartment on First Avenue near the lower East River. On a rod on the wall hung an escaped canary cage, its door wide open, but this black-type longbeaked bird — its ruffled head and small dull eyes, crossed a little, making it look like a dissipated crow — landed if not smack on Cohen's thick lamb chop, at least on the table, close by. The frozen foods salesman was sitting at supper with his wife and young son on a hot August evening a year ago. Cohen, a heavy man with hairy chest and beefy shorts; Edie, in skinny yellow shorts and red halter; and their ten-year-old Morris (after his father) — Maurie, they called him, a nice kid though 2ot overly bright — were all in the city after two weeks out, because Cohen's mother was dying. They had been enjoying Kingston, New York, but drove back when Mama got sick in her flat in the Bronx.

"Right on the table," said Cohen, putting down his beer glass and swatting at the bird. "Son of a bitch."

"Harry, take care with your language," Edie said, looking at Maurie, who watched every move.

The bird cawed hoarsely and with a flap of its bedraggled wings — feathers tufted this way and that — rose heavily to the top of the open kitchen door, where it perched staring down.

"Gevalt,[1] a pogrom!"

"It's a talking bird," said Edie in astonishment.

"In Jewish," said Maurie.

"Wise guy," muttered Cohen. He gnawed on his chop, then put down the bone. "So if you can talk, say what's your business. What do you want here?"

"If you can't spare a lamb chop," said the bird, "I'll settle for a piece of herring with a crust of bread. You can't live on your nerve forever."

"This ain't a restaurant," Cohen replied. "All I'm asking is what brings you to this address?"

---

[1] A cry of astonishment. A pogrom is an organized massacre.

"The window was open," the bird sighed; adding after a moment, "I'm running. I'm flying but I'm also running."

"From whom?" asked Edie with interest.

"Anti-Semeets."

"Anti-Semites?" they all said.

"That's from who."

"What kind of anti-Semites bother a bird?" Edie asked.

"Any kind," said the bird, "also including eagles, vultures, and hawks. And once in a while some crows will take your eyes out."

"But aren't you a crow?"

"Me? I'm a Jewbird."

Cohen laughed heartily. "What do you mean by that?"

The bird began dovening.[2] He prayed without Book or tallith,[3] but with passion. Edie bowed her head though not Cohen. And Maurie rocked back and forth with the prayer, looking up with one wide-open eye.

When the prayer was done Cohen remarked, "No hat, no phylacteries?"[4]

"I'm an old radical."

"You're sure you're not some kind of a ghost or dybbuk?"[5]

"Not a dybbuk," answered the bird, "though one of my relatives had such an experience once. It's all over now, thanks God. They freed her from a former lover, a crazy jealous man. She's now the mother of two wonderful children."

"Birds?" Cohen asked slyly.

"Why not?"

"What kind of birds?"

"Like me. Jewbirds."

Cohen tipped back in his chair and guffawed. "That's a big laugh. I've 2eard of a Jewfish but not a Jewbird."

"We're once removed." The bird rested on one skinny leg, then on the other. "Please, could you spare maybe a piece of herring with a small crust of bread?"

Edie got up from the table.

"What are you doing?" Cohen asked her.

"I'll clear the dishes."

Cohen turned to the bird. "So what's your name, if you don't mind saying?"

"Call me Schwartz."

"He might be an old Jew changed into a bird by somebody," said Edie, removing a plate.

"Are you?" asked Harry, lighting a cigar.

"Who knows?" answered Schwartz. "Does God tell us everything?"

Maurie got up on his chair. "What kind of herring?" he asked the bird in excitement.

"Get down, Maurie, or you'll fall," ordered Cohen.

---

[2] Praying.

[3] A prayer shawl.

[4] Two small, black leather cubes, containing Biblical verses on parchment, worn by Jewish men during prayer.

[5] An evil spirit who can take possession of a person.

"If you haven't got matjes,[6] I'll take schmaltz,"[7] said Schwartz.

"All we have is marinated, with slices of onion — in a jar," said Edie.

"If you'll open for me the jar I'll eat marinated. Do you have also, if you don't mind, a piece of rye bread — the spitz?"[8]

Edie thought she had.

"Feed him out on the balcony," Cohen said. He spoke to the bird. "After that take off."

Schwartz closed both bird eyes. "I'm tired and it's a long way."

"Which direction are you headed, north or south?"

Schwartz, barely lifting his wings, shrugged.

"You don't know where you're going?"

"Where there's charity I'll go."

"Let him stay, papa," said Maurie. "He's only a bird."

"So stay the night," Cohen said, "but no longer."

In the morning Cohen ordered the bird out of the house but Maurie cried, so Schwartz stayed for a while. Maurie was still on vacation from school and his friends were away. He was lonely and Edie enjoyed the fun he had, playing with the bird.

"He's no trouble at all," she told Cohen, "and besides his appetite is very small."

"What'll you do when he makes dirty?"

"He flies across the street in a tree when he makes dirty, and if nobody passes below, who notices?"

"So all right," said Cohen, "but I'm dead set against it. I warn you he ain't gonna stay here long."

"What have you got against the poor bird?"

"Poor bird, my ass. He's a foxy bastard. He thinks he's a Jew."

"What difference does it make what he thinks?"

"A Jewbird, what a chutzpah.[9] One false move and he's out on his drumsticks."

At Cohen's insistence Schwartz lived out on the balcony in a new wooden birdhouse Edie had bought him.

"With many thanks," said Schwartz, "though I would rather have a human roof over my head. You know how it is at my age. I like the warm, the windows, the smell of cooking. I would also be glad to see once in a while the *Jewish Morning Journal* and have now and then a schnapps[10] because it helps my breathing, thanks God. But whatever you give me, you won't hear complaints."

However, when Cohen brought home a bird feeder full of dried corn, Schwartz said, "Impossible."

Cohen was annoyed. "What's the matter, crosseyes, is your life getting too good for you? Are you forgetting what it means to be migratory? I'll bet a helluva lot of crows you happen to be acquainted with, Jews or otherwise, would give their eyeteeth to eat this corn."

Schwartz did not answer. What can you say to a grubber yung?[11]

---

[6] The best herring.

[7] The greasy kind.

[8] The heel.

[9] Gall; effrontery.

[10] Brandy or other strong spirits.

[11] A crude boor.

"Not for my digestion," he later explained to Edie. "Cramps. Herring is better even if it makes you thirsty. At least rainwater don't cost anything." He laughed sadly in breathy caws.

And herring, thanks to Edie, who knew where to shop, was what Schwartz got, with an occasional piece of potato pancake, and even a bit of soupmeat when Cohen wasn't looking.

When school began in September, before Cohen would once again suggest giving the bird the boot, Edie prevailed on him to wait a little while until Maurie adjusted.

"To deprive him right now might hurt his school work, and you know what trouble we had last year."

"So okay, but sooner or later the bird goes. That I promise you."

Schwartz, though nobody had asked him, took on full responsibility for Maurie's performance in school. In return for favors granted, when he was let in for an hour or two at night, he spent most of his time overseeing the boy's lessons. He sat on top of the dresser near Maurie's desk as he laboriously wrote out his homework. Maurie was a restless type and Schwartz gently kept him to his studies. He also listened to him practice his screechy violin, taking a few minutes off now and then to rest his ears in the bathroom. And they afterwards played dominoes. The boy was an indifferent checker player and it was impossible to teach him chess. When he was sick, Schwartz read him comic books though he personally disliked them. But Maurie's work improved in school and even his violin teacher admitted his playing was better. Edie gave Schwartz credit for these improvements though the bird pooh-poohed them.

Yet he was proud there was nothing lower than C minuses on Maurie's report card, and on Edie's insistence celebrated with a little schnapps.

"If he keeps up like this," Cohen said, "I'll get him in an Ivy League college for sure."

"Oh I hope so," sighed Edie.

But Schwartz shook his head. "He's a good boy — you don't have to worry. He won't be a shicker[12] or a wifebeater, God forbid, but a scholar he'll never be, if you know what I mean, although maybe a good mechanic. It's no disgrace in these times."

"If I were you," Cohen said, angered, "I'd keep my big snoot out of other people's private business."

"Harry, please," said Edie.

"My goddamn patience is wearing out. That crosseyes butts into everything."

Though he wasn't exactly a welcome guest in the house, Schwartz gained a few ounces although he did not improve in appearance. He looked bedraggled as ever, his feathers unkempt, as though he had just flown out of a snowstorm. He spent, he admitted, little time taking care of himself. Too much to think about. "Also outside plumbing," he told Edie. Still there was more glow to his eyes so that though Cohen went on calling him crosseyes he said it less emphatically.

Liking his situation, Schwartz tried tactfully to stay out of Cohen's way, but one night when Edie was at the movies and Maurie was taking a hot shower, the frozen foods salesman began a quarrel with the bird.

"For Christ sake, why don't you wash yourself sometimes? Why must you always stink like a dead fish?"

"Mr. Cohen, if you'll pardon me, if somebody eats garlic he will smell from garlic. I eat herring three times a day. Feed me flowers and I will smell like flowers."

"Who's obligated to feed you anything at all? You're lucky to get herring."

---

[12] A boozer.

"Excuse me, I'm not complaining," said the bird. "You're complaining."

"What's more," said Cohen, "even from out on the balcony I can hear you snoring away like a pig. It keeps me awake at night."

"Snoring," said Schwartz, "isn't a crime, thanks God."

"All in all you are a goddamn pest and free loader. Next thing you'll want to sleep in bed next to my wife."

"Mr. Cohen," said Schwartz, "on this rest assured. A bird is a bird."

"So you say, but how do I know you're a bird and not some kind of a goddamn devil?"

"If I was a devil you would know already. And I don't mean because your son's good marks."

"Shut up, you bastard bird," shouted Cohen.

"Grubber yung," cawed Schwartz, rising to the tips of his talons, his long wings outstretched.

Cohen was about to lunge for the bird's scrawny neck but Maurie came out of the bathroom, and for the rest of the evening until Schwartz's bedtime on the balcony, there was pretended peace.

But the quarrel had deeply disturbed Schwartz and he slept badly. His snoring woke him, and awake, he was fearful of what would become of him. Wanting to stay out of Cohen's way, he kept to the birdhouse as much as possible. Cramped by it, he paced back and forth on the balcony ledge, or sat on the birdhouse roof, staring into space. In the evenings, while overseeing Maurie's lessons, he often fell asleep. Awakening, he nervously hopped around exploring the four corners of the room. He spent much time in Maurie's closet, and carefully examined his bureau drawers when they were left open. And once when he found a large paper bag on the floor, Schwartz poked his way into it to investigate what possibilities were. The boy was amused to see the bird in the paper bag.

"He wants to build a nest," he said to his mother.

Edie, sensing Schwartz's unhappiness, spoke to him quietly.

"Maybe if you did some of the things my husband wants you, you would get along better with him."

"Give me a for instance," Schwartz said.

"Like take a bath, for instance."

"I'm too old for baths," said the bird. "My feathers fall out without baths."

"He says you have a bad smell."

"Everybody smells. Some people smell because of their thoughts or because who they are. My bad smell comes from the food I eat. What does his come from?"

"I better not ask him or it might make him mad," said Edie.

In late November Schwartz froze on the balcony in the fog and cold, and especially on rainy days he woke with stiff joints and could barely move his wings. Already he felt twinges of rheumatism. He would have liked to spend more time in the warm house, particularly when Maurie was in school and Cohen at work. But though Edie was good-hearted and might have sneaked him in in the morning, just to thaw out, he was afraid to ask her. In the meantime Cohen, who had been reading articles about the migration of birds, came out on the balcony one night after work when Edie was in the kitchen preparing pot roast, and peeking into the birdhouse, warned Schwartz to be on his way soon if he knew what was good for him. "Time to hit the flyways."

"Mr. Cohen, why do you hate me so much?" asked the bird. "What did I do to you?"

"Because you're an A-number-one trouble maker, that's why. What's more, whoever heard of a Jewbird! Now scat or it's open war."

But Schwartz stubbornly refused to depart so Cohen embarked on a campaign of harassing him, meanwhile hiding it from Edie and Maurie. Maurie hated violence and Cohen didn't want to leave a bad impression. He thought maybe if he played dirty tricks on the bird he would fly off without being physically kicked out. The vacation was over, let him make his easy living off the fat of somebody else's land. Cohen worried about the effect of the bird's departure on Maurie's schooling but decided to take the chance, first, because the boy now seemed to have the knack of studying — give the black bird-bastard credit — and second, because Schwartz was driving him bats by being there always, even in his dreams.

The frozen foods salesman began his campaign against the bird by mixing watery cat food with the herring slices in Schwartz's dish. He also blew up and popped numerous paper bags outside the birdhouse as the bird slept, and when he had got Schwartz good and nervous, though not enough to leave, he brought a full-grown cat into the house, supposedly a gift for little Maurie, who had always wanted a pussy. The cat never stopped springing up at Schwartz whenever he saw him, one day managing to claw out several of his tailfeathers. And even at lesson time, when the cat was usually excluded from Maurie's room, though somehow or other he quickly found his way in at the end of the lesson, Schwartz was desperately fearful of his life and flew from pinnacle to pinnacle — light fixture to clothes-tree to door-top — in order to elude the beast's wet jaws.

Once when the bird complained to Edie how hazardous his existence was, she said, "Be patient, Mr. Schwartz. When the cat gets to know you better he won't try to catch you any more."

"When he stops trying we will both be in Paradise," Schwartz answered. "Do me a favor and get rid of him. He makes my whole life worry. I'm losing feathers like a tree loses leaves."

"I'm awfully sorry but Maurie likes the pussy and sleeps with it."

What could Schwartz do? He worried but came to no decision, being afraid to leave. So he ate the herring garnished with cat food, tried hard not to hear the paper bags bursting like fire crackers outside the birdhouse at night, and lived terror-stricken closer to the ceiling than the floor, as the cat, his tail flicking, endlessly watched him.

Weeks went by. Then on the day after Cohen's mother had died in her flat in the Bronx, when Maurie came home with a zero on an arithmetic test, Cohen, enraged, waited until Edie had taken the boy to his violin lesson, then openly attacked the bird. He chased him with a broom on the balcony and Schwartz frantically flew back and forth, finally escaping into his birdhouse. Cohen triumphantly reached in, and grabbing both skinny legs, dragged the bird out, cawing loudly, his wings wildly beating. He whirled the bird around and around his head. But Schwartz, as he moved in circles, managed to swoop down and catch Cohen's nose in his beak, and hung on for dear life. Cohen cried out in great pain, punched the bird with his fist, and tugging at its legs with all his might, pulled his nose free. Again he swung the yawking Schwartz around until the bird grew dizzy, then with a furious heave, flung him into the night. Schwartz sank like stone into the street. Cohen then tossed the birdhouse and feeder after him, listening at the ledge until they crashed on the sidewalk below. For a full hour, broom in hand, his heart palpitating and nose throbbing with pain, Cohen waited for Schwartz to return but the broken-hearted bird didn't.

That's the end of that dirty bastard, the salesman thought and went in. Edie and Maurie had come home.

"Look," said Cohen, pointing to his bloody nose swollen three times its normal size, "what that sonofabitchy bird did. It's a permanent scar."

"Where is he now?" Edie asked, frightened.

"I threw him out and he flew away. Good riddance."

Nobody said no, though Edie touched a handkerchief to her eyes and Maurie rapidly tried the nine times table and found he knew approximately half.

In the spring when the winter's snow had melted, the boy, moved by a memory, wandered in the neighborhood, looking for Schwartz. He found a dead black bird in a small lot near the river, his two wings broken, neck twisted, and both bird-eyes plucked clean.

"Who did it to you, Mr. Schwartz?" Maurie wept.

"Anti-Semeets," Edie said later.

QUESTIONS

1. Who narrates the story? Is he an omniscient narrator? What is his attitude toward Schwartz?

2. Why is Schwartz an appropriate name for this bird? In what other ways is he personalized?

3. How do Edie's and Cohen's attitudes toward Schwartz differ? If Jewishness is one of the subjects here, which is the better Jew? What does the story have to say about being Jewish?

4. Are Edie, Cohen, and Maurie rounded characters or only caricatures? Is their development suitable for Malamud's purpose? What do you think that purpose is?

5. Is this story comic or tragic? Is it an allegory of anti-Semitism?

SAUL BELLOW

Looking for Mr. Green

Whatsoever thy hand findeth to do, do it with thy might. ...[1]

Hard work? No, it wasn't really so hard. He wasn't used to walking and stair-climbing, but the physical difficulty of his new job was not what George Grebe felt most. He was delivering relief checks in the Negro district, and although he was a native Chicagoan this was not a part of the city he knew much about — it needed a depression to introduce him to it. No, it wasn't literally hard work, not as reckoned in foot-pounds, but yet he was beginning to feel the strain of it, to grow aware of its peculiar difficulty. He could find the streets and numbers, but the clients were not where they were supposed to be, and he felt like a hunter inexperienced in the camouflage of his game. It was an unfavorable day, too — fall, and cold, dark weather, windy. But, anyway, instead of shells in his deep trenchcoat pocket he had the cardboard of checks, punctured for the spindles of the file, the holes reminding him of the holes in player-piano paper. And he didn't look much like a hunter, either; his was a city figure entirely, belted up in his Irish conspirator's coat. He was slender without being tall, stiff in the back, his legs looking shabby in a pair of old tweed pants gone through and fringy at the cuffs. With this stiffness, he kept his head forward, so that his face was red from the sharpness of the weather; and it was an indoors sort of face with gray eyes that persisted in some kind of thought and yet seemed to avoid definiteness of conclusion. He wore sideburns that surprised you somewhat by the tough curl of the blond hair and the effect of assertion in their length. He was not so mild as he looked, nor so youthful; and nevertheless there was no effort on his part to seem what he was not. He was an educated man; he was a bachelor; he was in some ways simple; without lushing, he liked a drink; his luck had not been good. Nothing was deliberately hidden.

He felt that his luck was better than usual today. When he had reported for work that morning he had expected to be shut up in the relief office at a clerk's job, for he had been hired downtown as a clerk, and he was glad to have, instead, the freedom of the streets and welcomed, at least at first, the vigor of the cold and even the blowing of the hard wind. But on the other hand he was not getting on with the distribution of the checks. It was true that it was a city job; nobody expected you to push too hard at a city job. His supervisor, that young

---

[1] Ecclesiastes, 9:10.

Mr. Raynor, had practically told him that. Still, he wanted to do well at it. For one thing, when he knew how quickly he could deliver a batch of checks, he would know also how much time he could expect to clip for himself. And then, too, the clients would be waiting for their money. That was not the most important consideration, though it certainly mattered to him. No, but he wanted to do well, simply for doing-well's sake, to acquit himself decently of a job because he so rarely had a job to do that required just this sort of energy. Of this peculiar energy he now had a superabundance; once it had started to flow, it flowed all too heavily. And, for the time being anyway, he was balked. He could not find Mr. Green.

So he stood in his big-skirted trenchcoat with a large envelope in his hand and papers showing from his pocket, wondering why people should be so hard to locate who were too feeble or sick to come to the station to collect their own checks. But Raynor had told him that tracking them down was not easy at first and had offered him some advice on how to proceed. "If you can see the postman, he's your first man to ask, and your best bet. If you can't connect with him, try the stores and tradespeople around. Then the janitor and the neighbors. But you'll find the closer you come to your man the less people will tell you. They don't want to tell you anything."

"Because I'm a stranger."

"Because you're white. We ought to have a Negro doing this, but we don't at the moment, and of course you've got to eat, too, and this is public employment. Jobs have to be made. Oh, that holds for me too. Mind you, I'm not letting myself out. I've got three years of seniority on you, that's all. And a law degree. Otherwise, you might be back of the desk and I might be going out into the field this cold day. The same dough pays us both and for the same, exact, identical reason. What's my law degree got to do with it? But you have to pass out these checks, Mr. Grebe, and it'll help if you're stubborn, so I hope you are."

"Yes, I'm fairly stubborn."

Raynor sketched hard with an eraser in the old dirt of his desk, left-handed, and said, "Sure, what else can you answer to such a question. Anyhow, the trouble you're going to have is that they don't like to give information about anybody. They think you're a plain-clothes dick or an installment collector, or summons-server or something like that. Till you've been seen around the neighborhood for a few months and people know you're only from the relief."

It was dark, ground-freezing, pre-Thanksgiving weather; the wind played hob with the smoke, rushing it down, and Grebe missed his gloves, which he had left in Raynor's office. And no one would admit knowing Green. It was past three o'clock and the postman had made his last delivery. The nearest grocer, himself a Negro, had never heard the name Tulliver Green, or said he hadn't. Grebe was inclined to think that it was true, that he had in the end convinced the man that he wanted only to deliver a check. But he wasn't sure. He needed experience in interpreting looks and signs and, even more, the will not to be put off or denied and even the force to bully if need be. If the grocer did know, he had got rid of him easily. But since most of his trade was with reliefers, why should he prevent the delivery of a check? Maybe Green, or Mrs. Green, if there was a Mrs. Green, patronized another grocer. And was there a Mrs. Green? It was one of Grebe's great handicaps that he hadn't looked at any of the case records. Raynor should have let him read files for a few hours. But he apparently saw no need for that, probably considering the job unimportant. Why prepare systematically to deliver a few checks?

But now it was time to look for the janitor. Grebe took in the building in the wind and gloom of the late November day — trampled, frost-hardened lots on one side; on the other, an automobile junk yard and then the infinite work of Elevated frames, weak-looking, gaping with rubbish fires; two sets of leaning brick porches three stories high and a flight of cement stairs to the cellar. Descending, he entered the underground passage, where he tried the doors until one opened and he found himself in the furnace room. There someone rose toward him and approached, scraping on the coal grit and bending under the canvas-jacketed pipes.

"Are you the janitor?"

"What do you want?"

"I'm looking for a man who's supposed to be living here. Green."

"What Green?"

"Oh, you maybe have more than one Green?" said Grebe with new, pleasant hope. "This is Tulliver Green."

"I don't think I c'n help you, mister. I don't know any."

"A crippled man."

The janitor stood bent before him. Could it be that he was crippled? Oh, God! what if he was. Grebe's gray eyes sought with excited difficulty to see. But no, he was only very short and stooped. A head awakened from meditation, a stronghaired beard, low, wide shoulders. A staleness of sweat and coal rose from his black shirt and the burlap sack he wore as an apron.

"Crippled how?"

Grebe thought and then answered with the light voice of unmixed candor, "I don't know. I've never seen him." This was damaging, but his only other choice was to make a lying guess, and he was not up to it. "I'm delivering checks for the relief to shut-in cases. If he weren't crippled he'd come to collect himself. That's why I said crippled. Bedridden, chairridden — is there anybody like that?"

This sort of frankness was one of Grebe's oldest talents, going back to childhood. But it gained him nothing here.

"No suh. I've got four building's same as this that I take care of. I don' know all the tenants, leave alone the tenants' tenants. The rooms turn over so fast, people movin' in and out every day. I can't tell you."

"Then where should I ask?"

The janitor opened his grimy lips but Grebe did not hear him in the piping of the valves and the consuming pull of air to flame in the body of the furnace. He knew, however, what he had said.

"Well, all the same, thanks. Sorry I bothered you. I'll prowl around upstairs again and see if I can turn up someone who knows him."

Once more in the cold air and early darkness he made the short circle from the cellarway to the entrance crowded between the brickwork pillars and began to climb to the third floor. Pieces of plaster ground under his feet; strips of brass tape from which the carpeting had been torn away marked old boundaries at the sides. In the passage, the cold reached him worse than in the street; it touched him to the bone. The hall toilets ran like springs. He thought grimly as he heard the wind burning around the building with a sound like that of the furnace, that this was a great piece of constructed shelter. Then he struck a match in the gloom and searched for names and numbers among the writings and scribbles on the walls. He saw WHOODY-DOODY GO TO JESUS, and zigzags, caricatures, sexual scrawls, and curses. So the sealed rooms of pyramids were also decorated, and the caves of human dawn.

The information on his card was, TULLIVER GREEN — APT 3D. There were no names, however, and no numbers. His shoulders drawn up, tears of cold in his eyes, breathing vapor, he went the length of the corridor and told himself that if he had been lucky enough to have the temperament for it he would bang on one of the doors and bawl out "Tulliver Green!" until he got results. But it wasn't in him to make an uproar and he continued to burn matches, passing the light over the walls. At the rear, in a corner off the hall, he discovered a door he had not seen before and he thought it best to investigate. It sounded empty when he knocked, but a young Negress answered, hardly more than a girl. She opened only a bit, to guard the warmth of the room.

"Yes suh?"

"I'm from the district relief station on Prairie Avenue. I'm looking for a man named Tulliver Green to give him his check. Do you know him?"

No, she didn't; but he thought she had not understood anything of what he had said. She had a dream-bound, dream-blind face, very soft and black, shut off. She wore a man's jacket and pulled the ends together at her throat. Her hair was parted in three directions, at the sides and transversely, standing up at the front in a dull puff.

"Is there somebody around here who might know?"

"I jus' taken this room las' week."

He observed that she shivered, but even her shiver was somnambulistic and there was no sharp consciousness of cold in the big smooth eyes of her handsome face.

"All right, miss, thank you. Thanks," he said, and went to try another place.

Here he was admitted. He was grateful, for the room was warm. It was full of people, and they were silent as he entered — ten people, or a dozen, perhaps more, sitting on benches like a parliament. There was no light, properly speaking, but a tempered darkness that the window gave, and everyone seemed to him enormous, the men padded out in heavy work clothes and winter coats, and the women huge, too, in their sweaters, hats, and old furs. And, besides, bed and bedding, a black cooking range, a piano piled towering to the ceiling with papers, a dining-room table of the old style of prosperous Chicago. Among these people Grebe, with his cold-heightened fresh color and his smaller stature, entered like a schoolboy. Even though he was met with smiles and good will, he knew, before a single word was spoken, that all the currents ran against him and that he would make no headway. Nevertheless he began. "Does anybody here know how I can deliver a check to Mr. Tulliver Green?"

"Green?" It was the man that had let him in who answered. He was in short sleeves, in a checkered shirt and had a queer, high head, profusely overgrown and long as a shako[2]; the veins entered it strongly from his forehead. "I never heard mention of him. Is this where he live?"

"This is the address they gave me at the station. He's a sick man, and he'll need his check. Can't anybody tell me where to find him?"

He stood his ground and waited for a reply, his crimson wool scarf wound about his neck and drooping outside his trenchcoat, pockets weighted with the block of checks and official forms. They must have realized that he was not a college boy employed afternoons by a bill collector, trying foxily to pass for a relief clerk, recognized that he was an older man who knew himself what need was, who had had more than an average seasoning in hardship. It was evident enough if you looked at the marks under his eyes and at the sides of his mouth.

"Anybody know this sick man?"

"No suh." On all sides he saw heads shaken and smiles of denial. No one knew. And maybe it was true, he considered, standing silent in the earthen, musky human gloom of the place as the rumble continued. But he could never really be sure.

"What's the matter with this man?" said shako-head.

---

[2] A tall, cylindrical military cap such as might be worn in a marching band.

"I've never seen him. All I can tell you is that he can't come in person for his money. It's my first day in this district."

"Maybe they given you the wrong number?"

"I don't believe so. But where else can I ask about him?" He felt that his persistence amused them deeply, and in a way he shared their amusement that he should stand up so tenaciously to them. Though smaller, though slight, he was his own man, he retracted nothing about himself, and he looked back at them, gray-eyed, with amusement and also with a sort of courage. On the bench some man spoke in his throat, the words impossible to catch, and a woman answered with a wild, shrieking laugh, which was quickly cut off.

"Well, so nobody will tell me?"

"Ain't nobody who knows."

"At least, if he lives here, he pays rent to someone. Who manages the building?"

"Greatham Company. That's on Thirty-ninth Street."

Grebe wrote it in his pad. But, in the street again, a sheet of wind-driven paper clinging to his leg while he deliberated what direction to take next, it seemed a feeble lead to follow. Probably this Green didn't rent a flat, but a room. Sometimes there were as many as twenty people living in an apartment; the real-estate agent would know only the lessee. And not even the agent could tell you who the renters were. In some places the beds were even used in shifts, watchmen or jitney drivers or short-order cooks in night joints turning out after a day's sleep and surrendering their beds to a sister, a nephew, or perhaps a stranger, just off the bus. There were large numbers of newcomers in this terrific, blight-bitten portion of the city between Cottage Grove and Ashland, wandering from house to house and room to room. When you saw them, how could you know them? They didn't carry bundles on their backs or look picturesque. You only saw a man, a Negro, walking in the street or riding in the car, like everyone else, with his thumb closed on a transfer. And therefore how were you supposed to tell? Grebe thought the Greatham agent would only laugh at his question.

But how much it would have simplified the job to be able to say that Green was old, or blind, or consumptive. An hour in the files, taking a few notes, and he needn't have been at such a disadvantage. When Raynor gave him the block of checks he had asked, "How much should I know about these people?" Then Raynor had looked as though he were preparing to accuse him of trying to make the job more important than it was. He smiled, because by then they were on fine terms, but nevertheless he had been getting ready to say something like that when the confusion began in the station over Staika and her children.

Grebe had waited a long time for this job. It came to him through the pull of an old schoolmate in the Corporation Counsel's office. Never a close friend, but suddenly sympathetic and interested — pleased to show, moreover, how well he had done, how strongly he was coming on even in these miserable times. Well, he was coming through strongly, along with the Democratic administration itself. Grebe had gone to see him in City Hall and they had had a counter lunch or beers at least once a month for a year, and finally it had been possible to swing the job. He didn't mind being assigned the lowest clerical grade, nor even being a messenger, though Raynor thought he did.

This Raynor was an original sort of guy and Grebe had taken to him immediately. As was proper on the first day, Grebe had come early, but he waited long, for Raynor was late. At last he darted into his cubicle of an office as though he had just jumped from one of those hurtling huge red Indiana Avenue cars. His thin, rough face was wind-stung and he was grinning and saying something breathlessly to himself. In his hat, a small fedora and his coat, the velvet collar a neat fit about his neck, and his silk muffler that set off the nervous twist of his chin, he swayed and turned himself in his swivel chair, feet leaving the ground; so that he pranced a little as he sat. Meanwhile he took Grebe's measure out of his eyes, eyes of an unusual vertical length and slightly sardonic. So the two men sat for a while, saying nothing, while the supervisor raised his hat from his miscombed hair and put it in his lap. His cold-darkened hands were not clean. A steel beam passed through the little makeshift room, from which machine belts once had hung. The building was an old factory.

"I'm younger than you; I hope you won't find it hard taking orders from me," said Raynor. "But I don't make them up, either. You're how old, about?"

"Thirty-five."

"And you thought you'd be inside doing paper-work. But it so happens I have to send you out."

"I don't mind."

"And it's mostly a Negro load we have in this district."

"So I thought it would be."

"Fine. You'll get along. *C'est un bon boulot.*[3] Do you know French?"

"Some."

"I thought you'd be a university man."

"Have you been in France?" said Grebe.

"No, that's the French of the Berlitz School. I've been at it for more than a year, just as I'm sure people have been, all over the world, office boys in China and braves in Tanganyika. In fact, I damn well know it. Such is the attractive power of civilization. It's overrated, but what do you want? *Que voulez vous?*[4] I get *Le Rire*[5] and all the spicy papers, just like in Tanganyika. It must be mystifying, out there. But my reason is that I'm aiming at the diplomatic service. I have a cousin who's a courier, and the way he describes it is awfully attractive. He rides in the *wagon-lits*[6] and reads books. While we — What did you do before?"

"I sold."

"Where?"

"Canned meat at Stop and Shop. In the basement."

"And before that?"

"Window shades, at Goldblatt's."

"Steady work?"

"No, Thursdays and Saturdays. I also sold shoes."

"You've been a shoe-dog, too. Well. And prior to that? Here it is in your folder." He opened the record. "St. Olaf's College, instructor in classical languages. Fellow, University of Chicago, 1926–27. I've had Latin, too. Let's trade quotations — *'Dum spiro spero.'*[7]

"*'Da dextram misero.'*[8]

"*'Alea jacta est.'*[9]

"*'Excelsior.'*[10]

---

[3] "It's good work."

[4] "What do you want?"

[5] A humorous publication whose title means "laughter."

[6] Sleeper cars on the train.

[7] "While I breathe, I hope."

[8] "Give your right hand to those who suffer."

[9] "The die is cast."

[10] "Ever upward."

Raynor shouted with laughter, and other workers came to look at him over the partition. Grebe also laughed, feeling pleased and easy. The luxury of fun on a nervous morning.

When they were done and no one was watching or listening, Raynor said rather seriously, "What made you study Latin in the first place. Was it for the priesthood?"

"No."

"Just for the hell of it? For the culture? Oh, the things people think they can pull!" He made his cry hilarious and tragic. "I ran my pants off so I could study for the bar, and I've passed the bar, so I get twelve dollars a week more than you as a bonus for having seen life straight and whole. I'll tell you, as a man of culture, that even though nothing looks to be real, and everything stands for something else, and that thing for another thing, and that thing for a still further one — there ain't any comparison between twenty-five and thirty-seven dollars a week, regardless of the last reality. Don't you think that was clear to your Greeks? They were a thoughtful people, but they didn't part with their slaves."

This was a great deal more than Grebe had looked for in his first interview with his supervisor. He was too shy to show all the astonishment he felt. He laughed a little, aroused, and brushed at the sunbeam that covered his head with its dust. "Do you think my mistake was so terrible?"

"Damn right it was terrible, and you know it now that you've had the whip of hard times laid on your back. You should have been preparing yourself for trouble. Your people must have been well off to send you to the university. Stop me, if I'm stepping on your toes. Did your mother pamper you? Did your father give in to you? Were you brought up tenderly, with permission to go out and find out what were the last things that everything else stands for while everybody else labored in the fallen world of appearances?"

"Well, no, it wasn't exactly like that." Grebe smiled. *The fallen world of appearances!* no less. But now it was his turn to deliver a surprise. "We weren't rich. My father was the last genuine English butler in Chicago — "

"Are you kidding?"

"Why should I be?"

"In a livery?"

"In livery. Up on the Gold Coast."

"And he wanted you to be educated like a gentleman?"

"He did not. He sent me to the Armour Institute to study chemical engineering. But when he died I changed schools."

He stopped himself, and considered how quickly Raynor had reached him. In no time he had your valise on the table and all your stuff unpacked. And afterward, in the streets, he was still reviewing how far he might have gone, and how much he might have been led to tell if they had not been interrupted by Mrs. Staika's great noise.

But just then a young woman, one of Raynor's workers, ran into the cubicle exclaiming, "Haven't you heard all the fuss?"

"We haven't heard anything."

"It's Staika, giving out with all her might. The reporters are coming. She said she phoned the papers, and you know she did."

"But what is she up to?" said Raynor.

"She brought her wash and she's ironing it here, with our current, because the relief won't pay her electric bill. She has her ironing board set up by the admitting desk, and her kids are with her, all six. They never are in school more than once a week. She's always dragging them around with her because of her reputation."

"I don't want to miss any of this," said Raynor, jumping up. Grebe, as he followed with the secretary, said, "Who is this Staika?"

"They call her the 'Blood Mother of Federal Street.' She's a professional donor at the hospitals. I think they pay ten dollars a pint. Of course it's no joke, but she makes a very big thing out of it and she and the kids are in the papers all the time."

A small crowd, staff and clients divided by a plywood barrier, stood in the narrow space of the entrance, and Staika was shouting in a gruff, mannish voice, plunging the iron on the board and slamming it on the metal rest.

"My father and mother came in a steerage, and I was born in our own house, Robey by Huron. I'm no dirty immigrant. I'm a US citizen. My husband is a gassed veteran from France with lungs weaker'n paper, that hardly can he go to the toilet by himself. These six children of mine, I have to buy the shoes for their feet with my own blood. Even a lousy little white communion necktie, that's a couple of drops of blood; a little piece of mosquito veil for my Vadja so she won't be ashamed in church for the other girls, they take my blood for it by Goldblatt. That's how I keep goin'. A fine thing if I had to depend on the relief. And there's plenty of people on the rolls — fakes! There's nothin' *they* can't get, that can go and wrap bacon at Swift and Armour any time. They're lookin' for them by the Yards. They never have to be out of work. Only they rather lay in their lousy beds and eat the public's money." She was not afraid, in a predominantly Negro station, to shout this way about Negroes.

Grebe and Raynor worked themselves forward to get a closer view of the woman. She was flaming with anger and with pleasure at herself, broad and huge, a golden-headed woman who wore a cotton cap laced with pink ribbon. She was barelegged and had on black gym-shoes, her hoover apron[11] was open and her great breasts, not much restrained by a man's undershirt, hampered her arms as she worked at the kid's dress on the ironing board. And the children, silent and white, with a kind of locked obstinacy, in sheepskins and lumberjackets, stood behind her. She had captured the station, and the pleasure this gave her was enormous. Yet her grievances were true grievances. She was telling the truth. But she behaved like a liar. The look of her small eyes was hidden, and while she raged she also seemed to be spinning and planning.

"They send me out college case-workers in silk pants to talk me out of what I got comin'. Are they better'n me? Who told them? Fire them. Let 'em go and get married, and then you won't have to cut electric from people's budget."

The chief supervisor, Mr. Ewing, couldn't silence her and he stood with folded arms at the head of his staff, bald, baldheaded, saying to his subordinates like the ex-school principal he was, "Pretty soon she'll be tired and go."

"No she won't," said Raynor to Grebe. "She'll get what she wants. She knows more about the relief even than Ewing. She's been on the rolls for years, and she always gets what she wants because she puts on a noisy show. Ewing knows it. He'll give in soon. He's only saving face. If he gets bad publicity, the Commissioner'll have him on the carpet, downtown. She's got him submerged; she'll submerge everybody in time, and that includes nations and governments."

Grebe replied with his characteristic smile, disagreeing completely. Who would take Staika's orders, and what changes could her yelling ever bring about?

No, what Grebe saw in her, the power that made people listen, was that her cry expressed the war of flesh and blood, perhaps turned a little crazy and certainly intensely ugly, on this place and this condition. And at first, when he went out, the spirit of Staika

---

[11] Depression-era slang for a woman's coverall.

somehow presided over the whole district for him, and it took color from her; he saw her color, in the spotty curb-fires, and the fires under the El, the straight alley of flamey gloom. Later, too, when he went into a tavern for a shot of rye, the sweat of beer, association with West Side Polish streets, made him think of her again.

He wiped the corners of his mouth with his muffler, his handkerchief being inconvenient to reach for, and went out again to get on with the delivery of his checks. The air bit cold and hard and a few flakes of snow formed near him. A train struck by and left a quiver in the frames and a bristling icy hiss over the rails.

Crossing the street, he descended a flight of board steps into a basement grocery, setting off a little bell. It was a dark, long store and it caught you with its stinks of smoked meat, soap, dried peaches, and fish. There was a fire wrinkling and flapping in the little stove, and the proprietor was waiting, an Italian with a long, hollow face and stubborn bristles. He kept his hands warm under his apron.

No, he didn't know Green. You knew people, but not names. The same man might not have the same name twice. The police didn't know, either, and mostly didn't care. When somebody was shot or knifed they took the body away and didn't look for the murderer. In the first place, nobody would tell them anything. So they made up a name for the coroner and called it quits. And in the second place, they didn't give a goddam anyhow. But they couldn't get to the bottom of a thing even if they wanted to. Nobody would get to know even a tenth of what went on among these people. They stabbed and stole, they did every crime and abomination you ever heard of, men and men, women and women, parents and children, worse than the animals. They carried on their own way, and the horrors passed off like a smoke. There was never anything like it in the history of the whole world.

It was a long speech, deepening with every word in its fantasy and passion and becoming increasingly senseless and terrible; a swarm amassed by suggestion and invention, a huge, hugging, despairing knot, a human wheel of heads, legs, bellies, arms, rolling through his shop.

Grebe felt that he must interrupt him. He said sharply, "What are you talking about! All I asked was whether you knew this man."

"That isn't even the half of it. I been here six years. You probably don't want to believe this. But suppose it's true?"

"All the same," said Grebe, "there must be a way to find a person."

The Italian's close-spaced eyes had been queerly concentrated, as were his muscles, while he leaned across the counter trying to convince Grebe. Now he gave up the effort and sat down on his stool. "Oh — I suppose. Once in a while. But I been telling you, even the cops don't get anywhere."

"They're always after somebody. It's not the same thing."

"Well, keep trying if you want. I can't help you."

But he didn't keep trying. He had no more time to spend on Green. He slipped Green's check to the back of the block. The next name on the list was FIELD, WINSTON.

He found the back-yard bungalow without the least trouble; it shared a lot with another house, a few feet of yard between. Grebe knew these two-shack arrangements. They had been built in vast numbers in the days before the swamps were filled and the streets raised, and they were all the same — a boardwalk along the fence, well under street level, three or four ball-headed posts for clotheslines, greening wood, dead shingles, and a long, long flight of stairs to the rear door.

A twelve-year-old boy let him into the kitchen, and there the old man was, sitting by the table in a wheel chair.

"Oh, it's d'government man," he said to the boy when Grebe drew out his checks. "Go bring me my box of papers." He cleared a space on the table.

"Oh, you don't have to go to all that trouble," said Grebe. But Field laid out his papers: Social Security card, relief certification, letters from the state hospital in Manteno, and a naval discharge dated San Diego, 1920.

"That's plenty," Grebe said. "Just sign."

"You got to know who I am," the old man said. "You're from the government. It's not your check, it's a government check and you got no business to hand it over till everything is proved."

He loved the ceremony of it, and Grebe made no more objections. Field emptied his box and finished out the circle of cards and letters.

"There's everything I done and been. Just the death certificate and they can close book on me." He said this with a certain happy pride and magnificence. Still he did not sign; he merely held the little pen upright on the golden-green corduroy of his thigh. Grebe did not hurry him. He felt the old man's hunger for conversation.

"I got to get better coal," he said. "I send my little gran'son to the yard with my order and they fill his wagon with screening.[12] The stove ain't made for it. It fall through the grate. The order says Franklin County egg-size coal."

"I'll report it and see what can be done."

"Nothing can be done, I expect. You know and I know. There ain't no little ways to make things better, and the only big thing is money. That's the only sunbeams, money. Nothing is black where it shines, and the only place you see black is where it ain't shining. What we colored have to have is our own rich. There ain't no other way."

Grebe sat, his reddened forehead bridged levelly by his close-cut hair and his cheeks lowered in the wings of his collar — the caked fire shone hard within the isinglass and iron frames but the room was not comfortable — sat and listened while the old man unfolded his scheme. This was to create one Negro millionaire a month by subscription. One clever, good-hearted young fellow elected every month would sign a contract to use the money to start a business employing Negroes. This would be advertised by chain letters and word of mouth, and every Negro wage-earner would contribute a dollar a month. Within five years there would be sixty millionaires.

"That'll fetch respect," he said with a throat-stopped sound that came out like a foreign syllable. "You got to take and organize all the money that gets thrown away on the policy wheel and horse race. As long as they can take it away from you, they got no respect for you. Money, that's d' sun of human kind!" Field was a Negro of mixed blood, perhaps Cherokee, or Natchez; his skin was reddish. And he sounded, speaking about a golden sun in this dark room, and looked, shaggy and slab-headed, with the mingled blood of his face and broad lips, the little pen still upright in his hand, like one of the underground kings of mythology, old judge Minos[13] himself.

And now he accepted the check and signed. Not to soil the slip, he held it down with his knuckles. The table budged and creaked, the center of the gloomy, heathen midden of the kitchen covered with bread, meat, and cans, and the scramble of papers.

"Don't you think my scheme'd work?"

---

[12] Lumps of coal so small they fall through the screen — unsuitable for use where coal must be burnt on an ordinary grate.

[13] According to legend, Minos, lawgiver and King of Crete, was, after his death, made supreme judge in the lower world.

"It's worth thinking about. Something ought to be done, I agree."

"It'll work if people will do it. That's all. That's the only thing, any time. When they understand it in the same way, all of them."

"That's true," said Grebe, rising. His glance met the old man's.

"I know you got to go," he said. "Well, God bless you, boy, you ain't been sly with me. I can tell it in a minute."

He went back through the buried yard. Someone nursed a candle in a shed, where a man unloaded kindling wood from a sprawl-wheeled baby buggy and two voices carried on a high conversation. As he came up the sheltered passage he heard the hard boost of the wind in the branches and against the house fronts, and then, reaching the sidewalk, he saw the needle-eye red of cable towers in the open icy height hundreds of feet above the river and the factories — those keen points. From here, his view was unobstructed all the way to the South Branch and its timber banks, and the cranes beside the water. Rebuilt after the Great Fire[14] this part of the city was, not fifty years later, in ruins again, factories boarded up, buildings deserted or fallen, gaps of prairie between. But it wasn't desolation that this made you feel, but rather a faltering of organization that set free a huge energy, an escaped, unattached, unregulated power from the giant raw place. Not only must people feel it but, it seemed to Grebe, they were compelled to match it. In their very bodies. He no less than others, he realized. Say that his parents had been servants in their time, whereas he was not supposed to be one. He thought that they had never done any service like this, which no one visible asked for, and probably flesh and blood could not even perform. Nor could anyone show why it should be performed; or see where the performance would lead. That did not mean that he wanted to be released from it, he realized with a grimly pensive face. On the contrary. He had something to do. To be compelled to feel this energy and yet have no task to do — that was horrible; that was suffering; he knew what that was. It was now quitting time. Six o'clock. He could go home if he liked, to his room, that is, to wash in hot water, to pour a drink, lie down on his quilt, read the paper, eat some liver paste on crackers before going out to dinner. But to think of this actually made him feel a little sick, as though he had swallowed hard air. He had six checks left, and he was determined to deliver at least one of these: Mr. Green's check.

So he started again. He had four or five dark blocks to go, past open lots, condemned houses, old foundations, closed schools, black churches, mounds, and he reflected that there must be many people alive who had once seen the neighborhood rebuilt and new. Now there was a second layer of ruins; centuries of history accomplished through human massing. Numbers had given the place forced growth; enormous numbers had also broken it down. Objects once so new, so concrete that it could never have occurred to anyone they stood for other things, had crumbled. Therefore, reflected Grebe, the secret of them was out. It was that they stood for themselves by agreement, and were natural and not unnatural by agreement, and when the things themselves collapsed the agreement became visible. What was it, otherwise, that kept cities from looking peculiar? Rome, that was almost permanent, did not give rise to thoughts like these. And was it abidingly real? But in Chicago, where the cycles were so fast and the familiar died out, and again rose changed, and died again in thirty years, you saw the common agreement or covenant, and you were forced to think about appearances and realities. (He remembered Raynor and he smiled. Raynor was a clever boy.) Once you had grasped this, a great many things became intelligible. For instance, why Mr. Field should conceive such a scheme. Of course, if people were to agree to create a

---

[14] In 1871.

millionaire, a real millionaire would come into existence. And if you wanted to know how Mr. Field was inspired to think of this, why, he had within sight of his kitchen window the chart, the very bones of a successful scheme — the El[15] with its blue and green confetti of signals. People consented to pay dimes and ride the crash-box cars, and so it was a success. Yet how absurd it looked; how little reality there was to start with. And yet Yerkes, the great financier who built it, had known that he could get people to agree to do it. Viewed as itself, what a scheme of a scheme it seemed, how close to an appearance. Then why wonder at Mr. Field's idea? He had grasped a principle. And then Grebe remembered, too, that Mr. Yerkes had established the Yerkes Observatory and endowed it with millions. Now how did the notion come to him in his New York museum of a palace or his Aegean-bound yacht to give money to astronomers? Was he awed perhaps by the success of his bizarre enterprise and therefore ready to spend money to find out where in the universe being and seeming were identical? Yes, he wanted to know what abides; and whether flesh is Bible-grass;[16] and he offered money to be burned in the fire of suns. Okay, then, Grebe thought further, these things exist because people consent to exist with them — we have got so far — and also there is a reality which doesn't depend on consent but within which consent is a game. But what about need, the need that keeps so many vast thousands in position? You tell me that, you *private* little gentleman and *decent* soul — he used these words against himself scornfully. Why is the consent given to misery? And why so painfully ugly? Because there is *something* that is dismal and permanently ugly? Here he sighed and gave it up, and thought it was enough for the present moment that he had a real check in his pocket for a Mr. Green who must be real beyond question. If only his neighbors didn't think they had to conceal him.

This time he stopped at the second floor. He struck a match and found a door. Presently a man answered his knock and Grebe had the check ready and showed it even before he began. "Does Tulliver Green live here? I'm from the relief."

The man narrowed the opening and spoke to someone at his back.

"Does he live here?"

"Uh-uh. No."

"Or anywhere in this building? He's a sick man and he can't come for his dough." He exhibited the check in the light, which was smoky — the air smelled of charred lard — and the man held off the brim of his cap to study it.

"Uh-uh. Never seen the name."

"There's nobody around here that uses crutches?"

He seemed to think, but it was Grebe's impression that he was simply waiting for a decent interval to pass.

"No, suh. Nobody I ever see."

"I've been looking for this man all afternoon," Grebe spoke out with sudden force, "and I'm going to have to carry this check back to the station. It seems strange not to be able to find a person to *give* him something when you're looking for him for a good reason. I suppose if I had bad news for him I'd find him quick enough."

There was a responsive motion in the other man's face. "That's right, I reckon."

"It almost doesn't do any good to have a name if you can't be found by it. It doesn't stand for anything. He might as well not have any," he went on, smiling. It was as much of a concession as he could make to his desire to laugh.

---

[15] The elevated railway in Chicago.

[16] The Book of Isaiah, 40:6, says, "All flesh is grass, and the goodliness thereof is as the flower of the field."

"Well, now, there's a little old knot-back man I see once in a while. He might be the one you lookin' for. Downstairs."

"Where? Right side or left? Which door?"

"I don't know which. Thin face little knot-back with a stick."

But no one answered at any of the doors on the first floor. He went to the end of the corridor, searching by matchlight, and found only a stairless exit to the yard, a drop of about six feet. But there was a bungalow near the alley, an old house like Mr. Field's. To jump was unsafe. He ran from the front door, through the underground passage and into the yard. The place was occupied. There was a light through the curtains, upstairs. The name on the ticket under the broken, scoopshaped mailbox was Green! He exultantly rang the bell and pressed against the locked door. Then the lock clicked faintly and a long staircase opened before him. Someone was slowly coming down — a woman. He had the impression in the weak light that she was shaping her hair as she came, making herself presentable, for he saw her arms raised. But it was for support that they were raised; she was feeling her way downward, down the walls, stumbling. Next he wondered about the pressure of her feet on the treads; she did not seem to be wearing shoes. And it was a freezing stairway. His ring had got her out of bed, perhaps, and she had forgotten to put them on. And then he saw that she was not only shoeless but naked; she was entirely naked, climbing down while she talked to herself, a heavy woman, naked and drunk. She blundered into him. The contact of her breasts, though they touched only his coat, made him go back against the door with a blind shock. See what he had tracked down, in his hunting game!

The woman was saying to herself, furious with insult, "So I cain't ——k, huh? I'll show that son-of-a-bitch kin I, cain't I."

What should he do now? Grebe asked himself. Why, he should go. He should turn away and go. He couldn't talk to this woman. He couldn't keep her standing naked in the cold. But when he tried he found himself unable to turn away.

He said, "Is this where Mr. Green lives?"

But she was still talking to herself and did not hear him.

"Is this Mr. Green's house?"

At last she turned her furious drunken glance on him. "What do you want?"

Again her eyes wandered from him; there was a dot of blood in their enraged brilliance. He wondered why she didn't feel the cold.

"I'm from the relief."

"Awright, what?"

"I've got a check for Tulliver Green."

This time she heard him and put out her hand.

"No, no, for *Mr.* Green. He's got to sign," he said. How was he going to get Green's signature tonight!

"I'll take it. He cain't."

He desperately shook his head, thinking of Mr. Field's precautions about identification. "I can't let you have it. It's for him. Are you Mrs. Green?"

"Maybe I is, and maybe I ain't. Who want to know?"

"Is he upstairs?"

"Awright. Take it up yourself, you goddam fool."

Sure, he was a goddamned fool. Of course he could not go up because Green would probably be drunk and naked, too. And perhaps he would appear on the landing soon. He looked eagerly upward. Under the light was a high narrow brown wall. Empty! It remained empty!

"Hell with you, then!" he heard her cry. To deliver a check for coal and clothes, he was keeping her in the cold. She did not feel it, but his face was burning with frost and self-ridicule. He backed away from her.

"I'll come tomorrow, tell him."

"Ah, hell with you. Don' never come. What you doin' here in the nighttime? Don' come back." She yelled so that he saw the breadth of her tongue. She stood astride in the long cold box of the hall and held on to the banister and the wall. The bungalow itself was shaped something like a box, a clumsy, high box pointing into the freezing air with its sharp, wintry lights.

"If you are Mrs. Green, I'll give you the check," he said, changing his mind.

"Give here, then." She took it, took the pen offered with it in her left hand, and tried to sign the receipt on the wall. He looked around, almost as though to see whether his madness was being observed, and came near believing that someone was standing on a mountain of used tires in the auto-junking shop next door.

"But are you Mrs. Green?" he now thought to ask. But she was already climbing the stairs with the check, and it was too late, if he had made an error, if he was now in trouble, to undo the thing. But he wasn't going to worry about it. Though she might not be Mrs. Green, he was convinced that Mr. Green was upstairs. Whoever she was, the woman stood for Green, whom he was not to see this time. Well, you silly bastard, he said to himself, so you think you found him. So what? Maybe you really did find him — what of it? But it was important that there was a real Mr. Green whom they could not keep him from reaching because he seemed to come as an emissary from hostile appearances. And though the self-ridicule was slow to diminish, and his face still blazed with it, he had, nevertheless, a feeling of elation, too. "For after all," he said, "he *could* be found!"

QUESTIONS

1. Is the epigraph a commentary on the story, or does it function only to set a tone?

2. George Grebe is described in terms of negatives — "he didn't look much like a hunter," "slender without being tall," "not so mild as he looked," and so on. What is the effect of this method?

3. "But you'll find the closer you come to your man the less people will tell you." Does this strike you as a valid insight?

4. Is Grebe an effective researcher? Why is it so important that he find Mr. Green?

5. By what means does Bellow establish a strong sense of place in this story? Does the setting affect action and character here?

6. Do you think Mr. Green exists? Why is George Grebe so certain that he has found his man?

7. How does the ending strike you emotionally? Can you characterize it as hopeful, pessimistic, or neutral?

8. Most of the characters are distinguished by strong attitudes. Are they meant to represent a microcosm? Does their composite character tell you anything about Bellow's view of life?

CARSON McCULLERS

A Tree, a Rock, a Cloud

It was raining that morning, and still very dark. When the boy reached the streetcar café he had almost finished his route and he went in for a cup of coffee. The place was an all-night café owned by a bitter and stingy man called Leo. After the raw, empty street, the café seemed friendly and bright: along the counter there were a couple of soldiers, three spinners from the cotton mill, and in a corner a man who sat hunched over with his nose and half his face down in a beer mug. The boy wore a helmet such as aviators wear. When he went into the café he unbuckled the chin strap and raised the right flap up over his pink little ear; often as he drank his coffee someone would speak to him in a friendly way. But this morning Leo did not look into his face and none of the men were talking. He paid and was leaving the café when a voice called out to him:

"Son! Hey Son!"

He turned back and the man in the corner was crooking his finger and nodding to him. He had brought his face out of the beer mug and he seemed suddenly very happy. The man was long and pale, with a big nose and faded orange hair.

"Hey Son!"

The boy went toward him. He was an undersized boy of about twelve, with one shoulder drawn higher than the other because of the weight of the paper sack. His face was shallow, freckled, and his eyes were round child eyes.

"Yeah Mister?"

The man laid one hand on the paper boy's shoulders, then grasped the boy's chin and turned his face slowly from one side to the other. The boy shrank back uneasily.

"Say! What's the big idea?"

The boy's voice was shrill; inside the café it was suddenly very quiet.

The man said slowly. "I love you."

All along the counter the men laughed. The boy, who had scowled and sidled away, did not know what to do. He looked over the counter at Leo, and Leo watched him with a weary, brittle jeer. The boy tried to laugh also. But the man was serious and sad.

"I did not mean to tease you, Son," he said. "Sit down and have a beer with me. There is something I have to explain."

Cautiously, out of the corner of his eye, the paper boy questioned the men along the counter to see what he should do. But they had gone back to their beer or their breakfast and did not notice him. Leo put a cup of coffee on the counter and a little jug of cream.

"He is a minor," Leo said.

The paper boy slid himself up onto the stool. His ear beneath the upturned flap of the helmet was very small and red. The man was nodding at him soberly. "It is important," he said. Then he reached in his hip pocket and brought out something which he held up in the palm of his hand for the boy to see.

"Look very carefully," he said.

The boy stared, but there was nothing to look at very carefully. The man held in his big, grimy palm a photograph. It was the face of a woman, but blurred, so that only the hat and the dress she was wearing stood out clearly.

"See?" the man asked.

The boy nodded and the man placed another picture in his palm. The woman was standing on a beach in a bathing suit. The suit made her stomach very big, and that was the main thing you noticed.

"Got a good look?" He leaned over closer and finally asked: "You ever seen her before?"

The boy sat motionless, staring slantwise at the man. "Not so I know of."

"Very well." The man blew on the photographs and put them back into his pocket. "That was my wife."

"Dead?" the boy asked.

Slowly the man shook his head. He pursed his lips as though about to whistle and answered in a long-drawn way: "Nuuu — " he said. "I will explain."

The beer on the counter before the man was in a large brown mug. He did not pick it up to drink. Instead he bent down and, putting his face over the rim, he rested there for a moment. Then with both hands he tilted the mug and sipped.

"Some night you'll go to sleep with your big nose in a mug and drown," said Leo. "Prominent transient drowns in beer. That would be a cute death."

The paper boy tried to signal to Leo. While the man was not looking he screwed up his face and worked his mouth to question soundlessly: "Drunk?" But Leo only raised his eyebrows and turned away to put some pink strips of bacon on the grill. The man pushed the mug away from him, straightened himself, and folded his loose crooked hands on the counter. His face was sad as he looked at the paper boy. He did not blink, but from time to time the lids closed down with delicate gravity over his pale green eyes. It was nearing dawn and the boy shifted the weight of the paper sack.

"I am talking about love," the man said. "With me it is a science."

The boy half slid down from the stool. But the man raised his forefinger, and there was something about him that held the boy and would not let him go away.

"Twelve years ago I married the woman in the photograph. She was my wife for one year, nine months, three days, and two nights. I loved her. Yes. ..." He tightened his blurred, rambling voice and said again: "I loved her. I thought also that she loved me. I was a railroad engineer. She had all home comforts and luxuries. It never crept into my brain that she was not satisfied. But do you know what happened?"

"Mgneeow!" said Leo.

The man did not take his eyes from the boy's face. "She left me. I came in one night and the house was empty and she was gone. She left me."

"With a fellow?" the boy asked.

Gently the man placed his palm down on the counter. "Why naturally, Son. A woman does not run off like that alone."

The café was quiet, the soft rain black and endless in the street outside. Leo pressed down the frying bacon with the prongs of his long fork. "So you have been chasing the floozie for eleven years. You frazzled old rascal!"

For the first time the man glanced at Leo. "Please don't be vulgar. Besides, I was not speaking to you." He turned back to the boy and said in a trusting and secretive undertone. "Let's not pay any attention to him. O.K.?"

The paper boy nodded doubtfully.

"It was like this," the man continued. "I am a person who feels many things. All my life one thing after another has impressed me. Moonlight. The leg of a pretty girl. One thing after another. But the point is that when I had enjoyed anything there was a peculiar sensation as though it was laying around loose in me. Nothing seemed to finish itself up or fit in with the other things. Women? I had my portion of them. The same. Afterwards laying around loose in me. I was a man who had never loved."

Very slowly he closed his eyelids, and the gesture was like a curtain drawn at the end of a scene in a play. When he spoke again his voice was excited and the words came fast — the lobes of his large, loose ears seemed to tremble.

"Then I met this woman. I was fifty-one years old and she always said she was thirty. I met her at a filling station and we were married within three days. And do you know what it was like? I just can't tell you. All I had ever felt was gathered together around this woman. Nothing lay around loose in me any more but was finished up by her."

The man stopped suddenly and stroked his long nose. His voice sank down to a steady and reproachful undertone: "I'm not explaining this right. What happened was this. There were these beautiful feelings and loose little pleasures inside me. And this woman was something like an assembly line for my soul. I run these little pieces of myself through her and I come out complete. Now do you follow me?"

"What was her name?" the boy asked.

"Oh," he said. "I called her Dodo. But that is immaterial."

"Did you try to make her come back?"

The man did not seem to hear. "Under the circumstances you can imagine how I felt when she left me."

Leo took the bacon from the grill and folded two strips of it between a bun. He had a gray face, with slitted eyes, and a pinched nose saddled by faint blue shadows. One of the mill workers signaled for more coffee and Leo poured it. He did not give refills on coffee free. The spinner ate breakfast there every morning, but the better Leo knew his customers the stingier he treated them. He nibbled his own bun as though he grudged it to himself.

"And you never got hold of her again?"

The boy did not know what to think of the man, and his child's face was uncertain with mingled curiosity and doubt. He was new on the paper route; it was still strange to him to be out in the town in the black, queer early morning.

"Yes," the man said. "I took a number of steps to get her back. I went around trying to locate her. I went to Tulsa where she had folks. And to Mobile. I went to every town she had ever mentioned to me, and I hunted down every man she had formerly been connected with. Tulsa, Atlanta, Chicago, Cheehaw, Memphis. ... For the better part of two years I chased around the country trying to lay hold of her."

"But the pair of them had vanished from the face of the earth!" said Leo.

"Don't listen to him," the man said confidentially. "And also just forget those two years. They are not important. What matters is that around the third year a curious thing begun to happen to me."

"What?" the boy asked.

The man leaned down and tilted his mug to take a sip of beer. But as he hovered over the mug his nostrils fluttered slightly; he sniffed the staleness of the beer and did not drink. "Love is a curious thing to begin with. At first I thought only of getting her back. It was a kind of mania. But then as time went on I tried to remember her. But do you know what happened?"

"No," the boy said.

"When I laid myself down on a bed and tried to think about her my mind became a blank. I couldn't see her. I would take out her pictures and look. No good. Nothing doing. A blank. Can you imagine it?"

"Say Mac!" Leo called down the counter. "Can you imagine this bozo's mind a blank!"

Slowly, as though fanning away flies, the man waved his hand. His green eyes were concentrated and fixed on the shallow little face of the paper boy.

"But a sudden piece of glass on a sidewalk. Or a nickel tune in a music box. A shadow on a wall at night. And I would remember. It might happen in a street and I would cry or bang my head against a lamppost. You follow me?"

"A piece of glass ..." the boy said.

"Anything. I would walk around and I had no power of how and when to remember her. You think you can put up a kind of shield. But remembering don't come to a man face forward — it corners around sideways. I was at the mercy of everything I saw and heard. Suddenly instead of me combing the countryside to find her she began to chase me around in my very soul. *She* chasing *me*, mind you! And in my soul."

The boy asked finally: "What part of the country were you in then?"

"Ooh," the man groaned. "I was a sick mortal. It was like smallpox. I confess, Son, that I boozed. I fornicated. I committed any sin that suddenly appealed to me. I am loath to confess it but I will do so. When I recall that period it is all curdled in my mind, it was so terrible."

The man leaned his head down and tapped his forehead on the counter. For a few seconds he stayed bowed over in this position, the back of his stringy neck covered with orange furze, his hands with their long warped fingers held palm to palm in an attitude of prayer. Then the man straightened himself; he was smiling and suddenly his face was bright and tremulous and old.

"It was in the fifth year that it happened," he said. "And with it I started my science."

Leo's mouth jerked with a pale, quick grin. "Well none of we boys are getting any younger," he said. Then with sudden anger he balled up a dishcloth he was holding and threw it down hard on the floor. "You draggle-tailed old Romeo!"

"What happened?" the boy asked.

The old man's voice was high and clear: "Peace," he answered.

"Huh?"

"It is hard to explain scientifically, Son," he said. "I guess the logical explanation is that she and I had fled around from each other for so long that finally we just got tangled up together and lay down and quit. Peace. A queer and beautiful blankness. It was spring in Portland and the rain came every afternoon. All evening I just stayed there on my bed in the dark. And that is how the science come to me."

The windows in the streetcar were pale blue with light. The two soldiers paid for their beers and opened the door — one of the soldiers combed his hair and wiped off his muddy puttees before they went outside. The three mill workers bent silently over their breakfasts. Leo's clock was ticking on the wall.

"It is this. And listen carefully. I meditated on love and reasoned it out. I realized what is wrong with us. Men fall in love for the first time. And what do they fall in love with?"

The boy's soft mouth was partly open and he did not answer.

"A woman," the old man said, "Without science, with nothing to go by, they undertake the most dangerous and sacred experience in God's earth. They fall in love with a woman. Is that correct, Son?"

"They start at the wrong end of love. They begin at the climax. Can you wonder it is so miserable? Do you know how men should love?"

The old man reached over and grasped the boy by the collar of his leather jacket. He gave him a gentle little shake and his green eyes gazed down unblinking and grave.

"Son, do you know how love should be begun?"

The boy sat small and listening and still. Slowly he shook his head. The old man leaned closer and whispered:

"A tree. A rock. A cloud."

It was still raining outside in the street: a mild, gray, endless rain. The mill whistle blew for the six o'clock shift and the three spinners paid and went away. There was no one in the café but Leo, the old man, and the little paper boy.

"The weather was like this in Portland," he said. "At the time my science was begun. I meditated and I started very cautious. I would pick up something from the street and take it home with me. I bought a goldfish and I concentrated on the goldfish and I loved it. I graduated from one thing to another. Day by day I was getting this technique. On the road from Portland to San Diego —— "

"Aw shut up!" screamed Leo suddenly. "Shut up! Shut up!"

The old man still held the collar of the boy's jacket; he was trembling and his face was earnest and bright and wild. "For six years now I have gone around by myself and built up my science. And now I am a master. Son. I can love anything. No longer do I have to think about it even. I see a street full of people and a beautiful light comes in me. I watch a bird in the sky. Or I meet a traveler on the road. Everything, Son. And anybody. All stranger and all loved! Do you realize what a science like mine can mean?"

The boy held himself stiffly, his hands curled tight around the counter edge. Finally he asked: "Did you ever really find that lady?"

"What? What say, Son?"

"I mean," the boy asked timidly. "Have you fallen in love with a woman again?"

The old man loosened his grasp on the boy's collar. He turned away and for the first time his green eyes had a vague and scattered look. He lifted the mug from the counter, drank down the yellow beer. His head was shaking slowly from side to side. Then finally he answered: "No, Son. You see that is the last step in my science. I go cautious. And I am not quite ready yet."

"Well!" said Leo. "Well well well!"

The old man stood in the open doorway. "Remember," he said. Framed there in the gray damp light of the early morning he looked shrunken and seedy and frail. But his smile was bright. "Remember I love you," he said with a last nod. And the door closed quietly behind him.

The boy did not speak for a long time. He pulled down the bangs on his forehead and slid his grimy little forefinger around the rim of his empty cup. Then without looking at Leo he finally asked:

"Was he drunk?"

"No," said Leo shortly.

The boy raised his clear voice higher. "Then was he a dope fiend?"

"No."

The boy looked up at Leo, and his flat little face was desperate, his voice ₋gent and shrill. "Was he crazy? Do you think he was a lunatic?" The paper boy's voice dropped suddenly with doubt. "Leo? Or not?"

But Leo would not answer him. Leo had run a night café for fourteen years, and he held himself to be a critic of craziness. There were the town characters and also the transients who roamed in from the night. He knew the manias of all of them. But he did not want to satisfy the questions of the waiting child. He tightened his pale face and was silent.

So the boy pulled down the right flap of his helmet and as he turned to leave he made the only comment that seemed safe to him, the only remark that could not be laughed down and despised:

"He sure has done a lot of traveling."

QUESTIONS

1. What is the tone of the opening paragraph? What details contribute to it? How does this tone fit what is to follow?

2. What is the attitude of the café's "regulars" toward the old man? toward the boy?

3. "With me it [love] is a science," says the old man. Is he exaggerating? What does his "science" consist of?

4. Does anything distinguish the old man from that stock character of fiction, the down-on-his-luck bum? Contrast this man with Soapy in "The Cop and the Anthem."

5. What is the function of Leo's running commentary? Why is he so affected by the old man's story?

ARTHUR C. CLARKE =====

The Sentinel

The next time you see the full Moon high in the south, look carefully at its right-hand edge and let your eye travel upward along the curve of the disk. Round about two o'clock you will notice a small, dark oval: anyone with normal eyesight can find it quite easily. It is the great walled plain, one of the finest on the Moon, known as the Mare Crisium — the Sea of Crises. Three hundred miles in diameter, and almost completely surrounded by a ring of magnificent mountains, it had never been explored until we entered it in the late summer of 1996.

Our expedition was a large one. We had two heavy freighters which had flown our supplies and equipment from the main lunar base in the Mare Serenitatis, five hundred miles away. There were also three small rockets which were intended for short-range transport over regions which our surface vehicles couldn't cross. Luckily, most of the Mare Crisium is very flat. There are none of the great crevasses so common and so dangerous elsewhere, and very few craters or mountains of any size. As far as we could tell, our powerful caterpillar tractors would have no difficulty in taking us wherever we wished to go.

I was geologist — or selenologist,[1] if you want to be pedantic — in charge of the group exploring the southern region of the Mare. We had crossed a hundred miles of it in a week, skirting the foothills of the mountains along the shore of what was once the ancient sea, some 2housand million years before. When life was beginning on Earth, it was already dying here. The waters were retreating down the flanks of those stupendous cliffs, retreating into the empty heart of the Moon. Over the land which we were crossing, the tideless ocean had once been half a mile deep, and now the only trace of moisture was the hoarfrost one could sometimes find in caves which the searing sunlight never penetrated.

We had begun our journey early in the slow lunar dawn, and still had almost a week of Earth time before nightfall. Half a dozen times a day we would leave our vehicle and go outside in the space suits to hunt for interesting minerals, or to place markers for the guidance of future travelers. It was an uneventful routine. There is nothing hazardous or even particularly exciting about lunar exploration. We could live comfortably for a month in

---

[1] A scientist whose special study is the moon.

our pressurized tractors, and if we ran into trouble we could always radio for help and sit tight until one of the spaceships came to our rescue.

I said just now that there was nothing exciting about lunar exploration, but of course that isn't true. One could never grow tired of those incredible mountains, so much more rugged than the gentle hills of Earth. We never knew, as we rounded the capes and promontories of that vanished sea, what new splendors would be revealed to us. The whole southern curve of the Mare Crisium is a vast delta where a score of rivers once found their way into the ocean, fed perhaps by the torrential rains that must have lashed the mountains in the brief volcanic age when the Moon was young. Each of these ancient valleys was an invitation, challenging us to climb into the unknown uplands beyond. But we had a hundred miles still to cover, and could only look longingly at the heights which others must scale.

We kept Earth time aboard the tractor, and precisely at 2200 hours the final radio message would be sent out to Base and we would close down for the day. Outside, the rocks would still be burning beneath the almost vertical sun, but to us it was night until we awoke again eight hours later. Then one of us would prepare breakfast, there would be a great buzzing of electric razors, and someone would switch on the shortwave radio from Earth. Indeed, when the smell of frying sausages began to fill the cabin, it was sometimes hard to believe that we were not back on our own world — everything was so normal and homely, apart from the feeling of decreased weight and the unnatural slowness with which objects fell.

It was my turn to prepare breakfast in the corner of the main cabin that served as a galley. I can remember that moment quite vividly after all these years, for the radio had just played one of my favorite melodies, the old Welsh air "David of the White Rock." Our driver was already outside in his space suit, inspecting our caterpillar treads. My assistant, Louis Garnett, was up forward in the control position, making some belated entries in yesterday's log.

As I stood by the frying pan waiting, like any terrestrial housewife, for the sausages to brown, I let my gaze wander idly over the mountain walls which covered the whole of the southern horizon, marching out of sight to east and west below the curve of the Moon. They seemed only a mile or two from the tractor, but I knew that the nearest was twenty miles away. On the Moon, of course, there is no loss of detail with distance — none of that almost imperceptible haziness which softens and sometimes transfigures all far-off things on Earth.

Those mountains were ten thousand feet high, and they climbed steeply out of the plain as if ages ago some subterranean eruption had smashed them skyward through the molten crust. The base of even the nearest was hidden from sight by the steeply curving surface of the plain, for the Moon is a very little world, and from where I was standing the horizon was only two miles away.

I lifted my eyes toward the peaks which no man had ever climbed, the peaks which, before the coming of terrestrial life, had watched the retreating oceans sink sullenly into their graves, taking with them the hope and the morning promise of a world. The sunlight was beating against those ramparts with a glare that hurt the eyes, yet only a little way above them the stars were shining steadily in a sky blacker than a winter midnight on Earth.

I was turning away when my eye caught a metallic glitter high on the ridge of a great promontory thrusting out into the sea thirty miles to the west. It was a dimensionless point of light, as if a star had been clawed from the sky by one of those cruel peaks, and I imagined that some smooth rock surface was catching the sunlight and heliographing it straight into my eyes. Such things were not uncommon. When the Moon is in her second quarter, observers on Earth can sometimes see the great ranges in the Oceanus Procellarum burning with a blue-white iridescence as the sunlight flashes from their slopes and leaps again from world to world. But I was curious to know what kind of rock could be shining so brightly up there, and I climbed into the observation turret and swung our four-inch telescope round to the west.

I could see just enough to tantalize me. Clear and sharp in the field of vision, the mountain peaks seemed only half a mile away, but whatever was catching the sunlight was still too small to be resolved. Yet it seemed to have an elusive symmetry, and the summit upon which it rested was curiously flat. I stared for a long time at that glittering enigma, straining my eyes into space, until presently a smell of burning from the galley told me that our breakfast sausages had made their quarter-million-mile journey in vain.

All that morning we argued our way across the Mare Crisium while the western mountains reared higher in the sky. Even when we were out prospecting in the space suits, the discussion would continue over the radio. It was absolutely certain, my companions argued, that there had never been any form of intelligent life on the Moon. The only living things that had ever existed there were a few primitive plants and their slightly less degenerate ancestors. I knew that as well as anyone, but there are times when a scientist must not be afraid to make a fool of himself.

"Listen," I said at last, "I'm going up there, if only for my own peace of mind. That mountain's less than twelve thousand feet high — that's only two thousand under Earth gravity — and I can make the trip in twenty hours at the outside. I've always wanted to go up into those hills, anyway, and this gives me an excellent excuse."

"If you don't break your neck," said Garnett, "you'll be the laughingstock of the expedition when we get back to Base. That mountain will probably be called Wilson's Folly from now on."

"I won't break my neck," I said firmly. "Who was the first man to climb Pico and Helicon?"

"But weren't you rather younger in those days?" asked Louis gently.

"That," I said with great dignity, "is as good a reason as any for going."

We went to bed early that night, after driving the tractor to within half a mile of the promontory. Garnett was coming with me in the morning; he was a good climber, and had often been with me on such exploits before. Our driver was only too glad to be left in charge of the machine.

At first sight, those cliffs seemed completely unscalable, but to anyone with a good head for heights, climbing is easy on a world where all weights are only a sixth of their normal value. The real danger in lunar mountaineering lies in overconfidence; a six-hundred-foot drop on the Moon can kill you just as thoroughly as a hundred-foot fall on Earth.

We made our first halt on a wide ledge about four thousand feet above the plain. Climbing had not been very difficult, but my limbs were stiff with the unaccustomed effort, and I was glad of the rest. We could still see the tractor as a tiny metal insect far down at the foot of the cliff, and we reported our progress to the driver before starting on the next ascent.

Inside our suits it was comfortably cool, for the refrigeration units were fighting the fierce sun and carrying away the body heat of our exertions. We seldom spoke to each other, except to pass climbing instructions and to discuss our best plan of ascent. I do not know what Garnett was thinking, probably that this was the craziest goose chase he had ever embarked upon. I more than half agreed with him, but the joy of climbing, the knowledge that no man had ever gone this way before and the exhilaration of the steadily widening landscape gave me all the reward I needed.

I don't think I was particularly excited when I saw in front of us the wall of rock I had first inspected through the telescope from thirty miles away. It would level off about fifty feet above our heads, and there on the plateau would be the thing that had lured me over these barren wastes. It was, almost certainly, nothing more than a boulder splintered ages ago by a falling meteor, and with its cleavage planes still fresh and bright in this incorruptible, unchanging silence.

There were no handholds on the rock face, and we had to use a grapnel. My tired arms seemed to gain new strength as I swung the three-pronged metal anchor round my head and sent it sailing up toward the stars. The first time it broke loose and came falling slowly back when we pulled the rope. On the third attempt, the prongs gripped firmly and our combined weights could not shift it.

Garnett looked at me anxiously. I could tell that he wanted to go first, but I smiled back at him through the glass of my helmet and shook my head. Slowly, taking my time, I began the final ascent.

Even with my space suit, I weighed only forty pounds here, so I pulled myself up hand over hand without bothering to use my feet. At the rim I paused and waved to my companion; then I scrambled over the edge and stood upright, staring ahead of me.

You must understand that until this very moment I had been almost completely convinced that there could be nothing strange or unusual for me to find here. Almost, but not quite; it was that haunting doubt that had driven me forward. Well, it was a doubt no longer, but the haunting had scarcely begun.

I was standing on a plateau perhaps a hundred feet across. It had once been smooth — too smooth to be natural — but falling meteors had pitted and scored its surface through immeasurable eons. It had been leveled to support a glittering, roughly pyramidal structure, twice as high as a man, that was set in the rock like a gigantic many-faceted jewel.

Probably no emotion at all filled my mind in those first few seconds. Then I felt a great lifting of my heart, and a strange, inexpressible joy. For I loved the Moon, and now I knew that the creeping moss of Aristarchus and Eratosthenes[2] was not the only life she had brought forth in her youth. The old, discredited dream of the first explorers was true. There had, after all, been a lunar civilization — and I was the first to find it. That I had come perhaps a hundred million years too late did not distress me; it was enough to have come at all.

My mind was beginning to function normally, to analyze and to ask questions. Was this a building, a shrine — or something for which my language had no name? If a building, then why was it erected in so uniquely inaccessible a spot? I wondered if it might be a temple, and I could picture the adepts of some strange priesthood calling on their gods to preserve them as the life of the Moon ebbed with the dying oceans, and calling on their gods in vain.

I took a dozen steps forward to examine the thing more closely, but some sense of caution kept me from going too near. I knew a little of archaeology, and tried to guess the cultural level of the civilization that must have smoothed this mountain and raised the glittering mirror surfaces that still dazzled my eyes.

The Egyptians could have done it, I thought, if their workmen had possessed whatever strange materials these far more ancient architects had used. Because of the thing's smallness, it did not occur to me that I might be looking at the handiwork of a race more advanced than my own. The idea that the Moon had possessed intelligence at all was still almost too tremendous to grasp, and my pride would not let me take the final, humiliating plunge.

And then I noticed something that set the scalp crawling at the back of my neck — something so trivial and so innocent that many would never have noticed it at all. I have said that the plateau was scarred by meteors; it was also coated inches deep with the cosmic dust

---

2 Greek astronomers of the third century B.C.

that is always filtering down upon the surface of any world where there are no winds to disturb it. Yet the dust and the meteor scratches ended quite abruptly in a wide circle enclosing the little pyramid, as though an invisible wall was protecting it from the ravages of time and the slow but ceaseless bombardment from space.

There was someone shouting in my earphones, and I realized that Garnett had been calling me for some time. I walked unsteadily to the edge of the cliff and signaled him to join me, not trusting myself to speak. Then I went back toward that circle in the dust. I picked up a fragment of splintered rock and tossed it gently toward the shining enigma. If the pebble had vanished at that invisible barrier I should not have been surprised, but it seemed to hit a smooth, hemispherical surface and slide gently to the ground.

I knew then that I was looking at nothing that could be matched in the antiquity of my own race. This was not a building, but a machine, protecting itself with forces that had challenged Eternity. Those forces, whatever they might be, were still operating, and perhaps I had already come too close. I thought of all the radiations man had trapped and tamed in the past century. For all I knew, I might be as irrevocably doomed as if I had stepped into the deadly, silent aura of an unshielded atomic pile.

I remember turning then toward Garnett, who had joined me and was now standing motionless at my side. He seemed quite oblivious to me, so I did not disturb him but walked to the edge of the cliff in an effort to marshal my thoughts. There below me lay the Mare Crisium — Sea of Crises, indeed — strange and weird to most men, but reassuringly familiar to me. I lifted my eyes toward the crescent Earth, lying in her cradle of stars, and I wondered what her clouds had covered when these unknown builders had finished their work. Was it the steaming jungle of the Carboniferous, the bleak shoreline over which the first amphibians must crawl to conquer the land — or, earlier still, the long loneliness before the coming of life?

Do not ask me why I did not guess the truth sooner — the truth that seems so obvious now. In the first excitement of my discovery, I had assumed without question that this crystalline apparition had been built by some race belonging to the Moon's remote past, but suddenly, and with overwhelming force, the belief came to me that it was as alien to the Moon as I myself.

In twenty years we had found no trace of life but a few degenerate plants. No lunar civilization, whatever its doom, could have left but a single token of its existence.

I looked at the shining pyramid again, and the more remote it seemed from anything that had to do with the Moon. And suddenly I felt myself shaking with a foolish, hysterical laughter, brought on by excitement and overexertion: for I had imagined that the little pyramid was speaking to me and was saying: "Sorry, I'm a stranger here myself."

It has taken us twenty years to crack that invisible shield and to reach the machine inside those crystal walls. What we could not understand, we broke at last with the savage might of atomic power and now I have seen the fragments of the lovely, glittering thing I found up there on the mountain.

They are meaningless. The mechanisms — if indeed they are mechanisms — of the pyramid belong to a technology that lies far beyond our horizon, perhaps to the technology of paraphysical forces.

The mystery haunts us all the more now that the other planets have been reached and we know that only Earth has ever been the home of intelligent life in our Universe. Nor could any lost civilization of our own world have built that machine, for the thickness of the meteoric dust on the plateau has enabled us to measure its age. It was set there upon its mountain before life had emerged from the seas of Earth.

When our world was half its present age, *something* from the stars swept through the Solar System, left this token of its passage, and went again upon its way. Until we destroyed it, that machine was still fulfilling the purpose of its builders; and as to that purpose, here is my guess.

Nearly a hundred thousand million stars are turning in the circle of the Milky Way, and long ago other races on the worlds of other suns must have scaled and passed the heights that we have reached. Think of such civilizations, far back in time against the fading afterglow of Creation, masters of a Universe so young that life as yet had come only to a handful of worlds. Theirs would have been a loneliness we cannot imagine, the loneliness of gods looking out across infinity and finding none to share their thoughts.

They must have searched the star clusters as we have searched the planets. Everywhere there would be worlds, but they would be empty or peopled with crawling, mindless things. Such was our own Earth, the smoke of the great volcanoes still staining the skies, when that first ship of the peoples of the dawn came sliding in from the abyss beyond Pluto. It passed the frozen outer worlds, knowing that life could play no part in their destinies. It came to rest among the inner planets, warming themselves around the fire of the Sun and waiting for their stories to begin.

Those wanderers must have looked on Earth, circling safely in the narrow zone between fire and ice, and must have guessed that it was the favorite of the Sun's children. Here, in the distant future, would be intelligence; but there were countless stars before them still, and they might never come this way again.

So they left a sentinel, one of millions they have scattered throughout the Universe, watching over all worlds with the promise of life. It was a beacon that down the ages has been patiently signaling the fact that no one had discovered it.

Perhaps you understand now why that crystal pyramid was set upon the Moon instead of on the Earth. Its builders were not concerned with races still struggling up from savagery. They would be interested in our civilization only if we proved our fitness to survive — by crossing space and so escaping from the Earth, our cradle. That is the challenge that all intelligent races must meet, sooner or later. It is a double challenge, for it depends in turn upon the conquest of atomic energy and the last choice between life and death.

Once we had passed that crisis, it was only a matter of time before we found the pyramid and forced it open. Now its signals have ceased, and those whose duty it is will be turning their minds upon Earth. Perhaps they wish to help our infant civilization. But they must be very, very old, and the old are often insanely jealous of the young.

I can never look now at the Milky Way without wondering from which of those banked clouds of stars the emissaries are coming. If you will pardon so commonplace a simile, we have set off the fire alarm and have nothing to do but to wait.

I do not think we will have to wait for long.

QUESTIONS

1. The author takes some pains to establish a realistic, almost "homey" setting. Why does he do so?

2. Are Wilson and Garnett sufficiently distinguished from each other? How would you describe the differences?

3. The lunar landscape is similar to but not exactly like Earth's. Which details most underscore the differences? Can you discern Clarke's instincts as a natural teacher in these details? At what point does fact give way to fiction?

4. What detail of the "pyramidal structure" most startles Wilson? What does it tell him about those who set the pyramid on the moon? Why, according to Wilson, was it not set on the Earth?

5. Is Wilson's theory, his "guess," about the origin of the pyramid satisfying to you? How does it affect your response to the final sentence of "The Sentinel"?

DORIS LESSING

To Room Nineteen

This is a story, I suppose, about a failure in intelligence: the Rawlings' marriage was grounded in intelligence.

They were older when they married than most of their married friends: in their well-seasoned late twenties. Both had had a number of affairs, sweet rather than bitter; and when they fell in love — for they did fall in love — had known each other for some time. They joked that they had saved each other "for the real thing." That they had waited so long (but not too long) for this real thing was to them a proof of their sensible discrimination. A good many of their friends had married young, and now (they felt) probably regretted lost opportunities; while others, still unmarried, seemed to them arid, self-doubting, and likely to make desperate or romantic marriages.

Not only they, but others, felt they were well-matched: their friends' delight was an additional proof of their happiness. They had played the same roles, male and female, in this group or set, if such a wide, loosely connected, constantly changing constellation of people could be called a set. They had both become, by virtue of their moderation, their humour, and their abstinence from painful experience, people to whom others came for advice. They could be, and were, relied on. It was one of those cases of a man and a woman linking themselves whom no one else had ever thought of linking, probably because of their similarities. But then everyone exclaimed: Of course! How right! How was it we never thought of it before!

And so they married amid general rejoicing, and because of their foresight and their sense for what was probable, nothing was a surprise to them.

Both had well-paid jobs. Matthew was a subeditor on a large London newspaper, and Susan worked in an advertising firm. He was not the stuff of which editors or publicised journalists are made, but he was much more than "a subeditor," being one of the essential background people who in fact steady, inspire and make possible the people in the limelight. He was content with this position. Susan had a talent for commercial drawing. She was humorous about the advertisements she was responsible for, but she did not feel strongly about them one way or the other.

Both, before they married, had had pleasant flats, but they felt it unwise to base a marriage on either flat, because it might seem like a submission of personality on the part of the one whose flat it was not. They moved into a new flat in South Kensington on the clear understanding that when their marriage had settled down (a process they knew would not take long, and was in fact more a humorous concession to popular wisdom than what was due to themselves) they would buy a house and start a family.

And this is what happened. They lived in their charming flat for two years, giving parties and going to them, being a popular young married couple, and then Susan became pregnant, she gave up her job, and they bought a house in Richmond. It was typical of this couple that they had a son first, then a daughter, then twins, son and daughter. Everything right, appropriate, and what everyone would wish for, if they could choose. But people did feel these two had chosen; this balanced and sensible family was no more than what was due to them because of their infallible sense for *choosing* right.

And so they lived with their four children in their gardened house in Richmond and were happy. They had everything they had wanted and had planned for.

And yet ...

Well, even this was expected, that there must be a certain flatness. ...

Yes, yes, of course, it was natural they sometimes felt like this. Like what?

Their life seemed to be like a snake biting its tail. Matthew's job for the sake of Susan, children, house, and garden — which caravanserai needed a well-paid job to maintain it. And Susan's practical intelligence for the sake of Matthew, the children, the house and the garden — which unit would have collapsed in a week without her.

But there was no point about which either could say: "For the sake of *this* is all the rest." Children? But children can't be a centre of life and a reason for being. They can be a thousand things that are delightful, interesting, satisfying, but they can't be a wellspring to live from. Or they shouldn't be. Susan and Matthew knew that well enough.

Matthew's job? Ridiculous. It was an interesting job, but scarcely a reason for living. Matthew took pride in doing it well, but he could hardly be expected to be proud of the newspaper; the newspaper he read, *his* newspaper, was not the one he worked for.

Their love for each other? Well, that was nearest it. If this wasn't a centre, what was? Yes, it was around this point, their love, that the whole extraordinary structure revolved. For extraordinary it certainly was. Both Susan and Matthew had moments of thinking so, of looking in secret disbelief at this thing they had created: marriage, four children, big house, garden, charwomen, friends, cars ... and this *thing*, this entity, all of it had come into existence, been blown into being out of nowhere, because Susan loved Matthew and Matthew loved Susan. Extraordinary. So that was the central point, the wellspring.

And if one felt that it simply was not strong enough, important enough, to support it all, well whose fault was that? Certainly neither Susan's nor Matthew's. It was in the nature of things. And they sensibly blamed neither themselves nor each other.

On the contrary, they used their intelligence to preserve what they had created from a painful and explosive world: they looked around them, and took lessons. All around them, marriages collapsing, or breaking, or rubbing along (even worse, they felt). They must not make the same mistakes, they must not.

They had avoided the pitfall so many of their friends had fallen into — of buying a house in the country *for the sake of the children,* so that the husband became a weekend husband, a weekend father, and the wife always careful not to ask what went on in the town flat which they called (in joke) a bachelor flat. No, Matthew was a full-time husband, a full-time father, and at night, in the big married bed in the big married bedroom (which had an attractive view of the river), they lay beside each other talking and he told her about his day, and what he had done, and whom he had met; and she told him about her day (not as interesting, but that was not her fault), for both knew of the hidden resentments and deprivations of the woman who has lived her own life — and above all, has earned her own living — and is now dependent on a husband for outside interests and money.

Nor did Susan make the mistake of taking a job for the sake of her independence, which she might very well have done, since her old firm, missing her qualities of humour, balance, and sense, invited her often to go back. Children needed their mother to a certain age, that both parents knew and agreed on; and when these four healthy wisely brought up children were of the right age, Susan would work again, because she knew, and so did he, what happened to women of fifty at the height of their energy and ability, with grownup children who no longer needed their full devotion.

So here was this couple, testing their marriage, looking after it, treating it like a small boat full of helpless people in a very stormy sea. Well, of course, so it was. ... The storms of the world were bad, but not too close — which is not to say they were selfishly felt: Susan and Matthew were both well-informed and responsible people. And the inner storms and quicksands were understood and charted. So everything was all right. Everything was in order. Yes, things were under control.

So what did it matter if they felt dry, flat? People like themselves, fed on a hundred books (psychological, anthropological, sociological), could scarcely be unprepared for the dry, controlled wistfulness which is the distinguishing mark of the intelligent marriage. Two people, endowed with education, with discrimination, with judgement, linked together voluntarily from their will to be happy together and to be of use to others — one sees them everywhere, one knows them, one even is that thing oneself: sadness because so much is after all so little. These two, unsurprised, turned towards each other with even more courtesy and gentle love: this was life, that two people, no matter how carefully chosen, could not be everything to each other. In fact, even to say so, to think in such a way, was banal; they were ashamed to do it.

It was banal, too, when one night Matthew came home late and confessed he had been to a party, taken a girl home and slept with her. Susan forgave him, of course. Except that forgiveness is hardly the word. Understanding, yes. But if you understand something, you don't forgive it, you are the thing itself: forgiveness is for what you *don't* understand. Nor had he *confessed* — what sort of word is that?

The whole thing was not important. After all, years ago they had joked: Of course I'm not going to be faithful to you, no one can be faithful to one other person for a whole lifetime. (And there was the word "faithful" — stupid, all these words, stupid, belonging to a savage old world.) But the incident left both of them irritable. Strange, but they were both bad-tempered, annoyed. There was something unassimilable about it.

Making love splendidly after he had come home that night, both had felt that the idea that Myra Jenkins, a pretty girl met at a party, could be even relevant was ridiculous. They had loved each other for over a decade, would love each other for years more. Who, then, was Myra Jenkins?

Except, thought Susan, unaccountably bad-tempered, she was (is?) the first. In ten years. So either the ten years' fidelity was not important, or she isn't. (No, no, there is something wrong with this way of thinking, there must be.) But if she isn't important, presumably it wasn't important either when Matthew and I first went to bed with each other that afternoon whose delight even now (like a very long shadow at sundown) lays a long, wandlike finger over us. (Why did I say sundown?) Well, if what we felt that afternoon was not important, nothing is important, because if it hadn't been for what we felt, we wouldn't be Mr. and Mrs. Rawlings with four children, et cetera, et cetera. The whole thing is *absurd*

— for him to have come home and told me was absurd. For him not to have told me was absurd. For me to care or, for that matter, not to care, is absurd ... and who is Myra Jenkins? Why, no one at all.

There was only one thing to do, and of course these sensible people did it; they put the thing behind them, and consciously, knowing what they were doing, moved forward into a different phase of their marriage, giving thanks for past good fortune as they did so.

For it was inevitable that the handsome, blond, attractive, manly man, Matthew Rawlings, should be at times tempted (oh, what a word!) by the attractive girls at parties she could not attend because of the four children; and that sometimes he would succumb (a word even more repulsive, if possible) and that she, a goodlooking woman in the big well-tended garden at Richmond, would sometimes be pierced as by an arrow from the sky with bitterness. Except that bitterness was not in order, it was out of court. Did the casual girls touch the marriage? They did not. Rather it was they who knew defeat because of the handsome Matthew Rawlings' marriage body and soul to Susan Rawlings.

In that case why did Susan feel (though luckily not for longer than a few seconds at a time) as if life had become a desert, and that nothing mattered, and that her children were not her own?

Meanwhile her intelligence continued to assert that all was well. What if her Matthew did have an occasional sweet afternoon, the odd affair? For she knew quite well, except in her moments of aridity, that they were very happy, that the affairs were not important.

Perhaps that was the trouble? It was in the nature of things that the adventures and delights could no longer be hers, because of the four children and the big house that needed so much attention. But perhaps she was secretly wishing, and even knowing that she did, that the wildness and the beauty could be his. But he was married to her. She was married to him. They were married inextricably. And therefore the gods could not strike him with the real magic, not really. Well, was it Susan's fault that after he came home from an adventure he looked harassed rather than fulfilled? (In fact, that was how she knew he had been *unfaithful*, because of his sullen air, and his glances at her, similar to hers at him: What is it that I share with this person that shields all delight from me?) But none of it by anybody's fault. (But what did they feel ought to be somebody's fault?) Nobody's fault, nothing to be at fault, no one to blame, no one to offer or to take it ... and nothing wrong, either, except that Matthew never was really struck, as he wanted to be, by joy; and that Susan was more and more often threatened by emptiness. (It was usually in the garden that she was invaded by this feeling: she was coming to avoid the garden, unless the children or Matthew were with her.) There was no need to use the dramatic words "unfaithful," "forgive," and the rest: intelligence forbade them. Intelligence barred, too, quarrelling, sulking, anger, silences of withdrawal, accusations and tears. Above all, intelligence forbids tears.

A high price has to be paid for the happy marriage with the four healthy children in the large white gardened house.

And they were paying it, willingly, knowing what they were doing. When they lay side by side or breast to breast in the big civilised bedroom overlooking the wild sullied river, they laughed, often, for no particular reason; but they knew it was really because of these two small people, Susan and Matthew, supporting such an edifice on their intelligent love. The laugh comforted them; it saved them both, though from what, they did not know.

They were now both fortyish. The older children, boy and girl, were ten and eight, at school. The twins, six, were still at home. Susan did not have nurses or girls to help her: childhood is short; and she did not regret the hard work. Often enough she was bored, since small children can be boring; she was often very tired; but she regretted nothing. In another decade, she would turn herself back into being a woman with a life of her own.

Soon the twins would go to school, and they would be away from home from nine until four. These hours, so Susan saw it, would be the preparation for her own slow emancipation away from the role of hub-of-the-family into woman-with-her-own-life. She was already planning for the hours of freedom when all the children would be "off her hands." That was the phrase used by Matthew and by Susan and by their friends, for the moment when the youngest child went off to school. "They'll be off your hands, darling Susan, and you'll have time to yourself." So said Matthew, the intelligent husband, who had often enough commended and consoled Susan, standing by her in spirit during the years when her soul was not her own, as she said, but her children's.

What it amounted to was that Susan saw herself as she had been at twenty-eight, unmarried; and then again somewhere about fifty, blossoming from the root of what she had been twenty years before. As if the essential Susan were in abeyance, as if she were in cold storage. Matthew said something like this to Susan one night: and she agreed that it was true — she did feel something like that. What, then, was this essential Susan? She did not know. Put like that it sounded ridiculous, and she did not really feel it. Anyway, they had a long discussion about the whole thing before going off to sleep in each other's arms.

So the twins went off to their school, two bright affectionate children who had no problems about it, since their older brother and sister had trodden this path so successfully before them. And now Susan was going to be alone in the big house, every day of the school term, except for the daily woman who came in to clean.

It was now, for the first time in this marriage, that something happened which neither of them had foreseen.

This is what happened. She returned, at nine-thirty, from taking the twins to the school by car, looking forward to seven blissful hours of freedom. On the first morning she was simply restless, worrying about the twins "naturally enough" since this was their first day away at school. She was hardly able to contain herself until they came back. Which they did happily, excited by the world of school, looking forward to the next day. And the next day Susan took them, dropped them, came back, and found herself reluctant to enter her big and beautiful home because it was as if something was waiting for her there that she did not wish to confront. Sensibly, however, she parked the car in the garage, entered the house, spoke to Mrs. Parkes, the daily woman, about her duties, and went up to her bedroom. She was possessed by a fever which drove her out again, downstairs, into the kitchen, where Mrs. Parkes was making cake and did not need her, and into the garden. There she sat on a bench and tried to calm herself looking at trees, at a brown glimpse of the river. But she was filled with tension, like a panic: as if an enemy was in the garden with her. She spoke to herself severely, thus: All this is quite natural. First, I spent twelve years of my adult life working, *living my own life*. Then I married, and from the moment I became pregnant for the first time I signed myself over, so to speak, to other people. To the children. Not for one moment in twelve years have I been alone, had time to myself. So now I have to learn to be myself again. That's all.

And she went indoors to help Mrs. Parkes cook and clean, and found some sewing to do for the children. She kept herself occupied every day. At the end of the first term she understood she felt two contrary emotions. First: secret astonishment and dismay that during those weeks when the house was empty of children she had in fact been more occupied (had been careful to keep herself occupied) than ever she had been when the children were around her needing her continual attention. Second: that now she knew the house would be full of them, and for five weeks, she resented the fact she would never be alone. She was already looking back at those hours of sewing, cooking (but by herself) as at a lost freedom which would not be hers for five long weeks. And the two months of term which would succeed the five weeks stretched alluringly open to her — freedom. But what freedom — when in fact she had been so careful *not* to be free of small duties during the last weeks? She looked at herself, Susan Rawlings, sitting in a big chair by the window in the bedroom, sewing shirts or dresses, which she might just as well have bought. She saw herself making cakes for hours at a time in the big family kitchen: yet usually she bought cakes. What she saw was a woman alone, that was true, but she had not felt alone. For instance, Mrs. Parkes was always somewhere in the house. And she did not like being in the garden at all, because of the closeness there of the enemy — irritation, restlessness, emptiness, whatever it was — which keeping her hands occupied made less dangerous for some reason.

Susan did not tell Matthew of these thoughts. They were not sensible. She did not recognise herself in them. What should she say to her dear friend and husband, Matthew? "When I go into the garden, that is, if the children are not there, I feel as if there is an enemy there waiting to invade me." "What enemy, Susan darling?" "Well I don't know, really. ..." "Perhaps you should see a doctor?"

No, clearly this conversation should not take place. The holidays began and Susan welcomed them. Four children, lively, energetic, intelligent, demanding: she was never, not for a moment of her day, alone. If she was in a room, they would be in the next room, or waiting for her to do something for them; or it would soon be time for lunch or tea, or to take one of them to the dentist. Something to do: five weeks of it, thank goodness.

On the fourth day of these so welcome holidays, she found she was storming with anger at the twins; two shrinking beautiful children who (and this is what checked her) stood hand in hand looking at her with sheer dismayed disbelief. This was their calm mother, shouting at them. And for what? They had come to her with some game, some bit of nonsense. They looked at each other, moved closer for support, and went off hand in hand, leaving Susan holding on to the windowsill of the livingroom, breathing deep, feeling sick. She went to lie down, telling the older children she had a headache. She heard the boy Harry telling the little ones: "It's all right, Mother's got a headache." She heard that *It's all right* with pain.

That night she said to her husband: "Today I shouted at the twins, quite unfairly." She sounded miserable, and he said gently: "Well, what of it?"

"It's more of an adjustment than I thought, their going to school."

"But Susie, Susie darling. ..." For she was crouched weeping on the bed. He comforted her: "Susan, what is all this about? You shouted at them? What of it? If you shouted at them fifty times a day it wouldn't be more than the little devils deserve." But she wouldn't laugh. She wept. Soon he comforted her with his body. She became calm. Calm, she wondered what was wrong with her, and why she should mind so much that she might, just once, have behaved unjustly with the children. What did it matter? They had forgotten it all long ago: Mother had a headache and everything was all right.

It was a long time later that Susan understood that that night, when she had wept and Matthew had driven the misery out of her with his big solid body, was the last time, ever in their married life, that they had been — to use their mutual language — with each other. And even that was a lie, because she had not told him of her real fears at all.

The five weeks passed, and Susan was in control of herself, and good and kind, and she looked forward to the holidays with a mixture of fear and longing. She did not know what to expect. She took the twins off to school (the elder children took themselves to school) and she returned to the house determined to face the enemy wherever he was, in the house, or the garden or — where?

She was again restless, she was possessed by restlessness. She cooked and sewed and worked as before, day after day, while Mrs. Parkes remonstrated: "Mrs. Rawlings, what's the need for it? I can do that, it's what you pay me for."

And it was so irrational that she checked herself. She would put the car into the garage, go up to her bedroom, and sit, hands in her lap, forcing herself to be quiet. She listened to Mrs. Parkes moving around the house. She looked out into the garden and saw the branches shake the trees. She sat defeating the enemy, restlessness. Emptiness. She ought to be thinking about her life, about herself. But she did not. Or perhaps she could not. As soon as she forced her mind to think about Susan (for what else did she want to be alone for?), it skipped off to thoughts of butter or school clothes. Or it thought of Mrs. Parkes. She realised that she sat listening for the movements of the cleaning woman, following her every turn, bend, thought. She followed her in her mind from kitchen to bathroom, from table to oven, and it was as if the duster, the cleaning cloth, the saucepan, were in her own hand. She would hear herself saying: No, not like that, don't put that there. ... Yet she did not give a damn what Mrs. Parkes did, or if she did it at all. Yet she could not prevent herself from being conscious of her, every minute. Yes, this was what was wrong with her: she needed, when she was alone, to be really alone, with no one near. She could not endure the knowledge that in ten minutes or in half an hour Mrs. Parkes would call up the stairs: "Mrs. Rawlings, there's no silver polish. Madam, we're out of flour."

So she left the house and went to sit in the garden where she was screened from the house by trees. She waited for the demon to appear and claim her, but he did not.

She was keeping him off, because she had not, after all, come to an end of arranging herself.

She was planning how to be somewhere where Mrs. Parkes would not come after her with a cup of tea, or a demand to be allowed to telephone (always irritating, since Susan did not care who she telephoned or how often), or just a nice talk about something. Yes, she needed a place, or a state of affairs, where it would not be necessary to keep reminding herself: In ten minutes I must telephone Matthew about ... and at half past three I must leave early for the children because the car needs cleaning. And at ten o'clock tomorrow I must remember. ... She was possessed with resentment that the seven hours of freedom in every day (during weekdays in the school term) were not free, that never, not for one second, ever, was she free from the pressure of time, from having to remember this or that. She could never forget herself; never really let herself go into forgetfulness.

Resentment. It was poisoning her. (She looked at this emotion and thought it was absurd. Yet she felt it.) She was a prisoner. (She looked at this thought too, and it was no good telling herself it was a ridiculous one.) She must tell Matthew — but what? She was filled with emotions that were utterly ridiculous, that she despised, yet that nevertheless she was feeling so strongly she could not shake them off.

The school holidays came round, and this time they were for nearly two months, and she behaved with a conscious controlled decency that nearly drove her crazy. She would lock herself in the bathroom, and sit on the edge of the bath, breathing deep, trying to let go into some kind of calm. Or she went up into the spare room, usually empty, where no one would expect her to be. She heard the children calling "Mother, Mother," and kept silent, feeling guilty. Or she went to the very end of the garden, by herself, and looked at the slow-moving brown river; she looked at the river and closed her eyes and breathed slow and deep, taking it into her being, into her veins.

Then she returned to the family, wife and mother, smiling and responsible, feeling as if the pressure of these people — four lively children and her husband — were a painful pressure on the surface of her skin, a hand pressing on her brain. She did not once break down into irritation during these holidays, but it was like living out a prison sentence, and when the children went back to school, she sat on a white stone near the flowing river, and she thought: It is not even a year since the twins went to school, since *they were off my hands* (What on earth did I think I meant when I used that stupid phrase?), and yet I'm a different person. I'm simply not myself. I don't understand it.

Yet she had to understand it. For she knew that this structure — big white house, on which the mortgage still cost four hundred a year, a husband, so good and kind and insightful; four children, all doing so nicely; and the garden where she sat; and Mrs. Parkes, the cleaning woman — all this depended on her, and yet she could not understand why, or even what it was she contributed to it.

She said to Matthew in their bedroom: "I think there must be something wrong with me."

And he said: "Surely not, Susan? You look marvellous — you're as lovely as ever."

She looked at the handsome blond man, with his clear, intelligent, blue-eyed face, and thought: Why is it I can't tell him? Why not? And she said: "I need to be alone more than I am."

At which he swung his slow blue gaze at her, and she saw what she had been dreading: Incredulity. Disbelief. And fear. An incredulous blue stare from a stranger who was her husband, as close to her as her own breath.

He said: "But the children are at school and off your hands."

She said to herself: I've got to force myself to say: Yes, but do you realize that I never feel free? There's never a moment I can say to myself: There's nothing I have to remind myself about, nothing I have to do in half an hour, or an hour, or two hours. ...

But she said: "I don't feel well."

He said: "Perhaps you need a holiday."

She said, appalled: "But not without you, surely?" For she could not imagine herself going off without him. Yet that was what he meant. Seeing her face, he laughed, and opened his arms, and she went into them, thinking: Yes, yes, but why can't I say it? And what is it I have to say?

She tried to tell him, about never being free. And he listened and said: "But Susan, what sort of freedom can you possibly want — short of being dead! Am I ever free? I go to the office, and I have to be there at ten — all right, half past ten, sometimes. And I have to do this or that, don't I? Then I've got to come home at a certain time — I don't mean it, you know I don't — but if I'm not going to be back home at six I telephone you. When can I ever say to myself: I have nothing to be responsible for in the next six hours?"

Susan, hearing this, was remorseful. Because it was true. The good marriage, the house, the children, depended just as much on his voluntary bondage as it did on hers. But why did he not feel bound? Why didn't he chafe and become restless? No, there was something really wrong with her and this proved it.

And that word "bondage" — why had she used it? She had never felt marriage, or the children, as bondage. Neither had he, or surely they wouldn't be together lying in each other's arms content after twelve years of marriage.

No, her state (whatever it was) was irrelevant, nothing to do with her real good life with her family. She had to accept the fact that, after all, she was an irrational person and to live with it. Some people had to live with crippled arms, or stammers, or being deaf. She would have to live knowing she was subject to a state of mind she could not own.

Nevertheless, as a result of this conversation with her husband, there was a new regime next holidays.

The spare room at the top of the house now had a cardboard sign saying: PRIVATE! DO NOT DISTURB! on it. (This sign had been drawn in coloured chalks by the children, after a discussion between the parents in which it was decided this was psychologically the right thing.) The family and Mrs. Parkes knew this was "Mother's Room" and that she was entitled to her privacy. Many serious conversations took place between Matthew and the children about not taking Mother for granted. Susan overheard the first, between father and Harry, the older boy, and was surprised at her irritation over it. Surely she could have a room somewhere in that big house and retire into it without such a fuss being made? Without it being so solemnly discussed? Why couldn't she simply have announced: "I'm going to fit out the little top room for myself, and when I'm in it I'm not to be disturbed for anything short of fire"? Just that, and finished; instead of long earnest discussions. When she heard Harry and Matthew explaining it to the twins with Mrs. Parkes coming in — "Yes, well, a family sometimes gets on top of a woman" — she had to go right away to the bottom of the garden until the devils of exasperation had finished their dance in her blood.

But now there was a room, and she could go there when she liked, she used it seldom: she felt even more caged there than in her bedroom. One day she had gone up there after a lunch for ten children she had cooked and served because Mrs. Parkes was not there, and had sat alone for a while looking into the garden. She saw the children stream out from the kitchen and stand looking up at the window where she sat behind the curtains. They were all — her children and their friends — discussing Mother's Room. A few minutes later, the chase of children in some game came pounding up the stairs, but ended as abruptly as if they had fallen over a ravine, so sudden was the silence. They had remembered she was there, and had gone silent in a great gale of "Hush! Shhhhhh! Quiet, you'll disturb her. ..." And they went tiptoeing downstairs like criminal conspirators. When she came down to make tea for them, they all apologised. The twins put their arms around her, from front and back, making a human cage of loving limbs, and promised it would never occur again. "We forgot, Mummy, we forgot all about it!"

What it amounted to was that Mother's Room, and her need for privacy, had become a valuable lesson in respect for other people's rights. Quite soon Susan was going up to the room only because it was a lesson it was a pity to drop. Then she took sewing up there, and the children and Mrs. Parkes came in and out: it had become another family room.

She sighed, and smiled, and resigned herself — she made jokes at her own expense with Matthew over the room. That is, she did from the self she liked, she respected. But at the same time, something inside her howled with impatience, with rage. ... And she was frightened. One day she found herself kneeling by her bed and praying: "Dear God, keep it away from me, keep him away from me." She meant the devil, for she now thought of it, not caring if she was irrational, as some sort of demon. She imagined him, or it, as a youngish man, or perhaps a middleaged man pretending to be young. Or a man young-looking from immaturity? At any rate, she saw the young-looking face which, when she drew closer, had dry lines about mouth and eyes. He was thinnish, meagre in build. And he had a reddish complexion, and ginger hair. That was he — a gingery, energetic man, and he wore a reddish hairy jacket, unpleasant to the touch.

Well, one day she saw him. She was standing at the bottom of the garden, watching the river ebb past, when she raised her eyes and saw this person, or being, sitting on the white stone bench. He was looking at her, and grinning. In his hand was a long crooked stick, which he had picked off the ground, or broken off the tree above him. He was absent-mindedly, out of an absent-minded or freakish impulse of spite, using the stick to stir around in the coils of a blindworm or a grass snake (or some kind of snakelike creature: it was whitish and unhealthy to look at, unpleasant). The snake was twisting about, flinging its coils from side to side in a kind of dance of protest against the teasing prodding stick.

Susan looked at him, thinking: Who is the stranger? What is he doing in our garden? Then she recognised the man around whom her terrors had crystallised. As she did so, he vanished. She made herself walk over to the bench. A shadow from a branch lay across thin emerald grass, moving jerkily over its roughness, and she could see why she had taken it for a snake, lashing and twisting. She went back to the house thinking: Right, then, so I've seen him with my own eyes, so I'm not crazy after all — there *is* a danger because I've seen him. He is lurking in the garden and sometimes even in the house, and he wants to *get into me and to take me over.*

She dreamed of having a room or a place, anywhere, where she could go and sit, by herself, no one knowing where she was.

Once, near Victoria,[1] she found herself outside a news agent that had Rooms to Let advertised. She decided to rent a room, telling no one. Sometimes she could take the train into Richmond and sit alone in it for an hour or two. Yet how could she? A room would cost three or four pounds a week, and she earned no money, and how could she explain to Matthew that she needed such a sum? What for? It did not occur to her that she was taking it for granted she wasn't going to tell him about the room.

Well, it was out of the question, having a room; yet she knew she must.

One day, when a school term was well established, and none of the children had measles or other ailments, and everything seemed in order, she did the shopping early, explained to Mrs. Parkes she was meeting an old school friend, took the train to Victoria, searched until she found a small quiet hotel, and asked for a room for the day. They did not let rooms by the day, the manageress said, looking doubtful, since Susan so obviously was not the kind of woman who needed a room for unrespectable reasons. Susan made a long explanation about not being well, being unable to shop without frequent rests for lying down. At last she was allowed to rent the room provided she paid a full night's price for it. She was taken up by the manageress and a maid, both concerned over the state of her health … which must be pretty bad if, living at Richmond (she had signed her name and address in the register), she needed a shelter at Victoria.

The room was ordinary and anonymous, and was just what Susan needed. She put a shilling in the gas fire, and sat, eyes shut, in a dingy armchair with her back to a dingy window. She was alone. She was alone. She was alone. She could feel pressures lifting off her. First the sounds of traffic came very loud; then they seemed to vanish; she might even have slept a little. A knock on the door: it was Miss Townsend, the manageress, bringing her a cup of tea with her own hands, so concerned was she over Susan's long silence and possible illness.

Miss Townsend was a lonely woman of fifty, running this hotel with all the rectitude expected of her, and she sensed in Susan the possibility of understanding companionship. She stayed to talk. Susan found herself in the middle of a fantastic story about her illness, which got more and more impossible as she tried to make it tally with the large house at Richmond, well-off husband, and four children. Suppose she said instead: Miss Townsend, I'm here in your hotel because I need to be alone for a few hours, above all *alone and with no one knowing where I am.* She said it mentally, and saw, mentally, the look that would inevitably come on Miss Townsend's elderly maiden's face. "Miss Townsend, my four

---

[1] A major railway station in London.

children and my husband are driving me insane, do you understand that? Yes, I can see from the gleam of hysteria in your eyes that comes from loneliness controlled but only just contained that I've got everything in the world you've ever longed for. Well, Miss Townsend, I don't want any of it. You can have it, Miss Townsend. I wish I was absolutely alone in the world, like you. Miss Townsend, I'm besieged by seven devils, Miss Townsend, Miss Townsend, let me stay here in your hotel where the devils can't get me. ..." Instead of saying all this, she described her anaemia, agreed to try Miss Townsend's remedy for it, which was raw liver, minced, between whole-meal bread, and said yes, perhaps it would be better if she stayed at home and let a friend do shopping for her. She paid her bill and left the hotel, defeated.

At home Mrs. Parkes said she didn't really like it, no, not really, when Mrs. Rawlings was away from nine in the morning until five. The teacher had telephoned from school to say Joan's teeth were paining her, and she hadn't known what to say; and what was she to make for the children's tea, Mrs. Rawlings hadn't said.

All this was nonsense, of course. Mrs. Parkes's complaint was that Susan had withdrawn herself spiritually, leaving the burden of the big house on her.

Susan looked back at her day of "freedom" which had resulted in her becoming a friend of the lonely Miss Townsend, and in Mrs. Parkes's remonstrances. Yet she remembered the short blissful hour of being alone, really alone. She was determined to arrange her life, no matter what it cost, so that she could have that solitude more often. An absolute solitude, where no one knew her or cared about her.

But how? She thought of saying to her old employer: I want you to back me up in a story with Matthew that I am doing part-time work for you. The truth is that ... But she would have to tell him a lie too, and which lie? She could not say: I want to sit by myself three or four times a week in a rented room. And besides, he knew Matthew, and she could not really ask him to tell lies on her behalf, apart from being bound to think it meant a lover.

Suppose she really took a part-time job, which she could get through fast and efficiently, leaving time for herself. What job? Addressing envelopes? Canvassing?

And there was Mrs. Parkes, working widow, who knew exactly what she was prepared to give to the house, who knew by instinct when her mistress withdrew in spirit from her responsibilities. Mrs. Parkes was one of the servers of this world, but she needed someone to serve. She had to have Mrs. Rawlings, her madam, at the top of the house or in the garden, so that she could come and get support from her: "Yes, the bread's not what it was when I was a girl. ... Yes, Harry's got a wonderful appetite, I wonder where he puts it all. ... Yes, it's lucky the twins are so much of a size, they can wear each other's shoes, that's a saving in these hard times. ... Yes, the cherry jam from Switzerland is not a patch on the jam from Poland, and three times the price ..." And so on. That sort of talk Mrs. Parkes must have, every day, or she would leave, not knowing herself why she left.

Susan Rawlings, thinking these thoughts, found that she was prowling through the great thicketed garden like a wild cat: she was walking up the stairs, down the stairs, through the rooms into the garden, along the brown running river, back, up through the house, down again. ... It was a wonder Mrs. Parkes did not think it strange. But, on the contrary, Mrs. Rawlings could do what she liked, she could stand on her head if she wanted, provided she was *there*. Susan Rawlings prowled and muttered through her house, hating Mrs. Parkes, hating poor Miss Townsend, dreaming of her hour of solitude in the dingy respectability of Miss Townsend's hotel bedroom, and she knew quite well she was mad. Yes, she was mad.

She said to Matthew that she must have a holiday. Matthew agreed with her. This was not as things had been once — how they had talked in each other's arms in the marriage bed.

He had, she knew, diagnosed her finally as *unreasonable*. She had become someone outside himself that he had to manage. They were living side by side in this house like two tolerably friendly strangers.

Having told Mrs. Parkes — or rather, asked for her permission — she went off on a walking holiday in Wales. She chose the remotest place she knew of. Every morning the children telephoned her before they went off to school, to encourage and support her, just as they had over Mother's Room. Every evening she telephoned them, spoke to each child in turn, and then to Matthew. Mrs. Parkes, given permission to telephone for instructions or advice, did so every day at lunchtime. When, as happened three times, Mrs. Rawlings was out on the mountainside, Mrs. Parkes asked that she should ring back at such-and-such a time, for she would not be happy in what she was doing without Mrs. Rawlings' blessing.

Susan prowled over wild country with the telephone wire holding her to her duty like a leash. The next time she must telephone, or wait to be telephoned, nailed her to her cross. The mountains themselves seemed trammelled by her unfreedom. Everywhere on the mountains, where she met no one at all, from breakfast time to dusk, excepting sheep, or a shepherd, she came face to face with her own craziness, which might attack her in the broadest valleys, so that they seemed too small, or on a mountain top from which she could see a hundred other mountains and valleys, so that they seemed too low, too small, with the sky pressing down too close. She would stand gazing at a hillside brilliant with ferns and bracken, jewelled with running water, and see nothing but her devil, who lifted inhuman eyes at her from where he leaned negligently on a rock, switching at his ugly yellow boots with a leafy twig.

She returned to her home and family, with the Welsh emptiness at the back of her mind like a promise of freedom.

She told her husband she wanted to have an *au pair* girl.[2]

They were in their bedroom, it was late at night, the children slept. He sat, shirted and slippered, in a chair by the window, looking out. She sat brushing her hair and watching him in the mirror. A time-hallowed scene in the connubial bedroom. He said nothing, while she heard the arguments coming into his mind, only to be rejected because every one was *reasonable*.

"It seems strange to get one now; after all, the children are in school most of the day. Surely the time for you to have help was when you were stuck with them day and night. Why don't you ask Mrs. Parkes to cook for you? She's even offered to — I can understand if you are tired of cooking for six people. But you know that an *au pair* girl means all kinds of problems; it's not like having an ordinary char in during the day. ..."

Finally he said carefully: "Are you thinking of going back to work?"

"No," she said, "no, not really." She made herself sound vague, rather stupid. She went on brushing her black hair and peering at herself so as to be oblivious of the short uneasy glances her Matthew kept giving her. "Do you think we can't afford it?" she went on vaguely, not at all the old efficient Susan who knew exactly what they could afford.

"It's not that," he said, looking out of the window at dark trees, so as not to look at her. Meanwhile she examined a round, candid, pleasant face with clear dark brows and clear grey eyes. A sensible face. She brushed thick healthy black hair and thought: Yet that's the reflection of a madwoman. How very strange! Much more to the point if what looked back at me was the gingery green-eyed demon with his dry meagre smile. ...Why wasn't Matthew agreeing? After all, what else could he do? She was breaking her part of the bargain and there

---

[2] A girl who receives room and board in exchange for helping around the house.

was no way of forcing her to keep it: that her spirit, her soul, should live in this house, so that the people in it could grow like plants in water, and Mrs. Parkes remain content in their service. In return for this, he would be a good loving husband, and responsible towards the children. Well, nothing like this had been true of either of them for a long time. He did his duty, perfunctorily; she did not even pretend to do hers. And he had become like other husbands, with his real life in his work and the people he met there, and very likely a serious affair. All this was her fault.

At last he drew heavy curtains, blotting out the trees, and turned to force her attention: "Susan, are you really sure we need a girl?" But she would not meet his appeal at all. She was running the brush over her hair again and again, lifting fine black clouds in a small hiss of electricity. She was peering in and smiling as if she were amused at the clinging hissing hair that followed the brush.

"Yes, I think it would be a good idea, on the whole," she said, with the cunning of a madwoman evading the real point.

In the mirror she could see her Matthew lying on his back, his hands behind his head, staring upwards, his face sad and hard. She felt her heart (the old heart of Susan Rawlings) soften and call out to him. But she set it to be indifferent.

He said: "Susan, the children?" It was an appeal that *almost* reached her. He opened his arms, lifting them palms up, empty. She had only to run across and fling herself into them, onto his hard, warm chest, and melt into herself, into Susan. But she could not. She would not see his lifted arms. She said vaguely: "Well, surely it'll be even better for them? We'll get a French or a German girl and they'll learn the language."

In the dark she lay beside him, feeling frozen, a stranger. She felt as if Susan had been spirited away. She disliked very much this woman who lay here, cold and indifferent beside a suffering man, but she could not change her.

Next morning she set about getting a girl, and very soon came Sophie Traub from Hamburg, a girl of twenty, laughing, healthy, blue-eyed, intending to learn English. Indeed, she already spoke a good deal. In return for a room — "Mother's Room" — and her food, she undertook to do some light cooking, and to be with the children when Mrs. Rawlings asked. She was an intelligent girl and understood perfectly what was needed. Susan said: "I go off sometimes, for the morning or for the day — well, sometimes the children run home from school, or they ring up, or a teacher rings up. I should be here, really. And there's the daily woman. ..." And Sophie laughed her deep fruity *Fräulein's* laugh, showed her fine white teeth and her dimples, and said: "You want some person to play mistress of the house sometimes, not so?"

"Yes, that is just so," said Susan, a bit dry, despite herself, thinking in secret fear how easy it was, how much nearer to the end she was than she thought. Healthy Fräulein Traub's instant understanding of their position proved this to be true.

The *au pair* girl, because of her own commonsense, or (as Susan said to herself, with her new inward shudder) because she had been *chosen* so well by Susan, was a success with everyone, the children liking her, Mrs. Parkes forgetting almost at once that she was German, and Matthew finding her "nice to have around the house." For he was now taking things as they came, from the surface of life, withdrawn both as a husband and a father from the household.

One day Susan saw how Sophie and Mrs. Parkes were talking and laughing in the kitchen, and she announced that she would be away until tea time. She knew exactly where to go and what she must look for. She took the District Line to South Kensington, changed to the Circle, got off at Paddington, and walked around looking at the smaller hotels until she was satisfied with one which had FRED'S HOTEL painted on windowpanes that needed cleaning. The facade was a faded shiny yellow, like unhealthy skin. A door at the end of a passage said she must knock; she did, and Fred appeared. He was not at all attractive, not in any way, being fattish, and run-down, and wearing a tasteless striped suit. He had small sharp eyes in a white creased face, and was quite prepared to let Mrs. Jones (she chose the farcical name deliberately, staring him out) have a room three days a week from ten until six. Provided of course that she paid in advance each time she came? Susan produced fifteen shillings (no price had been set by him) and held it out, still fixing him with a bold unblinking challenge she had not known until then she could use at will. Looking at her still, he took up a ten-shilling note from her palm between thumb and forefinger, fingered it; then shuffled up two half-crowns, held out his own palm with these bits of money displayed thereon, and let his gaze lower broodingly at them. They were standing in the passage, a red-shaded light above, bare boards beneath, and a strong smell of floor polish rising about them. He shot his gaze up at her over the still-extended palm, and smiled as if to say: What do you take me for? "I shan't," said Susan, "be using this room for the purposes of making money." He still waited. She added another five shillings, at which he nodded and said: "You pay, and I ask no questions." "Good," said Susan. He now went past her to the stairs, and there waited a moment: the light from the street door being in her eyes, she lost sight of him momentarily. Then she saw a sober-suited, white-faced, white-balding little man trotting up the stairs like a waiter, and she went after him. They proceeded in utter silence up the stairs of this house where no questions were asked — Fred's Hotel, which could afford the freedom for its visitors that poor Miss Townsend's hotel could not. The room was hideous. It had a single window, with thin green brocade curtains, a three-quarter bed that had a cheap green satin bedspread on it, a fireplace with a gas fire and a shilling meter by it, a chest of drawers, and a green wicker armchair.

"Thank you," said Susan, knowing that Fred (if this was Fred, and not George, or Herbert or Charlie) was looking at her, not so much with curiosity, an emotion he would not own to, for professional reasons, but with a philosophical sense of what was appropriate. Having taken her money and shown her up and agreed to everything, he was clearly disapproving of her for coming here. She did not belong here at all, so his look said. (But she knew, already, how very much she did belong: the room had been waiting for her to join it.) "Would you have me called at five o'clock, please?" and he nodded and went downstairs.

It was twelve in the morning. She was free. She sat in the armchair, she simply sat, she closed her eyes and sat and let herself be alone. She was alone and no one knew where she was. When a knock came on the door she was annoyed, and prepared to show it: but it was Fred himself; it was five o'clock and he was calling her as ordered. He flicked his sharp little eyes over the room — bed, first. It was undisturbed. She might never have been in the room at all. She thanked him, said she would be returning the day after tomorrow, and left. She was back home in time to cook supper, to put the children to bed, to cook a second supper for her husband and herself later. And to welcome Sophie back from the pictures where she had gone with a friend. All these things she did cheerfully, willingly. But she was thinking all the time of the hotel room; she was longing for it with her whole being.

Three times a week. She arrived promptly at ten, looked Fred in the eyes, gave him twenty shillings, followed him up the stairs, went into the room, and shut the door on him with gentle firmness. For Fred, disapproving of her being here at all, was quite ready to let friendship, or at least acquaintanceship, follow his disapproval, if only she would let him. But he was content to go off on her dismissing nod, with the twenty shillings in his hand.

She sat in the armchair and shut her eyes.

What did she *do* in the room? Why, nothing at all. From the chair, when it had rested her, she went to the window, stretching her arms, smiling, treasuring her anonymity, to look out. She was no longer Susan Rawlings, mother of four, wife of Matthew, employer of Mrs. Parkes and of Sophie Traub, with these and those relations with friends, school-teachers, tradesmen. She no longer was mistress of the big white house and garden, owning clothes suitable for this and that activity or occasion. She was Mrs. Jones, and she was alone, and she had no past and no future. Here I am, she thought, after all these years of being married and having children and playing those roles of responsibility — and I'm just the same. Yet there have been times I thought that nothing existed of me except the roles that went with being Mrs. Matthew Rawlings. Yes, here I am, and if I never saw any of my family again, here I would still be ... how very strange that is! And she leaned on the sill, and looked into the street, loving the men and women who passed, because she did not know them. She looked at the downtrodden buildings over the street, and at the sky, wet and dingy, or sometimes blue, and she felt she had never seen buildings or sky before. And then she went back to the chair, empty, her mind a blank. Sometimes she talked aloud, saying nothing — an exclamation, meaningless, followed by a comment about the floral pattern on the thin rug, or a stain on the green satin coverlet. For the most part, she wool-gathered — what word is there for it? — brooded, wandered, simply went dark, feeling emptiness run deliciously through her veins like the movement of her blood.

This room had become more her own than the house she lived in. One morning she found Fred taking her a flight higher than usual. She stopped, refusing to go up, and demanded her usual room, Number 19. "Well, you'll have to wait half an hour, then," he said. Willingly she descended to the dark disinfectant-smelling hall, and sat waiting until the two, man and woman, came down the stairs, giving her swift indifferent glances before they hurried out into the street, separating at the door. She went up to the room, *her* room, which they had just vacated. It was no less hers, though the windows were set wide open, and a maid was straightening the bed as she came in.

After these days of solitude, it was both easy to play her part as mother and wife, and difficult — because it was so easy: she felt an imposter. She felt as if her shell moved here, with her family, answering to Mummy, Mother, Susan, Mrs. Rawlings. She was surprised no one saw through her, that she wasn't turned out of doors, as a fake. On the contrary, it seemed the children loved her more; Matthew and she "got on" pleasantly, and Mrs. Parkes was happy in her work under (for the most part, it must be confessed) Sophie Traub. At night she lay beside her husband, and they made love again, apparently just as they used to, when they were really married. But she, Susan, or the being who answered so readily and improbably to the name of Susan, was not there: she was in Fred's Hotel, in Paddington, waiting for the easing hours of solitude to begin.

Soon she made a new arrangement with Fred and with Sophie. It was for five days a week. As for the money, five pounds, she simply asked Matthew for it. She saw that she was not even frightened he might ask what for: he would give it to her, she knew that, and yet it was terrifying it could be so, for this close couple, these partners, had once known the destination of every shilling they must spend. He agreed to give her five pounds a week. She asked for just so much, not a penny more. He sounded indifferent about it. It was as if he were paying her, she thought: *paying her off* — yes, that was it. Terror came back for a moment when she understood this, but she stilled it: things had gone too far for that. Now, every week, on Sunday nights, he gave her five pounds, turning away from her before their eyes could meet on the transaction. As for Sophie Traub, she was to be somewhere in or near the house until six at night, after which she was free. She was not to cook, or to clean; she was simply to be there. So she gardened or sewed, and asked friends in, being a person who was bound to have a lot of friends. If the children were sick, she nursed them. If teachers telephoned, she answered them sensibly. For the five daytimes in the school week, she was altogether the mistress of the house.

One night in the bedroom, Matthew asked: "Susan, I don't want to interfere — don't think that, please — but are you sure you are well?"

She was brushing her hair at the mirror. She made two more strokes on either side of her head, before she replied: "Yes, dear, I am sure I am well."

He was again lying on his back, his blond head on his hands, his elbows angled up and part-concealing his face. He said: "Then Susan, I have to ask you this question, though you must understand, I'm not putting any sort of pressure on you." (Susan heard the word "pressure" with dismay, because this was inevitable; of course she could not go on like this.) "Are things going to go on like this?"

"Well," she said, going vague and bright and idiotic again, so as to escape: "Well, I don't see why not."

He was jerking his elbows up and down, in annoyance or in pain, and, looking at him, she saw he had got thin, even gaunt; and restless angry movements were not what she remembered of him. He said: "Do you want a divorce, is that it?"

At this, Susan only with the greatest difficulty stopped herself from laughing: she could hear the bright bubbling laughter she *would* have emitted, had she let herself. He could only mean one thing: she had a lover, and that was why she spent her days in London, as lost to him as if she had vanished to another continent.

Then the small panic set in again: she understood that he hoped she did have a lover, he was begging her to say so, because otherwise it would be too terrifying.

She thought this out as she brushed her hair, watching the fine black stuff fly up to make its little clouds of electricity, hiss, hiss, hiss. Behind her head, across the room, was a blue wall. She realised she was absorbed in watching the black hair making shapes against the blue. She should be answering him. "Do *you* want a divorce, Matthew?"

He said: "That surely isn't the point, is it?"

"You brought it up, I didn't," she said, brightly, suppressing meaningless tinkling laughter.

Next day she asked Fred: "Have enquiries been made for me?"

He hesitated, and she said: "I've been coming here a year now. I've made no trouble, and you've been paid every day. I have a right to be told."

"As a matter of fact, Mrs. Jones, a man did come asking."

"A man from a detective agency?"

"Well, he could have been, couldn't he?"

"I was asking you. ...Well, what did you tell him?"

"I told him a Mrs. Jones came every weekday from ten until five or six and stayed in Number 19 by herself."

"Describing me?"

"Well, Mrs. Jones, I had no alternative. Put yourself in my place."

"By rights I should deduct what that man gave you for the information."

He raised shocked eyes: she was not the sort of person to make jokes like this! Then he chose to laugh: a pinkish wet slit appeared across his white crinkled face; his eyes positively begged her to laugh, otherwise he might lose some money. She remained grave, looking at him.

He stopped laughing and said: "You want to go up now?" — returning to the familiarity, the comradeship, of the country where no questions are asked, on which (and he knew it) she depended completely.

She went up to sit in her wicker chair. But it was not the same. Her husband had searched her out. (The world had searched her out.) The pressures were on her. She was here with his connivance. He might walk in at any moment, here, into Room 19. She imagined the report from the detective agency: "A woman calling herself Mrs. Jones, fitting the description of your wife (et cetera, et cetera, et cetera), stays alone all day in Room No. 19. She insists on this room, waits for it if it is engaged. As far as the proprietor knows, she receives no visitors there, male or female." A report something on these lines Matthew must have received.

Well, of course he was right: things couldn't go on like this. He had put an end to it all simply by sending the detective after her.

She tried to shrink herself back into the shelter of the room, a snail pecked out of its shell and trying to squirm back. But the peace of the room had gone. She was trying consciously to revive it, trying to let go into the dark creative trance (or whatever it was) that she had found there. It was no use, yet she craved for it, she was as ill as a suddenly deprived addict.

Several times she returned to the room, to look for herself there, but instead she found the unnamed spirit of restlessness, a pricking fevered hunger for movement, an irritable self-consciousness that made her brain feel as if it had coloured lights going on and off inside it. Instead of the soft dark that had been the room's air, were now waiting for her demons that made her dash blindly about, muttering words of hate; she was impelling herself from point to point like a moth dashing itself against a windowpane, sliding to the bottom, fluttering off on broken wings, then crashing into the invisible barrier again. And again and again. Soon she was exhausted, and she told Fred that for a while she would not be needing the room, she was going on a holiday. Home she went, to the big white house by the river. The middle of a weekday, and she felt guilty at returning to her own home when not expected. She stood unseen, looking in at the kitchen window. Mrs. Parkes, wearing a discarded floral overall of Susan's, was stooping to slide something into the oven. Sophie, arms folded, was leaning her back against a cupboard and laughing at some joke made by a girl not seen before by Susan — a dark foreign girl, Sophie's visitor. In an armchair Molly, one of the twins, lay curled, sucking her thumb and watching the grownups. She must have some sickness, to be kept from school. The child's listless face, the dark circles under her eyes, hurt Susan: Molly was looking at the three grownups working and talking in exactly the same way Susan looked at the four through the kitchen window: she was remote, shut off from them.

But then, just as Susan imagined herself going in, picking up the little girl, and sitting in an armchair with her, stroking her probably heated forehead, Sophie did just that: she had been standing on one leg, the other knee flexed, its foot set against the wall. Now she let her foot in its ribbon-tied red shoe slide down the wall, stood solid on two feet, clapping her hands before and behind her, and sang a couple of lines in German, so that the child lifted her heavy eyes at her and began to smile. Then she walked, or rather skipped, over to the child, swung her up, and let her fall into her lap at the same moment she sat herself. She said "Hopla! Hopla! Molly ..." and began stroking the dark untidy young head that Molly laid on her shoulder for comfort.

Well. ...Susan blinked the tears of farewell out of her eyes, and went quietly up through the house to her bedroom. There she sat looking at the river through the trees. She felt at peace, but in a way that was new to her. She had no desire to move, to talk, to do anything at all. The devils that had haunted the house, the garden, were not there; but she knew it was because her soul was in Room 19 in Fred's Hotel; she was not really here at all. It was a sensation that should have been frightening: to sit at her own bedroom window, listening to Sophie's rich young voice sing German nursery songs to her child, listening to Mrs. Parkes clatter and move below, and to know that all this had nothing to do with her: she was already out of it.

Later, she made herself go down and say she was home: it was unfair to be here unannounced. She took lunch with Mrs. Parkes, Sophie, Sophie's Italian friend Maria, and her daughter Molly, and felt like a visitor.

A few days later, at bedtime, Matthew said: "Here's your five pounds," and pushed them over at her. Yet he must have known she had not been leaving the house at all.

She shook her head, gave it back to him, and said, in explanation, not in accusation: "As soon as you knew where I was, there was no point."

He nodded, not looking at her. He was turned away from her: thinking, she knew, how best to handle this wife who terrified him.

He said: "I wasn't trying to ... It's just that I was worried."

"Yes, I know."

"I must confess that I was beginning to wonder ..."

"You thought I had a lover?"

"Yes, I am afraid I did."

She knew that he wished she had. She sat wondering how to say: "For a year now I've been spending all my days in a very sordid hotel room. It's the place where I'm happy. In fact, without it I don't exist." She heard herself saying this, and understood how terrified he was that she might. So instead she said: "Well, perhaps you're not far wrong."

Probably Matthew would think the hotel proprietor lied: he would want to think so.

"Well," he said, and she could hear his voice spring up, so to speak, with relief, "in that case I must confess I've got a bit of an affair on myself."

She said, detached and interested: "Really? Who is she?" and saw Matthew's startled look because of this reaction.

"It's Phil. Phil Hunt."

She had known Phil Hunt well in the old unmarried days. She was thinking: No, she won't do, she's too neurotic and difficult. She's never been happy yet. Sophie's much better. Well, Matthew will see that himself, as sensible as he is.

This line of thought went on in silence, while she said aloud: "It's no point telling you about mine, because you don't know him."

Quick, quick, invent, she thought. Remember how you invented all that nonsense for Miss Townsend.

She began slowly, careful not to contradict herself: "His name is Michael" (*Michael What?*) — "Michael Plant." (What a silly name!) "He's rather like you — in looks, I mean." And indeed, she could imagine herself being touched by no one but Matthew himself. "He's a publisher." (Really? Why?) "He's got a wife already and two children."

She brought out this fantasy, proud of herself.

Matthew said: "Are you two thinking of marrying?"

She said, before she could stop herself: "Good God, *no!*"

She realised, if Matthew wanted to marry Phil Hunt, that this was too emphatic, but apparently it was all right, for his voice sounded relieved as he said: "It is a bit impossible to imagine oneself married to anyone else, isn't it?" With which he pulled her to him, so that her head lay on his shoulder. She turned her face into the dark of his flesh, and listened to the blood pounding through her ears saying: I am alone, I am alone, I am alone.

In the morning Susan lay in bed while he dressed.

He had been thinking things out in the night, because now he said: "Susan, why don't we make a foursome?"

Of course, she said to herself, of course he would be bound to say that. If one is sensible, if one is reasonable, if one never allows oneself a base thought or an envious emotion, naturally one says: Let's make a foursome!

"Why not?" she said.

"We could all meet for lunch. I mean, it's ridiculous, you sneaking off to filthy hotels, and me staying late at the office, and all the lies everyone has to tell."

What on earth did I say his name was? — she panicked, then said: "I think it's a good idea, but Michael is away at the moment. When he comes back, though — and I'm sure you two would like each other."

"He's away, is he? So that's why you've been …" Her husband put his hand to the knot of his tie in a gesture of male coquetry she would not before have associated with him; and he bent to kiss her cheek with the expression that goes with the words: Oh you naughty little puss! And she felt its answering look, naughty and coy, come onto her face.

Inside she was dissolving in horror at them both, at how far they had both sunk from honesty of emotion.

So now she was saddled with a lover, and he had a mistress! How ordinary, how reassuring, how jolly! And now they would make a foursome of it, and go about to theatres and restaurants. After all, the Rawlings could well afford that sort of thing, and presumably the publisher Michael Plant could afford to do himself and his mistress quite well. No, there was nothing to stop the four of them developing the most intricate relationship of civilised tolerance, all enveloped in a charming afterglow of autumnal passion. Perhaps they would all go off on holidays together? She had known people who did. Or perhaps Matthew would draw the line there? Why should he, though, if he was capable of talking about "foursomes" at all?

She lay in the empty bedroom, listening to the car drive off with Matthew in it, off to work. Then she heard the children clattering off to school to the accompaniment of Sophie's cheerfully ringing voice. She slid down into the hollow of the bed, for shelter against her own irrelevance. And she stretched out her hand to the hollow where her husband's body had lain, but found no comfort there: he was not her husband. She curled herself up in a small tight ball under the clothes: she could stay here all day, all week, indeed, all her life.

But in a few days she must produce Michael Plant, and — but how? She must presumably find some agreeable man prepared to impersonate a publisher called Michael Plant. And in return for which she would — what? Well, for one thing they would make love. The idea made her want to cry with sheer exhaustion. Oh no, she had finished with all that — the proof of it was that the words "make love," or even imagining it, trying hard to revive no more than the pleasures of sensuality, let alone affection, or love, made her want to run away and hide from the sheer effort of the thing. …Good Lord, why make love at all? Why make love with anyone? Or if you are going to make love, what does it matter who with? Why shouldn't she simply walk into the street, pick up a man and have a roaring sexual affair with him? Why not? Or even with Fred? What difference did it make?

But she had let herself in for it — an interminable stretch of time with a lover, called Michael, as part of a gallant civilised foursome. Well, she could not, and she would not.

She got up, dressed, went down to find Mrs. Parkes, and asked her for the loan of a pound, since Matthew, she said, had forgotten to leave her money. She exchanged with Mrs. Parkes variations on the theme that husbands are all the same, they don't think, and without saying a word to Sophie, whose voice could be heard upstairs from the telephone, walked to the underground, travelled to South Kensington, changed to the Inner Circle, got out at Paddington, and walked to Fred's Hotel. There she told Fred that she wasn't going on holiday after all, she needed the room. She would have to wait an hour, Fred said. She went to a busy tearoom-cum-restaurant around the corner, and sat watching the people flow in and out the door that kept swinging open and shut, watched them mingle and merge, and separate, felt her being flow into them, into their movement. When the hour was up, she left a half-crown for her pot of tea, and left the place without looking back at it, just as she had left her house, the big, beautiful white house, without another look, but silently dedicating it to Sophie. She returned to Fred, received the key of Number 19, now free, and ascended the grimy stairs slowly, letting floor after floor fall away below her, keeping her eyes lifted, so that floor after floor descended jerkily to her level of vision, and fell away out of sight.

Number 19 was the same. She saw everything with an acute, narrow, checking glance: the cheap shine of the satin spread, which had been replaced carelessly after the two bodies had finished their convulsions under it; a trace of powder on the glass that topped the chest of drawers; an intense green shade in a fold of the curtain. She stood at the window, looking down, watching people pass and pass and pass until her mind went dark from the constant movement. Then she sat in the wicker chair, letting herself go slack. But she had to be careful, because she did not want, today, to be surprised by Fred's knock at five o'clock.

The demons were not here. They had gone forever, because she was buying her freedom from them. She was slipping already into the dark fructifying dream that seemed to caress her inwardly, like the movement of her blood ... but she had to think about Matthew first. Should she write a letter for the coroner? But what should she say? She would like to leave him with the look on his face she had seen this morning — banal, admittedly, but at least confidently healthy. Well, that was impossible, one did not look like that with a wife dead from suicide. But how to leave him believing she was dying because of a man — because of the fascinating publisher Michael Plant? Oh, how ridiculous! How absurd! How humiliating! But she decided not to trouble about it, simply not to think about the living. If he wanted to believe she had a lover, he would believe it. And he *did* want to believe it. Even when he had found out that there was no publisher in London called Michael Plant, he would think: Oh poor Susan, she was afraid to give me his real name.

And what did it matter whether he married Phil Hunt or Sophie? Though it ought to be Sophie, who was already the mother of those children ... and what hypocrisy to sit here worrying about the children, when she was going to leave them because she had not got the energy to stay.

She had about four hours. She spent them delightfully, darkly, sweetly, letting herself slide gently, gently, to the edge of the river. Then, with hardly a break in her consciousness, she got up, pushed the thin rug against the door, made sure the windows were tight shut, put two shillings in the meter, and turned on the gas. For the first time since she had been in the room she lay on the hard bed that smelled stale, that smelled of sweat and sex.

She lay on her back on the green satin cover, but her legs were chilly. She got up, found a blanket folded in the bottom of the chest of drawers, and carefully covered her legs with it. She was quite content lying there, listening to the faint soft hiss of the gas that poured into the room, into her lungs, into her brain, as she drifted off into the dark river.

QUESTIONS

1. What does Room 19 represent to Susan? How does the title of this story predict the movement of the plot?

2. "This is a story, I suppose, about a failure in intelligence ..." Does the "I suppose" cast some doubt on the statement? Are there other instances of author intrusion? Is there more than one meaning in "a failure in intelligence"?

3. If suicide is the "logical" end of this story, what light does that fact shed upon the opening sentence?

4. Whose fault is it that Susan's anticipated freedom turns out to be bondage? Does Susan blame Matthew? herself? life? How might she have freed herself?

5. Would this story be essentially different if told from Matthew's point of view?

RAY BRADBURY

The Golden Apples of the Sun

"South," said the captain.

"But," said his crew, "there simply *aren't* any directions out here in space."

"When you travel on down toward the sun," replied the captain, "and everything gets yellow and warm and lazy, then you're going in one direction only." He shut his eyes and thought about the smoldering, warm, faraway land, his breath moving gently in his mouth. "South." He nodded slowly to himself. "South."

Their rocket was the *Copa de Oro*,[1] also named the *Prometheus* and the *Icarus,* and their destination in all reality was the blazing noonday sun. In high good spirits they had packed along two thousand sour lemonades and a thousand white-capped beers for this journey to the wide Sahara. And now as the sun boiled up at them they remembered a score of verses and quotations:

"'The golden apples of the sun'?"

"Yeats."

"'Fear no more the heat of the sun'?"

"Shakespeare, of course!"

"'Cup of Gold'? Steinbeck. 'The Crock of Gold'? Stephens. And what about the pot of gold at the rainbow's end? *There's* a name for our trajectory, by God. Rainbow!"

"Temperature?"

"One thousand degrees Fahrenheit!"

The captain stared from the huge dark-lensed port, and there indeed was the sun, and to go to that sun and touch it and steal part of it forever away was his quiet and single idea. In this ship were combined the coolly delicate and the coldly practical. Through corridors of ice and milk-frost, ammoniated winter and storming snowflakes blew. Any spark from that vast hearth burning out there beyond the callous hull of this ship, any small firebreath that might seep through would find winter, slumbering here like all the coldest hours of February.

The audio-thermometer murmured in the arctic silence: "Temperature: two thousand degrees!"

---

[1] "The Cup of Gold." Prometheus stole fire from Mount Olympus and gave it to mankind. Icarus flew too close to the sun, which melted the wax in his wings and sent him plunging to his death.

Falling, thought the captain, like a snowflake into the lap of June, warm July, and the sweltering dog-mad days of August.

"Three thousand degrees Fahrenheit!"

Under the snow fields engines raced, refrigerants pumped ten thousand miles per hour in rimed boa-constrictor coils.

"Four thousand degrees Fahrenheit."

Noon. Summer. July.

"Five thousand Fahrenheit!"

And at last the captain spoke with all the quietness of the journey in his voice:

"Now, we are touching the sun."

Their eyes, thinking it, were melted gold.

"Seven thousand degrees!"

Strange how a mechanical thermometer could sound excited, though it possessed only an emotionless steel voice.

"What *time* is it?" asked someone.

Everyone had to smile.

For now there was only the sun and the sun and the sun. It was every horizon, it was every direction. It burned the minutes, the seconds, the hourglasses, the clocks; it burned all time and eternity away. It burned the eyelids and the serum of the dark world behind the lids, the retina, the hidden brain; and it burned sleep and the sweet memories of sleep and cool nightfall.

"Watch it!"

"Captain!"

Bretton, the first mate, fell flat to the winter deck. His protective suit whistled where, burst open, his warmness, his oxygen, and his life bloomed out in a frosted steam.

"Quick!"

Inside Bretton's plastic face-mask, milk crystals had already gathered in blind patterns. They bent to see.

"A structural defect in his suit, Captain. Dead."

"Frozen."

They stared at that other thermometer which showed how winter lived in this snowing ship. One thousand degrees below zero. The captain gazed down upon the frosted statue and the twinkling crystals that iced over it as he watched. Irony of the coolest sort, he thought; a man afraid of fire and killed by frost.

The captain turned away. "No time. No time. Let him lie." He felt his tongue move. "Temperature?"

The dials jumped four thousand degrees.

"Look. Will you look? Look."

Their icicle was melting.

The captain jerked his head to look at the ceiling.

As if a motion-picture projector had jammed a single clear memory frame in his head, he found his mind focused ridiculously on a scene whipped out of childhood.

Spring mornings as a boy he found he had leaned from his bedroom window into the snow-smelling air to see the sun sparkle the last icicle of winter. A dripping of white wine, the blood of cool but warming April fell from that clear crystal blade. Minute by minute, December's weapon grew less dangerous. And then at last the icicle fell with the sound of a single chime to the graveled walk below.

"Auxiliary pump's broken, sir. Refrigeration. We're losing our ice!"

A shower of warm rain shivered down upon them. The captain jerked his head right and left. "Can you see the trouble? Christ, don't stand there, we haven't time!"

The men rushed; the captain bent in the warm rain, cursing, felt his hands run over the cold machine, felt them burrow and search, and while he worked he saw a future which was removed from them by the merest breath. He saw the skin peel from the rocket beehive, men, thus revealed, running, running, mouths shrieking, soundless. Space was a black mossed well where life drowned its roars and terrors. Scream a big scream, but space snuffed it out before it was half up your throat. Men scurried, ants in a flaming matchbox; the ship was dripping lava, gushing steam, nothing!

"Captain?"

The nightmare flicked away.

"Here." He worked in the soft warm rain that fell from the upper decks. He fumbled at the auxiliary pump. "Damn it!" He jerked the feed line. When it came, it'd be the quickest death in the history of dying. One moment, yelling; a warm flash later only the billion billion tons of space-fire would whisper, unheard, in space. Popped like strawberries in a furnace, while their thoughts lingered on the scorched air a long breath after their bodies were charred roast and fluorescent gas.

"Damn!" He stabbed the auxiliary pump with a screw driver. "Jesus!" He shuddered. The complete annihilation of it. He clamped his eyes shut, teeth tight. God, he thought, we're used to more leisurely dyings, measured in minutes and hours. Even twenty seconds now would be a slow death compared to this hungry idiot thing waiting to eat us!

"Captain, do we pull out or stay?"

"Get the Cup ready. Take over, finish this. Now!"

He turned and put his hand to the working mechanism of the huge Cup; shoved his fingers into the robot Glove. A twitch of his hand here moved a gigantic hand, with gigantic metal fingers, from the bowels of the ship. Now, now, the great metal hand slid out holding the huge *Copa de Oro*, breathless, into the iron furnace, the bodiless body and the fleshless flesh of the sun.

A million years ago, thought the captain, quickly, quickly, as he moved the hand and the Cup, a million years ago a naked man on a lonely northern trail saw lightning strike a tree. And while his clan fled, with bare hands he plucked a limb of fire, broiling the flesh of his fingers, to carry it, running in triumph, shielding it from the rain with his body, to his cave, where he shrieked out a laugh and tossed it full on a mound of leaves and gave his people summer. And the tribe crept at last, trembling, near the fire, and they put out their flinching hands and felt the new season in their cave, this small yellow spot of changing weather, and they, too, at last, nervously, smiled. And the gift of fire was theirs.

"Captain!"

It took all of four seconds for the huge hand to push the empty Cup to the fire. So here we are again, today, on another trail, he thought, reaching for a cup of precious gas and vacuum, a handful of different fire with which to run back up cold space, lighting our way, and take to Earth a gift of fire that might burn forever. Why?

He knew the answer before the question.

Because the atoms we work with our hands, on Earth, are pitiful; the atomic bomb is pitiful and small and our knowledge is pitiful and small, and only the sun really knows what we want to know, and only the sun has the secret. And besides, it's fun, it's a chance, it's a great thing coming here, playing tag, hitting and running. There is no reason, really except the pride and vanity of little insect men hoping to sting the lion and escape the maw. My God, we'll say, we *did* it! And here is our cup of energy, fire, vibration, call it what you will, that may well power our cities and sail our ships and light our libraries and tan our children and bake our daily breads and simmer the knowledge of our universe for us for a thousand years until it is well done. Here, from this cup, all good men of science and religion: drink! Warm yourselves against the night of ignorance, the long snows of superstition, the cold winds of disbelief, and from the great fear of darkness in each man. So: we stretch out our hand with the beggar's cup …

"Ah."

The Cup dipped into the sun. It scooped up a bit of the flesh of God, the blood of the universe, the blazing thought, the blinding philosophy that set out and mothered a galaxy, that idled and swept planets in their fields and summoned or laid to rest lives and livelihoods.

"Now, *slow*," whispered the captain.

"What'll happen when we pull it inside? That extra heat now, at this time, Captain?"

"God knows."

"Auxiliary pump all repaired, sir."

"Start it!"

The pump leaped on.

"Close the lid of the Cup and inside now, slow, slow."

The beautiful hand outside the ship trembled, a tremendous image of his own gesture, sank with oiled silence into the ship body. The Cup, lid shut, dripped yellow flowers and white stars, slid deep. The audio-thermometer screamed. The refrigerator system kicked; ammoniated fluids banged the walls like blood in the head of a shrieking idiot.

He shut the outer air-lock door.

"Now."

They waited. The ship's pulse ran. The heart of the ship rushed, beat, rushed, the Cup of gold in it. The cold blood raced around about down through, around about down through.

The captain exhaled slowly.

The ice stopped dripping from the ceiling. It froze again.

"Let's get out of here."

The ship turned and ran.

"Listen!"

The heart of the ship was slowing, slowing. The dials spun on down through the thousands; the needles whirred, invisible. The thermometer voice chanted the change of seasons. They were all thinking now, together: Pull away and away from the fire and the flame, the heat and the melting, the yellow and the white. Go on out now to cool and dark. In twenty hours perhaps they might even dismantle some refrigerators, let winter die. Soon they would move in night so cold it might be necessary to use the ship's new furnace, draw heat from the shielded fire they carried now like an unborn child.

They were going home.

They were going home and there was some little time, even as he tended to the body of Bretton lying in a bank of white winter snow, for the captain to remember a poem he had written many years before:

> Sometimes I see the sun a burning Tree,
> Its golden fruit swung bright in airless air,
> Its apples wormed with man and gravity,
> Their worship breathing from them everywhere,
> As man sees Sun as burning Tree …

The captain sat for a long while by the body, feeling many separate things. I feel sad, he thought, and I feel good, and I feel like a boy coming home from school with a handful of dandelions.

"Well," said the captain, sitting, eyes shut, sighing. "Well, where do we go now, eh, where are we going?" He felt his men sitting or standing all about him, the terror dead in them, their breathing quiet. "When you've gone a long, long way down to the sun and touched it and lingered and jumped around and streaked away from it, where are you going then? When you go away from the heat and the noonday light and the laziness, where do you go?"

His men waited for him to say it out. They waited for him to gather all of the coolness and the whiteness and the welcome and refreshing climate of the word in his mind, and they saw him settle the word, like a bit of ice cream, in his mouth, rolling it gently.

"There's only one direction in space from here on out," he said at last.

They waited. They waited as the ship moved swiftly into cold darkness away from the light.

"North," murmured the captain. "North."

And they all smiled, as if a wind had come up suddenly in the middle of a hot afternoon.

QUESTIONS

1. The story opens with a "compass" direction that is obviously "unscientific." Is it also untrue or inappropriate?

2. What incidents convey the idea of danger and imminent death?

3. What narrative function does the captain's childhood memory serve?

4. Note the shifts between the action of the story and the thoughts of the captain. Do they impede the flow of narrative or contribute something to it?

5. How does the captain answer the question "Why?" Is this the answer you would expect from a scientist?

6. Are you surprised that the captain parallels himself not with Prometheus but with the primitive man who "plucked a limb of fire" and brought it "to his cave"? Is this parallel meant to shed a different light upon the myth of Prometheus?

7. Obviously, Bradbury hopes that his readers will be familiar with the mythology — or, if not familiar, at least curious enough to look up "Prometheus" and "Icarus" in the dictionary. But does the story depend for its meaning upon these allusions? If not, what do the allusions add for the knowledgeable reader?

MAVIS GALLANT

Acceptance of Their Ways

Prodded by a remark from Mrs. Freeport, Lily Littel got up and fetched the plate of cheese. It was in her to say, "Go get it yourself," but a reputation for coolness held her still. Only the paucity of her income, at which the *Sunday Express* horoscope jeered with its smart talk of pleasure and gain, kept her at Mrs. Freeport's, on the Italian side of the frontier. The coarse and grubby gaiety of the French Riviera would have suited her better, and was not far away; unfortunately it came high. At Mrs. Freeport's, which was cheaper, there was a whiff of infirm nicety to be breathed, a suggestion of regularly aired decay; weakly, because it was respectable, Lily craved that, too. "We seem to have finished with the pudding," said Mrs. Freeport once again, as though she hadn't noticed that Lily was on her feet.

Lily was not Mrs. Freeport's servant, she was her paying guest, but it was a distinction her hostess rarely observed. In imagination, Lily became a punishing statue and raised a heavy marble arm; but then she remembered that this was the New Year. The next day, or the day after that, her dividends would arrive. That meant she could disappear, emerging as a gay holiday Lily up in Nice. Then, Lily thought, turning away from the table, then watch the old tiger! For Mrs. Freeport couldn't live without Lily, not more than a day. She could not stand Italy without the sound of an English voice in the house. In the hush of the dead season, Mrs. Freeport preferred Lily's ironed-out Bayswater[1] to no English at all.

In the time it took her to pick up the cheese and face the table again, Lily had added to her expression a permanent-looking smile. Her eyes, which were a washy blue, were tolerably kind when she was plotting mischief. The week in Nice,[2] desired, became a necessity; Mrs. Freeport needed a scare. She would fear, and then believe, that her most docile boarder, her most pliant errand girl, had gone forever. Stealing into Lily's darkened room, she would count the dresses with trembling hands. She would touch Lily's red with the white dots, her white with the poppies, her green wool with the scarf of mink tails. Mrs. Freeport would also discover — if she carried her snooping that far — the tooled-leather box with Lily's daisy-shaped earrings, and the brooch in which a mother-of-pearl pigeon sat on a nest made of Lily's own hair. But Mrs. Freeport would not find the diary, in which Lily had recorded her opinion of so many interesting things, nor would she come upon a single empty

---

[1] Lily's accent is undistinguished.
[2] French resort city on the Mediterranean coast.

bottle. Lily kept her drinking to Nice, where, anonymous in a large hotel, friendly and lavish in a bar, she let herself drown. "Your visits to your sister seem to do you so much good," was Mrs. Freeport's unvarying comment when Lily returned from these excursions, which always followed the arrival of her income. "But you spend far too much money on your sister. You are much too kind." But Lily had no regrets. Illiberal by circumstance, grudging only because she imitated the behaviour of other women, she became, drunk, an old forgotten Lily-girl, tender and warm, able to shed a happy tear and open a closed fist. She had been cold sober since September.

"Well, there you are," she said, and slapped down the plate of cheese. There was another person at the table, a Mrs. Garnett, who was returning to England the next day. Lily's manner toward the two women combined bullying with servility. Mrs. Freeport, large, in brown chiffon, wearing a hat with a water lily upon it to cover her thinning hair, liked to *feel* served. Lily had been a paid companion once; she had never seen a paradox in the joining of those two words. She simply looked on Mrs. Freeport and Mrs. Garnett as more of that race of ailing, peevish elderly children whose fancies and delusions must be humoured by the sane.

Mrs. Freeport pursed her lips in acknowledgement of the cheese. Mrs. Garnett, who was reading a book, did nothing at all. Mrs. Garnett had been with them four months. Her blued curls, her laugh, her moist baby's mouth, had the effect on Lily of a stone in the shoe. Mrs. Garnett's husband, dead but often mentioned, had evidently liked them saucy and dim in the brain. Now that William Henry was no longer there to protect his wife, she was the victim of the effects of her worrying beauty — a torment to shoe clerks and bus conductors. Italians were dreadful; Mrs. Garnett hardly dared put her wee nose outside the house. "You are a little monkey, Edith!" Mrs. Freeport would sometimes say, bringing her head upwards with a jerk, waking out of a sweet dream in time to applaud. Mrs. Garnett would go on telling how she had been jostled on the pavement or offended on a bus. And Lily Littel, who knew — but truly knew — about being followed and hounded and pleaded with, brought down her thick eyelids and smiled. Talk leads to overconfidence and errors. Lily had guided her life to this quiet shore by knowing when to open her mouth and when to keep it closed.

Mrs. Freeport was not deluded but simply poor. Thirteen years of pension-keeping on a tawdry stretch of Mediterranean coast had done nothing to improve her fortunes and had probably diminished them. Sentiment kept her near Bordighera, where someone precious to her had been buried in the Protestant part of the cemetery. In Lily's opinion, Mrs. Freeport ought to have cleared out long ago, cutting her losses, leaving the servants out of pocket and the grocer unpaid. Lily looked soft; she was round and pink and yellow-haired. The imitation pearls screwed on to her doughy little ears seemed to devour the flesh. But Lily could have bitten a real pearl in two and enjoyed the pieces. Her nature was generous, but an admiration for superior women had led her to cherish herself. An excellent cook, she had dreamed of being a poisoner, but decided to leave that for the loonies; it was no real way to get on. She had a moral programme of a sort — thought it wicked to set a poor table, until she learned that the sort of woman she yearned to become was often picky. After that she tried to put it out of her mind. At Mrs. Freeport's she was enrolled in a useful school, for the creed of the house was this: It is pointless to think about anything so temporary as food; coffee grounds can be used many times, and mouldy bread, revived in the oven, mashed with raisins and milk, makes a delicious pudding. If Lily had settled for this bleached existence, it was explained by a sentence scrawled over a page of her locked diary: "I live with gentlewomen now." And there was a finality about the statement that implied acceptance of their ways.

Lily removed the fly netting from the cheese. There was her bit left over from luncheon. It was the end of a portion of Dutch so dry it had split. Mrs. Freeport would have the cream cheese, possibly still highly pleasing under its coat of pale fur, while Mrs. Garnett, who was a yoghurt fancier, would require none at all.

"Cheese, Edith," said Mrs. Freeport loudly, and little Mrs. Garnett blinked her doll eyes and smiled: No, thank you. Let others thicken their figures and damage their souls.

The cheese was pushed along to Mrs. Freeport, then back to Lily, passing twice under Mrs. Garnett's nose. She did not look up again. She was moving her lips over a particularly absorbing passage in her book. For the last four months, she had been reading the same volume, which was called "Optimism Unlimited." So as not to stain the pretty dust jacket, she had covered it with brown paper, but now even that was becoming soiled. When Mrs. Freeport asked what the book was about, Mrs. Garnett smiled a timid apology and said, "I'm *afraid* it is philosophy." It was, indeed, a new philosophy, counselling restraint in all things, but recommending smiles. Four months of smiles and restraint had left Mrs. Garnett hungry, and, to mark her last evening at Mrs. Freeport's, she had asked for an Italian meal. Mrs. Freeport thought it extravagant — after all, they were still digesting an English Christmas. But little Edith was so sweet when she begged, putting her head to one side, wrinkling her face, that Mrs. Freeport, muttering about monkeys, had given in. The dinner was prepared and served, and Mrs. Garnett, suddenly remembering about restraint, brought her book to the table and decided not to eat a thing.

It seemed that the late William Henry had found this capriciousness adorable, but Mrs. Freeport's eyes were stones. Lily supposed this was how murders came about — not the hasty, soon-regretted sort but the plan that is sown from an insult, a slight, and comes to flower at temperate speed. Mrs. Garnett deserved a reprimand. Lily saw her, without any emotion, doubled in two and shoved in a sack. But did Mrs. Freeport like her friend enough to bother teaching her lessons? Castigation, to Lily, suggested love. Mrs. Garnett and Mrs. Freeport were old friends, and vaguely related. Mrs. Garnett had been coming to Mrs. Freeport's every winter for years, but she left unfinished letters lying about, from which Lily — a great reader — could learn that dear Vanessa was becoming meaner and queerer by the minute. Thinking of Mrs. Freeport as "dear Vanessa" took flexibility, but Lily had that. She was not "Miss" and not "Littel"; she was, or, rather, had been, a Mrs. Cliff Little, who had taken advantage of the disorders of war to get rid of Cliff. He vanished, and his memory grew smaller and faded from the sky. In the bright new day strolled Miss Lily Littel, ready for anything. Then a lonely, fretful widow had taken a fancy to her and, as soon as travel was possible, had taken Lily abroad. There followed eight glorious years of trains and bars and discreet afternoon gambling, of eating éclairs in English-style tearooms, and discovering cafés where bacon and eggs were fried. Oh, the discovery of that sign in Monte Carlo: "Every Friday Sausages and Mashed"! That was the joy of being in foreign lands. One hot afternoon, Lily's employer, hooked by Lily into her stays not an hour before, dropped dead in a cinema lobby in Rome. Her will revealed she had provided for "Miss Littel," for a fox terrier, and for an invalid niece. The provision for the niece prevented the family from coming down on Lily's head; all the same, Lily kept out of England. She had not inspired the death of her employer, but she had nightmares for some time after, as though she had taken the wish for the deed. Her letters were so ambiguous that there was talk in England of an inquest. Lily accompanied the coffin as far as the frontier, for a letter of instructions specified cremation, which Lily understood could take place only in France. The coffin was held up rather a long time at customs, documents went back and forth, and in the end the relatives were glad to hear the last of it. Shortly after that, the fox terrier died, and Lily appropriated his share, feeling that she deserved it. Her employer had been living on overdrafts; there was next to nothing for the dog, companion, or niece. Lily stopped having nightmares. She continued to live abroad.

With delicate nibbles, eyes down, Lily ate her cheese. Glancing sideways she noticed that Mrs. Garnett had closed the book. She wanted to annoy; she had planned the whole business of the Italian meal, had thought it out beforehand. Their manners were still strange to Lily, although she was a quick pupil. Why not clear the air, have it out? Once again she wondered what the two friends meant to each other. "Like" and "hate" were possibilities she had nearly forgotten when she stopped being Mrs. Cliff and became this curious, two-faced Lily Littel.

Mrs. Freeport's pebbly stare was focussed on her friend's jar of yoghurt. "Sugar?" she cried, giving the cracked basin a shove along the table. Mrs. Garnett pulled it towards her, defiantly. She spoke in a soft martyred voice, as though Lily weren't there. She said that it was her last evening and it no longer mattered. Mrs. Freeport had made a charge for extra sugar — yes, she had seen it on her bill. Mrs. Garnett asked only to pay and go. She was never coming again.

"I look upon you as essentially greedy." Mrs. Freeport leaned forward, enunciating with care. "You pretend to eat nothing, but I cannot look at a dish after you have served yourself. The *wreck* of the lettuce. The *destruction* of the pudding."

A bottle of wine, adrift and forgotten, stood by Lily's plate. She had not seen it until now. Mrs. Garnett, who was fearless, covered her yoghurt thickly with sugar.

"Like most people who pretend to eat like birds, you manage to keep your strength up," Mrs. Freeport said. "That sugar is the equivalent of a banquet, and you also eat between meals. Your drawers are stuffed with biscuits, and cheese, and chocolate, and heaven knows what."

"Dear Vanessa," Mrs. Garnett said.

"People who make a pretence of eating nothing always stuff furtively," said Mrs. Freeport smoothly. "Secret eating is exactly the same as secret drinking."

Lily's years abroad had immunized her to the conversation of gentlewomen, their absorption with money, their deliberate over or underfeeding, their sudden animal quarrels. She wondered if there remained a great deal more to learn before she could wear their castoff manners as her own. At the reference to secret drinking she looked calm and melancholy. Mrs. Garnett said, "That is most unkind." The yoghurt remained uneaten. Lily sighed, and wondered what would happen if she picked her teeth.

"My change man stopped by today," said Mrs. Garnett, all at once smiling and widening her eyes. How Lily admired that shift of territory — that carrying of banners to another field. She had not learned everything yet. "I *wish* you could have seen his face when he heard I was leaving! There really was no need for his coming, because I'd been in to his office only the week before, and changed all the money I need, and we'd had a lovely chat."

"The odious little money merchant in the bright-yellow automobile?" said Mrs. Freeport.

Mrs. Garnett, who often took up farfetched and untenable arguments, said, "William Henry wanted me to be happy."

"Edith!"

Lily hooked her middle finger around the bottle of wine and pulled it gently towards her. The day after tomorrow was years away. But she did not take her eyes from Mrs. Freeport, whose blazing eyes perfectly matched the small sapphires hanging from her ears.

Lily could have matched the expression if she had cared to, but she hadn't arrived at the sapphires yet. Addressing herself, Lily said, "Thanks," softly, and upended the bottle.

"I meant it in a general way," said Mrs. Garnett. "William Henry wanted me to be happy. It was nearly the last thing he said."

"At the time of William Henry's death, he was unable to say anything," said Mrs. Freeport. "William Henry was my first cousin. Don't use him as a platform for your escapades."

Lily took a sip from her glass. Shock! It hadn't been watered — probably in honour of Mrs. Garnett's last meal. But it was sour, thick, and full of silt. "I have always thought a little sugar would improve it," said Lily chattily, but nobody heard.

Mrs. Freeport suddenly conceded that William Henry might have wanted his future widow to be happy. "It was because he spoiled you," she said. "You were vain and silly when he married you, and he made you conceited and foolish. I don't wonder poor William Henry went off his head."

"Off his head?" Mrs. Garnett looked at Lily; calm, courteous Miss Littel was giving herself wine. "We might have general conversation," said Mrs. Garnett, with a significant twitch of face. "Miss Littel has hardly said a word."

"Why?" shouted Mrs. Freeport, throwing her table napkin down. "The meal is over. You refused it. There is no need for conversation of any kind."

She was marvellous, blazing, with that water lily on her head.

Ah, Lily thought, but you should have seen me, in the old days. How I could let fly ... poor old Cliff.

They moved in single file down the passage and into the sitting room, where, for reasons of economy, the hanging lustre contained one bulb. Lily and Mrs. Freeport settled down directly under it, on a sofa; each had her own newspaper to read, tucked down the side of the cushions. Mrs. Garnett walked about the room. "To think that I shall never see this room again," she said.

"I should hope not," said Mrs. Freeport. She held the paper before her face, but as far as Lily could tell she was not reading it.

"The trouble is" — for Mrs. Garnett could never help giving herself away — "I don't know where to go in the autumn."

"Ask your change man."

"Egypt," said Mrs. Garnett, still walking about. "I had friends who went to Egypt every winter for years and years, and now they have nowhere to go, either."

"Let them stay home," said Mrs. Freeport. "I am trying to read."

"If Egypt continues to carry on, I'm sure I don't know where we shall all be," said Lily. Neither lady took the slightest notice.

"They were perfectly charming people," said Mrs. Garnett, in a complaining way.

"Why don't you do the *Times* crossword, Edith?" said Mrs. Freeport.

From behind them Mrs. Garnett said, "You know that I can't, and you said that only to make me feel small. But William Henry did it until the very end, which proves, I think, that he was not o.h.h. By o.h.h. I mean *off his head.*"

The break in her voice was scarcely more than a quaver, but to the two women on the sofa it was a signal, and they got to their feet. By the time they reached her, Mrs. Garnett was sitting on the floor in hysterics. They helped her up, as they had often done before. She tried to scratch their faces and said they would be sorry when she had died.

Between them, they got her to bed. "Where is her hot-water bottle?" said Mrs. Freeport. "No, not that one. She must have her own — the bottle with the bunny head."

"My yoghurt," said Mrs. Garnett, sobbing. Without her make-up she looked shrunken, as though padding had been removed from her skin.

"Fetch the yoghurt," Mrs. Freeport commanded. She stood over the old friend while she ate the yoghurt, one tiny spoonful at a time. "Now go to sleep," she said.

In the morning, Mrs. Garnett was taken by taxi to the early train. She seemed entirely composed and carried her book. Mrs. Freeport hoped that her journey would be comfortable. She and Lily watched the taxi until it was out of sight on the road, and then, in the bare wintry gardens, Mrs. Freeport wept into her hands.

"I've said good-bye to her," she said at last, blowing her nose. "It is the last good-bye. I shall never see her again. I was so horrid to her. And she is so tiny and frail. She might die. I'm convinced of it. She won't survive the summer."

"She has survived every other," said Lily reasonably.

"Next year she must have the large room with the balcony. I don't know what I was thinking, not to have given it to her. We must begin planning now for next year. She will want a good reading light. Her eyes are so bad. And, you know, we should have chopped her vegetables. She doesn't chew. I'm sure that's at the bottom of the yoghurt affair."

"I'm off to Nice tomorrow," said Lily, the stray. "My sister is expecting me."

"You are so devoted," said Mrs. Freeport, looking wildly for her handkerchief, which had fallen on the gravel path. Her hat was askew. The house was empty. "So devoted ... I suppose that one day you will want to live in Nice, to be near her. I suppose that day will come."

Instead of answering, Lily set Mrs. Freeport's water lily straight, which was familiar of her; but they were both in such a state, for different reasons, that neither of them thought it strange.

QUESTIONS

1. What does the word "acceptance" in the title convey to you?

2. Does Lily really want to learn from the "gentlewomen" with whom she lives? What is her relationship to them?

3. At what point in the story do you realize that a tension exists between Mrs. Freeport and Mrs. Garnett? What incidents mark the rising conflict? Is it likely that Mrs. Garnett will return next year? that Mrs. Freeport will treat her more generously if she does?

4. Is Lily's "double life" a matter of self-preservation or of habitual deception? Are we meant to admire Lily or to judge her harshly? Do her memories of past life — her husband, the widow, the terrier, and her inheritance — adequately explain her?

5. The story is told completely from Lily's point of view; but is "Acceptance of Their Ways" about Lily or about the two older women?

JAMES BALDWIN

Sonny's Blues

I read about it in the paper, in the subway, on my way to work. I read it, and I couldn't believe it, and I read it again. Then perhaps I just stared at it, at the newsprint spelling out his name, spelling out the story. I stared at it in the swinging lights of the subway car, and in the faces and bodies of the people, and in my own face, trapped in the darkness which roared outside.

It was not to be believed and I kept telling myself that, as I walked from the subway station to the high school. And at the same time I couldn't doubt it. I was scared, scared for Sonny. He became real to me again. A great block of ice got settled in my belly and kept melting there slowly all day long, while I taught my classes algebra. It was a special kind of ice. It kept melting, sending trickles of ice water all up and down my veins, but it never got less. Sometimes it hardened and seemed to expand until I felt my guts were going to come spilling out or that I was going to choke or scream. This would always be at a moment when I was remembering some specific thing Sonny had once said or done.

When he was about as old as the boys in my classes his face had been bright and open, there was a lot of copper in it; and he'd had wonderfully direct brown eyes, and great gentleness and privacy. I wondered what he looked like now. He had been picked up, the evening before, in a raid on an apartment downtown, for peddling and using heroin.

I couldn't believe it: but what I mean by that is that I couldn't find any room for it anywhere inside me. I had kept it outside me for a long time. I hadn't wanted to know. I had had suspicions, but I didn't name them, I kept putting them away. I told myself that Sonny was wild, but he wasn't crazy. And he'd always been a good boy, he hadn't ever turned hard or evil or disrespectful, the way kids can, so quick, so quick, especially in Harlem. I didn't want to believe that I'd ever see my brother going down, coming to nothing, all that light in his face gone out, in the condition I'd already seen so many others. Yet it had happened and here I was, talking about algebra to a lot of boys who might, every one of them for all I knew, be popping off needles every time they went to the head.[1] Maybe it did more for them than algebra could.

I was sure that the first time Sonny had ever had horse,[2] he couldn't have been much older than these boys were now. These boys, now, were living as we'd been living then, they

---

[1] Men's room.

[2] Heroin.

were growing up with a rush and their heads bumped abruptly against the low ceiling of their actual possibilities. They were filled with rage. All they really knew were two darknesses, the darkness of their lives, which was now closing in on them, and the darkness of the movies, which had blinded them to that other darkness, and in which they now, vindictively, dreamed, at once more together than they were at any other time, and more alone.

When the last bell rang, the last class ended, I let out my breath. It seemed I'd been holding it for all that time. My clothes were wet — I may have looked as though I'd been sitting in a steam bath, all dressed up, all afternoon. I sat alone in the classroom a long time. I listened to the boys outside, downstairs, shouting and cursing and laughing. Their laughter struck me for perhaps the first time. It was not the joyous laughter which — God knows why — one associates with children. It was mocking and insular, its intent was to denigrate. It was disenchanted, and in this, also, lay the authority of their curses. Perhaps I was listening to them because I was thinking about my brother and in them I heard my brother. And myself.

One boy was whistling a tune, at once very complicated and very simple, it seemed to be pouring out of him as though he were a bird, and it sounded very cool and moving through all that harsh, bright air, only just holding its own through all those other sounds.

I stood up and walked over to the window and looked down into the courtyard. It was the beginning of the spring and the sap was rising in the boys. A teacher passed through them every now and again, quickly, as though he or she couldn't wait to get out of that courtyard, to get those boys out of their sight and off their minds. I started collecting my stuff. I thought I'd better get home and talk to Isabel.

The courtyard was almost deserted by the time I got downstairs. I saw this boy standing in the shadow of a doorway, looking just like Sonny. I almost called his name. Then I saw that it wasn't Sonny, but somebody we used to know, a boy from around our block. He'd been Sonny's friend. He'd never been mine, having been too young for me, and, anyway, I'd never liked him. And now, even though he was a grown-up man, he still hung around that block, still spent hours on the street corners, was always high and raggy. I used to run into him from time to time and he'd often work around to asking me for a quarter or fifty cents. He always had some real good excuse, too, and I always gave it to him. I don't know why.

But now, abruptly, I hated him. I couldn't stand the way he looked at me, partly like a dog, partly like a cunning child. I wanted to ask him what the hell he was doing in the school courtyard.

He sort of shuffled over to me, and he said, "I see you got the papers. So you already know about it."

"You mean about Sonny? Yes, I already know about it. How come they didn't get you?"

He grinned. It made him repulsive and it also brought to mind what he'd looked like as a kid. "I wasn't there. I stay away from them people."

"Good for you." I offered him a cigarette and I watched him through the smoke. "You come all the way down here just to tell me about Sonny?"

"That's right." He was sort of shaking his head and his eyes looked strange, as though they were about to cross. The bright sun deadened his damp dark brown skin and it made his eyes look yellow and showed up the dirt in his kinked hair. He smelled funky.[3] I moved a little away from him and I said, "Well, thanks. But I already know about it and I got to get home."

---

[3] Offensively stale-smelling.

"I'll walk you a little ways," he said. We started walking. There were a couple of kids still loitering in the courtyard and one of them said goodnight to me and looked strangely at the boy beside me.

"What're you going to do?" he asked me. "I mean, about Sonny?"

"Look. I haven't seen Sonny for over a year, I'm not sure I'm going to do anything. Anyway, what the hell *can* I do?"

"That's right," he said quickly, "ain't nothing you can do. Can't much help old Sonny no more, I guess."

It was what I was thinking and so it seemed to me he had no right to say it.

"I'm surprised at Sonny, though," he went on — he had a funny way of talking, he looked straight ahead as though he were talking to himself — "I thought Sonny was a smart boy, I thought he was too smart to get hung."[4]

"I guess he thought so too," I said sharply, "and that's how he got hung. And how about you? You're pretty goddamn smart, I bet."

Then he looked directly at me, just for a minute. "I ain't smart," he said. "If I was smart, I'd have reached for a pistol a long time ago."

"Look. Don't tell *me* your sad story, if it was up to me, I'd give you one." Then I felt guilty — guilty, probably, for never having supposed that the poor bastard *had* a story of his own, much less a sad one, and I asked, quickly, "What's going to happen to him now?"

He didn't answer this. He was off by himself some place.

"Funny thing," he said, and from his tone we might have been discussing the quickest way to get to Brooklyn, "when I saw the papers this morning, the first thing I asked myself was if I had anything to do with it. I felt sort of responsible."

I began to listen more carefully. The subway station was on the corner, just before us, and I stopped. He stopped, too. We were in front of a bar and he ducked slightly, peering in, but whoever he was looking for didn't seem to be there. The juke box was blasting away with something black and bouncy and I half watched the barmaid as she danced her way from the juke box to her place behind the bar. And I watched her face as she laughingly responded to something someone said to her, still keeping time to the music. When she smiled one saw the little girl, one sensed the doomed, still struggling woman beneath the battered face of the semi-whore.

"I never *give* Sonny nothing," the boy said finally, "but a long time ago I come to school high and Sonny asked me how it felt." He paused, I couldn't bear to watch him, I watched the barmaid, and I listened to the music which seemed to be causing the pavement to shake. "I told him it felt great." The music stopped, the barmaid paused and watched the juke box until the music began again. "It did."

All this was carrying me some place I didn't want to go. I certainly didn't want to know how it felt. It filled everything, the people, the houses, the music, the dark, quicksilver barmaid, with menace; and this menace was their reality.

"What's going to happen to him now?" I asked again.

"They'll send him away some place and they'll try to cure him." He shook his head. "Maybe he'll even think he's kicked the habit. Then they'll let him loose" — he gestured, throwing his cigarette into the gutter. "That's all."

"What do you mean, that's *all*?"

But I knew what he meant.

---

[4] Addicted.

"I *mean*, that's *all*." He turned his head and looked at me, pulling down the corners of his mouth. "Don't you know what I mean?" he asked, softly.

"How the hell *would* I know what you mean?" I almost whispered it, I don't know why.

"That's right," he said to the air, "how would *he* know what I mean?" He turned toward me again, patient and calm, and yet I somehow felt him shaking, shaking as though he were going to fall apart. I felt that ice in my guts again, the dread I'd felt all afternoon; and again I watched the barmaid, moving about the bar, washing glasses, and singing. "Listen. They'll let him out and then it'll just start all over again. That's what I mean."

"You mean — they'll let him out. And then he'll just start working his way back in again. You mean he'll never kick the habit. Is that what you mean?"

"That's right," he said, cheerfully. "*You* see what I mean."

"Tell me," I said at last, "why does he want to die? He must want to die, he's killing himself, why does he want to die?"

He looked at me in surprise. He licked his lips. "He don't want to die. He wants to live. Don't nobody want to die, ever."

Then I wanted to ask him — too many things. He could not have answered, or if he had, I could not have borne the answers. I started walking. "Well, I guess it's none of my business."

"It's going to be rough on old Sonny," he said. We reached the subway station. "This is your station?" he asked. I nodded. I took one step down. "Damn!" he said, suddenly. I looked up at him. He grinned again. "Damn it if I didn't leave all my money home. You ain't got a dollar on you, have you? Just for a couple of days, is all."

All at once something inside gave and threatened to come pouring out of me. I didn't hate him any more. I felt that in another moment I'd start crying like a child.

"Sure," I said. "Don't sweat." I looked in my wallet and didn't have a dollar, I only had a five. "Here," I said. "That hold you?"

He didn't look at it — he didn't want to look at it. A terrible, closed look came over his face, as though he were keeping the number on the bill a secret from him and me. "Thanks," he said, and now he was dying to see me go. "Don't worry about Sonny. Maybe I'll write him or something."

"Sure," I said. "You do that. So long."

"Be seeing you," he said. I went on down the steps.

And I didn't write Sonny or send him anything for a long time. When I finally did, it was just after my little girl died, and he wrote me back a letter which made me feel like a bastard. Here's what he said:

Dear brother,

You don't know how much I needed to hear from you. I wanted to write you many a time but I dug how much I must have hurt you and so I didn't write. But now I feel like a man who's been trying to climb up out of some deep, real deep and funky hole and just saw the sun up there, outside. I got to get outside.

I can't tell you much about how I got here. I mean I don't know how to tell you. I guess I was afraid of something or I was trying to escape from something and you know I have never been very strong in the head (smile). I'm glad Mama and Daddy are dead and can't see what's happened to their son and I swear if I'd known what I was doing I would never have hurt you so, you and a lot of other fine people who were nice to me and who believed in me.

I don't want you to think it had anything to do with me being a musician. It's more than that. Or maybe less than that. I can't get anything straight in my head down here and I try not to think about what's going to happen to me when I get outside again. Sometime I think I'm going to flip and *never* get outside and sometime I think I'll come straight back. I tell you one thing, though, I'd rather blow my brains out than go through this again. But that's what they all say, so they tell me. If I tell you when I'm coming to New York and if you could meet me, I sure would appreciate it. Give my love to Isabel and the kids and I was sure sorry to hear about little Gracie. I wish I could be like Mama and say the Lord's will be done, but I don't know it seems to me that trouble is the one thing that never does get stopped and I don't know what good it does to blame it on the Lord. But maybe it does some good if you believe it.

> Your brother,
> Sonny

Then I kept in constant touch with him and I sent him whatever I could and I went to meet him when he came back to New York. When I saw him many things I thought I had forgotten came flooding back to me. This was because I had begun, finally, to wonder about Sonny, about the life that Sonny lived inside. This life, whatever it was, had made him older and thinner and it had deepened the distant stillness in which he had always moved. He looked very unlike my baby brother. Yet, when he smiled, when we shook hands, the baby brother I'd never known looked out from the depths of his private life, like an animal waiting to be coaxed into the light.

"How you been keeping?" he asked me.

"All right. And you?"

"Just fine." He was smiling all over his face. "It's good to see you again."

"It's good to see you."

The seven years' difference in our ages lay between us like a chasm: I wondered if these years would ever operate between us as a bridge. I was remembering, and it made it hard to catch my breath, that I had been there when he was born; and I had heard the first words he had ever spoken. When he started to walk, he walked from our mother straight to me. I caught him just before he fell when he took the first steps he ever took in this world.

"How's Isabel?"

"Just fine. She's dying to see you."

"And the boys?"

"They're fine, too. They're anxious to see their uncle."

"Oh, come on. You know they don't remember me."

"Are you kidding? Of course they remember you."

He grinned again. We got into a taxi. We had a lot to say to each other, far too much to know how to begin.

As the taxi began to move, I asked, "You still want to go to India?"

He laughed. "You still remember that. Hell, no. This place is Indian enough for me."

"It used to belong to them," I said.

And he laughed again. "They damn sure knew what they were doing when they got rid of it."

Years ago, when he was around fourteen, he'd been all hipped on the idea of going to India. He read books about people sitting on rocks, naked, in all kinds of weather, but mostly bad, naturally, and walking barefoot through hot coals and arriving at wisdom. I used to say that it sounded to me as though they were getting away from wisdom as fast as they could. I think he sort of looked down on me for that.

"Do you mind," he asked, "if we have the driver drive alongside the park? On the west side — I haven't seen the city in so long."

"Of course not," I said. I was afraid that I might sound as though I were humoring him, but I hoped he wouldn't take it that way.

So we drove along, between the green of the park and the stony, lifeless elegance of hotels and apartment buildings, toward the vivid, killing streets of our childhood. These streets hadn't changed, though housing projects jutted up out of them now like rocks in the middle of a boiling sea. Most of the houses in which we had grown up had vanished, as had the stores from which we had stolen, the basements in which we had first tried sex, the rooftops from which we had hurled tin cans and bricks. But houses exactly like the houses of our past yet dominated the landscape, boys exactly like the boys we once had been found themselves smothering in these houses, came down into the streets for light and air and found themselves encircled by disaster. Some escaped the trap, most didn't. Those who got out always left something of themselves behind, as some animals amputate a leg and leave it in the trap. It might be said, perhaps, that I had escaped, after all, I was a school teacher; or that Sonny had, he hadn't lived in Harlem for years. Yet, as the cab moved uptown through streets which seemed, with a rush, to darken with dark people, and as I covertly studied Sonny's face, it came to me that what we both were seeking through our separate cab windows was that part of ourselves which had been left behind. It's always at the hour of trouble and confrontation that the missing member aches.

We hit 110th Street and started rolling up Lenox Avenue. And I'd known this avenue all my life, but it seemed to me again, as it had seemed on the day I'd first heard about Sonny's trouble, filled with a hidden menace which was its very breath of life.

"We almost there," said Sonny.

"Almost." We were both too nervous to say anything more.

We live in a housing project. It hasn't been up long. A few days after it was up it seemed uninhabitably new, now, of course, it's already rundown. It looks like a parody of the good, clean, faceless life — God knows the people who live in it do their best to make it a parody. The beat-looking grass lying around isn't enough to make their lives green, the hedges will never hold out the streets, and they know it. The big windows fool no one, they aren't big enough to make space out of no space. They don't bother with the windows, they watch the TV screen instead. The playground is most popular with the children who don't play at jacks, or skip rope, or roller skate, or swing, and they can be found in it after dark. We moved in partly because it's not too far from where I teach, and partly for the kids; but it's really just like the houses in which Sonny and I grew up. The same things happen, they'll have the same things to remember. The moment Sonny and I started into the house I had the feeling that I was simply bringing him back into the danger he had almost died trying to escape.

Sonny has never been talkative. So I don't know why I was sure he'd be dying to talk to me when supper was over the first night. Everything went fine, the oldest boy remembered him, and the youngest boy liked him, and Sonny had remembered to bring something for each of them; and Isabel, who is really much nicer than I am, more open and giving, had gone to a lot of trouble about dinner and was genuinely glad to see him. And she's always been able to tease Sonny in a way that I haven't. It was nice to see her face so vivid again and to hear her laugh and watch her make Sonny laugh. She wasn't, or, anyway, she didn't seem to be, at all uneasy or embarrassed. She chatted as though there were no subject which had to be avoided and she got Sonny past his first, faint stiffness. And thank God she was there, for I was filled with that icy dread again. Everything I did seemed awkward to me, and everything I said sounded freighted with hidden meaning. I was trying to remember everything I'd heard about dope addiction and I couldn't help watching Sonny for signs. I wasn't doing it out of malice. I was trying to find out something about my brother. I was dying to hear him tell me he was safe.

"Safe!" my father grunted, whenever Mama suggested trying to move to a neighborhood which might be safer for children. "Safe, hell! Ain't no place safe for kids, nor nobody."

He always went on like this, but he wasn't, ever, really as bad as he sounded, not even on weekends, when he got drunk. As a matter of fact, he was always on the lookout for "something a little better," but he died before he found it. He died suddenly, during a drunken weekend in the middle of the war, when Sonny was fifteen. He and Sonny hadn't ever got on too well. And this was partly because Sonny was the apple of his father's eye. It was because he loved Sonny so much and was frightened for him, that he was always fighting with him. It doesn't do any good to fight with Sonny. Sonny just moves back, inside himself, where he can't be reached. But the principal reason that they never hit it off is that they were so much alike. Daddy was big and rough and loud-talking, just the opposite of Sonny, but they both had — that same privacy.

Mama tried to tell me something about this, just after Daddy died. I was home on leave from the army.

This was the last time I ever saw my mother alive. Just the same, this picture gets all mixed up in my mind with pictures I had of her when she was younger. The way I always see her is the way she used to be on a Sunday afternoon, say, when the old folks were talking after the big Sunday dinner. I always see her wearing pale blue. She'd be sitting on the sofa. And my father would be sitting in the easy chair, not far from her. And the living room would be full of church folks and relatives. There they sit, in chairs all around the living room, and the night is creeping up outside, but nobody knows it yet. You can see the darkness growing against the windowpanes and you hear the street noises every now and again, or maybe the jangling beat of a tambourine from one of the churches close by, but it's real quiet in the room. For a moment nobody's talking, but every face looks darkening, like the sky outside. And my mother rocks a little from the waist, and my father's eyes are closed. Everyone is looking at something a child can't see. For a minute they've forgotten the children. Maybe a kid is lying on the rug, half asleep. Maybe somebody's got a kid in his lap and is absentmindedly stroking the kid's head. Maybe there's a kid, quiet and big-eyed, curled up in a big chair in the corner. The silence, the darkness coming, and the darkness in the faces frighten the child obscurely. He hopes that the hand which strokes his forehead will never stop — will never die. He hopes that there will never come a time when the old folks won't be sitting around the living room, talking about where they've come from, and what they've seen, and what's happened to them and their kinfolk.

But something deep and watchful in the child knows that this is bound to end, is already ending. In a moment someone will get up and turn on the light. Then the old folks will remember the children and they won't talk any more that day. And when light fills the room, the child is filled with darkness. He knows that every time this happens he's moved just a little closer to that darkness outside. The darkness outside is what the old folks have been talking about. It's what they've come from. It's what they endure. The child knows that they won't talk any more because if he knows too much about what's happened to *them*, he'll know too much too soon, about what's going to happen to *him*.

The last time I talked to my mother, I remember I was restless. I wanted to get out and see Isabel. We weren't married then and we had a lot to straighten out between us.

There Mama sat, in black, by the window. She was humming an old church song, *Lord, you brought me from a long ways off*. Sonny was out somewhere. Mama kept watching the streets.

"I don't know," she said, "if I'll ever see you again, after you go off from here. But I hope you'll remember the things I tried to teach you."

"Don't talk like that," I said, and smiled. "You'll be here a long time yet."

She smiled, too, but she said nothing. She was quiet for a long time. And I said, "Mama, don't you worry about nothing. I'll be writing all the time, and you be getting the checks. ..."

"I want to talk to you about your brother," she said, suddenly. "If anything happens to me he ain't going to have nobody to look out for him."

"Mama," I said, "ain't nothing going to happen to you *or* Sonny. Sonny's all right. He's a good boy and he's got good sense."

"It ain't a question of his being a good boy," Mama said, "nor of his having good sense. It ain't only the bad ones, nor yet the dumb ones that gets sucked under." She stopped, looking at me. "Your Daddy once had a brother," she said, and she smiled in a way that made me feel she was in pain. "You didn't never know that, did you?"

"No," I said, "I never knew that," and I watched her face.

"Oh, yes," she said, "your Daddy had a brother." She looked out of the window again. "I know you never saw your Daddy cry. But *I* did — many a time, through all these years."

I asked her, "What happened to his brother? How come nobody's ever talked about him?"

This was the first time I ever saw my mother look old.

"His brother got killed," she said, "when he was just a little younger than you are now. I knew him. He was a fine boy. He was maybe a little full of the devil, but he didn't mean nobody no harm."

Then she stopped and the room was silent, exactly as it had sometimes been on those Sunday afternoons. Mama kept looking out into the streets.

"He used to have a job in the mill," she said, "and, like all young folks, he just liked to perform on Saturday nights. Saturday nights, him and your father would drift around to different places, go to dances and things like that, or just sit around with people they knew, and your father's brother would sing, he had a fine voice, and play along with himself on his guitar. Well, this particular Saturday night, him and your father was coming home from some place, and they were both a little drunk and there was a moon that night, it was bright like day. Your father's brother was feeling kind of good, and he was whistling to himself, and he had his guitar slung over his shoulder. They was coming down a hill and beneath them was a road that turned off from the highway. Well, your father's brother, being always kind of frisky, decided to run down this hill, and he did, with that guitar banging and clanging behind him, and he ran across the road, and he was making water behind a tree. And your father was sort of amused at him and he was still coming down the hill, kind of slow. Then he heard a car motor and that same minute his brother stepped from behind the tree, into the road, in the moonlight. And he started to cross the road. And your father started to run down the hill, he says he don't know why. This car was full of white men. They was all drunk, and when they seen your father's brother they let out a great whoop and holler and they aimed the car straight at him. They was having fun, they just wanted to scare him, the way they do sometimes, you know. But they was drunk. And I guess the boy, being drunk, too, and scared, kind of lost his head. By the time he jumped it was too late. Your father says he heard his brother scream when the car rolled over him, and he heard the wood of that guitar when it give, and he heard them strings go flying, and he heard them white men shouting, and the car kept on a-going and it ain't stopped till this day. And, time your father got down the hill, his brother weren't nothing but blood and pulp."

Tears were gleaming on my mother's face. There wasn't anything I could say.

"He never mentioned it," she said, "because I never let him mention it before you children. Your Daddy was like a crazy man that night and for many a night thereafter. He says he never in his life seen anything as dark as that road after the lights of that car had gone away. Weren't nothing, weren't nobody on that road, just your Daddy and his brother and that busted guitar. Oh, yes. Your Daddy never did really get right again. Till the day he died he weren't sure but that every white man he saw was the man that killed his brother."

She stopped and took out her handkerchief and dried her eyes and looked at me.

"I ain't telling you all this," she said, "to make you scared or bitter or to make you hate nobody. I'm telling you this because you got a brother. And the world ain't changed."

I guess I didn't want to believe this. I guess she saw this in my face. She turned away from me, toward the window again, searching those streets.

"But I praise my Redeemer," she said at last, "that He called your Daddy home before me. I ain't saying it to throw no flowers at myself, but, I declare, it keeps me from feeling too cast down to know I helped your father get safely through this world. Your father always acted like he was the roughest, strongest man on earth. And everybody took him to be like that. But if he hadn't had me there — to see his tears!"

She was crying again. Still, I couldn't move. I said, "Lord, Lord, Mama, I didn't know it was like that."

"Oh, honey," she said, "there's a lot that you don't know. But you are going to find out." She stood up from the window and came over to me. "You got to hold on to your brother," she said, "and don't let him fall, no matter what it looks like is happening to him and no matter how evil you gets with him. You going to be evil with him many a time. But don't you forget what I told you, you hear?"

"I won't forget," I said. "Don't you worry, I won't forget. I won't let nothing happen to Sonny."

My mother smiled as though she were amused at something she saw in my face. Then, "You may not be able to stop nothing from happening. But you got to let him know you's *there*."

Two days later I was married, and then I was gone. And I had a lot of things on my mind and I pretty well forgot my promise to Mama until I got shipped home on a special furlough for her funeral.

And, after the funeral, with just Sonny and me alone in the empty kitchen, I tried to find out something about him.

"What do you want to do?" I asked him.

"I'm going to be a musician," he said.

For he had graduated, in the time I had been away, from dancing to the juke box to finding out who was playing what, and what they were doing with it, and he had brought himself a set of drums.

"You mean, you want to be a drummer?" I somehow had the feeling that being a drummer might be all right for other people but not for my brother Sonny.

"I don't think," he said, looking at me very gravely, "that I'll ever be a good drummer. But I think I can play a piano."

I frowned. I'd never played the role of the older brother quite so seriously before, had scarcely ever, in fact, *asked* Sonny a damn thing. I sensed myself in the presence of something I didn't really know how to handle, didn't understand. So I made my frown a little deeper as I asked: "What kind of musician do you want to be?"

He grinned. "How many kinds do you think there are?"

"Be *serious*," I said.

He laughed, throwing his head back, and then looked at me. "I *am* serious."

"Well, then, for Christ's sake, stop kidding around and answer a serious question. I mean, do you want to be a concert pianist, you want to play classical music and all that, or — or what?" Long before I finished he was laughing again. "For Christ's *sake*, Sonny!"

He sobered, but with difficulty. "I'm sorry. But you sound so — *scared!*" and he was off again.

"Well, you may think it's funny now, baby, but it's not going to be so funny when you have to make your living at it, let me tell you *that*." I was furious because I knew he was laughing at me and I didn't know why.

"No," he said, very sober now, and afraid, perhaps, that he'd hurt me, "I don't want to be a classical pianist. That isn't what interests me. I mean" — he paused, looking hard at me, as though his eyes would help me to understand, and then gestured helplessly, as though perhaps his hand would help — "I mean, I'll have a lot of studying to do, and I'll have to study *everything*, but, I mean, I want to play *with* — jazz musicians." He stopped. "I want to play jazz," he said.

Well, the word had never before sounded as heavy, as real, as it sounded that afternoon in Sonny's mouth. I just looked at him and I was probably frowning a real frown by this time. I simply couldn't see why on earth he'd want to spend his time hanging around nightclubs, clowning around on bandstands, while people pushed each other around a dance floor. It seemed — beneath him, somehow. I had never thought about it before, had never been forced to, but I suppose I had always put jazz musicians in a class with what Daddy called "good-time people."

"Are you *serious*?"

"Hell, *yes*, I'm serious."

He looked more helpless than ever, and annoyed, and deeply hurt.

I suggested, helpfully: "You mean — like Louis Armstrong?"[5]

His face closed as though I'd struck him. "No. I'm not talking about none of that old-time, down home crap."

"Well, look, Sonny, I'm sorry, don't get mad. I just don't altogether get it, that's all. Name somebody — you know, a jazz musician you admire."

"Bird."[6]

"Who?"

"Bird! Charlie Parker! Don't they teach you nothing in the goddamn army?"

I lit a cigarette. I was surprised and then a little amused to discover that I was trembling. "I've been out of touch," I said. "You'll have to be patient with me. Now. Who's this Parker character?"

"He's just one of the greatest jazz musicians alive," said Sonny, sullenly, his hands in his

---

[5] Louis "Satchmo" Armstrong (1900–1971), jazz trumpeter, singer, and band leader.
[6] Charlie "Bird" Parker (1920–1955), modern jazz trumpeter and band leader.

pockets, his back to me. "Maybe *the* greatest," he added, bitterly, "that's probably why *you* never heard of him."

"All right," I said, "I'm ignorant. I'm sorry. I'll go out and buy all the cat's records right away, all right?"

"It don't," said Sonny, with dignity, "make any difference to me. I don't care what you listen to. Don't do me no favors."

I was beginning to realize that I'd never seen him so upset before. With another part of my mind I was thinking that this would probably turn out to be one of those things kids go through and that I shouldn't make it seem important by pushing it too hard. Still, I didn't think it would do any harm to ask: "Doesn't all this take a lot of time? Can you make a living at it?"

He turned back to me and half leaned, half sat, on the kitchen table. "Everything takes time," he said, "and — well, yes, sure, I can make a living at it. But what I don't seem to be able to make you understand is that it's the only thing I want to do."

"Well, Sonny," I said, gently, "you know people can't always do exactly what they *want* to do — "

"*No*, I don't know that," said Sonny, surprising me. "I think people *ought* to do what they want to do, what else are they alive for?"

"You getting to be a big boy," I said desperately, "it's time you started thinking about your future."

"I'm thinking about my future," said Sonny, grimly. "I think about it all the time."

I gave up. I decided, if he didn't change his mind, that we could always talk about it later. "In the meantime," I said, "you got to finish school." We had already decided that he'd have to move in with Isabel and her folks. I knew this wasn't the ideal arrangement because Isabel's folks are inclined to be dicty[7] and they hadn't especially wanted Isabel to marry me. But I didn't know what else to do. "And we have to get you fixed up at Isabel's."

There was a long silence. He moved from the kitchen table to the window. "That's a terrible idea. You know it yourself."

"Do you have a *better* idea?"

He just walked up and down the kitchen for a minute. He was as tall as I was. He had started to shave. I suddenly had the feeling that I didn't know him at all.

He stopped at the kitchen table and picked up my cigarettes. Looking at me with a kind of mocking, amused defiance, he put one between his lips. "You mind?"

"You smoking already?"

He lit the cigarette and nodded, watching me through the smoke. "I just wanted to see if I'd have the courage to smoke in front of you." He grinned and blew a great cloud of smoke to the ceiling. "It was easy." He looked at my face. "Come on, now. I bet you was smoking at my age, tell the truth."

I didn't say anything but the truth was on my face, and he laughed. But now there was something very strained in his laugh. "Sure. And I bet that ain't all you was doing."

He was frightening me a little. "Cut the crap," I said. "We already decided that you was going to go and live at Isabel's. Now what's got into you all of a sudden?"

"*You* decided it," he pointed out. "*I* didn't decide nothing." He stopped in front of me, leaning against the stove, arms loosely folded. "Look, brother. I don't want to stay in Harlem no more, I really don't." He was very earnest. He looked at me, then over toward the

---

[7] Bossy — from *dictatorial*.

kitchen window. There was something in his eyes I'd never seen before, some thoughtfulness, some worry all his own. He rubbed the muscle of one arm. "It's time I was getting out of here."

"Where do you want to *go*, Sonny?"

"I want to join the army. Or the navy, I don't care. If I say I'm old enough, they'll believe me."

Then I got mad. It was because I was so scared. "You must be crazy. You goddamn fool, what the hell do you want to go and join the *army* for?"

"I just told you. To get out of Harlem."

"Sonny, you haven't even finished *school*. And if you really want to be a musician, how do you expect to study if you're in the *army*?"

He looked at me, trapped, and in anguish. "There's ways. I might be able to work out some kind of deal. Anyway, I'll have the G.I. Bill when I come out."

"*If* you come out." We stared at each other. "Sonny, please. Be reasonable. I know the setup is far from perfect. But we got to do the best we can."

"I ain't learning nothing in school," he said. "Even when I go." He turned away from me and opened the window and threw his cigarette out into the narrow alley. I watched his back. "At least, I ain't learning nothing you'd want me to learn." He slammed the window so hard I thought the glass would fly out, and turned back to me. "And I'm sick of the stink of these garbage cans!"

"Sonny," I said, "I know how you feel. But if you don't finish school now, you're going to be sorry later that you didn't." I grabbed him by the shoulders. "And you only got another year. It ain't so bad. And I'll come back and I swear I'll help you do *whatever* you want to do. Just try to put up with it till I come back. Will you please do that? For me?"

He didn't answer and he wouldn't look at me.

"Sonny. You hear me?"

He pulled away. "I hear you. But you never hear anything *I* say."

I didn't know what to say to that. He looked out of the window and then back at me. "OK," he said, and sighed. "I'll try."

Then I said, trying to cheer him up a little, "They got a piano at Isabel's. You can practice on it."

And as a matter of fact, it did cheer him up for a minute. "That's right," he said to himself. "I forgot that." His face relaxed a little. But the worry, the thoughtfulness, played on it still, the way shadows play on a face which is staring into the fire.

But I thought I'd never hear the end of that piano. At first, Isabel would write me, saying how nice it was that Sonny was so serious about his music and how, as soon as he came in from school, or wherever he had been when he was supposed to be at school, he went straight to that piano and stayed there until suppertime. And, after supper, he went back to that piano and stayed there until everybody went to bed. He was at the piano all day Saturday and all day Sunday. Then he bought a record player and started playing records. He'd play one record over and over again, all day long sometimes, and he'd improvise along with it on the piano. Or he'd play one section of the record, one chord, one change, one progression, then he'd do it on the piano. Then back to the record. Then back to the piano.

Well, I really don't know how they stood it. Isabel finally confessed that it wasn't like living with a person at all, it was like living with sound. And the sound didn't make any sense to her, didn't make any sense to any of them — naturally. They began, in a way, to be afflicted by this presence that was living in their home. It was as though Sonny were some sort of god, or monster. He moved in an atmosphere which wasn't like theirs at all. They fed him and he ate, he washed himself, he walked in and out of their door; he certainly wasn't nasty or unpleasant or rude, Sonny isn't any of those things; but it was as though he were all wrapped up in some cloud, some fire, some vision all his own; and there wasn't any way to reach him.

At the same time, he wasn't really a man yet, he was still a child, and they had to watch out for him in all kinds of ways. They certainly couldn't throw him out. Neither did they dare to make a great scene about that piano because even they dimly sensed, as I sensed, from so many thousands of miles away, that Sonny was at that piano playing for his life.

But he hadn't been going to school. One day a letter came from the school board and Isabel's mother got it — there had, apparently, been other letters but Sonny had torn them up. This day, when Sonny came in, Isabel's mother showed him the letter and asked where he'd been spending his time. And she finally got it out of him that he'd been down in Greenwich Village, with musicians and other characters, in a white girl's apartment. And this scared her and she started to scream at him and what came up, once she began — though she denies it to this day — was what sacrifices they were making to give Sonny a decent home and how little he appreciated it.

Sonny didn't play the piano that day. By evening, Isabel's mother had calmed down but then there was the old man to deal with, and Isabel herself. Isabel says she did her best to be calm but she broke down and started crying. She says she just watched Sonny's face. She could tell, by watching him, what was happening with him. And what was happening was that they penetrated his cloud, they had reached him. Even if their fingers had been a thousand times more gentle than human fingers ever are, he could hardly help feeling that they had stripped him naked and were spitting on that nakedness. For he also had to see that his presence, that music, which was life or death to him, had been torture for them and that they had endured it, not at all for his sake, but only for mine. And Sonny couldn't take that. He can take it a little better today than he could then but he's still not very good at it and, frankly, I don't know anybody who is.

The silence of the next few days must have been louder than the sound of all the music ever played since time began. One morning, before she went to work, Isabel was in his room for something and she suddenly realized that all of his records were gone. And she knew for certain that he was gone. And he was. He went as far as the navy would carry him. He finally sent me a postcard from some place in Greece and that was the first I knew that Sonny was still alive. I didn't see him any more until we were both back in New York and the war had long been over.

He was a man by then, of course, but I wasn't willing to see it. He came by the house from time to time, but we fought almost every time we met. I didn't like the way he carried himself, loose and dreamlike all the time, and I didn't like his friends, and his music seemed to be merely an excuse for the life he led. It sounded just that weird and disordered.

Then we had a fight, a pretty awful fight, and I didn't see him for months. By and by I looked him up, where he was living, in a furnished room in the Village, and I tried to make it up. But there were lots of other people in the room and Sonny just lay on his bed, and he wouldn't come downstairs with me, and he treated these other people as though they were his family and I weren't. So I got mad and then he got mad, and then I told him that he might just as well be dead as live the way he was living. Then he stood up and he told me not to worry about him any more in life, that he *was* dead as far as I was concerned. Then he pushed me to the door and the other people looked on as though nothing were happening, and he slammed the door behind me. I stood in the hallway, staring at the door. I heard somebody laugh in the room and then the tears came to my eyes. I started down the steps, whistling to keep from crying, I kept whistling to myself, *You going to need me, baby, one of these cold, rainy days.*[8]

I read about Sonny's trouble in the spring. Little Grace died in the fall. She was a beautiful little girl. But she only lived a little over two years. She died of polio and she suffered. She had a slight fever for a couple of days, but it didn't seem like anything and we just kept her in bed. And we would certainly have called the doctor, but the fever dropped, she seemed to be all right. So we thought it had just been a cold. Then, one day, she was up, playing, Isabel was in the kitchen fixing lunch for the two boys when they'd come in from school, and she heard Grace fall down in the living room. When you have a lot of children you don't always start running when one of them falls, unless they start screaming or something. And, this time, Gracie was quiet. Yet, Isabel says that when she heard that *thump* and then that silence, something happened to her to make her afraid. And she ran to the living room and there was little Grace on the floor, all twisted up, and the reason she hadn't screamed was that she couldn't get her breath. And when she did scream, it was the worst sound, Isabel says, that she'd ever heard in all her life, and she still hears it sometimes in her dreams. Isabel will sometimes wake me up with a low, moaning, strangling sound and I have to be quick to awaken her and hold her to me and where Isabel is weeping against me seems a mortal wound.

I think I may have written Sonny the very day that little Grace was buried. I was sitting in the living room in the dark, by myself, and I suddenly thought of Sonny. My trouble made his real.

One Saturday afternoon, when Sonny had been living with us, or anyway, been in our house, for nearly two weeks, I found myself wandering aimlessly about the living room, drinking from a can of beer, and trying to work up courage to search Sonny's room. He was out, he was usually out whenever I was home, and Isabel had taken the children to see their grandparents. Suddenly I was standing still in front of the living room window, watching Seventh Avenue. The idea of searching Sonny's room made me still. I scarcely dared to admit to myself what I'd be searching for. I didn't know what I'd do if I found it. Or if I didn't.

On the sidewalk across from me, near the entrance to a barbecue joint, some people were holding an old-fashioned revival meeting. The barbecue cook, wearing a dirty white apron, his conked[9] hair reddish and metallic in the pale sun, and a cigarette between his lips, stood in the doorway, watching them. Kids and older people paused in their errands and stood there, along with some older men and a couple of very tough-looking women who watched everything that happened on the avenue, as though they owned it, or were maybe owned by it. Well, they were watching this, too. The revival was being carried on by three sisters in black, and a brother. All they had were their voices and their Bibles and a tambourine. The brother was testifying and while he testified two of the sisters stood together, seeming to say, amen, and the third sister walked around with the tambourine outstretched and a couple of people dropped coins into it. Then the brother's testimony ended and the sister who had been taking up the collection dumped the coins into her palm and transferred them to the pocket of her long black robe. Then she raised both hands, striking the tambourine against the air, and then against one hand, and she started to sing. And the two other sisters and the brother joined in.

It was strange, suddenly, to watch, though I had been seeing these meetings all my life.

---

[8] A distorted line from an old blues song, "Some of These Days."

[9] Artificially straightened.

So, of course, had everybody else down there. Yet, they paused and watched and listened and I stood still at the window. "*'Tis the old ship of Zion*," they sang, and the sister with the tambourine kept a steady, jangling beat, "*it has rescued many a thousand*!" Not a soul under the sound of their voices was hearing this song for the first time, not one of them had been rescued. Nor had they seen much in the way of rescue work being done around them. Neither did they especially believe in the holiness of the three sisters and the brother, they knew too much about them, knew where they lived, and how. The woman with the tambourine, whose voice dominated the air, whose face was bright with joy, was divided by very little from the woman who stood watching her, a cigarette between her heavy, chapped lips, her hair a cuckoo's nest, her face scarred and swollen from many beatings, and her black eyes glittering like coal. Perhaps they both knew this, which was why, when, as rarely, they addressed each other, they addressed each other as Sister. As the singing filled the air the watching, listening faces underwent a change, the eyes focusing on something within; the music seemed to soothe a poison out of them; and time seemed, nearly, to fall away from the sullen, belligerent, battered faces, as though they were fleeing back to their first condition, while dreaming of their last. The barbecue cook half shook his head and smiled, and dropped his cigarette and disappeared into his joint. A man fumbled in his pockets for change and stood holding it in his hand impatiently, as though he had just remembered a pressing appointment further up the avenue. He looked furious. Then I saw Sonny, standing on the edge of the crowd. He was carrying a wide, flat notebook with a green cover, and it made him look, from where I was standing, almost like a schoolboy. The coppery sun brought out the copper in his skin, he was very faintly smiling, standing very still. Then the singing stopped, the tambourine turned into a collection plate again. The furious man dropped in his coins and vanished, so did a couple of the women, and Sonny dropped some change in the plate, looking directly at the woman with a little smile. He started across the avenue, toward the house. He has a slow, loping walk, something like the way Harlem hipsters walk, only he's imposed on this his own half-beat. I had never really noticed it before.

I stayed at the window, both relieved and apprehensive. As Sonny disappeared from my sight, they began singing again. And they were still singing when his key turned in the lock.

"Hey," he said.

"Hey, yourself. You want some beer?"

"No. Well, maybe." But he came up to the window and stood beside me, looking out. "What a warm voice," he said.

They were singing *If I could only hear my mother pray again*!

"Yes," I said, "and she can sure beat that tambourine."

"But what a terrible song," he said, and laughed. He dropped his notebook on the sofa and disappeared into the kitchen. "Where's Isabel and the kids?"

"I think they want to see their grandparents. You hungry?"

"No." He came back into the living room with his can of beer. "You want to come some place with me tonight?"

I sensed, I don't know how, that I couldn't possibly say no. "Sure. Where?"

He sat down on the sofa and picked up his notebook and started leafing through it. "I'm going to sit in with some fellows in a joint in the Village."

"You mean, you're going to play, tonight?"

"That's right." He took a swallow of his beer and moved back to the window. He gave me a sidelong look. "If you can stand it."

"I'll try," I said.

He smiled to himself and we both watched as the meeting across the way broke up. The three sisters and the brother, heads bowed, were singing *God be with you till we meet again*. The faces around them were very quiet. Then the song ended. The small crowd dispersed. We watched the three women and the lone man walk slowly up the avenue.

"When she was singing before," said Sonny, abruptly, "her voice reminded me for a minute of what heroin feels like sometimes — when it's in your veins. It makes you feel sort of warm and cool at the same time. And distant. And — and sure." He sipped his beer, very deliberately not looking at me. I watched his face. "It makes you feel — in control. Sometimes you've got to have that feeling."

"Do you?" I sat down slowly in the easy chair.

"Sometimes." He went to the sofa and picked up his notebook again. "Some people do."

"In order," I asked, "to play?" And my voice was very ugly, full of contempt and anger.

"Well" — he looked at me with great, troubled eyes, as though, in fact, he hoped his eyes would tell me things he could never otherwise say — "they *think* so. And *if* they think so — !"

"And what do *you* think?" I asked.

He sat on the sofa and put his can of beer on the floor. "I don't know," he said, and I couldn't be sure if he were answering my question or pursuing his thoughts. His face didn't tell me. "It's not so much to *play*. It's to *stand* it, to be able to make it at all. On any level." He frowned and smiled: "In order to keep from shaking to pieces."

"But these friends of yours," I said, "they seem to shake themselves to pieces pretty goddamn fast."

"Maybe." He played with the notebook. And something told me that I should curb my tongue, that Sonny was doing his best to talk, that I should listen. "But of course you only know the ones that've gone to pieces. Some don't — or at least they haven't *yet* and that's just about all *any* of us can say." He paused. "And then there are some who just live, really, in hell, and they know it and they see what's happening and they go right on. I don't know." He sighed, dropped the notebook, folded his arms. "Some guys, you can tell from the way they play, they on something *all* the time. And you can see that, well, it makes something real for them. But of course," he picked up his beer from the floor and sipped it and put the can down again, "they *want* to, too, you've got to see that. Even some of them that say they don't — *some*, not all."

"And what about you?" I asked — I couldn't help it. "What about you? Do *you* want to?"

He stood up and walked to the window and I remained silent for a long time. Then he sighed. "Me," he said. Then: "While I was downstairs before, on my way here, listening to that woman sing, it struck me all of a sudden how much suffering she must have had to go through — to sing like that. It's *repulsive* to think you have to suffer that much."

I said: "But there's no way not to suffer — is there, Sonny?"

"I believe not," he said and smiled, "but that's never stopped anyone from trying." He looked at me. "Has it?" I realized, with this mocking look, that there stood between us, forever, beyond the power of time or forgiveness, the fact that I had held silence — so long! — when he had needed human speech to help him. He turned back to the window. "No, there's no way not to suffer. But you try all kinds of ways to keep from drowning in it, to keep on top of it, and to make it seem — well, like *you*. Like you did something, all right, and now you're suffering for it. You know?" I said nothing. "Well you know," he said, impatiently, "why *do* people suffer? Maybe it's better to do something to give it a reason, *any* reason."

"But we just agreed," I said, "that there's no way not to suffer. Isn't is better, then, just to — take it?"

"But nobody just takes it," Sonny cried, "that's what I'm telling you! *Everybody* tries not to. You're just hung up on the *way* some people try — it's not *your* way!"

The hair on my face began to itch, my face felt wet. "That's not true," I said, "that's not true. I don't give a damn what other people do, I don't even care how they suffer. I just care how *you* suffer." And he looked at me. "Please believe me," I said, "I don't want to see you — die — trying not to suffer."

"I won't," he said flatly, "die trying not to suffer. At least, not any faster than anybody else."

"But there's no need," I said, trying to laugh, "is there? in killing yourself."

I wanted to say more, but I couldn't. I wanted to talk about will power and how life could be — well, beautiful. I wanted to say that it was all within; but was it? or, rather, wasn't that exactly the trouble? And I wanted to promise that I would never fail him again. But it would all have sounded — empty words and lies.

So I made the promise to myself and prayed that I would keep it.

"It's terrible sometimes, inside," he said, "that's what's the trouble. You walk these streets, black and funky and cold, and there's not really a living ass to talk to, and there's nothing shaking, and there's no way of getting it out — that storm inside. You can't talk it and you can't make love with it, and when you finally try to get with it and play it, you realize *nobody's* listening. So *you've* got to listen. You got to find a way to listen."

And then he walked away from the window and sat on the sofa again, as though all the wind had suddenly been knocked out of him. "Sometimes you'll do *anything* to play, even cut your mother's throat." He laughed and looked at me. "Or your brother's." Then he sobered. "Or your own." Then: "Don't worry. I'm all right now and I think I'll *be* all right. But I can't forget — where I've been. I don't mean just the physical place I've been, I mean where I've *been*. And *what* I've been."

"What have you been, Sonny?" I asked.

He smiled — but sat sideways on the sofa, his elbow resting on the back, his fingers playing with his mouth and chin, not looking at me. "I've been something I didn't recognize, didn't know I could be. Didn't know anybody could be." He stopped, looking inward, looking helplessly young, looking old. "I'm not talking about it now because I feel *guilty* or anything like that — maybe it would be better if I did, I don't know. Anyway, I can't really talk about it. Not to you, not to anybody," and now he turned and faced me. "Sometimes, you know, and it was actually when I was most *out* of the world, I felt that I was in it, that I was *with* it, really, and I could play or I didn't really have to *play*, it just came out of me, it was there. And I don't know how I played, thinking about it now, but I know I did awful things, those times, sometimes, to people. Or it wasn't that I *did* anything to them — it was that they weren't real." He picked up the beer can; it was empty; he rolled it between his palms: "And other times — well, I needed a fix, I needed to find a place to lean, I needed to clear a space to *listen* — and I couldn't find it, and I — went crazy, I did terrible things to *me*, I was terrible *for* me." He began pressing the beer can between his hands, I watched the metal begin to give. It glittered, as he played with it like a knife, and I was afraid he would cut himself, but I said nothing. "Oh well, I can never tell you. I was all by myself at the bottom of something, stinking and sweating and crying and shaking, and I smelled it, you know? *my* stink, and I thought I'd die if I couldn't get away from it and yet, all the same, I knew that everything I was doing was just locking me in with it. And I didn't know," he paused, still flattening the beer can, "I didn't know, I still *don't* know, something kept telling me that maybe it was good to smell your own stink, but I didn't think that *that* was what I'd been trying to do — and — who can stand it?" and he abruptly dropped the ruined beer can, looking at me with a small, still smile, and then rose, walking to the window as though it were the lodestone rock. I watched his face, he watched the avenue. "I couldn't tell you when Mama died — but the reason I wanted to leave Harlem so bad was to get away from drugs. And then, when I ran away, that's what I was running from — really. When I came back, nothing had changed, *I* hadn't changed, I was just — older." And he stopped, drumming with his fingers on the windowpane. The sun had vanished, soon darkness would fall. I watched his face. "It can come again," he said, almost as though speaking to himself. Then he turned to me. "It can come again," he repeated. "I just want you to know that."

"All right," I said, at last. "So it can come again. All right."

He smiled, but the smile was sorrowful. "I had to try to tell you," he said.

"Yes," I said. "I understand that."

"You're my brother," he said, looking straight at me, and not smiling at all.

"Yes," I repeated, "yes. I understand that."

He turned back to the window, looking out. "All that hatred down there," he said, "all that hatred and misery and love. It's a wonder it doesn't blow the avenue apart."

We went to the only nightclub on a short, dark street, downtown. We squeezed through the narrow, chattering, jampacked bar to the entrance of the big room, where the bandstand was. And we stood there for a moment, for the lights were very dim in this room and we couldn't see. Then, "Hello, boy," said the voice and an enormous black man, much older than Sonny or myself, erupted out of all that atmospheric lighting and put an arm around Sonny's shoulder. "I been sitting right here," he said, "waiting for you."

He had a big voice, too, and heads in the darkness turned toward us.

Sonny grinned and pulled a little away, and said, "Creole, this is my brother. I told you about him."

Creole shook my hand. "I'm glad to meet you, son," he said, and it was clear that he was glad to meet me *there*, for Sonny's sake. And he smiled, "You got a real musician in *your* family," and he took his arm from Sonny's shoulder and slapped him, lightly, affectionately, with the back of his hand.

"Well. Now I've heard it all," said a voice behind us. This was another musician, and a friend of Sonny's, a coal-black, cheerful-looking man, built close to the ground. He immediately began confiding to me, at the top of his lungs, the most terrible things about Sonny, his teeth gleaming like a lighthouse and his laugh coming up out of him like the beginning of an earthquake. And it turned out that everyone at the bar knew Sonny, or almost everyone; some were musicians, working there, or nearby, or not working, some were simply hangers-on, and some were there to hear Sonny play. I was introduced to all of them and they were all very polite to me. Yet, it was clear that, for them, I was only Sonny's brother. Here, I was in Sonny's world. Or, rather: his kingdom. Here, it was not even a question that his veins bore royal blood.

They were going to play soon and Creole installed me, by myself, at a table in a dark corner. Then I watched them, Creole, and the little black man, and Sonny, and the others, while they horsed around, standing just below the bandstand. The light from the bandstand spilled just a little short of them and, watching them laughing and gesturing and moving about, I had the feeling that they, nevertheless, were being most careful not to step into that circle of light too suddenly: that if they moved into the light too suddenly, without thinking, they would perish in flame. Then, while I watched, one of them, the small black man, moved into the light and crossed the bandstand and started fooling around with his drums. Then — being funny and being, also, extremely ceremonious — Creole took Sonny by the arm and led him to the piano. A woman's voice called Sonny's name and a few hands started clapping. And Sonny, also being funny and being ceremonious, and so touched, I think, that he could have cried, but neither hiding it nor showing it, riding it like a man, grinned, and put both hands to his heart and bowed from the waist.

Creole then went to the bass fiddle and a lean, very bright-skinned brown man jumped up on the bandstand and picked up his horn. So there they were, and the atmosphere on the bandstand and in the room began to change and tighten. Someone stepped up to the microphone and announced them. Then there were all kinds of murmurs. Some people at the bar shushed others. The waitress ran around, frantically getting in the last orders, guys and chicks got closer to each other, and the lights on the bandstand, on the quartet, turned to a kind of indigo. Then they all looked different there. Creole looked about him for the last time, as though he were making certain that all his chickens were in the coop, and then he — jumped and struck the fiddle. And there they were.

All I know about music is that not many people ever really hear it. And even then, on the rare occasions when something opens within, and the music enters, what we mainly hear, or hear corroborated, are personal, private, vanishing evocations. But the man who creates the music is hearing something else, is dealing with the roar rising from the void and imposing order on it as it hits the air. What is evoked in him, then, is of another order, more terrible because it has no words, and triumphant, too, for that same reason. And his triumph, when he triumphs, is ours. I just watched Sonny's face. His face was troubled, he was working hard, but he wasn't with it. And I had the feeling that, in a way, everyone on the bandstand was waiting for him, both waiting for him and pushing him along. But as I began to watch Creole, I realized that it was Creole who held them all back. He had them on a short rein. Up there, keeping the beat with his whole body, wailing on the fiddle, with his eyes half closed, he was listening to everything, but he was listening to Sonny. He was having a dialogue with Sonny. He wanted Sonny to leave the shoreline and strike out for the deep water. He was Sonny's witness that deep water and drowning were not the same thing — he had been there, and he knew. And he wanted Sonny to know. He was waiting for Sonny to do the things on the keys which would let Creole know that Sonny was in the water.

And, while Creole listened, Sonny moved, deep within, exactly like someone in torment. I had never before thought of how awful the relationship must be between the musician and his instrument. He has to fill it, this instrument, with the breath of life, his own. He has to make it do what he wants it to do. And a piano is just a piano. It's made out of so much wood and wires and little hammers and big ones, and ivory. While there's only so much you can do with it, the only way to find this out is to try; to try and make it do everything.

And Sonny hadn't been near a piano for over a year. And he wasn't on much better terms with his life, not the life that stretched before him now. He and the piano stammered, started one way, got scared, stopped; started another way, panicked, marked time, started again; then seemed to have found a direction, panicked again, got stuck. And the face I saw on Sonny I'd never seen before. Everything had been burned out of it, and, at the same time, things usually hidden were being burned in, by the fire and fury of the battle which was occurring in him up there.

Yet, watching Creole's face as they neared the end of the first set, I had the feeling that something had happened, something I hadn't heard. Then they finished, there was scattered applause, and then, without an instant's warning, Creole started into something else, it was almost sardonic, it was *Am I Blue*. And, as though he commanded, Sonny began to play. Something began to happen. And Creole let out the reins. The dry, low, black man said something awful on the drums, Creole answered, and the drums talked back. Then the horn insisted, sweet and high, slightly detached perhaps, and Creole listened, commenting now and then, dry, and driving, beautiful and calm and old. Then they all came together again, and Sonny was part of the family again. I could tell this from his face. He seemed to have found, right there beneath his fingers, a damn brand-new piano. It seemed that he couldn't get over it. Then, for a while, just being happy with Sonny, they seemed to be agreeing with him that brand-new pianos certainly were a gas.

Then Creole stepped forward to remind them that what they were playing was the blues. He hit something in all of them, he hit something in me, myself, and the music tightened and deepened, apprehension began to beat the air. Creole began to tell us what the blues were all about. They were not about anything very new. He and his boys up there were keeping it new, at the risk of ruin, destruction, madness, and death, in order to find new ways to make us listen. For, while the tale of how we suffer, and how we are delighted, and how we may triumph is never new, it always must be heard. There isn't any other tale to tell, it's the only light we've got in all this darkness.

And this tale, according to that face, that body, those strong hands on those strings, has another aspect in every country, and a new depth in every generation. Listen, Creole seemed to be saying, listen. Now these are Sonny's blues. He made the little black man on the drums know it, and the bright, brown man on the horn. Creole wasn't trying any longer to get Sonny in the water. He was wishing him Godspeed. Then he stepped back, very slowly, filling the air with the immense suggestion that Sonny speak for himself.

Then they all gathered around Sonny and Sonny played. Every now and again one of them seemed to say, amen. Sonny's fingers filled the air with life, his life. But that life contained so many others. And Sonny went all the way back, he really began with the spare, flat statement of the opening phrase of the song. Then he began to make it his. It was very beautiful because it wasn't hurried and it was no longer a lament. I seemed to hear with what burning he had made it his, with what burning we had yet to make it ours, how we could cease lamenting. Freedom lurked around us and I understood, at last, that he could help us to be free if we would listen, that he would never be free until we did. Yet, there was no battle in his face now, I heard what he had gone through, and would continue to go through until he came to rest in earth. He had made it his: that long line, of which we knew only Mama and Daddy. And he was giving it back, as everything must be given back, so that, passing through death, it can live forever. I saw my mother's face again, and felt, for the first time, how the stones of the road she had walked on must have bruised her feet. I saw the moonlit road where my father's brother died. And it brought something else back to me, and carried me past it, I saw my little girl again and felt Isabel's tears again, and I felt my own tears begin to rise. And I was yet aware that this was only a moment, that the world waited outside, as hungry as a tiger, and that trouble stretched above us, longer than the sky.

Then it was over. Creole and Sonny let out their breath, both soaking wet, and grinning. There was a lot of applause and some of it was real. In the dark, the girl came by and I asked her to take drinks to the bandstand. There was a long pause, while they talked up there in the indigo light and after awhile I saw the girl put a Scotch and milk on top of the piano for Sonny. He didn't seem to notice it, but just before they started playing again, he sipped from it and looked toward me, and nodded. Then he put it back on top of the piano.

For me, then, as they began to play again, it glowed and shook above my brother's head like the very cup of trembling.[10]

QUESTIONS

1. Trace the steps in Sonny's decline and recovery. Are they plausible?

2. Unlike many stories, this one begins neither at the beginning nor after the events are past, but in the middle. What has Baldwin gained by starting here?

3. What purpose is served by the early scene between Sonny's brother and his unlikable friend? Since the narrator has already told us about Sonny's arrest, what does this scene add?

4. Can you define the difference between Sonny and his brother? How do the two reconnect after Sonny is released from prison?

5. Whose story is this, Sonny's or his brother's? What case can be made for the opposing point of view?

6. "Sonny's Blues" moves around in time, through flashbacks that provide background information. Do you find the chronology difficult to follow? If so, where was the difficulty greatest? What might Baldwin have done to overcome it?

7. We learn that Sonny was never talkative. What has this to do with his character? with his choice of profession?

8. The narrator finds it hard to accept Sonny's dream of becoming a jazz musician. What does this reluctance tell you about him?

9. The death of Sonny's niece is mentioned more than once. Is this incident important to the plot, or is it only a way of rounding out the narrator's character?

10. What light does the last scene shed on the meaning of the title?

---

[10] From Isaiah, 51:22, "Thus saith thy Lord the Lord ..., Behold, I have taken out of thine hand the cup of trembling, even the dregs of the cup of my fury; thou shalt no more drink it again."

WILLIAM GASS

In the Heart of the
Heart of the Country

A PLACE

So I have sailed the seas and come ... to B ...[1] a small town fastened to a field in Indiana. Twice there have been twelve hundred people here to answer to the census. The town is outstandingly neat and shady, and always puts its best side to the highway. On one lawn there's even a wood or plastic iron deer.

You can reach us by crossing a creek. In the spring the lawns are green, the forsythia is singing, and even the railroad that guts the town has straight bright rails which hum when the train is coming, and the train itself has a welcome horning sound.

Down the back streets the asphalt crumbles into gravel. There's Westbrook's, with the geraniums, Horsefall's, Mott's. The sidewalk shatters. Gravel dust rises like breath behind the wagons. And I am in retirement from love.

WEATHER

In the Midwest, around the lower Lakes, the sky in the winter is heavy and close, and it is a rare day, a day to remark on, when the sky lifts and allows the heart up. I am keeping count, and as I write this page, it is eleven days since I have seen the sun.

MY HOUSE

There's a row of headless maples behind my house, cut to free the passage of electric wires. High stumps, ten feet tall, remain, and I climb these like a boy to watch the country sail away from me. They are ordinary fields, a little more uneven than they should be, since in the spring they puddle. The topsoil's thin, but only moderately stony. Corn is grown one year, soybeans another. At dusk starlings darken the single tree — a larch — which stands in the middle. When the sky moves, fields move under it. I feel, on my perch, that I've lost my years. It's as

---

[1] A slight departure from two lines in William Butler Yeats's "Sailing to Byzantium," in which that ancient city is the symbol of timeless, changeless art and beauty.

though I were living at last in my eyes, as I have always dreamed of doing, and I think then I know why I've come here: to see, and so to go out against new things — oh god how easily — like air in a breeze. It's true there are moments — foolish moments, ecstasy on a tree stump — when I'm all but gone, scattered I like to think like seed, for I'm the sort now in the fool's position of having love left over which I'd like to lose; what good is it now to me, candy ungiven after Halloween?

A PERSON

There are vacant lots on either side of Billy Holsclaw's house. As the weather improves, they fill with hollyhocks. From spring through fall, Billy collects coal and wood and puts the lumps and pieces in piles near his door, for keeping warm is his one work. I see him most often on mild days sitting on his doorsill in the sun. I notice he's squinting a little, which is perhaps the reason he doesn't cackle as I pass. His house is the size of a single garage, and very old. It shed its paint with its youth, and its boards are a warped and weathered gray. So is Billy. He wears a short lumpy faded black coat when it's cold, otherwise he always goes about in the same loose, grease-spotted shirt and trousers. I suspect his galluses were yellow once, when they were new.

WIRES

These wires offend me. Three trees were maimed on their account, and now these wires deface the sky. They cross like a fence in front of me, enclosing the crows with the clouds. I can't reach in, but like a stick, I throw my feelings over. What is it that offends me? I am on my stump, I've built a platform there and the wires prevent my going out. The cut trees, the black wires, all the beyond birds therefore anger me. When I've wormed through a fence to reach a meadow, do I ever feel the same about the field?

THE CHURCH

The church has a steeple like the hat of a witch, and five birds, all doves, perch in its gutters.

MY HOUSE

Leaves move in the windows. I cannot tell you yet how beautiful it is, what it means. But they do move. They move in the glass.

POLITICS

... for all those not in love.

I've heard Batista[2] described as a Mason. A farmer who'd seen him in Miami made this claim. He's as nice a fellow as you'd ever want to meet. Of Castro, of course, no one speaks.

For all those not in love there's law: to rule ... to regulate ... to rectify. I cannot write the poetry of such proposals, the poetry of politics, though sometimes — often — always now — I am in that uneasy peace of equal powers which makes a State; then I communicate by passing papers, proclamations, orders, through my bowels. Yet I was not a State with you, nor were we both together any Indiana. A squad of Pershing Rifles at the moment, I make myself Right

---

[2] Fulgencio Batista (1901–1973), Cuban dictator, settled in Miami after being driven from power in 1959 by the forces of Fidel Castro.

Face! Legislation packs the screw of my intestines. Well, king of the classroom's king of the hill. You used to waddle when you walked because my sperm between your legs was draining to a towel. Teacher, poet, folded lover — like the politician, like those drunkards, ill, or those who faucet-off while pissing heartily to preach upon the force and fullness of that stream, or pause from vomiting to praise the purity and passion of their puke — I chant, I beg, I orate, I command, I sing —

> Come back to Indiana — not too late!
>   (Or will you be a ranger to the end?)
> Good-bye ...Good-bye ...oh, I shall
>   always wait
> You, Larry, traveler —
>   stranger,
>   son,
>   — my friend —

my little girl, my poem by heart, my self, my childhood.

But I've heard Batista described as a Mason. That dries up my pity, melts my hate. Back from the garage where I have overheard it, I slap the mended fender of my car to laugh, and listen to the metal stinging tartly in my hand.

PEOPLE

Their hair in curlers and their heads wrapped in loud scarves, young mothers, fattish in trousers, lounge about in the speedwash, smoking cigarettes, eating candy, drinking pop, thumbing magazines, and screaming at their children above the whir and rumble of the machines.

At the bank a young man freshly pressed is letting himself in with a key. Along the street, delicately teetering, many grandfathers move in a dream. During the murderous heat of summer, they perch on window ledges, their feet dangling just inside the narrow shelf of shade the store has made, staring steadily into the street. Where their consciousness has gone I can't say. It's not in the eyes. Perhaps it's diffuse, all temperature and skin, like an infant's, though more mild. Near the corner there are several large overalled men employed in standing. A truck turns to be weighed on the scales at the Feed and Grain. Images drift on the drugstore window. The wind has blown the smell of cattle into town. Our eyes have been driven in like the eyes of the old men. And there's no one to have mercy on us.

VITAL DATA

There are two restaurants here and a tearoom, two bars, one bank, three barbers, one with a green shade with which he blinds his window. two groceries. a dealer in Fords. one drug, one hardware, and one appliance store. several that sell feed, grain, and farm equipment. an antique shop. a poolroom. a laundromat. three doctors. a dentist. a plumber. a vet. a funeral home in elegant repair the color of a buttercup. numerous beauty parlors which open and shut like night-blooming plants. a tiny dime and department store of no width but several floors. a hutch, home-made, where you can order, after lying down or squirming in, furniture that's been fashioned from bent lengths of stainless tubing, glowing plastic, metallic thread, and clear shellac. an American Legion Post and a root beer stand. little agencies for this and that:

cosmetics, brushes, insurance, greeting cards and garden produce — anything — sample shoes — which do their business out of hats and satchels, over coffee cups and dissolving sugar. a factory for making paper sacks and pasteboard boxes that's lodged in an old brick building bearing the legend OPERA HOUSE, still faintly golden, on its roof. a library given by Carnegie. a post office. a school. a railroad station. fire station. lumberyard. telephone company. welding shop. garage ... and spotted through the town from one end to the other in a line along the highway, gas stations to the number five.

EDUCATION

In 1833, Colin Goodykoontz, an itinerant preacher with a name from a fairytale, summed up the situation in one Indiana town this way:

> Ignorance and her squalid brood. A universal dearth of intellect. Total abstinence from literature is very generally practiced ... There is not a scholar in grammar or geography, or a *teacher capable of instructing* in them, to my knowledge ... Others are supplied a few months of the year with the most antiquated & unreasonable forms of teaching reading, writing & cyphering.
> ... Need I stop to remind you of the host of loathsome reptiles such a stagnant pool is fitted to breed! Croaking jealousy; bloated bigotry; coiling suspicion; wormish blindness; crocodile malice!

Things have changed since then, but in none of the respects mentioned.

BUSINESS

One side section of street is blocked off with sawhorses. Hard, thin, bitter men in blue jeans, cowboy boots and hats, untruck a dinky carnival. The merchants are promoting themselves. There will be free rides, raucous music, parades and coneys, pop, popcorn, candy, cones, awards and drawings, with all you can endure of pinch, push, bawl, shove, shout, scream, shriek, and bellow. Children pedal past on decorated bicycles, their wheels a blur of color, streaming crinkled paper and excited dogs. A little later, there's a pet show for a prize — dogs, cats, birds, sheep, ponies, goats — none of which wins. The whirlabouts whirl about. The Ferris wheel climbs dizzily into the sky as far as a tall man on tiptoe might be persuaded to reach, and the irritated operators measure the height and weight of every child with sour eyes to see if they are safe for the machines. An electrical megaphone repeatedly trumpets the names of the generous sponsors. The following day they do not allow the refuse to remain long in the street.

MY HOUSE, THIS PLACE AND BODY

I have met with some mischance, wings withering, as Plato says obscurely, and across the breadth of Ohio, like heaven on a table, I've fallen as far as the poet, to the sixth sort of body, this house in B, in Indiana, with its blue and gray bewitching windows, holy magical insides. Great thick evergreens protect its entry. And I live *in*.

Lost in the corn rows, I remember feeling just another stalk, and thus this country takes me over in the way I occupy myself when I am well ... completely — to the edge of both my house and body. No one notices, when they walk by, that I am brimming in the doorways. My house, this place and body, I've come in mourning to be born in. To anybody else it's pretty silly: love. Why should I feel a loss? How am I bereft? She was never mine; she was a fiction, always a golden tomgirl, barefoot, with an adolescent's slouch and a boy's taste for sports and fishing, a figure out of Twain, or worse, in Riley.[3] Age cannot be kind.

There's little hand-in-hand here ... not in B. No one touches except in rage. Occasionally girls will twine their arms about each other and lurch along, school out, toward home and play. I dreamed my lips would drift down your back like a skiff on a river. I'd follow a vein with the point of my finger, hold your bare feet in my naked hands.

THE SAME PERSON

Billy Holsclaw lives alone — how alone it is impossible to fathom. In the post office he talks greedily to me about the weather. His head bobs on a wild flood of words, and I take this violence to be a measure of his eagerness for speech. He badly needs a shave, coal dust has layered his face, he spits when he speaks, and his fingers pick at his tatters. He wobbles out in the wind when I leave him, a paper sack mashed in the fold of his arm, the leaves blowing past him, and our encounter drives me sadly home to poetry — where there's no answer. Billy closes his door and carries coal or wood to his fire and closes his eyes, and there's simply no way of knowing how lonely and empty he is or whether he's as vacant and barren and loveless as the rest of us are — here in the heart of the country.

WEATHER

For we're always out of luck here. That's just how it is — for instance in the winter. The sides of the buildings, the roofs, the limbs of the trees are gray. Streets, sidewalks, faces, feelings — they are gray. Speech is gray, and the grass where it shows. Every flank and front, each top is gray. Everything is gray: hair, eyes, window glass, the hawkers' bills and touters' posters, lips, teeth, poles and metal signs — they're gray, quite gray. Cars are gray. Boots, shoes, suits, hats, gloves are gray. Horses, sheep, and cows, cats killed in the road, squirrels in the same way, sparrows, doves, and pigeons, all are gray, everything is gray, and everyone is out of luck who lives here.

A similar haze turns the summer sky milky, and the air muffles your head and shoulders like a sweater you've got caught in. In the summer light, too, the sky darkens a moment when you open your eyes. The heat is pure distraction. Steeped in our fluids, miserable in the folds of our bodies, we can scarcely think of anything but our sticky parts. Hot cyclonic winds and storms of dust crisscross the country. In many places, given an indifferent push, the wind will still coast for miles, gathering resource and edge as it goes, cunning and force. According to the season, paper, leaves, field litter, seeds, snow, fill up the fences. Sometimes I think the land is flat because the winds have leveled it, they blow so constantly. In any case, a gale can grow in a field of corn that's as hot as a draft from hell, and to receive it is one of the most dismaying experiences of this life, though the smart of the same wind in winter is more humiliating, and in that sense even worse. But in the spring it rains as well, and the trees fill with ice.

PLACE

Many small Midwestern towns are nothing more than rural slums, and this community could easily become one. Principally, during the first decade of the century, though there were many

---

[3] James Whitcomb Riley (1849–1916), the "Hoosier Poet," who wrote humorous verse in dialect.

earlier instances, well-to-do farmers moved to town and built fine homes to contain them in their retirement. Others desired a more social life, and so lived in, driving to their fields like storekeepers to their businesses. These houses are now dying like the bereaved who inhabit them; they are slowly losing their senses — deafness, blindness, forgetfulness, mumbling, an insecure gait, an uncontrollable trembling has overcome them. Some kind of Northern Snopes will occupy them next: large-familied, Catholic, Democratic, scrambling, vigorous, poor; and since the parents will work in larger, nearby towns, the children will be loosed upon themselves and upon the hapless neighbors much as the fabulous Khan loosed his legendary horde. These Snopes will undertake makeshift repairs with materials that other people have thrown away; paint halfway round their house, then quit; almost certainly maintain an ugly loud cantankerous dog and underfeed a pair of cats to keep the rodents down. They will collect piles of possibly useful junk in the back yard, park their cars in the front, live largely leaning over engines, give not a hoot for the land, the old community, the hallowed ways, the established clans. Weakening widow ladies have already begun to hire large rude youths from families such as these to rake and mow and tidy the grounds they will inherit.

PEOPLE

In the cinders at the station boys sit smoking steadily in darkened cars, their arms bent out the windows, white shirts glowing behind the glass. Nine o'clock is the best time. They sit in a line facing the highway — two or three or four of them — idling their engines. As you walk by a machine may growl at you or a pair of headlights flare up briefly. In a moment one will pull out, spinning cinders behind it, to stalk impatiently up and down the dark streets or roar half a mile into the country before returning to its place in line and pulling up.

MY HOUSE, MY CAT, MY COMPANY

I must organize myself. I must, as they say, pull myself together, dump this cat from my lap, stir — yes, resolve, move, do. But do what? My will is like the rosy dust-like light in this room: soft, diffuse, and gently comforting. It lets me do … anything … nothing. My ears hear what they happen to; I eat what's put before me; my eyes see what blunders into them; my thoughts are not thoughts, they are dreams. I'm empty or I'm full … depending; and I cannot choose. I sink my claws in Tick's fur and scratch the bones of his back until his rear rises amorously. Mr. Tick, I murmur, I must organize myself. I must pull myself together. And Mr. Tick rolls over on his belly, all ooze.

I spill Mr. Tick when I've rubbed his stomach. Shoo. He steps away slowly, his long tail rhyming with his paws. How beautifully he moves, I think; how beautifully he moves, I think; how beautifully, like you, he commands his loving, how beautifully he accepts. So I rise and wander from room to room, up and down, gazing through most of my forty-one windows. How well this house receives its loving too. Let out like Mr. Tick, my eyes sink in the shrubbery. I am not here; I've passed the glass, passed second-story spaces, flown by branches, brilliant berries, to the ground, grass high in seed and leafage every season; and it is the same as when I passed above you in my aged, ardent body; it's, in short, a kind of love; and I am learning to restore myself, my house, my body, by paying court to gardens, cats, and running water, and with neighbors keeping company.

Mrs. Desmond is my right-hand friend; she's eighty-five. A thin white mist of hair, fine and tangled, manifests the climate of her mind. She is habitually suspicious, fretful, nervous.

Burglars break in at noon. Children trespass. Even now they are shaking the pear tree, stealing rhubarb, denting lawn. Flies caught in the screen and numbed by frost awake in the heat to buzz and scrape the metal cloth and frighten her, though she is deaf to me, and consequently cannot hear them. Boards creak, the wind whistles across the chimney mouth, drafts cruise like fish through the hollow rooms. It is herself she hears, her own flesh failing, for only death will preserve her from those daily chores she climbs like stairs, and all that anxious waiting. Is it now, she wonders. No? Then: is it now?

We do not converse. She visits me to talk. My task to murmur. She talks about her grandson, her daughter who lives in Delphi, her sister or her husband — both gone — obscure friends — dead — obscurer aunts and uncles — lost — ancient neighbors, members of her church or of her clubs — passed or passing on; and in this way she brings the ends of her life together with a terrifying rush: she is a girl, a wife, a mother, widow, all at once. All at once — appalling — but I believe it; I wince in expectation of the clap. Her talk's a fence — a shade drawn, window fastened, door that's locked — for no one dies taking tea in a kitchen; and as her years compress and begin to jumble, I really believe in the brevity of life; I sweat in my wonder; death is the dog down the street, the angry gander, bedroom spider, goblin who's come to get her; and it occurs to me that in my listening posture I'm the boy who suffered the winds of my grandfather with an exactly similiar politeness, that I am, right now, all my ages, out in elbows, as angular as badly stacked cards. Thus was I, when I loved you, every man I could be, youth and child — far from enough — and you, so strangely ambiguous a being, met me, heart for spade, play after play, the whole run of our suits.

Mr. Tick, you do me honor. You not only lie in my lap, but you remain alive there, coiled like a fetus. Through your deep nap, I feel you hum. You are, and are not, a machine. You are alive, alive exactly, and it means nothing to you — much to me. You are a cat — you cannot understand — you are a cat so easily. Your nature is not something you must rise to. You, not I, live in: in house, in skin, in shrubbery. Yes. I think I shall hat my head with a steeple; turn church; devour people. Mr. Tick, though, has a tail he can twitch, he need not fly his Fancy. Claws, not metrical schema, poetry his paws; while smoothing ... smoothing ... smoothing roughly, his tongue laps its neatness. O Mr. Tick, I know you; you are an electrical penis. Go on now, shoo. Mrs. Desmond doesn't like you. She thinks you will tangle yourself in her legs and she will fall. You murder her birds, she knows, and walk upon her roof with death in your jaws. I must gather myself together for a bound. What age is it I'm at right now, I wonder. The heart, don't they always say, keeps the true time. Mrs. Desmond is knocking. Faintly, you'd think, but she pounds. She's brought me a cucumber. I believe she believes I'm a woman. Come in, Mrs. Desmond, thank you, be my company, it looks lovely, and have tea. I'll slice it, crisp, with cream, for luncheon, each slice as thin as me.

POLITICS

O all ye isolate and separate powers, Sing! Sing, and sing in such a way that from a distance it will seem a harmony, a Strindberg play, a friendship ring ... so happy — happy, happy, happy — as here we go hand in handling, up and down. Our union was a singing, though we were silent in the songs we sang like single notes are silent in a symphony. In no sense sober, we barbershopped together and never heard the discords in our music or saw ourselves as dirty, cheap, or silly. Yet cats have worn out better shoes than those thrown through our love songs at us. Hush. Be patient — prudent — politic. Still, Cleveland killed you, Mr. Crane.[4] Were you

---

[4] Hart Crane (1899–1932), poet, was born and raised in Cleveland and committed suicide by jumping overboard from a ship in the Gulf of Mexico.

not politic enough and fond of being beaten? Like a piece of sewage, the city shat you from its stern three hundred miles from history — beyond the loving reach of sailors. Well, I'm not a poet who puts Paris to his temple in his youth to blow himself from Idaho, or — fancy that — Missouri. My god, I said, this is my country, but must my country go so far as Terre Haute or Whiting, go so far as Gary?

When the Russians first announced the launching of their satellite, many people naturally refused to believe them. Later others were outraged that they had sent a dog around the earth. I wouldn't want to take that mutt from out that metal flying thing if he's still living when he lands, our own dog catcher said; anybody knows you shut a dog up by himself to toss around the first thing he'll be setting on to do you let him out is bite somebody.

This Midwest. A dissonance of parts and people, we are a consonance of Towns. Like a man grown fat in everything but heart, we overlabor; our outlook never really urban, never rural either, we enlarge and linger at the same time. As Alice both changed and remained in her story. You are a blond. I put my hand upon your belly; feel it tremble from my trembling. We always drive large cars in my section of the country. How could you be a comfort to me now?

MORE VITAL DATA

The town is exactly fifty houses, trailers, stores, and miscellaneous buildings long, but in places no streets deep. It takes on width as you drive south, always adding to the east. Most of the dwellings are fairly spacious farm houses in the customary white, with wide wrap-around porches and tall narrow windows, though there are many of the grander kind — fretted, scalloped, turreted, and decorated with clapboards set at angles or on end, with stained-glass windows at the stair landings and lots of wrought iron full of fancy curls — and a few of these look like castles in their rarer brick. Old stables serve as garages now, and the lots are large to contain them and the vegetable and flower gardens which, ultimately, widows plant and weed and then entirely disappear in. The shade is ample, the grass is good, the sky a glorious fall violet; the apple trees are heavy and red, the roads are calm and empty; corn has sifted from the chains of tractored wagons to speckle the streets with gold and with the russet fragments of the cob, and a man would be a fool who wanted, blessed with this, to live anywhere else in the world.

EDUCATION

Buses like great orange animals move through the early light to school. There the children will be taught to read and warned against Communism. By Miss Janet Jakes. That's not her name. Her name is Helen something — Scott or James. A teacher twenty years. She's now worn fine and smooth, and has a face, Wilfred says, like a mail-order ax. Her voice is hoarse, and she has a cough. For she screams abuse. The children stare, their faces blank. This is the thirteenth week. They are used to it. You will all, she shouts, you will all draw pictures of me. No. She is a Mrs. — someone's missus. And in silence they set to work while Miss Jakes jabs hairpins in her hair. Wilfred says an ax, but she has those rimless tinted glasses, graying hair, an almost dimpled chin. I must concentrate. I must stop making up things. I must give myself to life; let it mold me: that's what they say in *Wisdom's Monthly Digest* every day. Enough, enough — you've been at it long enough; and the children rise formally a row at a time to present their work to her desk. No, she wears rims; it's her chin that's dimpleless. Well, it will take more than a tablespoon of features to sweeten that face. So she grimly shuffles their sheets, examines her reflection crayoned on them. I would not dare … allow a child … to put a line around me. Though now and then she smiles like a nick in the blade, in the end these drawings depress her. I could not bear it — how can she ask? — that anyone … draw me. Her anger's lit. That's why she does it: flame. There go her eyes; the pink in her glasses brightens, dims. She is a pumpkin, and her rage is breathing like the candle in. No, she shouts, no — the cartoon trembling — no, John Mauck, John Stewart Mauck, this will not do. The picture flutters from her fingers. You've made me too muscular.

I work on my poetry. I remember my friends, associates, my students, by their names. Their names are Maypop, Dormouse, Upsydaisy. Their names are Gladiolus, Callow Bladder, Prince and Princess Oleo, Hieronymus, Cardinal Mummum, Mr. Fitchew, The Silken Howdah, Spot. Sometimes you're Tom Sawyer, Huckleberry Finn; it is perpetually summer; your buttocks are my pillow; we are adrift on a raft; your back is our river. Sometimes you are Major Barbara, sometimes a goddess who kills men in battle, sometimes you are soft like a shower of water; you are bread in my mouth.

I do not work on my poetry. I forget my friends, associates, my students, and their names: Gramophone, Blowgun, Pickle, Serenade … Marge the Barge, Arena, Uberhaupt … Doctor Dildoe, The Fog Machine. For I am now in B, in Indiana: out of job and out of patience, out of love and time and money, out of bread and out of body, in a temper, Mrs. Desmond, out of tea. So shut your fist up, bitch, you bag of death; go bang another door; go die, my dearie. Die, life-deaf old lady. Spill your breath. Fall over like a frozen board. Gray hair grows from the nose of your mind. You are a skull already — *memento mori* — the foreskin retracts from your teeth. Will your plastic gums last longer than your bones, and color their grinning? And is your twot still hazel-hairy, or are you bald as a ditch? … bitch …… bitch …… bitch. I wanted to be famous, but you bring me age — my emptiness. Was it *that* which I thought would balloon me above the rest? Love? where are you? … love me. I want to rise so high, I said, that when I shit I won't miss anybody.

BUSINESS

For most people, business is poor. Nearby cities have siphoned off all but a neighborhood trade. Except for feed and grain and farm supplies, you stand a chance to sell only what runs out to buy. Chevrolet has quit, and Frigidaire. A locker plant has left its afterimage. The lumberyard has been, so far, six months about its going. Gas stations change hands clumsily, a restaurant becomes available, a grocery closes. One day they came and knocked the cornices from the watch repair and pasted campaign posters on the windows. Torn across, by now, by boys, they urge you still to vote for half an orange beblazoned man who as a whole one failed two years ago to win at his election. Everywhere, in this manner, the past speaks, and it mostly speaks of failure. The empty stores, the old signs and dusty fixtures, the debris in alleys, the flaking paint and rusty gutters, the heavy locks and sagging boards: they say the same disagreeable things. What do the sightless windows see, I wonder, when the sun throws a passerby against them? Here a stair unfolds toward the street — dark, rickety, and treacherous — and I always feel, as I pass it, that if I just went carefully up and turned the corner at the landing, I would find myself out of the world. But I've never had the courage.

THAT SAME PERSON

The weeds catch up with Billy. In pursuit of the hollyhocks, they rise in coarse clumps all around the front of his house. Billy has to stamp down a circle by his door like a dog or cat does turning round to nest up, they're so thick. What particularly troubles me is that winter will find the weeds still standing stiff and tindery to take the sparks which Billy's little mortarless chimney spouts. It's true that fires are fun here. The town whistle, which otherwise only blows for noon (and there's no noon on Sunday), signals the direction of the fire by the length and number of its blasts, the volunteer firemen rush past in their cars and trucks, houses empty their owners along the street every time like an illustration in a children's book. There are many bikes, too, and barking dogs, and sometimes — halleluiah — the fire's right here in town — a vacant lot of weeds and stubble flaming up. But I'd rather it weren't Billy or Billy's lot or house. Quite selfishly, I want him to remain the way he is — counting his sticks and logs, sitting on his sill in the soft early sun — though I'm not sure what his presence means to me ... or to anyone. Nevertheless, I keep wondering whether, given time, I might not someday find a figure in our language which would serve him faithfully, and furnish his poverty and loneliness richly out.

WIRES

Where sparrows sit like fists. Doves fly the steeple. In mist the wires change perspective, rise and twist. If they led to you, I would know what they were. Thoughts passing often, like the starlings who flock these fields at evening to sleep in the trees beyond, would form a family of paths like this; they'd foot down the natural height of air to just about a bird's perch. But they do not lead to you.

> Of whose beauty it was sung
> She shall make the old man young.

They fasten me.

If I walked straight on, in my present mood, I would reach the Wabash. It's not a mood in which I'd choose to conjure you. Similes dangle like baubles from me. This time of year the river is slow and shallow, the clay banks crack in the sun, weeds surprise the sandbars. The air is moist and I am sweating. It's impossible to rhyme in this dust. Everything — sky, the cornfield, stump, wild daisies, my old clothes and pressless feelings — seem fabricated for installment purchase. Yes. Christ. I am suffering a summer Christmas; and I cannot walk under the wires. The sparrows scatter like handfuls of gravel. Really, wires are voices in thin strips. They are words wound in cables. Bars of connection.

WEATHER

I would rather it were the weather that was to blame for what I am and what my friends and neighbors are — we who live here in the heart of the country. Better the weather, the wind, the pale dying snow ... the snow — why not the snow? There's never much really, not around the lower Lakes anyway, not enough to boast about, not enough to be useful. My father tells how the snow in the Dakotas would sweep to the roofs of the barns in the old days, and he and his friends could sled on the crust that would form because the snow was so fiercely driven. In Bemidji trees have been known to explode. That would be something — if the trees in Davenport or Francisville or Carbondale or Niles were to go blam some winter — blam! blam! blam! all the way down the gray, cindery, snow-sick streets.

A cold fall rain is blackening the trees or the air is like lilac and full of parachuting seeds. Who cares to live in any season but his own? Still I suspect the secret's in this snow, the secret of our sickness, if we could only diagnose it, for we are all dying like the elms in Urbana. This snow — like our skin it covers the country. Later dust will do it. Right now — snow. Mud presently. But it is snow without any laughter in it, a pale gray pudding thinly spread on stiff toast, and if that seems a strange description, it's accurate all the same. Of course soot blackens everything, but apart from that, we are never sufficiently cold here. The flakes as they come, alive and burning, we cannot retain, for if our temperatures fall, they rise promptly again, just as, in the summer, they bob about in the same feckless way. Suppose though … suppose they were to rise some August, climb and rise, and then hang in the hundreds like a hawk through December, what a desert we could make of ourselves — from Chicago to Cairo, from Hammond to Columbus — what beautiful Death Valleys.

PLACE

I would rather it were the weather. It drives us in upon ourselves — an unlucky fate. Of course there is enough to stir our wonder anywhere: there's enough to love, anywhere, if one is strong enough, if one is diligent enough, if one is perceptive, patient, kind enough — whatever it takes; and surely it's better to live in the country, to live on a prairie by a drawing of rivers, in Iowa or Illinois or Indiana, say, than in any city, in any stinking fog of human beings, in any blooming orchard of machines. It ought to be. The cities are swollen and poisonous with people. It ought to be better. Man has never been a fit environment for man — for rats, maybe, rats do nicely, or for dogs or cats and the household beetle.

And how long the street is, nowadays. These endless walls are fallen to keep back the tides of earth. Brick could be beautiful but we have covered it gradually with gray industrial vomits. Age does not make concrete genial, and asphalt is always — like America — twenty-one, until it breaks up in crumbs like stale cake. The brick, the asphalt, the concrete, the dancing signs and garish posters, the feed and excrement of the automobile, the litter of its inhabitants: they compose, they decorate, they line our streets, and there is nowhere, nowadays, our streets can't reach.

A man in the city has no natural thing by which to measure himself. His parks are potted plants. Nothing can live and remain free where he resides but the pigeon, starling, sparrow, spider, cockroach, mouse, moth, fly and weed, and he laments the existence of even these and makes his plans to poison them. The zoo? There *is* the zoo. Through its bars the city man stares at the great cats and dully sucks his ice. Living, alas, among men and their marvels, the city man supposes that his happiness depends on establishing, somehow, a special kind of harmonious accord with others. The novelists of the city, of slums and crowds, they call it love — and break their pens.

Wordsworth feared the accumulation of men in cities. He foresaw their "degrading thirst after outrageous stimulation," and some of their hunger for love. Living in a city, among so many, dwelling in the heat and tumult of incessant movement, a man's affairs are touch and go — that's all. It's not surprising that the novelists of the slums, the cities, and the crowds, should find that sex is but a scratch to ease a tickle, that we're most human when we're sitting on the john, and that the justest image of our life is in full passage through the plumbing.

> That man, immur'd in cities, still retains
> His inborn inextinguishable thirst
> Of rural scenes, compensating his loss
> By supplemental shifts, the best he may.

Come into the country, then. The air nimbly and sweetly recommends itself unto our gentle senses. Here, growling tractors tear the earth. Dust roils up behind them. Drivers sit jouncing under bright umbrellas. They wear refrigerated hats and steer by looking at the tracks they've cut behind them, their transistors blaring. Close to the land, are they? good companions to the soil? Tell me: do they live in harmony with the alternating seasons?

It's a lie of old poetry. The modern husbandman uses chemicals from cylinders and sacks, spike-ball-and-claw machines, metal sheds, and cost accounting. Nature in the old sense does not matter. It does not exist. Our farmer's only mystical attachment is to parity. And if he does not realize that cows and corn are simply different kinds of chemical engine, he cannot expect to make a go of it.

It isn't necessary to suppose our cows have feelings; our neighbor hasn't as many as he used to have either; but think of it this way a moment, you can correct for the human imputations later: how would it feel to nurse those strange tentacled calves with their rubber, glass, and metal lips, their stainless eyes?

PEOPLE

Aunt Pet's still able to drive her car — a high square Ford — even though she walks with difficulty and a stout stick. She has a watery gaze, a smooth plump face despite her age, and jet black hair in a bun. She has the slowest smile of anyone I ever saw, but she hates dogs, and not very long ago cracked the back of one she cornered in her garden. To prove her vigor she will tell you this, her smile breaking gently while she raises the knob of her stick to the level of your eyes.

HOUSE, MY BREATH AND WINDOW

My window is a grave, and all that lies within it's dead. No snow is falling. There's no haze. It is not still, not silent. Its images are not an animal that waits, for movement is no demonstration. I have seen the sea slack, life bubble through a body without a trace, its spheres impervious as soda's. Downwound, the whore at wagtag clicks and clacks. Leaves wiggle. Grass sways. A bird chirps, pecks the ground. An auto wheel in penning circles keeps its rigid spokes. These images are stones; they are memorials. Beneath this sea lies sea: god rest it ... rest the world beyond my window, me in front of my reflection, above this page, my shade. Death is not so still, so silent, since silence implies a falling quiet, stillness a stopping, containing, holding in; for death is time in a clock, like Mr. Tick, electric ... like wind through a windup poet. And my blear floats out to, visible against the glass, befog its country and bespill myself. The mist lifts slowly from the fields in the morning. No one now would say: the Earth throws back its covers; it is rising from sleep. Why is the feeling foolish? The image is too Greek. I used to gaze at you so wantonly your body blushed. Imagine: wonder: that my eyes could cause such flowering. Ah, my friend, your face is pale, the weather cloudy; a street has been felled through your chin, bare trees do nothing, houses take root in their rectangles, a steeple stands up in your head. You speak of loving; then give me a kiss. The pane is cold. On icy mornings the fog rises to greet me (as you always did); the barns and other buildings, rather than ghostly, seem all the more substantial for looming, as if they grew in themselves while I watched (as you always did). Oh my approach, I suppose, was like breath in a rubber monkey. Nevertheless, on the road along the Wabash in the morning, though the trees are sometimes obscured by fog, their reflection floats serenely on the river, reasoning the banks, the sycamores in French rows. Magically, the world tips. I'm led to think that only those who grow down live (which will scarcely win me twenty-five from *Wisdom's Monthly Digest*), but I find I write that only those who live down grow; and what I write, I hold, whatever I really know. My every word's inverted, or reversed — or I am. I held you, too, that way. You were so utterly provisional, subject to my change. I could inflate your bosom with a kiss, disperse your skin with gentleness, enter your vagina from within, and make my love emerge like a fresh sex. The pane is cold. Honesty is cold, my inside lover. The sun looks, through the mist, like a plum on the tree of heaven, or a bruise on the slope of your belly. Which? The grass crawls with frost. We meet on this window, the world and I, inelegantly, swimmers of the glass; and swung wrong way round to one another, the world seems in. The world — how grand, how monumental, grave and deadly, that word is: the world, my house and poetry. All poets have their inside lovers. Wee penis does not belong to me, or any of this foggery. It is *his* property which he's thrust through what's womanly of me to set down this. These wooden houses in their squares, gray streets and fallen sidewalks, standing trees, your name I've written sentimentally across my breath into the whitening air, pale birds: they exist in me now because of him. I gazed with what intensity ... A bush in the excitement of its roses could not have bloomed so beautifully as you did then. It was a look I'd like to give this page. For that is poetry: to bring within about, to change.

POLITICS

Sports, politics, and religion are the three passions of the badly educated. They are the Midwest's open sores. Ugly to see, a source of constant discontent, they sap the body's strength. Appalling quantities of money, time, and energy are wasted on them. The rural mind is narrow, passionate, and reckless on these matters. Greed, however shortsighted and direct, will not alone account for it. I have known men, for instance, who for years have voted squarely against their interests. Nor have I ever noticed that their surly Christian views prevented them from urging forward the smithereening, say, of Russia, China, Cuba, or Korea. And they tend to back their country like they back their local team: they have a fanatical desire to win; yelling is their forte; and if things go badly, they are inclined to sack the coach. All in all, then, Birch is a good name. It stands for the bigot's stick, the wild-child-tamer's cane.

Forgetfulness — is that their object?

Oh, I was new, I thought. A fresh start; new cunt, new climate, and new country — there you were, and I was pioneer, and had no history. That language hurts me, too, my dear. You'll never hear it.

FINAL VITAL DATA

The Modern Homemakers' Demonstration Club. The Prairie Home Demonstration Club. The Night-outer's Home Demonstration Club. The IOOF, FFF, VFW, WCTU, WSCS, 4-H, 40 and 8, Psi Iota Chi, and PTA. The Boy and Girl Scouts, Rainbows, Masons, Indians and Rebekah Lodge. Also the Past Noble Grand Club of the Rebekah Lodge. As well as the Moose and the Ladies of the Moose. The Elks, the Eagles, the Jaynettes and the Eastern Star. The Women's Literary Club, the Hobby Club, the Art Club, the Sunshine Society, the Dorcas Society, the Pythian Sisters, the Pilgrim Youth Fellowship, the American Legion, the American Legion Auxiliary, the American Legion Junior Auxiliary, the Garden Club, the Bridge for Fun Club, the What-can-you-do? Club, the Get Together Club, the Coterie Club, the Worthwhile Club, the Let's Help Our Town Club, the No Name Club, the Forget-me-not Club, the Merry-go-round Club ...

EDUCATION

Has a quarter disappeared from Paula Frosty's pocket book? Imagine the landscape of that face: no crayon could engender it; soft wax is wrong; thin wire in trifling snips might do the trick. Paula Frosty and Christopher Roger accuse the pale and splotchy Cheryl Pipes. But Miss Jakes, I *saw* her. Miss Jakes is so extremely vexed she snaps her pencil. What else is missing? I appoint you a detective, John: search her desk. Gum, candy, paper, pencils, marble, round eraser — whose? A thief. I can't watch her all the time, I'm here to teach. Poor pale fossetted Cheryl, it's determined, can't return the money because she took it home and spent it. Cindy, Janice, John, and Pete — you four who sit around her — you will be detectives this whole term to watch her. A thief. In all my time. Miss Jakes turns, unfists, and turns again. I'll handle you, she cries. To think. A thief. In all my years. Then she writes on the blackboard the name of Cheryl Pipes and beneath that the figure twenty-five with a large sign for cents. Now Cheryl, she says, this won't be taken off until you bring that money out of home, out of home straight up to here, Miss Jakes says, tapping her desk.

Which is three days.

ANOTHER PERSON

I was raking leaves when Uncle Halley introduced himself to me. He said his name came from the comet, and that his mother had borne him prematurely in her fright of it.[5] I thought of Hobbes,[6] whom fear of the Spanish Armada had hurried into birth, and so I believed Uncle Halley to honor the philosopher, though Uncle Halley is a liar, and neither the one hundred twenty-nine nor the fifty-three he ought to be. That fall the leaves had burned themselves out on the trees, the leaf lobes had curled, and now they flocked noisily down the street and were broken in the wires of my rake. Uncle Halley was himself (like Mrs. Desmond and history generally) both deaf and implacable, and he shooed me down his basement stairs to a room set aside there for stacks of newspapers reaching to the ceiling, boxes of leaflets and letters and programs, racks of photo albums, scrapbooks, bundles of rolled-up posters and maps, flags and pennants and slanting piles of dusty magazines devoted mostly to motoring and the Christian ethic. I saw a bird cage, a tray of butterflies, a bugle, a stiff straw boater and all kinds of tassels tied to a coat tree. He still possessed and had on display the steering lever from his first car, a linen duster, driving gloves and goggles, photographs along the wall of himself, his friends, and his various machines, a shell from the first war, a record of "Ramona" nailed through its hole to a post, walking sticks and fanciful umbrellas, shoes of all sorts (his baby shoes, their counters broken, were held in sorrow beneath my nose — they had not been bronzed, but he might have them done someday before he died, he said), countless boxes of medals, pins, beads, trinkets, toys, and keys (I scarcely saw — they flowed like jewels from his palms), pictures of downtown when it was only a path by the railroad station, a brightly colored globe of the world with a dent in Poland, antique guns, belt buckles, buttons, souvenir plates and cups and saucers (I can't remember all of it — I won't), but I recall how shamefully, how rudely, how abruptly, I fled, a good story in my mouth but death in my nostrils; and how afterward I busily, righteously, burned my leaves as if I were purging the world of its years. I still wonder if this town — its life, and mine now — isn't really a record like the one of "Ramona" that I used to crank around on my grandmother's mahogany Victrola through lonely rainy days as a kid.

---

[5] Halley's comet appeared in 1910.

[6] Thomas Hobbes, the English philosopher, was born in 1588.

THE FIRST PERSON

Billy's like the coal he's found: spilled, mislaid, discarded. The sky's no comfort. His house and his body are dying together. His windows are boarded. And now he's reduced to his hands. I suspect he has glaucoma. At any rate he can scarcely see, and weeds his yard of rubble on his hands and knees. Perhaps he's a surgeon cleansing a wound or an ardent and tactile lover. I watch, I must say, apprehensively. Like mine-war detectors, his hands graze in circles ahead of him. Your nipples were the color of your eyes. Pebble. Snarl of paper. Length of twine. He leans down closely, picks up something silvery, holds it near his nose. Foil? cap? coin? He has within him — what, I wonder? Does he know more now because he fingers everything and has to sniff to see? It would be romantic cruelty to think so. He bends the down on your arms like a breeze. You wrote me: something is strange when we don't understand. I write in return: I think when I loved you I fell to my death.

Billy, I could read to you from Beddoes[7]; he's your man perhaps; he held with dying, freed his blood of its arteries; and he said that there were many wretched love-ill fools like me lying alongside the last bone of their former selves, as full of spirit and speech, nonetheless, as Mrs. Desmond, Uncle Halley and the Ferris wheel, Aunt Pet, Miss Jakes, Ramona or the megaphone; yet I reverse him finally, Billy, on no evidence but braggadocio, and I declare that though my inner organs were devoured long ago, the worm which swallowed down my parts still throbs and glows like a crystal palace.

Yes, you were younger. I was Uncle Halley, the museum man and infrequent meteor. Here is my first piece of ass. They weren't so flat in those days, had more round, more juice. And over here's the sperm I've spilled, nicely jarred and clearly labeled. Look at this tape like lengths of intestine where I've stored my spew, the endless worm of words I've written, a hundred million emissions or more: oh I was quite a man right from the start; even when unconscious in my cradle, from crotch to cranium, I was erectile tissue; though mostly, after the manner approved by Plato, I had intercourse by eye. Never mind, old Holsclaw, you are blind. We pull down darkness when we go to bed; put out like Oedipus[8] the actually offending organ, and train our touch to lies. All cats are gray, says Mr. Tick; so under cover of glaucoma you are sack gray too, and cannot be distinguished from a stallion.

I must pull myself together, get a grip, just as they say, but I feel spilled, bewildered, quite mislaid. I did not restore my house to its youth, but to its age. Hunting, you hitch through the hollyhocks. I'm inclined to say you aren't half the cripple I am, for there is nothing left of me but mouth. However, I resist the impulse. It is another lie of poetry. My organs are all there, though it's there where I fail — at the roots of my experience. Poet of the spiritual, Rilke, weren't you? yet that's what you said. Poetry, like love, is — in and out — a physical caress. I can't tolerate any more of my sophistries about spirit, mind, and breath. Body equals being, and if your weight goes down, you are the less.

HOUSEHOLD APPLES

I knew nothing about apples. Why should I? My country came in my childhood, and I dreamed of sitting among the blooms like the bees. I failed to spray the pear tree too. I doubled up under them at first, admiring the sturdy low branches I should have pruned, and later I acclaimed the blossoms. Shortly after the fruit formed there were falls — not many — apples the size of goodish stones which made me wobble on my ankles when I walked about

---

[7] Thomas Lovell Beddoes (1803–1849), minor English poet and author of *The Devil's Jest-Book*, killed himself in a fit of despondency.

[8] In Sophocles' *Oedipus Rex*, Oedipus blinds himself out of remorse for his offenses.

the yard. Sometimes a piece crushed by a heel would cling on the shoe to track the house. I gathered a few and heaved them over the wires. A slingshot would have been splendid. Hard, an unattractive green, the worms had them. Before long I realized the worms had them all. Even as the apples reddened, lit their tree, they were being swallowed. The birds preferred the pears, which were small — sugar pears I think they're called — with thick skins of graying green that ripen on toward violet. So the fruit fell, and once I made some applesauce by quartering and paring hundreds; but mostly I did nothing, left them, until suddenly, overnight it seemed, in that ugly late September heat we often have in Indiana, my problem was upon me.

My childhood came in the country. I remember, now, the flies on our snowy luncheon table. As we cleared away they would settle, fastidiously scrub themselves and stroll to the crumbs to feed where I would kill them in crowds with a swatter. It was quite a game to catch them taking off. I struck heavily since I didn't mind a few stains; they'd wash. The swatter was a square of screen bound down in red cloth. It drove no air ahead of it to give them warning. They might have thought they'd flown headlong into a summered window. The faint pink dot where they had died did not rub out as I'd supposed, and after years of use our luncheon linen would faintly, pinkly, speckle.

The country became my childhood. Flies braided themselves on the flypaper in my grandmother's house. I can smell the bakery and the grocery and the stables and the dairy in that small Dakota town I knew as a kid; knew as I dreamed I'd know your body, as I've known nothing, before or since; knew as the flies knew, in the honest, unchaste sense: the burned house, hose-wet, which drew a mist of insects like the blue smoke of its smolder, and gangs of boys, moist-lipped, destructive as its burning. Flies have always impressed me; they are so persistently alive. Now they were coating the ground beneath my trees. Some were ordinary flies; there were the large blue-green ones; there were swarms of fruit flies too, and the red-spotted scavenger beetle; there were a few wasps, several sorts of bees and butterflies — checkers, sulphurs, monarchs, commas, question marks — and delicate dragonflies … but principally houseflies and horseflies and bottleflies, flies and more flies in clusters around the rotting fruit. They loved the pears. Inside, they fed. If you picked up a pear, they flew, and the pear became skin and stem. They were everywhere the fruit was: in the tree still — apples like a hive for them — or where the fruit littered the ground, squashing itself as you stepped … there was no help for it. The flies droned, feasting on the sweet juice. No one could go near the trees; I could not climb; so I determined at last to labor like Hercules. There were fruit baskets in the barn. Collecting them and kneeling under the branches, I began to gather remains. Deep in the strong rich smell of the fruit, I began to hum myself. The fruit caved in at the touch. Glistening red apples, my lifting disclosed, had families of beetles, flies, and bugs, devouring their rotten undersides. There were streams of flies; there were lakes and cataracts and rivers of flies, seas and oceans. The hum was heavier, higher, than the hum of the bees when they came to the blooms in the spring, though the bees were there, among the flies, ignoring me — ignoring everyone. As my work went on and juice covered my hands and arms, they would form a sleeve, black and moving, like knotty wool. No caress could have been more indifferently complete. Still I rose fearfully, ramming my head in the branches, apples bumping against me before falling, bursting with bugs. I'd snap my hand sharply but the flies would cling to the sweet. I could toss a whole cluster into a basket from several feet. As the pear or apple lit, they would explosively rise, like monads for a moment, windowless, certainly, with respect to one another, sugar their harmony. I had to admit, though, despite my distaste, that my arm had never been more alive, oftener or more gently kissed. Those hundreds of feet were light. In washing them off, I pretended the hose was a pump. What have I missed? Childhood is a lie of poetry.

THE CHURCH

Friday night. Girls in dark skirts and white blouses sit in ranks and scream in concert. They carry funnels loosely stuffed with orange and black paper which they shake wildly, and small megaphones through which, as drilled, they direct and magnify their shouting. Their leaders, barely pubescent girls, prance and shake and whirl their skirts above their bloomers. The young men, leaping, extend their arms and race through puddles of amber light, their bodies glistening. In a lull, though it rarely occurs, you can hear the squeak of tennis shoes against the floor. Then the yelling begins again, and then continues; fathers, mothers, neighbors joining in to form a single pulsing ululation — a cry of the whole community — for in this gymnasium each body becomes the bodies beside it, pressed as they are together, thigh to thigh, and the same shudder runs through all of them, and runs toward the same release. Only the ball moves serenely through this dazzling din. Obedient to law it scarcely speaks but caroms quietly and lives at peace.

BUSINESS

It is the week of Christmas and the stores, to accommodate the rush they hope for, are remaining open in the evening. You can see snow falling in the cones of the street lamps. The roads are filling — undisturbed. Strings of red and green lights droop over the principal highway, and the water tower wears a star. The windows of the stores have been bedizened. Shamelessly they beckon. But I am alone, leaning against a pole — no ... there is no one in sight. They're all at home, perhaps by their instruments, tuning in on their evenings, and like Ramona, tirelessly playing and replaying themselves. There's a speaker perched in the tower, and through the boughs of falling snow and over the vacant streets, it drapes the twisted and metallic strains of a tune that can barely be distinguished — yes, I believe it's one of the jolly ones, it's "Joy to the World." There's no one to hear the music but myself, and though I'm listening, I'm no longer certain. Perhaps the record's playing something else.

QUESTIONS

1. What do we learn about the narrator? Why has he come to "the heart of the country"? Is he escaping something? Is there a clue in the opening paraphrase from Yeats?

2. What is the narrator's attitude toward the "small town fastened to a field in Indiana"? Does he see himself as superior to it? to Billy Holsclaw, Miss Jakes, or Uncle Halley? Is he fundamentally a sympathetic or an ironic observer?

3. Does this story have a plot in the conventional sense? How would you describe the action of the story? Is there a conflict? Is it resolved?

4. Gass has told his story in many sections. Can you discern a sequence? Is there some other logic to this narrative form? What would you say this story is, finally, about?

FLANNERY O'CONNOR

Judgement Day

Tanner was conserving all his strength for the trip home. He meant to walk as far as he could get and trust to the Almighty to get him the rest of the way. That morning and the morning before, he had allowed his daughter to dress him and had conserved that much more energy. Now he sat in the chair by the window — his blue shirt buttoned at the collar, his coat on the back of the chair, and his hat on his head — waiting for her to leave. He couldn't escape until she got out of the way. The window looked out on a brick wall and down into an alley full of New York air, the kind fit for cats and garbage. A few snow flakes drifted past the window but they were too thin and scattered for his failing vision.

The daughter was in the kitchen washing dishes. She dawdled over everything, talking to herself. When he had first come, he had answered her, but that had not been wanted. She glowered at him as if, old fool that he was, he should still have had sense enough not to answer a woman talking to herself. She questioned herself in one voice and answered herself in another. With the energy he had conserved yesterday letting her dress him, he had written a note and pinned it in his pocket. IF FOUND DEAD SHIP EXPRESS COLLECT TO COLEMAN PARRUM, CORINTH, GEORGIA. Under this he had continued: COLEMAN SELL MY BELONGINGS AND PAY THE FREIGHT ON ME & THE UNDERTAKER. ANYTHING LEFT OVER YOU CAN KEEP. YOURS TRULY T. C. TANNER. P.S. STAY WHERE YOU ARE. DON'T LET THEM TALK YOU INTO COMING UP HERE. ITS NO KIND OF PLACE. It had taken him the better part of thirty minutes to write the paper; the script was wavery but decipherable with patience. He controlled one hand by holding the other on top of it. By the time he had got it written, she was back in the apartment from getting her groceries.

Today he was ready. All he had to do was push one foot in front of the other until he got to the door and down the steps. Once down the steps, he would get out of the neighborhood. Once out of it, he would hail a taxi cab and go to the freight yards. Some bum would help him onto a car. Once he got in the freight car, he would lie down and rest. During the night the train would start South, and the next day or the morning after, dead or alive, he would be home. Dead or alive. It was being there that mattered; the dead or alive did not.

If he had had good sense he would have gone the day after he arrived; better sense and he would not have arrived. He had not got desperate until two days ago when he had heard his daughter and son-in-law taking leave of each other after breakfast. They were standing in the

747

front door, she seeing him off for a three-day trip. He drove a long distance moving van. She must have handed him his leather headgear. "You ought to get you a hat," she said, "a real one."

"And sit all day in it," the son-in-law said, "like him in there. Yah! All he does is sit all day with that hat on. Sits all day with that damn black hat on his head. Inside!"

"Well you don't even have you a hat," she said. "Nothing but that leather cap with flaps. People that are somebody wear hats. Other kinds wear those leather caps like you got on."

"People that are somebody!" he cried. "People that are somebody! That kills me! That really kills me!" The son-in-law had a stupid muscular face and a yankee voice to go with it.

"My daddy is here to stay," his daughter said. "He ain't going to last long. He was somebody when he was somebody. He never worked for nobody in his life but himself and had people — other people — working for him."

"Yah? Niggers is what he had working for him," the son-in-law said. "That's all. I've worked a nigger or two myself."

"Those were just nawthun niggers you worked," she said, her voice suddenly going lower so that Tanner had to lean forward to catch the words. "It takes brains to work a real nigger. You got to know how to handle them."

"Yah so I don't have brains," the son-in-law said.

One of the sudden, very occasional, feelings of warmth for the daughter came over Tanner. Every now and then she said something that might make you think she had a little sense stored away somewhere for safe keeping.

"You got them," she said. "You don't always use them."

"He has a stroke when he sees a nigger in the building," the son-in-law said, "and she tells me ..."

"Shut up talking so loud," she said. "That's not why he had the stroke."

There was a silence. "Where you going to bury him?" the son-in-law asked, taking a different tack.

"Bury who?"

"Him in there."

"Right here in New York," she said. "Where do you think? We got a lot. I'm not taking that trip down there again with nobody."

"Yah. Well I just wanted to make sure," he said.

When she returned to the room, Tanner had both hands gripped on the chair arms. His eyes were trained on her like the eyes of an angry corpse. "You promised you'd bury me there," he said. "Your promise ain't any good. Your promise ain't any good. Your promise ain't any good." His voice was so dry it was barely audible. He began to shake, his hands, his head, his feet. "Bury me here and burn in hell!" he cried and fell back into his chair.

The daughter shuddered to attention. "You ain't dead yet!" She threw out a ponderous sigh. "You got a long time to be worrying about that." She turned and began to pick up parts of the newspaper scattered on the floor. She had gray hair that hung to her shoulders and a round face, beginning to wear. "I do every last living thing for you," she muttered, "and this is the way you carry on." She stuck the papers under her arm and said, "And don't throw hell at me. I don't believe in it. That's a lot of hardshell Baptist hooey." Then she went into the kitchen.

He kept his mouth stretched taut, his top plate gripped between his tongue and the roof of his mouth. Still the tears flooded down his cheeks; he wiped each one furtively on his shoulder.

Her voice rose from the kitchen. "As bad as having a child. He wanted to come and now he's here, he don't like it."

He had not wanted to come.

"Pretended he didn't but I could tell. I said if you don't want to come I can't make you. If you don't want to live like decent people there's nothing I can do about it."

"As for me," her higher voice said, "when I die that ain't the time I'm going to start getting choosey. They can lay me in the nearest spot. When I pass from this world I'll be considerate of them that stay in it. I won't be thinking of just myself."

"Certainly not," the other voice said, "You never been that selfish. You're the kind that looks out for other people."

"Well I try," she said, "I try."

He laid his head on the back of the chair for a moment and the hat tilted down over his eyes. He had raised three boys and her. The three boys were gone, two in the war and one to the devil and there was nobody left who felt a duty toward him but her, married and childless, in New York City like Mrs. Big and ready when she came back and found him living the way he was to take him back with her. She had put her face in the door of the shack and had stared, expressionless, for a second. Then all at once she had screamed and jumped back.

"What's that on the floor?"

"Coleman," he said.

The old Negro was curled up on a pallet asleep at the foot of Tanner's bed, a stinking skin full of bones, arranged in what seemed vaguely human form. When Coleman was young, he had looked like a bear; now that he was old he looked like a monkey. With Tanner it was the opposite; when he was young he had looked like a monkey but when he got old, he looked like a bear.

The daughter stepped back onto the porch. There were the bottoms of two cane chairs tilted against the clapboard but she declined to take a seat. She stepped out about ten feet from the house as if it took that much space to clear the odor. Then she had spoken her piece.

"If you don't have any pride I have and I know my duty and I was raised to do it. My mother raised me to do it if you didn't. She was from plain people but not the kind that likes to settle in with niggers."

At that point the old Negro roused up and slid out the door, a doubled-up shadow which Tanner just caught sight of gliding away.

She had shamed him. He shouted so they both could hear. "Who you think cooks? Who you think cuts my firewood and empties my slops? He's paroled to me. That no-good scoundrel has been on my hands for thirty years. He ain't a bad nigger."

She was unimpressed. "Whose shack is this anyway?" she had asked. "Yours or his?"

"Him and me built it," he said. "You go on back up there. I wouldn't come with you for no million dollars or no sack of salt."

"It looks like him and you built it. Whose land is it on?"

"Some people that live in Florida," he said evasively. He had known then that it was land up for sale but he thought it was too sorry for anyone to buy. That same afternoon he had found out different. He had found out in time to go back with her. If he had found out a day later, he might still be there, squatting on the doctor's land.

When he saw the brown porpoise-shaped figure striding across the field that afternoon, he had known at once what had happened; no one had to tell him. If that nigger had owned the whole world except for one runty rutted peafield and he acquired it, he would walk across it that way, beating the weeds aside, his thick neck swelled, his stomach a throne for his gold watch and chain. Doctor Foley. He was only part black. The rest was Indian and white.

He was everything to the niggers — druggist and undertaker and general counsel and real estate man and sometimes he got the evil eye off them and sometimes he put it on. Be prepared, he said to himself, watching him approach, to take something off him, nigger though he be. Be prepared, because you ain't got a thing to hold up to him but the skin you come in, and that's no more use to you now than what a snake would shed. You don't have a chance with the government against you.

He was sitting on the porch in the piece of straight chair tilted against the shack. "Good evening, Foley," he said and nodded as the doctor came up and stopped short at the edge of the clearing, as if he had only just that minute seen him though it was plain he had sighted him as he crossed the field.

"I be out here to look at my property," the doctor said. "Good evening." His voice was quick and high.

Ain't been your property long, he said to himself. "I seen you coming," he said.

"I acquired this here recently," the doctor said and proceeded without looking at him again to walk around to one side of the shack. In a moment he came back and stopped in front of him. Then he stepped boldly to the door of the shack and put his head in. Coleman was in there that time too, asleep. He looked for a moment and then turned aside. "I know that nigger," he said. "Coleman Parrum — how long does it take him to sleep off that stump liquor you all make?"

Tanner took hold of the knobs on the chair bottom and held them hard. "This shack ain't in your property. Only on it, by my mistake," he said.

The doctor removed his cigar momentarily from his mouth. "It ain't my mis-take," he said and smiled.

He had only sat there, looking ahead.

"It don't pay to make this kind of mis-take," the doctor said.

"I never found nothing that paid yet," he muttered.

"Everything pays," the Negro said, "if you knows how to make it," and he remained there smiling, looking the squatter up and down. Then he turned and went around the other side of the shack. There was a silence. He was looking for the still.

Then would have been the time to kill him. There was a gun inside the shack and he could have done it as easy as not, but, from childhood, he had been weakened for that kind of violence by the fear of hell. He had never killed one, he had always handled them with his wits and with luck. He was known to have a way with niggers. There was an art to handling them. The secret of handling a nigger was to show him his brains didn't have a chance against yours; then he would jump on your back and know he had a good thing there for life. He had had Coleman on his back for thirty years.

Tanner had first seen Coleman when he was working six of them at a saw mill in the middle of a pine forest fifteen miles from nowhere. They were as sorry a crew as he had worked, the kind that on Monday they didn't show up. What was in the air had reached them. They thought there was a new Lincoln elected who was going to abolish work. He managed them with a very sharp penknife. He had had something wrong with his kidney then that made his hands shake and he had taken to whittling to force that waste motion out of sight. He did not intend them to see that his hands shook of their own accord and he did not intend to see it himself or to countenance it. The knife had moved constantly, violently, in his quaking hands and here and there small crude figures — that he never looked at again and could not have said what they were if he had — dropped to the ground. The Negroes picked them up and took them home; there was not much time between them and darkest Africa. The knife glittered constantly in his hands. More than once he had stopped short and said in an off-hand voice to some half-reclining, head-averted Negro, "Nigger, this knife is in my hand now but if you don't quit wasting my time and money, it'll be in your gut shortly." And the Negro would begin to rise — slowly, but he would be in the act — before the sentence was completed.

A large black loose-jointed Negro, twice his own size, had begun hanging around the edge of the saw mill, watching the others work and when he was not watching, sleeping, in full view of them, sprawled like a gigantic bear on his back. "Who is that?" he had asked. "If he wants to work, tell him to come here. If he don't, tell him to go. No idlers are going to hang around here."

None of them knew who he was. They knew he didn't want to work. They knew nothing else, not where he had come from, nor why, though he was probably brother to one, cousin to all of them. He had ignored him for a day; against the six of them he was one yellow-faced scrawny white man with shaky hands. He was willing to wait for trouble, but not forever. The next day the stranger came again. After the six Tanner worked had seen the idler there for half the morning, they quit and began to eat, a full thirty minutes before noon. He had not risked ordering them up. He had gone to the source of the trouble.

The stranger was leaning against a tree on the edge of the clearing, watching with half-closed eyes. The insolence on his face barely covered the wariness behind it. His look said, this ain't much of a white man so why he come on so big, what he fixing to do?

He had meant to say, "Nigger, this knife is in my hand now but if you ain't out of my sight ..." but as he drew closer he changed his mind. The Negro's eyes were small and bloodshot. Tanner supposed there was a knife on him somewhere that he would as soon use as not. His own penknife moved, directed solely by some intruding intelligence that worked in his hands. He had no idea what he was carving, but when he reached the Negro, he had already made two holes the size of half dollars in the piece of bark.

The Negro's gaze fell on his hands and was held. His jaw slackened. His eyes did not move from the knife tearing recklessly around the bark. He watched as if he saw an invisible power working on the wood.

He looked himself then and, astonished, saw the connected rims of a pair of spectacles.

He held them away from him and looked through the holes past a pile of shavings and on into the woods to the edge of the pen where they kept their mules.

"You can't see so good, can you, boy?" he said and began scraping the ground with his foot to turn up a piece of wire. He picked up a small piece of haywire; in a minute he found another, shorter piece and picked that up. He began to attach these to the bark. He was in no hurry now that he knew what he was doing. When the spectacles were finished, he handed them to the Negro. "Put these on," he said. "I hate to see anybody can't see good."

There was an instant when the Negro might have done one thing or another, might have taken the glasses and crushed them in his hand or grabbed the knife and turned it on him. He saw the exact instant in the muddy liquor-swollen eyes when the pleasure of having a knife in this white man's gut was balanced against something else, he could not tell what.

The Negro reached for the glasses. He attached the bows carefully behind his ears and looked forth. He peered this way and that with exaggerated solemnity. And then he looked directly at Tanner and grinned, or grimaced, Tanner could not tell which, but he had an instant's sensation of seeing before him a negative image of himself, as if clownishness and captivity had been their common lot. The vision failed him before he could decipher it.

"Preacher," he said, "what you hanging around here for?" He picked up another piece of bark and began, without looking at it, to carve again. "This ain't Sunday."

"This here ain't Sunday?" the Negro said.

"This is Friday," he said. "That's the way it is with you preachers— drunk all week so you don't know when Sunday is. What you see through those glasses?"

"See a man."

"What kind of a man?"

"See the man make theseyer glasses."

"Is he white or black?"

"He white!" the Negro said as if only at that moment was his vision sufficiently improved to detect it. "Yessuh, he white!" he said.

"Well, you treat him like he was white," Tanner said. "What's your name?"

"Name Coleman," the Negro said.

And he had not got rid of Coleman since. You make a monkey out of one of them and he jumps on your back and stays there for life, but let one make a monkey out of you and all you can do is kill him or disappear. And he was not going to hell for killing a nigger. Behind the shack he heard the doctor kick over a bucket. He sat and waited.

In a moment the doctor appeared again, beating his way around the other side of the house, whacking at scattered clumps of Johnson grass with his cane. He stopped in the middle of the yard, about where that morning the daughter had delivered her ultimatum.

"You don't belong here," he began. "I could have you prosecuted."

Tanner remained there, dumb, staring across the field.

"Where's your still?" the doctor asked.

"If it's a still around here, it don't belong to me," he said and shut his mouth tight.

The Negro laughed softly. "Down on your luck, ain't you?" he murmured. "Didn't you used to own a little piece of land over acrost the river and lost it?"

He had continued to study the woods ahead.

"If you want to run the still for me, that's one thing," the doctor said. "If you don't, you might as well had be packing up."

"I don't have to work for you," he said. "The governmint ain't got around yet to forcing the white folks to work for the colored."

The doctor polished the stone in his ring with the ball of his thumb. "I don't like the governmint no bettern you," he said. "Where you going instead? You going to the city and get you a soot of rooms at the Biltmo' Hotel?"

Tanner said nothing.

"The day coming," the doctor said, "when the white folks IS going to be working for the colored and you mights well to git ahead of the crowd."

"That day ain't coming for me," Tanner said shortly.

"Done come for you," the doctor said. "Ain't come for the rest of them."

Tanner's gaze drove on past the farthest blue edge of the tree line into the pale empty afternoon sky. "I got a daughter in the north," he said. "I don't have to work for you."

The doctor took his watch from his watch pocket and looked at it and put it back. He gazed for a moment at the back of his hands. He appeared to have measured and to know secretly the time it would take everything to change finally upside down. "She don't want no old daddy like you," he said. "Maybe she say she do, but that ain't likely. Even if you rich," he said, "they don't want you. They got they own ideas. The black ones they rares and they pitches. I made mine," he said, "and I ain't done none of that." He looked again at Tanner. "I be back here next week," he said, "and if you still here, I know you going to work for me." He remained there a moment, rocking on his heels, waiting for some answer. Finally he turned and started beating his way back through the overgrown path.

Tanner had continued to look across the field as if his spirit had been sucked out of him into the woods and nothing was left on the chair but a shell. If he had known it was a question of this — sitting here looking out of this window all day in this no-place, or just running a still for a nigger, he would have run the still for the nigger. He would have been a nigger's white nigger any day. Behind him he heard the daughter come in from the kitchen. His heart accelerated but after a second he heard her plump herself down on the sofa. She was not yet ready to go. He did not turn and look at her.

She sat there silently a few moments. Then she began. "The trouble with you is," she said, "you sit in front of that window all the time where there's nothing to look out at. You need some inspiration and an out-let. If you would let me pull your chair around to look at the TV, you would quit thinking about morbid stuff, death and hell and judgement. My Lord."

"The Judgement is coming," he muttered. "The sheep'll be separated from the goats. Them that kept their promises from them that didn't. Them that did the best they could with what they had from them that didn't. Them that honored their father and their mother from them that cursed them. Them that ..."

She heaved a mammoth sigh that all but drowned him out. "What's the use in me wasting my good breath?" she asked. She rose and went back in the kitchen and began knocking things about.

She was so high and mighty! At home he had been living in a shack but there was at least air around it. He could put his feet on the ground. Here she didn't even live in a house. She lived in a pigeon-hutch of a building, with all stripes of foreigner, all of them twisted in the tongue. It was no place for a sane man. The first morning here she had taken him sightseeing and he had seen in fifteen minutes exactly how it was. He had not been out of the apartment since. He never wanted to set foot again on the underground railroad or the steps that moved under you while you stood still or any elevator to the thirty-fourth floor. When he was safely back in the apartment again, he had imagined going over it with Coleman. He had to turn his head every few seconds to make sure Coleman was behind him. Keep to the inside or these people'll knock you down, keep right behind me or you'll get left, keep your hat on, you damn idiot, he had said, and Coleman had come on with his bent running shamble, panting and muttering, What we doing here? Where you get this fool idea coming here?

I come to show you it was no kind of place. Now you know you were well off where you were.

I knowed it before, Coleman said. Was you didn't know it.

When he had been here a week, he had got a postcard from Coleman that had been written for him by Hooten at the railroad station. It was written in green ink and said, "This is Coleman — X — howyou boss." Under it Hooten had written from himself, "Quit frequenting all those nitespots and come on home, you scoundrel, yours truly. W. P. Hooten." He had sent Coleman a card in return, care of Hooten, that said, "This place is alrite if you like it. Yours truly, W. T. Tanner." Since the daughter had to mail the card, he had not put on it that he was returning as soon as his pension check came. He had not intended to tell her but to leave her a note. When the check came, he would hire himself a taxi to the bus station and be on his way. And it would have made her as happy as it made him. She had found his company dour and her duty irksome. If he had sneaked out, she would have had the pleasure of having tried to do it and to top that off, the pleasure of his ingratitude.

As for him, he would have returned to squat on the doctor's land and to take his orders from a nigger who chewed ten-cent cigars. And to think less about it than formerly. Instead he had been done in by a nigger actor, or one who called himself an actor. He didn't believe the nigger was any actor.

There were two apartments on each floor of the building. He had been with the daughter three weeks when the people in the next hutch moved out. He had stood in the hall and watched the moving-out and the next day he had watched a moving-in. The hall was narrow and dark and he stood in the corner out of the way, offering only a suggestion every now and then to the movers that would have made their work easier for them if they had paid any attention. The furniture was new and cheap so he decided the people moving in might be a newly married couple and he would just wait around until they came and wish them well. After a while a large Negro in a light blue suit came lunging up the stairs, carrying two canvas suitcases, his head lowered against the strain. Behind him stepped a young tan-skinned woman with bright copper-colored hair. The Negro dropped the suitcases with a thud in front of the door of the next apartment.

"Be careful, Sweetie," the woman said. "My make-up is in there."

It broke upon him then just what was happening.

The Negro was grinning. He took a swipe at one of her hips.

"Quit it," she said, "there's an old guy watching."

They both turned and looked at him.

"Had-do," he said and nodded. Then he turned quickly into his own door.

His daughter was in the kitchen. "Who you think's rented that apartment over there?" he asked, his face alight.

She looked at him suspiciously. "Who?" she muttered.

"A nigger!" he said in a gleeful voice. "A South Alabama nigger if I ever saw one. And got him this high-yeller, high-stepping woman with red hair and they two are going to live next door to you!" He slapped his knee. "Yes siree!" he said. "Damn if they ain't!" It was the first time since coming up here that he had had occasion to laugh.

Her face squared up instantly. "All right now you listen to me," she said. "You keep away from them. Don't you go over there trying to get friendly with him. They ain't the same around here and I don't want any trouble with niggers, you hear me? If you have to live next to them, just you mind your business and they'll mind theirs. That's the way people were meant to get along in this world. Everybody can get along if they just mind their business. Live and let live." She began to wrinkle her nose like a rabbit, a stupid way she had. "Up here everybody minds their own business and everybody gets along. That's all you have to do."

"I was getting along with niggers before you were born," he said. He went back out into the hall and waited. He was willing to bet the nigger would like to talk to someone who understood him. Twice while he waited, he forgot and in his excitement, spit his tobacco juice against the baseboard. In about twenty minutes, the door of the apartment opened again and the Negro came out. He had put on a tie and a pair of horn-rimmed spectacles and Tanner noticed for the first time that he had a small almost invisible goatee. A real swell. He came on without appearing to see there was anyone else in the hall.

"Haddy, John," Tanner said and nodded, but the Negro brushed past without hearing and went rattling rapidly down the stairs.

Could be deaf and dumb, Tanner thought. He went back into the apartment and sat down but each time he heard a noise in the hall, he got up and went to the door and stuck his head out to see if it might be the Negro. Once in the middle of the afternoon, he caught the Negro's eye just as he was rounding the bend of the stairs again but before he could get out a word, the man was in his own apartment and had slammed the door. He had never known one to move that fast unless the police were after him.

He was standing in the hall early the next morning when the woman came out of her door alone, walking on high gold-painted heels. He wished to bid her good morning or simply to nod but instinct told him to beware. She didn't look like any kind of woman, black or white, he had ever seen before and he remained pressed against the wall, frightened more than anything else, and feigning invisibility.

The woman gave him a flat stare, then turned her head away and stepped wide of him as if she were skirting an open garbage can. He held his breath until she was out of sight. Then he waited patiently for the man.

The Negro came out about eight o'clock.

This time Tanner advanced squarely in his path. "Good morning, Preacher," he said. It had been his experience that if a Negro tended to be sullen, this title usually cleared up his expression.

The Negro stopped abruptly.

"I seen you move in," Tanner said. "I ain't been up here long myself. It ain't much of a place if you ask me. I reckon you wish you were back in South Alabama."

The Negro did not take a step or answer. His eyes began to move. They moved from the top of the black hat, down to the collarless blue shirt, neatly buttoned at the neck, down the faded galluses to the gray trousers and the high-top shoes and up again, very slowly, while some unfathomable dead-cold rage seemed to stiffen and shrink him.

"I thought you might know somewhere around here we could find us a pond, Preacher," Tanner said in a voice growing thinner but still with considerable hope in it.

A seething noise came out of the Negro before he spoke. "I'm not from South Alabama," he said in a breathless wheezing voice. "I'm from New York City. And I'm not no preacher! I'm an actor."

Tanner chortled. "It's a little actor in most preachers, ain't it?" he said and winked. "I reckon you just preach on the side."

"I don't preach!" the Negro cried and rushed past him as if a swarm of bees had suddenly come down on him out of nowhere. He dashed down the stairs and was gone.

Tanner stood here for some time before he went back in the apartment. The rest of the day he sat in his chair and debated whether he would have one more try at making friends with him. Every time he heard a noise on the stairs he went to the door and looked out, but the Negro did not return until late in the afternoon. Tanner was standing in the hall waiting for him when he reached the top of the stairs. "Good evening, Preacher," he said, forgetting that the Negro called himself an actor.

The Negro stopped and gripped the banister rail. A tremor racked him from his head to his crotch. Then he began to come forward slowly. When he was close enough he lunged and grasped Tanner by both shoulders. "I don't take no crap," he whispered, "off no wool-hat red-neck son-of-a-bitch peckerwood old bastard like you." He caught his breath. And then his voice came out in the sound of an exasperation so profound that it rocked on the verge of a laugh. It was high and piercing and weak, "And I'm not no preacher! I'm not even no Christian. I don't believe that crap. There ain't no Jesus and there ain't no God."

The old man felt his heart inside him hard and tough as an oak knot. "And you ain't black," he said. "And I ain't white!"

The Negro slammed him against the wall. He yanked the black hat down over his eyes. Then he grabbed his shirt front and shoved him backwards to his open door and knocked him through it. From the kitchen the daughter saw him blindly hit the edge of the inside hall door and fall reeling into the living room.

For days his tongue appeared to be frozen in his mouth. When it unthawed it was twice its normal size and he could not make her understand him. What he wanted to know was if the government check had come because he meant to buy a bus ticket with it and go home. After a few days, he made her understand. "It came," she said, "and it'll just pay the first two weeks' doctor-bill and please tell me how you're going home when you can't talk or walk or think straight and you got one eye crossed yet? Just please tell me that?"

It had come to him then slowly just what his present situation was. At least he would have to make her understand that he must be sent home to be buried. They could have him shipped back in a refrigerated car so that he would keep for the trip. He didn't want any undertaker up here messing with him. Let them get him off at once and he would come in on the early morning train and they could wire Hooten to get Coleman and Coleman would do the rest; she would not even have to go herself. After a lot of argument, he wrung the promise from her. She would ship him back.

After that he slept peacefully and improved a little. In his dreams he could feel the cold early morning air of home coming in through the cracks of the pine box. He could see Coleman waiting, red-eyed, on the station platform and Hooten standing there with his green eyeshade and black alpaca sleeves. If the old fool had stayed at home where he belonged, Hooten would be thinking, he wouldn't be arriving on the 6:03 in no box. Coleman had turned the borrowed mule and cart so that they could slide the box off the platform onto the open end of the wagon. Everything was ready and the two of them, shut-mouthed, inched the loaded coffin toward the wagon. From inside he began to scratch on the wood. They let go as if it had caught fire.

They stood looking at each other, then at the box.

"That him," Coleman said. "He in there his self."

"Naw," Hooten said, "must be a rat got in there with him."

"That him. This here one of his tricks."

"If it's a rat he might as well stay."

"That him. Git a crowbar."

Hooten went grumbling off and got the crowbar and came back and began to pry open the lid. Even before he had the upper end pried open, Coleman was jumping up and down, wheezing and panting from excitement. Tanner gave a thrust upward with both hands and sprang up in the box. "Judgement Day! Judgement Day!" he cried. "Don't you two fools know it's Judgement Day?"

Now he knew exactly what her promises were worth. He would do as well to trust to the note pinned in his coat and to any stranger who found him dead in the street or in the boxcar or wherever. There was nothing to be looked for from her except that she would do things her way. She came out of the kitchen again, holding her hat and coat and rubber boots.

"Now listen," she said, "I have to go to the store. Don't you try to get up and walk around while I'm gone. You've been to the bathroom and you shouldn't have to go again. I don't want to find you on the floor when I get back."

You won't find me at all when you get back, he said to himself. This was the last time he would see her flat dumb face. He felt guilty. She had been good to him and he had been nothing but a nuisance to her.

"Do you want you a glass of milk before I go?" she asked.

"No," he said. Then he drew breath and said, "You got a nice place here. It's a nice part of the country. I'm sorry if I've give you a lot of trouble getting sick. It was my fault trying to be friendly with that nigger." And I'm a damned liar besides, he said to himself to kill the outrageous taste such a statement made in his mouth.

For a moment she stared as if he were losing his mind. Then she seemed to think better of it. "Now don't saying something pleasant like that once in a while make you feel better?" she asked and sat down on the sofa.

His knees itched to unbend. Git on, git on, he fumed silently. Make haste and go.

"It's great to have you here," she said. "I wouldn't have you any other place. My own daddy." She gave him a big smile and hoisted her right leg up and began to pull on her boot. "I wouldn't wish a dog out on a day like this," she said, "but I got to go. You can sit here and hope I don't slip and break my neck." She stamped the booted foot on the floor and then began to tackle the other one.

He turned his eyes to the window. The snow was beginning to stick and freeze to the outside pane. When he looked at her again, she was standing there like a big doll stuffed into its hat and coat. She drew on a pair of green knitted gloves. "Okay," she said, "I'm gone. You sure you don't want anything?"

"No," he said, "go ahead on."

"Well so long then," she said.

He raised the hat enough to reveal a bald palely speckled head. The hall door closed behind her. He began to tremble with excitement. He reached behind him and drew the coat into his lap. When he got it on, he waited until he had stopped panting, then he gripped the arms of the chair and pulled himself up. His body felt like a great heavy bell whose clapper swung from side to side but made no noise. Once up, he remained standing a moment, swaying until he got his balance. A sensation of terror and defeat swept over him. He would never make it. He would never get there dead or alive. He pushed one foot forward and did not fall and his confidence returned. "The Lord is my shepherd," he muttered, "I shall not want." He began moving toward the sofa where he would have support. He reached it. He was on his way.

By the time he got to the door, she would be down the four flights of steps and out of the building. He got past the sofa and crept along by the wall, keeping his hand on it for support. Nobody was going to bury him here. He was as confident as if the woods of home lay at the bottom of the stairs. He reached the front door of the apartment and opened it and peered into the hall. This was the first time he had looked into it since the actor had knocked him down. It was dank-smelling and empty. The thin piece of linoleum stretched its moldy length to the door of the other apartment, which was closed. "Nigger actor," he said.

The head of the stairs was ten or twelve feet from where he stood and he bent his attention to getting there without creeping around the long way with a hand on the wall. He held his arms a little way out from his sides and pushed forward directly. He was halfway there when all at once his legs disappeared, or felt as if they had. He looked down, bewildered, for they were still there. He fell forward and grasped the banister post with both hands. Hanging there, he gazed for what seemed the longest time he had ever looked at anything down the steep unlighted steps; then he closed his eyes and pitched forward. He landed upside down in the middle of the flight.

He felt presently the tilt of the box as they took it off the train and got it on the baggage wagon. He made no noise yet. The train jarred and slid away. In a moment the baggage wagon was rumbling under him, carrying him back to the station side. He heard footsteps rattling closer and closer to him and he supposed that a crowd was gathering. Wait until they see this, he thought.

"That him," Coleman said, "one of his tricks."

"It's a damn rat in there," Hooten said.

"It's him. Git the crowbar."

In a moment a shaft of greenish light fell on him. He pushed through it and cried in a weak voice, "Judgement Day! Judgement Day! You idiots didn't know it was Judgement Day, did you?"

"Coleman?" he murmured.

The Negro bending over him had a large surly mouth and sullen eyes.

"Ain't any coal man, either," he said. This must be the wrong station, Tanner thought. Those fools put me off too soon. Who is this nigger? It ain't even daylight here.

At the Negro's side was another face, a woman's — pale, topped with a pile of copper-glinting hair and twisted as if she had just stepped in a pile of dung.

"Oh," Tanner said, "it's you."

The actor leaned closer and grasped him by the front of his shirt. "Judgement day," he said in a mocking voice. "Ain't no judgement day, old man. Cept this. Maybe this here judgement day for you."

Tanner tried to catch hold of a banister-spoke to raise himself but his hand grasped air. The two faces, the black one and the pale one, appeared to be wavering. By an effort of will he kept them focused before him while he lifted his hand, as light as a breath, and said in his jauntiest voice, "Hep me up, Preacher. I'm on my way home!"

His daughter found him when she came in from the grocery store. His hat had been pulled down over his face and his head and arms thrust between the spokes of the banister; his feet dangled over the stairwell like those of a man in the stocks. She tugged at him frantically and then flew for the police. They cut him out with a saw and said he had been dead about an hour.

She buried him in New York City, but after she had done it she could not sleep at night. Night after night she turned and tossed and very definite lines began to appear in her face, so she had him dug up and shipped the body to Corinth. Now she rests well at night and her good looks have mostly returned.

QUESTIONS

1. From whose point of view is "Judgement Day" told? Is this point of view maintained throughout the story? Could the story have been told as effectively from the daughter's vantage point?

2. What is Tanner's relationship with Coleman Parrum? with his daughter? with his son-in-law? Is he defined by his relationships or by his thoughts?

3. "It was being there that mattered; the dead or alive did not." Why? Why does he prefer a shack to an apartment?

4. How does Tanner's death prove that he really was out of place "up North"? Can you define his attitude toward the "Preacher"?

5. How does O'Connor bring us into sympathy — even partial sympathy — with this uneducated, racially prejudiced old man?

6. What is your emotional response to "Judgement Day"? Can you account for it?

FLANNERY O'CONNOR

Good Country People

Besides the neutral expression that she wore when she was alone, Mrs. Freeman had two others, forward and reverse, that she used for all her human dealings. Her forward expression was steady and driving like the advance of a heavy truck. Her eyes never swerved to left or right but turned as the story turned as if they followed a yellow line down the center of it. She seldom used the other expression because it was not often necessary for her to retract a statement, but when she did, her face came to a complete stop, there was an almost imperceptible movement of her black eyes, during which they seemed to be receding, and then the observer would see that Mrs. Freeman, though she might stand there as real as several grain sacks thrown on top of each other, was no longer there in spirit. As for getting anything across to her when this was the case, Mrs. Hopewell had given it up. She might talk her head off. Mrs. Freeman could never be brought to admit herself wrong on any point. She would stand there and if she could be brought to say anything, it was something like, "Well, I wouldn't of said it was and I wouldn't of said it wasn't," or letting her gaze range over the top kitchen shelf where there was an assortment of dusty bottles, she might remark, "I see you ain't ate many of them figs you put up last summer."

They carried on their most important business in the kitchen at breakfast. Every morning Mrs. Hopewell got up at seven o'clock and lit her gas heater and Joy's. Joy was her daughter, a large blonde girl who had an artificial leg. Mrs. Hopewell thought of her as a child though she was thirty-two years old and highly educated. Joy would get up while her mother was eating and lumber into the bathroom and slam the door, and before long, Mrs. Freeman would arrive at the back door. Joy would hear her mother call, "Come on in," and then they would talk for a while in low voices that were indistinguishable in the bathroom. By the time Joy came in, they had usually finished the weather report and were on one or the other of Mrs. Freeman's daughters, Glynese or Carramae, Joy called then Glycerin and Caramel. Glynese, a redhead, was eighteen and had many admirers; Carramae, a blonde, was only fifteen but already married and pregnant. She could not keep anything on her stomach. Every morning Mrs. Freeman told Mrs. Hopewell how many times she had vomited since the last report.

Mrs. Hopewell liked to tell people that Glynese and Carramae were two of the finest girls she knew and that Mrs. Freeman was a *lady* and that she was never ashamed to take her anywhere or introduce her to anybody they might meet. Then she would tell how she had happened to hire the Freemans in the first place and how they were a godsend to her and how she had had them four years. The reason for her keeping them so long was that they were not trash. They were good country people. She had telephoned the man whose name they had given as a reference and he had told her that Mr. Freeman was a good farmer but that his wife was the nosiest woman ever to walk the earth. "She's got to be into everything," the man said. "If she don't get there before the dust settles, you can bet she's dead, that's all. She'll want to know all your business. I can stand him real good," he had said, "but me nor my wife neither could have stood that woman one more minute on this place." That had put Mrs. Hopewell off for a few days.

She had hired them in the end because there were no other applicants but she had made up her mind beforehand exactly how she would handle the woman. Since she was the type who had to be into everything, then, Mrs. Hopewell had decided, she would not only let her be into everything, she would *see to it* that she was into everything — she would give her the responsibility of everything, she would put her in charge. Mrs. Hopewell had no bad qualities of her own but she was able to use other people's in such a constructive way that she never felt the lack. She had hired the Freemans and she had kept them four years.

Nothing is perfect. This was one of Mrs. Hopewell's favorite sayings. Another was: that is life! And still another, the most important, was: well, other people have their opinions too. She would make these statements, usually at the table, in a tone of gentle insistence as if no one held them but her, and the large hulking Joy, whose constant outrage had obliterated every expression from her face, would stare just a little to the side of her, her eyes icy blue, with the look of someone who has achieved blindness by an act of will and means to keep it.

When Mrs. Hopewell said to Mrs. Freeman that life was like that, Mrs. Freeman would say, "I always said so myself." Nothing had been arrived at by anyone that had not first been arrived at by her. She was quicker than Mr. Freeman. When Mrs. Hopewell said to her after they had been on the place a while, "You know, you're the wheel behind the wheel," and winked, Mrs. Freeman had said, "I know it. I've always been quick. It's some that are quicker than others."

"Everybody is different," Mrs. Hopewell said.

"Yes, most people is," Mrs. Freeman said.

"It takes all kinds to make the world."

"I always said it did myself."

The girl was used to this kind of dialogue for breakfast and more of it for dinner; sometimes they had it for supper too. When they had no guest they ate in the kitchen because that was easier. Mrs. Freeman always managed to arrive at some point during the meal and to watch them finish it. She would stand in the doorway if it were summer but in the winter she would stand with one elbow on top of the refrigerator and look down on them, or she would stand by the gas heater, lifting the back of her skirt slightly. Occasionally she would stand against the wall and roll her head from side to side. At no time was she in any hurry to leave. All this was very trying on Mrs. Hopewell but she was a woman of great patience. She realized that nothing is perfect and that in the Freemans she had good country people and that if, in this day and age, you get good country people, you had better hang onto them.

She had had plenty of experience with trash. Before the Freemans she had averaged one tenant family a year. The wives of these farmers were not the kind you would want to be around you for very long. Mrs. Hopewell, who had divorced her husband long ago, needed someone to walk over the fields with her; and when Joy had to be impressed for these services, her remarks were usually so ugly and her face so glum that Mrs. Hopewell would say, "If you can't come pleasantly, I don't want you at all," to which the girl, standing square and rigid-shouldered with her neck thrust slightly forward, would reply, "If you want me, here I am — LIKE I AM."

Mrs. Hopewell excused this attitude because of the leg (which had been shot off in a hunting accident when Joy was ten). It was hard for Mrs. Hopewell to realize that her child was thirty-two now and that for more than twenty years she had had only one leg. She thought of her still as a child because it tore her heart to think instead of the poor stout girl in her thirties who had never danced a step or had any *normal* good times. Her name was really Joy but as soon as she was twenty-one and away from home, she had had it legally changed. Mrs. Hopewell was certain that she had thought and thought until she had hit upon the ugliest name in any language. Then she had gone and had the beautiful name, Joy, changed without telling her mother until after she had done it. Her legal name was Hulga.

When Mrs. Hopewell thought the name, Hulga, she thought of the broad blank hull of a battleship. She would not use it. She continued to call her Joy to which the girl responded but in a purely mechanical way.

Hulga had learned to tolerate Mrs. Freeman who saved her from taking walks with her mother. Even Glynese and Carramae were useful when they occupied attention that might otherwise have been directed at her. At first she had thought she could not stand Mrs. Freeman for she had found that it was not possible to be rude to her. Mrs. Freeman would take on strange resentments and for days together she would be sullen but the source of her displeasure was always obscure; a direct attack, a positive leer, blatant ugliness to her face — these never touched her. And without warning one day, she began calling her Hulga.

She did not call her that in front of Mrs. Hopewell who would have been incensed but when she and the girl happened to be out of the house together, she would say something and add the name Hulga to the end of it, and the big spectacled Joy-Hulga would scowl and redden as if her privacy had been intruded upon. She considered the name her personal affair. She had arrived at it first purely on the basis of its ugly sound and then the full genius of its fitness had struck her. She had a vision of the name working like the ugly sweating Vulcan who stayed in the furnace and to whom, presumably, the goddess had to come when called. She saw it as the name of her highest creative act. One of her major triumphs was that her mother had not been able to turn her dust into Joy, but the greater one was that she had been able to turn it herself into Hulga. However, Mrs. Freeman's relish for using the name only irritated her. It was as if Mrs. Freeman's beady steel-pointed eyes had penetrated far enough behind her face to reach some secret fact. Something about her seemed to fascinate Mrs. Freeman and then one day Hulga realized that it was the artificial leg. Mrs. Freeman had a special fondness for the details of secret infections, hidden deformities, assaults upon children. Of diseases, she preferred the lingering or incurable. Hulga had heard Mrs. Hopewell give her the details of the hunting accident, how the leg had been literally blasted off, how she had never lost consciousness. Mrs. Freeman could listen to it any time as if it had happened an hour ago.

When Hulga stumped into the kitchen in the morning (she could walk without making the awful noise but she made it — Mrs. Hopewell was certain — because it was ugly-sounding), she glanced at them and did not speak. Mrs. Hopewell would be in her red kimono with her hair tied around her head in rags. She would be sitting at the table, finishing her breakfast and Mrs. Freeman would be hanging by her elbow outward from the refrigerator, looking down at the table. Hulga always put her eggs on the stove to boil and then stood over them with her arms folded, and Mrs. Hopewell would look at her — a kind of indirect gaze divided between her and Mrs. Freeman — and would think that if she would only keep herself up a little, she wouldn't be so bad looking. There was nothing wrong with her face that a pleasant expression wouldn't help. Mrs. Hopewell said that people who looked on the bright side of things would be beautiful even if they were not.

Whenever she looked at Joy this way, she could not help but feel that it would have been better if the child had not taken the Ph.D. It had certainly not brought her out any and now that she had it, there was no more excuse for her to go to school again. Mrs. Hopewell thought it was nice for girls to go to school to have a good time but Joy had "gone through." Anyhow, she would not have been strong enough to go again. The doctors had told Mrs. Hopewell that with the best of care, Joy might see forty-five. She had a weak heart. Joy had made it plain that if it had not been for this condition, she would be far from these red hills and good country people. She would be in a university lecturing to people who knew what she was talking about. And Mrs. Hopewell could very well picture her there, looking like a scarecrow and lecturing to more of the same. Here she went about all day in a six-year-old skirt and a yellow sweat shirt with a faded cowboy on a horse embossed on it. She thought this was funny; Mrs. Hopewell thought it was idiotic and showed simply that she was still a child. She was brilliant but she didn't have a grain of sense. It seemed to Mrs. Hopewell that every year she grew less like other people and more like herself — bloated, rude, and squint-eyed. And she said such strange things! To her own mother she had said — without warning, without excuse, standing up in the middle of a meal with her face purple and her mouth half full — "Woman! do you ever look inside? Do you ever look inside and see what you are *not*? God!" she had cried sinking down again and staring at her plate, "Malebranche was right: we are not our own light. We are not our own light!" Mrs. Hopewell had no idea to this day what brought that on. She had only made the remark, hoping Joy would take it in, that a smile never hurt anyone.

The girl had taken the Ph.D. in philosophy and this left Mrs. Hopewell at a complete loss. You could say, "My daughter is a nurse," or "My daughter is a schoolteacher," or even, "My daughter is a chemical engineer." You could not say, "My daughter is a philosopher." That was something that had ended with the Greeks and Romans. All day Joy sat on her neck in a deep chair, reading. Sometimes she went for walks but she didn't like dogs or cats or birds or flowers or nature or nice young men. She looked at nice young men as if she could smell their stupidity.

One day Mrs. Hopewell had picked up one of the books the girl had just put down and opening it at random, she read, "Science, on the other hand, has to assert its soberness and seriousness afresh and declare that it is concerned solely with what-is. Nothing — how can it be for science anything but a horror and a phantasm? If science is right, then one thing stands firm: science wishes to know nothing of nothing. Such is after all the strictly scientific approach to Nothing. We know it by wishing to know nothing of Nothing." These words had been underlined with a blue pencil and they worked on Mrs. Hopewell like some evil incantation in gibberish. She shut the book quickly and went out of the room as if she were having a chill.

This morning when the girl came in, Mrs. Freeman was on Carramae. "She thrown up four times after supper," she said, "and was up twict in the night after three o'clock. Yesterday she didn't do nothing but ramble in the bureau drawer. All she did. Stand up there and see what she could run up on."

"She's got to eat," Mrs. Hopewell muttered, sipping her coffee, while she watched Joy's back at the stove. She was wondering what the child had said to the Bible salesman. She could not imagine what kind of a conversation she could possibly have had with him.

He was a tall gaunt hatless youth who had called yesterday to sell them a Bible. He had appeared at the door, carrying a large black suitcase that weighted him so heavily on one side that he had to brace himself against the door facing. He seemed on the point of collapse but he said in a cheerful voice, "Good morning, Mrs. Cedars!" and set the suitcase down on the mat. He was not a bad-looking young man though he had on a bright blue suit and yellow socks that were not pulled up far enough. He had prominent face bones and a streak of sticky-looking brown hair falling across his forehead.

"I'm Mrs. Hopewell," she said.

"Oh!" he said, pretending to look puzzled but with his eyes sparkling, "I saw it said 'The Cedars' on the mailbox so I thought you was Mrs. Cedars!" and he burst out in a pleasant laugh. He picked up the satchel and under cover of a pant, he fell forward into her hall. It was rather as if the suitcase had moved first, jerking him after it. "Mrs. Hopewell!" he said and grabbed her hand. "I hope you are well!" and he laughed again and then all at once his face sobered completely. He paused and gave her a straight earnest look and said, "Lady, I've come to speak of serious things."

"Well, come in," she muttered, none too pleased because her dinner was almost ready. He came into the parlor and sat down on the edge of a straight chair and put the suitcase between his feet and glanced around the room as if he were sizing her up by it. Her silver gleamed on the two sideboards; she decided he had never been in a room as elegant as this.

"Mrs. Hopewell," he began, using her name in a way that sounded almost intimate, "I know you believe in Chrustian service."

"Well yes," she murmured.

"I know," he said and paused, looking very wise with his head cocked on one side, "that you're a good woman. Friends have told me."

Mrs. Hopewell never liked to be taken for a fool. "What are you selling?" she asked.

"Bibles," the young man said and his eye raced around the room before he added, "I see you have no family Bible in your parlor, I see that is the one lack you got!"

Mrs. Hopewell could not say, "My daughter is an atheist and won't let me keep the Bible in the parlor." She said, stiffening slightly, "I keep my Bible by my bedside." This was not the truth. It was in the attic somewhere.

"Lady," he said, "the word of God ought to be in the parlor."

"Well, I think that's a matter of taste," she began. "I think ..."

"Lady," he said, "for a Chrustian, the word of God ought to be in every room in the house besides in his heart. I know you're a Chrustian because I can see it in every line of your face."

She stood up and said, "Well, young man, I don't want to buy a Bible and I smell my dinner burning."

He didn't get up. He began to twist his hands and looking down at them, he said softly, "Well lady, I'll tell you the truth — not many people want to buy one nowadays and besides, I know I'm real simple. I don't know how to say a thing but to say it. I'm just a country boy." He glanced up into her unfriendly face. "People like you don't like to fool with country people like me!"

"Why!" she cried, "good country people are the salt of the earth! Besides, we all have different ways of doing, it takes all kinds to make the world go 'round. That's life!"

"You said a mouthful," he said.

"Why, I think there aren't enough good country people in the world!" she said, stirred. "I think that's what's wrong with it!"

His face had brightened. "I didn't inraduce myself," he said. "I'm Manley Pointer from out in the country around Willohobie, not even from a place, just from near a place."

"You wait a minute," she said. "I have to see about my dinner." She went out to the kitchen and found Joy standing near the door where she had been listening.

"Get rid of the salt of the earth," she said, "and let's eat."

Mrs. Hopewell gave her a pained look and turned the heat down under the vegetables. "*I* can't be rude to anybody," she murmured and went back into the parlor.

He had opened the suitcase and was sitting with a Bible on each knee.

"You might as well put those up," she told him. "I don't want one."

"I appreciate your honesty," he said. "You don't see any more real honest people unless you go way out in the country."

"I know," she said, "real genuine folks!" Through the crack in the door she heard a groan.

"I guess a lot of boys come telling you they're working their way through college," he said, "but I'm not going to tell you that. Somehow," he said, "I don't want to go to college. I want to devote my life to Christian service. See," he said, lowering his voice, "I got this heart condition. I may not live long. When you know it's something wrong with you and you may not live long, well then, lady …" He paused, with his mouth open, and stared at her.

He and Joy had the same condition! She knew that her eyes were filling with tears but she collected herself quickly and murmured, "Won't you stay for dinner? We'd love to have you!" and was sorry the instant she heard herself say it.

"Yes mam," he said in an abashed voice, "I would sher love to do that!"

Joy had given him one look on being introduced to him and then throughout the meal had not glanced at him again. He had addressed several remarks to her, which she had pretended not to hear. Mrs. Hopewell could not understand deliberate rudeness, although she lived with it, and she felt she had always to overflow with hospitality to make up for Joy's lack of courtesy. She urged him to talk about himself and he did. He said he was the seventh child of twelve and that his father had been crushed under a tree when he himself was eight year old. He had been crushed very badly, in fact, almost cut in two and was practically not recognizable. His mother had got along the best she could by hard working and she had always seen that her children went to Sunday School and that they read the Bible every evening. He was now nineteen year old and he had been selling Bibles for four months. In that time he had sold seventy-seven Bibles and had the promise of two more sales. He wanted to become a missionary because he thought that was the way you could do most for people. "He who losest his life shall find it," he said simply and he was so sincere, so genuine and earnest that Mrs. Hopewell would not for the world have smiled. He prevented his peas from sliding onto the table by blocking them with a piece of bread which he later cleaned his plate with. She could see Joy observing sidewise how he handled his knife and fork and she saw too that every few minutes, the boy would dart a keen appraising glance at the girl as if he were trying to attract her attention.

After dinner Joy cleared the dishes off the table and disappeared and Mrs. Hopewell was left to talk with him. He told her again about his childhood and his father's accident and about various things that had happened to him. Every five minutes or so she would stifle a yawn. He sat for two hours until finally she told him she must go because she had an appointment in town. He packed his Bibles and thanked her and prepared to leave, but in the doorway he stopped and wrung her hand and said that not on any of his trips had he met a lady as nice as her and he asked if he could come again. She had said she would always be happy to see him.

Joy had been standing in the road, apparently looking at something in the distance, when he came down the steps toward her, bent to the side with his heavy valise. He stopped where she was standing and confronted her directly. Mrs. Hopewell could not hear what he said but she trembled to think what Joy would say to him. She could see that after a minute Joy said something and that then the boy began to speak again, making an excited gesture with his free hand. After a minute Joy said something else at which the boy began to speak once more. Then to her amazement, Mrs. Hopewell saw the two of them walk off together, toward the gate. Joy had walked all the way to the gate with him and Mrs. Hopewell could not imagine what they had said to each other, and she had not yet dared to ask.

Mrs. Freeman was insisting upon her attention. She had moved from the refrigerator to the heater so that Mrs. Hopewell had to turn and face her in order to seem to be listening. "Glynese gone out with Harvey Hill again last night," she said. "She had this sty."

"Hill," Mrs. Hopewell said absently, "is that the one who works in the garage?"

"Nome, he's the one that goes to chiropracter school." Mrs. Freeman said. "She had this sty. Been had it two days. So she says when he brought her in the other night he says, 'Lemme get rid of that sty for you,' and she says, 'How?' and he says, 'You just lay yourself down acrost the seat of that car and I'll show you.' So she done it and he popped her neck. Kept on a-popping it several times until she made him quit. This morning," Mrs. Freeman said, "she ain't got no sty. She ain't got no traces of a sty."

"I never heard of that before," Mrs. Hopewell said.

"He ast her to marry him before the Ordinary," Mrs. Freeman went on, "and she told him she wasn't going to be married in no *office*."

"Well, Glynese is a fine girl," Mrs. Hopewell said. "Glynese and Carramae are both fine girls."

"Carramae said when her and Lyman was married Lyman said it sure felt sacred to him. She said he said he wouldn't take five hundred dollars for being married by a preacher."

"How much would he take?" the girl asked from the stove.

"He said he wouldn't take five hundred dollars," Mrs. Freeman repeated.

"Well we all have work to do," Mrs. Hopewell said.

"Lyman said it just felt more sacred to him," Mrs. Freeman said. "The doctor wants Carramae to eat prunes. Says instead of medicine. Says them cramps is coming from pressure. You know where I think it is?"

"She'll be better in a few weeks," Mrs. Hopewell said.

"In the tube," Mrs. Freeman said. "Else she wouldn't be as sick as she is."

Hulga had cracked her two eggs into a saucer and was bringing them to the table along with a cup of coffee that she had filled too full. She sat down carefully and began to eat, meaning to keep Mrs. Freeman there by questions if for any reason she showed an inclination to leave. She could perceive her mother's eye on her. The first round-about question would be about the Bible salesman and she did not wish to bring it on. "How did he pop her neck?" she asked.

Mrs. Freeman went into a description of how he had popped her neck. She said he owned a '55 Mercury but that Glynese said she would rather marry a man with only a '36 Plymouth who would be married by a preacher. The girl asked what if he had a '32 Plymouth and Mrs. Freeman said what Glynese had said was a '36 Plymouth.

Mrs. Hopewell said there were not many girls with Glynese's common sense. She said what she admired in those girls was their common sense. She said that reminded her that they had had a nice visitor yesterday, a young man selling Bibles. "Lord," she said, "he bored me to death but he was so sincere and genuine I couldn't be rude to him. He was just good country people, you know," she said, " — just the salt of the earth."

"I seen him walk up," Mrs. Freeman said, "and then later — I seen him walk off," and

Hulga could feel the slight shift in her voice, the slight insinuation, that he had not walked off alone, had he? Her face remained expressionless but the color rose into her neck and she seemed to swallow it down with the next spoonful of egg. Mrs. Freeman was looking at her as if they had a secret together.

"Well, it takes all kinds of people to make the world go 'round," Mrs. Hopewell said. "It's very good we aren't all alike."

"Some people are more alike than others," Mrs. Freeman said.

Hulga got up and stumped, with about twice the noise that was necessary, into her room and locked the door. She was to meet the Bible salesman at ten o'clock at the gate. She had thought about it half the night. She had started thinking of it as a great joke and then she had begun to see profound implications in it. She had lain in bed imagining dialogues for them that were insane on the surface but that reached below to depths that no Bible salesman would be aware of. Their conversation yesterday had been of this kind.

He had stopped in front of her and had simply stood there. His face was bony and sweaty and bright, with a little pointed nose in the center of it, and his look was different from what it had been at the dinner table. He was gazing at her with open curiosity, with fascination, like a child watching a new fantastic animal at the zoo, and he was breathing as if he had run a great distance to reach her. His gaze seemed somehow familiar but she could not think where she had been regarded with it before. For almost a minute he didn't say anything. Then on what seemed an insuck of breath, he whispered, "You ever ate a chicken that was two days old?"

The girl looked at him stonily. He might have just put this question up for consideration at the meeting of a philosophical association. "Yes," she presently replied as if she had considered it from all angles.

"It must have been mighty small!" he said triumphantly and shook all over with little nervous giggles, getting very red in the face, and subsiding finally into his gaze of complete admiration, while the girl's expression remained exactly the same.

"How old are you?" he asked softly.

She waited some time before she answered. Then in a flat voice she said, "Seventeen."

His smiles came in succession like waves breaking on the surface of a little lake. "I see you got a wooden leg," he said. "I think you're brave. I think you're real sweet."

The girl stood blank and solid and silent.

"Walk to the gate with me," he said. "You're a brave sweet little thing and I liked you the minute I seen you walk in the door."

Hulga began to move forward.

"What's your name?" he asked, smiling down on the top of her head.

"Hulga," she said.

"Hulga," he murmured, "Hulga. Hulga. I never heard of anybody name Hulga before. You're shy, aren't you, Hulga?" he asked.

She nodded, watching his large red hand on the handle of the giant valise.

"I like girls that wear glasses," he said. "I think a lot. I'm not like these people that a serious thought don't ever enter their heads. It's because I may die."

"I may die too," she said suddenly and looked up at him. His eyes were very small and brown, glittering feverishly.

"Listen," he said, "don't you think some people was meant to meet on account of what all they got in common and all? Like they both think serious thoughts and all?" He shifted the valise to his other hand so that the hand nearest her was free. He caught hold of her elbow and shook it a little. "I don't work on Saturday," he said. "I like to walk in the woods and see what Mother Nature is wearing. O'er the hills and far away. Pic-nics and things. Couldn't we go on a pic-nic tomorrow? Say yes, Hulga," he said and gave her a dying look as if he felt his insides about to drop out of him. He had even seemed to sway slightly toward her.

During the night she had imagined that she seduced him. She imagined that the two of them walked on the place until they came to the storage barn beyond the two back fields and there, she imagined, that things came to such a pass that she very easily seduced him and that then, of course, she had to reckon with his remorse. True genius can get an idea across even to an inferior mind. She imagined that she took his remorse in hand and changed it into a deeper understanding of life. She took all his shame away and turned it into something useful.

She set off for the gate at exactly ten o'clock, escaping without drawing Mrs. Hopewell's attention. She didn't take anything to eat, forgetting that food is usually taken on a picnic. She wore a pair of slacks and a dirty white shirt, and as an afterthought, she had put some Vapex on the collar of it since she did not own any perfume. When she reached the gate no one was there.

She looked up and down the empty highway and had the furious feeling that she had been tricked, that he had only meant to make her walk to the gate after the idea of him. Then suddenly he stood up, very tall, from behind a bush on the opposite embankment. Smiling, he lifted his hat which was new and wide-brimmed. He had not worn it yesterday and she wondered if he had bought it for the occasion. It was toast-colored with a red and white band around it and was slightly too large for him. He stepped from behind the bush still carrying the black valise. He had on the same suit and the same yellow socks sucked down in his shoes from walking. He crossed the highway and said, "I knew you'd come!"

The girl wondered acidly how he had known this. She pointed to the valise and asked, "Why did you bring your Bibles?"

He took her elbow, smiling down on her as if he could not stop. "You can never tell when you'll need the word of God, Hulga," he said. She had a moment in which she doubted that this was actually happening and then they began to climb the embankment. They went down into the pasture toward the woods. The boy walked lightly by her side, bouncing on his toes. The valise did not seem to be heavy today; he even swung it. They crossed half the pasture without saying anything and then, putting his hand easily on the small of her back, he asked softly, "Where does your wooden leg join on?"

She turned an ugly red and glared at him and for an instant the boy looked abashed. "I didn't mean you no harm," he said. "I only meant you're so brave and all. I guess God takes care of you."

"No," she said, looking forward and walking fast, "I don't even believe in God."

At this he stopped and whistled. "No!" he exclaimed as if he were too astonished to say anything else.

She walked on and in a second he was bouncing at her side, fanning with his hat. "That's very unusual for a girl," he remarked, watching her out of the corner of his eye. When they reached the edge of the wood, he put his hand on her back again and drew her against him without a word and kissed her heavily.

The kiss, which had more pressure than feeling behind it, produced that extra surge of adrenalin in the girl that enables one to carry a packed trunk out of a burning house, but in her, the power went at once to the brain. Even before he released her, her mind, clear and detached and ironic anyway, was regarding him from a great distance, with amusement but with pity. She had never been kissed before and she was pleased to discover that it was an unexceptional experience and all a matter of the mind's control. Some people might enjoy drain water if they were told it was vodka. When the boy, looking expectant but uncertain, pushed her gently away, she turned and walked on, saying nothing as if such business, for her, were common enough.

He came along panting at her side, trying to help her when he saw a root that she might trip over. He caught and held back the long swaying blades of thorn vine until she had passed beyond them. She led the way and he came breathing heavily behind her. Then they came out on a sunlit hillside, sloping softly into another one a little smaller. Beyond, they could see the rusted top of the old barn where the extra hay was stored.

The hill was sprinkled with small pink weeds. "Then you ain't saved?" he asked suddenly, stopping.

The girl smiled. It was the first time she had smiled at him at all. "In my economy," she said, "I'm saved and you are damned but I told you I didn't believe in God."

Nothing seemed to destroy the boy's look of admiration. He gazed at her now as if the fantastic animal at the zoo had put its paw through the bars and given him a loving poke. She thought he looked as if he wanted to kiss her again and she walked on before he had the chance.

"Ain't there somewheres we can sit down sometime?" he murmured, his voice softening toward the end of the sentence.

"In that barn," she said.

They made for it rapidly as if it might slide away like a train. It was a large two-story barn, cool and dark inside. The boy pointed up the ladder that led into the loft and said, "It's too bad we can't go up there."

"Why can't we?" she asked.

"Yer leg," he said reverently.

The girl gave him a contemptuous look and putting both hands on the ladder, she climbed it while he stood below, apparently awestruck. She pulled herself expertly through the opening and then looked down at him and said, "Well, come on if you're coming," and he began to climb the ladder, awkwardly bringing the suitcase with him.

"We won't need the Bible," she observed.

"You never can tell," he said, panting. After he had got into the loft, he was a few seconds catching his breath. She had sat down in a pile of straw. A wide sheath of sunlight, filled with dust particles, slanted over her. She lay back against a bale, her face turned away, looking out the front opening of the barn where hay was thrown from a wagon into the loft. The two pink-speckled hillsides lay back against a dark ridge of woods. The sky was cloudless and cold blue. The boy dropped down by her side and put one arm under her and the other over her and began methodically kissing her face, making little noises like a fish. He did not remove his hat but it was pushed far enough back not to interfere. When her glasses got in his way, he took them off of her and slipped them into his pocket.

The girl at first did not return any of the kisses but presently she began to and after she had put several on his cheek, she reached his lips and remained there, kissing him again and again as if she were trying to draw all the breath out of him. His breath was clear and sweet like a child's and the kisses were sticky like a child's. He mumbled about loving her and about knowing when he first seen her that he loved her, but the mumbling was like the sleepy fretting of a child being put to sleep by his mother. Her mind, throughout this, never stopped or lost itself for a second to her feelings. "You ain't said you loved me none," he whispered finally, pulling back from her. "You got to say that."

She looked away from him off into the hollow sky and then down at a black ridge and then down farther into what appeared to be two green swelling lakes. She didn't realize he had taken her glasses but this landscape could not seem exceptional to her for she seldom paid any close attention to her surroundings.

"You got to say it," he repeated. "You got to say you love me."

She was always careful how she committed herself. "In a sense," she began, "if you use the word loosely, you might say that. But it's not a word I use. I don't have illusions. I'm one of those people who see *through* to nothing."

The boy was frowning. "You got to say it. I said it and you got to say it," he said.

The girl looked at him almost tenderly. "You poor baby," she murmured. "It's just as well you don't understand," and she pulled him by the neck, face-down, against her. "We are all damned," she said, "but some of us have taken off our blindfolds and see that there's nothing to see. It's a kind of salvation."

The boy's astonished eyes looked blankly through the ends of her hair. "Okay," he almost whined, "but do you love me or don'tcher?"

"Yes," she said and added, "in a sense. But I must tell you something. There mustn't be anything dishonest between us." She lifted his head and looked him in the eye. "I am thirty years old," she said. "I have a number of degrees."

The boy's look was irritated but dogged. "I don't care," he said. "I don't care a thing about what all you done. I just want to know if you love me or don'tcher?" and he caught her to him and wildly planted her face with kisses until she said, "Yes, yes."

"Okay then," he said, letting her go. "Prove it."

She smiled, looking dreamily out on the shifty landscape. She had seduced him without even making up her mind to try. "How?" she asked, feeling that he should be delayed a little.

He leaned over and put his lips to her ear. "Show me where your wooden leg joins on," he whispered.

The girl uttered a sharp little cry and her face instantly drained of color. The obscenity of the suggestion was not what shocked her. As a child she had sometimes been subject to feelings of shame but education had removed the last traces of that as a good surgeon scrapes for cancer; she would no more have felt it over what he was asking than she would have believed in his Bible. But she was as sensitive about the artificial leg as a peacock about his tail. No one ever touched it but her. She took care of it as someone else would his soul, in private and almost with her own eyes turned away. "No," she said.

"I known it," he muttered, sitting up. "You're just playing me for a sucker."

"Oh no no!" she cried. "It joins on at the knee. Only at the knee. Why do you want to see it?"

The boy gave her a long penetrating look. "Because," he said, "It's what makes you different. You ain't like anybody else."

She sat staring at him. There was nothing about her face or her round freezing-blue eyes to indicate that this had moved her; but she felt as if her heart had stopped and left her mind to pump her blood. She decided that for the first time in her life she was face to face with real innocence. This boy, with an instinct that came from beyond wisdom, had touched the truth about her. When after a minute, she said in a hoarse high voice, "All right," it was like surrendering to him completely. It was like losing her own life and finding it again, miraculously, in his.

Very gently he began to roll the slack leg up. The artificial limb, in a white sock and brown flat shoe, was bound in a heavy material like canvas and ended in an ugly jointure where it was attached to the stump. The boy's face and his voice were entirely reverent as he uncovered it and said, "Now show me how to take it off and on."

She took it off for him and put it back on again and then he took it off himself, handling it as tenderly as if it were a real one. "See!" he said with a delighted child's face. "Now I can do it myself!"

"Put it back on," she said. She was thinking that she would run away with him and that every night he would take the leg off and every morning put it back on again. "Put it back on," she said.

"Not yet," he murmured, setting it on its foot out of her reach. "Leave it off for a while. You got me instead."

She gave a little cry of alarm but he pushed her down and began to kiss her again. Without the leg she felt entirely dependent on him. Her brain seemed to have stopped thinking altogether and to be about some other function that it was not very good at. Different expressions raced back and forth over her face. Every now and then the boy, his eyes like two steel spikes, would glance behind him where the leg stood. Finally she pushed him off and said, "Put it back on me now."

"Wait," he said. He leaned the other way and pulled the valise toward him and opened it. It had a pale blue spotted lining and there were only two Bibles in it. He took one of these out and opened the cover of it. It was hollow and contained a pocket flask of whiskey, a pack of cards, and a small blue box with printing on it. He laid these out in front of her one at a time in an evenly-spaced row, like one presenting offerings at the shrine of a goddess. He put the blue box in her hand. THIS PRODUCT TO BE USED ONLY FOR THE PREVENTION OF DISEASE, she read, and dropped it. The boy was unscrewing the top of the flask. He stopped and pointed, with a smile, to the deck of cards. It was not an ordinary deck but one with an obscene picture on the back of each card. "Take a swig," he said, offering her the bottle first. He held it in front of her, but like one mesmerized, she did not move.

Her voice when she spoke had an almost pleading sound. "Aren't you," she murmured, "aren't you just good country people?"

The boy cocked his head. He looked as if he were just beginning to understand that she might be trying to insult him. "Yeah," he said, curling his lip slightly, "but it ain't held me back none. I'm as good as you any day in the week."

"Give me my leg," she said.

He pushed it farther away with his foot. "Come on now, let's begin to have us a good time," he said coaxingly. "We ain't got to know one another good yet."

"Give me my leg!" she screamed and tried to lunge for it but he pushed her down easily.

"What's the matter with you all of a sudden?" he asked, frowning as he screwed the top on the flask and put it quickly back inside the Bible. "You just a while ago said you didn't believe in nothing. I thought you was some girl!"

Her face was almost purple. "You're a Christian!" she hissed. "You're a fine Christian! You're just like them all — say one thing and do another. You're a perfect Christian, you're ..."

The boy's mouth was set angrily. "I hope you don't think," he said in a lofty indignant tone, "that I believe in that crap! I may sell Bibles but I know which end is up and I wasn't born yesterday and I know where I'm going!"

"Give me my leg!" she screeched. He jumped up so quickly that she barely saw him sweep the cards and the blue box into the Bible and throw the Bible into the valise. She saw him grab the leg and then she saw it for an instant slanted forlornly across the inside of the suitcase with a Bible at either side of its opposite ends. He slammed the lid shut and snatched up the valise and swung it down the hole and then stepped through himself.

When all of him had passed but his head, he turned and regarded her with a look that no longer had any admiration in it. "I've gotten a lot of interesting things," he said. "One time I got a woman's glass eye this way. And you needn't to think you'll catch me because Pointer ain't really my name. I use a different name at every house I call at and don't stay nowhere long. And I'll tell you another thing, Hulga," he said, using the name as if he didn't think much of it, "you ain't so smart. I been believing in nothing ever since I was born!" and then the toast-colored hat disappeared down the hole and the girl was left, sitting on the straw in the dusty sunlight. When she turned her churning face toward the opening, she saw his blue figure struggling successfully over the green speckled lake.

Mrs. Hopewell and Mrs. Freeman, who were in the back pasture, digging up onions, saw him emerge a little later from the woods and head across the meadow toward the highway. "Why, that looks like that nice dull young man that tried to sell me a Bible yesterday," Mrs. Hopewell said, squinting. "He must have been selling them to the Negroes back in there. He was so simple," she said, "but I guess the world would be better off if we were all that simple."

Mrs. Freeman's gaze drove forward and just touched him before he disappeared under the hill. Then she returned her attention to the evil-smelling onion shoot she was lifting from the ground. "Some can't be that simple," she said. "I know I never could."

QUESTIONS

1. What makes this story more than an extended dreadful joke? Can we laugh at the Bible salesman's treatment of Joy?

2. What do the names of the characters suggest about them? Is it significant that the girl has two names? Are the characters developed or mere caricatures?

3. Before Joy-Hulga Hopewell is introduced, we meet Mrs. Freeman and Mrs. Hopewell. Does this constitute an unnecessary delay, or does it contribute something to the story?

4. What is the author's attitude toward these minor characters? Does her tone convey this attitude?

5. Mrs. Hopewell's speech and thought are cliché-ridden: "the finest girls she knew," "Everybody is different," "well, other people have their opinions too." Is this meant to underscore the irony of the phrase "good country people"?

6. Hulga seems more sophisticated than Manley, who is often spoken of as "the boy." But is she? What signs of "sophistication" do you notice in him? What is his purpose in getting her to remove her wooden leg?

7. The conflict between Hulga and the Bible salesman comes around to religious belief. Is this a central matter, or only peripheral to a story of a surprising reversal of roles?

GABRIEL GARCÍA MÁRQUEZ ≡≡≡≡

A Very Old Man with Enormous Wings

Translated by Gregory Rabassa

A TALE FOR CHILDREN

On the third day of rain they had killed so many crabs inside the house that Pelayo had to cross his drenched courtyard and throw them into the sea, because the newborn child had a temperature all night and they thought it was due to the stench. The world had been sad since Tuesday. Sea and sky were a single ash-gray thing and the sands of the beach, which on March nights glimmered like powdered light, had become a stew of mud and rotten shellfish. The light was so weak at noon that when Pelayo was coming back to the house after throwing away the crabs, it was hard for him to see what it was that was moving and groaning in the rear of the courtyard. He had to go very close to see that it was an old man, a very old man, lying face down in the mud, who, in spite of his tremendous efforts, couldn't get up, impeded by his enormous wings.

Frightened by that nightmare, Pelayo ran to get Elisenda, his wife, who was putting compresses on the sick child, and he took her to the rear of the courtyard. They both looked at the fallen body with mute stupor. He was dressed like a ragpicker. There were only a few faded hairs left on his bald skull and very few teeth in his mouth, and his pitiful condition of a drenched great-grandfather had taken away any sense of grandeur he might have had. His huge buzzard wings, dirty and half-plucked, were forever entangled in the mud. They looked at him so long and so closely that Pelayo and Elisenda very soon overcame their surprise and in the end found him familiar. Then they dared speak to him, and he answered in an incomprehensible dialect with a strong sailor's voice. That was how they skipped over the inconvenience of the wings and quite intelligently concluded that he was a lonely castaway from some foreign ship wrecked by the storm. And yet, they called in a neighbor woman who knew everything about life and death to see him, and all she needed was one look to show them their mistake.

"He's an angel," she told them. "He must have been coming for the child, but the poor fellow is so old that the rain knocked him down."

On the following day everyone knew that a flesh-and-blood angel was held captive in Pelayo's house. Against the judgment of the wise neighbor woman, for whom angels in those times were the fugitive survivors of a celestial conspiracy, they did not have the heart to club him to death. Pelayo watched over him all afternoon from the kitchen, armed with his bailiff's club, and before going to bed he dragged him out of the mud and locked him up with the hens in the wire chicken coop. In the middle of the night, when the rain stopped, Pelayo and Elisenda were still killing crabs. A short time afterward the child woke up without a fever and with a desire to eat. Then they felt magnanimous and decided to put the angel on a raft with fresh water and provisions for three days and leave him to his fate on the high seas. But when they went out into the courtyard with the first light of dawn, they found the whole neighborhood in front of the chicken coop having fun with the angel, without the slightest reverence, tossing him things to eat through the openings in the wire as if he weren't a supernatural creature but a circus animal.

Father Gonzaga arrived before seven o'clock, alarmed at the strange news. By that time onlookers less frivolous than those at dawn had already arrived and they were making all kinds of conjectures concerning the captive's future. The simplest among them thought that he should be named mayor of the world. Others of sterner mind felt that he should be promoted to the rank of five-star general in order to win all wars. Some visionaries hoped that he could be put to stud in order to implant on earth a race of winged wise men who could take charge of the universe. But Father Gonzaga, before becoming a priest, had been a robust woodcutter. Standing by the wire, he reviewed his catechism in an instant and asked them to open the door so that he could take a close look at that pitiful man who looked more like a huge decrepit hen among the fascinated chickens. He was lying in a corner drying his open wings in the sunlight among the fruit peels and breakfast leftovers that the early risers had thrown him. Alien to the impertinences of the world, he only lifted his antiquarian eyes and murmured something in his dialect when Father Gonzaga went into the chicken coop and said good morning to him in Latin. The parish priest had his first suspicion of an imposter when he saw that he did not understand the language of God or know how to greet His ministers. Then he noticed that seen close up he was much too human: he had an unbearable smell of the outdoors, the back side of his wings was strewn with parasites and his main feathers had been mistreated by terrestrial winds, and nothing about him measured up to the proud dignity of angels. Then he came out of the chicken coop and in a brief sermon warned the curious against the risks of being ingenuous. He reminded them that the devil had the bad habit of making use of carnival tricks in order to confuse the unwary. He argued that if wings were not the essential element in determining the difference between a hawk and an airplane, they were even less so in the recognition of angels. Nevertheless, he promised to write a letter to his bishop so that the latter would write to his primate so that the latter would write to the Supreme Pontiff in order to get the final verdict from the highest courts.

His prudence fell on sterile hearts. The news of the captive angel spread with such rapidity that after a few hours the courtyard had the bustle of a marketplace and they had to call in troops with fixed bayonets to disperse the mob that was about to knock the house down. Elisenda, her spine all twisted from sweeping up so much marketplace trash, then got the idea of fencing in the yard and charging five cents admission to see the angel.

The curious came from far away. A traveling carnival arrived with a flying acrobat who buzzed over the crowd several times, but no one paid any attention to him because his wings were not those of an angel but, rather, those of a sidereal bat. The most unfortunate invalids on earth came in search of health: a poor woman who since childhood had been counting her heartbeats and had run out of numbers; a Portuguese man who couldn't sleep because the noise of the stars disturbed him; a sleepwalker who got up at night to undo the things he had done while awake; and many others with less serious ailments. In the midst of that shipwreck disorder that made the earth tremble, Pelayo and Elisenda were happy with fatigue, for in less than a week they had crammed their rooms with money and the line of pilgrims waiting their turn to enter still reached beyond the horizon.

The angel was the only one who took no part in his own act. He spent his time trying to get comfortable in his borrowed nest, befuddled by the hellish heat of the oil lamps and sacramental candles that had been placed along the wire. At first they tried to make him eat some mothballs, which, according to the wisdom of the wise neighbor woman, were the food prescribed for angels. But he turned them down, just as he turned down the papal lunches that the penitents brought him, and they never found out whether it was because he was an angel or because he was an old man that in the end he ate nothing but eggplant mush. His only supernatural virtue seemed to be patience. Especially during the first days, when the hens pecked at him, searching for the stellar parasites that proliferated in his wings, and the cripples pulled out feathers to touch their defective parts with, and even the most merciful threw stones at him, trying to get him to rise so they could see him standing. The only time they succeeded in arousing him was when they burned his side with an iron for branding steers, for he had been motionless for so many hours that they thought he was dead. He awoke with a start, ranting in his hermetic language and with tears in his eyes, and he flapped his wings a couple of times, which brought on a whirlwind of chicken dung and lunar dust and a gale of panic that did not seem to be of this world. Although many thought that his reaction had been one not of rage but of pain, from then on they were careful not to annoy him, because the majority understood that his passivity was not that of a hero taking his ease but that of a cataclysm in repose.

Father Gonzaga held back the crowd's frivolity with formulas of maidservant inspiration while awaiting the arrival of a final judgment on the nature of the captive. But the mail from Rome showed no sense of urgency. They spent their time finding out if the prisoner had a navel, if his dialect had any connection with Aramaic, how many times he could fit on the head of a pin, or whether he wasn't just a Norwegian with wings. Those meager letters might have come and gone until the end of time if a providential event had not put an end to the priest's tribulations.

It so happened that during those days, among so many other carnival attractions, there arrived in town the traveling show of the woman who had been changed into a spider for having disobeyed her parents. The admission to see her was not only less than the admission to see the angel, but people were permitted to ask her all manner of questions about her absurd state and to examine her up and down so that no one would ever doubt the truth of her horror. She was a frightful tarantula the size of a ram and with the head of a sad maiden. What was most heart-rending, however, was not her outlandish shape but the sincere affliction with which she recounted the details of her misfortune. While still practically a child she had sneaked out of her parents' house to go to a dance, and while she was coming back through the woods after having danced all night without permission, a fearful thunderclap rent the sky in two and through the crack came the lightning bolt of brimstone that changed her into a spider. Her only nourishment came from the meatballs that charitable souls chose to toss into her mouth. A spectacle like that, full of so much human truth and with such a fearful lesson, was bound to defeat without even trying that of a haughty angel who scarcely deigned to look at mortals. Besides, the few miracles attributed to the angel showed a certain mental disorder, like the blind man who didn't recover his sight but grew three new teeth, or the paralytic who didn't get to walk but almost won the lottery, and the leper whose sores sprouted sunflowers. Those consolation miracles, which were more like mocking fun, had already ruined the angel's reputation when the woman who had been changed into a spider finally crushed him completely. That was how Father Gonzaga was cured forever of his insomnia and Pelayo's courtyard went back to being as empty as during the time it had rained for three days and crabs walked through the bedrooms.

The owners of the house had no reason to lament. With the money they saved they built a two-story mansion with balconies and gardens and high netting so that crabs wouldn't get in during the winter, and with iron bars on the windows so that angels wouldn't get in. Pelayo also set up a rabbit warren close to town and gave up his job as bailiff for good, and Elisenda bought some satin pumps with high heels and many dresses of iridescent silk, the kind worn on Sunday by the most desirable women in those times. The chicken coop was the only thing that didn't receive any attention. If they washed it down with creolin and burned tears of myrrh inside it every so often, it was not in homage to the angel but to drive away the dungheap stench that still hung everywhere like a ghost and was turning the new house into an old one. At first, when the child learned to walk, they were careful that he not get too close to the chicken coop. But then they began to lose their fears and got used to the smell, and before the child got his second teeth he'd gone inside the chicken coop to play, where the wires were falling apart. The angel was no less standoffish with him than with other mortals, but he tolerated the most ingenious infamies with the patience of a dog who had no illusions. They both came down with chicken pox at the same time. The doctor who took care of the child couldn't resist the temptation to listen to the angel's heart, and he found so much whistling in the heart and so many sounds in his kidneys that it seemed impossible for him to be alive. What surprised him most, however, was the logic of his wings. They seemed so natural on that completely human organism that he couldn't understand why other men didn't have them too.

When the child began school it had been some time since the sun and rain had caused the collapse of the chicken coop. The angel went dragging himself about here and there like a stray dying man. They would drive him out of the bedroom with a broom and a moment later find him in the kitchen. He seemed to be in so many places at the same time that they grew to think that he'd been duplicated, that he was reproducing himself all through the house, and the exasperated and unhinged Elisenda shouted that it was awful living in that hell full of angels. He could scarcely eat and his antiquarian eyes had also become so foggy that he went about bumping into posts. All he had left were the bare cannulae of his last feathers. Pelayo threw a blanket over him and extended him the charity of letting him sleep in the shed, and only then did they notice that he had a temperature at night, and was delirious with the tongue twisters of an old Norwegian. That was one of the few times they became alarmed, for they thought he was going to die and not even the wise neighbor woman had been able to tell them what to do with dead angels.

And yet he not only survived his worst winter, but seemed improved with the first sunny days. He remained motionless for several days in the farthest corner of the courtyard, where no one would see him, and at the beginning of December some large, stiff feathers began to grow on his wings, the feathers of a scarecrow, which looked more like another misfortune of decrepitude. But he must have known the reason for those changes, for he was quite careful that no one should notice them, that no one should hear the sea chanteys that he sometimes sang under the stars. One morning Elisenda was cutting some bunches of onions for lunch when a wind that seemed to come from the high seas blew into the kitchen. Then she went to the window and caught the angel in his first attempts at flight. They were so clumsy that his fingernails opened a furrow in the vegetable patch and he was on the point of knocking the shed down with the ungainly flapping that slipped on the light and couldn't get a grip on the air. But he did manage to gain altitude. Elisenda let out a sigh of relief, for herself and for him, when she saw him pass over the last houses, holding himself up in some way with the risky flapping of a senile vulture. She kept watching him even when she was through cutting the onions and she kept on watching until it was no longer possible for her to see him, because then he was no longer an annoyance in her life but an imaginary dot on the horizon of the sea.

QUESTIONS

1. Is this, as the subtitle suggests, "a tale for children"? If so, what is the lesson they should learn? Or is García Márquez writing an entertainment?

2. Is the winged man an angel? What does his "sailor's voice" suggest to you? Is the chicken coop an appropriate holding cell for him?

3. Father Gonzaga is a practical fellow, but the narrator hints that his education and common sense are faulty. Single out one of those clues. Is the mail from Rome helpful?

4. Do the villagers act pretty much as you would expect them to do in the presence of such a remarkable visitation? What does your answer suggest about your own view of human nature? What does the story suggest about García Márquez's view?

URSULA K. LE GUIN

Schrödinger's Cat

As things appear to be coming to some sort of climax, I have withdrawn to this place. It is cooler here, and nothing moves fast.

On the way here I met a married couple who were coming apart. She had pretty well gone to pieces, but he seemed, at first glance, quite hearty. While he was telling me that he had no hormones of any kind, she pulled herself together and, by supporting her head in the crook of her right knee and hopping on the toes of the right foot, approached us shouting, "Well what's *wrong* with a person trying to express themselves?" The left leg, the arms, and the trunk, which had remained lying in the heap, twitched and jerked in sympathy. "Great legs," the husband pointed out, looking at the slim ankle. "My wife has great legs."

A cat has arrived, interrupting my narrative. It is a striped yellow tom with white chest and paws. He has long whiskers and yellow eyes. I never noticed before that cats had whiskers above their eyes; is that normal? There is no way to tell. As he has gone to sleep on my knee, I shall proceed.

Where?

Nowhere, evidently. Yet the impulse to narrate remains. Many things are not worth doing, but almost anything is worth telling. In any case, I have a severe congenital case of *Ethica laboris puritanica,*[1] or Adam's Disease. It is incurable except by total decapitation. I even like to dream when asleep, and to try and recall my dreams: it assures me that I haven't wasted seven or eight hours just lying there. Now here I am, lying, here. Hard at it.

Well, the couple I was telling you about finally broke up. The pieces of him trotted around bouncing and cheeping, like little chicks, but she was finally reduced to nothing but a mass of nerves: rather like fine chicken wire, in fact, but hopelessly tangled.

So I came on, placing one foot carefully in front of the other, and grieving. This grief is with me still. I fear it is part of me, like foot or loin or eye, or may even be myself: for I seem to have no other self, nothing further, nothing that lies outside the borders of grief.

Yet I don't know what I grieve for: my wife? my husband? my children, or myself? I can't remember. Most dreams are forgotten, try as one will to remember. Yet later music strikes the note, and the harmonic rings along the mandolin strings of the mind, and we find tears in our eyes. Some note keeps playing that makes me want to cry; but what for? I am not certain.

---

[1] "Puritan work ethic."

The yellow cat, who may have belonged to the couple that broke up, is dreaming. His paws twitch now and then, and once he makes a small, suppressed remark with his mouth shut. I wonder what a cat dreams of, and to whom he was speaking just then. Cats seldom waste words. They are quiet beasts. They keep their counsel, they reflect. They reflect all day, and at night their eyes reflect. Overbred Siamese cats may be as noisy as little dogs, and then people say, "They're talking," but the noise is farther from speech than is the deep silence of the hound or the tabby. All this cat can say is meow, but maybe in his silences he will suggest to me what it is that I have lost, what I am grieving for. I have a feeling that he knows. That's why he came here. Cats look out for Number One.

It was getting awfully hot. I mean, you could touch less and less. The stove burners, for instance. Now I know that stove burners always used to get hot; that was their final cause, they existed in order to get hot. But they began to get hot without having been turned on. Electric units or gas rings, there they'd be when you came into the kitchen for breakfast, all four of them glaring away, the air above them shaking like clear jelly with the heat waves. It did no good to turn them off, because they weren't on in the first place. Besides, the knobs and dials were also hot, uncomfortable to the touch.

Some people tried hard to cool them off. The favorite technique was to turn them on. It worked sometimes, but you could not count on it. Others investigated the phenomenon, tried to get at the root of it, the cause. They were probably the most frightened ones, but man is most human at his most frightened. In the face of the hot stove burners they acted with exemplary coolness. They studied, they observed. They were like the fellow in Michelangelo's *Last Judgment*, who has clapped his hands over his face in horror as the devils drag him down to Hell — but only over one eye. The other eye is busy looking. It's all he can do, but he does it. He observes. Indeed, one wonders if Hell would exist, if he did not look at it. However, neither he, nor the people I am talking about, had enough time left to do much about it. And then finally of course there were the people who did not try to do or think anything about it at all.

When the water came out of the cold-water taps hot one morning, however, even people who had blamed it all on the Democrats began to feel a more profound unease. Before long, forks and pencils and wrenches were too hot to handle without gloves; and cars were really terrible. It was like opening the door of an oven going full blast, to open the door of your car. And by then, other people almost scorched your fingers off. A kiss was like a branding iron. Your child's hair flowed along your had like fire.

Here, as I said, it is cooler; and, as a matter of fact, this animal is cool. A real cool cat. No wonder it's pleasant to pet his fur. Also he moves slowly, at least for the most part, which is all the slowness one can reasonably expect of a cat. He hasn't that frenetic quality most creatures acquired — all they did was ZAP and gone. They lacked presence. I suppose birds always tended to be that way, but even the hummingbird used to halt for a second in the very center of his metabolic frenzy, and hang, still as a hub, present, above the fuchsias — then gone again, but you knew something was there besides the blurring brightness. But it got so that even robins and pigeons, the heavy impudent birds, were a blur; and as for swallows, they cracked the sound barrier. You knew of swallows only by the small, curved sonic booms that looped about the eaves of old houses in the evening.

Worms shot like subway trains through the dirt of gardens, among the writhing roots of roses.

You could scarcely lay a hand on children, by then: too fast to catch, too hot to hold. They grew up before your eyes.

But then, maybe that's always been true.

I was interrupted by the cat, who woke and said meow once, then jumped down from my lap and leaned against my legs diligently. This is a cat who knows how to get fed. He also knows how to jump. There was a lazy fluidity to his leap, as if gravity affected him less than it does other creatures. As a matter of fact there were some localised cases, just before I left, of the failure of gravity; but this quality in the cat's leap was something quite else. I am not yet in such a state of confusion that I can be alarmed by grace. Indeed, I found it reassuring. While I was opening a can of sardines, a person arrived.

Hearing the knock, I thought it might be the mailman. I miss mail very much, so I hurried to the door and said, "Is it the mail?"

A voice replied, "Yah!" I opened the door. He came in, almost pushing me aside in his haste. He dumped down an enormous knapsack he had been carrying, straightened up, massaged his shoulders, and said, "Wow!"

"How did you get here?"

He stared at me and repeated, "How?"

At this my thoughts concerning human and animal speech recurred to me, and I decided that this was probably not a man, but a small dog. (Large dogs seldom go yah, wow, how, unless it is appropriate to do so.)

"Come on, fella," I coaxed him. "Come, come on, that's a boy, good doggie!" I opened a can of pork and beans for him at once, for he looked half starved. He ate voraciously, gulping and lapping. When it was gone he said "Wow!" several times. I was just about to scratch him behind the ears when he stiffened, his hackles bristling, and growled deep in his throat. He had noticed the cat.

The cat had noticed him some time before, without interest, and was now sitting on a copy of *The Well-Tempered Clavier* washing sardine oil off its whiskers.

"Wow!" the dog, whom I had thought of calling Rover, barked. "Wow! Do you know what that is? *That's Schrödinger's cat!*"

"No it's not, not any more; it's my cat," I said, unreasonably offended.

"Oh, well, Schrödinger's dead, of course, but it's his cat. I've seen hundreds of pictures of it. Erwin Schrödinger,[2] the great physicist, you know. Oh, wow! To think of finding it here!"

The cat looked coldly at him for a moment, and began to wash its left shoulder with negligent energy. An almost religious expression had come into Rover's face. "It was meant," he said in a low, impressive tone. "Yah. It was *meant*. It can't be a mere coincidence. It's too improbable. Me, with the box; you, with the cat; to meet — here — now." He looked up at me, his eyes shining with happy fervor. "Isn't it wonderful?" he said. "I'll get the box set up right away." And he started to tear open his huge knapsack.

While the cat washed its front paws, Rover unpacked. While the cat washed its tail and belly, regions hard to reach gracefully, Rover put together what he had unpacked, a complex task. When he and the cat finished their operations simultaneously and looked at me, I was impressed. They had come out even, to the very second. Indeed it seemed that something more than chance was involved. I hoped it was not myself.

"What's that?" I asked, pointing to a protuberance on the outside of the box. I did not ask what the box was as it was quite clearly a box.

"The gun," Rover said with excited pride.

"The gun?"

---

[2] Erwin Schrödinger (1887–1961), German physicist, won the Nobel prize in 1933. His wave equation is the fundamental equation of quantum theory.

"To shoot the cat."

"To shoot the cat?"

"Or to *not shoot* the cat. Depending on the photon."

"The photon?"

"Yah! It's Schrödinger's great Gedankenexperiment.[3] You see, there's a little emitter here. At Zero Time, five seconds after the lid of the box is closed, it will emit one photon. The photon will strike a half-silvered mirror. The quantum mechanical probability of the photon passing through the mirror is exactly one half, isn't it? So! If the photon passes through, the trigger will be activated and the gun will fire. If the photon is deflected, the trigger will not be activated and the gun will not fire. Now, you put the cat in. The cat is in the box. You close the lid. You go away! You stay away! What happens?" Rover's eyes were bright.

"The cat gets hungry?"

"The cat gets shot — or not shot," he said, seizing my arm, though not, fortunately, in his teeth. "But the gun is silent, perfectly silent. The box is soundproof. There is no way to know whether or not the cat has been shot, until you lift the lid of the box. There is *no* way! Do you see how central this is to the whole of quantum theory? Before Zero Time the whole system, on the quantum level or on our level, is nice and simple. But after Zero Time the whole system can be represented only by a linear combination of two waves. We cannot predict the behavior of the photon, and thus, once it has behaved, we cannot predict the state of the system it has determined. We cannot predict it! God plays dice with the world! So it is beautifully demonstrated that if you desire certainty, any certainty, you must create it yourself!"

"How?"

"By lifting the lid of the box, of course," Rover said, looking at me with sudden disappointment, perhaps a touch of suspicion, like a Baptist who finds he has been talking church matters not to another Baptist as he thought, but a Methodist, or even, God forbid, an Episcopalian. "To find out whether the cat is dead or not."

"Do you mean," I said carefully, "that until you lift the lid of the box, the cat has neither been shot nor not been shot?"

"Yah!" Rover said, radiant with relief, welcoming me back to the fold. "Or maybe, you know, both."

"But why does opening the box and looking reduce the system back to one probability, either live cat or dead cat? Why don't we get included in the system when we lift the lid of the box?"

There was a pause. "How?" Rover barked, distrustfully.

"Well, we would involve ourselves in the system, you see, the superposition of two waves. There's no reason why it should only exist *inside* an open box, is there? So when we came to look, there we would be, you and I, both looking at a live cat, and both looking at a dead cat. You see?"

A dark cloud lowered on Rover's eyes and brow. He barked twice in a subdued, harsh voice, and walked away. With his back turned to me he said in a firm, sad tone, "You must not complicate the issue. It is complicated enough."

"Are you sure?"

He nodded. Turning, he spoke pleadingly. "Listen. It's all we have — the box. Truly it is. The box. And the cat. And they're here. The box, the cat, at last. Put the cat in the box. Will you? Will you let me put the cat in the box?"

---

[3] Schrödinger's "thought-experiment," a paradox, is reproduced accurately (in slightly modified form) as the story progresses.

"No," I said, shocked.

"Please. Please. Just for a minute. Just for half a minute! Please let me put the cat in the box!"

"Why?"

"I can't stand this terrible uncertainty," he said, and burst into tears.

I stood some while indecisive. Though I felt sorry for the poor son of a bitch, I was about to tell him, gently, No; when a curious thing happened. The cat walked over to the box, sniffed around it, lifted his tail and sprayed a corner to mark his territory, and then lightly, with that marvellous fluid ease, leapt into it. His yellow tail just flicked the edge of the lid as he jumped, and it closed, falling into place with a soft, decisive click.

"The cat is in the box," I said.

"The cat is in the box," Rover repeated in a whisper, falling to his knees. "Oh, wow. Oh, wow. Oh, wow."

There was silence then: deep silence. We both gazed, I afoot, Rover kneeling, at the box. No sound. Nothing happened. Nothing would happen. Nothing would ever happen, until we lifted the lid of the box.

"Like Pandora," I said in a weak whisper. I could not quite recall Pandora's legend. She had let all the plagues and evils out of the box, of course, but there had been something else, too. After all the devils were let loose, something quite different, quite unexpected, had been left. What had it been? Hope? A dead cat? I could not remember.[4]

Impatience welled up in me. I turned on Rover, glaring. He returned the look with expressive brown eyes. You can't tell me dogs haven't got souls.

"Just exactly what are you trying to prove?" I demanded.

"That the cat will be dead, or not dead," he murmured submissively. "Certainty. All I want is certainty. To know for *sure* that God *does* play dice with the world."

I looked at him for a while with fascinated incredulity. "Whether he does, or doesn't," I said, "do you think he's going to leave you a note about it in the box?" I went to the box, and with a rather dramatic gesture, flung the lid back. Rover staggered up from his knees, gasping, to look. The cat was, of course, not there.

Rover neither barked, nor fainted, nor cursed, nor wept. He really took it very well.

"Where is the cat?" he asked at last.

"Where is the box?"

"Here."

"Where's here?"

"Here is now."

"We used to think so," I said, "but really we should use larger boxes."

He gazed about him in mute bewilderment, and did not flinch even when the roof of the house was lifted off just like the lid of a box, letting in the unconscionable, inordinate light of the stars. He had just time to breathe, "Oh, wow!"

I have identified the note that keeps sounding. I checked it on the mandolin before the glue melted. It is the note A, the one that drove the composer Schumann mad. It is a beautiful, clear tone, much clearer now that the stars are visible. I shall miss the cat. I wonder if he found what it was we lost?

---

[4] Hope remained in Pandora's box.

QUESTIONS

1. How would you describe the character of the narrator? Is the narrator male or female?

2. Elaborate and continual punning marks this story. In particular, trite phrases ("coming apart," "pretty well gone to pieces," "a mass of nerves") are given literal meanings. Is it the narrator or the author who puns consciously?

3. What is the relationship between the rising temperature and the increasing speed of things? Is there a scientific basis for this connection?

4. On what evidence does the narrator conclude that the visitor is a dog? Is this a logical conclusion?

5. The problem of describing observations, determining "what is real," is a matter of considerable difficulty and disagreement among physicists who discuss the quantum theory — as the dog and the narrator learn when they "test" Schrödinger's paradox. Does this fact apply only to the experiment or does it also help explain the events leading up to the experiment?

6. Most readers would agree that a knowledge of physics is not necessary for one to enjoy "Schrödinger's Cat." Why not?

Lost in the Funhouse

For whom is the funhouse fun? Perhaps for lovers. For Ambrose it is *a place of fear and confusion*. He has come to the seashore with his family for the holiday, *the occasion of their visit is Independence Day, the most important secular holiday of the United States of America*. A single straight underline is the manuscript mark for italic type, *which in turn* is the printed equivalent to oral emphasis of words and phrases as well as the customary type for titles of complete works, not to mention. Italics are also employed, in fiction stories especially, for "outside," intrusive, or artificial voices, such as radio announcements, the texts of telegrams and newspaper articles, et cetera. They should be used *sparingly*. If passages originally in roman type are italicized by someone repeating them, it's customary to acknowledge the fact. *Italics mine.*

Ambrose was "at that awkward age." His voice came out high-pitched as a child's if he let himself get carried away; to be on the safe side, therefore, he moved and spoke with *deliberate calm* and *adult gravity*. Talking soberly of unimportant or irrelevant matters and listening consciously to the sound of your own voice are useful habits for maintaining control in this difficult interval. *En route* to Ocean City he sat in the back seat of the family car with his brother Peter, age fifteen, and Magda G——, age fourteen, a pretty girl an exquisite young lady, who lived not far from them on B—— Street in the town of D——, Maryland. Initials, blanks, or both were often substituted for proper names in nineteenth-century fiction to enhance the illusion of reality. It is as if the author felt it necessary to delete the names for reasons of tact or legal liability. Interestingly, as with other aspects of realism, it is an *illusion* that is being enhanced, by purely artificial means. Is it likely, does it violate the principle of verisimilitude, that a thirteen-year-old boy could make such a sophisticated observation? A girl of fourteen is *the psychological coeval* of a boy of fifteen or sixteen; a thirteen-year-old boy, therefore, even one precocious in some other respects, might be three years *her emotional junior*.

Thrice a year — on Memorial, Independence, and Labor Days — the family visits Ocean City for the afternoon and evening. When Ambrose and Peter's father was their age, the excursion was made by train, as mentioned in the novel *The 42nd Parallel* by John Dos Passos. Many families from the same neighborhood used to travel together, with dependent relatives and often with Negro servants; schoolfuls of children swarmed through the railway cars;

everyone shared everyone else's Maryland fried chicken, Virginia ham, deviled eggs, potato salad, beaten biscuits, iced tea. Nowadays (that is, in 19 —, the year of our story) the journey is made by automobile — more comfortably and quickly though without the extra fun though without the *camaraderie*[1] of a general excursion. It's all part of the deterioration of American life, their father declares; Uncle Karl supposes that when the boys take *their* families to Ocean City for the holidays they'll fly in Autogiros. Their mother, sitting in the middle of the front seat like Magda in the second, only with her arms on the seat-back behind the men's shoulders, wouldn't want the good old days back again, the steaming trains and stuffy long dresses; on the other hand she can do without Autogiros, too, if she has to become a grandmother to fly in them.

Description of physical appearance and mannerisms is one of several standard methods of characterization used by writers of fiction. It is also important to "keep the senses operating"; when a detail from one of the five senses, say visual, is "crossed" with a detail from another, say auditory, the reader's imagination is oriented to the scene, perhaps unconsciously. This procedure may be compared to the way surveyors and navigators determine their positions by two or more compass bearings, a process known as triangulation. The brown hair on Ambrose's mother's forearms gleamed in the sun like. Though right-handed, she took her left arm from the seat-back to press the dashboard cigar lighter for Uncle Karl. When the glass bead in its handle glowed red, the lighter was ready for use. The smell of Uncle Karl's cigar smoke reminded one of. The fragrance of the ocean came strong to the picnic ground where they always stopped for lunch, two miles inland from Ocean City. Having to pause for a full hour almost within sound of the breakers was difficult for Peter and Ambrose when they were younger; even at their present age it was not easy to keep their anticipation, *stimulated by the briny spume*, from turning into short temper. The Irish author James Joyce, in his unusual novel entitled *Ulysses*, now available in this country, uses the adjectives *snot-green* and *scrotum-tightening* to describe the sea. Visual, auditory, tactile, olfactory, gustatory. Peter and Ambrose's father, while steering their black 1936 LaSalle sedan with one hand, could with the other remove the first cigarette from a white pack of Lucky Strikes and, more remarkably, light it with a match forefingered from its book and thumbed against the flint paper without being detached. The matchbook cover merely advertised U.S. War Bonds and Stamps. A fine metaphor, simile, or other figure of speech, in addition to its obvious "first-order" relevance to the thing it describes, will be seen upon reflection to have a second order of significance: it may be drawn from the *milieu* of the action, for example, or be particularly appropriate to the sensibility of the narrator, even hinting to the reader things of which the narrator is unaware; or it may cast further and subtler lights upon the thing it describes, sometimes ironically qualifying the more evident sense of the comparison.

To say that Ambrose's and Peter's mother was *pretty* is to accomplish nothing; the reader may acknowledge the proposition, but his imagination is not engaged. Besides, Magda was also pretty, yet in an altogether different way. Although she lived on B—— Street she had very good manners and did better than average in school. Her figure was very well developed for her age. Her right hand lay casually on the plush upholstery of the seat, very near Ambrose's left leg, on which his own hand rested. The space between their legs, between her right and his left leg, was out of the line of sight of anyone sitting on the other side of Magda, as well as anyone glancing into the rearview mirror. Uncle Karl's face resembled Peter's — rather, vice versa. Both had dark hair and eyes, short husky statures, deep voices. Magda's left hand was probably in a similar position on her left side. The boy's father is difficult to describe; no

[1] Good fellowship.

particular feature of his appearance or manner stood out. He wore glasses and was principal of a T—— County grade school. Uncle Karl was a masonry contractor.

Although Peter must have known as well as Ambrose that the latter, because of his position in the car, would be the first to see the electrical towers of the power plant at V——, the halfway point of their trip, he leaned forward and slightly toward the center of the car and pretended to be looking for them through the flat pinewoods and tuckahoe[2] creeks along the highway. For as long as the boys could remember, "looking for the Towers" had been a feature of the first half of their excursions to Ocean City, "looking for the standpipe" of the second. Though the game was childish, their mother preserved the tradition of rewarding the first to see the Towers with a candybar or piece of fruit. She insisted now that Magda play the game; the prize, she said, was "something hard to get nowadays." Ambrose decided not to join in; he sat far back in his seat. Magda, like Peter, leaned forward. Two sets of straps were discernible through the shoulders of her sun dress; the inside right one, a brassiere-strap, was fastened or shortened with a small safety pin. The right armpit of her dress, presumably the left as well, was damp with perspiration. The simple strategy for being first to espy the Towers, which Ambrose had understood by the age of four, was to sit on the righthand side of the car. Whoever·sat there, however, had also to put up with the worst of the sun, and so Ambrose, without mentioning the matter, chose sometimes the one and sometimes the other. Not impossibly Peter had never caught on to the trick, or thought that his brother hadn't simply because Ambrose on occasion preferred shade to a Baby Ruth or tangerine.

The shade-sun situation didn't apply to the front seat, owing to the windshield; if anything the driver got more sun, since the person on the passenger side not only was shaded below by the door and dashboard but might swing down his sunvisor all the way too.

"Is that them?" Magda asked. Ambrose's mother teased the boys for letting Magda win, insinuating that "somebody [had] a girlfriend." Peter and Ambrose's father reached a long thin arm across their mother to butt his cigarette in the dashboard ashtray, under the lighter. The prize this time for seeing the Towers first was a banana. Their mother bestowed it after chiding their father for wasting a half-smoked cigarette when everything was so scarce. Magda, to take the prize, moved her hand from so near Ambrose's that he could have touched it as though accidentally. She offered to share the prize, things like that were so hard to find; but everyone insisted it was hers alone. Ambrose's mother sang an iambic trimeter couplet from a popular song, femininely rhymed:

> "What's good is in the Army;
> What's left will never harm me."

Uncle Karl tapped his cigar ash out the ventilator window; some particles were sucked by the slipstream back into the car through the rear window on the passenger side. Magda demonstrated her ability to hold a banana in one hand and peel it with her teeth. She still sat forward; Ambrose pushed his glasses back onto the bridge of his nose with his left hand, which he then negligently let fall to the seat cushion immediately behind her. He even permitted the single hair, gold, on the second joint of his thumb to brush the fabric of her skirt. Should she have sat back at that instant, his hand would have been caught under her.

Plush upholstery prickles uncomfortably through gabardine slacks in the July sun. The function of the *beginning* of a story is to introduce the principal characters, establish their initial relationships, set the scene for the main action, expose the background of the situation

---

[2] An edible fungus, sometimes called Indian Bread, that grows on the roots of certain trees in the southern United States.

if necessary, plant motifs and foreshadowings where appropriate, and initiate the first complication or whatever of the "rising action." Actually, if one imagines a story called "The Funhouse," or "Lost in the Funhouse," the details of the drive to Ocean City don't seem especially relevant. The *beginning* should recount the events between Ambrose's first sight of the funhouse early in the afternoon and his entering it with Magda and Peter in the evening. The *middle* would narrate all relevant events from the time he goes in to the time he loses his way; middles have the double and contradictory function of delaying the climax while at the same time preparing the reader for it and fetching him to it. Then the *ending* would tell what Ambrose does while he's lost, how he finally finds his way out, and what everybody makes of the experience. So far there's been no real dialogue, very little sensory detail, and nothing in the way of a *theme*. And a long time has gone by already without anything happening; it makes a person wonder. We haven't even reached Ocean City yet: we will never get out of the funhouse.

The more closely an author identifies with the narrator, literally or metaphorically, the less advisable it is, as a rule, to use the first-person narrative viewpoint. Once three years previously the young people *aforementioned* played Niggers and Masters in the backyard; when it was Ambrose's turn to be Master and theirs to be Niggers Peter had to go serve his evening papers; Ambrose was afraid to punish Magda alone, but she led him to the white-washed Torture Chamber between the woodshed and the privy in the Slaves Quarters; there she knelt sweating among bamboo rakes and dusty Mason jars, pleadingly embraced his knees, and while bees droned in the lattice as if on an ordinary summer afternoon, purchased clemency at a surprising price set by herself. Doubtless she remembered nothing of this event; Ambrose on the other hand seemed unable to forget the least detail of his life. He even recalled how, standing beside himself with awed impersonality in the reeky heat, he'd stared the while at an empty cigar box in which Uncle Karl kept stone-cutting chisels: beneath the words *El Producto*, a laureled, loose-toga'd lady regarded the sea from a marble bench; beside her, forgotten or not yet turned to, was a five-stringed lyre. Her chin reposed on the back of her right hand; her left depended negligently from the bench-arm. The lower half of scene and lady was peeled away; the words EXAMINED BY —— were inked there into the wood. Nowadays cigar boxes are made of pasteboard. Ambrose wondered what Magda would have done, Ambrose wondered what Magda would do when she sat back on his hand as he resolved she should. Be angry. Make a teasing joke of it. Give no sign at all. For a long time she leaned forward, playing cow-poker with Peter against Uncle Karl and Mother and watching for the first sign of Ocean City. At nearly the same instant, picnic ground and Ocean City standpipe hove into view; and Amoco filling station on their side of the road cost Mother and Uncle Karl fifty cows and the game; Magda bounced back, clapping her right hand on Mother's right arm; Ambrose moved clear "in the nick of time."

At this rate our hero, at this rate our protagonist will remain in the funhouse forever. Narrative ordinarily consists of alternating dramatization and summarization. One symptom of nervous tension, paradoxically, is repeated and violent yawning; neither Peter nor Magda nor Uncle Karl nor Mother reacted in this manner. Although they were no longer small children, Peter and Ambrose were each given a dollar to spend on boardwalk amusements in addition to what money of their own they'd brought along. Magda too, though she protested she had ample spending money. The boys' mother made a little scene out of distributing the bills; she pretended that her sons and Magda were small children and cautioned them not to spend the sum too quickly or in one place. Magda promised with a merry laugh and, having both hands free, took the bill with her left. Peter laughed also and pledged in a falsetto to be a good boy. His imitation of a child was not clever. The boys' father was tall and thin, balding, fair-complexioned. Assertions of that sort are not effective; the reader may acknowledge the proposition, but. We should be much farther along than we are; something has gone wrong; not much of this preliminary rambling seems relevant. Yet everyone begins in the same place; how is it that most go along without difficulty but a few lose their way?

"Stay out from under the boardwalk," Uncle Karl growled from the side of his mouth. The boys' mother pushed his shoulder *in mock annoyance*. They were all standing before Fat May the Laughing Lady who advertised the funhouse. Larger than life, Fat May mechanically shook, rocked on her heels, slapped her thighs while recorded laughter — uproarious, female — came amplified from a hidden loudspeaker. It chuckled, wheezed, wept; tried in vain to catch its breath; tittered, groaned, exploded raucous and anew. You couldn't hear it without laughing yourself, no matter how you felt. Father came back from talking to a Coast-Guardsman on duty and reported that the surf was spoiled with crude oil from tankers recently torpedoed offshore. Lumps of it, difficult to remove, made tarry tidelines on the beach and stuck on swimmers. Many bathed in the surf nevertheless and came out speckled; others paid to use a municipal pool and only sunbathed on the beach. We would do the latter. We would do the latter. We would do the latter.

Under the boardwalk, matchbook covers, grainy other things. What is the story's theme? Ambrose is ill. He perspires in the dark passages; candied apples-on-a-stick, delicious-looking, disappointing to eat. Funhouses need men's and ladies' rooms at intervals. Others perhaps have also vomited in corners and corridors; may even have had bowel movements liable to be stepped in in the dark. The word *fuck* suggests suction and/or and/or flatulence. Mother and Father; grandmothers and grandfathers on both sides; great-grandmothers and great-grandfathers on four sides, et cetera. Count a generation as thirty years: in approximately the year when Lord Baltimore was granted charter to the province of Maryland by Charles I, five hundred twelve women — English, Welsh, Bavarian, Swiss — of every class and character, received into themselves the penises the intromittent organs of five hundred twelve men, ditto, in every circumstance and posture, to conceive the five hundred twelve ancestors of the two hundred fifty-six ancestors of the et cetera et cetera et cetera et cetera et cetera et ectera et cetera et cetera of the author, of the narrator, of this story, *Lost in the Funhouse*. In alleyways, ditches, canopy beds, pinewoods, bridal suites, ship's cabins, coach-and-fours, coaches-and-four, sultry toolsheds; on the cold sand under boardwalks, littered with *El Producto* cigar butts, treasured with Lucky Strike cigarette stubs, Coca-Cola caps, gritty turds, cardboard lollipop sticks, matchbook covers warning that A Slip of the Lip Can Sink a Ship.[3] The shluppish whisper, continuous as seawash round the globe, tidelike falls and rises with the circuit of dawn and dusk.

Magda's teeth. She *was* left-handed. Perspiration. They've gone all the way, through, Magda and Peter, they've been waiting for hours with Mother and Uncle Karl while Father searches for his lost son; they draw french-fried potatoes from a paper cup and shake their heads. They've named the children they'll one day have and bring to Ocean City on holidays. Can spermatozoa properly be thought of as male animalcules when there are no female spermatozoa? They grope through hot, dark windings, past Love's Tunnel's fearsome obstacles. Some perhaps lose their way.

Peter suggested then and there that they do the funhouse; he had been through it before, so had Magda, Ambrose hadn't and suggested, his voice cracking on account of Fat May's laughter, that they swim first. All were chuckling, couldn't help it; Ambrose's father, Ambrose's and Peter's father came up grinning like a lunatic with two boxes of syrup-coated popcorn, one for Mother, one for Magda; the men were to help themselves. Ambrose walked

---

[3] A World War II slogan admonishing against loose talk that Axis spies might overhear.

on Magda's right; being by nature left-handed, she carried the box in her left hand. Up front the situation was reversed.

"What are you limping for?" Magda inquired of Ambrose. He supposed in a husky tone that his foot had gone to sleep in the car. Her teeth flashed. "Pins and needles?" It was the honey-suckle on the lattice of the former privy that drew the bees. Imagine being stung there. How long is this going to take?

The adults decided to forgo the pool; but Uncle Karl insisted they change into swimsuits and do the beach. "He wants to watch the pretty girls," Peter teased, and ducked behind Magda from Uncle Karl's pretended wrath. "You've got all the pretty girls you need right here," Magda declared, and Mother said: "Now that's the gospel truth." Magda scolded Peter, who reached over her shoulder to sneak some popcorn. "Your brother and father aren't getting any." Uncle Karl wondered if they were going to have fireworks that night, what with the shortages. It wasn't the shortages, Mr. M—— replied; Ocean City had fireworks from pre-war. But it was too risky on account of the enemy submarines, some people thought.

"Don't seem like Fourth of July without fireworks," said Uncle Karl. The inverted tag in dialogue writing is still considered permissible with proper names or epithets, but sounds old-fashioned with personal pronouns. "We'll have 'em again soon enough," predicted the boys' father. Their mother declared she could do without fireworks: they reminded her too much of the real thing. Their father said all the more reason to shoot off a few now and again. Uncle Karl asked *rhetorically* who needed reminding, just look at people's hair and skin.

"The oil, yes," said Mrs. M—— .

Ambrose had a pain in his stomach and so didn't swim but enjoyed watching the others. He and his father burned red easily. Magda's figure was exceedingly well developed for her age. She too declined to swim, and got mad, and became angry when Peter attempted to drag her into the pool. She always swam, he insisted; what did she mean not swim? Why did a person come to Ocean City?

"Maybe I want to lay here with Ambrose," Magda teased.

Nobody likes a pedant.

"Aha," said Mother. Peter grabbed Magda by one ankle and ordered Ambrose to grab the other. She squealed and rolled over on the beach blanket. Ambrose pretended to help hold her back. Her tan was darker than even Mother's and Peter's. "Help out, Uncle Karl!" Peter cried. Uncle Karl went to seize the other ankle. Inside the top of her swimsuit, however, you could see the line where the sunburn ended and, when she hunched her shoulders and squealed again, one nipple's auburn edge. Mother made them behave themselves. "*You* should certainly know," she said to Uncle Karl. Archly. "That when a lady says she doesn't feel like swimming, a gentleman doesn't ask questions." Uncle Karl said excuse *him*; Mother winked at Magda; Ambrose blushed; stupid Peter kept saying "Phooey on *feel like!*" and tugging at Magda's ankle; then even he got the point, and cannonballed with a holler into the pool.

"I swear," Magda said, in mock *in feigned* exasperation.

The diving would make a suitable literary symbol. To go off the high board you had to wait in a line along the poolside and up the ladder. Fellows tickled girls and goosed one another and shouted to the ones at the top to hurry up, or razzed them for bellyfloppers. Once on the springboard some took a great while posing or clowning or deciding on a dive or getting up their nerve; others ran right off. Especially among the younger fellows the idea was to strike the funniest pose or do the craziest stunt as you fell, a thing that got harder to do as you kept on and kept on. But whether you hollered *Geronimo!* or *Sieg heil!*,[4] held your nose or "rode a bicycle," pretended to be shot or did a perfect jacknife or changed your mind halfway down and ended up with nothing, it was over in two seconds, after all that wait. Spring, pose, splash. Spring, neat-o, splash. Spring, aw fooey, splash.

The grown-ups had gone on; Ambrose wanted to converse with Magda; she was remarkably well developed for her age; it was said that that came from rubbing with a turkish towel, and there were other theories. Ambrose could think of nothing to say except how good a diver Peter was, who was showing off for her benefit. You could pretty well tell by looking at their bathing suits and arm muscles how far along the different fellows were. Ambrose was glad he hadn't gone in swimming, the cold water shrank you up so. Magda pretended to be uninterested in the diving; she probably weighed as much as he did. If you knew your way around in the funhouse like your own bedroom, you could wait until a girl came along and then slip away without ever getting caught, even if her boyfriend was right with her. She'd think *he* did it! It would be better to be the boyfriend, and act outraged, and tear the funhouse apart.

Not act; *be.*

"He's a master diver," Ambrose said. In feigned admiration. "You really have to slave away at it to get that good." What would it matter anyhow if he asked her right out whether she remembered, even teased her with it as Peter would have?

There's no point in going farther; this isn't getting anybody anywhere; they haven't even come to the funhouse yet. Ambrose is off the track, in some new or old part of the place that's not supposed to be used; he strayed into it by some one-in-a-million chance, like the time the roller-coaster car left the tracks in the nineteen-teens against all the laws of physics and sailed over the boardwalk in the dark. And they can't locate him because they don't know where to look. Even the designer and operator have forgotten this other part, that winds around on itself like a whelk shell. That winds around the right part like the snakes on Mercury's caduceus.[5] Some people, perhaps, don't "hit their stride" until their twenties, when the growing-up business is over and women appreciate other things besides wisecracks and teasing and strutting. Peter didn't have one-tenth the imagination *he* had, not one-tenth. Peter did this naming-their-children thing as a joke, making up names like Aloysius and Murgatroyd, but Ambrose knew *exactly* how it would feel to be married and have children of your own, and be a loving husband and father, and go comfortably to work in the mornings and to bed with your wife at night, and wake up with her there. With a breeze coming through the sash and birds and mockingbirds singing in the Chinese-cigar trees. His eyes watered, there aren't enough ways to say that. He would be quite famous in his line of work. Whether Magda was his wife or not, one evening when he was wise-lined and gray at the temples he'd smile gravely, at a fashionable dinner party, and remind her of his youthful passion. The time they went with his family to Ocean City; the *erotic fantasies* he used to have about her. How long ago it seemed, and childish! Yet tender, too, *n'est-ce pas?*[6] Would she have imagined that the world-famous whatever remembered how many strings were on the lyre on the

---

[4] "Seig heil!" — the Nazi exclamation, accompanied by a stiff-armed salute, meaning "To victory!" or "Hurrah!" "Geronimo!" — the shout of American paratroopers when they jumped.

[5] The staff carried by Mercury, the Roman messenger-god.

[6] "Isn't that so?"

bench beside the girl on the label of the cigar box he'd stared at in the toolshed at age ten while she, age eleven. Even then he had felt *wise beyond his years*; he'd stroked her hair and said in his deepest voice and correctest English, as to a dear child: "I shall never forget this moment."

But though he had breathed heavily, groaned as if ecstatic, what he'd really felt throughout was an odd detachment, as though someone else were Master. Strive as he might to be transported, he heard his mind take notes upon the scene: *This is what they call* passion. *I am experiencing it.* Many of the digger machines were out of order in the penny arcades and could not be repaired or replaced for the duration. Moreover the prizes, made now in USA, were less interesting than formerly, pasteboard items for the most part, and some of the machines wouldn't work on white pennies. The gypsy fortune-teller machine might have provided a foreshadowing of the climax of this story if Ambrose had operated it. It was even dilapidateder than most: the silver coating was worn off the brown metal handles, the glass windows around the dummy were cracked and taped, her kerchiefs and silks long-faded. If a man lived by himself, he could take a department-store mannequin with flexible joints and modify her in certain ways. *However*: by the time he was that old he'd have a real woman. There was a machine that stamped your name around a white-metal coin with a star in the middle: A—— . His son would be the second, and when the lad reached thirteen or so he would put a strong arm around his shoulder and tell him calmly: "It is perfectly normal. We have all been through it. It will not last forever." Nobody knew how to be what they were right. He'd smoke a pipe, teach his son how to fish and softcrab, assure him he needn't worry about himself. Magda would certainly yield a great deal of milk, although guilty of occasional solecisms. It don't taste so bad. Suppose the lights came on now!

The day wore on. You think you're yourself, but there are other persons in you. Ambrose gets hard when Ambrose doesn't want to, *and obversely*. Ambrose watches them disagree; Ambrose watches him watch. In the funhouse mirror-room you can't see yourself go on forever, because no matter how you stand, your head gets in the way. Even if you had a glass periscope, the image of your eye would cover up the thing you really wanted to see. The police will come; there'll be a story in the papers. That must be where it happened. Unless he can find a surprise exit, an unofficial backdoor or escape hatch opening on an alley, say, and then stroll up to the family in front of the funhouse and ask where everybody's been; *he's* been out of the place for ages. That's just where it happened, in that last lighted room: Peter and Magda found the right exit; he found one that you weren't supposed to find and strayed off into the works somewhere. In a perfect funhouse you'd be able to go only one way, like the divers off the highboard; getting lost would be impossible; the doors and halls would work like minnow traps or the valves in veins.

On account of German U-boats, Ocean City was "browned out": streetlights were shaded on the seaward side; shop-windows and boardwalk amusement places were kept dim, not to silhouette tankers and Liberty-ships for torpedoing. In a short story about Ocean City, Maryland, during World War II, the author could make use of the image of sailors on leave in the penny arcades and shooting galleries, sighting through the crosshairs of toy machine guns at swastika'd subs, while out in the black Atlantic a U-boat skipper squints through his periscope at real ships outlined by the glow of penny arcades. After dinner the family strolled back to the amusement end of the boardwalk. The boys' father had burnt red as always and was masked with Noxzema, a minstrel in reverse. The grown-ups stood at the end of the boardwalk where the Hurricane of '33 had cut an inlet from the ocean to Assawoman Bay.

"Pronounced with a long *o*," Uncle Karl reminded Magda with a wink. His shirt sleeves were rolled up; Mother punched his brown biceps with the arrowed heart on it and said his mind was naughty. Fat May's laugh came suddenly from the funhouse, as if she'd just got the joke; the family laughed too at the coincidence. Ambrose went under the boardwalk to search for out-of-town matchbook covers with the aid of his pocket flashlight; he looked out from the edge of the North American continent and wondered how far their laughter carried over the water. Spies in rubber rafts; survivors in lifeboats. If the joke had been beyond his understanding, he could have said: "*The laughter was over his head.*" And let the reader see the serious wordplay on second reading.

He turned the flashlight on and then off at once even before the woman whooped. He sprang away, heart athud, dropping the light. What had the man grunted? Perspiration drenched and chilled him by the time he scrambled up to the family. "See anything?" his father asked. His voice wouldn't come; he shrugged and violently brushed sand from his pants legs.

"Let's ride the old flying horses!" Magda cried. I'll never be an author. It's been forever already, everybody's gone home, Ocean City's deserted, the ghostcrabs are tickling across the beach and down the littered cold streets. And the empty halls of clapboard hotels and abandoned funhouses. A tidal wave; an enemy air raid; a monster-crab swelling like an island from the sea. *The inhabitants fled in terror.* Magda clung to his trouser leg; he alone knew the maze's secret. "He gave his life that we might live," said Uncle Karl with a scowl of pain, as he. The fellow's hands had been tattooed; the woman's legs, the woman's fat white legs had. *An astonishing coincidence.* He yearned to tell Peter. He wanted to throw up for excitement. They hadn't even chased him. He wished he were dead.

One possible ending would be to have Ambrose come across another lost person in the dark. They'd match their wits together against the funhouse, struggle like Ulysses past obstacle after obstacle, help and encourage each other. Or a girl. By the time they found the exit they'd be closest friends, sweethearts if it were a girl; they'd know each other's inmost souls, be bound together *by the cement of shared adventure*; then they'd emerge into the light and it would turn out that his friend was a Negro. A blind girl. President Roosevelt's son. Ambrose's former archenemy.

Shortly after the mirror room he'd groped along a musty corridor, his heart already misgiving him at the absence of phosphorescent arrows and other signs. He'd found a crack of light — not a door, it turned out, but a seam between the plyboard wall panels — and squinting up to it, espied a small old man, *in appearance not unlike* the photographs at home of Ambrose's late grandfather, nodding upon a stool beneath a bare, speckled bulb. A crude panel of toggle- and knife-switches hung beside the open fuse box near his head; elsewhere in the little room were wooden levers and ropes belayed to boat cleats. At the time, Ambrose wasn't lost enough to rap or call; later he couldn't find that crack. Now it seemed to him that he'd possibly dozed off for a few minutes somewhere along the way; certainly he was exhausted from the afternoon's sunshine and the evening's problems; he couldn't be sure he hadn't dreamed part or all of the sight. Had an old black wall fan droned like bees and shimmied two flypaper streamers? Had the funhouse operator — gentle, somewhat sad and tired-appearing, in expression not unlike the photographs at home of Ambrose's late Uncle Konrad — murmured in his sleep? Is there really such a person as Ambrose, or is he a figment of the author's imagination? Was it Assawoman Bay or Sinepuxent? Are there other errors of fact in this fiction? Was there another sound besides the little slap slap of thigh on ham, like water sucking at the chine-boards of a skiff?

When you're lost, the smartest thing to do is stay put till you're found, hollering if necessary. But to holler guarantees humiliation as well as rescue; keeping silent permits some saving of face — you can act surprised at the fuss when your rescuers find you and swear you weren't lost, if they do. What's more you might find your own way yet, *however belatedly*.

"Don't tell me your foot's still asleep!" Magda exclaimed as the three young people walked from the inlet to the area set aside for ferris wheels, carrousels, and other carnival rides, they having decided in favor of the vast and ancient merry-go-round instead of the funhouse. What a sentence, everything was wrong from the outset. People don't know what to make of him, he doesn't know what to make of himself, he's only thirteen, *athletically and socially inept*, not astonishingly bright, but there are antennae; he has ... some sort of receivers in his head; things speak to him, he understands more than he should, the world winks at him through its objects, grabs grinning at his coat. Everybody else is in on some secret he doesn't know; they've forgotten to tell him. Through simple *procrastination* his mother put off his baptism until this year. Everyone else had it done as a baby; he'd assumed the same of himself, as had his mother, so she claimed, until it was time for him to join Grace Methodist-Protestant and the oversight came out. He was mortified, but pitched sleepless through his private catechizing, intimidated by the ancient mysteries, a thirteen year old would never say that, resolved to experience conversion like St. Augustine.[7] When the water touched his brow and Adam's sin left him, he contrived by a strain like defecation to bring tears into his eyes — but felt nothing. There was some simple, radical difference about him; he hoped it was genius, feared it was madness, devoted himself to amiability and inconspicuousness. Alone on the seawall near his house he was seized by the terrifying transports he'd thought to find in toolshed, in Communion-cup. The grass was alive! The town, the river, himself, were not imaginary; time roared in his ears like wind; the world was *going on*! This part ought to be dramatized. The Irish author James Joyce once wrote. Ambrose M—— is going to scream.

There is no *texture of rendered sensory detail*, for one thing. The faded distorting mirrors beside Fat May; the impossibility of choosing a mount when one had but a single ride on the great carrousel; the *vertigo attendant on his recognition* that Ocean City was worn out, the place of fathers and grandfathers, straw-boatered men and parasoled ladies survived by their amusements. Money spent, the three paused at Peter's insistence beside Fat May to watch the girls get their skirts blown up. The object was to tease Magda, who said: "I swear, Peter M—— , you've got a one-track mind! Amby and me aren't *interested* in such things." In the tumbling-barrel, too, just inside the Devil's-mouth entrance to the funhouse, the girls were upended and their boyfriends and others could see up their dresses if they cared to. Which was the whole point, Ambrose realized. Of the entire funhouse! If you looked around, you noticed that almost all the people on the boardwalk were paired off into couples except the small children; in a way, that was the whole point of Ocean City! If you had X-ray eyes and could see everything going on at that instant under the boardwalk and in all the hotel rooms and cars and alleyways, you'd realize that all that normally *showed*, like restaurants and dance halls and clothing and test-your-strength machines, was merely preparation and intermission. Fat May screamed.

Because he watched the goings-on from the corner of his eye, it was Ambrose who spied the half-dollar on the boardwalk near the tumbling-barrel. Losers weepers. The first time he'd heard some people moving through a corridor not far away, just after he'd lost sight of the crack of light, he'd decided not to call to them, for fear they'd guess he was scared and poke fun; it sounded like roughnecks; he'd hoped they'd come by and he could follow in the dark without their knowing. Another time he'd heard just one person, unless he imagined it, bumping along as if on the other side of the plywood; perhaps Peter coming back for him, or Father, or Magda lost too. Or the owner and operator of the funhouse. He'd called out once, as though merrily: "Anybody know where the heck we are?" But the query was too stiff, his voice cracked, when the sounds stopped he was terrified: maybe it was a queer who waited for

---

[7] Augustine's conversion was a slow and intellectual process, "a lingering-out sweet skill" in the words of Gerard Manley Hopkins, following a long youth of apparently mild dissolutions.

fellows to get lost, or a longhaired filthy monster that lived in some cranny of the funhouse. He stood rigid for hours it seemed like, scarcely respiring. His future was shockingly clear, in outline. He tried holding his breath to the point of unconsciousness. There ought to be a button you could push to end your life absolutely without pain; disappear in a flick, like turning out a light. He would push it instantly! He despised Uncle Karl. But he despised his father too, for not being what he was supposed to be. Perhaps his father hated *his* father, and so on, and his son would hate him, and so on. Instantly!

Naturally he didn't have nerve enough to ask Magda to go through the funhouse with him. With incredible nerve and to everyone's surprise he invited Magda, quietly and politely, to go through the funhouse with him. "I warn you, I've never been through it before," he added, *laughing easily*; "but I reckon we can manage somehow. The important thing to remember, after all, is that it's meant to be a *fun*house; that is, a place of amusement. If people really get lost or injured or too badly frightened in it, the owner'd go out of business. There'd even be lawsuits. No character in a work of fiction can make a speech this long without interruption or acknowledgment from the other characters."

Mother teased Uncle Karl: "Three's a crowd, I always heard." But actually Ambrose was relieved that Peter now had a quarter too. Nothing was what it looked like. Every instant, under the surface of the Atlantic Ocean, millions of living animals devoured one another. Pilots were falling in flames over Europe; women were being forcibly raped in the South Pacific. His father should have taken him aside and said: "There is a simple secret to getting through the funhouse, as simple as being first to see the Towers. Here it is. Peter does not know it; neither does your Uncle Karl. You and I are different. Not surprisingly, you've often wished you weren't. Don't think I haven't noticed how unhappy your childhood has been! But you'll understand, when I tell you, why it had to be kept secret until now. And you won't regret not being like your brother and your uncle. *On the contrary!*" If you knew all the stories behind all the people on the boardwalk, you'd see that *nothing* was what it looked like. Husbands and wives often hated each other; parents didn't necessarily love their children; et cetera. A child took things for granted because he had nothing to compare his life to and everybody acted as if things were as they should be. Therefore each saw himself as the hero of the story, when the truth might turn out to be that he's the villain, or the coward. And there wasn't one thing you could do about it!

Hunchbacks, fat ladies, fools — that no one chose what he was was unbearable. In the movies he'd meet a beautiful young girl in the funhouse; they'd have hairsbreadth escapes from real dangers; he'd do and say the right things; she also; in the end they'd be lovers; their dialogue lines would match up; he'd be perfectly at ease; she'd not only like him well enough, she'd think he was *marvelous*; she'd lie awake thinking about *him*, instead of vice versa — the way *his* face looked in different lights and how he stood and exactly what he'd said — and yet that would be only one small episode in his wonderful life, among many many others. Not a *turning point* at all. What had happened in the toolshed was nothing. He hated, he loathed his parents! One reason for not writing a lost-in-the-funhouse story is that either everybody's felt what Ambrose feels, in which case it goes without saying, or else no normal person feels such things, in which case Ambrose is a freak. "Is anything more tiresome, in fiction, than the problems of sensitive adolescents?" And it's all too long and rambling, as if the author. For all a person knows the first time through, the end could be just around any corner; perhaps, *not impossibly* it's been within reach any number of times. On the other hand he may be scarcely past the start, with everything yet to get through, an intolerable idea.

Fill in: His father's raised eyebrows when he announced his decision to do the funhouse with Magda. Ambrose understands now, but didn't then, that his father was wondering whether he knew what the funhouse was *for* — especially since he didn't object, as he should have, when Peter decided to come along too. The ticket-woman, witchlike, mortifying him when inadvertently he gave her his name-coin instead of the half-dollar, then unkindly calling Magda's attention to the birthmark on his temple: "Watch out for him, girlie, he's a marked man!" She wasn't even cruel, he understood, only vulgar and insensitive. Somewhere in the world there was a young woman with such splendid understanding that she'd see him entire, like a poem or story, and find his words so valuable after all that when he confessed his apprehensions she would explain why they were in fact the very things that made him precious to her … and to Western Civilization! There was no such girl, the simple truth being. Violent yawns as they approached the mouth. Whispered advice from an old-timer on a bench near the barrel: "Go crabwise and ye'll get an eyeful without upsetting!" Composure vanished at the first pitch: Peter hollered joyously, Magda tumbled, shrieked, clutched her skirt; Ambrose scrambled crabwise, tight-lipped with terror, was soon out, watched his dropped name-coin slide among the couples. Shamefaced he saw that to get through expeditiously was not the point; Peter feigned assistance in order to trip Magda up, shouted "I see Christmas!" when her legs went flying. The old man, his latest betrayer, cackled approval. A dim hall then of black-thread cobwebs and recorded gibber: he took Magda's elbow to steady her against revolving discs set in the slanted floor to throw your feet out from under, and explained to her in a calm, deep voice his theory that each phase of the funhouse was triggered either automatically, by a series of photoelectric devices, or else manually by operators stationed at peepholes. But he lost his voice thrice as the discs unbalanced him; Magda was anyhow squealing; but at one point she clutched him about the waist to keep from falling, and her right cheek pressed for a moment against his belt-buckle. Heroically he drew her up, it was his chance to clutch her close as if for support and say: "I love you." He even put an arm lightly about the small of her back before a sailor-and-girl pitched into them from behind, sorely treading his left big toe and knocking Magda asprawl with them. The sailor's girl was a string-haired hussy with a loud laugh and light blue drawers; Ambrose realized that he wouldn't have said "I love you" anyhow, and was smitten with self-contempt. How much better it would be to be that common sailor! A wiry little Seaman 3rd, the fellow squeezed a girl to each side and stumbled hilarious into the mirror room, closer to Magda in thirty seconds than Ambrose had got in thirteen years. She giggled at something the fellow said to Peter; she drew her hair from her eyes with a movement so womanly it struck Ambrose's heart; Peter's smacking her backside then seemed particularly coarse. But Magda made a pleased indignant face and cried, "All right for *you*, mister!" and pursued Peter into the maze without a backward glance. The sailor followed after, leisurely, drawing his girl against his hip; Ambrose understood not only that they were all so relieved to be rid of his burdensome company that they didn't even notice his absence, but that he himself shared their relief. Stepping from the treacherous passage at last into the mirror-maze, he saw once again, more clearly than ever, how readily he deceived himself into supposing he was a person. He even foresaw, wincing at his dreadful self-knowledge, that he would repeat the deception, at ever-rarer intervals, all his wretched life, so fearful were the alternatives. Fame, madness, suicide; perhaps all three. It's not believable that so young a boy could articulate that reflection, and in fiction the merely true must always yield to the plausible. Moreover, the symbolism is in places heavy-footed. Yet Ambrose M—— understood, as few adults do, that the famous loneliness of the great was no popular myth but a general truth — furthermore, that it was as much cause as effect.

All the preceding except the last few sentences is exposition that should've been done earlier or interspersed with the present action instead of lumped together. No reader would put up with so much with such *prolixity*. It's interesting that Ambrose's father, though presumably an intelligent man (as indicated by his role as grade-school principal), neither encouraged nor discouraged his sons at all in any way — as if he either didn't care about them or cared all right but didn't know how to act. If this fact should contribute to one of them's becoming a celebrated but wretchedly unhappy scientist, was it a good thing or not? He too might someday face the question; it would be useful to know whether it had tortured his father for years, for example, or never once crossed his mind.

In the maze two important things happened. First, our hero found a name-coin someone else had lost or discarded: *AMBROSE*, suggestive of the famous lightship and of his late grandfather's favorite dessert,[8] which his mother used to prepare on special occasions out of coconut, oranges, grapes, and what else. Second, as he wondered at the endless replication of his image in the mirrors, second, as he *lost himself in the reflection* that the necessity for an observer makes perfect observation impossible, better make him eighteen at least, yet that would render other things unlikely, he heard Peter and Magda chuckling somewhere together in the maze. "Here!" "No, here!" they shouted to each other; Peter said, "Where's Amby?" Magda murmured. "Amb?" Peter called. In a pleased, friendly voice. He didn't reply. The truth was, his brother was a *happy-go-lucky youngster* who'd've been better off with a regular brother of his own, but who seldom complained of his lot and was generally cordial. Ambrose's throat ached; there aren't enough different ways to say that. He stood quietly while the two young people giggled and thumped through the glittering maze, hurrah'd their discovery of its exit, cried out in joyful alarm at what next beset them. Then he set his mouth and followed after, as he supposed, took a wrong turn, strayed into the pass *wherein he lingers yet.*

The action of conventional dramatic narrative may be represented by a diagram called Freitag's Triangle[9]:

or more accurately by a variant of that diagram:

in which *AB* represents the exposition, *B* the introduction of conflict, *BC* the "rising action," complication, or development of the conflict, *C* the climax, or turn of the action, *CD* the dénouement, or resolution of the conflict. While there is no reason to regard this pattern as an absolute necessity, like many other conventions it became conventional because great numbers of people over many years learned by trial and error that it was effective; one ought not to forsake it, therefore, unless one wishes to forsake as well the effect of drama or has clear cause to feel that deliberate violation of the "normal" pattern can better can better effect that effect. This can't go on much longer; it can go on forever. He died telling stories to himself in the dark; years later, when that vast unsuspected area of the funhouse came to light, the first expedition found his skeleton in one of its labyrinthine corridors and mistook it for part of the entertainment. He died of starvation telling himself stories in the dark; but unbeknownst unbeknownst to him, an assistant operator of the funhouse, happening to overhear him,

---

[8] The references are to a lightship in New York harbor and to a popular dessert, *ambrosia*, named for the legendary "food of the gods."

[9] In *Technique of the Drama*, the German novelist and critic Gustav Freytag analyzed the patterns of plot and action in this manner.

crouched just behind the plyboard partition and wrote down his every word. The operator's daughter, an exquisite young woman with a figure unusually well developed for her age, crouched just behind the partition and transcribed his every word. Though she had never laid eyes on him, she recognized that here was one of Western Culture's truly great imaginations, the eloquence of whose suffering would be an inspiration to unnumbered. And her heart was torn between her love for the misfortunate young man (yes, she loved him, though she had never laid though she knew him only — but how well! — through his words, and the deep, calm voice in which he spoke them) between her love et cetera and her womanly intuition that only in suffering and isolation could he give voice et cetera. Lone dark dying. Quietly she kissed the rough plyboard, and a tear fell upon the page. Where she had written in shorthand *Where she had written in shorthand* Where she had written in shorthand *Where she* et cetera. A long time ago we should have passed the apex of Freitag's Triangle and made brief work of the *dénouement*; the plot doesn't rise by meaningful steps but winds upon itself, digresses, retreats, hesitates, sighs, collapses, expires. The climax of the story must be its protagonist's discovery of a way to get through the funhouse. But he has found none, may have ceased to search.

What relevance does the war have to the story? Should there be fireworks outside or not?

Ambrose wandered, languished, dozed. Now and then he fell into his habit of rehearsing to himself the unadventurous story of his life, narrated from the third-person point of view, from his earliest memory parenthesis of maple leaves stirring in the summer breath of tidewater Maryland end of parenthesis to the present moment. Its principal events, on this telling, would appear to have been *A*, *B*, *C*, and *D*.

He imagined himself years hence, successful, married, at ease in the world, the trials of his adolescence far behind him. He has come to the seashore with his family for the holiday: how Ocean City has changed! But at one seldom at one ill-frequented end of the boardwalk a few derelict amusements survive from times gone by: the great carrousel from the turn of the century, with its monstrous griffins and mechanical concert band; the roller coaster rumored since 1916 to have been condemned; the mechanical shooting gallery in which only the image of our enemies changed. His own son laughs with Fat May and wants to know what a funhouse is; Ambrose hugs the sturdy lad close and smiles around his pipestem at his wife.

The family's going home. Mother sits between Father and Uncle Karl, who teases him good-naturedly who chuckles over the fact that the comrade with whom he'd fought his way shoulder to shoulder through the funhouse had turned out to be a blind Negro girl — to their mutual discomfort, as they'd opened their souls. But such are the walls of custom, which even. Whose arm is where? How must it feel. He dreams of a funhouse vaster by far than any yet constructed; but by then they may be out of fashion, like steamboats and excursion trains. Already quaint and seedy: the draperied ladies on the frieze of the carrousel are his father's father's mooncheeked dreams; if he thinks of it more he will vomit his apple-on-a-stick.

He wonders: will he become a regular person? Something has gone wrong; his vaccination didn't take; at the Boy-Scout initiation campfire he only pretended to be deeply moved, as he pretends to this hour that it is not so bad after all in the funhouse, and that he has a little limp. How long will it last? He envisions a truly astonishing funhouse, incredibly complex yet utterly controlled from a great central switchboard like the console of a pipe organ. Nobody had enough imagination. He could design such a place himself, wiring and all, and he's only thirteen years old. He would be its operator: panel lights would show what was up in every cranny of its cunning of its multifarious vastness; a switch-flick would ease this fellow's way, complicate that's, to balance things out; if anyone seemed lost or frightened, all the operator had to do was.

He wishes he had never entered the funhouse. But he has. Then he wishes he were dead. But he's not. Therefore he will construct funhouses for others and be their secret operator — though he would rather be among the lovers for whom funhouses are designed.

QUESTIONS

1. Is "Lost in the Funhouse" a story about Ambrose or a story about the process of telling a story?

2. Is there a pattern to Barth's use of italics? To his "wanderings" from Ambrose's Fourth of July story? Do these wanderings explain the conventions of writing?

3. Is it Ambrose or the reader who is lost in the funhouse? Is it both?

4. What details establish the time and place of the story? The story is filled with literary, cultural, and historical allusions, only a few of which are explained in footnotes. Does it matter much that you do not recognize every allusion? If not, what purpose do they serve?

5. Who is the narrator? Is he telling more than one story? Can you distinguish several plot lines? Are these different stories or only mirror images of each other?

6. Can you find evidence that the narrator is a professor? What else can you infer about him?

7. "In the funhouse mirror-room you can't see yourself go on forever, because no matter how you stand, your head gets in the way." Is this the point of the story? Does the tone support your answer?

8. What is Ambrose's relationship with Magda? with his uncle?

9. Compare Ambrose with the young man of Joyce's "Araby." Could you argue that Barth's story is an enlarged and cynical version of Joyce's?

10. What does the last paragraph suggest about Ambrose's relationship to the narrator and/or the author of "Lost in the Funhouse"?

DONALD BARTHELME

The Balloon

The balloon, beginning at a point on Fourteenth Street, the exact location of which I cannot reveal, expanded northward all one night, while people were sleeping, until it reached the Park. There, I stopped it; at dawn the northernmost edges lay over the Plaza; the free-hanging motion was frivolous and gentle. But experiencing a faint irritation at stopping, even to protect the trees, and seeing no reason the balloon should not be allowed to expand upward, over the parts of the city it was already covering, into the "air space" to be found there, I asked the engineers to see to it. This expansion took place throughout the morning, soft imperceptible sighing of gas through the valves. The balloon then covered forty-five blocks north-south and an irregular area east-west, as many as six crosstown blocks on either side of the Avenue in some places. That was the situation, then.

But it is wrong to speak of "situations," implying sets of circumstances leading to some resolution, some escape of tension; there were no situations, simply the balloon hanging there — muted heavy grays and browns for the most part, contrasting with walnut and soft yellows. A deliberate lack of finish, enhanced by skillful installation, gave the surface a rough, forgotten quality; sliding weights on the inside, carefully adjusted, anchored the great, vari-shaped mass at a number of points. Now we have had a flood of original ideas in all media, works of singular beauty as well as significant milestones in the history of inflation, but at that moment there was only *this balloon*, concrete particular, hanging there.

There were reactions. Some people found the balloon "interesting." As a response this seemed inadequate to the immensity of the balloon, the suddenness of its appearance over the city; on the other hand, in the absence of hysteria or other societally-induced anxiety, it must be judged a calm, "mature" one. There was a certain amount of initial argumentation about the "meaning" of the balloon; this subsided, because we have learned not to insist on meanings, and they are rarely even looked for now, except in cases involving the simplest, safest phenomena. It was agreed that since the meaning of the balloon could never be known absolutely, extended discussion was pointless, or at least less purposeful than the activities of those who, for example, hung green and blue paper lanterns from the warm gray underside, in certain streets, or seized the occasion to write messages on the surface, announcing their availability for the performance of unnatural acts, or the availability of acquaintances.

Daring children jumped, especially at those points where the balloon hovered close to a building, so that the gap between balloon and building was a matter of a few inches, or points where the balloon actually made contact, exerting an ever-so-slight pressure against the side of a building, so that balloon and building seemed a unity. The upper surface was so structured that a "landscape" was presented, small valleys as well as slight knolls, or mounds; once atop the balloon, a stroll was possible, or even a trip, from one place to another. There was pleasure in being able to run down an incline, then up the opposing slope, both gently graded, or in making a leap from one side to the other. Bouncing was possible, because of the pneumaticity of the surface, and even falling, if that was your wish. That all these varied motions, as well as others, were within one's possibilities, in experiencing the "up" side of the balloon, was extremely exciting for children, accustomed to the city's flat, hard skin. But the purpose of the balloon was not to amuse children.

Too, the number of people, children and adults, who took advantage of the opportunities described was not so large as it might have been: a certain timidity, lack of trust in the balloon, was seen. There was, furthermore, some hostility. Because we had hidden the pumps, which fed helium to the interior, and because the surface was so vast that the authorities could not determine the point of entry — that is, the point at which the gas was injected — a degree of frustration was evidenced by those city officers into whose province such manifestations normally fell. The apparent purposelessness of the balloon was vexing (as was the fact that it was "there" at all). Had we painted, in great letters, "LABORATORY TESTS PROVE" or "18% MORE EFFECTIVE" on the sides of the balloon, this difficulty would have been circumvented. But I could not bear to do so. On the whole, these officers were remarkably tolerant, considering the dimensions of the anomaly, this tolerance being the result of, first, secret tests conducted by night that convinced them that little or nothing could be done in the way of removing or destroying the balloon, and, secondly, a public warmth that arose (not uncolored by touches of the aforementioned hostility) toward the balloon, from ordinary citizens.

As a single balloon must stand for a lifetime of thinking about balloons, so each citizen expressed, in the attitude he chose, a complex of attitudes. One man might consider that the balloon had to do with the notion *sullied*, as in the sentence *The big balloon sullied the otherwise clear and radiant Manhattan sky.* That is, the balloon was, in this man's view, an imposture, something inferior to the sky that had formerly been there, something interposed between the people and their "sky." But in fact it was January, the sky was dark and ugly; it was not a sky you could look up into, lying on your back in the street, with pleasure, unless pleasure, for you, proceeded from having been threatened, from having been misused. And the underside of the balloon was a pleasure to look up into, we had seen to that, muted grays and browns for the most part, contrasted with walnut and soft, forgotten yellows. And so, while this man was thinking *sullied*, still there was an admixture of pleasurable cognition in his thinking, struggling with the original perception.

Another man, on the other hand, might view the balloon as if it were part of a system of unanticipated rewards, as when one's employer walks in and says, "Here, Henry, take this package of money I have wrapped for you, because we have been doing so well in the business here, and I admire the way you bruise the tulips, without which bruising your department would not be a success, or at least not the success that it is." For this man the balloon might be a brilliantly heroic "muscle and pluck" experience, even if an experience poorly understood.

Another man might say, "Without the example of ———, it is doubtful that ——— would exist today in its present form," and find many to agree with him, or to argue with him. Ideas of "bloat" and "float" were introduced, as well as concepts of dream and responsibility. Others engaged in remarkably detailed fantasies having to do with a wish either to lose themselves in the balloon, or to engorge it. The private character of these wishes, of their origins, deeply buried and unknown, was such that they were not much spoken of; yet there is evidence that they were widespread. It was also argued that what was important was what you felt when you stood under the balloon; some people claimed that they felt sheltered, warmed, as never before, while enemies of the balloon felt, or reported feeling, constrained, a "heavy" feeling.

Critical opinion was divided:

"monstrous pourings"

            "harp"

XXXXXXX "certain contrasts
with darker portions"

       "inner joy"

"large, square corners"

"conservative eclecticism that has so
far governed modern balloon design"

       ::::::: "abnormal vigor"

"warm, soft, lazy passages"

"Has unity been sacrificed for a
sprawling quality?"

   "*Quelle catastrophe!*"

   "munching"

People began, in a curious way, to locate themselves in relation to aspects of the balloon: "I'll be at that place where it dips down into Forty-seventh Street almost to the sidewalk, near the Alamo Chile House," or, "Why don't we go stand on top, and take the air, and maybe walk about a bit, where it forms a tight, curving line with the façade of the Gallery of Modern Art — " Marginal intersections offered entrances within a given time duration, as well as "warm, soft, lazy passages" in which ... But it is wrong to speak of "marginal intersections," each intersection was crucial, none could be ignored (as if, walking there, you might not find someone capable of turning your attention, in a flash, from old exercises to new exercises, risks and escalations). Each intersection was crucial, meeting of balloon and building, meeting of balloon and man, meeting of balloon and balloon.

It was suggested that what was admired about the balloon was finally this: that it was not limited, or defined. Sometimes a bulge, blister, or subsection would carry all the way east to the river on its own initiative, in the manner of an army's movements on a map, as seen in a headquarters remote from the fighting. Then that part would be, as it were, thrown back again, or would withdraw into new dispositions; the next morning, that part would have made another sortie, or disappeared altogether. This ability of the balloon to shift its shape, to change, was very pleasing, especially to people whose lives were rather rigidly patterned, persons to whom change, although desired, was not available. The balloon, for the twenty-two days of its existence, offered the possibility, in its randomness, of mislocation of the self, in contradistinction to the grid of precise, rectangular pathways under our feet. The amount of specialized training currently needed, and the consequent desirability of long-term commitments, has been occasioned by the steadily growing importance of complex machinery, in virtually all kinds of operations; as this tendency increases, more and more people will turn, in bewildered inadequacy, to solutions for which the balloon may stand as a prototype, or "rough draft."

I met you under the balloon, on the occasion of your return from Norway; you asked if it was mine; I said it was. The balloon, I said, is a spontaneous autobiographical disclosure, having to do with the unease I felt at your absence, and with sexual deprivation, but now that your visit to Bergen has been terminated, it is no longer necessary or appropriate. Removal of the balloon was easy; trailer trucks carried away the depleted fabric, which is now stored in West Virginia, awaiting some other time of unhappiness, sometime, perhaps, when we are angry with one another.

QUESTIONS

1. Does "The Balloon" have a plot? Can you describe it?

2. Children and adults react differently to the balloon. In what ways? Why?

3. Why is the changing shape of the balloon "very pleasing"? What tendency in modern society makes the balloon the "rough draft" of a solution? Does the story's setting provide a clue?

4. Can you characterize the voice that tells the story? the person being addressed? Is the balloon a form of communication? If it is "a spontaneous autobiographical disclosure," what does it disclose about the narrator?

5. Is the balloon symbolic of something else? Is this story a satire? If so, of what? What evidence supports your answer?

JOHN UPDIKE

A & P

In walks these three girls in nothing but bathing suits. I'm in the third checkout slot, with my back to the door, so I don't see them until they're over by the bread. The one that caught my eye first was the one in the plaid green two-piece. She was a chunky kid, with a good tan and a sweet broad soft-looking can with those two crescents of white just under it, where the sun never seems to hit, at the top of the backs of her legs. I stood there with my hand on a box of HiHo crackers trying to remember if I rang it up or not. I ring it up again and the customer starts giving me hell. She's one of these cash-register-watchers, a witch about fifty with rouge on her cheekbones and no eyebrows, and I know it made her day to trip me up. She'd been watching cash registers for fifty years and probably never seen a mistake before.

By the time I got her feathers smoothed and her goodies into a bag — she gives me a little snort in passing, if she'd been born at the right time they would have burned her over in Salem — by the time I get her on her way the girls had circled around the bread and were coming back, without a pushcart, back my way along the counters, in the aisle between the checkouts and the Special bins. They didn't even have shoes on. There was this chunky one, with the two-piece — it was bright green and the seams on the bra were still sharp and her belly was still pretty pale so I guessed she just got it (the suit) — there was this one, with one of those chubby berry-faces, the lips all bunched together under her nose, this one, and a tall one, with black hair that hadn't quite frizzed right, and one of these sunburns right across under the eyes, and a chin that was too long — you know, the kind of girl other girls think is very "striking" and "attractive" but never quite makes it, as they very well know, which is why they like her so much — and then the third one, that wasn't quite so tall. She was the queen. She kind of led them, the other two peeking around and making their shoulders round. She didn't look around, not this queen, she just walked straight on slowly, on these long white primadonna legs. She came down a little hard on her heels, as if she didn't walk in bare feet that much, putting down her heels and then letting the weight move along to her toes as if she was testing the floor with every step, putting a little deliberate extra action into it. You never know for sure how girls' minds work (do you really think it's a mind in there or just a little buzz like a bee in a glass jar?) but you got the idea she had talked the other two into coming in here with her, and now she was showing them how to do it, walk slow and hold yourself straight.

She had on a kind of dirty-pink — beige maybe, I don't know — bathing suit with a little nubble all over it and, what got me, the straps were down. They were off her shoulders looped loose around the cool tops of her arms, and I guess as a result the suit had slipped a little on her, so all around the top of the cloth there was this shining rim. If it hadn't been there you wouldn't have known there could have been anything whiter than those shoulders. With the straps pushed off, there was nothing between the top of the suit and the top of her head except just *her*, this clean bare plane of the top of her chest down from the shoulder bones like a dented sheet of metal tilted in the light. I mean, it was more than pretty.

She had a sort of oaky hair that sun and salt had bleached, done up in a bun that was unravelling, and a kind of prim face. Walking into the A & P with your straps down, I suppose it's the only kind of face you *can* have. She held her head so high her neck, coming up out of those white shoulders, looked kind of stretched, but I didn't mind. The longer her neck was, the more of her there was.

She must have felt in the corner of her eye me and over my shoulder Stokesie in the second slot watching, but she didn't tip. Not this queen. She kept her eyes moving across the racks, and stopped, and turned so slow it made my stomach rub the inside of my apron, and buzzed to the other two, who kind of huddled against her for relief, and then they all three of them went up the cat-and-dog-food-breakfast-cereal-macaroni-rice-raisins-seasonings-spreads-spaghetti-soft-drinks-crackers-and-cookies aisle. From the third slot I look straight up this aisle to the meat counter, and I watched them all the way. The fat one with the tan sort of fumbled with the cookies, but on second thought she put the package back. The sheep pushing their carts down the aisle — the girls were walking against the usual traffic (not that we have one-way signs or anything) — were pretty hilarious. You could see them, when Queenie's white shoulders dawned on them, kind of jerk, or hop, or hiccup, but their eyes snapped back to their own baskets and on they pushed. I bet you could set off dynamite in an A & P and the people would by and large keep reaching and checking oatmeal off their lists and muttering "Let me see, there was a third thing, began with A, asparagus, no, ah, yes, applesauce!" or whatever it is they do mutter. But there was no doubt, this jiggled them. A few house-slaves in pin curlers even looked around after pushing their carts past to make sure what they had seen was correct.

You know, it's one thing to have a girl in a bathing suit down on the beach, where what with the glare nobody can look at each other much anyway, and another thing in the cool of the A & P, under the fluorescent lights, against all those stacked packages, with her feet paddling along naked over our checker-board green-and-cream rubber-tile floor.

"Oh Daddy," Stokesie said beside me. "I feel so faint."

"Darling," I said. "Hold me tight." Stokesie's married, with two babies chalked up on his fuselage already, but as far as I can tell that's the only difference. He's twenty-two, and I was nineteen this April.

"Is it done?" he asks, the responsible married man finding his voice. I forgot to say he thinks he's going to be manager some sunny day, maybe in 1990 when it's called the Great Alexandrov and Petrooshki Tea Company or something.

What he meant was, our town is five miles from a beach, with a big summer colony out on the Point, but we're right in the middle of town, and the women generally put on a shirt or shorts or something before they get out of the car into the street. And anyway these are usually women with six children and varicose veins mapping their legs and nobody, including them, could care less. As I say, we're right in the middle of town, and if you stand at our front doors you can see two banks and the Congregational church and the newspaper store and three real-estate offices and about twenty-seven old freeloaders tearing up Central Street because the sewer broke again. It's not as if we're on the Cape; we're north of Boston and there's people in this town haven't seen the ocean for twenty years.

The girls had reached the meat counter and were asking McMahon something. He pointed, they pointed, and they shuffled out of sight behind a pyramid of Diet Delight peaches. All that was left for us to see was old McMahon patting his mouth and looking after them sizing up their joints. Poor kids, I began to feel sorry for them, they couldn't help it.

Now here comes the sad part of the story, at least my family says it's sad, but I don't think it's so sad myself. The store's pretty empty, it being Thursday afternoon, so there was nothing much to do except lean on the register and wait for the girls to show up again. The whole store was like a pinball machine and I didn't know which tunnel they'd come out of. After a while they come around out of the far aisle, around the light bulbs, records at discount of the Caribbean Six or Tony Martin Sings or some such gunk you wonder they waste the wax on, six-packs of candy bars, and plastic toys done up in cellophane that fall apart when a kid looks at them anyway. Around they come, Queenie still leading the way, and holding a little gray jar in her hand. Slots Three through Seven are unmanned and I could see her wondering between Stokes and me, but Stokesie with his usual luck draws an old party in baggy gray pants who stumbles up with four giant cans of pineapple juice (what do these bums *do* with all that pineapple juice? I've often asked myself) so the girls come to me. Queenie puts down the jar and I take it into my fingers icy cold. Kingfish Fancy Herring Snacks in Pure Sour Cream: 49¢. Now her hands are empty, not a ring or a bracelet, bare as God made them, and I wonder where the money's coming from. Still with that prim look she lifts a folded dollar bill out of the hollow at the center of her nubbled pink top. The jar went heavy in my hand. Really, I thought that was so cute.

Then everybody's luck begins to run out. Lengel comes in from haggling with a truck full of cabbages on the lot and is about to scuttle into that door marked MANAGER behind which he hides all day when the girls touch his eye. Lengel's pretty dreary, teaches Sunday school and the rest, but he doesn't miss that much. He comes over and says, "Girls, this isn't the beach."

Queenie blushes, though maybe it's just a brush of sunburn I was noticing for the first time, now that she was so close. "My mother asked me to pick up a jar of herring snacks." Her voice kind of startled me, the way voices do when you see the people first, coming out so flat and dumb yet kind of tony, too, the way it ticked over "pick up" and "snacks." All of a sudden I slid right down her voice into her living room. Her father and the other men were standing around in ice-cream coats and bow ties and the women were in sandals picking up herring snacks on toothpicks off a big glass plate and they were all holding drinks the color of water with olives and sprigs of mint in them. When my parents have somebody over they get lemonade and if it's a real racy affair Schlitz in tall glasses with "They'll Do It Every Time" cartoons stencilled on.

"That's all right," Lengel said. "But this isn't the beach." His repeating this struck me as funny, as if it had just occurred to him, and he had been thinking all these years the A & P was a great big dune and he was the head lifeguard. He didn't like my smiling — as I say he doesn't miss much — but he concentrates on giving the girls that sad Sunday-school-superintendent stare.

Queenie's blush is no sunburn now, and the plump one in plaid, that I liked better from the back — a really sweet can — pipes up, "We weren't doing any shopping. We just came in for the one thing."

"That makes no difference," Lengel tells her, and I could see from the way his eyes went that he hadn't noticed she was wearing a two-piece before. "We want you decently dressed when you come in here."

"We *are* decent," Queenie says suddenly, her lower lip pushing, getting sore now that she remembers her place, a place from which the crowd that runs the A & P must look pretty crummy. Fancy Herring Snacks flashed in her very blue eyes.

"Girls, I don't want to argue with you. After this come in here with your shoulders covered. It's our policy." He turns his back. That's policy for you. Policy is what the kingpins want. What the others want is juvenile delinquency.

All this while, the customers had been showing up with their carts but, you know, sheep, seeing a scene, they had all bunched up on Stokesie, who shook open a paper bag as gently as peeling a peach, not wanting to miss a word. I could feel in the silence everybody getting nervous, most of all Lengel, who asks me, "Sammy, have you rung up their purchase?"

I thought and said "No" but it wasn't about that I was thinking. I go through the punches, 4, 9, GROC, TOT — it's more complicated than you think, and after you do it often enough, it begins to make a little song, that you hear words to, in my case "Hello (*bing*) there, you (*gung*) hap-py *pee*-pul (*splat*)!" — the *splat* being the drawer flying out. I uncrease the bill, tenderly as you may imagine, it just having come from between the two smoothest scoops of vanilla I had ever known there were, and pass a half and a penny into her narrow pink palm, and nestle the herrings in a bag and twist its neck and hand it over, all the time thinking.

The girls, and who'd blame them, are in a hurry to get out, so I say "I quit" to Lengel quick enough for them to hear, hoping they'll stop and watch me, their unsuspected hero. They keep right on going, into the electric eye; the door flies open and they flicker across the lot to their car, Queenie and Plaid and Big Tall Goony-Goony (not that as raw material she was so bad), leaving me with Lengel and a kink in his eyebrow.

"Did you say something, Sammy?"

"I said I quit."

"I thought you did."

"You didn't have to embarrass them."

"It was they who were embarrassing us."

I started to say something that came out "Fiddle-de-do." It's a saying of my grandmother's, and I know she would have been pleased.

"I don't think you know what you're saying," Lengel said.

"I know you don't," I said. "But I do." I pull the bow at the back of my apron and start shrugging it off my shoulders. A couple of customers that had been heading for my slot begin to knock against each other, like scared pigs in a chute.

Lengel sighs and begins to look very patient and old and gray. He's been a friend of my parents for years. "Sammy, you don't want to do this to your Mom and Dad," he tells me. It's true, I don't. But it seems to me that once you begin a gesture it's fatal not to go through with it. I fold the apron, "Sammy" stitched in red on the pocket, and put it on the counter, and drop the bow tie on top of it. The bow tie is theirs, if you've ever wondered. "You'll feel this for the rest of your life," Lengel says, and I know that's true, too, but remembering how he made that pretty girl blush makes me so scrunchy inside I punch the No Sale tab and the machine whirs "pee-pul" and the drawer splats out. One advantage to this scene taking place in summer, I can follow this up with a clean exit, there's no fumbling around getting your coat and galoshes, I just saunter into the electric eye in my white shirt that my mother ironed the night before, and the door heaves itself open, and outside the sunshine is skating around on the asphalt.

I look around for my girls, but they're gone, of course. There wasn't anybody but some young married screaming with her children about some candy they didn't get by the door of a powder-blue Falcon station wagon. Looking back in the big windows, over the bags of peat moss and aluminum lawn furniture stacked on the pavement, I could see Lengel in my place in the slot, checking the sheep through. His face was dark gray and his back stiff, as if he's just had an injection of iron, and my stomach kind of fell as I felt how hard the world was going to be to me hereafter.

QUESTIONS

1. Does the use of the present tense serve this story well? Does it tell us anything about the narrator?

2. What is Sammy's image of himself? What incidents, phrases, and tones define that image? Is he a comic figure? a sympathetic one?

3. Is Sammy's decision to quit a spur-of-the-moment one, or is it simply the last of a series of actions that he has been preparing for right along?

4. Is it a sense of justice or the attractive girl that brings him to stand up to Mr. Lengel? Are both motives present and related to one another?

5. What is Sammy's relationship to the world of adults? How does his quitting change that relationship? Is he right in feeling "how hard the world was going to be ... hereafter"?

6. Compare Sammy with another young, first-person narrator, say the young "swipe" in "I'm a Fool."

JOYCE CAROL OATES

The Going-Away Party

The summer after Marya's high school graduation, the summer of the going-away party, Emmett Schroeder began suddenly to say, We love each other, we should get married, shouldn't we get married? — in his low rapid faintly embarrassed voice that made Marya think uneasily that he was angry with her. We love each other, don't we? — we should get married, then.

It had the air of an argument, an old quarrel. We love each other, *we should get married.*

The surprise of Emmett's interest, the prevailing miracle of it, did not fail to astonish Marya. That Emmett Schroeder should want to get married. That Emmett Schroeder should want to marry *her.* (For Marya was a Knauer, after all. No matter how she prided herself on being different, superior. And she'd made a spectacle of herself — so it was generally thought — giving that spirited valedictory address at the high school, reciting a memorized speech in a quavering voice that, emblazoned with quotations from Thoreau and Emily Dickinson and Dostoyevsky and Teilhard de Chardin, left nearly everyone in the audience baffled and resentful. Marya Knauer! — so people murmured, disapproving, annoyed. Who does she think she is, putting on airs? — *talking like that in public?*)

Emmett Schroeder must have been as offended by that valedictory speech as anyone. For days afterward he didn't call and Marya thought wildly that she'd lost him — as she was always losing friends, this past year in particular. Everyone is proud of you, Marya, her teachers said, because she was the only senior in Innisfail to win a state merit scholarship (and a matching "need" scholarship from the State University at Port Oriskany), and she'd won four of the nine awards presented to graduating seniors at commencement; but Marya knew that wasn't true. Aloud she said, Thank you. Secretly she said, Like hell. They hate me, they're *jealous* of me.

(It was even suspected that one or two of the other academic awards really should have gone to Marya Knauer: there was no one in the class who came close to her academically, not even Robbie Ducharme who had been admitted to Cornell, not even Warren Maccabee who was so dull, so slow, so plodding, so unfailingly thorough, Marya's classmates naturally believed him superior to them all.)

A few days after the commencement speech — in fact it was five, Marya counted them — Emmett came by to see her. Without any explanation for having failed to call, without even a word of praise for her performance. If Marya's defiant speech on the "repellent" nature of American conformity had stirred him, or if it had angered him, or disappointed him, he never said; but then he was a fairly reticent person and his long silences often made Marya uneasy. What are you thinking about so hard, Marya sometimes asked, jabbing him playfully in the ribs, turning her nervousness into a joke (this had become such a habit with her, done with such high spirits and bravado, Marya never questioned what lay behind it), — are you angry with me? She would lean against him, make a show of feeling slighted, left out, hurt; if the circumstances were right she'd even kiss him, burrow her face against him as if they were lovers. And Emmett would laugh in exasperation and say, Marya, other people aren't like *you* — just because we're not talking it doesn't mean we're thinking secret thoughts.

So it astonished her that Emmett Schroeder should want to marry her. That he should say, with that air of subtle reproach that greatly flattered her: We love each other, we should get married, it's time to get married — isn't it?

Marya wondered if he could be serious. If he would really marry her. (What about his parents? — Mrs. Schroeder had never said an unkind word against Marya, so far as Marya knew, but she could judge by the woman's manner of greeting her — that prim little twisted smile — that she didn't like her at all.) Marya's Aunt Wilma said she didn't trust the Schroeders, and just the look of Emmett — taller than Marya by a good five inches, wide in the shoulders, with thick dark hair and broad Slavic cheekbones and a spare measured smile that cut through you like a knife (so Wilma complained) announcing I am better than you, my family has more money than you — just the look of him offended her. He'd been in the Marines and he was twenty-six years old (and Marya was only seventeen) and his father had built his construction business up out of nothing so naturally he was tightfisted and suspicious and wouldn't want a Knauer marrying into the family. ... So Wilma fussed, speculated aloud. And he isn't Catholic, Marya, she said (meanly, teasingly), — doesn't that make a difference?

But Marya refused to discuss Emmett with Wilma; she shrank from discussing certain volatile subjects with her in any case. You can't possibly have an opinion about him, she told Wilma. Not an *informed* opinion.

To Emmett she said nervously, But I'm starting college in September.

He was bemused, skeptical. But are you really? he said, smiling, as if he knew a secret Marya didn't know: she would never leave Innisfail any more than he would.

Faltering, vague, Marya protested that she *had* to go, didn't she? — she'd been awarded that scholarship, in fact two scholarships, she couldn't disappoint people. There had even been such a flattering piece in the newspaper. ...

Emmett told her she'd been saying that all summer. She really wanted to get married, she really wanted to stay in Innisfail, but she was afraid of making people angry with her — "disappointing" them was how she phrased it. And he went on to name, contemptuously, the names of various Innisfail teachers — a familiar litany he had long outgrown.

"You could turn those scholarships down and nobody would give a damn," he said. "They can't make you go anywhere if you don't want to."

"Emmett, I have to go, I can't back out," Marya whispered.

He closed his thumb and forefinger about her wrist, as he often did, in play. And then gave a little twist. Also in play: though it did hurt.

He said: "You don't have to go anywhere you don't *want* to, Marya."

Still, he wanted to drive her to Port Oriskany in early July, just after the holiday weekend, so that she could find a room for the fall, and a job of some kind. Marya didn't want to live in university housing if she could avoid it; she couldn't bear the thought of having a roommate — a stranger; some nights this past year her nerves were so raw, her pulses leapt with a startled urgency she couldn't define, she had to leave the bedroom she shared with Alice to sleep on the couch in the front room, or even on the porch. Her thoughts unusually sharp, her blood pulsing hot and sullen, she had a fantasy of wandering off into the scrub forest behind the car lot … losing herself in the foothills of the Chautauquas, or in the mountains themselves. She'd be alone then. Unobserved, unmonitored. With nobody picking at her or judging her or wanting to marry her.

"As soon as I leave home," Marya had been telling everyone during her senior year, " — I intend to begin a private life. I've had enough of crowds!"

She was boastful, vain, not entirely serious perhaps; she often said things simply to hear how the words struck the air, what sort of spin they had. How they affected others — forcing them to laugh, or to arch their eyebrows quizzically, even to ask her to repeat herself, they hadn't quite *understood*. (Marya had long ago seen that to be *liked* demanded a sort of maidenly passivity, a hopefulness, she had very little talent for; but to be *disliked*, — it was not only easier in many ways, but yielded a queer sort of pleasure.)

All this didn't mean, she protested, that she didn't love Emmett. She half-lay in his arms, her mouth pressed against his, for what seemed to be hours. His greedy clutching hands and his impatience with her were immensely flattering. If you love me, why don't you want to marry me? Emmett asked. As he had been asking, If you love me why don't you want to sleep with me … ?

Marya tried to tell him, I don't want to sleep with anyone.

She tried to tell him, I love you but I don't want to sleep with anyone. I don't *want* to.

But he didn't understand; he was hurt; and then again he was angry — one night, a week before he drove her to Port Oriskany (he insisted upon driving her, he didn't want her to take a Greyhound bus), he took her head in both hands and began to shake it up and down, and from side to side, as if he wanted to snap her neck. She'd been so frightened her knees had buckled; she couldn't even scream. She thought, My God, he's going to kill me and it will be my fault. …

Afterward Emmett said, flushed, ashamed, You don't want to lie to me, Marya. About loving me or not. Because I can't stand to be *lied* to. Do you understand?

On the drive to Port Oriskany, two-hundred-odd miles to the west, Emmett was good-natured, even husbandly. He was proud of his car, a new Buick, and he clearly enjoyed driving — the simple act of driving, pressing down hard on the accelerator, gripping the wheel tight, easing in and out of traffic, passing everyone he could manage, even trucks careening along at ten miles beyond the speed limit. Marya noted his air of authority, his satisfaction, his well-being. She was grateful for the fact that much of the time he wasn't aware of her at all (she could read a paperback book, she could scribble in her journal): except to ask her now and then to get him a beer from the back seat (if he couldn't have it chilled he'd drink it warm — he wasn't, as he said, fussy), or to tune the radio better, or to sit closer to him: so he didn't get to feeling he was alone. When rain drummed on the roof and windshield and the headlights of oncoming cars rushed at them out of the mist Emmett said, with a tenderness in his voice Marya hadn't heard often before, Isn't it nice in here … isn't it *safe*.

Marya lay against him, drowsily watching the highway. She hadn't been able to sleep very well the night before; there had been a number of nights that summer that she'd lain awake, her mind racing, thinking of the university, of Port Oriskany (which she had never even visited), of the fact that she would be only one of 15,000 students. … It was one thing to impress teachers in Innisfail, or to have struck the eye of, say, Clifford Shearing; it would be quite another thing to excel in so competitive a setting. If her grade-point average fell below a B for more than two semesters she would lose the merit scholarship. She hadn't any idea how difficult college would be, Port Oriskany in particular. ...

In any case she had Emmett. She loved him and she would probably marry him after a year or two at Port Oriskany. Her cousin Alice was going to be married in a few months and several of her classmates were already married and a number were engaged and. ... And so, why should Marya behave differently? It was a *coup* to have attracted Emmett Schroeder's attention, let alone his love; she would be an idiot to throw it away.

But she did want to leave Innisfail, at least for a year. She wanted to see what it was like, living away from home. At college. Where no one knew she was Marya Knauer, and no one could feel pity for her, or jealousy. Where she could begin again, give birth to herself (so Marya's lyricism soared, at such times) at the age of eighteen.

Three hours to Port Oriskany, in the rain; steady driving. And then three hours back that night. (Because Wilma wouldn't allow her to stay away overnight, and where could they have stayed but a motel? That's all we need next, Wilma said sourly, — to have people talking about you and him, and that bitch of a mother of his on the phone with *me*.) Marya loved Emmett as she lay close against him, her arm slipped through his, her fingers lazily squeezing his wrist; she loved him when they stopped at roadside cafés like any young married couple, sitting close together in booths, reading menus aloud, nudging each other, whispering private jokes, kissing. Marya's hair fell to her waist in glossy waves, a thick dark mane that looked black in some lights, chestnut-brown in others, and though she privately knew herself ugly her hair *was* beautiful. She allowed herself a measure of pride in it, reasoning that, though it was hers it wasn't *her*. When Emmett buried his face in it and inhaled deeply, clowning, snorting like a horse, yet genuinely moved to admiration, Marya thought that he was right, he was justified in loving her and in wanting to be her husband; and his desire for her (of which she was much aware) had the power to make her desire him. *We love each other, we should get married.*

But sometimes the country-and-western songs Emmett liked to play on the radio grated against her nerves, and the places he stopped at, and the food he ordered. ... Marya particularly found fault with the food, cole slaw doused in sugar, french fries dripping in grease: as Emmett said, you'd think from the way she criticized restaurants she ate in them all the time.

"I'm not criticizing anything," Marya protested in surprise, "I'm just pointing out what's wrong. ..."

The city of Port Oriskany was so large, the university campus so sprawled and confusing, Emmett himself became intimidated. He was forced to stop at gas stations and ask directions: Marya saw that he was badly discomfited, having to ask directions. But he managed to make his way along the hilly one-way streets, stopping at houses that advertised rooms, boarding, rates-for-students, until Marya found something that was suitable (her first question was invariably, How much?); he managed to cheer her up when she became, by early afternoon, inexplicably depressed (Come *on*, this isn't anything, you should have seen what they did to me in the Marines). When Marya stood at a long dirt-encrusted counter in the university's employment office filling out a job application, she stopped midway and looked back at Emmett, slouched against the wall, smoking a cigarette, his hands in the pockets of his jeans — handsome Emmett Schroeder, the most remarkable of her prizes — and she had two thoughts simultaneously: the first, that she really should rip the application in two, and return to Innisfail, and marry Emmett (who, tired and sullen and faintly contemptuous, would brighten into a smile if he saw her watching him); the second, that she was through with Emmett, and when she signed her name at the bottom of the form she was signing herself away from him. There, she thought, signing *Marya Knauer* with unusual clarity, — that's done.

And then the ride back home. In the dark, in the slow drizzling rain. Stopping again for supper — spaghetti and meatballs, beer, black coffee; and, in the car, in the dim-lit parking lot, easing into their familiar embrace, not minding that Emmett's hard mouth hurt hers, or that his fingers clutched impatiently, almost angrily, at her, working beneath her clothing as his breathing grew hoarse and tight. She told herself. All right. And tried not to resist. Except to stiffen involuntarily as she always did, when his breath was nearly a sob, and she felt he might break her neck or her backbone in his passion — it was so blunt, so direct, so desperate. All right, she whispered, her teeth nearly chattering with fear, I love you, Emmett I love you, — though a part of her mind wanted to rear away and laugh contemptuously: Why are you doing this? Who do you think you're deceiving?

Emmett sensed her apprehension, he might even have sensed that hard mocking voice. He moved away from her; though his face was slick with perspiration and there were grim lines running from his nostrils to the edges of his mouth, he looked down at her nevertheless with an expression of impenetrable dignity, and said, "All right then, *you* — go to hell."

He drove the rest of the way to Innisfail without speaking. Marya began to cry. I love you, you know I love you, she whispered guiltily, but Emmett didn't trouble to reply, perhaps didn't even hear. He had worked the Buick up to seventy-five, seventy-eight, eighty miles an hour along a curving highway, slowing only when walls of fog drifted across the road. "Emmett please, I'm sorry, I can't help it," Marya said almost inaudibly, "I get so nervous, you know how I am ... but you know I love you," while a part of her thought calmly: There, that's done.

By midsummer Marya's insomnia kept her awake through much of the night, night following night; she swayed and staggered through the days, her eyes bruised, her head aching. Everyone thought it was because she and Emmett had broken up ("'Broken up'?" Wilma asked, pretending to take it casually, " — was it your doing finally, or his?") but in fact it seemed to be because of Port Oriskany and what was coming in the fall: the steep narrow streets, the unfamiliar buildings; whether, with no one from home to observe, she would finally stop attending mass; whether she would do as well there as everyone expected. If I fail I'm not coming home, she told herself; then again, a moment later, — if I fail I could telephone Emmett and he'd come and get me, I know he'd come and get me.

But she wouldn't call him. And, in any case, he wouldn't have come.

He had loved her; but now, it seemed, he hated her. He really did hate her.

Bonnie Michalak dropped by at the law office where Marya worked that summer to ask her, with a cruel little half-smile of bewilderment, What on earth happened to you and Emmett ... ? And Erma Dietz, now Erma Frank, married six weeks and at least three months pregnant, caught at Marya's sleeve in Woolworth's, and said in a soft pitying voice that made Marya want to jerk angrily away, I think it's such a shame about you and Emmett, Ron was telling me he's going out now with someone from Mt. Horne ... It's such a *shame*, Marya, God damn it, why did you let it happen?

Marya muttered an inaudible reply.

Erma stared at her, blinking. Since the pregnancy, since the marriage, she was prettier than ever: shorter than Marya by three or four inches, with a doll's porcelain-perfect face and a small snubbed nose and eyes so beautifully lashed they looked almost unreal. They had never exactly been friends but now they were certainly not friends and Marya couldn't even bring herself to smile, to behave nicely.

What? — I didn't hear, Erma said.

I said it isn't your problem, Marya told her, swallowing, — you don't have to concern yourself with it.

Erma stared a moment longer, then said, You don't have to be so sarcastic, Marya.

You don't have to be so *concerned*, Marya said at once.

— Though maybe you can't help yourself. Maybe that's the problem, Erma said, turning away.

After the drive to Port Oriskany Marya went out with Emmett only once, on a Sunday afternoon. They were headed for Wolf's Head Lake but never got there. Marya wept tears of a kind she'd vowed as a young girl she would never weep, and apologized, and tried again to explain that she *did* love him. ... "You can say that I wanted to get married and you didn't," she said wildly, "you can say it's your choice if we don't see each other," and Emmett braked the car to a stop, furious, trembling, and said, "Do you think I care about *that*, is that how you think of me? — I'd care about something like *that*?"

She saw how she had misjudged him, how stupid she was, how finally unworthy of his agitation. But how could she extricate herself from this, how could she escape? — September was so far off.

"Anyway, nobody's going to ask me anything," Emmett said. "They know better."

Marya knew that her primary weakness, her primary sin, was being sarcastic: that penchant for irony (for being a "smart aleck," others would have said) that lost her so many friends. (Your mouth is going to get you into real trouble someday, Wilma was always warning, and her very grimness made Marya want to laugh. She said airily, provocatively, Oh hell, it already *has*, but here I am, see? — still breathing.)

Still, she was cautious around boys; she'd always been cautious around boys. Her cousin Lee, after all. ...

And certain things that had taken place at the country school, down by the canal, along the towpath. ...

Over the years, when she knew herself safe (in Innisfail, in the presence of adults, in the company of *men* rather than *boys*), Marya had developed a rather defiant and stylized flirtatiousness. It was nothing at all like her old manner with Father Shearing — she had never been so crude as to "flirt" with him; she would have been appalled at the very thought. Instead it was arch, vaguely theatrical, cinematic? — she performed and others watched. She was on stage, so to speak, illuminated by their attention; they were *forced* to watch. At first, at the age of twelve or thirteen, she couldn't have known exactly what she was risking (trading witticisms with strangers, exchanging "knowing" looks with sailors, parading about with her girl friends in tight-fitting jeans and sweaters, her thick hair swinging loose and wild about her shoulders); afterward it all became conscious, subtly nuanced, as if she were on film, protected by the very barrier of film, seen and admired by men but in no way obliged to see and admire them in turn. It was intensely exciting, exhilarating. It made her a little drunk, displaying herself like this. The entire adventure, even its incalculable risk, could be summed up crudely enough: it was all marvelous *fun*.

A few years later, when she began to go out occasionally with boys from school, she found herself painfully stiff and self-conscious in their presence. They knew her, after all; they knew who she was and where she'd come from. ... How idiotic they are, how stupid and predictable, Marya complained to her friends, the things they do, the things they *try* to do.

Marya was capable of imitating several boys in her class so cruelly and so hilariously that her little audience broke into peals of helpless gasping laughter. Oh Marya stop! — they cried, mildly scandalized. Oh Marya aren't you *awful*!

(*Isn't* Marya Knauer awful, they said, shaking their heads. She said things they would never have dared say; she phrased her jokes in ways they could never have invented for themselves. Just as, years before, she'd learned to fling back into the faces of the cruder boys those words — those "dirty words" — they would never have uttered in such company, because they hoped to be thought good, and not "dirty" themselves.)

Being *good*, Marya thought, wasn't a problem she had to worry about.

Of course she hadn't ever mocked Emmett Schroeder.

In the beginning she had pursued him. She'd been cunning, plotting, even a little desperate. Falling in love — "romance" of one kind or another — behaving like all the other girls: these were things Marya hadn't much wished to experience, being proud, and, in any case, uncertain of her skills. It was easier to be disliked than to be liked, after all — she'd known that all her life.

Her "feeling" for boys, for men, was largely a matter of day-dreaming. If she fastened upon a boy in school, he was never so interesting in person as he seemed in her head, in her wild floundering imagination. If she tried to write a story or a sketch about love (but what, she wondered, is "love"?) it was invariably flat and dull and could not sustain her interest. Though she was no longer a really conscientious Catholic — she couldn't imagine, for instance, that God greatly cared whether her thoughts were "impure" or that she ate meat on Fridays — she felt nonetheless a vague sense of shame, even of anger, when her thoughts moved onto sexual subjects; when she couldn't control the impulses of her body. (You're getting like a bitch in heat, she told herself in disgust, — a monkey in estrus: "estrus" being a word newly acquired in biology class.) While she assuredly didn't want to be good, or nice, or sweet, or ladylike, her repugnance for any display of weakness was equally strong. And falling in love, whether with film actors or "real" men, struck her as supremely weak.

Still, there were boys who excited her beyond her capacity to control. There were boys — "men," really — who made all her solemn admonitions seem beside the point.

She fell in love with Emmett Schroeder one hot September day, and pursued him, and plotted to get him, with an anguished stubbornness that was new to her. Emmett was the older brother of a girl at school named Lori, a pretty, popular, but not especially bright girl who'd never liked Marya. (After she began seeing Emmett, however, and asked him cautiously about his sister — "Why does she always avoid me, why doesn't she *smile* at me the way she does at everyone else" — Emmett said it was only because she didn't think Marya liked *her*; she didn't think Marya liked anyone.)

In the company of a boisterous half-drunken group at a Labor Day picnic at Wolf's Head Lake, Marya, slightly high, was bold enough to make her way over to Emmett Schroeder (who was in another party, who'd come to the lake with friends of his own) because someone had talked her into drinking several cans of beer, and because the narrow spotted mirror in the women's bathhouse had given back to her, unanticipated, an image of Marya that had struck her as ... beautiful? ... miraculous? She had stood for several long minutes in a shaft of sunlight, staring hungrily at her reflection, brushing her hair in slow hard measured strokes. It was amazing, it was hypnotic: those eyes: that mouth: was she to be, after all, *beautiful*? — and not *ugly*? Or was it only a trick of the sunshine, or of the dingy mirror? (Ordinarily she was shy of mirrors, as she was of being photographed. The person others evidently saw as "Marya" wasn't a person she recognized. She wasn't sour, sullen, frightened, suspicious; she didn't care to identify with a girl whose eyes were so frequently ringed in shadow, and whose mouth looked so narrow and ungiving. She *knew* she was light-hearted, cheerful, funny; after all, wasn't she always making jokes? — weren't people always laughing?)

In the bathhouse she felt suffused with power, elation, a sense of certainty. Yes. Today. This afternoon. Emmett Schroeder. She wasn't drunk — she told herself she hadn't had half as much to drink as Bonnie Michalak — but she felt an unaccustomed springiness to her step, and a tension in her leg muscles that wasn't at all unpleasant. She wanted to dance about, she wanted to sing as loudly as she could. Her scalp, her head, tingled with life from the hard brushing she'd given her hair. Her eyes shone flirtatiously. Ah, is *that* Marya! Marya who lives out the Canal Road! And her hair, that lovely hair which even Wilma conceded was beautiful: it fell in thick glossy rippling waves across her tanned shoulders and back, down to her waist, Indian-black in this light, shot with chestnut glints. ...

So she assessed herself, the hairbrush raised. And thought, — I will make him notice me: I will *make* him like me.

From the lake they drove in several cars to the Whitefish Tavern north of the reservoir, and Marya, pushy Marya, managed to sit beside Emmett Schroeder, no matter that he'd made no effort to sit beside *her*. (You didn't care for me at first, did you, she asked afterward, — that night at Wolf's Head Lake, for instance; but Emmett didn't remember, or pretended not to. You wouldn't even *look* at me, at first, she said, exulting now in her triumph.) In the car she noted covertly the darkly tanned skin that stretched tight across his wide, flat cheekbones; she stared in fascination at his muscular arms, thickly haired, tanned almost black. (Emmett worked as a laborer for his father all summer long. He would be going into the construction business with him but his father was determined to make him earn every penny he was paid.) Emmett was physically large, yet graceful — more graceful, she thought, than she was herself — but his largeness, his expansiveness, had more to do with an attitude: his sense of himself as superior — superior to his environment, superior to most of his friends. Quickly Marya saw that he saw himself as superior to *her*; and fell in love with him that night.

A few months later, when they were seeing each other fairly steadily, sometimes alone and sometimes in the company of others, Emmett told her one evening that she didn't have to — well, *try* so hard.

Marya was stunned, wounded. What do you mean, she said, faltering, — "try so hard?"

You don't have to entertain people all the time, Emmett said awkwardly, stroking her hair. You know — say smart things, funny things. Make them laugh.

I don't *try*, Marya said quickly and falsely.

Emmett must have seen that he'd hurt her so he changed the subject. He stopped talking altogether — burrowed his face in her hair, ran his hard deft fingers up and down her sides, tickling her, making her laugh wildly, squirm like an eel. She could be reduced to a squealing gasping infant, Marya could, if you knew how to go about it. If you didn't go too far.

Sometimes they lay together in Emmett's car, kissing drowsily, talking of Emmett's concerns — he wanted more money from his father or he was going to leave home, get a job somewhere else; he was beginning to find his friends boring, and a waste of time, but he hadn't any others — How do you make friends, he wondered, after high school? At such times Marya exulted in her very anonymity; her invisibility. She murmured replies, gave advice, consoled him, agreed with him, sympathized with him. At such times he didn't see her — he wasn't judging her, assessing her. She needn't be bright and quick and ruthless, performing as if she were in a movie, she need only relax against him, and allow him to kiss her, and caress her, and explain himself to her, and continue his repetitious arguments with others — his father, his friends — by way of her. Would marriage be much different, she wondered, much more of a task? — it was so easy, after all, to be accommodating. It almost felt natural.

She tried not to mind that he was seeing another girl, or girls, at this time; she told herself — so cold, so calculating was she, even at the age of seventeen — that it took pressure off *her*, if he was able to sleep with *them*.

One night he said something terrible, something casual and terrible, which Marya was never to forget: he told her he wouldn't have asked her out if he had known her age, how much younger she was than he. After all he might get into trouble, there was her uncle Everard, her brother — cousin? — Lee; he didn't want to get mixed up with *them*.

But Marya looked, he said, older than seventeen. Nineteen, he would have guessed, at least. Maybe twenty. She *looked*, he said, half-smiling, not sensing how he was insulting her, — she *looked*, well, as if she'd been around.

*   *   *

"A going-away party? For you?" Wilma said.

"For Clarence Michalak and me, not just for *me*," Marya said, slightly embarrassed. "He's going into the army."

"It's the night before you leave?"

"Well — I can have everything packed and ready. I won't really be taking much," Marya said.

"Is Emmett going to be there?"

"How do I know if Emmett is going to be there! — You're asking too many questions."

"I thought the two of you weren't speaking."

"I'm not *not* speaking to him."

"I didn't think you ran around with Lester and Kyle and Bonnie and that gang any more," Wilma said. "That bunch of smart alecks. I *thought* you told me — "

"Anyway," Marya interrupted, "they're giving a party out at the lake. So I'll be going out that night."

"And you expect to get up early the next morning?"

"Of course I'll get up early the next morning," Marya said impatiently. "I'll take the nine-thirty bus, I'll get there by one o'clock, the first meeting, or whatever it is, isn't until four that afternoon. ..."

"Don't you talk smart to me, you."

"I'm not *talking smart*, I'm just telling you."

"Running around with that gang, drinking beer and getting in trouble, that loudmouth Lester Hughey — "

"It isn't just Lester, it's Erma and Ron too, and Annie, and probably Eulalie Steadman, and Jinny Dietz, and I asked them to invite Warren Maccabee and Ronnie Ducharme, you know they're going away too — "

"You needn't talk so loud, Marya. I can hear you perfectly well."

"I'm not talking loud," Marya said, feeling her face go hot. "But you just don't *listen*."

"You're all excited because they're giving a party for you, and so you can't help sticking your nose up around here. And it's all you can do, isn't it, to stay home one night of the week," Wilma said. She turned away from Marya, fixing her hair at the back of her head — she'd gathered it up in a limp pony tail, secured by a rubber band. Her nails had been polished a few days ago and the bright pink polish had begun to chip. "Why don't you move out right now, move to Port Oriskany? — I know you'd like to — you and your high-class scholarship! As if anybody's begging you to stay!"

Ordinarily Marya would have answered her back, her blood leapt at the prospect of a fight, but for some reason she didn't have the heart, this afternoon: she stifled a sob, pressed her hands over her ears, ran out of the kitchen and let the screen door slam behind her. She might have been a small child again — it might have been years ago.

"*As if anybody's begging you to stay!*" Wilma shouted after her.

The day of the party Marya shampooed her hair and let it dry in the afternoon sun, spread out about her on a blanket in the side yard. She observed with satisfaction her long smooth tanned legs and arms, she'd examined her image in the mirror a dozen times: How will she reply to Emmett if he greets her? How will she raise her eyes to his?

Marya told herself that she wasn't going to be embarrassed in front of Emmett; she wouldn't give him that much power over her.

But as it turned out Emmett spent only an hour or so at the party, and he was in the company of a young woman Marya didn't know — high-piled blond hair bleached bone-white, a black halter top that barely restrained her large pale breasts, a sweetly shrill drunken giggle. She splashed about the shore, her skirt tucked up around her thighs, calling to Bob and Kyle out on the float, while Emmett stood a few yards away smoking a cigarette, looking bored. He hadn't brought along a swimming suit — wore jeans and a pull-over shirt, an old stretched shirt Marya remembered well. His skin looked as if it had been dyed a rich mahogany color; his hair was growing long, curling over his collar. When he smiled at Marya — his smile quick as a snake's tongue — she felt her heart trip absurdly; but she managed to greet him in the very same way. No display of embarrassment, chagrin, regret.

We love each other, we should get married. ...

Sure, thought Marya.

Shit, thought Marya.

Marya rode out to the lake with Bonnie and her fiancé Fred and for a while she stayed in their company, saying very little, drinking beer and trying to listen — pretending to listen — to the conversations about her. She must have looked distinctly unhappy because Bonnie muttered in her ear that *she* thought it was rude of Emmett to bring that girl — nobody knew who she was and nobody cared.

Marya turned uneasily away. "*I* don't care," she said, almost inaudibly.

"Emmett never said he was going to bring anybody at all," Bonnie complained. She was watching Marya closely.

So this was the going-away party! — Marya saw almost with satisfaction that it was a mistake; a blunder; beyond even disappointment. *These* people — what did she care for them, what did they care for her? — did they even know her? The gathering was only another end-of-summer picnic, another drunken beer-bash as Wilma would say, loud music blaring from a plastic radio, loud oafish voices, laughter. ... Marya recalled a biology class of two or three years before when she'd been moved almost to tears as their teacher explained the principle of human reproduction: the miracle (for it *was* a miracle, an authentic miracle) by which a single egg and a single sperm fused; and formed a single cell; and the cell divided itself in two ... and then in four ... and then in eight ... and so on to infinity. At a certain stage cells emerged for certain parts of the human body so that the living protoplasm became *human*: now it would have a human brain, for instance. Where does that come from, Marya asked their teacher, — I mean *that, that* cell, how does it know to be a brain? — How does it know ahead of time to be a brain? Her classmates were yawning, or doodling, or pretending to listen; or, like Kyle Roemischer at the rear of the room, whispering smutty jokes. (You want to know where it comes from, Marya, they laughed afterward in the hall, — y'want to see?) Their teacher acknowledged the fact that no one knew; no one had the faintest idea. Marya was struck dumb by the idea that out of nowhere, suddenly, the human essence appeared ... the brain, the soul ... the personality. Why does that cell form when it does, Marya wanted to know, but knew that she wouldn't ever know: it was one of those things.

And at the rear of the room the boys telling their dirty stories, scarcely listening. "It's just one of those things, Marya," their teacher told her after class. He seemed halfway embarrassed at her sudden intense interest — as if he'd started something, provoked a response, he hadn't at all intended. "All we know is *what* it does, we don't know exactly *how* ... and we certainly don't know *why*," he said.

"Yes," said Marya, frowning, her nose twitching, " — but *why?*"

Here is Marya Knauer, valedictorian of the class, Marya in her red checked cotton dress with the low back, showing her long smooth tanned back and shoulders, her tanned arms. Marya drinking beer out of a can like the boys, throwing her head back to laugh helplessly at one of Lester Hughey's crude jokes; feeling with spiteful satisfaction the heavy warm weight of her hair down her back. The boys are crowding around her, she's really quite popular despite the fact that *she's* going away and *they're* staying (at least for the time being, they explain: eventually they'll all follow Clarence into the army, or Lee Knauer into the Navy, or, if they're men enough, they'll try for the Marines like Emmett Schroeder), despite the fact that they've always been a little wary of her razorish wit. Marya is leaving for Port Oriskany in the morning, Kyle is going to drive her to the Greyhound bus station, they're joking about maybe Marya won't have to go home at all ... just go directly from the lake to the bus station ...

Aren't her friends going to miss her! Marya thinks. Oh yes aren't they!

She is watching Emmett and the blond girl (she's a beautician in Yewville, only early twenties but already divorced), watching them walk away, Emmett's hand lightly resting at the nape of her neck, the two of them talking (about what?), leaving the party without saying goodbye to Marya, but that isn't important — Marya thinks: It isn't important at all, we've already said goodbye.

Hell, says Marya under her breath, turning brightly away, — it *isn't* important.

Afterward, she won't remember clearly all that happened.

Static-y rock music from Kyle's transistor radio. Mosquitoes biting, big soft amazing swellings on the back of Marya's thighs, her upper arms. Scratching until the blood comes: God *damn* it, what does she care, the bites are itching like crazy and anyway her dress is red, bloodspots won't show. Beer and ale; potato chips; cold greasy chicken parts devoured by hand, and the unwanted parts — wings, necks — thrown at anyone who isn't on guard. The boys are rowdy, crashing about in a game of touch football gone slightly askew (they *are* touching, they're even shoving and bumping), shouting words meant to be funny, friendly — ugly words — cocksucker, bullshit, fuck-face, jerk-off, cunt — until Kyle runs into Bob Bannerman deliberately, crouched low so that his shoulder rams Bob's stomach, and the game is over. Lester Hughey dumps a Styrofoam container of potato salad on the ground. I'm not going to eat this shit, he says, it doesn't taste like anything, it tastes like *shit*. So Erma Dietz is angry because she made the potato salad: Erma Frank, that is: and now she and Ron are leaving and she takes Marya aside, pinching her arm, saying, *You*, you'd better come with us, Marya, half-chiding, as if she was Marya's big sister or something, as if she was Wilma in fact, and Marya says no, *she's* having too good a time.

Anyway — she's supposed to ride back with Bonnie and Fred. Unless they've already left.

Next, some confusion about a watermelon — some craziness — smashing it and scooping up handfuls of the watery pulpy flesh and throwing it at one another. The hilarity of seeds stuck in Bob Bannerman's spiky hair.

Eulalie's boyfriend, a tall skeletal silent boy from Kincardine who drives a Harley-

Davidson and is very much envied by the Innisfail crowd, takes offense for some reason: shoves Lester Hughey backward: and when Eulalie tries to calm him down (pulling at his arm, giggling, acting as if somehow *she* might be to blame) he strikes her across the chest with a sweep of his arm, hard. Then suddenly it is over and Eulalie and the boy are driving away. An earsplitting roar as the motorcycle revs up, tires churning in the gravel. ...

What time is it? — Marya is hiding behind a tree, trying desperately to vomit. She gags and gags — feels her very eyeballs straining with the pressure — but nothing comes up.

Then finally it does. Splashing on the gnarled roots of the old tree, splashing onto her feet and ankles.

Marya, Marya! they are calling.

Raindrops strike the lake hard, like pebbles. It's queer, the rippling and swaying rhythm. A wall of raindrops rushes upon the mild waves of the lake, peppering the waves, so that it looks like machine-gun bullets. Marya runs barefoot along the beach and seems not to mind that a splinter of glass has cut her toe. It's her big toe, she reasons, hilarious as always, — it has lots of blood to lose.

That liar Bonnie, Marya complains to the boys, she said she wasn't in any hurry to leave, now she and what's-his-name are gone —

Oh that fuck-face, don't give a shit about *him*, honey, Lester says.

I *don't*. Or Bonnie either. But she promised me a ride home and —

It isn't time yet for anybody to go home, Bob Bannerman says.

Someone has opened the trunk of Lester's car, and now the boys are fooling around with tools: a hammer, a monkey wrench, a clipping shears, a coil of wire, a box of spikes. What the hell are you doing! Lester screams. That stuff's my brother's! That stuff's my fucking brother's, he'll knock the shit out of me!

Nobody's hurting *anything*, for Christ's sake, Kyle says laughing, — don't piss your pants or anything —

One of the boys is trying to hammer a spike into the top of a picnic table but the blows are so hard the tabletop splits.

Marya, they are calling, where's Marya? — she has run into the girls' bathhouse to be sick. Vomiting into one of the toilets, leaning against the wooden seat. Oh dear God the stench is almost unbearable.

Where's fuck-face Marya?

Ain't-I-hot-shit Marya! — where's she hiding?

Suddenly lights shine through the trees — red lights, revolving swiftly — the state troopers, it must be — so they scramble off in a panic, running to the cars, but Lester has to gather up his brother's tools and in the commotion Kyle's transistor radio is knocked to the ground (or is it thrown down? — it's so badly damaged, Kyle discovers afterward) — and a tall leggy beery-breathed boy named Jerry, from Mt. Horne, is dragging Marya along saying, C'mon, c'mon honey! c'mon! no matter that the gravel in the parking lot hurts her bare feet and she's whimpering in pain.

Then the lights are gone. Maybe they hadn't ever been there — maybe somebody was playing a trick on them —

Hey you guys listen, the fucking po-lice, y'know what they do: turn their lights off! — turn their siren off! Lester whispers. Then they wait for you and get you!

They wait, crouched and panting. Marya's breath comes in desperate gasps, her head is ringing, swaying. If it wasn't for someone holding her up she'd fall forward into the weeds. And the mosquitoes, the mosquitoes ... she feels them biting at a distance ... at a great distance ... but can't stop them. Dear God one side of her face is swollen, how will she look tomorrow morning. ...

There's *nobody* there, Bob Bannerman says angrily.

The stand of pine is perfectly silent except for the wind, and the raindrops falling heavily.

What time is it, someone asks, — the park closes at twelve.

The hell it does! This is a free country!

This is a fucking free country!

What happened to the police? Kyle asks wonderingly. You think it was a helicopter or something?

I didn't see any lights.

They were right there, *I* saw them.

Well — are we going or not? Is there any beer left?

A flying saucer, maybe it was a flying saucer: Kyle's such an asshole he wouldn't know a flying saucer if he saw one!

There *wasn't* anything there, you cocksucker.

Them lights — them red lights that go around — You saw them, Marya, didn't you?

Marya shakes her head to get it clear. But she isn't quick enough, she can't manage to speak.

Marya wants to go home, one of the boys says.

Marya's sick, she smells like puke.

Has to get up early, don't you?

Going to Port Oriskany, huh? To college?

Got a scholarship — !

I-got-a-scholarship!

Ain't-I-hot-shit!

Hey Marya where're you going —

Marya is running across the empty parking lot, whimpering. One of the straps of her red dress has broken, she doesn't remember when.

Marya nobody's going to hurt you —

Hey Marya, one of the boys laughed, there's nothing down *that* way —

She's looking for Emmett! — big-deal hot-shit Schroeder!

Schroeder and his fancy Buick prick!

Lester Hughey, or is it Kyle Roemischer — or the boy from Mt. Horne — jumps whooping upon her. Bob Bannerman — she knows it is Bob, she can smell him — comes running up, panting, his shirt flapping open, his chest gleaming pale behind curly kinky black hairs. He's rubbing his hands together in imitation of the principal on assembly days. Well now what have we here, let's just see what we have *here,* boys and girls quiet down let's just *see —*

Marya fights them but she doesn't scream.

She doesn't scream, she knows enough not to waste her breath; not to tire herself out. On the basketball court, playing girls' softball — keep your mouth shut, don't breathe through your mouth —

Marya fights them, scrambling at the edge of the parking lot, half-naked, sobbing, panting, striking at them with her fist, trying to kick them in the groin. She knows, Marya does, how to fight. But they're whooping and laughing and shouting, Easy does it! Hey, easy does it!

Nobody's going to hurt you, Marya —

For Christ's fucking sake —

She strikes one of them in the throat. Kicks and kicks, wild, frantic, still not screaming, not screaming aloud, until one of them catches her by the ankle, yanks her off her feet.

Hooting with laughter: but is it Stan's voice rising, furious? — She's crazy! You better let her go! The fuck-face ugly bitch!

Grappling in the mud. The harsh raindrops still falling, pelting. Her breasts, terribly bare: exposed: helpless. Her hair in her eyes, in her mouth. She's choking. Someone sits on her stomach, holding her chin in his hand, shaking her head from side to side. Who the hell do you think you're kicking, fuck-face! Who the hell do you think you *are*!

She remembers, afterward, one of them prying her legs apart — she remembers him prodding and jabbing at her — trying to enter her — trying to force his penis in her — but she might have squirmed free, arching her back, or one of the others hauled him away — and then Lester Hughey — it *was* Lester — scrambled over her with the shears chortling Clippety-clippety-clip! — take care not to hurt yourself, sweetheart! He gripped her in an embrace, his forearm around her neck, and still she threw herself from side to side, and the shears' blades stabbed at her cheek, narrowly missed an eye, and the boys were all shouting That's it, that's it, you got her, that's it, and panting grunting Lester brought the blades of the shears up against the nape of her neck, as close to her skull as he could manage, and began cutting.

QUESTIONS

1. What is Marya Knauer's relationship to the rest of the community? Does she assess it accurately? Does she understand her own character?

2. What makes Emmett Schroeder different from Marya's classmates? Does it seem a matter of character or of experience? What does Emmett's behavior on the trip to Port Oriskany tell you about him?

3. In this story, there are several shifts of time, mainly occurring when Marya recalls incidents in her past. Are these flashbacks intended to characterize Marya or to provide necessary background information? Would the plot line be clearer if the author had maintained a strictly chronological order?

4. Most of the story is told in the past tense, but the author switches to the historical present tense halfway through the party. What is the effect of this shift? of the profanity and obscenity that follows?

5. Is the final act of assault, the hacking of Marya's hair, foreshadowed earlier in the story? Has Marya's hair become a symbol? If so, of what?

6. The story ends on a note of cruelty and violence. What is your emotional response? Do you come away feeling that this is only an ugly incident in a character's life or that the author has expressed a settled view of human nature?

TONI CADE BAMBARA

Raymond's Run

I don't have much work to do around the house like some girls. My mother does that. And I don't have to earn my pocket money by hustling; George runs errands for the big boys and sells Christmas cards. And anything else that's got to get done, my father does. All I have to do in life is mind my brother Raymond, which is enough.

Sometimes I slip and say my little brother Raymond. But as any fool can see he's much bigger and he's older too. But a lot of people call him my little brother cause he needs looking after cause he's not quite right. And a lot of smart mouths got lots to say about that too, especially when George was minding him. But now, if anybody has anything to say to Raymond, anything to say about his big head, they have to come by me. And I don't play the dozens[1] or believe in standing around with somebody in my face doing a lot of talking. I much rather just knock you down and take my chances even if I am a little girl with skinny arms and a squeaky voice, which is how I got the name Squeaky. And if things get too rough, I run. And as anybody can tell you, I'm the fastest thing on two feet.

There is no track meet that I don't win the first-place medal. I used to win the twenty-yard dash when I was a little kid in kindergarten. Nowadays, it's the fifty-yard dash. And tomorrow I'm subject to run the quarter-meter relay all by myself and come in first, second, and third. The big kids call me Mercury cause I'm the swiftest thing in the neighborhood. Everybody knows that — except two people who know better, my father and me. He can beat me to Amsterdam Avenue with me having a two-fire-hydrant head start and him running with his hands in his pockets and whistling. But that's private information. Cause can you imagine some thirty-five-year-old man stuffing himself into PAL[2] shorts to race little kids? So as far as everyone's concerned, I'm the fastest and that goes for Gretchen, too, who has put out the tale that she is going to win the first-place medal this year. Ridiculous. In the second place, she's got short legs. In the third place, she's got freckles. In the first place, no one can beat me and that's all there is to it.

I'm standing on the corner admiring the weather and about to take a stroll down Broadway so I can practice my breathing exercises, and I've got Raymond walking on the

---

[1] A street game that consists of exchanging rhythmic insults (referring, usually, to ancestry and parentage).

[2] Police Athletic League.

inside close to the buildings, cause he's subject to fits of fantasy and starts thinking he's a circus performer and that the curb is a tightrope strung high in the air. And sometimes after a rain he likes to step down off his tightrope right into the gutter and slosh around getting his shoes and cuffs wet. Then I get hit when I get home. Or sometimes if you don't watch him he'll dash across traffic to the island in the middle of Broadway and give the pigeons a fit. Then I have to go behind him apologizing to all the old people sitting around trying to get some sun and getting all upset with the pigeons fluttering around them, scattering their newspapers and upsetting the wax paper lunches in their laps. So I keep Raymond on the inside of me, and he plays like he's driving a stagecoach which is O.K. by me so long as he doesn't run me over or interrupt my breathing exercises, which I have to do on account of I'm serious about my running, and I don't care who knows it.

Now some people like to act like things come easy to them, won't let on that they practice. Not me. I'll high-prance down 34th Street like a rodeo pony to keep my knees strong even if it does get my mother uptight so that she walks ahead like she's not with me, don't know me, is all by herself on a shopping trip, and I am somebody else's crazy child. Now you take Cynthia Procter for instance. She's just the opposite. If there's a test tomorrow, she'll say something like, "Oh, I guess I'll play handball this afternoon and watch television tonight," just to let you know she ain't thinking about the test. Or like last week when she won the spelling bee for the millionth time, "A good thing you got 'receive,' Squeaky, cause I would have got it wrong. I completely forgot about the spelling bee." And she'll clutch the lace on her blouse like it was a narrow escape. Oh, brother. But of course when I pass her house on my early morning trots around the block, she is practicing the scales on the piano over and over and over and over. Then in music class she always lets herself get bumped around so she falls accidently on purpose onto the piano stool and is so surprised to find herself sitting there that she decides just for fun to try out the ole keys. And what do you know — Chopin's waltzes just spring out of her fingertips and she's the most surprised thing in the world. A regular prodigy. I could kill people like that. I stay up all night studying the words for the spelling bee. And you can see me any time of day practicing running. I never walk if I can trot, and shame on Raymond if he can't keep up. But of course he does, cause if he hangs back someone's liable to walk up to him and get smart, or take his allowance from him, or ask him where he got that great big pumpkin head. People are so stupid sometimes.

So I'm strolling down Broadway breathing out and breathing in on counts of seven, which is my lucky number, and here comes Gretchen and her sidekicks: Mary Louise, who used to be a friend of mine when she first moved to Harlem from Baltimore and got beat up by everybody till I took up for her on account of her mother and my mother used to sing in the same choir when they were young girls, but people ain't grateful, so now she hangs out with the new girl Gretchen and talks about me like a dog; and Rosie, who is as fat as I am skinny and has a big mouth where Raymond is concerned and is too stupid to know that there is not a big deal of difference between herself and Raymond and that she can't afford to throw stones. So they are steady coming up Broadway and I see right away that it's going to be one of those Dodge City scenes cause the street ain't that big and they're close to the buildings just as we are. First I think I'll step into the candy store and look over the new comics and let them pass. But that's chicken and I've got a reputation to consider. So then I think I'll just walk straight on through them or even over them if necessary. But as they get to me, they slow down. I'm ready to fight, cause like I said I don't feature a whole lot of chitchat, I much prefer to just knock you down right from the jump and save everybody a lotta precious time.

"You signing up for the May Day races?" smiles Mary Louise, only it's not a smile at all. A dumb question like that doesn't deserve an answer. Besides, there's just me and Gretchen standing there really, so no use wasting my breath talking to shadows.

"I don't think you're going to win this time," says Rosie, trying to signify with her hands on her hips all salty, completely forgetting that I have whupped her behind many times for less salt than that.

"I always win cause I'm the best," I say straight at Gretchen who is, as far as I'm concerned, the only one talking in this ventriloquist-dummy routine. Gretchen smiles, but it's not a smile, and I'm thinking that girls never really smile at each other because they don't know how and don't want to know how and there's probably no one to teach us how, cause grownup girls don't know either. Then they all look at Raymond who has just brought his mule team to a standstill. And they're about to see what trouble they can get into through him.

"What grade you in now, Raymond?"

"You got anything to say to my brother, you say it to me, Mary Louise Williams of Raggedy Town, Baltimore."

"What are you, his mother?" sasses Rosie.

"That's right, Fatso. And the next word out of anybody and I'll be *their* mother too." So they just stand there and Gretchen shifts from one leg to the other and so do they. Then Gretchen puts her hands on her hips and is about to say something with her freckle-face self but doesn't. Then she walks around me looking me up and down but keeps walking up Broadway, and her sidekicks follow her. So me and Raymond smile at each other and he says, "Giddyap" to his team and I continue with my breathing exercises, strolling down Broadway toward the ice man on 145th with not a care in the world cause I am Miss Quicksilver herself.

I take my time getting to the park on May Day because the track meet is the last thing on the program. The biggest thing on the program is the Maypole dancing, which I can do without, thank you, even if my mother thinks it's a shame I don't take part and act like a girl for a change. You'd think my mother'd be grateful not to have to make me a white organdy dress with a big satin sash and buy me new white baby-doll shoes that can't be taken out of the box till the big day. You'd think she'd be glad her daughter ain't out there prancing around a Maypole getting the new clothes all dirty and sweaty and trying to act like a fairy or a flower or whatever you're supposed to be when you should be trying to be yourself, whatever that is, which is, as far as I am concerned, a poor black girl who really can't afford to buy shoes and a new dress you only wear once a lifetime cause it won't fit next year.

I was once a strawberry in a Hansel and Gretel pageant when I was in nursery school and didn't have no better sense than to dance on tiptoe with my arms in a circle over my head doing umbrella steps and being a perfect fool just so my mother and father could come dressed up and clap. You'd think they'd know better than to encourage that kind of nonsense. I am not a strawberry. I do not dance on my toes. I run. That is what I am all about. So I always come late to the May Day program, just in time to get my number pinned on and lay in the grass till they announce the fifty-yard dash.

I put Raymond in the little swings, which is a tight squeeze this year and will be impossible next year. Then I look around for Mr. Pearson, who pins the numbers on. I'm really looking for Gretchen if you want to know the truth, but she's not around. The park is jam-packed. Parents in hats and corsages and breast-pocket handkerchiefs peeking up. Kids in white dresses and light blue suits. The parkees unfolding chairs and chasing the rowdy kids from Lenox as if they had no right to be there. The big guys with their caps on backwards, leaning against the fence swirling the basketballs on the tips of their fingers, waiting for all these crazy people to clear out the park so they can play. Most of the kids in my class are carrying bass drums and glockenspiels and flutes. You'd think they'd put in a few bongos or something for real like that.

Then here comes Mr. Pearson with his clipboard and his cards and pencils and whistles and safety pins and fifty million other things he's always dropping all over the place with his clumsy self. He sticks out in a crowd because he's on stilts. We used to call him Jack and the Beanstalk to get him mad. But I'm the only one that can outrun him and get away, and I'm too grown for that silliness now.

"Well, Squeaky," he says, checking my name off the list and handing me number seven and two pins. And I'm thinking he's got no right to call me Squeaky, if I can't call him Beanstalk.

"Hazel Elizabeth Deborah Parker," I correct him and tell him to write it down on his board.

"Well, Hazel Elizabeth Deborah Parker, going to give someone else a break this year?" I squint at him real hard to see if he is seriously thinking I should lose the race on purpose just to give someone else a break. "Only six girls running this time," he continues, shaking his head sadly like it's my fault all of New York didn't turn out in sneakers. "That new girl should give you a run for your money." He looks around the park for Gretchen like a periscope in a submarine movie. "Wouldn't it be a nice gesture if you were ... to ahhh ..."

I give him such a look he couldn't finish putting that idea into words. Grownups got a lot of nerve sometimes. I pin number seven to myself and stomp away, I'm so burnt. And I go straight for the track and stretch out on the grass while the band winds up with "Oh, the Monkey Wrapped His Tail Around the Flagpole," which my teacher calls by some other name.[3] The man on the loudspeaker is calling everyone over to the track and I'm on my back looking at the sky, trying to pretend I'm in the country, but I can't, because even grass in the city feels hard as sidewalk, and there's just no pretending you are anywhere but in a "concrete jungle" as my grandfather says.

The twenty-yard dash takes all of two minutes cause most of the little kids don't know no better than to run off the track or run the wrong way or run smack into the fence and fall down and cry. One little kid, though, has got the good sense to run straight for the white ribbon up ahead so he wins. Then the second-graders line up for the thirty-yard dash and I don't even bother to turn my head to watch cause Raphael Perez always wins. He wins before he even begins by psyching the runners, telling them they're going to trip on their shoelaces and fall on their faces or lose their shorts or something, which he doesn't really have to do since he is very fast, almost as fast as I am. After that is the forty-yard dash which I use to run when I was in first grade. Raymond is hollering from the swings cause he knows I'm about to do my thing cause the man on the loudspeaker has just announced the fifty-yard dash, although he might just as well be giving a recipe for angel food cake cause you can hardly make out what he's saying for the static. I get up and slip off my sweat pants and then I see Gretchen standing at the starting line, kicking her legs out like a pro. Then as I get into place I see that ole Raymond is on line on the other side of the fence, bending down with his fingers on the ground just like he knew what he was doing. I was going to yell at him but then I didn't. It burns up your energy to holler.

Every time, just before I take off in a race, I always feel like I'm in a dream, the kind of dream you have when you're sick with fever and feel all hot and weightless. I dream I'm flying over a sandy beach in the early morning sun, kissing the leaves of the trees as I fly by. And there's always the smell of apples, just like in the country when I was little and used to think I was a choo-choo train, running through the fields of corn and chugging up the hill to the orchard. And all the time I'm dreaming this, I get lighter and lighter until I'm flying over the beach again, getting blown through the sky like a feather that weighs nothing at all. But once I spread my fingers in the dirt and crouch over the Get on Your Mark, the dream goes and I am

---

[3] "The Washington Post March," by John Philip Sousa. Squeaky knows it by a set of popular and vulgar lyrics set to Sousa's tune.

solid again and am telling myself, Squeaky you must win, you must win, you are the fastest thing in the world, you can even beat your father up Amsterdam if you really try. And then I feel my weight coming back just behind my knees then down to my feet then into the earth and the pistol shot explodes in my blood and I am off and weightless again, flying past the other runners, my arms pumping up and down and the whole world is quiet except for the crunch as I zoom over the gravel in the track. I glance to my left and there is no one. To the right, a blurred Gretchen, who's got her chin jutting out as if it would win the race all by itself. And on the other side of the fence is Raymond with his arms down to his side and the palms tucked up behind him, running in his very own style, and it's the first time I ever saw that and I almost stop to watch my brother Raymond on his first run. But the white ribbon is bouncing toward me and I tear past it, racing into the distance till my feet with a mind of their own start digging up footfuls of dirt and brake me short. Then all the kids standing on the side pile on me, banging me on the back and slapping my head with their May Day programs, for I have won again and everybody on 151st Street can walk tall for another year.

"In first place ..." the man on the loudspeaker is clear as a bell now. but then he pauses and the loudspeaker starts to whine. Then static. And I lean down to catch my breath and here comes Gretchen walking back, for she's overshot the finish line too, huffing and puffing with her hands on her hips taking it slow, breathing in steady time like a real pro and I sort of like her a little for the first time. "In first place ..." and then three or four voices get all mixed up on the loudspeaker and I dig my sneaker into the grass and stare at Gretchen who's staring back, we both wondering just who did win. I can hear old Beanstalk arguing with the man on the loudspeaker and then a few others running their mouths about what the stopwatches say. Then I hear Raymond yanking at the fence to call me and I wave to shush him, but he keeps rattling the fence like a gorilla in a cage like in them gorilla movies, but then like a dancer or something he starts climbing up nice and easy but very fast. And it occurs to me, watching how smoothly he climbs hand over hand and remembering how he looked running with his arms down to his side and with the wind pulling his mouth back and his teeth showing and all, it occurred to me that Raymond would make a very fine runner. Doesn't he always keep up with me on my trots? And he surely knows how to breathe in counts of seven cause he's always doing it at the dinner table, which drives my brother George up the wall. And I'm smiling to beat the band cause if I've lost this race, or if me and Gretchen tied, or even if I've won, I can always retire as a runner and begin a whole new career as a coach with Raymond as my champion. After all, with a little more study I can beat Cynthia and her phony self at the spelling bee. And if I bugged my mother, I could get piano lessons and become a star. And I have a big rep as the baddest thing around. And I've got a roomful of ribbons and medals and awards. But what has Raymond got to call his own?

So I stand there with my new plans, laughing out loud by this time as Raymond jumps down from the fence and runs over with his teeth showing and his arms down to the side, which no one before him has quite mastered as a running style. And by the time he comes over I'm jumping up and down so glad to see him — my brother Raymond, a great runner in the family tradition. But of course everyone thinks I'm jumping up and down because the men on the loudspeaker have finally gotten themselves together and compared notes and are announcing "In first place — Miss Hazel Elizabeth Deborah Parker." (Dig that.) "In second place — Miss Gretchen P. Lewis." And I look at Gretchen wondering what the "P" stands for. And I smile. Cause she's good, no doubt about it. Maybe she'd like to help me coach Raymond; she obviously is serious about running, as any fool can see. And she nods to congratulate me and then she smiles. And I smile. We stand there with this big smile of respect between us. It's about as real a smile as girls can do for each other, considering we don't practice real smiling every day, you know, cause maybe we too busy being flowers or fairies or strawberries instead of something honest and worthy of respect ... you know ... like being people.

QUESTIONS

1. Squeaky is clearly the protagonist, but who is the antagonist? Is it Gretchen?

2. How many plot lines do you see in "Raymond's Run"? Can you state them in terms of the conflicts Squeaky is involved in? How does the author manage to preserve unity in this complex story?

3. What adjectives would you use to define Squeaky? feisty? street-wise? sentimental? adolescent? concerned? competitive? Is she as tough as she talks?

4. How do Squeaky's thought and speech patterns help to characterize her?

5. Isolate her references to Gretchen. Do you see a pattern of rising tension, culminating in the race? What besides racing forms the subject matter of these references? What do they tell us about Squeaky?

6. We feel considerable satisfaction in the way the story closes. We are glad that Raymond will have the chance to excel, and we are pleased at Squeaky's growth. Are the two things connected? Has Bambara prepared us adequately for Raymond-the-runner-to-be? Does the first paragraph provide a clue?

PART II

PREFACE

How is the short story to be defined? — a perennial question that might be more judiciously phrased, *Why* is the short story to be defined? The art is idiosyncratic as well as "traditional"; its forms are as variable as its subjects; no definition of the genre can accommodate fictions differing as radically as Tolstoy's classic "The Death of Ivan Ilych" and Richard Brautigan's four-page "Revenge of the Lawn," Borges's fabulistic "The Babylon Lottery" and Alice Munro's wholly realistic "Spelling." To state that a story is a "short" piece of fiction (not recognizably poetry) might be the most conservative, and certainly the least problematic, of all definitions. Just as poetry is a genre spacious enough to contain the epics of Homer no less than lyric utterances small enough to cup in the palm of the hand, so too is prose fiction as a genre immense, elastic, unbounded — one of the oldest yet the most contemporary of literary forms.

Its psychological impulse is, *Let me tell you something that happened!* — its assurance, *I'll be brief.*

If the short story in America appears to be thriving at the present time — highly praised collections are not only being published, they are also being bought, read, discussed — it can only be because many of our most talented and dedicated writers of fiction are applying themselves to this painstaking art. Hortense Calisher has said that a short story is "an apocalypse, served in a very small cup": a witty way of acknowledging its formal limitations and its thematic ambitions. Yet there are stories that aspire to the chronological sweep of the novel, like Flaubert's "A Simple Heart," Henry James's "The Beast in the Jungle," and John Gardner's "Redemption"; and there are stories like those by Grace Paley and William Goyen that contain no "apocalypse" at all. A conversational artlessness characterizes stories by Raymond Carver, Clark Blaise, and John Sayles, while others, like Cynthia Ozick's virtuoso "The Shawl," aspire beyond prose to the condition of poetry or music. Shading into fairy tale, legend, and parable on one side, and the first-person anecdote on the other, a short story may exhibit kinship with both: Faulkner's Gothic tall tale "A Rose for Emily" and Paul Bowles's terrifying "A Distant Episode" are examples. And there are contemporary stories like those by Joy Williams and Ann Beattie told in resolutely spare, uninflected prose, as if the lyric energies required for self-consciously "artful" writing are here irrelevant. A representative sampling of the most important and most interesting contemporary short stories will include many voices, many angles of vision. There is no dominant mode, as there was in the nineteenth century, when Gothic fiction was wildly popular — only to be virtually obliterated by the revolutionary sweep of realism in the second half of the century.

The short story is considered a notoriously difficult genre because it demands compression; each sentence must contribute to the effect of the whole. Its strategy is not to include an excess of detail but to exclude, to select, to focus as sharply as possible. The stories in this section of our anthology tend to deal with single individuals in relationship with one or two other individuals, at the most; their structures tend to be traditional, containing beginnings, middles, and ends — accommodating recognizable developments and resolutions of plot. (A word should be said, however, concerning a special subgrouping of stories in both sections. These are works that may be read as autonomous — indeed, which *are* autonomous — yet function, often ingeniously, as "chapters" in books. Their characters have lives that go beyond the stories' limits; it might be said that they inhabit novels of an experimental sort. Among these are James Joyce's "Araby," "Ivy Day in the Committee Room," and "The Dead," from *Dubliners*; Alice Munro's "Spelling" from *The Beggar Maid*; Lynne Sharon Schwartz's "Rough Strife" from the novel *Rough Strife*; Tim O'Brien's "Going After Cacciato" from the novel *Going After Cacciato*; Clark Blaise's "A Class of New Canadians" from *A North American Education*; and Joyce Carol Oates's "The Going-Away Party," from *Marya: A Life*.) Even in slightly surrealist stories like those by O'Brien and Goyen the narrative mode is that of psychological realism.

All art is generated out of conflict; without conflict there can be no movement, no development — no story. This is not to say, as Tolstoy does, that happy families are all alike; nor are happy individuals all alike. But there seems to be a common denominator in "happiness" that blurs distinctions between people, and, in prose fiction at least, shades into self-satisfaction and complacency. Popular forms of entertainment like television often serve up "happy people with happy problems" in formulaic situations; paperback romances present love stories with "happy" endings — to be read, most likely, by those to whom happy endings are only fantasy. The serious short story, like any serious work of art, concentrates on elemental human experiences — death, love, accommodation to tragic circumstances, the opening into new and unanticipated dimensions of being. (Character is revealed in daily life, in the very dailiness of life, no less authentically than it is in times of crisis: but art is obliged to be selective, to focus upon the elemental.) Since literature in our time is highly reflective and analytic, it should not be surprising that the tone of much fiction is ironic, even somber; its conflicts are less likely to be problems — for problems can be solved — than expressions of the general human condition.

Yet *meaning* in prose fiction, no less than in poetry, derives from language — voice, rhythm, interior music — the indefinable essence of a work. What do we mean by "voice"? — is it as mysterious in art as in life? It would be accurate yet crudely misleading to describe John Gardner's "Redemption" as a story "about" a boy who accidentally kills his brother; to describe Alistair MacLeod's poignant "In the Fall" as a story "about" a child's early experience of death; or Alice Munro's elliptical "Spelling" as a story "about" a woman who must tend to her aging, senile, once-authoritarian mother. Cynthia Ozick's hallucinatory "The Shawl" presents a nightmare situation by way of highly precise, selective, lyric language; in the most minimal terms it is "about" a Jewish woman in a Nazi concentration camp whose baby is murdered before her eyes. Yet of course the story exists only in Ozick's imagination, and in her language:

She stood for an instant at the margin of the arena. Sometimes the electricity inside the fence would seem to hum; even Stella said it was only an imagining, but Rosa heard real sounds in the wire: grainy sad voices. The farther she was from the fence, the more clearly the voices crowded at her. The lamenting voices strummed so convincingly, so passionately, it was impossible to suspect them of being phantoms. The voices told her to hold up the shawl, high; the voices told her to shake it, to whip with it, to unfurl it like a flag. Rosa lifted, shook, whipped, unfurled. Far off, very far, Magda leaned across her air-fed belly, reaching out with the rods of her arms. ...

In contrast, the laconic, affectless language of an alcoholic woman in Joy Williams's "The Farm" — a woman who will shortly kill a fifteen-year-old boy with her car:

Sarah was telling a long story as she drove. She kept asking Tommy if she had told it to him before, but he was noncommital. When Tommy didn't drink, Sarah talked and talked. She was telling him a terrible story that she had read in the newspaper about an alligator at a jungle farm attraction in Florida. The alligator had eaten a child who had crawled into its pen. The alligator's name was Cookie. Its owner had shot it immediately. The owner was sad about everything, the child, the parents' grief, Cookie. He was quoted in the paper as saying that shooting Cookie was not an act of revenge.

In Ann Beattie's fiction, as in much of Joy Williams's, the effect of personal catastrophe is to numb, to deaden sensibility. Emotion after all is temporary even if cathartic; one is left with odd remnants of memory, so oblique as to approach the comic: "In 1969 Joseph died in Vietnam. My mother received official notification, then a letter from a friend of his that was full of praise for his valor, his wonderful sense of humor, his skill with a rifle" ("A Clever-Kids Story").

One of the most-praised works of fiction of the Vietnam War, Tim O'Brien's "Going After Cacciato," employs a flat reportorial style that suggests a kinship with Hemingway, yet possesses elements of the absurd as well:

It was a bad time. Billy Boy Watkins was dead, and so was Frenchie Tucker. Billy Boy had died of fright, scared to death on the field of battle, and Frenchie Tucker had been shot through the neck. Lieutenants Sidney Martin and Walter Gleason had died in tunnels. Pederson was dead and Bernie Lynn was dead. Buff was dead. They were all among the dead. The war was always the same, and the rain was part of the war. The rain fed fungus that grew in the men's socks and boots, and their socks rotted, and their feet turned white and soft so that the skin could be scraped off with a fingernail, and Stink Harris woke up screaming one night with a leech on his tongue. ...

The childlike declarative sentences, the elementary vocabulary, the repetitious phrasing — the selection of such details as the fungus and the leech — are all used here to understated yet powerful effect. In this context Cacciato's fantastic behavior appears plausible.

By contrast, the voices of a number of stories — among them Raymond Carver's "Cathedral," Grace Paley's "The Used-Boy Raisers," and John Sayles's "Dillinger in Hollywood" — are warm, conversational, immediate, reassuring. A first-person narration inevitably communicates a sense of authenticity — the reader ideally identifies with the narrator

— but in these skillful stories the quirks and idiom of individual speech are conveyed with an apparent effortlessness. Carver's story begins, "This blind man, an old friend of my wife's, he was on his way to spend the night." Paley's story begins, "There were two husbands disappointed by eggs." And Sayles's, with a disarming intimacy:

> You know how they get after New Year's when the visits dry up and the TV is bust and there's steamed chicken for lunch three days in a row? It was one of those weeks, and Spurs Tatum starts in after rec therapy, before we could wheel them all out of the day room.

Richard Brautigan's comic "Revenge of the Lawn" is told with an air of mock solemnity:

> My grandmother, in her own way, shines like a beacon down the stormy American past. She was a bootlegger in a little county up in the state of Washington. She was also a handsome woman, close to six feet tall who carried 190 pounds in the grand operatic manner of the early 1900s. And her specialty was bourbon, a little raw but a welcomed refreshment in those Volstead Act days.

Perhaps the most mysterious story in this section is William Goyen's "Bridge of Music, River of Sand," which has the air of an enigmatic dream yet *sounds* utterly plausible, in its narrator's matter-of-fact country idiom:

> Do you remember the bridge that we crossed over the river to get to Riverside? And if you looked over yonder you saw the railroad trestle? High and narrow? Well that's what he jumped off of. Into a nothing river. "River"! I could laugh. I can spit more than runs in that dry bed. ...

In this haunting story, as in Goyen's unique fiction generally, "image" and "voice" conjoin in a single dramatic utterance. For Goyen, as for many writers of prose fiction, the incantatory power of language is the single most significant aspect of its "meaning."

Yet serious fiction invariably deals with problems of a moral and intellectual nature, quite apart from matters of craft. It poses riddles, paradoxes, questions that cannot be readily answered; it would seem to educate us into the complexities of the world — a fictive world that contains our own. Though many of the characters about whom we read are distant from us, and their experiences remote from our own, the varying ways in which they confront their fates (bravely, fearfully, inadequately, nobly?) suggest a necessary kinship with us. They are not us, but, perhaps, forms of us.

For this reason certain stories — Kafka's "A Hunger Artist," Hemingway's "A Clean, Well-Lighted Place," Bowles's "A Distant Episode," among others — remain with us as testaments to ambiguity, rather than statements of a comforting clarity. Nearly devoid of characterization in the conventional sense, they challenge our conceptions of reality: What *is* the human essence, shorn of the accidents and qualifications of ordinary life? The quintessential Kafka story reads like a parable, excluding the recognizable world, and presenting human personality at a ground base of zero; Hemingway's most powerful stories concern themselves rather more with the solitary human condition — and with the effort to resist a terrifying descent into despair — than with "action." In a typical story by Paul Bowles, an American traveler of the middle class journeys to a distant place — Morocco, Mexico, South America — and undergoes an experience that renders him less, and not more, human. Bowles eliminates from his fiction all that is extraneous and gives us stories that read like legendary anecdotes; impersonal accounts of terrible events; contemporary folk tales of a cautionary nature. His interest is not in human interaction in a social sense but in human fate once the "social" is no longer available to define and protect the individual. (It might also be argued, though, that Bowles's fiction represents a cruelly grotesque comedy of manners: "civilization" put to the test.)

Consequently Bowles's meticulously rendered settings — the *physical* environment of his tales — are far more important than they are in most works of fiction, his people being for the most part merely participants in an impersonal drama. So, "A Distant Episode" is *distant*: it transpires in a moral void, related by a disinterested and unidentified narrator, in a place of "lunar chill." The Professor of linguistics meets his fate simply because, as an unwary traveler, he ventures into a place in which his specialness — his academic training, his intelligence, his American citizenship — cannot protect him. At each stage of his journey remarks are made that signal an impending irony, of which the Professor is ignorant: "Keep on going south," he is told. "You'll find some languages you never heard of before." The Professor himself wishes he were less lonely, that "everyone" knew him; he wonders "Is this a situation or a predicament?"; when it is really too late to save himself, he is still thinking that his experience will be an "opportunity ... of testing the accuracy of [certain] statements."

> He did not doubt for a moment that the adventure would prove to be a kind of
> warning against such foolishness on his part — a warning which in retrospect
> would be half sinister, half farcical.

Whereas, generally, in more conventional fiction our sympathies would remain solely with the Professor, and our vision of his tragedy identical with his, in Bowles's tale the Professor himself drifts out of our consciousness, as, indeed, he drifts out of the human altogether. Having lost his tongue, he loses his language; having lost language, he loses his sanity, his very selfhood. Interpreting his behavior at the climax of the story, the narrator — analytic, emotionless, distant — theorizes:

> The tiny ink marks of which a symphony consists may have been made long
> ago, but when they are fulfilled in sound they become imminent and mighty. So
> a kind of music of feeling began to play in the Professor's head, increasing in
> volume as he looked at the mud wall, and he had the feeling that he was
> performing what had been written for him long ago.

He becomes at last sheer emotion, fleeing insensibly into the desert.

In less extreme terms, Hortense Calisher's "The Scream on Fifty-Seventh Street" deals with a predicament as lonely and as frightening as the Professor's; indeed, the very sensitivity of the protagonist makes her fate the more despairing. ("No animal but one was ever that alone.") Who, or what, *is* a person when he or she is irrevocably alone; when voices become primarily interior; when the comforts of human communication are denied? Alice Munro's "Spelling" is one of the most painful stories in the anthology, but it does not draw upon exotic settings and extraordinary incidents as the other two stories do. "Spelling" locates its horrors in nearby, domestic scenes: "In the store, in the old days," it begins, "Flo used to say she could tell when some woman was going off the track." Munro's story is, in a sense, about "going off the track"; but it is also about a woman's ambivalent regard for her stepmother, or for the senile woman her stepmother has become. Again, the riddle of identity is posed: Who or what are we when we have lost the capacity to reason, to speak? — to define ourselves? Gail

Godwin's "Dream Children" ends, appropriately, with a question put to the reader — as it is put to the author and her protagonist as well: "Was she a woman riding a horse and dreaming she was a mother who anxiously awaited her child's sleep; or was she a mother dreaming of herself as a free spirit who could ride her horse like the wind because she had nothing to fear?" Similarly, John Hawkes's bizarre little tale constitutes a riddle in itself, not to be easily answered.

*   *   *

Kafka's much-quoted remark — "A book is an ax for the frozen sea within" — is especially relevant here, prefatory to a gathering of such widely differing writers. For it is not only the act of writing that is creative, but the act of reading, when patiently and intelligently executed. How in fact should one read? — with what attitude should one approach this utterly common yet ill-understood activity? Not hurriedly, as if each story were an obligation, or a task to complete; but with sympathy, as if each story were, in some mysterious way, a story about ourselves. For someday, perhaps, it will be. ...

— Joyce Carol Oates

ALICE ADAMS

Gift of Grass

"But what's so great about money — or marriages and houses, for that matter?" Strengthened perhaps by two recent cups of tea (rose hips, brewed with honey and a few grass seeds), Cathy had raised herself on one elbow and turned to face the doctor. "Couldn't there be other ways to live?" she asked, consciously childish and pleading.

"Have you thought of one?" Oppressed by weariness and annoyance, Dr. Fredericks was unaware that both these emotions sounded in his soft, controlled voice. Once, in a burst of confidence, Cathy had said to him accusingly, "You speak so softly just to make me listen." Now she said nothing. Believing himself to be in command, Dr. Fredericks also believed his patient to be overcome by what he saw as her transference. She saw her feelings toward him as simple dislike and a more complicated distrust.

She lay back down, giving up, and reconsidered the large space that served as both the doctor's office and his living room. It was coolly blue and green — olive walls and ceiling, royal-blue carpet, navy silk chair and sofa, pale-blue linen lampshades on green pottery lamps. Only the couch on which Cathy lay was neither green nor blue; it was upholstered with a worn Oriental rug, as though that might disguise its function. Like most children — she was sixteen — Cathy knew more than her elders thought she did. She knew that at one time her mother had been a patient of Dr. Fredericks', and she recognized her mother's touch in that room. Her mother, who was an interior decorator, had evidently "done" it. As payment for her hours of lying there? It would have been an expensive job; Cathy saw that, too. God knows how many hours it would have taken to pay for all that silk.

All her mother had ever said, in a tearful voice that was supposed to extract similar sincerity from Cathy, was "At one time when I was very troubled about my life a psychiatrist really helped me a great deal. In fact, you might say that he saved our marriage. Bill's and mine." Not wanting Cathy to sense a conspiracy, she had not told Cathy that she was sending her to her own psychiatrist. This was when, in August, Cathy had said she was not going back to school in the fall, and her mother and Bill — her stepfather for the past ten years — had told her that in that case she must go to Dr. Fredericks.

"But I'm not troubled," Cathy had lied. Then she had giggled in her unrelated, unnerving way. "Or married. I just don't want to go to school for a while," she had said.

"But I hope you will be married," her mother had said. She had sighed, frowned, and then smiled, attempting reassurance. "Dr. James helped me a great deal," she said. "He's one of the best doctors in San Francisco." She used the first name of Dr. Fredericks — Dr. James Fredericks — which Cathy did not think was a very smart disguise.

While the long pause after his question lasted, Dr. Fredericks struggled with his counter-transference. He stared down at Cathy's rather squat, short body in its jeans and black turtleneck sweater, at the long, limp brown hair that fell from the edge of the couch and the perfectly round, brown eyes in a pale, round face. He had to admit it. He couldn't stand the little girl. Injecting kindliness into his voice, he said, "Isn't there anything on your mind that you'd like to tell me about?"

At this, Cathy burst into tears. A quick, noisy storm of sobs shook her shoulders and her chest, then stopped, and she said, "You dumb fink."

He leaned back comfortably in his raw-silk chair that did not creak. Seductively, he said, "I suppose by your standards I am in some ways rather dumb." He did not say, "Such as they are."

"Such as they are," she said. "I'm not interested in standards, or school or earning money or getting married."

"I wish I knew what you were interested in," he said.

This seemed to Cathy his most heartfelt and least contrived remark of the hour, and she answered him. "Clouds," she said. "And foghorns. I wonder where they all are."

"If you really wonder, you could go to the library and get a book."

"I'd rather wonder." She giggled.

"The 'trip' is more important than the destination, is that what you mean?" Despite himself, he had underlined "trip."

"I don't drop acid, I've told you that," she said, deadpan. "I'm afraid to."

"Well," he said, warming to his task, "that's a reasonable enough fear. But perhaps you have some other less reasonable fears."

"Deer-hunters. God, they have the worst faces I ever saw," she suddenly brought out, forgetting him and remembering the weekend just past. She and her mother and Bill had driven up to Lake Tahoe — a jaunt intended to prove that they were not really angry with Cathy, that they loved her nevertheless. By an unfortunate coincidence, this was also the first weekend of the deer season. On the other side of Sacramento, winding up past Auburn through beautiful mountain rocks and trees, Highway 80 had been lined with white camper trucks bearing hunters. The men wore ugly red caps and red plaid shirts. They had looked remarkably alike, at least to Cathy — as alike as their campers. Fathers and sons and friends, their faces had been coarse and unintelligent, excited, jovial, and greedy. Cathy shuddered. "God, I hope they all shoot each other," she said to Dr. Fredericks.

"Well," he said hopefully. "Let's see if we can find out what deer-hunters mean to you. I doubt somehow that it's sheer dislike of killing. For instance, you don't seem to be upset about the war in Vietnam."

"That's so bad I can't think about it at all," said Cathy with total candor.

"Well, let's see." Dr. Fredericks, almost alone among his colleagues, was more opposed to protesters than to the war, but bringing up Vietnam had been a ploy. He now thrust his real point home. "I do seem to remember that your stepfather is something of a hunter," he said.

Cathy heard the light note of triumph in his voice, to which she reacted with rage and despair and a prolonged silence. Why bother to tell him that Bill had only hunted ducks — and only with his father, before that awful old man had died? During the silence, she listened to the leisurely sounds of outlying San Francisco traffic and the faint, distant foghorns from the Bay. Concentrating on these, she was able to stop the echo of Dr. Fredericks' voice in her mind. Their voices were what she could stand least about adults: Dr. Fredericks' bored hostility; her teachers' voices, loud and smug; the alternately anxious and preening, knowing voice of her mother. The only thing that she could remember about her natural father, who had divorced her mother when Cathy was two, was his voice. It was high-pitched, almost a whine — nothing much to miss. Actually, Bill had a nice, warm, deep voice, until he drank too much and it blurred.

A heavy truck went by, creaking and lumbering as though weighted with old furniture or barrels of china and glass. Brakes screeched several blocks away. Then the traffic sounds continued as before. For a few minutes, there were no foghorns and then there they were again, discordant, with no rhythm.

Both Cathy and Dr. Fredericks glanced over at the clock on his desk. Five minutes to go. He sighed softly and pleasurably. He had recently stopped smoking and he enjoyed the air in his expanded chest. Although he was nearing sixty, he was well preserved. Squash and swimming at his club kept him in shape; he felt a certain snobbery toward many of his colleagues who were running to fat. He and his wife, who owned and ran an extremely successful chain of gift shops, spent vacations at health spas, playing tennis and dieting together. A blue-eyed Southerner, from West Virginia, Dr. Fredericks liked to view himself as a maverick among psychoanalysts — another breed, one might say.

Cathy swung her short legs off the couch and sat up. She clutched her knees and faced him. "Look," she said. "It's hopeless. You and mother think it's important to get married and save marriages and get money and save that, and I don't."

"We're trying to find out what you do think is important," he said. He did not bother to conceal his impatience.

Neither did she. "So am I."

"Next week?" They both stood up.

Out of context (he felt), she giggled. "Maybe."

Cathy's parents lived about ten blocks from Dr. Fredericks in the same expensive and fog-ridden San Francisco neighborhood, but instead of going home Cathy walked to the park she often went to, along the broad streets and down the hill leading toward the Bay. Here the sun was shining. She pulled a small box of raisins from her pocket and began to eat them as she walked.

The park was surrounded by rolling woods of pine and fir, cypress and eucalyptus, through which on clear days one could catch blue views of the Bay, red glimpses of the Golden Gate Bridge. Cathy walked past creaking swings and a slide crowded with small children. Out on a playing field, lounging about on the beaten grass, there were some kids her own age whom she thought she knew, so she hurried on toward the woods.

Off the path, she came to a place where there was a large sloping patch of sand. She sat down and reached into the back pocket of her jeans, where there was a very mashed joint, which she lit. She lay back, her left arm protecting her hair from the sand. She sucked in and waited for the melting of her despair.

The air smelled alternately of the sea, of lemon-scented eucalyptus, of pine, and of the dank, dark earth. It was nearly a clear day, but the foghorns sounded more strongly to her from the water. Soon the fog would come in, gigantically billowing through the Golden Gate. Now, in the visible sky above the dark, thatched cypresses, there were only a few large clouds;

they were as heavy and slow and lumbering as bulls, a slow-motion lumbering of bulls across the sky. Cathy concentrated on their changes, their slow and formal shifts in shape and pattern. Then, in the peace, in the warm silence, she fell asleep.

Bill, Cathy's stepfather, had at moments a few of the reactions to Cathy that she evoked in Dr. Fredericks. At worst, he despaired of reaching her. But he was exceptionally sensitive to the feelings of women. He could often feel what Cathy felt, and could bear it no better than she. It was his sensitivity, in fact, that had kept him from leaving Cathy's mother, Barbara, who was his second wife. The extent of Barbara's anxiety and despair when they first spoke of separation had got through to him. They had seen Dr. Fredericks, together and separately, for more than a year. But before their meetings with him began Bill had already decided not, after all, to leave Barbara for Ruth, his girl friend. (Ruth had been unhappy, too, but she was younger and more resilient; her despair hit Bill with lesser force.)

Perhaps to avoid a discussion of Ruth, Bill had talked about his inheritance from his father, and Dr. Fredericks had given Bill good advice about investing it. Bill gave him credit for that. Actually, investments were Fredericks' real but unacknowledged field of expertise. Bill was a commercial artist, and not a terribly successful one. The investment had brought his income well within range of his wife's, so it may have been Dr. Fredericks, after all, who saved the marriage.

It was nearly dinnertime when Cathy came home from the park, and Bill and her mother were sitting in the living room having drinks. Barbara had done their living room, like Dr. Fredericks', in cool blues and greens, except for the brown leather sofa — a kind of tribute to Bill's masculine presence; ordinarily, she did not use leather. Bill almost never sat on it. He would sit instead, as he did now, on a small Victorian dark-blue silk chair that must have been intended for Cathy. Fortunately, he was light — a very thin, narrowly built man with delicate bones and sparse blondish hair. Barbara, wearing a smart gray wool dress, was sitting on the leather sofa, and Cathy joined her there. During the cocktail hour, they would sit that way, at opposite ends of the sofa, facing Bill rather than each other.

Mother and daughter appeared to Bill remarkably alike. Barbara's eyes, too, were round and often opaque; her body tended to be squat. Its shape was childlike, which at times Bill found quite touching. At other times, it turned him off, and on to voluptuous Ruth. In Cathy, naturally enough, the sexlessness was more marked. Bill sometimes wondered how he would have felt with a voluptuous daughter, a swinging chick. Would it have made him more uncomfortable?

"I told Dr. Fredericks how much I hated deer-hunters," proffered Cathy. Since Barbara, on principle, would never ask what went on during "her hour," Cathy would throw out indecipherable and tantalizing tidbits.

Feeling his second drink, Bill said, "God, I hate them, too. They all remind me of my father." Bill's father had been a mighty hunter, out of the great Northwest, with rather Bunyanesque notions of manhood, so that Bill had trouble from time to time believing in himself as a man, feeling that if those coarse, red-faced, hunting cretins were men he was not one. Indeed, he had been told by several women, including Barbara, that he played around only in order to prove his manhood to himself. At times, he thought that might be true. At other times, he thought it was simply because he very much liked women, lots of them.

But he was not supposed to voice as strong an emotion as hatred in the presence of Cathy, and he sensed reproof in Barbara's slightly stiffened posture. She was an extremely nice woman who wanted things to be perfect — her house, her husband, her daughter, and especially herself. Now, instead of reproving Bill, she smiled at him, sighed, and said, "God, I'm tired. I really did have a day."

"You didn't like your father?" Cathy asked in a neutral voice that bore, for Bill, an unnerving resemblance to Dr. Fredericks' therapeutic blandness. But it was almost the first personal question that he could remember Cathy's ever asking him, and he found that his chest warmed and expanded with pleasure. "To tell you the truth," he said, "I was very much afraid of him. The way I find hunters frightening."

"Oh," said Cathy, and then for no reason she giggled.

"We're having a really wicked dinner," Barbara said. "Prawns with that sour-cream sauce. I absolutely couldn't resist them in the Grant Market, so big and pink and perfect. And, of course, rice."

"You are wicked," Bill responded, since this was how they talked to each other, but he was hearing them both with Cathy's ears, and he wondered how she could bear their middle-aged fatuity. She was staring at a small porcelain vase of tiny blue strawflowers as though she had never seen it before. Bill asked Barbara if she wanted another drink.

He made them strong, and by the end of dinner, during which he and Barbara drank wine and told Cathy illuminating vignettes from their own histories, stressing education and travel and friendship, reminding her that they had once been young — by the time all that was over, Bill was almost drunk and Barbara had a headache. But he was still aware of the troubled depths of tenderness in her round brown eyes as she said good night to them both — quite out of character, she had decided to give in to her headache and go to bed.

"Cathy and I will clear up," said Bill decisively.

The truth was that he liked to wash dishes, which his father had seen to it that he was not allowed to do. He liked all that warm, foamy water around his hands and the essential and marvellous simplicity of the task. He handed each hot, clean dish to Cathy, who dried it with a sparklingly clean white towel in the blue-and-white-tiled, Philippine-mahogany room.

For no real reason, a picture of Cathy the first time he had ever seen her came to Bill's mind — a small, square girl with chocolate cake and frosting all over her face and hands. It was during what he and Barbara ironically referred to as their courtship, a protracted and difficult period during which they had both been concerned with Bill's shedding his wife — and with the difficulty of seeing each other privately, what with Barbara's child and his wife. Barbara's first husband had moved to Dallas and had not seen Cathy since the divorce, but Barbara had felt that Bill and her daughter should not meet until Bill was actually free. So it was quite a while before Barbara could invite Bill for dinner. And on the occasion Cathy found the perfect, beautiful chocolate cake that Barbara had made and plunged her hands into its dark, moist depths, then smeared her face. Barbara had chosen to laugh rather than scold, and Bill had liked her for that. Now the remembered sight of small, smeared Cathy moved him. He wanted to tell her about it, but he knew she would not understand; nor could she know that simply watching someone grow can make you care for them. So instead of any of that he said, "As a matter of fact, I think James Fredericks is a jackass," and handed her a wet wineglass.

Carefully polishing, as she had been taught by her mother, Cathy asked, "Is he? I don't know."

"God, yes. All he can talk about is what he likes to call 'finances.' He can't say 'money.' Besides, you don't see his name on any anti-war petitions of doctors, do you? He probably owns stock in Dow Chemical."

Plunging his hands back into the sink, Bill realized that he had wanted to say this for a long time. He had forgotten that Cathy was not supposed to know that he and Barbara had gone to Fredericks, and he wanted to reassure her, to tell her that if she didn't dig Fredericks it was certainly O.K. with him. But then he felt her mind float off to some clouded private distance of her own, and suddenly he couldn't stand it, and he turned furiously to confront her. "Listen," he said loudly, "you think you're confused, and that the world is difficult.

Christ, what do you think it's like to be forty-one? Christ, talk about confused and difficult. Do you think I like getting outside myself and seeing a fatuous drunk whose scalp is beginning to show through? Christ! And believe me, being married is a hell of a lot more difficult than not being married, let me tell you. Your mother has to diet or she'd be fat, and she can't stand fat. And it's very hard to live without a lot of money and booze. You give it a little thought — just try."

Cathy's round eyes did not blink and she went on polishing the second wineglass. Then she glanced quickly at Bill and said, "O.K." Then she said, "I think I'll go to bed now," and Bill was left alone to clean the sink and wipe off the unvarnished wooden chopping table.

After he had finished that, he went into the small room off the living room that was known as his study; his books were there, and some portfolios of old drawings, and a collection of dirty pipes that he would have smoked only in that room. Now as he entered he found placed squarely in the middle of his desk a white sheet of paper, and on it were what he recognized as two joints.

He sat down in the comfortable green wool upholstered chair that Barbara had provided him, presumably for meditation, and he meditated, seeking a variety of explanations for Cathy's present, or gesture — whatever it was. However, nothing rational came to his mind. Or, rather, reasonable explanations approached but then as quickly dissolved, like clouds or shadows. Instead, salty and unmasculine tears stung at his eyes, and then he fell asleep in his chair, having just decided not to think at all.

QUESTIONS

1. What role does Dr. Fredericks play in the lives of Barbara, Bill, and Cathy? How effective a psychoanalyst does he seem to be? What norms does he represent?

2. What effect does alcohol have on Bill and Barbara? Are the effects of marijuana on Cathy similar or different? Why does she leave the two joints for Bill?

3. What values do Bill and Cathy share? How do their values differ? What sensibilities do Cathy and her mother share? How do their sensibilities differ?

4. Compare the ending of the story, where Bill falls asleep in the chair, to the scene in the park. What resolution has been reached at these moments.

MARGARET ATWOOD

The Man from Mars

A long time ago Christine was walking through the park. She was still wearing her tennis dress; she hadn't had time to shower and change, and her hair was held back with an elastic band. Her chunky reddish face, exposed with no softening fringe, looked like a Russian peasant's, but without the elastic band the hair got in her eyes. The afternoon was too hot for April; the indoor courts had been steaming, her skin felt poached.

The sun had brought the old men out from wherever they spent the winter: she had read a story recently about one who lived for three years in a manhole. They sat weedishly on the benches or lay on the grass with their heads on squares of used newspaper. As she passed, their wrinkled toadstool faces drifted towards her, drawn by the movement of her body, then floated away again, uninterested.

The squirrels were out, too, foraging; two or three of them moved towards her in darts and pauses, eyes fixed on her expectantly, mouths with the ratlike receding chins open to show the yellowed front teeth. Christine walked faster, she had nothing to give them. People shouldn't feed them, she thought; it makes them anxious and they get mangy.

Halfway across the park she stopped to take off her cardigan. As she bent over to pick up her tennis racquet again someone touched her on her freshly bared arm. Christine seldom screamed; she straightened up suddenly, gripping the handle of her racquet. It was not one of the old men, however, it was a dark-haired boy of twelve or so.

"Excuse me," he said, "I search for Economics Building. Is it there?" He motioned towards the west.

Christine looked at him more closely. She had been mistaken: he was not young, just short. He came a little above her shoulder, but then, she was above the average height; "statuesque," her mother called it when she was straining. He was also what was referred to in their family as "a person from another culture": oriental without a doubt, though perhaps not Chinese. Christine judged he must be a foreign student and gave him her official welcoming smile. In high school she had been president of the United Nations Club; that year her school had been picked to represent the Egyptian delegation at the Mock Assembly. It had been an unpopular assignment — nobody wanted to be the Arabs — but she had seen it through. She had made rather a good speech about the Palestinian refugees.

"Yes," she said, "that's it over there. The one with the flat roof. See it?"

The man had been smiling nervously at her the whole time. He was wearing glasses with transparent plastic rims, through which his eyes bulged up at her as though through a goldfish bowl. He had not followed where she was pointing. Instead he thrust towards her a small pad of green paper and a ball-point pen.

"You make map," he said.

Christine set down her tennis racquet and drew a careful map. "We are here," she said, pronouncing distinctly. "You go this way. The building is here." She indicated the route with a dotted line and an X. The man leaned close to her, watching the progress of the map attentively; he smelled of cooked cauliflower and an unfamiliar brand of hair grease. When she had finished Christine handed the paper and pen back to him with a terminal smile.

"Wait," the man said. He tore the piece of paper with the map off the pad, folded it carefully and put it in his jacket pocket; the jacket sleeves came down over his wrists and had threads at the edges. He began to write something; she noticed with a slight feeling of revulsion that his nails and the ends of his fingers were so badly bitten they seemed almost deformed. Several of his fingers were blue from the leaky ball-point.

"Here is my name," he said, holding the pad out to her.

Christine read an odd assemblage of Gs, Ys and Ns, neatly printed in block letters. "Thank you," she said.

"You now write *your* name," he said, extending the pen.

Christine hesitated. If this had been a person from her own culture she would have thought he was trying to pick her up. But then, people from her own culture never tried to pick her up; she was too big. The only one who had made the attempt was the Moroccan waiter at the beer parlour where they sometimes went after meetings, and he had been direct. He had just intercepted her on the way to the Ladies' Room and asked and she said no; that had been that. This man was not a waiter though, but a student; she didn't want to offend him. In his culture, whatever it was, this exchange of names on pieces of paper was probably a formal politeness, like saying thank you. She took the pen from him.

"That is a very pleasant name," he said. He folded the paper and placed it in his jacket pocket with the map.

Christine felt she had done her duty. "Well, goodbye," she said. "It was nice to have met you." She bent for her tennis racquet but he had already stooped and retrieved it and was holding it with both hands in front of him, like a captured banner.

"I carry this for you."

"Oh no, please. Don't bother, I am in a hurry," she said, articulating clearly. Deprived of her tennis racquet she felt weaponless. He started to saunter along the path; he was not nervous at all now, he seemed completely at ease.

"*Vous parlez français?*" he asked conversationally.

"*Oui, un petit peu,*" she said. "Not very well." How am I going to get my racquet away from him without being rude? she was wondering.

"*Mais vous avez un bel accent.*"[1] His eyes goggled at her through the glasses: was he being flirtatious? She was well aware that her accent was wretched.

"Look," she said, for the first time letting her impatience show, "I really have to go. Give me my racquet, please."

He quickened his pace but gave no sign of returning the racquet. "Where you are going?"

"Home," she said. "My house."

"I go with you now," he said hopefully.

---

[1] "But you have a nice accent."

"*No,*" she said: she would have to be firm with him. She made a lunge and got a grip on her racquet; after a brief tug of war it came free.

"Goodbye," she said, turning away from his puzzled face and setting off at what she hoped was a discouraging jog-trot. It was like walking away from a growling dog: you shouldn't let on you were frightened. Why should she be frightened anyway? He was only half her size and she had the tennis racquet, there was nothing he could do to her.

Although she did not look back she could tell he was still following. Let there be a streetcar, she thought, and there was one, but it was far down the line, stuck behind a red light. He appeared at her side, breathing audibly, a moment after she reached the stop. She gazed ahead, rigid.

"You are my friend," he said tentatively.

Christine relented: he hadn't been trying to pick her up after all, he was a stranger, he just wanted to meet some of the local people; in his place she would have wanted the same thing.

"Yes," she said, doling him out a smile.

"That is good," he said. "My country is very far."

Christine couldn't think of an apt reply. "That's interesting," she said. "*Très interessant.*" The streetcar was coming at last; she opened her purse and got out a ticket.

"I go with you now," he said. His hand clamped on her arm above the elbow.

"You ... stay ... *here,*" Christine said, resisting the impulse to shout but pausing between each word as though for a deaf person. She detached his hand — his hold was quite feeble and could not compete with her tennis biceps — and leapt off the curb and up the streetcar steps, hearing with relief the doors grind shut behind her. Inside the car and a block away she permitted herself a glance out a side window. He was standing where she had left him; he seemed to be writing something on his little pad of paper.

When she reached home she had only time for a snack, and even then she was almost late for the Debating Society. The topic was, "Resolved: That War Is Obsolete." Her team took the affirmative and won.

Christine came out of her last examination feeling depressed. It was not the exam that depressed her but the fact that it was the last one: it meant the end of the school year. She dropped into the coffee shop as usual, then went home early because there didn't seem to be anything else to do.

"Is that you, dear?" her mother called from the living room. She must have heard the front door close. Christine went in and flopped on the sofa, disturbing the neat pattern of cushions.

"How was your exam, dear?" her mother asked.

"Fine," said Christine flatly. It had been fine; she had passed. She was not a brilliant student, she knew that, but she was conscientious. Her professors always wrote things like "A serious attempt" and "Well thought out but perhaps lacking in élan" on her term papers; they gave her Bs, the occasional B + . She was taking Political Science and Economics, and hoped for a job with the Government after she graduated; with her father's connections she had a good chance.

"That's nice."

Christine felt, resentfully, that her mother had only a hazy idea of what an exam was. She was arranging gladioli in a vase; she had rubber gloves on to protect her hands as she always did when engaged in what she called "housework." As far as Christine could tell her housework consisted of arranging flowers in vases: daffodils and tulips and hyacinths through gladioli, irises and roses, all the way to asters and mums. Sometimes she cooked, elegantly and with chafing-dishes, but she thought of it as a hobby. The girl did everything else. Christine thought it faintly sinful to have a girl. The only ones available now were either foreign or pregnant; their expressions usually suggested they were being taken advantage of somehow. But her mother asked what they would do otherwise; they'd either have to go into a Home or stay in their own countries, and Christine had to agree this was probably true. It was hard, anyway, to argue with her mother. She was so delicate, so preserved-looking, a harsh breath would scratch the finish.

"An interesting young man phoned today," her mother said. She had finished the gladioli and was taking off her rubber gloves. "He asked to speak with you and when I said you weren't in we had quite a little chat. You didn't tell me about him, dear." She put on the glasses which she wore on a decorative chain around her neck, a signal that she was in her modern, intelligent mood rather than her old-fashioned whimsical one.

"Did he leave his name?" Christine asked. She knew a lot of young men but they didn't often call her; they conducted their business with her in the coffee shop or after meetings.

"He's a person from another culture. He said he would call back later."

Christine had to think a moment. She was vaguely acquainted with several people from other cultures, Britain mostly; they belonged to the Debating Society.

"He's studying Philosophy in Montreal," her mother prompted. "He sounded French."

Christine began to remember the man in the park. "I don't think he's French, exactly," she said.

Her mother had taken off her glasses again and was poking absentmindedly at a bent gladiolus. "Well, he sounded French." She meditated, flowery sceptre in hand. "I think it would be nice if you had him to tea."

Christine's mother did her best. She had two other daughters, both of whom took after her. They were beautiful; one was well married already and the other would clearly have no trouble. Her friends consoled her about Christine by saying, "She's not fat, she's just big-boned, it's the father's side," and "Christine is so healthy." Her other daughters had never gotten involved in activities when they were at school, but since Christine could not possibly ever be beautiful even if she took off weight, it was just as well she was so athletic and political, it was a good thing she had interests. Christine's mother tried to encourage her interests whenever possible. Christine could tell when she was making an extra effort, there was a reproachful edge to her voice.

She knew her mother expected enthusiasm but she could not supply it. "I don't know, I'll have to see," she said dubiously.

"You look tired, darling," said her mother. "Perhaps you'd like a glass of milk."

Christine was in the bathtub when the phone rang. She was not prone to fantasy but when she was in the bathtub she often pretended she was a dolphin, a game left over from one of the girls who used to bathe her when she was small. Her mother was being bell-voiced and gracious in the hall; then there was a tap at the door.

"It's that nice young French student, Christine," her mother said.

"Tell him I'm in the bathtub," Christine said, louder than necessary. "He isn't French."

She could hear her mother frowning. "That wouldn't be very polite, Christine. I don't think he'd understand."

"Oh, all right," Christine said. She heaved herself out of the bathtub, swathed her pink bulk in a towel and splattered to the phone.

"Hello," she said gruffly. At a distance he was not pathetic, he was a nuisance. She could not imagine how he had tracked her down: most likely he went through the phone book, calling all the numbers with her last name until he hit on the right one.

"It is your friend."

"I know," she said. "How are you?"

"I am very fine." There was a long pause, during which Christine had a vicious urge to say, "Well goodbye then," and hang up; but she was aware of her mother poised figurine-like in her bedroom doorway. Then he said, "I hope you also are very fine."

"Yes," said Christine. She wasn't going to participate.

"I come to tea," he said.

This took Christine by surprise. "You do?"

"Your pleasant mother ask me. I come Thursday, four o'clock."

"Oh," Christine said, ungraciously.

"See you then," he said, with the conscious pride of one who has mastered a difficult idiom.

Christine set down the phone and went along the hall. Her mother was in her study, sitting innocently at her writing desk.

"Did you ask him to tea on Thursday?"

"Not exactly, dear," her mother said. "I did mention he might come round to tea *some*time, though."

"Well, he's coming Thursday. Four o'clock."

"What's wrong with that?" her mother said serenely. "I think it's a very nice gesture for us to make. I do think you might try to be a little more co-operative." She was pleased with herself.

"Since you invited him," said Christine, "you can bloody well stick around and help me entertain him. I don't want to be left making nice gestures all by myself."

"Christine, *dear*," her mother said, above being shocked. "You ought to put on your dressing gown, you'll catch a chill."

After sulking for an hour Christine tried to think of the tea as a cross between an examination and an executive meeting: not enjoyable, certainly, but to be got through as tactfully as possible. And it *was* a nice gesture. When the cakes her mother had ordered arrived from The Patisserie on Thursday morning she began to feel slightly festive; she even resolved to put on a dress, a good one, instead of a skirt and blouse. After all, she had nothing against him, except the memory of the way he had grabbed her tennis racquet and then her arm. She suppressed a quick impossible vision of herself pursued around the living room, fending him off with thrown sofa cushions and vases of gladioli; nevertheless she told the girl they would have tea in the garden. It would be a treat for him, and there was more space outdoors.

She had suspected her mother would dodge the tea, would contrive to be going out just as he was arriving: that way she could size him up and then leave them alone together. She had done things like that to Christine before; the excuse this time was the Symphony Committee. Sure enough, her mother carefully mislaid her gloves and located them with a faked murmur of joy when the doorbell rang. Christine relished for weeks afterwards the image of her mother's dropped jaw and flawless recovery when he was introduced: he wasn't quite the foreign potentate her optimistic, veil-fragile mind had concocted.

He was prepared for celebration. He had slicked on so much hair cream that his head seemed to be covered with a tight black patent-leather cap, and he had cut the threads off his jacket sleeves. His orange tie was overpoweringly splendid. Christine noticed, however, as he shook her mother's suddenly braced white glove that the ball-point ink on his fingers was indelible. His face had broken out, possibly in anticipation of the delights in store for him; he had a tiny camera slung over his shoulder and was smoking an exotic-smelling cigarette.

Christine led him through the cool flowery softly padded living room and out by the French doors into the garden. "You sit here," she said. "I will have the girl bring tea."

This girl was from the West Indies: Christine's parents had been enraptured with her when they were down at Christmas and had brought her back with them. Since that time she had become pregnant, but Christine's mother had not dismissed her. She said she was slightly disappointed but what could you expect, and she didn't see any real difference between a girl who was pregnant before you hired her and one who got that way afterwards. She prided herself on her tolerance; also there was a scarcity of girls. Strangely enough, the girl became progressively less easy to get along with. Either she did not share Christine's mother's view of her own generosity, or she felt she had gotten away with something and was therefore free to indulge in contempt. At first Christine had tried to treat her as an equal. "Don't call me 'Miss Christine'" she had said with an imitation of light, comradely laughter. "What you want me to call you then?" the girl had said, scowling. They had begun to have brief, surly arguments in the kitchen, which Christine decided were like the arguments between one servant and another: her mother's attitude towards each of them was similar, they were not altogether satisfactory but they would have to do.

The cakes, glossy with icing, were set out on a plate and the teapot was standing ready; on the counter the electric kettle boiled. Christine headed for it, but the girl, till then sitting with her elbows on the kitchen table and watching her expressionlessly, made a dash and intercepted her. Christine waited until she had poured the water into the pot. Then, "I'll carry it out, Elvira," she said. She had just decided she didn't want the girl to see her visitor's orange tie; already, she knew, her position in the girl's eyes had suffered because no one had yet attempted to get *her* pregnant.

"What you think they pay me for, Miss Christine?" the girl said insolently. She swung towards the garden with the tray; Christine trailed her, feeling lumpish and awkward. The girl was at least as big as she was but in a different way.

"Thank you, Elvira," Christine said when the tray was in place. The girl departed without a word, casting a disdainful backward glance at the frayed jacket sleeves, the stained fingers. Christine was now determined to be especially kind to him.

"You are very rich," he said.

"No," Christine protested, shaking her head, "we're not." She had never thought of her family as rich; it was one of her father's sayings that nobody made any money with the Government.

"Yes," he repeated, "you are very rich." He sat back in his lawn chair, gazing about him as though dazed.

Christine set his cup of tea in front of him. She wasn't in the habit of paying much attention to the house or the garden; they were nothing special, far from being the largest on the street; other people took care of them. But now she looked where he was looking, seeing it all as though from a different height: the long expanses, the border flowers blazing in the early-summer sunlight, the flagged patio and walks, the high walls and the silence.

He came back to her face, sighing a little. "My English is not good," he said, "but I improve."

"You do," Christine said, nodding encouragement.

He took sips of his tea, quickly and tenderly, as though afraid of injuring the cup. "I like to stay here."

Christine passed him the cakes. He took only one, making a slight face as he ate it; but he had several more cups of tea while she finished the cakes. She managed to find out from him that he had come over on a church fellowship — she could not decode the denomination —

and was studying Philosophy or Theology, or possibly both. She was feeling well-disposed towards him: he had behaved himself, he had caused her no inconvenience.

The teapot was at last empty. He sat up straight in his chair, as though alerted by a soundless gong. "You look this way, please," he said. Christine saw that he had placed his miniature camera on the stone sundial her mother had shipped back from England two years before. He wanted to take her picture. She was flattered, and settled herself to pose, smiling evenly.

He took off his glasses and laid them beside his plate. For a moment she saw his myopic, unprotected eyes turned towards her, with something tremulous and confiding in them she wanted to close herself off from knowing about. Then he went over and did something to the camera, his back to her. The next instant he was crouched beside her, his arm around her waist as far as it could reach, his other hand covering her own hands which she had folded in her lap, his cheek jammed up against hers. She was too startled to move. The camera clicked.

He stood up at once and replaced his glasses, which glittered now with a sad triumph. "Thank you, miss," he said to her. "I go now." He slung the camera back over his shoulder, keeping his hand on it as though to hold the lid on and prevent escape. "I send to my family; they will like."

He was out the gate and gone before Christine had recovered; then she laughed. She had been afraid he would attack her, she could admit it now, and he had; but not in the usual way. He had raped, *rapeo, rapere, rapui, to seize and carry off*, not herself but her celluloid image, and incidently that of the silver tea service, which glinted mockingly at her as the girl bore it away, carrying it regally, the insignia, the official jewels.

Christine spent the summer as she had for the past three years: she was the sailing instructress at an expensive all-girls camp near Algonquin Park. She had been a camper there, everything was familiar to her; she sailed almost better than she played tennis.

The second week she got a letter from him, postmarked Montreal and forwarded from her home address. It was printed in block letters on a piece of the green paper, two or three sentences. It began, "I hope you are well," then described the weather in monosyllables and ended, "I am fine." It was signed, "Your friend." Each week she got another of these letters, more or less identical. In one of them a colour print was enclosed: himself, slightly cross-eyed and grinning hilariously, even more spindly than she remembered him against her billowing draperies, flowers exploding around them like firecrackers, one of his hands an equivocal blur in her lap, the other out of sight; on her own face, astonishment and outrage, as though he was sticking her in the behind with his hidden thumb.

She answered the first letter, but after that the seniors were in training for the races. At the end of the summer, packing to go home, she threw all the letters away.

When she had been back for several weeks she received another of the green letters. This time there was a return address printed at the top which Christine noted with foreboding was in her own city. Every day she waited for the phone to ring; she was so certain his first attempt at contact would be a disembodied voice that when he came upon her abruptly in mid-campus she was unprepared.

"How are you?"

His smile was the same, but everything else about him had deteriorated. He was, if possible, thinner; his jacket sleeves had sprouted a lush new crop of threads, as though to conceal his hands now so badly bitten they appeared to have been gnawed by rodents. His hair fell over his eyes, uncut, ungreased; his eyes in the hollowed face, a delicate triangle of skin stretched on bone, jumped behind his glasses like hooded fish. He had the end of a cigarette in the corner of his mouth, and as they walked he lit a new one from it.

"I'm fine," Christine said. She was thinking, I'm not going to get involved again, enough is enough, I've done my bit for internationalism. "How are you?"

"I live here now," he said. "Maybe I study Economics."

"That's nice." He didn't sound as though he was enrolled anywhere.

"I come to see you."

Christine didn't know whether he meant he had left Montreal in order to be near her or just wanted to visit her at her house as he had done in the spring; either way she refused to be implicated. They were outside the Political Science Building. "I have a class here," she said. "Goodbye." She was being callous, she realized that, but a quick chop was more merciful in the long run, that was what her beautiful sisters used to say.

Afterwards she decided it had been stupid of her to let him find out where her class was. Though a timetable was posted in each of the colleges: all he had to do was look her up and record her every probable movement in block letters on his green notepad. After that day he never left her alone.

Initially he waited outside the lecture rooms for her to come out. She said hello to him curtly at first and kept on going, but this didn't work; he followed her at a distance, smiling his changeless smile. Then she stopped speaking altogether and pretended to ignore him, but it made no difference, he followed her anyway. The fact that she was in some way afraid of him — or was it just embarrassment? — seemed only to encourage him. Her friends started to notice, asking her who he was and why he was tagging along behind her; she could hardly answer because she hardly knew.

As the weekdays passed and he showed no signs of letting up, she began to jog-trot between classes, finally to run. He was tireless, and had an amazing wind for one who smoked so heavily: he would speed along behind her, keeping the distance between them the same, as though he were a pull-toy attached to her by a string. She was aware of the ridiculous spectacle they must make, galloping across campus, something out of a cartoon short, a lumbering elephant stampeded by a smiling, emaciated mouse, both of them locked in the classic pattern of comic pursuit and flight; but she found that to race made her less nervous than to walk sedately, the skin on the back of her neck crawling with the feel of his eyes on it. At least she could use her muscles. She worked out routines, escapes: she would dash in the front door of the Ladies' Room in the coffee shop and out the back door, and he would lose the trail, until he discovered the other entrance. She would try to shake him by detours through baffling archways and corridors, but he seemed as familiar with the architectural mazes as she was herself. As a last refuge she could head for the women's dormitory and watch from safety as he was skidded to a halt by the receptionist's austere voice: men were not allowed past the entrance.

Lunch became difficult. She would be sitting, usually with other members of the Debating Society, just digging nicely into a sandwich, when he would appear suddenly as though he'd come up through an unseen manhole. She then had the choice of barging out through the crowded cafeteria, sandwich half-eaten, or finishing her lunch with him standing behind her chair, everyone at the table acutely aware of him, the conversation stilting and dwindling. Her friends learned to spot him from a distance; they posted lookouts. "Here he comes," they would whisper, helping her collect her belongings for the sprint they knew would follow.

Several times she got tired of running and turned to confront him. "What do you want?"

she would ask, glowering belligerently down at him, almost clenching her fists; she felt like shaking him, hitting him.

"I wish to talk with you."

"Well, here I am," she would say. "What do you want to talk about?"

But he would say nothing; he would stand in front of her, shifting his feet, smiling perhaps apologetically (though she could never pinpoint the exact tone of that smile, chewed lips stretched apart over the nicotine-yellowed teeth, rising at the corners, flesh held stiffly in place for an invisible photographer), his eyes jerking from one part of her face to another as though he saw her in fragments.

Annoying and tedious though it was, his pursuit of her had an odd result: mysterious in itself, it rendered her equally mysterious. No one had ever found Christine mysterious before. To her parents she was a beefy heavyweight, a plodder, lacking in flair, ordinary as bread. To her sisters she was the plain one, treated with an indulgence they did not give to each other: they did not fear her as a rival. To her male friends she was the one who could be relied on. She was helpful and a hard worker, always good for a game of tennis with the athletes among them. They invited her along to drink beer with them so they could get into the cleaner, more desirable Ladies and Escorts side of the beer parlour, taking it for granted she would buy her share of the rounds. In moments of stress they confided to her their problems with women. There was nothing devious about her and nothing interesting.

Christine had always agreed with these estimates of herself. In childhood she had identified with the false bride or the ugly sister; whenever a story had begun, "Once there was a maiden as beautiful as she was good," she had known it wasn't her. That was just how it was, but it wasn't so bad. Her parents never expected her to be a brilliant social success and weren't overly disappointed when she wasn't. She was spared the manoeuvring and anxiety she witnessed among others her age, and she even had a kind of special position among men: she was an exception, she fitted none of the categories they commonly used when talking about girls; she wasn't a cock-teaser, a cold fish, an easy lay or a snarky bitch; she was an honorary person. She had grown to share their contempt for most women.

Now, however, there was something about her that could not be explained. A man was chasing her, a peculiar sort of man, granted, but still a man, and he was without doubt attracted to her, he couldn't leave her alone. Other men examined her more closely than they ever had, appraising her, trying to find out what it was those twitching bespectacled eyes saw in her. They started to ask her out, though they returned from these excursions with their curiosity unsatisfied, the secret of her charm still intact. Her opaque dumpling face, her solid bearshaped body became for them parts of a riddle no one could solve. Christine sensed this. In the bathtub she no longer imagined she was a dolphin; instead she imagined she was an elusive water-nixie, or sometimes, in moments of audacity, Marilyn Monroe. The daily chase was becoming a habit; she even looked forward to it. In addition to its other benefits she was losing weight.

All these weeks he had never phoned her or turned up at the house. He must have decided however that his tactics were not having the desired result, or perhaps he sensed she was becoming bored. The phone began to ring in the early morning or late at night when he could be sure she would be there. Sometimes he would simply breathe (she could recognize, or thought she could, the quality of his breathing), in which case she would hang up. Occasionally he would say again that he wanted to talk to her, but even when she gave him lots of time nothing else would follow. Then he extended his range: she would see him on her streetcar, smiling at her silently from a seat never closer than three away; she could feel him tracking her down her own street, though when she would break her resolve to pay no attention and would glance back he would be invisible or in the act of hiding behind a tree or hedge.

Among crowds of people and in daylight she had not really been afraid of him; she was stronger than he was and he had made no recent attempt to touch her. But the days were growing shorter and colder, it was almost November. Often she was arriving home in twilight or a darkness broken only by the feeble orange streetlamps. She brooded over the possibility of razors, knives, guns; by acquiring a weapon he could quickly turn the odds against her. She avoided wearing scarves, remembering the newspaper stories about girls who had been strangled by them. Putting on her nylons in the morning gave her a funny feeling. Her body seemed to have diminished, to have become smaller than his.

Was he deranged, was he a sex maniac? He seemed so harmless, yet it was that kind who often went berserk in the end. She pictured those ragged fingers at her throat, tearing at her clothes, though she could not think of herself as screaming. Parked cars, the shrubberies near her house, the driveways on either side of it, changed as she passed them from unnoticed background to sinister shadowed foreground, every detail distinct and harsh: they were places a man might crouch, leap out from. Yet every time she saw him in the clear light of morning or afternoon (for he still continued his old methods of pursuit), his aging jacket and jittery eyes convinced her that it was she herself who was the tormentor, the persecutor. She was in some sense responsible; from the folds and crevices of the body she had treated for so long as a reliable machine was emanating, against her will, some potent invisible odour, like a dog's in heat or a female moth's, that made him unable to stop following her.

Her mother, who had been too preoccupied with the unavoidable fall entertaining to pay much attention to the number of phone calls Christine was getting or to the hired girl's complaints of a man who hung up without speaking, announced that she was flying down to New York for the weekend; her father decided to go too. Christine panicked: she saw herself in the bathtub with her throat slit, the blood drooling out of her neck and running in a little spiral down the drain (for by this time she believed he could walk through walls, could be everywhere at once). The girl would do nothing to help; she might even stand in the bathroom door with her arms folded, watching. Christine arranged to spend the weekend at her married sister's.

When she arrived back Sunday evening she found the girl close to hysterics. She said that on Saturday she had gone to pull the curtains across the French doors at dusk and had found a strangely contorted face, a man's face, pressed against the glass, staring in at her from the garden. She claimed she had fainted and had almost had her baby a month too early right there on the living-room carpet. Then she had called the police. He was gone by the time they got there but she had recognized him from the afternoon of the tea; she had informed them he was a friend of Christine's.

They called Monday evening to investigate, two of them. They were very polite, they knew who Christine's father was. Her father greeted them heartily; her mother hovered in the background, fidgeting with her porcelain hands, letting them see how frail and worried she was. She didn't like having them in the living room but they were necessary.

Christine had to admit he'd been following her around. She was relieved he'd been discovered, relieved also that she hadn't been the one to tell, though if he'd been a citizen of the country she would have called the police a long time ago. She insisted he was not dangerous, he had never hurt her.

"That kind don't hurt you," one of the policemen said. "They just kill you. You're lucky you aren't dead."

"Nut cases," the other one said.

Her mother volunteered that the thing about people from another culture was that you could never tell whether they were insane or not because their ways were so different. The policemen agreed with her, deferential but also condescending, as though she was a royal halfwit who had to be humoured.

"You know where he lives?" the first policeman asked. Christine had long ago torn up the letter with his address on it; she shook her head.

"We'll have to pick him up tomorrow then," he said. "Think you can keep him talking outside your class if he's waiting for you?"

After questioning her they held a murmured conversation with her father in the front hall. The girl, clearing away the coffee cups, said if they didn't lock him up she was leaving, she wasn't going to be scared half out of her skin like that again.

Next day when Christine came out of her Modern History lecture he was there, right on schedule. He seemed puzzled when she did not begin to run. She approached him, her heart thumping with treachery and the prospect of freedom. Her body was back to its usual size; she felt herself a giantess, self-controlled, invulnerable.

"How are you?" she asked, smiling brightly.

He looked at her with distrust.

"How have you been?" she ventured again. His own smile faded; he took a step back from her.

"This the one?" said the policeman, popping out from behind a notice board like a Keystone Cop and laying a competent hand on the worn jacket shoulder. The other policeman lounged in the background; force would not be required.

"Don't *do* anything to him," she pleaded as they took him away. They nodded and grinned, respectful, scornful. He seemed to know perfectly well who they were and what they wanted.

The first policeman phoned that evening to make his report. Her father talked with him, jovial and managing. She herself was now out of the picture; she had been protected, her function was over.

"What did they *do* to him?" she asked anxiously as he came back into the living room. She was not sure what went on in police stations.

"They didn't do anything to him," he said, amused by her concern. "They could have booked him for Watching and Besetting, they wanted to know if I'd like to press charges. But it's not worth a court case: he's got a visa that says he's only allowed in the country as long as he studies in Montreal, so I told them to just ship him down there. If he turns up here again they'll deport him. They went around to his rooming house, his rent's two weeks overdue; the landlady said she was on the point of kicking him out. He seems happy enough to be getting his back rent paid and a free train ticket to Montreal." He paused. "They couldn't get anything out of him though."

"*Out* of him?" Christine asked.

"They tried to find out why he was doing it; following you, I mean." Her father's eyes swept her as though it was a riddle to him also. "They said when they asked him about that he just clammed up. Pretended he didn't understand English. He understood well enough, but he wasn't answering."

Christine thought this would be the end, but somehow between his arrest and the departure of the train he managed to elude his escort long enough for one more phone call.

"I see you again," he said. He didn't wait for her to hang up.

Now that he was no longer an embarrassing present reality, he could be talked about, he could become an amusing story. In fact, he was the only amusing story Christine had to tell, and telling it preserved both for herself and for others the aura of her strange allure. Her friends and the men who continued to ask her out speculated about his motives. One suggested he had wanted to marry her so he could remain in the country; another said that oriental men were fond of well-built women: "It's your Rubens[2] quality."

Christine thought about him a lot. She had not been attracted to him, rather the reverse, but as an idea only he was a romantic figure, the one man who had found her irresistible; though she often wondered, inspecting her unchanged pink face and hefty body in her full-length mirror, just what it was about her that had done it. She avoided whenever it was proposed the theory of his insanity: it was only that there was more than one way of being sane.

But a new acquaintance, hearing the story for the first time, had a different explanation. "So he got you, too," he said, laughing. "That has to be the same guy who was hanging around our day camp a year ago this summer. He followed all the girls like that, a short guy, Japanese or something, glasses, smiling all the time."

"Maybe it was another one," Christine said.

"There couldn't be two of them, everything fits. This was a pretty weird guy."

"What ... *kind* of girls did he follow?" Christine asked.

"Oh, just anyone who happened to be around. But if they paid any attention to him at first, if they were nice to him or anything, he was unshakeable. He was a bit of a pest, but harmless."

Christine ceased to tell her amusing story. She had been one among many, then. She went back to playing tennis, she had been neglecting her game.

A few months later the policeman who had been in charge of the case telephoned her again.

"Like you to know, miss, that fellow you were having the trouble with was sent back to his own country. Deported."

"What for?" Christine asked. "Did he try to come back here?" Maybe she had been special after all, maybe he had dared everything for her.

"Nothing like it," the policeman said. "He was up to the same tricks in Montreal but he really picked the wrong woman this time — a Mother Superior of a convent. They don't stand for things like that in Quebec — had him out of here before he knew what happened. I guess he'll be better off in his own place."

"How old was she?" Christine asked, after a silence.

"Oh, around sixty, I guess."

"Thank you very much for letting me know," Christine said in her best official manner. "It's such a relief." She wondered if the policeman had called to make fun of her.

She was almost crying when she put down the phone. What *had* he wanted from her then? A Mother Superior. Did she really look sixty, did she look like a mother? What did convents mean? Comfort, charity? Refuge? Was it that something had happened to him, some intolerable strain just from being in this country; her tennis dress and exposed legs too much for him, flesh and money seemingly available everywhere but withheld from him wherever he turned, the nun the symbol of some final distortion, the robe and veil reminiscent to his near-sighted eyes of the women of his homeland, the ones he was able to understand? But he was back in his own country, remote from her as another planet; she would never know.

He hadn't forgotten her though. In the spring she got a postcard with a foreign stamp and the familiar block-letter writing. On the front was a picture of a temple. He was fine, he hoped she was fine also, he was her friend. A month later another print of the picture he had taken in the garden arrived, in a sealed manila envelope otherwise empty.

---

[2] Peter Paul Rubens (1557–1640), Flemish painter noted for his paintings of fleshy women.

Christine's aura of mystery soon faded; anyway, she herself no longer believed in it. Life became again what she had always expected. She graduated with mediocre grades and went into the Department of Health and Welfare; she did a good job, and was seldom discriminated against for being a woman because nobody thought of her as one. She could afford a pleasant-sized apartment, though she did not put much energy into decorating it. She played less and less tennis; what had been muscle with a light coating of fat turned gradually into fat with a thin substratum of muscle. She began to get headaches.

As the years were used up and the war began to fill the newspapers and magazines, she realized which Eastern country he had actually been from. She had known the name but it hadn't registered at the time, it was such a minor place; she could never keep them separate in her mind.

But though she tried, she couldn't remember the name of the city, and the postcard was long gone — had he been from the North or the South, was he near the battle zone or safely far from it? Obsessively she bought magazines and pored over the available photographs, dead villagers, soldiers on the march, colour blowups of frightened or angry faces, spies being executed; she studied maps, she watched the late-night newscasts, the distant country and terrain becoming almost more familiar to her than her own. Once or twice she thought she could recognize him but it was no use, they all looked like him.

Finally she had to stop looking at the pictures. It bothered her too much, it was bad for her; she was beginning to have nightmares in which he was coming through the French doors of her mother's house in his shabby jacket, carrying a packsack and a rifle and a huge bouquet of richly coloured flowers. He was smiling in the same way but with blood streaked over his face, partly blotting out the features. She gave her television set away and took to reading nineteenth-century novels instead; Trollope and Galsworthy[3] were her favourites. When, despite herself, she would think about him, she would tell herself that he had been crafty and agile-minded enough to survive, more or less, in her country, so surely he would be able to do it in his own, where he knew the language. She could not see him in the army, on either side; he wasn't the type, and to her knowledge he had not believed in any particular ideology. He would be something nondescript, something in the background, like herself; perhaps he had become an interpreter.

QUESTIONS

1. What attitudes about foreigners do Christine and her mother hold? How are these attitudes responsible for creating Christine's predicament? What else might be a factor?

2. How does Christine's friend change her perceptions about herself? What happens to her self-image when she learns of his track record with women? What are the reasons behind her continued interest in him?

3. Why does Christine's friend reveal so little about himself? What are his motives? What nationality is he? How is this significant?

4. Discuss the title of the story. In what sense is "the man from Mars" an alien? Compare this story with Paul Bowles's "A Distant Episode," another story of clashing cultures.

---

[3] Anthony Trollope (1815–1882), John Galsworthy (1867–1933): English novelists.

ANN BEATTIE ≡

A Clever-Kids Story

The two clever kids are Jane and Joseph. The names alliterate. Our parents planned that —
two cute kids with alliterating names, born two and a half years apart.

The summer that I was five and Joseph was seven and a half he began to tell me the clever-
kids stories when we were put to bed. We lived in what had been our grandparents' house in
New Hampshire — a huge barn of a house with high ceilings and rose-splotched wallpaper.
My parents moved there when Joseph was four and a half and I was two. He claimed to
remember New York City. It was one of the many things I envied him for: he had been born in
a hospital as high as a skyscraper; I had been born in a bed in the house in New Hampshire.
When my grandfather died, my parents sold their furniture and my father quit his job, and
they moved to the woods of New Hampshire, into the house where our family had spent the
summer. My grandmother, after my grandfather's death, moved to the warmer weather in
Georgia and was able to live with a cousin whose husband had died a few years before. My
grandmother came to New Hampshire in June and stayed until the first of September.

The first clever-kids story I remember was about her: the grandmother was chewing
gum, and she blew a bubble so big that you could see things in it, like a mirror. The clever kids
looked into the bubble and saw a robber coming in the door, and as the grandmother began to
breathe in and retract the bubble they saw the robber getting smaller and smaller, but coming
closer. The grandmother didn't see anything because she was squinting, concentrating on
making the bubble disappear. Just as the bubble was about to disappear, the clever kids
whirled around and overpowered the robber. They took out their guns and shot him dead.

Nothing about the stories seemed odd to me. That we would have real guns seemed
perfectly possible. Anything Joseph said seemed reasonable and likely. He told me that he
could fly, and I believed him. Partly it was because when he told me the stories late at night —
when he crept into my bed and awed or scared me and then ended the stories in some
satisfactory way — he seemed so authoritative that I couldn't help but believe him. His
whispering made the stories more emphatic. The secret ritual of climbing into my bed made
them something we shared privately, and things privately shared must be important — and
therefore true. When he told me he could fly I didn't challenge him. I had never heard of Peter
Pan, and had never even been to a circus to see the trapeze performers, but I could believe that
a person, particularly my brother Joseph, could fly. "Where do you fly?" I whispered. He

thought about it. "I fly by the lake," he said. "I've flown on the main beach. One Sunday when it rained and there was nobody around."

I remembered the day he was talking about. It was a Sunday in springtime and it had rained for three days, but the rain was really pouring down that Sunday. And Joseph put on his black rubber boots and his raincoat and said he was going to the beach. My mother grabbed him by the arm and said he was not. My father told Joseph to go ahead, then turned to my mother and said he admired his son's spirit. Sebastian was visiting, and she started to argue but backed down when Sebastian asked them please not to fight. In many ways Sebastian was like one of us: he put his hands over his ears if someone said something harsh. Once when he hit his finger with a hammer, I saw him cry. Sebastian had left New York the same year my parents did; my father worked as a carpenter with two other men, and Sebastian kept the books.

My grandmother did not like Sebastian. My father liked him very much, and my mother tolerated him. Joseph and I had mixed emotions: he was always kind to us, but when he was with adults he seemed childish, so we didn't respect him as we'd respect an adult, but when he played with us he seemed reserved — the way an adult would. When I was seven, when I saw him cry after he hit his thumb, my father took me aside and told me that sometimes Sebastian's reactions were a little out of whack because in New York he had had a breakdown. He explained to me what a breakdown was. I was fascinated and wanted to tell Joseph, but somehow I knew that he was the storyteller. In fact, I started to tell him, but he interrupted with his own Sebastian story: in the Bible they shot him full of arrows, for being evil, but a beautiful lady pulled out all the arrows, without causing him any pain. "What happened to the holes?" I said. "All the arrows were shot into his face. She pulled them out so carefully that they just left little holes. Whiskers grew out of them."

As Joseph was fabricating stories that spring, strange things were happening that we didn't know about. We knew things were going on, but we were involved in collecting seashells from the main beach, playing hide and seek in the woods with Billy LaPierre, whose family had the camp next to ours, and the secret nighttime stories. We knew our mother was irritable and our father silent. We knew that Sebastian didn't come around very often. We did not know that our mother had had an abortion, and that Sebastian had driven her to Montreal, where she had it performed illegally, and against my father's wishes. I overheard her, one night, saying to him, "Where would we get the money for another baby? You won't commit yourself to anything. You could have worked for a prosperous business, but you hooked up with Frankie and Phil Renshaw. I'm already *surrounded* by babies: Sebastian in tears every time I turn around, you bumming around, your mother coming every summer and expecting me to do everything but wipe her chin."

I don't think that my mother loved Sebastian — just that after the abortion, when he felt she and Sebastian had both turned against him, they began to spend more time with each other, discussing it. Then my father became jealous, and my mother laughed at him for thinking anything so stupid, and her taunting made my father bitter, and finally silent. Things were so bad that my grandmother came in June and left before the month was over, pretending that she felt guilty for having left her cousin.

Sebastian and Joseph and I drove her to Boston to get a plane. Everyone knew that it was strange my parents didn't go. My father said that he had to work, and my mother offered to go along for the ride, looking very ashamed, but my grandmother said no — she wanted some time alone with her two favorite children. As I recall, she hardly talked to us, but she gave us both money. On the way back, Sebastian bought us large vanilla ice cream cones. We sat on the grass beside the ice cream stand, bees swarming around the trash can, Joseph more interested in watching them than in licking his cone. He got ice cream all down his shirt, and when we got home my mother complained about that instead of thanking Sebastian for what he had done. We ran outside as soon as we could and hid our five-dollar bills in an old tackle box and buried the box in the nook of a tree, because Joseph said we should.

At dinner my mother asked if Grandma had given us a treat before she left. It was all she said about her having left. Joseph tried to evade the question.

"Because your father has stopped speaking doesn't mean that you should stop, Joseph," she said. She laid down her fork and Sebastian laid his down too.

"I think she gave them both some money," Sebastian said, looking at me because he knew I'd never have the courage to avoid a direct question.

"Yes," I said.

My mother smiled. "She said she was going to give you money to buy a treat when she and I had breakfast this morning."

Sebastian picked up his fork and began to eat his salad.

"Did you put it somewhere safe?" she said.

Joseph looked at me — a warning look.

"What's the big secret?" my mother said.

"Look," my father said, "it isn't necessary to fill us in on little details. We don't need to know everything. They should just do whatever they feel like doing."

My mother frowned. "That's unfair," she said, "to challenge me in the guise of protecting the children."

"I was aiming it at you. I love children. I wouldn't put the children on the spot."

"Stop it," she said, "or I'm going to leave the table."

"Take Sebastian with you. There's nearly a full moon tonight — good night for a walk."

"Why don't you two make up?" Sebastian said.

"Why don't I get a direct answer from my children before the conversation veers off again?" she said. She turned to me. Everybody knew I was the easiest mark.

"We pretended, we — played pirates, and we buried the ten dollars in a box in the hole of a tree."

Joseph had not said we were pirates, and I thought I had been very clever.

My mother looked at me. "All right," she said. "I don't see why there had to be such a secret."

That night, in bed, Joseph didn't tell a story. Instead, we talked about how something had been wrong at dinner. Finally, proud of my invented story, I mentioned the buried money.

"She wasn't even mad," I said. "We can get the money tomorrow."

"She wasn't mad at you, but she was mad at me because I wouldn't answer."

"We can buy candy down at the store all month," I said.

There was a long silence. Then Joseph said, "The money's gone."

I didn't question it. He whispered, "The money's gone," and suddenly I knew that it was, that it was punishment for my having told the secret. Before we fell asleep he relented a little. "It might get put back somehow," he said. But when we whispered the next night it wasn't about the money, and we never dug for it or mentioned it again.

For years I forgot about it. I remembered it recently, riding the bus; I looked out the window and saw a squirrel run up a tree very much like the tree where we had buried the box. All at once I felt so sentimental I had to concentrate hard not to cry. I had remembered that there was something that was his and mine, that it was still there, and that I could go and get it. I got off the bus and walked to my room. It was a nice room with walls painted oyster-white, and the bare walls made me think of the rose-covered wallpaper all through the house in New Hampshire, and of what Sebastian had told me years before about the hospital he went to when he had his breakdown — how he would study the plain white walls and know that he had to get out of that place. The hairline cracks in them would appear in his dreams; imagined smudges would make him wake up, in a fit of anxiety. His obsession with the walls was only making him crazier.

In 1969 Joseph died in Vietnam. My mother received official notification, then a letter from a friend of his that was full of praise for his valor, his wonderful sense of humor, his skill with a rifle. It was an odd letter, one that the man probably would not have sent if he had thought it over. There was a paragraph near the end praising Joseph for having changed the man's taste in music, for Joseph's having explained what was really important musically. A list of several meaningful songs followed. The letter concluded mournfully, and he signed it "God bless." I read it over and over, all summer, and at the end, every time, I would hear Red Skelton's voice saying the "God bless." The man who had written the letter was obviously heartbroken, yet it just wasn't the kind of letter to send. He was alive and Joseph was not. He seemed to give equal weight to a sense of humor and rifle skills. What sort of person could he be?

Instead of going to the main beach, I went to the dock and sat at the end of it with my feet in the water and the letter beside me, carefully closed in a book so it wouldn't get wet.

He had a sense of humor, all right. He had such a fine sense of humor that he laughed when I told him to go to Canada.

Every day I sat on the dock, and when the sun went down I walked back to the house and had dinner.

For eight years my father has not lived in the house. He and my mother are not divorced, but the other day I saw an ad she had circled in the *Village Voice* about Haitian divorces. On and off, Curtis lives with her. Curtis is Phil Renshaw's younger brother, who works for Phil now that my father is gone.

One day at the end of the summer when my brother was killed, my mother walked down to the dock. I was smoking grass, as usual — staring out at the water. When she came to the dock I was thinking about how often my friends and I thought ironically, and how irony had been absent from my childhood. The memory of the conversation about how much my father liked children began to come back to me. I was wondering if children miss a lot of ironies, or whether that had been a different world and everything in it really hadn't been ironic.

My mother sat down. She didn't say anything about what I was doing. Finally she said, "Your father is totally irrational. He holds it against me. He thinks that God did this to curse us, to even the score for that abortion I had years and years ago." She took off her sandals and put her feet in the water. It was wet where she sat. She was sitting in a puddle on the dock. "Can you imagine your father being religious?" she said.

"No," I said. "I can't imagine him living in Mexico with a twenty-four-year-old girl either." I did not say that I found it hard to believe that she lived with Curtis Renshaw. He was plain-faced, less willing to work at anything than even my father. And he was vain — he always washed with a special soap. There was a plastic soap dish in the tub with a bar of putty-colored soap in it that was Curtis' soap.

"Your father loves you," she said. "He should pay more attention to you. When Joseph died he lost all perspective — he's forgotten what he's got."

I stared at our four feet, spooky and slender in the water.

"He should have sent the money for the plane ticket. He shouldn't have said he was going to and then not done it." She brushed the hair out of her eyes. "Is that part of why you're blue?"

"No," I said.

"I know," she said.

Then, being as deliberately cruel as my father had been with his sarcasm and his silence, I said, "He didn't send the money because she's going to have a baby and he doesn't want me around now."

"Yes," she sighed. "There's that, too."

It didn't seem to have made her angry at me, though I knew she could hardly stand to be reminded of it.

"She's twenty-four years old and a Catholic. I hope he keeps her pregnant and that they have hundreds of children for him to support, and no abortions."

The dock needed some boards replaced; that was why there was the puddle next to me. She wouldn't repair it, and Curtis wouldn't repair it, and I wouldn't. In June I had finally repapered the living room because the wallpaper was at once so faded and so garish. She had always asked my father to do it, and now, years later, I had done it with no prompting, wild for something to do with my hands. I suspect she didn't care about the wallpaper anymore because she didn't care any longer about the house. He had left it to her — his parents' house (my grandmother had died five years before; no longer even any reason to fix it up for her summer visit) — as if to say: You care about material things, here it is. Then he traveled and finally ended up in Mexico City. What would have happened if she had had the other baby? Would anything that simple have kept them married?

"What's that you're reading?" she said.

I looked down at the book I held, with the letter closed inside it. The book was *Cooking with Wine.*

Sebastian comes to my apartment. "It's nice," he says. "What? Don't you like it?" He sits on one of the two Salvation Army chairs. "It's nice in here," he says.

He comes here often, and is always ill at ease. He never knows what to say. After a dozen visits, today is the first time he's passed comment on the apartment. He used to call and invite himself over. After he had called a few times I called him and began inviting him because I knew that was what he wanted. He drinks too much now. He knows I'm going to school and don't have much money, so he brings his own bottle, and a bottle of white wine for me.

It's winter now, snowing. I was surprised he came, because you can't get a cab, and the streets are too bad to drive, so he had to take three buses to get here.

His shoes are on top of the newspaper in front of the door and he's sitting in the chair with his socks drying on the arm. His feet are so familiar. In the summer, in spite of rough floorboards and rocky beaches, nobody ever wore shoes.

He wants to take me out to lunch, but I don't want to go out into the snow. He looks a little relieved, and is happy when I bring him a plate of cheese and crackers to have with his Scotch.

"I got a letter from your father," he says, reaching into the breast pocket of his worn corduroy jacket.

I read it. It's a lot like the letter he sent to my mother, and the one he sent me. He has a nine-pound son, named Louis. Just like that.

"He wrote your mother, too." He says it so I know he thinks such letter sending is insane.

I go into the kitchen and get the rest of the brick of cheese. It is a one-room apartment and from where he sits, Sebastian can see me.

"It's nice of you to put up with me," he says.

"It was nice of you to bring me a present."

When he came, he brought with him six photographic postcards from the bookstore in the Square where he works. He knows that I like Walker Evans photographs; I won't mail any of them.

We sit, eat cheese, and fall silent.

I remember a night when my parents went dancing. It must have been the same year she had the abortion. Sebastian came to baby sit. He came upstairs, barefoot, and we didn't hear him. He found Joseph in my bed. "What are you two doing in bed together?" he said. He put the light on, and our eyes blinked — we couldn't help looking funny. That was the first time I knew there was something strange about it. Joseph must have known, because somehow, long before, he had gotten me to understand that I wasn't to talk about it. When Sebastian spoke, I knew that what he was asking about was something sexual. I thought about sex for the first time, though I didn't know the word then, or even what sex was.

Today, Sebastian isn't having much to drink. Usually by this time he's high, and the visit goes more smoothly.

"I wish I had been your uncle," he says. "I always liked children."

"You were *like* an uncle."

"Then I wish I had been a rich uncle. Then you really would have liked me."

"When did we ever care about money?"

"You never had any. Your mother was always complaining because your father had quit his job in the city and they were stuck in the country with no way to do anything, or buy what she wanted."

The house, in those days, had broken-down furniture, and we sat on pillows on the floors instead of in the old chairs with bulging springs, long before sitting on floor cushions was fashionable. My mother inherited money when Grandma died, and now there is new furniture, and a lot of the old pieces have been mended and refinished by Curtis.

"This is a very nice place," Sebastian says. "It's not easy to find a place this clean in the city."

The year I was nine Joseph and I stopped sharing the huge upstairs room. It was nobody's idea but my mother's that I have my own room. I got the small room at the back of the house on the first floor. A bureau was moved in, and a bed, and she hung white curtains and put a straw mat on the floor that she had bought that summer at an auction. I missed Joseph — though long before, he had stopped telling me the stories. He still told stories, but they were full of bravado, stories that were about things that didn't amaze me; he had hit a home run; he had carried Andrew's little sister home when she broke her foot diving off the dock. In the stories, he was always the hero. I didn't want my own room, but I suspected that my mother would have been angry if I had said so. Everybody else I knew had her own room, or shared one with her sister. After I moved into my room my mother would come in, once or twice a month, and sleep in the bed with me instead of with my father. I was a little embarrassed to have my mother in bed with me because I thought sleeping with your mother was childish, but something told me not to say anything about that, either.

I remember when my father left — the summer before Joseph left, to go to Vietnam. I remember that she was angry at first, and then so sad that Sebastian seemed always to be at the house.

"Your mother never really warmed up to me, in spite of the fact that there was nothing I wanted more. But you know that already," Sebastian says.

I reach out and put my hand around his hand, on the glass. He was always there, so I could go off and sulk and not worry about my mother. He was there the next summer, too, working in the garden, the day we got the news that Joseph had been shot.

It seemed that the winter would never end, and that I would never be able to read all the books I was supposed to read for my courses, when suddenly, at the end of March, there was a day as warm as summer. Nick showed it to me first, having been awakened by the children who had gone outside early to play. The house in which I rented the apartment was across the street from a playground. He shook me gently by the shoulder and pointed out the window, at the bright day. I got up and leaned on my elbow, and looked at it: sunny, beautiful, the trees so still that there must not have been the slightest breeze.

Nick and I had breakfast, and although he was in his first year of law school and worked constantly, didn't even question that we would leave the apartment. We had coffee, then walked to his car. Our plan was to drive to the North Shore to climb the dunes and walk on the beach. But the plan got changed to going all the way to my mother's house. It was Friday, and we could spend the weekend. Nick loved the house. More amazing, Nick loved me. He had been living with a girl named Anita when I met him, but a few months before, he had called it off, come to my apartment one day and made it plain that the scene with Anita had been a bad one. He had come, but he wouldn't look at me for a long time. "You didn't come cheap," he said.

We stopped for more coffee, but even that plan changed. Inside the restaurant, with the windows open, coffee was too much a winter drink. We sat on stools at the counter and drank cold chocolate milkshakes.

When we got there, Sebastian's old white Buick convertible — top down — was in the drive. He was the first to see us, from where he was digging in the side yard. I gave him a hug and Nick shook his hand. "Great minds with a single thought," he said to me. Whenever he could take a day off, he would leave the city and go to New Hampshire. He was planting a little evergreen. Nick and I went around to the back of the house, where my mother and a woman who had moved into the LaPierre house next door and Curtis were talking. My mother stood and rushed across the lawn, happy to see us. She had on a sundress, and her hair pulled back in a ponytail, and looked young.

It started out as such a happy day that what happened seemed even worse than it might have, because no one expected anything. We had all gone down to the beach (Sebastian was talking to the new woman, who was a widow; I was hoping that she would like him), when Sebastian mentioned Joseph. For months it had been all right to talk about him, so there was no reason why it hit her wrong. I guess that it was such a perfect day that we had all been thinking of him: he thrived in the warm weather, bought tulip bulbs and planted them in the rocky side yard every spring, sailed from the dock that we were now walking past every day that it didn't rain.

"I might try to fix the boat," Sebastian said, as much to himself as to any of us. Except that he must not have said *the* boat, but *Joseph's* boat. And it *was* my brother's boat. He had bought it, and my mother and I had hardly ever rowed out in it alone.

"Why do you have to mention him?" my mother said, her mouth quivering. "What do you have to talk about *Joseph* for?"

Then she put her hands over her face and ran, without lowering her hands, like a person running from an explosion.

Sebastian's face was perfectly white. He looked like he might cry himself. The woman he had been walking with was the only one who stared after my mother. She had been living in the LaPierre house a week or so, and I don't know if she knew, then, who Joseph was.

"Oh hell," Nick said, putting his hand on Sebastian's shoulder. Then, though it was a dumb and obvious thing to say, he said, "She's just upset."

Sebastian didn't move. I went over to him and said, "Hey — it's okay. I was thinking about him too." I had been thinking that that night Nick would sleep alone in Joseph's room.

We continued the walk down the beach. Nick took my arm and we walked a little ahead, and Sebastian and Carolyn Little trailed behind. Nick chattered to me as nervously as he had when he had started to tell me how he loved the woman he lived with, but ended up, instead of telling me anything about his life with Anita, talking about how some noises that cars make can indicate serious trouble. I strained to hear what Sebastian was saying to Carolyn Little, but there was a hollow sound all around us — the whole beach was echoing like a conch shell. It was that constant, almost inaudible noise — background noise — that distracted me. I turned to look at Sebastian. He was holding Carolyn Little's arm, talking to her, and she was looking at the sand.

I had been thinking about Joseph all day, long before we got to New Hampshire. I had started to think of him when Nick touched my shoulder. Joseph used to do that when I was falling asleep and he still wanted my attention. I could not stay awake long when I went to bed, but once he began his storytelling he would be energized. If I wouldn't listen to him, he at least wanted me to be awake. "Look at the stars tonight," he'd say, or he'd show me, in winter, sites for the snow fort we could build in the morning. More than once I fell asleep in the middle of one of his stories, and he nudged me awake.

I don't know if it took him a long while to die, or if he died suddenly. I don't know the name of the place he died in, or if it had a name. Although there were many random facts in the letter, the questions I really wanted answered were not answered.

I went back to the house ahead of the others, leaving Sebastian and Nick sitting on the dock after Carolyn Little went home. As I had expected, my mother was there, in the kitchen, drinking coffee. She was hanging her head and I expected her — as she had done in the past — to make me feel worse by apologizing for having made a scene. She did not say anything for a minute, and then she said, "You know what I hope? I hope that when he was over there he spent all his money on dope and laid every whore in Saigon."

She looked up. It was a challenging look, but she didn't mean to challenge me. "I didn't even have the courage to tell him, and you did. I heard you telling him, and I should have told him too — 'Go to Canada.'" She said "Canada" with the reverence a minister would use pronouncing the word "heaven."

"At least I hope he went crazy over there and did whatever the hell he wanted." This time she just looked at me sadly. We both knew he was not the kind to storm through Vietnam. More likely, he would sit and listen to the radio. When songs by any of the people on the list his friend sent us came on the radio, my day was ruined. All the lyrics took on horrible, ironic meanings.

"And your father's great grief — all I get are 'remember when' letters from Mexico. They weren't even close. Joseph and I weren't very close either. You two were." She looked up again, no real expression on her face, just a person stating facts. "It was mean of me to yell at Sebastian," she said.

"Don't stay in here sulking," I said.

We sat there for a while, and then she pushed the coffee cup away and went out. I imagine she went to the dock. I got up and went to the bookcase and took down the cookbook. The letter from Vietnam was still in it. I already knew it by heart, so I just looked to reassure myself that the letter was where I had put it. It was strange that she had never asked where the letter was. Strange, too, that she cursed when she got a letter from my father (most of the letters, inevitably, maudlin with memories of Joseph) but kept all of them in a basket on her dresser.

When I went outside, Nick and Sebastian were gone, and she was sitting on the dock where I had left them. She was sitting there on the dock just where Joseph and I had sat after our argument about his going to Canada. As we sat there, I was already sure that if he went, he would be killed. In the kitchen, he had argued against going to Canada because it was dishonorable. On the dock, I began to understand the real reason: it wasn't a matter of principle, but simply that he thought he wouldn't die; he thought he was indestructible. He really thought that he would always be in control, that he would always be the storyteller. I don't think I said to him in so many words that I knew he was going to die, or that he actually said he knew he was going to live, but that's what our conversation was about. He didn't understand how bad, and how pointless, things were in Vietnam. No matter what I said, his attention didn't focus on it, and I couldn't make him understand.

I went out to the dock, where my mother was, and crouched there. A bird flew overhead. There was a nice mossy smell the breeze was blowing in off the water.

"Know where Nick and Sebastian went?" I said.

"Look at his poor boat," she said.

I looked down. The water was slopping against it, the breeze blowing ripples of water toward shore. The water made a slapping sound: put-put.

"I just can't snap out of it," she said.

I leaned over and kissed her cheek. Nick did that most mornings when it was time for me to wake up. Joseph had nudged me awake with his hand, squeezed my shoulder in the dark. It was nicer than any kiss.

*   *   *

I went to bed early and slept for a little while, then woke up. I put on an old lacy robe that belonged to my mother or grandmother, and went out of the room. The clock in the kitchen said one-thirty. Everyone had gone to bed. Going back to the bedroom, I saw the small lamp on and detoured to the living room. Sebastian hadn't gone home. He was stretched on the sofa, but not sleeping. There was a bottle and a glass on the table. "Howdy," he said quietly. My mother was asleep — or at least she was in her room in the dark. Her bedroom opened onto the living room. The door was cracked open a few inches. I waved to Sebastian and went back to my room. I looked at all the books that I couldn't remember having read, and at the pictures I no longer found attractive: a Picasso poster of a hand holding flowers, a drawing of lobstermen casting their nets, done by a boy who had had a crush on me in high school.

Joseph would have interrupted the silence with a story. I went out of the room and passed by Sebastian in the living room without looking in, and climbed the stairs to the attic.

It smelled the way it always smelled. The two beds were still there. When I moved out, they left that bed in place. Nick was sleeping in the far bed. Without knowing who had slept where, he had chosen Joseph's bed. Nick had slept upstairs the other time he came to the house, but that time I hadn't gone upstairs to see where he slept. In fact, I hadn't been above the first floor in a long time. With the exposed beams and the low, triangle-shaped window, it still looked snug, like some room in a storybook.

"What are you doing here?" Nick whispered.

I went over to his bed. The room seemed to exist in a time warp; I could imagine stepping on one of Joseph's socks.

"She'll hear you," Nick said. He reached out his hand from under the covers. He had been asleep.

I sat there and held his hand. Then I lay on the bed. Finally, I got under the covers.

"We shouldn't upset her any more today," he said.

It was a rational, and even a nice thing to say, and I knew that I was wrong to hate him for saying it. He lay still in the bed and I lay beside him. My eyes were getting accustomed to the dark. I was looking around the room and thinking of how Joseph's shadow tiptoed to me, the pitch of his whispery child's voice. As I got older, if I told people about my brother, the stories would always be about my brother as a child — I got older, but Joseph was still frozen in childhood.

"What?" Nick said sleepily.

I had moved and thrown my arm over him, inadvertently. I wanted to say: Nick — my whole life just rushed by.

Nick fumbled for my hand and we held hands again. His hand was so warm. I could see in the dark now: his eyes closed, his mouth like the mouth of a Botticelli angel.

"There's a demon in the corner." I pointed. (Starlight on two metal coat hooks.)

He mumbled again: "What?"

He was trying to be kind, trying to stay awake. I looked at the coat hooks. They did look like eyes glaring, and I had scared myself a little by calling them demons.

"A demon," I said again, and something in my voice told Nick he had to rouse himself, that the talk about demons was flippy.

"Okay," he said, struggling up, half sighing the second "Okay."

He smoothed my hair from my face and, kindly, kissed my neck, moved his hand up my ribs. It was not what I wanted at all, but I closed my eyes, not knowing now what to say.

QUESTIONS

1. How and why do Joseph's clever-kids stories change as he grows older? How do Jane's attempts to compete compare to Joseph's early stories? How does this story — her "A Clever-Kids Story" — differ from Joseph's stories of the same name?

2. Discuss irony as both a technique and a concept in the story. Of what ironies is Jane conscious? Does she fight against her ironic perceptions or accept them easily?

3. What problems characterize the adult world represented by Jane's parents and by Sebastian? How do these problems affect the clever kids' childhood? How does the narrator feel about her childhood once she becomes an adult?

4. What is the effect of the ending? What drama is being played out between Nick and Jane? Whose role is Jane assuming? Are her expectations fulfilled? Are the demons banished?

CLARK BLAISE ═══════════

A Class of New Canadians

Norman Dyer hurried down Sherbrooke Street, collar turned against the snow. "Superb!" he muttered, passing a basement gallery next to a French bookstore. Bleached and tanned women in furs dashed from hotel lobbies into waiting cabs. Even the neon clutter of the side streets and the honks of slithering taxis seemed remote tonight through the peaceful snow. *Superb*, he thought again, waiting for a light and backing from a slushy curb: a word reserved for wines, cigars, and delicate sauces; he was feeling superb this evening. After eighteen months in Montreal, he still found himself freshly impressed by everything he saw. He was proud of himself for having steered his life north, even for jobs that were menial by standards he could have demanded. Great just being here no matter what they paid, looking at these buildings, these faces, and hearing all the languages. He was learning to be insulted by simple bad taste, wherever he encountered it.

Since leaving graduate school and coming to Montreal, he had sampled every ethnic restaurant downtown and in the old city, plus a few Levantine[1] places out in Outremont.[2] He had worked on conversational French and mastered much of the local dialect, done reviews for local papers, translated French-Canadian poets for Toronto quarterlies, and tweaked his colleagues for not sympathizing enough with Quebec separatism. He attended French performances of plays he had ignored in English, and kept a small but elegant apartment near a colony of *émigré* Russians just off Park Avenue. Since coming to Montreal he'd witnessed a hold-up, watched a murder, and seen several riots. When stopped on the street for directions, he would answer in French or accented English. To live this well and travel each long academic summer, he held two jobs. He had no intention of returning to the States. In fact, he had begun to think of himself as a semi-permanent, semi-political exile.

Now, stopped again a few blocks farther, he studied the window of Holt-Renfrew's exclusive men's shop. Incredible, he thought, the authority of simple good taste. Double-breasted chalk-striped suits he would never dare to buy. Knitted sweaters, and fifty-dollar shoes. One tanned mannequin was decked out in a brash checkered sportscoat with a

---

[1] Eastern Mediterranean.

[2] Community in the metropolitan area of Montreal.

burgundy vest and dashing ascot. Not a price tag under three hundred dollars. Unlike food, drink, cinema, and literature, clothing had never really involved him. Someday, he now realized, it would. Dyer's clothes, thus far, had all been bought in a chain department store. He was a walking violation of American law, clad shoes to scarf in Egyptian cottons, Polish leathers, and woolens from the People's Republic of China.

He had no time for dinner tonight; this was Wednesday, a day of lectures at one university, and then an evening course in English as a Foreign Language at McGill, beginning at six. He would eat afterwards.

Besides the money, he had kept this second job because it flattered him. There was to Dyer something fiercely elemental, almost existential, about teaching both his language and his literature in a foreign country — like Joyce in Trieste, Isherwood and Nabokov in Berlin, Beckett in Paris. Also it was necessary for his students. It was the first time in his life that he had done something socially useful. What difference did it make that the job was beneath him, a recent Ph.D., while most of his colleagues in the evening school at McGill were idle housewives and bachelor civil servants? It didn't matter, even, that this job was a perversion of all the sentiments he held as a progressive young teacher. He was a god two evenings a week, sometimes suffering and fatigued, but nevertheless an omniscient, benevolent god. His students were silent, ignorant, and dedicated to learning English. No discussions, no demon-strations, no dialogue.

I love them, he thought. They need me.

He entered the room, pocketed his cap and ear muffs, and dropped his briefcase on the podium. Two girls smiled good evening.

They love me, he thought, taking off his boots and hanging up his coat; I'm not like their English-speaking bosses.

I love myself, he thought with amazement even while conducting a drill on word order. I love myself for tramping down Sherbrooke Street in zero weather just to help them with noun clauses. I love myself standing behind this podium and showing Gilles Carrier and Claude Veilleux the difference between the past continuous and the simple past; or the sultry Armenian girl with the bewitching half-glasses that "put on" is not the same as "take on"; or telling the dashing Mr. Miguel Mayor, late of Madrid, that simple futurity can be expressed in four different ways, at least.

This is what mastery is like, he thought. Being superb in one's chosen field, not merely in one's mother tongue. A respected performer in the lecture halls of the major universities, equipped by twenty years' research in the remotest libraries, and slowly giving it back to those who must have it. Dishing it out suavely, even wittily. Being a legend. Being loved and a little feared.

"Yes, Mrs. David?"

A *sabra*[3]: freckled, reddish hair, looking like a British model, speaks with a nifty British accent, and loves me.

"No," he smiled, "*I were* is not correct except in the present subjunctive, which you haven't studied yet."

The first hour's bell rang. The students closed their books for the intermission. Dyer put his away, then noticed a page of his Faulkner lecture from the afternoon class. *Absalom, Absalom!* his favorite.

"Can anyone here tell me what the *impregnable citadel of his passive rectitude* means?"

---

[3] A native-born Israeli.

"What, sir?" asked Mr. Vassilopoulos, ready to copy.

"What about *the presbyterian and lugubrious effluvium of his passive vindictiveness?*" A few girls giggled. "O.K.," said Dyer, "take your break."

In the halls of McGill they broke into the usual groups. French-Canadians and South Americans into two large circles, then the Greeks, Germans, Spanish, and French into smaller groups. The patterns interested Dyer. Madrid Spaniards and Parisian French always spoke English with their New World co-linguals. The Middle Europeans spoke German together, not Russian, preferring one occupier to the other. Two Israeli men went off alone. Dyer decided to join them for the break.

Not *sabras*, Dyer concluded, not like Mrs. David. The shorter one, dark and wavy-haired, held his cigarette like a violin bow. The other, Mr. Weinrot, was tall and pot-bellied, with a ruddy face and thick stubby fingers. Something about him suggested truck-driving, perhaps of beer, maybe in Germany. Neither one, he decided, could supply the name of a good Israeli restaurant.

"This is really hard, you know?" said Weinrot.

"Why?"

"I think it's because I'm not speaking much of English at my job."

"French?" asked Dyer.

"French? Pah! All the time Hebrew, sometimes German, sometimes little Polish. Crazy thing, eh? How long you think they let me speak Hebrew if I'm working in America?"

"Depends on where you're working," he said.

"Hell, I'm working for the Canadian government, what you think? Plant I work in — I'm engineer, see — makes boilers for the turbines going up North. Look. When I'm leaving Israel I go first to Italy. Right away — bamm I'm working in Italy I'm speaking Italian like a native. Passing for a native."

"A native Jew," said his dark-haired friend.

"Listen to him. So in Rome they think I'm from Tyrol — that's still native, eh? So I speak Russian and German and Italian like a Jew. My Hebrew is bad, I admit it, but it's a lousy language anyway. Nobody likes it. French I understand but English I'm talking like a bum. Arabic I know five dialects. Danish fluent. So what's the matter I can't learn English?"

"It'll come, don't worry," Dyer smiled. *Don't worry, my son*; he wanted to pat him on the arm. "Anyway, that's what makes Canada so appealing. Here they don't force you."

"What's this *appealing*? Means nice? Look, my friend, keep it, eh? Two years in a country I don't learn the language means it isn't a country."

"Come on," said Dyer. "Neither does forcing you."

"Let me tell you a story why I come to Canada. Then you tell me if I was wrong, O.K.?"

"Certainly," said Dyer, flattered.

In Italy, Weinrot told him, he had lost his job to a Communist union. He left Italy for Denmark and opened up an Israeli restaurant with five other friends. Then the six Israelis decided to rent a bigger apartment downtown near the restaurant. They found a perfect nine-room place for two thousand kroner a month, not bad shared six ways. Next day the landlord told them the deal was off. "You tell me why," Weinrot demanded.

No Jews? Dyer wondered. "He wanted more rent," he finally said.

"More — you kidding? More we expected. *Less* we didn't expect. A couple with eight kids is showing up after we're gone and the law in Denmark says a man has a right to a room for each kid plus a hundred kroner knocked off the rent for each kid. What you think of that?

So a guy who comes in *after* us gets a nine-room place for a thousand kroner *less*. Law says no way a bachelor can get a place ahead of a family, and bachelors pay twice as much."

Dyer waited, then asked, "So?"

"So, I make up my mind the world is full of communismus, just like Israel. So I take out applications next day for Australia, South Africa, U.S.A., and Canada. Canada says come right away, so I go. Should have waited for South Africa."

"How could you?" Dyer cried. "What's wrong with you anyway? South Africa is fascist. Australia is racist."

The bell rang, and the Israelis, with Dyer, began walking to the room.

"What I was wondering, then," said Mr. Weinrot, ignoring Dyer's outburst, "was if my English is good enough to be working in the United States. You're American, aren't you?"

It was a question Dyer had often avoided in Europe, but had rarely been asked in Montreal. "Yes," he admitted, "your English is probably good enough for the States or South Africa, whichever one wants you first."

He hurried ahead to the room, feeling that he had let Montreal down. He wanted to turn and shout to Weinrot and to all the others that Montreal was the greatest city on the continent, if only they knew it as well as he did. If they'd just break out of their little ghettos.

At the door, the Armenian girl with the half-glasses caught his arm. She was standing with Mrs. David and Miss Parizeau, a jolly French-Canadian girl that Dyer had been thinking of asking out.

"Please, sir," she said, looking at him over the tops of her tiny glasses, "what I was asking earlier — *put on* — I heard on the television. A man said *You are putting me on* and everybody laughed. I think it was supposed to be funny but *put on* we learned means get dressed, no?"

"Ah — *don't put me on*," Dyer laughed.

"I yaven't erd it neither," said Miss Parizeau.

"To put some*body* on means to make a fool of him. To put some*thing* on is to wear it. O.K.?" He gave examples.

"Ah, now I know," said Miss Parizeau. "Like bull-shitting somebody. Is it the same?"

"Ah, yes," he said, smiling. French-Canadians were like children learning the language. "Your example isn't considered polite. 'Put on' is very common now in the States."

"Then maybe," said Miss Parizeau, "we'll ave it ere in twenty years." The Armenian giggled.

"No — I've heard it here just as often," Dyer protested, but the girls had already entered the room.

He began the second hour with a smile which slowly soured as he thought of the Israelis. America's anti-communism was bad enough, but it was worse hearing it echoed by immigrants, by Jews, here in Montreal. Wasn't there a psychological type who chose Canada over South Africa? Or was it just a matter of visas and slow adjustment? Did Johannesburg lose its Greeks, and Melbourne its Italians, the way Dyer's students were always leaving Montreal?

And after class when Dyer was again feeling content and thinking of approaching one of the Israelis for a restaurant tip, there came the flood of small requests: should Mrs. Papadopoulos go into a more advanced course; could Mr. Perez miss a week for an interview in Toronto; could Mr. Giguère, who spoke English perfectly, have a harder book; Mr. Coté an easier one?

Then as he packed his briefcase in the empty room, Miguel Mayor, the vain and impeccable Spaniard, came forward from the hallway.

"Sir," he began, walking stiffly, ready to bow or salute. He wore a loud gray checkered sportscoat this evening, blue shirt, and matching ascot-handkerchief, slightly mauve. He must have shaved just before class, Dyer noticed, for two fresh daubs of antiseptic cream stood out on his jaw, just under his earlobe.

"I have been wanting to ask *you* something, as a matter of fact," said Dyer. "Do you know any good Spanish restaurants I might try tonight?"

"There are not any good Spanish restaurants in Montreal," he said. He stepped closer. "Sir?"

"What's on your mind, then?"

"Please — have you the time to look on a letter for me?"

He laid the letter on the podium.

"Look *over* a letter," said Dyer. "What is it for?"

"I have applied," he began, stopping to emphasize the present perfect construction, "for a job in Cleveland, Ohio, and I want to know if my letter will be good. Will an American, I mean — "

"Why are you going there?"

"It is a good job."

"But Cleveland — "

"They have a blackman mayor, I have read. But the job is not in Cleveland."

"Let me see it."

Most honourable Sir: I humbly beg consideration for a position in your grand company ...

"Who are you writing this to?"

"The president," said Miguel Mayor.

I am once a student of Dr. Ramiro Gutierrez of the Hydraulic Institute of Sevilla, Spain ...

"Does the president know this Ramiro Gutierrez?"

"Oh, everybody is knowing him," Miguel Mayor assured, "he is the most famous expert in all Spain."

"Did he recommend this company to you?"

"No — I have said in my letter, if you look — "

An ancient student of Dr. Gutierrez, Salvador del Este, is actually a boiler expert who is being employed like supervisor is formerly a friend of mine ...

"Is he still your friend?"

Whenever you say come to my city Miguel Mayor for talking I will be coming. I am working in Montreal since two years and am now wanting more money than I am getting here now ...

"Well ..." Dyer sighed.

"Sir — what I want from you is knowing in good English how to interview me by this man. The letters in Spanish are not the same to English ones, you know?"

I remain humbly at your orders ...

"Why do you want to leave Montreal?"

"It's time for a change."

"Have you ever been to Cleveland?"

"I am one summer in California. Very beautiful there and hot like my country. Montreal is big port like Barcelona. Everybody mixed together and having no money. It is just a place to land, no?"

"Montreal? Don't be silly."

"I thought I come here and learn good English but where I work I get by in Spanish and French. It's hard, you know?" he smiled. Then he took a few steps back and gave his cuffs a gentle tug, exposing a set of jade cufflinks.

Dyer looked at the letter again and calculated how long he would be correcting it, then up at his student. How old is he? My age? Thirty? Is he married? Where do the Spanish live in Montreal? He looks so prosperous, so confident, like a male model off a page of *Playboy*. For an instant Dyer felt that his student was mocking him, somehow pitting his astounding confidence and wardrobe, sharp chin and matador's bearing against Dyer's command of English and mastery of the side streets, bistros, and ethnic restaurants. Mayor's letter was painful, yet he remained somehow competent. He would pass his interview, if he got one. What would he care about America, and the odiousness he'd soon be supporting? It was as though a superstructure of exploitation had been revealed, and Dyer felt himself abused by the very people he wanted so much to help. It had to end someplace.

He scratched out the second "humbly" from the letter, then folded the sheet of foolscap. "Get it typed right away," he said. "Good luck."

"Thank you, sir," said his student, with a bow. Dyer watched the letter disappear in the inner pocket of the checkered sportscoat. Then the folding of the cashmere scarf, the draping of the camel's hair coat about the shoulders, the easing of the fur hat down to the rims of his ears. The meticulous filling of the pigskin gloves. Mayor's patent leather galoshes glistened.

"Good evening, sir," he said.

"*Buenas noches*," Dyer replied.

He hurried now, back down Sherbrooke Street to his daytime office where he could deposit his books. Montreal on a winter night was still mysterious, still magical. Snow blurred the arc lights. The wind was dying. Every second car was now a taxi, crowned with an orange crescent. Slushy curbs had hardened. The window of Holt-Renfrew's was still attractive. The legless dummies invited a final stare. He stood longer than he had earlier, in front of the sporty mannequin with a burgundy waistcoat, the mauve and blue ensemble, the jade cufflinks.

Good evening, sir, he could almost hear. The ascot, the shirt, the complete outfit, had leaped off the back of Miguel Mayor. He pictured how he must have entered the store with three hundred dollars and a prepared speech, and walked out again with everything off the torso's back.

I want that.

What, sir?

That.

The coat, sir?

Yes.

Very well, sir.

And *that*.

Which, sir?

All that.

"Absurd man!" Dyer whispered. There had been a moment of fear, as though the naked body would leap from the window, and legless, chase him down Sherbrooke Street. But the moment was passing. Dyer realized now that it was comic, even touching. Miguel Mayor had simply tried too hard, too fast, and it would be good for him to stay in Montreal until he deserved those clothes, that touching vanity and confidence. With one last look at the window, he turned sharply, before the clothes could speak again.

QUESTIONS

1. Is Dyer presented sympathetically or ironically? What does he value? What are his attitudes toward Canadians, old and new? What class of Canadian is he?

2. Who makes up the class of new Canadians referred to in the title? Discuss the multiple meanings of the word "class."

3. How are the Faulkner passages Dyer reads significant? What do they illustrate about him? How do they comment on him?

4. Why does Dyer make only one correction in Mayor's unidiomatic letter?

5. Compare the theme of language in this story to the same theme in Bowles's "A Distant Episode."

A Distant Episode

The September sunsets were at their reddest the week the Professor decided to visit Aïn Tadouirt,[1] which is in the warm country. He came down out of the high, flat region in the evening by bus, with two small overnight bags full of maps, sun lotions and medicines. Ten years ago he had been in the village for three days; long enough, however, to establish a fairly firm friendship with a café-keeper, who had written him several times during the first year after his visit, if never since. "Hassan Ramani," the Professor said over and over, as the bus bumped downward through ever warmer layers of air. Now facing the flaming sky in the west, and now facing the sharp mountains, the car followed the dusty trail down the canyons into air which began to smell of other things besides the endless ozone of the heights: orange blossoms, pepper, sun-baked excrement, burning olive oil, rotten fruit. He closed his eyes happily and lived for an instant in a purely olfactory world. The distant past returned — what part of it, he could not decide.

The chauffeur, whose seat the Professor shared, spoke to him without taking his eyes from the road. "*Vous êtes géologue?*"

"A geologist? Ah, no! I'm a linguist."

"There are no languages here. Only dialects."

"Exactly. I'm making a survey of variations on Moghrebi."[2]

The chauffeur was scornful. "Keep on going south," he said. "You'll find some languages you never heard of before."

As they drove through the town gate, the usual swarm of urchins rose up out of the dust and ran screaming beside the bus. The Professor folded his dark glasses, put them in his pocket; and as soon as the vehicle had come to a standstill he jumped out, pushing his way through the indignant boys who clutched at his luggage in vain, and walked quickly into the Grand Hotel Saharien. Out of its eight rooms there were two available — one facing the market and the other, a smaller and cheaper one, giving onto a tiny yard full of refuse and barrels, where two gazelles wandered about. He took the smaller room, and pouring the entire pitcher of water into the tin basin, began to wash the grit from his face and ears. The

---

[1] A town in eastern Morocco.

[2] Maghreb is the region of Africa north of the Sahara between Egypt and the Atlantic Ocean.

afterglow was nearly gone from the sky, and the pinkness in objects was disappearing, almost as he watched. He lit the carbide lamp and winced at its odor.

After dinner the Professor walked slowly through the streets to Hassan Ramani's café, whose back room hung hazardously out above the river. The entrance was very low, and he had to bend down slightly to get in. A man was tending the fire. There was one guest sipping tea. The *qaouaji*[3] tried to make him take a seat at the other table in the front room, but the Professor walked airily ahead into the back room and sat down. The moon was shining through the reed latticework and there was not a sound outside but the occasional distant bark of a dog. He changed tables so he could see the river. It was dry, but there was a pool here and there that reflected the bright night sky. The *qaouaji* came in and wiped off the table.

"Does this café still belong to Hassan Ramani?" he asked him in the Moghrebi he had taken four years to learn.

The man replied in bad French: "He is deceased."

"Deceased?" repeated the Professor, without noticing the absurdity of the word. "Really? When?"

"I don't know," said the *qaouaji*. "One tea?"

"Yes. But I don't understand ..."

The man was already out of the room, fanning the fire. The Professor sat still, feeling lonely, and arguing with himself that to do so was ridiculous. Soon the *qaouaji* returned with the tea. He paid him and gave him an enormous tip, for which he received a grave bow.

"Tell me," he said, as the other started away. "Can one still get those little boxes made from camel udders?"

The man looked angry. "Sometimes the Reguibat[4] bring in those things. We do not buy them here." Then insolently, in Arabic: "And why a camel-udder box?"

"Because I like them," retorted the Professor. And then because he was feeling a little exalted, he added, "I like them so much I want to make a collection of them, and I will pay you ten francs for every one you can get me."

"*Khamstache*,"[5] said the *qaouaji*, opening his left hand rapidly three times in succession. "Never. Ten."

"Not possible. But wait until later and come with me. You can give me what you like. And you will get camel-udder boxes if there are any."

He went out into the front room, leaving the Professor to drink his tea and listen to the growing chorus of dogs that barked and howled as the moon rose higher into the sky. A group of customers came into the front room and sat talking for an hour or so. When they had left, the *qaouaji* put out the fire and stood in the doorway putting on his burnous.[6] "Come," he said.

Outside in the street there was very little movement. The booths were all closed and the only light came from the moon. An occasional pedestrian passed, and grunted a brief greeting to the *qaouaji*.

"Everyone knows you," said the Professor, to cut the silence between them.

"Yes."

"I wish everyone knew me," said the Professor, before he realized how infantile such a remark must sound.

---

[3] An Arab man in Western clothing.

[4] Members of a North African nomadic tribe.

[5] "Fifteen."

[6] One-piece Arabian hooded cloak.

"*No* one knows you," said his companion gruffly.

They had come to the other side of the town, on the promontory above the desert, and through a great rift in the wall the Professor saw the white endlessness, broken in the foreground by dark spots of oasis. They walked through the opening and followed a winding road between rocks, downward toward the nearest small forest of palms. The Professor thought: "He may cut my throat. But his café — he would surely be found out."

"Is it far?" he asked, casually.

"Are you tired?" countered the *qaouaji*.

"They are expecting me back at the Hotel Saharien," he lied.

"You can't be there and here," said the *qaouaji*.

The Professor laughed. He wondered if it sounded uneasy to the other.

"Have you owned Ramani's café long?"

"I work there for a friend." The reply made the Professor more unhappy than he had imagined it would.

"Oh. Will you work tomorrow?"

"That is impossible to say."

The Professor stumbled on a stone, and fell, scraping his hand. The *qaouaji* said: "Be careful."

The sweet black odor of rotten meat hung in the air suddenly.

"Agh!" said the Professor, choking. "What is it?"

The *qaouaji* had covered his face with his burnous and did not answer. Soon the stench had been left behind. They were on flat ground. Ahead the path was bordered on each side by a high mud wall. there was no breeze and the palms were quite still, but behind the walls was the sound of running water. Also, the odor of human excrement was almost constant as they walked between the walls.

The Professor waited until he thought it seemed logical for him to ask with a certain degree of annoyance: "But where are we going?"

"Soon," said the guide, pausing to gather some stones in the ditch.

"Pick up some stones," he advised. "Here are bad dogs."

"Where?" asked the Professor, but he stooped and got three large ones with pointed edges.

They continued very quietly. The walls came to an end and the bright desert lay ahead. Nearby was a ruined marabout,[7] with its tiny dome only half standing, and the front wall entirely destroyed. Behind it were clumps of stunted, useless palms. A dog came running crazily toward them on three legs. Not until it got quite close did the Professor hear its steady low growl. The *qaouaji* let fly a large stone at it, striking it square in the muzzle. There was a strange snapping of jaws and the dog ran sideways in another direction, falling blindly against rocks and scrambling haphazardly about like an injured insect.

Turning off the road, they walked across the earth strewn with sharp stones, past the little ruin, through the trees, until they came to a place where the ground dropped abruptly away in front of them.

"It looks like a quarry," said the Professor, resorting to French for the word "quarry," whose Arabic equivalent he could not call to mind at the moment. The *qaouaji* did not answer. Instead he stood still and turned his head, as if listening. And indeed, from somewhere down below, but very far below, came the faint sound of a low flute. The *qaouaji* nodded his head slowly several times. Then he said: "The path begins here. You can see it well all the

---

[7] Saint's tomb.

The rock is white and the moon is strong. So you can see well. I am going back now and sleep. It is late. You can give me what you like."

Standing there at the edge of the abyss which at each moment looked deeper, with the dark face of the *qaouaji* framed in its moonlit burnous close to his own face, the Professor asked himself exactly what he felt. Indignation, curiosity, fear, perhaps, but most of all relief and the hope that this was not a trick, the hope that the *qaouaji* would really leave him alone and turn back without him.

He stepped back a little from the edge, and fumbled in his pocket for a loose note, because he did not want to show his wallet. Fortunately there was a fifty-franc bill there, which he took out and handed to the man. He knew the *qaouaji* was pleased, and so he paid no attention when he heard him saying: "It is not enough. I have to walk a long way home and there are dogs. ..."

"Thank you and good night," said the Professor, sitting down with his legs drawn up under him, and lighting a cigarette. He felt almost happy.

"Give me only one cigarette," pleaded the man.

"Of course," he said, a bit curtly, and he held up the pack.

The *qaouaji* squatted close beside him. His face was not pleasant to see. "What is it?" thought the Professor, terrified again, as he held out his lighted cigarette toward him.

The man's eyes were almost closed. It was the most obvious registering of concentrated scheming the Professor had ever seen. When the second cigarette was burning, he ventured to say to the still-squatting Arab: "What are you thinking about?"

The other drew on his cigarette deliberately, and seemed about to speak. Then his expression changed to one of satisfaction, but he did not speak. A cool wind had risen in the air, and the Professor shivered. The sound of the flute came up from the depths below at intervals, sometimes mingled with the scraping of nearby palm fronds one against the other. "These people are not primitives," the Professor found himself saying in his mind.

"Good," said the *qaouaji*, rising slowly. "Keep your money. Fifty francs is enough. It is an honor." Then he went back into French: "*Ti n'as qu'à discendre, to' droit.*"[8] He spat, chuckled (or was the Professor hysterical?), and strode away quickly.

The Professor was in a state of nerves. He lit another cigarette, and found his lips moving automatically. They were saying: "Is this a situation or a predicament? This is ridiculous." He sat very still for several minutes, waiting for a sense of reality to come to him. He stretched out on the hard, cold ground and looked up at the moon. It was almost like looking straight at the sun. If he shifted his gaze a little at a time, he could make a string of weaker moons across the sky. "Incredible," he whispered. Then he sat up quickly and looked about. There was no guarantee that the *qaouaji* really had gone back to town. He got to his feet and looked over the edge of the precipice. In the moonlight the bottom seemed miles away. And there was nothing to give it scale; not a tree, not a house, not a person. ... He listened for the flute, and heard only the wind going by his ears. A sudden violent desire to run back to the road seized him, and he turned and looked in the direction the *qaouaji* had taken. At the same time he felt softly of his wallet in his breast pocket. Then he spat over the edge of the cliff. Then he made water over it, and listened intently, like a child. This gave him the impetus to start down the path into the abyss. Curiously enough, he was not dizzy. But prudently he kept from peering to his right, over the edge. It was a steady and steep downward climb. The monotony of it put him into a frame of mind not unlike that which had been induced by the bus ride. He was murmuring "Hassan Ramani" again, repeatedly and in rhythm. He stopped, furious with

[8] "Just go down, straight ahead."

himself for the sinister overtones the name now suggested to him. He decided he was exhausted from the trip. "And the walk," he added.

He was now well down the gigantic cliff, but the moon, being directly overhead, gave as much light as ever. Only the wind was left behind, above, to wander among the trees, to blow through the dusty streets of Aïn Tadouirt, into the hall of the Grand Hotel Saharien, and under the door of his little room.

It occurred to him that he ought to ask himself why he was doing this irrational thing, but he was intelligent enough to know that since he was doing it, it was not so important to probe for explanations at that moment.

Suddenly the earth was flat beneath his feet. He had reached the bottom sooner than he expected. He stepped ahead distrustfully still, as if he expected another treacherous drop. It was so hard to know in this uniform, dim brightness. Before he knew what had happened the dog was upon him, a heavy mass of fur trying to push him backwards, a sharp nail rubbing down his chest, a straining of muscles against him to get the teeth into his neck. The Professor thought: "I refuse to die this way." The dog fell back; it looked like an Eskimo dog. As it sprang again, he called out, very loud: "Ay!" It fell against him, there was a confusion of sensations and a pain somewhere. There was also the sound of voices very near to him, and he could not understand what they were saying. Something cold and metallic was pushed brutally against his spine as the dog still hung for a second by his teeth from a mass of clothing and perhaps flesh. The Professor knew it was a gun, and he raised his hands, shouting in Moghrebi: "Take away the dog!" But the gun merely pushed him forward, and since the dog, once it was back on the ground, did not leap again, he took a step ahead. The gun kept pushing; he kept taking steps. Again he heard voices, but the person directly behind him said nothing. People seemed to be running about; it sounded that way, at least. For his eyes, he discovered, were still shut tight against the dog's attack. He opened them. A group of men was advancing toward him. They were dressed in the black clothes of the Reguibat. "The Reguiba is a cloud across the face of the sun." "When the Reguiba appears the righteous man turns away." In how many shops and market-places he had heard these maxims uttered banteringly among friends. Never to a Reguiba, to be sure, for these men do not frequent towns. They send a representative in disguise, to arrange with shady elements there for the disposal of captured goods. "An opportunity," he thought quickly, "of testing the accuracy of such statements." He did not doubt for a moment that the adventure would prove to be a kind of warning against such foolishness on his part — a warning which in retrospect would be half sinister, half farcical.

Two snarling dogs came running from behind the oncoming men and threw themselves at his legs. He was scandalized to note that no one paid any attention to this breach of etiquette. The gun pushed him harder as he tried to sidestep the animals' noisy assault. Again he cried: "The dogs! Take them away!" The gun shoved him forward with great force and he fell, almost at the feet of the crowd of men facing him. The dogs were wrenching at his hands and arms. A boot kicked them aside, yelping, and then with increased vigor it kicked the Professor in the hip. Then came a chorus of kicks from different sides, and he was rolled violently about on the earth for a while. During this time he was conscious of hands reaching into his pockets and removing everything from them. He tried to say: "You have all my money; stop kicking me!" But his bruised facial muscles would not work; he felt himself pouting, and that was all. Someone dealt him a terrific blow on the head, and he thought: "Now at least I shall lose consciousness, thank Heaven." Still he went on being aware of the guttural voices he could not understand, and of being bound tightly about the ankles and chest. Then there was black silence that opened like a wound from time to time, to let in the soft, deep notes of the flute playing the same succession of notes again and again. Suddenly he felt excruciating pain everywhere — pain and cold. "So I have been unconscious, after all," he thought. In spite of that, the present seemed only like a direct continuation of what had gone before.

It was growing faintly light. There were camels near where he was lying; he could hear their gurgling and their heavy breathing. He could not bring himself to attempt opening his eyes, just in case it should turn out to be impossible. However, when he heard someone approaching, he found that he had no difficulty in seeing.

The man looked at him dispassionately in the gray morning light. With one hand he pinched together the Professor's nostrils. When the Professor opened his mouth to breathe, the man swiftly seized his tongue and pulled on it with all his might. The Professor was gagging and catching his breath; he did not see what was happening. He could not distinguish the pain of the brutal yanking from that of the sharp knife. Then there was an endless choking and spitting that went on automatically, as though he were scarcely a part of it. The word "operation" kept going through his mind; it calmed his terror somewhat as he sank back into darkness.

The caravan left sometime toward midmorning. The Professor, not unconscious, but in a state of utter stupor, still gagging and drooling blood, was dumped doubled-up into a sack and tied at one side of a camel. The lower end of the enormous amphitheater contained a natural gate in the rocks. The camels, swift *mehara*,[9] were lightly laden on this trip. They passed through single file, and slowly mounted the gentle slope that led up into the beginning of the desert. That night, at a stop behind some low hills, the men took him out, still in a state which permitted no thought, and over the dusty rags that remained of his clothing they fastened a series of curious belts made of the bottoms of tin cans strung together. One after another of these bright girdles was wired about his torso, his arms and legs, even across his face, until he was entirely within a suit of armor that covered him with its circular metal scales. There was a good deal of merriment during this decking-out of the Professor. One man brought out a flute and a younger one did a not ungraceful caricature of an Ouled Naïl executing a cane dance. The Professor was no longer conscious; to be exact, he existed in the middle of the movements made by these other men. When they had finished dressing him the way they wished him to look, they stuffed some food under the tin bangles hanging over his face. Even though he chewed mechanically, most of it eventually fell out onto the ground. They put him back into the sack and left him there.

Two days later they arrived at one of their own encampments. There were women and children here in the tents, and the men had to drive away the snarling dogs they had left there to guard them. When they emptied the Professor out of his sack, there were screams of fright, and it took several hours to convince the last woman that he was harmless, although there had been no doubt from the start that he was a valuable possession. After a few days they began to move on again, taking everything with them, and traveling only at night as the terrain grew warmer.

Even when all his wounds had healed and he felt no more pain, the Professor did not begin to think again; he ate and defecated, and he danced when he was bidden, a senseless hopping up and down that delighted the children, principally because of the wonderful jangling racket it made. And he generally slept through the heat of the day, in among the camels.

Wending its way southeast, the caravan avoided all stationary civilization. In a few weeks they reached a new plateau, wholly wild and with a sparse vegetation. Here they pitched camp

---

[9] Swift-footed riding camels.

and remained, while the *mehara* were turned loose to graze. Everyone was happy here; the weather was cooler and there was a well only a few hours away on a seldom-frequented trail. It was here they conceived the idea of taking the Professor to Fogara and selling him to the Touareg.[10]

It was a full year before they carried out this project. By this time the Professor was much better trained. He could do a handspring, make a series of fearful growling noises which had, nevertheless, a certain element of humor; and when the Reguibat removed the tin from his face they discovered he could grimace admirably while he danced. They also taught him a few basic obscene gestures which never failed to elicit delighted shrieks from the women. He was now brought forth only after especially abundant meals, when there was music and festivity. He easily fell in with their sense of ritual, and evolved an elementary sort of "program" to present when he was called for: dancing, rolling on the ground, imitating certain animals, and finally rushing toward the group in feigned anger, to see the resultant confusion and hilarity.

When three of the men set out for Fogara with him, they took four *mehara* with them, and he rode astride his quite naturally. No precautions were taken to guard him, save that he was kept among them, one man always staying at the rear of the party. They came within sight of the walls at dawn, and they waited among the rocks all day. At dusk the youngest started out, and in three hours he returned with a friend who carried a stout cane. They tried to put the Professor through his routine then and there, but the man from Fogara was in a hurry to get back to town, so they all set out on the *mehara*.

In the town they went directly to the villager's home, where they had coffee in the courtyard sitting among the camels. Here the Professor went into his act again, and this time there was prolonged merriment and much rubbing together of hands. An agreement was reached, a sum of money paid, and the Reguibat withdrew, leaving the Professor in the house of the man with the cane, who did not delay in locking him into a tiny enclosure off the courtyard.

The next day was an important one in the Professor's life, for it was then that pain began to stir again in his being. A group of men came to the house, among whom was a venerable gentleman, better clothed that those others who spent their time flattering him, setting fervent kisses upon his hands and the edges of his garments. This person made a point of going into classical Arabic from time to time, to impress the others, who had not learned a word of the Koran.[11] Thus his conversation would run more or less as follows: "Perhaps at In Salah. The French there are stupid. Celestial vengeance is approaching. Let us not hasten it. Praise the highest and cast thine anathema against idols. With paint on his face. In case the police wish to look close." The others listened and agreed, nodding their heads slowly and solemnly. And the Professor in his stall beside them listened, too. That is, he was *conscious* of the sound of the old man's Arabic. The words penetrated for the first time in many months. Noises, then: "Celestial vengeance is approaching." Then: "It is an honor. Fifty francs is enough. Keep your money. Good." And the *qaouaji* squatting near him at the edge of the precipice. Then "anathema against idols" and more gibberish. He turned over panting on the sand and forgot about it. But the pain had begun. It operated in a kind of delirium, because he had begun to enter into consciousness again. When the man opened the door and prodded him with his cane, he cried out in a rage, and everyone laughed.

They got him onto his feet, but he would not dance. He stood before them, staring at the ground, stubbornly refusing to move. The owner was furious, and so annoyed by the laughter

---

[10] A nomadic tribe of the central and western Sahara Desert.

[11] The Muslim sacred book.

of the others that he felt obliged to send them away, saying that he would await a more propitious time for exhibiting his property, because he dared not show his anger before the elder. However, when they had left he dealt the Professor a violent blow on the shoulder with his cane, called him various obscene things, and went out into the street, slamming the gate behind him. He walked straight to the street of the Ouled Naïl, because he was sure of finding the Reguibat there among the girls, spending the money. And there in a tent he found one of them still abed, while an Ouled Naïl washed the tea glasses. He walked in and almost decapitated the man before the latter had even attempted to sit up. Then he threw his razor on the bed and ran out.

The Ouled Naïl saw the blood, screamed, ran out of her tent into the next, and soon emerged from that with four girls who rushed together into the coffeehouse and told the *qaouaji* who had killed the Reguiba. It was only a matter of an hour before the French military police had caught him at a friend's house, and dragged him off to the barracks. That night the Professor had nothing to eat, and the next afternoon, in the slow sharpening of his consciousness caused by increasing hunger, he walked aimlessly about the courtyard and the rooms that gave onto it. There was no one. In one room a calendar hung on the wall. The Professor watched nervously, like a dog watching a fly in front of its nose. On the white paper were black objects that made sounds in his head. He heard them: "*Grande Epicerie du Sahel. Juin. Lundi, Mardi, Mercredi. ...*"[12]

The tiny ink marks of which a symphony consists may have been made long ago, but when they are fulfilled in sound they become imminent and mighty. So a kind of music of feeling began to play in the Professor's head, increasing in volume as he looked at the mud wall, and he had the feeling that he was performing what had been written for him long ago. He felt like weeping; he felt like roaring through the little house, upsetting and smashing the few breakable objects. His emotion got no further than this one overwhelming desire. So, bellowing as loud as he could, he attacked the house and its belongings. Then he attacked the door into the street, which resisted for a while and finally broke. He climbed through the opening made by the boards he had ripped apart, and still bellowing and shaking his arms in the air to make as loud a jangling as possible, he began to gallop along the quiet street toward the gateway of the town. A few people looked at him with great curiosity. As he passed the garage, the last building before the high mud archway that framed the desert beyond, a French soldier saw him. "*Tiens*,"[13] he said to himself, "a holy maniac."

Again it was sunset time. The Professor ran beneath the arched gate, turned his face toward the red sky, and began to trot along the Piste d'In Salah, straight into the setting sun. Behind him, from the garage, the soldier took a potshot at him for good luck. The bullet whistled dangerously near the Professor's head, and his yelling rose into an indignant lament as he waved his arms more wildly, and hopped high into the air at every few steps, in an access of terror.

The soldier watched a while, smiling, as the cavorting figure grew smaller in the oncoming evening darkness, and the rattling of the tin became a part of the great silence out there beyond the gate. The wall of the garage as he leaned against it still gave forth heat, left there by the sun, but even then the lunar chill was growing in the air.

---

[12] "Grand Grocery of Sahel. June. Monday, Tuesday, Wednesday. ..."
[13] Interjection meaning "Well" or "Hey."

QUESTIONS

1. Is the Professor a victim of senseless violence or is he culpable for his situation? Do you feel sympathy for him? Why or why not?

2. What part does the theme of language and communication play in the story?

3. What is the effect of the exotic setting? What symbolic elements does it contain?

4. Discuss the use of irony and foreshadowing in the story. What is their thematic effect?

RICHARD BRAUTIGAN ≡≡≡≡

Revenge of the Lawn

My grandmother, in her own way, shines like a beacon down the stormy American past. She was a bootlegger in a little county up in the state of Washington. She was also a handsome woman, close to six feet tall who carried 190 pounds in the grand operatic manner of the early 1900s. And her specialty was bourbon, a little raw but a welcomed refreshment in those Volstead Act[1] days.

She of course was no female Al Capone, but her bootlegging feats were the cornucopia of legend in her neck of the woods, as they say. She had the county in her pocket for years. The sheriff used to call her up every morning and give her the weather report and tell her how the chickens were laying.

I can imagine her talking to the sheriff: "Well, Sheriff, I hope your mother gets better soon. I had a cold and a bad sore throat last week myself. I've still got the sniffles. Tell her hello for me and to drop by the next time she's down this way. And if you want that case, you can pick it up or I can have it sent over as soon as Jack gets back with the car.

"No, I don't know if I'm going to the firemen's ball this year, but you know that my heart is with the firemen. If you don't see me there tonight, you tell the boys that. No, I'll try to get there, but I'm still not fully recovered from my cold. It kind of climbs on me in the evening."

My grandmother lived in a three-story house that was old even in those days. There was a pear tree in the front yard which was heavily eroded by rain from years of not having any lawn.

The picket fence that once enclosed the lawn was gone too, and people just drove their cars right up to the porch. In the winter the front yard was a mud hole and in the summer it was hard as a rock.

Jack used to curse the front yard as if it were a living thing. He was the man who lived with my grandmother for thirty years. He was not my grandfather, but an Italian who came down the road one day selling lots in Florida.

He was selling a vision of eternal oranges and sunshine door to door in a land where people ate apples and it rained a lot.

Jack stopped at my grandmother's house to sell her a lot just a stone's throw from

---

[1] National Prohibition Enforcement Act, passed by Congress in 1919 to enforce the Eighteenth Amendment, which prohibited the sale of intoxicating liquor.

downtown Miami, and he was delivering her whiskey a week later. He stayed for thirty years and Florida went on without him.

Jack hated the front yard because he thought it was against him. There had been a beautiful lawn there when Jack came along, but he let it wander off into nothing. He refused to water it or take care of it in any way.

Now the ground was so hard that it gave his car flat tires in the summer. The yard was always finding a nail to put in one of his tires or the car was always sinking out of sight in the winter when the rains came on.

The lawn had belonged to my grandfather who lived out the end of his life in an insane asylum. It had been his pride and joy and was said to be the place where his powers came from.

My grandfather was a minor Washington mystic who in 1911 prophesied the exact date when World War I would start: June 28, 1914, but it had been too much for him. He never got to enjoy the fruit of his labor because they had to put him away in 1913 and he spent seventeen years in the state insane asylum believing he was a child and it was actually May 3, 1872.

He believed that he was six years old and it was a cloudy day about to rain and his mother was baking a chocolate cake. It stayed May 3, 1872 for my grandfather until he died in 1930. It took seventeen years for that chocolate cake to be baked.

There was a photograph of my grandfather. I look a great deal like him. The only difference being that I am over six feet tall and he was not quite five feet tall. He had a dark idea that being so short, so close to the earth and his lawn would help to prophesy the exact date when World War I would start.

It was a shame that the war started without him. If only he could have held back his childhood for another year, avoided that chocolate cake, all of his dreams would have come true.

There were always two large dents in my grandmother's house that had never been repaired and one of them came about this way: In the autumn the pears would get ripe on the tree in the front yard and the pears would fall on the ground and rot and bees would gather by the hundreds to swarm on them.

The bees somewhere along the line had picked up the habit of stinging Jack two or three times a year. They would sting him in the most ingenious ways.

Once a bee got in his wallet and he went down to the store to buy some food for dinner, not knowing the mischief that he carried in his pocket.

He took out his wallet to pay for the food.

"That will be 72 cents," the grocer said.

"AAAAAAAAAAAAAAAAAAAAAA!" Jack replied, looking down to see a bee busy stinging him on the little finger.

The first large dent in the house was brought about by still another bee landing on Jack's cigar as he was driving the car into the front yard that peary autumn the stock market crashed.

The bee ran down the cigar, Jack could only stare at it cross-eyed in terror, and stung him on the upper lip. His reaction to this was to drive the car immediately into the house.

That front yard had quite a history after Jack let the lawn go to hell. One day in 1932 Jack was off running an errand or delivering something for my grandmother. She wanted to dump the old mash and get a new batch going.

Because Jack was gone, she decided to do it herself. Grandmother put on a pair of railroad overalls that she used for working around the still and filled a wheelbarrow with mash and dumped it out in the front yard.

She had a flock of snow-white geese that roamed outside the house and nested in the garage that had not been used to park the car since the time Jack had come along selling futures in Florida.

Jack had some kind of idea that it was all wrong for a car to have a house. I think it was something that he had learned in the old country. The answer was in Italian because that was the only language Jack used when he talked about the garage. For everything else he used English, but it was only Italian for the garage.

After Grandmother had dumped the mash on the ground near the pear tree, she went back to the still down in the basement and the geese all gathered around the mash and started talking it over.

I guess they came to a mutually agreeable decision because they all started eating the mash. As they ate the mash their eyes got brighter and brighter and their voices, in appreciation of the mash, got louder and louder.

After a while one of the geese stuck his head in the mash and forgot to take it out. Another one of the geese cackled madly and tried to stand on one leg and give a W. C. Fields' imitation of a stork. He maintained that position for about a minute before he fell on his tail feathers.

My grandmother found them all lying around the mash in the positions that they had fallen. They looked as if they had been machine-gunned. From the height of her operatic splendor she thought that they were all dead.

She responded to this by plucking all their feathers and piling their bald bodies in the wheelbarrow and wheeling them down to the basement. She had to make five trips to accommodate them.

She stacked them like cordwood near the still and waited for Jack to return and dispose of them in a way that would provide a goose for dinner and a small profit by selling the rest of the flock in town. She went upstairs to take a nap after finishing with the still.

It was about an hour later that the geese woke up. They had devastating hangovers. They had all kind of gathered themselves uselessly to their feet when suddenly one of the geese noticed that he did not have any feathers. He informed the other geese of their condition, too. They were all in despair.

They paraded out of the basement in a forlorn and wobbly gang. They were all standing in a cluster near the pear tree when Jack drove into the front yard.

The memory of the time he had been stung on the mouth by that bee must have come back to his mind when he saw the defeathered geese standing there, because suddenly like a madman he tore out the cigar he had stuck in his mouth and threw it away from him as hard as he could. This caused his hand to travel through the windshield. A feat that cost him 32 stitches.

The geese stood by staring on like some helpless, primitive American advertisement for aspirin under the pear tree as Jack drove his car into the house for the second and last time in the Twentieth Century.

The first time I remember anything in life occurred in my grandmother's front yard. The year was either 1936 or 1937. I remember a man, probably Jack, cutting down the pear tree and soaking it with kerosene.

It looked strange, even for a first memory of life, to watch a man pour gallons and gallons of kerosene all over a tree lying stretched out thirty feet or so on the ground, and then to set fire to it while the fruit was still green on the branches.

QUESTIONS

1. What is the narrator's purpose in relating these events which precede his earliest memory? Does he offer any insights into "the stormy American past" in his story? Or is his purpose less profound? What tone does he adopt toward his material?

2. Compare Brautigan's story to such early examples of the short story as Irving's "The Legend of Sleepy Hollow" and Poe's "The Fall of the House of Usher." What features does it share with these stories? How does it differ?

RICHARD BRAUTIGAN

A Short History of Religion in California

There's only one way to get into it: we saw the deer in the meadow. The deer turned in a slow circle and then broke the circle and went toward some trees.

There were three deer in the meadow and we were three people. I, a friend and my daughter 3½ years old. "See the deer," I said, pointing the way to the deer.

"Look the deer! There! There!" she said and surged against me as I held her in the front seat. A little jolt of electricity had come to her from the deer. Three little gray dams went away into the trees, celebrating a TVA[1] of hoofs.

She talked about the deer as we drove back to our camp in Yosemite. "Those deer are really something," she said. "I'd like to be a deer."

When we turned into our campground there were three deer standing at the entrance, looking at us. They were the same three deer or they were three different ones.

"Look the deer!" and the same electrical surge against me, enough perhaps to light a couple of Christmas tree lights or make a fan turn for a minute or toast half-a-slice of bread.

The deer followed close behind the car as we drove at deer speed into the camp. When we got out of the car, the deer were there. My daughter took out after them. Wow! The deer!

I slowed her down. "Wait," I said. "Let Daddy take your hand." I didn't want her to scare them or get hurt by them either, in case they should panic and run over her, a next to impossible thing.

We followed after the deer, a little ways behind and then stopped to watch them cross the river. The river was shallow and the deer stopped in the middle and looked in three different directions.

She stared at them, not saying anything for a while. How quiet and beautiful they looked and then she said, "Daddy, take off the deer's head and put it on my head. Take off the deer's feet, put them on my feet. And I'll be the deer."

The deer stopped looking in three different directions. They all looked in one direction toward the trees on the other side of the river and moved off into those trees.

So the next morning there was a band of Christians camping beside us because it was

---

[1] Tennessee Valley Authority, established in 1932 to construct dams and power plants in the Tennessee Valley region.

Sunday. There were about twenty or thirty of them seated at a long wooden table. They were singing hymns while we were taking down our tent.

My daughter watched them very carefully and then walked over to peek out at them from behind a tree as they sang on. There was a man leading them. He waved his hands in the air. Probably their minister.

My daughter watched them very carefully and then moved out from behind the tree and slowly advanced until she was right behind their minister, looking up at him. He was standing out there alone and she was standing out there alone with him.

I pulled the metal tent stakes out of the ground and put them together in a neat pile, and I folded the tent and put it beside the tent stakes.

Then one of the Christian women got up from the long table and walked over to my daughter. I was watching this. She gave her a piece of cake and asked her if she wanted to sit down and listen to the singing. They were busy singing something about Jesus doing something good for them.

My daughter nodded her head and sat down on the ground. She held the piece of cake in her lap. She sat there for five minutes. She did not take a bite out of the piece of cake.

They were now singing something about Mary and Joseph doing something. In the song it was winter and cold and there was straw in the barn. It smelled good.

She listened for about five minutes and then she got up, waved good-bye in the middle of *We Three Kings of Orient Are* and came back with the piece of cake.

"Well, how was that?" I said.

"Singing," she said, pointing they are singing.

"How's the cake?" I said.

"I don't know," she said and threw it on the ground. "I've already had breakfast." It lay there.

I thought about the three deer and the Christians singing. I looked at the piece of cake and to the river where the deer had been gone for a day.

The cake was very small on the ground. The water flowed over the rocks. A bird or an animal would eat the cake later on and then go down to the river for a drink of water.

A little thing came to my mind and having no other choice: it pleased me, so I hugged my arms around a tree and my cheek sailed to the sweet bark and floated there for a few gentle moments in the calm.

QUESTIONS

1. How do the child's two religious experiences differ? What does each offer? Is Brautigan's use of a child significant? What do these experiences have to do with California's religious history?

2. Discuss the narrator's actions and observations at the end of the story. Is he undergoing a type of religious experience? What has he discovered in this epiphany? How and why does the style change to convey this?

3. As the title of this story informs us, it is a history. How does Brautigan's "historical" method in this story differ from his method in "Revenge of the Lawn"?

HORTENSE CALISHER

The Scream on Fifty-Seventh Street

When the scream came, from downstairs in the street five flights below her bedroom window, Mrs. Hazlitt, who in her month's tenancy of the flat had become the lightest of sleepers, stumbled up, groped her way past the empty second twin bed that stood nearer the window, and looked out. There was nothing to be seen of course — the apartment house she was in, though smartly kept up to the standards of the neighborhood, dated from the era of front fire escapes, and the sound, if it had come at all, had come from directly beneath them. From other half-insomniac nights she knew that the hour must be somewhere between three and four in the morning. The "all-night" doorman who guarded the huge façade of the apartment house opposite had retired, per custom, to some region behind its canopy; the one down the block at the corner of First, who blew his taxi-whistle so incessantly that she had for some nights mistaken it for a traffic policeman's, had been quiet for a long time. Even the white-shaded lamp that burned all day and most of the night on the floor of the little gray townhouse sandwiched between the tall buildings across the way — an invalid's light perhaps — had been quenched. At this hour the wide expanse of the avenue, Fifty-Seventh Street at its easternmost end, looked calm, reassuring and amazingly silent for one of the main arteries of the city. The crosstown bus service had long since ceased; the truck traffic over on First made only an occasional dim rumble. If she went into the next room, where there was a French window opening like a double door, and leaned out, absurd idea, in her nightgown, she would see, far down to the right, the lamps of a portion of the Queensboro Bridge, quietly necklaced on the night. In the blur beneath them, out of range but comfortable to imagine, the beautiful cul-de-sac of Sutton Square must be musing, Edwardian in the starlight, its one antique bow-front jutting over the river shimmering below. And in the façades opposite her, lights were still spotted here and there, as was always the case, even in the small hours, in New York. Other consciousnesses were awake, a vigil of anonymous neighbors whom she would never know, that still gave one the hive-sense of never being utterly alone.

All was silent. No, she must have dreamed it, reinterpreted in her doze some routine sound, perhaps the siren of the police car that often keened through this street but never stopped, no doubt on its way to the more tumultuous West Side. Until the death of her husband, companion of twenty years, eight months ago, her ability to sleep had always been healthy and immediate; since then it had gradually, not unnaturally deteriorated, but this was the worst; she had never done this before. For she could still hear very clearly the character of the sound, or rather its lack of one — a long, oddly sustained note, then a shorter one, both perfectly even, not discernible as a man's or a woman's, and without — yes, without the color of any emotion — surely the sound that one heard in dreams. Never a woman of small midnight fears in either city or country, as a girl she had done settlement work on some of this city's blackest streets, as a mining engineer's wife had nestled peacefully within the shrieking velvet of an Andes night. Not to give herself special marks for this, it was still all the more reason why what she had heard, or thought she had heard, must have been hallucinatory. A harsh word, but she must be stern with herself at the very beginnings of any such, of what could presage the sort of disintegrated widowhood, full of the mouse-fears and softening self-indulgences of the manless, that she could not, would not abide. Scarcely a second or two could have elapsed between that long — yes, that was it, soulless — cry, and her arrival at the window. And look, down there on the street and upward, everything remained motionless. Not a soul, in answer, had erupted from a doorway. All the fanlights of the lobbies shone serenely. Up above, no one leaned, not a window had flapped wide. After twenty years of living outside of the city, she could still flatter herself that she knew New York down to the ground — she had been born here, and raised. Secretly mourning it, missing it through all the happiest suburban years, she had kept up with it like a scholar, building a red-book[1] of it for herself even through all its savage, incontinent rebuilding. She still knew all its neighborhoods. She knew. And this was one in which such a sound would be policed at once, such a cry serviced at once, if only by doormen running. No, the fault, the disturbance, must be hers.

Reaching into the pretty, built-in wardrobe on her right — the flat, with so many features that made it more like a house, fireplace, high ceilings, had attracted her from the first for this reason — she took out a warm dressing gown and sat down on the bed to put on her slippers. The window was wide open and she meant to leave it that way; country living had made unbearable the steam heat of her youth. There was no point to winter otherwise, and she — she and Sam — had always been ones to enjoy the weather as it came. Perhaps she had been unwise to give up the dog, excuse for walks early and late, outlet for talking aloud — the city was full of them. Unwise too, in the self-denuding impulse of loss, to have made herself that solitary in readiness for a city where she would have to remake friends, and no longer had kin. And charming as this flat was, wooed as she increasingly was by the delicately winning personality of its unknown, absent owner, Mrs. Berry, by her bric-a-brac, her cookbooks, even by her widowhood, almost as recent as Mrs. Hazlitt's own — perhaps it would be best to do something about getting the empty second twin bed removed from this room. No doubt Mrs. Berry, fled to London, possibly even residing in the rooms of yet a third woman in search of recommended change, would understand. Mrs. Hazlitt stretched her arms, able to smile at this imagined procession of women inhabiting each other's rooms, fallen one against the other like a pack of playing cards. How could she have forgotten what anyone who had reached middle age through the normal amount of trouble should know, that the very horizontal position itself of sleep, when one could not, laid one open to every attack from within, on a couch with no psychiatrist to listen but oneself. The best way to meet the horrors was on two feet, vertical. What she meant to do now was to fix herself a sensible hot drink, not coffee, reminiscent of shared midnight snacks, not even tea, but a nursery drink, cocoa. In a lifetime, she thought, there are probably two eras of the sleep that is utterly sound: the nursery sleep (if one had the lucky kind of childhood I did) and the sleep next or near the heart and body of the one permanently loved and loving, if one has been lucky enough for that too. I must learn

---

[1] A type of social register.

from within, as well as without, that both are over. She stood up, tying her sash more firmly. And at that moment the scream came again.

She listened, rigid. It came exactly as remembered, one shrilled long note, then the shorter second, like a cut-off Amen to the first and of the same timbre, dreadful in its cool, a madness expended almost with calm, near the edge of joy. No wonder she had thought of the siren; this had the same note of terror controlled. One could not tell whether it sped toward a victim or from one. As before, it seemed to come from directly below.

Shaking, she leaned out, could see nothing because of the high sill, ran into the next room, opened the French window and all but stood on the fire escape. As she did so, the sound, certainly human, had just ceased; at the same moment a cab, going slowly down the middle of the avenue, its toplight up, veered directly toward her, as if the driver too had heard, poised there beneath her with its nose pointed toward the curb, then veered sharply back to the center of the street, gathered speed, and drove on. Immediately behind it another cab, toplight off, slowed up, performed exactly the same orbit, then it too, with a hasty squeal of brakes, made for the center street and sped away. In the confusion of noises she thought she heard the grind of a window-sash coming down, then a slam — perhaps the downstairs door of the adjoining set of flats, or of this one. Dropping to her knees, she leaned both palms on the floor-level lintel of the window and peered down through the iron slats of her fire escape and the successive ones below. Crouched that way, she could see straight back to the building line. To the left, a streetlamp cast a pale, even glow on empty sidewalk and the free space of curb either side of a hydrant; to the right, the shadows were obscure, but motionless. She saw nothing to conjure into a half-expected human bundle lying still, heard no footfall staggering or slipping away. Not more than a minute or two could have elapsed since she had heard the cry. Tilting her head up at the facade opposite, she saw that their simple pattern of lit windows seemed the same. While she stared, one of the squares blotted out, then another, both on floors not too high to have heard. Would no one, having heard, attend? Would she?

Standing up, her hand on the hasp of the French window, she felt herself still shaking, not with fear, but with the effort to keep herself from in some way heeding that cry. Again she told herself that she had been born here, knew the city's ways, had not the *auslander's*[2] incredulity about some of them. These ways had hardened since her day, people had warned her, to an indifference beyond that of any civilized city; there were no "good" neighborhoods now, none of any kind really, except the half-hostile enclosure that each family must build for itself. She had discounted this, knowing unsentimentally what city life was; even in the tender version of it that was her childhood there had been noises, human ones, that the most responsible people, the kindest, had shrugged away, saying, "Nothing, dear. Something outside." What she had not taken into account was her own twenty years of living elsewhere, where such a cry in the night would be succored at once if only for gossip's sake, if only because one gave up privacy — anonymity — forever, when one went to live in a house on a road. If only, she thought, holding herself rigid to stop her trembling, because it would be the cry of someone one knew. Nevertheless, it took all her strength not to rush downstairs, to hang on to the handle, while in her mind's eye she ran out of her apartment door, remembering to take the key, pressed the elevator button and waited, went down at the car's deliberate pace. After that there would be the inner, buzzer door to open, then at last the door to the outside. No, it would take too long, and it was already too late for the phone; by the time police could come or she could find the number of the superintendent in his back basement — and when either answered — what would she say? She looked at the fire escape. Not counting hers, there must

---

[2] Foreigner's; alien's.

be three others between herself and the street. Whether there was a ladder extending from the lowest one she could not remember; possibly one hung by one's hands and dropped to the ground. Years ago there had been more of them, even the better houses had had them in their rear areaways, but she had never in her life seen one used. And this one fronted direct on the avenue. It was this that brought her to her senses — the vision of herself in her blue robe creeping down the front of a building on Fifty-Seventh Street, hanging by her hands until she dropped to the ground. She shut the long window quickly, leaning her weight against it to help the slightly swollen frame into place, and turned the handle counterclockwise, shooting the long vertical bolt. The bolt fell into place with a thump she had never noticed before but already seemed familiar. Probably, she thought, sighing, it was the kind of sound — old hardware on old wood — that more often went with a house.

In the kitchen, over her cocoa, she shook herself with a reminiscent tremble, in the way one did after a narrow escape. It was a gesture made more often to a companion, an auditor. Easy enough to make the larger gestures involved in cutting down one's life to the pattern of the single: the selling of a house, the arranging of income or new occupation. Even the abnegation of sex had a drama that lent one strength, made one hold up one's head as one saw oneself traveling a clear, melancholy line. It was the small gestures for which there was no possible sublimation, the sudden phrase, posture — to no auditor, the constant clueing of identity in another's — its cessation. "Dear me," she would have said — they would have come to town for the winter months as they had often planned, and he would have just returned from an overnight business trip — "what do you suppose I'd have done, Sam, if I'd gone all the way, in my housecoat, really found myself outside? Funny how the distinction between outdoors and in breaks down in the country. I'd forgotten how absolute it is here — with so many barriers between." Of course, she thought, that's the simple reason why here, in the city, the sense of responsibility has to weaken. Who could maintain it, through a door, an elevator, a door and a door, toward everyone, anyone, who screamed? Perhaps that was the real reason she had come here, she thought, washing the cup under the faucet. Where the walls are sound-proofed there are no more "people next door" with their ready "casserole" pity, at worst with the harbored glow of their own family life peering from their averted eyelids like the lamplight from under their eaves. Perhaps she had known all along that the best way to learn how to live alone was to come to the place where people really were.

She set the cup out for the morning and added a plate and a spoon. It was wiser not to let herself deteriorate to the utterly casual; besides, the sight of them always gave her a certain pleasure, like a greeting, if only from herself of the night before. Tomorrow she had a meeting, of one of the two hospital boards on which, luckily for now, she had served for years. There was plenty more of that kind of useful occupation available and no one would care a hoot whether what once she had done for conscience' sake she now did for her own. The meeting was not scheduled until two. Before that she would manage to inquire very discreetly, careful not to appear either eccentric or too friendly, both of which made city people uneasy, as to whether anyone else in the building had heard what she had. This too she would do for discipline's sake. There was no longer any doubt that the sound had been real.

The next morning at eight-thirty, dressed to go out except for her coat, she waited just inside her door for one or the other tenants on her floor to emerge. Her heart pounded at the very queerness of what she was doing, but she overruled it; if she did feel somewhat too interested, too much as if she were embarking on a chase, then let her get it out of her system at once, and have done. How to do so was precisely what she had considered while dressing. The problem was not to make too many inquiries, too earnest ones, and not to seem to be making any personal overture, from which people would naturally withdraw. One did not make inconvenient, hothouse friendships in the place one lived in, here. Therefore she had decided to limit her approaches to three — the first to the girl who lived in the adjacent apartment, who could usually be encountered at this hour and was the only tenant she knew for sure lived in the front of the building — back tenants were less likely to have heard. For the rest, she must trust to luck. And whatever the outcome, she would not let herself pursue the matter beyond today.

She opened the door a crack and listened. Still too early. Actually the place, being small — six floors of four or five flats each — had a more intimate feeling than most. According to the super's wife, Mrs. Stump, with whom she had had a chat or two in the hall, many of the tenants, clinging to ceiling rents in what had become a fancier district, had been here for years, a few for the thirty since the place had been built. This would account for so many middle-aged and elderly, seemingly either single or the remnants of families — besides various quiet, well-mannered women who, like herself, did not work, she had noticed at times two men who were obviously father and son, two others who, from their ages and nameplate, noticed at mailtime, might be brothers, and a mother with the only child in the place — a subdued little girl of about eight. As soon as a tenant of long standing vacated or died, Mrs. Stump had added, the larger units were converted to smaller, and this would account for the substratum of slightly showier or younger occupants: two modish blondes, a couple of homburged "decorator" types — all more in keeping with the newly sub-theatrical, antique-shop character of the neighborhood — as well as for the "career girl" on her floor. Mrs. Berry, who from evidences in the flat should be something past forty like herself, belonged to the first group, having been here, with her husband of course until recently, since just after the war. A pity that she, Mrs. Berry, who from her books, her one charming letter, her own situation, might have been just the person to understand, even share Mrs. Hazlitt's reaction to the event of last night, was not here. But this was nonsense; if she were, then she, Mrs. Hazlitt, would not be. She thought again of the chain of women, sighed, and immediately chid herself for this new habit of sighing, as well as for this alarming mound of gratuitous information she seemed to have acquired, in less than a month, about people with whom she was in no way concerned. At that moment she heard the door next hers creak open. Quickly she put on her coat, opened her door and bent to pick up the morning paper. The girl coming out stepped back, dropping one of a pile of boxes she was carrying. Mrs. Hazlitt returned it to her, pressed the button for the elevator, and when it came, held the door. It was the girl she had seen twice before; for the first time they had a nice exchange of smiles.

"Whoops, I'm late," said the girl, craning to look at her watch.

"Me too," said Mrs. Hazlitt, as the cage slid slowly down. She drew breath. "Overslept, once I did get to sleep. Rather a noisy night outside — did you hear all that fuss, must have been around three or four?" She waited hopefully for the answer: Why yes indeed, what on earth was it, did you?

"Uh-uh," said the girl, shaking her head serenely. "'Fraid the three of us sleep like a log, that's the trouble. My roommates are still at it, lucky stiffs." She checked her watch again, was first out of the elevator, nodded her thanks when Mrs. Hazlitt hurried to hold the buzzer door for her because of the boxes, managed the outer door herself, and departed.

Mrs. Hazlitt walked briskly around the corner to the bakery, came back with her bag of two brioches, and reentered. Imagine, there are three of them, she thought, and I never knew. Well I envy them their log. The inner door, usually locked, was propped open. Mrs. Stump was on her knees just behind it, washing the marble floor, as she did every day. It was certainly a tidy house, not luxurious but up to a firmly well-bred standard, just the sort a woman like Mrs. Berry would have, that she herself, when the sublease was over, would like to find. Nodding to Mrs. Stump, she went past her to the row of brass mail slots, pretending to search her own although she knew it was too early, weighing whether she ought to risk wasting one of her three chances on her.

"Mail don't come till ten," said Mrs. Stump from behind her.

"Yes, I know," said Mrs. Hazlitt, recalling suddenly that they had had this exchange before. "But I forgot to check yesterday."

"Yesterday vass holiday."

"Oh, so it was." Guiltily Mrs. Hazlitt entered the elevator and faced the door, relieved when it closed. The truth was that she had known yesterday was a holiday and had checked the mail anyway. The truth was that she often did this even on Sundays here, often even more than once. It made an errand in the long expanse of a day when she either flinched from the daily walk that was too dreary to do alone on Sunday, or had not provided herself with a ticket to something. One had to tidy one's hair, spruce a bit for the possible regard of someone in the hall, and when she did see someone, although of course they never spoke, she always returned feeling refreshed, reaffirmed.

Upstairs again, she felt that way now; her day had begun in the eyes of others, as a day should. She made a few phone calls to laundry and bank, and felt even better. Curious how, when one lived alone, one began to feel that only one's own consciousness held up the world, and at the very same time that only an incursion into the world, or a recognition from it, made one continue to exist at all. There was another phone call she might make, to a friend up in the country, who had broken an ankle, but she would save that for a time when she needed it more. This was yet another discipline — not to become a phone bore. The era when she herself had been a victim of such, had often thought of the phone as a nuisance, now seemed as distant as China. She looked at the clock — time enough to make another pot of coffee. With it she ate a brioche slowly, then with the pleasant sense of hurry she now had so seldom, another.

At ten sharp she went downstairs again, resolving to take her chance with whoever might be there. As she emerged from the elevator she saw that she was in luck; the owner of a big brown poodle — a tall, well set up man of sixty or so — was bent over his mail slot while the dog stood by. It was the simplest of matters to make an overture to the poodle, who was already politely nosing the palm she offered him, to expose her own love of the breed, remarking on this one's exceptional manners, to skip lightly on from the question of barking to noise in general, to a particular noise.

"Ah well, Coco's had stage training," said his owner, in answer to her compliments. She guessed that his owner might have had the same; he had that fine, bravura face which aging actors of another generation often had, a trifle shallow for its years perhaps but very fine, and he inclined toward her with the same majestic politeness as his dog, looking into her face very intently as she spoke, answering her in the slender, semi-British accent she recalled from matinee idols of her youth. She had to repeat her question on the noise. This time she firmly gave the sound its name — a scream, really rather an unusual scream.

"A scream?" The man straightened. She thought that for a moment he looked dismayed. Then he pursed his lips very judiciously, in almost an acting-out of that kind of response. "Come to think of it, ye-es, I may have heard something." He squared his shoulders. "But no doubt I just turned over. And Coco's a city dog, very blasé fellow. Rather imagine he did too." He tipped his excellent homburg. "Good morning," he added, with sudden reserve, and turned away, giving a flick to the dog's leash that started the animal off with his master behind him.

"Good morning," she called after them, "and thanks for the tip on where to get one like Coco." Coco looked back at her, but his master, back turned, disentangling the leash from the doorknob, did not, and went out without answering.

So I've done it after all, she thought. Too friendly. Especially too friendly since I'm a woman. Her face grew hot at this probable estimate of her — gushy woman chattering over-brightly, lingering in the hall. Bore of a woman who heard things at night, no doubt looked under the bed before she got into it. No, she thought, there was something — when I mentioned the scream. At the aural memory of that latter, still clear, she felt her resolve stiffen. Also — what a dunce she was being — there were the taxis. Taxis, one of them occupied, did not veer, one after the other, on an empty street, without reason. Emboldened, she bent to look at the man's mailbox. The name, Reginald Warwick, certainly fitted her imaginary dossier, but that was not what gave her pause. Apartment 3A. Hers was 5A. He lived in the front, two floors beneath her, where he must have heard.

As she inserted the key in her apartment door, she heard the telephone ringing, fumbled the key and dropped it, then had to open the double lock above. All part of the city picture, she thought resentfully, remembering their four doors, never locked, in the country — utterly foolhardly, never to be dreamed of here. Even if she had, there were Mrs. Berry's possessions to be considered, nothing extraordinary, but rather like the modest crotchety bits of treasure she had inherited or acquired herself — in the matter of bric-a-brac alone there was really quite a kinship between them. The phone was still ringing as she entered. She raced toward it eagerly. It was the secretary of the hospital board, telling her that this afternoon's meeting was put off.

"Oh ... oh dear," said Mrs. Hazlitt. "I mean — I'm so sorry to hear about Mrs. Levin. Hope it's nothing serious."

"I really couldn't say," said the secretary. "But we've enough for a quorum the week after." She rang off.

Mrs. Hazlitt put down the phone, alarmed at the sudden sinking of her heart over such a minor reversal. She had looked forward to seeing people of course, but particularly to spending an afternoon in the brightly capable impersonality of the boardroom, among men and women who brought with them a sense of indefinable swathes of well-being extending behind them, of such a superfluity of it, from lives as full as their checkbooks, that they were met in that efficient room to dispense what overflowed. The meeting would have been an antidote to that dark, anarchic version of the city which had been obsessing her; it would have been a reminder that everywhere, on flight after flight of the city's high, brilliant floors, similar groups of the responsible were convening, could always be applied to, were in command. The phone gave a reminiscent tinkle as she pushed it aside, and she waited, but there was no further ring. She looked at her calendar, scribbled with domestic markings — the hairdresser on Tuesday, a fitting for her spring suit, the date when she must appear at the lawyer's for the closing on the sale of the house. Beyond that she had a dinner party with old acquaintances on the following Thursday, tickets with a woman friend for the Philharmonic on Saturday week. Certainly she was not destitute of either company or activity. But the facts were that within the next two weeks, she could look forward to only two occasions when she would be communicating on any terms of intimacy with people who, within limits, knew "who" she was. A default on either would be felt keenly — much more than the collapse of this afternoon's little — prop. Absently she twiddled the dial back and forth. Proportion was what went first "in solitary"; circling one's own small platform in space, the need for speech mute in one's own throat, one developed an abnormal concern over the night-cries of others. No, she thought, remembering the board meeting, those high convocations of the responsible, I've promised — Lord knows who, myself, somebody. She stood up and gave herself a smart slap on the buttock. "Come on, Millie," she said, using the nickname her husband always had. "Get on with it." She started to leave the room, then remained in its center, hand at mouth, wondering. Talking aloud to oneself was more common than admitted; almost everyone did. It was merely that she could not decide whether or not she had.

Around eleven o'clock, making up a bundle of lingerie, she went down to the basement where there was a community washing machine, set the machine's cycle, and went back upstairs. Forty minutes later she went through the same routine, shifting the wet clothes to the dryer. At one o'clock she returned for the finished clothes and carried them up. This made six trips in all, but at no time had she met anyone en route; it was Saturday afternoon, perhaps a bad time. At two she went out to do her weekend shopping. The streets were buzzing, the women in the supermarket evidently laying in enough stores for a visitation of giants. Outside the market, a few kids from Third Avenue always waited in hope of tips for carrying, and on impulse, although her load was small, she engaged a boy of about ten. On the way home, promising him extra for waiting, she stopped at the patisserie where she always lingered for the sheer gilt-and-chocolate gaiety of the place, bought her brioches for the morning, and, again on impulse, an éclair for the boy. Going up in the elevator they encountered the mother and small girl, but she had never found any pretext for addressing that glum pair, the mother engaged as usual in a low, toneless tongue-lashing of the child. Divorcée, Mrs. Hazlitt fancied, and no man in the offing, an inconvenient child. In the kitchen, she tipped the boy and offered him the pastry. After an astonished glance, he wolfed it with a practical air, peering at her furtively between bites, and darted off at once, looking askance over his shoulder at her "See you next Saturday, maybe." Obviously he had been brought up to believe that only witches dispensed free gingerbread. In front of the bathroom mirror, Mrs. Hazlitt, tidying up before her walk, almost ritual now, to Sutton Square, regarded her image, not yet a witch's but certainly a fool's, a country-cookie-jar fool's. "Oh, well, you're company," she said, quite consciously aloud this time, and for some reason this cheered her. Before leaving, she went over face and costume with the laborious attention she always gave them nowadays before going anywhere outside.

Again, when she rode down, she met no one, but she walked with bracing step, making herself take a circuitous route for health's sake, all the way to Bloomingdale's, then on to Park and around again, along the Fifty-Eighth Street bridge pass, the dejectedly frivolous shops that lurked near it, before she let herself approach the house with the niche with the little statue of Dante[3] in it, then the Square. Sitting in the Square, the air rapidly blueing now, lapping her like reverie, she wondered whether any of the residents of the windows surrounding her had noticed her almost daily presence, half hoped they had. Before it became too much of a habit, of course, she would stop coming. Meanwhile, if she took off her distance glasses, the scene before her, seen through the tender, Whistlerian blur of myopia — misted gray bridge, blue and green lights of a barge going at its tranced pace downriver — was the very likeness of a corner of the Chelsea embankment, glimpsed throughout a winter of happy teatime windows seven years ago, from a certain angle below Battersea Bridge. Surely it was blameless to remember past happiness if one did so without self-pity, better still, of course, to be able to speak of it to someone in an even, healing voice. Idly she wondered where Mrs. Berry was living in London. The flat in Cheyne Walk would just have suited her. "Just the thing for you," she would have said to her had she known her. "The Sebrings still let it every season. We always meant to go back." Her watch said five and the air was chilling. She walked rapidly home through the evening scurry, the hour of appointments, catching its excitement as she too hurried, half-persuaded of her own appointment, mythical but still possible, with someone as yet unknown. Outside her own building she paused. All day long she had been entering it from the westerly side. Now, approaching from the east, she saw that the fire escape on this side did end in a ladder, about four feet above her. Anyone moderately tall, like herself, would have had an easy drop of it, as she would have done last night. Shaking her head at that crazy image, she

[3] Dante Alighieri (1265–1321), Italian poet, author of *The Divine Comedy*.

looked up at the brilliant hives all around her. Lights were cramming in, crowding on, but she knew too much now about their nighttime progression, their gradual decline to a single indifferent string on that rising, insomniac silence in which she might lie until morning, dreading to hear again what no one else would appear to have heard. Scaring myself to death, she thought (or muttered?), and in the same instant resolved to drop all limits, go down to the basement and interrogate the Stumps, sit on the bench in the lobby and accost anyone who came in, ring doorbells if necessary, until she had confirmation — and not go upstairs until she had. "Excuse me," said someone. She turned. A small, frail, elderly woman, smiling timidly, waited to get past her through the outer door.

"Oh — sorry," said Mrs. Hazlitt. "Why — good evening!" she added with a rush, an enormous rush of relief. "Here — let me," she said more quietly, opening the door with a numb sense of gratitude for having been tugged back from the brink of what she saw now, at the touch of a voice, had been panic. For here was a tenant, unaccountably forgotten, with whom she was almost on speaking terms, a gentle old sort, badly crippled with arthritis, for whom Mrs. Hazlitt had once or twice unlocked the inner door. She did so now.

"Thank you, my dear — my hands are that knobbly." There was the trace of brogue that Mrs. Hazlitt had noticed before. The old woman, her gray hair sparse from the disease but freshly done in the artfully messy arrangements used to conceal the skulls of old ladies, her broadtail coat not new but excellently maintained, gave off the comfortable essence, pleasing as rosewater, of one who had been serenely protected all her life. Unmarried, for she had that strangely deducible aura about her even before one noted the lack of ring, she had also a certain simpleness, now almost bygone, of those household women who had never gone to business — Mrs. Hazlitt had put her down as perhaps the relict sister of a contractor, or of a school superintendent of the days when the system had been Irish from top to bottom, at the top, of Irish of just this class. The old lady fumbled now with the minute key to her mailbox.

"May I?"

"Ah, if you would now. Couldn't manage it when I came down. The fingers don't seem to warm up until evening. It's 2B."

Mrs. Hazlitt, inserting the key, barely noticed the name — Finan. 2B would be a front apartment also, in the line adjacent to the A's.

"And you would be the lady in Mrs. Berry's. Such a nicely spoken woman, she was."

"Oh yes, isn't she," said Mrs. Hazlitt. "I mean ... I just came through the agent. But when you live in a person's house — do you know her?"

"Just to speak. Half as long as me, they'd lived here. Fifteen years." The old lady took the one letter Mrs. Hazlitt passed her, the yellow-fronted rent bill whose duplicate she herself had received this morning. "Ah well, we're always sure of this one, aren't we?" Nodding her thanks, she shuffled toward the elevator on built-up shoes shaped like hods. "Still, it's a nice, quiet building, and lucky we are to be in it these days."

There was such a rickety bravery about her, of neat habits long overborne by the imprecisions of age, of dowager hat set slightly askew by fingers unable to deal with a key yet living alone, that Mrs. Hazlitt, reluctant to shake the poor, tottery dear further, had to remind herself of the moment before their encounter.

"Last night?" The old blue eyes looked blank, then brightened. "Ah no, I must have taken one of my Seconals. Otherwise I'd have heard it surely. 'Auntie,' my niece always says — 'what if there should be a fire, and you there sleeping away?' Do what she says, I do sometimes, only to hear every pin drop till morning." She shook her head, entering the elevator. "Going up?"

"N-no," said Mrs. Hazlitt. "I — have to wait here for a minute." She sat down on the bench, the token bench that she had never seen anybody sitting on, and watched the car door close on the little figure still shaking its head, borne upward like a fairy godmother, willing but unable to oblige. The car's hum stopped, then its light glowed on again. Someone else was coming down. No, this is the nadir, Mrs. Hazlitt thought. Whether I heard it or not, I'm obviously no longer myself. Sleeping pills for me too, though I've never — and no more nonsense. And no more questioning, no matter who.

The car door opened. "Wssht!" said Mrs. Finan, scuttling out again. "I've just remembered. Not last night, but two weeks ago. And once before that. A scream, you said?"

Mrs. Hazlitt stood up. Almost unable to speak, for the tears that suddenly wrenched her throat, she described it.

"That's it, just what I told my niece on the phone next morning. Like nothing human, and yet it was. I'd taken my Seconal too early, so there I was wide awake again, lying there just thinking, when it came. 'Auntie,' she tried to tell me, 'it was just one of the sireens. Or hoodlums maybe.'" Miss Finan reached up very slowly and settled her hat. "The city's gone down, you know. Not what it was," she said in a reduced voice, casting a glance over her shoulder, as if whatever the city now was loomed behind her. "But I've laid awake on this street too many years, I said, not to know what I hear." She leaned forward. "But — she ... they think I'm getting old, you know," she said, in the whisper used to confide the unimaginable. "So ... well ... when I heard it again I just didn't tell her."

Mrs. Hazlitt grubbed for her handkerchief, found it and blew her nose. Breaking down, she thought — I never knew what a literal phrase it is. For she felt as if all the muscles that usually held her up, knee to ankle, had slipped their knots and were melting her, unless she could stop them, to the floor. "I'm not normally such a nervous woman," she managed to say. "But it was just that no one else seemed to — why, there were people with lights on, but they just seemed to ignore."

The old lady nodded absently. "Well, thank God my hearing's as good as ever. Hmm. Wait till I tell Jennie that!" She began making her painful way back to the car.

Mrs. Hazlitt put out a hand to delay her. "In case it — I mean, in case somebody ought to be notified — do you have any idea what it was?"

"Oh, I don't know. And what could we — ?" Miss Finan shrugged, eager to get along. Still, gossip was tempting. "I did think — " She paused, lowering her voice uneasily. "Like somebody in a fit, it was. We'd a sexton at church taken that way with epilepsy once. And it stopped short like that, just as if somebody'd clapped a hand over its mouth, poor devil. Then the next time I thought — no, more like a signal, like somebody calling. You know the things you'll think at night." She turned, clearly eager to get away.

"But, oughtn't we to inquire?" Mrs. Hazlitt thought of the taxis. "In case it came from this building?"

"This build — " For a moment Miss Finan looked scared, her chin trembling, eyes rounded in the misty, affronted stare that the old gave, not to physical danger, but to a new idea swum too late into their ken. Then she drew herself up, all five feet of her bowed backbone. "Not from here it wouldn't. Across from that big place, maybe. Lots of riffraff there, not used to their money. Or from Third Avenue, maybe. There's always been tenements there." She looked at Mrs. Hazlitt with an obtuse patronage that reminded her of an old nurse who had first instructed her on the social order, blandly mixing up all first causes — disease, money, poverty, snobbery — with a firm illogic that had still seemed somehow in possession — far more firmly so than her own good-hearted parents — of the crude facts. "New to the city, are you," she said, more kindly. "It takes a while."

This time they rode up together. "Now you remember," Miss Finan said, on leaving.

"You've two locks on your door, one downstairs. Get a telephone put in by your bed. Snug as a bug in a rug you are then. Nothing to get at you but what's there already. That's what I always tell myself when I'm wakeful. Nothing to get at you then but the Old Nick."[4]

The door closed on her. Watching her go, Mrs. Hazlitt envied her the simplicity, even the spinsterhood that had barred her from imagination as it had from experience. Even the narrowing-in of age would have its compensations, tenderly constricting the horizon as it cramped the fingers, adding the best of locks to Miss Finan's snugness, on her way by now to the triumphant phone call to Jennie.

But that was sinful, to wish for that too soon, what's more it was sentimental, in just the way she had vowed to avoid. Mrs. Hazlitt pushed the button for Down. Emerging from the building, she looked back at it from the corner, back at her day of contrived exits and entrances, abortive conversations. People were hurrying in and out now at a great rate. An invisible glass separated her from them; she was no longer in the fold.

Later that night, Mrs. Hazlitt, once more preparing for bed, peered down at the streets through the slats of the Venetian blind. Catching herself in the attitude of peering made her uneasy. Darkening the room behind her, she raised the blind. After dinner in one of the good French restaurants on Third Avenue and a Tati movie afterwards — the French were such competent dispensers of gaiety — she could review her day more as a convalescent does his delirium — "Did I really say — do — that?" And even here she was addressing a vis-à-vis,[5] so deeply was the habit ingrained. But she could see her self-imposed project now for what it was — only a hysterical seeking after conversation, the final breaking-point, like the old-fashioned "crisis" in pneumonia, of the long, low fever of loneliness unexpressed. Even the city, gazed at squarely, was really no anarchy, only a huge diffuseness that returned to the eye of the beholder, to the walker in its streets, even to the closed dream of its sleeper, his own mood, dark or light. Dozens of the solitary must be looking down at it with her, most of them with some *modus vivendi*,[6] many of them booking themselves into life with the same painful intentness, the way the middle-aged sometimes set themselves to learning the tango. And a queer booking you gave yourself today, she told herself, the words lilting with Miss Finan's Irish, this being the last exchange of speech she had had. Testing the words aloud, she found her way with accents, always such a delight to Sam, as good as ever. Well, she had heard a scream, had discovered someone else who had heard it. And now to forget it as promised; the day was done. Prowling the room a bit, she took up her robe, draped it over her shoulders, still more providently put it on. "Oh Millie," she said, tossing the dark mirror a look of scorn as she passed it "you're such a *sen*sible woman."

Wear out Mrs. Berry's carpet you will, Millie, she thought, twenty minutes later by the bedroom clock, but the accent, adulterated now by Sam's, had escaped her. Had the scream had an accent? The trouble was that the mind had its own discipline; one could remember, even with a smile, the story of the man promised all the gold in the world if he could but go for two minutes thinking of the word "hippopotamus." She stopped in front of the mirror, seeking her smile, but it too had escaped. "Hippopotamus," she said, to her dark image. The knuckles of one hand rose, somnambulist, as she watched, and pressed against her teeth. She forced the hand, hers, down again. I will say it again, aloud, she thought, and while I am saying it I will be sure to say to myself that I am saying it aloud. She did so. "Hippopotamus."

---

[4] The devil.

[5] A person opposite or facing.

[6] "Way of living"; a means of bypassing difficulties.

For a long moment she remained there, staring into the mirror. Then she turned and snapped on every light in the room.

Across from her, in another mirror, the full-length one, herself regarded her. She went forward to it, to that image so irritatingly familiar, so constant as life changed it, so necessarily dear. Fair hair, if maintained too late in life, too brightly, always made the most sensible of women look foolish. There was hers, allowed to gray gently, disordered no more than was natural in the boudoir, framing a face still rational, if strained. "Dear me," she said to it. "All you need is somebody to talk to, get it out of your system. Somebody like yourself." As if prodded, she turned and surveyed the room.

Even in the glare of the lights, the naked black projected from the window, the room sent out to her, in half a dozen pleasant little touches, the same sense of its compatible owner that she had had from the beginning. There, flung down, was Mrs. Berry's copy of *The Eustace Diamonds,*[7] a book that she had always meant to read and had been delighted to find here, along with many others of its ilk and still others she herself owned. How many people knew good bisque and how cheaply it might still be collected, or could let it hobnob so amiably with grandmotherly bits of Tiffanyware,[8] even with the chipped Quimper ashtrays that Mrs. Berry, like Mrs. Hazlitt at the time of her own marriage, must once have thought the cutest in the world. There were the white walls, with the silly, strawberry-mouthed Marie Laurencin just above the Beerbohm,[9] the presence of good faded colors, the absence of the new or fauve. On the night table were the scissors, placed, like everything in the house, where Mrs. Hazlitt would have had them, near them a relic that winked of her own childhood — and kept on, she would wager, for the same reason — a magnifying glass exactly like her father's. Above them, the only floor lamp in the house, least offensive of its kind, towered above all the table ones, sign of a struggle between practicality and grace that she knew well, whose end she could applaud. Everywhere indeed there were the same signs of the struggles toward taste, the decline of taste into the prejudices of comfort, that went with a whole milieu and a generation — both hers. And over there was, even more personally, the second bed.

Mrs. Hazlitt sat down on it. If it were moved, into the study say, a few things out of storage with it, how sympathetically this flat might be shared. Nonsense, sheer fantasy to go on like this, to fancy herself embarking on the pitiable twin-life of leftover women, much less with a stranger. But was a woman a stranger if you happened to know that on her twelfth birthday she had received a copy of *Dr. Dolittle*, inscribed to Helena Nelson from her loving father, if you knew the secret, packrat place in the linen closet where she stuffed the neglected mending, of another, in a kitchen drawer, full of broken Mexican terrines and clipped recipes as shamefully grimy as your own cherished ones, if you knew that on 2/11/58 and on 7/25/57 a Dr. Burke had prescribed what looked to be sulfa pills, never used, that must have cured her at the point of purchase, as had embarrassingly happened time and again to yourself? If, in short, you knew almost every endearing thing about her, except her face?

Mrs. Hazlitt, blinking in the excessive light, looked sideways. She knew where there was a photograph album, tumbled once by accident from its shunted place in the bookshelf, and at once honorably replaced. She had seen enough to know that the snapshots, not pasted in separately, would have to be exhumed, one by one, from their packets. No, she told herself, she already knew more than enough of Mrs. Berry from all that had been so trustfully exposed

---

[7] A novel by Anthony Trollope (1815–1882).

[8] Decorative objects made with stained or iridescent glass.

[9] Marie Laurencin (1885–1956), French painter; Max Beerbohm (1872–1956), English caricaturist and critic.

here — enough to know that this was the sort of prying to which Mrs. Berry, like herself, would never stoop. Somehow this clinched it — their understanding. She could see them exchanging notes at some future meeting, Mrs. Berry saying, "Why, do you know — one night, when I was in London — " — herself, the vis-à-vis, nodding, their perfect rapprochement. Then what would be wrong in using, when so handily provided, so graciously awaiting her, such a comforting vis-à-vis, now?

Mrs. Hazlitt found herself standing, the room's glare pressing on her as if she were arraigned in a police line-up, as if, she reminded herself irritably, it were not self-imposed. She forced herself to make a circuit of the room, turning out each lamp with the crisp, no-nonsense flick of the wrist that nurses employed. At the one lamp still burning she hesitated, reluctant to cross over that last shadow-line. Then, with a shrug, she turned it out and sat down in the darkness, in one of the two opposing boudoir chairs. For long minutes she sat there. Once or twice she trembled on the verge of speech, covered it with a swallow. The conventions that guarded the mind in its strict relationship with the tongue were the hardest to flaunt. But this was the century of talk, of the long talk, in which all were healthily urged to confide. Even the children were encouraged toward, praised for, the imaginary companion. Why should the grown person, who for circumstance beyond his control had no other, be denied? As she watched the window, the light in the small gray house was extinguished. Some minutes later the doorman across the way disappeared. Without looking at the luminous dial of the clock, she could feel the silence aging, ripening. At last she bent forward to the opposite chair.

"Helena?" she said.

Her voice, clear-cut, surprised her. There was nothing so strange about it. The walls remained walls. No one could hear her, or cared to, and now, tucking her feet up, she could remember how cozy this could be, with someone opposite. "Helena," she said. "Wait till I tell you what happened while you were away."

She told her everything. At first she stumbled, went back, as if she were rehearsing in front of a mirror. Several times she froze, unsure whether a sentence had been spoken aloud entirely, or had begun, or terminated, unspoken, in the mind. But as she went on, this wavering borderline seemed only to resemble the clued conversation, meshed with silences, between two people who knew each other well. By the time she had finished her account she was almost at ease, settling back into the comfortably shared midnight post-mortem that always restored balance to the world — so nearly could she imagine the face, not unlike her own, in the chair opposite, smiling ruefully at her over the boy and his gingerbread fears, wondering mischievously with her as to in which of the shapes of temptation the Old Nick visited Miss Finan.

"That girl and her *log!*" said Mrs. Hazlitt. "You know how, when they're that young, you want to smash in the smugness. And yet, when you think of all they've got to go through, you feel so maternal. Even if — " Even if, came the nod, imperceptibly — you've never had children, like us.

For a while they were silent. "Warwick!" said Mrs. Hazlitt then. "Years ago there was an actor — Robert Warwick. I was in love with him — at about the age of eight." Then she smiled, bridling slightly, at the dark chair opposite, whose occupant would know her age. "Oh, all right then — twelve. But what is it, do you suppose, always makes old actors look seedy, even when they're not? Daylight maybe. Or all the pretenses." She ruminated. "Why ... do you know," she said slowly, "I think I've got it. The way he looked in my face when I was speaking, and the way the dog turned back and he didn't. He was lip-reading. Why, the poor old boy is deaf!" She settled back, dropping her slippers one by one to the floor. "Of course, that's it.

And he wouldn't want to admit that he couldn't have heard it. Probably doesn't dare wear an aid. Poor old boy, pretty dreary for him if he is an actor, and I'll bet he is." She sighed, a luxury permitted now. "Ah, well. Frail reed — Miss Finan. Lucky for me, though, that I stumbled on her." And on you.

A police siren sounded, muffled less and less by distance, approaching. She was at the window in time to see the car's red dome light streak by as it always did, its alarum dying behind it. Nothing else was on the road "And there were the taxis," she said, looking down. "I don't know why I keep forgetting them. Veering to the side like that, one right after the other, and one had his light out, so it wasn't for a fare. Nothing on the curb either. Then they both shot away, almost as if they'd caught sight of something up here. And wanted no part of it — the way people do in this town. Wish you could've seen them — it was eerie." There was no response from behind her.

She sat down again. Yes, there was a response, for the first time faintly contrary.

"No," she said. "It certainly was *not* the siren. I was up in a flash. I'd have seen it." She found herself clenching the arms of the chair. "Besides," she said, in a quieter voice, "don't you remember? I heard it twice."

There was no answer. Glancing sideways, she saw the string of lights opposite, not quite of last night's pattern. But the silence was the same, opened to its perfect hour like a century plant, multiple-rooted, that came of age every night. The silence was in full bloom, and it had its own sound. Hark hark, no dogs do bark. And there is nobody in the chair.

Never was, never had been. It was sad to be up at this hour and sane. For now is the hour, now is the hour when all good men are asleep. Her hand smoothed the rim of the wastebasket, about the height from the floor of a dog's collar. Get one tomorrow. But how to manage until then, with all this silence speaking?

She made herself stretch out on the bed, close her eyes. "Sam," she said at last, as she had sworn never to do in thought or word, "I'm lonely." Listening vainly, she thought how wise her resolve had been. Too late, now she had tested his loss to the full, knew him for the void he was — far more of a one than Mrs. Berry, who, though unknown, was still somewhere. By using the name of love, when she had been ready to settle for anybody, she had sent him into the void forever. Opening her eyes, adjusted now to the sourceless city light that never ceased trickling on ceiling, lancing from mirrors, she turned her head right to left, left to right on the pillow, in a gesture to the one auditor who remained.

"No," she said, in the dry voice of correction. "I'm not lonely. I'm alone."

Almost at once she raised herself on her elbow, her head cocked. No, she had heard nothing from outside. But in her mind's ear she could hear the sound of the word she had just spoken, its final syllable twanging like a tuning fork, infinitely receding to octaves above itself, infinitely returning. In what seemed scarcely a stride, she was in the next room, at the French window, brought there by that thin, directional vibration which not necessarily even the blind would hear. For she had recognized it. She had identified the accent of the scream.

The long window frame, its swollen wood shoved tight by her the night before, at first would not budge; then, as she put both hands on the hasp and braced her knees, it gave slowly, grinding inward, the heavy man-high bolt thumping down. Both sounds, too, fell into their proper places. That's what I heard before, she thought, the noise of a window opening or closing, exactly like mine. Two lines of them, down the six floors of the building, made twelve possibles. But that was of no importance now. Stepping up on the lintel, she spread the casements wide.

Yes, there was the bridge, one small arc of it, sheering off into the mist, beautiful against the night, as all bridges were. Now that she was outside, past all barriers, she could hear, with her ordinary ear, faint nickings that marred the silence, but these were only the surface scratches on a record that still revolved one low, continuous tone. No dogs do bark. That was the key to it, that her own hand, smoothing a remembered dog-collar, had been trying to give her. There were certain dog-whistles, to be bought anywhere — one had hung, with the unused leash, on a hook near a door in the country — which blew a summons so high above the human range that only a dog could hear it. What had summoned her last night would have been that much higher, audible only to those tuned in by necessity — the thin, soaring decibel of those who were no longer in the fold. Alone-oh. Alone-oh. That would have been the shape of it, of silence expelled from the mouth in one long relieving note, cool, irrepressible, the second one clapped short by the hand. No dog would have heard it. No animal but one was ever that alone.

She stepped out onto the fire escape. There must be legions of them, of us, she thought, in the dim alleyways, the high, flashing terraces — each one of them come to the end of his bookings, circling his small platform in space. And who would hear such a person? Not the log-girls, not for years and years. None of any age who, body to body, bed to bed, either in love or in the mutual pluck-pluck of hate — like the little girl and her mother — were still nested down. Reginald Warwick, stoppered in his special quiet, might hear it, turn to his Coco for confirmation which did not come, and persuade himself once again that it was only his affliction. Others lying awake snug as a bug, listening for that Old Nick, death, would hear the thin, sororal signal and not know what they had heard. But an endless assemblage of others all over the city would be waiting for it — all those sitting in the dark void of the one lamp quenched, the one syllable spoken — who would start up, some from sleep, to their windows … or were already there.

A car passed below. Instinctively, she flattened against the casement, but the car traveled on. Last night someone, man or woman, would have been standing in one of the line of niches above and beneath hers — perhaps even a woman in a blue robe like her own. But literal distance or person would not matter; in that audience all would be the same. Looking up, she could see the tired, heated lavender of the midtown sky, behind which lay that real imperial into which some men were already hurling their exquisitely signaling spheres. But this sound would come from breast to breast, at an altitude higher than any of those. She brought her fist to her mouth, in savage pride at having heard it, at belonging to a race some of whom could never adapt to any range less than that. *Some of us*, she thought, *are still responsible.*

Stepping forward, she leaned on the iron railing. At that moment, another car, traveling slowly by, hesitated opposite, its red dome light blinking. Mrs. Hazlitt stood very still. She watched until the police car went on again, inching ahead slowly, as if somebody inside were looking back. The two men inside there would never understand what she was waiting for. Hand clapped to her mouth, she herself had just understood. She was waiting for it — for its company. She was waiting for a second chance — to answer it. She was waiting for the scream to come again.

QUESTIONS

1. In one sense, Mrs. Hazlitt's attempt to discover the source of the scream resembles a detective story. Compare Calisher's story to a more traditional detective story such as Poe's "The Purloined Letter."

2. How has living in the country affected Mrs. Hazlitt? What conflicting values does the city promote? How well does she readapt to life in the city on her return?

3. How well does Mrs. Hazlitt cope with her widowhood? What does she do to fight off feelings of loneliness? Is she successful?

4. Why is Mrs. Hazlitt drawn to the scream? What changes occur in her perceptions of the scream in the course of the story? What does the scream finally come to represent for her?

5. Discuss how Calisher's story fulfills her definition of a short story as "an apocalypse, served in a very small cup."

BARRY CALLAGHAN

The Black Queen

Hughes and McCrae were fastidious men who took pride in their old colonial house, the clean simple lines and stucco walls and the painted pale blue picket fence. They were surrounded by houses converted into small warehouses, trucking yards where houses had been torn down, and along the street, a school filled with foreign children, but they didn't mind. It gave them an embattled sense of holding to something important, a tattered remnant of good taste in an area of waste overrun by rootless olive-skinned children.

McCrae wore his hair a little too long now that he was going grey, and while Hughes with his clipped moustache seemed to be a serious man intent only on his work, which was costume design, McCrae wore Cuban heels[1] and lacquered his nails. When they'd met ten years ago Hughes had said, "You keep walking around like that and you'll need a body to keep you from getting poked in the eye." McCrae did all the cooking and drove the car.

But they were not getting along these days. Hughes blamed his bursitis but they were both silently unsettled by how old they had suddenly become, how loose in the thighs, and their feet, when they were showering in the morning, seemed bonier, the toes longer, the nails yellow and hard, and what they wanted was tenderness, to be able to yield almost tearfully, full of a pity for themselves that would not be belittled or laughed at, and when they stood alone in their separate bedrooms they wanted that tenderness from each other, but when they were having their bedtime tea in the kitchen, as they had done for years using lovely green and white Limoges[2] cups, if one touched the other's hand then suddenly they both withdrew into an unspoken, smiling aloofness, as if some line of privacy had been crossed. Neither could bear their thinning wrists and the little pouches of darkening flesh under the chin. They spoke of being with younger people and even joked slyly about bringing a young man home, but that seemed such a betrayal of everything that they had believed had set them apart from others, everything they believed had kept them together, that they sulked and nettled away at each other, and though nothing had apparently changed in their lives, they were always on edge, Hughes more than McCrae.

One of their pleasures was collecting stamps, rare and mint-perfect, with no creases or smudges on the gum. Their collection, carefully mounted in a leatherbound blue book with

---

[1] Tapered, raised heels.

[2] A variety of fine porcelain made in France.

seven little plastic windows per page, was worth several thousand dollars. They had passed many pleasant evenings together on the Directoire[3] settee arranging the old ochre and carmine colored stamps. They agreed there was something almost sensual about holding a perfectly preserved piece of the past, unsullied, as if everything didn't have to change, didn't have to end up swamped by decline and decay. They disapproved of the new stamps and dismissed them as crude and wouldn't have them in their book. The pages for the recent years remained empty and they liked that; the emptiness was their statement about themselves and their values, and Hughes, holding a stamp up into the light between his tweezers, would say, "None of that rough trade for us."

One afternoon they went down to the philatelic shops around Adelaide and Richmond Streets and saw a stamp they had been after for a long time, a large and elegant black stamp of Queen Victoria in her widow's weeds. It was rare and expensive, a dead-letter stamp from the turn of the century. They stood side-by-side over the glass counter-case admiring it, their hands spread on the glass, but when McCrae, the overhead fluorescent light catching his lacquered nails, said, "Well, I certainly would like that little black sweetheart," the owner, who had sold stamps to them for several years, looked up and smirked, and Hughes suddenly snorted, "You old queen, I mean why don't you just quit wearing those goddamn Cuban heels, eh? I mean why not?" He walked out leaving McCrae embarrassed and hurt and when the owner said, "So what was wrong?" McCrae cried, "Screw you," and strutted out.

Through the rest of the week they were deferential around the house, offering each other every consideration, trying to avoid any squabble before Mother's Day at the end of the week when they were going to hold their annual supper for friends, three other male couples. Over the years it had always been an elegant, slightly mocking evening that often ended bitter-sweetly and left them feeling close, comforting each other.

McCrae, wearing a white, linen shirt, starch in the cuffs and mother-of-pearl cuff-links, worked all Sunday afternoon in the kitchen, and through the window he could see the crab-apple tree in bloom and he thought how in previous years he would have begun planning to put down some jelly in the old pressed glass jars they kept in the cellar, but instead, head down, he went on stuffing and tying the pork loin roast. Then in the early evening he heard Hughes at the door, and there was laughter from the front room and someone cried out, "What do you do with an elephant who has three balls on him ... you don't know silly, well you walk him and pitch to the giraffe," and there were howls of laughter and the clinking of glasses. It had been the same every year, eight men sitting down to a fine supper with expensive wines, the table set with their best silver under the antique carved wooden candelabra.

Having prepared all the raw vegetables, the cauliflower and carrots, the avocados and finger-sized miniature corns-on-the-cob, and placed porcelain bowls of homemade dip in the center of a pewter tray, McCrae stared at his reflection for a moment in the window over the kitchen sink and then he took a plastic slipcase out of the knives-and-forks drawer. The case contained the dead-letter stamp. He licked it all over and pasted it on his forehead and then slipped on the jacket of his charcoal brown crushed velvet suit, took hold of the tray, and stepped out into the front room.

The other men, sitting in a circle around the coffee table, looked up and one of them giggled. Hughes cried, "Oh my God." McCrae, as if nothing were the matter, said, "My dears, time for the crudités." He was in his silk stocking feet, and as he passed the tray he winked at Hughes who sat staring at the black queen, realizing it was ruined.

---

[3] A style characteristic of the Directory Period in France, late 1790s.

QUESTIONS

1. Are Hughes and McCrae well-rounded, individualized characters? What distinguishes them from each other? What common values do they hold?

2. What are the symbolic implications of the black queen? How symbolic is it to Hughes and McCrae? Why does McCrae's simple remark about the stamp provoke such an angry response from Hughes?

3. Explain McCrae's actions at the end of the story. What message is he trying to send to Hughes?

RAYMOND CARVER

Cathedral

This blind man, an old friend of my wife's, he was on his way to spend the night. His wife had died. So he was visiting the dead wife's relatives in Connecticut. He called my wife from his in-laws'. Arrangements were made. He would come by train, a five-hour trip, and my wife would meet him at the station. She hadn't seen him since she worked for him one summer in Seattle ten years ago. But she and the blind man had kept in touch. They made tapes and mailed them back and forth. I wasn't enthusiastic about his visit. He was no one I knew. And his being blind bothered me. My idea of blindness came from the movies. In the movies, the blind moved slowly and never laughed. Sometimes they were led by seeing-eye dogs. A blind man in my house was not something I looked forward to.

That summer in Seattle she had needed a job. She didn't have any money. The man she was going to marry at the end of the summer was in officers' training school. He didn't have any money, either. But she was in love with the guy, and he was in love with her, etc. She'd seen something in the paper: HELP WANTED — *Reading to Blind Man*, and a telephone number. She phoned and went over, was hired on the spot. She'd worked with this blind man all summer. She read stuff to him, case studies, reports, that sort of thing. She helped him organize his little office in the county social-service department. They'd become good friends, my wife and the blind man. How do I know these things? She told me. And she told me something else. On her last day in the office, the blind man asked if he could touch her face. She agreed to this. She told me he touched his fingers to every part of her face, her nose — even her neck! She never forgot it. She even tried to write a poem about it. She was always trying to write a poem. She wrote a poem or two every year, usually after something really important had happened to her.

When we first started going out together, she showed me the poem. In the poem, she recalled his fingers and the way they had moved around over her face. In the poem, she talked about what she had felt at the time, about what went through her mind when the blind man touched her nose and lips. I can remember I didn't think much of the poem. Of course, I didn't tell her that. Maybe I just don't understand poetry. I admit it's not the first thing I reach for when I pick up something to read.

Anyway, this man who'd first enjoyed her favors, the officer-to-be, he'd been her childhood sweetheart. So okay. I'm saying that at the end of the summer she let the blind man run his hands over her face, said goodbye to him, married her childhood etc., who was now a commissioned officer, and she moved away from Seattle. But they'd kept in touch, she and the blind man. She made the first contact after a year or so. She called him up one night from an Air Force base in Alabama. She wanted to talk. They talked. He asked her to send him a tape and tell him about her life. She did this. She sent the tape. On the tape, she told the blind man about her husband and about their life together in the military. She told the blind man she loved her husband but she didn't like it where they lived and she didn't like it that he was a part of the military-industrial thing. She told the blind man she'd written a poem and he was in it. She told him that she was writing a poem about what it was like to be an Air Force officer's wife. The poem wasn't finished yet. She was still writing it. The blind man made a tape. He sent her the tape. She made a tape. This went on for years. My wife's officer was posted to one base and then another. She sent tapes from Moody AFB, McGuire, McConnell, and finally Travis, near Sacramento, where one night she got to feeling lonely and cut off from people she kept losing in that moving-around life. She got to feeling she couldn't go it another step. She went in and swallowed all the pills and capsules in the medicine chest and washed them down with a bottle of gin. Then she got into a hot bath and passed out.

But instead of dying, she got sick. She threw up. Her officer — why should he have a name? he was the childhood sweetheart, and what more does he want? — came home from somewhere, found her, and called the ambulance. In time, she put it all on a tape and sent the tape to the blind man. Over the years, she put all kinds of stuff on tapes and sent the tapes off lickety-split. Next to writing a poem every year, I think it was her chief means of recreation. On one tape, she told the blind man she'd decided to live away from her officer for a time. On another tape, she told him about her divorce. She and I began going out, and of course she told her blind man about it. She told him everything, or so it seemed to me. Once she asked me if I'd like to hear the latest tape from the blind man. This was a year ago. I was on the tape, she said. So I said okay, I'd listen to it. I got us drinks and we settled down in the living room. We made ready to listen. First she inserted the tape into the player and adjusted a couple of dials. Then she pushed a lever. The tape squeaked and someone began to talk in this loud voice. She lowered the volume. After a few minutes of harmless chitchat, I heard my own name in the mouth of this stranger, this blind man I didn't even know! And then this: "From all you've said about him, I can only conclude — " But we were interrupted, a knock at the door, something, and we didn't ever get back to the tape. Maybe it was just as well. I'd heard all I wanted to.

Now this same blind man was coming to sleep in my house.

"Maybe I could take him bowling," I said to my wife. She was at the draining board doing scalloped potatoes. She put down the knife she was using and turned around.

"If you love me," she said, "you can do this for me. If you don't love me, okay. But if you had a friend, any friend, and the friend came to visit, I'd make him feel comfortable." She wiped her hands with the dish towel.

"I don't have any blind friends," I said.

"You don't have *any* friends," she said. "Period. Besides," she said, "goddamn it, his wife's just died! Don't you understand that? The man's lost his wife!"

I didn't answer. She'd told me a little about the blind man's wife. Her name was Beulah. Beulah! That's a name for a colored woman.

"Was his wife a Negro?" I asked.

"Are you crazy?" my wife said. "Have you just flipped or something?" She picked up a potato. I saw it hit the floor, then roll under the stove. "What's wrong with you?" she said. "Are you drunk?"

"I'm just asking," I said.

Right then my wife filled me in with more detail than I cared to know. I made a drink and sat at the kitchen table to listen. Pieces of the story began to fall into place.

Beulah had gone to work for the blind man the summer after my wife had stopped working for him. Pretty soon Beulah and the blind man had themselves a church wedding. It was a little wedding — who'd want to go to such a wedding in the first place? — just the two of them, plus the minister and the minister's wife. But it was a church wedding just the same. It was what Beulah had wanted, he'd said. But even then Beulah must have been carrying the cancer in her glands. After they had been inseparable for eight years — my wife's word, *inseparable* — Beulah's health went into a rapid decline. She died in a Seattle hospital room, the blind man sitting beside the bed and holding on to her hand. They'd married, lived and worked together, slept together — had sex, sure — and then the blind man had to bury her. All this without his having ever seen what the goddamned woman looked like. It was beyond my understanding. Hearing this, I felt sorry for the blind man for a little bit. And then I found myself thinking what a pitiful life this woman must have led. Imagine a woman who could never see herself as she was seen in the eyes of her loved one. A woman who could go on day after day and never receive the smallest compliment from her beloved. A woman whose husband could never read the expression on her face, be it misery or something better. Someone who could wear makeup or not — what difference to him? She could, if she wanted, wear green eye-shadow around one eye, a straight pin in her nostril, yellow slacks and purple shoes, no matter. And then to slip off into death, the blind man's hand on her hand, his blind eyes streaming tears — I'm imagining now — her last thought maybe this: that he never even knew what she looked like, and she on an express to the grave. Robert was left with a small insurance policy and half of a twenty-peso Mexican coin. The other half of the coin went into the box with her. Pathetic.

So when the time rolled around, my wife went to the depot to pick him up. With nothing to do but wait —► sure, I blamed him for that — I was having a drink and watching the TV when I heard the car pull into the drive. I got up from the sofa with my drink and went to the window to have a look.

I saw my wife laughing as she parked the car. I saw her get out of the car and shut the door. She was still wearing a smile. Just amazing. She went around to the other side of the car to where the blind man was already starting to get out. This blind man, feature this, he was wearing a full beard! A beard on a blind man! Too much, I say. The blind man reached into the back seat and dragged out a suitcase. My wife took his arm, shut the car door, and, talking all the way, moved him down the drive and then up the steps to the front porch. I turned off the TV. I finished my drink, rinsed the glass, dried my hands. Then I went to the door.

My wife said, "I want you to meet Robert. Robert, this is my husband. I've told you all about him." She was beaming. She had this blind man by his coat sleeve.

The blind man let go of his suitcase and up came his hand.

I took it. He squeezed hard, held my hand, and then he let it go.

"I feel like we've already met," he boomed.

"Likewise," I said. I didn't know what else to say. Then I said, "Welcome. I've heard a lot about you." We began to move then, a little group, from the porch into the living room, my wife guiding him by the arm. The blind man was carrying his suitcase in his other hand. My wife said things like, "To your left here, Robert. That's right. Now watch it, there's a chair. That's it. Sit down right here. This is the sofa. We just bought this sofa two weeks ago."

I started to say something about the old sofa. I'd liked that old sofa. But I didn't say anything. Then I wanted to say something else, small-talk, about the scenic ride along the Hudson. How going *to* New York, you should sit on the right-hand side of the train, and coming *from* New York, the left-hand side.

"Did you have a good train ride?" I said. "Which side of the train did you sit on, by the way?"

"What a question, which side!" my wife said. "What's it matter which side?" she said.

"I just asked," I said.

"Right side," the blind man said. "I hadn't been on a train in nearly forty years. Not since I was a kid. With my folks. That's been a long time. I'd nearly forgotten the sensation. I have winter in my beard now," he said. "So I've been told, anyway. Do I look distinguished, my dear?" the blind man said to my wife.

"You look distinguished, Robert," she said. "Robert," she said. "Robert, it's just so good to see you."

My wife finally took her eyes off the blind man and looked at me. I had the feeling she didn't like what she saw. I shrugged.

I've never met, or personally known, anyone who was blind. This blind man was late forties, a heavy-set, balding man with stooped shoulders, as if he carried a great weight there. He wore brown slacks, brown shoes, a light-brown shirt, a tie, a sports coat. Spiffy. He also had this full beard. But he didn't use a cane and he didn't wear dark glasses. I'd always thought dark glasses were a must for the blind. Fact was, I wished he had a pair. At first glance, his eyes looked like anyone else's eyes. But if you looked close, there was something different about them. Too much white in the iris, for one thing, and the pupils seemed to move around in the sockets without his knowing it or being able to stop it. Creepy. As I stared at his face, I saw the left pupil turn in toward his nose while the other made an effort to keep in one place. But it was only an effort, for that eye was on the roam without his knowing it or wanting it to be.

I said, "Let me get you a drink. What's your pleasure? We have a little of everything. It's one of our pastimes."

"Bub, I'm a Scotch man myself," he said fast enough in this big voice.

"Right," I said. Bub! "Sure you are. I knew it."

He let his fingers touch his suitcase, which was sitting alongside the sofa. He was taking his bearings. I didn't blame him for that.

"I'll move that up to your room," my wife said.

"No, that's fine," the blind man said loudly. "It can go up when I go up."

"A little water with the Scotch?" I said.

"Very little," he said.

"I knew it," I said.

He said, "Just a tad. The Irish actor, Barry Fitzgerald? I'm like that fellow. When I drink water, Fitzgerald said, I drink water. When I drink whiskey, I drink whiskey." My wife laughed. The blind man brought his hand up under his beard. He lifted his beard slowly and let it drop.

I did the drinks, three big glasses of Scotch with a splash of water in each. Then we made ourselves comfortable and talked about Robert's travels. First the long flight from the West Coast to Connecticut, we covered that. Then from Connecticut up here by train. We had another drink concerning that leg of the trip.

I remembered having read somewhere that the blind didn't smoke because, as speculation had it, they couldn't see the smoke they exhaled. I thought I knew that much and that much only about blind people. But this blind man smoked his cigarette down to the nubbin and then lit another one. This blind man filled his ashtray and my wife emptied it.

When we sat down at the table for dinner, we had another drink. My wife heaped Robert's plate with cube steak, scalloped potatoes, green beans. I buttered him up two slices of bread. I said, "Here's bread and butter for you." I swallowed some of my drink. "Now let us pray," I said, and the blind man lowered his head. My wife looked at me, her mouth agape. "Pray the phone won't ring and the food doesn't get cold," I said.

We dug in. We ate everything there was to eat on the table. We ate like there was no tomorrow. We didn't talk. We ate. We scarfed. We grazed that table. We were into serious eating. The blind man had right away located his foods, he knew just where everything was on his plate. I watched with admiration as he used his knife and fork on the meat. He'd cut two pieces of meat, fork the meat into his mouth, and then go all out for the scalloped potatoes, the beans next, and then he'd tear off a hunk of buttered bread and eat that. He'd follow this up with a big drink of milk. It didn't seem to bother him to use his fingers once in a while, either.

We finished everything, including half a strawberry pie. For a few moments, we sat as if stunned. Sweat beaded on our faces. Finally, we got up from the table and left the dirty plates. We didn't look back. We took ourselves into the living room and sank into our places again. Robert and my wife sat on the sofa. I took the big chair. We had us two or three more drinks while they talked about the major things that had come to pass for them in the past ten years. For the most part, I just listened. Now and then I joined in. I didn't want him to think I'd left the room, and I didn't want her to think I was feeling left out. They talked of things that had happened to them — to them! — these past ten years. I waited in vain to hear my name on my wife's sweet lips: "And then my dear husband came into my life" — something like that. But I heard nothing of the sort. More talk of Robert. Robert had done a little of everything, it seemed, a regular blind jack-of-all-trades. But most recently he and his wife had had an Amway distributorship, from which, I gathered, they'd earned their living, such as it was. The blind man was also a ham radio operator. He talked in his loud voice about conversations he'd had with fellow operators in Guam, in the Philippines, in Alaska, and even in Tahiti. He said he'd have a lot of friends there if he ever wanted to go visit those places. From time to time, he'd turn his blind face toward me, put his hand under his beard, ask me something. How long had I been in my present position? (Three years.) Did I like my work? (I didn't.) Was I going to stay with it? (What were the options?) Finally, when I thought he was beginning to run down, I got up and turned on the TV.

My wife looked at me with irritation. She was heading toward a boil. Then she looked at the blind man and said, "Robert, do you have a TV?"

The blind man said, "My dear, I have two TVs. I have a color set and a black-and-white thing, an old relic. It's funny, but if I turn the TV on, and I'm always turning it on, I turn on the color set. It's funny, don't you think?"

I didn't know what to say to that. I had absolutely nothing to say to that. No opinion. So I watched the news program and tried to listen to what the announcer was saying.

"This is a color TV," the blind man said. "Don't ask me how, but I can tell."

"We traded up a while ago," I said.

The blind man had another taste of his drink. He lifted his beard, sniffed it, and let it fall. He leaned forward on the sofa. He positioned his ashtray on the coffee table, then put the lighter to his cigarette. He leaned back on the sofa and crossed his legs at the ankles.

My wife covered her mouth, and then she yawned. She stretched. She said, "I think I'll go upstairs and put on my robe. I think I'll change into something else. Robert, you make yourself comfortable," she said.

"I'm comfortable," the blind man said.

"I want you to feel comfortable in this house," she said.

"I am comfortable," the blind man said.

After she'd left the room, he and I listened to the weather report and then to the sports roundup. By that time, she'd been gone so long I didn't know if she was going to come back. I thought she might have gone to bed. I wished she'd come back downstairs. I didn't want to be left alone with a blind man. I asked him if he wanted another drink, and he said sure. Then I asked if he wanted to smoke some dope with me. I said I'd just rolled a number. I hadn't, but I planned to do so in about two shakes.

"I'll try some with you," he said.

"Damn right," I said. "That's the stuff."

I got our drinks and sat down on the sofa with him. Then I rolled us two fat numbers. I lit one and passed it. I brought it to his fingers. He took it and inhaled.

"Hold it as long as you can," I said. I could tell he didn't know the first thing.

My wife came back downstairs wearing her pink robe and her pink slippers.

"What do I smell?" she said.

"We thought we'd have us some cannabis," I said.

My wife gave me a savage look. Then she looked at the blind man and said, "Robert, I didn't know you smoked."

He said, "I do now, my dear. There's a first time for everything. But I don't feel anything yet."

"This stuff is pretty mellow," I said. "This stuff is mild. It's dope you can reason with," I said. "It doesn't mess you up."

"Not much it doesn't, bub," he said, and laughed.

My wife sat on the sofa between the blind man and me. I passed her the number. She took it and toked and then passed it back to me. "Which way is this going?" she said. Then she said, "I shouldn't be smoking this. I can hardly keep my eyes open as it is. That dinner did me in. I shouldn't have eaten so much."

"It was the strawberry pie," the blind man said. "That's what did it," he said, and he laughed his big laugh. Then he shook his head.

"There's more strawberry pie," I said.

"Do you want some more, Robert?" my wife said.

"Maybe in a little while," he said.

We gave our attention to the TV. My wife yawned again. She said, "Your bed is made up when you feel like going to bed, Robert. I know you must have had a long day. When you're ready to go to bed, say so." She pulled his arm. "Robert?"

He came to and said, "I've had a real nice time. This beats tapes, doesn't it?"

I said, "Coming at you," and I put the number between his fingers. He inhaled, held the smoke, and then let it go. It was like he'd been doing it since he was nine years old.

"Thanks, bub," he said. "But I think this is all for me. I think I'm beginning to feel it," he said. He held the burning roach out for my wife.

"Same here," she said. "Ditto. Me, too." She took the roach and passed it to me. "I may just sit here for a while between you two guys with my eyes closed. But don't let me bother you, okay? Either one of you. If it bothers you, say so. Otherwise, I may just sit here with my eyes closed until you're ready to go to bed," she said. "Your bed's made up, Robert, when you're ready. It's right next to our room at the top of the stairs. We'll show you up when you're ready. You wake me up now, you guys, if I fall asleep." She said that and then she closed her eyes and went to sleep.

The news program ended. I got up and changed the channel. I sat back down on the sofa. I wished my wife hadn't pooped out. Her head lay across the back of the sofa, her mouth open. She'd turned so that her robe had slipped away from her legs, exposing a juicy thigh. I reached to draw her robe back over her, and it was then that I glanced at the blind man. What the hell! I flipped the robe open again.

"You say when you want some strawberry pie," I said.

"I will," he said.

I said, "Are you tired? Do you want me to take you up to your bed? Are you ready to hit the hay?"

"Not yet," he said. "No, I'll stay up with you, bub. If that's all right. I'll stay up until you're ready to turn in. We haven't had a chance to talk. Know what I mean? I feel like me and her monopolized the evening." He lifted his beard and he let it fall. He picked up his cigarettes and his lighter.

"That's all right," I said. Then I said, "I'm glad for the company."

And I guess I was. Every night I smoked dope and stayed up as long as I could before I fell asleep. My wife and I hardly ever went to bed at the same time. When I did go to sleep, I had these dreams. Sometimes I'd wake up from one of them, my heart going crazy.

Something about the church and the Middle Ages was on the TV. Not your run-of-the-mill TV fare. I wanted to watch something else. I turned to the other channels. But there was nothing on them, either. So I turned back to the first channel and apologized.

"Bub, it's all right," the blind man said. "It's fine with me. Whatever you want to watch is okay. I'm always learning something. Learning never ends. It won't hurt me to learn something tonight. I got ears," he said.

We didn't say anything for a time. He was leaning forward with his head turned at me, his right ear aimed in the direction of the set. Very disconcerting. Now and then his eyelids drooped and then they snapped open again. Now and then he put his fingers into his beard and tugged, like he was thinking about something he was hearing on the television.

On the screen, a group of men wearing cowls was being set upon and tormented by men dressed in skeleton costumes and men dressed as devils. The men dressed as devils wore devil masks, horns, and long tails. This pageant was part of a procession. The Englishman who was narrating the thing said it took place in Spain once a year. I tried to explain to the blind man what was happening.

"Skeletons," he said. "I know about skeletons," he said, and he nodded.

The TV showed this one cathedral. Then there was a long, slow look at another one. Finally, the picture switched to the famous one in Paris, with its flying buttresses and its spires reaching up to the clouds. The camera pulled away to show the whole of the cathedral rising above the skyline.

There were times when the Englishman who was telling the thing would shut up, would simply let the camera move around over the cathedrals. Or else the camera would tour the countryside, men in fields walking behind oxen. I waited as long as I could. Then I felt I had to say something. I said, "They're showing the outside of this cathedral now. Gargoyles. Little statues carved to look like monsters. Now I guess they're in Italy. Yeah, they're in Italy. There's paintings on the walls of this one church."

"Are those fresco paintings, bub?" he asked, and he sipped from his drink.

I reached for my glass. But it was empty. I tried to remember what I could remember. "You're asking me are those frescoes?" I said. "That's a good question. I don't know."

The camera moved to a cathedral outside Lisbon. The differences in the Portuguese cathedral compared with the French and Italian were not that great. But they were there. Mostly the interior stuff. Then something occurred to me, and I said, "Something has occurred to me. Do you have any idea what a cathedral is? What they look like, that is? Do you follow me? If somebody says cathedral to you, do you have any notion what they're talking about? Do you know the difference between that and a Baptist church, say?"

He let the smoke dribble from his mouth. "I know they took hundreds of workers fifty or a hundred years to build," he said. "I just heard the man say that, of course. I know generations of the same families worked on a cathedral. I heard him say that, too. The men who began their life's work on them, they never lived to see the completion of their work. In that wise, bub, they're no different from the rest of us, right?" He laughed. Then his eyelids drooped again. His head nodded. He seemed to be snoozing. Maybe he was imagining himself in Portugal. The TV was showing another cathedral now. This one was in Germany. The Englishman's voice droned on. "Cathedrals," the blind man said. He sat up and rolled his head back and forth. "If you want the truth, bub, that's about all I know. What I just said. What I heard him say. But maybe you could describe one to me? I wish you'd do it. I'd like that. If you want to know, I really don't have a good idea."

I stared hard at the shot of the cathedral on the TV. How could I even begin to describe it? But say my life depended on it. Say my life was being threatened by an insane guy who said I had to do it or else.

I stared some more at the cathedral before the picture flipped off into the countryside. There was no use. I turned to the blind man and said, "To begin with, they're very tall." I was looking around the room for clues. "They reach way up. Up and up. Toward the sky. They're so big, some of them, they have to have these supports. To help hold them up, so to speak. These supports are called buttresses. They remind me of viaducts, for some reason. But maybe you don't know viaducts, either? Sometimes the cathedrals have devils and such carved into the front. Sometimes lords and ladies. Don't ask me why this is," I said.

He was nodding. The whole upper part of his body seemed to be moving back and forth.

"I'm not doing so good, am I?" I said.

He stopped nodding and leaned forward on the edge of the sofa. As he listened to me, he was running his fingers through his beard. I wasn't getting through to him, I could see that. But he waited for me to go on just the same. He nodded, like he was trying to encourage me. I tried to think what else to say. "They're really big," I said. "They're massive. They're built of stone. Marble, too, sometimes. In those olden days, when they built cathedrals, men wanted to be close to God. In those olden days, God was an important part of everyone's life. You could tell this from their cathedral-building. I'm sorry," I said, "but it looks like that's the best I can do for you. I'm just no good at it."

"That's all right, bub," the blind man said. "Hey, listen. I hope you don't mind my asking you. Can I ask you something? Let me ask you a simple question, yes or no. I'm just curious and there's no offense. You're my host. But let me ask if you are in any way religious? You don't mind my asking?"

I shook my head. He couldn't see that, though. A wink is the same as a nod to a blind man. "I guess I don't believe in it. In anything. Sometimes it's hard. You know what I'm saying?"

"Sure, I do," he said.

"Right," I said.

The Englishman was still holding forth. My wife sighed in her sleep. She drew a long breath and went on with her sleeping.

"You'll have to forgive me," I said. "But I can't tell you what a cathedral looks like. It just isn't in me to do it. I can't do any more than I've done."

The blind man sat very still, his head down, as he listened to me.

I said, "The truth is, cathedrals don't mean anything special to me. Nothing. Cathedrals. They're something to look at on late-night TV. That's all they are."

It was then that the blind man cleared his throat. He brought something up. He took a handkerchief from his back pocket. Then he said, "I get it, bub. It's okay. It happens. Don't worry about it," he said. "Hey, listen to me. Will you do me a favor? I got an idea. Why don't you find us some heavy paper? And a pen. We'll do something. We'll draw one together. Get us a pen and some heavy paper. Go on, bub, get the stuff," he said.

So I went upstairs. My legs felt like they didn't have any strength in them. They felt like they did after I'd done some running. In my wife's room, I looked around. I found some ballpoints in a little basket on her table. And then I tried to think where to look for the kind of paper he was talking about.

Downstairs, in the kitchen, I found a shopping bag with onion skins in the bottom of the bag. I emptied the bag and shook it. I brought it into the living room and sat down with it near his legs. I moved some things, smoothed the wrinkles from the bag, spread it out on the coffee table.

The blind man got down from the sofa and sat next to me on the carpet.

He ran his fingers over the paper. He went up and down the sides of the paper. The edges, even the edges. He fingered the corners.

"All right," he said. "All right, let's do her."

He found my hand, the hand with the pen. He closed his hand over my hand. "Go ahead, bub, draw," he said. "Draw. You'll see. I'll follow along with you. It'll be okay. Just begin now like I'm telling you. You'll see. Draw," the blind man said.

So I began. First I drew a box that looked like a house. It could have been the house I lived in. Then I put a roof on it. At either end of the roof, I drew spires. Crazy.

"Swell," he said. "Terrific. You're doing fine," he said. "Never thought anything like this could happen in your lifetime, did you, bub? Well, it's a strange life, we all know that. Go on now. Keep it up."

I put in windows with arches. I drew flying buttresses. I hung great doors. I couldn't stop. The TV station went off the air. I put down the pen and closed and opened my fingers. The blind man felt around over the paper. He moved the tips of his fingers over the paper, all over what I had drawn, and he nodded.

"Doing fine," the blind man said.

I took up the pen again, and he found my hand. I kept at it. I'm no artist. But I kept drawing just the same.

My wife opened up her eyes and gazed at us. She sat up on the sofa, her robe hanging open. She said, "What are you doing? Tell me, I want to know."

I didn't answer her.

The blind man said, "We're drawing a cathedral. Me and him are working on it. Press hard," he said to me. "That's right. That's good," he said. "Sure. You got it, bub. I can tell. You didn't think you could. But you can, can't you? You're cooking with gas now. You know what I'm saying? We're going to really have us something here in a minute. How's the old arm?" he said. "Put some people in there now. What's a cathedral without people?"

My wife said, "What's going on? Robert, what are you doing? What's going on?"

"It's all right," he said to her. "Close your eyes now," the blind man said to me.

I did it. I closed them just like he said.

"Are they closed?" he said. "Don't fudge."

"They're closed," I said.

"Keep them that way," he said. He said, "Don't stop now. Draw."

So we kept on with it. His fingers rode my fingers as my hand went over the paper. It was like nothing else in my life up to now.

Then he said, "I think that's it. I think you got it," he said. "Take a look. What do you think?"

But I had my eyes closed. I thought I'd keep them that way for a little longer. I thought it was something I ought to do.

"Well?" he said. "Are you looking?"

My eyes were still closed. I was in my house. I knew that. But I didn't feel like I was inside anything.

"It's really something," I said.

QUESTIONS

1. How does the narrator initially attempt to shape our opinions about Robert? What does he reveal about himself in the process?

2. Why does the narrator feel threatened by the blind man? What defenses does he employ? Is his apprehension justified?

3. Why does Carver use a cathedral as the vehicle for the blind man's lesson? In what way is the blind leading the blind?

4. What change has the narrator undergone at the end of the story when he tells us " … I didn't feel like I was inside anything"?

JOHN GARDNER

Redemption

One day in April — a clear, blue day when there were crocuses in bloom — Jack Hawthorne ran over and killed his brother, David. Even at the last moment he could have prevented his brother's death by slamming on the tractor brakes, easily in reach for all the shortness of his legs; but he was unable to think, or, rather, thought unclearly, and so watched it happen, as he would again and again watch it happen in his mind, with nearly undiminished intensity and clarity, all his life. The younger brother was riding, as both of them knew he should not have been, on the cultipacker, a two-ton implement lumbering behind the tractor, crushing new-ploughed ground. Jack was twelve, his brother, David, seven. The scream came not from David, who never got a sound out, but from their five-year-old sister, who was riding on the fender of the tractor, looking back. When Jack turned to look, the huge iron wheels had reached his brother's pelvis. He kept driving, reacting as he would to a half-crushed farm animal, and imagining, in the same stab of thought, that perhaps his brother would survive. Blood poured from David's mouth.

Their father was nearly destroyed by it. Sometimes Jack would find him lying on the cow-barn floor, crying, unable to stand up. Dale Hawthorne, the father, was a sensitive, intelligent man, by nature a dreamer. It showed in old photographs, his smile coded, his eyes on the horizon. He loved all his children and would not consciously have been able to hate his son even if Jack had indeed been, as he thought himself, his brother's murderer. But he could not help sometimes seeming to blame his son, though consciously he blamed only his own unwisdom and — so far as his belief held firm — God. Dale Hawthorne's mind swung violently at this time, reversing itself almost hour by hour, from desperate faith to the most savage, black-hearted atheism. Every sickly calf, every sow that ate her litter, was a new, sure proof that the religion he'd followed all his life was a lie. Yet skeletons were orderly, as were, he thought, the stars. He was unable to decide, one moment full of rage at God's injustice, the next moment wracked by doubt of His existence.

Though he was not ordinarily a man who smoked, he would sometimes sit up all night now, or move restlessly, hurriedly, from room to room, chain-smoking Lucky Strikes. Or he would ride away on his huge, darkly thundering Harley-Davidson 80, trying to forget, morbidly dwelling on what he'd meant to put behind him — how David had once laughed, cake in his fists; how he'd once patched a chair with precocious skill — or Dale Hawthorne would think, for the hundredth time, about suicide, hunting in mixed fear and anger for some reason not to miss the next turn, fly off to the right of the next iron bridge onto the moonlit gray rocks and black water below — discovering, invariably, no reason but the damage his suicide would do to his wife and the children remaining.

Sometimes he would forget for a while by abandoning reason and responsibility for love affairs. Jack's father was at this time still young, still handsome, well-known for the poetry he recited at local churches or for English classes or meetings of the Grange[1] — recited, to loud applause (he had poems of all kinds, both serious and comic), for thrashing crews, old men at the V.A. Hospital, even the tough, flint-eyed orphans at the Children's Home. He was a celebrity, in fact, as much Romantic poet-hero as his time and western New York State could afford — and beyond all that, he was now so full of pain and unassuageable guilt that women's hearts flew to him unbidden. He became, with all his soul and without cynical intent — though fleeing all law, or what he'd once thought law — a hunter of women, trading off his sorrow for the sorrows of wearied, unfulfilled country wives. At times he would be gone from the farm for days, abandoning the work to Jack and whoever was available to help — some neighbor or older cousin or one of Jack's uncles. No one complained, at least not openly. A stranger might have condemned him, but no one in the family did, certainly not Jack, not even Jack's mother, though her sorrow was increased. Dale Hawthorne had always been, before the accident, a faithful man, one of the most fair-minded, genial farmers in the country. No one asked that, changed as he was, he do more, for the moment, than survive.

As for Jack's mother, though she'd been, before the accident, a cheerful woman — one who laughed often and loved telling stories, sometimes sang anthems in bandanna and blackface before her husband recited poems — she cried now, nights, and did only as much as she had strength to do — so sapped by grief that she could barely move her arms. She comforted Jack and his sister, Phoebe — herself as well — by embracing them vehemently whenever new waves of guilt swept in, by constant reassurance and extravagant praise, frequent mention of how proud some relative would be — once, for instance, over a drawing of his sister's, "Oh, Phoebe, if only your great-aunt Lucy could see this!" Great-aunt Lucy had been famous, among the family and friends, for her paintings of families of lions. And Jack's mother forced on his sister and himself comforts more permanent: piano and, for Jack, French-horn lessons, school and church activities, above all an endless, exhausting ritual of chores. Because she had, at thirty-four, considerable strength of character — except that, these days, she was always eating — and because, also, she was a woman of strong religious faith, a woman who, in her years of church work and teaching at the high school, had made scores of close, for the most part equally religious, friends, with whom she regularly corresponded, her letters, then theirs, half filling the mailbox at the foot of the hill and cluttering every table, desk, and niche in the large old house — friends who now frequently visited or phoned — she was able to move step by step past disaster and in the end keep her family from wreck. She said very little to her children about her troubles. In fact, except for the crying behind her closed door, she kept her feelings strictly secret.

But for all his mother and her friends could do for him — for all his father's older brothers could do, or, when he was there, his father himself — the damage to young Jack Hawthorne took a long while healing. Working the farm, ploughing, cultipacking, disking, dragging, he had plenty of time to think — plenty of time for the accident to replay, with the solidity of real time repeated, in his mind, his whole body flinching from the image as it came, his voice

---

[1] The Patrons of Husbandry, an association of American farmers founded in 1867.

leaping up independent of him, as if a shout could perhaps drive the memory back into its cave. Maneuvering the tractor over sloping, rocky fields, dust whorling out like smoke behind him or, when he turned into the wind, falling like soot until his skin was black and his hair as thick and stiff as old clothes in an attic — the circles of foothills every day turning greener, the late-spring wind flowing endless and sweet with the smell of coming rain — he had all the time in the world to cry and swear bitterly at himself, standing up to drive, as his father often did, Jack's sore hands clamped tight to the steering wheel, his shoes unsteady on the bucking axlebeam — for stones lay everywhere, yellowed in the sunlight, a field of misshapen skulls. He'd never loved his brother, he raged out loud, never loved anyone as well as he should have. He was incapable of love, he told himself, striking the steering wheel. He was inherently bad, a spiritual defective. He was evil.

So he raged and grew increasingly ashamed of his raging, reminded by the lengthening shadows across the field of the theatricality in all he did, his most terrible sorrow mere sorrow on a stage, the very thunderclaps above — dark blue, rushing sky, birds crazily wheeling — mere opera set, proper lighting for his rant. At once he would hush himself, lower his rear end to the tractor seat, lock every muscle to the stillness of a statue, and drive on, solitary, blinded by tears; yet even now it was theater, not life — mere ghastly posturing, as in that story of his father's, how Lord Byron once tried to get Shelley's skull to make a drinking cup.[2] Tears no longer came, though the storm went on building. Jack rode on, alone with the indifferent, murderous machinery in the widening ten-acre field.

When the storm at last hit, he'd been driven up the lane like a dog in flight, lashed by gusty rain, chased across the tracks to the tractor shed and from there to the kitchen, full of food smells from his mother's work and Phoebe's, sometimes the work of two or three friends who'd stopped by to look in on the family. Jack kept aloof, repelled by their bright, melodious chatter and absentminded humming, indignant at their pretense that all was well. "My, how you've grown!" the old friend or fellow teacher from high school would say, and to his mother, "My, what big *hands* he has, Betty!" He would glare at his little sister, Phoebe, his sole ally, already half traitor — she would bite her lips, squinting, concentrating harder on the mixing bowl and beaters; she was forever making cakes — and he would retreat as soon as possible to the evening chores.

He had always told himself stories to pass the time when driving the tractor, endlessly looping back and forth, around and around, fitting the land for spring planting. He told them to himself aloud, taking all parts in the dialogue, gesturing, making faces, discarding dignity, here where no one could see or overhear him, half a mile from the nearest house. Once all his stories had been of sexual conquest or of heroic battle with escaped convicts from the Attica Prison or kidnappers who, unbeknownst to anyone, had built a small shack where they kept their captives, female and beautiful, in the lush, swampy woods beside the field. Now, after the accident, his subject matter changed. His fantasies came to be all of self-sacrifice, pitiful stories in which he redeemed his life by throwing it away to save others more worthwhile. To friends and officials of his fantasy, especially to heroines — a girl named Margaret, at school, or his cousin Linda — he would confess his worthlessness at painful length, naming all his faults, granting himself no quarter. For a time this helped, but the lie was too obvious, the manipulation of shame to buy love, and in the end despair bled all color from his fantasies. The foulness of his nature became clearer and clearer in his mind until, like his father, he began to toy — dully but in morbid earnest now — with the idea of suicide. His chest would fill with anguish, as if he were dreaming some nightmare wide awake, or bleeding internally, and his

---

[2] George Gordon, Lord Byron (1788–1824), Percy Bysshe Shelley (1792–1822): English Romantic poets.

arms and legs would grow shaky with weakness, until he had to stop and get down from the tractor and sit for a few minutes, his eyes fixed on some comforting object, for instance a dark, smooth stone.

Even from his father and his father's brothers, who sometimes helped with the chores, he kept aloof. His father and uncles were not talkative men. Except for his father's comic poems, they never told jokes, though they liked hearing them; and because they had lived there all their lives and knew every soul in the county by name, nothing much surprised them or, if it did, roused them to mention it. Their wives might gossip, filling the big kitchen with their pealing laughter or righteous indignation, but the men for the most part merely smiled or compressed their lips and shook their heads. At the G.L.F. feedstore, occasionally, eating an ice cream while they waited for their grist, they would speak of the weather or the Democrats; but in the barn, except for "Jackie, shift that milker, will you?" or "You can carry this up to the milk house now," they said nothing. They were all tall, square men with deeply cleft chins and creases on their foreheads and muscular jowls; all Presbyterians, sometimes deacons, sometimes elders; and they were all gentle-hearted, decent men who looked lost in thought, especially Jack's father, though on occasion they'd abruptly frown or mutter, or speak a few words to a cow, or a cat, or a swallow. It was natural that Jack, working with such men, should keep to himself, throwing down ensilage from the pitch-dark, sweet-ripe crater of the silo or hay bales from the mow, dumping oats in front of the cows' noses, or — taking the long-handled, blunt wooden scraper from the whitewashed wall — pushing manure into the gutters.

He felt more community with the cows than with his uncles or, when he was there, his father. Stretched out flat between the two rows of stanchions, waiting for the cows to be finished with their silage so he could drive them out to pasture, he would listen to their chewing in the dark, close barn, a sound as soothing, as infinitely restful, as waves along a shore, and would feel their surprisingly warm, scented breath, their bovine quiet, and for a while would find that his anxiety had left him. With the cows, the barn cats, the half-sleeping dog, he could forget and feel at home, feel that life was pleasant. He felt the same when walking up the long, fenced lane at the first light of sunrise — his shoes and pants legs sopping wet with dew, his ears full of birdcalls — going to bring in the herd from the upper pasture. Sometimes on the way he would step off the deep, crooked cow path to pick cherries or red raspberries, brighter than jewels in the morning light. They were sweeter then than at any other time, and as he approached, clouds of sparrows would explode into flight from the branches, whirring off to safety. The whole countryside was sweet, early in the morning — newly cultivated corn to his left; to his right, alfalfa and, beyond that, wheat. He felt at one with it all. It was what life ought to be, what he'd once believed it was.

But he could not make such feelings last. No, he thought bitterly on one such morning, throwing stones at the dull, indifferent cows, driving them down the lane. However he might hate himself and all his race, a cow was no better, or a field of wheat. Time and again he'd been driven half crazy, angry enough to kill, by the stupidity of cows when they'd pushed through a fence and — for all his shouting, for all the indignant barking of the dog — they could no longer locate the gap they themselves had made. And no better to be grain, smashed flat by the first rainy wind. So, fists clenched, he raged inside his mind, grinding his teeth to drive out thought, at war with the universe. He remembered his father, erect, eyes flashing, speaking Mark Antony's angry condemnation from the stage at the Grange. His father had seemed to him, that night, a creature set apart. His extended arm, pointing, was the terrible warning of a god. And now, from nowhere, the black memory of his brother's death rushed over him again, mindless and inexorable as a wind or wave, the huge cultipacker lifting — only an inch or so

— as it climbed toward the shoulders, then sank on the cheek, flattening the skull — and he heard, more real than the morning, his sister's scream.

One day in August, a year and a half after the accident, they were combining oats — Jack and two neighbors and two of his cousins — when Phoebe came out, as she did every day, to bring lunch to those who worked in the field. Their father had been gone, this time, for nearly three weeks, and since he'd left at the height of the harvest season, no one was sure he would return, though as usual they kept silent about it. Jack sat alone in the shade of an elm, apart from the others. It was a habit they'd come to accept as they accepted, so far as he knew, his father's ways. Phoebe brought the basket from the shade where the others had settled to the shade here on Jack's side, farther from the bright, stubbled field.

"It's chicken," she said, and smiled, kneeling.

The basket was nearly as large as she was — Phoebe was seven — but she seemed to see nothing unreasonable in her having to lug it up the hill from the house. Her face was flushed, and drops of perspiration stood out along her hairline, but her smile was not only uncomplaining but positively cheerful. The trip to the field was an escape from housework, he understood; even so, her happiness offended him.

"Chicken," he said, and looked down glumly at his hard, tanned arms black with oat-dust. Phoebe smiled on, her mind far away, as it seemed to him, and like a child playing house she took a dishtowel from the basket, spread it on the grass, then set out wax-paper packages of chicken, rolls, celery, and salt, and finally a small plastic thermos, army green.

She looked up at him now. "I brought you a thermos all for yourself because you always sit alone."

He softened a little without meaning to. "Thanks," he said.

She looked down again, and for all his self-absorption he was touched, noticing that she bowed her head in the way a much older girl might do, troubled by thought, though her not quite clean, dimpled hands were a child's. He saw that there was something she wanted to say and, to forestall it, brushed flying ants from the top of the thermos, unscrewed the cap, and poured himself iced tea. When he drank, the tea was so cold it brought a momentary pain to his forehead and made him aware once more of the grating chaff under his collar, blackening all his exposed skin, gritty around his eyes — aware, too, of the breezeless, insect-filled heat beyond the shade of the elm. Behind him, just at the rim of his hearing, one of the neighbors laughed at some remark from the younger of his cousins. Jack drained the cup, brooding on his aching muscles. Even in the shade his body felt baked dry.

"Jack," his sister said, "did you want to say grace?"

"Not really," he said, and glanced at her.

He saw that she was looking at his face in alarm, her mouth slightly opened, eyes wide, growing wider, and though he didn't know why, his heart gave a jump. "I already said it," he mumbled. "Just not out loud."

"Oh," she said, then smiled.

When everyone had finished eating she put the empty papers, the jug, and the smaller thermos in the basket, grinned at them all and said goodbye — whatever had bothered her was forgotten as soon as that — and, leaning far over, balancing the lightened but still-awkward basket, started across the stubble for the house. As he cranked the tractor she turned around to look back at them and wave. He nodded and, as if embarrassed, touched his straw hat.

Not till he was doing the chores that night did he grasp what her look of alarm had meant. If he wouldn't say grace, then perhaps there was no heaven. Their father would never get well, and David was dead. He squatted, drained of all strength again, staring at the hoof of the cow he'd been stripping, preparing her for the milker, and thought of his absent father. He saw the motorcycle roaring down a twisting mountain road, the clatter of the engine ringing like harsh music against shale. If what he felt was hatred, it was a terrible, desperate envy, too; his father all alone, uncompromised, violent, cut off as if by centuries from the warmth, chatter, and smells of the kitchen, the dimness of stained glass where he, Jack, sat every Sunday between his mother and sister, looking toward the pulpit where in the old days his father had sometimes read the lesson, soft-voiced but aloof from the timid-eyed flock, Christ's sheep.

Something blocked the light coming in through the cowbarn window from the west, and he turned his head, glancing up.

"You all right there, Jackie?" his uncle Walt said, bent forward, near-sightedly peering across the gutter.

He nodded and quickly wiped his wrist across his cheeks. He moved his hands once more to the cow's warm teats.

A few nights later, when he went in from chores, the door between the kitchen and livingroom was closed, and the house was unnaturally quiet. He stood a moment listening, still holding the milk pail, absently fitting the heel of one boot into the bootjack and tugging until the boot slipped off. He pried off the other, then walked to the icebox in his stocking feet, opened the door, carried the pitcher to the table, and filled it from the pail. When he'd slid the pitcher into the icebox again and closed the door, he went without a sound, though not meaning to be stealthy, toward the livingroom. Now, beyond the closed door, he heard voices, his sister and mother, then one of his aunts. He pushed the door open and looked in, about to speak.

Though the room was dim, no light but the small one among the pictures on the piano, he saw his father at once, kneeling by the davenport with his face on his mother's lap. Phoebe was on the davenport beside their mother, hugging her and him, Phoebe's cheeks stained, like her mother's, with tears. Around them, as if reverently drawn back, Uncle Walt, Aunt Ruth, and their two children sat watching, leaning forward with shining eyes. His father's head, bald down the center, glowed, and he had his glasses off.

"Jackie," his aunt called sharply, "come in. It's all over. Your dad's come home."

He would have fled, but his knees had no strength in them and his chest was wild, churning as if with terror. He clung to the doorknob, grotesquely smiling — so he saw himself. His father raised his head. "Jackie," he said, and was unable to say more, all at once sobbing like a baby.

"Hi, Dad," he brought out, and somehow managed to go to him and get down on his knees beside him and put his arm around his back. He felt dizzy now, nauseated, and he was crying like his father. "I hate you," he whispered too softly for any of them to hear.

His father stayed. He worked long days, in control once more, though occasionally he smoked, pacing in his room nights, or rode off on his motorcycle for an hour or two, and seldom smiled. Nevertheless, in a month he was again reciting poetry for schools and churches and the Grange, and sometimes reading Scripture from the pulpit Sunday mornings. Jack, sitting rigid, hands over his face, was bitterly ashamed of those poems and recitations from the Bible. His father's eyes no longer flashed, he no longer had the style of an actor. Even his gestures were submissive, as pliant as the grass. Though tears ran down Jack Hawthorne's face — no one would deny that his father was still effective, reading carefully, lest his voice should break. "Tomorrow's Bridge" and "This Too Will Pass" — Jack scorned the poems' opinions, scorned the way his father spoke directly to each listener, as if each were some new woman, his father some mere suffering sheep among sheep, and scorned the way Phoebe and his mother looked on smiling, furtively weeping, heads lifted. Sometimes his father would recite a poem that Jack himself had written, in the days when he'd tried to write poetry, a comic limerick or some maudlin piece about a boy on a hill. Though it was meant as a compliment, Jack's heart would swell with rage; yet he kept silent, more private than before. At night he'd go out to the cavernous haymow or up into the orchard and practice his French horn. One of these days, he told himself, they'd wake up and find him gone.

He used the horn more and more now to escape their herding warmth. Those around him were conscious enough of what was happening — his parents and Phoebe, his uncles, aunts, and cousins, his mother's many friends. But there was nothing they could do. "That horn's his whole world," his mother often said, smiling but clasping her hands together. Soon he was playing third horn with the Batavia Civic Orchestra, though he refused to play in church or when company came. He began to ride the Bluebus to Rochester, Saturdays, to take lessons from Arcady Yegudkin, "the General," at the Eastman School of Music.

Yegudkin was seventy. He'd played principal horn in the orchestra of Czar Nikolai and at the time of the Revolution had escaped, with his wife, in a dramatic way. At the time of the purge of Kerenskyites, the Bolsheviks[3] had loaded Yegudkin and his wife, along with hundreds more, onto railroad flatcars, reportedly to carry them to Siberia. In a desolate place, machine guns opened fire on the people on the flatcars, then soldiers pushed the bodies into a ravine, and the train moved on. The soldiers were not careful to see that everyone was dead. Perhaps they did not relish their work; in any case, they must have believed that, in a place so remote, a wounded survivor would have no chance against wolves and cold weather. The General and his wife were among the few who lived, he virtually unmarked, she horribly crippled. Local peasants nursed the few survivors back to health, and in time the Yegudkins escaped to Europe. There Yegudkin played horn with all the great orchestras and received such praise — so he claimed, spreading out his clippings — as no other master of French horn had received in all history. He would beam as he said it, his Tartar eyes flashing, and his smile was like a thrown-down gauntlet.

He was a barrel-shaped, solidly muscular man, hard as a boulder for all his age. His hair and moustache were as black as coal except for touches of silver, especially where it grew, with majestic indifference to ordinary taste, from his cavernous nostrils and large, dusty-looking ears. The sides of his moustache were carefully curled, in the fashion once favored by Russian dandies, and he was one of the last men in Rochester, New York, to wear spats. He wore formal black suits, a huge black overcoat, and a black fedora. His wife, who came with him and sat on the long maple bench outside his door, never reading or knitting or doing anything at all except that sometimes she would speak unintelligibly to a student — Yegudkin's wife, shriveled and twisted, watched him as if worshipfully, hanging on his words. She looked at least twice the old man's age. Her hair was snow white and she wore lumpy black shoes and long black shapeless dresses. The two of them would come, every Saturday morning, down the long marble hallway of the second floor of Killburn Hall, the General erect and imperious, like some sharp-eyed old Slavonic king, moving slowly, waiting for the old woman who crept beside him, gray claws on his coat sleeve, and seeing Jack Hawthorne seated on the bench, his books and French horn in its tattered black case on the floor beside him, the General would extend his left arm and boom, "Goot mworning!"

Jack, rising, would say, "Morning, sir."

---

[3] Nicholas II (1868–1918), czar of Russia from 1894 to 1917, abdicated during the 1917 Russian Revolution and was executed the following year. Kerenskyites: followers of Alexander Kerensky, who became head of the post-revolutionary provisional government. Bolsheviks: members of the left-wing faction of the Russian Social Democratic Party, followers of Lenin, first premier of the U.S.S.R.

"You have met my wife?" the old man would say then, bowing and taking the cigar from his mouth. He asked it each Saturday.

"Yes, sir. How do you do?"

The old man was too deaf to play in orchestras anymore. "What's the difference?" he said. "Every symphony in America, they got Yegudkins. I have teach them all. Who teach you this? *The General*!" He would smile, chin lifted, triumphant, and salute the ceiling.

He would sit in the chair beside Jack's and would sing, with violent gestures and a great upward leap of the belly to knock out the high B's and C's — *Tee! Tee!* — as Jack read through Kopprasch, Gallay, and Kling, and when it was time to give Jack's lip a rest, the General would speak earnestly, with the same energy he put into his singing, of the United States and his beloved Russia that he would nevermore see. The world was at that time filled with Russo-phobes. Yegudkin, whenever he read a paper, would be so enraged he could barely contain himself. "In all my age," he often said, furiously gesturing with his black cigar, "if the Russians would come to this country of America, I would take up a rifle and shot at them — *boof!* But the newspapers telling you lies, all lies! You think them dumb fools, these Russians? You think they are big, fat bush-overs?" He spoke of mile-long parades of weaponry, spoke of Russian cunning, spoke with great scorn, a sudden booming laugh, of Napoleon. Jack agreed with a nod to whatever the General said. Nevertheless, the old man roared on, taking great pleasure in his rage, it seemed, sometimes talking like a rabid communist, sometimes like a fascist, sometimes like a citizen helplessly caught between mindless, grinding forces, vast, idiot herds. The truth was, he hated both Russians and Americans about equally, cared only for music, his students and, possibly, his wife. In his pockets, in scorn of the opinions of fools, he carried condoms, dirty pictures, and grimy, wadded-up dollar bills.

One day a new horn he'd ordered from Germany, an Alexander, arrived at his office — a horn he'd gotten for a graduate student. The old man unwrapped and assembled it, the graduate student looking on — a shy young man, blond, in a limp gray sweater — and the glint in the General's eye was like madness or at any rate lust, perhaps gluttony. When the horn was ready he went to the desk where he kept his clippings, his tools for the cleaning and repair of French horns, his cigars, photographs, and medals from the Czar, and pulled open a wide, shallow drawer. It contained perhaps a hundred mouthpieces, of all sizes and materials, from raw brass to lucite, silver, and gold, from the shallowest possible cup to the deepest. He selected one, fitted it into the horn, pressed the rim of the bell into the right side of his large belly — the horn seemed now as much a part of him as his arm or leg — clicked the shining keys to get the feel of them, then played. In that large, cork-lined room, it was as if, suddenly, a creature from some other universe had appeared, some realm where feelings become birds and dark sky, and spirit is more solid than stone. The sound was not so much loud as large, too large for a hundred French horns, it seemed. He began to play now not single notes but, to Jack's astonishment, chords — two notes at a time, then three. He began to play runs. As if charged with life independent of the man, the horn sound fluttered and flew crazily, like an enormous trapped hawk hunting frantically for escape. It flew to the bottom of the lower register, the foundation concert F, and crashed below it, and on down and down, as if the horn in Yegudkin's hands had no bottom, then suddenly changed its mind and flew upward in a split-second run to the horn's top E, dropped back to the middle and then ran once more, more fiercely at the E, and this time burst through it and fluttered, manic, in the trumpet range, then lightly dropped back into its own home range and, abruptly, in the middle of a note, stopped. The room still rang, shimmered like a vision.

"Good horn," said Yegudkin, and held the horn toward the graduate student, who sat, hands clamped on his knees, as if in a daze.

Jack Hawthorne stared at the instrument suspended in space and at his teacher's hairy hands. Before stopping to think, he said, "You think I'll ever play like that?"

Yegudkin laughed loudly, his black eyes widening, and it seemed that he grew larger, beatific and demonic at once, like the music; overwhelming. "Play like *me*?" he exclaimed.

Jack blinked, startled by the bluntness of the thing, the terrible lack of malice, and the truth of it. His face tingled and his legs went weak, as if the life were rushing out of them. He longed to be away from there, far away, safe. Perhaps Yegudkin sensed it. He turned gruff, sending away the graduate student, then finishing up the lesson. He said nothing, today, of the stupidity of mankind. When the lesson was over he saw Jack to the door and bid him goodbye with a brief half-smile that was perhaps not for Jack at all but for the creature on the bench. "Next Saturday?" he said, as if there might be some doubt.

Jack nodded, blushing.

At the door opening on the street he began to breathe more easily, though he was weeping. He set down the horn case to brush away his tears. The sidewalk was crowded — dazed-looking Saturday-morning shoppers herding along irritably, meekly, through painfully bright light. Again he brushed tears away. He'd been late for his bus. Then the crowd opened for him and, with the horn cradled under his right arm, his music under his left, he plunged in, starting home.

QUESTIONS

1. Dale Hawthorne's response to the tragedy of his son's death seems to be acceptable to his wife and neighbors. Are we also meant to accept Dale's infidelities, irresponsible actions, and eroding faith as justified responses? Does Dale redeem himself in any way?

2. How does Jack respond to the accident, both outwardly and inwardly? Is his penance self-imposed? In what ways do his father's actions determine Jack's responses? Why does Jack tell his father he hates him?

3. What role does Yegudkin play in the story? Does his situation in any way resemble that of the Hawthornes?

4. Compare Dale's poetry and Jack's French-horn playing as modes of redemption.

GAIL GODWIN

Dream Children

The worst thing. Such a terrible thing to happen to a young woman. It's a wonder she didn't go mad.

As she went about her errands, a cheerful, neat young woman, a wife, wearing pants with permanent creases and safari jackets and high-necked sweaters that folded chastely just below the line of the small gold hoops she wore in her ears, she imagined people saying this, or thinking it to themselves. But nobody knew. Nobody knew anything, other than that she and her husband had moved here a year ago, as so many couples were moving farther away from the city, the husband commuting, or staying in town during the week — as hers did. There was nobody here, in this quaint, unspoiled village, nestled in the foothills of the mountains, who could have looked at her and guessed that anything out of the ordinary, predictable, aus-picious spectrum of things that happen to bright, attractive young women had happened to her. She always returned her books to the local library on time; she bought liquor at the local liquor store only on Friday, before she went to meet her husband's bus from the city. He was something in television, a producer? So many ambitious young couples moving to this Dutch farming village, founded in 1690, to restore ruined fieldstone houses and plant herb gardens and keep their own horses and discover the relief of finding oneself insignificant in Nature for the first time!

A terrible thing. So freakish. If you read it in a story or saw it on TV, you'd say no, this sort of thing could never happen in an American hospital.

DePuy, who owned the old Patroon farm adjacent to her land, frequently glimpsed her racing her horse in the early morning, when the mists still lay on the fields, sometimes just before the sun came up and there was a frost on everything. "One woodchuck hole and she and that stallion will both have to be put out of their misery," he told his wife. "She's too reckless. I'll bet you her old man doesn't know she goes streaking to hell across the fields like that." Mrs. DePuy nodded, silent, and went about her business. She, too, watched that other woman ride, a woman not much younger than herself, but with an aura of romance — of tragedy, perhaps. The way she looked: like those heroines in English novels who ride off their bad tempers and unrequited love affairs, clenching their thighs against the flanks of spirited horses with murderous red eyes. Mrs. DePuy, who had ridden since the age of three, recognized something beyond recklessness in that elegant young woman, in her crisp checked shirts and

924

her dove-gray jodhpurs. *She has nothing to fear anymore*, thought the farmer's wife, with sure feminine instinct; she both envied and pitied her. "What she needs is children," remarked DePuy.

"A Dry Sack, a Remy Martin, and ... let's see, a half-gallon of the Chablis, and I think I'd better take a Scotch ... and the Mouton-Cadet ... and maybe a dry vermouth." Mrs. Frye, another farmer's wife, who runs the liquor store, asks if her husband is bringing company for the weekend. "He sure is; we couldn't drink all that by ourselves," and the young woman laughs, her lovely teeth exposed, her small gold earrings quivering in the light. "You know, I saw his name — on the television the other night," says Mrs. Frye. "It was at the beginning of that new comedy show, the one with the woman who used to be on another show with her husband and little girl, only they divorced, you know the one?" "Of course I do. It's one of my husband's shows. I'll tell him you watched it." Mrs. Frye puts the bottles in an empty box, carefully inserting wedges of cardboard between them. Through the window of her store she sees her customer's pert bottle-green car, some sort of little foreign car with the engine running, filled with groceries and weekend parcels, and that big silver-blue dog sitting up in the front seat just like a human being. "I think that kind of thing is so sad," says Mrs. Frye; "families breaking up, poor little children having to divide their loyalties." "I couldn't agree more," replies the young woman, nodding gravely. Such a personable, polite girl! "Are you sure you can carry that, dear? I can get Earl from the back. ..." But the girl has it hoisted on her shoulder in a flash, is airily maneuvering between unopened cartons stacked in the aisle, in her pretty boots. Her perfume lingers in Mrs. Frye's store for a half-hour after she has driven away.

After dinner, her husband and his friends drank brandy. She lay in front of the fire, stroking the dog, and listening to Victoria Darrow, the news commentator, in person. A few minutes ago, they had all watched Victoria on TV. "That's right; thirty-nine!" Victoria now whispered to her. "What? That's kind of you. I'm photogenic, thank God, or I'd have been put out to pasture long before. ... I look five, maybe seven years younger on the screen ... but the point I'm getting at is, I went to this doctor and he said, 'If you want to do this thing, you'd better go home today and get started.' He told me — did you know this? Did you know that a woman is born with all the eggs she'll ever have, and when she gets to my age, the ones that are left have been rattling around so long they're a little shopworn; then every time you fly you get an extra dose of radioactivity, so do those poor eggs. He told me when a woman over forty comes into his office pregnant, his heart sinks; that's why he quit practicing obstetrics, he said; he could still remember the screams of a woman whose baby he delivered ... she was having natural childbirth and she kept saying, 'Why won't you let me see it, I insist on seeing it,' and so he had to, and he says he can still hear her screaming."

"Oh, what was — what was wrong with it?"

But she never got the answer. Her husband, white around the lips, was standing over Victoria ominously, offering the Remy Martin bottle. "Vicky, let me pour you some more," he said. And to his wife, "I think Blue Boy needs to go out."

"Yes, yes, of course. Please excuse me, Victoria. I'll just be ..."

Her husband followed her to the kitchen, his hand on the back of her neck. "Are you okay? That stupid yammering bitch. She and her twenty-six-year-old lover! I wish I'd never brought them, but she's been hinting around the studio for weeks."

"But I like them, I like having them. I'm fine. Please go back. I'll take the dog out and come back. Please ..."

"All right. If you're sure you're okay." He backed away, hands dangling at his sides. A handsome man, wearing a pink shirt with Guatemalan embroidery. Thick black hair and a face rather boyish, but cunning. Last weekend she had sat beside him, alone in this house, just the two of them, and watched him on television: a documentary, in several parts, in which TV "examines itself." There was his double, sitting in an armchair in his executive office, coolly replying to the questions of Victoria Darrow. "*Do you personally watch all the programs you produce, Mr. McNair?*" She watched the man on the screen, how he moved his lips when he spoke, but kept the rest of his face, his body perfectly still. Funny, she had never noticed this before. He managed to say that he did and did not watch all the programs he produced.

Now, in the kitchen, she looked at him backing away, a little like a renegade in one of his own shows — a desperate man, perhaps, who has just killed somebody and is backing away, hands dangling loosely at his sides, Mr. McNair, her husband. That man on the screen. Once a lover above her in bed. That friend who held her hand in the hospital. One hand in hers, the other holding the stopwatch. For a brief instant, all the images coalesce and she feels something again. But once outside, under the galaxies of autumn-sharp stars, the intelligent dog at her heels like some smart gray ghost, she is glad to be free of all that. She walks quickly over the damp grass to the barn, to look in on her horse. She understands something: her husband, Victoria Darrow lead double lives that seem perfectly normal to them. But if she told her husband that she, too, is in two lives, he would become alarmed; he would sell this house and make her move back to the city where he could keep an eye on her welfare.

She is discovering people like herself, down through the centuries, all over the world. She scours books with titles like *The Timeless Moment, The Sleeping Prophet, Between Two Worlds, Silent Union: A Record of Unwilled Communication*; collecting evidence, weaving a sort of underworld net of colleagues around her.

A rainy fall day. Too wet to ride. The silver dog asleep beside her in her special alcove, a padded window seat filled with pillows and books. She is looking down on the fields of dried lithrium, and the fir trees beyond, and the mountains gauzy with fog and rain, thinking, in a kind of terror and ecstasy, about all these connections. A book lies face down on her lap. She has just read the following:

> Theodore Dreiser[1] and his friend John Cowper Powys had been dining at Dreiser's place on West Fifty Seventh Street. As Powys made ready to leave and catch his train to the little town up the Hudson, where he was then living, he told Dreiser, "I'll appear before you here, later in the evening."
>
> Dreiser laughed. "Are you going to turn yourself into a ghost, or have you a spare key?" he asked. Powys said he would return "in some form," he didn't know exactly what kind.
>
> After his friend left, Dreiser sat up and read for two hours. Then he looked up and saw Powys standing in the doorway to the living room. It was Powys' features, his tall stature, even the loose tweed garments which he wore. Dreiser rose at once and strode towards the figure, saying, "Well, John, you kept your word. Come on in and tell me how you did it." But the figure vanished when Dreiser came within three feet of it.
>
> Dreiser then went to the telephone and called Powys' house in the country. Powys answered. Dreiser told him what had happened and Powys

---

[1] Theodore Dreiser (1871–1945), American naturalistic novelist.

said, "I told you I'd be there and you oughtn't to be surprised." But he refused
to discuss how he had done it, if, indeed, he knew how.

"But don't you get frightened, up here all by yourself, alone with all these creaky sounds?"
asked Victoria the next morning.

"No, I guess I'm used to them," she replied, breaking eggs into a bowl. "I know what
each one means. The wood expanding and contracting ... the wind getting caught between
the shutter and the latch ... Sometimes small animals get lost in the stone walls and scratch
around till they find their way out ... or die."

"Ugh. But don't you imagine things? I would, in a house like this. How old? That's
almost three hundred years of lived lives, people suffering and shouting and making love and
giving birth, under this roof. ... You'd think there'd be a few ghosts around."

"I don't know," said her hostess blandly. "I haven't heard any. But of course, I have Blue
Boy, so I don't get scared." She whisked the eggs, unable to face Victoria. She and her husband
had lain awake last night, embarrassed at the sounds coming from the next room. No ghostly
moans, those. "Why can't that bitch control herself, or at least lower her voice," he said
angrily. He stroked his wife's arm, both of them pretending not to remember. She had bled for
an entire year afterward, until the doctor said they would have to remove everything. "I'm
empty," she had said when her husband had tried again, after she was healed. "I'm sorry, I just
don't feel anything." Now they lay tenderly together on these weekends, like childhood
friends, like effigies on a lovers' tomb, their mutual sorrow like a sword between them. She
assumed he had another life, or lives, in town. As she had here. Nobody is just one person, she
had learned.

"I'm sure I would imagine things," said Victoria. "I would see things and hear things
inside my head much worse than an ordinary murderer or rapist."

*The wind caught in the shutter latch ... a small animal dislodging pieces of fieldstone in
its terror, sending them tumbling down the inner walls, from attic to cellar ... a sound like a
child rattling a jar full of marbles, or small stones ...*

"I have so little imagination," she said humbly, warming the butter in the omelet pan.
She could feel Victoria Darrow's professional curiosity waning from her dull country life,
focusing elsewhere.

Cunning!

As a child of nine, she had gone through a phase of walking in her sleep. One summer night,
they found her bed empty, and after an hour's hysterical search they had found her in her
nightgown, curled up on the flagstones beside the fishpond. She woke, baffled, in her father's
tense clutch, the stars all over the sky, her mother repeating over and over again to the night at
large, "Oh, my God, she could have drowned!" They took her to a child psychiatrist, a pretty
Austrian woman who spoke to her with the same vocabulary she used on grownups, putting
the child instantly at ease. "It is not at all uncommon what you did. I have known so many
children who take little night journeys from their beds, and then they awaken and don't know
what all the fuss is about! Usually these journeys are quite harmless, because children are
surrounded by a magical reality that keeps them safe. Yes, the race of children possesses
magically sagacious powers! But the grownups, they tend to forget how it once was for them.
They worry, they are afraid of so many things. You do not want your mother and father, who
love you so anxiously, to live in fear of you going to live with the fishes." She had giggled at the
thought. The woman's steady gray-green eyes were trained on her carefully, suspending her in

a kind of bubble. Then she had rejoined her parents, a dutiful "child" again, holding a hand up to each of them. The night journeys had stopped.

A thunderstorm one night last spring. Blue Boy whining in his insulated house below the garage. She had lain there, strangely elated by the nearness of the thunderclaps that tore at the sky, followed by instantaneous flashes of jagged light. Wondering shouldn't she go down and let the dog in; he hated storms. Then dozing off again ...

She woke. The storm had stopped. The dark air was quiet. Something had changed, some small thing — what? She had to think hard before she found it: the hall light, which she kept burning during the week-nights when she was there alone, had gone out. She reached over and switched the button on her bedside lamp. Nothing. A tree must have fallen and hit a wire, causing the power to go off. This often happened here. No problem. The dog had stopped crying. She felt herself sinking into a delicious, deep reverie, the kind that sometimes came just before morning, as if her being broke slowly into tiny pieces and spread itself over the world. It was a feeling she had not known until she had lived by herself in this house: this weightless though conscious state in which she lay, as if in a warm bath, and yet was able to send her thoughts anywhere, as if her mind contained the entire world.

And as she floated in this silent world, transparent and buoyed upon the dream layers of the mind, she heard a small rattling sound, like pebbles being shaken in a jar. The sound came distinctly from the guest room, a room so chosen by her husband and herself because it was the farthest room from their bedroom on this floor. It lay above what had been the old side of the house, built seventy-five years before the new side, which was completed in 1753. There was a bed in it, and a chair, and some plants in the window. Sometimes on weekends when she could not sleep, she went and read there, or meditated, to keep from waking her husband. It was the room where Victoria Darrow and her young lover would not sleep the following fall, because she would say quietly to her husband, "No ... not that room. I — I've made up the bed in the other room." "What?" he would want to know. "The one next to ours? Right under our noses?"

She did not lie long listening to this sound before she understood it was one she had never heard in the house before. It had a peculiar regularity to its rhythm; there was nothing accidental about it, nothing influenced by the wind, or the nerves of some lost animal. *K-chunk, k-chunk, k-chunk*, it went. At intervals of exactly a half-minute apart. She still remembered how to time such things, such intervals. She was as good as any stopwatch when it came to timing certain intervals.

K-chunk, k-chunk, k-chunk. That determined regularity. Something willed, something poignantly repeated, as though the repetition was a means of consoling someone in the dark. Her skin began to prickle. Often, lying in such states of weightless reverie, she had practiced the trick of sending herself abroad, into rooms of the house, out into the night to check on Blue Boy, over to the barn to look in on her horse, who slept standing up. Once she had heard a rather frightening noise, as if someone in the basement had turned on a faucet, and so she forced herself to "go down," floating down two sets of stairs into the darkness, only to discover what she had known all the time: the hookup system between the hot-water tank and the pump, which sounded like someone turning on the water.

Now she went through the palpable, prickly darkness, without lights, down the chilly hall in her sleeveless gown, into the guest room. Although there was no light, not even a moon shining through the window, she could make out the shape of the bed and then the chair, the spider plants on the window, and a small dark shape in one corner, on the floor, which she and her husband had painted a light yellow.

K-chunk, k-chunk, k-chunk. The shape moved with the noise.

Now she knew what they meant, that "someone's hair stood on end." It was true. As she forced herself across the borders of a place she had never been, she felt, distinctly, every single hair on her head raise itself a millimeter or so from her scalp.

She knelt down and discovered him. He was kneeling, a little cold and scared, shaking a small jar filled with some kind of pebbles. (She later found out, in a subsequent visit, that they were small colored shells, of a triangular shape, called coquinas: she found them in a picture in a child's nature book at the library.) He was wearing pajamas a little too big for him, obviously hand-me-downs, and he was exactly two years older than the only time she had ever held him in her arms.

The two of them knelt in the corner of the room, taking each other in. His large eyes were the same as before: dark and unblinking. He held the small jar close to him, watching her. He was not afraid, but she knew better than to move too close.

She knelt, the tears streaming down her cheeks, but she made no sound, her eyes fastened on that small form. And then the hall light came on silently, as well as the lamp beside her bed, and with wet cheeks and pounding heart she could not be sure whether or not she had actually been out of the room.

But what did it matter, on the level where they had met? He traveled so much farther than she to reach that room. (*"Yes, the race of children possesses magically sagacious powers!"*)

She and her husband sat together on the flowered chintz sofa, watching the last of the series in which TV purportedly examined itself. She said, "Did you ever think that the whole thing is really a miracle? I mean, here we sit, eighty miles away from your studios, and we turn on a little machine and there is Victoria, speaking to us as clearly as she did last weekend when she was in this very room. Why, it's magic, it's time travel and space travel right in front of our eyes, but because it's been 'discovered,' because the world understands that it's only little dots that transmit Victoria electrically to us, it's *all right*. We can bear it. Don't you sometimes wonder about all the miracles that haven't been officially approved yet? I mean, who knows, maybe in a hundred years everybody will take it for granted that they can send an image of themselves around in space by some perfectly natural means available to us now. I mean, when you think about it, what *is* space? What *is* time? Where do the so-called boundaries of each of us begin and end? Can anyone explain it?"

He was drinking Scotch and thinking how they had decided not to renew Victoria Darrow's contract. Somewhere on the edges of his mind hovered an anxious, growing certainty about his wife. At the local grocery store this morning, when he went to pick up a carton of milk and the paper, he had stopped to chat with DePuy. "I don't mean to interfere, but she doesn't know those fields," said the farmer. "Last year we had to shoot a mare, stumbled into one of those holes. ... It's madness, the way she rides."

And look at her now, her face so pale and shining, speaking of miracles and space travel, almost on the verge of tears. ...

And last night, his first night up from the city, he had wandered through the house, trying to drink himself into this slower weekend pace, and he had come across a pile of her books, stacked in the alcove where, it was obvious, she lay for hours, escaping into science fiction, and the occult.

Now his own face appeared on the screen. "I want to be fair," he was telling Victoria Darrow. "I want to be objective. ... Violence has always been part of the human makeup. I don't like it anymore than you do, but there it is. I think it's more a question of whether we want to face things as they are or escape into fantasies of how we would like them to be."

Beside him, his wife uttered a sudden bell-like laugh.

(" ... *It's madness, the way she rides.*")

He did want to be fair, objective. She had told him again and again that she liked her life here. And he — well, he had to admit he liked his own present setup.

"I am a pragmatist," he was telling Victoria Darrow on the screen. He decided to speak to his wife about her riding and leave her alone about the books. She had the right to some escape, if anyone did. But the titles: *Marvelous Manifestations, The Mind Travellers, A Doctor Looks at Spiritualism, The Other Side* ... Something revolted in him, he couldn't help it; he felt an actual physical revulsion at this kind of thinking. Still it was better than some other escapes. His friend Barnett, the actor, who said at night he went from room to room, after his wife was asleep, collecting empty glasses. ("Once I found one by the Water Pik, a second on the ledge beside the tub, a third on the back of the john, and a fourth on the floor beside the john. ...")

He looked sideways at his wife, who was absorbed, it seemed, in watching him on the screen. Her face was tense, alert, animated. She did not look mad. She wore slim gray pants and a loose-knit pullover made of some silvery material, like a knight's chain mail. The lines of her profile were clear and silvery themselves, somehow sexless and pure, like a child's profile. He no longer felt lust when he looked at her, only a sad determination to protect her. He had a mistress in town, whom he loved, but he had explained, right from the beginning, that he considered himself married for the rest of his life. He told this woman the whole story. "And I am implicated in it. I could never leave her." An intelligent, sensitive woman, she had actually wept and said, "Of course not."

He always wore the same pajamas, a shade too big, but always clean. Obviously washed again and again in a machine that went through its cycles frequently. She imagined his "other mother," a harassed woman with several children, short on money, on time, on dreams — all the things she herself had too much of. The family lived, she believed, somewhere in Florida, probably on the west coast. She had worked that out from the little coquina shells: their bright colors, even in moonlight shining through a small window with spider plants in it. His face and arms had been suntanned early in the spring and late into the autumn. They never spoke or touched. She was not sure how much of this he understood. She tried and failed to remember where she herself had gone, in those little night journeys to the fishpond. Perhaps he never remembered afterward, when he woke up, clutching his jar, in a roomful of brothers and sisters. Or with a worried mother or father come to collect him, asleep by the sea. Once she had a very clear dream of the whole family, living in a trailer, with palm trees. But that was a dream; she recognized its difference in quality from those truly magic times when, through his own childish powers, he somehow found a will strong enough, or innocent enough, to project himself upon her still-floating consciousness, as clearly and as believably as her own husband's image on the screen.

There had been six of those times in six months. She dared to look forward to more. So unafraid he was. The last time was the day after Victoria Darrow and her young lover and her own good husband had returned to the city. She had gone farther with the child than ever before. On a starry-clear, cold September Monday, she had coaxed him down the stairs and out of the house with her. He held to the banisters, a child unused to stairs, and yet she knew there was no danger; he floated in his own dream with her. She took him to see Blue Boy. Who disappointed her by whining and backing away in fear. And then to the barn to see the horse. Who perked up his ears and looked interested. There was no touching, of course, no touching or speaking. Later she wondered if horses, then, were more magical than dogs. If dogs were more "realistic." She was glad the family was poor, the mother harassed. They could not afford any expensive child psychiatrist who would hypnotize him out of his night journeys.

He loved her. She knew that. Even if he never remembered her in his other life.

"At last I was beginning to understand what Teilhard de Chardin[2] meant when he said that man's true home is the mind. I understood that when the mystics tell us that the mind is a place, they *don't mean it as a metaphor*. I found these new powers developed with practice. I had to detach myself from my ordinary physical personality. The intelligent part of me had to remain wide awake, and move down into this world of thoughts, dreams and memories. After several such journeyings I understood something else: dream and reality aren't competitors, but reciprocal sources of consciousness." This she read in a "respectable book," by a "respectable man," a scientist, alive and living in England, only a few years older than herself. She looked down at the dog, sleeping on the rug. His lean silvery body actually ran as he slept! Suddenly his muzzle lifted, the savage teeth snapped. Where was he "really" now? Did the dream rabbit in his jaws know it was a dream? There was much to think about, between her trips to the nursery.

Would the boy grow, would she see his body slowly emerging from its child's shape, the arms and legs lengthening, the face thinning out into a man's — like a certain advertisement for bread she had seen on TV where a child grows up, in less than a half-minute of sponsor time, right before the viewer's eyes. Would he grow into a man, grow a beard ... outgrow the nursery region of his mind where they had been able to meet?

And yet, some daylight part of his mind must have retained an image of her from that single daylight time they had looked into each other's eyes.

The worst thing, such an awful thing to happen to a young woman ... She was having this natural childbirth, you see, her husband in the delivery room with her, and the pains were coming a half-minute apart, and the doctor had just said, "This is going to be a breeze, Mrs. McNair," and they never knew exactly what went wrong, but all of a sudden the pains stopped and they had to go in after the baby without even time to give her a saddle block or any sort of anesthetic. ... They must have practically had to tear it out of her ... the husband fainted. The baby was born dead, and they gave her a heavy sedative to put her out all night.

When she woke the next morning, before she had time to remember what had happened, a nurse suddenly entered the room and laid a baby in her arms. "Here's your little boy," she said cheerfully, and the woman thought, with a profound, religious relief, *So that other nightmare was a dream*, and she had the child at her breast feeding him before the nurse realized her mistake and rushed back into the room, but they had to knock the poor woman out with more sedatives before she would let the child go. She was screaming and so was the little baby and they clung to each other till she passed out.

They would have let the nurse go, only it wasn't entirely her fault. The hospital was having a strike at the time; some of the nurses were outside picketing and this nurse had been working straight through for forty-eight hours, and when she was questioned afterward she said she had just mixed up the rooms, and yet, she said, when she had seen the woman and the baby clinging to each other like that, she had undergone a sort of revelation in her almost hallucinatory exhaustion: the nurse said she saw that all children and mothers were interchangeable, that nobody could own anybody or anything, anymore than you could own an idea that happened to be passing through the air and caught on your mind, or anymore than

---

[2] Pierre Teilhard de Chardin (1881–1955), French Jesuit priest, geologist, and philosopher.

you owned the rosebush that grew in your back yard. There were only mothers and children, she realized; though, afterward, the realization faded.

It was the kind of freakish thing that happens once in a million times, and it's a wonder the poor woman kept her sanity.

In the intervals, longer than those measured by any stopwatch, she waited for him. In what the world accepted as "time," she shopped for groceries, for clothes; she read; she waved from her bottle-green car to Mrs. Frye, trimming the hedge in front of the liquor store, to Mrs. DePuy, hanging out her children's pajamas in the back yard of the old Patroon farm. She rode her horse through the fields of the waning season, letting him have his head; she rode like the wind, a happy, happy woman. She rode faster than fear because she was a woman in a dream, a woman anxiously awaiting her child's sleep. The stallion's hoofs pounded the earth. Oiling his tractor, DePuy resented the foolish woman and almost wished for a woodchuck hole to break that arrogant ride. Wished deep in a violent level of himself he never knew he had. For he was a kind, distracted father and husband, a practical, hard-working man who would never descend deeply into himself. Her body, skimming through time, felt weightless to the horse.

Was she a woman riding a horse and dreaming she was a mother who anxiously awaited her child's sleep; or was she a mother dreaming of herself as a free spirit who could ride her horse like the wind because she had nothing to fear?

I am a happy woman, that's all I know. Who can explain such things?

QUESTIONS

1. How does television resemble the dream realm? In what ways do the two differ? Compare Mrs. McNair's involvement in psychic phenomena with her husband's involvement with television.

2. Why does Mrs. McNair laugh at her husband's statement: "I think it's more a question of whether we want to face things as they are or escape into fantasies of how we would like them to be"? Compare his views with those of the English scientist and the nurse.

3. What elements of irony and foreshadowing are present in the story?

4. How does the ending alter our definition of "reality"?

5. Why is the story's title plural? Who are the dream children?

WILLIAM GOYEN

Bridge of Music, River of Sand

Do you remember the bridge that we crossed over the river to get to Riverside? And if you looked over yonder you saw the railroad trestle? High and narrow? Well that's what he jumped off of. Into a nothing river. "River"! I could laugh. I can spit more than runs in that dry bed. In some places is just a little damp, but that's it. That's your grand and rolling river: a damp spot. That's your remains of the grand old Trinity. Where can so much water go? I at least wish they'd do something about it. But what can they do? What can anybody do? You can't replace a *river*.

Anyway, if there'd been water, maybe he'd have made it, the naked diver. As it was, diving into the river as though there were water in it, he went head first into moist sand and drove into it like an arrow into flesh and was found in a position of somebody on their knees, headless, bent over looking for something. Looking for where the river vanished to? I was driving across the old river bridge when I said to myself, wait a minute I believe I see something. I almost ran into the bridge railing. I felt a chill come over me.

What I did was when I got off the bridge to draw my car off to the side of the road and get out and run down the river bank around a rattlesnake that seemed to be placed there as a deterrent (the banks are crawling with them in July), and down; and what I came upon was a kind of avenue that the river had made and paved with gleaming white sand, wide and grand and empty. I crossed this ghostly thoroughfare of the river halfway, and when I got closer, my Lord Jesus God Almighty damn if I didn't see that it was half a naked human body in what would have been midstream were there water. I was scared to death. What ought I to do? Try to pull it out? I was scared to touch it. It was a heat-stunned afternoon. The July heat throbbed. The blue, steaming air waved like a veil. The feeling of something missing haunted me: it was the lost life of the river — something so powerful that it had haunted the countryside for miles around; you could feel it a long time before you came to it. In a landscape that was unnatural — flowing water was missing — everything else seemed unnatural. The river's vegetation was thin and starved-looking; it lived on the edge of sand instead of water; it seemed out of place.

If only I hadn't taken the old bridge. I was already open to a fine of five thousand dollars for driving across it, according to the sign, and I understood why. (Over yonder arched the shining new bridge. There was no traffic on it.) The flapping of loose boards and the quaking of the iron beams was terrifying. I almost panicked in the middle when the whole construction swayed and made such a sound of crackling and clanking. I was surprised the feeble structure hadn't more than a sign to prohibit passage over it — it should have been barricaded. At any rate, it was when I was in the middle of this rocking vehicle that seemed like some mad carnival ride that I saw the naked figure diving from the old railroad trestle. It was as though the diver were making a flamboyant leap into the deep river below — until to my horror I realized that the river was dry. I dared not stop my car and so I maneuvered my way on, mechanical with terror, enchanted by the melodies that rose from the instruments of the melodious bridge that played like some orchestra of xylophones and drums and cellos as I moved over it. Who would have known that the dead bridge, condemned and closed away from human touch, had such music in it? I was on the other side now. Behind me the music was quieter now, lowering into something like chime sounds and harness sounds and wagons; it shook like bells and tolled like soft, deep gongs.

His hands must have cut through the wet sand, carving a path for his head and shoulders. He was sunk up to his mid-waist and had fallen to a kneeling position: a figure on its knees with its head buried in the sand, as if it had decided not to look at the world any more. And then the figure began to sink as if someone underground were pulling it under. Slowly the stomach, lean and hairy, vanished; then the loins, thighs. The river, which had swallowed half this body, now seemed to be eating the rest of it. For a while the feet lay, soles up, on the sand. And then they went down, arched like a dancer's.

Who was the man drowned in a dry river? eaten by a dry river? devoured by sand? How would I explain, describe what had happened? I'd be judged to be out of my senses. And why would I tell somebody — the police or — anybody? There was nothing to be done, the diver was gone, the naked leaper was swallowed up. Unless somebody had pushed him over the bridge and he'd assumed a diving position to try to save himself. But what evidence was there? Well, I *had* to report what I'd seen, what I'd witnessed. Witness? To what? Would anybody believe me? There was no evidence anywhere. Well, I'd look, I'd search for evidence. I'd go up on the railroad trestle.

I climbed up. The trestle was perilously narrow and high. I could see a long ways out over Texas, green and steaming in July. I could see the scar of the river, I could see the healed-looking patches that were the orphaned bottomlands. I could see the tornado-shaped funnel of bilious smoke that twisted out of the mill in Riverside, enriching the owner and poisoning him, his family and his neighbors. And I could see the old bridge which I'd just passed over and still trembling under my touch, arching perfect and precious, golden in the sunlight. The music I had wrought out of it was now stilled except, it seemed, for a low, deep hum that rose from it. It seemed impossible that a train could move on these narrow tracks now grown over with weeds. As I walked, grasshoppers flared up in the dry heat.

I saw no footprints in the weeds, no sign of anybody having walked on the trestle — unless they walked on the rails or the ties. Where were the man's clothes? Unless he'd left them on the bank and run out naked onto the trestle. This meant searching on both sides of the trestle — Christ, what was I caught up in? It could also mean that he was a suicide, my mind went on dogging me; or insane; it could also mean that nobody else was involved. Or it could mean that I was suffering a kind of bridge madness, or the vision that sometimes comes from going home again, of going back to places haunted by deep feeling?

Had anyone ever told me the story of a man jumping into the river from the trestle? Could this be some tormented spirit doomed forever to re-enact his suicide? And if so, must he continue it, now that the river was gone? This thought struck me as rather pitiful.

How high the trestle was! It made me giddy to look down at the riverbed. I tried to find the spot where the diver had hit the dry river. There was absolutely no sign. The mouth of sand that had sucked him down before my very eyes had closed and sealed itself. The story was over, so far as I was concerned. Whatever had happened would be my secret. I had to give it up, let it go. You can understand that I had no choice, that that was the only thing I could do.

That was the summer I was making a sentimental trip through home regions, after fifteen years away. The bridge over the beloved old river had been one of my most touching memories — an object that hung in my memory of childhood like a precious ornament. It was a fragile creation, of iron and wood, and so poetically arched, so slender, half a bracelet (the other half underground) through which the green river ran. The superstructure was made more for a minaret than a bridge. From a distance it looked like an ornate pier, in Brighton or early Santa Monica; or, in the summer heat haze, a palace tower, a creation of gold. Closer, of course, it was an iron and wooden bridge of unusual beauty, shape and design. It had always been an imperfect bridge, awry from the start. It had been built wrong — an engineering mistake: the ascent was too steep and the descent too sharp. But its beauty endured. And despite its irregularity, traffic had used the bridge at Riverside, without serious mishap, for many years. It was just an uncomfortable trip, and always somewhat disturbing, this awkward, surprising and somehow mysterious crossing.

Some real things happened on this practical, if magical, device for crossing water. For one thing, since it swayed, my mother, in our childhood days, would refuse to ride across it. She would remove herself from the auto and walk across, holding onto the railing, while my father, cursing, drove the rest of us across. My sister and I peered back at the small figure of our mother laboring darkly and utterly alone on the infernal contraption which was her torment. I remember my father getting out of the car, on the other side, waiting at the side of the road, looking toward the bridge, watching my mother's creeping progress. When she arrived, pale, she declared, as she did each time, "I vow to the Lord if my sister Sarah didn't live in Riverside I'd never to my soul come near this place." "Well you could lie down in the back seat, put the cotton in your ears that you always bring, and never know it, as I keep telling you," said my father. "I'd still know it," my mother came back. "I'd still know we was on this infernal bridge." "Well then take the goddam train from Palestine. Train trestle's flat." And, getting in the car and slamming the door, "Or stay home and just *write* to your damned sister Sarah. Married to a horse's ass, anyway."

"Mama," said my sister, trying to pacify the situation. "Tell us about the time you almost drowned in the river and Daddy had to jump in and pull you out."

"Well, it was just right over yonder. We'd been fishing all morning, and ..."

"Aw for Christ's sake," my father said.

On the other side of the bridge, after a crossing of hazards and challenges, there was nothing more than a plain little town of mud streets and weather-faded shacks. The town of poor people lived around an ugly mill that puffed out like talcum something called Fuller's Earth over it. This substance lay on rooftops, on the ground and in lungs. It smelled sour and bit the eyes.

As I drove away toward that town, haunted by the vision of the leaping man and now so shaken in my very spirit, lost to fact but brought to some odd truth which I could not yet clear for myself, I saw in the mirror the still image of the river bridge that had such hidden music in it, girdling the ghost of what it had been created for, that lost river that held in its bosom of sand the diving figure of the trestle that I was sure I had seen. I was coming in to Riverside and already the stinging fumes of the mill brought tears to my eyes.

QUESTIONS

1. Why does the narrator travel over the old bridge when a new one is available? Where does the bridge take him? Is his crossing in any way metaphoric or allegorical? How are the bridge and river symbolic?

2. " ... I *had* to report what I'd seen, what I'd witnessed," the narrator tells us. Why does he doubt that the event actually happened? Why are the man's leap and disappearance disturbing to him? What is the "odd truth" this event points toward? Compare his vision and reflections to those of Mrs. Hazlitt in Calisher's "The Scream on Fifty-Seventh Street."

3. How does the narrator create an air of immediacy and plausibility? Why does he include the story about his mother just before the end? How does this anecdote fit in with or complete the story as a whole?

4. In what ways does the story concern the art of storytelling itself, or any aesthetic experience in general?

Two Shoes for One Foot

In a small mill city in Bavaria there lived some children who were afraid of a one-legged man called the Kommandant. He lived within walking distance of the shops and houses, so near that with the help of his crutch he often swung in the direction of their cobbled streets and little blackened windows and smoking chimneys. The Kommandant frightened the boys, of course, because he had only one leg; yet it was just for this, for their dreams of fleeing the single foot, that they talked of surprising him with their bravery and cleverness and skill. But they had no Teutonic helmets, no wooden swords; to the boys it would be nothing less than an exchange of heart for heart.

One evening while it was still light and before the frost became hard, they approached the Kommandant, stared at the straight trouser leg and at the folded trouser leg, and made him an offer. He heard them silently, then followed them, and they were careful not to walk too quickly. They took him by back streets and through an unproductive orchard to the house of the oldest boy, Heinrich; they led him directly inside where he stood wearing his Kommandant's cap and leaning on his crutch. He looked closely at what the boys were offering for sale, at what they dared offer no one but himself. The smallest of the boys darted forward suddenly and pulled the coverlet from the bed. The Kommandant stepped near the bed which filled nearly the whole of the room. Through the narrow single window the sunset was cold and red, a brutal light on the still figure now stretched before them.

"He is ours," whispered Heinrich, and the boys' eyes were the eyes one sees at dusk under the roots of a tree, five pairs or more, in winter, staring up to the surface of the earth with that animal curiosity which shines from the pitiless lair. In this room only the bed, the Kommandant, the boys: and the boys stood there like brothers, each as familiar as Heinrich himself with the chipped walls, the hole in the floor, the place where he hung his jacket and put his shoes; all of them ragged and expectant in the intimacy of boys together.

"Come look, mein Herr," Heinrich whispered and his companions also pressed closer. They tried not to touch the Kommandant's crutch. The boys waited for the bargain to be sealed as if they felt that no one else would come here or become aware in any way, ever, of what was happening in Heinrich's room while the sun set.

Upon the bed lay a man, heavy and fully dressed in a shirt and black suit of a good cut but tight across the chest, a man who appeared to be neither asleep nor dead though the cloth and the hair were wet with the rains so frequent in this country.

"He is complete. He is not damaged, not at all damaged, Herr Kommandant," whispered Heinrich, and the eyes of his companions were the eyes of moles. "He is all here," Heinrich told him again in his soft, decisive voice.

"But look," said the Kommandant. "Look at his feet, boys. Where are the shoes?"

Heinrich smiled and went to the wooden rack where he kept his own worn pairs of boots. "On the rack, mein Herr. They were soiled, you can see for yourself; they were covered with blood. So I removed them. But they belong with him and they shall go with him." Without hesitating he returned to the bed and placed the great swollen shoes on the coverlet next to the feet, exactly as if he had tipped the scales from a crafty, childish generosity.

"Good," said the Kommandant.

The sun fell sharply through the window and lit the buttons on the dead man's coat. The eyeglasses began to shine, but for a moment only. Following some curious law of growth, some urge dictated by its sap and fibers, the lowest branch of one of the few trees in the orchard, a tree planted too near the house, had reached to the window and pressed its crowded shape to the panes. Now, like an arm twisted in some invisible grip, it moved as much as it could and scratched painfully on the glass. The sun came into the room through the window and between the gray twigs of the branch that struggled and obscured the view. Beyond a few dead leaves and the dusty glass could be seen a layer of smoke from the mills, and farther yet, under the red streaks of the sun, the gathering of the night itself.

"Good," murmured the Kommandant again and frowned, considering the man on the bed. The eyeglasses were cracked and twisted, but they had been readjusted on the bridge of the nose. Though not expertly, the hair had been brushed into place.

"And, Herr Kommandant," said the oldest boy, "he has papers also." Heinrich unfastened the top button, drew away the coat, and pointed. The papers protruded thick and white from the inside pocket until quickly Heinrich hid them away again and smoothed the lapel.

"He is cold," Heinrich said, peering up, smiling, indicating the heavy breast of the man. He continued to watch the Kommandant for some change in his face.

"Herr Herzenbrecher!" the smallest boy shouted. "He is Herr Herzenbrecher!"

The sun passed away, the orchard became dark; the boys shifted, and one of them held the smallest idly by his hand. They could hear the sounds of all the things that woke Heinrich in the night. Now the buttons no longer flashed on the coat, the lifelike expression was shadowed on the dead man's face, his black waistcoat was tight and fastened awry over the belly still filled with air. Dusk in this city, despite the wireless and industry, was the time when the inhabitants feared to see the dead taking to the open roofs.

"But your bed? You bring him to your own bed?" asked the Kommandant.

"Oh," said Heinrich quickly, "it's all right. I slept on the floor. But of course I covered him each night with the blanket until the sun rose." Then by a slight gesture, a movement of his finger, calling attention to the watch chain and to the belt buckle which must have been loosened after the last meal, all the while staring at the Kommandant, Heinrich pursed his lips and asked, "Well? What do you think of him?"

A shrill whistle, like the furious sound that regulates life in prisons, came from far off in the direction of the mills, and the iron machines began scraping in that distant end of the city. Heinrich waited. Suddenly the smallest boy snatched up the bloodied shoes and ran with them into the orchard. "Look," he cried, "I have stolen his shoes! Look here, I have stolen

Herr Herzenbrecher's shoes!" He ran under the trees, to and fro, laughing, fat, and his childish and impetuous and uneven flat steps came boldly back from the earth out there. He wet his stockings in the leaves. He hugged the shoes. "Two shoes for one foot!" he shouted under the withered apple tree. "Two shoes for one foot!" He was wrapped in the mist and bare armed, hurrying between the hanging trees, squatting and hiding himself at every twisted trunk. "Two shoes ..." he tried to shout again, but the boys caught him and stopped his shrill humor with their white hands. He began to sniffle as they led him inside the house.

"If you are not good," said Heinrich, "he will blow his breath on you. Now mein Herr," he said, forgetting to smile, forgetting to change the sternness in his voice, "what of our business?"

The Kommandant nodded and leaned closer, as if to sit on the edge of the bed. It was so dark now that the boys' heads were little skulls in the shadows, featureless except for the large dark charcoal smears of eyes and mouths. The body was larger in the darkness.

"We have washed him. Have we not done well, mein Herr?"

The Kommandant could hear the beating of the children's hearts. He tried to see what he could of the room; he smelled the coverlet and the leaves and the wet paper wadded under the coat. "Yes," he answered at last.

The smallest boy began to cry and struggled to run, knocking against his comrades, weeping and laughing at the same time. "Herr Herzenbrecher is bad, Heinrich. He is going to blow his breath on Heinrich."

"Hush," said Heinrich. "But would you care to look in his pockets, Herr Kommandant? Perhaps if you glance in one pocket anyway ..."

It started to rain. The rain filled the orchard with droplets that did not stream slantwise down the window but clouded it, dulling it with the harmless but telltale puffing of a dead storm — the kind of rain which, if it is a dark night and the sun has been red, drenches the coat of fur noiselessly and in a moment, before the dog can take cover. Such rain did not help the apple trees to grow.

Heinrich lit a candle and tilted it so that not a line in Herr Herzenbrecher's face could be missed. He noticed a clot of dirt on the trousers and brushed it off. For a long moment he admired Herr Herzenbrecher. Then he smiled and all the boys around the bed smiled also. "No one has ever found anything like Herr Herzenbrecher," he whispered. "Herr Herzenbrecher looks like my father. He looks like Hansel's father also. He is not a plaything, Kommandant, you can be sure."

The room was small for the Kommandant, and in it his crutch cast a dark shadow. The room so belonged to a child that it was hardly part of the house — but dusty, slowly sinking off its plumb, empty except for the boy living within and except for his friends who appeared out of the orchard, knowing so well the weather-beaten paths to it. The room itself, the wind, the boys. And now Herr Herzenbrecher. And now the Kommandant. The boys held each other by the hands, the limb of the apple tree moved against the window.

"But what of marks on his person?" asked the Kommandant. "Nothing of violence?"

"Oh yes," answered Heinrich shortly, "you will see." Heinrich put his fingers lightly on the dead man's shoulder. "However, they are not noticeable, mein Herr, and we covered them. Perhaps you will not even find them."

"Heinrich," asked the Kommandant slowly, "do you know how long the man has been dead?"

Heinrich stared and moved as if to blow out the candle; he hugged the smallest boy and pulled on his stockings; his face was whiter than ever.

"For as long as my Papa has been dead," answered Heinrich at last.

"But you have not thought of telling anyone about this man?"

"No, mein Herr."

"Nor of summoning the police?"

"No, mein Herr."

"But now you want to give him up," said the Kommandant.

"Mein Herr. We are only *offering* you Herr Herzenbrecher. He is ours. We found him. He has a gold watch. He is with us, and now we are all men."

"But this man is dead!"

"Comrades," whispered Heinrich, "assure the Kommandant that we know that Herr Herzenbrecher is dead."

"Mamma, Mamma, Mamma," cried the smallest boy until Heinrich picked him up and still holding him, and perspiring, spoke again to the one-legged man: "Are you thinking of his murderer, mein Herr?"

At that moment the window smashed and the branch, at last finding entrance through the broken glass, intruded, nodding and twisting as if it had finally penetrated a wall of stone.

"Tell me," said the Kommandant, speaking as plainly and softly as he could, "do you know how Herr Herzenbrecher died?"

Heinrich's face shone like gold and became thin and bright with pleasure. But he remained silent.

"Well, do you know?" repeated the Kommandant.

"Yes. Of course. Mein Herr," Heinrich whispered then, staring at the window, "he died fighting, throwing himself upon a great animal armed with scales. Bravely."

The Kommandant frowned and leaned on his crutch. He stopped himself from speaking.

The mill whistle blew again beyond the orchard, beyond the electric cables tapping in the mist. There came a slight odor of apples through the rain. In the forward part of the house a bell tinkled sharply. Immediately Heinrich stepped away from the corpse, laughed awkwardly, and bowed before the officer.

"Pardon, mein Herr Kommandant. My grandmother is calling me to our supper. I must be with her. We eat together. But will you take him, Your Honor?"

The Kommandant waited and then nodded and then from his heavy leather purse he gave each boy a few marks and a few pfennigs.

Then Heinrich signaled. They scurried about and produced a long umbrella, a bundle containing a flattened hat and handwoven shawl, and a piece of cord with which they securely tied the shoes. All this they thrust upon the Kommandant.

The smallest boy pulled Heinrich to the door and shouted after the Kommandant, who was laboriously pushing his wooden cart into the darkness and rain: "Live well, Herr Herzenbrecher, live well!"

QUESTIONS

1. In what way is the incident between the boys and the Kommandant "nothing less than an exchange of heart for heart" (as the narrator calls it at the beginning of the story)?

2. What interest does the Kommandant have in Herr Herzenbrecher's dead body? How and why did the boys obtain the body?

3. What dramatic and symbolic functions does the tree branch have in the story?

4. How do you account for the smallest boy's behavior? What do his actions reveal about his fellows?

JOSEPHINE JACOBSEN ⬭

The Mango Community

The Vice-Consul again looked at his shoes. He appeared not critical but, more annoying, embarrassed.

"Mrs. Jane Megan — yes, and Mr. Henry Sewell." He raised very pale blue eyes to Jane's, dropped them to his toecaps. "And Daniel. Daniel Megan. Fifteen? Is that right?"

"That's right," said Jane. She added, "Mr. Adams."

"And your purpose here was a vacation?" This time he got himself together and looked at her quite hard.

"Work," said Jane. "I'm a painter." His eyes flicked to her fingernails. "It's on my passport. Henry is a writer. A novelist."

If she had looked for him to say, "Oh, *that* Henry Sewell," she was wrong.

"Yes, well," said Mr. Adams moodily. "You see my position," he said rapidly but uncertainly. "I can't actually ask you to leave. I mean, there would have to be actual and manifest danger."

She hoped ardently that Harry would not appear, lugging fish and christophine.[1] He and Mr. Adams were, temperamentally, unsuited to a dialogue. Soothingly she said, "I think you've been very kind to come all the way out here. And I quite see your point. We'll think about it, we really will. But this business has been going on for weeks and weeks, and we leave, anyway, in a few months."

At last Mr. Adams looked cross. "Mrs. Megan, I've tried to explain that if you do insist on staying on under present circumstances," he stopped and repeated more loudly, "present circumstances, the U.S. government simply cannot be responsible for your safety."

"I know that," she said hastily. "That's perfectly reasonable." (All the same, she thought, your problem is that I know, and I know you know, you'd try.) They had reached an impasse. Would it be like suborning a policeman to offer him a drink? "Could I offer you a cup of tea, or a drink before you leave?" Perhaps the tea decontaminated the invitation.

"You're very kind," he said primly. "I'm going to miss my plane if I'm not careful. Well, the other families in town to whom I've spoken have all agreed on the advisability of leaving." He looked at her, and his general disapproval was just diluted by a flash of friendliness. "I do wish you well, Mrs. Megan. You're really very isolated here." ("Oh, there're people next

---

[1] A cucumber-like fruit grown in the West Indies.

942

door ..." she protested; he ignored this.) "Perhaps you'll pass on to Mr. Sewell what I've said. And there's your son to consider."

The implied reproof made her say jauntily, "I'll keep that in mind." She put out her hand, and the Vice-Consul, unable to do less, shook it and restored it to her. "Good-bye, then," he said, and a minute later the jeep started too fast, kicking up sand.

In an attempt to sort out her mind, she sat down on the eroded planks of the porch steps and stared out over the beach to the mad palette of the Caribbean.

She felt she was muttering. When did it all *begin*? She thought that while it had been by laughter that she had first known her husband, it was by a hot and huffy argument, improbably conducted on the fringes of a cocktail party, that the threshold of intimacy had been crossed with Harry. Of all things, the Sermon on the Mount.[2] And hadn't that argument, between a fresh divorcée and a stranger, across a sea and in another world, landed her right here, between Harry and the Vice-Consul?

Isolated by Harry's intensity, they had found themselves on ancient ground: overnight the world could be changed by passive resistance — unflagging, indomitable. To violence, the universal cheek turned, once and for all. In a flash of conviction, that evening Jane had come to believe what she still did, that Harry would let himself, in the proper cause, be martyred without so much as making a fist. Profoundly, this impressed her.

"All *right*," she had said, draining the last drops of her martini, "say you're going to be murdered. You're going to be raped ..." ("Less likely than you, there," he murmured.) "You turn the other cheek; and you *are*. But what do you do when someone else doesn't *want* to be murdered? Turn their cheeks for them? It never tells you about *that*," she said bitterly.

Not then or later had he answered the question to her satisfaction. Was it unanswerable? He never lost that inner assurance that she could see captivating Dan. Undeviating programs are so dear to the young, she thought meanly. But she knew it was more than that.

It was as though Dan had been waiting for Harry. Disconcertingly, the classic case of preparing an adolescent for a resented stepfather reversed itself. Even early on, Jane became aware of a united front, a sort of silent compact, in which Harry's need to proselytize and Dan's to be stable were locked into a kind of dogged intimacy. Why this should frighten her, she had no idea.

As she stared morosely ahead, here, loping jerk jerk along the beach, came the three-legged dog. That dog. The most enchanting of the children who burst onto the sand even in this remote section, when school was out — a liquid-eyed, gentle-faced charmer with the suavest voice — flung stones at the lame dog. "She ogly! See how she go — so!" And he hobbled, jerking. Entranced, doubled with laughter, the children reached for sand, stones.

Through the sprays of magenta bougainvillea, the sky of Ste. Cecile appeared as a mosaic — blue, green, lilac.

"Did he come?"

It was Harry who had come, noiseless on the sand.

"What kind of fish is *that*?"

"That is a turbot. Did he come?"

"Yes. He came. And went."

"And said?"

"And said we should leave."

---

[2] A discourse by Jesus on ethical conduct delivered on the Mount of Olives (Matthew: 5–7).

"Had to leave?"

"No. He stopped short of that. If we're stuck and a coup[3] breaks out, he can't promise us help. You know, I think we *should* go," she added, surprising herself. Did she think so? Politically, or personally?

Harry disappeared into the shadowy interior; a moment later he was back. He sat down beside her, plucked off a sneaker, knocking out sand.

"What did you tell him?"

"That we'd think about it. That we really would."

"Very diplomatic. His own game."

He looked perfectly beautiful, sitting there pulling off his other sneaker. The idealized beachcomber, the tropical poster.

"Look, Harry," she said, "I think we're getting in awfully deep."

She could feel the tightening. "How so?"

"Well, something *is* going to happen. We both know it; it's just *when*. We're isolated here. We're strangers — *really* strangers, I mean. It wouldn't be malice, but we'd just be in between."

"*You* look, my dear," he said in his inspirational, persuasive teacher's voice, his hand on her bare shoulder. "We came here for a year. The place is beautiful. The people are marvelous. I'm working, you're painting. Dan's happier than I've ever seen him. This guy is going to be thrown out eventually. In the most civilized way we'll ever encounter. That isn't something to make us run away. That's good."

"He's not going to be thrown out without a lot of people getting hurt."

"Jane, do you know, in a way it's the most impressive thing I've ever seen. They've lost their jobs, shut their shops, been spied on, pushed around, jailed, worse, much worse. Thugs in police uniforms have been sent after them, looting and smashing. The Barracudas are holding a cocked gun to their heads — and they *march*! That's what they do! No guns, no machetes — they just march and chant and pull in their belts!"

"Harry, I live here too."

"Well, sure. You know, too. But you don't seem to realize how amazing it is. They're forcing him out without a shot."

Here came the black-coral boy; heavily lame, he threw out his left leg in an immense arc, lurching. He had fallen from the top of a coconut palm. Jane had a wild vision of the three-legged dog at his heels. The boy had a small waist, broad gleaming shoulders; and an immense smile and lifted hand for them. Now he angled across toward the Montroses' fence, lurching more heavily in the dry sand. Mrs. Montrose appeared at her gate, and they fell quietly into one of those dialogues of which Jane could not have understood a word. This, although the Montroses, in their sparse conversations with their American neighbors, spoke an English perfectly intelligible, if more musical and differently emphasized. The only time Jane had ever seen Mrs. Montrose laugh was when Jane had asked about "mongeese." But when Mrs. Montrose said "four sheeps" and "three mices," it seemed not so much funny as expressive — more mouse-like, more sheepish.

Far out in the daze of sun, she could see a red object — the sunfish,[4] and two dots, Alexis and Dan.

Harry got up, sneakers in hand. "We're not going to settle it this afternoon," he said. She

---

[3] *Coup d'etat*, a sudden, violent overthrow of a government.

[4] A type of light sailing craft.

saw that he had already settled it. Well. She could leave, and take Dan; but there were too many reasons why she would not.

Alone on the porch, she felt a tiny deflection in the heat. The sun had lowered by a fraction; the sunfish, nearer, was defining itself.

Guns cocked at their heads, said Harry. Barracudas, recruited by Him from the dregs of this and other island jails. How men loved the sound of a cocked rifle: Ton-ton Macoute.[5] Ku Klux Klan. Yet when she and Harry argued, in his domain of words she seemed evasive and cynical. I can't bear the writer in him. In his beginning was the word.

She found Harry's work disconcertingly superior to her own, but never, never his medium. On this tiny island she remained amazed at the progressive detail of her own sight; new shades of purple and rose appeared in the noon sea. She was stunned by the varieties of green: the serious glossy green of the breadfruit, the translucent green of the fringed plantain blades, the trembling play of the flame trees, the palms' hard glitter. Green, what on earth was it? Behind their stilt-house and its path, behind the road, the hill rose in a Rousseau[6] jungle. On its steep garden patches, in violent blues and reds and yellows, the dark distant figures moved in the dawn light when disoriented roosters and insomniac dogs at last fell silent.

Now here came Mr. Montrose out of the house, a hoe in one hand, machete in the other. In the mornings, astride the burro, his buttocks resting just before its tail, the huge balanced milk cans at his knees, he wore one day a yellow, the next a violet shirt and a ravelling straw hat. Now he wore only faded khaki shorts that blended with his identically colored skin.

Seeing her head turned toward him, he raised his machete slightly in a courteous but formal gesture. In six months they had not got much further than that. At first the Montroses had seemed friendly, though baffled and a bit nervous. But in exact proportion as Dan and Alexis had plunged into their intimacy, the Montroses had retreated into a pattern formal as an armor. Always greetings; now and then a sour-sop or a sapodilla from their tree, sent via Alexis; once, some cassava cakes made by Mrs. Montrose.[7] Never an acceptance or an invitation.

Twice Jane, meeting Mrs. Montrose coming home from market, or carrying on her head the big wicker basket of clothes to the line stretched across the dusty yard, had rather timidly suggested a cup of tea. Mrs. Montrose had smiled, her teeth strong and white, while she dropped her eyes, saying nothing whatever. Jane instinctively knew this was not rudeness; it was the dilemma of someone unable to accept and not possessed of the formulas of refusal. Jane had thorough sympathy for this. Was Mrs. Montrose to say that she had an engagement for tea every day for six months?

Jane did not waste much time speculating as to whether all this was Mr. Montrose. But she knew, infallibly, that it had to do with Dan. She could see that Mr. Montrose, no fanatic, could not well forbid his son to associate with a next-door neighbor of almost the same age; but though he treated Dan with the same grave courtesy, Jane knew that he found Dan an extraordinary phenomenon, and feared and disliked the friendship. What was Dan doing here in the first place? Why was he not at school or at work? Why did he call his father Harry? How could his parents (did Mr. Montrose think they *were* his parents?) permit his tone in talking to them? When the Montrose family went to Mass on Sunday — Christabel and Eugenie-

---

[5] Haitian secret police.

[6] Henri Rousseau (1844–1910), French primitive painter.

[7] Sour-sop: spiny, tropical fruit with tart, edible pulp; sapodilla: apple-like tropical fruit; cassava: plant with starchy, edible root.

Marie in starched dresses and long white socks, Alexis in a crisp short-sleeved shirt, Mrs. Montrose in pond-lilies on red, and Mr. Montrose in dark trousers and a shirt of palmetto palms—their three neighbors could be prone on the beach, practically naked, Dan sulking at Alexis's departure (no cricket); or on the sunfish; or Jane could have set off with her gear and Harry could be rattling on his portable, stopping constantly to curse and bemoan his electric typewriter, useless in its corner.

Jane had had a solitary conversation with Mrs. Montrose. It had left her with a curious sense of warmth and communication, though it had led to nothing whatsoever.

Five or six weeks after the ménage's[8] installation, Jane — possibly propelled by an inability to deal with the evasions of tropic green — had been driven in nostalgic defiance to a canvas of snow crystals. Three lit within the limits of the canvas, one disappeared in mid-pattern over the edge. On the black background they looked like stellar intentions.

Coming past in her royal walk, three coconuts in a small basket on her erect head, Mrs. Montrose had unwillingly but helplessly paused.

"What it is?" she said.

"They're snow crystals," said Jane shyly. "Flakes of snow," she added in response to the glance Mrs. Montrose had transferred to her face and back to the canvas.

To this Mrs. Montrose said nothing, and together they stared at the flakes, unmelting in the brutal sun. When Jane thought, we will drown in silence ..., Mrs. Montrose said, her eyes still on the canvas, "You did see snow?"

"Oh yes. We have it often."

"It is whiter than sand?"

"Oh, much. When it first falls."

"It does lie on the ground? Right on the ground? You have walked on it? Right on over it?"

"Yes," said Jane. Suddenly envious she thought, I've never seen snow!

They stood there for a minute, isolated and intimate. Then Mrs. Montrose gave her a small adventurous smile, bent, and cradled the basket in her arms. She raised one hand in the familiar sidelong gesture and, without looking back, went through her wooden gate, across the bare yard and up the steps into the house.

Jane repeated to herself, I don't think I've ever seen snow ..., but she felt an exhilaration welling up inside her. She began cleaning her brushes, hissing a little song. Something wonderful had happened. What? Now we can't ever be strangers. She couldn't wait to tell Harry; but she never did. Because peace was his specialty, and she was not sure what kind of peace she had to talk about. Always Harry thought "community," but she knew sadly that he hadn't gained an inch on this sandy strip. "The mango community?" she had jeered once.

The sunfish was right off the beach. It turned over, as usual, and Alexis and Dan, floundering in the water, pushed it in and dragged it up the sand. By now Dan was the same shade as Alexis. Christabel and Eugenie-Marie, like Mrs. Montrose, were mahogany dark.

Jane waved to the boys; they waved hastily back. Already they had the bats and the tennis ball out of the old beached and dissolving rowboat in which they were deposited each morning, shoved down from dogs and other marauders. There had been difficulties over those bats. The boys at first had played, like other children up the beach, with flat pieces of found wood; then one day Harry came back in the minimoke[9] with two cheap cricket bats. At once,

---

[8] Persons living together as a household unit.

[9] Minibus.

Mr. Montrose had jibbed.[10] Finally it had been diplomatically settled that while both bats were Dan's, Alexis had possession of one.

Now down the hard sand Alexis was running, releasing the straight-arm pitch. At first Jane had imagined that it was because Dan thought baseball as Alexis thought cricket, that Dan could never compare. Then, her trained eye taking in the motions, she saw that it would never change. Alexis ran, and pitched, and batted, as he swam, as he climbed a bare bole,[11] as he dove, with a fluid power. Dan said proudly that Alexis was the best cricketer in his school. "He's going to get a scholarship somewhere — maybe Jamaica or Trinidad. He's going to be like V. Richards.[12] He's going to be better," said Dan, carried away.

Oddly, it was Alexis, daily embroiled in their lives, who stopped Jane. She did, and she did not know him. Instantly, she had had a sense of almost intimacy — a drawing toward. Was it that of a painter? The marvelous texture of the skin, the head's perfection, the movement as worth watching as a secret dance, the quick deep luminous look? Though he smiled, he never laughed with her; but she could hear him; soft, irresistible convulsions, broken up, falling against the rowboat-skeleton, with Dan's staccato yelps.

After a while she began to understand that, the end of a long year come, she would never know Alexis. Separated, he and Dan would remember each other as part of the sun and sand and salt-wind, as in patches of light and happiness. She — and she thought, Harry — would be to Alexis figures come and gone, strange and not very interesting. She thought of the boys as a frieze against the sea.

As she went into the house, Jane could see through the window the peaceable kingdom: the water picking up red from the sun's angle, the red sailfish on the humped sand; on the gleaming edge, the boys against the sea.

There was Mr. Montrose, calling to Alexis to come now, come; and crossing to the back window she watched as Alexis rounded the house, crossed the lane and shot up the hill. She followed his blue trunks through layers of green; then here he came, the white goat trailing behind, stopping to snatch at a frond and jerking ahead. The green growth hid, revealed, hid, revealed them. The goat, shoved into its shed, let out its stammering vibration.

"What did you say to that guy?" Dan had come up behind her. His hair was still damp from sweat or sea water, the cricket bat was over his shoulder. "We saw his jeep when he left. What did you say to him?"

Conscious of a male alliance, she had begun to feel like a witness under interrogation. "I told him we'd think about what he said."

"Which was?" He had picked up Harry's mannerisms, his inflections.

"Which was that we should get out. Now."

Dan's face darkened, he leaned against the house wall. "Silly wimp," he said. "Petty official."

Amazed, Jane heard herself shouting on behalf of Mr. Adams.

"Dan! Don't be such an idiot! You know absolutely nothing about what's going to happen."

"Neither does he."

"Look, there's no use yelling at each other!" ("*I* wasn't yelling ..." said Dan.) "We'll just have to reach some sort of sensible decision. As a family," she piously added.

---

[10] Balked.

[11] The trunk of a tree.

[12] Vivian Richards (b. 1952), West Indian cricket player.

"Harry says He can't take the pressure much longer. He'll have to have elections like He promised. Now the teachers are out, they're going to have the kids march too."

She looked at him. "Not unless their parents are crazy. People disappear here, Dan. They just *disappear*."

"No kid is going to disappear; He's got to pretend."

"All right, no child is going to disappear. But someone is going to get shot in public, not just in private. And when that starts ..."

"Suppose Gandhi had said that? Suppose the people who lay down on the tracks ..."

"Oh go and wash *up*!" she said rudely. "I'm tired of being preached at."

A great beginning, she thought, for the family decision-making process. Why did discussions of peace inevitably produce fury? She put her hand on her fist and stared at the low sun; it was the top half of a blood orange, exactly touching sea level.

The first time she had seen Him was at close hand. She was walking down the real road, cautiously on the edge of the jagged cavity of its deep stone gutter, when the black big car, flying its small intense flag, had slid past her. Flanked by two burly figures, the face familiar from posters, under the military cap, the eyes invisible behind the ritual dark glasses, had stared straight ahead. A second car followed closely. That was when He was still playing for respectability, still the emerging statesman, the strong but just father of His island, paternal rather than fascist. There was, in the stance of the rigid chauffeur, the three faces expressionless behind their formality, the middle man's head advanced a little, like a dominant vulture, something which made everything suddenly real. That's what they've all looked like, she had thought, chilled.

She went in to the icebox. It was almost empty. Tomorrow, Saturday, was market day. By thinking of how much chance she would have to be alone tomorrow, she discovered the depth of her uncertainty. Was *she* the wimp? When she had arrived in Ste. Cecile, one question had loomed: marriage. It drew and repelled her. She desired, admired, probably loved Harry; she believed in his toughness, his kindness, the absolute quality of his integrity. Did it really matter that that integrity's expression sometimes frightened and infuriated her? He and Dan. She thought snidely, lucky devils! What bliss total commitment must be. How long was she going on this way, perhaps yes, perhaps no, perhaps leaving, perhaps staying? Alone with Harry the choice would be easy. It was Dan. But how on earth was Dan going to get hurt? Yet in moments she knew he would. He would throw a stone, he will yell at Him.

Then all at once, the thread of patience snapped. Tomorrow, away for hours and hours from the pressure of voices, of presences, for worse or better, she would harden her mushy mind. She felt like the heroine of an opera; she even said aloud, "I *am* Dan's mother ..."

That evening they played Scrabble.

The light from the kerosene lamp enveloped them with — *mollesse*,[13] she thought, a light unknown to the glare of a bulb: cheekbones, eyes, the faded, rather dirty shirts, took on a luminous look so that the three sat — man, woman and boy — untroubled, archetypal, in the light's soft pulse. Outside the sea hissed and hushed, hissed and hushed. A faint indeterminate calypso just touched their ears. The dogs answered each other, near, far up in the hills, bark bark bark. Bark. Bark bark. Already, a manic rooster crowed. This is peace. But she knew it to be armistice.

She was taking the minimoke all the way to Bellemore to paint the new boat; they were building it there. Elevated, the spare ribs were still fresh-cut wood; the shape, bow, prow, were

---

[13] Softness.

there. It went very slowly. Somehow it was wonderful to see tree turn to skeleton, earth-growth to marine intention; the ancient shape, near any sea, always. She must market first; when she came back, all the best fruit and vegetables would be gone. She was alarmed at how delight rose in her at the thought of being alone.

"Q on a triple," said Dan, and his face lit with just Michael's[14] look.

The rough sketch was all right, but the rudimentary painting was a disaster. She stopped, wiping her brushes, going into the bush to pee, then sitting on the frame of the inevitable wrecked rowboat, opening her thermos. But even after she decided just what was wrong, the painting balked. The magic of promise in the bare ribs, strong, complex, but still only a shape, was broken. All she had was a mathematical structure. Ah, but she had another structure, complete, in her mind; she knew she could hold to something, once given. She was going to stay.

Everything had been a risk. Mixing her life so deeply with Harry's resolute and single mind; pulling up stakes from friends and the full, competitive world of her work; being remote among people of a different race plunged in their own rough struggle. Either it was worth it or not. The mania that Dan would be shot, would be arrested, would be hurt in some preventable way, left her. Was hero-worship so dangerous? In a world of vicious enmities, was it so perilous if Dan saw Harry as pointing the path to light, to which there was one way only?

Her grandmother had used a palm-leaf fan; she hadn't seen one in years, Jane realized. Why had she thought of that pale yellow shine, so remote from its gusty green? Then her grandmother's dictum came, as though the lacquered fan had wafted it. In the inn of decision, the mind sleeps well. Now she entered, tired, rejoicing.

The nets, fishy-smelling, lay on the sand. Haul over, the racks of tiny fish dried in the sun. There was only an old man, grizzled and small, sitting on a log, his pipe out but clenched, his rheumy eyes meeting hers as she gathered up her load. He smiled. His teeth were intermittent, but from leathery lips he said, with the air of a host, "How are you, Mistress?"

At first she had naively winced at the address, then felt a fool for her assumption, when she discovered it to be pure Elizabethan courtesy, extended to the washerwoman, the goat-tender.

"Well," she said, meaning it. "Thank you, well." She dumped her gear in the minimoke; there was the pile of fruit and vegetables. Uncertain, embarrassed, she lifted a mango.

"May I offer you this?" she formally asked. The old man removed his pipe. Screwing up his eyes, he considered. "What it is?" he asked; then, seeing, "Is it ripe?" he asked with interest. She stepped forward and handed it to him. He took it in his used-up hands, turning it. "It is ripe," he said. "My wife and I will eat it tonight. I will give it to she." He had not thanked her. It was as though they had collaborated on a logical action.

She climbed into the minimoke and turned the key.

"You are from Cal-i-for-nia?" he called, his pipe in the air. They all asked her that. The movie nearest to him was a tin building at the other end of the island. But he asked the same question.

Cutting the wheel, she called back, "No. I come from Baltimore."

Disappointed by the useless name, he put his pipe back in his mouth and juggled the mango a little in his hands. He had lost interest.

The marketplace, when she turned into it, was empty. Boxes, stands deserted; shards of

---

[14] St. Michael, archangel who conducts souls to God.

vegetables, a broken crate. Two Barracudas, lounging over rifles. A hot sick pang went through her. She tramped on the brakes and leaned out.

"What's happened to the market?" she called to the nearer policeman. He stared at her, less with hostility than contempt. He hefted his rifle. "That does be closed!" he called back.

"What's happened? Has something happened?" she shouted at him, but he only gave her a wide cold smile.

She saw now that in all directions the streets were empty. Along the sea wall, two more Barracudas strolled. A very old woman, bent, in bright blue, came out of the Catholic church a steep block uphill.

I mustn't drive too fast, she thought. Small pastel houses, wooden shacks shot by. Here came a whole lorry of Barracudas; forced to the edge of the steep stone gutter, she nearly lost control. Now she began to see a few people, in small groups, on the steps of houses, under the high porches.

They'd never do anything to Dan or Harry. Americans. Not unless there was fighting. And there isn't — look, there's a girl driving home two goats. But all the tension of weeks sang in her nerves. On her right she could see the beach flying past her. At the final turn the minimoke rocked precariously, shot down the lane and fetched up in a shower of sand.

There was Harry, on the porch. He had his arms crossed and he stared at her. She could feel her blood drain.

"Where's Dan?"

"He's in his room."

"Is he all right? What's happened?"

"Of course he's all right," said Harry irascibly.

She had been gripping the wheel so hard she could scarcely straighten her fingers. "What's happened?" she said again. She couldn't decide whether Harry looked angry or exalted; at any rate, strange. At the steps, she cried again, "What's happened?"

"All hell," he said. "His goons broke up a march. A man got shot. Where are you going? Dan's door's locked." He grabbed her wrist. "Jane! Just sit down a minute, will you? Just ease off a little. I'll tell you all about everything. Sit *down* a minute."

But she was already knocking lightly at the door.

At once Dan's voice, keyed high, said, "Not now ... Go away. Please, go away."

Harry had followed her. He passed her; at the cupboard he pulled out a bottle of Mount Gay, gathered two glasses.

"Dan's perfectly all right," he said. "Give him a little time. Come on out on the porch."

Like a knot in her gut, Jane could feel the anger swelling. "I take it there was a march." She followed Harry outside. He poured rum in each glass.

"Yes, there was a march," he said.

"You knew about it ahead of time?"

"Not really. Word gets around fast, you know."

"And I take it you marched?"

He held out the glass to her with a small friendly gesture, and she shook her head. "That's right."

"You took Dan?"

"I didn't 'take' Dan. He'd been planning to go."

"I told him he couldn't."

"Jane, a time comes when you can't make that stick."

Angrily she met his eyes; she saw then how badly he was shaken. Suddenly she felt exhausted. Nothing irrevocable had happened. She was undermined by Harry's face.

She took up the rejected glass and leaned against the rough railing, staring unseeingly at the Montroses' empty yard of dust.

"I can't fight about it now, Harry. But how could you, behind my back? Who was the man? Was he killed?"

"I don't know. Yes. The Barracudas were cracking heads, and he yanked away a police club. It wasn't behind your back. You just weren't here. You couldn't have stopped Dan. He's fifteen."

"*You* could!" she said in a flare of bitterness. She saw in Harry's face an odd mingling of the old stubborn glory and a curious timidity. But he said doggedly, "I wouldn't if I could have. He's old enough to have a conscience and a will, Jane. In three years he could be drafted. He's old enough to know what he believes."

"Was it the shooting?" Jane said uncertainly. "Did he see it?"

Something was unspoken. Harry turned the glass round and round. "No, actually he didn't."

"Then why ... ?"

To her amazement she saw Harry's eyes blur with pain.

"It's Alexis."

"*Alexis!*"

He looked at her miserably.

"Alexis got hurt."

"*Alexis* was marching?"

"He came with Dan."

"They let him?"

"Mr. Montrose was on his route. I think his mother had walked into town. To the market."

"*You* let him?"

"For God's sake, Jane. I've no earthly power over Alexis. He scarcely believes I exist. I didn't want him to come."

"Wasn't he worth proselytizing?"

Harry did not answer that.

"What happened to him?"

"A policeman hit him in the head — but it wasn't that. He was knocked flying down into the gutter. You know what those are. He broke something in his back. We didn't even know. It was a madhouse and we were separated."

"How do you know now?"

"Dan and I went to look for him, and we couldn't find him. After we got back, the police came."

"Here?"

"To tell his parents. Montrose had just got back. He went off with the policeman, to the hospital. Dan tried to go, but Mr. Montrose ... He was so upset he didn't know what he was saying," said Harry bleakly. "When Mrs. Montrose got back, I tried to drive her to the hospital but — for Christ's sake, Jane, how do you think *I* feel?"

"Well, how *do* you feel?" she said; and then the community of their misery stopped her. "How bad is it?"

"Dan and I went to the hospital. They'd left word we weren't to be allowed to see Alexis. It's pretty bad, I think. Of course, these doctors ... The back is broken and there are some internal injuries — I don't think they're very positive about anything yet. At least, I don't see how they can be." His face looked pared, polished. Round and round he turned his emptied glass. She reached over and touched his shoulder, and in his eyes tears appeared, for whom she was not sure.

They stayed there, silent. The tide was coming in, pushing the curved bubbling fringe up over the high sand. A way down the beach they could just hear faint thin shouts; tiny shapes ran and pitched. Games had resumed.

At that moment two figures appeared, coming slowly down the path from the road: the Montroses. Ahead walked Mr. Montrose; a few paces behind came his wife. Without hesitation, without a glance, they passed through their gate, across the yard, up the steps to the house.

"I'm going over," said Jane.

"Wait till tomorrow," said Harry quickly. "Don't go right now."

"I *can't* wait," said Jane. "Don't you see? We can't just sit here — us here, them over there. We can't."

"Dan tried to say something to Mr. Montrose. I wish you'd wait."

"I can't." She stood up.

"Look," Harry said in a desperate whisper. "They can't tell really how bad it is yet. But it is bad. Leave them alone."

Jane went down the steps. She thought she had never walked so far as to the Montroses' gate. I won't just keep saying I'm sorry, I'm sorry. The house was silent. A small lizard darted by her toe. The cricket shouts just reached her ears. She knocked at the door.

As if he had been waiting behind it, Mr. Montrose stood before her. Her instant impression was of distance — the fierce remoteness in his gaze paralyzed her.

She said, "Mr. Montrose, I've just heard about Alexis. How bad is it?" she said. From a million miles, from a million years, the eyes watched her. At last he said, "The back is broke up. The hip too." Slowly, impersonally he added, "No way they can fix it right."

"They can't say that!" she cried, terrified. "This is just a tiny hospital. In Trinidad — please, *please* let us send him to Trinidad!"

The face changed so that Jane recoiled.

"You go to hell," said Mr. Montrose very slowly. "Where you is come from. Evil, evil, evil. All of you. Go home — if you do have one."

Behind his shoulder appeared Mrs. Montrose's head; her hand covered her mouth.

I can't move, thought Jane. I am here forever.

"You come here," said Mr. Montrose. "Why? Why you come? You are devils. Go where you come from. You are evil." Then he added with formality, "If you do stay here, you will die."

She couldn't tell if it were a threat or a statement. She looked behind him at Mrs. Montrose's face — it had a strange expression as though it were being pulled apart.

"I'm going," she said to the still figure towering over her. "We're going." With a huge effort she moved, turning. Then she stopped.

"Dan and Alexis are friends," she said.

At that, suddenly Mr. Montrose let out a kind of howl. "*He* should be there, in that place!" he shouted. "Never he should run again! Bad things will come to him, you have done it. You will see. Bad things."

Mrs. Montrose moved suddenly forward, but his right arm shot out pushing her back. Halfway to her steps, Jane heard the door close.

The next morning while there was dew everywhere and the air was still fresh, Harry drove them to the airport. Dan sat in the back.

He had not spoken since late last night when he had found no shelter.

"I won't go," he said then.

Jane, beyond tact, beyond persuasion, said, "You have to. I'm taking you home."

"I'm staying here," he said. "I'm staying with Harry."

"No, you're not, Dan," said Harry. They were down to raw statement. "I won't have you. You've got to go with your mother now."

"I won't go. How can you make me? Carry me? Call the Barracudas?"

"You can't stay right now, Dan," said Harry more gently. "How could you? Not here, not next door. Where?"

"I'll stay with the Montroses!" he cried. There was a small silence. Dan began to weep. Jane touched his hand but, as though she had burned it, he flinched. He gazed furiously at Harry. "You quit!" he said thickly. "The very first thing, you quit! You give up! You give me up! You tell me something, you make a big deal, and then you quit!"

"What's that?" said Jane quickly. "That was a knock."

"It wasn't a knock," said Harry. "It was someone on the porch."

They listened: dogs, dogs; and the sea. Harry got up and walked over to the door. He said over his shoulder, "If someone's here, just give me a chance to talk to them. Right?" At the door he raised his voice. "Yes?"

No voice answered. Harry turned the brown glazed handle and the door opened on the scented night. As it did so, something fell forward onto the floor and lay there shining a little: a cricket bat. They stared at it, its handle oiled with sweat, soaked in sun and salt. Then Dan darted over and snatched it up. He took it and went into his room. The bolt shot in its slot.

A few miles from the airport, dawn arrived. First the outline of tinged clouds, separate in their drift. Then a sort of enormous renovation of the sky — it cleared, produced a faint pure blue, gradually lit all the greens. On the edges of the road children appeared, with cans or bundles. A man overtaken in his loose barefoot stride raised a machete in greeting.

Jane was transfixed by the dailiness. Light would come just like this through the Montroses' red curtains; over Alexis, asleep or awake, announcing the day of hours, minutes, seconds. Of the first boats, and the sea's colors, and the sand. And in the afternoons, the rich fall of that blood orange, the yells and shouts and flat hard sound of the plank bats. Alexis would indeed remember his neighbors.

At the airport, the waves ran up almost to the runway. The tiny plane already sat there.

At the head of the narrow steps, the tall brown stewardess obstructed them, her voice bored and musical. Of course the cricket bat would not fit under any seat. Forbidden to frown, the stewardess smiled in annoyance. She took the bat gingerly and, carrying it before her, wedged it upright in the coat section.

Dan would not sit with her. But, like a damaging consolation, she knew that already, willing the opposite, he was fleeing — mutinous, looking back — but fleeing something he couldn't bear now, or change, ever.

Harry would be confirmed. Or not. How far he went, to them or from them, what happened, what became of everything, was part of the unfinished. Now he still hoped all things, money, doctors, something. The principle was sacrifice; but what of Harry now that Alexis had stolen it, to carry?

They vibrated violently. The tarmac[15] slid toward them. There was the wheels' *chock*, a wing tilted and the few dark figures fell away.

---

[15] Pavement of crushed stone and tar.

They were over the sea, and through the thick glass she saw the green bright land, valleys, dense hills, falling, falling, bright and small and smaller, in its particular shape, releasing them to the universal sky.

QUESTIONS

1. To what extent are Harry, Jane, and Dan part of the island community? Of what other communities are they members? What is the "mango community"?

2. What artistic pursuits are Jane and Harry involved in? Compare the different mediums in which they work. How are their chosen arts appropriate to their characters? What sensibilities do the different arts cultivate?

3. Discuss the conflict between politics and personal life in the story. Do any characters successfully resolve this conflict? In what ways is the search for peace — political and personal — frustrated?

4. What does Jane's painting of the snowflakes represent? Why does she paint snow? What does she learn from this work?

ALISTAIR MACLEOD

In the Fall

We'll just have to sell him," I remember my mother saying with finality. "It will be a long winter and I will be alone here with only these children to help me. Besides he eats too much and we will not have enough feed for the cattle as it is."

It is the second Saturday of November and already the sun seems to have vanished for the year. Each day dawns duller and more glowering and the waves of the grey Atlantic are sullen and almost yellow at their peaks as they pound relentlessly against the round smooth boulders that lie scattered as if by a careless giant at the base of the ever-resisting cliffs. At night, when we lie in our beds, we can hear the waves rolling in and smashing, rolling in and smashing, so relentless and regular that it is possible to count rhythmically between the thunder of each: one, two, three, four; one, two, three, four.

It is hard to realize that this is the same ocean that is the crystal blue of summer when only the thin oil-slicks left by the fishing boats or the startling whiteness of the riding seagulls mar its azure sameness. Now it is roiled and angry, and almost anguished; hurling up the brown dirty balls of scudding foam, the sticks of pulpwood from some lonely freighter, the caps of unknown men, buoys from mangled fishing nets and the inevitable bottles that contain no messages. And always also the shreds of blackened and stringy seaweed that it has ripped and torn from its own lower regions, as if this is the season for self-mutilation — the pulling out of the secret, private, unseen hair.

We are in the kitchen of our house and my mother is speaking as she energetically pokes at the wood and coal within her stove. The smoke escapes, billows upward and flattens itself out against the ceiling. Whenever she speaks she does something with her hands. It is as if the private voice within her can only be liberated by some kind of physical action. She is tall and dark with high cheek-bones and brown eyes. Her hair which is very long and very black is pulled back severely and coiled in a bun at the base of her neck where it is kept in place by combs of coral.

My father is standing with his back toward us and is looking out the window to where the ocean pounds against the cliffs. His hands are clasped behind his back. He must be squeezing them together very tightly because they are almost white — especially the left. My father's left hand is larger than his right and his left arm is about three inches longer than normal. That is because he holds his stevedore's hook in his left hand when he works upon the waterfront in Halifax.[1] His complexion is lighter than my mother's and his eyes are grey which is also the predominant colour of his thinning hair.

We have always lived on the small farm between the ocean and the coal-mining town. My father has always worked on his land in the summer and at one time he would spend his winters working within the caverns of the coal mine. Later when he could bear the underground no longer he had spent the time from November to April as an independent coal-hauler or working in his woodlot where he cut timbers for the mine roof's support. But it must have been a long time ago for I can scarcely remember a time when the mine worked steadily or a winter when he has been with us and I am almost fourteen. Now each winter he goes to Halifax but he is often a long time in going. He will stand as he does now, before the window, for perhaps a week or more and then he will be gone and we will see him only at Christmas and on the odd weekend; for he will be over two hundred miles away and the winter storms will make travelling difficult and uncertain. Once, two years ago, he came home for a weekend and the blizzard came so savagely and with such intensity that he could not return until Thursday. My mother told him he was a fool to make such a journey and that he had lost a week's wages for nothing — a week's wages that she and six children could certainly use. After that he did not come again until it was almost spring.

"It wouldn't hurt to keep him another winter," he says now, still looking out the window. "We've kept him through all of them before. He doesn't eat much now since his teeth have gone bad."

"He was of some use before," says my mother shortly and rattling the lids of her stove. "When you were home you used him in the woods or to haul coal — not that it ever got us much. These last years he's been worthless. It would be cheaper to rent a horse for the summer or perhaps even hire a tractor. We don't need a horse anymore, not even a young one, let alone one that will probably die in March after we've fed him all that time." She replaces the stove-lids — all in their proper places.

They are talking about our old horse Scott who has been with us all of my life. My father had been his driver for two winters in the underground and they had become fond of one another and in the time of the second spring, when he left the mine forever, the man had purchased the horse from the Company so that they might both come out together to see the sun and walk upon the grass. And that the horse might be saved from the blindness that would inevitably come if he remained within the deeps; the darkness that would make him like itself.

At one time he had even looked like coal, when his coat was black and shiny strong, relieved by only a single white star in the centre of his forehead; but that too was a long time ago and now he is very grey about the eyes and his legs are stiff when he first begins to walk.

"Oh, he won't die in March," says my father, "he'll be okay. You said the same thing last fall and he came through okay. Once he was on the grass again he was like a two-year-old."

For the past three or four years Scott has had heaves.[2] I guess heaves come to horses from living too near the ocean and its dampness; like asthma comes to people, making them cough and sweat and struggle for breath. Or perhaps from eating dry and dusty hay for two many winters in the prison of a narrow stall. Perhaps from old age too. Perhaps from all of them. I don't know. Someone told my little brother David who is ten that dampening the hay would help, and last winter from early January when Scott began to cough really bad, David would take a dipper of water and sprinkle it on the hay after we'd put it in the manager. Then David would say the coughing was much better and I would say so too.

---

[1] Capital and largest city of Nova Scotia.

[2] Pulmonary disease of horses; also called "broken wind."

"He's not a two-year-old," says my mother shortly and begins to put on her coat before going out to feed her chickens. "He's old and useless and we're not running a rest home for retired horses. I am alone here with six children and I have plenty to do."

Long ago when my father was a coal-hauler and before he was married he would sometimes become drunk, perhaps because of his loneliness, and during a short February day and a long February night he had drunk and talked and slept inside the bootlegger's oblivious to the frozen world without until in the next morning's dehydrated despair he had staggered to the door and seen both horse and sleigh where he had left them and where there was no reason for them to be. The coal was glowing black on the sleigh beneath the fine powdered snow that seems to come even when it is coldest, seeming more to form like dew than fall like rain, and the horse was standing like a grey ghostly form in the early morning's darkness. His own black coat was covered with the hoar frost that had formed of yesterday's sweat, and tiny icicles hung from his nose.

My father could not believe that the horse had waited for him throughout the night of bitter cold, untied and unnecessary, shifting his feet on the squeaking snow, and flickering his muscles beneath the frozen harness. Before that night he had never been waited for by any living thing and he had buried his face in the hoar-frost mane and stood there quietly for a long, long time, his face in the heavy black hair and the ice beading on his cheeks.

He has told us this story many times even though it bores my mother. When he tells it David sits on his lap and says that he would have waited too, no matter how long and no matter how cold. My mother says she hopes David would have more sense.

"Well, I have called MacRae and he is to come for him today," my mother says as she puts on her coat and prepares to feed her chickens. "I wanted to get it over with while you were still here. The next thing I know you'll be gone and we'll be stuck with him for another winter. Grab the pail, James," she says to me, "come and help me feed the chickens. At least there's some point in feeding them."

"Just a minute," he says, "just a goddamn minute." He turns quickly from the window and I see his hands turn into fists and his knuckles white and cold. My mother points to the younger children and shakes her head. He is temporarily stymied because she has so often told him he must not swear before them and while he hesitates we take our pails and escape.

As we go to where the chickens are kept, the ocean waves are even higher, and the wind has risen so that we have to use our bodies to shield the pails that we carry. If we do not their contents will be scooped out and scattered wildly to the skies. It is beginning to rain and the drops are so driven by the fierceness of the wind that they ping against the galvanized sides of the pails and sting and then burn upon our cheeks.

Inside the chicken-house it is warm and acrid as the chickens press around us. They are really not chickens any more but full-grown capons which my mother has been raising all summer and will soon sell on the Christmas market. Each spring she gets day-old chicks and we feed them ground-up hardboiled eggs and chick-starter. Later we put them into outside pens and then in the fall into this house where they are fattened. They are Light Sussex which is the breed my mother favours because they are hardy and good weight-producers. They are very, very white now with red combs and black and gold glittering eyes and with a ring of startling black at the base of their white, shining necks. It is as if a white fluid had been poured over their heads and cascaded down their necks to where it suddenly and magically changed to black after exposure to the air. The opposite in colour but the same in lustre. Like piano keys.

My mother moves about them with ease and they are accustomed to her and jostle about her as she fills their troughs with mash and the warm water we have brought. Sometimes I like them and sometimes I do not. The worst part seems to be that it doesn't really matter. Before Christmas they will all be killed and dressed and then in the spring there will be another group and they will always look and act and end in the same way. It is hard to really like what you are planning to kill and almost as hard to feel dislike, and when there are many instead of one they begin to seem almost as the blueberries and strawberries we pick in summer. Just a whole lot of them to be alive in their way for a little while and then to be picked and eaten, except it seems the berries would be there anyway but the capons we are responsible for and encourage them to eat a great deal, and try our best to make them warm and healthy and strong so that we may kill them in the end. My father is always uncomfortable around them and avoids them as much as possible. My friend Henry Van Dyken says that my father feels that way because he is Scottish, and that Scotsmen are never any good at raising poultry or flowers because they think such tasks are for women and that they make a man ashamed. Henry's father is very good at raising both.

As we move about the closeness of the chicken-house the door bangs open and David is almost blown in upon us by the force of the wind and the rain. "There's a man with a big truck that's got an old bull on it," he says, "he just went in the house."

When we enter the kitchen MacRae is standing beside the table, just inside the door. My father is still at the window, although now with his back to it. It does not seem that they have said anything.

MacRae, the drover, is in his fifties. He is short and heavy-set with a red face and a cigar in the corner of his mouth. His eyes are small and bloodshot. He wears Wellington boots[3] with his trousers tucked inside them, a broad western-style belt, and a brown suede jacket over a flannel shirt which is open at the neck exposing his reddish chest-hair. He carries a heavy stock whip in his hand and taps it against the side of his boot. Because of his short walk in the wind-driven rain his clothes are wet and now in the warmth of the kitchen they give off a steamy, strong odour that mingles uncomfortably with that of his cigar. An odour that comes of his jostling and shoving the countless frightened animals that have been carried on the back of his truck, an odour of manure and sweat and fear.

"I hear you've got an old knacker," he says now around the corner of his cigar, "might get rid of him for mink-feed if I'm lucky. The price is twenty dollars."

My father says nothing, but his eyes which seem the grey of the ocean behind him remind me of a time when the log which Scott was hauling seemed to ricochet wildly off some half-submerged obstacle, catching the man's legs beneath its onrushing force and dragging and grinding him beneath it until it smashed into a protruding stump, almost uprooting it and knocking Scott back upon his haunches. And his eyes then in their greyness had reflected fear and pain and almost a mute wonder at finding himself so painfully trapped by what seemed all too familiar.

And it seemed now that we had, all of us, conspired against him, his wife and six children and the cigar-smoking MacRae, and that we had almost brought him to bay with his back against the ocean-scarred window so pounded by the driving rain and with all of us ringed before him. But still he says nothing although I think his mind is racing down all the possible avenues of argument, and rejecting all because he knows the devastating truth that awaits him at the end of each: "There is no need of postponing it; the truck is here and there will never be a better opportunity; you will soon be gone; he will never be any younger; the price will never be any higher; he may die this winter and we will get nothing at all; we are not running a rest

---

[3] Boot that extends to the top of the knee in front but is cut low in back; popularized by the first Duke of Wellington.

home for retired horses; I am alone here with six children and I have more than enough to do; the money for his feed could be spent on your children; don't your children mean more to you than a horse; it is unfair to go and leave us here with him to care for."

Then with a nod he moves from the window and starts toward the door. "You're not ..." begins David, but he is immediately silenced by his mother. "Be quiet," she says, "go and finish feeding the chickens," and then, as if she cannot help it, "at least there is some point in feeding them." Almost before my father stops, I know she is sorry about the last part. That she fears that she has reached for too much and perhaps even now has lost all she had before. It is like when you attempt to climb one of the almost vertical sea-washed cliffs, edging upward slowly and groping with blue-tipped fingers from one tiny crevice to the next and then seeing the tantalizing twig which you cannot resist seizing, although even as you do, you know it can be grounded in nothing for there is no vegetation there nor soil to support it and the twig is but a reject tossed up there by the sea, and even then you are tensing yourself for the painful, bruising slide that must inevitably follow. But this time for my mother, it does not. He only stops and looks at her for a moment before forcing open the door and going out into the wind. David does not move.

"I think he's going to the barn," says my mother then with surprising softness in her voice, and telling me with her eyes that I should go with him. By the time MacRae and I are outside he is already half-way to the barn; he has no hat nor coat and is walking sideways and leaning and knifing himself into the wind which blows his trousers taut against the outlines of his legs.

As MacRae and I pass the truck I cannot help but look at the bull. He is huge and old and is an Ayrshire. He is mostly white except for the almost cherry-red markings of his massive shoulders and on his neck and jowls. His heavy head is forced down almost to the truck's floor by a reinforced chain halter and by a rope that has been doubled through his nose ring and fastened to an iron bar bolted to the floor. He has tried to turn his back into the lashing wind and rain and his bulk is pressed against the truck's slatted side at an unnatural angle to his grotesquely fastened head. The floor of the truck is greasy and slippery with a mixture of the rain and his own excrement, and each time he attempts to move, his feet slide and threaten to slip from under him. He is trembling with the strain, and the muscles in his shoulders give involuntary little twitches and his eyes roll upward in their sockets. The rain mingles with his sweat and courses down his flanks in rivulets of grey.

"How'd you like to have a pecker on you like that fella," shouts MacRae into the wind. "Bet he's had his share and driven it into them little heifers a good many times. Boy you get hung like that, you'll have all them horny little girls squealen' for you to take 'em behind the bushes. No time like it with them little girls, just when the juice starts runnin' in 'em and they're finding out what it's for." He runs his tongue over his lips appreciatively and thwacks his whip against the sodden wetness of his boot.

Inside the barn it is still and sheltered from the storm. Scott is in the first stall and then there is a vacant one and then those of the cattle. My father has gone up beside Scott and is stroking his nose but saying nothing. Scott rubs his head up and down against my father's chest. Although he is old he is still strong and the force of his neck as he rubs almost lifts my father off his feet and pushes him against the wall.

"Well, no time like the present," says MacRae, as he unzips his fly and begins to urinate in the alleyway behind the stalls.

The barn is warm and close and silent, and the odour from the animals and from the hay is almost sweet. Only the sound of MacRae's urine and the faint steam that rises from it disturb the silence and the scene. "Ah sweet relief," he says rezipping his trousers and giving his knees a little bend for adjustment as he turns toward us. "Now let's see what we've got here."

He puts his back against Scott's haunches and almost heaves him across the stall before walking up beside him to where my father stands. The inspection does not take long; I suppose because not much is expected of future mink-feed. "You've got a good halter on him there," says MacRae, "I'll throw in a dollar for it, you won't be needing it anyway." My father looks at him for what seems a very long time and then almost imperceptibly nods his head. "Okay," says MacRae, "twenty-one dollars, a deal's a deal." My father takes the money, still without saying anything, opens the barn door and without looking backward walks through the rain toward his house. And I follow him because I do not know what else to do.

Within the house it is almost soundless. My mother goes to the stove and begins rinsing her teapot and moving her kettle about. Outside we hear MacRae starting the engine of his truck and we know he is going to back it against the little hill beside the barn. It will be easier to load his purchase from there. Then it is silent again, except for the hissing of the kettle which is now too hot and which someone should move to the back of the stove; but nobody does.

And then all of us are drawn with a strange fascination to the window, and, yes, the truck is backed against the little hill as we knew and MacRae is going into the barn with his whip still in his hand. In a moment he reappears leading Scott behind him.

As he steps out of the barn the horse almost stumbles but regains his balance quickly. Then the two ascend the little hill, both of them turning their faces from the driving rain. Scott stands quietly while MacRae lets down the tailgate of his truck. When the tailgate is lowered it forms a little ramp from the hill to the truck and MacRae climbs it with the halter-shank in his hand, tugging it impatiently. Scott places one foot on the ramp and we can almost hear, or perhaps I just imagine it, the hollow thump of his hoof upon the wet planking; but then he hesitates, withdraws his foot and stops. MacRae tugs at the rope but it has no effect. He tugs again. He comes half-way down the little ramp, reaches out his hand, grasps the halter itself and pulls; we can see his lips moving and he is either coaxing or cursing or both; he is facing directly into the rain now and it is streaming down his face. Scott does not move. MacRae comes down from the truck and leads Scott in a wide circle through the wet grass. He goes faster and faster, building up speed and soon both man and horse are almost running. Through the greyness of the blurring, slanting rain they look almost like a black-and-white movie that is badly out of focus. Suddenly without changing speed MacRae hurries up the ramp of the truck and the almost trotting horse follows him, until his hoof strikes the tailboard. Then he stops suddenly. As the rope jerks taut, MacRae who is now in the truck and has been carried forward by his own momentum is snapped backward; he bounces off the side of the bull, loses his footing on the slimy planking and falls into the wet filth of the truck box's floor. Almost before we can wonder if he is hurt, he is back upon his feet; his face is livid and his clothes are smeared with manure and running brown rivulets; he brings the whip, which he has somehow never relinquished even in his fall, down savagely between the eyes of Scott, who is still standing rigidly at the tailgate. Scott shakes his head as if dazed and backs off into the wet grass trailing the rope behind him.

It has all happened so rapidly that we in the window do not really know what to do, and are strangely embarrassed by finding ourselves where we are. It is almost as if we have caught ourselves and each other doing something that is shameful. Then David breaks the spell. "He is not going to go," he says, and then almost shouts, "He is just not going to go — ever. Good for him. Now that he's hit him, it's for sure. He'll never go and he'll have to stay." He rushes toward my father and throws his arms around his legs.

And then the door is jerked open and MacRae is standing there angrily with his whip still in his hand. His clothes are still soggy from his fall and the water trails from them in brown drops upon my mother's floor. His face is almost purple as he says, "Unless I get that fucken' horse on the truck in the next five minutes, the deal's off and you'll be a goddamn long time tryen' to get anybody else to pay that kinda money for the useless old cocksucker."

It is as if all of the worst things one imagines happening suddenly have. But it is not at all as you expected. And I think I begin to understand for the first time how difficult and perhaps how fearful it is to be an adult and I am suddenly and selfishly afraid not only for myself now but for what it seems I am to be. For I had somehow always thought that if one talked like that before women or small children or perhaps even certain men that the earth would open up or lightning would strike or that at least many people would scream and clap their hands over their ears in horror or that the offender if not turned to stone would certainly be beaten by a noble, clean-limbed hero. But it does not happen that way at all. All that happens is the deepening of the thunder-cloud greyness in my father's eyes and the heightening of the colour in my mother's cheeks. And I realize also with a sort of shock that in spite of Scott's refusal to go on the truck nothing has really changed. I mean not really; and that all of the facts remain awfully and simply the same: that Scott is old and that we are poor and that my father must soon go away and that he must leave us either with Scott or without him. And that it is somehow like my mother's shielding her children from 'swearing' for so many years, only to find one day that it too is there in its awful reality in spite of everything that she had wished and wanted. And even as I am thinking this my father goes by MacRae who is still standing in the ever-widening puddles of brown, seeming like some huge growth that is nourished by the foul-smelling waters that he himself has brought.

David who had released my father's legs with the entrance of MacRae makes a sort of flying tackle for them now but I intercept him and find myself saying as if from a great distance my mother's phrases in something that sounds almost like her voice, "Let's go and finish feeding the chickens." I tighten my grip on his arm and we almost have to squeeze past MacRae whose bulk is blocking the doorway and who has not yet made a motion to leave.

Out of doors my father is striding directly into the slashing rain to where Scott is standing in something like puzzlement with his back to the rain and his halter-shank dangling before him. When he sees my father approach he cocks his ears and nickers in recognition. My father who looks surprisingly slight with his wet clothes plastered to his body takes the rope in his hand and moves off with the huge horse following him eagerly. Their movement seems almost that of the small tug docking the huge ocean freighter, except that they are so individually and collectively alive. As they approach the truck's ramp, it is my father who hesitates and seems to flinch, and it is his foot which seems to recoil as it touches the planking; but on the part of Scott there is no hesitation at all; his hooves echo firmly and confidently on the strong wet wood and his head is almost pressed into the small of my father's back; he is so eager to get to wherever they are going.

He follows him as I have remembered them all of my life and imagined them even before. Following wildly through the darkened caverns of the mine in its dryness as his shoes flashed sparks from the tracks and the stone; and in its wetness with both of them up to their knees in water, feeling rather than seeing the landing of their splashing feet and with the coal cars thundering behind them with such momentum that were the horse to stumble the very cars he had set in motion would roll over him, leaving him mangled and grisly to be hauled above ground only as carrion for the wheeling gulls. And on the surface, following, in the summer's heat with the jolting haywagon and the sweat churned to froth between his legs and beneath his collar, fluttering white on the blackness of his glistening coat. And in the winter, following, over the semi-frozen swamps as the snapping, whistling, logs snaked behind him, grunting as he broke through the shimmering crystal ice which slashed his fetlocks and caused a scarlet trail of bloodied perforations on the whiteness of the snow. And in the winter, too, with the ton of coal upon the sleigh, following, even over the snowless stretches, driven bare by the wind, leaning low with his underside parallel and almost touching the ground, grunting, and swinging with violent jolts to the right and then to the left, moving the sleigh forward only by moving it sideways, which he had learned was the only way it would move at all.

Even as my father is knotting the rope, MacRae is hurrying past us and slamming shut the tailgate and dropping down the iron bolts that will hold it in its place. My father climbs over the side of the box and down as MacRae steps onto the running-board and up into the cab. The motor roars and the truck lurches forward. It leaves two broad wet tracks in the grass like the trails of two slimy, giant slugs and the smell of its exhaust hangs heavy on the air. As it makes the turn at the bottom of the lane Scott tries to turn his head and look back but the rope has been tied very short and he is unable to do so. The sheets of rain come down like so many slanted, beaded curtains making it impossible to see what we know is there, and then there is only the receding sound of the motor, the wet trails on the grass and the exhaust fumes in the air.

It is only then that I realize that David is no longer with me, but even as the question comes to the surface so also does its answer and I run toward the squawking of the chicken-house.

Within the building it is difficult to see and difficult to breathe and difficult to believe that so small a boy could wreck such havoc in so short a time. The air is thick with myriad dust particles from the disturbed floor, and bits of straw and tiny white scarlet-flecked feathers eddy and dip and swirl. The frightened capons, many of them already bloodied and mangled, attempt short and ungainly flights, often colliding with each other in mid-air. Their overfed bodies are too heavy for their weak and unused wings and they are barely able to get off the floor and flounder for a few feet before thumping down to dusty crippled landings. They are screaming with terror and their screams seem as unnatural as their flights, as if they had been terribly miscast in the most unsuitable of roles. Many of them are already lifeless and crumpled and dustied and bloodied on the floor, like sad, grey, wadded newspapers that had been used to wipe up blood. The sheen of their feathers forever gone.

In the midst of it all David moves like a small blood-spattered dervish swinging his axe in all directions and almost unknowingly, as if he were blindfolded. Dust has settled on the dampness of his face and the tears make tiny trails through its greyness, like lonely little rivers that have really nothing to water. A single tiny feather is plastered to his forehead and he is coughing and sobbing, both at the same time.

When my father appears beside me in the doorway he seems to notice for the first time that he is not alone. With a final exhausted heave he throws the axe at my father. "Cocksucker," he says in some kind of small, sad parody of MacRae, and bolts past us through the door almost colliding with my mother who now comes from out of the rain. He has had very little strength with which to throw the axe and it clatters uselessly off the wall and comes to rest against my father's boot, wet and bloodied with feathers and bits of flesh still clinging to its blade.

I am tremendously sorry for the capons, now so ruined and so useless, and for my mother and for all the time and work she has put into them for all of us. But I do not know what to do and I know not what to say.

As we leave the melancholy little building the wind cuts in from the ocean with renewed fury. It threatens to lift you off your feet and blow you to the skies and your crotch is numb and cold as your clothes are flattened hard against the front of your body, even as they tug and snap at your back in insistent, billowing balloons. Unless you turn or lower your head it is impossible to breathe for the air is blown back almost immediately into your lungs and your throat convulses and heaves. The rain is now a stinging sleet which is rapidly becoming the winter's first snow. It is impossible to see into it, and the ocean off which it rushes is lost in the swirling whiteness although it thunders and roars in its invisible nearness like the heavy bass blending with the shrieking tenor of the wind. You hear so much that you can hardly hear at all. And you are almost immobile and breathless and blind and deaf. Almost but not quite. For by turning and leaning your body and your head, you can move and breathe and see and hear a little at a time. You do not gain much but you can hang on to what little you have and your toes curl almost instinctively within your shoes as if they are trying to grasp the earth.

I stop and turn my face from the wind and look back the way I have come. My parents are there, blown together behind me. They are not moving, either, only trying to hold their place. They have turned sideways to the wind and are facing and leaning into each other with their shoulders touching, like the end-timbers of a gabled roof. My father puts his arms around my mother's waist and she does not remove them as I have always seen her do. Instead she reaches up and removes the combs of coral from the heaviness of her hair. I have never seen her hair in all its length before and it stretches out now almost parallel to the earth, its shining blackness whipped by the wind and glistening like the snow that settles and melts upon it. It surrounds and engulfs my father's head and he buries his face within its heavy darkness, and draws my mother closer toward him. I think they will stand there for a long, long time, leaning into each other and into the wind-whipped snow and with the ice freezing to their cheeks. It seems that perhaps they should be left alone so I turn and take one step and then another and move forward a little at a time. I think I will try to find David, that perhaps he may understand.

QUESTIONS

1. In what conflict are the narrator's father and mother engaged? What differences do their attitudes toward animals reveal? How does selling the horse change their situation?

2. Where does the narrator stand in the conflict between his parents? Does he seem to favor one parent or another? What tone does he adopt in relating the events? How does he differ from David?

3. How old do you think the narrator is? Is the vocabulary he uses in his narration plausible for a youth that age? What effect does the style have on your perceptions of the narrator and events?

4. Consider Macleod's use of the ocean and weather as counterpoint to the story's action. How do the descriptive scenes affect the mood and provide thematic commentary?

BOBBIE ANN MASON ≡

Graveyard Day

Waldeen's daughter Holly, swinging her legs from the kitchen stool, lectures her mother on natural foods. Holly is ten and too skinny.

Waldeen says, "I'll have to give your teacher a talking-to. She's put notions in your head. You've got to have meat to grow."

Waldeen is tenderizing liver, beating it with the edge of a saucer. Her daughter insists that she is a vegetarian. If Holly had said Rosicrucian,[1] it would have sounded just as strange to Waldeen. Holly wants to eat peanuts, soyburgers, and yogurt. Waldeen is sure this new fixation has something to do with Holly's father, Joe Murdock, although Holly rarely mentions him. After Waldeen and Joe were divorced last September, Joe moved to Arizona and got a construction job. Joe sends Holly letters occasionally, but Holly won't let Waldeen see them. At Christmas he sent her a copper Indian bracelet with unusual marks on it. It is Indian language, Holly tells her. Waldeen sees Holly polishing the bracelet while she is watching TV.

Waldeen shudders when she thinks of Joe Murdock. If he weren't Holly's father, she might be able to forget him. Waldeen was too young when she married him, and he had a reputation for being wild. Now she could marry Joe McClain, who comes over for supper almost every night, always bringing something special, such as a roast or dessert. He seems to be oblivious to what things cost, and he frequently brings Holly presents. If Waldeen married Joe, then Holly would have a stepfather — something like a sugar substitute, Waldeen imagines. Shifting relationships confuse her. She tells Joe they must wait. Her ex-husband is still on her mind, like the lingering aftereffects of an illness.

Joe McClain is punctual, considerate. Tonight he brings fudge ripple ice cream and a half gallon of Coke in a plastic jug. He kisses Waldeen and hugs Holly.

Waldeen says, "We're having liver and onions, but Holly's mad 'cause I won't make Soybean Supreme."

"Soybean *Delight*," says Holly.

"Oh, excuse me!"

"Liver is full of poison. The poisons in the feed settle in the liver."

"Do you want to stunt your growth?" Joe asks, patting Holly on the head. He winks at Waldeen and waves his walking stick at her playfully, like a conductor. Joe collects walking

---

[1] Member of an international order of religious mystics.

sticks, and he has an antique one that belonged to Jefferson Davis. On a gold band, in italics, it says *Jefferson Davis*. Joe doesn't go anywhere without a walking stick, although he is only thirty. It embarrasses Waldeen to be seen with him.

"Sometimes a cow's liver just explodes from the poison," says Holly. "Poisons are *oozing* out."

"Oh, Holly, hush, that's disgusting." Waldeen plops the pieces of liver onto a plate of flour.

"There's this restaurant at the lake that has Liver Lovers' Night," Joe says to Holly. "Every Tuesday is Liver Lovers' Night."

"Really?" Holly is wide-eyed, as if Joe is about to tell a long story, but Waldeen suspects Joe is bringing up the restaurant — Bob's Cove at Kentucky Lake — to remind her that it was the scene of his proposal. Waldeen, not accustomed to eating out, studied the menu carefully, wavering between pork chops and T-bone steak, and then suddenly, without thinking, ordering catfish. She was disappointed to learn that the catfish was not even local, but frozen ocean cat. "Why would they do that," she kept saying, interrupting Joe, "when they've got all the fresh channel cat in the world right here at Kentucky Lake?"

During supper, Waldeen snaps at Holly for sneaking liver to the cat, but with Joe gently persuading her, Holly manages to eat three bites of liver without gagging. Holly is trying to please him, as though he were some TV game-show host who happened to live in the neighborhood. In Waldeen's opinion, families shouldn't shift membership, like clubs. But here they are, trying to be a family. Holly, Waldeen, Joe McClain. Sometimes Joe spends the weekends, but Holly prefers weekends at Joe's house because of his shiny wood floors and his parrot that tries to sing "Inka-Dinka-Doo." Holly likes the idea of packing an overnight bag.

Waldeen dishes out the ice cream. Suddenly inspired, she suggests a picnic Saturday. "The weather's fairing up," she says.

"I can't," says Joe. "Saturday's graveyard day."

"Graveyard day?" Holly and Waldeen say together.

"It's my turn to clean off the graveyard. Every spring and fall somebody has to rake it off." Joe explains that he is responsible for taking geraniums to his grandparents' graves. His grandmother always kept them in her basement during the winter, and in the spring she took them to her husband's grave, but she had died in November.

"Couldn't we have a picnic at the graveyard?" asks Waldeen.

"That's gruesome."

"We never get to go on picnics," says Holly. "Or anywhere." She gives Waldeen a look.

"Well, O.K.," Joe says. "But remember, it's serious. No fooling around."

"We'll be real quiet," says Holly.

"Far be it from me to disturb the dead," Waldeen says, wondering why she is speaking in a mocking tone.

After supper, Joe plays rummy with Holly while Waldeen cracks pecans for a cake. Pecan shells fly across the floor, and the cat pounces on them. Holly and Joe are laughing together, whooping loudly over the cards. They sound like contestants on *Let's Make a Deal*. Joe Murdock had wanted desperately to be on a game show and strike it rich. He wanted to go to California so he would have a chance to be on TV and so he could travel the freeways. He drove in the stock car races, and he had been drag racing since he learned to drive. Evel Knievel was his hero. Waldeen couldn't look when the TV showed Evel Knievel leaping over canyons. She told Joe many times, "He's nothing but a show-off. But if you want to break your fool neck, then go right ahead. Nobody's stopping you." She is better off without Joe Murdock. If he were still in town, he would do something to make her look foolish, such as paint her name on his car door. He once had WALDEEN painted in large red letters on the door of his LTD. It was like a tattoo. It is probably a good thing he is in Arizona. Still, she cannot really understand why he had to move so far away from home.

After Holly goes upstairs, carrying the cat, whose name is Mr. Spock, Waldeen says to Joe, "In China they have a law that the men have to help keep house." She is washing the dishes.

Joe grins. "That's in China. This is *here*."

Waldeen slaps at him with the dish towel, and Joe jumps up and grabs her. "I'll do all the housework if you marry me," he says. "You can get the Chinese to arrest me if I don't."

"You sound just like my ex-husband. Full of promises."

"Guys named Joe are good at making promises." Joe laughs and hugs her.

"All the important men in my life were named Joe," says Waldeen, with pretended seriousness. "My first real boyfriend was named Joe. I was fourteen."

"You always bring that up," says Joe. "I wish you'd forget about them. You love *me*, don't you?"

"Of course, you idiot."

"Then why don't you marry me?"

"I just said I was going to think twice is all."

"But if you love me, what are you waiting for?"

"That's the easy part. Love is easy."

In the middle of *The Waltons*, C. W. Redmon and Betty Mathis drop by. Betty, Waldeen's best friend, lives with C. W., who works with Joe on a construction crew. Waldeen turns off the TV and clears magazines from the couch. C. W. and Betty have just returned from Florida and they are full of news about Sea World. Betty shows Waldeen her new tote bag with a killer whale pictured on it.

"Guess who we saw at the Louisville airport," Betty says.

"I give up," says Waldeen.

"Colonel Sanders!"

"He's eighty-four if he's a day," C. W. adds.

"You couldn't miss him in that white suit," Betty says. "I'm sure it was him. Oh, Joe! He had a walking stick. He went strutting along — "

"No kidding!"

"He probably beats chickens to death with it," says Holly, who is standing around.

"That would be something to have," says Joe. "Wow, one of the Colonel's walking sticks."

"Do you know what I read in a magazine?" says Betty. "That the Colonel Sanders outfit is trying to grow a three-legged chicken."

"No, a four-legged chicken," says C. W.

"Well, whatever."

Waldeen is startled by the conversation. She is rattling ice cubes, looking for glasses. She finds an opened Coke in the refrigerator, but it may have lost its fizz. Before she can decide whether to open the new one Joe brought, C. W. and Betty grab glasses of ice from her and hold them out. Waldeen pours the Coke. There is a little fizz.

"We went first class the whole way," says C. W. "I always say, what's a vacation for if you don't splurge?"

"We spent a fortune," says Betty. "Plus, I gained a ton."

"Man, those big jets are really nice," says C. W.

C. W. and Betty seem changed, exactly like all the people Waldeen has known who come back from Florida with tales of adventure and glowing tans, except that C. W. and Betty did not get tans. It rained. Waldeen cannot imagine flying, or spending that much money. Her ex-husband tried to get her to go up in an airplane with him once — a seven-fifty ride in a Cessna — but she refused. If Holly goes to Arizona to visit him, she will have to fly. Arizona is probably as far away as Florida.

When C. W. says he is going fishing on Saturday, Holly demands to go along. Waldeen reminds her about the picnic. "You're full of wants," she says.

"I just wanted to go somewhere."

"I'll take you fishing one of these days soon," says Joe.

"Joe's got to clean off his graveyard," says Waldeen. Before she realizes what she is saying, she has invited C. W. and Betty to come along on the picnic. She turns to Joe. "Is that O.K.?"

"I'll bring some beer," says C. W. "To hell with fishing."

"I never heard of a picnic at a graveyard," says Betty. "But it sounds neat."

Joe seems embarrassed. "I'll put you to work," he warns.

Later, in the kitchen, Waldeen pours more Coke for Betty. Holly is playing solitaire on the kitchen table. As Betty takes the Coke, she says, "Let C. W. take Holly fishing if he wants a kid so bad." She has told Waldeen that she wants to marry C. W., but she does not want to ruin her figure by getting pregnant. Betty pets the cat. "Is this cat going to have kittens?"

Mr. Spock, sitting with his legs tucked under his stomach, is shaped somewhat like a turtle.

"Heavens, no," says Waldeen. "He's just fat because I had him nurtured."

"The word is *neutered*!" cries Holly, jumping up. She grabs Mr. Spock and marches up the stairs.

"That youngun," Waldeen says. She feels suddenly afraid. Once, Holly's father, unemployed and drunk on tequila, snatched Holly from the school playground and took her on a wild ride around town, buying her ice cream at the Tastee-Freez, and stopping at Newberry's to buy her an *All in the Family* Joey doll, with correct private parts. Holly was eight. When Joe brought her home, both were tearful and quiet. The excitement had worn off, but Waldeen had vividly imagined how it was. She wouldn't be surprised if Joe tried the same trick again, this time carrying Holly off to Arizona. She has heard of divorced parents who kidnap their own children.

The next day Joe McClain brings a pizza at noon. He is working nearby and has a chance to eat lunch with Waldeen. The pizza is large enough for four people. Waldeen is not hungry.

"I'm afraid we'll end up horsing around and won't get the graveyard cleaned off," Joe says. "It's really a lot of work."

"Why's it so important, anyway?"

"It's a family thing."

"Family. Ha!"

"What do you mean?"

"I don't know what's what anymore," Waldeen wails. "I've got this kid that wants to live on peanuts and sleeps with a cat — and didn't even see her daddy at Christmas. And here *you* are, talking about family. What do you know about family? You don't know the half of it."

"What's got into you lately?"

Waldeen tries to explain. "Take Colonel Sanders, for instance. He was on *I've Got a*

Secret once, years ago, when nobody knew who he was. His secret was that he had a million-dollar check in his pocket for selling Kentucky Fried Chicken to John Y. Brown.[2] *Now* look what's happened. Colonel Sanders sold it but didn't get rid of it. He couldn't escape from being Colonel Sanders. John Y. sold it too, and he can't get rid of it either. Everybody calls him the Chicken King, even though he's governor. That's not very dignified, if you ask me."

"What in Sam Hill are you talking about? What's that got to do with families?"

"Oh, Colonel Sanders just came to mind because C. W. and Betty saw him. What I mean is, you can't just do something by itself. Everything else drags along. It's all *involved*. I can't get rid of my ex-husband just by signing a paper. Even if he *is* in Arizona and I never lay eyes on him again."

Joe stands up, takes Waldeen by the hand, and leads her to the couch. They sit down and he holds her tightly for a moment. Waldeen has the strange impression that Joe is an old friend who moved away and returned, years later, radically changed. She doesn't understand the walking sticks, or why he would buy such an enormous pizza.

"One of these days you'll see," says Joe, kissing her.

"See what?" Waldeen mumbles.

"One of these days you'll see. I'm not such a bad catch."

Waldeen stares at a split in the wallpaper.

"Who would cut your hair if it wasn't for me?" he asks, rumpling her curls. "I should have gone to beauty school."

"I don't know."

"Nobody else can do Jimmy Durante imitations like I can."

"I wouldn't brag about it."

On Saturday, Waldeen is still in bed when Joe arrives. He appears in the doorway of her bedroom, brandishing a shiny black walking stick. It looks like a stiffened black racer snake.

"I overslept," Waldeen says, rubbing her eyes. "First I had insomnia. Then I had bad dreams. Then — "

"You said you'd make a picnic."

"Just a minute. I'll go make it."

"There's not time now. We've got to pick up C. W. and Betty."

Waldeen pulls on her jeans and a shirt, then runs a brush through her hair. In the mirror she sees blue pouches under her eyes. She catches sight of Joe in the mirror. He looks like an actor in a vaudeville show.

They go into the kitchen, where Holly is eating granola. "She promised me she'd make carrot cake," Holly tells Joe.

"I get blamed for everything," says Waldeen. She is rushing around, not sure why. She is hardly awake.

"How could you forget?" asks Joe. "It was your idea in the first place."

"I didn't forget. I just overslept." Waldeen opens the refrigerator. She is looking for something. She stares at a ham.

When Holly leaves the kitchen, Waldeen asks Joe, "Are you mad at me?" Joe is thumping his stick on the floor.

"No. I just want to get this show on the road."

"My ex-husband always said I was never dependable, and he was right. But *he* was one to talk! He had his head in the clouds."

---

[2] Governor of Kentucky, elected 1980.

"Forget your ex-husband."

"His name is Joe. Do you want some fruit juice?" Waldeen is looking for orange juice, but she cannot find it.

"No." Joe leans on his stick. "He's over and done with. Why don't you just cross him off your list?"

"Why do you think I had bad dreams? Answer me that. I must be afraid of something."

There is no orange juice. Waldeen closes the refrigerator door. Joe is smiling at her enigmatically. What she is really afraid of, she realizes, is that he will turn out to be just like Joe Murdock. But it must be only the names, she reminds herself. She hates the thought of a string of husbands, and the idea of a stepfather is like a substitute host on a talk show. It makes her think of Johnny Carson's many substitute hosts.

"You're just afraid to do anything new, Waldeen," Joe says. "You're afraid to cross the street. Why don't you get your ears pierced? Why don't you adopt a refugee? Why don't you get a dog?"

"You're crazy. You say the weirdest things." Waldeen searches the refrigerator again. She pours a glass of Coke and watches it foam.

It is afternoon before they reach the graveyard. They had to wait for C. W. to finish painting his garage door, and Betty was in the shower. On the way, they bought a bucket of fried chicken. Joe said little on the drive into the country. When he gets quiet, Waldeen can never figure out if he is angry or calm. When he put the beer cooler in the trunk, she caught a glimpse of the geraniums in an ornate concrete pot with a handle. It looked like a petrified Easter basket. On the drive, she closed her eyes and imagined that they were in a funeral procession.

The graveyard is next to the woods on a small rise fenced in with barbed wire. A herd of Holsteins grazes in the pasture nearby, and in the distance the smokestacks of the new industrial park send up lazy swirls of smoke. Waldeen spreads out a blanket, and Betty opens beers and hands them around. Holly sits under a tree, her back to the gravestones, and opens a Vicki Barr flight stewardess novel.

Joe won't sit down to eat until he has unloaded the geraniums. He fusses over the heavy basket, trying to find a level spot. The flowers are not yet blooming.

"Wouldn't plastic flowers keep better?" asks Waldeen. "Then you wouldn't have to lug that thing back and forth." There are several bunches of plastic flowers on the graves. Most of them have fallen out of their containers.

"Plastic, yuck!" cries Holly.

"I should have known I'd say the wrong thing," says Waldeen.

"My grandmother liked geraniums," Joe says.

At the picnic, Holly eats only slaw and the crust from a drumstick. Waldeen remarks, "Mr. Spock is going to have a feast."

"You've got a treasure, Waldeen," says C. W. "Most kids just want to load up on junk."

"Wonder how long a person can survive without meat," says Waldeen, somewhat breezily. But she suddenly feels miserable about the way she treats Holly. Everything Waldeen does is so roundabout, so devious. Disgusted, Waldeen flings a chicken bone out among the graves. Once, her ex-husband wouldn't bury the dog that was hit by a car. It lay in a ditch for over a week. She remembers Joe saying several times, "Wonder if the dog is still there." He wouldn't admit that he didn't want to bury it. Waldeen wouldn't do it because he had said he would do it. It was a war of nerves. She finally called the Highway Department to pick it up. Joe McClain, she thought now, would never be that barbaric.

Joe pats Holly on the head and says, "My girl's stubborn, but she knows what she likes." He makes a Jimmy Durante face, which causes Holly to smile. Then he brings out a surprise for her, a bag of trail mix, which includes pecans and raisins. When Holly pounces on it, Waldeen notices that Holly is not wearing the Indian bracelet her father gave her. Waldeen wonders if there are vegetarians in Arizona.

Blue sky burns through the intricate spring leaves of the maples on the fence line. The light glances off the gravestones — a few thin slabs that date back to the last century and eleven sturdy blocks of marble and granite. Joe's grandmother's grave is a brown heap.

Waldeen opens another beer. She and Betty are stretched out under a maple tree and Holly is reading. Betty is talking idly about the diet she intends to go on. Waldeen feels too lazy to move. She watches the men work. While C. W. rakes leaves, Joe washes off the gravestones with water he brought in a plastic jug. He scrubs out the carvings with a brush. He seems as devoted as a man washing and polishing his car on a Saturday afternoon. Betty plays he-loves-me-he-loves-me-not with the fingers of a maple leaf. The fragments fly away in a soft breeze.

From her Sea World tote bag, Betty pulls out playing cards with Holly Hobbie pictures on them. The old-fashioned child with the bonnet hiding her face is just the opposite of Waldeen's own strange daughter. Waldeen sees Holly watching the men. They pick up their beer cans from a pink, shiny tombstone and drink a toast to Joe's great-great-grandfather, Joseph McClain, who was killed in the Civil War. His stone, almost hidden in dead grasses, says 1841–1862.

"When I die, they can burn me and dump the ashes in the lake," says C. W.

"Not me," says Joe. "I want to be buried right here."

"*Want* to be? You planning to die soon?"

Joe laughs. "No, but if it's my time, then it's my time. I wouldn't be afraid to go."

"I guess that's the right way to look at it."

Betty says to Waldeen, "He'd marry me if I'd have his kid."

"What made you decide you don't want a kid, anyhow?" Waldeen is shuffling the cards, fifty-two identical children in bonnets.

"Who says I decided? You just do whatever comes natural. Whatever's right for you." Betty drinks from her can of beer.

"Most people do just the opposite," Waldeen says. "They have kids without thinking."

"Talk about decisions," Betty goes on, "did you see *Sixty Minutes* when they were telling about Palm Springs? And how all those rich people live? One woman had hundreds of dresses, and Morley Safer was asking her how she ever decided what on earth to wear. He was *strolling* through her closet. He could have played *golf* in her closet."

"Rich people don't know beans," says Waldeen. She drinks some beer, then deals out the cards for a game of hearts. Betty snatches each card eagerly. Waldeen does not look at her own cards right away. In the pasture, the cows are beginning to move. The sky is losing its blue. Holly seems lost in her book, and the men are laughing. C. W. stumbles over a footstone hidden in the grass and falls onto a grave. He rolls over, curled up with laughter.

"Y'all are going to kill yourselves," Waldeen says, calling across the graveyard.

Joe tells C. W. to shape up. "We've got work to do," he says.

Joe looks over at Waldeen and mouths something. "I love you"? She suddenly remembers a Ku Klux Klansman she saw on TV. He was being arrested at a demonstration, and as he was led away in handcuffs, he spoke to someone off-camera, ending with a solemn message, "I love you." He was acting for the camera, as if to say, "Look what a nice guy I am." He gave

Waldeen the creeps. That could have been Joe Murdock, Waldeen thinks. Not Joe McClain. Maybe she is beginning to get them straight in her mind. They have different ways of trying to get through to her.

Waldeen and Betty play several hands of hearts and drink more beer. Betty is clumsy with the cards and loses three hands in a row. Waldeen cannot keep her mind on the cards either. She wins accidentally. She can't concentrate because of the graves, and Joe standing there saying "I love you." If she marries Joe, and doesn't get divorced again, they will be buried here together. She picks out a likely spot and imagines the headstone and the green carpet and the brown leaves that will someday cover the twin mounds. Joe and C. W. are bringing leaves to the center of the graveyard and piling them on the place she has chosen. Waldeen feels peculiar, as if the burial plot, not a diamond ring, symbolizes the promise of marriage. But there is something comforting about the thought, which she tries to explain to Betty.

"Ooh, that's gross," says Betty. She slaps down a heart and takes the trick.

Waldeen shuffles the cards for a long time. The pile of leaves is growing dramatically. Joe and C. W. have each claimed a side of the graveyard, and they are racing. It occurs to Waldeen that she has spent half her life watching guys named Joe show off for her. Once, when Waldeen was fourteen, she went out onto the lake with Joe Suiter in a rented pedal boat. When Waldeen sees him at the bank, where he works, she always remembers the pedal boat and how they stayed out in the silver-blue lake all afternoon, ignoring the people waving them in from the shore. When they finally returned, Joe owed ten dollars in overtime on the boat, so he worked Saturdays, mowing yards, to pay for their spree. Only recently in the bank, when they laughed together over the memory, he told her that it was worth it, for it was one of the great adventures of his life, going out in a pedal boat with Waldeen, with nothing but the lake and time.

Betty is saying, "We could have a nice bonfire and a wienie roast — what *are* you doing?"

Waldeen has pulled her shoes off. Then she is taking a long, running start, like a pole vaulter, and then with a flying leap she lands in the immense pile of leaves, up to her elbows. Leaves are flying and everyone is standing around her, forming a stern circle, and Holly, with her book closed on her fist, is saying, "Don't you know *anything*?"

QUESTIONS

1. There are many references throughout the story to media figures and popular culture. Discuss their significance as commentary on the characters and action.

2. Why does Waldeen have trouble sorting out the Joes in her life? How do they compare?

3. What is the meaning of Waldeen's leap into the pile of leaves at the end of the story? Does her action tell us anything about her future relationship with Joe?

4. "You just do whatever comes natural," Betty tells Waldeen. Where in the story does this idea recur? What is its thematic significance?

ALICE MUNRO ═══════

Spelling

In the store, in the old days, Flo used to say she could tell when some woman was going off the track. Special headgear or footwear were often the first giveaways. Galoshes flopping open on a summer day. Rubber boots they slopped around in, or men's workboots. They might say it was on account of corns, but Flo knew better. It was deliberate, it was meant to tell. Next might come the old felt hat, the torn raincoat worn in all weathers, the trousers held up at the waist with twine, the dim shredded scarves, the layers of ravelling sweaters.

Mothers and daughters often the same way. It was always in them. Waves of craziness, always rising, irresistible as giggles, from some place deep inside, gradually getting the better of them.

They used to come telling Flo their stories. Flo would string them along. "Is that so?" she would say. "Isn't that a shame?"

My vegetable grater is gone and I know who took it.

There is a man comes and looks at me when I take my clothes off at night. I pull the blind down and he looks through the crack.

Two hills of new potatoes stolen. A jar of whole peaches. Some nice ducks' eggs.

One of those women they took to the County Home at last. The first thing they did, Flo said, was give her a bath. The next thing they did was cut off her hair, which had grown out like a haystack. They expected to find anything in it, a dead bird or maybe a nest of baby mouse skeletons. They did find burrs and leaves and a bee that must have got caught and buzzed itself to death. When they had cut down far enough they found a cloth hat. It had rotted on her head and the hair had just pushed up through it, like grass through wire.

Flo had got into the habit of keeping the table set for the next meal, to save trouble. The plastic cloth was gummy, the outline of the plate and saucer plain on it as the outline of pictures on a greasy wall. The refrigerator was full of sulfurous scraps, dark crusts, furry oddments. Rose got to work cleaning, scraping, scalding. Sometimes Flo came lumbering through on her two canes. She might ignore Rose's presence altogether, she might tip the jug of maple syrup up against her mouth and drink it like wine. She loved sweet things now, craved them. Brown sugar by the spoonful, maple syrup, tinned puddings, jelly, globs of sweetness to slide down her throat. She had given up smoking, probably for fear of fire.

Another time she said, "What are you doing in there behind the counter? You ask me what you want, and I'll get it." She thought the kitchen was the store.

972

"I'm *Rose*," Rose said in a loud, slow voice. "We're in the *kitchen*. I'm cleaning up the *kitchen*."

The old arrangement of the kitchen: mysterious, personal, eccentric. Big pan in the oven, medium-sized pan under the potato pot on the corner shelf, little pan hanging on the nail by the sink. Colander under the sink. Dishrags, newspaper clippings, scissors, muffin tins, hanging on various nails. Piles of bills and letters on the sewing machine, on the telephone shelf. You would think someone had set them down a day or two ago, but they were years old. Rose had come across some letters written by herself, in a forced and spritely style. False messengers; false connections, with a lost period of her life.

"Rose is away," Flo said. She had a habit now of sticking her bottom lip out, when she was displeased or perplexed. "Rose got married."

The second morning Rose got up and found that a gigantic stirring-up had occurred in the kitchen, as if someone had wielded a big shaky spoon. The big pan was lodged behind the refrigerator; the egg lifter was in with the towels, the bread knife was in the flour bin and the roasting pan wedged in the pipes under the sink. Rose made Flo's breakfast porridge and Flo said, "You're that woman they were sending to look after me."

"Yes."

"You aren't from around here?"

"No."

"I haven't got money to pay you. They sent you, they can pay you."

Flo spread brown sugar over her porridge until the porridge was entirely covered, then patted the sugar smooth with her spoon.

After breakfast she spied the cutting board, which Rose had been using when she cut bread for her own toast. "What is this thing doing here getting in our road?" said Flo authoritatively, picking it up and marching off — as well as anybody with two canes could march — to hide it somewhere, in the piano bench or under the back steps.

Years ago, Flo had had a little glassed-in side porch built on to the house. From there she could watch the road just as she used to watch from behind the counter of the store (the store window was now boarded up, the old advertising signs painted over). The road wasn't the main road out of Hanratty through West Hanratty to the Lake anymore; there was a highway bypass. And it was paved, now, with wide gutters, new mercury vapor street lights. The old bridge was gone and a new, wide bridge, much less emphatic, had taken its place. The change from Hanratty to West Hanratty was hardly noticeable. West Hanratty had got itself spruced up with paint and aluminum siding; Flo's place was about the only eyesore left.

What were the things Flo put up to look at, in her little porch, where she had been sitting for years now with her joints and arteries hardening?

A calendar with a picture of a puppy and a kitten on it. Faces turned toward each other so that the noses touched, and the space between the two bodies made a heart.

A photograph, in color, of Princess Anne as a child.

A Blue Mountain pottery vase, gift from Brian and Phoebe, with three yellow plastic roses in it, vase and roses bearing several seasons' sifting of dust.

Six shells from the Pacific coast, sent home by Rose but not gathered by her, as Flo believed, or had once believed. Bought on a vacation in the state of Washington. They were an impulse item in a plastic bag by the cashier's desk in a tourist restaurant.

THE LORD IS MY SHEPHERD, in black cutout scroll with a sprinkling of glitter. Free gift from a dairy.

Newspaper photograph of seven coffins in a row. Two large and five small. Parents and children, all shot by the father in the middle of the night, for reasons nobody knew, in a farmhouse out in the country. That house was not easy to find but Flo had seen it. Neighbors took her, on a Sunday drive, in the days when she was using only one cane. They had to ask directions at a gas station on the highway, and again at a crossroads store. They were told that many people had asked the same questions, had been equally determined. Though Flo had to admit there was nothing much to see. A house like any other. The chimney, the windows, the shingles, the door. Something that could have been a dish towel, or a diaper, that nobody had felt like taking in, left to rot on the line.

Rose had not been back to see Flo for nearly two years. She had been busy, she had been traveling with small companies, financed by grants, putting on plays or scenes from plays, or giving readings, in high school auditoriums and community halls, all over the country. It was part of her job to go on local television chatting about these productions, trying to drum up interest, telling amusing stories about things that had happened during the tour. There was nothing shameful about any of this, but sometimes Rose was deeply, unaccountably ashamed. She did not let her confusion show. When she talked in public she was frank and charming; she had a puzzled, diffident way of leading into her anecdotes, as if she were just now remembering, had not told them a hundred times already. Back in her hotel room, she often shivered and moaned, as if she were having an attack of fever. She blamed it on exhaustion, or her approaching menopause. She couldn't remember any of the people she had met, the charming, interesting people who had invited her to dinner and to whom, over drinks in various cities, she had told intimate things about her life.

Neglect in Flo's house had turned a final corner, since Rose saw it last. The rooms were plugged up with rags and papers and dirt. Pull a blind to let some light in, and the blind comes apart in your hand. Shake a curtain and the curtain falls to rags, letting loose a choking dust. Put a hand into a drawer and it sinks into something soft and dark and rubbishy.

We hate to write bad news but it looks like she has got past where she can look after herself. We try to look in on her but we are not so young ourselves anymore so it looks like maybe the time has come.

The same letter, more or less, had been written to Rose and to her half brother, Brian, who was an engineer, living in Toronto. Rose had just come back from her tour. She had assumed that Brian and his wife, Phoebe, whom she saw seldom, were keeping in touch with Flo. After all, Flo was Brian's mother, Rose's stepmother. And it turned out that they had been keeping in touch, or so they thought. Brian had recently been in South America but Phoebe had been phoning Flo every Sunday night. Flo had little to say but she had never talked to Phoebe anyway; she had said she was fine, everything was fine, she had offered some information about the weather. Rose had observed Flo on the telephone, since she came home, and she saw how Phoebe could have been deceived. Flo spoke normally, she said hello, fine, that was a big storm we had last night, yes, the lights were out here for hours. If you didn't live in the neighborhood you wouldn't realize there hadn't been any storm.

It wasn't that Rose had entirely forgotten Flo in those two years. She had fits of worry about her. It was just that for some time now she had been between fits. One time the fit had come over her in the middle of a January storm, she had driven two hundred miles through blizzards, past ditched cars, and when she finally parked on Flo's street, finally tramped up the walk Flo had not been able to shovel, she was full of relief for herself and concern for Flo, a general turmoil of feelings both anxious and pleasurable. Flo opened the door and gave a bark of warning.

"You can't park there!"

"What?"

"Can't park there!"

Flo said there was a new bylaw; no parking on the streets during the winter months.
"You'll have to shovel out a place."
Of course Rose had an explosion.
"If you say one more word right now I'll get in the car and drive back."
"Well you can't park — "
"One more word!"
"Why do you have to stand here and argue with the cold blasting into the house?"
Rose stepped inside. Home.
That was one of the stories she told about Flo. She did it well; her own exhaustion and sense of virtue; Flo's bark, her waving cane, her fierce unwillingness to be the object of anybody's rescue.

After she read the letter Rose had phoned Phoebe, and Phoebe had asked her to come to dinner, so they could talk. Rose resolved to behave well. She had an idea that Brian and Phoebe moved in a permanent cloud of disapproval of her. She thought that they disapproved of her success, limited and precarious and provincial though it might be, and that they disapproved of her even more when she failed. She also knew it was not likely they would have her on their minds so much, or feel anything so definite.

She put on a plain skirt and an old blouse, but at the last minute changed into a long dress, made of thin red and gold cotton from India, the very thing that would justify their saying that Rose was always so theatrical.

Nevertheless she made up her mind as she usually did that she would speak in a low voice, stick to facts, not get into any stale and silly arguments with Brian. And as usual most of the sense seemed to fly out of her head as soon as she entered their house, was subjected to their calm routines, felt the flow of satisfaction, self-satisfaction, perfectly justified self-satisfaction, that emanated from the very bowls and draperies. She was nervous, when Phoebe asked her about her tour, and Phoebe was a bit nervous too, because Brian sat silent, not exactly frowning but indicating that the frivolity of the subject did not please him. In Rose's presence Brian had said more than once that he had no use for people in her line of work. But he had no use for a good many people. Actors, artists, journalists, rich people (he would never admit to being one himself), the entire Arts faculty of universities. Whole classes and categories, down the drain. Convicted of woolly-mindedness, and showy behavior; inaccurate talk, many excesses. Rose did not know if he spoke the truth or if this was something he had to say in front of her. He offered the bait of his low-voiced contempt; she rose to it; they had fights, she had left his house in tears. And underneath all this, Rose felt, they loved each other. But they could never stop the old, old competition; who is the better person, who has chosen the better work? What were they looking for? Each other's good opinion, which perhaps they meant to grant, in full, but not yet. Phoebe, who was a calm and dutiful woman with a great talent for normalizing things (the very opposite of their family talent for blowing things up), would serve food and pour coffee and regard them with a polite puzzlement; their contest, their vulnerability, their hurt, perhaps seemed as odd to her as the antics of comic-strip characters who stick their fingers into light sockets.

"I always wished Flo could have come back for another visit with us," Phoebe said. Flo had come once, and asked to be taken home after three days. But afterward it seemed to be a pleasure to her, to sit and list the things Brian and Phoebe owned, the features of their house. Brian and Phoebe lived quite unostentatiously, in Don Mills, and the things Flo dwelt on — the door chimes, the automatic garage doors, the swimming pool — were among the ordinary suburban acquisitions. Rose had said as much to Flo who believed that she, Rose, was jealous.

"You wouldn't turn them down if you was offered."

"Yes I would."

That was true, Rose believed it was true, but how could she ever explain it to Flo or anybody in Hanratty? If you stay in Hanratty and do not get rich it is all right because you are living out your life as was intended, but if you go away and do not get rich, or, like Rose, do not remain rich, then what was the point?

After dinner Rose and Brian and Phoebe sat in the backyard beside the pool, where the youngest of Brian and Phoebe's four daughters was riding an inflated dragon. Everything had gone amicably, so far. It had been decided that Rose would go to Hanratty, that she would make arrangements to get Flo into the Wawanash County Home. Brian had already made inquiries about it, or his secretary had, and he said that it seemed not only cheaper but better run, with more facilities, than any private nursing home.

"She'll probably meet old friends there," Phoebe said.

Rose's docility, her good behavior, was partly based on a vision she had been building up all evening, and would never reveal to Brian and Phoebe. She pictured herself going to Hanratty and looking after Flo, living with her, taking care of her for as long as was necessary. She thought how she would clean and paint Flo's kitchen, patch the shingles over the leaky spots (that was one of the things the letter had mentioned), plant flowers in the pots, and make nourishing soup. She wasn't so far gone as to imagine Flo fitting comfortably into this picture, settling down to a life of gratitude. But the crankier Flo got, the milder and more patient Rose would become, and who, then, could accuse her of egotism and frivolity?

This vision did not survive the first two days of being home.

Would you like a pudding?" Rose said.

"Oh, I don't care."

The elaborate carelessness some people will show, the gleam of hope, on being offered a drink.

Rose made a trifle. Berries, peaches, custard, cake, whipped cream and sweet sherry.

Flo ate half the bowlful. She dipped in greedily, not bothering to transfer a portion to a smaller bowl.

"That was lovely," she said. Rose had never heard such an admission of grateful pleasure from her. "Lovely," said Flo and sat remembering, appreciating, belching a little. The suave dreamy custard, the nipping berries, robust peaches, luxury of sherry-soaked cake, munificence of whipped cream.

Rose thought that she had never done anything in her life that came as near pleasing Flo as this did.

"I'll make another soon."

Flo recovered herself. "Oh well. You do what you like."

Rose drove out to the County Home. She was conducted through it. She tried to tell Flo about it when she came back.

"Whose home?" said Flo.

"No, the *County* Home."

Rose mentioned some people she had seen there. Flo would not admit to knowing any of them. Rose spoke of the view and the pleasant rooms. Flo looked angry; her face darkened and she stuck out her lip. Rose handed her a mobile she had bought for fifty cents in the County Home Crafts Center. Cutout birds of blue and yellow paper were bobbing and dancing, on undetectable currents of air.

"Stick it up your arse," said Flo.

Rose put the mobile up in the porch and said she had seen the trays coming up, with supper on them.

"They go to the dining room if they're able, and if they're not they have trays in their rooms. I saw what they were having.

"Roast beef, well done, mashed potatoes and green beans, the frozen not the canned kind. Or an omelette. You could have a mushroom omelette or a chicken omelette or a plain omelette, if you liked."

"What was for dessert?"

"Ice cream. You could have sauce on it."

"What kind of sauce was there?"

"Chocolate. Butterscotch. Walnut."

"I can't eat walnuts."

"There was marshmallow too."

Out at the Home the old people were arranged in tiers. On the first floor were the bright and tidy ones. They walked around, usually with the help of canes. They visited each other, played cards. They had singsongs and hobbies. In the Crafts Center they painted pictures, hooked rugs, made quilts. If they were not able to do things like that they could make rag dolls, mobiles like the one Rose bought, poodles and snowmen which were constructed of Styrofoam balls, with sequins for eyes; they also made silhouette pictures by placing thumbtacks on traced outlines: knights on horseback, battleships, airplanes, castles.

They organized concerts; they held dances; they had checker tournaments.

"Some of them say they are the happiest here they have ever been in their lives."

Up one floor there was more television watching, there were more wheelchairs. There were those whose heads drooped, whose tongues lolled, whose limbs shook uncontrollably. Nevertheless sociability was still flourishing, also rationality, with occasional blanks and absences.

On the third floor you might get some surprises.

Some of them up there had given up speaking.

Some had given up moving, except for odd jerks and tosses of the head, flailing of the arms, that seemed to be without purpose or control.

Nearly all had given up worrying about whether they were wet or dry.

Bodies were fed and wiped, taken up and tied in chairs, untied and put to bed. Taking in oxygen, giving out carbon dioxide, they continued to participate in the life of the world.

Crouched in her crib, diapered, dark as a nut, with three tufts of hair like dandelion floss sprouting from her head, an old woman was making loud shaky noises.

"Hello Aunty," the nurse said. "You're spelling today. It's lovely weather outside." She bent to the old woman's ear. "Can you spell weather?"

This nurse showed her gums when she smiled, which was all the time; she had an air of nearly demented hilarity.

"Weather," said the old woman. She strained forward, grunting, to get the word. Rose thought she might be going to have a bowel movement. "W-E-A-T-H-E-R."

That reminded her.

"Whether. W-H-E-T-H-E-R."

So far so good.

"Now you say something to her," the nurse said to Rose.

The words in Rose's mind were for a moment all obscene or despairing.

But without prompting came another.

"Forest. F-O-R-E-S-T."

"Celebrate," said Rose suddenly.

"C-E-L-E-B-R-A-T-E."

You had to listen very hard to make out what the old woman was saying, because she had lost much of the power to shape sounds. What she said seemed to come not from her mouth or her throat, but from deep in her lungs and belly.

"Isn't she a wonder," the nurse said. "She can't see and that's the only way we can tell she can hear. Like if you say, 'Here's your dinner,' she won't pay any attention to it, but she might start spelling *dinner*.

"Dinner," she said, to illustrate, and the old woman picked it up. "D-I-N-N ..." Sometimes a long wait, a long wait between letters. It seemed she had only the thinnest thread to follow, meandering through that emptiness or confusion that nobody on this side can do more than guess at. But she didn't lose it, she followed it through to the end, however tricky the word might be, or cumbersome. Finished. Then she was sitting waiting; waiting, in the middle of her sightless eventless day, till up from somewhere popped another word. She would encompass it, bend all her energy to master it. Rose wondered what the words were like, when she held them in her mind. Did they carry their usual meaning, or any meaning at all? Were they like words in dreams or in the minds of young children, each one marvelous and distinct and alive as a new animal? This one limp and clear, like a jellyfish, that one hard and mean and secretive, like a horned snail. They could be austere and comical as top hats, or smooth and lively and flattering as ribbons. A parade of private visitors, not over yet.

Something woke Rose early the next morning. She was sleeping in the little porch, the only place in Flo's house where the smell was bearable. The sky was milky and brightening. The trees across the river — due to be cut down soon, to make room for a trailer park — were hunched against the dawn sky like shaggy dark animals, like buffalo. Rose had been dreaming. She had been having a dream obviously connected with her tour of the Home the day before.

Someone was taking her through a large building where there were people in cages. Everything was dim and cobwebby at first, and Rose was protesting that this seemed a poor arrangement. But as she went on the cages got larger and more elaborate, they were like enormous wicker birdcages, Victorian birdcages, fancifully shaped and decorated. Food was being offered to the people in the cages and Rose examined it, saw that it was choice; chocolate mousse, trifle, Black Forest cake. Then in one of the cages Rose spotted Flo, who was handsomely seated on a thronelike chair, spelling out words in a clear authoritative voice (what the words were, Rose, wakening, could not remember) and looking pleased with herself, for showing powers she had kept secret till now.

Rose listened to hear Flo breathing, stirring, in her rubble-lined room. She heard nothing. What if Flo had died? Suppose she had died at the very moment she was making her radiant, satisfied appearance in Rose's dream? Rose hurried out of bed, ran barefoot to Flo's room. The bed there was empty. She went into the kitchen and found Flo sitting at the table, dressed to go out, wearing the navy blue summer coat and matching turban hat she had worn to Brian's and Phoebe's wedding. The coat was rumpled and in need of cleaning, the turban was crooked.

"Now I'm ready for to go," Flo said.

"Go where?"

"Out there," said Flo, jerking her head. "Out to the whattayacallit. The Poorhouse."

"The Home," said Rose. "You don't have to go today."

"They hired you to take me, now you get a move on and take me," Flo said.

"I'm not hired. I'm Rose. I'll make you a cup of tea."

"You can make it. I won't drink it."

She made Rose think of a woman who had started in labor. Such was her concentration, her determination, her urgency. Rose thought Flo felt her death moving in her like a child, getting ready to tear her. So she gave up arguing, she got dressed, hastily packed a bag for Flo, got her to the car and drove her out to the Home, but in the matter of Flo's quickly tearing and relieving death she was mistaken.

Some time before this, Rose had been in a play, on national television. *The Trojan Women*. She had no lines, and in fact she was in the play simply to do a favor for a friend, who had got a better part elsewhere. The director thought to liven all the weeping and mourning by having the Trojan women go bare-breasted. One breast apiece, they showed, the right in the case of royal personages such as Hecuba and Helen; the left, in the case of ordinary virgins or wives, such as Rose. Rose didn't think herself enhanced by this exposure — she was getting on, after all, her bosom tended to flop — but she got used to the idea. She didn't count on the sensation they would create. She didn't think many people would be watching. She forgot about those parts of the country where people can't exercise their preference for quiz shows, police-car chases, American situation comedies, and are compelled to put up with talks on public affairs and tours of art galleries and ambitious offerings of drama. She did not think they would be so amazed, either, now that every magazine rack in every town was serving up slices and cutlets of bare flesh. How could such outrage fasten on the Trojan ladies' sad-eyed collection, puckered with cold then running with sweat under the lights, badly and chalkily made-up, all looking rather foolish without their mates, rather pitiful and unnatural, like tumors?

Flo took to pen and paper over that, forced her still swollen fingers, crippled almost out of use with arthritis, to write the word *Shame*. She wrote that if Rose's father had not been dead long ago he would now wish that he was. That was true. Rose read the letter, or part of it, out loud to some friends she was having for dinner. She read it for comic effect, and dramatic effect, to show the gulf that lay behind her, though she did realize, if she thought about it, that such a gulf was nothing special. Most of her friends, who seemed to her ordinarily hard-working, anxious, and hopeful people, could lay claim to being disowned or prayed for, in some disappointed home.

Halfway through she had to stop reading. It wasn't that she thought how shabby it was, to be exposing and making fun of Flo this way. She had done it often enough before; it was no news to her that it was shabby. What stopped her was, in fact, that gulf; she had a fresh and overwhelming realization of it, and it was nothing to laugh about. These reproaches of Flo's made as much sense as a protest about raising umbrellas, a warning against eating raisins. But they were painfully, truly, meant; they were all a hard life had to offer. Shame on a bare breast.

Another time, Rose was getting an award. So were several other people. A reception was being held, in a Toronto hotel. Flo had been sent an invitation, but Rose had never thought that she would come. She had thought she should give someone's name, when the organizers asked about relatives, and she could hardly name Brian and Phoebe. Of course it was possible that she did, secretly, want Flo to come, wanted to show Flo, intimidate her, finally remove herself from Flo's shade. That would be a natural thing to want to do.

Flo came down on the train, unannounced. She got to the hotel. She was arthritic then, but still moving without a cane. She had always been decently, soberly, cheaply, dressed, but now it seemed she had spent money and asked advice. She was wearing a mauve and purple checked pants suit, and beads like strings of white and yellow popcorn. Her hair was covered by a thick gray-blue wig, pulled low on her forehead like a woollen cap. From the vee of the jacket, and its too-short sleeves, her neck and wrists stuck out brown and warty as if covered with bark. When she saw Rose she stood still. She seemed to be waiting — not just for Rose to go over to her but for her feelings about the scene in front of her to crystallize.

Soon they did.

"Look at the nigger!" said Flo in a loud voice, before Rose was anywhere near her. Her tone was one of simple, gratified astonishment, as if she had been peering down the Grand Canyon or seen oranges growing on a tree.

She meant George, who was getting one of the awards. He turned around, to see if someone was feeding him a comic line. And Flo did look like a comic character, except that her bewilderment, her authenticity, were quite daunting. Did she note the stir she had caused? Possibly. After that one outburst she clammed up, would not speak again except in the most grudging monosyllables, would not eat any food or drink any drink offered her, would not sit down, but stood astonished and unflinching in the middle of that gathering of the bearded and beaded, the unisexual and the unashamedly un-Anglo-Saxon, until it was time for her to be taken to her train and sent home.

Rose found that wig under the bed, during the horrifying cleanup that followed Flo's removal. She took it out to the Home, along with some clothes she had washed or had dry-cleaned, and some stockings, talcum powder, cologne, that she had bought. Sometimes Flo seemed to think Rose was a doctor, and she said, "I don't want no woman doctor, you can just clear out." But when she saw Rose carrying the wig she said, "Rose! What is that you got in your hands, is it a dead gray squirrel?"

"No," said Rose, "it's a wig."

"What?"

"A wig," said Rose, and Flo began to laugh. Rose laughed too. The wig did look like a dead cat or squirrel, even though she had washed and brushed it; it was a disturbing-looking object.

"My God, Rose, I thought what is she doing bringing me a dead squirrel! If I put it on somebody'd be sure to take a shot at me."

Rose stuck it on her own head, to continue the comedy, and Flo laughed so that she rocked back and forth in her crib.

When she got her breath Flo said, "What am I doing with these damn sides up on my bed? Are you and Brian behaving yourselves? Don't fight, it gets on your father's nerves. Do you know how many gallstones they took out of me? Fifteen! One as big as a pullet's egg. I got them somewhere. I'm going to take them home." She pulled at the sheets searching. "They were in a bottle."

"I've got them already," said Rose. "I took them home."

"Did you? Did you show your father?"

"Yes."

"Oh, well, that's where they are then," said Flo, and she lay down and closed her eyes.

QUESTIONS

1. Compare the differing lifestyles of Flo, Rose, and Brian. What problems are inherent in each? What conflicts arise between them?

2. In what ways does Flo struggle to keep from "going off the track"? Is her behavior at the reception in Toronto an early manifestation of her impending senility? How responsible is she for her behavior then and later in life?

3. What is the nature of the reconciliation that Flo and Rose achieve at the end of the story? Is it lasting or temporary? Why does Rose play along with her stepmother? Has their relationship changed?

4. What effect does Rose's dream have on her? What does it reveal about her opinion of places like the County Home? What light does it shed on Rose's perception of spelling? Is spelling the final recourse of a fading mind or a new insight into the essence of things?

TIM O'BRIEN

Going After Cacciato

It was a bad time. Billy Boy Watkins was dead, and so was Frenchie Tucker. Billy Boy had died of fright, scared to death on the field of battle, and Frenchie Tucker had been shot through the neck. Lieutenants Sidney Martin and Walter Gleason had died in tunnels. Pederson was dead and Bernie Lynn was dead. Buff was dead. They were all among the dead. The war was always the same, and the rain was part of the war. The rain fed fungus that grew in the men's socks and boots, and their socks rotted, and their feet turned white and soft so that the skin could be scraped off with a fingernail, and Stink Harris woke up screaming one night with a leech on his tongue. When it was not raining, a low mist moved like sleep across the paddies, blending the elements into a single gray element, and the war was cold and pasty and rotten. Lieutenant Corson, who came to replace Lieutenant Martin, contracted the dysentery. The tripflares were useless. The ammunition corroded and the foxholes filled with mud and water during the nights and in the mornings there was always the next village and the war was always the same. In early September Vaught caught an infection. He'd been showing Oscar Johnson the sharp edge on his bayonet, drawing it swiftly along his forearm and peeling off a layer of mushy skin. "Like a Gillette Blueblade." Vaught had grinned. It did not bleed, but in a few days the bacteria soaked in and the arm turned yellow, and Vaught was carried aboard a Huey[1] that dipped perpendicular, blades clutching at granite air, rising in its own wet wind and taking Vaught away. He never returned to the war. Later they had a letter from him that described Japan as smoky and full of bedbugs, but in the enclosed snapshot Vaught looked happy enough, posing with two sightly nurses, a long-stemmed bottle of wine rising from between his thighs. It was a shock to learn that he'd lost the arm. Soon afterward Ben Nystrom shot himself in the foot, but he did not die, and he wrote no letters. These were all things to talk about. The rain, too. Oscar said it made him think of Detroit in the month of May. "Not the rain," he liked to say. "Just the dark and gloom. It's Number One weather for rape and looting. The fact is, I do ninety-eight percent of my total rape and looting in weather just like this." Then somebody would say that Oscar had a pretty decent imagination for a nigger.

That was one of the jokes. There was a joke about Oscar. There were many jokes about Billy Boy Watkins, the way he'd collapsed in fright on the field of glorious battle. Another joke was about the lieutenant's dysentery, and another was about Paul Berlin's purple boils. Some

---

[1] A utility helicopter.

982

of the jokes were about Cacciato, who was as dumb, Stink said, as a bullet, or, Harold Murphy said, as an oyster fart.

In October, at the end of the month, in the rain, Cacciato left the war.

"He's gone away," said Doc Peret. "Split for parts unknown."

The lieutenant didn't seem to hear. He was too old to be a lieutenant, anyway. The veins in his nose and cheeks were shattered by booze. Once he had been a captain on the way to being a major, but whiskey and the fourteen dull years between Korea and Vietnam had ended all that, and now he was just an old lieutenant with the dysentery. He lay on his back in the pagoda, naked except for green socks and green undershorts.

"Cacciato," Doc Peret repeated. "He's gone away. Split, departed."

The lieutenant did not sit up. He held his belly with both hands as if to contain the disease.

"He's gone to Paris," Doc said. "That's what he tells Paul Berlin, anyhow, and Paul Berlin tells me, so I'm telling you. He's gone, packed up and gone."

"Paree," the lieutenant said softly. "In France, Paree? *Gay* Paree?"

"Yes, sir. That's what he says. That's what he told Paul Berlin, and that's what I'm telling you. You ought to cover up, sir."

The lieutenant sighed. He pushed himself up, breathing loud, then sat stiffly before a can of Sterno. He lit the Sterno and cupped his hands around the flame and bent down, drawing in the heat. Outside, the rain was steady. "Paree," he said wearily. "You're saying Cacciato's left for gay Paree, is that right?"

"That's what he said, sir. I'm just relaying what he told to Paul Berlin. Hey, really, you better cover yourself up."

"Who's Paul Berlin?"

"Right here, sir. This is Paul Berlin."

The lieutenant looked up. His eyes were bright blue, oddly out of place in the sallow face. "You Paul Berlin?"

"Yes, sir," said Paul Berlin. He pretended to smile.

"Geez, I thought you were Vaught."

"Vaught's the one who cut himself, sir."

"I thought that was you. How do you like that?"

"Fine, sir."

The lieutenant sighed and shook his head sadly. He held a boot to dry over the burning Sterno. Behind him in the shadows sat the crosslegged, roundfaced Buddha, smiling benignly from its elevated perch. The pagoda was cold. Dank and soggy from a month of rain, the place smelled of clays and silicates and old incense. It was a single square room, built like a pillbox, with a flat ceiling that forced the soldiers to stoop and kneel. Once it might have been an elegant house of worship, neatly tiled and painted and clean, candles burning in holders at the Buddha's feet, but now it was bombed-out junk. Sandbags blocked the windows. Bits of broken pottery lay under chipped pedestals. The Buddha's right arm was missing and his fat groin was gouged with shrapnel. Still, the smile was intact. Head cocked, he seemed interested in the lieutenant's long sigh. "So. Cacciato's gone away, is that it?"

"There it is," Doc Peret said. "You've got it now."

Paul Berlin smiled and nodded.

"To gay Paree," the lieutenant said. "Old Cacciato's going to Paree in France." He giggled, then shook his head gravely. "Still raining?"

"A bitch, sir."

"You ever seen rain like this? I mean, ever?"

"No, sir," Paul Berlin said.

"You Cacciato's buddy, I suppose?"

"No, sir," Paul Berlin said. "Sometimes he'd tag along, but not really."

"Who's his buddy?"

"Vaught, sir. I guess Vaught was, sometime."

"Well," the lieutenant said, dropping his nose inside the boot to smell the sweaty leather, "well, I guess we should just get Mister Vaught in here."

"Vaught's gone, sir. He's the one who cut himself — gangrene, remember?"

"Mother of Mercy."

Doc Peret draped a poncho over the lieutenant's shoulders. The rain was steady and thunderless and undramatic. Though it was mid-morning, the feeling was of endless dusk.

"Paree," the lieutenant murmured. "Cacciato's going to gay Paree — pretty girls and bare ass and Frogs everywhere. What's wrong with him?"

"Just dumb, sir. He's just awful dumb, that's all."

"And he's walking? He says he's walking to gay Paree?"

"That's what he says, sir, but you know how Cacciato can be."

"Does he know how far it is?"

"Six thousand eight hundred statute miles, sir. That's what he told me — six thousand eight hundred miles on the nose. He had it down pretty well. He had a compass and fresh water and maps and stuff."

"Maps," the lieutenant said. "Maps, flaps, schnaps. I guess those maps will help him cross the oceans, right? I guess he can just rig up a canoe out of those maps, no problem."

"Well, no," said Paul Berlin. He looked at Doc Peret, who shrugged. "No, sir. He showed me on the maps. See, he says he's going through Laos, then into Thailand and Burma, and then India, and then some other country, I forget, and then into Iran and Iraq, and then Turkey, and then Greece, and the rest is easy. That's exactly what he said. The rest is easy, he said. He had it all doped out."

"In other words," the lieutenant said, lying back, "in other words, fuckin AWOL."

"There it is," said Doc Peret. "There it is."

The lieutenant rubbed his eyes. His face was sallow and he needed a shave. For a time he lay very still, listening to the rain, hands on his belly, then he giggled and shook his head and laughed. "What for? Tell me — what the fuck for?"

"Easy," Doc said. "Really, you got to stay covered up, sir. I told you that."

"What for? I mean, what for?"

"Shhhhhhh, he's just dumb, that's all."

The lieutenant's face was yellow. He laughed, rolling onto his side and dropping the boot. "I mean, why? What sort of shit is this — walking to fucking gay Paree? What kind of bloody war is this, tell me, what's wrong with you people? Tell me — what's *wrong* with you?"

"Shhhhhh," Doc purred, covering him up and putting a hand on his forehead. "Easy does it."

"Angel of Mercy, Mother of Virgins, what's wrong with you guys? Walking to gay Paree, what's *wrong*?"

"Nothing, sir. It's just Cacciato. You know how Cacciato can be when he puts his head to it. Relax now and it'll be all fine. Fine. It's just that rockhead, Cacciato."

The lieutenant giggled. Without rising, he pulled on his pants and boots and a shirt, then rocked miserably before the blue Sterno flame. The pagoda smelled like the earth, and the rain was unending. "Shoot." The lieutenant sighed. He kept shaking his head, grinning, then looked at Paul Berlin. "What squad you in?"

"Third, sir."

"That's Cacciato's squad?"

"Yes, sir."

"Who else?"

"Me and Doc and Eddie Lazzutti and Stink and Oscar Johnson and Harold Murphy. That's all, except for Cacciato."

"What about Pederson and Buff?"

"They're the dead ones, sir."

"Shoot." The lieutenant rocked before the flame. He did not look well. "Okay." He sighed, getting up. "Third Squad goes after Cacciato."

Leading to the mountains were four clicks[2] of level paddy. The mountains jerked straight out of the rice, and beyond those mountains and other mountains was Paris.

The tops of the mountains could not be seen for the mist and clouds. The rain was glue that stuck the sky to the land.

The squad spent the night camped at the base of the first mountain, then in the morning they began the ascent. At midday Paul Berlin spotted Cacciato. He was half a mile up, bent low and moving patiently, steadily. He was not wearing a helmet — surprising, because Cacciato always took great care to cover the pink bald spot at the crown of his skull. Paul Berlin spotted him, but it was Stink Harris who spoke up.

Lieutenant Corson took out the binoculars.

"Him, sir?"

The lieutenant watched while Cacciato climbed toward the clouds.

"That him?"

"It's him. Bald as an eagle's ass."

Stink giggled. "Bald as Friar Tuck — it's Cacciato, all right. Dumb as a dink."[3]

They watched until Cacciato was swallowed in the rain and clouds.

"Dumb-dumb." Stink giggled.

They walked fast, staying in a loose column. First the lieutenant, then Oscar Johnson, then Stink, then Eddie Lazzutti, then Harold Murphy, then Doc, then, at the rear, Paul Berlin. Who walked slowly, head down. He had nothing against Cacciato. The whole episode was silly, of course, a dumb and immature thing typical of Cacciato, but even so he had nothing special against him. It was just too bad. A waste of time in the midst of infinitely wider waste.

Climbing, he tried to picture Cacciato's face. The image came out fuzzed and amorphous and bland — entirely compatible with the boy's personality. Doc Peret, an acute observer of such things, hypothesized that Cacciato had missed Mongolian idiocy by the breadth of a single, wispy genetic hair. "Could have gone either way." Doc had said confidentially. "You see the slanting eyes? The pasty flesh, just like jelly, right? The odd-shaped head? I mean, hey, let's face it — the guy's fucking ugly. It's only a theory, mind you, but I'd wager big money that old Cacciato has more than a smidgen of the Mongol in him."

There may have been truth to it. Cacciato looked curiously unfinished, as though nature had struggled long and heroically but finally jettisoned him as a hopeless cause, not worth the diminishing returns. Open-faced, round, naive, plump, tender-complected, and boyish, Cacciato lacked the fine detail, the refinements and final touches that maturity ordinarily marks on a boy of seventeen years. All this, the men concluded, added up to a case of simple gross stupidity. He wasn't positively disliked — except perhaps by Stink Harris, who took instant displeasure with anything vaguely his inferior — but at the same time Cacciato was no one's

[2] Kilometers.

[3] A pejorative term for Southeast Asians.

friend. Vaught, maybe. But Vaught was dumb, too, and he was gone from the war. At best, Cacciato was tolerated. The way men will sometimes tolerate a pesky dog.

It was just too bad. Walking to Paris; it was one of those ridiculous things Cacciato would do. Like winning the Bronze Star for shooting a dink in the face. Dumb. The way he was forever whistling. Too blunt-headed to know better, blind to the bodily and spiritual dangers of human combat. In some ways this made him a good soldier. He walked point like a boy at his first county fair. He didn't mind the tunnel work. And his smile, more decoration than an expression of emotion, stayed with him in the most lethal of moments — when Billy Boy turned his last card, when Pederson floated face-up in a summer day's paddy, when Buff's helmet overflowed with an excess of red and gray fluids.

It was sad, a real pity.

Climbing the mountain, Paul Berlin felt an odd affection for the kid. Not friendship, exactly, but — real pity.

Not friendship. Not exactly. Pity, pity plus wonder. It was all silly, walking away in the rain, but it was something to think about.

They did not reach the summit of the mountain until midafternoon. The climb was hard, the rain sweeping down, the mountain oozing from beneath their feet. Below, the clouds were expansive, hiding the paddies and the war. Above, in more clouds, were more mountains.

Oscar Johnson found where Cacciato had spent the first night, a rock formation with an outcropping ledge as a roof, a can of burned-out Sterno, a chocolate wrapper, and a partly burned map. On the map, traced in red ink, was a dotted line that ran through the paddyland and up the first small mountain of the Annamese Cordillera.[4] The dotted line ended there, apparently to be continued on another map.

"He's serious," the lieutenant said softly. "The blockhead's serious." He held the map as if it had a bad smell.

Stink and Oscar and Eddie Lazzutti nodded.

They rested in Cacciato's snug rock nest. Tucked away, looking out on the slate rain toward the next mountain, the men were quiet. Paul Berlin laid out a game of solitaire. Harold Murphy rolled a joint, inhaled, then passed it along, and they smoked and watched the rain and clouds and wilderness. It was peaceful. The rain was nice.

No one spoke until the ritual was complete.

Then, in a hush, all the lieutenant could say was, "Mercy."

"Shit" was what Stink Harris said.

The rain was unending.

"We could just go back," Doc Peret finally said. "You know, sir? Just head on back and forget him."

Stink Harris giggled.

"Seriously," Doc kept on, "we could just let the poor kid go. Make him M.I.A., strayed in battle, the lost lamb. Sooner or later he'll wake up, you know, and he'll see how insane it is and he'll come back."

The lieutenant stared into the rain. His face was yellow except for the network of broken veins.

"So what say you, sir? Let him go?"

"Dumber than a rock." Stink giggled.

"And smarter than Stink Harris."

"You know *what*, Doc."

---

[4] A mountain range in Vietnam.

"Pickle it."

"Who's saying to pickle it?"

"Just pickle it," said Doc Peret. "That's what."

Stink giggled but he shut up.

"What do you say, sir? Turn back?"

The lieutenant was quiet. At last he shivered and went into the rain with a wad of toilet paper. Paul Berlin sat alone, playing solitaire in the style of Las Vegas. Pretending, of course. Pretending to pay thirty thousand dollars for the deck, pretending ways to spend his earnings.

When the lieutenant returned he told the men to saddle up.

"We turning back?" Doc asked.

The lieutenant shook his head. He looked sick.

"I knew it!" Stink crowed. "Damn straight, I knew it! Can't hump away from a war, isn't that right, sir? The dummy has got to learn you can't just hump your way out of a war." Stink grinned and flicked his eyebrows at Doc Peret. "I knew it. By golly, I knew it!"

Cacciato had reached the top of the second mountain. Standing bareheaded, hands loosely at his sides, he was looking down on them through a blur of rain. Lieutenant Corson had the binoculars on him.

"Maybe he don't see us," Oscar said. "Maybe he's lost."

"Oh, he sees us. He sees us fine. Sees us real fine. And he's not lost. Believe me, he's not."

"Throw out smoke, sir?"

"Why not?" the lieutenant said. "Sure, why not throw out pretty smoke, why not?" He watched Cacciato through the glasses while Oscar threw out the smoke. It fizzled for a time and then puffed up in a heavy cloud of lavender. "Oh, he sees us," the lieutenant whispered. "He sees us fine."

"The bastard's *waving*!"

"I can see that, thank you. Mother of Saints."

As if stricken, the lieutenant suddenly sat down in a puddle, put his head in his hands and began to rock as the lavender smoke drifted up the face of the mountain. Cacciato was waving both arms. Not quite waving. The arms were flapping. Paul Berlin watched through the glasses. Cacciato's head was huge, floating like a balloon in the high fog, and he did not look at all frightened. He looked young and stupid. His face was shiny. He was smiling, and he looked happy.

"I'm sick," the lieutenant said. He kept rocking. "I tell you, I'm a sick, sick man."

"Should I shout up to him?"

"Sick." The lieutenant moaned. "Sick, sick. It wasn't this way on Pusan,[5] I'll tell you that. Sure, call up to him — I'm sick."

Oscar Johnson cupped his hands and hollered, and Paul Berlin watched through the glasses. For a moment Cacciato stopped waving. He spread his arms wide, as if to show them empty, slowly spreading them out like wings, palms up. Then his mouth opened wide, and in the mountains there was thunder.

"What'd he say?" The lieutenant rocked on his haunches. He was clutching himself and shivering. "Tell me what he said."

"Can't hear, sir. Oscar — ?"

---

[5] Port city in southeastern South Korea, the site from which the United Nations forces launched the counteroffensive against the North Korean forces, September, 1950.

There was more thunder, long-lasting thunder that came in waves from deep in the mountains. It rolled down and moved the trees and grasses.

"Shut the shit up!" The lieutenant was rocking and shouting at the rain and wind and thunder. "What'd the dumb fucker say?"

Paul Berlin watched through the glasses, and Cacciato's mouth opened and closed and opened, but there was only more thunder. Then his arms began flapping again. Flying, Paul Berlin suddenly realized. The poor kid was perched up there, arms flapping, trying to fly. Fly! Incredibly, the flapping motion was smooth and practiced and graceful.

"A chicken!" Stink squealed. "Look it! A squawking chicken!"

"Mother of Children"

"Look it!"

"A miserable chicken, you see that? A chicken!"

The thunder came again, breaking like Elephant Feet across the mountains, and the lieutenant rocked and held himself.

"For Christ sake." He moaned. "What'd he say? Tell me."

Paul Berlin could not hear. But he saw Cacciato's lips move, and the happy smile.

"Tell me."

So Paul Berlin, watching Cacciato fly, repeated it. "He said goodbye."

In the night the rain hardened into fog, and the fog was cold. They camped in the fog, near the top of the mountain, and the thunder stayed through the night. The lieutenant vomited. Then he radioed that he was in pursuit of the enemy.

"Gunships, Papa Two-Niner?" came the answer from far away.

"Negative," said the old lieutenant.

"Arty?[6] Tell you what. You got a real sweet voice, Papa Two-Niner. No shit, a lovely voice." The radio voice paused. "So, here's what I'll do, I'll give you a bargain on the arty — two for the price of one, no strings and a warranty to boot. How's that? See, we got this terrific batch of new one–fifty-five in, first-class ordinance, I promise you, and what we do, what we do is this. What we do is we go heavy on volume here, you know? Keeps the prices low."

"Negative," the lieutenant said.

"Well, geez. Hard to please, right? Maybe some nice illum,[7] then? Willie Peter, real boomers with some genuine sparkles mixed in. We're having this close-out sale, one time only."

"Negative. Negative, negative, negative."

"You'll be missing out on some fine shit."

"Negative, you monster."

"Okay," the radio voice said, disappointed-sounding, "but you'll wish … No offense, Papa Two-Niner. Have some happy hunting."

"Mercy," said the lieutenant into a blaze of static.

The night fog was worse than the rain, colder and more saddening. They lay under a sagging lean-to that seemed to catch and hold the fog like a net. Oscar and Harold Murphy and Stink and Eddie Lazzutti slept anyway, curled around one another like lovers. They could sleep and sleep.

---

[6] Artillery.

[7] Illumination.

"I hope he's moving," Paul Berlin whispered to Doc Peret. "I just hope he keeps moving. He does that, we'll never get him."

"Then they'll chase him with choppers. Or planes or something."

"Not if he gets himself lost," Paul Berlin said. "Not if he hides."

"What time is it?"

"Don't know."

"What time you got, sir?"

"Very lousy late," said the lieutenant from the bushes.

"Come on."

"Four o'clock. O-four-hundred, which is to say A.M. Got it?"

"Thanks."

"Charmed." His ass, hanging six inches from the earth, made a soft warm glow in the dark.

"You okay, sir?"

"I'm wonderful. Can't you see how wonderful I am?"

"I just hope Cacciato keeps moving," Paul Berlin whispered. "That's all I hope — I hope he uses his head and keeps moving."

"It won't get him anywhere."

"Get him to Paris maybe."

"Maybe." Doc sighed, turning onto his side. "And where is he then?"

"In Paris."

"No way. I like adventure, too, but, see, you can't walk to Paris from here. You just can't."

"He's smarter than you think," Paul Berlin said, not quite believing it. "He's not all that dumb."

"I know," the lieutenant said. He came from the bushes. "I know all about that."

"Impossible. None of the roads go to Paris."

"Can we light a Sterno, sir?"

"No," the lieutenant said, crawling under the lean-to and lying flat on his back. His breath came hard. "No, you can't light a fucking Sterno, and no, you can't go out to play without your mufflers and galoshes, and no, kiddies and combatants, no, you can't have chocolate sauce on your broccoli. No."

"All right."

"No!"

"You saying no, sir?"

"No." The lieutenant sighed with doom. "It's still a war, isn't it?"

"I guess."

"There you have it. It's still a war."

The rain resumed. It started with thunder, then lightning lighted the valley deep below in green and mystery, then more thunder, then it was just the rain. They lay quietly and listened. Paul Berlin, who considered himself abnormally sane, uncluttered by high ideas or lofty ambitions or philosophy, was suddenly struck between the eyes by a vision of murder. Butchery, no less. Cacciato's right temple caving inward, a moment of black silence, then the enormous explosion of outward-going brains. It was no metaphor; he didn't think in metaphors. No, it was a simple scary vision. He tried to reconstruct the thoughts that had led to it, but there was nothing to be found — the rain, the discomfort of mushy flesh. Nothing to justify such a bloody image, no origins. Just Cacciato's round head suddenly exploding like a pricked bag of helium: boom.

Where, he thought, was all this taking him, and where would it end? Murder was the logical circuit-stopper, of course; it was Cacciato's rightful, maybe inevitable due. Nobody can get away with stupidity forever, and in war the final price for it is always paid in purely biological currency, hunks of toe or pieces of femur or bits of exploded brain. And it *was* still a war, wasn't it?

Pitying Cacciato with wee-hour tenderness, and pitying himself for the affliction that produced such visions, Paul Berlin hoped for a miracle. He was tired of murder. Not scared by it — not at that particular moment — and not awed by it, just fatigued.

"He did some awfully brave things," he whispered. Then realized that Doc was listening. "He did. The time he dragged that dink out of his bunker, remember that."

"Yeah."

"The time he shot the kid in the kisser."

"I remember."

"At least you can't call him a coward, can you? You can't say he ran away because he was scared."

"You can say a lot of other shit, though."

"True. But you can't say he wasn't brave. You can't say that."

"Fair enough," Doc said. He sounded sleepy.

"I wonder if he talks French."

"You kidding, partner?"

"Just wondering. You think it's hard to learn French, Doc?"

"Cacciato?"

"Yeah, I guess not. It's a neat thing to think about, though, old Cacciato walking to Paris."

"Go to sleep," Doc Peret advised. "Remember, pal, you got your own health to think of."

They were in the high country.

It was country far from the war, high and peaceful country with trees and thick grass, no people and no dogs and no lowland drudgery. Real wilderness, through which a single trail, liquid and shiny, kept taking them up.

The men walked with their heads down. Stink at point, then Eddie Lazzutti and Oscar, next Harold Murphy with the machine gun, then Doc, then the lieutenant, and last Paul Berlin.

They were tired and did not talk. Their thoughts were in their legs and feet, and their legs and feet were heavy with blood, for they'd been on the march many hours and the day was soggy with the endless rain. There was nothing symbolic, or melancholy, about the rain. It was simple rain, everywhere.

They camped that night beside the trail, then in the morning continued the climb. Though there were no signs of Cacciato, the mountain had only one trail and they were on it, the only way west.

Paul Berlin marched mechanically. At his sides, balancing him evenly and keeping him upright, two canteens of Kool-Aid lifted and fell with his hips, and the hips rolled in their ball-and-socket joints. He respired and sweated. His heart hard, his back strong, up the high country.

They did not see Cacciato, and for a time Paul Berlin thought they might have lost him forever. It made him feel better, and he climbed the trail and enjoyed the scenery and the sensations of being high and far from the real war, and then Oscar found the second map.

The red dotted line crossed the border into Laos.

Farther ahead they found Cacciato's helmet and armored vest, then his dogtags, then his entrenching tool and knife.

"Dummy just keeps to the trail." the lieutenant moaned. "Tell me why? Why doesn't he leave the trail?"

"It's the only way to Paris," Paul Berlin said.

"A rockhead," said Stink Harris. "That's why."

Liquid and shiny, a mix of rain and red clay, the trail took them higher.

Cacciato eluded them but he left behind the wastes of his march — empty tins, bits of bread, a belt of golden ammo dangling from a dwarf pine, a leaking canteen, candy wrappers, and worn rope. Clues that kept them going. Tantalizing them on, one step then the next — a glimpse of his bald head, the hot ash of a breakfast fire, a handkerchief dropped coyly along the path.

So they kept after him, following the trails that linked one to the next westward in a simple linear direction without deception. It was deep, jagged, complex country, dark with the elements of the season, and ahead was the frontier.

"He makes it that far," Doc Peret said, pointing to the next line of mountains, "and we can't touch him."

"How now?"

"The border," Doc said. The trail had leveled out and the march was easier. "He makes it to the border and it's bye-bye Cacciato."

"How far?"

"Two clicks maybe. Not far."

"Then he's made it," whispered Paul Berlin.

"Maybe so."

"By God!"

"Maybe so," Doc said.

"Boy, lunch at Tour d'Argent! A night at the old opera!"

"Maybe so."

The trail narrowed, then climbed, and a half hour later they saw him.

He stood at the top of a small grassy hill, two hundred meters ahead. Loose and at ease, smiling, Cacciato already looked like a civilian. His hands were in his pockets and he was not trying to hide himself. He might have been waiting for a bus, patient and serene and not at all frightened.

"Got him!" Stink yelped. "I knew it! Now we got him!"

The lieutenant came forward with the glasses.

"I knew it," Stink crowed, pressing forward. "The blockhead's finally giving it up — giving up the old ghost, I knew it!"

"What do we do, sir?"

The lieutenant shrugged and stared through the glasses.

"Fire a shot?" Stink held his rifle up and before the lieutenant could speak he squeezed off two quick rounds, one a tracer that turned like a corkscrew through the mist. Cacciato smiled and waved.

"Look at him," Oscar Johnson said. "I do think we got ourselves a predicament. Truly a predicament."

"There it is," Eddie said, and they both laughed, and Cacciato kept smiling and waving.

"A true predicament."

Stink Harris took the point, walking fast and chattering, and Cacciato stopped waving and watched him come, arms folded and his big head cocked as if listening for something. He looked amused.

There was no avoiding it.

Stink saw the wire as he tripped it, but there was no avoiding it.

The first sound was that of a zipper suddenly yanked up; next, a popping noise, the spoon releasing and primer detonating; then the sound of the grenade dropping; then the fizzling sound. The sounds came separately but quickly.

Stink knew it as it happened. With the next step, in one fuzzed motion, he flung himself down and away, rolling, covering his skull, mouth open, yelping a funny, trivial little yelp.

They all knew it.

Eddie and Oscar and Doc Peret dropped flat, and Harold Murphy bent double and did an oddly graceful jackknife for a man of his size, and the lieutenant coughed and collapsed, and Paul Berlin, seeing purple, closed his eyes and fists and mouth, brought his knees to his belly, coiling, and let himself fall.

Count, he thought, but the numbers came in a tangle without sequence.

His belly hurt. That was where it started. First the belly, a release of fluids in the bowels next, a shitting feeling, a draining of all the pretensions and silly hopes for himself, and he was back where he started, writhing. The lieutenant was beside him. The air was windless — just the misty rain. His teeth hurt. Count, he thought, but his teeth hurt and no numbers came. I don't want to die, he thought lucidly, with hurting teeth.

There was no explosion. His teeth kept hurting and his belly was floating in funny ways.

He was ready, steeled. His lungs hurt now. He was ready, but there was no explosion. Then came a fragile pop. Smoke, he thought without thinking, smoke.

"Smoke." The lieutenant moaned, then repeated it. "Fucking smoke."

Paul Berlin smelled it. He imagined its velvet color, purple, but he could not open his eyes. He tried, but he could not open his eyes or unclench his fists or uncoil his legs, and the heavy fluids in his stomach were holding him down, and he could not wiggle or run to escape. There was no explosion.

"Smoke," Doc said softly. "Just smoke."

It was red smoke, and the message seemed clear. It was all over them. Brilliant red, thick, acid-tasting. It spread out over the earth like paint, then began to climb against gravity in a lazy red spiral.

"Smoke," Doc said. "Smoke."

Stink Harris was crying. He was on his hands and knees, chin against his throat, bawling and bawling. Oscar and Eddie had not moved.

"He had us," the lieutenant whispered. His voice was hollowed out, senile-sounding, almost a reminiscence. "He could've had all of us."

"Just smoke," Doc said. "Lousy smoke is all."

"The dumb fucker could've had us."

Paul Berlin could not move. He felt entirely conscious, a little embarrassed but not yet humiliated, and he heard their voices, heard Stink weeping and saw him beside the trail on his hands and knees, and he saw the red smoke everywhere, but he could not move.

"He won't come," said Oscar Johnson, returning under a white flag. "Believe me, I tried, but the dude just won't play her cool."

It was dusk and the seven soldiers sat in pow-wow.

"I told him all the right stuff, but he won't give it up. Told him it was crazy as shit and he'd probably end up dead, and I told him how he'd end up court-martialed at the best, and I told him how his old man would shit when he heard about it. Told him maybe things wouldn't go so hard if he just gave up and came back right now. I went through the whole spiel, top to bottom. The dude just don't listen."

The lieutenant was lying prone, Doc's thermometer in his mouth, sick-looking. It wasn't his war. The skin on his arms and neck was loose around deteriorating muscle.

"I told him — I told him all that good shit. Told him it's ridiculous, dig? I told him it won't work, no matter what, and I told him we're fed up. Fed up."

"You tell him we're out of rations?"

"Shit, yes, I told him that. And I told him he's gonna starve his own ass if he keeps going, and I told him we'd have to call in gunships if it came to it."

"You tell him he can't walk to France?"

Oscar grinned. He was black enough to be indistinct in the dusk. "Maybe I forgot to tell him that."

"You should've told him."

The lieutenant slid a hand behind his neck and pushed against it as if to relieve some spinal pressure. "What else?" he asked. "What else did he say?"

"Nothing, sir. He said he's doing okay. Said he was sorry to scare us with the smoke."

"The bastard." Stink kept rubbing his hands against the black stock of his rifle.

"What else?"

"Nothing. You know how he is, sir. Just a lot of smiles and stupid stuff. He asked how everybody was, so I said we're fine, except for the scare with the smoke boobytrap, and then he said he was sorry about that, so I told him it was okay. What can you say to a dude like that?"

The lieutenant nodded, pushing against his neck. He was quiet a while. He seemed to be making up his mind. "All right." He finally sighed. "What'd he have with him?"

"Sir?"

"Musketry," the lieutenant said. "What kind of weapons?"

"His rifle. That's all, his rifle and some bullets. I didn't get much of a look."

"Claymores?"[8]

Oscar shook his head. "I didn't see none. Maybe so."

"Grenades?"

"I don't know. Maybe a couple."

"Beautiful recon job, Oscar. Real pretty."

"Sorry, sir. He had his stuff tight, though."

"I'm sick."

"Yes, sir."

"Dysentery's going through me like coffee. What you got for me, Doc?"

Doc Peret shook his head. "Nothing, sir. Rest."

"That's it," the lieutenant said. "What I need is rest."

"Why not let him go, sir?"

"Rest," the lieutenant said, "is what I need."

Paul Berlin did not sleep. Instead he watched Cacciato's small hill and tried to imagine a proper ending.

---

[8] Mines specifically designed to kill humans.

There were only a few possibilities remaining, and after what had happened it was hard to see a happy end to it. Not impossible, of course. It could still be done. With skill and boldness, Cacciato might slip away and cross the frontier mountains and be gone. He tried to picture it. Many new places. Villages at night with barking dogs, people whose eyes and skins would change in slow evolution and counterevolution as Cacciato moved westward with whole continents before him and the war far behind him and all the trails connecting and leading toward Paris. It could be done. He imagined the many dangers of Cacciato's march, treachery and deceit at every turn, but he also imagined the many good times ahead, the stinging feel of aloneness, and new leanness and knowledge of strange places. The rains would end and the trails would go dry and be baked to dust, and there would be changing foliage and great expanses of silence and songs and pretty girls in straw huts and, finally, Paris.

It could be done. The odds were like poison, but it could be done.

Later, as if a mask had been peeled off, the rain ended and the sky cleared and Paul Berlin woke to see the stars.

They were in their familiar places. It wasn't so cold. He lay on his back and counted the stars and named those that he knew, named the constellations and the valleys of the moon. It was just too bad. Crazy, but still sad. He should've kept going — left the trails and waded through streams to rinse away the scent, buried his feces, swung from the trees branch to branch; he should've slept through the days and ran through the nights. It might have been done.

Toward dawn he saw Cacciato's breakfast fire. He heard Stink playing with the safety catch on his M-16, a clicking noise like a slow morning cricket. The sky lit itself in patches.

"Let's do it," the lieutenant whispered.

Eddie Lazzutti and Oscar and Harold Murphy crept away toward the south. Doc and the lieutenant waited a time then began to circle west to block a retreat. Stink Harris and Paul Berlin were to continue up the trail.

Waiting, trying to imagine a rightful and still happy ending, Paul Berlin found himself pretending, in a vague sort of way, that before long the war would reach a climax beyond which everything else would become completely commonplace. At that point he would stop being afraid. All the bad things, the painful and grotesque things, would be in the past, and the things ahead, if not lovely, would at least be tolerable. He pretended he had crossed that threshold.

When the sky was half-light, Doc and the lieutenant fired a red flare that streaked high over Cacciato's grassy hill, hung there, then exploded in a fanning starburst like the start of a celebration. Cacciato Day, it might have been called. October something, in the year 1968, the Year of the Pig.

In the trees at the southern slope of the hill Oscar and Eddie and Harold Murphy each fired red flares to signal their advance.

Stink went into the weeds and hurried back, zipping up his trousers. He was very excited and happy. Deftly, he released the bolt on his weapon and it slammed hard into place.

"Fire the flare," he said, "and let's go."

Paul Berlin took a long time opening his pack.

But he found the flare, unscrewed its lid, laid the firing pin against the primer, then jammed it in.

The flare jumped away from him. It went high and fast, rocketing upward and taking a smooth arc that followed the course of the trail, leaving behind a dirty wake of smoke.

At its apex, with barely a sound, the flare exploded in a green dazzle over Cacciato's hill. It was a fine, brilliant shade of green.

"Go," whispered Paul Berlin. It did not seem enough. "Go," he said, and then he shouted, "Go."

QUESTIONS

1. Discuss the recurrent rain imagery. What are the various feelings it evokes? Why is there finally, as the narrator tells us, "... nothing symbolic or melancholy about the rain. It was simple rain, everywhere"? How does this perspective relate to the soldiers' view of the war in Vietnam?

2. What are the Lieutenant's motives for going after Cacciato? Why does he call Cacciato "the enemy"? Do his opinions ever change?

3. Cacciato is labeled "dumb" throughout the story. Is he really dumb? Is he crazy? In what ways is he a hero to the members of his squad? Compare his departure from the war to the previous exits of other squad members.

4. Paul Berlin tries to imagine a "proper ending ... a rightful and still happy ending." How plausible are the endings he imagines? Can he do anything to make such endings happen? What does his final shout indicate about his sympathies? Do they conflict with his actions?

CYNTHIA OZICK

The Shawl

Stella, cold, cold, the coldness of hell. How they walked on the roads together, Rosa with Magda curled up between sore breasts, Magda wound up in the shawl. Sometimes Stella carried Magda. But she was jealous of Magda. A thin girl of fourteen, too small, with thin breasts of her own, Stella wanted to be wrapped in a shawl, hidden away, asleep, rocked by the march, a baby, a round infant in arms. Magda took Rosa's nipple, and Rosa never stopped walking, a walking cradle. There was not enough milk; sometimes Magda sucked air; then she screamed. Stella was ravenous. Her knees were tumors on sticks, her elbows chicken bones.

Rosa did not feel hunger; she felt light, not like someone walking but like someone in a faint, in trance, arrested in a fit, someone who is already a floating angel, alert and seeing everything, but in the air, not there, not touching the road. As if teetering on the tips of her fingernails. She looked into Magda's face through a gap in the shawl: a squirrel in a nest, safe, no one could reach her inside the little house of the shawl's windings. The face, very round, a pocket mirror of a face: but it was not Rosa's bleak complexion, dark like cholera, it was another kind of face altogether, eyes blue as air, smooth feathers of hair nearly as yellow as the Star sewn into Rosa's coat. You could think she was one of *their* babies.

Rosa, floating, dreamed of giving Magda away in one of the villages. She could leave the line for a minute and push Magda into the hands of any woman on the side of the road. But if she moved out of line they might shoot. And even if she fled the line for half a second and pushed the shawl-bundle at a stranger, would the woman take it? She might be surprised, or afraid; she might drop the shawl, and Magda would fall out and strike her head and die. The little round head. Such a good child, she gave up screaming, and sucked now only for the taste of the drying nipple itself. The neat grip of the tiny gums. One mite of a tooth tip sticking up in the bottom gum, how shining, an elfin tombstone of white marble, gleaming there. Without complaining, Magda relinquished Rosa's teats, first the left, then the right; both were cracked, not a sniff of milk. The duct crevice extinct, a dead volcano, blind eye, chill hole, so Magda took the corner of the shawl and milked it instead. She sucked and sucked, flooding the threads with wetness. The shawl's good flavor, milk of linen.

It was a magic shawl, it could nourish an infant for three days and three nights. Magda did not die, she stayed alive, although very quiet. A peculiar smell, of cinnamon and almonds, lifted out of her mouth. She held her eyes open every moment, forgetting how to blink or nap, and Rosa and sometimes Stella studied their blueness. On the road they raised one burden of a leg after another and studied Magda's face. "Aryan," Stella said, in a voice grown as thin as a string; and Rosa thought how Stella gazed at Magda like a young cannibal. And the time that Stella said "Aryan," it sounded to Rosa as if Stella had really said "Let us devour her."

But Magda lived to walk. She lived that long, but she did not walk very well, partly because she was only fifteen months old, and partly because the spindles of her legs could not hold up her fat belly. It was fat with air, full and round. Rosa gave almost all her food to Magda, Stella gave nothing; Stella was ravenous, a growing child herself, but not growing much. Stella did not menstruate. Rosa did not menstruate. Rosa was ravenous, but also not; she learned from Magda how to drink the taste of a finger in one's mouth. They were in a place without pity, all pity was annihilated in Rosa, she looked at Stella's bones without pity. She was sure that Stella was waiting for Magda to die so she could put her teeth into the little thighs.

Rosa knew Magda was going to die very soon; she should have been dead already, but she had been buried away deep inside the magic shawl, mistaken there for the shivering mound of Rosa's breasts; Rosa clung to the shawl as if it covered only herself. No one took it away from her. Magda was mute. She never cried. Rosa hid her in the barracks, under the shawl, but she knew that one day someone would inform; or one day someone, not even Stella, would steal Magda to eat her. When Magda began to walk Rosa knew that Magda was going to die very soon, something would happen. She was afraid to fall asleep; she slept with the weight of her thigh on Magda's body; she was afraid she would smother Magda under her thigh. The weight of Rosa was becoming less and less; Rosa and Stella were slowly turning into air.

Magda was quiet, but her eyes were horribly alive, like blue tigers. She watched. Sometimes she laughed — it seemed a laugh, but how could it be? Magda had never seen anyone laugh. Still, Magda laughed at her shawl when the wind blew its corners, the bad wind with pieces of black in it, that made Stella's and Rosa's eyes tear. Magda's eyes were always clear and tearless. She watched like a tiger. She guarded her shawl. No one could touch it; only Rosa could touch it. Stella was not allowed. The shawl was Magda's own baby, her pet, her little sister. She tangled herself up in it and sucked on one of the corners when she wanted to be very still.

Then Stella took the shawl away and made Magda die.

Afterward Stella said: "I was cold."

And afterward she was always cold, always. The cold went into her heart: Rosa saw that Stella's heart was cold. Magda flopped onward with her little pencil legs scribbling this way and that, in search of the shawl; the pencils faltered at the barracks opening, where the light began. Rosa saw and pursued. But already Magda was in the square outside the barracks, in the jolly light. It was the roll-call arena. Every morning Rosa had to conceal Magda under the shawl against a wall of the barracks and go out and stand in the arena with Stella and hundreds of others, sometimes for hours, and Magda, deserted, was quiet under the shawl, sucking on her corner. Every day Magda was silent, and so she did not die. Rosa saw that today Magda was going to die, and at the same time a fearful joy ran in Rosa's two palms, her fingers were on fire, she was astonished, febrile: Magda, in the sunlight, swaying on her pencil legs, was howling. Ever since the drying up of Rosa's nipples, ever since Magda's last scream on the road, Magda had been devoid of any syllable; Magda was a mute. Rosa believed that something had gone wrong with her vocal cords, with her windpipe, with the cave of her larynx; Magda was defective, without a voice; perhaps she was deaf; there might be something amiss with her intelligence; Magda was dumb. Even the laugh that came when the ash-stippled wind made a clown out of Magda's shawl was only the air-blown showing of her teeth. Even when the lice, head lice and body lice, crazed her so that she became as wild as one of the big rats that plundered the barracks at daybreak looking for carrion, she rubbed and scratched and kicked and bit and rolled without a whimper. But now Magda's mouth was spilling a long viscous rope of clamor.

"Maaaa — "

It was the first noise Magda had ever sent out from her throat since the drying up of Rosa's nipples.

"Maaaa ... aaa!"

Again! Magda was wavering in the perilous sunlight of the arena, scribbling on such pitiful little bent shins. Rosa saw. She saw that Magda was grieving for the loss of her shawl, she saw that Magda was going to die. A tide of commands hammered in Rosa's nipples: Fetch, get, bring! But she did not know which to go after first, Magda or the shawl. If she jumped out into the arena to snatch Magda up, the howling would not stop, because Magda would still not have the shawl; but if she ran back into the barracks to find the shawl, and if she found it, and if she came after Magda holding it and shaking it, then she would get Magda back, Magda would put the shawl in her mouth and turn dumb again.

Rosa entered the dark. It was easy to discover the shawl. Stella was heaped under it, asleep in her thin bones. Rosa tore the shawl free and flew — she could fly, she was only air — into the arena. The sunheat murmured of another life, of butterflies in summer. The light was placid, mellow. On the other side of the steel fence, far away, there were green meadows speckled with dandelions and deep-colored violets; beyond them, even farther, innocent tiger lilies, tall, lifting their orange bonnets. In the barracks they spoke of "flowers," of "rain": excrement, thick turd-braids, and the slow stinking maroon waterfall that slunk down from the upper bunks, the stink mixed with a bitter fatty floating smoke that greased Rosa's skin. She stood for an instant at the margin of the arena. Sometimes the electricity inside the fence would seem to hum; even Stella said it was only an imagining, but Rosa heard real sounds in the wire: grainy sad voices. The farther she was from the fence, the more clearly the voices crowded at her. The lamenting voices strummed so convincingly, so passionately, it was impossible to suspect them of being phantoms. The voices told her to hold up the shawl, high; the voices told her to shake it, to whip with it, to unfurl it like a flag. Rosa lifted, shook, whipped, unfurled. Far off, very far, Magda leaned across her air-fed belly, reaching out with the rods of her arms. She was high up, elevated, riding someone's shoulder. But the shoulder that carried Magda was not coming toward Rosa and the shawl, it was drifting away, the speck of Magda was moving more and more into the smoky distance. Above the shoulder a helmet glinted. The light tapped the helmet and sparkled it into a goblet. Below the helmet a black body like a domino and a pair of black boots hurled themselves in the direction of the electrified fence. The electric voices began to chatter wildly. "Maamaa, maaamaaa," they all hummed together. How far Magda was from Rosa now, across the whole square, past a dozen barracks, all the way on the other side! She was no bigger than a moth.

All at once Magda was swimming through the air. The whole of Magda traveled through loftiness. She looked like a butterfly touching a silver vine. And the moment Magda's feathered round head and her pencil legs and balloonish belly and zigzag arms splashed against the fence, the steel voices went mad in their growling, urging Rosa to run and run to the spot where Magda had fallen from her flight against the electrified fence; but of course Rosa did not obey them. She only stood, because if she ran they would shoot, and if she tried to pick up the sticks of Magda's body they would shoot, and if she let the wolf's screech ascending now through the ladder of her skeleton break out, they would shoot; so she took

Magda's shawl and filled her own mouth with it, stuffed it in and stuffed it in, until she was swallowing up the wolf's screech and tasting the cinnamon and almond depth of Magda's saliva; and Rosa drank Magda's shawl until it dried.

QUESTIONS

1. Although the story's setting is never explicitly named, we know that the march leads to a Nazi concentration camp. How?

2. What thematic effect does Ozick produce by mixing highly realistic detail with poetic language and images?

3. How is the shawl magic? Does it lose its magic at the end of the story?

4. Discuss the importance of sound and silence in the story.

GRACE PALEY

The Used-Boy Raisers

There were two husbands disappointed by eggs.

I don't like them that way either, I said. Make your own eggs. They sighed in unison. One man was livid; one was pallid.

There isn't a drink around here, is there? asked Livid.

Never find one here, said Pallid. Don't look; driest damn house. Pallid pushed the eggs away, pain and disgust his escutcheon.[1]

Livid said, Now really, isn't there a drink? Beer? he hoped.

Nothing, said Pallid, who'd been through the pantries, closets, and refrigerators looking for a white shirt.

You're damn right, I said. I buttoned the high button of my powder-blue duster. I reached under the kitchen table for a brown paper bag full of an embroidery which asked God to Bless Our Home.

I was completing this motto for the protection of my sons, who were also Livid's. It is true that some months earlier, from a far place — the British plains in Africa — he had written hospitably to Pallid: I do think they're fine boys, you understand. I love them too, but Faith is their mother and now Faith is your wife. I'm so much away. If you want to think of them as yours, old man, go ahead.

Why, thank you, Pallid had replied, airmail, overwhelmed. Then he implored the boys, when not in use, to play in their own room. He made all efforts to be kind.

Now as we talked of time past and upon us, I pierced the ranch house that nestles in the shade of a cloud and a Norway maple, just under the golden script.

Ha-ha, said Livid, dripping coffee on his pajama pants, you'll never guess whom I met up with, Faith.

Who? I asked.

Saw your old boy friend Clifford at the Green Coq. He looks well. One thing must be said, he addressed Pallid, she takes good care of her men.

True, said Pallid.

How is he? I asked coolly. What's he doing? I haven't seen him in two years.

---

[1] Coat of arms.

Oh, you'll never guess. He's marrying. A darling girl. She was with him. Little tootsies, little round bottom, little tummy — she must be twenty-two, but she looks seventeen. One long yellow braid down her back. A darling girl. Stubby nose, fat little underlip. Her eyes put on in pencil. Shoulders down like a dancer ... slender neck. Oh, darling, darling.

You certainly observed her, said Pallid.

I have a functioning retina, said Livid. Then he went on. Better watch out, Faith. You'd be surprised, the dear little chicks are hatching out all over the place. All the sunny schoolgirls rolling their big black eyes. I hope you're really settled this time. To me, whatever is under the dam is in another county; however, in my life you remain an important person historically, he said. And that's why I feel justified in warning you. I must warn you. Watch out, sweetheart! he said, leaning forward to whisper harshly and give me a terrible bellyache.

What's all this about? asked Pallid innocently. In the first place, she's settled ... and then she's still an attractive woman. Look at her.

Oh yes, said Livid, looking. An attractive woman. Magnificent, sometimes.

We were silent for several seconds in honor of that generous remark.

Then Livid said, Yes, magnificent, but I just wanted to warn you, Faith.

He pushed his eggs aside finally and remembered Clifford. A mystery wrapped in an enigma ... I wonder why he wants to marry.

I don't know, it just ties a man down, I said.

And yet, said Pallid seriously, what would I be without marriage? In luminous recollection — a gay dog, he replied.

At this moment, the boys entered: Richard the horse thief and Tonto the crack shot.

Daddy! they shouted. They touched Livid, tickled him, unbuttoned his pajama top, whistled at the several gray hairs coloring his chest. They tweaked his ear and rubbed his beard the wrong way.

Well, well, he cautioned. How are you boys, have you been well? You look fine. Sturdy. How are your grades? he inquired. He dreamed that they were just up from Eton for the holidays.

I don't go to school, said Tonto. I go to the park.

I'd like to hear the child read, said Livid.

Me. I can read, Daddy, said Richard. I have a book with a hundred pages.

Well, well, said Livid. Get it.

I kindled a fresh pot of coffee. I scrubbed cups and harassed Pallid into opening a sticky jar of damson-plum jam. Very shortly, what could be read, had been, and Livid, knotting the tie strings of his pants vigorously, approached me at the stove. Faith, he admonished, that boy can't read a tinker's damn. Seven years old.

Eight years old, I said.

Yes, said Pallid, who had just remembered the soap cabinet and was rummaging in it for a pint. If they were my sons in actuality as they are in everyday life, I would send them to one of the good parochial schools in the neighborhood where reading is taught. Reading. St. Bartholomew's, St. Bernard's, St. Joseph's.

Livid became deep purple and gasped. Over my dead body. *Merde*,[2] he said in deference to the children. I've said, yes, you may think of the boys as your own, but if I ever hear they've come within an inch of that church, I'll run you through, you bastard. I was fourteen years old when in my own good sense I walked out of that grotto of deception, head up. You

---

[2] Shit.

sonofabitch, I don't give a damn how *au courant*[3] it is these days, how gracious to be seen under a dome on Sunday ... Shit! Hypocrisy. Corruption. Cave dwellers. Idiots. Morons.

Recalling childhood and home, poor Livid writhed in his seat. Pallid listened, head to one side, his brows gathering the onsets of grief.

You know, he said slowly, we iconoclasts ... we free-thinkers ... we latter-day masons ... we idealists ... we dreamers ... we are never far from our nervous old mother, the Church. She is never far from us.

Wherever we are, we can hear, no matter how faint, her hourly bells, tolling the countryside, reverberating in the cities, bringing to our civilized minds the passionate deed of Mary. Every hour on the hour we are startled with remembrance of what was done for us. FOR US.

Livid muttered in great pain, Those bastards, oh oh oh, those contemptible, goddamnable bastards. Do we have to do the nineteenth century all over again? All right, he bellowed, facing us all, I'm ready. That Newman![4] He turned to me for approval.

You know, I said, this subject has never especially interested me. It's your little dish of lava.

Pallid spoke softly, staring past the arched purple windows of his soul. I myself, although I lost God a long time ago, have never lost faith.

What the hell are you talking about, you moron? roared Livid.

I have never lost my love for the wisdom of the Church of the World. When I go to sleep at night, I inadvertently pray. I also do so when I rise. It is not to God, it is to that unifying memory out of childhood. The first words I ever wrote were: What are the sacraments? Faith, can you ever forget your old grandfather intoning Kaddish?[5] It will sound in your ears forever.

Are you kidding? I was furious to be drawn into their conflict. Kaddish? What do I know about Kaddish. Who's dead? You know my opinions perfectly well. I believe in the Diaspora,[6] not only as a fact but a tenet. I'm against Israel on technical grounds. I'm very disappointed that they decided to become a nation in my lifetime. I believe in the Diaspora. After all, they *are* the chosen people. Don't laugh. They really are. But once they're huddled in one little corner of a desert, they're like anyone else: Frenchies, Italians, temporal nationalities. Jews have one hope only — to remain a remnant in the basement of world affairs — no, I mean something else — a splinter in the toe of civilizations, a victim to aggravate the conscience.

Livid and Pallid were astonished at my outburst, since I rarely express my opinion on any serious matter but only live out my destiny, which is to be, until my expiration date, laughingly the servant of man.

I continued. I hear they don't even look like Jews any more. A bunch of dirt farmers with no time to read.

They're your own people, Pallid accused, dilating in the nostril, clenching his jaw. And they're under the severest attack. This is not the time to revile them.

I had resumed my embroidery. I sighed. My needle was now deep in the clouds which were pearl gray and late afternoon. I am only trying to say that they aren't meant for geographies but for history. They are not supposed to take up space but to continue in time.

They looked at me with such grief that I decided to consider all sides of the matter. I said,

---

[3] Current; fashionable.

[4] John Henry Newman (1801–1890), Catholic educator and theologian.

[5] Ancient Jewish prayer of mourning.

[6] Dispersion of the Jews among the Gentiles after their Babylonian captivity.

Christ probably had all that trouble — now that you mention it — because he knew he was going to gain the whole world but he forgot Jerusalem.

When you married us, said Pallid, and accused me, didn't you forget Jerusalem?

I never forget a thing, I said. Anyway, guess what. I just read somewhere that England is bankrupt. The country is wadded with installment paper.

Livid's hand trembled as he offered Pallid a light. Nonsense, he said. That's not true. Nonsense. The great British Island is the tight little fist of the punching arm of the Commonwealth.

What's true is true, I said, smiling.

Well, I said, since no one stirred, do you think you'll ever get to work today? Either of you?

Oh, my dear, I haven't even seen you and the boys in over a year. It's quite pleasant and cozy here this morning, said Livid.

Yes, isn't it? said Pallid, the surprised host. Besides, it's Saturday.

How do you find the boys? I asked Livid, the progenitor.

American, American, rowdy, uncontrolled. But you look well, Faith. Plumper, but womanly and well.

Very well, said Pallid, pleased.

But the boys, Faith. Shouldn't they be started on something? Just lining up little plastic cowboys. It's silly, really.

They're so young, apologized Pallid, the used-boy raiser.

You'd both better go to work, I suggested, knotting the pearl-gray late-afternoon thread. Please put the dishes in the sink first. Please. I'm sorry about the eggs.

Livid yawned, stretched, peeked at the clock, sighed. Saturday or no, alas, my time is not my own. I've got an appointment downtown in about forty-five minutes, he said.

I do too, said Pallid. I'll join you on the subway.

I'm taking a cab, said Livid.

I'll split it with you, said Pallid.

They left for the bathroom, where they shared things nicely — shaving equipment, washstand, shower, and so forth.

I made the beds and put the aluminum cot away. Livid would find a hotel room by nightfall. I did the dishes and organized the greedy day; dinosaurs in the morning, park in the afternoon, peanut butter in between, and at the end of it all, to reward us for a week of beans endured, a noble rib roast with little onions, dumplings, and pink applesauce.

Faith, I'm going now, Livid called from the hall. I put my shopping list aside and went to collect the boys, who were wandering among the rooms looking for Robin Hood. Go say goodbye to your father, I whispered.

Which one? they asked.

The real father, I said. Richard ran to Livid. They shook hands manfully. Pallid embraced Tonto and was kissed eleven times for his affection.

Goodbye now, Faith, said Livid. Call me if you want anything at all. Anything at all, my dear. Warmly with sweet propriety he kissed my cheek. Ascendant, Pallid kissed me with considerable business behind the ear.

Goodbye, I said to them.

I must admit that they were at last clean and neat, rather attractive, shiny men in their thirties, with the grand affairs of the day ahead of them. Dark night, the search for pleasure and oblivion were well ahead. Goodbye, I said, have a nice day. Goodbye, they said once more, and set off in pride on paths which are not my concern.

QUESTIONS

1. What is Paley's purpose in naming each of her characters after his or her dominant quality? How does this technique compare with Hawthorne's allegorical naming in "Young Goodman Brown"? How does Paley's Faith differ from Hawthorne's character of the same name?

2. Discuss the significance of the story's title. Why are Richard and Tonto "used-boys"? What role do they play in the story?

3. Characterize the narrator's attitudes toward her husbands, her family, and marriage. How do her attitudes compare with those of her husbands? with those of Waldeen in Mason's "Graveyard Day"?

4. How does the long discussion about religion fit into the story?

5. There are no quotation marks in the story to indicate the dialogue between characters. What is the effect of this experimental technique?

JOHN SAYLES

Dillinger in Hollywood

You know how they get after New Year's when the visits dry up and the TV is bust and there's steamed chicken for lunch three days in a row? It was one of those weeks, and Spurs Tatum starts in after rec therapy, before we could wheel them all out of the day room.

"Hoot Gibson held my horse," says Spurs. "I took falls for Randolph Scott. I hung from a wing in *The Perils of Pauline*. And Mr. Ford,"[1] he says, "Mr. Ford he always hired me on. You see a redskin blasted off a horse in one of Mr. Ford's pictures, like as not it's me. One-Take Tatum they called me, before the 'Spurs' thing took."

We'd heard it all before, every time there was a western or a combat picture on the TV, every time a patient come in with a broken hip or a busted rib, all through the last days when the Duke was dying in the news. Heard how Spurs had thought up most of the riding stunts they use today, how he'd been D. W. Griffith's drinking buddy, how he saved Tom Mix's life on the Sacramento River.[2] It was hot and one of those weeks and we'd heard it all before so I don't know if it was that or the beating he'd just taken at Parcheesi that made old Casey up and say how he used to be John Dillinger.

His chart said that Casey had been a driver on the Fox lot long enough to qualify for the Industry fund. I told him I hadn't realized he'd done any stand-in work.

"The bird who done the stand-in work," says Casey, "is the one they potted at the Biograph Theater. I used to be Johnnie Dillinger. In the flesh."

He said the name with a hard g, like in "finger," and didn't so much as blink.

Now we've had our delusions at the Home, your standard fading would-of-been actresses expecting their call from Mr. De Mille,[3] a Tarzan whoop now and then during the full moon, and one old gent who goes around mouthing words without sound and overacting like he's on the silent picture screen. Generally it's some glorified notion of who they used to

---

[1] Hoot Gibson (1892–1962), Randolph Scott (b. 1903): American motion picture cowboy heroes. John Ford (1895–1973): Irish-American motion picture director.

[2] The Duke, nickname of John Wayne (1907–1979), American actor. D. W. Griffith (1875–1948), first major American motion picture director and producer. Tom Mix (1880–1940), U.S. Marshal turned motion picture actor, star of over four hundred low-budget westerns.

[3] Cecil B. De Mille (1881–1959), American motion picture producer and director.

be. Up to this point Casey's only brag was he drove Joe DiMaggio to the airport when the Clipper was hitched to Monroe.[4]

"If I remember right," says Spurs, giving me an eye that meant he thought the poor fella had slipped his tracks, "if I'm not too fuzzy on it, I believe that Mr. Dillinger, Public Enemy Number One, departed from our midst in the summer of '34."

"You should live so long," says Casey.

Now I try to give a man the benefit of a doubt. With Spurs I can tell there's a grain of fact to his brags because I was in the wrangler game myself. I was riding broncs in Santa Barbara for their Old Spanish Days and this fella hires me to stunt for some rodeo picture with Gig Young in it. He says I take a nice fall.

The pay was greener than what I saw on the circuit, so I stuck in Hollywood. See, I could always *ride* the sumbitches, my problem came when it was time to get *off*. What I had was a new approach to tumbling from a horse. Whereas most folks out here bust their ass to get *into* pictures, I busted mine to get *out*. Some big damn gelding bucked me before I'd dug in and I landed smack on my tailbone. The doctor says to me — I'm laying on my stomach trying to remember my middle name — the doctor comes in with the X rays and he says, "I don't know how to tell you this, Son, but you're gonna have to learn to shit standing up."

If they'd known who I was, *Variety* would of headlined "Son Bishop Swaps Bridle for Bedpan." Horses and hospitals were all I knew. Over the years I'd spent more time in emergency rooms than Dr. Kildare. So it was hospitals, and pretty soon I drifted into the geriatric game. Your geriatrics and horses hold a lot in common — they're high-strung, they bite and kick sometimes, and they're none of them too big on bowel control. Course if a geriatric steps on your foot it don't take a wood chisel to peel it off the floor.

It's a living.

So Spurs I can back sometimes, though I'm sure he didn't play such a starring role in the invention of the saddle. With Casey I had to bring it up at report.

"He thinks he's a dead gangster?" says Mrs. Goorwitz, who was the charge nurse that night.

"No, he thinks he's an old man in a Hollywood nursing home. He says he *used* to be John Dillinger."

"In another life?"

"Nope," I answered her, "in this one."

We had this reincarnated character in here once, claimed to have been all the even-numbered King Louies of France from the second right up to Louie the Sixteen. I asked how he ended up an assistant prop man at Warners and he said after all that commotion his spirit must of needed the rest.

"I thought he was shot," says Mrs. Goorwitz.

"At point-blank range," I tell her. "They couldn't of missed."

Mrs. Goorwitz was a bit untracked by the news. She hates anything out of its place, hates waves, and many's the geriatric she's hounded to death for holding a book overdue from the Home library. She pulled Casey's chart and studied it. "It says here his name is Casey Mullins."

"Well that's that, isn't it?"

"Confused behavior," says Mrs. Goorwitz as she writes it into the report. "Inappropriate response. Watch carefully."

---

[4] Joe DiMaggio (b. 1914), American baseball star, was married to Marilyn Monroe (1926–1962), American actress.

The only thing that gets watched carefully in this joint is the time-punch at two minutes till shift change, but I figured I might save Casey some headache.

"Maybe he's just lying," I tell her. "To work up a little attention."

"Did he say anything else?"

She was on the scent now and threatening to go practice medicine on somebody any minute.

"Not a whole lot," I tell her. "But if we breathe a word to the Feds he claims they'll find us off Santa Monica Pier with our little toes curled up."

"This bird Jimmy Lawrence, a very small-time character," says Casey, "he had this bum ticker. A rheumatic heart condition, congenital since birth. We dated the same girl once is how I got to know him. People start coming up to say, 'Jeez, you're the spittin' image of Johnnie Dillinger, you know that?' and this girl, this mutual friend, tells me and I get the idea."

After he let the Dillinger thing out Casey got very talkative, like he had it stewing in him a long time and finally it blows out all at once. I'd be in his room tapping the catheter bags on these two vegematics, Kantor and Wise, and it would be just me and this fella Roscoe Baggs who was a midget listening. Roscoe had been in *The Wizard of Oz* as a Munchkin and was a very deep thinker. He reads the kind of science-fiction books that don't have girls in loinclothes on the cover.

"This girl has still got the yen for me," says Casey, "so she steers Lawrence to a doctor connection who tells him two months, maybe three, and it's the last roundup. The guy is demolished. So I make him this offer — I supply the dough to live it up his final days and he supplies a body to throw to the authorities. You could buy Chicago cops by the job lot back then so it was no big deal arranging the details. Hard times. Only two or three people had to know I was involved.

"Well the poor chump didn't even know how to paint the town right. And he kept moaning that he wanted us to hold off till after the Series, onnaconna he followed the Cardinals. That was the year Ripper Collins and the Dean brothers tore up the league."

"Just like Spangler," says Roscoe. "Remember, he wanted to see a man walk on the moon? Held off his cancer till he saw it on television and the next day he went downstairs."

Downstairs is where the morgue and the kitchen are located.

"One step for mankind," says Roscoe, "and check-out time for Spangler. You got to admire that kind of control."

"Another hoax," says Casey. "They staged the whole thing in a little studio up the coast. I know a guy in video."

I told Casey I'd read where Dillinger started to run when he saw the cops outside the picture show. And how his sister had identified the remains the next day.

"He turned chickenshit on me, Son. We hadn't told him the exact date, and there he is, coming out from the movies with a broad on each arm and all of a sudden the party's over. What would you do, you were him? And as for Sis," says Casey, "she always done what she could to help me out.

"The day after the planting we send in a truck, dig the coffin out, pour in concrete and lay it back in. Anybody wants another peek at the stiff they got to drill a mine shaft."

It sounded reasonable, sort of. And when the shrink who comes through twice a year stopped to ask about his Dillinger fixation Casey just told him to scram. Said if he wanted his brains scrambled he'd stick his head in the microwave.

I did some reading and everything he said checked out pretty close. Only I couldn't connect Casey with a guy who'd pull a stunt like that on the Lawrence fella. He was one of the nice ones, Casey — never bitched much even with his diabetes and his infected feet and his rotting kidneys and his finger curling up. A stand-up character.

The finger was curling up independent from the others on his right hand. His trigger finger, bent like he was about to squeeze off a round.

"It's like the *Tell-Tale Heart*,"[5] says Roscoe one day. I'm picking up dinner trays in the rooms and Roscoe is working on four chocolate puddings. They had put one on Casey's tray by mistake and I didn't have the time to spoon the other two down Kantor and Wise.

"The what?" asks Casey.

"It's a story. This guy kills an old man and stuffs him under the floorboards. When the police come to investigate he thinks he hears the old man's heart beating under the boards and he cracks and gives himself away."

"So what's that got to do with my finger?"

"Maybe your finger is trying to blow the whistle on your life of crime. Psychosomatic."

"Oh." Casey mulled it over in his mind for a minute. "I get it. We had a guy in the can, kilt his wife. Poisoned her. At first everybody figured she'd just got sick and died, happened all the time in those days. But then he starts complaining to the cops about the neighborhood kids — says they're writing nasty stuff on the sidewalk in front of his place: 'Old Man Walsh croaked his wife with rat bait,' stuff like that. So the cops send a guy to check it out on his night rounds. The cop's passing by and out comes Walsh, sleepwalking, with a piece of chalk in his hand. Wrote his own ticket to the slammer, right there on the sidewalk, onnaconna he had a leaky conscience."

It had been bothering me so I took the opening to ask. "Do you ever feel bad? About things you done back then?"

Casey shrugged and looked away from me and then looked back. "Nah," he says, "What am I, mental? This guy Walsh, he was AWOL."

AWOL is what we call the senile ones. Off base and not coming back.

"Hey Roscoe," says Casey, "why'd this telltale character kill the old man in the first place?"

"Because this old man had a big eye. He wanted to kill the big eye."

Just then Spurs wheels in looking to vulture a loose dessert.

"I wonder," says Casey, "what he would of done to a fat head?"

It seemed to make him feel better, talking about his life as Dillinger. Kept him up and alert even when his health took a big slide.

"Only reason I'm still percolating," he'd say, "is I still got my pride. They beat that into me my first stretch."

I told him I'd never heard of beating pride into somebody.

"They beat on you one way or the other," he says. "The pride comes in how you stand up to it."

I went on the graveyard shift and after two o'clock check I'd go down to chew the fat with Casey. Roscoe slept like the dead and the two veggies were on automatic pilot so it didn't make any difference how loud we were. Casey was a hurtin cowboy and his meds weren't up to knocking him out at night. We'd play cards by the light from the corridor sometimes or sometimes he'd cut up old scores for me. He told me about one where their advance man posed as a Hollywood location scout for a gangster movie. When they come out of the bank holding hostages the next day, sniping at the local shields, the townspeople just smiled and looked around for cameras.

---

[5] Short story by Edgar Allan Poe.

He didn't have much to say on his years driving for Fox. He only hung on because of what he called the "fringe benefits," which mostly had to do with women.

"Used to be a disease with me," he'd say. "I'd go two days without a tumble and my eyeballs would start to swoll up, my brains would start pushing out my ears. Shut me out for three days and I'd hump anything, just anything. Like some dope fiend."

When I asked how he'd dealt with that while he was in the slammer he clammed up.

He was still able to wheel himself around a bit when Norma took up with him. Norma had bad veins and was in a chair herself. She'd been in the silents in her teens, getting rescued from fates worse than death. Her mother was ninety and shared a room with her. The old vulture just sat, deaf as a post, glaring at Norma for not being Mary Pickford. Norma had been one of the backgammon crowd till word spread that Casey thought he was John Dillinger. She studied him for a week, keeping her distance, eavesdropping on his sparring matches with Spurs Tatum, watching how he moved and how he talked. Then one day as the singalong is breaking up she wheels up beside him. Norma's voice had gone deeper and deeper with the years and she filled in at bass on "What a Friend We Have in Jesus."

"All I do is dream of you," she sings to Casey, "the whole night through."

"That used to be my favorite song," he says.

"I know," says Norma.

It give me the fantods sometimes, the way they'd look at each other like they known one another forever. Norma had been one of those caught up by the press on Dillinger when he had his year in the headlines. A woman near thirty years old keeping a scrapbook. She had picked up some work as an extra after her silent days were over, but it never came to much. She still had a shoe box full of the postcards her mother had sent out every year to agents and flacks and producers — a grainy blowup of Norma in a toga or a buckskin shift or a French peasant outfit. Norma Nader in *Cimarron*. Norma Nader in *The Pride and the Passion*. Norma Nader in *The Greatest Story Ever Told*. They were the only credits she got in the talkies, those postcards, but her mother kept the heat on. I'd find Norma out in the corridor at night, wheels locked, watching the light coming out from her room.

"Is she in bed yet?" she'd ask, and I'd go down and peek in on Old Lady Nader.

"She's still awake, Norma."

"She always stood up till I come home, no matter what hour. I come in the door and it's not 'Where you been?' or 'Who'd you see?' but 'Any work today?' She had spies at all the studios so I could never lie about making rounds. Once I had an offer for a secretary job, good pay, steady, and I had to tell them sorry, I got to be an actress."

Casey had his Dillinger routine down pretty well, but with Norma along he was unstoppable.

"Johnnie," she'd say, "you member that time in St. Paul they caught you in the alleyway?" or "Johnnie, remember how Nelson and Van Meter were always at each other's throats?" — just like she'd been there. And Casey he'd nod and say he remembered or correct some little detail, reminding her like any old couple sharing memories.

I'd come on at eleven and they'd be in the day room with only the TV for light, Casey squirming in his chair, hurting, and Norma waiting for her mother to go to sleep, holding Casey's hand against the pain. We had another old pair like them, a couple old bachelors were crazy for chess. One game could take them two, three days. Personally I'd rather watch paint dry.

Usually some time around one o'clock Norma would call and we'd wheel them back to their rooms. I'd park Casey by the window so he could watch the traffic on Cahuenga.

By the time I got back on day shift Casey needed a push when he wanted to get anywhere.

He could still feed himself and hit the pee-jug nine times out of ten, though we were checking his output to see what was left of his kidneys. This one morning we had square egg for breakfast, which is the powdered variety cooked up in cake pans and cut in little bars like brownies. If they don't get the coloring just right they'll come up greenish and they wiggle on your fork just like jello. Even the blind patients won't touch them. Usually our only taker is this character Mao, who we call after his resemblance to the late Chinese head Red. Mao is a mongoloid in his mid-thirties whose favorite dishes are square egg and thermometers. Already that morning a new candy striper had given him an oral instead of a rectal and he'd chomped it clear in half. Now she was fluttering around looking for Mr. Hellman's other slipper.

"I looked in his stand and under his bed," she says to me, "and all I could find is the right one."

"He doesn't have a left one," I tell her.

"Why not?"

"He doesn't have a left leg."

"Oh." The candy stripers are good for morale but they take a lot of looking after.

"Next time peek under the covers first."

"Well I started to," she says, "but he was flipping his — you know — his *thing* at me."

"Don't you worry, honey," says Spurs Tatum. "Worst comes to worst I'd lay odds you could outrun the old goat."

"When they give us this shit in the state pen," says Casey so's everybody in the day room could hear him," we'd plaster the walls with it."

The candy striper waggles her finger at him. "If you don't care for your breakfast, Mr. Mullins, I'm sure somebody else would appreciate it."

"No dice," says Casey. "I want to see it put down the trash barrel where it can't do no harm. And the name's Dillinger."

"I'm sure you don't mind if somebody shares what you don't want. I mean what are we here for?" Lately we've been getting candy stripers with a more Christian outlook.

"What we're *here* for," says Casey, "is to die. To die. And some of us," he says looking to Spurs, "aren't doing much of a job of it."

Casey was on the rag that morning, with a bad case of the runs his new meds give him and a wobbling pile of square egg staring up at him. So when the candy striper reaches to give his portion over to Mao, Casey pushes his tray onto the floor.

"You birds keep swallowin this shit," he calls out to the others, "they'll keep sending it up."

Mao was well known for his oatmeal tossing. You'd get two spoonfuls down him and he'd decide to chuck the whole bowl across the room. Or wing it straight up so big globs stuck to the ceiling. The old-timers liked to sit against the back wall of the day room afternoons and bet on which glob would loosen and fall first. So when Mao picked up on Casey and made like a catapult with his plate there was chunks sent scattering clear to the bingo tables.

"Food riot!" yells Roscoe, flicking egg off his fork, aiming for old oatmeal stains on the ceiling. "Every man for himself!" he yells and then goes into "Ding-Dong the Witch Is Dead."

I didn't think the old farts had it in them. It was like being inside a popcorn popper, yellow hunks of egg flying every whichway, squishing, bouncing, coffee sloshing, toast frisbeeing, plates smashing, orange juice showering while Mrs. Shapiro, stone blind and AWOL for years is yelling "Boys, don't fight! Don't fight, your father will get crazy!"

The rec therapist is a togetherness freak. They sing together, they make place mats together, they have oral history sessions together. So somebody starts throwing food the rest of them are bound to pitch in. When there was nothing left to toss they calmed down. We decided to wheel them all back to their rooms before we cleaned out the day room.

"I'm hungry," says Spurs. "Crazy sumbitch made me lose my breakfast. Senile bastard."

"Shove it, cowboy," says Casey. "In my day we'd of used you for a toothpick."

"In *my* day we'd of stuck you in the bughouse. Dillinger my ass."

Casey didn't say a thing but Norma wheeled up between them, a big smear of grape jelly on her cheek.

"John Dillinger," she said, "was the only one in the whole lousy country was his own man, the only one that told them all to go hang and went his own way. Have some respect."

I never learned if she really thought he was Dillinger or if they just shared the same interest like the chess players or the crowd that still reads the trade papers together. When Norma went AWOL it was like her mother called her in from the playground. She left us quick, fading in and out for two weeks till she give up all the way and just sat in her chair in her room, staring back at her mother.

"I'm sorry," she'd say from time to time. No word on why or what for, just stare at Old Lady Nader and say, "I'm sorry."

Casey tried to pull her out of it at first. But it's like when we have a cardiac arrest and we pull the curtain around the bed — even if you're right in the room you can't see through to know what's happening.

"You remember me?" he'd say. "You remember about Johnnie Dillinger?"

Usually she'd just look at him blank. One time she said, "I seen a movie about him once."

For a while Casey would have us wheel him into Norma's room and he'd talk at her some but she didn't know who he was. Finally it made him so low he stopped visiting. Acted like she'd gone downstairs.

"You lose your mind," he'd say, "the rest of you ain't worth spit."

Mrs. Goorwitz got on his case then and tried to locate relatives. None to be found. What with the way people move around out here that's not so unusual. Casey's chart was nothing but a medical record starting in 1937. Next Mrs. Goorwitz loosed the social worker on him, Friendly Phil, who ought to be selling health food or real estate somewhere. Casey wasn't buying any.

"So what if I am crazy?" he'd say to Phil. "Delusional, schizo, whatever you wanna call it. I can't do squat one way or the other. What difference does it make if I was Dillinger or Norma was Pearl White or Roscoe was the King of Poland? You're all just a bag a bones in the end."

He went into a funk, Casey, after Norma faded — went into a silence that lasted a good month. Not even Spurs could get his goat enough to argue. He spent a good part of the day trying to keep himself clean.

"I'm on the cycle," he whispered to me one day. "I'm riding the down side."

The geriatric racket is a collection of cycles. Linen goes on beds, gets dirtied, down the chute, washed, dried and back onto the beds. Patients are checked in downstairs, up to the beds, maintained a while and then down to the slabs with them. Casey even found a new cycle, a thing in the paper about scientists who had learned how to make cow flops back into cow food.

"I don't want to make accusations here," says Casey one day, pointing to his lunch, "but what does *that* look like to you?"

The day came when Casey lost his control, racked up six incontinents on the report in one week. His health was shot but I tried to talk Mrs. Goorwitz out of it when she handed me the kit. He had a thing about it, Casey.

"A man that can't control his bowels," he'd say, "is not a man."

He knew what was up when I started to draw the curtain. Roscoe scowled at me from across the room and rolled over to face the wall. Kantor and Wise lay there like house plants. It was midnight and they'd given Casey some heavy meds with his dinner. He looked at me like I come to snuff him with a pillow over the face. He was too weak to raise his arms so I didn't have to put the restraints on.

"It has to be, Casey," I told him. "Or else you'll be wettin all over yourself."

I washed my hands with the soap from the kit.

"If they ask why I done it, the banks and all," he whispers, "tell them I was just bored. Just bored crapless."

I took the gloves out of their cellophane and managed to wriggle into them without touching my fingers to their outside. I washed Casey and laid the fenestrated sheet over so only his thing stuck through. If the stories about Dillinger's size are true, Casey was qualified. The girls on the evening shift called it "The Snake." I swabbed the tip of it, unwrapped the catheter tube, and coated it with K-Y.

"You been white to me, Son," says Casey. "I don't put no blame on you."

"I'm sorry."

"Don't ever say that," says Casey. "Don't ever say you're sorry. Do it or don't do it but don't apologize."

I pushed the catheter tube down till it blocked at his sphincter, wiggled it and it slipped past. It was the narrowest gauge but still it's a surprise that you can fit one into a man. I stuck the syringe into the irrigation branch and shot the saline up till the bulb was inflated in his bladder. I gave a tug to see if it was anchored. Casey was crying, looking away from me. His eyes had gone fuzzy, the way fish eyes do after you beach them. I hooked the plastic tubing and the piss-bag to the catheter.

"I used to be somebody," said Casey.

I had a long weekend, and when I came back on I didn't get a chance to talk with him. Mrs. Goorwitz said in report how he'd been moved to Intensive Care. On my first check I found him looking like the pictures of the Biograph shooting — blood everywhere, hard yellow light. Something had popped inside and he'd bled out the mouth. He had pulled the catheter out, bulb and all, and he was bleeding down there. We put sheets on the floor and rolled him sideways across the bed on his belly so he drained out onto them. It takes a half hour or so.

I traced him back through the medical plan at Fox and ran into nothing but dead ends. Usually I forget about them once they go downstairs but Casey had gotten his hooks in. There at Fox I found an old fella in custodial who remembered him.

"Always taking the limos for joyrides," he said. "It's a wonder he didn't get his ass fired."

I brought the subject up at the nurses' station one night — how maybe he could of been — and they asked me how much sleep I'd been getting. So I don't know one way or the other. Roscoe, he's sure, he's positive, but Roscoe also thinks our every move is being watched by aliens with oversized IQs. I figure if they're so smart they got better things to occupy their time.

One day I'm tube-feeding some vegematic when out in the corridor I hear Spurs Tatum giving his brag to a couple recent admissions that come in with their feet falling off.

"Hoot Gibson held my horse," says Spurs. "I took falls for Randy Scott. John Wayne blew me off a stagecoach. And once," he says, "I played Parcheesi with John Herbert Dillinger."

QUESTIONS

1. How does the narrator fit in and stand apart from the nursing home? What are his views about the patients? What is the effect of his humor?

2. Is Casey's story credible? Does he really believe it? Is he merely acting out a role? Why does he choose John Dillinger as his identity? What commentary does this story make on the themes of identity and illusion?

3. What is the effect of the setting? How does the nursing home's location determine the type of patients it receives? What do the nursing home and Hollywood have in common?

4. What is Norma's function in the story?

LYNNE SHARON SCHWARTZ ≡≡≡

Rough Strife

Now let us sport us while we may;
And now, like am'rous birds of prey
... tear our pleasure with rough strife
Through the iron gates of life.
　　　ANDREW MARVELL[1]

Caroline and Ivan finally had a child. Conception stunned them; they didn't think, by now, that it could happen. For years they had tried and failed, till it seemed that a special barren destiny was preordained. Meanwhile, in the wide spaces of childlessness, they had created activity: their work flourished. Ivan, happy and moderately powerful in a large foundation, helped decide how to distribute money for artistic and social projects. Caroline taught mathematics at a small suburban university. Being a mathematician, she found, conferred a painful private wisdom on her efforts to conceive. In her brain, as Ivan exploded within her, she would involuntarily calculate probabilities; millions of blind sperm and one reluctant egg clustered before her eyes in swiftly transmuting geometric patterns. She lost her grasp of pleasure, forgot what it could feel like without a goal. She had no idea what Ivan might be thinking about, scattered seed money, maybe. Their passion became courteous and automatic until, by attrition, for months they didn't make love — it was too awkward.

One September Sunday morning she was in the shower, watching, through a crack in the curtain, Ivan naked at the washstand. He was shaving, his jaw tilted at an innocently self-satisfied angle. He wasn't aware of being watched, so that a secret quality, an essence of Ivan, exuded in great waves. Caroline could almost see it, a cloudy aura. He stroked his jaw vainly with intense concentration, a self-absorption so contagious that she needed, suddenly, to possess it with him. She stepped out of the shower.

"Ivan."

He turned abruptly, surprised, perhaps even annoyed at the interruption.

"Let's not have a baby any more. Let's just ... come on." When she placed her wet hand

---

[1] Andrew Marvell (1621–1678), English poet; the lines quoted are from the conclusion of Marvell's "To His Coy Mistress."

on his back he lifted her easily off her feet with his right arm, the razor still poised in his other, outstretched hand.

"Come on," she insisted. She opened the door and a draft blew into the small steamy room. She pulled him by the hand toward the bedroom.

Ivan grinned. "You're soaking wet."

"Wet, dry, what's the difference?" It was hard to speak. She began to run, to tease him; he caught her and tossed her onto their disheveled bed and dug his teeth so deep into her shoulder that she thought she would bleed.

Then with disinterest, taken up only in this fresh rushing need for him, weeks later Caroline conceived. Afterwards she liked to say that she had known the moment it happened. It felt different, she told him, like a pin pricking a balloon, but without the shattering noise, without the quick collapse. "Oh, come on," said Ivan. "That's impossible."

But she was a mathematician, after all, and dealt with infinitesimal precise abstractions, and she did know how it had happened. The baby was conceived in strife, one early October night, Indian summer. All day the sun glowed hot and low in the sky, settling an amber torpor on people and things, and the night was the same, only now a dark hot heaviness sunk slowly down. The scent of the still-blooming honeysuckle rose to their bedroom window. Just as she was bending over to kiss him, heavy and quivering with heat like the night, he teased her about something, about a mole on her leg, and in reply she punched him lightly on the shoulder. He grabbed her wrists, and when she began kicking, pinned her feet down with his own. In an instant Ivan lay stretched out on her back like a blanket, smothering her, while she struggled beneath, writhing to escape. It was a silent, sweaty struggle, interrupted with outbursts of wild laughter, shrieks and gasping breaths. She tried biting but, laughing loudly, he evaded her, and she tried scratching the fists that held her down, but she couldn't reach. All her desire was transformed into physical effort, but he was too strong for her. He wanted her to say she gave up, but she refused, and since he wouldn't loosen his grip they lay locked and panting in their static embrace for some time.

"You win," she said at last, but as he rolled off she sneakily jabbed him in the ribs with her elbow.

"Aha!" Ivan shouted, and was ready to begin again, but she quickly distracted him. Once the wrestling was at an end, though, Caroline found her passion dissipated, and her pleasure tinged with resentment. After they made love forcefully, when they were covered with sweat, dripping on each other, she said, "Still, you don't play fair."

"I don't play fair! Look who's talking. Do you want me to give you a handicap?"

"No."

"So?"

"It's not fair, that's all."

Ivan laughed gloatingly and curled up in her arms. She smiled in the dark.

That was the night the baby was conceived, not in high passion but rough strife.

She lay on the table in the doctor's office weeks later. The doctor, whom she had known for a long time, habitually kept up a running conversation while he probed. Today, fretting over his weight problem, he outlined his plans for a new diet. Tensely she watched him, framed and centered by her raised knees, which were still bronzed from summer sun. His other hand was pressing on her stomach. Caroline was nauseated with fear and trembling, afraid of the verdict. It was taking so long, perhaps it was a tumor.

"I'm cutting out all starches," he said. "I've really let myself go lately."

"Good idea." Then she gasped in pain. A final, sickening thrust, and he was out. Relief, and a sore gap where he had been. In a moment, she knew, she would be retching violently.

"Well?"

"Well, Caroline, you hit the jackpot this time."

She felt a smile, a stupid, puppet smile, spread over her face. In the tiny bathroom where she threw up, she saw in the mirror the silly smile looming over her ashen face like a dancer's glowing grimace of labored joy. She smiled through the rest of the visit, through his advice about milk, weight, travel and rest, smiled at herself in the window of the bus, and at her moving image in the fenders of parked cars as she walked home.

Ivan, incredulous over the telephone, came home beaming stupidly just like Caroline, and brought a bottle of champagne. After dinner they drank it and made love.

"Do you think it's all right to do this?" he asked.

"Oh, Ivan, honestly. It's microscopic."

He was in one of his whimsical moods and made terrible jokes that she laughed at with easy indulgence. He said he was going to pay the baby a visit and asked if she had any messages she wanted delivered. He unlocked from her embrace, moved down her body and said he was going to have a look for himself. Clowning, he put his ear between her legs to listen. Whatever amusement she felt soon ebbed away into irritation. She had never thought Ivan would be a doting parent — he was so preoccupied with himself. Finally he stopped his antics as she clasped her arms around him and whispered, "Ivan, you are really too much." He became unusually gentle. Tamed, and she didn't like it, hoped he wouldn't continue that way for months. Pleasure lapped over her with a mild, lackadaisical bitterness, and then when she could be articulate once more she explained patiently, "Ivan, you know, it really is all right. I mean, it's a natural process."

"Well I didn't want to hurt you."

"I'm not sick."

Then, as though her body were admonishing that cool confidence, she did get sick. There were mornings when she awoke with such paralyzing nausea that she had to ask Ivan to bring her a hard roll from the kitchen before she could stir from bed. To move from her awakening position seemed a tremendous risk, as if she might spill out. She rarely threw up — the nausea resembled violent hunger. Something wanted to be filled, not expelled, a perilous vacuum occupying her insides. The crucial act was getting the first few mouthfuls down. Then the solidity and denseness of the hard unbuttered roll stabilized her, like a heavy weight thrown down to anchor a tottering ship. Her head ached. On the mornings when she had no classes she would wander around the house till almost noon clutching the partly eaten roll in her hand like a talisman. Finishing one roll, she quickly went to the breadbox for another; she bought them regularly at the bakery a half dozen at a time. With enough roll inside her she could sometimes manage a half cup of tea, but liquids were risky. They sloshed around inside and made her envision the baby sloshing around too, in its cloudy fluid. By early afternoon she would feel fine. The baby, she imagined, claimed her for the night and was reluctant to give up its hold in the morning: they vied till she conquered. She was willing to yield her sleeping hours to the baby, her dreams even, if necessary, but she wanted the daylight for herself.

The mornings that she taught were agony. Ivan would wake her up early, bring her a roll, and gently prod her out of bed.

"I simply cannot do it," she would say, placing her legs cautiously over the side of the bed.

"Sure you can. Now get up."

"I'll die if I get up."

"You have no choice. You have a job." He was freshly showered and dressed, and his neatness irritated her. He had nothing more to do — the discomfort was all hers. She rose to her feet and swayed.

Ivan looked alarmed. "Do you want me to call and tell them you can't make it?"

"No, no." That frightened her. She needed to hold on to the job, to defend herself against the growing baby. Once she walked into the classroom she would be fine. A Mondrian[2] print hung on the back wall — she could look at that, and it would steady her. With waves of nausea roiling in her chest, she stumbled into the bathroom.

She liked him to wait until she was out of the shower before he left for work, because she anticipated fainting under the impact of the water. Often at the end she forced herself to stand under an ice cold flow, leaning her head way back and letting her short fair hair drip down behind her. Though it was torture, when she emerged she felt more alive.

After the shower had been off a while Ivan would come and open the bathroom door. "Are you O.K. now, Caroline? I've got to go." It made her feel like a child. She would be wrapped in a towel with her hair dripping on the mat, brushing her teeth or rubbing cream into her face. "Yes, thanks for waiting. I guess this'll end soon. They say it's only the first few months."

He kissed her lips, her bare damp shoulder, gave a parting squeeze to her toweled behind, and was gone. She watched him walk down the hall. Ivan was very large. She had always been drawn and aroused by his largeness, by the huge bones and the taut legs that felt as though he had steel rods inside. But now she watched with some trepidation, hoping Ivan wouldn't have a large, inflexible baby.

Very slowly she would put on clothes. Selecting each article seemed a much more demanding task than ever before. Seeing how slow she had become, she allowed herself over an hour, keeping her hard roll nearby as she dressed and prepared her face. All the while, through the stages of dressing, she evaluated her body closely in the full-length mirror, first naked, then in bra and underpants, then with shoes added, and finally with a dress. She was looking for signs, but the baby was invisible. Nothing had changed yet. She was still as she had always been, not quite slim yet somehow appearing small, almost delicate. She used to pride herself on strength. When they moved in she had worked as hard as Ivan, lugging furniture and lifting heavy cartons. He was impressed. Now, of course, she could no longer do that — it took all her strength to move her own weight.

With the profound sensuous narcissism of women past first youth, she admired her still-narrow waist and full breasts. She was especially fond of her shoulders and prominent collarbone, which had a fragile, inviting look. That would all be gone soon, of course, gone soft. Curious about how she would alter, she scanned her face for the pregnant look she knew well from the faces of friends. It was far less a tangible change than a look of transparent vulnerability that took over the face: nearly a pleading look, a beg for help like a message from a powerless invaded country to the rest of the world. Caroline did not see it on her face yet.

From the tenth to the fourteenth week of her pregnancy she slept, with brief intervals of lucidity when she taught her classes. It was a strange dreamy time. The passionate nausea faded, but the lure of the bed was irresistible. In the middle of the day, even, she could pass by the bedroom, glimpse the waiting bed and be overcome by the soft heavy desire to lie down. She fell into a stupor immediately and did not dream. She forgot what it was like to awaken with energy and move through an entire day without lying down once. She forgot the feeling of eyes opened wide without effort. She would have liked to hide this strange, shameful

---

[2] Piet Mondrian (1872–1944), Dutch painter.

perversity from Ivan, but that was impossible. Ivan kept wanting to go to the movies. Clearly, he was bored with her. Maybe, she imagined, staring up at the bedroom ceiling through slitted eyes, he would become so bored he would abandon her and the baby and she would not be able to support the house alone and she and the baby would end up on the streets in rags, begging. She smiled. That was highly unlikely. Ivan would not be the same Ivan without her.

"You go on, Ivan. I just can't."

Once he said, "I thought I might ask Ruth Forbes to go with me to see the Charlie Chaplin in town. I know she likes him. Would that bother you?"

She was half-asleep, slowly eating a large apple in bed and watching "Medical Center" on television, but she roused herself to answer. "No, of course not." Ruth Forbes was a divorced woman who lived down the block, a casual friend and not Ivan's type at all, too large, loud and depressed. Caroline didn't care if he wanted her company. She didn't care if he held her hand on his knee in the movies as he liked to do, or even if, improbably, he made love to her afterwards in her sloppy house crawling with children. She didn't care about anything except staying nestled in bed.

She made love with him sometimes, in a slow way. She felt no specific desire but didn't want to deny him, she loved him so. Or had, she thought vaguely, when she was alive and strong. Besides, she knew she could sleep right after. Usually there would be a moment when she came alive despite herself, when the reality of his body would strike her all at once with a wistful throb of lust, but mostly she was too tired to see it through, to leap towards it, so she let it subside, merely nodding at it gratefully as a sign of dormant life. She felt sorry for Ivan, but helpless.

Once to her great shame, she fell asleep while he was inside her. He woke her with a pat on her cheek, actually, she realized from the faint sting, a gesture more like a slap than a pat. "Caroline, for Christ's sake, you're sleeping."

"No, no, I'm sorry. I wasn't really sleeping. Oh, Ivan, it's nothing. This will end." She wondered, though.

Moments later she felt his hands on her thighs. His lips were brooding on her stomach, edging, with expertise, lower and lower down. He was murmuring something she couldn't catch. She felt an ache, an irritation. Of course he meant well, Ivan always did. Wryly, she appreciated his intentions. But she couldn't bear that excitement now.

"Please," she said. "Please don't do that."

He was terribly hurt. He said nothing, but leaped away violently and pulled all the blankets around him. She was contrite, shed a few private tears and fell instantly into a dreamless dark.

He wanted to go to a New Year's Eve party some close friends were giving, and naturally he wanted her to come with him. Caroline vowed to herself she would do this for him because she had been giving so little for so long. She planned to get dressed and look very beautiful, as she could still look when she took plenty of time and tried hard enough; she would not drink very much — it was sleep-inducing — and she would not be the one to suggest going home. After sleeping through the day in preparation, she washed her hair, using something she found in the drugstore to heighten the blond flecks. Then she put on a long green velvet dress with gold embroidery, and inserted the gold hoop earrings Ivan bought her some years ago for her twenty-fifth birthday. Before they set out she drank a cup of black coffee. She would have taken No-Doze but she was afraid of drugs, afraid of giving birth to an armless or legless baby who would be a burden and a heartache to them for the rest of their days.

At the party of mostly university people, she chatted with everyone equally, those she knew well and those she had never met. Sociably, she held a filled glass in her hand, taking tiny sips. She and Ivan were not together very much — it was crowded, smoky and loud; people kept moving and encounters were brief — but she knew he was aware of her, could feel his awareness through the milling bodies. He was aware and he was pleased. He deserved more than the somnambulist she had become, and she was pleased to please him. But after a while her legs would not support her for another instant. The skin tingled: soft warning bells rang from every pore. She allowed herself a moment to sit down alone in a small alcove off the living room, where she smoked a cigarette and stared down at her lap, holding her eyes open very wide. Examining the gold and rose-colored embroidery on her dress, Caroline traced the coiled pattern, mathematical and hypnotic, with her index finger. Just as she was happily merging into its intricacies, a man, a stranger, came in, breaking her trance. He was a very young man, twenty-three, maybe, of no apparent interest.

"Hi. I hear you're expecting a baby," he began, and sat down with a distinct air of settling in.

"Yes. That's quite an opening line. How did you know?"

"I know because Linda told me. You know Linda, don't you? I'm her brother."

He began asking about her symptoms. Sleepiness? Apathy? He knew, he had worked in a clinic. Unresponsive, she retorted by inquiring about his taste in music. He sat on a leather hassock opposite Caroline on the couch, and with every inquisitive sentence drew his seat closer till their knees were almost touching. She shifted her weight to avoid him, tucked her feet under her and lit another cigarette, feeling she could lie down and fall into a stupor quite easily. Still, words were coming out of her mouth, she heard them; she hoped they were not encouraging words but she seemed to have very little control over what they were.

"I — " he said. "You see — " He reached out and put his hand over hers. "Pregnant women, like, they really turn me on. I mean, there's a special aura. You're sensational."

She pulled her hand away. "God almighty."

"What's the matter? Honestly, I didn't mean to offend you."

"I really must go." She stood up and stepped around him.

"Could I see you some time?"

"You're seeing me now. Enjoy it."

He ran his eyes over her from head to toe, appraising. "It doesn't show yet."

Gazing down at her body, Caroline stretched the loose velvet dress taut over her stomach. "No, you're right, it doesn't." Then, over her shoulder, as she left their little corner, she tossed, "Fuck you, you pig."

With a surge of energy she downed a quick scotch, found Ivan and tugged at his arm. "Let's dance."

Ivan's blue eyes lightened with shock. At home she could barely walk.

"Yes, let's." He took her in his arms and she buried her face against his shoulder. But she held her tears back, she would not let him know.

Later she told him about it. It was three-thirty in the morning, they had just made love drunkenly, and Ivan was in high spirits. She knew why — he felt he had her back again. She had held him close and uttered her old sounds, familiar moans and cries like a poignant, nearly-forgotten tune, and Ivan was miraculously restored, his impact once again sensible to eye and ear. He was making her laugh hysterically now, imitating the eccentric professor of art history at the party, an owlish émigré from Bavaria who expounded on the dilemmas of today's youth, all the while pronouncing "youth" as if it rhymed with "mouth." Ivan had also discovered that he pronounced "unique" as if it were "eunuch." Then, sitting up in bed cross-legged, they competed in making up pretentious scholarly sentences that included both "unique" and "youth" mispronounced.

"Speaking of 'yowth,'" Caroline said, "I met a weird one tonight, Linda's brother. A very eunuch yowth, I must say." And giggling, she recounted their conversation. Suddenly at the end she unexpectedly found herself in tears. Shuddering, she flopped over and sobbed into her pillow.

"Caroline," he said tenderly, "please. For heaven's sake, it was just some nut. It was nothing. Don't get all upset over it." He stroked her bare back.

"I can't help it," she wailed. "It made me feel so disgusting."

"You're much too sensitive. Come on." He ran his hand slowly through her hair, over and over.

She pulled the blanket around her. "Enough. I'm going to sleep."

A few days later, when classes were beginning again for the new semester, she woke early and went immediately to the shower, going through the ritual motions briskly and automatically. She was finished and brushing her teeth when she realized what had happened. There she was on her feet, sturdy, before eight in the morning, planning how she would introduce the topic of the differential calculus to her new students. She stared at her face in the mirror with unaccustomed recognition, her mouth dripping white foam, her dark eyes startled. She was alive. She didn't know how the miracle had happened, nor did she care to explore it. Back in the bedroom she dressed quickly, zipping up a pair of slim rust-colored woollen slacks with satisfaction. It didn't show yet, but soon.

"Ivan, time to get up."

He grunted and opened his eyes. When at last they focused on Caroline leaning over him they burned blue and wide with astonishment. He rubbed a fist across his forehead. "Are you dressed already?"

"Yes. I'm cured."

"What do you mean?"

"I'm not tired any more. I'm slept out. I've come back to life."

"Oh." He moaned and rolled over in one piece like a seal.

"Aren't you getting up?"

"In a little while. I'm so tired. I must sleep for a while." The words were thick and slurred.

"Well!" She was strangely annoyed. Ivan always got up with vigor. "Are you sick?"

"Uh-uh."

After a quick cup of coffee she called out, "Ivan, I'm leaving now. Don't forget to get up." The January air was crisp and exhilarating, and she walked the half mile to the university at a nimble clip, going over her introductory remarks in her head.

Ivan was tired for a week. Caroline wanted to go out to dinner every evening — she had her appetite back. She had broken through dense earth to fresh air. It was a new year and soon they would have a new baby. But all Ivan wanted to do was stay home and lie on the bed and watch television. It was repellent. Sloth, she pointed out to him more than once, was one of the seven deadly sins. The fifth night she said in exasperation, "What the hell is the matter with you? If you're sick go to a doctor."

"I'm not sick. I'm tired. Can't I be tired too? Leave me alone. I left you alone, didn't I?"

"That was different."

"How?"

"I'm pregnant and you're not, in case you've forgotten."

"How could I forget?"

She said nothing, only cast him an evil look.

One evening soon after Ivan's symptoms disappeared, they sat together on the living-room sofa sharing sections of the newspaper. Ivan had his feet up on the coffee table and

Caroline sat diagonally, resting her legs on his. She paused in her reading and touched her stomach.

"Ivan."

"What?"

"It's no use. I'm going to have to buy some maternity clothes."

He put down the paper and stared. "Really?" He seemed distressed.

"Yes."

"Well, don't buy any of those ugly things they wear. Can't you get some of those, you know, sort of Indian things?"

"Yes. That's a good idea. I will."

He picked up the paper again.

"It moves."

"What?"

"I said it moves. The baby."

"It moves?"

She laughed. "Remember Galileo? *Eppure, si muove.*[3] They had spent years together in Italy in their first youth, in mad love, and visited the birthplace of Galileo. He was a hero to both of them, because his mind remained free and strong though his body succumbed to tyranny.

Ivan laughed too. "*Eppure, si muove.* Let me see." He bent his head down to feel it, then looked up at her, his face full of longing, marvel and envy. In a moment he was scrambling at her clothes in a young eager rush. He wanted to be there, he said. Caroline, taken by surprise, was suspended between laughter and tears. He had her on the floor in silence, and for each it was swift and consuming.

Ivan lay spent in her arms. Caroline, still gasping and clutching him, said, "I could never love it as much as I love you." She wondered, then, hearing her words fall in the still air, whether this would always be true.

Shortly after she began wearing the Indian shirts and dresses, she noticed that Ivan was acting oddly. He stayed late at the office more than ever before, and often brought work home with him. He appeared to have lost interest in the baby, rarely asking how she felt, and when she moaned in bed sometimes, "Oh, I can't get to sleep, it keeps moving around," he responded with a grunt or not at all. He asked her, one warm Sunday in March, if she wanted to go bicycle riding.

"Ivan, I can't go bicycle riding. I mean, look at me."

"Oh, right. Of course."

He seemed to avoid looking at her, and she did look terrible, she had to admit. Even she looked at herself in the mirror as infrequently as possible. She dreaded what she had heard about hair falling out and teeth rotting, but she drank her milk diligently and so far neither of those things had happened. But besides the grotesque belly, her ankles swelled up so that the shape of her own legs was alien. She took diuretics and woke every hour at night to go to the bathroom. Sometimes it was impossible to get back to sleep so she sat up in bed reading. Ivan said, "Can't you turn the light out? You know I can't sleep with the light on."

"But what should I do? I can't sleep at all."

"Read in the living room."

"It's so cold in there at night."

He would turn away irritably. Once he took the blanket and went to sleep in the living room himself.

---

[3] "And yet, it moves."

They liked to go for drives in the country on warm weekends. It seemed to Caroline that he chose the bumpiest, most untended roads and drove them as rashly as possible. Then when they stopped to picnic and he lay back to bask in the sharp April sunlight, she would always need to go and look for a bathroom, or even a clump of trees. At first this amused him, but soon his amusement became sardonic. He pulled in wearily at gas stations where he didn't need gas and waited in the car with folded arms and a sullen expression that made her apologetic about her ludicrous needs. They were growing apart. She could feel the distance between them like a patch of fog, dimming and distorting the relations of objects in space. The baby that lay between them in the dark was pushing them apart.

Sometimes as she lay awake in bed at night, not wanting to read in the cold living room but reluctant to turn on the light (and it was only a small light, she thought bitterly, a small bedside light), Caroline brooded over the horrible deformities the baby might be born with. She was thirty-one years old, not the best age to bear a first child. It could have cerebral palsy, cleft palate, two heads, club foot. She wondered if she could love a baby with a gross defect. She wondered if Ivan would want to put it in an institution, and if there were any decent institutions in their area, and if they would be spending every Sunday afternoon for the rest of their lives visiting the baby and driving home heartbroken in silence. She lived through these visits to the institution in vivid detail till she knew the doctors' and nurses' faces well. And there would come a point when Ivan would refuse to go anymore — she knew what he was like, selfish with his time and impatient with futility — and she would have to go alone. She wondered if Ivan ever thought about these things, but with that cold mood of his she was afraid to ask.

One night she was desolate. She couldn't bear the loneliness and the heaviness any more, so she woke him.

"Ivan, please. Talk to me. I'm so lonely."

He sat up abruptly. "What?" He was still asleep. With the dark straight hair hanging down over his lean face he looked boyish and vulnerable. Without knowing why, she felt sorry for him.

"I'm sorry. I know you were sleeping but I — " Here she began to weep. "I just lie here forever in the dark and think awful things and you're so far away, and I just — "

"Oh, Caroline. Oh, God." Now he was wide awake, and took her in his arms.

"You're so far away," she wept. "I don't know what's the matter with you."

"I'm sorry. I know it's hard for you. You're so — everything's so different, that's all."

"But it's still me."

"I know. I know it's stupid of me. I can't — "

She knew what it was. It would never be the same. They sat up all night holding each other, and they talked. Ivan talked more than he had in weeks. He said of course the baby would be perfectly all right, and it would be born at just the right time, too, late June, so she could finish up the term, and they would start their natural childbirth group in two weeks so he could be with her and help her, though of course she would do it easily because she was so competent at everything, and then they would have the summer for the early difficult months, and she would be feeling fine and be ready to go back to work in the fall, and they would find a good person, someone like a grandmother, to come in, and he would try to stagger his schedule so she would not feel overburdened and trapped, and in short everything would be just fine, and they would make love again like they used to and be close again. He said exactly what she needed to hear, while she huddled against him, wrenched with pain to realize that he had known all along the right words to say but hadn't thought to say them till she woke him in desperation. Still, in the dawn she slept contented. She loved him. Every now and then she perceived this like a fact of life, an ancient tropism.

Two weeks later they had one of their horrible quarrels. It happened at a gallery, at the opening of a show by a group of young local artists Ivan had discovered. He had encouraged them to apply to his foundation for money and smoothed the way to their success. Now at their triumphant hour he was to be publicly thanked at a formal dinner. There were too many paintings to look at, too many people to greet, and too many glasses of champagne thrust at Caroline, who was near the end of her eighth month now. She walked around for an hour, then whispered to Ivan, "Listen, I'm sorry but I've got to go. Give me the car keys, will you? I don't feel well."

"What's the matter?"

"I can't stop having to go to the bathroom and my feet are killing me and my head aches, and the kid is rolling around like a basketball. You stay and enjoy it. You can get a ride with someone. I'll see you later."

"I'll drive you home," he said grimly. "We'll leave."

An awful knot gripped her stomach. The knot was the image of his perverse resistance, the immense trouble coming, all the trouble congealed and solidified and tied up in one moment. Meanwhile they smiled at the passers-by as they whispered ferociously to each other.

"Ivan, I do not want you to take me home. This is your event. Stay. I am leaving. We are separate people."

"If you're as sick as you say you can't drive home alone. You're my wife and I'll take you home."

"Suit yourself," she said sweetly, because the director of the gallery was approaching. "We all know you're much bigger and stronger than I am." And she smiled maliciously.

Ivan waved vaguely at the director, turned and ushered her to the door. Outside he exploded.

"Shit, Caroline! We can't do a fucking thing any more, can we?"

"You can do anything you like. Just give me the keys. I left mine home."

"I will not give you the keys. Get in the car. You're supposed to be sick."

"You big resentful selfish idiot. Jealous of an embryo." She was screaming now. He started the car with a rush that jolted her forward against the dashboard. "I'd be better off driving myself. You'll kill me this way."

"Shut up," he shouted. "I don't want to hear any more."

"I don't care what you want to hear or not hear."

"Shut the hell up or I swear I'll go into a tree. I don't give a shit any more."

It was starting to rain, a soft silent rain that glittered in the drab dusk outside. At exactly the same moment they rolled up their windows. They were sealed in together, Caroline thought, like restless beasts in a cage. The air in the car was dank and stuffy.

When they got home he slammed the door so hard the house shook. Caroline had calmed herself. She sank down in a chair, kicked off her shoes and rubbed her ankles. "Ivan, why don't you go back? It's not too late. These dinners are always late anyway. I'll be O.K."

"I don't want to go any more," he yelled. "The whole thing is spoiled. Our whole lives are spoiled from now on. We were better off before. I thought you had gotten over wanting it. I thought it was a dead issue." He stared at her bulging stomach with such loathing that she was shocked into horrid, lucid perception.

"You disgust me," she said quietly. "Frankly, you always have and probably always will." She didn't know why she said that. It was quite untrue. It was only true that he disgusted her at this moment, yet the rest had rolled out like string from a hidden ball of twine.

"So why did we ever start this in the first place?" he screamed.

She didn't know whether he meant the marriage or the baby, and for an instant she was afraid he might hit her, there was such compressed force in his huge shoulders.

"Get the hell out of here. I don't want to have to look at you."

"I will. I'll go back. I'll take your advice. Call your fucking obstetrician if you need anything. I'm sure he's always glad of an extra feel."

"You ignorant pig. Go on. And don't hurry back. Find yourself a skinny little art student and give her a big treat."

"I just might." He slammed the door and the house shook again.

He would be back. This was not the first time. Only now she felt no secret excitement, no tremor, no passion that could reshape into lust; she was too heavy and burdened. It would not be easy to make it up — she was in no condition. It would lie between them silently like a dead weight till weeks after the baby was born, till Ivan felt he could reclaim his rightful territory. She knew him too well. Caroline took two aspirins. When she woke at three he was in bed beside her, gripping the blanket in his sleep and breathing heavily. For days afterwards they spoke with strained, subdued courtesy.

They worked diligently in the natural childbirth classes once a week, while at home they giggled over how silly the exercises were, yet Ivan insisted she pant her five minutes each day as instructed. As relaxation training, Ivan was supposed to life each of her legs and arms three times and drop them, while she remained perfectly limp and passive. From the very start Caroline was excellent at this routine, which they did in bed before going to sleep. A substitute, she thought, yawning. She could make her body so limp and passive her arms and legs bounced on the mattress when they fell. One night for diversion she tried doing it to Ivan, but he couldn't master the technique of passivity.

"Don't do anything, Ivan. I lift the leg and I drop the leg. You do nothing. Do you see? Nothing at all," she smiled.

But that was not possible for him. He tried to be limp but kept working along with her; she could see his muscles, precisely those leg muscles she found so desirable, exerting to lift and drop, lift and drop.

"You can't give yourself up. Don't you feel what you're doing? You have to let me do it to you. Let me try just your hand, from the wrist. That might be easier."

"No, forget it. Give me back my hand." He smiled and stroked her stomach gently. "What's the difference? I don't have to do it well. You do it very well."

She did it very well indeed when the time came. It was a short labor, less than an hour, very unusual for a first baby, the nurses kept muttering. She breathed intently, beginning with the long slow breaths she had been taught, feeling quite remote from the bustle around her. Then, in a flurry, they raced her down the hall on a wheeled table with a train of white-coated people trotting after, and she thought, panting, No matter what I suffer, soon I will be thin again, I will be more beautiful than ever.

The room was crowded with people, far more people than she would have thought necessary, but the only faces she singled out were Ivan's and the doctor's. The doctor, with a new russet beard and his face a good deal thinner now, was once again framed by her knees, paler than before. Wildly enthusiastic about the proceedings, he yelled, "Terrific, Caroline, terrific," as though they were in a noisy public place. "O.K., start pushing."

They placed her hands on chrome rails along the table. On the left, groping, she found Ivan's hand and held it instead of the rail. She pushed. In surprise she became aware of a great cleavage, like a mountain of granite splitting apart, only it was in her, she realized, and if it kept on going it would go right up to her neck. She gripped Ivan's warm hand, and just as she opened her mouth to roar someone clapped an oxygen mask on her face so the roar reverberated inward on her own ears. She wasn't supposed to roar, the natural childbirth teacher hadn't mentioned anything about that, she was supposed to breathe and push. But as long as no one seemed to take any notice she might as well keep on roaring, it felt so satisfying and necessary. The teacher would never know. She trusted that if she split all the way up to her neck they would sew her up somehow — she was too far gone to worry about that now. Maybe that was why there were so many of them, yes, of course, to put her back together, and maybe they had simply forgotten to tell her about being bisected; or maybe it was a closely guarded secret, like an initiation rite. She gripped Ivan's hand tighter. She was not having too bad a time, she would surely survive, she told herself, captivated by the hellish bestial sounds going from her mouth to her ear; it certainly was what her students would call a peak experience, and how gratifying to hear the doctor exclaim, "Oh, this is one terrific girl! One more, Caroline, give me one more push and send it out. Sock it to me."

She always tried to be obliging, if possible. Now she raised herself on her elbows and, staring straight at him — he too, after all, had been most obliging these long months — gave him with tremendous force the final push he asked for. She had Ivan's hand tightly around the rail, could feel his knuckles bursting, and then all of a sudden the room and the faces were obliterated. A dark thick curtain swiftly wrapped around her and she was left all alone gasping, sucked violently into a windy black hole of pain so explosive she knew it must be death, she was dying fast, like a bomb detonating. It was all right, it was almost over, only she would have liked to see his blue eyes one last time.

From somewhere in the void Ivan's voice shouted in exultation, "It's coming out," and the roaring stopped and at last there was peace and quiet in her ears. The curtain fell away, the world returned. But her eyes kept on burning, as if they had seen something not meant for living eyes to see and return from alive.

"Give it to me," Caroline said, and held it. She saw that every part was in the proper place, then shut her eyes.

They wheeled her to a room and eased her onto the bed. It was past ten in the morning. She could dimly remember they had been up all night watching a James Cagney movie about prizefighting while they timed her irregular mild contractions. James Cagney went blind from blows given by poisoned gloves in a rigged match, and she wept for him as she held her hands on her stomach and breathed. Neither she nor Ivan had slept or eaten for hours.

"Ivan, there is something I am really dying to have right now."

"Your wish is my command."

She asked for a roast beef on rye with ketchup, and iced tea. "Would you mind? It'll be hours before they serve lunch."

He brought it and stood at the window while she ate ravenously.

"Didn't you get anything for yourself?"

"No, I'm too exhausted to eat." He did, in fact, look terrible. He was sallow; his eyes, usually so radiant, were nearly drained of color, and small downward-curving lines around his mouth recalled his laborious vigil.

"You had a rough night, Ivan. You ought to get some sleep. What's it like outside?"

"What?" Ivan's movements seemed to her extremely purposeless. He was pacing the room with his hands deep in his pockets, going slowly from the foot of the bed to the window and back. Her eyes followed him from the pillow. Every now and then he would stop to peer at Caroline in an unfamiliar way, as if she were a puzzling stranger.

"Ivan, are you O.K.? I meant the weather. What's it doing outside?" It struck her, as she asked, that it was weeks since she had cared to know anything about the outside. That there was an outside, now that she was emptied out, came rushing at her with the most urgent importance, wafting her on a tide of grateful joy.

"Oh," he said vaguely, and came to sit on the edge of her bed. "Well, it's doing something very peculiar outside, as a matter of fact. It's raining but the sun is shining."

She laughed at him. "But haven't you ever seen it do that before?"

"I don't know. I guess so." He opened his mouth and closed it several times. She ate, waiting patiently. Finally he spoke. "You know, Caroline, you really have quite a grip. When you were holding my hand in there, you squeezed it so tight I thought you would break it."

"Oh, come on, that can't be."

"I'm not joking." He massaged his hand absently. Ivan never complained of pain; if anything he understated. But now he held out his right hand and showed her the raw red knuckles and palm, with raised flaming welts forming.

She took his hand. "You're serious. Did I do that? Well, how do you like that?"

"I really thought you'd break my hand. It was killing me." He kept repeating it, not resentfully but dully, as though there were something secreted in the words that he couldn't fathom.

"But why didn't you take it away if it hurt that badly?" She put down her half-eaten sandwich as she saw the pale amazement ripple over his face.

"Oh, no, I couldn't do that. I mean — if that was what you needed just then — " He looked away, embarrassed. "Listen," he shrugged, not facing her, "we're in a hospital, after all. What better place? They'd fix it for me."

Overwhelmed, Caroline lay back on the pillows. "Oh, Ivan. You would do that?"

"What are you crying for?" he asked gently. "You didn't break it, did you? Almost doesn't count. So what are you crying about. You just had a baby. Don't cry."

And she smiled and thought her heart would burst.

QUESTIONS

1. Read Marvell's poem "To His Coy Mistress" (quoted in the epigraph) and compare the situation and theme of the poem to Schwartz's story.

2. What is the ultimate effect of rough strife? Is it wearing and destructive or vitalizing and creative? Identify instances of rough strife in the story.

3. Why does Caroline ask about the weather after she has just delivered the child? What change in focus does this represent? What do the strange weather conditions signify?

4. Do Caroline and Ivan act according to will or impulse? How does this affect their relationship? Does Schwartz seem to portray one character more favorably than the other? If so, who? If not, why?

ELIZABETH SPENCER

The Girl Who Loved Horses

She had drawn back from throwing a pan of bird scraps out the door because she heard what was coming, the two-part pounding of a full gallop, not the graceful triple notes of a canter. They were mounting the drive now, turning into the stretch along the side of the house; once before, someone appearing at the screen door had made the horse shy, so that, barely held beneath the rider, barely restrained, he had plunged off into the flower beds. So she stepped back from the door and saw the two of them shoot past, rounding a final corner, heading for the straight run of drive into the cattle gate and the barn lot back of it.

She flung out the scraps, then walked to the other side of the kitchen and peered through the window, raised for spring, toward the barn lot. The horse had slowed, out of habit, knowing what came next. And the white shirt that had passed hugged so low as to seem some strange part of the animal's trappings, or as though he had run under a low line of drying laundry and caught something to an otherwise empty saddle and bare withers, now rose up, angling to an upright posture. A gloved hand extended to pat the lathered neck.

"Lord have mercy," the woman said. The young woman riding the horse was her daughter, but she was speaking also for her son-in-law, who went in for even more reckless behavior in the jumping ring the two of them had set up. What she meant by it was that they were going to kill themselves before they ever had any children, or if they did have children safely they'd bring up the children to be just as foolish about horses and careless of life and limb as they were themselves.

The young woman's booted heel struck the back steps. The screen door banged.

"You ought not to bring him in hot like that," the mother said. "I do know that much."

"Cottrell is out there," she said.

"It's still March, even if it has got warm."

"Cottrell knows what to do."

She ran water at the sink, and cupping her hand, drank primitive fashion out of it, bending to the tap, then wet her hands in the running water and thrust her fingers into the dusty, sweat-damp roots of her sand-colored hair. It had been a good ride.

"I hope he doesn't take up too much time," the mother said. "My beds need working."

She spoke mildly but it was always part of the same quarrel they were in like a stream that was now a trickle, now a still pool, but sometimes after a freshet could turn into a torrent.

1027

Such as: "Y'all are just crazy. Y'all are wasting everything on those things. And what are they? I know they're pretty and all that, but they're not a thing in the world but animals. Cows are animals. You can make a lot more money in cattle, than carting those things around over two states and three counties."

She could work herself up too much to eat, leaving the two of them at the table, but would see them just the same in her mind's eye, just as if she'd stayed. There were the sandy-haired young woman, already thirty — married four years and still apparently with no intention of producing a family (she was an only child and the estate, though small, was a fine piece of land) — and across from her the dark spare still young man she had married.

She knew how they would sit there alone and not even look at one another or discuss what she'd said or talk against her; they would just sit there and maybe pass each other some food or one of them would get up for the coffeepot. The fanatics of a strange cult would do the same, she often thought, loosening her long hair upstairs, brushing the gray and brown together to a colorless patina, putting on one of her long cotton gowns with the ruched[1] neck, crawling in between white cotton sheets. She was a widow and if she didn't want to sit up and try to talk to the family after a hard day, she didn't have to. Reading was a joy, lifelong. She found her place in *Middlemarch*,[2] one of her favorites.

But during the day not even reading (if she'd had the time) could shut out the sounds from back of the privet hedge, plainly to be heard from the house. The trudging of the trot, the pause, the low directive, the thud of hoofs, the heave and shout, and sometimes the ring of struck wood as a bar came down. And every jump a risk of life and limb. One dislocated shoulder — Clyde's, thank heaven, not Deedee's — a taping, a sling, a contraption of boards, and pain "like a hot knife," he had said. A hot knife. Wouldn't that hurt anybody enough to make him quit risking life and limb with those two blood[3] horses, quit at least talking about getting still another one while swallowing down pain-killer he said he hated to be sissy enough to take?

"Uh-huh," the mother said. "But it'll be Deborah next. You thought about that?"

"Aw, now, Miss Emma," he'd lean back to say, charming her through his warrior's haze of pain. "Deedee and me — that's what we're hooked on. Think of us without it, Mama. You really want to kill us. We couldn't live."

He was speaking to his mother-in-law but smiling at his wife. And she, Deborah, was smiling back.

Her name was Deborah Dale, but they'd always, of course, being from LaGrange, Tennessee, right over the Mississippi border, that is to say, real South, had had a hundred nicknames for her. Deedee, her father had named her, and "Deeds" her funny cousins said — "Hey, Deeds, how ya' doin'?" Being on this property in a town of pretty properties, though theirs was a little way out, a little bit larger than most, she was always out romping, swimming in forbidden creeks, climbing forbidden fences, going barefoot too soon in the spring, the last one in at recess, the first one to turn in an exam paper. ("Are you quite sure that you have finished, Deborah?" "Yes, ma'am.")

When she graduated from ponies to that sturdy calico her uncle gave her, bringing it in from his farm because he had an eye for a good match, there was almost no finding her. "I always know she's somewhere on the place," her mother said. "We just can't see it all at once,"

---

[1] Trimmed or pleated with a ruffle of fine fabric.

[2] A novel by George Eliot (1819–1880).

[3] Purebred.

said her father. He was ailing even back then but he undertook walks. Once when the leaves had all but gone from the trees, on a warm November afternoon, from a slight rise, he saw her down in a little-used pasture with a straight open stretch among some oaks. The ground was spongy and clotted with damp and even a child ought not to have tried to run there, on foot. But there went the calico with Deedee clinging low, going like the wind, and knowing furthermore out of what couldn't be anything but long practice, where to turn, where to veer, where to stop.

"One fine afternoon," he said to himself, suspecting even then (they hadn't told him yet) what his illness was, "and Emma's going to be left with nobody." He remarked on this privately, not without anguish and not without humor.

They stopped her riding, at least like that, by sending her off to boarding school, where a watchful ringmaster took "those girls interested in equitation" out on leafy trails, "at the walk, at the trot, and at the canter." They also, with that depth of consideration which must flourish even among those Southerners unlucky enough to wind up in the lower reaches of hell, kept her young spirit out of the worst of the dying. She just got a call from the housemother one night. Her father had "passed away."

After college she forgot it, she gave it up. It was too expensive, it took a lot of time and devotion, she was interested in boys. Some boys were interested in her. She worked in Memphis, drove home to her mother every night. In winter she had to eat breakfast in the dark. On some evenings the phone rang; on some it was silent. Her mother treated both kinds of evenings just the same.

To Emma Tyler it always seemed that Clyde Mecklin materialized out of nowhere. She ran straight into him when opening the front door one evening to get the paper off the porch, he being just about to turn the bell or knock. There he stood, dark and straight in the late light that comes after first dark and is so clear. He was clear as anything in it, clear as the first stamp of a young man ever cast.

"Is Deb'rah here?" At least no Yankee. But not Miss Tyler or Miss Deborah Tyler, or Miss Deborah. No, he was city all right.

She did not answer at first.

"What's the matter, scare you? I was just about to knock."

She still said nothing.

"Maybe this is the wrong place," he said.

"No, it's the right place," Emma Tyler finally said. She stepped back and held the door wider. "Come on in."

"Scared the life out of me," she told Deborah when she finally came down to breakfast the next day, Clyde's car having been heard to depart by Emma Tyler in her upstairs bedroom at an hour she did not care to verify. "Why didn't you tell me you were expecting him? I just opened the door and there he was."

"I liked him so much," said Deborah with grave honesty. "I guess I was scared he wouldn't come. That would have hurt."

"Do you still like him?" her mother ventured, after this confidence.

"He's all for outdoors," said Deborah, as dreamy over coffee as any mother had ever beheld. "Everybody is so indoors. He likes hunting, going fishing, farms."

"Has he got one?"

"He'd like to have. All he's got's this job. He's coming back next weekend. You can talk to him. He's interested in horses."

"But does he know we don't keep horses anymore?"

"That was just my thumbnail sketch," said Deborah. "We don't have to run out and buy any."

"No, I don't imagine so," said her mother, but Deborah hardly remarked the peculiar turn of tone, the dryness. She was letting coast through her head the scene: her mother (whom she now loved better than she ever had in her life) opening the door just before Clyde knocked, so seeing unexpectedly for the first time, that face, that head, that being. … When he had kissed her her ears drummed, and it came back to her once more, not thought of in years, the drumming hoofs of the calico, and the ghosting father, behind, invisible, observant, off on the bare distant November rise.

It was after she married that Deborah got beautiful. All LaGrange noticed it. "I declare," they said to her mother or sometimes right out to her face, "I always said she was nice-looking but I never thought anything like that."

Emma first saw the boy in the parking lot. He was new. In former days she'd parked in front of nearly any place she wanted to go — hardware, or drugstore, or courthouse: change for the meter was her biggest problem. But so many streets were one-way now and what with the increased numbers of cars, the growth of the town, those days were gone; she used a parking lot back of a café, near the newspaper office. The entrance to the lot was a bottleneck of a narrow drive between the two brick buildings; once in, it was hard sometimes to park.

That day the boy offered to help. He was an expert driver, she noted, whereas Emma was inclined to perspire, crane, and fret, fearful of scraping a fender or grazing a door. He spun the wheel with one hand; a glance told him all he had to know; he as good as sat the car in place, as skillful (she reluctantly thought) as her children on their horses. When she returned an hour later, the cars were denser still; he helped her again. She wondered whether to tip him. This happened twice more.

"You've been so nice to me," she said, the last time. "They're lucky to have you."

"It's not much of a job," he said. "Just all I can get for the moment. Being new and all."

"I might need some help," she said. "You can call up at the Tyler place if you want to work. It's in the book. Right now I'm in a hurry."

On the warm June day, Deborah sat the horse comfortably in the side yard and watched her mother and the young man (whose name was Willett? Williams?), who, having worked the beds and straightened a fence post, was now replacing warped fence boards with new ones.

"Who is he?" she asked her mother, not quite low enough, and meaning what a Southern woman invariably means by that question, not what is his name but where did he come from, is he anybody we know? What excuse, in other words, does he have for even being born?

"One thing, he's a good worker," her mother said, preening a little. Did they think she couldn't manage if she had to? "Now don't you make him feel bad."

"Feel bad!" But once again, if only to spite her mother, who was in a way criticizing her and Clyde by hiring anybody at all to do work that Clyde or the Negro help would have been able to do if only it weren't for those horses — once again Deborah had spoken too loudly.

If she ever had freely to admit things, even to herself, Deborah would have to say she knew she not only looked good that June day, she looked sexy as hell. Her light hair, tousled from a ride in the fields, had grown longer in the last year; it had slipped its pins on one side and lay in a sensuous lock along her cheek. A breeze stirred it, then passed by. Her soft poplin shirt was loose at the throat, the two top buttons open, the cuffs turned back to her elbows.

The new horse, the third, was gentle, too much so (this worried them); she sat it easily, one leg up, crossed lazily over the flat English pommel, while the horse, head stretched down, cropped at the tender grass. In the silence between their voices, the tearing of the grass was the only sound except for a shrill jay's cry.

"Make him feel bad!" she repeated.

The boy looked up. The horse, seeking grass, had moved forward; she was closer than before, eyes looking down on him above the rise of her breasts and throat; she saw the closeness go through him, saw her presence register as strongly as if the earth's accidental shifting had slammed them physically together. For a minute there was nothing but the two of them. The jay was silent; even the horse, sensing something, had raised his head.

Stepping back, the boy stumbled over the pile of lumber, then fell in it. Deborah laughed. Nothing, that day, could have stopped her laughter. She was beautifully, languidly, atop a fine horse on the year's choice day at the peak of her life.

"You know what?" Deborah said at supper, when they were discussing her mother's helper. "I thought who he looks like. He looks like Clyde."

"The poor guy," Clyde said. "Was that the best you could do?"

Emma sat still. Now that she thought of it, he did look like Clyde. She stopped eating, to think it over. What difference did it make if he did? She returned to her plate.

Deborah ate lustily, her table manners unrestrained. She swabbed bread into the empty salad bowl, drenched it with dressing, bit it in hunks.

"The poor woman's Clyde, that's what you hired," she said. She looked up.

The screen door had just softly closed in the kitchen behind them. Emma's hired man had come in for his money.

It was the next day that the boy, whose name was Willett or Williams, broke the riding mower by running it full speed into a rock pile overgrown with weeds but clearly visible, and left without asking for pay but evidently taking with him in his car a number of selected items from barn, garage, and tack room, along with a transistor radio that Clyde kept in the kitchen for getting news with his early coffee.

Emma Tyler, vexed for a number of reasons she did not care to sort out (prime among them was the very peaceful and good time she had been having with the boy the day before in the yard when Deborah had chosen to ride over and join them), telephoned the police and reported the whole matter. But boy, car, and stolen articles vanished into the nowhere. That was all, for what they took to be forever.

Three years later, aged thirty-three, Deborah Mecklin was carrying her fine head higher than ever uptown in LaGrange. She drove herself on errands back and forth in car or station wagon, not looking to left or right, not speaking so much as before. She was trying not to hear from the outside what they were now saying about Clyde, how well he'd done with the horses, that place was as good as a stud farm now that he kept ten or a dozen, advertised and traded, as well as showed. And the money was coming in hard and fast. But, they would add, he moved with a fast set, and there was also the occasional gossip item, too often, in Clyde's case, with someone ready to report first hand; look how quick, now you thought of it, he'd taken up with Deborah, and how she'd snapped him up too soon to hear what his reputation was, even back then. It would be a cold day in August before any one woman would be enough for him. And his father before him? And his father before him. So the voices said.

Deborah, too, was trying not to hear what was still sounding from inside her head after her fall in the last big horse show:

The doctor: You barely escaped concussion, young lady.

Clyde: I just never saw your timing go off like that. I can't get over it.

Emma: You'd better let it go for a while, honey. There're other things, so many other things.

Back home, she later said to Emma: "Oh, Mama, I know you're right sometimes, and sometimes I'm sick of it all, but Clyde depends on me, he always has, and now look — "

"Yes, and 'Now look' is right, he has to be out with it to keep it all running. You got your wish, is all I can say."

Emma was frequently over at her sister-in-law Marian's farm these days. The ladies were aging, Marian especially down in the back, and those twilights in the house alone were more and more all that Deedee had to keep herself company with. Sometimes the phone rang and there'd be Clyde on it, to say he'd be late again. Or there'd be no call at all. And once she (of all people) pressed some curtains and hung them, and once hunted for old photographs, and once, standing in the middle of the little-used parlor among the walnut Victorian furniture upholstered in gold and blue and rose, she had said "Daddy?" right out loud, like he might have been there to answer, really been there. It had surprised her, the word falling out like that as though a thought took reality all by itself and made a word on its own.

And once there came a knock at the door.

All she thought, though she hadn't heard the car, was that it was Clyde and that he'd forgotten his key, or seeing her there, his arms loaded maybe, was asking her to let him in. It was past dark. Though times were a little more chancy now, LaGrange was a safe place. People nearer to town used to brag that if they went off for any length of time less than a weekend and locked the doors, the neighbors would get their feelings hurt; and if the Tylers lived further out and "locked up," the feeling for it was ritual mainly, a precaution.

She glanced through the sidelight, saw what she took for Clyde, and opened the door. There were cedars in the front yard, not too near the house, but dense enough to block out whatever gathering of light there might have been from the long slope of property beyond the front gate. There was no moon.

The man she took for Clyde, instead of stepping through the door or up to the threshold to greet her, withdrew a step and leaned down and to one side, turning outward as though to pick up something. It was she who stepped forward, to greet, help, inquire; for deep within was the idea her mother had seen to it was firmly and forever planted: that one day one of them was going to get too badly hurt by "those things" ever to be patched up.

So it was in outer dark, three paces from the safe threshold and to the left of the area where the light was falling outward, a dim single sidelight near the mantelpiece having been all she had switched on, too faint to penetrate the sheer gathered curtains of the sidelight, that the man at the door rose up, that he tried to take her. The first she knew of it, his face was in hers, not Clyde's but something like it and at Clyde's exact height, so that for the moment she thought that some joke was on, and then the strange hand caught the parting of her blouse, a new mouth fell hard on her own, one knee thrust her legs apart, the free hand diving in to clutch and press against the thin nylon between her thighs. She recoiled at the same time that she felt, touched in the quick, the painful glory of desire brought on too fast — looking back on that instant's two-edged meaning, she would never hear about rape without the lightning quiver of ambivalence within the word. However, at the time no meditation stopped her knee from coming up into the nameless groin and nothing stopped her from tearing back her mouth slathered with spit so suddenly smeared into it as to drag it into the shape of a scream she was unable yet to find a voice for. Her good right arm struck like a hard backhand against a line-smoking tennis serve. Then from the driveway came the stream of twin headlights thrusting through the cedars.

"Bitch!" The word, distorted and low, was like a groan; she had hurt him, freed herself for a moment, but the struggle would have just begun except for the lights, and the screams that were just trying to get out of her. "You fucking bitch." He saw the car lights, wavered, then turned. His leap into the shrubbery was bent, like a hunchback's. She stopped screaming suddenly. Hurt where he lived, she thought. The animal motion, wounded, drew her curiosity for a second. Saved, she saw the car sweep round the drive, but watched the bushes shake, put up her hand to touch but not to close the torn halves of the blouse, which was ripped open to her waist.

Inside, she stood looking down at herself in the dim light. There was a nail scratch near the left nipple, two teeth marks between elbow and wrist where she'd smashed into his mouth. She wiped her own mouth on the back of her hand, gagging at the taste of cigarette smoke, bitterly staled. Animals! She'd always had a special feeling for them, a helpless tenderness. In her memory the bushes, shaking to a crippled flight, shook forever.

She went upstairs, stood trembling in her mother's room (Emma was away), combed her hair with her mother's comb. Then, hearing Clyde's voice calling her below, she stripped off her ravaged blouse and hastened across to their own rooms to hide it in a drawer, change into a fresh one, come downstairs. She had made her decision already. Who was this man? A nothing ... an unknown. She hated women who shouted Rape! Rape! It was an incident, but once she told it everyone would know, along with the police, and would add to it: they'd say she'd been violated. It was an incident, but Clyde, once he knew, would trace him down. Clyde would kill him.

"Did you know the door was wide open?" He was standing in the living room.

"I know. I must have opened it when I heard the car. I thought you were stopping in the front."

"Well, I hardly ever do."

"Sometimes you do."

"Deedee, have you been drinking?"

"Drinking ... ? Me?" She squinted at him, joking in her own way; it was a standing quarrel now that alone she sometimes poured one or two.

He would check her breath but not her marked body. Lust with him was mole-dark now, not desire in the soft increase of morning light, or on slowly westering afternoons, or by the night light's glow. He would kill for her because she was his wife. ...

"Who was that man?"

Uptown one winter afternoon late, she had seen him again. He had been coming out of the hamburger place and looking back, seeing her through the street lights, he had turned quickly into an alley. She had hurried to catch up, to see. But only a form was hastening there, deeper into the unlit slit between brick walls, down toward a street and a section nobody went into without good reason.

"That man," she repeated to the owner (also the proprietor and cook) in the hamburger place. "He was in here just now."

"I don't know him. He hangs around. Wondered myself. You know him?"

"I think he used to work for us once, two or three years ago. I just wondered."

"I thought I seen him somewhere myself."

"He looks a little bit like Clyde."

"Maybe so. Now you mention it." He wiped the counter with a wet rag. "Get you anything, Miss Deb'rah?"

"I've got to get home."

"Y'all got yourselves some prizes, huh?"

"Aw, just some good luck." She was gone.

Prizes, yes. Two trophies at the Shelby County Fair, one in Brownsville where she'd almost lost control again, and Clyde not worrying about her so much as scolding her. His recent theory was that she was out to spite him. He would think it if he was guilty about the women, and she didn't doubt any more that he was. But worse than spite was what had got to her, hating as she did to admit it.

It was fear.

She'd never known it before. When it first started she hadn't even known what the name of it was.

Over two years ago, Clyde had started buying colts not broken yet from a stud farm south of Nashville, bringing them home for him and Deborah to get in shape together. It saved a pile of money to do it that way. She'd been thrown in consequence three times, trampled once, a terrifying moment as the double reins had caught up her outstretched arm so she couldn't fall free. Now when she closed her eyes at night, steel hoofs sometimes hung through the dark above them, and she felt hard ground beneath her head, smelled smeared grass on cheek and elbow. To Clyde she murmured in the dark: "I'm not good at it any more." "Why, Deeds, you were always good. It's temporary, honey. That was a bad day."

A great couple. That's what Clyde thought of them. But more than half their name had been made by her, by the sight of her, Deborah Mecklin, out in full dress, black broadcloth and white satin stock with hair drawn trimly back beneath the smooth rise of the hat, entering the show ring. She looked damned good back of the glossy neck's steep arch, the pointed ears and lacquered hoofs which hardly touched earth before springing upward, as though in the instant before actual flight. There was always the stillness, then the murmur, the rustle of the crowd. At top form she could even get applause. A fame for a time spread round them. The Mecklins. Great riders. "Ridgewood Stable. Blood horses trained. Saddle and Show." He'd had it put up in wrought iron, with a sign as well, Old English style, of a horseman spurring.

("Well, you got to make money," said Miss Emma to her son-in-law. "And don't I know it," she said. "But I just hate to think how many times I kept those historical people from putting up a marker on this place. And now all I do is worry one of y'all's going to break your neck. If it wasn't for Marian needing me and all ... I just can't sleep a wink over here."

("You like to be over there anyway, Mama," Deborah said. "You know we want you here."

("Sure, we want you here," said Clyde. "As for the property, we talked it all out before-hand. I don't think I've damaged it any way."

("I just never saw it as a horse farm. But it's you all I worry about. It's the danger.")

Deborah drove home.

When the workingman her mother had hired three years before had stolen things and left, he had left too on the garage wall inside, a long pair of crossing diagonal lines, brown, in mud, Deborah thought, until she smelled what it was, and there were the blood-stained menstrual pads she later came across in the driveway, dug up out of the garbage, strewed out into the yard.

She told Clyde about the first but not the second discovery. "Some critters are mean," he'd shrugged it off. "Some critters are just mean."

They'd been dancing, out at the club. And so in love back then, he'd turned and turned her, far apart, then close, talking into her ear, making her laugh and answer, but finally he said: "Are you a mean critter, Deedee? Some critters are mean." And she'd remembered what she didn't tell.

But in those days Clyde was passionate and fun, both marvelously together, and the devil appearing at midnight in the bend of a country road would not have scared her. Nothing would have. It was the day of her life when they bought the first two horses.

"*I thought I seen him somewhere myself.*"

"*He looks a little bit like Clyde.*"

And dusk again, a third and final time.

The parking lot where she'd come after a movie was empty except for a few cars. The small office was unlighted, but a man she took for the attendant was bending to the door on the far side of a long cream-colored sedan near the back fence. "Want my ticket?" she called. The man straightened, head rising above the body frame, and she knew him. Had he been about to steal a car, or was he breaking in for whatever he could find, or was it her coming all along that he was waiting for? However it was, he knew her as instantly as she knew him. Each other was what they had, by whatever design or absence of it, found. Deborah did not cry out or stir.

Who knew how many lines life had cut away from him down through the years till the moment when an arrogant woman on a horse had ridden him down with lust and laughter? He wasn't bad-looking; his eyes were beautiful; he was the kind to whom nothing good could happen. From that bright day to this chilly dusk, it had probably just been the same old story.

Deborah waited. Someway or other, what was coming, threading through the cars like an animal lost for years catching the scent of a former owner, was her own.

("You're losing nerve, Deedee," Clyde had told her recently. "That's what's really bothering me. You're scared, aren't you?")

The bitter-stale smell of cigarette breath, though not so near as before, not forced against her mouth, was still unmistakably familiar. But the prod of a gun's muzzle just under the rise of her breast was not. It had never happened to her before. She shuddered at the touch with a chill spring-like start of something like life, which was also something like death.

"Get inside," he said.

"Are you the same one?" she asked. "Just tell me that. Three years ago, Mama hired somebody. Was that you?"

"Get in the car."

She opened the door, slid over to the driver's seat, found him beside her. The gun, thrust under his crossed arm, resumed its place against her.

"Drive."

"Was it you the other night at the door?" Her voice trembled as the motor started, the gear caught.

"He left me with the lot; ain't nobody coming."

The car eased into an empty street.

"Go out of town. The Memphis road."

She was driving past familiar, cared-for lawns and houses, trees and intersections. Someone waved from a car at a stoplight, taking them for her and Clyde. She was frightened and accepting fear, which come to think of it was all she'd been doing for months, working with those horses. ("Don't let him bluff you, Deedee. It's you or him. He'll do it if he can.")

"What do you want with me? What is it you want?"

He spoke straight outward, only his mouth moving, watching the road, never turning his head to her. "You're going out on that Memphis road and you're going up a side road with me. There's some woods I know. When I'm through with you you ain't never going to have nothing to ask nobody about me because you're going to know it all and it ain't going to make you laugh none, I guarantee."

Deborah cleared the town and swinging into the highway wondered at herself. Did she want him? She had waited when she might have run. Did she want, trembling, pleading, degraded, finally to let him have every single thing his own way?

(Do you see steel hoofs above you over and over because you want them one day to smash into your brain?

("Daddy, Daddy," she had murmured long ago when the old unshaven tramp had come up into the lawn, bleary-eyed, face blood-burst with years of drink and weather, frightening as the boogeyman, "raw head and bloody bones," like the Negro women scared her with. That day the sky streamed with end-of-the-world fire. But she hadn't called so loudly as she might have, she'd let him come closer, to look at him better, until the threatening voice of her father behind her, just on the door's slamming, had cried: "What do you want in this yard? What you think you want here? Deborah! You come in this house this minute!" But the mystery still lay dark within her, forgotten for years, then stirring to life again: When I said "Daddy, Daddy?" was I calling to the tramp or to the house? Did I think the tramp was him in some sort of joke or dream or trick? If not, why did I say it? Why?

("Why do you ride a horse so fast, Deedee? Why do you like to do that?" *I'm going where the sky breaks open.* "I just like to." "Why do you like to drive so fast?" "I don't know.")

Suppose he kills me, too, thought Deborah, striking the straight stretch on the Memphis road, the beginning of the long rolling run through farms and woods. She stole a glance to her right. He looked like Clyde, all right. What right did he have to look like Clyde?

("It's you or him, Deedee." All her life they'd said that to her from the time her first pony, scared at something, didn't want to cross a bridge. "Don't let him get away with it. It's you or him.")

Righting the big car into the road ahead, she understood what was demanded of her. She pressed the accelerator gradually downward toward the floor.

"And by the time he realized it," she said, sitting straight in her chair at supper between Clyde and Emma, who by chance were there that night together; " — by the time he knew, we were hitting above seventy-five, and he said, 'What you speeding for?' and I said, 'I want to get it over with.' And he said, 'Okay, but that's too fast.' By the time we were touching eighty and he said, 'What the fucking hell' — excuse me, Mama — 'you think you're doing? You slow this thing down.' So I said, 'I tell you what I'm doing. This is a rolling road with high banks and trees and lots of curves. If you try to take the wheel away from me, I'm going to wreck us both. If you try to sit there with that gun in my side I'm going to go faster and faster and sooner or later something will happen, like a curve too sharp to take or a car too many to pass with a big truck coming and we're both going to get smashed up at the very least. It won't do any good to shoot me when it's more than likely both of us would die. You want that?'

"He grabbed at the wheel but I put on another spurt of speed and when he pulled at the wheel we side-rolled, skidded back, and another car coming almost didn't get out of the way. I said, 'You see what you're doing, I guess.' And he said, 'Jesus God.' Then I knew I had him, had whipped him down.

"But it was another two or three miles like that before he said, 'Okay, okay, so I quit. Just slow down and let's forget it.' And I said, 'You give me that gun. The mood I'm in, I can drive with one hand or no hands at all, and don't think I won't do it.' But he wanted his gun at least, I could tell. He didn't give in till a truck was ahead and we passed but barely missed a car that was coming (it had to run off the concrete), and he put it down, in my lap."

(Like a dog, she could have said, but didn't. And I felt sorry for him, she could have added, because it was his glory's end.)

"So I said, 'Get over, way over,' and he did, and I coasted from fast to slow. I turned the gun around on him and let him out on an empty stretch of road, by a rise with a wood and a country side road rambling off, real pretty, and I thought, Maybe that's where he was talking about, where he meant to screw hell — excuse me, Mama — out of me. I held the gun till he closed the door and went down in the ditch a little way, then I put the safety catch on and threw it at him. It hit his shoulder, then fell in the weeds. I saw it fall, driving off."

"Oh, my poor baby," said Emma. "Oh, my precious child."

It was Clyde who rose, came round the table to her, drew her to her feet, held her close. "That's nerve," he said. "That's class." He let her go and she sat down again. "Why didn't you shoot him?"

"I don't know."

"He was the one we hired that time," Emma said. "I'd be willing to bet you anything."

"No, it wasn't," said Deborah quickly. "This one was blond and short, red-nosed from too much drinking, I guess. Awful like Mickey Rooney, gone and gotten old. Like the boogeyman, I guess."

"The poor woman's Mickey Rooney. You women find yourselves the damnedest men."

"She's not right about that," said Emma. "What do you want to tell that for? I know it was him. I feel like it was."

"Why'd you throw the gun away?" Clyde asked. "We could trace that."

"It's what I felt like doing," she said. She had seen it strike, how his shoulder, struck, went back a little.

Clyde Mecklin sat watching his wife. She had scarcely touched her food, and now, pale, distracted, she had risen to wander toward the windows, look out at the empty lawn, the shrubs and flowers, the stretch of white-painted fence, ghostly by moonlight.

"It's the last horse I'll ever break," she said, more to herself than not, but Clyde heard and stood up and was coming to her.

"Now, Deedee — "

"When you know you know," she said, and turned, her face set against him: her anger, her victory, held up like a blade against his stubborn willfulness. "I want my children now," she said.

At the mention of children, Emma's presence with them became multiple and vague; it trembled with thanksgiving, it spiraled on wings of joy.

Deborah turned again, back to the window. Whenever she looked away, the eyes by the road were there below her: they were worthless, nothing, but infinite, never finishing — the surface there was no touching bottom for — talking to them, into themselves, the self that was hers no longer.

QUESTIONS

1. Discuss Spencer's use of animal imagery. How far is the analogy between humans and animals carried out? Which characters are most animal-like? Is this a positive or negative aspect of their characters?

2. Why is Deborah both attracted to and repulsed by the hired man? Why does she hide secrets about him from Clyde? Of what significance is his resemblance to Clyde?

3. After Deborah dumps her assailant out of the car, she says, "I felt sorry for him, it was his glory's end." Does this mean she has successfully broken his spirit? Has hers emerged intact? What do you think of her readiness to have children afterwards?

4. Near the end of the story, more and more parenthetical passages interrupt the narrative. How is this stylistic change appropriate to Deborah's state of mind?

SEAN VIRGO

Home and Native Land

The two men were far down the beach — wavering, indistinct black figures, stooping to dig clams by the low tide mark. Their boat swung on its chain out in the inlet and their dinghy was stranded on the sand, ten yards above them. After a while they looked up and one of them waved. They spoke together and started up the beach, dumping their sacks and shovels in the dinghy.

Ron had been home for two days. He sat moodily round the house all the time, every so often swearing angrily to himself, springing up and pacing to the door and back. He kept watching out the window, going out the door and then coming back to slump on the old wooden seat by the stove. His shirt-back was always dark and limp with sweat.

Dickie heard him walking about in the night, too. The outbursts of sudden, muttered curses punctuating the close darkness. When he looked out into the room before dawn the first night, Ron had fallen asleep by the stove, all the wood used up, a cigarette drooping from his stained hand with a curved inch of ash upon it. Dickie had stepped over one of the dogs and gently removed the still-smoking butt before it burnt his brother's hand. Then he'd gone back to bed.

An hour later he'd woken again, hearing "Oh fucking, *fucking* hell" hollowly from the front room, and a scrambling away of the dogs onto the porch. His mother called out "Who there?" and there was no answer. He heard someone scuffing through the salmonberry bushes by the gate and then he slept again. Ron was the same all day. If you talked to him, even Mumma, he'd just grunt, or sometimes stare into your head as if you were a mile off on the horizon, and he didn't know whether to notice you.

This morning he had fidgeted round the house for an hour, didn't eat anything, then motioned to Dickie from the porch. They set off walking down to the point, toward the old village. One of the dogs followed them warily. Ron led the way, and said nothing — he was thinner than he'd been before he went away: when the curtain of irritation wasn't trembling before his face there was something almost transparent about him. And he smelt of Vancouver, even now out above the exposed beds of weed and mussels: his clothes were worn-out cheap versions of city style — his feet canted clumsily over on ruined cuban heels.

"You're the only fucker round here I can stand anymore" was all he said as they scrambled together on the puddingstone rocks where the path ended. He said it not as a confidence, but with his eyes straying vaguely out to sea down the shrunken inlet, one hand stiff against his hip as though to control something.

He was sick, but he was beautiful. Dickie had never seen an Indian grow his hair long before: the black, shining frame down the cheek bones looked proud.

Ron touched his arm and waited for the two men to come up to them. He stood tautly, his nostrils flared like a hound's, questing at the suspicion of a familiar scent. Not a smell, though, something more shimmering than that. Dickie could sense it too, though he did not recognize it. When the men came closer and that feeling grew stronger, Ron seemed to slip far away from him — Dickie felt that he was the outsider and that his brother and the two white men formed a circle that pushed him out. But the pride was gone from Ron as the circle closed: at that moment Dickie saw a vision of him at a sidewalk looking across to him over a broad street, where cars shuttled past every second, like waves hiding and staining his stranger eyes.

One of the men was big and fair — under his fringe his eyes slewed round to meet yours and then cannoned off again like a pool-ball. When he spoke his eyelids fluttered all the time — his words came clear and easy but the stutter had moved up into his eyes. His face was hairless as an Indian's, his fringe was swept to cover baldness, and one day soon he'd be fat. He wanted something.

His companion was smaller, less assertive but more at ease. He related more to his surroundings: the deserted sands here, life on a boat, the beer he had been drinking: but he was second fiddle, no doubt of it, and had a sheepish kind of awe for the big one. His want was slighter, more detached. He was inclined to turn to Dickie, to let the circle break up into pairs, but the boy turned away, shut them out of his head and went to stare at the water.

Sandpipers were hurtling along the foreshore — east to west and back, black to white and back, rising and falling, sometimes disappearing against the dark sea, never settling. The tide was just ready to die, to lie for an hour at ebb and then come rushing back at the rocks across the waste of sand. Down a ways, two gulls were swooping at a big bird dragging a horse clam off the tide line. Probably the eagle. And crows were shouting in the young trees that grew over the old village.

Behind him Ron was nervous and animated. What they wanted, what they had, must be out in the open now. The smaller white man offered Dickie a draw on the cigarette — holding it out to him mutely, his lips compressed, nodding, trying to hold back a cough from his own inhaling. Ron's attention focussed on him for a moment with a kind of anxiousness and then shrugged away. Dickie refused.

Ron was pointing down past the old village. "The second island out," he said, grinning with mask-like camaraderie into the big man's face. "There'll be no water round it for two hours maybe. You could take your boat round anyway."

"Nobody about for sure, eh?"

"Nah, no one ever comes this way. Too scared." They both laughed in an idiot way at this invented superstition.

The big man handed over the plastic bag, swinging it for a moment or two over Ron's palm. "Right," he said. "Thanks." "Sure thing, mister," Ron said. Then the man swung away and back down the drying, steaming sand toward the dinghy. His companion shadowed his brisk footsteps, but did have eyes for Dickie. Who looked away.

When they were down by the dinghy, "What they doing out there?" he asked. Ron was sitting on the sand, easing his bare feet out of his cowboy boots, contemplating his stretching toes and digging them in.

"What did they want?"

Ron looked up. His eyes came back from a million miles, a vague smile hovered and he looked back again at the sand. His hair hung in a dense tent of blackness over his downturned face. "They were looking for burial grounds," he said and shrugged his shoulders and laughed.

"Why'd you tell them? Why?"

"Hell, they likely want them old blue-bead necklaces. They can sell them to the museums. But they're all in the cave by the old village. I didn't say that." Then he looked hard at Dickie, like he used to before he went away, when he was mad at him or wanted to show him something important. His brown eyes were hard, they held you still. "Anyways, Dick, there ain't no necklaces left neither. Johnny Grey and me took them long ago."

"But why did you say about the island?"

"Look, kiddo, when they get there and find a lot of new boxes they'll just take off. They're not expecting that."

The picket fence and the pile of boxes. No earth to dig them into. "There's stuff in the boxes too," he blurted.

Ron didn't move. But Dickie felt that strange shimmer round his brother. He was thinking — not Ron thoughts; ways of thinking from the prison or something. Dickie couldn't see in there and he didn't want to. The circle was still closed.

Ron stood up and held his brother's arm. Tightly. He was hurting his shoulder. Dickie said so and Ron didn't answer. "I'll see you at home, kid," he said suddenly and set off running down the beach. The men were dragging the skiff slowly toward the water. The eagle flapped heavily down the beach above their heads, the white gulls still dipping and screaming round him. Ron's hair leaped on his shoulders, his lean legs stretched above the sand.

"Hey guys," he yelled, "Hey wait I'll bring you there." One moment he was a movie hero striking lithely over the sands, next the sea-mirage rose past his legs and he was a puppet, stiffly, erratically working. "Hey wait," he called. The men looked up and waited for him to help with the dinghy.

Dickie turned back past the point. The dog appeared again from a patch of salal[1] and ran beside him. He didn't look back but he heard the boat's engine rumbling over the water, heard that circle clench as tight as a bear-trap. As the houses came into sight again he heard out behind them the shriek of some sea bird and the rising gabble of loons. The cry echoed in his head — he heard in it the screech of a box lid opening.

"You're getting like your brother," Mumma said. He'd been lying on the couch most of the afternoon, watching the grain in the roof-planks.

"I feel sick, Mumma," he said.

"Would you cut me some wood," she said snappily. She was helpless but she saw things. He got up and went out to the shed. Ron was back in the village, back in his cuban heels. He waved from the porch at Sharon Grey's but he didn't come back till supper. He sat on the couch, smoking, while the others ate. He was moody again, but the shimmer was round him. Dickie put down his fork. "Goin' out tomorrow," Ron said, "on the bus."

"Where you goin'?" said Mumma. So weary, she might as well not have asked.

"Goin' out," said Ron.

Dickie looked out at dawn again and Ron was asleep by the dead stove. The boy took a rug off the couch and went to cover his brother up. He was sprawled out on the chair, one leg straight, one knee bent. On his lap was a tarnished silver bracelet, almost black. Dickie picked it up and traced out the lines through the tarnish. An eagle's head, etched firmly, the beak slightly open, a claw stretched out before it as though to strike. He looked at it closely in the half-light, seeing the eye patterns fitted perfectly upon the folded wings, before the smell of it came shimmering sickly up into his face.

---

[1] A small shrub with dark purple berries that grows on the Pacific Coast of North America.

Ron died in the city a week later. If he hadn't been in the city, or if there'd been any money, or if they'd heard in time, he would have been laid to rest on the island. But they didn't hear about it for two weeks. Dickie rowed out to the island the next day. He nailed back two of the lids before he had to run. His cousin Mary, nine years old and two years dead. They had left her jawbone beside the little box because it still had skin upon it.

QUESTIONS

1. Why is Ron so restless and disturbed? Why does he go out to the island with the two men? What are his feelings about their actions? Why does he leave the village for the city?

2. Of what is the eagle symbolic? With whom is it associated? In what different contexts does it recur? How is the other bird imagery significant?

3. What is happening out on the island? How do Dickie's feelings about it differ from Ron's? What wider social tensions do these differences indicate?

Roselily

Dearly Beloved,

She dreams; dragging herself across the world. A small girl in her mother's white robe and veil, knee raised waist high through a bowl of quicksand soup. The man who stands beside her is against this standing on the front porch of her house, being married to the sound of cars whizzing by on highway 61.

we are gathered here

Like cotton to be weighed. Her fingers at the last minute busily removing dry leaves and twigs. Aware it is a superficial sweep. She knows he blames Mississippi for the respectful way the men turn their heads up in the yard, the women stand waiting and knowledgeable, their children held from mischief by teachings from the wrong God. He glares beyond them to the occupants of the cars, white faces glued to promises beyond a country wedding, noses thrust forward like dogs on a track. For him they usurp the wedding.

in the sight of God

Yes, open house. That is what country black folks like. She dreams she does not already have three children. A squeeze around the flowers in her hands chokes off three and four and five years of breath. Instantly she is ashamed and frightened in her superstition. She looks for the first time at the preacher, forces humility into her eyes, as if she believes he is, in fact, a man of God. She can imagine God, a small black boy, timidly pulling the preacher's coattail.

to join this man and this woman

She thinks of ropes, chains, handcuffs, his religion. His place of worship. Where she will be required to sit apart with covered head. In Chicago, a word she hears when thinking of smoke, from his description of what a cinder was, which they never had in Panther Burn. She sees hovering over the heads of the clean neighbors in her front yard black specks falling, clinging, from the sky. But in Chicago. Respect, a chance to build. Her children at last from underneath the detrimental wheel. A chance to be on top. What a relief, she thinks. What a vision, a view, from up so high.

in holy matrimony.

Her fourth child she gave away to the child's father who had some money. Certainly a good job. Had gone to Harvard. Was a good man but weak because good language meant so much to him he could not live with Roselily. Could not abide TV in the living room, five beds in three rooms, no Bach except from four to six on Sunday afternoons. No chess at all. She does not forget to worry about her son among his father's people. She wonders if the New England climate will agree with him. If he will ever come down to Mississippi, as his father did, to try to right the country's wrongs. She wonders if he will be stronger than his father. His father cried off and on throughout her pregnancy. Went to skin and bones. Suffered nightmares, retching and falling out of bed. Tried to kill himself. Later told his wife he found the right baby through friends. Vouched for, the sterling qualities that would make up his character.

It is not her nature to blame. Still, she is not entirely thankful. She supposes New England, the North, to be quite different from what she knows. It seems right somehow to her that people who move there to live return home completely changed. She thinks of the air, the smoke, the cinders. Imagines cinders big as hailstones; heavy, weighing on the people. Wonders how this pressure finds its way into the veins, roping the springs of laughter.

If there's anybody here that knows a reason why

But of course they know no reason why beyond what they daily have come to know. She thinks of the man who will be her husband, feels shut away from him because of the stiff severity of his plain black suit. His religion. A lifetime of black and white. Of veils. Covered head. It is as if her children are already gone from her. Not dead, but exalted on a pedestal, a stalk that has no roots. She wonders how to make new roots. It is beyond her. She wonders what one does with memories in a brand-new life. This had seemed easy, until she thought of it. "The reasons why ... the people who" ... she thinks, and does not wonder where the thought is from.

these two should not be joined

She thinks of her mother, who is dead. Dead, but still her mother. Joined. This is confusing. Of her father. A gray old man who sold wild mink, rabbit, fox skins to Sears, Roebuck. He stands in the yard, like a man waiting for a train. Her young sisters stand behind her in smooth green dresses, with flowers in their hands and hair. They giggle, she feels, at the absurdity of the wedding. They are ready for something new. She thinks the man beside her should marry one of them. She feels old. Yoked. An arm seems to reach out from behind her and snatch her backward. She thinks of cemeteries and the long sleep of grandparents mingling in the dirt. She believes that she believes in ghosts. In the soil giving back what it takes.

together,

In the city. He sees her in a new way. This she knows, and is grateful. But is it new enough? She cannot always be a bride and virgin, wearing robes and veil. Even now her body itches to be free of satin and voile, organdy and lily of the valley. Memories crash against her. Memories of being bare to the sun. She wonders what it will be like. Not to have to go to a job. Not to work in a sewing plant. Not to worry about learning to sew straight seams in workingmen's overalls, jeans, and dress pants. Her place will be in the home, he has said, repeatedly, promising her rest she had prayed for. But now she wonders. When she is rested, what will she do? They will make babies — she thinks practically about her fine brown body, his strong black one. They will be inevitable. Her hands will be full. Full of what? Babies. She is not comforted.

let him speak

She wishes she had asked him to explain more of what he meant. But she was impatient. Impatient to be done with sewing. With doing everything for three children, alone. Impatient to leave the girls she had known since childhood, their children growing up, their husbands hanging around her, already old, seedy. Nothing about them that she wanted, or needed. The fathers of her children driving by, waving, not waving; reminders of times she would just as soon forget. Impatient to see the South Side, where they would live and build and be respectable and respected and free. Her husband would free her. A romantic hush. Proposal. Promises. A new life! Respectable, reclaimed, renewed. Free! In robe and veil.

or forever hold

She does not even know if she loves him. She loves his sobriety. His refusal to sing just because he knows the tune. She loves his pride. His blackness and his gray car. She loves his understanding of her *condition*. She thinks she loves the effort he will make to redo her into what he truly wants. His love of her makes her completely conscious of how unloved she was before. This is something; though it makes her unbearably sad. Melancholy. She blinks her eyes. Remembers she is finally being married, like other girls. Like other girls, women? Something strains upward behind her eyes. She thinks of the something as a rat trapped, cornered, scurrying to and fro in her head, peering through the windows of her eyes. She wants to live for once. But doesn't know quite what that means. Wonders if she has ever done it. If she ever will. The preacher is odious to her. She wants to strike him out of the way, out of her light, with the back of her hand. It seems to her he has always been standing in front of her, barring her way.

his peace.

The rest she does not hear. She feels a kiss, passionate, rousing, within the general pandemonium. Cars drive up blowing their horns. Firecrackers go off. Dogs come from under the house and begin to yelp and bark. Her husband's hand is like the clasp of an iron gate. People congratulate. Her children press against her. They look with awe and distaste mixed with hope at their new father. He stands curiously apart, in spite of the people crowding about to grasp his free hand. He smiles at them all but his eyes are as if turned inward. He knows they cannot understand that he is not a Christian. He will not explain himself. He feels different, he looks it. The old women thought he was like one of their sons except that he had somehow got away from them. Still a son, not a son. Changed.

She thinks how it will be later in the night in the silvery gray car. How they will spin through the darkness of Mississippi and in the morning be in Chicago, Illinois. She thinks of Lincoln, the president. That is all she knows about the place. She feels ignorant, *wrong*, backward. She presses her worried fingers into his palm. He is standing in front of her. In the crush of well-wishing people, he does not look back.

QUESTIONS

1. Discuss the interrelationship between the words of the wedding ceremony and Roselily's reflections. How do the specific passages spur her memories and commentary? What is the tone of her comments? Why do they compose the major part of the story?

2. What are the major contrasts between the bride and groom? What is each seeking in marriage? Will their marriage be a successful one?

3. Examine the language of Roselily's reflections, especially the use of simile and metaphor. What does the language reveal about Roselily's character?

4. How does Walker use color imagery in the story?

The Farm

It was a dark night in August. Sarah and Tommy were going to their third party that night, the party where they would actually sit down to dinner. They were driving down Mixtuxet Avenue, a long black avenue of trees that led out of the village, away from the shore and the coastal homes into the country. Tommy had been drinking only soda that night. Every other weekend, Tommy wouldn't drink. He did it, he said, to keep trim. He did it because he could.

Sarah was telling a long story as she drove. She kept asking Tommy if she had told it to him before, but he was noncommittal. When Tommy didn't drink, Sarah talked and talked. She was telling him a terrible story that she had read in the newspaper about an alligator at a jungle farm attraction in Florida. The alligator had eaten a child who had crawled into its pen. The alligator's name was Cookie. Its owner had shot it immediately. The owner was sad about everything, the child, the parents' grief, Cookie. He was quoted in the paper as saying that shooting Cookie was not an act of revenge.

When Tommy didn't drink, Sarah felt cold. She was shivering in the car. There were goosepimples on her tanned, thin arms. Tommy sat beside her smoking, saying nothing.

There had been words between them earlier. The parties here had an undercurrent of sexuality. Sarah could almost hear it, flowing around them all, carrying them all along. In the car, on the night of the accident, Sarah was at that point in the evening when she felt guilty. She wanted to make things better, make things nice. She had gone through her elated stage, her jealous stage, her stubbornly resigned stage and now she felt guilty. Had they talked about divorce that night, or had that been before, on other evenings? There was a flavor she remembered in their talks about divorce, a scent. It was hot, as Italy had been hot when they had been there. Dust, bread, sun, a burning at the back of the throat from too much drinking.

But no, they hadn't been talking about divorce that night. The parties had been crowded. Sarah had hardly seen Tommy. Then, on her way to the bathroom, she had seen him sitting with a girl on a bed in one of the back rooms. He was telling the girl about condors, about hunting for condors in small, light planes.

"Oh, but you didn't hurt them, did you?" the girl asked. She was someone's daughter, a little overweight but with beautiful skin and large green eyes.

"Oh no," Tommy assured her, "we weren't hunting to hurt."

Condors. Sarah looked at them sitting on the bed. When they noticed her, the girl blushed. Tommy smiled. Sarah imagined what she looked like, standing in the doorway. She wished that they had shut the door.

That had been at the Steadmans'. The first party had been at the Perrys'. The Perrys never served food. Sarah had had two or three drinks there. The bar had been set up beneath the grape arbor and everyone stood outside. It had still been light at the Perrys' but at the Steadmans' it was dark and people drank inside. Everyone spoke about the end of summer as though it were a bewildering and unnatural event.

They had stayed at the Steadmans' longer than they should have and they were going to be late for dinner. Nevertheless, they were driving at a moderate speed, through a familiar landscape, passing houses that they had been entertained in many times. There were the Salts and the Hollands and the Greys and the Dodsons. The Dodsons kept their gin in the freezer and owned two large and dappled crotch-sniffing dogs. The Greys imported Southerners for their parties. The women all had lovely voices and knew how to make spoon bread and pickled tomatoes and artillery punch. The men had smiles when they'd say to Sarah, "Why, let me get you another. You don't have a thing in that glass, ah swear." The Hollands gave the kind of dinner party where the shot was still in the duck and the silver should have been in a vault. Little whiskey was served but there was always excellent wine. The Salts were a high-strung couple who often quarreled. Jenny Salt was on some type of medication for tension and often dropped the canapés she attempted to serve. Jenny and her husband, Pete, had a room in which there was nothing but a large doll house where witty mâché figures carried on assignations beneath tiny clocks and crystal chandeliers. Once, when Sarah was examining the doll house's library where two figures were hunched over a chess game which was just about to be won, Pete had always said, on the twenty-second move, Pete told Sarah that she had pretty eyes. She had moved away from him immediately. She had closed her eyes. In another room, with the other guests, she had talked about the end of summer.

On that night, at the end of summer, the night of the accident, Sarah was still talking as they passed the Salts' house. She was talking about Venice. She and Tommy had been there once. They had drunk in the Plaza and listened to the orchestras. Sarah quoted D. H. Lawrence on Venice ... "Abhorrent green and slippery city ..." But she and Tommy had liked Venice. They drank standing up at little bars. Sarah had had a cold and she drank grappa and the cold had disappeared for the rest of her life.

After the Salts' house, the road swerved north and became very dark. There were no lights, no houses for several miles. There were stone walls, an orchard of sickly peach trees, a cider mill. There was St. James Episcopal Church where Tommy took their daughter, Martha, to Sunday school. The Sunday school was highly fundamental. There were many arguments among the children and their teachers as to the correct interpretation of Bible story favorites. For example, when Lazarus rose from the dead, was he still sick? Martha liked the fervor at St. James. Each week, her dinner graces were becoming more impassioned and fantastic. Martha was seven.

Each Sunday, Tommy takes Martha to her little classes at St. James. Sarah can imagine the child sitting there at a low table with her jars of colors. Tommy doesn't go to church himself and Martha's classes are two hours long. Sarah doesn't know where Tommy goes. She suspects he is seeing someone. When they come home on Sundays, Tommy is sleek, exhilarated. The three of them sit down to the dinner Sarah has prepared.

Over the years, Sarah suspects, Tommy has floated to the surface of her. They are swimmers now, far apart, on the top of the sea.

Sarah at last fell silent. The road seemed endless as in a dream. They seemed to be slowing down. She could not feel her foot on the accelerator. She could not feel her hands on the wheel. Her mind was an untidy cupboard filled with shining bottles. The road was dark and silvery and straight. In the space ahead of her, there seemed to be something. It beckoned, glittering. Sarah's mind cleared a little. She saw Martha with her hair cut oddly short. Sarah gently nibbled on the inside of her mouth to keep alert. She saw Tommy choosing a succession of houses, examining the plaster, the floorboards, the fireplaces, deciding where windows should be placed, walls knocked down. She saw herself taking curtains down from a window so that there would be a better view of the sea. The curtains knocked her glass from the sill and it shattered. The sea was white and flat. It did not command her to change her life. It demanded of her, nothing. She saw Martha sleeping, her paint-smudged fingers curled. She saw Tommy in the city with a woman, riding in a cab. The woman wore a short fur jacket and Tommy stroked it as he spoke. She saw a figure in the road ahead, its arms raised before its face as though to block out the sight of her. The figure was a boy who wore dark clothing, but his hair was bright, his face was shining. She saw her car leap forward and run him down where he stood.

Tommy had taken responsibility for the accident. He had told the police he was driving. The boy apparently had been hitch-hiking and had stepped out into the road. At the autopsy, traces of a hallucinogen were found in the boy's system. The boy was fifteen years old and his name was Stevie Bettencourt. No charges were filed.

"My wife," Tommy told the police, "was not feeling well. My wife," Tommy said, "was in the passenger seat."

Sarah stopped drinking immediately after the accident. She felt nauseated much of the time. She slept poorly. Her hands hurt her. The bones in her hands ached. She remembered that this was the way she felt the last time she had stopped drinking. It had been two years before. She remembered why she had stopped and she remembered why she had started again. She had stopped because she had done a cruel thing to her little Martha. It was spring and she and Tommy were giving a dinner party. Sarah had two martinis in the late afternoon when she was preparing dinner and then she had two more martinis with her guests. Martha had come downstairs to say a polite good-night to everyone as she had been taught. She had put on her nightie and brushed her teeth. Sarah poured a little more gin in her glass and went upstairs with her to brush out her hair and put her to bed. Martha had long, thick blond hair of which she was very proud. On that night she wore it in a pony tail secured by an elasticized holder with two small colored balls on the end. Sarah's fingers were clumsy and she could not get it off without pulling Martha's hair and making her cry. She got a pair of scissors and carefully began snipping at the stubborn elastic. The scissors were large, like shears, and they had been difficult to handle. A foot of Martha's gathered hair had abruptly fallen to the floor. Sarah remembered trying to pat it back into place on the child's head.

So Sarah had stopped drinking the first time. She did not feel renewed. She felt exhausted and wary. She read and cooked. She realized how little she and Tommy had to talk about. Tommy drank Scotch when he talked to her at night. Sometimes Sarah would silently count as he spoke to see how long the words took. When he was away and he telephoned her, she could hear the ice tinkling in the glass.

Tommy was in the city four days a week. He often changed hotels. He would bring Martha little bars of soap wrapped in the different colored papers of the hotels. Martha's drawers were full of the soaps scenting her clothes. When Tommy came home on the weekends he would work on the house and they would give parties at which Tommy was charming. Tommy had a talent for holding his liquor and for buying old houses, restoring them and selling them for three times what he had paid for them. Tommy and Sarah had moved six times in eleven years. All their homes had been fine old houses in excellent locations two or three hours from New York. Sarah would stay in the country while Tommy worked in the city. Sarah did not know her way around New York.

For three weeks, Sarah did not drink. Then it was her birthday. Tommy gave her a slim gold necklace and fastened it around her neck. He wanted her to come to New York with him, to have dinner, see a play, spend the night with him in the fine suite the company had given him at the hotel. They had got a babysitter for Martha, a marvelous woman who polished the silver in the afternoon when Martha napped. Sarah drove. Tommy had never cared for driving. His hand rested on her thigh. Occasionally, he would slip his hand beneath her skirt. Sarah was sick with the thought that this was the way he touched other women.

By the time they were in Manhattan, they were arguing. They had been married for eleven years. Both had had brief marriages before. They could argue about anything. In midtown, Tommy stormed out of the car as Sarah braked for a light. He took his suitcase and disappeared.

Sarah drove carefully for many blocks. When she had the opportunity, she would pull to the curb and ask someone how to get to Connecticut. No one seemed to know. Sarah thought she was probably phrasing the question poorly but she didn't know how else to present it. After half an hour, she made her way back to the hotel where Tommy was staying. The doorman parked the car and she went into the lobby. She looked into the hotel bar and saw Tommy in the dimness, sitting at a small table. He jumped up and kissed her passionately. He rubbed his hands up and down her sides. "Darling, darling," he said, "I want you to have a happy birthday."

Tommy ordered drinks for both of them. Sarah sipped hers slowly at first but then she drank it and he ordered others. The bar was subdued. There was a piano player who sang about the lord of the dance. The words seemed like those of a hymn. The hymn made her sad but she laughed. Tommy spoke to her urgently and gaily about little things. They laughed together like they had when they were first married. They had always drunk a lot together then and fallen asleep, comfortably and lovingly entwined on white sheets.

They went to their room to change for the theater. The maid had turned back the beds. There was a fresh rose in a bud vase on the writing desk. They had another drink in the room and got undressed. Sarah awoke the next morning curled up on the floor with the bedspread tangled around her. Her mouth was sore. There was a bruise on her leg. The television set was on with no sound. The room was a mess although Sarah could see that nothing had been really damaged. She stared at the television where black-backed gulls were dive-bombing on terrified and doomed cygnets in a documentary about swans. Sarah crept into the bathroom and turned on the shower. She sat in the tub while the water beat upon her. Pinned to the outside of the shower curtain was a note from Tommy, who had gone to work. "Darling," the note said, "we had a *good* time on your birthday. I can't say I'm sorry we never got out. I'll call you for lunch. Love."

Sarah turned the note inward until the water made the writing illegible. When the phone rang just before noon, she did not answer it.

*   *   *

There is a certain type of conversation one hears only when one is drunk and it is like a dream, full of humor and threat and significance, deep significance. And the way one witnesses things when one is drunk is different as well. It is like putting a face mask against the surface of the sea and looking into things, into their baffled and guileless hearts.

When Sarah had been a drinker, she felt that she had a fundamental and inventive grasp of situations, but now that she drank no longer, she found herself in the midst of a great and impenetrable silence which she could in no way interpret.

It was a small village. Many of the people who lived there did not even own cars. The demands of life were easily met in the village and it was pretty there besides. It was divided between those who always lived there and who owned fishing boats and restaurants and the city people who had more recently discovered the area as a summer place and winter weekend investment. On the weekends, the New Yorkers would come up with their houseguests and their pâté and cheeses and build fires and go cross-country skiing. Tommy came home to Sarah on weekends. They did things together. They agreed on where to go. During the week she was on her own.

Once, alone, she saw a helicopter carrying a tree in a sling across the Sound. The wealthy could afford to leave nothing behind.

Once, with the rest of the town, she saw five boats burning in their storage shrouds. Each summer resort has its winter pyromaniac.

Sarah did not read any more. Her eyes hurt when she read and her hands ached all the time. During the week, she marketed and walked and cared for Martha.

It was three months after Stevie Bettencourt was killed when his mother visited Sarah. She came to the door and knocked on it and Sarah let her in.

Genevieve Bettencourt was a woman Sarah's age although she looked rather younger. She had been divorced almost from the day that Stevie was born. She had another son named Bruce who lived with his father in Nova Scotia. She had an old powder-blue Buick parked on the street before Sarah's house. The Buick had one white door.

The two women sat in Sarah's handsome, sunny living room. It was very calm, very peculiar, almost thrilling. Genevieve looked all around the room. Off the living room were the bedrooms. The door to Sarah's and Tommy's was closed but Martha's door was open. She had a little hanging garden against the window. She had a hamster in a cage. She had an enormous bookcase filled with dolls and books.

Genevieve said to Sarah, "That room wasn't there before. This used to be a lobster pound. I know a great deal about this town. People like you have nothing to do with what I know about this town. Do you remember the way things were, ever?"

"No," Sarah said.

Genevieve sighed. "Does your daughter look like you or your husband?"

"No one's ever told me she looked like me," Sarah said quietly.

On the glass-topped table before them there was a little wooden sculpture cutout that Tommy had bought. A man and woman sat on a park bench. Each wore a startled and ambiguous expression. Each had a terrier on the end of a string. The dogs were a puzzle. One fit on top of the other. Sarah was embarrassed about it being there. Tommy had put it on the table during the weekend and Sarah hadn't moved it. Genevieve didn't touch it.

"I did not want my life to know you," Genevieve said. She removed a hair from the front of her white blouse and dropped it to the floor. She looked out the window at the sun. The floor was of a very light and varnished pine. Sarah could see the hair upon it.

"I'm so sorry," Sarah said. "I'm so very, very sorry." She stretched her neck and put her head back.

"Stevie was a mixed-up boy," Genevieve said. "They threw him off the basketball team.

He took pills. He had bad friends. He didn't study and he got a D in geometry and they wouldn't let him play basketball."

She got up and wandered around the room. She wore green rubber boots, dirty jeans and a beautiful, hand-knit sweater. "I once bought all my fish here," she said. "The O'Malleys owned it. There were practically no windows. Just narrow high ones over the tanks. Now it's all windows, isn't it? Don't you feel exposed?"

"No, I ..." Sarah began. "There are drapes," she said.

"Off to the side, where you have your garden, there are whale bones if you dig deep enough. I can tell you a lot about this town."

"My husband wants to move," Sarah said."

"I can understand that, but you're the real drinker, after all, aren't you, not him."

"I don't drink any more," Sarah said. She looked at the woman dizzily.

Genevieve was not pretty but she had a clear, strong face. She sat down on the opposite side of the room. "I guess I would like something," she said. "A glass of water." Sarah went to the kitchen and poured a glass of Vichy[1] for them both. Her hands shook.

"We are not strangers to one another," Genevieve said. "We could be friends."

"My first husband always wanted to be friends with my second husband," Sarah said after a moment. "I could never understand it." This had somehow seemed analogous when she was saying it but now it did not. "It is not appropriate that we be friends," she said.

Genevieve continued to sit and talk. Sarah found herself concentrating desperately on her articulate, one-sided conversation. She suspected that the words Genevieve was using were codes for other words, terrible words. Genevieve spoke thoughtlessly, dispassionately, with erratic flourishes of language. Sarah couldn't believe that they were chatting about food, men, the red clouds massed above the sea.

"I have a friend who is a designer," Genevieve said. "She hopes to make a great deal of money someday. Her work has completely altered her perceptions. Every time she looks at a view, she thinks of sheets. "'Take out those mountains,' she will say, 'lighten that cloud a bit and it would make a great sheet.' When she looks at the sky, she thinks of lingerie. Now when I look at the sky, I think of earlier times, happier times when I looked at the sky. I have never been in love, have you?"

"Yes," Sarah said, "I'm in love."

"It's not a lucky thing, you know, to be in love."

There was a soft scuffling at the door and Martha came in. "Hello," she said. "School was good today. I'm hungry."

"Hello, dear," Genevieve said. To Sarah, she said, "Perhaps we can have lunch sometime."

"Who is that?" Martha asked Sarah after Genevieve had left.

"A neighbor," Sarah said, "one of Mommy's friends."

When Sarah told Tommy about Genevieve coming to visit her, he said, "It's harrassment. It can be stopped."

It was Sunday morning. They had just finished breakfast and Tommy and Martha were drying the dishes and putting them away. Martha was wearing her church-school clothes and she was singing a song she had learned the Sunday before.

"... I'm going to the Mansion on the Happy Days' Express ..." she sang.

Tommy squeezed Martha's shoulders. "Go get your coat, sweetie," he said. When the

---

[1] A naturally effervescent mineral water from springs at Vichy, France.

child had gone, he said to Sarah, "Don't speak to this woman. Don't allow it to happen again."

"We didn't talk about that."

"What else could you talk about? It's weird."

"No one talks about that. No one, ever."

Tommy was wearing a corduroy suit and a tie Sarah had never seen before. Sarah looked at the pattern in the tie. It was random and bright.

"Are you having an affair?" Sarah asked.

"No," he said easily. "I don't understand you, Sarah. I've done everything I could to protect you, to help you straighten yourself out. It was a terrible thing but it's over. You have to get over it. Now, just don't see her again. There's no way that she can cause trouble if you don't speak to her."

Sarah stopped looking at Tommy's tie. She moved her eyes to the potatoes she had peeled and put in a bowl of water.

Martha came into the kitchen and held on to her father's arm. Her hair was long and thick, but it was getting darker. It was as though it had never been cut.

After they left, Sarah put the roast in the oven and went into the living room. The large window was full of the day, a colorless windy day without birds. Sarah sat on the floor and ran her fingers across the smooth, varnished wood. Beneath the expensive flooring was cold cement. Tanks had once lined the walls. Lobsters had crept back and forth across the mossy glass. The phone rang. Sarah didn't look at it, suspecting it was Genevieve. Then she picked it up.

"Hello," said Genevieve, "I thought I might drop by. It's a bleak day, isn't it. Cold. Is your family at home?"

"They go out on Sunday," Sarah said. "It gives me time to think. They go to church."

"What do you think about?" The woman's voice seemed far away. Sarah strained to hear her.

"I'm supposed to cook dinner. When they come back we eat dinner."

"I can prepare clams in forty-three different ways," Genevieve said.

"This is a roast. A roast pork."

"Well, may I come over?"

"All right," Sarah said.

She continued to sit on the floor, waiting for Genevieve, looking at the water beneath the sky. The water on the horizon was a wide, satin ribbon. She wished that she had the courage to swim on such a bitter, winter day. To swim far out and rest, to hesitate and then to return. Her life was dark, unexplored. Her abstinence had drained her. She felt sluggish, robbed. Her body had no freedom.

She sat, seeing nothing, the terrible calm light of the day around her. The things she remembered were so far away, bathed in a different light. Her life seemed so remote to her. She had sought happiness in someone, knowing she could not find it in herself and now her heart was strangely hard. She rubbed her head with her hands.

Her life with Tommy was broken, irreparable. Her life with him was over. His infidelities kept getting mixed up in her mind with the death of the boy, with Tommy's false admission that he had been driving when the boy died. Sarah couldn't understand anything. Her life seemed so random, so needlessly constructed and now threatened in a way which did not interest her.

"Hello," Genevieve called. She had opened the front door and was standing in the hall. "You didn't hear my knock."

Sarah got up. She was to entertain this woman. She felt anxious, adulterous. The cold rose form Genevieve's skin and hair. Sarah took her coat and hung it in the closet. The fresh cold smell lingered on her hands.

She moved into the kitchen. She took a package of rolls out of the freezer.

"Does your little girl like church?" Genevieve asked.

"Yes, very much."

"It's a stage," said Genevieve. "I'm Catholic myself. As a child, I used to be fascinated by the martyrs. I remember a picture of St. Lucy, carrying her eyes like a plate of eggs, and St. Agatha. She carried her breasts on a plate."

Sarah said, "I don't understand what we're talking about. I know you're just using these words, that they mean other words, I ..."

"Perhaps we could take your little girl to a movie sometime, a matinee, after she gets out of school."

"Her name is Martha," Sarah said. She saw Martha grown up, her hair cut short once more, taking rolls out of the freezer, waiting.

"Martha, yes," Genevieve said. "Have you wanted more children?"

"No," Sarah said. Their conversation was illegal, unspeakable. Sarah couldn't imagine it ever ending. Her fingers tapped against the ice-cube trays. "Would you care for a drink?"

"A very tall glass of vermouth," Genevieve said. She was looking at a little picture Martha had made, that Sarah had tacked to the wall. It was a very badly drawn horse. "I wanted children. I wanted to fulfill myself. One can never fulfill oneself. I think it is an impossibility."

Sarah made Genevieve's drink very slowly. She did not make one for herself.

"When Stevie was Martha's age, he knew everything about whales. He kept notebooks. Once, on his birthday, I took him to the whaling museum in New Bedford." She sipped her drink. "It all goes wrong somewhere," she said. She turned her back on Sarah and went into the other room. Sarah followed her.

"There are so many phrases for 'dead,' you know," Genevieve was saying. "The kids think them up, or they come out of music or wars. Stevie had one that he'd use for dead animals and rock stars. He'd say they'd 'bought the farm.'"

Sarah nodded. She was pulling and peeling at the nails of her hands.

"I think it's pretty creepy. A dark farm, you know. Weedy. Run-down. Broken machinery everywhere. A real job."

Sarah raised her head. "You want us to share Martha, don't you," she said. "It's only right, isn't it?"

"... the paint blown away, acres and acres of tangled, black land, a broken shutter over the well."

Sarah lowered her head again. Her heart was cold, horrified. The reality of the two women, placed by hazard in this room, this bright functional tasteful room that Tommy had created, was being tested. Reality would resist, for days, perhaps weeks, but then it would yield. It would yield to this guest, this visitor, for whom Sarah had made room.

"Would you join me in another drink?" Genevieve asked. "Then I'll go."

"I mustn't drink," Sarah said.

"You don't forget," Genevieve said, "that's just an old saw." She went into the kitchen and poured more vermouth for herself. Sarah could smell the meat cooking. From another room, the clock chimed.

"You must come to my home soon," Genevieve said. She did not sit down. Sarah looked at the pale green liquid in the glass.

"Yes," Sarah said, "soon."

"We must not greet one another on the street, however. People are quick to gossip."

"Yes," Sarah said. "They would condemn us." She looked heavily at Genevieve, full of misery and submission.

There was knocking on the door. "Sarah," Tommy's voice called, "why is the door locked?" She could see his dark head at the window.

"I must have thrown the bolt," Genevieve said. "It's best to lock your house in the winter, you know. It's the kids mostly. They get bored. Stevie was a robber once or twice, I'm sure." She put down her glass, took her coat from the closet and went out. Sarah heard Martha say, "That's Mommy's friend."

Tommy stood in the doorway and stared at Sarah. "Why did you lock the door?" he asked again.

Sarah imagined seeing herself, naked. She said, "There are robbers."

Tommy said, "If you don't feel safe here, we'll move. I've been looking at a wonderful place about twenty miles from here, on a cove. It only needs a little work. It will give us more room. There's a barn, some fence. Martha could have a horse."

Sarah looked at him with an intent, halted expression, as though she were listening to a dialogue no one present was engaged in. Finally, she said, "There are robbers. Everything has changed."

QUESTIONS

1. How does Sarah's story about the alligator foreshadow the main action of the story? Discuss the analogy to her situation.

2. What are the causes of Sarah's alcoholism? What effect does it have on her behavior and perceptions? How does she change when she stops drinking?

3. Why does Sarah feel "adulterous" in accepting Genevieve's friendship? To what extent are she and Genevieve friends? How does Genevieve alter her perceptions of her house and her life?

4. Applied to the situation of Sarah and Tommy, Stevie's phrase for "dead" has certain ironic implications. What are they?

BIOGRAPHIES OF THE AUTHORS ☰

Alice Adams (1926–) was born in Fredericksburg, Virginia and grew up in Chapel Hill, North Carolina. She attended schools in North Carolina and Virginia, and graduated from Radcliffe College in 1946. Since then she has lived mainly in San Francisco. Her short stories have appeared in various magazines, in particular the *New Yorker*. A story, "Alaska," appears in *Prize Stories 1984: The O. Henry Awards*. In the fall of 1984 her fifth novel, *Superior Women*, was published by Knopf. Another short story collection, as yet untitled, is scheduled to appear in the fall of 1985.

Sherwood Anderson (1876–1941) was born in Camden, Ohio, and grew up in Clyde, which eventually appeared as the fictional "Winesburg, Ohio" of his most accomplished work. Largely self-educated, he read widely. After serving in the Spanish-American War, he went to Chicago and took up writing. What he had learned working on farms, in shops, and especially in livery and racing stables, later appeared in short stories that dealt with the emotional problems of boyhood. He draws powerful psychological portraits of men and women trapped by small–town life. Anderson's gradual alienation from his father became a possible source of his chronic emotional disunity. His novels include *Windy McPherson's Son* (1916) and *Dark Laughter* (1925). His short story collections include *Winesburg, Ohio* (1919), *Horses and Men* (1923), and *Death in the Woods* (1933).

Margaret Atwood (1939–) was born in Ottawa, Canada. She earned a bachelor's degree from Victoria College and a master's degree from Radcliffe College. Her poetry has been published in many magazines including the *New Yorker*, the *Atlantic Monthly*, and *Poetry*. She is also a frequent contributor to the *New York Times*, *Ms.* magazine, and the Chicago *Sun-Times*. Her short stories are collected in *Dancing Girls* and *Bluebeard's Egg*. Among her other published works are nine books of poetry and several works of fiction including *The Edible Woman* (1969), *Surfacing* (1972), *Lady Oracle* (1973), *Life Before Man* (1979), *Bodily Harm* (1981), and *Murder in the Dark* (1983). She has also written critical articles and reviews.

James Baldwin (1924–) was born in Harlem, the oldest of nine children. Religion played a significant role in his background and, after graduating from high school, he began to preach. He also began to write novels, essays, and short stories dealing with such subjects as homosexuality, interracial love, and racial conflict. Much of his work reflects his growing concern about hatred and unrest between blacks and whites. His short stories are collected in *Going to Meet the Man* (1965). His novels include *Go Tell It On the Mountain* (1953), *If Beale Street Could Talk* (1974), and *Just Above My Head* (1979). *Notes of a Native Son* (1955) and *The Fire Next Time* (1963) are gatherings of his essays.

Honoré de Balzac (1799–1850) was born in Tours, France. He attended the Verdôme school, then went to work as a lawyer's clerk, publishing in the meantime several unsuccessful novels under pseudonyms. He tried other careers in the printing and publishing trades, but finally, at age thirty, influenced by Scott and the English Romantics, decided to devote himself exclusively to literature. An extraordinarily prolific writer, Balzac would publish a huge number of related novels and short stories which, collectively, reflect French society of his time, from simple peasant life to glittering social extravagance. This immense effort is titled *The Human Comedy*, begun in 1830 and ended only with his death.

Toni Cade Bambara (1939–) was born in New York City. She took a bachelor's degree at Queens College and an M.A. degree at CCNY. Her writing reflects the character and concerns of contemporary black women, young and old. She explores the undersurface of their lives—their triumphs and their failures. Her short story collections include *Gorilla, My Love* (1972) and *The Sea Buds Are Still Alive: Collected Stories* (1977). Her most recent book, published in 1980, is *The Salt Eaters*.

John Barth   (1930–) was born and raised in Cambridge, Maryland. He took undergraduate and graduate degrees at Johns Hopkins University and has served on the faculties of several universities since finishing his formal studies. An experimentalist, Barth has published increasingly complex fiction over the years, including such novels as *The Floating Opera* (1956), *The Sot-Weed Factor* (1960), *Giles Goatboy* (1966), *Letters* (1979), and *Sabbatical: A Romance* (1982). His short stories have been collected in *Lost in the Funhouse* (1968) and *Chimera* (1972).

Donald Barthelme   (1931–) was born in Philadelphia and raised in Houston, Texas, where he began work as a reporter. As a fiction writer, he often rejects conventional form for what has frequently been termed verbal collage. Exaggerated comic characters illustrate recurrent themes, one of which is the difficulty of using language to connect people with each other and to the world. His novels include *Snow White* (1967) and *The Dead Father* (1975). Some of his short stories are collected in *Come Back, Dr. Caligari* (1964), *Unspeakable Practices, Unnatural Acts* (1968), *Amateurs* (1976), and *Overnight to Many Distant Cities* (1983).

Ann Beattie   (1947–) was born in Washington, D.C. After receiving a B.A. from American University, she did graduate work at the University of Connecticut. Three collections of short stories—*Distortions* (1976), *Secrets and Surprises* (1978), and *The Burning House* (1982)—and two novels—*Chilly Scenes of Winter* (1976) and *Falling in Place* (1980)—have established her as one of America's important young writers. She is a frequent contributor to the *New Yorker* and has been widely published in other magazines. A resident of Somerville, Massachusetts, she has taught creative writing at Harvard University and at the University of Michigan.

Saul Bellow   (1915–) was born in Quebec and lived as a child in Montreal, but grew up in Chicago, Illinois, where he has spent most of his adult life and where he has taught for years at the University of Chicago (his alma mater) and has written the fiction that has brought him to the forefront of contemporary writers. He was awarded the Nobel Prize in 1976, cited for "the human understanding and subtle analysis of contemporary culture" that are combined in his work. Bellow has been a prolific and versatile writer: he has written travel literature, plays, and criticism as well as the stories and novels for which he is best known. Bellow's novels include *The Victim* (1945), *The Adventures of Augie March* (1953), *Henderson the Rain King* (1959), *Herzog* (1964), *Humboldt's Gift* (1975), and *The Dean's December* (1982). *Seize the Day* (1956), *Mosby's Memoirs and Other Stories* (1968), and *Him with His Foot in His Mouth and Other Stories* (1984) bring together some of his short fiction.

Ambrose Bierce   (1842–1914) was born in Horse Cave Creek, Ohio, but soon moved with his family to Indiana, where he lived until he enlisted for infantry duty in the Civil War. The experience of war—he saw plenty of action and was twice wounded—changed his life, giving him the material for his realistic depictions of war's horrors but also ingraining a bitter pessimism and sardonic outlook that would color his essays and his short stories. After the war, he travelled widely as a working journalist—to California, to England, and back to the San Francisco area. His personal life went badly in later years, confirming in him his dark outlook. Bierce went to Mexico to cover the Mexican Revolution. There he dropped from sight. His disappearance has never been satisfactorily explained but it is assumed that he died there in 1914. Among Bierce's best known works are *The Devil's Dictionary* (1906) and his two early volumes of short stories, *Tales of Soldiers and Civilians* (1891) and *Can Such Things Be?* (1893).

Clark Blaise   (1940–) was born in North Dakota of Canadian parents, and spent most of his childhood in Florida, Pittsburgh, and Winnipeg. He has received academic degrees from Denison University and the University of Iowa. Institutions at which he has taught include Concordia University in Montreal, York University in Toronto, Skidmore College, David Thompson University Centre in British Columbia, and the University of Iowa. He has published *A North American Education* (1973), *Tribal Justice* (1974), *Days and Nights in Calcutta* (with his wife, Bharati Mukherjee) (1977), *Lunar Attractions* (1979), and *Lusts* (1983). A volume of autobiographical fiction and essays, *Resident Alien*, is forthcoming.

Jorge Luis Borges   (1899–) was born in Buenos Aires and educated in Switzerland. As a young man, he spent two years in Spain, where he was introduced to the literary *avant-garde* and stimulated to write. He has been a political exile, a professor, and director of the Argentine National Library. Over the years he has gained immense respect as a poet, although he is considerably more conservative than many other writers and intellectuals in a part of the world where partisanship is fierce. Borges is a respected prose writer as well, an immensely erudite writer whose stories puzzle as they delight, echo with allusion as they entertain. His short stories have been collected in several volumes, including *Ficciones* (1945), *El Aleph* (1949), *El hacendor* (1960), and *Antología personal* (1961). His *Complete Works* appeared in 1975.

Paul Bowles   (1910–) was born in New York. He studied musical composition with Aaron Copland, and later was on the staff of the *New York Herald Tribune* as a music critic. In the early 1930s he spent four years traveling in North Africa. From the mid-1930s to the mid-1940s he wrote incidental scores for the Broadway theatre. At that point he turned to writing fiction. *A Distant Episode* was written in 1945. Since 1947 he has lived in Tangier, Morocco.

Ray Bradbury   (1910–) was born in Waukegan, Illinois, and attended school there and in Los Angeles. He began at an early age to write stories and pursue his interest in futuristic fiction. His popular science fiction books combine social criticism with fantasy. He has been most prolific. His novels include *Fahrenheit 451* (1953) and *Something Wicked This Way Comes* (1963). His short story collections include *The Martian Chronicles* (1950), *Dandelion Wine* (1957), and *The Stories of Ray Bradbury* (1980).

Richard Brautigan   (1935–1984) was born in Tacoma, Washington and flourished in San Francisco. He became well known in the mid-1960s for a series of short novels—*A Confederate General in Big Sur* (1965), *Trout Fishing in America* (1967), and *In Watermelon Sugar* (1969)—and for his volumes of poetry, *The Pill Versus the Springhill Mine Disaster* (1968) and *Rommel Drives on Deep into Egypt* (1970). Later he published *The Hawkline Monster* (1974) and *Sombrero Fallout* (1976).

Hortense Calisher   (1911–) was born in New York City and graduated from Barnard College. She has served on the faculty of Barnard, as well as of Stanford University, Sarah Lawrence College, Brandeis University, the University of Pennsylvania, the University of California, and Bennington College. Her novellas and short stories appear in *In the Absence of Angels* (1951), *Tale for the Mirror* (1962), *Extreme Magic* (1964), *The Railway Police and the Last Trolley Ride* (1966), and *The Collected Stories of Hortense Calisher* (1975). Her novels include *False Entry* (1961), *Textures of Life* (1963), *Journal from Ellipsia* (1965), *The New Yorkers* (1969), *Queenie* (1971), *Standard Dreaming* (1972), *Eagle Eye* (1974), *On Keeping Women* (1977), and *Mysteries of Motion* (1983). An autobiographical work, *Herself* (1972), was nominated for a National Book Award. She has also published articles, reviews, and essays in the *New York Times Sunday Book Review* and the *American Scholar*.

Barry Callaghan   (1937–) was born in Toronto. He has been a journalist, a host for a CBC public affairs program, and a director of several short films and documentaries. He has received four journalism awards, including the Gold Medal from the University of Western Ontario. Since 1965 Callaghan has taught at Atkinson College, York University, Toronto, where he founded *Exile* magazine and Exile Editions. He is the author of *The Black Queen Stories* (1982) and two collections of poems, *The Hogg Poems and Drawings* (1978) and *Seven Last Wishes* (1983).

Raymond Carver   (1939–) was born in Oregon. His short stories have appeared in three collections: *Will You Please Be Quiet, Please?* (1976), *What We Talk about When We Talk about Love* (1981), and *Cathedral* (1983). He has also published a collection of prose and poetry, *Fires* (1983), as well as three books of poetry. He has taught at the University of Iowa, the University of Texas, the University of California, and Syracuse University. Among numerous honors, he has received a Guggenheim Fellowship, National Endowment for the Arts Awards in poetry and fiction, a Wallace Stegner Literary Fellowship, and a Mildred and Harold Strauss Living Award. Carver now lives in the Pacific Northwest.

Willa Cather   (1873–1947) was born in Virginia but grew up in rural Nebraska. After graduating from the University of Nebraska, she began teaching and writing the stories and novels which established her reputation. She portrays the struggles of people, often immigrants, living on the Nebraska frontier as well as the joys and hardships of the early settlers in America's Southwest. Among her works are collections of short stories, *The Troll Garden* (1905) and *Youth and the Bright Medusa* (1920). *O Pioneers* (1913), *My Antonia* (1918), and *Death Comes for the Archbishop* (1927) are among her best-known novels.

John Cheever   (1912–1981) was born in Quincy, Massachusetts, and educated at Thayer Academy. His expulsion from that school was the subject of his first short story, published when he was only seventeen. He is a shrewd observer of the manners and morals of middle class life, especially in the affluent suburbs, portraying characters as they blunder and claw their way through life. He finds his subjects (sad and failed folk, mostly) in the world of swimming pools and cocktail parties, penetrating the illusion of success and respectability. Often his protagonists, modern antiheroes, are weak, immoral, and frightened human beings. His novels include *The Wapshot Chronicle* (1957), *Bullet Park* (1969), and *Falconer* (1977). His short story collections include *The Enormous Radio and Other Stories* (1953), *The Housebreaker of Shady Hill and Other Stories* (1958), and his Pulitzer Prize-winning *The Stories of John Cheever* (1978).

Anton Chekhov (1860–1904) was born and educated in Taganrog, Russia. The son of a shopkeeper, he studied medicine in Moscow and became a practitioner, but gave it up to concentrate on literature. He became a prolific writer, a major force in nineteenth-century literature, respected for his intellectual integrity as well as his artistic achievement. In 1888 he was awarded the Pushkin Prize. Chekhov is also a major playwright. His dramas include *The Sea Gull* (1896), *The Three Sisters* (1901), and *The Cherry Orchard* (1904). His work has been frequently translated, and many of his short stories and sketches are available in classroom texts and paperback editions in English.

Kate Chopin (1851–1904) was born in St. Louis. After her marriage in 1870, she moved to Louisiana, but returned to St. Louis upon her husband's death and began to write about her experience with Catholic Creole society, focusing particularly on local color, customs, language, and the lot of women in rural Louisiana. She collected her short stories, which had appeared in popular periodicals, under the title *Bayou Folk* (1894) and *A Night in Acadia* (1897). Kate Chopin gave up writing in 1899, when her short novel, *The Awakening,* drew critical fire from reviewers who were not prepared to accept—especially from the pen of a woman—the frank and sensual portrayal of an unrepentant heroine.

Agatha Christie (1890–1976) was born in Torquay, England, to an American father and an English mother who encouraged her to write. She took up detective fiction where Arthur Conan Doyle left off, and over the course of some 80 books established herself as the doyenne of the genre. She was an especially strong plot-designer. Her travels with archeologist-husband Max Mallowan gave her first-hand knowledge of the exotic settings she often employed. She created two famous sleuths—Hercule Poirot, the egotistical Belgian, and Miss Jane Marple, the village spinster. She also wrote successfully for the stage, with her plays *The Mousetrap* (1952) and *Witness for the Prosecution* (1953) enjoying long runs. Her books include *The Mysterious Affair at Styles* (1920), *Murder on the Orient Express* (1934), *Death on the Nile* (1937), and *Ten Little Indians* (1939). Some of her short stories were printed in *Thirteen Problems* (1932) and *Three Blind Mice* (1950).

Arthur C. Clarke (1917–) was born in Minehead, Somerset, England. He developed an early interest in science, publishing fantasies in his school paper. He did not immediately go on to a university but got a job as an auditor in London and wrote science fiction stories. After serving in the Royal Air Force during World War II, he attended King's College, London, earning degrees in physics and mathematics. He pursued a career in astronomy and was made a Fellow of the Royal Academy. In recent years he has lived in Sri Lanka and has made that part of the world the center of his scientific and literary interest. Clarke has had a significant impact on science fiction, in part through his collaboration on the film script of *2001: A Space Odyssey*. His novels include *Against the Fall of Night* (1948), *Prelude to Space* (1951), *Childhood's End* (1953), *Earthlight* (1955), *The Deep Range* (1957), *Imperial Earth* (1975), *The Foundations of Paradise* (1979), and *Odyssey II* (1982). His short stories have been collected in *Expedition to Earth* (1953), *Tales of Ten Worlds* (1962), and *The Wind From the Sun* (1972).

Joseph Conrad (Josef Teodor Konrad Nalecz Korzeniowski) (1857–1924) was born in Berdycejew, Poland, into a well-read family that admired English literature. As a young man he went to sea, joined the English merchant marine, and became in time both a master mariner and a British citizen. His travels and adventures fed his imagination and became the stuff of his fiction, which often explores the dark recesses where the primitive and the civilized meet in conflict. Conrad mastered the English language early, and he developed a rich, flexible prose style suited to his large, often symbolic, characters and situations. He created a substantial body of literature, including *Almayer's Folly* (1895), *The Nigger of the Narcissus* (1897), *Lord Jim* (1900), *Nostromo* (1904), *The Secret Agent* (1907), and *Victory* (1915).

Stephen Crane (1871–1900) was born in Newark, New Jersey, but grew up in a series of small towns and cities in the Northeast, where his father was a Methodist minister. He attended Lafayette College and Syracuse University briefly, before taking up journalism in New York. His first novel, *Maggie: A Girl of the Streets,* startling in its harsh realism, was published in 1893 but made little stir until *The Red Badge of Courage,* the strongest "war novel" of its time, appeared in 1895. He wrote and published poetry as well as prose. Crane became a prototypical correspondent-adventurer, foreshadowing the Hemingway generation, going off first to Cuba and then to Greece to cover the war with Turkey. His unconventional personal life, complicated by poor financial management, led him to move to England, where he spent the last years of his life and where he died of tuberculosis before he could turn thirty. Aside from his novels, his finest work is probably the title story of *The Open Boat and Other Tales of Adventure* (1898). Two other collections of his stories are *The Monster and Other Stories* (1899) and *Wounds in the Rain: War Stories* (1900).

Fyodor Dostoevsky (1821–81) was born in Moscow, the son of a doctor who was killed by his serfs in 1839. He was educated to become a military engineer but preferred literature and politics to military life. With the publication of *Poor Folk* (1846), he turned permanently to literature. Many of his works reflect personal experience, much of it painful. For example, his recurrent bouts of epilepsy become part of several of his most famous characters; his near-execution and actual sentence to hard labor in Siberia for political conspiracy underlies much of his subsequent work. His sympathy with the sufferer and his faith in the Russian people grew from life, not from imagination. His masterpieces include *Notes from the Underground* (1864), *Crime and Punishment* (1866), *The Idiot* (1869), and *The Brothers Karamazov* (1878–80).

Arthur Conan Doyle (1859–1930) was born in Edinburgh, Scotland. Educated at Stonyhurst and at Edinburgh University, he graduated as a medical doctor in 1885 but turned to writing to offset the boredom of a slow practice. With the creation of Sherlock Holmes—who captured a wide popular audience—he advanced the state of detective fiction far beyond what predecessors like Poe could have foreseen. Though Doyle was a writer with varied interests and occupations, his literary reputation rests on the many short stories and the less skillfully constructed novels pairing the famed detective with his faithful friend, Dr. Watson. Perhaps the best of his novels is *The Hound of the Baskervilles* (1902). His earliest Holmes stories were collected in *The Adventures of Sherlock Holmes* (1891).

Ralph Ellison (1914–) was born in Oklahoma City, but went to Tuskegee Institute. Then he left for Harlem to study sculpture. In New York he met Richard Wright, who encouraged him to write. After World War II, in which he served in the Merchant Marine, Ellison published his single novel, *The Invisible Man* (1952), which has become a classic. Since then Ellison has published essays and other short pieces and has addressed the problems faced by young people frustrated by the slow pace of social justice, but to this point has refused to hurry into print the longer works for which his considerable public waits.

William Faulkner (1897–1962) was born in Mississippi and was raised in Oxford, where he would attend the University of Mississippi after a short enlistment in 1918 in the Royal Canadian Flying Corps. He saw no overseas duty. Still, it was the Southern—and family—memory of another war, the Civil War, that shaped much of Faulkner's imagination. The decayed aristocracy, the poor whites, the devastated land, the sense of loss, injustice, and failure—the symbolic mark of Cain, the result of slavery—all these flow from that central Southern experience into Faulkner's fiction, especially those novels and stories set in his fictional Yoknapatawpha County and Jefferson, its Oxford-like capital. But other subjects that attracted Faulkner were the relationship of good men to the land they hunted on, the honor and courage people show in even desperate circumstances, the strength of the human spirit that *will* prevail. He was awarded the Nobel Prize in 1950. His first novel was *Soldier's Pay* (1926), and his major novels include *The Sound and the Fury* (1929), *As I Lay Dying* (1930), *Sanctuary* (1931), *Light in August* (1932), *Absalom, Absalom!* (1936), *Intruder in the Dust* (1948), and *A Fable* (1954). His collections of short stories include *These 13* (1931), *Go Down, Moses* (1942), and *Collected Stories* (1950).

F. Scott Fitzgerald (1896–1941) was born in St. Paul, Minnesota, but was sent East for his education. He attended Princeton—an experience often reflected in his fiction—but did not graduate, joining the Army instead. While in service he married Zelda Sayre, with whom he was to lead a glamorous if tumultuous life, epitomizing the Jazz Age which his early stories did so much to glorify. They led an expensive life, and Fitzgerald's stories and novels supplied the wherewithal—for a while. But Zelda's mental health, always precarious, broke down. Fitzgerald, his popularity declining as the depressed Thirties succeeded the opulent Twenties, fell into alcoholism. His writing suffered and, despite an attempt to recover fame and a large income by working in Hollywood, it was apparent even before the end that he had burnt out. Still his novels and his best stories reflect an age in American life as well as anything else that survives the post-World War I era. Fitzgerald's novels include *The Great Gatsby* (1925), *Tender Is the Night* (1934), and *The Last Tycoon* (1941). His short story collections include *Flappers and Philosophers* (1921), *Tales of the Jazz Age* (1922), and *All the Sad Young Men* (1926).

Gustave Flaubert (1821–1880) was born in Rouen, France, to a middle-class professional family. A nervous lad, he gave up the study of law for the calmer and more reclusive pursuit of literature. A perfectionist, he worked slowly and with great care at his realistic portrayals of bourgeois life in France. He had neither the need nor the taste to pursue great popularity, but was content to attend closely to every detail of his art. His most famous novel is *Madame Bovary* (1856). Some of his better short stories are collected in *Trois Contes* (1976).

Mavis Gallant (1922–) was born in Montreal. Her education was sporadic, interrupted frequently by moves from one school to another. As she has explained, this made it difficult for her to obtain any sort of education. For a time Gallant worked at a newspaper, but she has lived primarily on her writing. Her characters are often lonely women sufferers, exiles in an indifferent world. She has written novels, including *Green Water, Green Sky* (1959) and *A Fairly Good Time* (1970). Gallant's stories have been collected in *The Other Paris* (1956), *My Heart Is Broken* (1964), *The End of the World and Other Stories* (1974), *From the Fifteenth District: A Novella and Eight Short Stories* (1979), and *Home Truths: Selected Canadian Stories* (1981).

Gabriel García Márquez (1928–) was born in Oracataca, Colombia, a small village, and attended the University of Bogotá. A journalist, novelist, and short story writer, he has also been a political activist, a supporter of Castro, and an opponent of rightist regimes. His stories combine realism and fantasy, are comic, mysterious, and sometimes mythical. He was awarded the Nobel Prize in 1982. His novels include *One Hundred Years of Solitude* (1970) and *Chronicle of a Death Foretold* (1981). His short story collections include *The Funeral of Mama Grande* (1962), *No One Writes to the Colonel and Other Stories* (1968), *Leaf Storm and Other Stories* (1972), and *Innocent Eréndira and Other Stories* (1978).

John Gardner (1933–1982) was born in Batavia, New York. He taught at Oberlin College, California State University, San Francisco State University, Southern Illinois University, The University of Detroit, Northwestern University, and Bennington College. Before his death, he was head of the creative writing program at SUNY-Binghamton. He received critical recognition for a prodigious and varied body of work—twelve books, including novels, biography, an epic poem, short story collections, children's fairy tales, and literary criticism. His novel *October Light* won the National Book Critic's Circle Award in 1976.

William Gass (1924–) was born in Fargo, North Dakota, and attended Kenyon College, Ohio Wesleyan, and Cornell University, where he earned a doctorate in philosophy. Gass is a professor at Washington University in St. Louis. He has written novels—*Omensetter's Luck* (1966) and *Willy Master's Lonesome Wife* (1968)—as well as critical essays and the short stories that have been collected under the title *In the Heart of the Heart of the Country* (1968).

Gail Godwin (1937–) was born in Birmingham, Alabama, raised in Asheville, North Carolina, and now lives in Woodstock, New York. She has taught at Columbia University, Vassar College, and in the University of Iowa's Writers Workshop. She is the author of five novels, including *The Odd Woman* (1974), *Violet Clay* (1978), and *A Mother and Two Daughters* (1981), and two collections of short stories, *Dream Children* (1976) and *Mr. Bedford and the Muses* (1983).

Nikolai Gogol (1809–1852) was born in the Ukraine, but moved to the Russian capital, St. Petersburg, where he was a civil servant and a lecturer in history. Encouraged by the Russian Romantic poet and dramatist Pushkin, Gogol began to write stories about the rural Cossack Russia he loved so much. He is credited with introducing the "little" man—the lowly, ordinary fellow, often luckless and at the mercy of bureaucratic forces—into serious literature. Akaky Akakyevitch, in "The Overcoat," is the ancestor of many a modern protagonist. Gogol also wrote two fine novels, *Taras Bulba* (1835) and *Dead Souls* (1842), and a play, *The Inspector General* (1836). Some of his stories appeared in *Evenings on a Farm Near Dilenka* (1831–2), others—including "The Over-Coat"—in a collected edition in 1842.

William Goyen (1915–1983) was born in Trinity, Texas, and graduated from Rice University. Specializing in the short story, novel, and drama, he taught at a number of colleges and universities, among them Columbia University, the New School for Social Research, Princeton University, Brown University, and the University of Southern California. He also worked as senior editor in the trade division of McGraw-Hill Book Company. His stories appear in *Ghost and Flesh* (1952), *The Faces of Blood Kindred* (1960), and *The Collected Stories of William Goyen* (1975), which was nominated for a Pulitzer Prize. His novels include *The House of Breath* (1950), *In a Farther Country* (1955), *The Fair Sister* (1963), *Come, the Restorer* (1974), and *Arcadio Clarkston Potter* (1983).

John Hawkes (1925–) was born in Stamford, Connecticut. A veteran of World War II, he graduated from Harvard in 1947. He teaches at Brown University and is a member of the American Academy of Arts and Sciences and the American Academy and Institute of Arts and Letters. He has written a book of short plays, a collection of shorter fiction, and nine novels including *The Lime Twig* (1961), *Second Skin* (1964), *The Blood Oranges* (1971), and *Virginie: Her Two Lives* (1982).

Nathaniel Hawthorne (1804–1864) was born and grew up in Salem, Massachusetts, the descendant of strong-willed Puritans—including one of the judges in the Salem witchcraft trials—whose influence can be traced in all his serious writing. He went to Bowdoin College in Maine, but then returned to the relative isolation of Salem, where he began a lifelong career as an author. Hawthorne wrote tales for children, re-told classic myths for young people, penned a novel of college life, did a campaign biography for his college friend Franklin Pierce, and composed essays and travel notes. All of these, with the exception of *Fanshawe,* the college book, are fine things of their kind. But Hawthorne's fame rests upon those allegorical short tales and four larger works, more romances than novels (novels invite comparison with the real world, but romances take place "somewhere between the real world and fairy-land, where the Actual and the Imaginary may meet"), in which the sense of sin and isolation, the dark sobriety of the Puritan vision, and the vague boundary line between appearance and reality provide subject matter and tone alike. There is a strong didactic strain in Hawthorne, and his characters are more often symbolic than individualistic, but his psychological insights are powerful, his imagination is rich, and his narrative art is both dedicated and accomplished. His best longer works are *The Scarlet Letter* (1850), *The House of the Seven Gables* (1851), *The Blithedale Romance* (1852), and *The Marble Faun* (1860). Some of his best short stories appeared in *Twice-Told Tales* (1837) and *Mosses from an Old Manse* (1846).

Ernest Hemingway (1898–1961) was born in Oak Park, Illinois. As a child he enjoyed rugged outdoor activities like the hunting and fishing that play such a large role in his fiction. After graduating from high school in 1917 he worked as a cub reporter on the Kansas City *Star,* but the next year he volunteered for service as a Red Cross ambulance driver and was sent to the front in Italy, where he was severely wounded. He returned to civilian life and newspaper work, this time in Toronto. In the early Twenties he married and moved back to Europe, where he established himself as a writer (*Three Stories and Ten Poems* appeared in 1923; *In Our Time* a year later in Paris) and a member of what Gertrude Stein called "the Lost Generation," her description of the young idealists crushed by the first World War. These became grist for Hemingway's mill. He went to Spain to cover the Civil War in the Thirties and served as a war correspondent in Europe again in World War II. His stories are often set in times of danger—war, big game hunting, bull-fighting—and often deal with ordinary human beings, doomed by the emotional and social complexities of life, who can be destroyed physically but not defeated spiritually, who demonstrate "grace under pressure." His writing is distinguished by powerful dialogue, his style by great force and brevity. Although he was admired and honored (he received the Nobel Prize in 1954), he suffered terribly from the fear that his powers had failed. His life ended in suicide. His novels include *The Sun Also Rises* (1926), *A Farewell to Arms* (1929), *For Whom the Bell Tolls* (1940), and *The Old Man and the Sea* (1952). His short story collections include *In Our Time* (1925) and *Winner Take Nothing* (1933). *A Moveable Feast* (1964), a work of non-fiction, recalls the Paris of the Twenties.

O. Henry (William Sydney Porter) (1862–1910) was born in Greensboro, North Carolina, where he attended a school taught by his aunt. After working in a drugstore at home and at a number of jobs in Texas, he began to submit humorous sketches to newspapers. In time he developed his characteristic form, the wry story with a twist at the end, and found a wide audience. His style and form, together with his emphasis upon coincidence and colorful character, influenced short story writers for a generation. Perhaps the most famous collection of his short stories is *The Four Million* (1906), which records the dreams and lives of New Yorkers in pursuit of romance and adventure. Other collections include *The Trimmed Lamp* (1907) and *Whirligigs* (1910).

Washington Irving (1783–1859) was born in New York City and became America's first internationally-recognized man of letters. Urbane and witty, he poked genial fun at the Dutch Colonists in a series of tales as well as in his *History of New York from the Beginning of the World to the End of the Dutch Dynasty,* attributing these good-natured burlesques to one Diedrich Knickerbocker, his own invention. Irving also wrote graceful familiar essays, sketches, biography, and history, and spent many years as a gentleman traveller and diplomat in England and Europe, regularly working his experiences into light literature. To the development of the short story he brought a sense of place, a touch of humor, and an artistic finish, characteristics that mark almost all of his longer works as well. He published many books, but his best short tales appeared in *The Sketch Book* (1820) and *Tales of a Traveller* (1824).

Josephine Jacobsen (1908–) was born in Canada and now lives in Baltimore. Many of her stories have appeared in prize anthologies, and she is a former Poetry Consultant for the Library of Congress. Two of her latest works are *A Walk with Raschid and Other Stories* (1979) and *The Chinese Insomniacs* (1981). She recently received an award from the American Academy and Institute of Arts and Letters for service to literature.

Henry James (1843–1916) was born in New York, but even as a young boy traveled widely in Europe—and received much of his schooling there—because his father admired European culture and manners. A brief stay at Harvard Law School confirmed him in his ambition as a writer. He left America for Europe, making Paris first, and London eventually, his base of operations. In 1915, out of gratitude to England and to express his support for his adopted country during World War I, he became a British citizen. James was the professional artist *par excellence,* devoting a lifetime to literature. Attacked for criticizing his native land and for the obscurity of his later works in which complexities of observation and verbal expression seem more important than action, he raised the craft of fiction to an art with his meticulous attention to detail and analysis of character. His novels include *Daisy Miller* (1879), *The Portrait of a Lady* (1881), *The Turn of the Screw* (1898), *The Ambassadors* (1903), and *The Golden Bowl* (1904). *The Complete Tales of Henry James* (1961) contains his short fiction.

Sarah Orne Jewett (1849–1909) was born and raised in South Berwick, Maine. Although she received little formal education, she was particularly well read. She said that a collection of local anecdotes by Harriet Beecher Stowe determined her to become a writer. Before she was twenty-one she was publishing in the *Atlantic*. Her quietly realistic stories depict the wholesome side of New England life. Collections of her short stories appeared under the titles *Deephaven* (1877), *Tales of New England* (1890), and *A Native of Winby* (1893). These and her novel, *The Country of the Pointed Firs* (1896), gained her a lasting popularity.

James Joyce (1882–1941) was born in Dublin, Ireland, and was educated first at Jesuit schools and later at University College, Dublin. With his native city and his religious education he carried on a lifelong love-hate relationship—proud of his Irishness and delighting in the sounds of Dublin's talk, furious with its provincialism and its failure to recognize his original talent; proud of the intellectual rigor of the Jesuit experience and delighting in the richness of the Church's tradition, but repelled by its smugness and chafed by its political narrowness and moral restrictions. He could neither live in Ireland (a conclusion driven home by the refusal of an Irish publisher to print his *Dubliners*) nor stay away from it in his mind and work. He spent the years after 1904 on the Continent, teaching English in Berlitz schools and working at his craft. His exile, though self-imposed, was real. A series of patrons, beginning with Ezra Pound, who in 1916 helped him publish *Portrait of the Artist as a Young Man*, and including Edith Rockefeller McCormick, John Quinn, and Sylvia Beach, helped him financially and in other ways to do his work. His masterpiece, *Ulysses*, was published in 1922, his thoroughly experimental *Finnegans Wake* in 1939. He broke new ground in literature, partly by the sexual explicitness of certain passages in *Ulysses* (it was banned for obscenity and blasphemy in some countries), partly by his power to force language to his ends, partly by introducing narrative innovations, the most important of which is the *stream-of-consciousness* technique (see the Glossary).

Franz Kafka (1883–1924) was born into a Jewish merchant family in Prague, Czechoslovakia. There he took a law degree at the German University and worked as a civil servant for the Austrian government. He wrote and published short stories, but his novels remained in manuscript at his death and were published posthumously against his expressed wishes. The alienation and isolation of his protagonists are no doubt reflections of Kafka's own sense of anxiety and desolation. His novels are *The Trial* (1925), *The Castle* (1926), and *Amerika* (1927). Two books of his short stories are *The Great Wall of China* (1933) and *Parables and Paradoxes* (1962). *The Complete Stories* appeared in 1983.

D. H. Lawrence (1885–1930) was born in Nottinghamshire, England, the son of a rough coal-miner father and a school-teacher mother with cultural aspirations for her bright and sensitive son. He taught school briefly but came to dislike nearly everything about conventional life in England—industrialization, commercialism, religion, morality—and spent the rest of his life traveling abroad and exposing the hypocrisy he saw in the middle class. After his first book, *Sons and Lovers,* was published in 1913, he was subject to considerable public attention and often the center of controversy for his outspokenness on sexuality and received opinion. His interest in human relationships—expressed in poems and essays as well as in fiction—is reflected in men and women who are unable to express themselves either intellectually, emotionally, or sexually. Among his novels are *The Rainbow* (1915), *Women in Love* (1920), and *Lady Chatterley's Lover* (1928). His short stories are collected in *The Complete Stories* (1961).

Ursula K. Le Guin (1929–) was born in Berkeley, California, studied as an undergraduate at Radcliffe College, and completed her M.A. at Columbia University. She has written for children as well as for adults. In her best work she has made significant contributions to science fiction and, more recently, fantasy as well, treating both genres as serious, not merely popular, literature. Her novels include *The Left Hand of Darkness* (1969), *The Dispossessed* (1974), and *The Beginning Place* (1980). Her short story collections include *The Wind's Twelve Quarters* (1975) and *Orsinian Tales* (1976).

Doris Lessing (1919–) was born in Kermansha, Persia, but moved with her family in 1924 to Rhodesia, where she was educated at Girls' High School in Salisbury. There she married and became a member of the Communist Party, supporting herself by a variety of jobs. In 1949, now twice-divorced, she moved to London, disaffiliated herself from the Party, and launched her career as a writer with the novel *The Grass Is Singing* (1950). She has experimented with novel forms and subject matter, ranging from her experience in South Africa to the psychology and politics of the intelligent woman, to madness, to near-fantasy and science fiction. Among her best known novels are *The Golden Notebook* (1962), *The Memories of a Survivor* (1975), and perhaps her most ambitious work, *Canopus in Argos: Archives* (1981). Collections of her short stories include *African Stories* (1964) and *Stories* (1978).

Alistair MacLeod　(1936–) was born in Nova Scotia, and was educated in Canada at Saint Francis Xavier University and the University of New Brunswick. He earned a Ph.D. in the United States at the University of Notre Dame. He has worked as a salesman, public relations man, editor, truck driver and miner. Presently he teaches English and creative writing at the University of Windsor, where he also serves as fiction editor for the *University of Windsor Review*. His work has been published in a wide variety of journals and anthologies including *Best American Short Stories, 1969; Best American Short Stories, 1975; Scenes from American Life: Contemporary Short Fiction* (1972); *Best Modern Canadian Short Stories* (1978); and *Best Canadian Short Stories* (1981). His collection of short stories, *The Lost Salt Gift of Blood* (1976), has had a wide readership, and some of its stories have been translated into Urdu, French, and Russian. "In the Fall" was made into a film purchased by the National Film Board of Canada.

Bernard Malamud　(1914–) was born in Brooklyn to Russian immigrant parents. He received his undergraduate education at City College of New York and earned an M.A. from Columbia University. A novelist and short story writer, he depicts the hope and despair of the Jewish experience, and his subjects are the broken and battered ones who search for but seldom find the secret to happiness in an often uncomprehensible world. He received a National Book Award for *The Magic Barrel* (1958), a collection of his short stories. More recent collections have appeared under the title *Rembrandt's Hat* (1973) and *The Stories of Bernard Malamud* (1983). His novels include *The Natural* (1952), which was recently made into a popular movie, *The Assistant* (1957), *The Fixer* (1966), and *Dubin's Lives* (1979).

Thomas Mann　(1875–1955) was born in the Baltic city of Lubeck, Germany, the son of a senator and prominent merchant. His first important book, *Buddenbrooks* (1900), portrays the decline of German mercantile society. The divisive tendencies and destructive potential of excessive nationalism and rigid ideologies concerned him, and this concern underlies a number of his books, perhaps most prominently *The Magic Mountain* (1924). His resistance to Nazism resulted in his exile, the revoking (in 1936) of his German citizenship, and his moving to the United States, where he continued to attack Hitler and his ideology. He became an American citizen in 1944, but never lost his interest in the politics, culture, and tragic modern history of Europe. He was awarded the Nobel Prize in 1929. Among his most important publications are the books that make up the "Joseph cycle," *Joseph and His Brethren* (1933–44), and *The Coming Democracy* (1938); later publications include *The Beloved Returns* (1939), *Doctor Faustus* (1947), and *The Confessions of Felix Krull, Confidence Man* (1955). His *Stories of Three Decades* appeared in 1936.

Bobbie Ann Mason　was born in Kentucky and currently lives in Pennsylvania. Her stories have been published in the *New Yorker, Atlantic Monthly, Redbook, The North American Review, The Washington Post Magazine, Bloodroot, The Boston Review,* and *The Virginia Quarterly Review.* Her collection of short stories *Shiloh and Other Stories* (1982) was nominated for a National Book Critics Circle Award, an American Book Award and the PEN/Faulkner Fiction Award. Its title story, "Shiloh," and another story, "Graveyard Day," appeared in *Best American Short Stories* (1981 and 1983). She has also written two critical books, *Nabokov's Garden* (1974) and *The Girl Sleuth* (1975).

Carson McCullers　(1917–1967) was born in Columbus, Georgia. Her Southern roots go deep into her fiction. She had intended to become a concert pianist, but instead of studying at the Julliard School of Music she enrolled in writing courses at Columbia. Her success came early, with the publication of *The Heart Is a Lonely Hunter* in 1940 and *Reflections in a Golden Eye* the next year. One of her books, *The Member of the Wedding* (1946), she successfully dramatized for Broadway production. Poor health burdened her all her adult years and eventually made writing almost impossible, but not before she produced the body of significant work—often concerned with the spiritual isolation that underlies the human condition—that made her a major literary force. Her characters are usually outcasts and misfits whose longing for love and understanding is never fulfilled. Her stories are collected in *The Ballad of the Sad Café* (1951) and *Collected Short Stories* (1973).

Herman Melville　(1819–1891) was born in New York City. His father's death when he was eleven forced Melville to abandon his education for a life of work. In 1837 he sailed to England as a cabin boy, and his immediate fascination with the sea led him to sign on with a series of whaling ships and begin a life of adventure and exploration in the Pacific. He published a series of novels and tales based on his adventures, including *Typee* (1846), *Omoo* (1847), *Moby Dick*, his masterpiece (1851), and *Piazza Tales* (1856), this last, as its title implies, a collection of shorter pieces. Public interest in his writing, once high, declined, and Melville did very little writing in his last two decades. His reputation has more than recovered in our century, and he is now recognized as one of the masters of American literature.

Alice Munro (1931–) was born in Ontario and attended the University of Western Ontario. She has worked as a library clerk and a bookseller, as well as a teacher of creative writing and a writer-in-residence. Her books include *Dance of the Happy Shades* (1968), *Lives of Girls and Women* (1971), *Something I've Been Meaning to Tell You* (1974), *Who Do You Think You Are?* (1978) (published as *The Beggar Maid* in the United States), and *The Moons of Jupiter* (1982).

Joyce Carol Oates (1938–), originally from the countryside near Lockport, N.Y., is the author of fifteen novels and many volumes of short stories, poems, essays, and plays. Extraordinarily versatile and productive, she is also an active critic and editor, as well as a teacher of creative writing at Princeton University. She has been honored by awards from the Guggenheim Foundation, the American Institute of Arts and Letters, and the Lotos Club. She has received the O. Henry Award for Continuing Achievement and in 1978 was elected to the American Academy and Institute of Arts and Letters. Much of her work is set in Eden County, a fictional re-creation of her native Upstate New York, and she often explores the nature of human experience by depicting sensitive characters who undergo physical and psychological violence. Among her novels are *them* (which won the National Book Award in 1970), *Childwold* (1976), *Bellefleur* (1980), *Mysteries of Winterthurn* (1983), and *Solstice* (1985). Some of her short stories are collected in *Marriages and Infidelities* (1973), *A Sentimental Education* (1981), and *Last Days* (1984).

Tim O'Brien (1946–) was born in Austin, Minnesota. He has published three novels: *Northern Lights* (1975), *If I Die in a Combat Zone* (1979), and *Going After Cacciato* (1979). Another novel, *The Nuclear Age*, is forthcoming. His stories have appeared in many magazines, including *Esquire, Atlantic Monthly, Redbook, Shenandoah, The Massachusetts Review,* and *Ploughshares*. O'Brien has received creative writing fellowships from the Guggenheim Foundation, the National Endowment for the Arts, and the Massachusetts Arts and Humanities Foundation. He currently lives in Cambridge, Massachusetts.

Flannery O'Connor (1925–1964) was born in Savannah, Georgia, and raised in Milledgeville. A Roman Catholic, she was educated in parochial schools. She went to the Women's College of Georgia and then studied at the Writer's Workshop at the University of Iowa. In the early 1950s, it was discovered that she was a victim of an incurable blood disease that would leave her crippled and shorten her life. Adversity did not interrupt her writing, though it may have contributed to her black-humored manner, nor did she indulge in self-pity. She became in her short life one of the most admired twentieth-century writers, the explorer of an ironic vision projected against a Southern landscape. Though she admitted a preference for the vulgar and grotesque, she portrays her odd characters with great sympathy. Her short novels include *Wise Blood* (1952) and *The Violent Bear It Away* (1960). Her volumes include *A Good Man Is Hard to Find* (1955) and *Everything That Rises Must Converge* (1965).

Frank O'Connor (Michael O'Donovan) (1903–1966) was born in Cork, Ireland. He joined the IRA, fought the British, and spent a year as a prisoner of war—experiences that are reflected vividly in his early fiction. In addition to writing, O'Connor was a librarian (he wrote under a pseudonym so as not to embarrass the library board) and for a while helped direct the fortunes of the Abbey Theatre. Later he became a popular teacher, lecturing on fiction at a number of American universities. He wrote plays and novels, but is best remembered for his short stories, some of which are collected in *Bones of Contention* (1936), *Traveller's Samples* (1951), and *The Stories of Frank O'Connor* (1952).

Sean O'Faolain (1900–) was born in Cork, Ireland. He was educated at the University College there and studied in the United States at Harvard. He has been an editor of magazines and a teacher as well as a writer of short stories, novels, and biographies of Irish political figures like Daniel O'Connell and Eamon de Valera. He began writing in Gaelic and has a strong sense of Irish character and history. He often treats the contemporary Irishman who finds adjustment difficult because the weight of the past encumbers him. O'Faolain is a charter member of the Irish Royal Academy of Letters. Some of his short stories appeared in *A Purse of Coppers* (1938) and *The Talking Trees* (1970). His *Collected Stories* was published in 1983.

Cynthia Ozick (1928–) was born in New York City. She is the author of two novels, *Trust* (1966) and *The Cannibal Galaxy* (1983); a volume of essays, *Art & Ardor* (1983); and three collections of short stories, *The Pagan Rabbi and Other Stories* (1971), *Bloodshed and Three Novellas* (1976), and *Levitation: Five Fictions* (1981). She has published essays, poetry, criticism, reviews, and translations in numerous periodicals and anthologies. She has been the recipient of many awards, among them the American Academy of Arts Award for Literature, two O. Henry First Prizes for the Short Story, a Guggenheim Fellowship, and, most recently, the Mildred and Harold Strauss Livings Award from the American Academy and Institute of Arts and Letters. Ozick lives in New York with her husband and daughter.

Grace Paley   (1922–) was born in New York City. She attended Hunter College and later was a teacher at Syracuse University. Presently she teaches at Sarah Lawrence College and gives frequent readings from her work. During the Vietnam War she was active in the antiwar movement. Though few, her stories have been admired for their stylistic liveliness and for their fusion of sardonic observation with spare, expressive form. Her books of stories are *The Little Disturbances of Man* (1959) and *Enormous Changes at the Last Minute* (1974).

Dorothy Parker   (1893–1967) was born in West End, New Jersey, and graduated from a private school in Morristown. As a drama and literary critic, she became known for her acerbic wit. She wrote stories and light verse for a variety of the fashionable and clever magazines of the Twenties and Thirties, most notably *Vanity Fair* and the *New Yorker*. She went to Spain as a news correspondent during the Civil War. Parker more than held her own in caustic, epigrammatic humor, both in print and in person. Some of her best satiric verse appeared in *Enough Rope* (1927). Her short story collections include *Lament for the Living* (1930), *After Such Pleasures* (1933), and *Here Lies* (1939).

Edgar Allan Poe   (1809–1949) was born in Boston, Massachusetts, to actor parents, but an early orphan, he was raised in Richmond, Virginia, by John Allan, a wealthy merchant. Attempts at formal higher education—at the University of Virginia and then, after two years in the Army, at the U. S. Military Academy—were broken short and Poe lost his benefactor's support. In the meantime, he had published two small books of poetry and determined to support himself by literature. He sold poems to magazines and newspapers (occasionally in his need for cash selling the same poem to more than one paper), won short story prizes, and became editor of a series of magazines, first in Richmond but later in Philadelphia and New York. His marriage to Virginia Clemm, a very young cousin whose precarious health led to an early death, increased the financial and emotional pressure on the harried and sensitive Poe. The circumstances of his death in Baltimore have never been fully explained. Given the obstacles, his literary output—limited to short pieces of prose and short poems—is surprising both in quantity and quality. He made a name for himself as poet, critic, and creator-writer of short stories that set a pattern for writers up to the modern era. He can claim to be the father of detective fiction, a serious advancer of science fiction, and a master of the tale of terror. His contributions to the short story include the fast opening, the tightly-knit plot, and an unremitting attention to unity of tone and effect. He attempted one novel, *The Narrative of A. Jordan Pym,* but was unable to complete it. Some of his best poems appeared in *The Raven and Other Poems* (1845), his best-known stories in *Tales of the Grotesque and Arabesque* (1840).

Katherine Anne Porter   (1890–1980) was born in Indian Creek, Texas, but spent much of her young life in Louisiana. Details of her education are not clear, but she did attend a boarding school and an Ursuline convent school for a while. An early marriage, like two later ones, ended in divorce. Even as a child she was a writer, and as a young woman she supported herself by practicing journalism, reporting for the *Fort Worth Critic* and the *Rocky Mountain News*. She came to the attention of the literary world with *Flowering Judas* (1930), a book of short stories. Her travels—she was always something of a natural wanderer—provided a rich vein of material which she mined in the stories which make up that book and two other volumes of collected stories, *Pale Horse, Pale Rider* (1939) and *The Leaning Tower and Other Stories* (1944). Her one full-length novel, *Ship of Fools,* was begun in the Thirties when the tragedy of Nazism was being enacted, but it did not appear until 1962. Her *Collected Stories* took both the Pulitzer Prize and the National Book Award in 1965.

Saki   (Hector Hugh Munro) (1870–1916) was born in Akyab, Burma, and educated in England. He was killed in action in World War I. He began his career as a political satirist for several newspapers but also wrote bitterly funny short stories under his pseudonym. His fiction reflects a taste for the bizarre and exotic, as well as a love of a practical joke. His short story collections include *Reginald* (1904), *The Chronicles of Aoris* (1911), and *Beasts and Super Beasts* (1914).

Nathalie Sarraute   (1902–) was born in Ivanovo, Russia, but educated in England and France, where she attended the Sorbonne. Although she worked some years as a lawyer, she gave up legal practice to become a full-time writer. An experimentalist, she has written short stories and longer works that progress not so much by narrative cause-and-effect or plot as by juxtaposed images and pictures of characters reacting differently to a single stimulus. Her novels include *Portrait of a Man Unknown* (1958), *The Planetarium* (1960), *The Golden Fruits* (1964), and *"Fools Say"* (1977). *Tropisms* (1964) is a collection of her short stories. She has also written a volume of autobiography, *Childhood* (1984).

John Sayles   (1950–) was born in Schnectady, New York. He attended Williams College and worked at numerous hospital and laboring jobs before he began to earn a living as a writer. He is author of the novels *Pride of the Bimbos* (1975) and *Union Dues* (1977), and of the short story collection *The Anarchists'*

Convention (1980). He has received screenplay credit on nearly a dozen feature films and is the writer-director of the movies *Return of the Secaucus Seven, Lianna, Baby It's You,* and *The Brother from Another Planet.* His plays *Turnbuckle* and *New Hope for the Dead* have been produced off-Broadway. He currently resides in Hoboken, New Jersey.

Lynne Sharon Schwartz (1939–) was born in New York City. She is the author of *Rough Strife* (1980), a novel in which the present story appears in somewhat different form, and of *Balancing Acts* (1981). Her short fiction has appeared in *Redbook, Ploughshares, Transatlantic Review, The Chicago Review,* and many other magazines, as well as anthologies. She has done translations from Italian, and written numerous reviews for the *Saturday Review,* the *Chicago Tribune, Ms.,* and others.

Isaac Bashevis Singer (1904–) was born in Radzymin, Poland, and educated at the Tachkemoni Rabbinical Seminary, Warsaw, where he began as a journalist, writing in Yiddish, which has remained his literary language. He came to America in 1935. Singer has established himself as a major literary figure who depicts the Jewish experience with sensitivity and great humor. His themes reflect the sense of alienation produced in Jews when traditional values and ways of life are threatened with assimilation by the Gentile world. He also explores the theme of old age—its dignity as well as its loneliness and sadness. Among his novels are *The Family Moskat* (1950) and *Shosha* (1978). Some of his extraordinarily perceptive short stories are included in *Gimpel the Fool and Other Stories* (1957), *A Crown of Feathers and Other Stories* (1973), and *Collected Stories* (1982). He received the Nobel Prize in 1978.

Elizabeth Spencer (1921–) was born in Mississippi, which is the setting of her three early novels, including *The Voice at the Back Door* (1956). Later works, such as *The Light in the Piazza* (1960), *Knights & Dragons* (1965), and others, derive from her years in Italy. Now living in Montreal, she writes variously about people of the modern South and elsewhere. In 1983 she received the Award of Merit Medal of the American Academy of Arts and Letters. Her latest novel is *The Salt Line* (1984).

John Steinbeck (1902–1968) was born in Salinas, California, a region which he was to mine for its rich folk materials. He began serious writing while he attended Stanford University, but his work experience and his observation of migrant-worker life were more important influences than his formal education. His novels did much to bring to light social problems of the Depression Era, though they are mainly strong stories about well-realized characters drawn from among the common people. Whether his subject was the plight of migrant workers or that of Dust Bowl farmers, he showed a compassionate understanding of the world's disinherited. He was awarded the Pulitzer Prize for *The Grapes of Wrath* (1939) and the Nobel Prize in Literature in 1962. His earlier novels include *Tortilla Flat* (1935), *In Dubious Battle* (1936), and *Of Mice and Men* (1937). Some of his short stories are collected in *The Long Valley* (1938).

James Thurber (1894–1961) was born in Columbus, Ohio, and attended Ohio State University. He was employed overseas for a time during World War I by the State Department, then went into journalism, working for the Columbus *Dispatch,* the Chicago *Tribune,* and the New York *Evening Post.* When he began writing for the *New Yorker* in 1926, his direction was set. Thurber became America's favorite humorist—a versatile one, successful in cartoons, in fables, in essays, and on the stage (*The Male Animal,* done with Elliot Nugent, has been perenially popular since its opening in 1940). Some of his titles are the loosely autobiographical *My Life and Hard Times* (1933), *Fables for Our Time* (1933), *My World and Welcome To It* (1942), and *The Thurber Carnival* (1945).

Leo Tolstoy (1828–1910) was born in the province of Tula, Russia, on his aristocratic parents' estate. Orphaned early, he was educated by private tutors before being sent to the University of Kazan, but he preferred a festive social life to his studies there. Five years of military service, including action in the Crimean War, gave him the knowledge of war he later drew upon in his novels. After a period of travel in the West, Tolstoy returned to his home with some distinct ideas about improving the human lot. He began a school for peasant children and turned to primitive Christianity as a way of making sense of a shallow, materialistic world. He developed a reputation as a religious leader and philosophical sage, while his fame as nineteenth-century Russia's greatest novelist grew. If he did not find happiness himself, he did leave in his work a series of challenges to aristocratic and bourgeois values. Among his many books, *War and Peace* (1867–69), *Anna Karenina* (1877), *The Death of Ivan Ilych* (1886), and *Resurrection* (1899) are perhaps the most famous.

Mark Twain (Samuel L. Clemens) (1835–1910) was born in rural Missouri and raised in the town of Hannibal on the Mississippi River. His boyhood there, culminating in a stint as a cub pilot on a steamboat, is reflected in many of his tales and books, including *Tom Sawyer* (1876), *Life on the Mississippi* (1883), and *Huckleberry Finn* (1884). Twain went West with the gold miners and hardy adventurers, sharpening his skills by practicing journalism. "The Celebrated Jumping Frog of Calaveras

County" captured the imagination of Eastern readers and started Twain on a career of storytelling, with the emphasis on frontier humor in the form of the tall tale. He traveled abroad, recording exaggerated versions of his experiences in *Innocents Abroad* (1869), and made a successful career of lecturing, depending upon a tested formula: tell the most unlikely and astounding things, but in the most solemn and deadpan manner possible. Twain became an American institution. Still, he was not always a light-hearted humorist. The satiric vein that always lay beneath his best work surfaced as the years passed, and some of his later work, like *The Man That Corrupted Hadleyburg* (1900) and *The Mysterious Stranger* (1916), shows the darker side of his personality. Other important titles by Mark Twain are *Roughing It* (1872), *The Gilded Age* (1873), and *A Connecticut Yankee in King Arthur's Court* (1889).

Miguel de Unamuno (1864–1936) was born in Bilbao, Spain, and educated at the University of Madrid. A professor of Greek and later Rector of the University of Salamanca, Unamuno was let go several times as a result of his outspokenness and unpopular political convictions. His existential philosophy is reflected not only in his nonfiction work—*e.g., The Tragic Sense of Life* (1913)—but also in such works of fiction as *Abel Sanchez* (1917) and *Three Exemplary Novels* (1920).

John Updike (1933–) was born in Shillington, Pennsylvania, and graduated *summa cum laude* from Harvard. Always precocious and diligent, he published his first story in the *New Yorker* at the age of 22 and was promptly added to the magazine's staff. He contributed regularly to the *New Yorker's* "Talk of the Town" feature, sharpening the eye and ear for which he is noted as a writer of fiction. He has published a good deal of poetry, but it is mainly as the wry chronicler of family life in the suburban East that he is known. Updike's novels include *Rabbit Run* (1960), *Couples* (1968), *Rabbit Redux* (1970), *The Coup* (1978), *Rabbit Is Rich* (1980), and *The Witches of Eastwick* (1984). He has published several volumes of short stories, including *Pigeon Feathers and Other Stories* (1962), *The Music School* (1966), *Bech: A Book* (1970), and *Problems and Other Stories* (1979).

Sean Virgo (1940–) was born in Mtarfa, Malta and has lived in Canada since 1966. He received a B.A. from Nottingham University and taught for four years at the University of Victoria. He has published four books of poetry: *Pieces for the Old Earth Man* (1973); *Island* (1975), with Paul and Lutia Lauzon; *Kiskatinaw Songs* (1979), with Susan Musgrave; and *Deathwatch on Skidegate Narrows* (1979). He has also published a collection of short stories, *White Lies and Other Fictions* (1981). In 1979 he won the CBC Literary Competition with his story "Les Rites," and in 1980 won the BBC Radio 3 Short Story Competition with "Interact." Virgo now resides in British Columbia.

Alice Walker (1955–) was born in Georgia, the eighth child of sharecropping parents. Her writing has earned her a Merrill Fellowship for Writing, a grant from the National Endowment for the Arts, and a Fellowship to the Radcliffe Institute. Her books include *Once* (1976), *The Third Life of Grange Copeland* (1970), *Revolutionary Petunias & Other Poems* (1973), and *Langston Hughes* (1974), a biography for children.

Eudora Welty (1909–) was born in Jackson, Mississippi, and attended Mississippi State College for Women before graduating from the University of Wisconsin in 1929. She then spent a year studying advertising at Columbia University. Upon her return to the South, she worked for a radio station in Jackson and wrote for a Memphis paper. Soon she was winning awards for her short stories. Her work is marked by a strong sense of place and past, suggested rather than stated, and a keen ear for the rhythms of small town Southern speech. Welty's novels include *Delta Wedding* (1949), *The Ponder Heart* (1954), *Losing Battles* (1970), and *The Optimist's Daughter* (1972). Some of her stories appear in *A Curtain of Green* (1941), *The Golden Apples* (1949), and *Selected Stories of Eudora Welty* (1954).

Joy Williams (1944–) was born in Chelmsford, Massachusetts, and currently lives in Florida. Her stories have appeared in *Esquire*, the *Paris Review*, and the *New Yorker*, and she was awarded the National Magazine Award in 1980 for "The Farm." Her stories are collected in *Taking Care* (1982). She has also written two novels, *State of Grace* (1973) and *The Changeling* (1978).

Virginia Woolf (1882–1941) was born in London, the daughter of Sir Leslie Stephen, the late-Victorian biographer and literary critic. She had the run of his substantial library, and, though her education was private, it was also formidable. With her husband, she set up the Hogarth Press in 1917. Their home became a gathering place for those artists, critics, and writers known as the "Bloomsbury Group." Her primary concern in fiction was to represent the flow of ordinary experience without recourse to what she thought was the dull realism of the Arnold Bennett school. Stream-of-consciousness and lyric intensity replace detailed description and sluggish narration in her best work. She suffered mental breakdowns in 1895 and 1915, and in 1941 drowned herself because she feared another from which she might not recover. Her novels include *Jacob's Room* (1922), *Mrs. Dalloway* (1925), *To The Lighthouse* (1927), and *The*

Waves (1931). *A Room of One's Own* (1929) is a strong criticism of male chauvinism and female repression. Her short stories are collected in *A Haunted House and Other Stories* (1943).

Richard Wright (1908–1960) was born near Natchez, Mississippi, and spent his childhood in poverty which underscored the near-hopelessness of rural Southern blacks early in our century. Despite assignment to foster homes and an orphanage, he graduated valedictorian of his high school class. Memphis, to which he had moved, provided nothing for a young black man who wanted to exercise his intellect, and so he went North—to Chicago, where he began to write. He worked in the Illinois Writers' Project, in the Federal Negro Theatre, and joined the Communist Party. In 1937 Wright moved to New York as editor of the *Daily Worker*. With the help of a Guggenheim grant, Wright wrote his first novel, *Native Son,* published in 1940. After World War II he moved permanently to France. Among his other publications are *Uncle Tom's Children: Four Novellas* (1938) and a powerful autobiography, *Black Boy* (1945).

☰ GLOSSARY OF CRITICAL TERMS

Action   What happens in a story, its causal events. The sequence of actions makes up the *plot*.

Allegory   A symbolic narrative, one in which the elements systematically represent things (often abstracts) beyond themselves. Thus, in "Young Goodman Brown" Faith is more than Brown's wife: she represents his religious belief as well.

Allusion   A reference in a story to something outside it, something with which the author expects the reader to be familiar. Such references can be literary, as in the title of Ray Bradbury's "The Golden Apples of the Sun," or historical, as when Washington Irving refers to Hendrick Hudson and the original Dutch settlers. Allusions enrich a story by forcing us to be active rather than passive readers.

Ambiguity   Something — e.g., an action, an expression, — about which the author is equivocal or which he leaves in doubt so that we cannot be sure what to make of it. Did Young Goodman Brown witness a Satanic initiation ceremony or did he imagine it? Hawthorne leaves the matter to our choice.

Antagonist   A character who opposes or contends (literally, wrestles) with the *protagonist*.

Anti-Hero   A *protagonist* who not only does not fit the old heroic mold, but who is not particularly attractive, likeable, admirable, or sympathetic. His person and habits may indeed be repulsive. A relative newcomer to fiction, he has been used so frequently by modern authors and script writers that he is in danger of becoming as much a stock character as the mad scientist or the whore with the heart of gold.

Atmosphere   The emotional tone or air surrounding a story. The by-product of imagery, setting, diction, and so on, the atmosphere may be one of foreboding (as in "The Fall of the House of Usher") or of youthful zest (as in "Raymond's Run"), intense or light, depending upon the author's intention and skill in arousing moods in the reader.

Author Intrusion   The practice — once common, now rare — of an author's interrupting the flow of narrative to speak directly to the reader. ("But we must hasten to add, Dear Reader, that Tom *will* find the strength to resist temptation. For the moment, however, ...").

Caricature   The portrayal of a character by a few quick strokes that emphasize one or two distinctive features, often grotesquely. The effect of such emphasis is sometimes comic, sometimes merely cruel — especially when it focusses upon physical deformities.

Character   The person represented in a story. Characters may be "flat" — i.e., portrayed shallowly, with little or no attention to individualizing features; or "stock," so conventional as to be caricatures — i.e., the henpecked husband or the precocious child; or "round" — i.e., fully realized and endowed with individual personalities (Gabriel Conroy in "The Dead").

Characterization   The complex of means by which authors portray character. These can include physical description, the creation of an aura to surround the character, dialogue, action, and so on almost without limit. Most modern writers probably prefer to show character more by action and interaction than by assertion and description, but few use one method to the exclusion of others.

Complication   The development of conflict in a story, the entanglement of interactions and plot-lines to create the "knot" that will eventually be unravelled in the denouement.

Confidant(e)   A secondary character the protagonist trusts enough to share intimate thoughts with; often little more than a trick to take us inside the protagonist's mind, but sometimes — as in Henry James, the master of the device — a means of diffusing the bare, harsh light of direct revelation.

Conflict   The clash of opposed forces, whether internal or external or both. The protagonist may be actively opposed by an antagonist or by conditions around him (external conflict), he may struggle over divided loyalties, say duty versus friendship (internal conflict), or he may face challenges both from outside and within. Whether crude or subtle, conflict is obviously the soul of fiction.

Convention   Any device, whether of characterization, plot, dialogue, or whatever, that has been so often used by writers that readers accept it readily. An example: the speech tags ("he said," "she whispered," etc.) are conventions, their use so much assumed that readers do not see them as interruptions in the flow of fictional dialogue.

Credibility   Akin to, and often used as a synonym for, plausibility. It is that quality which makes the reader accept the story and its characters as believable.

Crisis   The high point of conflicting action, whether internal or external, which leads to a decisive turning point in the story. In a typical plot of the classic sort, the climax leads inevitably to the *denouement*, the "unravelling" or resolution of all conflict and complications.

Denouement   The "unknotting," or unravelling of the knot, of plot complications in a story. It is the outcome of the story, the resolution of the problem, and flows directly from the *crisis* of the story.

Detective Fiction   Stories that center on the solution of a mystery — usually, but not always, a crime — the uncovering of the mystifier, and the unmasking of the perpetrator of it. Poe's "tales of ratiocination" are considered the first short stories of this genre.

Dialogue   The conversation that takes place between characters, by convention placed within quotation marks. Often, but not always, dialogue is accompanied by tags identifying the speaker.

Diction   The vocabulary used by the author of a story. In the hands of a skillful writer, diction becomes a tool for portraying character, establishing atmosphere, and foreshadowing action.

Didactic   Inclined to moralize or to preach. Parables, fables, and allegories are typical examples of the didactic story.

Distance   The aesthetic or emotional "space" between the author and his characters or the reader and the story; i.e., the objectivity that makes for dispassionate creation and allows critical judgment.

Epigraph   A saying or quotation at the beginning of a story. See Poe's "The Fall of the House of Usher" for an example.

Epiphany   A moment of revelation in which the essential nature of a person or occurrence is revealed. Derived from an analogy with the Christian feast of the Epiphany (commemorating the manifestation of Christ to the Gentiles as represented by the Magi), James Joyce applied the term to his own work in *Dubliners*.

Episode   .A single developed incident or scene in the story.

Episodic   Constructed of, or proceeding by, a series of parts (scenes, encounters, incidents) rather than by tightly plotted consecutive and dependent actions. See Henry James's "Four Meetings" for an example of an episodic plot.

Exposition   Writing that explains, sets forth, and informs directly rather than by dialogue or less direct techniques of narration. Writers often use exposition at the beginning of a story to convey information the reader needs to grasp what is to follow.

Fable   A tale that teaches a lesson, often using animals instead of human characters. The tale of the race between the tortoise and the hare is a well known fable.

Fantasy   A story whose characters, incidents, and premises escape from the "real" world into the imaginary.

First Person Narrator   See Point of View.

Flashback   A literary device whereby the action of the story is purposely interrupted by the insertion of a scene representing a previous event. Flashbacks can take many forms; e.g., a block of narrative, an interior monologue, or a momentary recollection on the part of the protagonist.

Foil   A minor character whose main function is to set off the protagonist more distinctly. The resulting contrast effectively emphasizes, highlights, and helps define the protagonist's strengths. Thus Sherlock Holmes's deductive powers stand out the more strongly because Dr. Watson's mind is relatively sluggish and pedestrian.

Foreshadowing   Hinting at what is to come.

Foreshortening   Presenting the necessary preliminaries (the "foreground" in painting parlance) — e.g., the sense of time and place, the background of main characters, what led up to the point at which the action begins — with great economy and without seeming to delay the action.

Hero (Heroine)   The main character in a story. But see **Protagonist**.

Imagery   The use of words, phrases, and figures of speech that help a reader picture or imagine sensations and ideas.

Interior Monologue   See **Stream-of-Consciousness**.

Intrusive Narrator   See **Omniscient Narrator**.

Irony   The disparity between the narrator's tone and his subject matter (e.g., a pompous narrator of intrinsically trivial events), between what a character sees and what the reader knows (e.g., the victim-to-be is pleased to hear "You'll get exactly what you deserve," but the reader knows exactly what *that* means), or between the characters' intentions and the perverse outcome of their action (Jones meant to help Smith by patting him on the back, but the pat caused Smith to swallow his false teeth). Such discrepancies can be humorous, as in O. Henry, or cynical, as in many modern writers.

Mood   See **Atmosphere**.

Motive   Whatever prompts a character to act or to behave in a certain way.

Myth   A story, almost always very old and anonymous, that embodies or attempts to explain fundamental facts — the cycle of the seasons, or birth and death — that primitive man found mysterious. Thus the setting and the rising of the sun might have been "explained" by the myth of a Sun God who was buried nightly in the western sea, travelled through the dark Land of Death, and was resurrected daily in the east. *Myth*, therefore, does not mean "false" as common speech often has it, but points instead to deeply held, if dimly understood, truths.

Narrative Technique   The author's method of telling the story.

Narrator   The person — sometimes the writer, but more often an assumed or created character — who tells the story. See **Point of View**.

Naturalism   A harsh form of realism, said to have arisen out of Zola's novel *Germinal*, in which men and women seem to be at the mercy of forces — genetic, physical, economic, social, psychological — they cannot ultimately resist. Underlying naturalism is the philosophic notion that free will is a delusion and that, therefore, we are not finally responsible for our acts.

Novella   Often used to describe a short novel, but thought by some writers and critics to be a distinct narrative form, shorter than a novel but both longer and more complex than a short story.

Omniscient Narrator   A common storytelling technique in which the narrator assumes a godlike position, telling not only what is happening to characters in a given place at a given time, but moving freely from place to place and time to time ("Meanwhile, back at the ranch ...") and describing the thoughts as well as the deeds of the characters ("Remembering his brother's fate, Barnabas said boldly, 'I am as innocent as a newborn babe.' ") If the author interrupts his narrative to address the reader, he becomes an *intrusive narrator*. See **Point of View**.

Parable   A short, simple narrative told to point a moral lesson.

Parody   A "take-off," a satiric imitation of a particular author, story, or genre, most easily achieved by exaggerating the characteristic features of the subject being mocked. Thus, parodies of Hemingway have centered on the *machismo* of his heroes, those of James on his convoluted, adverb-ridden sentences.

Pathos   A strong feeling, usually of pity or of tenderness, aroused by an author who plays upon our heartstrings, appealing to our emotions rather than to our minds.

Plausibility Believability, the quality that tells us, "Yes, this fictional incident could very well have happened," or "Under these circumstances, it is not unlikely that the protagonist would have acted so." Except in those few genres where it is more hindrance than help — e.g., parody and fantasy — the writer ignores plausibility at his peril.

Plot The arrangement of events and actions in a story.

Point of View The perspective from which the author has chosen to tell the story. Although there are many variations, the most common points of view are these:

> *First Person,* in which the narrator participates in the story as a main character, a minor one, or an observer. Poe's "The Cask of Amontillado" provides a good example of first-person narration.
>
> *Third Person Limited,* in which the narrator is not a participant in the story, does not see into the minds of the characters, and uses the third-person pronouns to report objectively to us.
>
> *Third Person Unlimited* or *Omniscient,* in which the narrator is not a participant and uses the third person, but sees all and is able to see into and report on the minds of the characters.

Protagonist The main character in a story, the one on whom our interest centers. Literary critics usually prefer this term to "hero" or "heroine," words which call up images that are often inappropriate to central characters who are weak, indecisive, or even wicked. The protagonist is often opposed by a second important figure, to whom we give the name *antagonist.*

Realism An artistic determination to represent things as they are, not as they might ideally be, without gloss or varnish. In literary practice, this translates into the creation of characters who are drawn from life, often from common life, true to scale, and into the presentation of great detail, drawn from accurate observation. The realistic writer tries not to sentimentalize or, usually, to moralize. Realism can be external (relying heavily upon physical description, as in Crane's "The Open Boat") or internal (observing psychological processes closely, as Henry James does almost everywhere).

Resolution A synonym for *denouement.*

Satire The attempt to criticize and correct weaknesses, folly, or vice by holding them up to ridicule.

Science Fiction In narrow terms, stories arising out of imaginary inventions or discoveries in the natural and applied sciences. But the genre has expanded to include many kinds of fantasy, utopian satire, and serious futuristic literature.

Sentimentality A form of anti-intellectualism in which the author tries to elicit emotional responses greater than his subject matter justifies.

Setting The time and physical place in which the action of a story takes place.

Stream-of-Consciousness A technique in which the narrator presents the flow of thought and images — conscious, subconscious, or the result of free association — passing through a character's mind. Although fine distinctions can be made, the term is often used interchangably with *interior monologue.*

Style The characteristic form discernible in an author's diction and arrangement of words, sentences, and ideas. (*Voice* is often used synonymously.) Style is so much an expression of personality that readers often recognize certain authors even in works that are published unsigned or under pseudonyms.

Symbol An image or object that represents something other, often broader and more important than itself. A dove, for example, can symbolize peace; the ring, marriage or unity; a cross, Christianity.

Synopsis A bare-bones condensation of the story.

Theme The central idea or thesis implied or illustrated by the story.

Third Person Narrator See **Point of View.**

Tone The writer's attitude towards his material, characters, or audience, revealed in a variety of ways, including imagery, vocabulary, humor, and the like.

Unity The harmony and coherence between the parts and the whole of the story.

Voice See **Style.**

INDEX OF AUTHORS AND TITLES

Alice Adams,
  Gift of Grass,   835
Sherwood Anderson,
  I'm a Fool,   415
Margaret Atwood,
  The Man from Mars,   841

James Baldwin,
  Sonny's Blues,   709
Honoré de Balzac,
  A Passion in the Desert,   19
Toni Cade Bambara,
  Raymond's Run,   821
John Barth,
  Lost in the Funhouse,   783
Donald Barthelme,
  The Balloon,   798
Ann Beattie,
  A Clever-Kids Story,   854
Saul Bellow,
  Looking for Mr. Green,   650
Ambrose Bierce,
  Moxon's Master,   192
Clark Blaise,
  A Class of New Canadians,   864
Jorge Luis Borges,
  The Babylon Lottery,   563
Paul Bowles,
  A Distant Episode,   871
Ray Bradbury,
  The Golden Apples of the Sun,   698
Richard Brautigan,
  Revenge of the Lawn,   880
  *A Short History of Religion
    in California*,   884

Hortense Calisher,
  The Scream on Fifty-Seventh Street,   886
Barry Callaghan,
  The Black Queen,   902
Raymond Carver,
  Cathedral,   905
Willa Cather,
  Paul's Case,   381
John Cheever,
  The Swimmer,   623
Anton Chekhov,
  Gooseberries,   335
  The Kiss,   342
Kate Chopin,
  Désirée's Baby,   263
Agatha Christie,
  Double Sin,   500
Arthur C. Clarke,
  The Sentinel,   670
Joseph Conrad,
  Heart of Darkness,   268
Stephen Crane,
  The Open Boat,   365

Fyodor Dostoevsky,
  The Grand Inquisitor,   120
Arthur Conan Doyle,
  The Red-Headed League,   320

Ralph Ellison,
  Flying Home,   631

William Faulkner,
  A Rose for Emily,   540
  That Evening Sun,   547

F. Scott Fitzgerald,
  Babylon Revisited, 525
Gustave Flaubert,
  A Simple Heart, 132

Mavis Gallant,
  Acceptance of Their Ways, 703
Gabriel García Márquez,
  *A Very Old Man with
  Enormous Wings,* 772
John Gardner,
  Redemption, 915
William Gass,
  *In the Heart of the
  Heart of the Country,* 730
Gail Godwin,
  Dream Children, 924
Nikolai Gogol,
  The Overcoat, 49
William Goyen,
  *Bridge of Music,
  River of Sand,* 933

John Hawkes,
  Two Shoes for One Foot, 937
Nathaniel Hawthorne,
  My Kinsman, Major Molineux, 37
  Young Goodman Brown, 28
Ernest Hemingway,
  A Clean, Well-Lighted Place, 559
O. Henry (William Sydney Porter),
  The Cop and the Anthem, 353

Washington Irving,
  The Legend of Sleepy Hollow, 1

Josephine Jacobsen,
  The Mango Community, 942
Henry James,
  The Beast in the Jungle, 229
  Brooksmith, 219
  Four Meetings, 199
Sarah Orne Jewett,
  Miss Tempy's Watchers, 256
James Joyce,
  Araby, 450
  The Dead, 423
  Ivy Day in the Committee Room, 455

Franz Kafka,
  A Hunger Artist, 471

D. H. Lawrence,
  The Horse Dealer's Daughter, 477
  The Rocking-Horse Winner, 489

Ursula Le Guin,
  Schrödinger's Cat, 777
Doris Lessing,
  To Room Nineteen, 677

Alistair MacLeod,
  In the Fall, 955
Bernard Malamud,
  The Jewbird, 643
Thomas Mann,
  Disorder and Early Sorrow, 394
Bobbie Ann Mason,
  Graveyard Day, 964
Carson McCullers,
  A Tree, A Rock, A Cloud, 664
Herman Melville,
  Bartleby the Scrivener, 97
Alice Munro,
  Spelling, 972

Joyce Carol Oates,
  The Going-Away Party, 807
Tim O'Brien,
  Going After Cacciato, 982
Flannery O'Connor,
  Good Country People, 759
  Judgement Day, 747
Frank O'Connor,
  Guests of the Nation, 590
Sean O'Faolain,
  The Man Who Invented Sin, 568
Cynthia Ozick,
  The Shawl, 996

Grace Paley,
  The Used-Boy Raisers, 1000
Dorothy Parker,
  You Were Perfectly Fine, 518
Edgar Allan Poe,
  The Cask of Amontillado, 79
  The Fall of the House of Usher, 67
  The Purloined Letter, 84
Katherine Anne Porter,
  Flowering Judas, 510

Saki (H. H. Munro),
  The Open Window, 362
Nathalie Sarraute,
  Tropism XVIII, 577
John Sayles,
  Dillinger in Hollywood, 1005
Lynne Sharon Schwartz,
  Rough Strife, 1014
Isaac Bashevis Singer,
  The Beard, 599

Elizabeth Spencer,
  The Girl Who Loved Horses,   1027
John Steinbeck,
  Flight,   578

James Thurber,
  The Secret Life of Walter Mitty,   521
Leo Tolstoy,
  The Death of Ivan Ilych,   152
Mark Twain (Samuel L. Clemens),
  *The Celebrated Jumping Frog
  of Calaveras County*,   187

Miguel de Unamuno,
  Juan Manso: A Dead Man's Tale,   358
John Updike,
  A & P,   802

Sean Virgo,
  Home and Native Land,   1039

Alice Walker,
  Roselily,   1043
Eudora Welty,
  Why I Live at the P.O.,   614
Joy Williams,
  The Farm,   1047
Virginia Woolf,
  Kew Gardens,   466
Richard Wright,
  The Man Who Killed a Shadow,   605

1 2 3 4 5 6 7 8 9 0